Library of America, a nonprofit organization,
champions our nation's cultural heritage
by publishing America's greatest writing in
authoritative new editions and providing resources
for readers to explore this rich, living legacy.

JOHN UPDIKE

NOVELS 1978–1984

The Coup
Rabbit Is Rich
The Witches of Eastwick

Christopher Carduff, *editor*

THE LIBRARY OF AMERICA

John Updike: Novels 1978–1984
is published with support from

THE GIORGI FAMILY FOUNDATION

Contents

THE COUP I

RABBIT IS RICH 245

THE WITCHES OF EASTWICK 667

APPENDIX
  Remarks upon accepting the National Book Critics
    Circle Award for Fiction for *Rabbit Is Rich* 941
  Remarks upon accepting the American Book Award
    for Fiction for *Rabbit Is Rich* 943
  "Special Message" to readers of the Franklin
    Library's Signed First Edition Society printing of
    The Witches of Eastwick 945

Chronology 951
Note on the Texts 982
Notes 988

THE COUP

TO MY MOTHER

fellow writer & lover of far lands

Acknowledgments

The Koran quotations are from the Penguin Classics translation by N. J. Dawood. The Melville lines at the head of Chapter IV come from "The House-top: A Night Piece," composed during the Draft Riots of July 1863 in New York City, when George Opdyke was mayor. The epigraph for Chapter VII is taken from an address given by Professor el-Calamawy at a conference on "Arab and American Cultures" that she and I attended in Washington in September of 1976. Professors George N. Atiyeh of The Library of Congress, G. Wesley Johnson of the University of California at Santa Barbara, and Carl R. Proffer of the University of Michigan have generously responded to requests for information. My African history derived from books by Basil Davidson, Robert W. July, E. Jefferson Murphy, Olivia Vlahos, J. W. Nyakatura, Alfred Guillaume, Paul Fordham, Colin Turnbull, Alan Moorehead, Leda Farrant, Jacques Berque, Roland Oliver, and J. D. Fage. For geography, I used the *National Geographic* magazine, children's books, *Beau Geste*, and travellers' accounts from Mungo Park to Evelyn Waugh, from René Caillié to John Gunther. Two out-of-the-way volumes of especial value were *The Politics of Natural Disaster: The Case of the Sahel Drought*, edited by Michael H. Glantz, and *Islam in West Africa*, by J. Spencer Trimingham. Thurston Clarke's *The Last Caravan*, a factual account of the Nigerien Tuareg during the 1968–74 drought, was published while I was retyping my manuscript, too late for me to benefit from more than a few details of its informational wealth. My wife, Martha, helped with the typing and, for the year in which she was this novel's sole reader, beautifully smiled upon it. Not that she, or any of the above, are responsible for irregularities in my engineering of *The Coup*.

J. U.

Does there not pass over man a space of time when his life is a blank?

—THE KORAN, sura 76

I

M Y COUNTRY of Kush, landlocked between the mongrelized, neo-capitalist puppet states of Zanj and Sahel, is
small for Africa, though larger than any two nations of Europe. Its northern half is Saharan; in the south, forming the
one boundary not drawn by a Frenchman's ruler, a single river
flows, the Grionde, making possible a meagre settled agriculture. Peanuts constitute the principal export crop: the doughty
legumes are shelled by the ton and crushed by village women
in immemorial mortars or else by antiquated presses manufactured in Lyons; then the barrelled oil is caravanned by camelback and treacherous truck to Dakar, where it is shipped to
Marseilles to become the basis of heavily perfumed and erot-
ically contoured soaps designed not for my naturally fragrant
and affectionate countrymen but for the antiseptic lavatories of
America—America, that fountainhead of obscenity and glut.
Our peanut oil travels westward the same distance as eastward
our ancestors plodded, their neck-shackles chafing down to
the jugular, in the care of Arab traders, to find from the flesh-
markets of Zanzibar eventual lodging in the harems and palace
guards of Persia and Chinese Turkestan. Thus Kush spreads
its transparent wings across the world. The ocean of desert
between the northern border and the Mediterranean littoral
once knew a trickling traffic in salt for gold, weight for weight;
now this void is disturbed only by Swedish playboys fleeing
cold boredom in Volvos that soon forfeit their seven coats of
paint to the rasp of sand and the roar of their engines to the
omnivorous howl of the harmattan. They are skeletons before
their batteries die. Would that Allah had so disposed of all infidel intruders!

To the south, beyond the Grionde, there is forest, nakedness, animals, fever, chaos. It bears no looking into. Whenever
a Kushite ventures into this region, he is stricken with *mal à
l'estomac.*

Kush is a land of delicate, delectable emptiness, named for a
vanished kingdom, the progeny of Kush, son of Ham, grandson of Noah. Their royalty, ousted from the upper Nile in the

5

fourth century by the Christian hordes of Axum, retreated from Meroë, fabled home of iron, into the wastes of Kordofan and Darfur, and farther westward still, pursued by dust devils along the parched savanna, erecting red cities soon indistinguishable from the rocks, until their empty shattered name, a shard of grandeur, was salvaged by our revolutionary council in 1968 and, replacing the hated designation of Noire, was bestowed upon this hollow starving nation as many miles as years removed from the original Kush, itself an echo: Africa held up a black mirror to Pharaonic Egypt, and the image was Kush.

The capital is Istiqlal, renamed in 1960, upon independence, and on prior maps called Cailliéville, in honor of the trans-Saharan traveller of 1828, who daubed his face brown, learned pidgin Arabic, and achieved European celebrity by smuggling himself into a caravan from Timbuctoo to Fez and doing what hundreds of unsung Berbers had been doing for centuries, maligning them as brutes even while he basked in the loud afterglow of their gullible hospitality. Previous to French organization of the territory of Noire in 1905 (checking a British thrust arising in the Sudan), the area on both sides of the river had been known, vaguely, as Wanjiji. An Arab trading town, Al-Abid, much shrunken from its former glory, huddles behind the vast white-and-green Palais de l'Administration des Noirs, modelled on the Louvre and now used in its various wings as offices for the present government, a People's Museum of Imperialist Atrocities, a girls' high school dedicated to the extirpation of the influences of Christian mission education, and a prison for the politically aberrant.

In area Kush measures 126,912,180 hectares. The population density comes to .03 per hectare. In the vast north it is virtually immeasurable. The distant glimpsed figure blends with the land as the blue hawk blends with the sky. There are twenty-two miles of railroad and one hundred seven of paved highway. Our national airline, Air Kush, consists of two Boeing 727s, stunning as they glitter above the also glittering tin shacks by the airfield. In addition to peanuts are grown millet, sorghum, cotton, yams, dates, tobacco, and indigo. The acacia trees yield some marketable gum arabic. The natives extract ingenious benefits from the baobab tree, weaving mats from its fibrous heart, ropes from its inner bark, brewing porridge and glue and a diaphoretic for dysentery from the pulp of its fruit, turning the elongated shells into water scoops, sucking the acidic and refreshing seeds, and even boiling the leaves, in desperate times, into a kind of spinach. When are times not desperate? Goats eat the little baobab trees, so there are only old giants. The herds of livestock maintained by the tribes of pastoral nomads have been dreadfully depleted by the drought. The last elephant north of the Grionde gave up its life and its ivory in 1959, with a bellow that still reverberates. "The toubabs took the big ears with them," is the popular saying. Both Sahel and Zanj possess quantities of bauxite, manganese, and other exploitable minerals, but aside from a streak of sulphur high in the Bulub Mountains the only known mineral deposit in Kush is the laterite that renders great tracts of earth unarable. (I am copying these facts from an old *Statesman's Year-Book*, freely, here where I sit in sight of the sea, so some of them may be obsolete.) In the north there were once cities of salt populated by slaves, who bred and worshipped and died amid the incessant cruel glisten; these mining settlements, supervised by the blue-clad Tuareg, are mere memories now. But even memory thins in this land, which suggests, on the map, an angular skull whose cranium is the empty desert. Along the lower irregular line of the jaw, carved by the wandering brown river, there was a king, the Lord of Wanjiji, whose physical body was a facet of God so radiant that a curtain of gold flakes protected the eyes of those entertained in audience from his glory; and this king, restored to the throne as a constitutional monarch in the wake of the *loi-cadre* of 1956 and compelled to abdicate after the revolution of 1968, has been all but forgotten. Conquerors and governments pass before the people as dim rumors, as entertainment in a hospital ward. Truly, mercy is interwoven with misery in the world wherever we glance.

Among the natural resources of Kush perhaps should be listed our diseases—an ample treasury which includes, besides famine and its edema and kwashiorkor, malaria, typhus, yellow fever, sleeping sickness, leprosy, bilharziasis, onchocerciasis, measles, and yaws. As these are combatted by the genius of science, human life itself becomes a disease of the overworked, eroded earth. The average life expectancy in Kush is thirty-seven years, the per capita gross national product $79, the literacy rate 6%. The official currency is the *lu*. The flag is a plain green field. The form of government is a constitutional monarchy with the constitution suspended and the monarch deposed. An eleven-man Suprême Counseil Révolutionnaire et Militaire pour l'Émergence serves as the executive arm of the government and also functions as its legislature. The pure and final socialism envisioned by Marx, the theocratic populism of Islam's periodic reform movements: these transcendent models guide the council in all decisions. SCRME's chairman, and the Commander-in-Chief of the Armed Forces, Minister of National Defense, and President of Kush was (*is*, the *Statesman's Year-Book* has it) Colonel Hakim Félix Ellelloû—that is to say, myself.

Yet a soldier's disciplined self-effacement, my Cartesian schooling, and the African's traditional abjuration of ego all constrain this account to keep to the third person. There are two selves: the one who acts, and the "I" who experiences. This latter is passive even in a whirlwind of the former's making, passive and guiltless and astonished. The historical performer bearing the name of Ellelloû was no less mysterious to me than to the American press wherein he was never presented save snidely and wherein his fall was celebrated with a veritable minstrelsy of anti-Negro, anti-Arab cartoons; in the same spirit the beer-crazed mob of American boobs cheers on any autumnal Saturday or Sunday the crunched leg of the unhome-team left tackle as he is stretchered off the field. Ellelloû's body and career carried me here, there, and I never knew why, but submitted.

We know this much of him: he was short, prim, and black. He was produced, in 1933, of the rape of a Salu woman by a Nubian raider. The Salu are a sedentary tribe in the peanut highlands of the west. His mother, a large, oppressively vital woman of the clan Amazeg, became the wife by inheritance of her husband's sister's husband, her own husband having been slaughtered the same night of her rape. The peanut lands are brown, the whispering feathery brown of the uprooted bushes as they dry, precious pods inward, in stacks two meters high, and Ellelloû from the first, perhaps taking his clue from these strange fruits that can mature only underground, showed a wish to merge with his surroundings. In the public eye he always wore brown, the tan of his military uniform, unadorned, as monotonous and uninsistent as the tan of the land itself, the savanna merging into desert. Even the rivers in Kush are brown, but for the blue moment when the torrents of a rainstorm boil murderously down a wadi; and the sudden verdure of the rainy season soon dons a cloak of dust. In conformity with the prejudices of the Prophet, Ellelloû resisted being photographed. Such tattered images, in sepia tints, as gathered fly specks in the shop windows and civic corridors of Istiqlal were hieratic and inexpressive. His one affectation of costume was the assumption, on some state occasions, of those particularly excluding and protective sunglasses whose odd trade name is NoIR. It was said that his anonymity was a weapon, for armed with it he would venture out among the populace as a spy and beggar, in the manner of the fabled Caliph Haroun ar-Raschid. Colonel Ellelloû was a devout Muslim. He had four wives, and left them all (it was said) unsatisfied, so consuming was his love for the arid land of Kush.

At the age of seventeen, to escape the constriction of village life, in whose order his illegitimacy and his mother's widowhood gave him a low place, he enlisted in the *Troupes coloniales* and eventually saw service in French Indochina prior to Colonel de Castries' defeat at Dienbienphu in 1954, by which time he had risen to the rank of sergeant. In battle he found himself possessed of a dead calm that to his superiors appeared commendable. In truth it was peanut behavior. Out of the tightest spot, even as when the hordes of General Giap outnumbered the defenders four to one and the Asiatic abhorrence of black skins was notoriously lethal to the *troupes noires*, Ellelloû had faith that the pull of fate would rescue him, if he be numb enough, and submit to being shelled. During the subsequent campaigns of his division, which was called into fratricidal struggle with the independence-seekers of Algeria, Ellelloû left no trace of himself on the military record. He re-emerges from the shadows around 1959, with the rank of major, as an attaché to King Edumu IV, Lord of Wanjiji. The Gallic imperialists' failure with Bao Dai had not totally soured their taste for puppet monarchs. The king was then in his sixties, and had spent a dozen years under house arrest by the colonial representatives of the Fourth Republic in retribution for his alleged

collaboration with the Vichy government of Noire and their
German sponsors, his shame doubled by the heroic example of
resistance offered by Félix Eboué of French Equatorial Africa to
the south. Ellelloû continued in close association with the king
and with the liberal-bourgeois-elitist administration to which
the king lent his tarnished authority, until the coup of 1968, in
which Ellelloû, though secondary to the well-mourned people's hero Major-General Jean-François Yakubu Soba, played
a decisive, if not conspicuous, part. He became Minister of
Information in 1969, Minister of Defense later that year, and
upon the successful assassination attempt upon General Soba
on the twelfth day of Ramadan, President. According to the
Statesman's Year-Book, he keeps an apartment within the gran-
diose government building erected by the French and another
in the military barracks at Sobaville. His wives are scattered in
four separate villas in the suburb still called, as it was in the days
of imperialist enslavement, Les Jardins. His domicilic policy is
apparently to be in no one place at any specific time. More than
this, of the legendary national leader and Third-World spokesman, is difficult to discover.

Why did the king love me? I ask myself this in anguish,
remembering his infinitely creased face surrounded by wiry
white hair and in color the sunken black of a dried fig, his way
of nodding and nodding as if his head were mounted on a
tremulously balanced pivot, his cackle of mirth and greed like a
fine box crushed underfoot, his preposterously bejewelled little
hands, so little thickened by labor as to seem two-dimensional,
so lightly gesturing, lifting in a wind of hopeless gaiety and
sadness such as lifts puffs of dust on the street. His pallid eyes,
not blue yet not brown either, a green, rather, blanched by
his blindness to a cat's shallow-backed yellow, always reminded
me that his royal line had come from the north, contemptuous
and foreign, however darkened—arrogant assailants, themselves in flight, bringing with them, worse than their personal
cruelties, the terrible idea of time, of history, of a revelation
receding inexorably, leaving us to live and die to no purpose,
in a state of nonsense. What did this blind man see when he
looked at me? I can only speculate that, amid so many possessed by their personal causes, by schemes of aggrandizement
for themselves and their clans and their wives' clans, I was a

blur of a new color, patriotism. This arbitrary and amorphous land descended to him from the French, this slice of earth with its boundaries sketched by an anonymous cartographer at the infamous Berlin Conference of 1885 and redrawn more firmly as a military zone for occupation a decade later, its pacification not complete until 1917 and its assets to this day mortgaged to La Banque de France and its beautiful brown thin people invisible on every map—what was it? The historic kingdom of Wanjiji had expanded and contracted like the stomach of some creature that does not eat for centuries; by the time the Gauls, at de Gaulle's mystical bidding, abandoned colonial rule and cast about for an agency wherewith to rule covertly, Wanjiji had shrunk to a name and a notion of infinite privilege in the head of one ancient prisoner. He, casting about in turn, saw in me, an exile returned with re-educated passions, what he failed to discern within himself: an idea of Kush.

In the Year of the Prophet 1393, which the comic arithmetic of the infidels numbers as 1973, at the end of the wet season, which had been dry, the President went to visit the king. The people thought the Lord of Wanjiji dead, executed with his ministers and his cousins those first tonic months of the Revolution, in the inner Cour de Justice, where now the girls of the Anti-Christian High School played hockey and volleyball. In truth King Edumu was held a secret captive in the Palais de l'Administration des Noirs, along the wall of whose endless corridors, at the level of a walking man's knuckles, ran a painted green strip like an interior horizon. The floor was speckled with flakes of lime fallen from the ceiling above, where the frosted foliations of Art Nouveau were a few of them unbroken. In the perpetual dusk of these halls soldiers saluted the dictator as he passed, and their whores with a whimper and a swirl of their rags hid in the doorways of offices become barracks. At this hour the smell of scorching feathers wafted from chambers where once clerks whose very mustaches appeared thin as penstrokes had scribbled a web of imaginary order. From the king's guarded apartment came a perfume of cloves and a drone of the Koran. The old man to relieve the boredom of his captivity and perhaps to curry favor with his fanatic captor had converted to the True Faith and for the hour before evening azan had read to him those suras which body forth Paradise. "*For the unbelievers We have prepared fetters and chains, and a blazing Fire. But the righteous shall drink of a cup tempered at the Camphor Fountain, a gushing spring at which the servants of Allah will refresh themselves. . . .*" The enchanting old villain formerly had taken pride in a barbarous animism of blood and substitution, and in the interstices of French supervision had exercised the fructifying privilege of royal murderousness. Young female attendants especially had fallen victims to his whim. And though their screams under the ax and the smothering pillows had escaped from the palace windows, there was never a shortage of nubile, trembling, onyx-skinned, heavy-breasted replacements, thrust forward not only by the sycophancy of their families but by something suicidal and, beneath their moist terror, voracious within themselves. "*Reclining there upon soft couches, they shall feel neither the scorching heat nor the biting cold. Trees will spread their shade around them, and fruits will hang in clusters over them.*" The king's cell was lit by a clay-colored slant of late sun. He knew Ellelloû's tread, and with a divinely scant gesture signalled his reader, a young Fula wearing upon his shaved head a plum-red fez, to be silent.

Never large, the king had shrunken. His little hooked nose alone had resisted the reshaping of time and sat in the center of his face like a single tart fruit being served on an outworn platter. His shallow yellow eyes shifted rapidly and still appeared to see. Indeed, an examining physician has reported that they remained sensitive to violent movement, and to a candle held close enough to singe his eyebrows.

"Splendor of Splendors," Ellelloû began, "thy unworthy agent greets thee."

"A beggar salutes a rich man," the king responded. "Why have you honored me, Ellelloû, and when will I be free?"

"When Allah the Compassionate deems thy people strong enough to endure the glory of thy reign."

They spoke in Arabic, until a more urgent tempo drove them to French. All their languages were second languages, since Wanj for the one and Salu for the other were tongues of the hut and the village council, taught by mothers and lost as the world expanded. All the languages they used, therefore, felt to them as clumsy masks their thoughts must put on.

"I am not asking to rule again," the king replied, "but merely to set my face beneath the stars."

"The very stars would enlist as your soldiers and put their spears to our throats; the people are parched, and your resurrection would set them afire."

"I cannot see the smile on your lips, Ellelloû, but I hear mockery twist your voice. State your purpose, and leave irony to Allah, in Whose sight we are mice in the gaze of a lion. Have you some business worth the ruin of an old beggar's peace?" He returned his hand to his lap with a papery grace that belied its burden of garnets and emeralds and silver filigree: the king sat in a *lungi* of striped white silk in a nest of pillows and bolsters, his wrists resting symmetrically on the knees of his folded legs. Around his brow was tied a riband of spun gold in token of the curtain of the unsurpassable metal that formerly had shielded from his radiations the mortals who came grovelling to him in petition. His hair, long uncut, stood far out from his head in wiry rays, a halo of wool, as awesome as comical. Ellelloû was reminded disagreeably of murky photographs he had seen in the Istiqlal underground press, *Nouvelles en noir et blanc*, of American "hippies," young scions of corporation lawyers and professional rabbis who, to dramatize the absurd sexual spree their reactionary drug-addled hearts confused with the needed real revolution, affected headbands in presumptuous emulation of the red men their forefathers had unceremoniously exterminated.

Seen in this light, the king appeared so vulnerably displaced, so gallantly ridiculous, that Ellelloû was moved to confess, as a wayward son to drunken father: "I have been north. My adventures there trouble me."

"Why do you seek to be troubled? A leader must not be divided within himself. He is the unmoved pivot, the frozen sun."

"The people starve. The rains now have failed for the fifth year. The herdsmen steal millet from their wives and children to feed the cattle; still the animals drop, and are fallen upon for the little meat left on their bones. I have seen vultures come to the feast and be themselves stoned and consumed. The people eat bats and mice, they eat skinks and scorpions, gerbils and termites; they glean the carcasses that even jackals leave. The hair of the children turns orange. Their eyes and bellies bulge. Their heads are shaped like the skulls of mummies baked in the sand. When they grow too weak to whimper, their silence is the worst."

"It anticipates the silence of Paradise," smiled the king.

As their own silence widened, Ellelloû felt he had failed. He felt himself at the center of a cosmic failure, his failure to communicate the reality of suffering at one with the cosmic refusal to prevent this suffering. Held mute in a moment without a pose, a mask, Ellelloû felt the terror of responsibility and looked about him for someone with whom to share it. The attendant who had been reading from the Book of Books sat cross-legged on a green satin cushion, eyes downcast, his thumb curved to turn the page. At a glance I saw in him a police officer, and knew that my conversation with the king would be reported in full to Michaelis Ezana, my Minister of the Interior. I knew too that the king would eventually offer words of wisdom to fill the void between us where his smile had feathered. In the days when I had been his courtier his words would overnight condense in my mind like dew on the underside of a leaf. My eye continued about his cell. Though it contained objects of pure gold and of the fanatic workmanship that only extreme poverty coupled with faith in an afterlife produces, it also held much that could be termed rubble—scraps of torn cloth, sticks of wood bound together as by a playful idiot, small pouches of spicy dust, visible bones and bits of once-living matter dried and darkened out of recognition, and a certain amount of sheer dirt, most conspicuous in the corners but some of it apparently with deliberation sprinkled recently on the inlaid lid of an ivory chest, on the head and knobby shoulders of a pot-bellied ebony idol, and on the carved saddle-seat of the sacred stool of Wanjiji. This last had been tucked into a corner at a tilt, one lion-foot having been broken and not repaired. How repair, indeed, so sacred an object? The workman's hands would uselessly tremble in such close proximity to the holy. Amulets—Koranic phrases, often inauthentic, in little bark or leather cylinders—were littered here and there, and empty bowls in which, before their liquid had evaporated, a soul had been captured. My soul, perhaps. How often, I wondered, had my death been rendered in mime, and the king's escape been effected via the fragile fabrications of *juju*? My palms prickled to think there were prayers of which I was the urgent object, prayers arising all over the land; like a massive transparent ball my terror, my responsibility, threatened to roll over me again. I flung my attention to the walls, where hung a number of framed portraits this king of eclectic sensibility had collected in the years of his constitutional reign, when he subscribed to Western magazines—de Gaulle, Nkrumah, Farouk, an etching of King Yohannes IV of Ethiopia, a poster of Elvis Presley in full sequinned regalia, Marilyn Monroe from a bed of polar bear skins making upward at the lens the crimson O of a kiss whose mock emotion led her to close her greasy eyelids, and a page torn from that magazine whose hearty name of *Life* did not save it from dying, torn roughly out but sumptuously framed, showing a female child dancer in patent-leather shoes poised in midstep with bright camera-conscious eyes upon a flight of stairs leading nowhere. At her side stood a pair of long legs in checked trousers belonging, it was my growing belief, to a black man whose hands were muffled in white gloves and whose head was cut off by the top of the page. The king caught my mind in mid-flight.

"The white devils," he said, "give grain. And milk transmuted to powder. And medicine that by a different magic might turn the children's hair black again."

Disturbed by the decapitated black dancer, I exclaimed, "Food from filthy hands is filth! The integrity of Kush rejects the charity of imperialist exploiters!"

"*Der Spatz in der Hand*, my old friends used to say, *ist besser als die Taube auf dem Dach.*"

"Gifts bring men, men bring bullets, bullets bring oppression. Africa has undergone this cycle often enough."

The king performed the dainty pragmatic shrug with which, in the days before the Revolution, he would have a page boy mutilated for dozing in an anteroom. "Your friends the Russians," he said, "are generous exporters of spies and last year's rockets. They themselves buy wheat from the Americans."

"Only to advance the revolution. The peasantry of America, seeing itself swindled, seethes on the verge of riot."

"The world is splitting in two," said the king, "but not in the way we were promised, not between the Red and the free but between the fat and the lean. In one place, the food rots; in another, the people starve. Why emphasize the unkind work of nature that keeps these halves apart?"

"I am not the creator of this Revolution but its instrument," I told the king. "It is not I but the will of Kush that rejects offal. A sick man must vomit or grow sicker. When the Revolution occurred, the task of the Conseil—of General Soba, and Ezana, and myself—"

The king nodded wearily, anticipating, his head on that delicate pivot, nodding, nodding.

"—was not to inspire the people but to protect from their enthusiasm the capitalist intriguers who under your protection had infested Istiqlal; but for our intervention they would have been slaughtered ere they could be expelled."

"Enough were slaughtered. And their thin-lipped wives taken alive for the harems of the socialist elite."

"A phrase without meaning," I said.

The king said, "Let me tell you of an event without meaning: the hand of the giver is outstretched, and that of the beggar remains closed."

"Begging has its holy place on the streets, not in the corridors of government."

"Daily, I beg for my freedom."

"Your freedom consists of being hidden. I envy you that freedom."

"And well you might. The deaths in the north are on your head." The king smiled, lifting those blind eyes which were like loci upon a plane of crazed crystal. "It is good. The people adore the Lord who asks them to die. Had I not been so tender a father to my children, had not my policies sheltered them from the rage of the absolute, they would not have turned their backs. Where there is poverty, there must be drama. Your rule will be long, Hakim Félix, if your heart does not soften."

I could not leave it like this. I pleaded, "The purity of Kush is its strength. In the lands of our oppressors the fat millions have forgotten how to live and look to the world's forsaken to remind them. The American crates piled at our borders stank of despair; I went there and ordered them burned."

"Reflections of so signal a deed have flickered even in this remotest of caves. I commend you, Colonel Ellèlloû, ruler of lava and ash. Only Satan has a like domain."

"Spoken like one of his legions, like one whose eyes are still closed to the light of the Prophet. Though you have taken upon yourself a pretense of Islam, your faith is centered across the Grionde, where terror and torture still reign, where *juju* still clouds the minds of men, as the tsetse fly poisons their blood. Here, the sky shows its face. There is one God, unknowable, without feature. Praise be to Allah, Lord of the Worlds."

"The Beneficent, the Merciful," the king responded. "You do an injustice to the sincerity of my adherence. I find Islam a beautifully practical religion, streamlined even, the newest thing in this line. But as to cruelty, the rain forest beyond the river holds none as rigorous as the fury of a jihad. I am blind, but not so blind as those righteous whose eyes roll upward, who kill and are killed to gain a Paradise of shade trees, as I hear in the Book." He gestured toward the reader, who remained impassive, quiet as a machine waiting to be activated; this police spy was young and smooth, his oval face rather feminine in its stolid fineness beneath the plum-colored fez. "Your sky," the king told me, "shines all day like the flat of a sword. The sky-spirit has come to hate the earth-spirit. Your land is cursed, unhappy Félix. You have cursed this land with your hatred of the world."

"I hate only the evil that is in the world."

"You burn its food while your subjects starve. And it is said you brought death in the north."

"An American committed suicide. We stood by helpless."

"That was an error. In Africa, one white death shrieks louder than a thousand black lives."

"You hear much, in your cave. I too have my ears, and they hear the people murmur that the old king somewhere lives, and drags the land with him into senility."

The king returned his heavy hand, gently as an ash drifts back to the hearth, to its site on his knee. "Then show me to the people in my vigor."

"What they say is true. You are old. You were old when I was young."

"Young and helpless: who was it who plucked you from the shadows where you had been hiding, hiding in such fear you had almost forgotten the languages of Kush, and set you at his side, in a resplendent new uniform, and taught you statecraft?"

"The question answers itself, my lord. And the fact that you have breath to ask it testifies sufficiently to my gratitude. Even when I was young, you lied to minimize your age, and a generation has grown whiskers since."

"What concern is my physical state to anyone but myself, since I am no longer king?"

"The people, though we seek to educate them, believe as did their fathers that there is no way to leave the royal stool but through the gate of blood. The natural death of a king is an abomination unto the state."

"And you? What do you believe?"

"I believe—I believe the debts between us have been paid."

"Then kill me. Kill me in the square by the Mosque of the Day of Disaster and show the people my head. Water the land with my blood. I have no fear. My ancestors bubble in the earth like *pombe* brewing. The thought of death is sweeter to me than honey dipped from the tree."

"The people will ask, Why was this not done before, in the morning of L'Émergence? The king's ministers and lackeys were relieved of the misery of their lives, why was he spared? Why for these five years of blight has Ellelloû kept the heart of reaction alive?"

The king said swiftly, "The answer is plain: out of love. Inopportune love, and the unpolitic loyalty of the fearful. Tell them, their colonel is a man who holds within himself many possibilities. Tell them, it is not they the ignorant who hug to themselves the bloody madness of *juju* but their leader as well, the progressive and passionate embodiment of Islamic Marxism, who to mitigate their suffering proposes nothing better than the murder of the decrepit old prisoner who was once the alleged chief of benighted, mythical Wanjiji!" The king laughed, a frightening crackling of his crystal plane, which Ellelloû in his orb of numbness felt to be a plane of his fate. The king spoke on, his little silken figure agitated, lifted upwards, as if by strings of song. "Tell them, the madness of the divine anoints their leader, rendering Kush the beacon of the Third World, the marvel and scandal of the capitalist press, the kindling of glee in a billion breasts! But remember, Colonel Ellellôu, murder me once, the dice have been thrown. There will be no more magic among the souvenirs of Noire." His tongue rattled and fell away to a whisper within the prolonged *r* of this abhorrent old name. His eyes, shallow-backed, reflected the last light from the window, the scabbing green-painted frame of which admitted as well the muezzins' twanging call to first prayer, *salāt al-maghrib*; it echoed under the cloudless sky as under a darkening dome of tile. "The day has begun," the king said. "Go to the mosque. The President must display his faith."

As Ellellôu walked down the corridor, where the smell of scorched feathers had thickened, and the muttering of the soldiers and their whores had grown richer and more conspiratorial, the pretty young reader's voice picked up the dropped thread: "*They shall be attended by boys graced with eternal youth, who to the beholder's eyes will seem like scattered pearls. When you gaze upon that scene you will behold a kingdom blissful and glorious.*"

They shall be arrayed in garments of fine green silk and rich brocade, and adorned with bracelets of silver. Their Lord will give them a pure beverage to drink. Indeed, it had been dry in the north. By noon of the first day's drive, our party of three having gathered in the Palais garage at dawn, the wideflung peanut fields broke up into scattered poor plantings of cassava and maize that scratched our eyes with their look of hopeless effort. The rarely glimpsed cultivator of those gravelly fields would lift a bony arm in greeting as our Mercedes poured past, trailing its illusory mountain of dust. The pisé rectangles of Istiqlal, their monotony of dried mud broken in the center of town by the wooden façades of Indian storefronts, a-swirl with Arabic and Hindi, and the concrete-and-glass abominations flauntingly imposed, before the Revolution, by the French and, since, by the East Germans, soon dissolved—once the tin shantytown of resettled nomads was behind us—into the low, somehow liquid horizon, its stony dun slumber scarcely disturbed by a distant cluster of thatched roofs encircled by euphorbia, or by the sullen looming of a roadside hovel, a rusted can on a stick advertising the poisonous and interdicted native beer. More than once we had to detour around a giraffe skeleton strung across the *piste*, the creature drawn there on its last legs by the thin mane of grass that in this desolation sprang up in response to the liquid that boiling radiators spilled in passing. Yet all morning we saw not another vehicle. As the heat of the high sun overpowered even our splendid machine's air-conditioning, Mtesa, my driver, pulled into a cluster of huts woven of thorn-strands over an armature of acacia boughs and compacted with mud; these shelters had hovered on the horizon for half an hour. Opuku, my bodyguard, rummaged through the napping inhabitants and found a withered crone who mumblingly muddled together some raffia mats for our repose and brought us grudging portions of oversalted cous-cous. The water from her calabash tasted sweet and may have been drugged, for we slept so soundly that we were awakened well after the time of *salāt al-'asr*, and then forcibly, by a young woman, naked but for her pointed nosepiece and throat-rings of rhino hair, who evidently wished to soothe us further with the gift of her charms, which had been rubbed to a noxious gleam with rancid butter. This sad and graceful slave received a kick from Opuku, a sleepy curse from Mtesa, and words of enlightenment from me in regard to the Prophet's extollation of chastity in women, and of his admonishments to men that they not abuse female orphans. Our afternoon prayers hastily performed, we offered the old woman a handful of paper *lu*, —so called, the malicious wit of the departing French had it, because they were circulated *in lieu* of hard currency. Upon being thunderously informed by bull-necked Opuku that I was President of the nation, with power of life and death over all Kushites, while in sober proof Mtesa drove up in the Mercedes with its fluttering flag of stark green on the fender, our venerable hostess sank to her knees wailing, closed her eyes against our largesse, and begged instead for mercy. This she received, in the form of our departure. We drove into the night, a night of creamy blue, without lights, or one wherein the occasional far speck of a campfire shone with the unaccountable watery beauty of a star. By prearrangement we were to spend the night in the region called Hulūl, at the secret Soviet installation there.

No road marked the way to the buried bunkers, and no

conspicuous ventilation shafts or entrance ports betrayed their presence. The occasional straggle of nomads with their camels and goats may have noticed that acres of the soil had been dislocated and reconstituted, or may even have stumbled across extrusions of cement and aluminum masked by plastic thornbushes and elephant grass; but when the nomad does not understand, he moves on, his mental narrowness complementing the width of his wandering life, which might derange more open minds. In a sense the land itself is forgetful, an evaporating pan out of which all things human rise into blue invisibility. Not far off, for instance, in the Hulūl Depression stood the red ruins of a structure called Hallāj, and no one remembered why it was so named, or what congregation had worshipped what god amid its now unroofed pillars.

Even the secret at hand had its inconsequential side. Three sets of MIRVed SS-9 ICBMs in their subterranean sheaths pointed north to the Mediterranean, west toward similar U.S. installations in the lackey territory of Sahel, and east to the remote Red Sea ports of Zanj, which in certain permutations of nuclear holocaust might become strategically significant enough to vaporize. Our Kushite rockets were "third wave" weaponry; that is, by the time they were utilized the major industrial and population centers would be erased from the globe. Like the players of a chess contest reduced to a few rooks, pawns, and the emblematic kings, the major powers, yawning over their brandy, would be pursuing a desultory end game, to determine which style of freedom—freedom from disorder, freedom from inhibition—would suffuse the spherical desert that remained. That world, amusing to contemplate, would not only be Saharan in aspect but would be dominated by underdamaged Africa, in long-armed partnership with Polynesians, Eskimos, Himalayan Orientals, and the descendants of British convicts in Australia. More amusingly still, Michaelis Ezana, a nagging doubter of our Soviet allies, maintained that the rockets were in truth dummies, sacks of local sand where the warheads should be, set here by solemn treaty merely to excite the opposite superpower to install, at burdensome expense, authentic missiles in neighboring Sahel. Whatever the case, a slab of earth eight meters wide and two thick lifted at the prearranged signal from our headlights (dim, undim, out, dim), and the party of Russian soldiers below rejoiced, amid the furious electricity of their vast bunker, at this diversion. In preparation for our visit they had all become drunk.

Mtesa and Opuku, blinking in amazement at this bubble of sun captured underground, were swamped with hairy embraces, Cyrillic barks, and splashing offers of vodka, which Opuku did not initially refuse. I informed them, in my loudest French, that "*N'alcoolisons pas, le Dieu de notre gens interdit cela*," and upon many repetitions of this baffling negation won for myself and my small party the right to respond in chalky Balkan mineral water (fetched from the sub-cellar) to their interminable toasts and to observe with sobriety this foreign enclave. The Russians had been here since the secret SAND (Soviet-Allied Nuclear Deterrents) talks of 1971 and in the two years since had amply furnished the bunker in the stuffy tsarist style of Soviet supercomfort, from the lamps with fringed shades and soapstone bases carved in the shape of tussling bears resting on runners of Ukrainian lace to the obligatory oil paintings of Lenin exhorting workers against a slanted sunset and Brezhnev charming with the luxuriance of his eyebrows a flowery crowd of Eurasiatic children. The linguist among them, a frail steel-bespectacled second lieutenant whose Arabic was smeared with an Iraqi accent and whose French sloshed in the galoshes of Russian *zhushes*, fell dead drunk in the midst of the banquet; we carried on with minimal toasts to the heroes of our respective races. "Lumumba," they would say, and I would answer, as their glasses were refilled, "*À* Stakhanov." "Nasser, *da*, Sadat, *nyet*" was met, amid uproarious applause, with "*Vive* Sholokov, *écrasez* Solzhenitsyn," to applause yet more tumultuous. My opposite number, Colonel Sirin, who in this single installation commanded perhaps the equivalent in expenditure of the entire annual military budget of Kush, discovered that I comprehended English and, no doubt more coarsely than he intended, proposed honor to "all good niggers." I responded with the seventy-seventh sura of the Koran (*"Woe on that day to the disbelievers! Begone to that Hell which you deny!"*) as translated into my native tongue of Salu, whose glottal rhythms enchanted the Reds in their dizziness. Our store of reciprocal heroes exhausted, the briefing blackboard was dragged forth and we matched toasts to the letters of our respective alphabets.

"Щ !" the colonel proposed, milking the explosive sound for its maximum richness.

I tactfully responded with the beautiful terminal form of "ق."

"ж ! !" he boasted, "*le plus belle* letter all over goddam world!"

I outdid him, I dare believe, gracefully proposing, "ح."

There was a presentation of medals, and a monumental picture-book of the treasures accumulated by the subterranean monks of Kiev, and then these strange men began to dance from a squatting position and in demonstration of manliness to chew their liquor glasses like so many biscuits. Since they were their own best audience for these feats, I persuaded a young and relatively sober aide to show us to our chambers. Several of the officers staggered along, and one especially burly Slav playfully planted a foot in Mtesa's backside as we knelt to our deferred *salāt al-ʿishā*.

Failing to fall asleep promptly within the smothering softness of the Soviet bed, with its brocaded canopy and its stony little packets for pillows, I reflected back upon the customs and the orgy we had been privileged to witness, and located along the borders of my memory an analogy that seemed clarifying: with their taut pallor, bristling hair devoid of a trace of a curl, oval eyes, short limbs, and tightly packed bodies whose muscular energy seemed drawn into a knot at the back of their necks, these Russians reminded me of nothing so much as the reckless, distasteful packs of wild swine that when I was a child would come north from the bogs by the river to despoil the vegetable plantings of our village. They had a bristling power and toughness, to be sure, but lacked both the weighty magic of the lion and the hippo and the weightless magic of the gazelle and the shrike, so that the slaughter of one with spears and stones, as he squealed and dodged—the boars were not easy to kill—took place in an incongruous hubbub of laughter. Even in death their eyes kept that rheumy glint whereby the hunted betray the pressures under which they live.

Once during the night the telephone in our overfurnished chamber rang. When I picked it up, there was no voice at the other end, nor was there a click. Through the long tunnel of silence I seemed to see into the center of the Kremlin, where terror never sleeps. And our hosts were up early to see us off. Their uniforms were fresh and correct, and their faces —those square semi-Asiatic faces that appear too big for their thin features—were shaved, betraying only in an abnormally keen sheen, a drained, thin-skinned look, their carousal of a few hours before. It was their rule never to stray aboveground, even when, before the famine became extreme, fresh milk and meat might have enhanced their diet of frozen and powdered provisions—as if even one slice of authentically rank native goat cheese would fatally contaminate this giant capsule, this hermetic offshoot of the insular motherland. In this they were unlike the Americans, who wandered everywhere like children, absurdly confident of being loved. Nor was the Soviet exclusiveness confident and inward, like that of the French. By the terms of their treaty—at their insistence, not ours—a soldier or technician found afoot in the open air was to be jailed and segregated from the populace. One's impression could only be of a power immensely timorous, a behemoth frightened of even such gaunt black mice as we poor citizens of Kush. We shook hands, the colonel and I. I thanked him for his hospitality, he thanked me for mine. He said Russia and Kush were brothers in progressivism and in the unanimous patriotism of their polyglot peoples. I responded to Colonel Sirin (his bespectacled interpreter being still abed comatose) as exactly as I could; our two peoples, I said, were possessed of an "*essence religieuse*" and our lands of "*les vacances magnifiques*." Mtesa and Opuku witnessed this unintelligible exchange wonderingly, and the Mercedes, coughing on its heady swig of Siberian diesel fuel, took us up the ramp, to the slab of desert that lifted on pneumatic hinges to admit scalding floods of light and to reveal again the shimmering horizons of our journey.

The Hulūl Depression, its gravels and crusty sands ruddy in color, as if the rivers that had long ago emptied into this cracked lakebed had been tinged with blood, gave way, while the sun climbed toward its incandescent apogee, to the foothills of the Bulub Mountains. The *piste* diminished to a winding track, treacherously pitted and strewn with a flinty scrabble that well challenged the mettle of our Michelin steel-belted

squint of these Yankees is muddled in with their something eternally puerile, awkward, winning, and hopeful. They want, these sons of the simultaneously most expansionist and most avowedly idealistic of power aggregations, to have all things both ways: to eat both the chicken and the egg, to be both triumphant and coddled, to seem both shrewd and ingenuous. I saw him as a child, in his parents' well-padded, musty home on some curving suburban street, squinting into the fragile glued frame of a model airplane, or licking the sweetened mounts of his stamp collection, unaware that, opening beneath him, an abyss in the carpet, a chute of time would bring him to the respectable adventurism of the foreign service and this evening moment, amid a mob of Tuareg, while a strip of saffron still lingered above the westward safety of Sahel. A stir of pity, like the first unease that will lead to vomit, I bit down. He was young on the ladder of power, still assigned to the negligible nations, the licorice and caramel and chocolate people in their little trays at the front of the store; hard work and no filching would take him, as his gray hair whitened and his sleek wife wrinkled, deeper into the store, to the back room where the wholesalers grunted, amid the aromas of burlap and vinegar, their pennywise accommodations. Better for him to have become a professor of Government at a small snowy Midwestern college. My mind's eye held his wife, who would be freckled and fair and already watching her weight and slightly hardened in the role of foreign service helpmate, too ready to repack the constantly pruned possessions, to adjust her manner to a new race of servants, to learn a new smattering of shopping phrases, to cater gaily, adroitly, and appropriately to those couples above them, below them, and beside them in the dance of legations and overseas offices. I even knew how she would make love: with abashed aggression, tense in her alleged equality of body, primed like a jammed bazooka on the pornographic plastic fetishes and sexual cookbooks of her white tribe and yet, when all cultural discounts are entered, with something of graciousness, of helpless feeling, of an authentic twist at the end. . . . The squirm of nausea again. I pictured their flat in Dakar or Lagos, their "starter house" in a suburb of Maryland or Virginia, with its glass tables and incessant electricity, an island of light carved from our darkness, and my pity ceased. I told the tall intruder,

"I am a citizen of Kush, delegated to ask why you are troubling our borders and what means this mountain of refuse?"

"This isn't refuse, pal—it's manna. Donated to your stricken area by the generosity of the American government and the American people acting in conjunction with the Food and Agriculture Organization of the United Nations. U.S. Air Force C-130s have been flying this stuff in to the emergency airfield in northern Sahel and I've been sent down here from the USAID office in Tangier at the urging of the FAO people in Rome to locate the bottleneck vis-à-vis distribution of the emergency aid to the needy areas of Kush and to expedite the matter. I've been sitting out here in the underside of nowhere frying my ass off for two weeks trying to contact somebody in authority. Whoever the hell you are, you're the best thing I've seen today."

"May I ask a few questions?"

"Shoot."

"Who was it, pray, who informed you of this supposed neediness?"

He touched his sunburned forehead and shoved back the sheaf of dry hair there. His suit, designed for cocktail parties on embassy lawns, had rumpled, out here in these badlands. His sweat had caked dark not only on his collar but along the hems of his pockets, wherever skin repeatedly touched cloth. "Who're you trying to kid?" he asked me. "These cats are *starving.* The whole world knows it, you can see 'em starve on the six o'clock news every night. The American people want to help. We know this country's socialist and xenophobic, we know Ellelloû's a schizoid paranoid; we don't give a fuck. This kind of humanitarian catastrophe cuts across the political lines, as far as my government's concerned."

"Are you aware," I asked him, "that your government's cattle vaccination project increased herd size even as the forage and water of this region were being exhausted?"

"I've read that in some report, but—"

"And that the deep wells drilled by foreign governments disrupted nomadic grazing patterns so that deserts have been created with the wells at their center? Are you aware, furthermore, that climatic conditions in this region have been the same for five years, that the 'humanitarian catastrophe' you speak of is to us the human condition?"

"O.K., O.K.—better late than never. We're here now, and what's the hang-up? I can't get anybody to talk to me."

At my back, the impatient murmur of the Tuareg intensified, and with it intensified, to fade quickly away, that misplaced barbershop sweetness. "I will talk to you," I said, raising my voice so that our audience might understand, at least, that I was on the attack. "I am Ellelloû. I speak for the people of Kush. The people of Kush reject capitalist intervention in all its guises. They have no place in their stomachs for the table scraps of a society both godless and oppressive. Offer your own blacks freedom before you pile boxes of carcinogenic trash on the holy soil of Kush!"

"Listen," he pleaded, "Zanj is taking tons of grain a day, and they have *Chinese advisers* over there. This thing cuts right through the political shit, and anyway don't yell at me, I marched for civil rights all through college."

"And have now been predictably co-opted," I said. "I am not as ignorant of your nation's methods as you may suppose. As to Zanj, I am told that you have favored its suffering citizens with tons of number two sorghum, a coarse grain grown for cattle fodder, which gives its human consumers violent diarrhea."

He shed some insolence at this information, and assumed a more confiding tone. "There've been some ball-ups, yeah, but don't forget these primitives are used to a high-protein diet of meat and milk. They eat better'n we do. We send what we have."

"I see," said I, gazing upward at the terrace of crates, fitfully illuminated by some torches that had been lit in the throng of witnesses at my back. *Korn Kurls* had been stamped across one whole tier, and *Total* in letters of great momentum repeated itself over and over on the wall of cardboard that reached into darkness, toward the blazing desert stars.

"Listen," the American was trying to sell me, "these break-fast cereals, with a little milk, sugar if you have it, are dynamite, don't knock 'em. You're chewing cactus roots, and we know it." In another tone, boyish and respectful, he asked, "You really Ellelloû? I love some of the things you wrote in exile. They were assigned in a Poli Sci course I took at Yale."

So he knew of my exile. My privacy was invaded. Confusion was upon me. I took off my sunglasses. The brightness of the lights shed by the torches was surprising. Should I be getting royalties? At the back of my skull the horde was chanting, "El-lelloû, Ellelloû. . . ." As if to escape a lynch mob, I stepped forward, across the invisible Sahel-Kush border, toward the dark mountain of aid. Seeing this political barrier breached, my American confided, "They really want this stuff," in a voice that implied the battle was over; I would sign some papers, his starchy bounty could be abandoned, he would be received into his wife's freckled bed in Tangier, and his superiors would commend him all the way back to Washington. Alas, there was no safety for him in my heart, or in this night. His pallor, now that night was altogether upon us, appeared eerie, formless, or rather having the form of a parasite shaped to conform to the sunless innards of a nobler, more independent creature. The nomads and their rabble of slaves with a giant rustling crossed the border after me, pressing us with their flapping torches into a semi-circle of space against the cliff of cardboard—cardboard, giant letters of the Roman alphabet, and polypropylene, for our benefactors shipped their inferior sorghum in transparent sacks, whose transparency revealed wood chips and dead mice and whose slippery surfaces reflected the torches, torches that highlighted also with red sparks the rungs of an aluminum lad-der set against the cliff, the drops of sweat on the American's parasite-gray neck, and the agitated eyeballs of the Tuareg. "Ellelloû, Ellelloû. . . ." As their murmur had conjured me from the desert, so I must conjure from within myself a gesture of leadership, an action.

Our toubab's slavish, hard-breathing, panic-suppressing de-meanor begged for cruelty. Scenting a "deal," a *détente*, he told me, "No kidding, there's a lot of real food value up there, I remember when they unloaded seeing Spam and powdered milk." He clambered up the ladder to look for these strata, while the Tuareg pressed closer, shaking their torches indig-nantly at such an act of levitation. I could scarcely hear his shouts: ". . . here you go . . . Carnation . . . add three parts water . . ."

"But we have no water!" I called up to him, trying, it seems now in hindsight, to buy time for both of us. "In Kush, water is more precious than blood!"

He was swallowed by darkness, between the torches and the stars. "No problem," his voice drifted down. "We'll bring in teams . . . green revolution . . . systems of portable trenching . . . a lily pond right where you're standing . . . here we go . . . no, that's cream of celery soup. . . ." His voice, pattering down upon them like a nonsensical angel's, had become an intolerable irritation to the Tuareg masses. As their torches drew nearer, the source of the voice could be seen, a white blur disappearing and reappearing, ever higher, among the escarpments and crevasses of combustible packaging.

Within my numbing orb of responsibility, my arm had become leaden; yet I lifted it high, and dropped it in solemn signal, so that the inevitable would appear to come from me.

Torches were touched to the base of the pyramid; it became a pyre. To his credit, the young American, when he saw the smoke and flames rising toward him, and all those slopes beneath him ringed by exultant Kushite patriots, did not cry out for mercy, or attempt to scramble and leap to a safety that was not there, but, rather, climbed to the pinnacle and, luridly illumined, awaited the martyrdom for which there must have been, in the training for foreign service provided by his insidious empire, some marginal expectation and religious preparation. We were surprised, how silently he died. Or were his cries merely drowned within the roar of the ballooning tent of flame that engulfed the treasure-heap his writhing figure for a final minute ornamented like a dark star? When he had stood beside me, I could smell on the victim, under the sweat of his long stale wait and the bland, oysterish odor of his earnestness, the house of his childhood, the musty halls, the cozy bathroom soaps, the glue of his adolescent hobbies, the aura of his alcoholic and sexually innocent parents, the ashtray scent of dissatisfaction. What dim wish to do right, hatched by the wavery blue light of the television set with its curious international shadows, had led him to the fatal edge of a safety that he imagined had no limits? I checked my heart's tremor with some verses from the Book, that foresees all and thereby encloses all: *On that day men shall become like scattered moths and the mountains like tufts of carded wool. On that day there shall be downcast faces, of men broken and worn out, burnt by a scorching fire, drinking from a seething fountain. On that day there shall be radiant faces, of men well-pleased with their labors, in a lofty garden.*

The Tuareg and their slaves were in a joyful tumult. Opuku and Mtesa came and guarded me from the confusion. There was a slithering in my palm of another, smaller hand. I saw that Kutunda, her broken lip scabbed, was still with me, that I had replaced Wadal as her protector.

Now the fire had taken its first giant draught, and our nostrils acknowledged the quantity of grain our triumphant gesture had consumed, for the scorched air was bathed in the benevolent aroma of baking bread; the desert night, as flakes of corrugated-cardboard ash plenteously drifted downward, knew the unaccustomed wonder of snow.

II

I N THE season the toubabs call fall, Colonel Ellelloû returned
to Istiqlal, his recessive mood deepened by an incident on
the straight road south of Hulūl, near the vanished city of
Haïr. The triangle of himself, Mtesa, and Opuku had been
squared by the addition of Kutunda, whose unwashed female
body brought to the interior of the Mercedes an altogether
new fragrance, overlaid upon the oily distant scent of German
workmanship, the clinging understink of camel dung, and the
haunting aroma of the dreadful bonfire, which had crept in the
windows and permeated the gray velour inexpungably as an
evil memory. They were silent for miles, as each brain whirred
its own wheels: Mtesa intent upon steering his marvellous
machine, Kutunda wondering what would become of her
and putting out through her shabby coussabe pungent feelers of fright and compliance, and Opuku apparently asleep, his
round skull scarcely lolling on his muscle-buttressed neck as
his dreams revolved (Ellelloû surmised from the man's moans
of unease) images of violence, of flame, of lust for the pale,
straight-nosed, black-clad nomad women. In Kush we never
cease dreaming of intercourse between dark and fair skin, between thick lips and thin lips, between wandering herdsman
and sedentary farmer.

The Mercedes had driven all night, to erase the fire from the
dark of our minds. Dawn had broken and passed. The landscape in the vicinity of Haïr is pink and flat, salty and shimmering; a dot in the distance dissolves or becomes a blood-colored
boulder the spaces themselves seem to hurl. Ellelloû in his
rumpled khaki was gazing forward through the windshield
over the shoulder of his driver while the head of the oblivious
Kutunda rested heavily on his shoulder. Then a dot placed at
the unsteady apex of the triangle the road's breadth dwindled
to—the horizon teetering upon its fulcrum, some bumpy paws
of the Bulub foothills being retracted on the right, a thorn-
mantled zareba just perceptible in the dusty depths to the left
—this dot enlarged with a speed out of proportion to that of
the Mercedes and declared itself, at a distance perhaps of two

kilometers, to be another vehicle. Within a few seconds, of time stretched like rubber by the laws of relativity, the alien vehicle was by, quick as the shadow of the wing of a hawk. Ellelloû marvelled, for the thing had appeared to be, not an explicable peanut lorry or piece of military transport, but a vehicle such as could not possibly be roaring along in Kush —that is, a large open-backed truck to whose flatbed were chained twin stacks of mechanically flattened bodies of once-bulbous, candy-colored American automobiles. Their engines had been removed, the space had been crushed wherein children had quarrelled, adolescents had made love, and oldsters had blinked mileage-mad holidays away.

In jerking his head to follow the truck's swift disappearance into the trembling pink folds of the north, Ellelloû awoke the fair Kutunda. For fairish, or merely dusky, she was, beneath the layers of dirt, with a round face and lips broad but not everted in form. Her lips as she attempted to respond to arousal seemed stuck by the mucilage of sleep to her small, rather inturned teeth. Her eyes widened, sensing Ellelloû's alarm. The colonel had grasped Mtesa's shoulder and, in the barking, shrill voice with which, over the state radio, he would announce some new austerity or reprisal, he was asking, "What was it? Did you see it?"

"Truck," the driver answered.

"What kind of truck?"

"Big. Fast. No speed limit out here."

"Did you ever see any other truck like it?"

The answer came after maddening deliberation. "No."

"Where do you think it came from?"

The driver shrugged. "Town."

"Istiqlal? Never. Where would it get those—those *things* it was carrying? Where was it taking them?"

"Maybe from Zanj going to Sahel. Or other way around."

"Who would let it through the border? Who would sell it fuel?"

Mtesa conceded, "Funny thing," but with no more concern than if he had seen an unusual bird at a water hole, or a bizarrely maimed beggar on the street. The ignorant see miracles every day.

It occurred to Ellelloû that Mtesa was bluffing, humoring him; he had seen nothing. He commanded, "Tell me what you saw. *What* funny thing?"

"Big truck toting squashed *voitures*."

"What kind of *voitures*?"

"Not Benzis."

Ellelloû slumped back defeated. He would have preferred that the truck have been his private hallucination. Better his own insanity, he reasoned, than that of the nation. The vision, if actual, placed upon him an unwelcome necessity to act, to cope with a strange invasion, for he knew that the affronting apparition was a commonplace sight on the clangorous, poisonous, dangerous highways of the United States. Kutunda, who had been asleep, and to whom the thing had been invisible, felt to occupy the only undistorted quadrant of the car, and in his weariness Ellelloû toppled into the comfortable vacancy of her fragrance of musk and dung, of smoke and hunger, of Kush.

Evidently upon his return to Istiqlal Ellelloû established Kutunda in an apartment above a basket-weaving shop whose real dealings were in hashish and khat; her presence here, and his suspicion of a conspiracy whose headquarters were in the capital, reinforced his habit of venturing disguised into the city, especially the disreputable section known as Hurriyah, which rises, like heaps of mud boxes stacked for removal, against the eastern wall of the vast Palais de l'Administration des Noirs, with its sixteen pilasters representing the sixteen most common verbs that require *être* instead of *avoir* as auxiliary in all compound tenses. Its façade is topped with eight marble statues of an unreal whiteness, uneroded in this climate, that symbolize the eight bourgeois virtures—*Assiduité, Économie, Médiocrité, Conjugalité, Tempérance, Optimisme, Dynamisme*, and *Modernité*. Its blank side glows in the dawn like the flank of an eternal, voluptuous promise heaving itself free of the earth, above the little roofs of thatch, cracked tile, and rock-weighted tin.

So it loomed in Ellelloû's eyes, as he blinked from the pallet he shared with Kutunda. In sleep her stringy, lustreless hair—so different from the soft and wiry curls that adorned, cut close or braided in ornate patterns, the skulls of Ellelloû's Salu sisters, and three of his four wives—had drifted stickily across her face; her hair held red streaks amid the black, and the kohl with which she had beautified her eyes had smudged. The dusty brown of her cheeks showed in the slant light linear shadows of a single diagonal tribal cicatrice, one on each cheekbone. The noises about them in the slum, the banging of calabashes and scraping of warm ashes and the unwrapping of hashish packets concealed in fasces of rattan below and the buzzing of children's recitation from the Koran school across the steep ochre alley, made it hard to return to sleep, his *salāt as-subh* performed, and Ellelloû lay there beside her hard-breathing unconsciousness like a thirsty man lying on the lip of a well, conscious that the nation was dying, that the beginnings of its day were the leavings of the night, that the dry sounds he heard, of rattling, scraping, unwrapping, reciting, were hopeless sounds, scavenging sounds, of chickens too thin to slaughter pecking at stones that would never be seeds. Allah Himself was dried-up and old, and had wandered away.

When Kutunda awoke, he asked her, "Would it help, to kill the king?"

She performed her duties in a pot and went about the room naked, carelessly mingling her limbs with the swords and sentinels of sun the horizontally slatted windows admitted in impalpable ranks. Shafts of radiant dust swirled like barber poles. The room was irregular in shape, with rafters of twisted tamarisk. The walls of hardened clay mirrored her skin, flickeringly, as, with the quickness of greed, with the slowness of delight, my mistress assembled the decorations and ornaments—the dab of antimony on each eyelid, the manacles of gold about her wrists, the heaped necklaces of fine beads tightly strung on zebra-tail hairs—allowable to the dictator's concubine. As a perquisite of this position, my waif set her jaw to give advice. Removed from the shadows of the tents and ditches of the north, Kutunda appeared older than when I had seduced her. Determined creases in her brow and about her pursed mouth betrayed some previous years of taking thought; vexations had worn their channels; perhaps a decade had passed since her first uncleanness. She had a squint; perhaps she needed glasses. "Tell me about this king," she said.

"He is feeble but clever, my captive and yet my protector, in some sense that made me reluctant to order his execution when L'Émergence broke forth, and when his violent death would have seemed unexceptional. All of Edumu's political and cultural conditioning tended to estrange him from the working classes and the peasantry. His regime was corrupt, in regard both to his personal tyranny—he was carelessly cruel in the antique, sensuous manner—and to the bourgeois ideology of his ministers, who to maintain their own prosperity within the pathetically unrepresentative elite were selling to the Americans what their fathers had sold to the French, who for that matter thought they still owned it. Their only maneuver, in the nation's war against misery, was to solicit, with much incidental bribery, another foreign concession, to build another glass hotel to function as a whorehouse for the *kafirs*. The difficulty with government in Africa, my dear Kutunda, is that in the absence of any considerable mercantile or industrial development the government is the only concentration of riches and therefore is monopolized by men who seek riches. The private vices of Edumu would have been trivial had his political orientation been correct, that is, had he offered in any way to overthrow the ancient patterns of adventurism and enlightened self-interest which were tolerable when moderated by the personal interplay of the small tribal unit but which are sheerly brutalizing when that interplay is outgrown. His conservatism, which I would rather describe as a feckless impotence, was masked by considerable personal charm, even kindliness to his chosen intimates, and by the smiling obscurantism of the hopeless cynic."

"The king," Kutunda said, her squint drawing her cheek-scars up, underlining what I perceived as a recalling of me to the business at hand, away from the rhetoric of "Poli Sci," with a seriousness that made me shudder in fear for Edumu, for this wanton woman (her odorousness now enriched by the spices and perfumes of the black-market shops) had a hard head for men's affairs, "the king is old?"

"Older than anyone knows, but not likely, I fear, to do us the favor of dying."

"That would be no favor," Kutunda said. "It would deprive the government of whatever appearance of incentive might be gained by his execution as a sky-criminal."

She used here a technical Sara term referring to an offender not against his fellow men but against the overarching harmony of common presumptions: "political criminal" might be our modern translation. Naked but for the bangles and unguents of beautification, Kutunda began to strut with the importance my ears lent her words. Her heels firmly struck the floor; her toes seemed to prolong her grip; her stride, back and forth in the little room, gave me cause to remember that her grandmother had been a leopard. Her legs were thick and slightly bowed; her buttocks had that delicious wobble of maturity. I began vaguely to long for sex. It stretched my bones, to think how much of my life had been spent listening to naked women talk. "One must look for the center of unhealth," she explained. "This center lies not, I think, within the king, who cannot help being the type of man he is, but within your mercy toward him."

"He took me up when I was less than a grain of sand, a soldier with falsified papers, and set me at his side. He made me a son, when he had fifty sons already. I would sooner spill the blood of my true father, a Nubian raider whose face vanished with the wind, than this old tyrant who forgave me everything, and still forgives."

"What have you done to forgive?"

"I was born of a rape. And now I govern a starving land."

"Why were your papers falsified?"

"Because the truth would have done me no good, nor will it benefit you."

Her sable eyes, that seemed to strain for focus, slid toward me, seeing that she had presumed. Her tongue moved on, more humoringly. "We must locate the center of the evil that makes the sky avoid the earth. They are lovers, the earth and the sky, and in the strength of their passion fly apart as quickly as they come together. They are like one of the white men's mighty machines; a single speck of evil will bring it to a halt. Now a demon does not occupy the entire body, but a pinhead point within it, for a demon has no necessary size, and must be small to fly. It may enter by a nostril or the anus, and take up residence in the gizzard or the little toe. Have you tortured the king, to find a spot where there is no pain? There the demon likely resides, and a heated dagger, thrust smartly in, will drive him out. But the surgery must be exact. Fingers make favorite burrows for the bad spirits; a reasonable precaution would be to slice off the old king's hands. I see you do not like that plan."

I had said nothing, merely attempted to visualize the event —the wrist veins pumping like the mouth of a jug, the eerie *Dasein* of the severed hand, still bearing its fingerprints, and the life-lines of its palm, though lifeless as wax.

Kutunda's head disappeared in her new green coussabe, one of several that had replaced the rags in which I had found her. Golden stitching of ecstatic concentricity stiffened its sleeves. Clothed, she became flirtatious and slimmer, and her gravely politic air dissolved into suggestions that were plainly malicious and jealous; she was jealous of my love for the king. "Cut off his testicles," she suggested, "and display them in the scales of the statue of Justice above the main portal of the Palais. *Wanjiji,*" she scornfully pronounced. "There has been no Wanjiji since my grandfather's time, and even then its men were famous for their cowardice and gluttony. In war they waited till the men of the other village were gone and then came in and butchered the children. Tear out his eyes and stuff them up his rectum, so they can spy out where his demon lives."

"A demon has come to live in *you,*" I observed, grabbing at the gaudy cloth as she swirled by. Her ankle-rings of bronze and silver tintinnabulated.

"God has nowhere to alight in Kush!" She dodged me, her lips snarled back from her inturned teeth. "On the highest peak there sits a wrinkled old man in a cell, guarded by a soldier in khaki who wishes to hide in the dust. So the Compassionate One flies on, His river flows on, the sky remains bright, and Kush remains barren. You need to make a show, Colonel Ellelloû, so Allah will notice us all. We are easy to forget. There must be blood. Blood is spirit, it draws down spirit. Dismember the king; tie his limbs to four stallions and give them the whip. His shrieks will dislodge the atom of evil and happiness will descend." She exposed her childish teeth in a grin, tilted her round head, and began to do up her greasy braids.

"Your plan has something to it," I heard myself concede, though at the thought of my patron's dismemberment my own limbs, their stir of lust ignored and dissipated, felt leaden.

Not that, at this stage of his disintegration, the colonel conspicuously neglected his official duties. He was generally at his desk, military green steel in his fanatically austere office on the corner of the Palais de l'Administration des Noirs overlooking Al-Abid—the rotting canopies of its dusty *souk*, its rickety wharves and pirogues slender as spears—for hours before Michaelis Ezana reported from his adjoining office, and the two drank together their morning chocolate and in their unending dialectical contention mapped the nation's path into the future.

Ezana was all facts and figures, a proponent of loans from the World Bank and grants from UNESCO, of schemes for dams and irrigation, of capital investments cleverly pried from the rivalry between the two superpowers (and that shadowy third, China, that has the size but not as it were the mass, the substance, to be called super), and more lately of hopes of financial rescue from their brethren in Islam, the oily, dollar-drunk sheiks of Kuwait and Qatar. At the outset of L'Émergence, Ellelloû had shared Ezana's enthusiasm for these manipulations of their sovereignty, as elaborate and phantasmal as the manipulations of the teeming spirit-world conducted by the witches and marabouts beyond the Grionde. But, seeing the plans come to nothing, or less than nothing—the expensive peanut-shelling equipment fall into disuse for want of repairmen, the wells drilled become the focus of a ravaged pasturage, the one dam constructed become the source of a plague of bilharzia-infested snails—Ellelloû had retreated from these impure involvements and watched with a sardonic detachment Ezana's energetic attempts to engage the world in the fortunes of Kush. The Minister of the Interior's habitual dress, formerly the rude khaki of a fighter for the people, now tended toward suits tailored in London, Milanese loafers, Parisian socks with rococo clocks, and, though silk was expressly forbidden to men by all the accreted moral authority of Islam, Hong Kong shirts of a suspicious suppleness; on his wrist he wore a Swiss watch of which the face, black, lit up with the hour and minute in Arabic numerals when a small side button was pressed. This watch fascinated his subordinates, who wondered where, in its scanty black depths, the device coiled the many minutes it was not called upon to display. So it was with Michaelis Ezana, who could produce whatever facts and figures were asked for, yet whose depths remained opaque. And scanty; for, however able and ambitious, Ezana utterly lacked that inward dimension, of ethical, numinous brooding, whereby a leader bulges outward from the uncertainties of his own ego and impresses a people. An observer seeing the two leaders bow their heads together in conference would have noticed that, though equally short and black, of the two Ezana gave more blackness back; blackness irrepressibly bounced and skidded off the spherical, luminous surfaces of his face. Whereas Ellelloû's was a mat black, the product of a long soaking-in. He tolerated Ezana because it was etched, on the crystal plane of things possible, that Ezana would never succeed him. Ellelloû's popularity, as reports drifted south of his flamboyant personal victory on behalf of the people against capitalist subversion, had surged to a height where suppositions of madness would not disturb it; so he dared, this morning, as the chocolate cooled at their elbows, to confide his visions to Ezana.

"Returning from the site of the repelled invasion," Ellelloû said, "in the region of Haïr, we saw a strange thing."

"A strange truck," Ezana quickly clarified. "As Minister of the Interior, Comrade, I have taken this sinister matter firmly in hand. The Bureau of Transport is at a loss. Of the two hundred twenty-six motored vehicles registered in Kush, seventy-seven of them public taxis and one hundred and four at the disposal of members of the government, the remaining forty-five registrants have been investigated and none answers to the description of a flatbed four-axle carrier of compressed scrap chassis."

"Who gave you, Comrade Ezana, such a complete description?"

"There were four of you in the automobile, of whom two, I believe, were awake. Draw your own conclusions."

Mtesa, a traitor?

Ezana smiled reassuringly. His plump fingers, loaded with gems like especially bright droplets of an enveloping lubricity, slid descriptively through the air. "The air of Kush is transparent, there are no secrets, only reticences," he said. "The truck is the thing. I cannot account for it. It is unaccountable."

"Also," Ellelloû ventured, comforted by the other's thoroughness, which brought all things shadowy into the light of numerical investigation, and might dispel even the dictator's unconfessed lassitude, "on the way north, in a gap of the Bulub hills, I glimpsed far off a golden arc, perhaps two golden arcs, I am not certain."

Ezana's fluid manner stiffened. "Did anyone other than yourself, my President, observe this apparition?"

"Neither Mtesa nor Opuku could confirm my sighting, though we halted the car and prowled the terrain for a vantage. Opuku had just pointed out the smoke of an encampment, and thus had drawn my gaze in that direction. If they had . . . one would have said . . . I thought . . . the region is strange."

"This was, I believe, the morning after your fatiguing night in the ICBM crib with the Russians, an experience in itself rather conducive to the unwilling suspension of reality."

"It was. But I was not so tired, nor so susceptible to the fumes of the alcohol spilled by uproarious barbarians, as to mistake my own eyesight. Could there be, I wonder, an ancient ruin in the vicinity, or an accessory Soviet installation the Minister of the Interior has omitted to acknowledge?"

"You are the Minister of Defense, and you know my opinion of this paramilitary foolery between the superparanoids. No need exists to double dummy rockets; and if it were the case why advertise the site with shining spires?"

"Not spires, arches."

"Whatever. The shimmer of the sand and the heated layers of air play strange tricks. Roul the desert devil delights in *trompe-l'œil*. Rest your mind, my President; I think the rumors of famine have troubled your peace of mind unduly."

"Rumors? They are facts."

"Exaggerated, moot facts. The Western press delights in making us appear incompetent. The nomads have always dragged our statistics down. Their way of life is archaic, wasteful, and destructive. Their absurd coinage of cattle has become ruinously clumsy. We must seize this opportunity to urbanize them. Already, the displaced nomads, and the sedentary farmers whose crops have failed or been consumed by the lawless herds, crowd to the edges of Istiqlal, where the tents and shacks, adjacent to the airport in full view of incoming flights, breed misery unalloyed by any suggestion of the picturesque. Their ancient nations have failed them; they are the citizens of our new nation, no longer of the Tuareg or the Salu or the Fulani or the Moundang but of Kush; Kush must reach down and house them, educate them, enlist them. This famine that so troubles you in truth is L'Émergence, given a fortuitous climatic dimension."

Ellelloû, though moved by echoes of his own rhetoric, asked, "Who will supply the wealth to house, educate, enlist as you describe?"

Ezana contemplated an upper corner of the room. "In the Ippi Rift," he began, "there is some interesting geology."

Ellelloû didn't hear. He had stood, to declaim, "The rich blocs each have client states whose prosperity is of more strategic moment than ours. Our place at the table will be the nethermost chair; let us remain standing, and at least trouble the conscience of the feast."

Impatience cinched shut the shining curves of Ezana's visage. "This feast has never had a conscience," he said. "We *are* at the table, Comrade, there is no helping it. There is no way a nation cannot live in the world. A man, yes, can withdraw into sainthood; but a nation of its very collective essence strives to prosper. A nation is like a plant; it is a lower thing than a man, not a higher, as you would have it."

"Yet the people look up, and must see something. You speak of the fortuitous; this is blasphemy. The famine exists, and therefore must have a meaning, both Marxist and divine. I think it means our revolution was not thorough enough; it left a pocket of reaction here in the Palais de l'Administration, on the floor below us, in the far wing. I know you know the king still lives. What would you say to his public execution?"

Michaelis Ezana shrugged. "I think it would be as an event not non-trivial. The king is already one with his ancestors."

Ellelloû warned, "It would horrify the world bourgeoisie, who are sentimental about monarchs. Their offers to bring us the benefits of their eight virtues might slacken, and your office would have less paper to handle."

Ezana repeated his shrug, exactly. "It would sever a strand

to the colonial past. He is your personal prisoner, deal with him as seems expedient." He reshuffled back into his briefcase the fanned papers—graphs, maps, computer print-outs—that again had failed to interest the President. Ellelloû sat down and sipped his chocolate, which had grown cool. But no mere tepidity had subverted its taste: there was something added and subtracted, something malty, ersatz, adulterate, mild, mellow, vitaminized. Ambushed by recognition, Ellelloû blurted out to Ezana the one word, "Ovaltine!"

Sittina, my third wife, lived in a villa among bushes of oleander, camel's-foot, and feathery bamboo, among children she no longer even pretended were mine and half-completed paintings, weavings abandoned in mid-stripe on the loom, and shimmering gowns which needed only to be hemmed to be finished. On the harpsichord, *The Well-Tempered Clavier* always stood open to the same fugue. She was too variously talented to push anything through to mastery. Soot-black, slender, the huge hoops of her earrings pierced through the tops of her cup-shaped ears rather than the lobes and touching one shoulder or another as she moved her lovely small tipped-back head, she was elevated and detached in her view of me, and I found this oddly confirming.

"So the Palais kitchen makes Ovaltine instead of pure Ghanaian chocolate for a change," she said. "What of it? You think you burned all the produce the Yankees are smuggling in? It's not that easy, they make tons more of junk every day. Don't worry about it, Félix. Face it, Africa is crazy about trading. Where else can you buy in the marketplace honest-to-God fingernail clippings? I mean, it's wild."

She said all this glancingly, over her shoulder, in her offhand American English. The daughter of a Tutsi chief, she had been sent in a time of Hutu massacre to a small all-black college in the state of Alabama, and indeed had set several sprint records there. The turn of her calves and the length of her thighs had won my heart, in the heyday of Edumu's restored rule, when she competed in the Noire Pan-African games of 1962. Though she had ever been in our marriage elusive, like the wind she raced with, I could never consider her a bad wife. Often in the bed of another, in my virile thirties, in the carefree Sixties, the thought of her pointed tits and trim bean-shaped buttocks had given me rise. Yet the reality of her was more mixed than the thought, the inner image of her. Sittina and I had not made love for four years, though the youngest of the glossy, long-skulled children that wobbled and prattled through the room, chased by parrots and pet patas monkeys, was under two. Sittina was wearing a loose-throated long-sleeved dashiki with rainbow-dyed culottes of crushed voile; they flapped and swayed with the movements of her wonderful impatient legs. She was engaged, in one of her abortive projects, with fashion design, and her outfit, so contemporary and timeless both, so Western and African, was one of her creations. But, she explained, between bursts of attention to the needful children—each of whom cast at me, in my unadorned khaki, the glance one gives a gardener or messenger boy who has come six steps too far into the house—that it was impossible nowadays to obtain cloth or even needles and thread, that there was nothing for sale in the markets but the cheapest sort of *merikani*, faded bolts the missionaries must have brought, and that since the Revolution had reduced the European community so drastically there were no customers anyway, the wives of the Kuwaitis never came out of their compounds, the Albanian women were stringy-haired savages smelling of wet wool, and that awful Mrs. Ezana—how can he stand her?, she's *such* a bluestocking—went everywhere barebreasted, as a sign of political undeviation. *Pas chic*, Sittina said. Her words had all the substance of a complaint but not, truly, the tone. I felt I had come on the afternoon of a visit to or by some lover; hence her benign, if abstracted and hurried, manner. She continued, "What are you doing about the drought? Even the price of a goat head is out of sight. A single cassava brings two hundred *lu*. You put some millet paste on the windowsill to curdle and in five minutes it's stolen. The refugees from the north come into town and rob —what else can the poor things do? My night guard had his throat slit the other night and walked home in a sulk. Don't ask me where *I* was, I forget. They took the stainless steel flatware and two of my old trophies but hadn't the sophistication to steal the Chagall." The Chagall, of the customary upside-down Jew smiling at a green moon, had been our wedding present from the king. Now it hung on the far wall between an Ife harvest-drama mask and a Somali saddle-cloth of an exceptionally elaborate pattern. Sittina, who bore the name of a Queen of Shendy, had furnished the spacious living-room of the villa in a scattered "artistic" style with sub-Saharan arti-facts whose solemn blacks and browns, whose surfaces of red-stained animal hide and hollowed gourd still redolent of the organic matrix from which they had been gently lifted by the last stage of manufacture consorted with the glib rectilinear-ity and mechanically perfect surfaces of the Danish armchairs and glass-and-aluminum coffee tables that had been salvaged from the pillage of the European quarters in 1968. The whole room, with its cracks and gaps and air of casual assemblage and incompleted intentions, seemed an insubstantial sham compared to a room I could suddenly remember, of white-painted moldings and unchipped knick-knacks, of impregna-ble snugness and immovable solidity, tight as the keel of a ship, carpeted wall to wall, crammed with upright, polished, nubbled, antimacassared furniture including a cabineted tele-vision set and a strange conical table of three platterlike shelves that held a gleaming trove of transparent paperweights con-taining in their centers crinkled paper or plastic flowers, evil eyes of all colors whose stare seemed a multiform sister to the grave gray-green Cyclops stare of the unlit television screen, all this furniture in this exotic far-off room sharing a feel-ing of breathless fumigated intrusion-proof cleanness that pressed on my chest as I waited for someone, love embodied, as perfect and white as the woodwork that embowered her, to descend the stairs; the varnished treads and slender balus-ters did a kind of pirouette at the foot of the stairs, a skillful cold whirl of carpentry that broke, by one of those irruptions to which my mind was lately prone, through the dusky mud tints of Sittina's villa, the tender fragility of things African, the friable dishes and idols and houses of earth moistened and shaped and dried again, of hides and reeds crumbling back to grass and dust, of the people themselves for their bright moment of laughter rising out of the clay and sinking again, into the featureless face of Allah, which it is the final bliss for believers to behold, through the seven veils of Paradise. My memory laid a cold curse on the present moment. Sittina's offhand beauty, the sense of suspension her mind spun, in the disarrayed room, as she waited for me to leave, so she could proceed with that life of uncompleted curves that amused her, underlined the desolation known only to those who live between two worlds.

But who, in the world, now, does not live between two worlds?

"I'm glad," I said to her, of the Chagall; and of the drought: "We are taking steps."

"God, Félix, the depression rolls off you like a stench."

"Sorry. Something about you touched me just then."

She made a swift movement, testing her hair, which was pulled back from her skull and intricately pinned by two dried fish spines. The women of Kush spare no pains to knit and knot their hair in extraordinary patterns. No doubt there is a Marxist explanation for this, having to do with a disproportion of available labor to available materials, all history testifying, with the tedious workmanship that crowds our museum cases, to a terrible excess of life, of time, that overruns all crannies as tropical tendrils embroider every inch of available light. Sittina's gesture had been flirtatious. She offered, haltingly, "I have an appointment to go out, but if my lord . . . has come in search of his . . . rights, I will stay. Cheerfully. It once . . . we . . . I am attempting to apologize for something I am not certain I caused. Until the Revolution, we were together enough. Is that not so?"

"It is so, Sittina. Your shadow in a dark room . . ." I could not finish, the memory slipped its sheath.

"Did I become an enemy of the people, that I had to be rebuffed?"

The recollection of her warm shadow, the sudden scissoring embrace of her long thighs, my hand underneath those taut buttocks, overlaid the stuffily immaculate living-room with its evil dance of balusters and staring glass *objets*, and I found myself too sliced, by successive waves of lost experience, to explain well what I did wish to share: "Under the old king, there was a kind of life possible, which we borrowed from him, his vitality and his unexamined assumption that he was right, right to demand and consume what so many strained to donate out of their poverty. When he was displaced, much that was let us say healthy and morally neutral went with him, inextricably

involved as it was with the corruption, the bourgeois feudal-
ism, the unpurged way of looking at things. You and I were
among the innocent sweepings. I am sorry."

She said, "I had forsaken my father for you, at a time when
he lived hunted in the mountains. When the tide of massacre
reversed, he beckoned me to take my place among the Tutsi as
a princess. I declined. And still I stay here with you, though all
Africa says you are crazy."

"Is that so?"

"It is so that they say it. The truth of what they say, I cannot
judge. Our traditions treat madness as sacred, and we look to
the sacred to rule us."

"The appointment you are about to keep, does it excite
you?"

"It did. Now you've confused me."

"Remember our trysts, under the stadium, when we were
children of the king?"

"The king, the king. *You* are king now."

"Do you still make that cooing noise, when you spread your
legs?"

"I have said, I will stay." She spat, a Tutsi courtesy.

"Go. My blood is heavy in me."

"I must say, you're spreading a lot of guilt around."

"Some day, when the land is healthy again, it would please
me to be enlisted among the men who serve you, Sittina."

"You deserted, when this army contained no body but
yours. And I understand you brought back a Sara wench from
the north, and have installed her above a basket shop."

"A matter of state, merely. The woman acts as my adviser."

"Ask me my advice"—her words kept rhythm with the vigor
of her circular motions as she wound a turban about her skull,
and finished with a swash around her throat—"and it would be
to give Kush back to old Edumu and the frogs and get some
decent pâté back in the shops."

"I liked what you said about madness," I said. "Did you
know," I went on, unwilling, somehow, to have this dishevelled
visit terminate, "that the British once had a plan of flooding
the entire Sahara, before they realized it was a plateau? They
thought it would fill like a bathtub because it was under the
Mediterranean on their maps!"

Sittina was setting off, swooping here and there to kiss her children like a black heron dipping her narrow head to catch fish; half-unthinkingly she finished by kissing her husband, the swoop and dip being minimal here, because the dictator of Kush was a mere six inches shorter than she. Her breath, snatched inwards in the exultation of her departure, smelled of anise. As she retreated, the cut of her culottes, and a lift given her figure by the addition of the turban, made her look high-assed.

"I love you," said Ellelloû, unheard.

The trial of the king proceeded smoothly. The revelation that he was still alive proved, surprisingly, to be no surprise. The populace had always sensed it. The monarch's health was still drunk in the palm-wine bars, in the narrow stalls where the faithful chew khat while the pagans swallow *barasa* and guinea-corn beer. Even in the public schools, in the lists of the Lords of Wanjiji, the reign of Edumu IV was learned with an open dash, without a date of termination.

For the sake of the foreign press, then, developments within the Palais de l'Administration des Noirs were staged through a successive lifting of veils of rumor. The first rumor was that the king had been living in exile across the river, among the loyal Wanj who continued their life of trading fish and hippo teeth for salt and juju beads under the remote rule of Captain Bokassa of former Oubangui-Shari. The next rumor was that the king had ill-advisedly crossed the Grionde to lead a revisionist, pro-monarchial coup; this preposterous attempt, founded on fantastical CIA intelligence that the people of Kush were disenchanted with L'Émergence and SCRME, of course failed, encountering on the north bank of the river the magnificent solidarity of the Kushite national conscience. The third rumor claimed that, amid terrific loss of life among his followers, the king was taken into custody, and (this was the fourth rumor) captured papers revealed that the severe food shortages of recent years had been caused not by the climate of Kush nor its bountiful soil but by royalist conspirators within the administration. According to the fifth rumor, Lieutenant-Colonel Michaelis Ezana was superbly extirpating these anti-people, pro-feudalist traitors from the Department of the Interior and the Bureau of Transport, which had been discovered exporting foodstuffs to neighboring Sahel, along whose border one massive illegal cache had been discovered and destroyed by the personal vigilance and action of Colonel Ellellou himself, in response to information provided by a female patriot, Kutunda Traorē, a *griot* of the doughty Sara tribe.

Mentioning Kutunda had been Ezana's idea, not mine. He had met her at my office, where she would visit me during the heat of the mid-day to enjoy the air-conditioning and to bring me lunch of peppered raw mutton and honied manioc from the Hurriyah market, and to borrow some *lu*. The rustle and intricate engraving of paper money delighted her innocence; in the village of her girlhood there had been, apart from heads of cattle, only two types of currency, both rare—giant bars of iron impossible for a woman to lift, and tiny round mirrors that, if dropped, were hard to find. Ezana spoke a rusty dialect of Sara, and spent hours with Kutunda, giggling and yelping over his own grammatical errors.

For the people of Kush, a pronouncement was promulgated:

TO ALL CITIZENS OF KUSH

Le Suprême Conseil Révolutionnaire et Militaire pour l'Émergence announces that miserable *Edumu* formerly known as *Lord of Wanjiji* has been found *Guilty of High Crimes and Misdemeanors* against the *People* and *Physical Environment* of *Kush*, leading to *Widespread Shortages*, *Dislocations*, and *Suffering*. The *National Honor of Kush* and the *Will of Allah* demand that *Justice* be *Done* to this *Reactionary and Discredited Exploiter of the Many*, Who in the course of his *Mockery of a Reign* appropriated to Himself the *Means of Production* and the *Headwaters of Revenue*, as well as *Wantonly* and without *Mercy* ordering the *Deaths and Ignominies* of those who served Him, and privately doubting to his *Intimates* the *One True God*, the *Compassionate* and *Merciful*, Whose *Prophet* is *Mohamet*. *A*foresaid *Edumu*'s Very *Presence* in the *Land* dilutes and *Undermines* the *Scientific Socialism of Kush*; this *Blot* upon *Our Flag* will be *Joyously Removed* the twelfth *Day* of *Shawwāl* in this Year *1393 A.H.*, in the Square of the *Mosque of the Day of Disaster*, within the *Holy Capital of Istiqlal.*

Colonel H. F. Ellellou
President of Kush
Chairman of SCRME

This announcement, printed on green placards, was posted on the walls of the city, and was chanted, in Arabic, Berber, French, Tamahaq, Salu, Sara, Tshi, and Ga, from the minarets of the mosques, from the windows of the Palais de l'Administration des Noirs, from the weathered wooden balconies of the Indian shops and the reed roofs of the riverside *souk*. Word had even been posted in the panoramic revolving restaurant of the glass skyscraper the East Germans had erected to the glory of socialism.

Yet the crowd that came to the execution was small. By midmorning the sun stood high and the clay of the square, packed by the passage of footsteps to the smoothness of ivory, was white to the eye and scalding to unsandalled feet. Several military trucks had been aligned and the sides removed, to make a platform for the ceremony. King Edumu, bobbing with the aftereffects of his interrogation, which had focussed on the soles of his feet, and blinking in this unaccustomed breadth of light, which penetrated even his crazed corneas, was led forth in white robes by some soldiers who, it was clear from their carriage and aura, had greeted this great day with tumblers of *kaikai*. The meagre throng, at least half of them children given a school holiday, attempted a cheer that ebbed into puzzled sullen silence as the king, his little body more than once having to be disentangled from his voluminous, luminous *lungi*, was lifted into position on the flatbed of the central truck, where Ellelloû, Ezana, and the nine other colonels were seated on folding chairs. A headblock had been hacked of blood-red camwood. The king stood awkwardly beside it, not knowing at first which way to face. Behind him, in a ragged arc doubled, as a rainbow is sometimes doubled, by an arc of parasols above it, wives and offspring and lesser government officials crowded the subsidiary trucks and even perched on the cab roofs. Of Ellelloû's four wives, none had deigned to appear, but Kutunda Traorē was present, resplendent in a cascading emerald *boubou* and a turban that Sittina had designed. Vivaciously speaking to one bureaucrat and then another, tossing her head and switching her hips, she had appointed herself the hostess of the occasion. Ellelloû searched her face vainly for traces of the smudged whore he had found among the well-diggers. Why, he wondered, generation after generation, century after century, must vulgarity repossess all the energy? Still, Kutunda's childish delight and stocky self-importance alone struck, in this atmosphere of embarrassed, underpopulated anticlimax, the ringing bronze note of gleeful release and public complicity he had hoped for.

Not quite alone; for there was another who entered unembarrassed into the occasion, and that was the king. Though crippled by age and inquisition, and more insecure in his gestures under the vacuous dome of sky than in the close-walled cells of his confinement, the king had the forms for his feelings. Beneath the glitter of his gold headband and the cloud of his unshorn wool his fig-dark features shone with formal courage. The little arc of his nose aimed, amid the insolent hubbub, in the direction of the citizenry. They, with the exception of a few children, had tucked themselves well back from the trucks, in the alley-mouths and beneath the café-awnings at the shady rim of the square. So far from continuous, a blanket of unified humanity as Ellellou had imagined, it was a crowd of clots, as recalcitrant-appearing perhaps as those clots of blood from which Allah first fashioned men. The king lifted his arms.

He spoke in no language that Ellellou knew. A few of the crowd, its drowsy buzzing ceased, stepped forward from the alleys and the awnings onto the blazing clay, better to hear; these were the ones who understood Wanj. Thus the blackest and most stoic faces sifted forward, leaving behind the brown, the reddish-tan, the merely dusky. The king in his blindness stared directly into the sun, orating.

"People of Wanj, rejoice with me! Today I go to join our ancestors, who live below, who are our blood! These mad soldiers who attempt to govern us are puppets of the ancestors, who dangle them a moment before they toss them aside. If their rule is just, why has the sky-god withheld rain these five years? They say Edumu is the center of the sickness, but when I was the Lord of Wanj and had bewitched the French with their little round hats to be my policemen and scribes, rain fell in abundance, and the palms poured their wine upon the ground, and there were not enough camels in Noire to carry our peanuts to Dakar! Of what am I accused by these poor soldiers, those apostles of '*le socialisme scientifique*' [for Wanj had no words for this concept]? Of black magic, of being '*un élément*

indésirable' within the fabled purity of Kush! I say Kush is a
fiction, an evil dream the white man had, and that those who
profess to govern her are twisted and bent double. They are in
truth white men, though their faces wear black masks. Look
at them as they sit behind me, with their fat wives and fatter
children! What have these men to do with you? Nothing. They
have come from afar, to steal and enslave. I challenge them by
the ancient code of Wanjiji: let him who accuses me execute
me! If a demon give his hand strength, then guilt shall travel
up his arm and become his soul's burden. If he falter, then I
will live, and those who speak Wanj will still have a Lord and a
living connection with the gods of their ancestors!"

The crowd hissed and murmured in its desultory way; the
sun, mounting higher, was draining purpose and clarity from
the holiday. Colonel Wambutti, who spoke Wanj, crouched
forward and murmured the gist of the king's words into Ellelloû's ear. The President promptly nodded, comprehending the
challenge. He stood and glanced about for the executioner's
sword.

Credit the now (in some quarters) discredited Ellelloû
with the grandeur of his response in this hour. Squeamishly
he had absented himself from the interrogations of the king,
and upon the occasion when the old man, his feet so flogged
their soles had become bubbles of livid flesh, had indeed confessed to conspiring with Roul the desert devil and with Jean-
Paul Chrêmeau, the Christian, alexandrine-indicting premier
of Sahel, to bring about drought and demoralization, Ellelloû
had been prowling the city disguised as an orange-seller; by
the time the President could be located and brought to the
dungeon, the king had recanted, and hurled at him an absurd
litany of American trade-names—"Coca-Cola! Polaroid! Chevrolet! IBM!" Indeed, the scandalized marabouts and professional torturers agreed, devils were at work here. Ellelloû had
gone pale at the outburst, and turned on his heel.

Not so now. A power beyond him descended and gave him
calm. He stepped lightly to the king's side.

The king said softly into the sun, "I know that step."

"Are you sure?"

The king did not turn his head, as if to avoid what glimmers of my face might come to him. He preferred to rest his

gaze in blank radiance. "Another saying came to me after our conversation."

"What was it, my Lord?"

"*Wer andern eine Grube gräbt, fällt selbst hinein.* Who digs the pit for others, falls in himself. It was said of their Führer, by my old friends."

"A pit awaits all of us. Yours is no deeper than others. You are simply at its lip."

"I was not thinking of myself, but of Colonel Ellelloû." He laughed; it was like a small fine box being crushed underfoot. His body smelled, faintly, of cloves.

"It is not I who acts," I said, "but Kush."

"Then, there can be no talk of mercy?"

"It is not a lesson I was well taught."

"Your teacher perhaps had too much to teach."

"It would be an impiety to usurp the prerogative of the Most Merciful. Why talk of mercy among men, when justice can be achieved?"

"Can it?"

"See." Behind his back I extended my hand. Opuku was holding the giant scimitar, taken for this ceremony from its case in the People's Museum of Imperialist Atrocities, for in the name of ethnic integrity the French had permitted executions in this classic manner until the importation of the guillotine, now also in the Museum. The Suprême Conseil had rejected the idea of bringing forth the guillotine for this state occasion as savoring of neo-colonialism. All of the executions during the early Émergence had been by firing squad. Blue smoke had risen from the inner courtyard of the Palais in rectangular clouds, like cloudy cakes released from a mold. Think of it. My mind in its exalted, distended condition had time to entertain many irrelevant images. Think of the blade of that guillotine, wrapped in straw and burlap to protect its edge, but perhaps gaps worked loose in the wrapping causing glints of reflection to fly across the desert as the pack-camel swayed on its way as it brought humanitarian murder to this remotest and least profitable heart of Africa.

The handle of the scimitar, bronze worked to imitate wound cord, nearly fell from my hand, so unexpectedly ponderous was the blade. In this life woven of illusions and insubstantial impressions it is gratifying to encounter heft, to touch the leaden center of things, the *is* at the center of *be*, the rock in Plato's cave. I thought of an orange. I lifted the sword high, so that the reflection from its flashing blade hurtled around the square like a hawk of lethal brightness, slicing the eyes of the crowd and the hardened clay of the façades, the shuttered fearful windows, the blanched, pegged walls and squat aspiring minaret of the Mosque of the Day of Disaster. In the glare of the sky the swooping reflections were swallowed, disgorged again upon the earth as the scimitar was lowered and steadied. A speech in response to the king's seemed called for.

"People of Kush! Be deaf to this criminal's blasphemies! Gladly your President takes into his hand the instrument of God's rectitude! Praise Him Who abides! *The unbelievers love this fleeting life too well, and thus prepare for themselves a heavy day of doom!* The day of doom has come to the alleged Lord of Wanjiji! He is an empty gourd, a mask without a face! When Edumu ruled, he gathered to himself riches that your labor created. He took to himself your most lissome women, and called your best land his own. The toubabs levied their taxes through the maze beneath his throne; under cover of his kingship the riches God has hidden in our mountains and our river were ferried away. Infidel harlots in countries of fog and clouds are adorned with our jewels because of this betrayer. Sentimental elements within the Suprême Conseil have preserved his life to this moment! This was a mistake, an abomination! God has cursed this land accordingly! By the sword in my hand I shall cleanse the land! Sacredly is it written: *Idolatry is worse than carnage.* Those of you who moved forward to hear the words of Wanj, hear these words! The Lord of Wanjiji is a clot of blood, a speck upon the purity of Kush. His life has been long and odious. He is cunning. His wisdom is barren. He has mocked Ellelloû. He has mocked the Revolution. I act now not as myself, not as Ellelloû, but as the breath of L'Émergence, blowing away a speck of dirt! God's will gives my arms strength! Behold, those who doubt!!"

Opuku meanwhile and one of the colonels—Colonel Batwa was my impression, an ex-prize fighter—attempted to bring the king to kneel and place his head on the saddle-shaped block of red camwood. The king in his blindness, or out of some notion of abused dignity, resisted; there was more kick in his old body than one would have thought; the crowd chuckled a bit. I could feel, through the pink mists my verbal frenzy had set to swirling in my skull, his sensations, his struggling stiff frailty; I entered in, was pushed and pulled among jostling shelves of muscular darkness, of dazzling not-seeing. My hair was gripped, a hardness knocked against my chin, sun-hot camwood scorched my throat. A smoky smell. The orange in my mind rolled away. The king's head had been arranged on the block. Looking down, I had become perilously tall. The path the scimitar must descend through air appeared a long flaw in crystal. A few drops of sweat glinted in the net of wrinkles on the nape of the old man's neck, bared as Opuku, perhaps rougher than need be (it crossed my mind), tugged forward for me the mass of Edumu's hair, matted and yellowish like a sheep's. I eyed my spot between two vertebrae. Incongruously, there entered my mind from afar the image of a candy apple, such as one buys at county fairs in Wisconsin—its tough glaze, its slender wooden stick, its little cap of coconut. The first bite is the most difficult. The king cleared his throat, as if to address one of us. But his thought went nowhere, a trickle in the hot sands of his terror, and an intense mechanical interest arose like a hiss of steam from the point between two cervical lumps where two wrinkles conveniently crossed. Opuku's hands gripped deeper into the wool, as if the king were tensing to struggle, and I saw that the moment I wanted with all my being behind me was still a fraction of a second ahead. The divine breath grunted into my chest and the scimitar descended. Though the blade struck through to the wood, the noise was clumsier, more multiple, than I had expected.

Sun. The clay of the square was accepting yet another day's merciless brilliance. An edge of green metal, unpainted where the paint had chipped the flatbed's crimped lip took my eye. I found I was waiting, in the pocket of sharp quiet before the crowd loosed an appalled, triumphant roar, for the king, as his throat-clearing had promised, to say another word.

The very ink in my pen coagulates at these memories.

Robust Opuku held up the king's head at arm's length, as the center of an opposing basketball team demonstrates his intimidating one-handed grip. Relief at the thing accomplished flowed through me, so I was slow to notice how little blood flowed from the severed head. This medically explicable fact

—the brain in its fury to live had drawn blood up into itself like a sponge—was to haunt the kingdom I had inherited. The king's eyes were blissfully closed, while his body in its silken white *lungi* flipped about with a hideous undirected strength, even the arms flailing. Opuku with a booted foot pressed the body flat, as the chopped throat, romantically rich in purples and blues, spilled blood sobbingly. There came uninvited into my mind the flat side of that candy apple, where it has rested while hardening, and where the sugary semi-elastic glaze was thickest. The taste of this glaze, bitten into, and its stubborn texture were as vivid to me as Kutunda's cry of joy, a thrilled fe-male keening less voluntary than a dog's howl, cutting through the stunned air. A host of gnats had come to drink.

So it seemed from the truck—gnats, blood, a crimped edge of metal, and irrelevant fairgrounds memories all compressed by the sunlight into one unfeeling, unmeaning moment, through which there coursed nevertheless a palpable liquid re-lief. From the vantage of the crowd, it looked far otherwise: Ellelloû's neat brown figure, sunglassless, stepped forward and with a leverlike stroke altered the quality of the smallest of the puppets posed on a makeshift stage. The head was held up. Then other puppets, unpredicted, appeared: blue-clad Tuareg, the lower halves of their faces covered by *tagilmusts*, perhaps twenty of them, on fine Arabian horses rode in from the east-ern side of the square, mingled with the khaki men on the green trucks, and after a tussle carried off the smaller of the king's two bodily remains.

Up close, Opuku received a slash on his arm, and Colonel Ezana's wife was the butt of an indecent suggestion; but the very speed of the attack (which had the crowd been as numer-ous as expected would have been disastrously impeded) and its apparently limited objective of carrying off the severed head enabled it to pass like a loud but harmless wind. Some of the crowd thought the episode merely a part of the governmental pageant that had been arranged.

Ellelloû with admirable presence of mind addressed those spectators that had not fled the scene. "Citizens of Kush! Fear not! The alleged Lord of Wanjiji is dead, his would-be rescuers have had to content themselves with the unspeakable refuse of his physical remains! His soul has gone to everlasting fire! The forces of imperialism and reaction have again been thwarted! There is no doubt that these brazen terrorists are hirelings of the American paper tiger, or perhaps fanatical capitalists disguised in the robes of the Tuareg! We of Le Suprême Conseil Révolutionnaire et Militaire pour l'Émergence laugh at their presumption and invite the socialized people of Kush to defecate upon their individualistic, entrepreneurial violence!! The loathsome theft shall be avenged, have no fear! Disperse to your homes, and prepare for the deluge! You have witnessed the enactment of a purgation profoundly pleasing to Allah, and deeply beneficial to our green and pleasant land!"

Ellelloû shouted all this, in a rapture of abandonment to the furious wind within him, that could be vented only into the imaginary ear of his nation, but in his private aspect knew that his accusations were problematical, for he had seen the eyes of the raider who had snatched the king's head from Opuku's slashed arm, and they were not the wolvish eyes of a Targui or a North American, frosted and blue, but amber and slant like the survival-minded eyes of wild swine. Also, Ellelloû, transfixed by his battle-calm, waiting through a microscopically lucid series of milliseconds to be tumbled like a rabbit by a lion, too tranquil to think of lifting his bloodied scimitar in self-defense, scented through the flurry of odors of unwashed flesh and Arabian horsehair a subtle sweetness chiming with his memories of the banquet in the rocket bunker. Vodka.

While the capital still buzzed of these portentous events (which the majority of the indolent populace had lacked the civic conscience to witness, and which, in the recounting to the unpatriotically absent, became unreal), Ellelloû descended into the Hurriyah district in the disguise of an orange-seller, to visit Kutunda. Now that the effects of the drought and famine were felt even in the metropolis, there were no oranges to sell, and the peddler instead offered to the echoing, anfractuous alleys the mere image of oranges, put into song:

> "*Round and firm as the breasts of one's beloved's younger sister,*
> *she who exposes her gums when she laughs,*
> *and spies from her pallet wondering when her time will come;*

to the touch delicately rough like one's own testicles,
stippled waxy hides tearable and acrid when torn,
staining one's fingers with the sharpest essence of the juice;

when the hide is scattered like thick rose petals,
the fruit is found partitioned in quarter-moons,
each in its papery baby skin dulcet as dust;

parted from its many brothers too greedily,
each segment will weep bright tears of juice,
foreshadowing the explosion in the consumer's mouth;

how sweet is the water of the juice! Our lips sting,
the rivers of our heart rush upward
to greet the miracle secreted in this symmetry!

And the color, what is the color? The color
is that strip of the heavens closest to the dunes
before the green flash announces the arrival of night."

For such a song, which the singer elaborated through many variations—evoking in some versions the navel and the crusty button at the poles of the orange, dwelling rhapsodically in others upon the tasteless mossy inside of the skin that holds the drops of nectar like jewels in a felt-lined case, and in still others upon the joys of spitting out the seeds—coins or cowries would be cast from the windows, appearing in his path like a sudden spatter of the rains that had failed to come, or paper notes would be thrust at him by servants sent out by the wealthy; for with the drying-up of merchandise to buy, *lu* had become plentiful, and many were in a cash sense wealthy. People would attempt to bribe him to sing a song of bananas, or couscous, or spring lamb turned on a spit with peppers and onions, but he would say No, he was a seller of oranges, and could conjure up only *their* image amply enough to banish the reality of hunger.

Kutunda was finding her quarters above the basket shop insufficient. Her new possessions—billowing clothes, bulky jewelry, inlaid tables, throw pillows, cuddly stuffed Steiff animals, mechanical beauty aids, a hair-blower and a WaterPik—were overwhelming the little pisé-walled room which a month ago had seemed such a grateful improvement over the exiguous spaces of a tent or a ditch. Ellelloû, removing the stained robes and net yoke of an orange-seller, noticed on her wrist a watch with a blank black face. "A gift," she admitted. "Look, you press here, and the numbers come up! It is what they call electronic wizardry."

"In exchange for what service to Ezana?"

"For my services to the state; my wisdom and counsel."

"In urging the murder of the helpless old king?"

"I merely urged what your heart had already decreed but lacked the courage to execute."

"Lacked the madness, I now think. What good has come of it? The sky is as blank as your watch-face, and horror clouds my heart. Since the day, Ezana is formal and correct with me; I feel he is standing clear of my ruin."

"Ezana will dodge as you turn. There is no leader left in Kush but my colonel. Let me show you the clothes I bought; the shopgirl said they were designed by a Tutsi princess." As she walked back and forth to her bulging cedar wardrobe, her heels thumped in the manner specifically enjoined by the twenty-fourth sura, *And let them not stamp their feet in walking so as to reveal their hidden trinkets*, the same sura that says consolingly, *Unclean women are for unclean men, and unclean men for unclean women*. She hurled one width of rainbow-dyed cloth over her head, wriggled it smooth, gazed at herself in the mirror with pursed lips, held a bloodstone earring against the lobe of one ear, and rejected the outfit by baring her tiny teeth, bowing her head, swinging her hands to the nape of her neck, giving the garment a sharp forward pull, and becoming naked again, her stout legs first. Her buttocks in the seriousness of this ritual had a tightened tuck, a flattening of their outward curve that touched me with its sign of pliant aging.

Yet, in bed, in darkness, my manhood recoiled from her familiar maneuvers of hands and mouth, grown since our desert courtship to fit my predilections as closely as a worn saddle fits its camel's humps. Now her mouth, moist as it was, burned; whenever my stalk verged upon response, upon enlargement and erection, the picture entered my mind of the king's severed neck, its pulsing plumbing suddenly sliced across and emptying itself, by spurts that seemed sluggish, into the crystalline vacancy of that moment before the Tuareg, too late, galloped into the square. The blood of mine that had been flowing to produce the engorgement of potency fell back, alarmed. "You are angry with me," Kutunda at last observed, weary of wanton exertions.

"Why would I be?"

"You mourn the king."

"Had the whim ever seized him, he would have done worse to me. He took me up, I think, because he was amused by my ambivalences. Even his mercies were sardonic. He sat on the world lightly, like the spider that is immune from the web's stickiness."

"Yet you found my hatred vulgar, and further bear against me the grudge men always bear against those women they have conquered. It is a puzzle: the men who need women hate them, and those who do not, like your comrade Ezana, do not."

"More your comrade than mine now. You have a magical timepiece to mirror his, and the two of you giggle in Sara, hatching my doom."

"*You* are hatching it," Kutunda said, as quickly as she had set an ornament to her ear and taken it away; yet she could not take this truth away, though from the pinch of her lips she wished she could. *Unclean*, we are all unclean, with our smudges of truth.

I said to her, in explanation of my impotence, "You have lost the good smell of dirt you had in the ditches of the north. Now you stink of French soap. I cannot make love through the fragrance of our exploiters."

"You are sad. Forgive me my fun with Ezana. He is an innocent man, but so full of words and ideas; his being practical gives us much to talk about. It is exciting. We talk of the refugee camps, of re-education, of irrigation, of eliciting capital investment from the superpowers and multi-national corporations, with low interest rates and twenty-year moratoriums."

"It is futile. We have nothing they need. We are no one's dominos. Tell me a story, Kutunda, to distract me from my shame, as you used to in the ditches, when you would come to me from poor limp Wadal." Remembering this man made me wonder, Could she be the source of impotence, driving her from man to man in an orgy of betrayal? These modern women have yet to evolve a modern male to service them.

She told me a strange tangled story, of intricate blasphemy, as once of Wadal urinating on the fetishes, only now of Michaelis Ezana, who beneath his buttery black outward form was Roul the desert devil, a creature of blanched bones and arbitrary flesh, who sets lakes all around us, yet renders the spot where we stand burningly dry. Men in their thirst bite their fingertips and suck the salty blood; they kill their camels and drink the mucoid fluid in the stomach of the carcass. In this guise Ezana rules Kush, driving the whirlwind of the Tuareg on before him, eroding the pious and egalitarian republic of his archenemy Colonel Ellelloû. In the remoteness of the Ippi Rift there is a city to rival Istiqlal; here men copulate with pangolins, and women allow hyraxes to enter their vaginas, and all the moisture that Allah had allotted for the land of Kush is kept in a giant transparent sack underground, entered through a cave mouth of golden arches, a wobbly sloshing bubble deeper than a gypsum mine, and descending into it Ezana takes the form of an octopus, and sucks screaming, drowning maidens into his beak, and awaits the maiden, a maiden dusky and fearless and virginal, with teeth dainty as seed-pearls, who with a scimitar of tourmaline will sever the octopus beak of Roul though he eject a cloud of ink; and then she will puncture the transparent sack so that water will flood the land, and the bones of her father's herds will come to life, lowing, and the tamarisk and *Mimosa ferruginea* will bloom, and camels will become intelligent dolphins, and what other turbulent nonsense Ellelloû was never to know, for he fell asleep, amid the sliding of Kutunda's solid limbs and the nightmare shapes her voice conjured up.

He was awoken at dawn by twin sharp needs: to urinate and to pray. His duties performed, he lay beside the woman; in her sleep her hair had made tentacles across her face and a trail of saliva from the corner of her lips gleamed indeed like some trace of a subaqueous struggle.

Through the slats at the foot of the pallet the white flank of the Palais de l'Administration des Noirs glowed pink and mute in the first flush of light. Thus, Ellelloû saw, loomed political power immemorially to the masses of men: a blank wall, a windowless palace that inscrutably shoulders us away.

Also he perceived that a new strange sound had come to mix with the scratching dry noises of the Hurriyah slum—ashes being scraped, calabashes clicking, the Koran being murmured. From somewhere under him music was arising, rasping muffled music of an alien rhythm, with words, repeated in the tireless ecstasy of religious chant, that seemed to say:

> "*Chuff, chuff,*
> *do it to me, baby,*
> *do it, do it.*
> *Momma don't mind what Daddy say,*
> *we're gonna rock the night away.*
> *Do it, do it,*
> *do it to me, baby,*
> *chuff, chuff, sho' enough,*
> *ohhhhh.*"

III

SOLDIERS AT the command of the government systematically searched the hovels of Hurriyah for transistor radios, cassette players, four-track hi-fi rigs, and any musical instrument other than the traditional tambourine, *alghaita, kakaki, hu-hu,* hour-glass drum, end-blown reed flute, or that single-stringed instrument, whose sounding box is a goatskin-covered calabash, called the *anzad*. Ellelloû at this point in time vigorously prosecuted the cause of cultural, ethical, and political purity in Kush. Any man caught urinating in a standing position, instead of squatting in the manner of Mohamet and his followers, was detained and interrogated until the offender could prove he was a pagan and not a Christian. Overzealous enlistees from the swaddled north seized and flogged young girls on the banks of the Grionde, under the impression that their bare breasts imitated decadent French fashions. The flocks of secretaries working within the corridors and anterooms of the Palais de l'Administration des Noirs were enjoined from wearing tight skirts and blouses; the corridors and anterooms were obediently thronged with loose *boubous* and *kangas*. Yet underneath these traditional wrappings, Colonel Ellelloû suspected, the women were wearing elastic Western underwear, spicy brands called Lollypop and Spanky.

Within the inner rooms of the Palais he and Ezana conferred not quite as usual; a new note, a post-coital irritability, had entered their discussions since the execution of the king. That had been Ellelloû's trump; Ezana still held his cards. Though for state occasions he still appeared in the revolutionary uniform of khaki, taking his place in the row of SCRME sub-colonels as alike as the ten digits of two gloves on their balcony or viewing platform, in the privacy of his office he had taken to wearing powder-blue or even salmon-pink leisure suits, with a knit shirt open at the neck and cuffless trousers of tremendous flare. The Marxist explanation for this flare, Ellelloû thought, would be the same as for a sultan's pantaloons, or a burgomaster's lace. He felt his own thin khaki tight on his back as he leaned forward, appearing to plead, in that tense voice which even when amplified by giant loudspeakers had something of the anxious, as of an impediment overcome, about it: "There is a conspiracy. The dreams of the people are being undermined."

Ezana smiled. "Or is it the dreams of the people that are doing the undermining?"

Ellellou said, "They would all acknowledge that we are on the right path, were it not for this cursèd, adventitious drought."

Ezana's smile contained one gold tooth, which seemed squarer than the others. "The drought cannot be adventitious and cursèd both. If we believe in curses, we do not believe in accidents. At any rate, my comrade, who in Kush denies that we are on the right path? Save for the paltry few imperialist quislings and extinct fossils enjoying re-education in what were once the wine cellars of the French? The security forces of the Department of the Interior, supplemented by antiterrorist squads of the Kushite army, have found no radios, no trucks loaded with crushed Fords and Chevrolets. True, in a closet of a Koran school, the troops unearthed a cache of bubble gum. But we have always known that there is a black market dealing in Western luxuries smuggled in from our doctrinally unsympathetic neighboring states, or lingering from our own lamentable pre-revolutionary era.

"Let us not, however," Ezana continued, and Ellellou marvelled at the inexhaustible smooth machinery of the man's mouth, that functioned within the resonating mellow hum of self-delight, "discuss trifles. Let us discuss peanuts. To natural disaster, my President, world geopolitics has added economic distress. The nub of it is, now that the Americans are no longer vexed by Vietnam and the Watergate imbroglio promises to remove from their chests the incubus of Nixon, they have woken to the fact, long patent to the rest of the world, that they as a race are morbidly fat. An orgy of dieting, jogging, tennis, and other narcissistic exercises has overtaken them, and—this is the *crux*—among the high-calorie casualties of their new regimen is the unsavory stuff called peanut butter. Apparently, spread on so-called 'crackers' and unappetizingly mixed with fruit-imitative chemical 'jellies' between slices of their deplorable rubbery bread, this paste formed a staple of the benighted masses' diet. Well, in the national lunge toward athletic slimness and eternal physical youth, less peanut butter is being consumed, and the peanut growers of their notoriously *apartheid* South are compelled to export.

"Nothing, Comrade Colonel," Ezana went on, with a louder and more urgent tone, seeing his auditor stir and threaten to interrupt, "more clearly advertises the American decline and coming collapse than this imperative need, contrary to all imperialist principles, to export raw materials. Nevertheless, for the time being, their surplus peanuts are underselling our own in Marseilles, and those farmers who at governmental urging devoted their land to a cash crop now wish they had grown millet and yams to feed their own children. Without the francs the peanuts would have brought, we lack the hard currency with which to procure replacement parts for the Czech dynamos, and electricity will fail in Istiqlal."

"Not a bad thing, perhaps," Colonel Ellellou offered, caressing his cup of chocolate, which he had tasted warily, and found unimpeachable. "Kush will revert to God's light, and not turn the night to uses inveighed against by Mohamet. *By the light of day, and by the fall of night, your Lord has not forsaken you.* What has electricity brought us, I ask, but godlessness and ever more dependence upon the Czech middlemen?"

Ezana's gold tooth flashed as he flipped a piece of yellow paper across his desk to the President. "Without the mercy of electricity," he said, "we would be deprived of communications such as this."

Ellellou read: REPLY SOONEST ALL INFO RELATING DISAPPEARANCE DONALD GIBES OFFICER USAID ACTING CONJUNCTION W/FAO AND WFP NEAR NW BORDER KUSH SEP 1973. URGENTEST. KLIPSPRINGER UNDRSCTRY DEPT STATE USA.

Ellellou said, "They must have meant Gibbs. Nobody is called Gibes in America."

"The probable," Ezana told him, "is not always the actual. In regard to this cable, what shall our government do?"

"No answer is more eloquent," Ellellou answered, "than no answer."

"Men may follow this piece of paper. And after the men, guns and airplanes. This Gibes was precious to somebody."

"Gibbs, it must be," Ellellou said. "Gibes is an insult."

"Be that as it may, if his government make this man's fate

a point of honor, the effects may be disproportionate, as so lamentably often proves true in affairs between nations. The Americans have not the Asian discretion of our friends the Soviets, who take such lasting pleasure in bullying the already subdued, and in surviving the incarceration of their own winters. The Americans have the chronic irritation of their incessant elections to goad them into false heroics, and if I understand them historically have reached that dangerous condition when a religion, to contradict its own sensation that it is dying, lashes out against others. Thus the Victorians flung their Christianity against the heathen of the world after Voltaire and Darwin had made its tenets ridiculous; thus the impoverished sultan of Morocco in 1591 hurled troops across the Sahara to occupy Gao and Timbuctoo, a conquest that profited him nothing and destroyed the Songhai empire forever."

"I do not know Americans," Ellelloû lied. "But I do not think that having just extricated themselves from the embrace of General Thieu they will risk themselves against the starvelings of Kush."

"Exactly not," Ezana agreed, with a pounce as jarring as disagreement. "Until the moralistic Vietnam misadventure fades, they will content themselves, like our ex-mentors the French, with selling hardware to all sides of local conflicts and keeping the peanut-oil supply lines open."

"In that matter of peanuts and electricity," Ellelloû ventured, "might the Banque de France consider another loan?"

"Interest on present loans, my good President, plus the salaries of our civil service, account for a hundred and eleven per cent of the Kush national budget."

Ellelloû's heart sank at the statistic.

But Ezana said, "Not to worry. These debits are in fact credits, for they persuade the capital-holding countries to hold us upright. Meanwhile, all capital drifts to the oil-exporting nations. From there, however, it drifts back to the countries that produce machinery and luxury goods. Praise Allah, we need no longer, in a sense, concern ourselves with money at all, for it exists above us in a fluid aurosphere, that mixes with the atmosphere, the stratosphere, and the ionosphere, blanketing us all with its invisible circulations."

"By these as by other circulations, it never rains on Kush."

"You exaggerate. There was an exceptionally heavy dew just this morning. In the global aurosphere there can be transient lows and highs, but by the laws of the gases nothing like a complete vacuum. Our turn will come; perhaps it is already coming."

"In the form of Big Stick telegrams." Ellellού found this conversation depressing, all the more deeply so because of Ezana's mental nimbleness. This man's twinkling joy in being among the elite was the opposite of infectious. To take pleasure in power seemed childish sacrilege. Power was reality, power was grief. Ellellού felt his heart falling down through the veils of semblance into the utter vacuity upon which all things rested. Lives, millions of lives, hung on Ellellού's will and dragged it down. The famine weighed upon him sickeningly. Energy had silted to the bottom of his soul. He had returned to this hypothetical slice of desert, steppe, and savanna grateful for its searing simplicity, on fire with the wish to seal off its perfection; but his will had not averted congestion—rather, had become an element within it, this confused, derivative congestion of the actual, of which Ezana, with his rapid fingers and shapely leisure suit, was the condensation, the gleaming dewdrop on the nettle of the nation.

"What if we respond," he was suggesting, tirelessly, of the cable, which in Ellellού's mind had already been consumed, and turned into snow like the first dry biting flakes that announced the November beginnings of the Wisconsin winters, when a second, white continent was imposed upon the green, brown first, "with a cable protesting CIA interference in the internal affairs of Kush, that is, their clumsy and ghoulish, how can we say, *caput*napping of the king, who was executed with full legality, by the Koranic and Marxist codes? We would have no trouble producing evidence of culpability; even the footprints they left on the dust showed a tread-pattern peculiar to American sneakers."

"They were on horseback."

"Several dismounted, in the flurry. Abundant clues fell from their pockets. Jackknives, dental floss."

"Overabundant," Ellellού said.

"We can send irrefutable wirephotos. Cheaper, we can leak glossies to *Nouvelles en noire et blanc*, to which every Western embassy subscribes."

"And yet," Ellellô said, "the one Targui who passed close to me had Russian breath. Beets and vodka."

Ezana shrugged. "There is a sweet green tea the Tuareg drink that smells similarly."

"And yet you say this was not the Tuareg, but the CIA."

"I do. This CIA, did it not arrange for the assassination of its own President and his brother? There is no fathoming their devious designs. They are a cancer that grows of its own mad purposes."

"This fury of anti-Americanism," Ellellô observed, "comes strangely from my Minister of the Interior."

Ezana spread his fingers, their nails manicured to a lunar lustre, upon his glass desktop as if to confess "the jig was up" and he would "level." He said, "I wish to discredit in advance rumors that may distract my President."

"Rumors of what?"

"Of a sad absurdity. Among the superstitious rabble of our poor retrograde nation, some say that the king's head, magically joined to its spiritual body, talks prophecies from a cave deep in the mountains."

Ellellô had not heard this rumor, and it lit his depression like a splinter of moon in the depths of a well. "Again," he pointed out, "something Russian in this. The Bulubs are proximate to the missile crib."

Ezana sat back, and sipped his chocolate, contemplating his President much as the black face of his wristwatch contemplated the turn of the heavens. Ellellô, his heart lightly racing at the possibility that the king had in some sense survived and therefore his own responsibility was in some sense mitigated, sipped his own chocolate. "Not the Bulub Mountains," Ezana told him, "but the Balak."

"The Balak? In the Bad Quarter?"

Ezana nodded complacently. "Where not even the *National Geographic* has been."

The Bad Quarter: the trackless northeastern quadrant that borders on Libya and Zanj. Neither scorpions nor thorns thrive there, not even the hardy *Hedysarum alhagi* eulogized by Caillié. Wide wadis remember ancient water, weird mesas have been whipped into shape by wicked, unwitnessed winds. By day the desert is so blindingly hot and pure the sands in some declivities have turned to molten glass; by night the frost cracks rocks with a typewriter staccato. Geometrically perfect alkali flats end as abruptly as floors at the base of metamorphic walls soaring as by reversed lava flow to crumpled crests where snow had been sighted by Victorian explorers, in a century more humid than ours. "I must go there," Ellelloû said, the will to do so being born in him as airily as a dust devil on the Square by the Mosque of the Day of Disaster; Ezana's complacence evaporated.

"I cannot advise that, my President," he said. "You are putting yourself at the mercy of fate."

"Where all men are, at all times."

"Some in more dignified postures than others."

"My posture is always, simply, one of service to my country."

"How can you serve your country by chasing phantoms?"

"How else?" It may be, Ellelloû reflected [and I now, with greater distinctness, write], that in the attenuation, desiccation, and death of religions the world over, a new religion is being formed in the indistinct hearts of men, a religion without a God, without prohibitions and compensatory assurances, a religion whose antipodes are motion and stasis, whose one rite is the exercise of energy, and in which exhausted forms like the quest, the vow, the expiation, and the attainment through suffering of wisdom are, emptied of content, put in the service of a pervasive expenditure whose ultimate purpose is entropy, whose immediate reward is fatigue, a blameless confusion, and sleep. Millions now enact the trials of this religion, without giving it a name, or attributing to themselves any virtue. That rumored cave, undoubtedly a trap, which Ezana for some devious reason wished me to avoid, though he would enjoy the freedom of my being away from Istiqlal, beckoned to me; my whim as man, my duty as President, compelled me there. For have not African tyrants been traditionally strangers to their domains, and should not ideal rule attempt to harmonize not only the powers, forces, and factions within the boundaries but the vacancies as well, the hallucinations, the lost hopes, the dim peoples feeble as ropes of sand?

Yet Ellelloû was slow to depart, and remained in Istiqlal all the month of Shawwāl, which the Salu call the moon of hesitation. The Tuareg *iklān*, whom the Western press unfairly referred to as slaves, pried loose cakes of salt from the crusted bed of Lake Hulūl and brought them south to trade for smelt, yams, amulets, and the aphrodisiac powder whose principal ingredient was ground rhinoceros horn. Michaelis Ezana zealously watched the economic indicators for signs that this annual salt harvest might be reversing the long Kushite recession.

One day Ellelloû, in full panoply of state, the solid green national flag fluttering from the fender of his Mercedes, visited his first wife, Kadongolimi, at her overcrowded villa in Les Jardins.

He was met at the door by a bony bare-chested man with the slant eyes and taut coffee skin of the Hausa; though the hour was eleven in the morning, this fellow was already drunk on palm wine, and Ellelloû identified him as a son-in-law. Within the villa, the rooms had been so bestrewn with goat hides and raffia and the ceilings so blackened with the smoke of cooking-fires that the atmospheric tang duplicated that of the dictator's native village, where he had wed Kadongolimi at the age of sixteen. Children, some of them presumably his grandchildren, teemed and shrilled through the battered, notched, bedaubed doorways of the villa; the louvers and latches of the windows had been smashed and jammed so that a hut darkness reigned in rooms designed as if to admit the colorful kind light of southern France. The smells of rancid butter, roasted peanuts, pounded millet, salted fish, and human eliminations mixed in an airy porridge that Ellelloû's nostrils, after a minute of adjustment, found delicious: the smell of being Salu. He unbuttoned the top button of his khaki shirt and wondered why he didn't visit Kadongolimi more often. Here was earth-strength.

A chastely and utterly naked young woman came and took his hand, with a naturalness that only a daughter could bring. He fished for her name and came up with only the memory of her face, with its arching little braids and slightly drooping Kadongolimi-like lips, mounted on a shorter, chubbier body, without this swaying adolescent slimness. She led him through the maze of clatter and clamor, the rooms alive with squatting groups and pairs mending, stirring, crying, feeding, scolding, crooning, loving, and breathing, all under the sanction of the fibrous, staring fetishes of hacked wood and stolen fur and feathers, supernatural presences not repugnant or ridiculous in their setting but one with the mats, the grinding stones, the wide bowls and tall pestles, not disposed decoratively as in Sittina's eclectic villa but here used as the furniture of daily life, brown and rough as a seed pod splitting to let new life through. His old tongue came back to him, spoken with that accent of overemphasis peculiar to his native stretch of the pea-nut lands, with the swallowed *l*'s and pop-eyed clacks of his mother's people. Nephews, daughters-in-law, totem brothers, sisters by second wives of half-uncles greeted Ellelloû, and all in that ironical jubilant voice implying what a fine rich joke he, a Salu, had imposed upon the alien tribes in becoming the chief of this nation imagined by the white men, and thereby poten-tially appropriating all its spoils to their family use. For there lay no doubt, in the faces of these his relatives, that through all the disguises a shifting world forced on him he remained one of them, that nothing the world could offer Ellelloû to drink, no nectar nor elixir, would compare with the love he had siphoned from their pool of common blood. And it was true, at least, that since he had taken office this villa had absorbed the villas to the right and left of it and become a sprawling village compound in the heart of Les Jardins, lacking only the spherical granaries of whitened mud looped around the huts like giant pearls.

His naked daughter led him across a courtyard where the flagstones had been pried up to form baking ovens. Across the way, through a cloister, Kadongolimi had established se-date quarters, darkened and fragrant, where she held court to the hosts of her progeny. She had grown fat as a queen termite, and spent hours propped in a half-reclining position in an aluminum-and-airfoam chaise longue the white occupi-ers of this villa, great sunners and users of Bain de Soleil, had abandoned when one day the servants no longer answered their clapping and instead a boy of a soldier appeared and announced that they, being the wrong color now, had been deposed from the Istiqlal elite. Kadongolimi when she took possession had had the chaise longue dragged indoors and made it her daybed. Two docile tots fanned her bulk with palm fronds. Her cheeks were marked with the semi-circular tattoos that, until outlawed by SCRME, identified and beautified the

brides of the Salu. Her earlobes had been pierced and distended to receive fist-sized scrolls of gold on days of festivity
and pomp; today, empty, her lobes hung like loops of thick
black shoestring to her shoulders. She lifted a pink hand, a
pulpy-petalled small flower put forth by a swollen old limb.
"Bini," she said. "You look like carrion. What is eating at you?"

She called him "Bini," his Amazeg name, by which she had
known him since the age when he had squirmed down from
his mother's hip and begun to walk. Kadongolimi was four
years older than he. When he was five, she was a leggy screech-
ing personage of nine, bossy as a mother. A cousin, her hands
had rattled on his skull in the courteous search for lice. When
they married, she had been a woman for a third of her life, and
the shuddering, rustling bushes of her experience interposed
between them their first nights. Her superiority never left them
but became enjoyable. Ellelloû in her presence floated as in
an oily bath, underestimated, weightless, coy. To Kadongolimi
he would always be a child who had just left his mother's hip.
There being no chair in the room, he squatted down on his
hams, plucked a twig from a bush poking through a hole in the
wall, and began to clean his teeth.

"The gods," he answered diffidently, tasting the twig. Some
substratum in the phloem or xylem savored smartly of those
little glossy red American candies prevalent in wintertime, that
relenting time of winter when the icicles crash from the eaves
and the black streets shine with the melting of drifts.

"You should never have forsaken the gods of our fathers,"
Kadongolimi told him, gingerly shifting her pontifical weight
in the precarious hammock of aluminum.

"What had they given our fathers," Ellelloû asked his wife,
"but terror and torpor, so the slavers Arab and Christian alike
did with us as we did with animals? They had the wheel, the
gun; we had *juju*."

"Have you forgotten so soon? The gods gave life to every
shadow, every leaf. Everywhere we looked, there was spirit.
At every turn of our lives, spirit greeted us. We knew how to
dance, awake or asleep. No misery could touch the music in us.
Let other men die in chains; we lived. Bini, as a boy you were
always active, always pretending to be something else. A bird,

a snake. You went away to fight in the white man's wars and came back from across the sea colder than a white man, for at least he gets drunk and he fucks."

Ellelloû nodded and smiled and tasted the twig, moving it from tooth to tooth. She had said these things before, and would say them again. His replies too had the predictability of song. He said, "I returned with the true God in my heart, the Lord of the Worlds, the Owner of the Day of Judgment. I brought back to Kush the God half of its souls already worshipped."

"The empty half, the cruel half. This God of Mohamet is a no-God, an eraser of gods; He cannot be believed in, for He has no attributes and is nowhere. What is believed in in our land, what gives consolation, is what remains of the old gods, the traces that have not been erased. They are around us everywhere, in pieces. What grows, grows because they are in the stem. Where a place is holy, it is holy because they live in the stones. They are like us, uncountable. The God who made us all made us and turned his back. He is out of the picture, he does not want to be bothered. It is the little gods that make the connections, that bring love and food and relief from pain. They are in the *gris-gris* the leper wears around his neck. They are in the scraps of cloth the widow ties to the fire bush. They are in the dust, they are so many." Her great black arm, with a gleaming wart in the crease of the elbow, dropped at her side; she flung a pinch of dust at her squatting husband.

Perhaps the twig he was chewing contained in the inner bark an hallucinogen, for the dust seemed to grow in the air, to become a jinni, a devil, with boneless hands and too many fingers: the spectre of the drought. Kadongolimi laughed, exposing toothless gums.

"How are the children?" he asked.

"Bini, we had no children, they all sprouted from other men. You were a boy who had no idea where his *kiki* should go. Then you returned from the land of the toubabs a twisted man and took younger wives. The long-legged Sittina, who has led you such a chase, and the One Who Is Always Wrapped. Then the idiot child Sheba, and now I hear there is yet another, a slut from the desert."

"Kadongolimi, let not your grievances, which are somewhat real, destroy all other reality. The children born before the French conscripted me to defend their plantations in Asia surely were mine, though their names escape me."

"You were not conscripted, you enlisted. You fled."

"You had grown huge, in your flesh and in your demands."

"Bini, you always fantasized. You left me slender as a bamboo."

"And returned to find you big as a baobab."

"Seven years later, how could I be unchanged? You avoided me. You avoided me because you knew I would discover the secrets of your absence. I discovered them anyway."

"Spare me hearing them. Sell them to Michaelis Ezana. He has set up a talking head in the Bad Quarter to discredit my regime. I am going there to confront this marvel."

Pity leaped in her, as a frog disturbs a pond. "My poor Bini, why not stay in Istiqlal, and rule as other leaders do—give your cousins assistant ministerships, and conduct border disputes with other nations to distract us from our poverty?"

"Poverty is not the name of it. A barefoot man is not poor until he sees others wearing shoes. Then he feels shame. Shame is the name of it. Shame is being smuggled into Kush. A blow is needed, to reawaken our righteous austerity."

Kadongolimi said, "You killed the king."

"Imperfectly. Ezana manipulates the body."

"Why do you blame Ezana?"

"I feel him all about me, obstructing my dreams."

"Reality obstructs your dreams. Ezana wishes only to administer a reasonable state."

"A state such as Kush is too thin to be administered except by gestures. When we effected the Revolution, we discovered a strange thing. There was nothing to revolutionize. Our Minister of Industry looked for factories to nationalize, and there were none. The Minister of Agriculture sought out the large land holdings to seize and subdivide, and found that most of the land was in a legal sense unowned. There was poverty but no oppression; how could this be? There were fishing villages, peanut farmers, mammy markets, goats, elephant grass, camels and cattle and wells. We dug deeper wells, that we could do, and that proved a disaster, for the herds then did not move on but stayed until the grassland around the wells had been grazed to dust. We sought to restore autonomy to the people, in the form of citizens' councils and elections with pictographic ballots, but they had never surrendered autonomy in their minds. The French had been an apparition, a bright passing parade. The French had educated a few *assimilés*, given them jobs, paid them in francs, and taxed them. They were taxing themselves, to govern themselves. It was exquisitely circular, like their famous logic, like their villanelles. Ezana does not see this. He admired the French, he admires the polluting Americans and their new running dogs the Chinese. He mocks our allies the Russians, whose torpid monism throbs in tune with our own. He hired Russian double agents to impersonate Tuareg, so I would become confused. He has seduced my Sara protégée with promises of an office of her own, and typing lessons, and contact lenses! Forgive me, Kadongolimi, for troubling your repose with this tirade. I feel sore beset, infiltrated. I can appear thus disarmed only with you. Only you knew me as I was, hoeing the peanut fields, and playing *ohwari* by the hour. You remember my mother, her violence. My father, his absence. My brothers, their clamor and greed. My uncle Anu, his lopsided smile and lasciviousness, that extended even to she-goats, and the leg, its nerves severed by a Nubian bayonet, that compelled him to become a carver of masks. I came to ask after our seed, our children. That silent girl with budding breasts who led me in, was she ours? We last clasped a dozen years ago, and she would be not younger than that. Kadongolimi, remember the games we would play—I the lion, you the gazelle?"

"I remember less each year I lie here, forgotten by my husband. I remember a boy who didn't know where his *kiki* should go."

Ah, Ellelloû. He was stricken with the unsatisfiable desire to rescue this his first woman from the sarcophagus of fat into which she had been lowered and sealed, to have her come forth as again half of the young lithe couple they had been, amid curtains of green, the conical roofs and circular granaries of their village scattered like dewdrops along a web of paths that threaded outward into cassava patches and pastures yielding to the broad peanut fields with their elusive musky fragrance of starch. And when the wind blew, the grasslands beyond whitened in clusters of racing pallor like racing deer, white-throated, white-rumped waterbuck and the oryx with his slim slant horns. Giraffes would come into the peanut fields from the acacia plains and with splayed front legs and lowered necks feed from the tops of the drying stacks, and be chased away by the boys of the village clapping together bowls and pestles and rattling gourds. Drifting like clouds the giraffes would canter away, their distant mild faces unblaming, the orbs of their great eyes more luminous than the moon. In this village, where all was open and predetermined and contiguous and blessed, Kadongolimi had confided to him in the dappled shelter of sun-soaked bushes the smell of her pleasure, the taste of her sweat. In harvest season they would hollow caves in the heaped mountains of uprooted, drying peanut plants. The skin of her back took a hatched imprint. She had been careless of herself, bestowing her body wherever she was admired with the proper courtesies, the requisite hours of dancing, heels stamping the earth, the ceremonial sleeplessness. But when betrothed to Bini she drew upon herself, with the shaved skull and crescent tattoos, the dignity of a bespoken woman. He remembered the long arc of cranium the shaving exposed, and the silver curve of sun upon it when she came, still wet from her ritual bathing, to be accepted by his mother as her daughter. By the forms of the marriage, which lasted days, Kadongolimi curled on a mat like a newborn while her mother-in-law touched her lips with milk symbolic of her own. Bini watched this awestruck by its implication of a solemn continuum of women, above him, around him, always. And he remembered how the shaved skull thrust forward Kadongolimi's face, the insolent long jaw, the heavy lips like numb, dangerous fruit. He remembered her ears, then delicate and perforated to receive only the smallest rods of gold. And in their own hut her soft muffled salty smell, and her genitals simple as a cowrie. While he slept, the morning outside resounding to the blows of her pounding millet to meal, for him, her husband. Sun shuddered in the heaved fan of chaff. The depth of lost time made him dizzy; he stood, spitting out the twig. His thighs ached, their muscles stretched by the unaccustomed squat.

Kadongolimi, too, met resistance, seeking to arise. The naked girl, who had been standing unnoticed in the shadows, stepped forward; Ellelloû, startled by the motion, turned his head, and his gaze was splashed by the sun-saturated bougainvillea the vanished colonists had planted in the patio, now gone wild. He and the girl raised Kadongolimi to her feet; the woman gasped, astonished to find her spirit wrapped in so much inertia, in the weight that sagged as if to crack his arms and shoulders and then swayed away onto the slender girl, whose breasts were the shape of freshly started anthills.

"Tell me," Ellelloû whispered to his wife, "is she not ours?"

"Oh, Bini," she grunted. The effort of standing nearly smothered her words. "You are the father of us all. What matters the paternity of this good child? You yourself were born of a whirlwind. She loves you. We love you. In this house you will be welcome when all else crumbles. Only be not too long. In your absence, weeds spring up. Even the earth forgets."

One bright day Ellelloû, walking the streets in the stiff blue disguise of a government messenger boy, saw, along one of the narrow sandy lanes that zigzagged down from Hurriyah, a Muslim woman wearing freaky sunglasses. Unlike his severe NoIRs, they were round-square in shape, oversized, attached to the temples below center, and more darkly tinted at the top of the lens than at the bottom. Otherwise she was wearing the traditional black *buibui* of Muslim women, thong sandals, and a veil. She disappeared into a doorway before Ellelloû could halt her and ask at what illegal and subversive market she had made her purchase. He would have cited to her the holy verse, *Unbelievers shield their eyes; the truth continues to blaze.*

In the void created by her vanishing there blossomed then the memory of a tree of sunglasses he had seen when new in the land of the devils, in 1954, he a young deserter enrolled as a special student at a liberal arts college in the optimistic city of Franchise, Wisconsin. He had wandered on that September day, its slanting sunlight peppered with sprinkles of scarlet in the ponderous green of these North American trees, among a thousand white students, through the questionnaires and queues of college enrollment, and across the wide main street, as a-whirl with traffic as a dance of knives, to the awninged bookstore, where in accordance with his course requirements he loaded up with Tom Paine, the Federalist papers, the

Arthur Schlesingers, a typographically frenzied scrapbook of masterly American prose, a lethally heavy economics text in a falsely smiling cover of waxen blue, and empty notebooks that he himself was to scribble full of lectured wisdom, their covers mottled like long-rotten wood and their pages suggesting fields of endless thin irrigation ditches. His purchases left him thirsty. From under the awning next to the bookstore he glimpsed through a wide pane of reflection-shuffling glass, above a jumble of faded cardboard totems, a counter that promised some kind of drink, perhaps a silvery *arak* or, in accordance with the symbols advertising sun-tan lotion, palm wine. Ellellou was not then the devout and abstemious Muslim he became. He entered. The hazards and betrayals of military service and his remarkable flight, which had taken him from Dakar, where he was to have been reassigned to the Algerian struggle, to Marseilles and then London and Toronto, where he was hidden in the French-speaking ghetto behind Queen Street, had not prepared him for the interior of this American drugstore, these walls and racks crowded with intensely captive spirits, passionate, bright, and shrill, their cries for the release of purchase multiplied by the systematic madness of industrial plenty. Boxes contained little jars, little jars contained capsules, capsules contained powders and fluids that contained relief, catharsis, magic so potent, as advertised by their packaging, that young Hakim feared they might explode in his face. In another area there were intricate instruments, sealed upon cardboard with transparent bubbles, for the plucking and curling and indeed torturing of female hair, and next to these implements blunt-nosed scissors, children's crayons, paper punches and yo-yos and, farther on, rows of Mars Bars and Good 'n' Plenties and Milky Ways laid to bed in box after box proximate to a rack of toothbrushes, dental floss, and abrasive ointments phallically packaged and chemically fortified to resist the very decay that these celestial candies, marshalled inexorably as soldiers on a parade ground, were manufactured to generate. Hakim's instinct was to smash, to disarray this multifaceted machine, this drugstore, so unlike the chaste and arcane *pharmacies* of Caillliéville, where the sallow Frenchman in his lime-green smock guarded his goods behind a chest-high counter showing only a few phials of colored water. This place was more like a

witch's hut of murky oddments hurled to infinity by omnipresent mirrors, even mirrors overhead, circular suspended convex
mirrors which foreshortened into dwarves the slack-faced toubab sons and daughters as they shuffled along these artificially
cooled aisles like drugged worshippers selecting a pious trinket
or potion from the garish variety of aids to self-worship. Sickly
music flowed from invisible tubes in the walls. Hakim, in the
loose brown suit of an overweight separatist who ran a bistro in
colonized Ontario, paused before an upright rack of tall cards,
vulgar and facetious, yet which these U.S. indigenes in their
ancient freedom were apparently meant to mail to one another
in ritualized insult; many of the cards had a tactile element,
a piece of fuzz glued to a bit of cartoon clothing, a passage
of cardboard raised in the manner of hammered trays from
Baghdad, and even, in some of the cards, a hole that appeared
to reveal something indecent (*un derrière*), which, when one
opened the card, was revealed as something innocuous (a plate
of pink ice cream).

"Don't touch."

"*Pardon?*"

He identified the voice as arising in the loose-skinned throat
of a scrawny besmocked oldster, prodigiously pallid, his forehead blotched by some evidently non-tropical skin disease.
"Hands off, young fella. Get those cards dirty, they ain't worth
nothin' to nobody."

"*Je vois.*" Dirty? Moving away, he nearly bumped into a tree
of sunglasses. Less a tree, in truth, than a bush, the height of a
man, armored in many dark eyes. The whole thing sluggishly,
unsteadily rotated. Bini, the future Ellelloû, quickly put his
dirty hands behind his back, to display to the querulous attendant that it was not he who was touching this prodigious, fragile array, causing it to tremble. It was, he saw, a young white
woman on the other side. With impatient authoritative jerks
of her slender bare arms she was pushing at the rack to make
it disgorge the, for her, ideal pair of sunglasses. She plucked
out a pair with flared tinsel frames, set them deftly but rather
roughly on her thin-lipped, decisive face, and sharply asked
Hakim, "Whaddeya think?"

"*Charmante,*" he brought out, when he realized she was
addressing him.

She replaced the frames, not in the slot where she had found them, and seized a pair with rims of pale-blue plastic, the lenses also blue. These, blanketing the upper half of her face, emphasized the chiselled prettiness of her mouth and the angry-seeming spatter of freckles across her nose. "Not so good," he said, remembering to speak English this time. "Too much blue."

The girl put on a third pair, and this time smiled—a fierce quick smile that pounced upon the space between her pointed chin and bone-straight nose—for when I solemnly looked to give my third verdict, the dark lenses were mirrors, and what I saw, my brown suit swallowed by the two receding drugstores packed into the girl's mocking sockets, was myself, badly shaven, badly dressed, bug-eyed with youth and fright. Her name was Candace. We were to meet often, as fellow freshmen, and became lovers. She was blond. When her summer's freckles faded, her whiteness was so powdery I imagined I could lick it off.

"Our parched lips sting / and the rivers of our heart rush upward / to greet the vivid juice of symmetry," Elleloû sang, climbing the narrow brick stairs that ascended to the second floor from the panelled and bossed ancient doorway, so low even he had to stoop, that stood beside the doorway into the basketry-and-hashish shop like an overdressed child beside its preoccupied mother; the shop door stood ajar, yielding to the nameless itinerant seller of images of oranges a murky glimpse of the shop's proprietor leaning forward from beneath his overhanging wilderness of drying raffia and completed but unshaped weaves to exchange with a customer shrouded in rags an elongate packet for a sheaf of rustling, dust-colored *lu*. Beneath the customer's ragged hem Elleloû glimpsed, or imagined he glimpsed, denim cuffs and the coarse arabesque of platform soles. A tourist, perhaps. Ezana's figures (the Ministry of the Interior had jurisdiction over the Bureau of Tourism) showed that tourists, against all discouragements, were arriving in ever greater numbers, to feast their eyes upon the disaster of the famine, to immerse themselves in the peace of a place on the crumbling edge of nothingness. *Eradicate tourism*: he made the mental note, and tapped the three syllables of his name, El/lel/loû, on Kutunda's door, beneath the brass anti-burglary lock she had recently installed. *Eradicate property*, he thought, *eradicate theft.*

Kutunda was dressed, for it was mid-morning, in the trim Dacron skirt and jacket, with secretarial upsweep and sensible dearth of bangles, in which she reported to her office in the Palais de l'Administation des Noirs. And Ellelloû had seen her flitting in and out of Ezana's office wearing reading glasses like two half-moons cradled on their backs; when she gazed level across their tops, her brown, nearly black eyes appeared startled, her brain beating time behind them and the inquisitive, interrupted arch of her eyebrows also offending him, for she had taken to plucking only the hairs between them, whereas in the desert, with a flint for a razor, she had for beauty's sake painfully scraped them to a thin line. When women cease to beautify, Marx warns, an economic threat is posed to men. "I have an appointment," she told him, as if in truth and not in disguise he was a seller of oranges, with none to sell.

"With your President. Now," Ellelloû told her. "Take off that absurd capitalist costume."

Her tone slipped to a more deferential notch as she offered, "I can put myself at your service any time after lunch, my lord."

"*Allah reprieves no soul when its term is ended*," he quoted, and slipped from his own costume. A fearful reluctance, for she had been imbued with un-Kushite ideals of punctuality, dragged at her hand as together they undid the buttoned, zippered work of the past hour's dressing. The uncovering of her brassiere, and the prim clean underpants, excited him; in the America he had known, a lust had attached to these radiantly laundered undergarments greater than that assigned the naked body, which had confusing associations of aesthetic beauty and the inviolability of marble. Her eyes unaided by spectacles perceived the sign and sceptre of his having been stirred; the dictator bade her, still in her elastic underwear, to kneel to him. Amusement flavoring her indignation, Kutunda with her generous mouth, whose lips had the width but not the eversion of the blacker maidens of the Grionde, and whose little inturned teeth tingled like stars in the night of his nerves, rhythmically swallowed him; their silhouettes, as shallow in relief as figures on a Pharaoh's wall, were almost motionless in the full-length mirror she had installed, between two of the big armoires she had bought to hold her swelling wealth of clothes. In addition to these, silk-lined and papered outside with reproductions of *La chasse de la licorne* and other Flemish *menues verdures*, Swiss reproductions so fine one could see every thread of the tapestries, Kutunda had acquired a steel desk supporting what appeared to be a dictating machine, plus tiers of plastic in-out trays, and flanking this desk two new powder-gray four-drawer filing cabinets, so that when Ellelloû elected to drive home the seed his skillful and by now inspired mistress had brought to the verge of light, it was not easy to find a space of floor in which to execute his decision; the dramatic tug whereby he removed her underpants also brought his elbow into sharp contact with an edge of metal and tears to his eyes. The red thought, *Sex is atrocity*, flashed into his mind, along with the holy text, *Impatience is the very stuff which man is made of.* He pushed on; down among the steel handles and jutting drawers he recovered the earthy closeness, if not the satisfactorily rank aromas, of their first love-bouts, in the gritty ditches of unsuccessful wells. He laughed as her guttural cries exactly fitted his recollections.

"My President," she said, when her breathing eased; "has found himself again."

"One finds many things thought to be lost, in the preparations for a trip."

"A trip again? It's just a few months since you went north to the border and repelled the American invasion."

"And rescued the lovely Kutunda."

"And rescued the lovely Kutunda," she repeated mechanically. She was throwing on clothes and glancing at her wristwatch, pinching it to redden its face with numbers.

"What appointment with Ezana and his underlings," Ellelloû asked, "can take such precedence over your adored?"

"You take everything so personally," the wench accused, retightening her chignon and snatching up her briefcase. "I adore you, but it's not much of a career, is it, sitting around above a hash shop waiting to turn on the adoration? Michaelis gives me things to do; I can't really read yet, but I can talk on the telephone, and almost every day now I have these fascinating conversations with a woman whose Sara is quite fluent but really so funnily accented, I have to control myself from laughing sometimes—she phones all the way from Washington nearly every morning, I forget what hour it is their time, I really can't see why the imperialists don't have the same time we do, they must be going to bed at dawn and having lunch under the stars. Michaelis has tried to explain a thousand times, he says the world is round like an orange, and spins, and the sun is another orange—"

"What do you talk about, with this woman from Washington?"

"Oh, anything, we just warm the line up. She tells me what the weather is like, and how long the lines are at the gas stations, and what a nice man Mr. Agnew was, always so well-spoken and well-groomed"—she glanced about wildly, looking for something she lost, and then found it, the alligator case containing her reading glasses—"and then Mr. Klipspringer comes on and talks to Michaelis."

"And what does this lackey of the oppressors say to Colonel Ezana?" I asked, my fury, which pressed inside my head like corked champagne, defizzed by the melancholy observation that she no longer moved like the great-granddaughter of a leopard, but more electrically, twitchily, like a modern woman connected to a variety of energy-sources. Her nobly stout legs, with their calloused, broadened heels and pantherlike thighs, had been slimmed, by some (I imagined) calibrated diet whose pseudo-medical niceties were catered to even in the depths of our famine.

"Oh, I don't know, they talk in English, I suppose about the reparations—"

"Reparations?"

My doxy was frightened, seeing that these matters, which had become commonplace in her bureaucratic life, were a scandal to me; feigning, this time, a search, she with her briefcase and Dacron suit and trim legs and taut shiny hair from which all sand and mutton grease had been rinsed, looking everywhere but into my face, backpedalled and dodged about the cluttered, compressed room, before whose door I stood guard, soldierly though naked, a small brown man not really weary of being deceived. The knot of guilt in my belly needed still more digestive acid.

"My President surely knows," Kutunda fluttered, "of the negotiations concerning the American, Gibbs, who immolated
himself on the pile of contraband either in madness or in protest of his nation's continued efforts to subvert Southeast Asia,
or of American complicity in the recent renewed Israeli assault
upon Arab integrity. Apparently at college he had been radical.
His widow wants his ashes. At the moment, if my understanding is accurate, and it may well not be, in exchange for the
ashes and an apology to President Chrêmeau, whose territory
was violated—"

"Never! He violated ours by giving the white devils free
passage."

"And you know, of course, about the Koran in Braille."

"Braille?"

"A wonderful invention," Kutunda explained with innocent enthusiasm, "that enables the blind to read with their
hands. As his part of the bargain Klipspringer is going to ship
thousands—ten thousand, twenty thousand, he's waiting for
Michaelis to pull together the 1970 census figures—and along
with them twenty or thirty absolutely apolitical instructors in
this alphabet, you tattoo it onto the paper, I've felt some, it
tingles, you can't see it but you can feel it, for a study center
they would be willing to put up in Istiqlal, on the site of the
USIS library that got burned down in the coup five years ago.
It's quite dramatic-looking, I've seen blueprints, concrete
wings supported by polyurethaned nylon cables, and stainless
steel letters all across the front, naming it for, they wondered
if you'd object, the old king Edumu, because he was blind.
You must know about it. Hasn't Klipspringer talked to you
over the phone too? He talks to me, sometimes, before Michaelis comes on, only his Arabic is about as simple as mine,
he gets me to giggling. Please don't frown. Klipspringer absolutely promises there won't be any CIA people among the
Braille instructors, he hates the CIA more than we do, he says
they've gone and pre-empted the policy-making powers of
Congress, whatever that means, and nobody in Washington
will have them to any parties. You did know all of this, didn't
you? Tell me you're just teasing."

"I never tease my Kutunda, because she tells me such
good stories. Take a message, if you will, to my old comrade

Lieutenant-Colonel, once Corporal, Ezana. Tell him it has come to my attention that he verily *is* Roul, the desert devil."

"And I can go? That's super. I haven't missed too much of the meeting, it was going to be a slide show and those are always slow to set up. Klipspringer has sent us a whole crate of carousels showing agriculture and irrigation in the Negev. You could come too. You could give me a ride. Don't you have anything to do up at the Palais? We could make love after lunch if you wanted, I'm sorry if I seemed preoccupied this morning, you caught me at a bad time, but I didn't fake my climax, I swear it. It was a beautiful climax, really. Only my President can lead me so utterly to forget myself, I am led to the brink of another world, and grow terrified lest I fall in and be annihilated. It's neat."

It heartened me to see the desert child in her revived, wheedling and winsome, at the thought of a ride in my Mercedes.

"I'll drop you on the way," I said. "I still have my morning prayers to do."

The little Mosque of the Clots of Blood was obscurely placed in the east of Al-Abid, from which remote section the Palais showed its unfinished side, the unstuccoed mud bricks crumbling cariously. Here the land becomes flat and the space between the square earth houses, the *tembes*, widens, and tufts of dry grass where footsteps neglect to tread evoke the savanna that once flourished here, before goats and God killed it. The mosque has no minaret, and protruding support timbers stick from its sides like toothpicks from an olive. All civic prestige was a century ago transferred to the Mosque of the Day of Disaster; but within the vacant court a limestone fountain whose worn lip was edged with a raised inscription that could be made out to be the first verse of the ninety-sixth sura, *Recite in the name of your Lord, the Creator, who created man from clots of blood*, offered through all the hours of the days and nights of our drought fresh water for the ablutions of the pious. From what source? Touching my hands to the reverently incised stone, then to the startling running cool crystal of the liquid, then to my lips and eyelids in the prescribed manner, I thought of thirst, of its passion greater than any other save the passion for pain to cease, and of the unknown men, their names and bones now lost as thoroughly as grains of sand underfoot in Istiqlal, who had dug down to this undying spring, where so few chose to come.

The interior of the Mosque of the Clots of Blood was empty, always empty but for the senile imam at the five appointed prayers of the day, between which appointments it stood open to the unpopulated peace of Allah. *Turn up your eyes: can you detect a single flaw?* The wall containing the mihrab had been covered with a pale-blue tile, patternless. I knelt; prostrated myself; repeated the *rak'a* thrice; then sat back on my heels, my hands at rest on my thighs, and let the meditative backwash of prayer move through me, purifying.

In America my friends, late at night, confidential and searching on wine and beer, for hashish then was known only to musicians, would inquire about my religion, proposing the possibility—to their minds, an empirical certainty—that God did not exist, as if this possibility rendered futile the exercises of my piety, which to their minds appeared a wasted enterprise, a bad investment. My faith was not then beyond being troubled, and if in those small inebriated hours I gazed down within myself I saw many shifting transparencies and at the bottom of them no distinct and certain God. Indeed on the rational level many contra-indications could be espied. But then the God of our Koran is the last God to be born, a furious Last Gasp that set the tongue of the Prophet to whirling in terror and whose mystics have whirled ever since, a God Who cuts like a hot knife through the polyheaded pictorial absurdities of the Hindu and the Catholic, the Methodist and the fetishist, a God without qualities; so perhaps belief in Him also lacks qualities. Some of our Sufis have divulged that at the height of purity in which Godhead dwells existence and the lack of it are trivial quibbles; the distinction amid that radiance looms imperceptible. What can be purer than nonexistence? What more soothing and scourging? Allah's option is to exist or not; mine, to worship or not. No fervor overtops that which arises from contact with the Absolute, though the contact be all one way. The wall of pale-blue tiles echoed the repose and equilibrium within me, a silence never heard in lands of doubt and mockery.

Blue tile. A single fly, whose motions showed supernatural

intelligence in their avoidance of repetition and any curve that might be broken down as geometric. My mind flowed with this fly into emptiness. I saw what I must do. It was a step along transparent stairs. All praise be to Allah, the Magnificent, the Merciful. A single small window, the scallops of its arch half-crumbled into dazzling dust, showed the depth and strength of the blue day besieging in vain the little mosque's thick walls. My gaze drank these tiles.

Ezana looked up, surprised to see me, more surprised to see Opuku and Mtesa behind me. It was not our usual hour for consultation. In the hour of dusk, he had put on a sashed robe of paisley silk and was sipping from a tall glass in which a slice of lime floated, while the air conditioner purred at his ear. He was reading a book, an American novel, no doubt concerning the grotesque sexual misadventures of a Jewish intellectual or a self-liberated woman. Its contents were making him smile, and the smile was slow to leave his face. His manner remained mellow well into our conversation. He lifted his feet, slippered in Italian leather, from the Moroccan hassock where they rested and would have risen in greeting had I not signalled him to stay at ease. "I have come to be briefed," I said, "upon the negotiations with the Americans that I understand are proceeding."

"Not negotiations, conversations," he said. "This fellow Klipspringer is rather hard to cut short, he is so—what do you Americans say?—*giving*."

"You Americans?"

"Forgive me, my President, *the* Americans. You have just walked into this book I am reading, full of these poor benighted bourgeoisie struggling to psychoanalyze the universe. I am tasting this trash the better to understand our enemy. They are a strange lost race, poorer than they know. I wonder if we of the Third World might not have eventually to welcome them among us—they too have a deficient balance of trade, a high unemployment rate, an agricultural bias in the national temperament, and the need for a protectionist tariff if their struggling native industries are not to be overwhelmed by the superior efficiency and skill of the old Axis powers. Indeed, Comrade President, at a time when the Arabs have all the capital, the Siberians and the Brazilians all the undeveloped resources, and the Chinese all the ideological zeal, one wonders if in the interests of global stability a grant of aid to the United States might not be a prudent apportionment within our next year's national budget. I jest, of course."

"Of course. Yet it does sound as though this Klipspringer has all too amiably insinuated confusions into the mind of my chief minister. These people are pirates. Without the use of a single soldier their economy sucks wealth from the world, in the service of a rapacious, wholly trivial and wasteful consumerism. My order was, in answer to their overtures, no answer."

"But no answer is an answer, which goads the interrogator. By discussing, we are delaying, and dissolving. This wretched Gibbs has not been mentioned for days. We cannot pretend the Americans do not exist; they have leverage upon the French, and if the French cease to underwrite our peanuts we cease to exist in the world."

"Or begin to exist in a better world."

"Also, as my Colonel knows, some reactionary elements evaded our revolution and took refuge in Sahel; an infusion of American arms might turn these ridiculous dissidents into an invading force, which would find our borders permeable and our population, however loyal to the name of Ellelloû, desperately weakened by drought."

"Hungry men make good soldiers," I pointed out. "When it comes to battle, the poor retain a golden weapon: they have little to lose. Their lives are a shabby anteroom in the palace of the afterlife. The Prophet's vivid Paradise is our atomic bomb; under its blast the poor toubabs shrivel like insects clinging to soulless existence. *Of the life to come they are heedless.* As to the French, they are too busy stuffing their money down the throat of the Concorde to look up; the entire wealth of a nation of misers has been swallowed by this aeronautical goose. Forget the infidels, they are mired in materialism and its swinish extinction of spirit. Defiance is our safest as well as noblest policy."

"Even your shy friends the Soviets," Ezana pursued, "are not exempt from American influence, now that the unspoken standoff has been translated into *détente.*"

"What has driven you, Comrade, so low, into this slime of *Realpolitik*? I will save you from the demon you have inhaled.

If another call from this Klipspringer is honored with courtesy, the cables to the Palais shall be cut on my order."

His face, all hemispheres and highlights, went dull with disappointment. His gold tooth winked out; his lower teeth showed in a grimace of grief. "But tomorrow we were to discuss the possibility of an addition to the Braille Library, a leprosarium dedicated to the memory of my father. Yours, I know, was a whirlwind, a pinch of fertilizing dust; my father I knew and loved. He had been a warrior, then, as the French pacification spread, a ferryman, at a bend of the Grionde where the banks draw close. Perhaps because of his ventures to the southern side, he contracted leprosy in midlife, turned silver and perished limb by limb. His nose, his fingers. I watched it transpire. My present dignity and the indignation that enrolled me in the Revolution alike stem from a vow he extracted from me with his final breaths. I vowed that I would climb high into the order of things, that other citizens of Noire would never have to endure suffering and humiliation as unmitigated as his."

"Better, perhaps, to have vowed to face your own end with less complaining than, from the sound of it, your progenitor."

Ezana blinked away this insult to his father. He leaned forward from his easy chair, to confide his message urgently, to press its warmth into the sinuous channels of my ear. My comrade in his foppish accoutrements became more naked to me than since the fury and fear of L'Émergence, and that aftermath in which we conspired together to do away with the empty-headed Soba. Ezana said to me, "The world is not what it was. There is no longer any deep necessity to suffer. The only lesson suffering ever gave was how to endure more suffering. What gives men pain, with some lingering exceptions, can now be cured. Smallpox, even in our bedevilled land, is being encircled and exterminated. We know what children need in their bellies, even when we cannot put it there. The fading of an afterlife—for it has faded, my friend Ellelloû, however you churn your heart—has made this life more to be cherished. When all is said and done about the persisting violence on our planet, and the pronouncements of SCRME are set against the fulminations of *Nouvelles en noire et blanc*, the fact remains that the violence, relatively, is small, and deliberately kept small by the powers that could make it big. War has been reduced to the status of criminal activity—it is no longer the sport of gentlemen. This is a great thing, this loss of respectability. We feel it everywhere, even in the vacancies of Kush. Hatred on the national scale has become insincere. The self-righteousness has vanished, that justified great slaughter. The units of race and tribe, sect and nation, by which men identified themselves and organized their youth into armies no longer attract blind loyalty; the Cubans and Belgians, the Peruvians and Indonesians, all mingle at our Palais receptions, lusting after one another's wives and complaining alike about the tedium of the diplomatic service in this Allah-forsaken penalty post of a backwater. Such interplay betokens an increase of humane pragmatism and a decrease of demented energy that makes my vow to redeem my father's life inevitable of success."

"These units you disparage," I said, "were mankind's building blocks. If they dissolve, we have a heap of dust, of individual atoms. This is not peace, but entropy. Like all comfortable cowards, Comrade Ezana, you overvalue peace. Is it possible," I asked, "that some principle of contention is intrinsic to Nature, from the first contentious thrust of bare existence against the sublime, original void? The serene heavens, as witnessed by astronomers, shine by grace of explosion and consumption on a scale unthinkable, and the glazed surface of marble or the demure velvet of a maiden's eyelid are by the dissections of particle physics a frenzy of whirling and a titanic tension of incompatible charges. You and I, for additional example, have long been at odds, and the government of Kush has been born of the dialectical space between us. Out of the useful war between us, a synthesis has emerged; a synthesis, for a while at least, does package the conflicting energies that met within it."

Ezana's fingers, forced apart by the thick rings upon them, spread wider, in careful thought, upon the glass of his desktop. "I sometimes wonder, my President, if even the fruitful diagrams of Marx do schematic justice to the topology of a world where the Soviet proletariat conducts a black market in blue jeans while the children of the capitalist middle class manufacture bombs and jovial posters of Mao."

"Or where," I added, "the chief minister of a radical junta holds subversive conversations with the American secret intelligence and attempts to infect his own President with the false, sentimental, atheistical pluralism acquired thereby."

Ezana's rejoinder was aborted, for Kutunda, her secretarial suit concealed, as per government regulations, in a flowing *boubou*, burst into Ezana's office accompanied by an oval-faced young man whom I recognized, through the veil of his formal blandness, as the young Fula policeman who had read the Koran to the king. He still wore his plum-colored fez, but the white vest and pantaloons of the high-servant caste had been exchanged for a tapered shirt of needle-fine stripes and taupe slacks of indecently close tailoring about his hips yet so wide at the cuff only the square enamelled-looking tips of his shoes were unenveloped. Both Kutunda and he were holding full glasses and returning to a species of party. She also held a box of those salty biscuits called HiHo, and her young escort a red-rimmed crescent of Edam cheese. They had returned, however, to witness their host's being taken into custody by Mtesa and Opuku, at my command, as a traitor to the state, and as a wearer of silk. Ezana was confined to the king's old rooms in the barracks wing of the Palais de l'Administration des Noirs, above the floor occupied by the People's Museum of Imperialist Atrocities and within earshot of the shrieks of the Istiqlal Anti-Christian High School for Girls volleyball team.

His protests, his pleas, would fatigue me to scribble. One of them was, "My President, if you incarcerate your Chief Minister, and simultaneously proceed with your individualistic, entrepreneurial pilgrimage to the rumored cave in the Balak Massif, you will leave Kush without a head of state!"

I doubted that Kush would notice, but to be on the safe side, and to demonstrate to Ezana my liberated, inspired powers of decision, I turned to the young fez-wearing spy and appointed him Acting Minister of the Interior, Chief of the Bureau of Transport, Co-ordinator of Forests and Fisheries, and Chairman of the Board of Tourism. Kutunda, I said, would instruct him in his duties.

Duties, duties. Before I could depart it was necessary that I visit my second wife, that I press my little thornbush to my bosom. She lived, the Muffled One, in a shuttered villa in the most venerable part of Les Jardins, where the plane and chestnut trees imported by the *colons* had grown tall in the fifty wet years prior to 1968, only to falter, droop, and die in the five years since. Their blanched skeletons, brutally cropped in the Gallic manner, lined the curving avenues. Candace's villa had been rankly overgrown, but the drought had done some work of pruning where the hand of man had been idle; a sapless, leafless *Petrea volubilis* made its desiccated way along cracks in the stucco façade, clutching the shutters with splintering fingers and spiralling up the little Ionic pillars of the front portico. The vine had been prying loose the tiles from the portico roof when its life had been arrested. My ring of chimes produced a strange rustling noise within, but Candace was at the door quickly, as if she had been watching my approach through the blind walls.

Or perhaps she had been about to go out, for she was muffled head to toe in a dull black *buibui* with the addition of a face-veil that covered even her brow. A scattering of holes smaller than the holes in a cabbage-grater permitted her to see, in speckled fashion. Perhaps some retrograde corner of Afghanistan or Yemen still holds a crazed old spice merchant, sheik, or bandit who keeps his concubines thus; but in Istiqlal, where socialist progressivism had reinforced the traditional insouciance of African womanhood, such a costume had to be taken as an irony, a sour joke upon me.

"Holy Christ, look who it isn't," her voice exclaimed through the layers of muslin.

Behind her stood a big Songhai maid with a basket on her arm. This girl's face showed alarm at my visit; to her I was the ghost of authority, and her ultimate employer. Candy had no other servant, and not because of any penuriousness of mine. In the early years of our marriage, when I had lived with her half, then a third, of my time, the household was appropriately staffed. As my visits dwindled, she bade the attendants drop away, racing through the housework once a month, even poking in the vegetable patch, until the sun nearly smothered her. Now she and her girl were going out shopping; but since Candy almost never purchased anything, preferring to order all non-perishable goods from the United States by mail-order, I could only conclude that the purpose of these expeditions was to display herself, muffled, as a mystery and, among

rumormongers, a national scandal. People said that Ellellou
had mutilated this wife in a passion, or to satisfy a perverse
sexual need had married a monster of deformity.

"You have your fucking nerve," she continued, "showing up
here in your little soldier outfit as if I owe you anything but
a—a good kick in the balls."

Her native inhibitions had given pause to the phrase that her
native freedom of speech and, now, her feminist consciousness
of genital oppression had suggested. But Candace was not a
ball-kicker, she was a heart-stabber.

"My adored," I said, "I have come to bid thee good-bye. I
am about to walk the edge of my fate, and may fall off."

My Islamic courtesies of course infuriated her. "Don't give
me any of this Kismet crap," she said. "I knew you when you
couldn't tell the Koran from the Sears Roebuck catalogue." As
if in recoil from this stab, she angrily turned, my pillar of cloth,
and it was alarming, how closely her back resembled her front.
In full purdah she seemed less a person than a growth, a kind of
gray asparagus. Candace waved the frightened Songhai away,
with that jerky embarrassed roughness of those who think their
servants should be their friends, and let herself drop wearily
into an imitation Chippendale armchair ordered from Grand
Rapids. She had tried to reconstitute, in this French villa spun
of sub-Saharan materials, the rectilinear waterproof comfort of
a Wisconsin living-room. But the tile floor, the *banco* walls, the
rattan furniture betrayed the illusion, which termites and the
breakage occasioned by our terrible dryness had further undermined. Without removing any of her wrappings, Candace put
her sandalled feet up on a curly-maple butler's tray table whose
leaves had warped and loosened in the weather. Where her parents might have had a pair of painted-porcelain mallards with
their hollow backs bedding narcissus bulbs rooted in pebbles,
she had set an earthen dish holding some unshelled peanuts. I
took one, cracked it, and ate it. There is a sweetness, a docile
pithy soul-quality of taste, to our Kushian goobers that I have
never met elsewhere. "Well, chief," my wife said, "how's top-
level tricks? Chopping old Edumu's noggin off didn't seem to
raise the humidity any."

"These spiritual balances are not easy to strike. I have put
Michaelis Ezana into the king's old cell, which might make

the difference. He has been compromising the honor of our country with your ex-compatriots."

"Poor guy, probably just trying to bring a little rationale into Ellellou's heaven on earth."

"Tell me," I countered, "the rationale of the Universe, and I will order my heaven accordingly."

"Don't go undergraduate on me," Candace said. "That's how you got me into this hellhole, being all winsome and philosophical, building the no-nations up from scratch. Scratch is the word. Scratch is where you start, and scratch is where you end. God, it's hot in this damn bag."

"Take off the veil," I suggested. "Your joke is wasted on your forbearing husband."

"Joke, my ass," she said, and my own nervousness eased at the hardening of her voice, certain as daybreak to go harder and higher. "Who was it who smuggled me in in wraps in the first place? Who was it used to tell reporters I was a *zawiya* Berber too pious to be seen? And then after those rotten Pan-African games leaked it around that Sittina was his second wife instead of his third? Who was it, Mr. Double-*l* double-*l oo*, who put me deeper into wraps when came the Revolution and every Yank in Istiqlal was shipped back to Ellis Island? Christ, if you don't think I wouldn't have been over-goddam-joyed to go back with the rest of them where you can have a drink of water without lifting out the centipedes first and bowing toward smelly Mecca five times a day and having to kick starving kids out of your way every time you walk the goat, you have another think coming. But oh no, not me, crazy old Candy, all A's in Poli Sci but loyal as a mutt out of class, crazy, conditioned to be some man's slave, sitting here watching my fucking life melt away, and you call it a joke. You *would*," Candace said, and undid her head wraps with furious counterclockwise motions. A trembling white hand unclasped her veil.

Her face. Much as I had first seen it, without the mirroring sunglasses, the receding aisles of evil goods, her cheeks still round and firm, her chin pointed, her nose bone-white, bone-straight. She even smiled, her fierce quick smile, in relief at her head's being free. "Christ, I can breathe," she said. Flaxen wisps looped in damp deshabille onto her flushed brow; from the corners of her blue eyes, the milky blue-green of beryl,

fanned vexed wrinkles that could have been produced, in another life, by laughter. Her powder-pale skin was still young;
it had not suffered in my country as it would have in her own,
had not been baked and whipped by the sun of golf courses
and poolside patios and glaring shopping center parking lots
in these years when, as the Wrapped One, she had sheltered
herself amid the mysteries of Istiqlal. I was glad of this. Watching her unwind her headshawl, and then unveil, I remembered
how I had seen her naked, and the memory of her body moving pale, loose, and lithe in the neon-tinged darkness of an off-
campus room numbed me so that had all the world's sorrow
been at this moment funnelled into my poor narrow being I
would not have felt an iota more: I was full.

With the air she could now breathe she had launched a
bitchy monologue. "How *is* dear Sittina? Still chasing cock
and playing Bach? And my big momma Kadongolimi? You still
mosey round to your old *awa* for your fix of tribal juice? And
that other idiot, little Sheba—has she learned to chew with her
mouth shut yet? But you like that, don't you? You like these
dyed-in-the-wool down-home Kushy types, don't you? Hakim
Happy Ellelloû, de mon ob de *pee*ple. De mon what om, right?
Well here's one cunt that hates your guts, buster. You better
stick a stamp on me and send me home."

"You belong here."

"Divorce me. It's easy. All you have to do is say '*Tallaqtuki*'
three times. Come on, say it. One, two— Divorce me and
you'll have a slot for this new twat, what's her name."

"Kutunda. Our connection is entirely official. As to you,
my beloved Candace, my personal attachment aside, you serve
a purpose for the nation. There is pressure on our borders.
When the Day of Disaster comes, I can point to you as proof
that the President of Kush is anti-imperialist but by no means
anti-American."

"You don't know what you are, you poor little spook. You
are the most narcissistic, chauvinistic, megalomaniacal, cata-
tonic schizoid creep this creepy continent ever conjured up.
And that's saying a lot."

Her clinical epithets reminded me of her book-club books
—the warping, fading, termite-riddled stacks and rows of volumes imported from her native land, popular psychology and
sociology mostly. How to succeed, how to be saved, how to

survive the mid-life crisis, how to find fulfillment within femininity, how to be free, how to love, how to face death, how to
harness your fantasies, how to make dollars in your spare time
—the endless self-help and self-exploration of a performance-
oriented race that has never settled within itself the fundamental question of what a man *is*. A man is a clot of blood. Hopeful
books, they disintegrated rapidly in this climate; she had run
out of shelf space and stacked this literary foreign aid on the
floor, where our great sub-continent of insects hollowed out
the covers from underneath, their invisible chewing a rerun
of the chewing of her eyes as she read away the monotonous
succession of her days, weeks, and years.

Candace was on her feet and speechifying. "I hate you. I
hate this place. I hate the heat, the bugs, the mud. Nothing
lasts here, and nothing changes. The clothes when you wash
them dry like cardboard. A dead rat on the floor is a skeleton by noon. I'm thirsty all the time, aren't *you*? Happy"—the
nickname she gave me in college—"I'm *sink*ing, and I can't *do*
anything about it. I'm seeing the only shrink in Istiqlal and he
shrugs and says, 'Why don't you just *leave*?' I tell him, 'I *can't*,
I'm married to the *Pres*ident!'"

Her straw-blond, straw-bright hair fell forward as if to
veil her sobbing; my impulse to reach and offer comfort was
checked only by my certain knowledge that this offer would
fail, that my loving touch would feed her anger as the books
on how to be happy fed her unhappiness.

She lifted her head, her eyes red-rimmed but abruptly dry. In
the simple bold style with which she had once asked me, "How
do I look?," she asked, "Can't you get me out of this?"

"*This*, as perhaps your friend the Freudian marabout has
already suggested, is you. You have chosen. I am powerless
to alter your choices. When we were in your land, not mine,
it was you who courted me, and I in my poverty, my strangeness, my blackness, was slow to respond. I was afraid of the
consequences. You were heedless. Your heart demanded. So
be it. Here you are. Had you allowed me, fifteen years ago,
to give you the children I then wanted, your son would be
taller than you now, and your daughters would be cheerful
company."

"Shit on that," Candace mumbled. "I wasn't sure. You
weren't either. We didn't want to take on that responsibility,

everything was difficult enough, we knew what we were doing might not work."

"You didn't wish," Ellelloû told her, "to become the mother of Africans."

"It's not that simple, and you know it. You were different once we got here, you didn't make me feel secure. Big Momma had you half the time, and then you got so thick with the king. Anyway, I didn't always use the diaphragm, either, and nothing happened. Maybe one of us is sterile. Your other wives, are those children yours? We should have discussed things like this years ago. Where were you?"

"Tending to duty." The primness of Ellelloû's answer indicated that the conversation had exhausted its usefulness for him. He had suffered enough recrimination to fuel his departure.

Sensing him about to slip away, Candace clung and asked, "If I tried to go home, would you stop me?"

"As your husband, I would indulge you in all things. As father, however, of all the citizens of Kush, I would feel obliged to discourage defection. In this time of crisis and dearth, our human resources must be conserved. Border patrols have been instituted to confine the nomads. Every peanut caravan as it departs includes a quota of spies and enforcers. I wish the imperialist press, which describes our socialist order as a squalid police state, to receive no malicious hint confirming rumors of maladministration within Kush. Your presence," Ellelloû told his wife, "is especially cherished here. Let me add that Opuku's brother, whom you have not met, nor would I wish it, has in his patriotic love of order developed a number of interesting ways to inflict discomfort without leaving any mark upon the body. I confide this to you in a spirit of tenderness and affection."

The white woman's eyes blazed; the rims of her lips wrinkled with tension. "You sadistic little turd. When I think of what I wanted to give you. You know what everybody at college used to say to me? They said I was crazy to put myself at the mercy of a Negro."

"You needed to prove them right," Ellelloû said, bothered by a certain poignant twist in her body, as in some late-Hellenic robed statues, implying the erotic axis of the body within, and within that an ambivalent torque of the soul—in Candace's case, between taunting and plea, a regret that even in her extremity of rage she should taunt her husband with the blackness that had made him fascinating and herself noble and the two of them together undergraduate stars at McCarthy College, in that distant city of Franchise.

"I shouldn't tell you this, but you know what Professor Craven used to say to me? I won't say it."

"Say it, if it will help you."

"He said, Today's slave, tomorrow's tyrant."

"Excellent. By the same token, Today's liberal, tomorrow's bigot. You could have had Professor Craven, you could have been for a time his reigning student concubine, but you chose to slight him."

"He was married."

"So was I."

"I couldn't believe it. When I met Kadongolimi here, when I saw she really existed, I nearly died. How could you *do* that to me?—have such a big fat wife. I thought you were making her up. We were in America. You were so touching, such a ragamuffin."

Ellelloû slapped her, so little did he like being reminded of the pathetic figure he had cut in those days. Lest she think the blow had been unconsidered, he repeated it; the pink stain on her cheek glowed wider than his hand as it deepened to red. She would have twisted quite away had he not held her shoulders. Her pose reminded him now of those thin-lipped, supernaturally cool Flemish Virgins impassive, with averted eyes, beside a pointed arch giving upon a tiny crowded turquoise landscape. The rift of sorrow in him widened. Terrible, he thought, that rebuke had come upon her not for any of her insults but for a moment of innocent openness, remembering a ragamuffin. "Believe this then," Ellelloû told her harshly, in apology. "For your safety: you are my wife. For your comfort: this will pass. I will not always be President."

Colonel Ellelloû finally departed from Istiqlal in the last month, Dhū 'l-Hijja, of that troubled year. The afternoon temperature in the square of the Mosque of the Day of Disaster was 112° F., 44.4° C. The dictator took with him, along with the faithful Opuku and Mtesa, his fourth wife, Sheba.

IV

Beneath the stars the roofy desert spreads
Vacant as Libya.

—HERMAN MELVILLE, 1863

THE REGION called the Balak is the size of France, if Alsace-Lorraine had been permanently conceded to Germany and by the same treaty Belgium had been annexed. Arab traders as early as the year 400 A.H. noted a peculiarity of these barren heights which European adventurers of the nineteenth century A.D., such as Heinrich Barth and Gustav Nachtigal, confirmed: a local absence of color. The sky here is white, and the earth, in contrast to the vivid ochres, reds, and mauves of the northwest quadrant of Kush, shows in its rocks and dunes, its playas and wadis, its *reg*, *erg*, and *hammada*, only dreary varieties of gray. The valleys of molten glass have already been mentioned; the low xerophytic growth has, by the process of natural selection, subdued its natural green to a tint fainter than that of the palm leaves in a faded oleograph of the Holy Land. Here bloom, famously, the world's dullest flowers; here white scorpions and black snakes live off one another's eggs. Travellers have provoked skepticism by reporting how even the gaudiest goods and garb are gradually drained to monochrome in the slow climb through the Massif; dear Sheba, laden with gold and coral, copper and jasper, lapis lazuli and chrysoprase, her eyelids daubed with antimony and her fingernails with henna, her exquisite *chocolat-sans-lait* body wrapped in silver-embroidered indigo, scarlet, and turquoise, even her feet clad in sandals whose parrot green chimed with the parrot-belly pink of her toenails, day by day was overlaid with deeper and deeper layers of the dust of colorlessness. Her skin, glossy as coal, shed its purple highlights; the palms of her hands no longer lifted to release glimpses of lilac; even her tongue seemed no longer red, lolling in the velvet orifice her careless jaw revealed as she incessantly chewed kola nuts. Her teeth and the whites of her eyes in this atmosphere gleamed more brilliant than ever, and the flaring edges of her lips and nostrils were emphasized as by an ink-laden fine quill. The stem of her neck, the virtuoso arabesques of her sullen profile, and the perfect, burnished crimpings of her ears all looked limned and shaded by an artist whose effects the addition of color would have muddied. Sheba was petite, the only one of my wives smaller than I, and her beauty was sharpened to a blueprint precision, the immaculate mechanics of a butterfly husk, with this removal of the rainbow.

Four hundred kilometers from Al-Abid the *piste* dwindled to an impassable trail between ashen rocks. We left the grayer-than-ever Mercedes to Opuku and Mtesa and joined, in the guise of a detribalized *anzad* player and her protector, a caravan carrying (we gathered) from Ouagadougou or Niamey to a contraband depot on the Zanj border a medley of sinister goods. The caravan leader was a hirsute, jittery brute of the Kel-ulli tribe; Sidi Mukhtar was his name and his person abundantly mixed what the intrepid Barth called the three traditional Arab qualities of *rejela* (valor), *sirge* (thievishness), and *dhiyafa* (hospitality). Sheba—who was kittenish at first—and I peeked whenever we could into the camel-bags, where we found such contraband as hallucinogenic khat, firearms of Czech and Mexican manufacture, plastic sandals from Japan, transistor radios assembled on such low-wage platforms as Singapore and Hong Kong, and boxes and boxes of Bic pens, Venus pencils, and Eberhard Faber typewriter erasers. There were also wooden crates of what Sheba thought would be bullets and grenades but when we pried a slat loose proved to be black ribbons on metal spools, white correction cartridges, and steely, spherical, UFOish IBM type elements for not only the Arabic alphabet but for the 276 characters of Amharic and the antique squiggles of Geez. Had Sidi Mukhtar known of our prowlings he would have staked us to an anthill and left us to shrivel like banana skins cast aside. Or so he said. Actually, the caravan was a loose, good-natured federation of likeminded individual mercantile entrepreneurs, in the best traditions of African humanism; the sole severity came in the distribution of the water, which was done with an iron hand.

Our days began at night. We were awakened beneath the stars—the stars! in the midnight absolute that arched above

the Balak the constellations hung inflamed like chandeliers—
and made our way, tinkling and sighing and snorting, toward
the pearl dawn whose blush was as delicate as the pink tinge in
nacre, to that point in mid-morning when the camels began to
squat down simply of despair. The camel is an engaging creature spiritually: he proceeds steadily to the breaking-point beyond which he cannot go at all, and then, like as not, he is apt
to squat down, blink, take one more breath through his rubbery nostrils, and die. We were supposed to sleep in our tents
through the torrid mid-day, but in fact it was difficult, with
the whistle of the wind in the peg-ropes, and a sense of restless
activity outside (presences of sand that yet muttered and cast
man-shaped shadows on the translucent tent-sides), and our
thirsty anticipation of the water that would be dispensed at
dusk. The water skins, the *zemzimayas*, were brought around
by an evil-smelling henchman of Sidi Mukhtar's; he determined our quotas by counting the bobs of our Adam's apples,
and never failed to jostle Sheba's succulent breasts in tearing
the leather canteen from her hands.

To pass the dazed, insomniac afternoons Sheba and I would
attempt to make love, but grains of sand interposed and
abraded our venereal membranes. The sand here was strange,
black and white like salt and pepper, and at moments seemed
an immense page of print too tiny to read. She would lie with
her head on my belly, gently blowing me, or else play the *anzad* and sing, while I softly beat time on the hollows of my
abdomen:

> "*Do it to me, baby,*
> *do it if you can.*
> *If I can't have a drink of water,*
> *I'd as soon suck off a man.*"

The sun beat upon the squares of camel hide above us so hard
as to render them thin as oiled paper held up to candlelight;
in our writhings we sought the shadow of each other's bodies.
There would enter my mind those streams and shady gardens
old, harried Mohamet conjured up in the after-hours babble
of his mid-life crisis to lead the mulish Meccans away from
their stony idols and female deities, and, more persistently still,
of the soda fountain of the Franchise drugstore, named if I

remembered correctly Oasis Pharmaceuticals and Sundries, where I had first met Candace, amid that frightful hectoring of brightly packaged newnesses, beside the baleful tree of sunglasses. And while Sheba's dear head, the lustrous hair of which she braided no two days with the same intricacy, rested stickily on my stomach and her ash-colored, thirst-swollen tongue loyally teased my absent-minded penis, my thoughts would swim through rivers of lemonade rickeys, lime phosphates that dripped their fizzing overflow into the chrome grate below the taps, Coca-Cola brewed out of syrup upon chips of ice, 7 Ups paler than water itself, and that mysterious dark challenger to the imperial Coke, the swarthy, enigmatic Pepsi, with whom I felt an underdog's empathy. Milkshakes were in those days of plenty so lavishly prepared that the counter-boy, ingloriously dubbed the "soda jerk," served them in two containers, one of cloudy, hefty glass and the other of the chill futuristic metal in which the sudsy marvel had been churned. These "soda jerks," I came to understand, were recruited from the adolescent ranks of the "townies"—that is, the permanent residents of Franchise, refugees from subsistence farming in the main, every last one of them white and Gentile, as opposed to those of us smuggled in academic gowns into the community as students at McCarthy College, whose brick pinnacles and massy treetops hovered above the gravelly flat roofs of the "towny" business section like the upper levels of a ziggurat, where only gods and priests feeding dead kings dare venture. Emerging, blinking, from Oasis Pharmaceuticals, my mind's eye confronted, between me and that ivy-shaggy campus corner opposite, the breadth of Commerce Street, with its dangling traffic light and surging traffic of opulent automobiles. Everything in America, through that middle bulge of the Fifties, seemed to this interloper fat, abundant, and bubblelike, from the fenders of the cars to the cranium of the President. Franchise was a middle-sized city of 35,000. Its main street ran straight as an arrow, disused trolley tracks still embedded in its center. Its few factories, mostly devoted to paper manufacture, were out of sight down by the lake, whose breezes they tainted with the chemical overflow of the pulping process. The lake had been left, with that romantic *douceur* the Americans trail in the wake of their rapacities, its Indian name, Timmebago, though the bestowers of that name had been long since scourged from its shores by gunfire, firewater, and smallpox.

In the summer, the brightness of which lasted into October, the merchants of Franchise lowered awnings above their store-fronts, and the virtually continuous strip of scalloped shadow laid along the dazzling wide sidewalk now merged with the stifling shade of the tent as I lay there flooded in my thirst by remembrance; my mind's eye, hesitantly, fearfully, look-ing both ways twice, crossed the dangerous street and hus-tled into the deep green closures of the college. Beneath the stately arches of the elms and the more horizontal branches of the oaks and copper beeches the spaces appeared subaqueous and we students, elongated as by refraction, silent swimmers. In this aquarium light the academic buildings seemed plaster temples lowered into our element as ornaments, with solid insides and painted-on windows; the pillared Classics build-ing looked especially fake. Then the wheel of North American weather turned and there came an elemental change: the roof of elm-leaves was golden, and falling, and letting in sky, and the leaves were burning in great piles tended by the college grounds crew, grizzled old townies who ogled our girls; the autumnal fragrance of leaf-smoke overpowered the caustic emissions of the paper mills and recalled to young Félix the patches of brush that were cleared for cassava and maize by the women of his village. They would sing, chopping, uproot-ing, bending from the waist in unison beneath that African sky whose vastness was so subtly distant a brother to the vast-ness of the farm-country sky the straight main street dissolved into, past the hedges, the lawns, the Victorian-Gothic faculty housing. Above silver silos and corn rows and rolling meadows studded with fat cows, the platinum clouds piled one on top of another in a triumphant, vaporous wealth. In Africa, the clouds ran like herds of wildebeest, strung-out and gray, has-tening, always, to get somewhere else, in this savanna that had to be vast, for in any one place it was poor. Then, the carousel of seasons turning again, fire became air, the leaves blew all away; all was black and white, black twigs on white sky, black men on white earth, and Candy was waiting, waiting for her Happy, at the dark cave mouth of Livingstone Hall, her snow-bright bangs set off by a knitted scarf the red of Christmas ribbon. Her mother had knitted this scarf, and the matching red mittens with which Candy was hugging her mold-colored notebooks and big Ec text with its slick cover of smiling blue tighter to her chest as if for warmth. Snow was all about like a mirage, a liftingness in the bottom of Happy's vision that made the automobiles sing in chains and lowered window-sills to the level of the ground. This was truly another world, that had bred another race of men to make their way, barking joyously, through this illusory element, this starry mud. One handful of those tiny ice-feathers would bite into his face now, would dissolve his lips and open his throat again, so he could croak a word of love to Sheba. Kissed, Candy would hurry him into the cave, where the radiators were hurling heat recklessly against the cold that entered with them through the double doors, the linoleum floors dirty with melted footprints and tracked-in fragments—matches, gum wrappers, the little red strip that pulled open a cigarette pack—of the culture of paper and radiant waste around them.

I must have dozed. When I awoke, Sheba's head was heavy on my sandy belly or my Ec textbook was open in my lap to the dour visage of Adam Smith or a chart of the decline in the purchasing power of the guilder since 1450. A few more minutes, the lecture would end, and I could have my noon beer in the Badger Cafe. There were luncheonettes, ice-cream parlors, and bars in the city blocks around the campus; in these we would gather, these islands of warmth in the ocean of cold, and talk, Candy and I and her friends. A number of her friends were American Negroes, then beginning to be called Afro-Americans; she was one of those white women who cannot leave black men alone. No mark of Cain or Ham identifies such a female, but some questing chromosome within holds her sexually fast to the tarbaby. Candy's parents in her child-hood had had colored cooks and maids, and at the side of these corpulent, didactic, floury-handed mammies the child had felt a cherishing and security absent from the hysterically neat rooms of the house beyond the kitchen. This had been in Chicago; at about the time of what in Africa they call a wom-an's first uncleanness her father moved his insurance agency to Oshkosh. Chicago's black circumambience thinned to an off-center pocket of paperworkers, ex-slaves whose escape had stopped short of Canada. And in all-white Franchise any dark faces must belong to McCarthy students: flip, coffee-colored Barry Little from Kalamazoo; Muslimized, bitter-black Oscar X from Chicago's South Side; quiet, cinnamon-and-ginger Turnip Schwarz up the river from East St. Louis. Med Jhabvala, with his pointed beard and fluting, female voice, and myopic, beautiful Wendy Miyamoto, from San Francisco, who got 99s on all her exams and rarely said a word, completed our shadowy circle. There was even an Indian on campus, a Dakota called Charlie Crippled Steer, who stalked along in fur-lined earflaps and threw things at track meets; he sat at our table once in a while, but did not like us. He did not like anybody, striding the snowy diagonals of our walks with a frozen grimace, his mouth a sad slash, his eyes small as currants. These marginal Americans fascinated me. But amid the maddening slapping of the tent flaps in the mindless wind, the overheard snuffling of stoic camels and the clangorous harangues of desperately bored camel-drivers, my flickering memories of that exotic Wisconsin seemed bits of a Fifties movie, with its studiously recruited cross-section meant to emblemize the melting pot, the fertile and level moral prairie of American goodness. This prairie's harvest celebration came at McCarthy each November, in the Thanksgiving football game against our arch-rival, Pusey Baptist, an even more northerly academic village of virgins and bruisers that, for the four years of my undergraduate career, was four times narrowly defeated—in 1954 by an intercepted pass, in 1955 by a goal-line stand, in 1956 by a heroic, dodging, arhythmical, incredible end run by a sandy-haired instant legend who next year died uncomplainingly of leukemia, and in 1957, most thrillingly for us non-gringos, by a field goal kicked sideways, soccer style, from the forty-three-yard line by a Peruvian general's degenerate son, who had gone out for the team as a way of making homosexual contacts. Memory, enough! Never-to-be-entered-again spaces the mind has hollowed out! The pom-poms! The beer kegs! The single-throated roaring in the concrete bowl, named Kellogg Stadium for its benefactor corporation and irreverently nicknamed the Breakfast Dish. And seen from high above through the vapor of tens of thousands of breaths, those synchronized American cheerleaders, a row of M's ("Give me an M," they would implore), yelling in the zero weather for victory as nakedly as Zulus ("Give me a *C!*"), their cheeks flaming ("Give me a *C, A, R!*"), their breasts pouncing as in rapid succession each dropped to one knee and shot forth an arm. *Rah!*

I licked my lips, remembering the beer in the frats afterward, where the Pusey Baptists were invited to drown their annual sorrow, and the rugs stank like swamps of hops, and the exceptional co-ed, liberated without a restraining philosophy of liberation, liquidly consigned herself, in a ratty upstairs chamber, with hip-hoisted skirt and discarded underpants, to a line-up of groggy, beefy ejaculators. Sheba shifted her head, and our skins where melted together threatened to tear. She lay her head beside my arm, her jaw ajar, and with a gray tongue licked the sweat from my pores.

Was I happy? They called me so, but in truth the studies were hard. I had been granted a scholarship from some nefarious reserve of laundered and retitled government money, and had to keep up my grades, and in addition worked as waiter and short-order cook in various eating establishments within a walk of the McCarthy campus, including a Howard Johnson's, with its dummy minaret, on the thru-traffic edge of Franchise. I did not work in any of the places where my circle of friends gathered. I did not want them embarrassed by having me serve them. I did not want them to hear the towny waitresses and kitchen goons call me, not entirely without affection, Grease, Sambo, or Flapjack.

Where was I? The Off-Campus Luncheonette was foggy with cigarette smoke and thermal-interface steam, with the plinging of pinball and the twanging of Patti Page; the Pure Dairy Products Ice Cream Parlor had twirled-wire chairs and round marbletop tables whose butter-pecan-streaked-with-blueberry surfaces camouflaged the slopped excess of our gooey sundaes and viscid, frothy sodas; the Badger Cafe offered sawdust on the floor and high-backed booths of dark-stained plywood. Here we would badger Oscar X about his remarkable faith. "You mean to say," Turnip Schwarz would insist in that Southern accent of gently prolonged incredulity, "that this Mr. Yacub *really* persuaded *exactly* fifty-nine thousand nine hundred and ninety-nine black people to this Isle of Patmos in order to breed some obnoxious race of white devils that none of these participants would ever live to see and that none of them would want to *be* anyway?"

Oscar X usually wore brown suits and a white shirt with tie, and spoke in a diction of acquired precision, neatly baring his teeth at the close of each rebuttal. "It did not happen all at once. It took, according to the Prophet Mr. Farrad Muhammad, two hundred years of regulated eugenics to create a brown race from the black, two hundred more to produce from that a red race, two hundred more to produce a race of yellow folk"—a crisp little nod here to Wendy, silent on her side of the booth—"and from this a final deuce of centuries to the ultimate generation and supreme insult to Allah, the blond, blue-eyed, hairy-assed devils, who went nude on all fours and lived in trees, as all the textbooks tell us."

"Friend," Barry Little told Oscar X, "that is the pathetic sort of horseshit with which the common nigger has been scrambling his brains in this land all along. You can't breed a race in a couple generations, you need a million years; and what the textbooks tell us for that matter is that the black man isn't the oldest thing, he is the newest thing in *Homo sapiens*, the latest improved model. This here Muhammad Fraud of yours had read a little *Reader's Digest* anthropology and had the Bible shouted at him by his momma and that was all the information plus his misery that he *had*."

Esmeralda Miller was the only black woman at McCarthy. Her father was a dentist in a small city in upstate New York and she claimed she was a Marxist, in these days when that was a deadly serious thing to do. She was flat-chested and ash-colored and spoke in a level lustreless way, inflexible and indifferent, bored by arguing, the possessor of the flat truth. "You're both talking about alienation, man's alienation from his species being, and you can't talk about that without talking about the self-estrangement induced by forced labor. These racial categories are archaic, they have nothing to do with the class struggle; the black bourgeoisie, where it exists, is as oppressive, and in the last analysis as inevitably self-destructive, as the white, and now we have to add the yellow. Look at Liberia."

Wendy unexpectedly spoke. "Yet didn't Lenin point out that Western capitalism has forestalled its doom by the exploitation, through colonial imperialism, of the natural resources and cheap labor of the non-white peoples?"

"The white man is the devil," Oscar X broke back in. "He is a deliberately manufactured synthetic devil who is so disgusting the black man had to herd him across the Arabian desert and put him in those cold dark European Ice Age caves so he wouldn't destroy the world with his devilish mischief, and that is the proven historical truth, because that is where the white man came from; he was filling those caves full of gnawed-over bones while the black man down south was putting up those Pyramids easy as pie. These are *facts*."

The door of the café opened, admitting cold air and Candy. "Here comes pinktoes," Barry Little muttered. She fetched her own chair and sat at a corner of the already crowded table. The faint flurry of greetings died to a silence until Hakim Félix al-Bini cleared his throat and continued the conversation.

"It seems to me," he said, "the truth of a mythology should not be judged evidentially piece by piece but by its *gestalt* result. This Mr. Yacub, with his big head and his resemblance to Frankenstein, seems more than we need, from the standpoint of plausibility; but then so do Hitler, and Joan of Arc, and Jesus. They existed. Many things exist, and our dreams tell us many more exist, or exist elsewhere. What matters in a myth, a belief, is, Does it fit the facts, as it were, backwards? Does it enable us to live, to keep going? Yacub seems implausible but it does seem true, as we look around, that the white man is, as Oscar says, a devil."

Candy blushed, right to the neck of her sweater. "I should resent this," she said, "except you're all so nice."

"We are not nice," Barry Little said. "We are rapist apes."

"White people don't mean to be devils."

"No devil does," Hakim Félix told her. "But that is your tragedy, not ours." He took pity. "I was thinking less of lovely American co-eds than of my French commanding officers. They wear stiff dark uniforms and boxes on their heads and they shriek and slap their African soldiers as if they are possessed. Even the way they move, in angry little jerks, suggests dead men animated by devils. What we call a *zombi*." He was annoyed at her, for she had distracted him, with her complicated human situation of a white woman compelled to mingle with blacks, from some urgent general truth his mind had almost framed.

Barry Little had turned to Oscar X again. "The U.S. Negro has peddled horseshit to Ol' Massah so long he can't stop peddling it to himself. Until he gets up off his shiny ass and starts playing the game he can keep squatting right at the bottom of the heap. The game is, grab. That's why we've come to school, to learn to grab. There's only one way up, and that's worm your way. Sister Esmeralda of the Communist Storefront Evangelical Association and I agree about one thing at least: forget your color, colored man. Your dollar's as green as the next."

Turnip Schwarz said, "Willy Mays hit that ball over the fence, that's four bases for him too."

"You are one thousand per cent off your greedy heads," replied Oscar X. "Without the Brotherhood of Islam or some such, the single black man in any Northern city is less than nobody. He is not there, he is a *hole*. When a brother of ours in Temple Two is pulled in by the devil police, we go show up at the station in our nice quiet suits and that brother gets legal attention. He is not bopped. Those devils tuck their clubs away and put on smiles, because they see *power*."

"You can have power without superstition," Esmeralda said.

"*No*," the future Ellelloû said; the word "suits" had reminded him of what he had wanted to say. "It takes a mountain of myth to make even a grain of difference. It takes Mr. Yacub and the Isle of Patmos to make a man in the ghetto put on a suit. Oscar, you say Allah showed up in Detroit in 1930 in the person of a raincoat peddler called W. D. Fard and then disappeared in 1934; the Christians say He showed up in Jerusalem in the year 30 and then disappeared in the year 33. What is the result of these incredible rumors? Slaves lift their heads a fraction of an inch higher. Is this enough result? It is. Nothing less will produce any result at all. The dictatorship of the proletariat, the divinity of this or that itinerant—the crucial question isn't Can you prove it? but Does it give us a handle on the reality that otherwise would overwhelm us?" His voice sounded strained, reaching. But he discovered in the faces in the booth that his high-pitched oratory was not absurd, or not only absurd. Of course he had in his mind not the parochial concerns of these Americans—even the poorest of them rich by African standards—but the dim idea, stirring, of distant Kush. Candy placed her pale hand upon his and patted it, in consolation for an impossible future, or to recall him to this moment, these foreign accents, these abundant beverages, this cozy bar, this "bull session."

Shots rang out beyond the tent, barking and then whining, spanking the sand in spurts. The rifles of the caravan guards, old M-16s bought at discount, were not slow to answer, through a thatch of grunts and scuffling. Men raced by. Shadows flickered on the tent sides. The silent comedy of men fighting for their lives. Ellellou pressed Sheba beneath him, rolling her off the mat into a sandy corner where an assassin would not be likely to aim. His brain moved in the lazy logical notches that crisis activated in him, the synapses huge as lightning. He saw with microscopic clarity the glistening impasto of sweat and sand on Sheba's neck, noted that a necklace of fine lapis lazuli beads had been broken by the violence of his protective action. He calculated the odds that his identity had been detected, decided they were 50–50 (Mtesa, who had told Ezana of the mysterious truck, was the negative binary pole), and, given a prevalent co-efficient of danger, decided to stay in the tent, in his opaque, bullet-permeable prism of anonymity, rather than make a break into the wind, the dust, the shouts, the colorlessness. He amused himself, in the space between volleys of bullets, with searching amid the sand granules for the tiny lapis lazuli beads Sheba had shed, which would have been easier to find had their sparkling blue not ebbed from them. He sifted in his inner ear the friendly gunshots from those of the raiders, and heard the latter describing an arc that was coming no closer, that indeed was receding, into the desert reaches of the level truth that nothing matters in our human scale, for Allah truly is great. *Takbīr!*

This phrase had dawned in its grandeur for Ellellou not in his animist village but far from home, where the clubby minority students of McCarthy College had in the cheerful, smoky, bibulous flush of youthful egoism and sexual undercurrent forged the personal armament that would hold off the white man's encircling, sniping world. Through Oscar X young Hakim rediscovered Islam, travelling with the black American to the mother shrine, Elijah Muhammad's Temple Two in Chicago, or to the nearer, less majestic Temple Three in Milwaukee. Amid these conservatively suited brothers and reserved, chastely gowned and turbanned sisters, the future Ellelloû, welcomed and yet set apart as an African, found reminiscence of his deserted continent's dignity, its empty skies and savannas, its beautiful browns.

Subsequent palavering in the stirred-up caravan failed to discover any purpose to the raid. Nothing was taken, not so much as a camel-bag. A number of empty bottles—Московская, they said, Особая Водка—dropped by the shouting, shooting camel-riders muffled in *tagilmusts* had the hollow glitter of a deliberate clue. "Either," the President confided to Sheba, "they were Tuareg drunk on CIA bribes, or CIA operatives wishing to seem to be disguised Russians, or Russians who with the clumsy effrontery of these telltale leavings wish to suggest that they are CIA operatives."

Sidi Mukhtar had another thought. "You know," he said, "still slave-raiders in Balak."

Ellelloû scoffed. "That all died out with Tippu Tib."

"Not all," the caravan leader said, some hidden cause for humor creasing the withered rascal's features. "More selective now. Quality market instead of quantity."

"But who would they be after?" Ellelloû asked, feigning innocence of the knowledge that he himself, the President, was the caravan's prize.

Sidi Mukhtar winked toward the disguised dictator's tent. "Fine woman," he said simply.

Shadows, angels, dangers, trucks on the road, radio waves in the air slip by us. The incident had the quality, an impalpable slithering-by, of those Wisconsin nights when, outside in the snow no whiter than Candy's hips and flanks as they gleamed within the erotic turmoil of bedsheets, a siren went by, bleating and beating blue upon the bricks, the ivy, the windowsills, the steeples and silos of sleeping Franchise. In their senior year Candy had received permission to rent a room off-campus, with another girl, who for erotic reasons of her own was much in Green Bay. The room, above a realtor's office, was until this intrusion of blue black and white. The black lover would lift himself on an arm, the white beloved would lift her head, to recall him to their act, their intimacy, which had nothing to do with the tumult of which a fragment had poured past, and of which other fragments—the pulsing red lights of fire engines or of an ambulance—would in a minute follow. In this minute the frames of the prints, the mirrors, the wallpaper pattern in this room showed gray, gray on gray, the brightest gray the rectangles of the windowpanes that sealed them off from the world outside, whose murderous confusions swept by like the giant wings of a snowstorm. Their love, their mingled moistures, their breathing was suspended while the sirens passed. Were the police coming for him? He was aware that in some of these States skins of different colors rubbing was a crime. For his penis in her vagina there could be a rope around his neck. Nor did the Black Muslims condone copulating out of the faith, let alone with a blue-eyed she-devil. It was a conflict-making delight of his years here, being driven by Oscar X through the white man's fat landscape in a battered but capacious and powerful '49 Oldsmobile, while the radio poured forth Dinah Washington and Kay Starr, heading toward a temple of Islam in the slums of some Midwestern metropolis, where they might be frisked by grim Irish police or held up at knifepoint by unconverted juvenile delinquents of their own color. Dangers everywhere, slipping and sliding by.

Félix had perceived through the shadows a stain of blood on the bedsheet. Indeed, she had felt different tonight, not her usual just-tight-enough lubricity, but her wetness somehow rougher than usual, clotted. Unclean. Involuntarily he had grimaced, and had been told, "You should thank God. Up to this morning I was afraid I was pregnant."

"Wow," he said, Americanized.

She wanted to squeeze even more intimacy out of the revelation, to win more praise, for a fear endured. "Is that all you can say? You know, it's a rotten thing, to be a woman. You can't run away from your body. And the worst thing—"

"The worst thing, dear Candy?"

"Never mind."

"The worst thing was, you didn't want to be carrying a black baby?"

"No, I'd rather like that, as a matter of fact."

"Then what was this worst thing?"

"I won't tell you." She left the bed to get a cigarette. In the room whose dimness seemed a cubic volume of smoke, her body, crossed to the bureau, was pale, loose, lithe. She struck a match. A red glow formed the center of her voice. "I wasn't sure who the father was."

A police car bleated in the white night, more distantly. It did not take very many minutes of verbal struggle, as he remembered the incident, for him to elicit from her that the other possible father had been Craven.

Sheba had been too stoned to feel much alarm during the raid. As the spanking, whining sound of rifle fire receded, and violent silhouettes ceased to be projected through the dim prism-shaped volume of the tent, she bit my shoulder to suggest that I could withdraw the protective mass of my body from on top of hers. She shook some of the sand from her elaborate coiffure of tiny braids pinned into parabolas, and to revive herself for the night's trek popped a kola nut. With slack-jawed rapture she chewed, dyeing the inside of her mouth a deeper shade of gray. Along with her supply of Liberian kola nuts she had a bundle of Ethiopian khat and, for back-up, some Iranian bhang. Her gentle spirit rarely descended to earth.

Her robes hanging loose, her squat showed me between the parted roundnesses of the thighs her exquisite genitals, underparts profiled in two bulges, the cleft barely masked by the gauze of a thousand perfect circlets. Seeing me stare, Sheba laughed and, without abandoning the rapture of kola-chewing, urinated on the desert sand. In my madness of thirst, of love, I reached forward with cupped hands to rescue some of the liquid, though I knew from tales of other travellers that urine was as acid as lemon juice. It haunted my mouth for a burning hour. I went outside to discuss the raid. Sidi Mukhtar showed me the vodka bottles in the sun, their highlights hot as laser beams. I returned to the tent, where sweet Sheba, mellower, sang to the melancholy creak of her *anzad*:

> "*Do it to me, baby,*
> *do it, do it.*
> *Take that cold knife from its sheath,*

stick it in me underneath,
backwards, frontwards,
down my throat,
this trip has gone on
too long."

My responsive song, to which I kept time by tapping the
pummel of my camel-saddle, concerned oranges, an orange
imagined this time as shrivelled, and so infested by insects
it hums like a spherical transistor radio, until its substance
is consumed and the shell, brittle and stippled, shatters, like
a clay myrrh-holder from ancient Meroë. Our fellows in the
caravan, wearying of cursing the raiders and vowing highly
anatomical revenge, gathered at the tent-flap, and tossed in
to us fistfuls of obsolete coinage, cowrie shells and tiny mirrors, and pre-devaluation *lu* with its Swiss-tooled profile of
King Edumu, his head as bodiless on these coins as it was
in reality. The caravan drivers, porters, guards, navigators,
blacksmiths, leather-workers, translators, accountants, and
quality-controllers all lusted growlingly after my Sheba, who
contrived while laying double- and triple-stopped fingerings
upon the neck of the *anzad* simultaneously to expose one
bare foot and braceleted ankle. These men, their faces mere
slivers of baked skin and decayed teeth showing through the
folds of their *galabiehs* and *keffiyehs*, crowded too close, and,
feeling challenged, I pushed one. He fell like a stick lightly
stuck in the sand, and fainted; so weakened were we all by the
hardships of the Balak. Then came at last the water bag, the
swallowed streams of paradise, the rogue's lascivious nudge of
my wife's pendulous breasts, the sunset prayers, the saddling
up, the by now automatically deft repacking of our armful
of effects into capacious *khoorgs*, the tying fast of the rolled
tent-hides. Our camels suffered their cinched burdens with a
thirupping of their lips and a batting of their Disneyesque eyelashes. From afar Sidi Mukhtar hallooed. The moon showed
its silver crescent. The night's advance had begun.

These details are not easy to reconstruct, as I write where I
do, with its distractions of traffic, its *ombrelles* and promenad-
ing protégés, its tall drinks of orange Fanta and seltzer water
braced with a squid-squirt of anisette. But in the listening half

of my brain a certain jointed, clanking rhythm of our days remains, a succession of ordained small concussions, refastenings,
bucklings, and halloos as they passed down the line, avowing
our readiness to march, with certain death the penalty for falling out of our musical chain of snorting, swaying camels and
cajoling, whirling guides.

But O the desert stars! What propinquous glories! Tremulous globes overseeing our shadowy progress with their utter silence. More than chandeliers, chandeliers of chandeliers.
Um al-Nujūm, the Mother of Stars, ran as a central vein, a
luminous rift, within a sky, black as a jeweller's display velvet,
that everywhere yielded, to the patient, astounded eye, more
stars, so that the smallest interval between two luminaries was
subdivided, and subdivided again, by the appearance of new
points, leading awed scrutiny inward to a scale by which the
blur in Andromeda became an oval immensity whose particle
suns could be numbered. Under such a filigree our papery line
of silhouettes passed, camel-bells softly chuckling, through
the nocturnal escarpments and craters, wearily disturbing the
undisturbed sand. Sheets of lava rose around us like apparitions, eruptions through a crystalline mantle whose splinters
had lain for aeons where they fell. Abundant sandstone testified to a Paleozoic ocean; deeply cut dry canyons proved that
once in some ghostly humid time great rivers had watered
the Massif. Scaley defiles, of shale a-gleam as if wet, suddenly
gave way to giddying views, immense gray bowls of emptiness sweeping to the next jagged, starlit range. What meant so
much inhuman splendor? *But when the earth is crushed to fine
dust, and your Lord comes down with the angels in their ranks,
and Hell is brought near—on that day man will remember his
deeds.* My life by those lunar perspectives became a focus of
terror, an infinitely small point nevertheless enormously hollow, a precipitous intrusion of some substance totally alien
and unwelcome, into these rocks, these fantastic orbs of fire,
this treacherous ground of sand. I could not have withstood
the solitude, the monotony, the huge idiocy of this barren
earth, had not Sheba been by my side, sullen and warm. I
loved in her what the others, the cruel illiterates of the desert,
scented—her vacancy. Where another woman had an interior,
a political space that sent its emissaries out to bargain for her

body and her honor, Sheba had a space that asked no tending, that supported a nomadic traffic of music and drugs. Such a woman is an orphan of Allah, a sacred object. Sheba never questioned, never reflected. I said to her, "The stars. Are they not terrible?"

"No. Why?"

"So vast, so distant. Each is a sun, so distant that its light, travelling faster than the fastest jinni, takes years to reach our eyes."

"Even if such a lie were true, how would it affect us?"

"It means we are less than dust in the scheme of things."

She shrugged. "What can be done, then?"

"Nothing, but to pray that it not be so."

"So that is why you pray."

"For that, and to reassure the people of Kush."

"But you do not believe?"

"For a Muslim, unbelief is like a third eye. Impossible."

We swayed in silence. Our fatigue was a tower to which each night added another tier. I said, "And do you know, there are laws all about us? Laws of energy and light, laws that set these rocks here, and determined their shape, and their slant. Once an ocean lay down many grains of sand; once the bodies of more small creatures than there are stars above us laid down their skeletons to form islands, great shoals, which volcanoes lifted up, and then the wind wore down again, and water that rained, and flowed, and vanished. Once all this was green, and men hunted elephants and antelope, and drew pictures of themselves on the rocks."

"Show me such a picture."

"They are hard to find. I have seen them in books."

"Things can be made up and put into books. I want to see a picture on a rock."

"I will hope to show you one. But what I am saying is more than that once men hunted and even fished here. I am saying that perhaps again this will be true, and we will be forgotten, all of us forgotten, of less account than the camels whose hides make up our tents. Past and future are immense around us, they are part of the laws I speak of, that are more exact than anything you know, they are like those rocks that when you split them come away exactly flat. Everything obeys these laws.

Things grow by these laws, and things die by them. They are what make us die. We are caught inside them, like birds in a cage—no, like insects in a cage that is all bars, that has no space inside, like a piece of rotten wood, only not rotten but hard, harder than the hardest rock. And the rock, one single rock, stretches out to those stars, and beyond, for in truth they seem very close, and there is a blackness beyond, where those same laws continue, and continue to crush us, finer than the finest dust, finer than the antimony you use to make your eyelids gray. Help me, Sheba. I am sinking."

"I do what I can. But you make what I do seem very little."

"No, it is much."

After a pause, while the feet of our steeds slithered on the cold sand, she asked me, "When do you think we will reach our destination?"

"We will reach it," I told her, "when there is no farther to go."

"And how will we know when that is?"

"The drought," I told her, "will have ended."

In the home of Candace's parents, where she took me late in our freshman year, the white woodwork was like a cage also. I marvelled at the tightness, the finish. Her father came toward me from rooms away, a big man with Candy's beryl eyes and gray hair so thin and light it wandered across his skull as he gestured. I had the impression that his bigness was composed of many soft places, bubbles in his flesh where alcohol had fermented and expanded; he shook my hand with too much force, overcarrying. "So you're the young man my daughter has been raving about," he said.

Raving? I looked at Candy's pointed polite face, whose straight fine nose had come from her mother; I had just met the lady, who seemed afraid. Maybe the something bloated and patchy about the Dad was fear too. We were all afraid. I was alarmed, as the house opened to me—its woodwork interlocked like the lattice of an elaborate trap; its pale, splashy, furtively scintillating wallpaper; its deep, fruit-colored, step-squelching carpets; its astonishing living-room, long and white, two white sofas flanking a white marble coffee table bearing porcelain ashtrays and a set of brass scales holding white lilies whose never-wilt lustre was too good to be true.

And what were these little saucers, with tiny straight sides and bottoms of cork, scattered everywhere, on broad sofa arms and circular end tables, as if some giant had bestowed on the room the largesse of his intricate, oversize coinage?

"Daddy, I wouldn't say 'raving,'" Candy corrected, embarrassed, her face, that I now perceived as a clash of genes, blushing.

"Rave is what she does, Mr.— I don't want to mispronounce."

"Call me Felix," I said, Anglicizing the *é*. I wondered if I should sit, and would the sofa swallow me like some clothy crocodile? Often in America, in drugstores and traffic jams, I had the sensation of being within a bright, voracious, many-toothed maw. The Cunninghams' living-room had puddles of cosmetic odor here and there. As in the old cinema palace on Commerce Street, a heroic stagnation had overtaken decor. Seating myself on the edge of the bottomlessly spongy sofa, I touched the brass scales and, sure enough, discovered a refusal to tip. Once an honest artifact, it had been polished, welded, and loaded with plastic lilies. Fixed forever, like that strange Christian heaven, where nothing happened, not even the courtship of houris.

"*Asseyez-vous*," Mrs. Cunningham had suggested, with a smile touchingly like her daughter's, only somehow uneven, as if Candy's quick smile had been crumpled up and then retrieved and smoothed and pasted over a basic frown.

But when I responded, in textbook French, complimenting my hostess on the beauty of her room and its florid and cinematic appointments, her visage went as blank as that of the enamelled shepherdess on the mantel, frozen in a pose of alert unheeding vis-à-vis the fluting shepherd in the exactly corresponding mantel position. Between them stood an impressive clock with a pendulum of mercury rods, and its action may have been interfering, on their chilly elfin plane, with the call of the shepherd's piping. The fireplace itself, the hearth whose symbolic domestic centrality was so primitive that even I might have found here a familiar resonance, was swept as clean as a shower stall and ornamented with unscathed brass andirons supporting three perfect birch logs that would never be burned.

Mr. Cunningham restored the conversation to solid English.

"Feelicks, if I'm not being too personal, what's your major going to be at McCarthy?"

"Freshmen are not required to declare, but I had thought Government, with a minor in French Literature."

"French Literature, what the hell use would that be to your people? Government, I can see. Good luck with it."

"In the strange climate of my native land, Mr. Cunningham, the literature the French brought us may transplant better than the political institutions. There is a dryness in Racine, a harshness in Villon, that suits our case. In French Indochina, not many years ago, I had the experience of trading memorized sonnets by Ronsard with a prisoner of war, a terrorist who was later executed. In the less developed quarters of the world, the power politics of the West can be brushed aside, but its culture is pernicious."

"*Can*dy," Mrs. Cunningham began with the overemphasis of the shy, having seated herself in a wing chair patterned in cabbage-sized roses, her lean shins laid gracefully, diagonally together with a dainty self-conscious "sexiness" that reminded me of her daughter . . . who had vanished! *Horreur!* Where? I could hear her voice dimly giggling in some far reach of the house. She had gone upstairs, it later transpired, to talk with her "kid" brother; or was it into the kitchen, to renew acquaintance with the Cunninghams' colored cook? At any rate, she had left me alone with her terrifying pale parents, the female of whom was posed in mid-sentence, and who now settled on the verb she had paused to locate among her treasury of "nice" things—"al*lud*ed to your romantic adventures."

"Not romantic, Madame; dreary, truly. The French in exchange for their poems asked that we fight in other poor countries. I obliged them in Indochina, for it took me out of my native village; when it came to Algeria, where the rebels were fellow Africans, I became a rebel myself, and deserted."

"Oh dear," Mrs. Cunningham said. "Can you ever go back?"

"Not until the colonial power departs. But this may happen within the decade. All it needs is a politician in Paris who is willing to act as a mortician. In the meantime, I enjoy your amazing country as a dream from which I will some day wake miraculously refreshed."

"There's a question I'm rarin' to ask you," Mr. Cunningham

said, rising ominously, but not to throttle me, as his growling tone for a second implied to my alert nerves, but to move to a tall cabinet and get himself another drink, from a square bottle whose first name was Jack, or was it Jim? The riddle of my own name he informally solved with, "How about *you*, fella?"

My mouth was indeed dry, from unease. "A glass of water, if it's no trouble."

He threatened to balk. "Plain water?" Then his mind embraced my response, as something he might have expected, from an underprivileged delegate from the childlike underworld. "Wouldn't you rather have a 7 Up? Or a Schlitz?"

I would have, and brushed from my own mind the mirage of a beer sitting golden on a dark table of the Badger Cafe; but I felt the family dinner ahead of me streteh like a long trek through a bristling wilderness of glass and silver and brittle remarks, and had resolved upon sobriety as my safeguard. Also there was some silent satisfaction in impeding this big white devil's determination to be hospitable. "Just water, if you please," I insisted.

"Your religion, I suppose?"

"Several of them."

"Some ice in it?" he asked.

"No ice," I said, again against my desires, but in conformity with an ideal austerity I had grown like a carapace, in which to weather this occasion.

"Alice," he said, with unexpected euphony; his obedient wife arose—the shepherdess *did* hear the shepherd—and went into the kitchen, which seemed to be, by one of those inscrutable jurisdictions whereby American couples order the apparent anarchy of their marriages, her province. Mr. Cunningham, freshly reinforced by his bottled cohort, pursued his interesting question, which was, "What do you make of our American colored people?"

I had already enough converse with the disciples of Elijah Muhammad to hear the word "colored" as strange, but this strangeness was swallowed by the expanding strangeness of the preceding "our." I looked at my feet, for I was travelling in treacherous territory. My search for an answer was needless, for Mr. Cunningham was providing it.

"What can we do," he was asking me, "to help these people?

They move into a nice neighborhood and turn it into a jungle. You pour millions of state money in and it goes up in smoke. Our American cities are being absolutely destroyed. Detroit used to be a great town. They've turned it into a hellhole, you get mugged by these kids right in Hudson's, the downtown is a wasteland. Chicago's going the same way. Hyde Park, all around the university, these lovely homes, a white girl can't walk her dog after supper without a knife in her stocking. The Near North Side's a little better, but two blocks in from the Lake you're taking your life in your hands. Why do you think I moved the family up to Oshkosh? I lost forty grand a year by leaving the city. But hell, the rates on real estate were going out of sight, the only way to get your money out of some of those neighborhoods was burn 'em down. Cars, anybody who keeps a car on the street should have his head examined. They wouldn't just steal 'em, they'd smash 'em up—pure spite. What's *eat*ing the bastards? You'd love to know."

Mrs. Cunningham returned with the water, in a glass with a silver rim, and I thought of desert water holes, the brackishness, the camel prints in the mud, the bacterial slime that somehow even across the burning sands manages to find its live way.

Mr. Cunningham's tone tightened a little, with his wife's return. There was this flattering about his tirade: that he was addressing me as a fellow sufferer, that the heat of his grievance had burned away my visible color. He went on, "I've had my knocks up here, trying to make a name coming in cold in the middle of life; but at least I'm not afraid my daughter's going to be raped and don't have to lock the car every time I stop to take a piss at a gas station."

"Frank," Alice said.

"Sorry, there, but I guess even over in the Sahara you know what a piss is."

"*Nous buvons le pissat*," I said, smiling.

"Exactly," he said, slipping a glance of small triumph into his wife. "Anyway, where was I? Yeah, my question: What's the solution for these people?"

"Provide them useful work?"

Made in all timidity, this suggestion seemed to tip him toward fury. His patchy look intensified, his hair fluffed straight up. "Christ, they won't take the jobs there are, they'd rather rake in welfare. Your average Chicago jigaboo, he's too smart to dirty his paws; if he can't pimp or hustle drugs, or land some desk job with dingbat Daley, he'll just get his woman pregnant and watch the cash roll in."

"That is—what do you call it?—American individualism, is it not? And enterprise, of an unforeseen sort."

He stared at me. He was beginning to see me. "Christ, if that's enterprise, let's give it all over to the Russians. They've got the answer. Concentration camps."

"Daddy, you promised you wouldn't," Candy cried; for she had come down the stairs, freshly brushed, her face alight with the happiness of "home," her crimson lips renewed, her rounded slim body bouncy as a cheerleader's, in a cashmere sweater and a pleated wool skirt, which swirled as she swung herself around the newel post whose carpentered pirouette I had admired upon entering.

"Wouldn't what, dear?" her mother asked, as if straining to hear, in this room of silent clocks and chiming resemblances.

"Wouldn't bother Happy about the Chicago blacks."

"Not just Chicago," her father protested, "it's lousy everywhere. Even L.A., they're pulling it under. Hell, Chicago at least has a political machine, to make payoffs and keep some kind of lid on. In a city like Newark, they've just taken over. They've done to Newark what we did to Hiroshima. Grass doesn't even grow where they are. They are the curse of this country, I tell you, no offense to our friend here."

"Daddy, you are so ignorant and prejudiced I just can't even cry about it anymore. I didn't want to bring Happy here but Mother said I must. You make me *very* ashamed in front of him."

"Happy, hell, he's out of it. He's an African, at least they got some pride over there. As he says, they have their own culture. The poor colored in this country, they got nothing but what they steal." And he not quite drunkenly winked at me. It crossed my mind that I, as an African, was being thanked because I had not come over here to stay and raise the automotive insurance rates with my thievery; more, he saw me as the embodiment of the mother continent that yearned, he hoped, to take the Afro-Americans back into a friendly, oozy chaos.

"Exactly," I said, and stood. "Nothing but what they steal." In the rebellious act of standing I changed my perspective on the room, and was freshly overwhelmed by its *exotisme*, its fantasy, the false flowers and fires, the melting-iceberg shapes of its furniture, its whiteness and coldness and magnificent sterility; the emptiness, in short, of its lavish fullness, besprinkled with those inexplicable cork coins.

[I express this badly. The wet ring from a glass of Fanta has blurred my manuscript. I long to get back to the Bad Quarter of Kush, and the spaces of my dear doomed Sheba.]

The "kid" brother had followed Candy downstairs. Frank Jr. was a furtive, semi-obese child of fourteen—old enough, in my village, for the long house—whose complexion showed the ravages of sleeping alone, night after night, in an over-heated room with teddy bears, felt pennants, and dotted Swiss curtains. The smile he grudged me displayed a barbarous, no doubt painful tooth-armor of silver and steel. His limp dank handshake savored of masturbatory rites. His eyes were fishy with boredom, and he tried to talk to me about basketball, of which I knew, despite my color, nothing. For this family occasion the child had put on a shirt and tie; the collar and knot cut cruelly into the doughy flesh of his neck. I thought, Here is the inheritor of capitalism and imperialism, of the Crusades and the spinning jenny. Yet he did not so much seem Mr. Cunningham in embryo as Mr. Cunningham, with his quirky bravado, desperate wish to be liked, and somehow innocently thinned and scattered hair, seemed a decaying, jerry-built expansion of his son. I perceived that a man, in America, is a failed boy.

Then a black woman came into the alabaster archway of the living-room. For all the frills of her uniform, she looked familiar, with her heavy lower lip and fattening charms. Her uncanny resemblance to Kadongolimi was reinforced by her manner, which implied that she had had many opportunities in life and might well, with equal contentment, be elsewhere. "Dinner, ma'am." We all stood, in obedience to our queenly servant.

But before we went in, Mrs. Cunningham, with a predatory deftness that showed a whole new piece of her equipment for survival, had silently as a pickpocket knifed behind me and placed my empty water glass, which I had set down in the center of an end table beside a sofa arm, securely within one of the little cork-and-silver saucers. Of course. They were "coasters," which in the friendly bars of Franchise took the form of simple discs of advertisement-imprinted blotting paper. By such sudden darts into the henceforth obvious, anthropology proceeds.

Oscar X took the future Elleloû to meetings of the Nation of Islam; they disliked the term Black Muslims, though both "black" and "Muslim" seemed canonical. Temple Three, in Milwaukee, was two hours to the south, but another rushing, radio-flooded hour, in that many-knobbed, much-rusted, lavishly chromate guzzler of *essence* called, I thought oddly in a nation obsessed with the new, an Olds, took us to Temple Two, in Chicago, where the Messenger of Allah himself could be heard. He spoke in a murmur, a small delicate man with some resemblance, I was to notice when I awoke in Noire, to Edumu IV, Lord of Wanjiji. The Messenger wore an embroidered gold fez. He was a frail little filament who burned with a pure hatred when he thought of white men and lit up our hearts. He spoke of the white man's "tricknology." He told us that the black man in America had been so brainwashed by the blue-eyed devils he was mentally, morally, and spiritually dead. He spoke of a nation of black men, carved from the side of America like a blood-warm steak from the side of an Ethiopian steer, that would exist on a par with the other nations of the world. He rehearsed the services the black man had performed for his slavemasters in the United States, from cooking their meals and suckling their babies (yes) to building their levees and fighting their wars (yes indeed). He mocked the civil-rights movements, the "sitting-in," "lying-in," "sliding-in," "begging-in," to unite with a slavemaster who on the one hand demands separate schools, beaches, and toilets and on the other hand through the agency of rape had so mongrelized the American black man that not a member of this audience was the true ebony color of his African fathers. "Little Lamb!" souls in our crowd would cry out, and "*Teach*, Messenger!" The litany of wrongs never wearied him, this shambling gold-fezzed foreshadow of my king. At his mention of rape, I would find myself crying. At his mention of the tribe

of Shabazz, for which the word "Negro" was a false and malicious label, I would find myself exultant. At his amazed soft
recounting of some newly arisen marvel of devilish hypocrisy,
such as the then recent Supreme Court decision which told
black men they were integrated and thus opened them up to
the sheriff's dogs when they were such fools as to take their little scrubbed and pigtailed daughters to school, or such ancient
marvels of Christian tricknology as the mixing of slaves in the
lots as they were sold so that no two spoke the same language
or remembered the same gods, so that no idol remained to
these slaves but the white devil's blue-eyed, yellow-haired, historically grotesque Jesus, I would find myself wild with visions
of what must be done, of sleeping millions to be awakened
from their brainwashing, of new nations founded on the rock
of vengeance and led by such quiet brown hate-inspired men
as this, our Messenger.

And on Tuesday nights (Unity Nights) or Friday nights
(Civilization Nights) it was pleasant to mingle, and even to be
cosseted as an African with a smattering of Arabic, among the
beige-gowned women and dark-suited men who had redeemed
themselves from the flash and ruin of the ghetto. Ex-criminals,
many of them, they moved with the severity of *sous-officiers*,
and I realized that, in this era when the magic wand is hollow
and all wizards, chiefs, and Pharaohs went tumbling under the
gun's miraculous bark, the army is the sole serious institution
left—all others are low comedy and vacuous costumery. The
army must rule. The United States takes noisy pride in its sack-
suited government of lawyers and fixers, but the bulky blue
army of police is what the citizen confronts. Their patrol cars
bleat past every lulled couple's fornication nest. Their baby-
faced officers waddle across Commerce Street with waistfuls
of leather-swaddled armaments. Beyond these blue men, for
my black friends, the government was a gossamer of headlines
spun like fresh cobwebs each morning, and brushed away by
noon. I perceived this then: government is mythological in nature. These stepchildren of Islam were seeking to concoct a
counter-myth. "*Al-salāmu ʿalaykum!*" The Messenger's greeting rolled back: "*Wa-ʿalaykum al-salām!*" I had never heard
Arabic, which in Africa stings like a whip wielded by slavers
and schoolteachers, spoken so sweetly as here, in America, in
the flat rote accents of children of janitors and sharecroppers,

who had memorized their few phrases as the passwords into self-reliance and dignity. *Takbīr!* God is great! *Mā shā' allah:* it is as God wills.

If our non-alcoholic fruit punches, and the porkless delicacies prepared by the ankle-weary work-day kitchen slaves of white homes, all had a flavor of charade, it was a purposeful earnest charade, and with altogether another taste too, a sacred spicy something that prickled in my nostrils and made me, enacting my own charade as an authentic Child of the Book, feel more exalted, more serenely myself, than I did, in this treacherous land of *kafirs*, anywhere else.

Although Oscar X, I years later learned, gave up the Faith in disgust at the Messenger's well-authenticated sexual lapses, and some of my chaste sisters have put on again the white robes of the Christian choir, and my earnest lean-faced brothers (their eyes glittering above their cheekbones like snipers levelling their sights, their dangerous nervousness sheathed in the quiet devil-garb of corporation lawyers and FBI men) have re-enlisted in the guerrilla war of the streets—though the Nation of Islam took a mortal wound when it became Malcolm's killer, and the Afro-American's misery moved on in its search for the revolutionary instrument, those ghetto temples were for me a birthplace. The Messenger disclosed to me riches that were, unbeknownst, mine. He taught me that the evils I had witnessed were not accidental but intrinsic. He showed me that the world is our enslaver, and that the path to freedom is the path of abnegation. He taught me nationhood, purity, and hatred: for hatred is the source of all strengths, and its fruit is change, as love is the source of debility, and its fruit is passive replication of what already too numerously exists.

At temple meetings, on vacation from Candy Cunningham and McCarthy College with their noble schemes for my transformation into a white-headed, lily-livered black man, I was free to imagine myself in an absolutist form. Crystals of dreaming erected within me, and the nation of Kush as it exists is the residue of those crystals.

The terrain became more mountainous; the patches of thornbush, the scant tufts of the world's dullest flowers, no longer could draw the least excuse for life from the gray rocks, the black air. At night the sound of dry ice shattering rocks gave staccato echo to the scrabble of the camels trying to keep their footing on millennial accumulations of scree. We rattled as we went, and Sheba's *anzad* (varied now and then by an end-blown flute that doubled as a dildo in the face of my impotence) eerily harmonized with the stony music our passage struck from the resonant minerals and crystals jutting around us. Haematite, magnetite, kassiterite, wolframite, muscovite, mispickel, and feldspars cast their glints by moonlight. I recalled Ezana's dark geological allusions, and wondered how my old Minister of the Interior was faring in captivity. We had shared the same *caserne*, heard together the call, "*Aux armes! Aux armes! Les Diables Jaunes!*" Sentimental reflections of all sorts coursed through my weary soul. The moons waxed and waned; Dhū 'l-Hijja became Muharram, Muharram became Safar, or else I had lost count. The waterhole scouts ranged away from the caravan for days, and some never returned. The moment was approaching when Sheba and I must leave the caravan and seek out the cave where the head of Edumu IV reportedly babbled oracles.

In the vicinity of the cave, Sidi Mukhtar told us, European rock doves had gathered, and now one or two of these birds, gray, but with points of lustre on the head and throat that bubbled up, in this monochromatic climate, to the verge of iridescence, could be seen at dusk and dawn, dotting a distant slope of speckled asphalt-colored shale like pigeons in the lee of chimneys on city roofs. Up and down we wound our way through alleylike passes so narrow the sky was reduced to the width of a river above our heads. The ordeal was aging Sheba: the baby fat of trust had fallen from her cheeks; some of the looks she darted at me sideways, through the asynchronous heaving of our camels' humps, were positively dubious.

"Do you love me?" Candy would ask.

"Tell me what you mean by love," young Hakim would counter, his emotional defenses well fortified by the years of arid book-learning: from Plato to Einstein, a steady explosion, the sheltering gods all shattered.

"What do you mean, what do I mean?"

Follow-up emergency vehicles wailed by on the street below. Their spinning red lights dyed the icicles at the window a bloody red: fangs of a deep-throated growl. "To what extent," he pursued, "is your so-called love for me love of yourself, yourself in the Promethean stance of doing the forbidden, that is, of loving me?"

"To what extent, I could ask in turn, is your fucking me revenging yourself on the white world?"

"Is that what your parents suggest?"

"They don't know. They don't ask. After a certain age it's easier for them to forget you have a body. Marriage would be the only crunch."

"Indeed."

"What do you mean, 'Indeed'?"

"I mean, indeed, marriage would be a crunch." He changed the subject, so firmly she would know it was being changed. "This fucking to avenge oneself, I think that is an American style. I do not have, that I can detect, the sexual sense of outrage that our friends Oscar and Turnip and Barry bear toward the white man, whom they call, simply, the Man. The brown-faced Arabs were butchering and carrying off my people while the French were innocently constructing Chartres. The Tuareg have been more ruthless still. They are white, beneath their blue robes. In my land the black man is the Man, who performs generation after generation the super stunt of continuing to exist, to multiply among the pain and the heat. Noire is a river where others come to fish, but they do not swim with us."

"Touch me while you talk. Please, Happy."

He touched her white flank, from which the reflected red pulsing had ebbed. "In the village," he said, in his weariness surrendering to the first words that came, "we were always touching one another, uncles and sisters and friends, and then at thirteen the boys earn the right to sleep as an age-set, in the long house. I often think of your brother, the sadness of him sleeping alone, in a room all his. To emerge from such solitude into sexuality must be a great arrival, greater than in other nations, too poor to have so many rooms. And then the middle-aged of America do not touch either. At the end, the nurses and doctors handle you. It is a sign the darkness of the womb is being approached again."

She turned her back and her skin felt cold as a snake's. She had wanted to talk about marriage.

Pyrolusite, goethite, antimonite, quartz: Sidi Mukhtar
named the crystals, winking. "Much treasure." He tapped the
cliff. He had once fallen in with Rommel's armies and been
trained in geology, in *Erdwissenschaft*. He had grown fond of
the *anzad* player and her little protector. He was sorry to see
them leave the caravan. But the dread time had come.

At the same moment, Ellelloû later learned from reliable
sources, Michaelis Ezana was making his way through the
midnight corridors of the Palais de l'Administration des Noirs.
He had persuaded his guards, two Golo simpletons who had
been shifted from the rat-killing detail at one of the surplus-
peanut mounds on the plains near Al-Abid, that a six o'clock
martini was a kind of internal ablution which should, for ultimate purity, be taken with the *salāt al-maghrib*. Day by day
he increased the proportion of gin to vermouth to the point
where the stout fellows, hardened imbibers of honey beer,
toppled. His way was clear. As once before in these pages, as
perceived from this same window, the muezzins' twanging call
echoed under the cloudless sky as under a darkening dome of
tile. Rather than risk confrontation with the soldiers and their
doxies quartered in the fourth-floor corridor, who, if not fully
alerted to the *nuancé* shifts of inner-circle leadership in Kush,
certainly had caught the smoky whiff of *tabu* that now attached
to Ezana, he, by a series of ripping, knotting, and measuring
actions that like certain of these sentences were maddeningly
distended by seemingly imperative refinements and elabora-
tions in the middle, constructed a rope of caftans and agals
and descended, through the silver kiss of the last moon of Safar, down the wall, in his terrified descent accompanied by his
indifferent shadow, a faint large bat-shape whose feet touched
his abrasively. Ezana attained, without the makeshift rope's
breaking, a window of the third floor, which housed the People's Museum of Imperialist Atrocities. As he had in descending prayed, the window was unfastened; or, rather, the catch
had long since come loose from the wood, baked by the daily
heat to the friability of clay. He pushed it open with a crackle
and, trembling, dropped to the floor inside.

Few visited the Museum but nostalgic reactionaries. The
leather trappings on the French parade harness had been nibbled and consumed by the starving. The little model, meant

to scandalize with its penury, of the typical servants' hut *circa* 1910 had been carefully dismantled and smuggled outside to serve as shelter for a family of Istiqlal's urban homeless. The torturing apparatus, dominated by a gaunt dental drill, and the guillotine, Gothic pinnacle of Gallic justice, cast the longest shadows as the Minister of the Interior stole barefoot among the dusty museum cases. The cases contained lumps of rubber and gypsum and other raw materials gouged from Noire by naked workers (shown in a miniature tableau, balsawood bodies expiring of exhaustion at the mouth of a papier-mâché mine) paid a few centimes a day. An entire case was filled with centimes. Another case held only imperialist mustaches and monocles; these latter winked as Ezana's shadow soundlessly passed. The next case held emptied bottles of the *colons'* ungodly poisons—absinthe, cognac, champagne, Perrier water; their glimmer was doused and rekindled again as Ezana, his heart thumping, slid by. In other cases, more darkly, lurked Bibles and missals in their pernicious range of sizes and languages; displayed with them, wittily, were the ledgers of the army of the profiteers, the plantation managers, the concessionnaires, the export-import agencies, the factors of European cloth and cutlery in the remote villages, the shipping lines that creakily plied the Grionde. Ezana had once made a study of these ledgers, and after some consultation with Ellellou had suppressed this curious finding: none showed a profit. On paper, colonialism was a distinctly losing venture. The cost of the armies, the administrators, the flags, the forts, the bullets, the roads, the quinine, the imported knives, forks, and spoons, quite outweighed the grudging haul of raw materials and taxes elicited from the unprincipled, evasive chiefs and stubbornly inefficient populace. The most rapacious exploiter of them all, King Leopold, who permitted appalling atrocities in an attempt to balance his books, had to be rescued from bankruptcy. As the colonies were jettisoned into independence, the ledgers of the metropolitan capitals registered distinct relief. The most *outré* region of *la France, d'Outremer*, Noire, had been, in Paris, a minor statistical nuisance.

Why, then, had the oppressors come? As Ezana moved barefoot through the deserted museum, the nagging question merged with the discomfort in his feet, their soles,

for too many years cradled in Italian leather, made tender
by the daring descent down the rough inner face of the Palais.
The Europeans had come, it seemed, out of simple jealousy;
the Portuguese had a fort or two, so the Danes and Dutch
had to have forts. Egypt fell to the British, so the French had
to have the Sahara; because the British had Nigeria, the Germans had to have Tanganyika. But what, then, was there to
do with these vast tracts? Drain swamps, shoot elephants,
plant cocoa, clear the way for missionaries. In Noire these
activities had been carried forward in the most attenuated
way: there were few swamps, and fewer elephants. Nevertheless the Gauls had gone through the motions, and a handful of Frenchmen who at home would have been outcasts
here established, on the backs of blacks little more aware of
their presence than of flies on their skins, a precarious, shrill
self-importance. A case in the museum held whips, ranging
from the brutal *cicotte*, a length of hippo hide for flogging
plantation workers into line, to the dainty silken *fouet* with
which a regional administrator's wife could chastise one of
her maidservants, knots having been artfully braided into the
ends of the threads. The next case contained obscene accessories of a brothel in Hurriyah maintained for white militia
and laborers by the dusky *autochtones*. Contact, of a sort, had
been made. Civilization like an avalanche of sludge had collapsed into the blank clean places of the maps. Skins rubbed
as among sleepers with shut lids, thrashing and tugging at
the covers. Along one dark wall there were great maps of the
sub-Saharan empires, Songhai and Mali and Kanem-Bornu;
these too had been imposed from beyond and their rise and
fall punctuated by the severing of many an ear, hand, and
head. On this same wall hung daguerreotypes gone coppery
and quaint, of frilly picnics in the bush, of military parades
aligning multitudinous buttons, of a painter in the goatee
and slack white shirt of the *fin de siècle* scrupulously loading
his easel with an Impressionist rendering of a beehive hut
and a baobab tree. Stealthily past these images of an out-of-
date intermingling Ezana crept, pondering the meaning of
colonialism, the impossibility that a nation with the sublime
literature and cuisine of France would subdue a scruffy sixth
of an ungrateful continent in order to create flattering jobs

for a few adventurous dregs, and the concomitant possibility that now this great land of Kush existed solely to give
employment to a few revolutionary elitists like himself. The
memorials of imperial atrocities stretched out their shadows
as if not to let him go as he eased back the massive hexagonal
bolt on a door beneath an oil portrait of Governor Faidherbe, action shots of the Hourst expedition, and photostats
of especially atrocious pages from Colonel Toutée's famous
diary. Ezana let himself stealthily into the corridor. It was
empty. The flaking white ceiling, the green molding at the
level of his hand, diminished toward infinity. Ghostly in his
dirty prisoner's robe, his eyes bugging in his curvilinear face,
his wristwatch holding the exact time to the second behind
its own black face, Ezana moved close to the wall, pondering Ellelloû, his leader's far journey, the unlikelihood that he
would reach his destination. He pondered his own survival,
weighed the odds against a Palais coup.

But Ezana had no wish to lead. To advise, to raise quiet
objections while chocolate quietly cooled, to train typists, sign
directives, pull rafts of allied statistics from the consoles of filing cabinets, to see a nation and all its nebulous load of baffled
human consciousness reduced to rigorous alignments of nouns
and numbers, and furthermore to dress like a dignitary, to appear on an odd denomination of postage stamp, and to have
an embezzled fortune banked against the Day of Disaster in
a numbered Swiss account—all this he liked, but not to lead.
A leader is one who, out of madness or goodness, volunteers
to take upon himself the woe of a people. There are few men
so foolish; hence the erratic quality of leadership in the world.
Ezana furthermore didn't see that leadership was very productive or progressive; the results that truly changed the condition
of mankind were achieved by anonymous men, accumulators
of correct facts and minute improvements, men of unspectacu-
lar gifts who add the culminating touch and arrive at the nearly
obvious conclusion while the charismatic sloganeers and lightning rods of the media go through their symbolic motions—
paper gods consumed by the primeval conflagration of human
curiosity. They could be scrapped in a minute, but there would
always be a place for a man like him.

He crept along the corridor, and came at last to a stairway.

Day-Glo-orange arrows pointed down and signs in six languages said DOWN ONLY. Ezana had reason to ask himself if
indeed he did have a place. In his cheap robe of old *merikani*,
its folds tapping his shaking knees and spherical buttocks, he
felt transposed into that spatially vague afterlife so monotonously guaranteed by the rambling Mohamet. Did the stairway go down to the girls' high school or to the prison where
dissident rural chiefs and adolescents addicted to contraband
comic books underwent laborious courses of political reeduca-
tion, with seminars on the Thousand Uses of the Peanut and
the Thought of Josef Stalin thrown in for second offenders?
Ezana had no business in either of these places; his education
felt complete. Against all official indications he took the stairway up, to the floor where his old offices were. The image of
his old suite—the shag carpet, the glass-topped desk, the In
basket, the Out basket, and the little tree of rubber stamps
beside the postage scales—burned in his mind like an oasis in
the imagination of a desert traveller. Once seated in that place,
he could regrasp the levers of government. Ellelloû, however
far away, would feel the nation rumble under his feet, the gears
of progress re-engaged. The contretemps concerning Gibbs
and Klipspringer would pass like a woman's petulance. He and
Ellelloû needed one another as the earth needs the sky, as the
traveller needs the camel. One determines, the other implements. Already Ezana was beginning to feel snug, nestled back
into place and reconnected to the power terminals.

    The first thing he must implement, he saw with sudden exec-
utive clarity, was the cooling of Klipspringer. These Americans,
they talk in billions, but turn out to have been "brainstorm-
ing." No matter: the quick winds of Washington would blow
him away, and another bargainer would take his place. As for
the Russians, he would work to rid Kush of their boisterous
mischief. Obstructionists and familiars of confusion, profiteers
of all disarray, they were behind this melancholy distraction of
the President, Ezana had no doubt. The superparanoids, he
had once amusingly called the world's present subdividers. He
found them both gross, compared to the old imperialist powers, who in their chilly country houses and baroque chancel-
leries at least had partitioned the outgunned continents while
being served delicacies beside which borscht and hamburger
were so much dogfood. He was hungry, Ezana realized.

He wound his way through three echoing turns of the cast-iron spiral stairs and came to a door of riveted plates, each stamped with Art Nouveau efflorations. These noodly motifs the French had brought, along with military science, the metric system, and punctilio. This door swung open at a touch. Why? Ezana wondered if his guards might have awoken from their comas and alerted the authorities. But what authorities? The carpeted corridors, with their water-coolers and framed citations for bureaucratic excellence, their cork bulletin boards shingled with yellowing, curling inter-office memos and facetiously annotated clippings from *Nouvelles en noire et blanc*, were empty at this hour, like a valley whose inhabitants have fled before the rumored invader could materialize. The narrow door of Ellelloû's ascetic office was shut, its frosted glass inscrutable, intact, dark.

But behind the larger glass of Ezana's own office door, two dozen steps along the corridor, past a circular table holding copies of Cuban and Bulgarian magazines whose covers featured tawny beauties beaded with water on the beaches of the Black and Caribbean seas, a light burned. A guttural laugh, as from a ditch, arose within. He put his ear—abnormally small and infolded, even for a black man—against the glass. He heard beneath Kutunda's laugh another voice, male, loudly at ease. They were waiting for him, a party was in progress. Delicately Ezana opened the door and moved through his old anteroom to the inner office. There he was greeted by the dazzling sight of Kutunda in lacy red underwear, her hair bleached platinum and teased to a bouffant mass, bringing a wire basket of papers, like a cocktail waitress bringing hors d'œuvres, to the man behind the desk. This was the oval-faced young man who had once read the Koran to the king; he still wore his plum-colored fez and his expression of dense ebony calm, though in his hand was held, black and white and faintly blue, a gun.

"We need each other," he told Michaelis Ezana.

V

Esmeralda Miller was an interesting color, a gray as of iron filings so fine the eye could not detect the individual grains. In Hakim's fancy the tint, which savored of manufacture, was a by-product of her beliefs, her economic determinism. At the same time she was an attractive, ectomorphic young woman, with a lean prognathous face, almond-shaped eyes framed in pink plastic spectacles, and a bewitching way of thoughtfully swaying her jaw, as if testing molar crowns her father had made for her. "What are you trying to achieve?" she would ask the young deserter from Noire, across the table in the Off-Campus Luncheonette, or later in the Pure Dairy Products Ice Cream Parlor, or later still in the Badger Cafe, with its beer-soaked sawdust on the floor, and its bubbling, phosphorescent advertisements. "Messing around with this deluded bitch Candy."

"Achieve? That's a rather other-directed way of putting it. What did Freud say? Pleasure is the removal of tension. There is a tension that screwing her relieves. No doubt the sex has a component of vengeance, of tasting evil, of stealing Charlie's prize, et cetera. From her side, kindred craziness. Still, we get along."

"She's no prize, is what you can't see. She put the move on you in the first place. You just took it. You've been taking it for years, now, and she's got marriage in her eye. What happens when you graduate?"

"I have told her, more than once, that I am married."

"To some old black cow in the heart of nowhere? This white girl no more cares about that woman than a bug under a rock. She doesn't believe she exists, and neither do I. Anyway, who says you're ever going back? Let's face it, Haps, you're American as apple pandowdy. I try to talk sense to you friend to friend, and you give me back David Riesman and overheard Freud. I love ya."

This last was said as lightly as these words can be said, as Bob Hope or Clark Gable says them, but Félix took them in, and understood her advice now as propaganda. He began to play with her. "As a Muslim, I am entitled to four wives."

142

"Shit. You're about as Muslim as I am Daddy Warbucks. I hope that stuff hasn't taken you in; it's just our usual native storefront I'm-comin'-home-Jesus routine, with a few funny phrases thrown in. *Inshallah*, Walla-Walla."

"I don't mock your faith," he said stiffly. "Anyway, you're wrong about my never going back. You don't follow the African news in the back pages. The British have given in to Nkrumah, and de Gaulle has been brought to power to end the Algerian war. Only de Gaulle can face down the military."

"God, you're impossible when you get on your great men kick. De Gaulle is just Ike with a bigger nose; they are bal*loons*. History is happening under*neath*. When the oppressed peoples rise *up*, they will just *take*. Meanwhile, nobody is giving them anything. France can bleed all it wants, international capital won't *let* it let go."

"International capital, I believe, has decided colonies are obsolete. The companies themselves, and their insidious products, are the new armies."

"The proletariat—"

"The proletariat, there is no proletariat. Show me the proletariat here. You have the blacks, kept in ghettos because of a superstitious horror of their skins, their rolling eyes, their whiplike penises—"

"Some are stubby," Esmeralda said.

"You have the Indians," Félix went on, "who never knew what hit 'em. And you have the white workers, who Marx to the contrary are thoroughly enrolled in consumerism, making junk and buying junk, drinking junk and driving junk. That is the revolution, surely—the triumph of the unnecessary. If Marx could see his English proletariat now, he wouldn't recognize such softness, such silliness, soaked through and through with ale and the telly. He thought the proletariat was a sponge that would have to be squeezed until a revolution ran out. What happened instead is it sopped up some of the surplus its labor had created and bloated, in a spongy way. There is a kind of poisonous mush abroad in the planet, Esmeralda, and the Muslims aren't quite wrong about its being devilish. It crowds out the good, it makes goodness impossible. Great fanatics can no longer arise; they are swamped by distractions."

"There you go, into obscurantism again. Ideas go back to basics. Food and shelter and clothing, medicine and transportation and the rest of it. Everybody has the same needs, but ninety per cent of the world's wealth is in the hands of ten per cent of the world's people. A revolution has to come."

"Movements have to come. Marx was right, the world is a machine; but he thought some parts, the parts he named, moved while the rest held still. I see two major motions in the world now. There is this seeping down and outwards of Euro-American consumerism. And there is this groping upwards of the dusky underdog. But a third motion encompasses both. As the poor man reaches upwards, the ground is sinking beneath his feet, he is sinking in the spreading poverty, the muchness of humanity divided into the same weary constant, the over-used, overpopulated world." He sipped his beer; its bubbles reminded him: "In my boyhood the giraffes, the elephants, the lions were familiar deities, come to play on the horizon of our world. Soon there will be no animals left bigger than men. Then, only cockroaches, rats, and men. So these gestures of economics are like the reaching gestures on Géricault's painting of the raft of the *Medusa*, gestures that will never grasp their objects, because the raft is sinking. Your Communism is such a failed gesture. In the industrialized countries of Western Europe, where Marx reasoned the uprising must come, the Communist party officials wear suits with vests, and sidle forward for their share, as you Americans say, of the pie."

Her silence, during which she appeared to be focusing closely upon his lips, emboldened him to continue, in what he fancied a Dostoevskian vein: "The age of any revolution is five years. After that, either its participants have wandered off, dismayed by failure, or else have succeeded and become an establishment, generally more tyrannous than the one they displaced. We Africans like de Gaulle. He reminds us of the giraffe, of the gods that no longer visit us. He will make a revolution, not from underneath but from above; give him five years. Algeria will get its independence, and with it, because the French are imperious and demand absolute logic of themselves, all the vast lesser bits of French West Africa, even my empty, un-loved Noire. That is how history happens, in fits of impatience. Then de Gaulle will be thrown aside, like Robespierre; or else become a fussy old man losing quarrels with his Parliament. No matter; by then I will have returned. *Au revoir, les États-Unis!* Farewell, Esmeralda!"

The future Ellelloû had a strange sensation, sometimes, in talking to these Americans, black or white: their faces were units in a foreign language, they inhabited a stratum of reality, a slant of thought, so remote from his own that in the effort to be understood he grew dizzy. Esmeralda's solemn gray face, with that touch of languid sexuality working at the rounded points of her jaws, seemed across the table a chasm or a well he was looking straight down into, where his own head was distantly, waveringly mirrored.

She said, "You should write some of that up and send it to *The Journal of Underdeveloped Political Thought*."

The journal was really called *Political Thought in the Under-developed Nations*, and was published by a group of suspect liberals and malcontented expatriates in an adjacent Mid-western state, one also shaped like a mitten. Hakim took her advice, spinning out in a few long caffeine-crazed nights between terms that little string of articles mentioned sixteen years later, with unintended provocative effect, by the unfortunate Gibbs. They comprised in Hakim's mind the third triumph of his undergraduate career. The second had been his near-election, missing by four votes (his four black friends, he suspected), as Campus Organizer of Pep. His first had been his seduction of Candy.

"You really taking that bitch back with you?" Esmeralda asked.

He toyed with his empty beer glass, wondering if he should have another. "I had not thought so."

"Good luck, black boy, losing her. These white chicks like to call the tune; leave off the loving, they holler rape."

"My native land would seem a barren place to Candace." The balusters of her staircase, the claustrophobic comfort of her father's living-room, swirled through his mind, as he exposed his lower teeth in reflection, conscious of Esmeralda's abnormally intent focus upon his lips. Her stare was numbing his gums.

"Somebody that strong-headed and spoiled thinks she could melt the North Pole if she went there. That's the weakness of a ruling class, they can't take in adverse information. How do you feel about Craven?"

He flipped the little cardboard coaster, idly, to the side without an advertisement. "Unhappy. I believe there have been tender passages between them."

"You can bet your ass on that. She'll fuck anything as long as it's not a boy her own age, race, and income bracket. That's *her* revolution. Haps, she's bad news. She's tough, and she's cold. What *is* the magic? You've been making yourself conspicuous with that girl since you set foot on free soil."

He thought of Candy, her pink cheeks, her red knitted head-scarf, her neurotic sharp smile, and of how, coming up to her along a diagonal path, standing next to her in the cold, he felt airy and towering. He told Esmeralda, "It's like eating snow." Even this seemed too much a confession, a betrayal; he became angry with his interrogator. "Why should I come to this country to sleep with a black woman?" he asked her explosively. "My country is nothing but black women." Still in that squeezed voice of anger, he said, "How about another beer?"

"Beer back at the YCC," Esmeralda mumbled, submissively. The Young Communist Club kept two rooms in an asbestos-shingled tenement house on a back street of Franchise, for a rent that, though beyond the means of the meagre membership, was somehow met. Esmeralda could count, this night as on most nights, on having the place to herself. They walked along pavements packed with snow, only the heads of the parking meters protruding from the drifts, the whiteness hardened to ice and tinted by neon signs and the half-lit display windows of closed shops, ungrated in those safe days, even the windows of jewelry stores. Back from Commerce Street the pavements were erratically shovelled, so for some stretches, where a widow lived, or a family that had fallen below the social norms, glossy mounds had to be traversed on little paths, worn by the boots of schoolchildren. Candy for this weekend had gone away with her family, skiing in the Laurentians. The YCC quarters were identified only by the initials. No hammer and sickle, no red star. There had been problems with broken windows. Esmeralda turned up the heat. A mattress on the floor did for a bed. The term "crash pad" had not yet been invented. Esmeralda's body, naked on the sheetless ticking, was the same slate hue her face was, an even soft gray that moved him, taken with her stringy hips and underdeveloped breasts; the slaver's sperm, it seemed, had entered her blood line to steal shine from her skin, and joyful African protuberance from her body. When she left the bed, instead of glimmering in the darkened room like a candle, she vanished. What Félix liked best about these American seductions was not the exchange of salivas and juices but the post-coitus, the ritual cigarettes and the standing around in the kitchen rummaging up something to eat, their exploited genitals lit up by the sudden glow of the refrigerator, its polychrome wealth of beer cans, yogurt cups, frozen vegetables, packets of cheese and luncheon meats and other good bottled, wrapped, and encapsulated things. The young Communists, like any frat, kept a sweet, starchy, and spotty larder. To Hakim, reared on nuts and porridges, this gentle, naked pecking after food—Esmeralda concocted herself a sandwich of peanut butter and marshmallow fluff—savored of home and soothed the acerb aftereffects of the tragic act of love. She had had no climax, and he had been distracted by the giant red poster of Lenin, goateed and pince-nezed, staring upwards with the prophetic fury of a scholar who has just found his name misspelled in a footnote. "She ain't even taught you how to screw," Esmeralda said, pleased to have an additional score on Candy, and depressing her lover with the hint that their fornication, in such romantic surroundings, had been merely an extension of a propaganda campaign. To an extent, it worked; he looked more kindly upon Marx thereafter, as Marx, from a poster on the other wall, grandfatherly and unfoolable, had looked kindly down upon the heaving buttocks of the future Ellelloû.

The time had come for them to leave the caravan. The flinty passes had widened and the Massif now tipped downwards toward the highlands of Zanj and, weeks to the northeast, the southwest corner of Egypt. We thanked Sidi Mukhtar with a purse of hundred-*lu* pieces. Feeling that our relationship, though extended in time, had been less close emotionally than it might have been, I confided that I and my beautiful bride (as amorous, I further confided in coarse Berber, as she was shapely) had peeked into some of the caravan's cases and discovered their unexpected contents. His grin displaying the rift between his front teeth, and lifting a pearl-sized wart nestled in the flange of one nostril, our leader explained the eventual destination of the office supplies: Iran. "The Shahanshah," he said, "has much wish to modernize. In his hurry he buy typewriters from West Germans and paper from Swedes and then discover only one type spool fit typewriter, only one type eraser not smudge paper. American know-how meanwhile achieve obsolescence such that only fitting spool stockpiled in Accra as aid-in-goods when cocoa market collapse. Formula of typewriter eraser held secret and cunning capitalists double, redouble price when Shah push up oil price to finance purchase of jet fighters, computer software, and moon rocks. French however operating through puppet corporations in Dahomey have secured formula as part of multi-billion-franc deferred-interest somatic-collateral package and erect eraser factory near gum arabic plantations. Much borax also in deal, smuggled by way of Ouagadougou. Now Sadat has agreed to let goods across Nile if Shahanshah agrees to make anti-Israeli statement and buy ten thousand tickets to *son-et-lumière* show at Sphinx."

I did not believe the rogue's garbled story, but deemed it prudent to suppress my doubts. Instead, I repeated our appreciation of his *rejela* (valor) and *dhiyafa* (hospitality), said that his skill at navigating through the perils of the Balak argued a pious intimacy with the purposes of Allah, and, by way of parting compliment, confided, "Unbeknownst to you, you have been transporting, in the guise of two mendicant musicians, the President of Kush and one of his First Ladies. *Je suis Ellelloú.*"

"*Je sais, je sais,*" Sidi Mukhtar responded out of his bag of tongues, his face in merriment twitching like the skin of a sand lizard just emerged from his hole. "Otherwise, I kill. We see Benzi following us before mountains become too bad. Super car, gives ride free of sway."

"Why would you have killed me?" It is perhaps part of my inheritance from the communally tender, multi-generational, intra-supportive village of my upbringing to be always astonished that any real harm lurks in the world.

The third component of Sidi Mukhtar's personality, his *sirge* (thievishness), shuffled cheerfully to the fore. He answered me, "To sell Madame to the Yemenis. Good posh black girls, with correct long neck and hollow back, very hard to come by. Only shoddy slaves come on market now. Mostly drug addicts from bourgeois European families, decadent riff-raff looking for security. Yemenis, Saudis need intelligent slaves, to operate electrical appliances."

Here, too, I doubted the mercantile tall tale, and distrusted the note of socialist snobbery he had injected, presumably to please me. His men loaded our camels with sacks of dried dates and sloshing skins of water. We exchanged farewells: my "*Allah Ma'ak*" for his "*Aghrub 'Anni.*" The caravan, our home for these moons, shuffled, clanked, and sighed its way out of sight, as the tepid dawn washed away the shadows of the night and, with them, the stars. An hour later, we discovered that the villain had given us not water in our *zemzimayas* but wine, which our religion forbade us to drink, though from its bouquet it was a fair vintage; a lot of sturdy Bordeaux found its way into our trade routes, brought back to Dakar in the peanut-oil tankers as ballast.

Glimpses of rock doves led us upwards and leftwards, into a porous region of caves. At this height color crept back, first by way of iridescent hints in the birds' feathers, next in the rainbow-shimmer on the oil-smooth face of an overhanging rock. We passed through pastel moments much as Esmeralda and I had paced a gallery of neon auras on the way to our betrayal of pale Candace. Sheba rode a camel of the coveted *azrem* shade—a pinkish eggshell, dun toward the tail and white in the huge eyelashes that fringed the iris of glacial blue. My own steed was a mud-brown gelding with a worrisomely depressed hump and a nagging habit of clearing his throat. The pads of their feet, evolved for the *erg*'s slipping sands, split on the rocky trails, and as the days wore on we often dismounted and walked beside them, winding our way upwards, led by the bubbling coo of coral-footed doves. The geology was strange. Certain summits appeared to have been molded by a giant, ill-tempered child, finger-furrows distinct and some petrified depressions holding the whirling ridges of what seemed a thumbprint. The terrain felt formed by play, of an idiotic sort that left no clues to the logic of the game. A frozen bulbousness—double-dip, Reddi-wip accumulations of weathered lava topped by such gravitational anomalies as natural arches and big boulders balanced on smaller—gave way to cleavages and scree as geometrically finicking as the debris of a machinist's shop. Amid these splits and frolicsome tumblings, caves abounded; where the caves multiplied, so did the paintings left by the mysterious happy herdsmen and hunters of the Green Sahara. Centuries of calm sunlight had not faded their sheltered ochres and indigos. Wild buffalo bore between their horns little round marks like shrunken halos; their hunters were depicted with skins the color of oranges and enlarged heads round as the helmets of space travellers. In a deep cave a galloping goddess, daintily horned, a shower of grain between her antennae like static, rose to the domed ceiling, carrying up with her the steatopygial silhouettes of naked mortals, running also, overlaid and scattered like leaves in agitation slipping from a tree. Brown, gray, custard, pepper, cinnamon: the colors of our African cookery depicted, with the primitive painter's numinous, nervous precision, the varieties of cattle, as the herding culture replaced the hunting. These very herds, no doubt, had helped turn the grassland from green to tan, to dust, to nothing.

Sheba, gaunt now as a ballerina, her sumptuous costume in tatters from which color had forever fled, her intricate necklaces of lapis lazuli and jasper and of coral from a shore where milk-warm waves lapped life into quivery barnacles fallen bit by bit along our way, wanted to stay in a cool dim cave, and die. We had drunk the sardonic wine on the second day, blaspheming against our bodies, and had vomited accordingly. The dried fruit stuck in our throats like ash; her dear tongue was swollen like the body of a frog in the dried mud of an exhausted water hole; she spoke indistinctly, but I understood her to say that she was dizzy, and that her skull had a sun of pain in it. Begging her to rise and stumble another kilometer forward with me, stooping down and with my own depleted strength tugging at her resistless limbs, I thought of all the women I had led into such a wilderness, a promised green land of love that then had turned infertile, beneath the monomaniacal eye of my ambition, my wish to create a nation, to create a nation as a pedestal for myself, my pathetic self. The whites of her eyes, rolling upwards in a delirious faint, had become an astonishing golden color, as in the hollow head with which a mummified Pharaoh is helmeted for *his* spaceflight, the golden eyes inset with onyx irises that have been stolen.

"Do it to me, baby, do it, do it," I crooned, to tease her back to life, to bring her back from mummification into the moist full skin of the girl I had met strolling the alleys of Istiqlal, her svelte jaws methodically chewing uppers and downers, kola and khat, her ear pressed to a transistor radio tuned to the perfidious pop-rock stations of Brazzaville, the same *Plus Haute Quarantaine* over and over. I had been in the disguise of a gum-seller, little packets of Chiclets that sold two for a *lu*, or for a kiss in lieu of that. At the first touch of her lips I knew Sheba had the mouth for me. Now those satin cushions, the upper even more generously stuffed than the lower, were split, the skin at the edges of the split blackened as if deliberately singed, and the pale inner lining, next to her gums, blued by the onset of cyanosis.

"My . . . Lord," she pronounced. "Divorce . . . me."

"Never," I said, and managed to work her limp body onto my shoulders. I carried her from the cave to the camels, who were waiting with that impeccable poise of their species, conserving their inner resources. But as I dropped her diminished weight across the embroidered saddle cloth of her beautiful *azrem* mount, the creature died. It did not even keel over, but held in death its sitting position; the head on its long neck simply rested on the rocky trail, and twisted gently as the muscles relaxed. Its albino lashes lowered like drawgates.

Was this the end? *Never*, I repeated to myself. All of the nubile women in our land of Kush, above the lowest social stratum, carry a dagger with which to stab their own hearts if their honor is compromised, ere the rapist can work his will. My mother, alas, had had no such implement, but Sheba did. I plucked it, its blade of Damascus steel and handle of polished chalcedony, from the bindings of her bosom and cut open the dead camel's stomach, so we could drink the brackish green water secreted there. With this liquid I called Sheba back to life; she shuddered and wept, and as her strength returned cursed me in the astonishingly vile language which flows so easily from the lips of even the prettiest of the younger generation. As she gave out these signs of restored vitality, I loaded our baggage onto our surviving camel, my mudcolored mount, with his housemaid's knees and smoker's hack. He accepted Sheba's weight—*Takbīr!*—and I shuffled beside them on foot.

Vistas loomed, through clefts and apertures worn by wind erosion, of a hazed sea of sand so far below us as to be another planet; the prospect was westward, to the Ippi Rift Valley that runs north and south through the center of my great land. Closer to our eyes, petrophagous lichen silvered the relative damp of some shadows, and an inverted dwarf species of thornbush (*Alhagi inversum*) adorned the underside of ledges. The quality of the rock-paintings, too, was subtly changing; daubed ground ochre and charcoal paste gave way to a furry, swirling technique of primary colors sprayed from a can. Swastikas, stylized genitals, and curious forms involving circles attached to crosses or arrows or circumscribing a kind of airplane replaced the magical representations of Green Sahara's vanished animists. Some of the hieroglyphs could be read: ROCKETS, CLASS OF '55, GAY IS GOOD, REVOLUCIÓN AHORA, QUÉBEC LIBRE, HELTER SKELTER, FAT CITY. The letters of this last were themselves fat; this style was prevalent. Many of the inscriptions had been overlaid: the simple sign STOP had been amended to STOP WAR and then an antipacifist had scratched out the S. Some inviting surfaces were muddy with a mad tangle of colors, defying all decipherment, even if Sheba and I had had the stomach for it, which we did not. For our drink of camel bile had turned our bowels queasy. She had become the gray of the cardboard that stiffens a fresh ream of paper. I too, at this oxygen-scant altitude, under the vertical gaze of noon, on this leaden planet, could go on no farther. We half-toppled, half-crawled into the scribbled mouth of a cave, that seemed to be the entrance, a kind of kiosk, to a subterranean system in whose depths, unless my senses of smell and hearing betrayed me, cold flowers were being sold and pinball was being played.

The camel accompanied us inside, and was the first to fall asleep. Then Sheba succumbed to oblivion, her head, that little snug sack of loyalty, resting on my arm. The green demon of nausea churning within kept me from sleeping instantly; as my eyes adjusted to the gloom I saw that our shelter and, it seemed likely, tomb had once been a bower of love, and still was love's memorial. TEX LOVES RITA, a wall opposite proclaimed, and from this same wall, and those adjacent, the names of many more thronged like clouds of the damned to my attention, not all of them written in the flatfooted alphabet Roman imperialism marched through Europe, but many in our own incomparably dancing Arabic script, and some in the chunky formations of St. Cyril, the flowerets of lowercase Greek, Asia's busy bamboolike brushstrokes, and the staring, rectilinear symbols of Tiffinagh, that traces Tamachek onto the sand. So many names, so much love, so many cries uttered on the verge of *la petite mort*, so much sperm; my stomach sickened, and the blood ebbed from my head. But before I lapsed, in tune with Sheba's breathing, into the sleep that might be our last, I noticed, on a rock above her head this indelible legend: HAPPY LOVES CANDY.

"*What* did your father say?"

"It's not as if he talks about you a lot, he doesn't. He used to ask a lot of questions, he was very interested in you. He thought you could tell him the secret, of how the blacks can be the way they are, of why they don't love this country the way he does."

"His and theirs aren't the same country. They're as different as Heaven and Hell."

"I *know* that, Happy, don't argue with *me*. I'm just trying to be *him* for a minute. My goodness, you're touchy these days."

"Pre-partum blues," he suggested, in his lover's weary voice. The snow had melted, refroze, and finally receded for the last of the four times he would witness this beautiful North American relenting; their graduation approached.

"And *carp*ing," Candy continued, unmollified. "At times you sound exactly like Esmeralda. Fucked her lately?"

He said nothing. He realized that to assure her that he had not slept with Esmeralda after the occasion that Candy had, with the astonishing nose that white women have for infractions of their property rights, sniffed out and goaded him to confess, would be to repaint in newly vivid colors this baleful lapse, and to renew Candy's hyperbolic anger and grief. Her overreaction had baffled and then frightened him. He had tapped, all innocently, a source of passion, of human power, unknown to Africa. In the village, the bushes had every night quivered with casual pairings. He had taken Kadongolimi's many previous lovers into his arms along with her tattoos. The episode with Esmeralda had been painless, instructive, more healthful than another beer, and on the whole less intimate, in terms of penetration of his nervous system, than would have been a trip to her father the dentist. Really, Candy had punished him too severely for this walk through the snow; her copious tears over the event had dried to an unending sarcasm, a baring of fangs in her voice. These toubabs were indeed poison; he had less trouble believing, as W. D. Fard has proclaimed, that these blue-eyed animals, once engendered, had to be banished, a race of snarling, howling wolves, to the icy caves of Europe. Candy would get a wolvish look at the thought of his infidelity. Her lips would go parched; her eyes would turn lifeless, cold, and small. She would begin to talk about the sacrifices she had made for him. Her whole life had been ruined, it seemed, by the injection of his sperm. Yet, paradoxically, not a drop of that sperm must be spilled out of her body. She had rights. She had put herself in great social peril. She, she.

She told him, "I can't trust you at all anymore. You two can sneak off into the bushes any time. You have such wonderful things in common. You both hate whites. You both have rhythm. I bet you talk about me, don't you? You call me pinktoes."

"*Please*," he said, embarrassed for her.

She did not notice this, in her zeal to embarrass him. "Don't you find her bony?" she asked. "And pedantic? And—well, *dreary*? So just barely middle-class? Think of her father, drilling all those teeth."

"As opposed to glorious yours, selling all those policies."

"Sneer at Daddy if you must, he'd do anything in the world for Mother and me. He'd kill for us, if he had to."

"Or just for the pleasure of killing."

Tears turned her eyelids pink. She set her arms stickily around his neck, proud of those tears, of her hot close breath. "Happy, this isn't us. What's gone wrong?"

You have gone wrong. You must let go. He suppressed these

words, patiently asking once more, "What did your father say, exactly?"

"He was horrible," she sobbed. "Just horrible." Holding her, he was reminded of how, in an intermission of soldiering, he, a young husband not out of his teens, had held one of Kadongolimi's babies, that had been born while he was a year away, against his chest, and patted it to ease its colic, its inner demons, and this infant wished upon him had burped air; the women gathered around like a single-bodied black continuum had praised this little hiccup. So Candy now wanted to be praised for her sobs. "He said," she forced out, "he'd kill you if you tried to marry me."

"Marry you? And what did you say to that, darling?"

"I said"—a shudder, a big gulp, a sob, and then—"he couldn't stop us, we'd elope."

In his sleep with Sheba, Ellelloû rotated, his robes entangled beneath him and enfolding lumpy pockets of the white dust of the cave floor. He was aware through his dreams of these lumps and of her body, sunk in forgetfulness but now and then roused to rotate like his own, two carcasses turned on parallel spits, touching with a rustle, their hunger and thirst borne by shrivelled organs submerged beneath the reach of pain. Yet no submergence quite concealed from that mass of sporadic lights, colors, and linkages that was his immortal consciousness the fact of this proximate woman, her scent and sadness and the warm skin beneath her own robes, that had come through the Balak faded as by too scalding a wash. His sleeping brain acknowledged the certain graciousness of her accompanying him, though from the Marxist standpoint it could be maintained that she had no choice, it was accompany him or wander the streets as a waif of poverty. But what was this, this trek through silicon and starlight and now this death in a cavern strewn with condoms and Kleenexes and other sedimented evidences of love, but poverty? In Ellelloû's sleep an arch of pity and sorrowful gratitude built itself from his beating heart to this his rib, his mate, enclosing as in a crypt Sheba's body, her yielding lips, her blue-black brow smooth and round as a dome of tile. Then a scent of vodka was at his nostrils, and water was at his lips.

"*Prosnis', chernozhopyi!*" a Targui was shouting in my ear; and my first waking thought was that of course it must have been the Russians who stole the head of the king, for only they would have been so anthropologically obtuse within their own passionate, isolate culture and prodigious territories as not to know that the Tuareg were the traditional enemies of Wanjiji, holding the riverine kingdom in thrall when they were strong, retreating back into the desert when they were weaker. The Tuareg could not help but regard us as slaves, and we them as devils, devils from the desert, howling like the harmattan, their mouths masked because they had no jaws, just gaping throats that spewed vile yells and cruelty. These Tuareg succoring me had their mouths and noses swaddled; nothing showed but their wolvish pale eyes, and their muffled voices.

"*Eta chernaya pizd a nichevo zhivchik, a?*"

"*Spokoino, u nikh u vsekh sifilis.*"

They muttered as if I had no ears. One of them wore steel-rimmed spectacles; when his comrades noticed I was awake, he began to address me in his slurred Iraqi Arabic and, his vocabulary failing, his sloshy French. "Rise up, Mr. President!" he cried through the haze of languages. "You are near the end of your journey! The path has been made easier! *Vive* Kush! *Vive le peuple et la fraternité socialiste et islamique! Écrasez l'infâme capitaliste, monopolisé, et très, très décadent!*"

Several Tuareg women, their naked faces impassive, the wrists and ankles dyed blue, were laving Sheba's feet and re-braiding her hair; though my dear girl flickered toward me a feeble smile, her eyes, under a helpless pressure, kept closing, the lids freshly anointed with antimony.

It was true, the upward path had been made easier. The steepness declined, as the summit neared, and an asphalt strip, wide enough for a golf cart, with green-painted pipe railings on the side of a precipitous falling-off, had been engineered where the natural trail might have seemed impassably rugged. Yellow signs advised FALLING ROCK and ORYX CROSSING, and others advertised our growing closeness to the ORACLE'S CAVE, to LA TÊTE QUI PARLE, to Мавзолей Эдуму Четвертого. My old brown baggage camel, who had been fed a barrel of Ukrainian millet (or could it have been Nebraska sorghum?), fairly danced on his threadbare legs as he bouncingly bore along the sumptuous little body of Sheba, who had been slipped a few kola nuts and was chewing through a high. I felt, as one does after too deep a sleep, uncaught-up with myself: the physical half hurried along to expectancy's accelerated heartbeat, while the spiritual man loitered behind in a fog, groping for the reason for his shadowy, guilty sensation of something undone, of something disastrous due. The path, briskly engineered through the rose-colored cliffs and abysses, was crossed by a newly built funicular railway; the crossing-marking, X, reminded me of something unpleasant I have always wanted to forget.

"You are crazy," Oscar X firmly, patiently stated, as if reciting a memorized speech. "You are what the Messenger terms a black man with a white man's head. Man, you are sad. You are evil and you are sad. I wash my hands of you. I wish to wipe you from my mind. *Anā lā a'rifuka*. The Nation of Islam is one thousand per cent opposed to what you are undertaking. The mixture of the races is a crime against purity. The Word of God unambiguously proclaims, sooner a black man mate with a lazy shit-smeared sow or the female of the alligator species than entrust his ebony penis to the snatch of a white devil mare."

Félix imagined in the floridity of this indictment a simultaneous undercutting, a self-mocking. But he detected no humor or mercy in Oscar's face. People when they go behind the curtain of a creed become unknown. He said, "You know Candy. You like her."

"I have tolerated her," Oscar said. "But I have not liked her. She is the offspring of the stock that has enslaved us, that spits on us whenever it chooses. This woman has spit upon you, and you don't have the mother wit to wipe your fucking face." He sipped his Ovaltine and came up with a scummy lip.

Barry Little tried to help, telling Félix, "She was raised too clean. She needs to get down into it, but doesn't want to get real dirt on herself. So she tells herself a story in the dark. In her mind, you are the pimp and the customers both. That's a way these upper-class sheltered girls get their kicks, it's nothing personal in regards to you. Make it personal and permanent, that would be a big mistake. I'm not saying white and black can't live together, they *got* to, this separate black nation old Elijah Poole keeps plugging is fantastical purely. But in this particular case, of you and little Miss Cunningham, I'm saying that would be one fantasy on top of another. You don't know America, and she don't know Africa."

"Perhaps we know each other."

"You know each other in the dark," Barry said. "Out in the light, what do you see? Her momma's a washrag and her daddy's a redneck who'd fry your ass if he could find the button. Kiss her good-bye, you'd be doing her a favor as well as yourself. I'm not talking black or brown, I'm trying to talk to you straight. If you and she were both green in color, I'd have my doubts about the personalities."

"No such thing as color blind," Turnip Schwarz interposed. "No such thing."

Esmeralda said indignantly, "You're all talking to this boy as though he had a choice. Any choice he ever had he threw away. He's been hustled. He's in over his head and can't say No now."

"Just get on the plane to Timbuctoo, the way to say No," Turnip said.

Félix felt hemmed in, shoved, in the businesslike American manner. He resented their attempt to pry him open and meddle in the fate he was nurturing within; he could not explain to them how delicately all the truths they advanced were built into his plan, were included in the sprawling, devious budget that in the end would balance. It was true, Candy had come upon him and was sweeping him along; but we can propel ourselves only a little way out of ourselves and for the rest must play with the forces beyond us that impinge. He gazed steadily at Oscar and said, "I have been reading the Book of Books, as the Messenger advises. *Women are your fields: go, then, into your fields as you please.*"

Oscar blinked, and quoted back: "*You shall not wed pagan women, unless they embrace the faith. A believing slave-girl is better than an idolatress, although she may please you.*"

"Jesus preserve us," Esmeralda breathed. Candy had come in at the door of the luncheonette; even at a distance, through the smoke and jangle, the future Ellelloû could see she had been crying. More trouble with her parents, or Craven, or some other white spokesmen. She came toward their black table timidly now, sensing that here too she was abhorred. Yet in honor of spring she had put on a forsythia-yellow sweater and a pleated white skirt. Félix lifted from his chair as a tide toward the moon.

Oscar X stood up angrily. "I will not contaminate myself any longer," he stated so all could hear, "by consorting with mongrel clowns and lackeys of the doomed devil-race." To Félix he said, again with the precision of something rehearsed, "*L'anatu Allāhi ʿalayka*." He walked out, taking with him Temple Two and Temple Three, the joyful car rides together, the Brotherhood. His curse Félix felt as a blast of heat upon his face, the heat whose first wave had been, in infancy, the absence of his father. He felt this heat as Allah. Allah is the essential seriousness of things, their irreversibility. Our friends all die to us, some before we are born.

Let us step back a moment, onto the spongy turf of psychohistorical speculation. There was in our young hero (not so young as he appeared to his clamorous advisers; by 1958 he was going on twenty-six) an adsorptive chemical will that made him adhere to just those surfaces that would have repelled him: he took away from the United States not only the frightened body of Candy Cunningham in a blue linen suit but the Nation of Islam, internalized as a certain shade of beige idealism mixed of severity, xenophobia, decency, and isolation. As New World immigrants preserve in their ethnic neighborhoods folk dances and items of cuisine that in the old country have become obsolete, so Ellelloû held to a desiccated, stylized version of the faith that meanwhile failed for Oscar X, who fell away in the mid-Sixties, when the scandals of the Messenger's sexual strayings (not one but two secretaries pregnant!) unfolded to a bloody climax in the gunning-down of his schismatic Chief Minister Malcolm in New York City, on West 166th Street. So the Nation of Islam was just another gangland after all. In the strength of his disillusion Oscar became a trainee with the Chicago police, and with unfeigned enthusiasm helped bop long-haired protester heads at the 1968 Democratic Convention, at the same time as his repudiated brother was fomenting the revolution that overthrew Edumu IV and brought Islamic socialism to Noire, renamed Kush.

Now the path was continuously paved, and littered with bits of paper—torn tickets and Popsicle wrappers. The pigeons were thick about us, throbbling and strutting in their streetwise self-importance, too full of crushed Fritos and dropped popcorn to flutter away. The first people we saw were Chinese

—a small close flock of official visitors, in their blue-gray many-pocketed pajamas, their mass-produced wire-frame spectacles (no doubt of identical prescription) resting on the fat of their cheeks as they smilingly squinted up from their guidebooks toward something on high we could not yet see. We had come upon them around a corner and, as if the dusty spectacle of the disguised President and his delectable, stoned consort on foot and camelback respectively had been organized for them as an additional local wonder, they obligingly switched, in a unified motion, their twinkling attention full upon us. These tourists appeared amazed when the weary camel plodded straight toward them, rippling his upper lip contemptuously, forcing them to break formation and crowd to the sides of the path. They joked among themselves in their curious pitch-chirping.

How had these Confucians come here? The question was answered by the next turn in the path, which revealed a parking lot blasted from the outcroppings and holding six or seven large tourist buses, some striped like zebras and others spotted like giraffes. Emblazoned on their sides was the name of a Zanj tourist agency, the same which in other directions exposed to the stupefied gaze of aliens, through smoky-blue windows that bathed our Africa in perpetual twilight, the oceanic herds of the Tanzanian grasslands, Lalibela's cathedrals carved from solid rock, the inexhaustible salt quarries of the Danakil Depression, and what other bleak marvels were exploitable in this continent whose most majestic feature is the relative absence of Man. To such buses the Zanj border was not far away, and evidently the entrepreneurs found no insurmountable obstacle there. I must create one. "I will close the border," I confided to Sheba. "This is an atrocity."

"I think it's an improvement," she said languidly, from within her trip. "Can I have another lemonade?"

We had patronized a refreshment stand manned by a detribalized Djerma, offering beverages in all bubbling colors. "The delicate ecology of the Balak," I told her, "is being devastated."

"There's lots left," she pointed out.

"One germ can kill a giant," I explained to her, vowing, "I'll have old Komomo's hide for this."

Wamphumel Komomo, President-for-Life of Zanj: height six foot six, weight three hundred seventy pounds. He wore (and still wears, but for my own peace of mind let this description be consigned to the past tense) garish robes so intricately worked each sleeve cost a seamstress her sight and a crown that consisted of a cheetah's snarling skull, gilded. Worse, he was a flirt. The British had taught him this. They had flirted with him by capturing him when he was a guerrilla leader, placing him in prison, scheduling his execution, and then, when the rising tides of freedom forced them to decamp, suddenly installing him as President, in return for his promise not to expel the white settler community from the fertile highlands and along the little seacoast. The shape of Zanj reached out to include its miserable Red Sea port like a child touching wet paint while looking the other way. The bulk of Zanj was as infertile, unprofitable, and stately as Kush. But old Komomo, with his picturesque regalia of catskins, ornamental welts, and medals from the lesser European armies, tirelessly flirted with the international community, inviting the Americans in to build him a desalination plant and then expelling them, inviting the Russians in to train his air force and then expelling them, milking even the Australians and the post-Sukarno Indonesians for their dollop of aid, their stretch of highway, their phosphate refinery, or mile-high broadcasting antenna. Now his pets were the Chinese, who were building him a railway from his nasty little port to the preposterous new capital he had ordained in the interior, Komomo-glorifying Zanjomo, its street-plan cribbed from Baron Haussmann, its government buildings based on photos of forgotten World Fairs, its central adornment a mock-heroic bronze stalagmite bearing Komomo's shifty features in imitation of Rodin's *Balzac* and likely to survive the model's death for one week, by which time the old nepotist's competing sons-in-law will have melted it down for bullets. Not a tuck in his patriarchal robes ungarnished by private gain, which he extracted from the toubab corporations as blithely as his forebears the cannibal chiefs extracted *hongo* from the Arab slavers, Komomo flirted moreover with all the elements within his country, appearing in ostrich feathers in a veldt village and a hardhat in a magnesium mine, placating the Africa Firsters by taxing the Indian shopkeepers and placating the Asian community with public readings from the Upanishads, balancing his denunciations of Ian Smith and the still-exclusivist Zanj Athletic Club with frequent photographs of himself embracing some visiting devil or local "landowner" and "business leader," touting with scrupulously equal decibels the "tribal integrity" of "our great African masses" and the "total impartiality" of "our color-blind Constitution." The American press loved this artful clown; in their rotogravures he looked like a negative print of Santa Claus. Now he was flooding my purified, penniless but proud country with animalistic buses stuffed full of third-echelon Chou Shmoes, German shutterbugs, British spinsters, bargain-seeking Bulgarians, curious Danes, Italian archaeologists, and trip-crazed American collegians bribed by their soused and adulterous parents to get out of the house and let capitalism collapse in peace—all to see a dead head in the dead center of the Bad Quarter.

At the next turn of the path, as the bridle burned in my hands, so hard was it being tugged by my pack camel in the frisky throes of restored vitality, I could see a polychrome, polyglot little mob gathered at the mouth of what must be the cave. It looked artificial, but badly made, like a department-store window display, besprinkled with greenish glitter-dust. It is said that God, as he created these mountains of the Balak, worked in haste. It is also said that the royalty of Kush, chased from Meroë by the Christian hordes of Axum, may have come this way, constructing as they went cities scarcely distinguishable from the rocks. Or perhaps—a third possibility—the unsubtle Soviets, having selected this as the site from which to broadcast slander against the incorruptible President of Kush, had with their usual heavy hand engineered the locale to resemble one of those concrete medleys of domes and parapets that speak to their huddling hearts.

One of Dr. Frederic (without the *k*, yes) Craven's courses in the Government Department of McCarthy College was "U.S. *vs.* USSR: Two Wayward Children of the Enlightenment." Another course was "Plato to Pound: Totalitarianism as the Refuge of Superior Minds." There was a sardonic touch, too, to his seminars: "Bureaucratic Continuity During Political Crises" studied, with use of original documents, phenomena such as the adjudication of misdemeanors and traffic fines during the

French Revolution and mail delivery during the American War Between the States. "Weak or Strong?: The Presidency from Fillmore to the Second Harrison" took the paradoxical position that American history would have been much the same if the opponents of these Chief Executives had been elected instead, and that the average man fared better under Pierce and Grant than under Lincoln. He also taught the only course that touched upon the darkest continent: "The Persistence of the Pharaonic Ideal in the Sudanic Kingdoms from 600 to 1600 A.D." Félix and Candace took this course together; their shoulder-rubbing proximity during lectures gave the lecturer pain. Candy was one of Craven's "pets." In that sinister way of American intellectual men, he had grown handsomer with age, his boyishly gaunt figure filling out without ceasing to be essentially youthful; kept tendony by tennis and tan by sailing through September on the cerulean, polluted surface of Lake Timmebago, he had created in time a kind of vertical harem of undergraduate mistresses, whom graduation disposed of without his even having to provide a dismissive dowry. Candy, apparently, in some interstice or worn spot of her harassed liaison with the future Ellelloû, had placed herself among Craven's concubines, and had renewed the relationship when the young African—understandably, to all but her—had waffled or responded sluggishly to her female call for a "commitment" that translated into elopement, bigamy, and for all he knew, American arrest and incarceration. One warm day deep in the reign of Dwight Eisenhower, Craven invited the black student to his office, a cozy cave lined with leaning gray government manuals and smelling of the peculiarly sweet pipe smoke it was one of Craven's vanities to emit. He offered Félix a low seat on his Naugahyde seducer's couch but the youth, his manner stiff with a wary dignity, took instead a hard straight chair whose seat, all but the edge, was loaded with blue exam booklets. End of term was at hand.

"Hakim Félix," the professor began, evidently imagining this mode of address was swankily parallel to use, in Russian, of the patronymic, "let me begin by confessing some slight disappointment in your exam. You had the facts down pat, but, if I may say so, you seemed to show less gut feeling for the African ethos than some of the middle-class white kids in the course.

Miss Cunningham, for instance, wrote an essay on kinship that damn near made me cry."

The student perched still farther forward on the overburdened chair. "Africa is large," was the best excuse he could offer for his curious failure. "Also, the French did not encourage our ethos, they were intent upon inculcating their own."

"Well," Craven briskly conceded, sucking lip-smackingly upon his pipestem, releasing a blue wraith of saccharine alter ego, "far be it from me to out-African an African. There was nothing strictly wrong, just my nebulous sense of something missing."

"Perhaps that is the very African ingredient."

Craven closed his pale, rather too mobile lips upon the amber of his pipestem. He did not relish fancy thinking not his own. "I asked you in, though, not to talk about that but to wish you well, really. Can you tell me your plans, Félix?"

"I plan to return, sir. The U.S. immigration officials have never been happy with my status here, though the college has been most liberal and supportive. In Noire, King Edumu, placed back on his throne—placed, I should say strictly, on a throne he never before occupied—in the wake of Guy Mollet's *loi-cadre* proclamation two years ago, has instituted a policy of amnesty toward political criminals under colonialism. And now that de Gaulle has offered the territories either internal autonomy with assistance or complete autonomy without, I think a new era is even more decisively under way, and I will be able to rejoin the military, and serve the new nation, without fear."

"There is no politics without fear," Craven said, "as there is no organization without coercion. However, I wish you well. Have *you* no fear, may I ask, of having lost touch, these four years, with the realities of your own people?"

"As your examination suggests I have. I do not know. My guess is, America will fade for me as even the most intense dreams fade, and in any case the realities of my people are not static, but in the process of transformation. Perhaps I can help create new realities."

"Perhaps." The pipe came into even more elaborate play, the amber stem pointing this way and that as Craven knocked, blew into, and rapidly reamed this little instrument of pleasure. "Will America fade, I wonder, so rapidly if you take a piece of it with you? A living piece. You know to whom I refer."

"I do, and assume your concern is for my political future. Rest easy, I beg you. The new President of Sahel, a poet of sorts, has for wife a *minette* from Lyons. The mighty Suleiman, as you well know, made his queen Roxelana, a consort of Russian blood paler than even the lovely strawberry-blond Mrs. Craven, to whom I hope you will forward my parting regards."

"I will," he said, in unwilled echo of his broken wedding vows.

"Surely," the student meekly persisted, "distinctions in tint of skin have no priority in the world that my professors, you foremost, have taught me must be welded into one, lest the nuclear holocaust transpire. I have come here in innocence, anxious to learn, and part of my American experience has been to fall in love; how could it have been otherwise? This is the land where love is broadcast with the free hand of Johnny Appleseed."

"Be that as it may"—one of Craven's favorite phrases, while he searched for his place in the lecture—"in the instance I have in mind, sentimental exogamist though I am bound to be, I can see, frankly, little good. The female is spoiled, neurotic, headstrong, and too young to know her own mind. You are older, a man of some experience, though I sometimes wonder if your experiences as you describe them do not partake of the fabulous. Why could you not be, for example, an American from, say, Detroit, who affects a French accent and the prissy African manner? That would explain why, in your examination, you showed so little feel for the, shall we say, heart of the matter."

"Might it be the instructor who lacks the feel? Africa is not only log drums and sand dunes; we have cities, we have history, which you proposed to teach. We have languages, more than any other continent. We are a melting pot that will not boil over with the addition of one more female Caucasian. I think in your intelligence you have made an idea of blackness; when you look at me, you see an idea, and ideas do not talk back, ideas do not lust for the unlikely, ideas do not carry away the professor's—what do they say, in comic books?—'date bait.'"

"You speak as though you are the abductor. The impression I gather from your friends, *mon bon Félix*, is that you are the abducted."

"If by my friends you mean Esmeralda and Oscar, they have their own points of view, their own reasons for jealousy and malice. I cannot really see why you are bothering to hector a student on the subject of his personal life. If you have a claim to exert over Miss Cunningham, or a proposal to make to her alternative to mine, then do so; otherwise, let her join in silence the ranks of your lovely one-time students."

"Your welfare concerns me as well as Candy's."

"Let me ask you this: were I a Swiss or a Swede or even a pale-skinned Tibetan, would you be so concerned? Would you, even if you were, presume to call me in, like some shoeshine boy who has applied the wrong color polish?"

"I resent your implication. I have friends of every race; I was a vocal supporter of the civil rights movement long before it became fashionable. I am a charter member of the Franchise Fair Housing Committee. The fact that you and she are black and white is not the issue. Your education here has been an utter waste if you imagine that it is."

"My education here has been strange," Félix told Craven, contemplating with loathing the toubab's dry, prematurely gray hair; his soft broad lips like two worms bloodless and bloated; his complacent, ever youthful eyes. This man, the African thought, sails on the black waters of the world's suffering; the future Ellelloû announced, "Your warnings about myself and Candy are not altogether foolish. Nevertheless, I will take her with me."

"Why on earth?"

"Two reasons at least. Because she wishes it, and because you do not. She has asked to be rescued, to be lifted from the sickly sweetness of her life in this sickening-rich country and replanted in an environment less damaged. Though you would all, black and white, deny her this, I will grant it. I will grant her freedom, in the style of your heroes, with their powdered hair and rouged faces, the Founding Fathers; Liberty or Death is the slogan you fling from your ivied fortress, your so-called Department of Government; I fling it back, demonstrating that your instruction has not been entirely wasted upon me. I thank you, Professor Craven. Good luck in your Cold War, your battle against Sputnik. Good luck in your magnificent campaign of seduction of ignorant virgins, so as to avoid looking into the ravishing eyes of the loyal, sorrowing Mrs. Craven."

Craven's white face had gone whiter, realizing through the sweetish pipesmoke that he was closeted with a demagogue. The dictator, remembering the incident, one of a number of better-forgotten run-ins obstructing his departure with Candy from America, realized that Craven (who had given him, in petty retaliation for this interview, on a postcard that took seven months to arrive in the then Cailliéville, a B− for the course) had somewhat resembled the martyred Gibbs.

The Kush International Airport, a single runway east of Al-Abid, shimmers like a mirage amid the whistling-thorn. The tires of planes touching down frequently explode from the heat. Zebu, before the drought reduced the herds to hides and bones, were a sometime hazard. Now, the government has erected a two-meter aluminum fence to protect incoming visitors from the squalid, disease-infested emergency camps of refugee pastoralists from the deserted savanna. The glinting fence and the riveted wings of the Air Kush 727 and the great metallic sheet of cloudless sky contracted to pained pinpricks the pupils of the two Americans disembarking and exchanging greetings with the three-person welcoming committee: an oval-faced young Fula wearing a fez; a shorter plumper older African affecting Italian shoes, an English suit in the flared mod cut, and a wristwatch without a face; and a fetching if slightly stocky Sara woman accoutered in seersucker and secretarial half-glasses resting on her bosom, hung from a wildebeest-hair cord about her neck. Had the encounter been witnessed by an interested observer (instead of by the indifferent, wraithlike mechanics in sagging gray coveralls drifting through the haze of hunger, heat, and jet fuel fumes) he might have deduced that a reunion among long-separated kin had been effected. In truth, there was a similarity between the effusive welcomers and the greedily welcomed, though the former were solid black and the latter all-American. There were two, a man and a woman. The woman was blond, not in the flaxen way of Candy but brassily, glintingly, with a tinge of tangerine; her peach-colored suit was too hot for this climate and a rose flush overspread her face in the first minute, before she was completely down the shimmering metal stairs. Shadows below her eyes, emphasized by dents near the bridge of her nose, testified to the fatigue of her just-endured journey and perhaps to her recently suffered grief.

This was Angelica Gibbs, whom I had widowed. For all her fatigue, she gave off, in my vision of this encounter where I was absent, that American freshness which never ceased to delight my eyes on the McCarthy campus, that air of headlong progress, the uptilted chin cleaving gaily through the subarboreal shade, a freshness born of fearlessness born in turn of inner certainty of being justly blessed with health and love. She winced but would not wilt in the brightness of Kush— a constant lightning, an incessant noon. She shook hands with Ezana, Kutunda, and the (among his other titles) Acting Chairman of the Board of Tourism. Her manner was polite, timid, tired, tentative. Not so the manner of the man with her, a short plump man with heavy lids, liquid and lively brown eyes, a hairline mustache waxed to two thornlike points, and graying hair parted as centrally as his mustache. His limbs were short and his center of gravity seemed low, so that nothing could topple him, not even the uproarious embraces of Michaelis Ezana as the two joked like spiritual brothers at last corporally united, Klipspringer (for it was he) egging the hilarity on with his farcical Arabic and worse Sara. Kutunda was enchanted into guttural giggles by the apparition, out of the tinny-voiced telephone, of this magical man who had libraries in his pocket and who pretended the world was round as an orange. Mrs. Gibbs, her youthful face prematurely consigned to a widow's watchful sobriety, and the young Acting (among other responsibilities) Minister of the Interior, were the most reserved, but were willing, even they, to pin the enthusiasm of hope to this sun-swept intermingling, as the giant turbines of the 727 died, whined to a silence, and the less prestigious passengers—shabby Moroccan merchants carrying carpetbags, black chieftains as languidly scornful as rock stars, waxen-faced alcoholic Belgian mercenaries on their furtive way south, Japanese salesmen of telecommunication components, nationless agents of the hydrocarbon cartels, plump disaster bureaucrats from the UN, Jehovah's Witness missionaries from New Zealand, and other motes of the mercantile and messianic riffraff that has always drifted across the monotonously unanswered question our continent poses—poked their heads from the plane, squinted, and tumbled down the stairs.

"Welcome to the People's Republic of Kush," said Ezana in his Oxonian English accent.

"Looks like the country north of Vegas," Klipspringer told him. "My sinuses feel better already. Washington's a freezing swamp this time of year." He spoke with the pith of memos. "God!" He rapturously inhaled. "Heaven!"

He smoothed back his already smooth hair and beamed toward the aluminum fence, behind which children fought rats for morsels. There was no such thing as garbage in refugee camps.

Klipspringer's black counterpart, as if dancing for his life, which in a way he was, for he had arranged this meeting on sufferance of my interim appointees, made expansive ushering gestures toward the black official Cadillac which had been specially borrowed from the running dogs of Sahel for the occasion. The Mercedes was shadowing me, and the old official Citroën had ceased to go up and down on its pneumatic springs and rattled worse than a Dahomey taxi.

"In my country," Ezana told him, "there once were two seasons, dry and rainy. Now there is one."

"Where is the poverty?" Mrs. Gibbs asked Kutunda.

Kutunda looked toward Ezana to decipher the gibberish. "Nowhere," he prompted her in Sara. Presiding above this friendly confusion was the serene oval face and sleek fez of the Acting Co-ordinator of Forests and Fisheries, who now, having been rehearsed in some ceremonial English, bowed above the short, pink, hopeful, jet-lagged Americans and said with exquisite intonation, "Good-bye."

"Hello, he means," Ezana interjected. "A greatly gifted administrator, a superb student of the Koran, but untrained in your language, which is an exotic one to most of our people."

Hearing the word "Koran," this Chief of the Bureau of Transport amended his greeting, "*Al-Salāmu ʿAlaykum*," and at the touch of these satin syllables Angelica Gibbs thrilled.

Dear lady, why are you one of this quintet gathered, in the haze of my mind's eye, to make alliance against Colonel Ellelloû, who wanders more kilometers away than there are footprints on the moon, seeking to isolate the germ of the curse on his land? *Can he who follows the guidance of his Lord be compared to him who is led by his appetites and whose foul deeds seem fair to him?* I "zero in" on your face, dear Mrs. Gibbs, you mother of fatherless sons, you trekker through endless supermarket aisles and gargantuan consumer of milk and gasoline. How can you hate me—me, a fatherless son? I am so little. Your face is vast; powder has silted into the pores; years have gently webbed your beauty; disillusion has subtly dimmed the once-blue lakes of your eye-whites, the sensitive black of your pupils; there is a girlish, anxious tousle to your hair. I want to hide amid its ruddy roots, from shame at having caused you distress, at having displaced your far-flung arrangements with the world, all the filaments of your careful socio-economic compromise at a blow wiped away. Your great face, conjured from afar by the mystery of your unctuous, scrambling husband's death, turns a moment, before eclipse within the shadows of the Cadillac, toward the miraculously blank Kushite sky; your face is then blanched by solar fury as well as fatigue, and I, your invisible enemy, see, beneath your lifted upper lip, halfway down one of your splendid American incisors, a tooth bared by a vagary of thought and incandescent in the sun, a speck, no bigger than a *bi*, no bigger than the dot on a *bi*, a speck of lipstick, a clot of blood.

As, both on foot now, amid the lengthening shadows of the hour of sunset prayer, we moved upwards to the domed cave, Sheba surprised me by talking. "My lord, my husband: must this be?"

"My dear Sheba, we have travelled to the verge of death so we may arrive at this point."

"So you say; but perhaps the travelling, our hardships and our survival of them, was what was necessary for my lord's purpose: to purify his life and redeem his land."

"If that were so, then rain would be falling."

"Rain in the Balak would be empty noise on stone: perhaps beyond the southern horizon, where the savanna waits to be green again, rain falls."

"When rain falls in Kush, my blood will know it."

"My blood, too, talks. It tells me to be afraid."

"What could my Sheba fear? Her President is with her, and the Mercedes follows always behind, with Mtesa and Opuku and their machine guns."

"My President, I think," the girl said, her coiffure restored and her necklace resplendent yet the normal elastic sway of her walk still hobbled, as she made her way with bent, reluctant steps, "has no cause to fear. He does not love his life, and such men travel enchanted through the adventures they bring upon others. But I, I have not lived two decades, and am a woman, and my life is of the earth; though I have given my blood to the earth, it has not yet given me a child, and such peace as I have must come in the chewing of kola nuts and khat, and in the music which lifts one's soul a little free of sadness."

"I am sorry you are sad. A thousand girls in Istiqlal would exult in the honor of your position."

"The honor has been empty, but I embrace it still. My lord is the touch of Allah to me. Even when my tongue was so swollen I feared I would choke, I adored him. But here, amid these strangers, at the mouth of this artificial wonder, we enter an area of transgression. I wish I were back on the streets of Hurriyah, digging the scene and thinking of nothing."

"You sense this is a trap. But I have no choice but to enter it. I am the key that must dare to lose itself in the lock."

"Forgive me, but I do not fear for you, but for myself. That raid by the Tuareg, I was not so dazed I did not wonder if it was not for me they had come. And then those Tuareg that gave us water, I felt their lust. Our caravan driver said, the Yemenis are starving for slaves. I have value, else my lord would not have stolen me from the streets."

Her shoulders gave a limp doleful shrug as I hugged her. "How foolish and conceited my little queen has become! Always thinking of herself! Anyway, the Yemenis keep their slaves now in little air-conditioned ranch houses, with kitchenettes, door chimes, and a rumpus room with a dartboard!"

Yet, though I tried to tease her fear to nothing, her fresh self-expressiveness—her attempt to become an independently anxious and defensive individual—sexually excited me, so that, that night, my member, adamant as an adolescent's, penetrated the gently resistant darkness of a woman, troubled and palpable in her fear. My explosion of seed felt engendering, as her hips heaved to receive me deeper, on the oversoft, antiseptic motel bed, and then rolled, instantly, into sleep. For an hour, I caressed Sheba's shoulders, sheathed shoulder blades, and relaxed buttocks as if tenderly to seal a pledge into her body. Of the events that followed none more enduringly torments me than my never knowing if my instinct was correct, and whether or not a little Ellelloû, wrinkled, innocent, and indignant, nine months later bubbled into this world's scorching atmosphere out of my fourth wife's beautiful blue-black loins.

We had to spend the night because the cave was closed. Indeed we were lucky to find a room in the shabbily constructed tourists' lodge, with its paper-thin partitions and dubious desk clerk. As we had made the last turn on the golfcart path through the lengthening lavender shadows, the matching frocks and mocking glances of a pack of Northern European schoolgirls poured past us on either side, and beyond them we saw a green steel grate inarguably drawn across the cave-mouth, saying FERMÉ, مغلق, Θ, Закрът. In smaller type beneath, we read, OUVERT *de 9 h à 12 h, de 14 h à 17 h. Billets d'entrée 50 lu.* At nine the next morning, therefore, having breakfasted at one of the concessionaire stands that had sprung up like fungi on the spot, vending croissants and caviar, teriyaki and chili, kebab and hot dogs from beneath a chorus of umbrellas, Sheba and I joined the polyglot, vacuously titillated crowd waiting for admission. Among its members I noticed Mtesa and Opuku, standing slightly apart in their uniforms, which appeared fresh. Under cover of the bustle as the green shutter-gate was slowly cranked upwards, and a clammy waft of cold air breathed from the mysteries within, I sidled up to Mtesa and asked, "How did you get the Mercedes up those gorges?"

He stared at me almost impudently; he was growing a little mustache. "No need," he said. "Broad road up from plains. Well-marked, all tourist services. You came scenic way."

A bell rang, and the crowd pushed forward. Sheba clung to my side in the jostling, sudden darkness. Concrete stairs and ramps alleviated but did not entirely eliminate the treacherous unevenness of the cavern floor. Small spotlights illuminated noteworthy graffiti and, at one spot, a cluster of Silurian mollusc fossils whose sea bed had been gradually lifted into this arid altitude. The oracle was situated in an artfully framed recess; chains held back the curious from close inspection. *La tête du roi*, which as we stared slowly gathered to itself a greenish glow derived (I surmised) from the illuminatory expressionism of the Moscow Arts Theatre, seemed at first one more rough, cracked rocky protuberance among the many others that filled the recess like buds of subaqueous coral, like the polyps the electron microscope reveals in the smoothest matter. Then its details dawned.

Edumu's head, so small in life, had grown larger in death. Its eyes were closed, its lips lax and drooping on one side, perhaps deformed by the force of its severance. I had never chopped off a head before, and one of the disappointments of the Tuareg capture had been my subsequent inability to check my craftsmanship. I had kept my wrists firm and paused at the top. The blow had felt smooth and well-angled, considering my state of nervous tension and the muscular inhibition it induces.

A wreath of white cloth, reminiscent of the old king's *lungi*, enwrapped the sliced throat, and a kind of altar of Plexiglas demonstrated with its transparence that no body existed beneath the head. The head's expression was, well, drab. I was reminded of the dusty relics of grandeur in his cell, though the symbolic riband of gold on his forehead took glitter from the rheostatted spotlight. His foolish ecstatic halo of wiry white wool had been tidied and diminished; undertakers never get the hair quite right. When Edumu's eyelids lifted, the crowd gasped and Sheba grasped my hand so hard I felt a metacarpal snap. The pain lost itself, however, in my wonder at the old king's shallow-backed eyes. The crazed pallor of the irises was unmistakably his, *but these eyes saw*. Rather than drifting skywards as they used to in our interviews, they focused out upon us—upon *me*, it seemed—levelly. Fighting down the vomitus of superstitious terror rising in my craw, I reasoned that in this detail the enemies of my state had forfeited credibility.

The head's lips moved with the slight stiffness of an engine starting in the morning. "Patriotic citizens of Kush," it creakily addressed the rapt crowd, "there is great evil among you. A greatly evil man, whose name is known to you all, and whose face is known to few."

He and I had chosen my name together, laughing, on an evening in the Palais when he thought the Revolution was a joke, and he would be released from detention when its first wave of bluster was by.

"This man," the head continued, the mechanical action of its lips now uncannily corresponding to the drifting way Edumu had talked, as if a kind of wind blew in and out of his heart, "pretends to unite the multitudinous races and religions of Kush against the capitalist toubabs, the fascist Americans who carry forward the cause of international capitalism on behalf of the world's rapacious minority of blue-eyed white devils." Yes, his voice had slightly shifted, in the drafty chambers of my associations, to that of the Messenger, droning on softly in Chicago's Temple Two, a little brown precipitate of centuries of wrong, a gentle concentration of hate.

The head kept talking, with a sudden shrill jump in the amperage of the electrical system that, I realized, was picking up and broadcasting the vibrations of the lungless voice-box. "This man, while proclaiming hatred of the Americans, is in fact American at heart, having been poisoned by four years spent there after deserting the *Troupes coloniales*. He is profoundly unclean. One of his wives is American, the wife who is called the All Wrapped Up. Because of his black skin, he was subjected to discrimination and confusing emotional experiences in the land of the devils, and his political war, which causes him to burn gifts of food and assassinate those functionaries who bring these gifts, is in truth a war within himself, for which the innocent multitudes suffer. He has projected upon the artificial nation of Kush his own furious though ambivalent will; the citizens of this poor nation are prisoners of his imagination, and the barren landscape, where children and cattle starve, mirrors his exhausted spirit. He has grown weary of seeming to hate what he loves. Just as nostalgia leaks into his reverie, while he dozes above the drawingboard of the People's Revolution so vividly blueprinted by our heroic Soviet allies, so traces of decadent, doomed capitalist consumerism creep into the life-fabric of the noble, beautiful, and intrinsically pure Kushite peasants and workers."

I felt the hand of a hack writer had intruded these phrases into the tape and exclaimed aloud the Berber word for still-fresh camel dung. My neighbors in the throng shushed me angrily, having been thus far held fascinated by the head's analysis of our internal difficulties.

"Wrongly," the head continued, with a new decibel shift, dropping the voice into a more plaintive timbre, "was I, a harmless and cynical figurehead at worst, sacrificed to the welfare of the state. The head that should have rolled belongs to Colonel Hakim Félix Elleloû. Even as his public self puts on a wrathful show of extirpating traces of foreign contamination, his private self, operating upon the innocent vacancy of our sublime but susceptible territory, engenders new outbreaks of the disease. Even now an entire American boom town, with false fronts, brazen bubble-gum-blowing whores, and *pombe*-dispensing saloons has materialized within the Ippi Rift, above a reservoir of water stored in porous sandstone since the beginning of time against the coming of the Mahdi. Destroy this evil city, citizens of Kush! But unless you destroy its source, the repressed affections and idle dreaming of your shadowy leader, other excrescences will spring up instead, and your children will continue to harken to rock music, your wives will secretly desire to expose their ankles, and your brother, with whom you have shared your last curd of goat cheese, will succumb to the profit motive and become a soulless robot of greed and usury, a cog in a machine driven by economic forces beyond all human appeal! Citizens of Kush: Overthrow Elleloû! Overthrow Elleloû, and rain will fall!"

I looked about me to see a citizen of Kush, and of course there were none to be seen, only foreigners, adventurers, curiosity-seekers whose minds had already darted ahead to the next sight, the return to the bus, the probability of finding a rest room without a long line. The head was concluding, its lips clearly out of sync, "This has been a vision vouchsafed to me in Paradise, where the veil is lifted from the eyes of men. It comes to you courtesy of Soviet technology. Thank you for your attention. Feel free to wander about the cave, only do not touch the prehistoric Saharan art work, which the moisture of your breath is gradually eroding. For your further entertainment a slide show depicting the Kush national heritage will be shown on the wall behind me."

VI

THE PRESIDENT, all later accounts agree, had endured the diatribe with dignity. Only when the slide show began did he forcefully intervene. Clad, remember, in the tattered *gala-bieh* of a desert wanderer—an assistant musician, a sideman—Ellelloû stepped over the chain while the first slides exploded from the projector: Kodachrome fixations of dunes, of peanut pyramids, of the hydroelectric dam beloved of Michaelis Ezana, of feathery tribal dances along the muddy Grionde, of pirogues, of shambas, of a camel ruminating and a muffled Targui glowering before the unexpected background of Istiqlal's East German skyscraper. Taking abruptly distorted fragments of these images on his back and writhing shoulders, he ripped the head by its fleece from its roots of color-coded wiring cleverly threaded through the top sheet of Plexiglas, which was perforated two-ply. Sparks—green, orange—flew. Fear and astonishment made a momentary circle of peace around the desecrator.

Edumu's head shocked Ellelloû's haptic sense with its weight, far less than when filled with watery brains and blood, and its texture, which combined those of paper and wax, dead in such different ways. The skull had been enlarged, to receive so much mechanical and electronic apparatus: another Sovietism, the dictator reasoned—for with their superior miniaturization techniques the Americans could have fitted all this into the skull of a mole. Yet, despite the small distortion of scale, Ellelloû, hugging the head to his chest to break the last stubborn connections, found tears smarting in his eyes, for in life this head, mounted atop the closest approximation to a father the barren world had allowed him, had never been held by him thus, and the act discovered the desire. They had been two of a kind, small cool men more sensitive than was efficient to the split between body and mind, between thought and deed. The king had prepared him to rule, though it had meant his own ouster. "A king must be a stranger," he had told his ambitious attaché. "His function is to take upon himself the resentment of his people for their misery." *A king must be a stranger:* this truth, peculiarly African, rustled in Ellelloû's own skull while the desecrated other pressed its little fig of a nose, rubbery in reconstruction, against his hushed heart. Then the affronted electronic engineers, and a motley guard clad in indigo Tuareg robes and green soldiers' uniforms, burst from their hidden places and encircled him with intent to kill.

Russian, Wanj, Arabic, Tamachek were shouted; Ellelloû's *galabieh* was rudely tugged and Edumu's head was torn from his arms, though the riband of gold, the dwindled veil of a sacred presence, remained in his fist. His captors, pressing close about him, had terrible breaths: not only vodka but the spoiled yeast of native beer and the sourness of millet porridge licked from dusty fingers mingled fiercely in the captive's face, along with an unaccountable distant sweet tang, of barbershop hair-oil.

"*Je suis Ellelloû*," he said, repeatedly, for his first assertion was not heard, or else his accent was not understood. He was struck beside the ear; a scarlet numbness overspread his face from that portion; he was spat upon, mistily; his arms were pinioned and his wrists twisted as an unseen other struggled with his fingers for the golden headband.

The pressure ceased, the uproar was quelled. Opuku and Mtesa had stepped forward, gleaming in the nakedness of power, Opuku's machine gun a beautiful *mitrailleuse* after a design by Berthier, oiled like a Nubian whore, and Mtesa's .44 magnum scarcely less enchanting. A patriotic poster was unfurled beside Ellelloû's face; the crowd of tourists, comprehending little and cowering back from the violence, applauded as if this comparison were part of the show, of the Kush national heritage. Indeed, the slide show had automatically continued throughout, planting a Berber grin squarely upon the grimace of a furious technician, and the next instant projecting upon our struggle the pastoral peace of a herd of sheep overgrazing the Hulūl Depression. Due to the poor photogravure of the poster, my identity was unsettled until one of the Soviets came forward and shook my hand; I recognized, amid the cocoa-paste of his absurd disguise as a nomad, the shallow, tilted, alert, hunted yellowish eyes of his race. "Colonel Ellelloû," he said, "*je présume*."

"Colonel Sirin," I remembered.

"Death to the people's enemies and revisionist counter-revolutionaries wherever they may be found," he said, through his translator, who had appeared at his side in the baggy costume of a bespectacled Maoist sightseer.

"Just so," I said, and nodded toward the dreary relic of Edumu IV where it lay on the cavern floor, one more piece of debris, debunked, inoperative, a prop at the back of the stage. "Have you asked yourself," I asked the colonel, "if your perpetration of this charade does not constitute a serious breach of the treaties between our two great democratic nations?"

The colonel shrugged and talked at Russian length, words that were translated as, "It is very boring, in the bunker. As part of *détente*, our government has instructed us to mingle more freely with the local populations."

"There was no population here, until your contraption attracted it. Even so, the audience is composed of day-trippers from Zanj, with whom our border will be henceforth closed. Your plot has served to put a little profit into old Komomo's pocket, but has left the loyal citizens of Kush unmoved."

"Not quite unmoved, Comrade; for the First Citizen of Kush has personally come far to attend to the oracle, as we knew he would." The colonel was shedding his shamed face and costumed unease, and his affectation of omniscience rankled in conjunction with the recalled ordeal of his bunker hospitality—his drunken toastmaking, his materialist clichés, his atheistical mockery. The Koran says, *Woe to those who debar others from the path of Allah and seek to make it crooked*. And the king had once advised me, *Enemies are a spiritual treasure, allies a practical burden*. In his swinish Slavic fashion my ally, confident that the joke of his devious interferences was now shared, debonairly lit a Космос cigarette, that went ill with his rags and his paint. It came to me that in addition to closing the Zanj border I should abrogate the missile treaty, as Ezana had often advised: thus I was thinking fondly of Ezana at the very moment, give or take a minute, when he was falling in love, over cocktails and freeze-dried peanuts, with Mrs. Gibbs, her brassy hair playing Ping-Pong with points of light in Mr. Klipspringer's freely administered bourbon. The wires leading into my head were as many as those into the dismantled king's.

I told the smirking colonel opposite, "And the oracle spoke a great deal of facile, impudent, and traitorous nonsense, in the style of that messiah of bourgeois self-seeking, the Zionist Sigmund Freud."

"The oracle spouted not only psychology, but geography as well—did you not notice?"

"The rumor of the metropolis in the Ippi Rift I take to be as phantasmal as the gadget's analysis of the President's neurotic sublimations."

"Not a metropolis, but a small industrial city, of the type you call—" Consultation with his translator finally produced the word, "upstate."

"With variegated housing and charming recreational sites," the translator added.

"Not an encampment of beggars could exist there," I told them, "but that the Minister of my Interior would have informed me. In our sublime vacancy even the birth of a camel makes vibrations."

The colonel smiled, and flakes of cocoa-paste fell from his cheeks. "The Minister of your Interior you have judged, correctly, to be a traitor. Also he is a man who dislikes friction. Your Soviet friends, however, remain true to the Revolution. In alerting you to danger, we have gone to some lengths to avoid your official channels, which are rotten with revisionist spies."

Ellelloû saw that truly he must travel on, westward to the Ippi Rift; but as this new leaf of adventure unfolded before him he felt only an exhaustion, the weariness of the destined, who must run a long track to arrive at what should have been theirs from the start: an identity, a fate. His trip to the Balak had been, in its wantonness, its simplifying hardships, freedom; his trip down from the Massif, by the unscenic highway, in the air-conditioned Mercedes, without his beloved Sheba, heartsick duty. Sheba had vanished in the tumult that had surrounded his uprooting of the head; in what shadows and by what hands she had been seized remained mysteries. The Russians, anxious to dispel the suddenly hysterical President's threats of abrogation and anarchy, had assisted in the furious search. Every cranny of the cave was probed; the apparatus of audio-visual illusion was overturned; the technicians' lockers were ransacked, even the refrigerators in the cafeteria, even the caviar barrels. She was not in the cave.

She had been taken outside, then. The clefts of the rocks were searched, while pigeons wheeled overhead and Ellelloû

in an agony of remembrance relived running his fingers along
the clefts of her body, recalled amid the mineral wilderness
the wistful thin melody of her *anzad*, the rounded perfection of her glossy shoulders and blue-black thighs, the velvet
caress of her lips on his indifferent member, her stoned docility and soft intermittent plea that there must be a better
life than this. The *taste* of her, Ellelloû remembered, the kola
in her kisses and the salt of her female secretions that mixed
with the alkaline dryness of borax when, on the dirt beneath
the stars, he would perform cunnilingus. The fast food and
soft drink stands were one by one overturned and smashed as
at Ellelloû's command the Kushite soldiers the Soviets with
usurped authority had enlisted joined the frantic search. *Divorce me*, she had begged, after telling him, *You make what I
do seem very little*. The tourist buses, wheeling in the parking
lots with their squealing loads of curiosity-seekers from Dorset
and Canton, were halted, and the passengers made to stand
with their arms above their heads in the now-vicious noon-
ward sun, as small in the sky as a pea, as a white-hot bullet.
"Beat them," Ellelloû commanded. "Rape them!" The soldiers, bewildered teen-agers fresh from the peanut fields and
the fishing villages, attempted in their innocence to obey, but
the beatings were feeble and the objects of rape, withered and
twittery in their long-sleeved English gardening dresses and
floppy rose-gathering hats, were unappetizing. Russian engineers, galvanized by Ellelloû's fury, went through the buses
with measuring tapes and hand computers, hoping to deduce
a space where the priceless bride might be concealed. Tires
were slashed, windshields smashed. The drivers, detribalized
Zanjians preening hitherto on their trousered power to steer
machines bigger than elephants, were pummelled for the fun
of it. "Destroy!" the dictator cried, to the consternation of the
Soviet colonel. "Destroy everything in this vicinity not created
by the hand of God!"

"But the concrete walkways—"

"Shall be reduced to rubble. All this was imposed without
my authority; by my authority all traces of desecration shall be
removed."

"We obtained permits," the Russian sputtered. "The new
head of the Department of Forests and Fisheries—all forms in

order—a boon to future travellers—Eurodollars." His translator was struggling to keep up.

"Travellers," Ellelloû sweepingly replied, "were never meant
to trivialize these peaks. But find me my Sheba unharmed,
Colonel Sirin, and we will let this amusement park endure as
a memorial to the happy event. Otherwise by my decree its
desolation shall forever objectify the desolation of my heart."

"I offer a theory," the translator said in his own words,
whether couched in sloshy French or muddy Arabic, I forget. "There were among us some authentic Tuareg, acting
as advisers, scouts, and regional experts." In the exhilaration
of speaking his own thoughts he went on, "Do you know,
some say—it is very interesting—the Tuareg are descended
from Christian medieval crusaders who strayed; hence their
frequent use of the cross as decoration, and their chivalric refusal to work with their hands?"

"That is interesting," Ellelloû agreed. "Where are these *kafirs*?"

It was soon discovered, amidst the swirling dust of poured
concrete being pulverized and immobilized buses being overturned, that there were only false Tuareg, that the true had
fled.

"They will sell her to the Yemenis!" Ellelloû cried.

"If so," the translator offered, "that too is not without historical interest, for Yemen was, in Biblical times, the land of
Sheba. Perhaps she will feel at home there."

She would have a kitchenette, a frozen food locker, a little ranch house with chimes for a doorbell and Muzak piped
into the den. She would wear an apron and house slippers, she
would learn to push a vacuum cleaner. She would forget him;
he would shrink to the size of a *bi* in her mind. The strong man
wept. Ellelloû ordered Opuku to line up all the tourists and
machine-gun them.

His child, like himself, would have a rumor, a gust of wind,
for a father. This fantasy, that he had impregnated the *disparue*
Sheba, hardened to a conviction as, having left the contrite Soviets in charge of restoring their developed hectare of the Balak
to its pristine condition, Ellelloû descended in the Mercedes
westward toward the Ippi Rift. The hum of the highway dulled
his ears. His mind was carried back to the times when he and

Oscar X and some one or two others (such as John 46X, who had kicked the heroin habit with the aid of Allah, had tried out for defensive lineman with the Packers, and had shoulders as broad as Opuku's, so when he came along Félix had to sit in the back seat) would descend south from Franchise to worship at the temple in Milwaukee or, an hour farther to the south, the Holy of Holies in Chicago. The green fields of Wisconsin would swing past like the swells of a soft sea. The white barns and silver silos bespoke an America where they in their gas-guzzling, mufflerless Olds were a devilish impurity, black corpuscles cruising along America's veins, past heaves of soil that, though casual as the shrugs of an ocean, had been memorized by farmers' footsteps, generation after generation. Over the car radio came Doris Day and twanging country plaints and, as the city neared, Dinah Washington and the rickety, jolly, hot-from-the-cozy-dark black man's jazz. Those tinkling notes never failed to catch the edge of the wave. Set on a ridge with the pride of a castle, a gaunt gabled farmhouse kept company with its one big tree. Poverty had roofed a house here and there with a patchwork of discounted shingles six different colors. Félix was fascinated by the power-line towers, steel skeletons whose shape suggested giants daintily holding threads of pure force in tiny arms hanging straight down, insulators. The delicate grandeur of their latticed forms repeated to the rolling horizon, and in moments the swiftly altering perspective from the back seat stamped one upon the other; such moments, like those of *déjà vu*, were thrilling, with a resonance beyond their visual proof that the towers diminished along a perfectly straight line. And Félix felt a meaning too in the backs of billboards, visible on the left, slatted structures solemnly designed, cut, trussed, and nailed to carry a commercial message fleetingly; one billboard had a curved silhouette which a backwards glance revealed to be that of a pickle, and another the outline, ominous when seen from afar, of a steer advertising his own demise through the channels of a local steakhouse. In the occasional distance a water-tower stood on its long legs like a Martian invader puzzling what to do next. In winter these fields turned white, white sprinkled with the black calligraphy of snow fences and leafless trees, a landscape as void of growth as the one his gray car was endlessly speeding through, gobbling one horizon only to be faced with an identical other. At times the dictator wanted to flog his country for being so senselessly vast. The day arched like a blinding headache above their endless meal of kilometers.

Ellelloû, alone in the back seat, his motionlessness a mask for his suffocating struggle with the resurging, undownable fact of Sheba's absence, was slow to sense the constraint in the car, a tension and disapproval emanating from the back of Opuku's round bald skull, connected to the mass of his shoulders by a glistening pyramidal neck. Ellelloû recalled that he had never heard machine-gun fire, though he had ordered some. He leaned forward and asked, "The tourists—did they die well?"

Opuku held silent.

Ellelloû persisted, "Or did they die ignobly, begging and cackling for mercy? Pigs." He quoted, "*When the Hour of Doom overtakes them, the wrongdoers will swear that they had stayed away but one hour.*"

Opuku confessed, "I didn't shoot them. I told them, Run away into the rocks. Those too frightened and feeble hid behind buses."

Ellelloû, his heart engulfed by rhythmic waves of grief, asked his bodyguard why he had thus betrayed L'Émergence. The motions of his heart, when he focused upon them, were like the attempts of a man with clumsy mechanical hands to drown in a bucket of bendable, skidding plastic a cat crazy to live.

"No betrayal," Opuku said. "Those poor toubabs just dragged in by Zanj tourist package. Old ladies. Gentlemen marabouts."

"Capitalist vermin," Ellelloû replied apathetically, gazing out the window at the streaming void. "Warmongers and exploiters."

"Slant-eyes too," Mtesa pointed out.

"Nixon-lovers," was the reply, still lacking in spirit. But he did not like Mtesa's siding with Opuku. Their little counter-revolution must be quelled. The President took his eyes from the congenial dun vacancy visible and sought to ignite with a spark of his old fervor the predictable kindling of his rhetoric. "You had the gun in your hands and their faces before you," he told Opuku, "and pity intervened. Pity is our African vice. We pitied Mungo Park, we pitied Livingstone, we pitied the

Portuguese and let them all live to enslave us." A sickening clothy memory, of Sheba mounted on her pink camel in full regalia, squeezed his body down, so his discourse continued in a higher pitch. "Imagine yourself a statistic on a toubab's accounting sheet, and further imagine that by inking you out, you and a thousand others, he can save a dollar, a shilling, a franc or even a *lu* on the so-called bottom line. Do you imagine, Lieutenant Opuku, that *his* finger will hesitate to pull *that* particular trigger? No, the ink will flow. You will be Xed out by Exxon, engulfed by Gulf, crushed by the U.S., disenfranchised by France, not only you but your entire loving nation of succulent wives, loyal brothers, righteous fathers, and agèd but still amusing mothers. All inked out, absolutely, without the merest flourish of compunction. In the vocabulary of profit there is no word for 'pity.' So your squeamish refusal to follow my distinct orders was a laughable freak, a butterfly from the moon, speaking an incomprehensible language to these deaf and dumb earthlings, who have no hearts, whose bodies are compounded of minerals utterly foreign to your own elastic arteries and stalwart bones. These people consist entirely of numbers; pulling the trigger of your government-financed— I am obliged to point out—machine gun, your superb Berthier *mitrailleuse*, would have constituted an act of erasure impeccable in its innocence, as well as being a gift of obedience pleasing to your President, and a polite enough message that even old addle-pated Komomo, the king clown of pan-African confusion, might have comprehended. Opuku, remember the Book: *Mohamet is Allah's apostle. Those who follow him are ruthless to the unbelievers but merciful to one another.*"

Ellelloû sank back into the velour, exhausted. He tucked little remembered bits of Sheba—her earrings, the fleshy bump in the center of her upper lip—around himself like ends and corners of a blanket. But he could not doze; the tension in the car remained. Opuku smoked a plastic-tipped cigarillo, having sulkily removed the highly crinkly wrapper, and Mtesa steered unswervingly through the flatnesses of the Ihoö, a plain of hardened talcum hammered to its present form by millennia of the sun's stagnant fury. In such a world Ellelloû's mind could fashion no shelter for itself; though his eyelids closed. He saw green fields, the slatted backs of billboards, and heard Mtesa suddenly grunt.

"Another truck?" Ellelloû asked. He was resigned, now, to such wonders multiplying.

"No truck, sir. Look to the left."

Perhaps seven kilometers to the south, a lost city shimmered —one of the red cities that, some archaeologists believe, the refugee royalty of conquered Kush erected in what was then grassland. Others thought they were Christian monasteries, whose cells were later used to house the harems of wilderness sheiks expatriate from Darfur. The stones of the walls, blue-speckled bricks it takes two modern men to lift, are silent, and for all their solidity have crumbled, so that at this distance, to Ellelloû's eyes, which also were not what they once were, they suggested that ring of fragile shred which remains when a wasps' nest is knocked down. Out of this ragged papery rim rose, still intact and scarcely weathered, hewn from imperishable indigenous stone, a monolithic stairway leading nowhere.

Meanwhile (to extrapolate), at a choice table of the Afrikafreiheitswursthaus the East Germans had installed on the top story of their skyscraper, Mrs. Gibbs, Mr. Klipspringer, Michaelis Ezana, Kutunda Traoře, and the young police spy in the plum-colored fez were enjoying a glittering luncheon. Ezana was happy, in his element among the twinkling imported cutlery and crystal steins, talkative, giddy on Liebfraumilch, and in love with the brassy-haired American widow, whose natural grief was underlined by stomach troubles and an ear problem originating in the imperfectly pressurized Air Kush 727. Ezana was showing off his African cynicism and gift of tongues, and though his coquetry was wasted upon its object, it was enjoyed by her benignly smiling, heavy-lidded, delicately mustachioed escort, the professionally patient Mr. Klipspringer.

"Your Mr. Nixon," Ezana prattled in his musical, trippingly accented English, "I do not think this Watergate matter should do him any harm. How could such a puny *contretemps* offset his stirring accomplishments of the last six months? He has ceased to bomb Cambodia, renewed relations with Egypt, created trustworthy governments in Chile and in Greece, provided himself with a new Vice-President as tall and handsome if not as eloquent as the old, and enhanced the American economy by arranging with the Arabs to double the price of oil.

Truly, a charismatic dynamo, who has fascinated the American people again in the workings of their own democracy."

Klipspringer chuckled. This man, what good nature, what tireless tact! "Maybe so, Mike," he allowed. "But from where I sit he looks like a loser."

"Indeed, a loser in a narrow sense; but reflect upon the purgative value of a leader who unravels before a nation's riveted eyes. If he falls, he will carry your nation's woes with him into the abyss. Twice recently, if I mistake not, your federation has been humiliated, by the North Vietnamese with their mortars, by the Arabs with their embargo. What more poetic and profoundly satisfying"—here he bestowed a dazzling, ignored smile upon the American widow, who was studying her plate wondering what, exactly, had gone into this sausage— "psychotherapy, if my term is correct, than the evisceration of a President, out of whom tumble in majestic abundance tapes, forgeries, falsified income taxes, and mealy-mouthed lies? This is theatre in the best African tradition, wherein the actor is actually slain!"

"Your own President, where is he?" asked Angelica Gibbs, prodding herself out of absorption with her own, obscurely troubled interior.

Ezana translated the inquiry into Sara for Kutunda and Fula for the man in the fez, who both laughed, that wicked bubbling African laughter connecting directly with the underworld; it rang in Ezana's ears as a permutation of his own intoxication with this tired-looking, diarrhetic angel who had come from afar to sit opposite him across the Afrikafreiheitswursthaus's laundered linen.

Instead of answering her, he lifted a fork before his face and said through its thoughtfully twirled tines, "The channels of the mind, it may be, like those of our nostrils, have small hairs —cilia, is that the word? If we think always one way, these lie down and grow stiff and cease to perform their cleansing function. The essence of sanity, it has often been my reflection, is the entertainment of opposite possibilities: to think the contrary of what has been customarily thought, and thus to raise these little—cilia, am I wrong?—on end, so they can perform again in unimpeachable fashion their cleansing function. You want examples. If we believe that Allah is almighty, let us suppose that Allah is non-existent. If we have been assured that America is a nasty place, let us consider that it is a happy place."

"It's the place for me," Mr. Klipspringer cheerfully interposed, "and I've been to Hell and gone. When I see that old soapy-looking Capitol dome from the window of the jet, I think, *This is it. This is me.*"

Ezana would not cease his flirting with the poor fatigued Mrs. Gibbs. "Now your President," he informed her, "is a master of such alternations of assumption. Let us suppose, he says, that China is not a bad place but a good place, a friendly place. We have many pleasant Chinese restaurants in the United States, he reasons, perhaps China is equally pleasant. Or let us suppose, he says, that the way to rule is not to lead and inspire the people but to hide from them, to absent oneself increasingly, like the ancient Tiberius, who frolicked upon his island while Jesus Christ was spreading subversion—are my facts correct?"

"I never heard it put quite that way, Mike," Klipspringer said, closing his lips then upon the wetted end of a Cuban cigar, which had cost him twenty *lu* in a basket shop where stacks of them were rotting, and crossing his eyes to ignite the other end with a propane-flame lighter. The man in the red fez noticed the lighter with admiration, and Klipspringer passed it to him. "It's yours," he said, with a soft chop of his manicured plump hand. And, with further delightful gratuity, blew a perfect smoke ring, that came spinning from beneath his pert mustache like a new-fangled missile.

"Our President also," Ezana continued to the pallid American beauty, "rules by mystical dissociation of sensibility, if I understand the phrase. Leaving the development of a plausible pragmaticism to those of us that stay behind in fallible Istiqlal, he explores the wider land for omens, to discover the religious source of the drought."

The man in the red fez, who was growing to understand more English than the others expected, interrupted with a spate of local language to which Ezana listened at first amusedly, then with some gravity. By a smart soft chop of his hand the speaker indicated he wished Ezana to translate.

"He says," Ezana told Klipspringer, "there is no drought. The nomads have survived many worse, by loaning their cattle to sedentary farmers in the south and reclaiming them when the dry sahel recovers again. The introduction of the cash-crop economy at the behest of the French has made this system difficult. The farmers no longer traffic with nomads, they need paper money to buy their wives Japanese sandals and transistor radios. And he says furthermore the well-meaning white men drilled wells and vaccinated against rinderpest, and this increased herd size to the point where desert was formed by the livestock. He says there is no drought, just bad ecology."

Klipspringer's eyebrows were elegant silvery structures, trimmed but not overtrimmed, riding up and down on the emotions behind his brow like the vessels of Ra on eddies of spirit. They had arched high, lifting his heavy careful lids; in the space thus cleared his liquid brown eyes poured forth to the faces at the table all their luminous gift of caring. His baritone trembled with emotion. "Mike," he said, "you tell the man for me, No problem. Our technical boys can mop up any mess technology creates. All you need here is a little developmental input, some dams in the wadis and some extensive replanting with the high-energy pampas grass the guys in the green revolution have come up with. You have a beautiful country here, basically, and we're prepared to make a sizeable commitment to its future. You tell the man we're very sensitive to the ecological end of things, not to worry. They were worried in Alaska and now they've stopped worrying. The caribou've never been better off. Miracles are an everyday business for our boys."

"I want this murderer brought to justice!" Mrs. Gibbs suddenly cried from the depths of her sorrow and impatience, her queasiness and interrupted sexuality. "I want Don avenged." Baring her teeth, she exposed a fleck of lipstick on one incisor.

Klipspringer put his hand adroitly over hers. "Angelica, revenge isn't part of the international picture. Internationally speaking, revenge is a no-no. What we have instead are realignments."

"Madame is a guest of the state," Ezana reassured her. "It pains me to think she should be denied anything she desires in Kush."

Kutunda, jealous of her former patron's infatuation with this freckled she-devil from the land where ice grows downward, launched into a long story of how she had been taken captive by Ellelloû; he had broken into her hut where she slept, the chaste daughter of a widely respected *dibia*, and had desecrated her body with his urine so that, unmarriageable, she had no choice but to become his concubine. He kept her in a closet, illiterate, and compelled her to perform unclean acts; he even refused to give her typing lessons. The young man in the fez, whose Sara was nearly as good as his Fula, expressed rapture at her telling; he choked back his laughter, lest he miss a word. Ezana's Sara was not fluent enough to follow the torrent of vigorous and redolent idioms, and he contented himself with saying brusquely, at the tale's end, to the white widow, "This lady, a cultural attaché, also has grievances against our President. It is regrettably true, he has committed many unpopular actions in the last half-year. His inspirations are not always happy. He put to death our old king, whom many of the river-folk superstitiously venerated."

"Where is he? Where *is* he?" Angelica all but screamed.

"He has ventured, you might say, upon a good-will mission," Ezana said, glancing at the black face of his wristwatch, as if space as well as time were packed into its shallow depths, like life in a coil of DNA. "It is hard to say where."

"Where—iss—*ee*?" the Acting Minister of the Interior suddenly enunciated, in halting but vivid English. "Ee—iss—*here!*"

Everyone laughed, except Mrs. Gibbs, and Ezana turned to Klipspringer. "Let us discuss what you call our expanding relations. If the Braille Institute is to be built, it must be by local laborers, enlisted from our new masses of the urban unemployed, and following an indigenous design, in conformity with African humanism."

The American diplomat lowered his eyelids and rounded his cigar ash on the rim of the plate holding a few discreet shreds of sauerkraut and the rubbery tied ends of his consumed knackwurst. "You bet," he said. "Maybe with a little *souk*like string of shops, boutiques and travel agencies, nothing noisy, along the ground-level mall. We want to help you become yourselves. A settled identity is the foundation of freedom. An unsettled nation is an enemy of freedom. A nation hates America because it hates itself. A progressive, thriving nation, whatever

its racial balance and political persuasion, loves America because, frankly, in my not so unprejudiced opinion, but the facts
pretty well bear me out, America is downright lovable. America
loves all peoples and wants them to be happy, because America loves happiness. Mr. Ezana, you and the boss-man here"
—his hand chopped toward the wearer of the plum-colored
fez, who obligingly smiled and underneath the table squeezed
Kutunda's knee so hard her own smile widened with pain—
"may wonder why the American revolution has lasted nearly
two hundred years, and yours is limping after only five. The answer is, All our Founding Fathers promised was the pursuit of
happiness. Our people are still pursuing it, they'll never catch
up to it; if they did, they'd turn right around and blame the
Revolution. That's the secret, if you follow me."

"Ed, cut it out," Mrs. Gibbs said. "What are you doing
about Don?"

"We're working on that," he assured her. "First you said you
wanted his ashes, now you want revenge."

"There is a city," Ezana offered, "perhaps prematurely
named, we might instead call Gibbsville."

"Where is this city?" she asked.

A spark of communication ran around the ring of faces, and
Ezana sadly confessed, "We are not at liberty to divulge."

She looked at her companions at the table and saw through
her tears black faces smilingly sealed upon secrets, secrets.

Ezana looked at her and saw beyond the brassy toss of her
hair, through the tilted plate glass set there to make a panorama
around the restaurant, at such a height above the city no odor
or peep of misery could arise, Istiqlal to the southeast: the bristling rectilinear business section directly underneath the skyscraper, narrow polychrome boxes whose sides were scrawled
with lettering in many languages including even the native
Hindi of the shopowners; the rows of camels and bicycles teth-
ered and parked in the clay square of the Mosque of the Day
of Disaster; the mosque itself, its minaret a dusky phallus, its
dome a blue-tiled breast; the boulevards the French had diagonally cut through the maze of mud rhomboids and irregular
alleyways; the dead chestnuts and poplars lining the boulevards
and resting like a tenebrous cloud upon the pastel villas of Les
Jardins; the scrappy glinting quilt of the shantytown at Al-Abid;

to the left, the airport and the slender road to Sobaville; to the right, the venerable jumbled hump of Hurriyah lifted like a coy shoulder into the rosy cliff of the west wing of the Palais de l'Administration des Noirs; beyond, the *souk* and the rickety dock and the pirogues; and farther beyond, a black curve of the blue Grionde. *I love you, I love you* ran through Michaelis Ezana's mind dizzily, and the white woman's weary queasy face, the merriment arising between the red fez and Kutunda's bleached hair, the American's blanketing gray confidence that all would be taken care of—all merged in this embracing, spiralling, panoramic feeling. In Kush, the politics of love was being born.

The Ippi Rift is a global curiosity that hides itself among the valleys of Northern Europe, belches forth its tensions at Mount Etna and the Valle del Bove, slips beneath the Mediterranean, and continues south to the vicinity of Johannesburg. Astronauts in their orbits see it plainer than China's Great Wall. Those who live in it do not see it at all. According to the theory of continental drift, the Rift marks the line along which Africa will eventually break in two—not, as would seem from a human standpoint sensible, along an east-west axis, so that the Islamic/Caucasoid third would separate from the predominantly Negroid area south of the fifteenth parallel, but longitudinally, with all our latitudinal diversity of race and climate not only preserved but duplicated. The lengthy fault, whose incidents include the Øresund, the political division of the Germanies, Lake Tanganyika, and the Kimberly diamond fields, excites geological aberrations, and there have long been rumors of oddities—oases, rumblings, auroras—in its vicinity as it cleaves the otherwise featureless desolation of central Kush.

Nevertheless, the President of the nation was surprised, on the second day of his droning, mournful ride with the sulky Opuku and the evasive Mtesa, by the bulge of emerald that jumped through their windshield at a turning of their descent, in second gear, down the steep, pink-gray slope of the Rift's eastern bank.

In some parts of the world this green would have been a simple suburban lawn; here it appeared with an evil intensity, as a sudden face of Roul. Back upon the lawn crouched a menacing fabrication, a low "ranch" house, a façade of bricks gratuitously whitened in splotches and of aluminum siding that feigned the wooden condition of clapboards. Similar, though not quite identical, houses were arrayed along both sides of this road, which had become one of those curbed asphalt curves real-estate developers dub "crescents." Lawn sprinklers hurled rainbows against the crystalline aridity of the air. Otherwise there was no sign of life, not even a lone postman. The children must be at school, the housewives at the supermarket. Or else the whole development was a mock-up constructed to torment him. Ellelloû felt a skimpiness, a threadbare name-less something as of those towns that come and go while the passenger dozes above the road map in his lap and the driver fiddles with the radio, seeking a nonreligious station. *As for the unbelievers, their works are like a mirage in a desert. The thirsty traveller thinks it is water, but when he comes nearer he finds that it is nothing. He finds Allah there, who pays him back in full.* Too soon, considering the spaces the city-builders had at their disposal, the crescents yielded to an unlovely straightaway with supermarkets and trash dumps and low windowless go-go dives. In the front seat, Mtesa and Opuku were becoming noisy; they had never before seen gasoline stations with plastic twirlers, or ice-cream stands in the shape of a sundae cup, with a painted cherry on top doubling as an air-conditioner vent. Or the golden parabolas of a McDonald's, a meagre hutch of an eatery dwarfed by both its monumental self-advertisement and its striped lake of a parking lot. The sight of these wonders at first caused them to mutter and then to jubilate aloud, hi-lariously, as people will laugh with terrified exhilaration when immersed in the mist and tumult of a waterfall.

The straightaway thickened into a drab little "downtown," with pavements and traffic lights. Here, the sight of their coun-trymen wearing cowboy hats, blue jeans, tie-dyed T-shirts, and summer-weight business suits provoked even louder delight, infuriatingly, for Ellelloû was trying to plan his attack, to screen out the superfluous, to concentrate. He put on his NoIR sun-glasses. The Mercedes had slowed to a stop-and-go crawl. A young girl, younger and coarser than Sheba, but with a touch of the ruminating insouciance Ellelloû painfully remembered, strolled past beneath the awnings, beside the parking meters, wearing an apricot halter tied high, tattered denim cut-offs the buttocks of which were patched with two faded cotton heart-shapes, and shiny-green platforms ten centimeters thick at the heels. She was chewing bubble gum with all of her brain.

Opuku leaned out and called to her in demotic Arabic, "Where you goin', little girl?"

"Wherever you ain't, fat man," was her answer, capped by a popped bubble, which sprung forth fresh hilarity from the two soldiers.

The girl, who had delivered her rebuff with yet that languid provocative sideways tug of the eyes that Kushite women affect in potentially compromising social intercourse, was strolling past the window of a *cinq et dix*, and the ill-assorted much-ness of its windows—the gimmicky, plasticky, ball-and-jacky, tacky, distinctly dusty abundance of these toys, tools, hobby helps, and cardboard games—agitated Ellelloû's breast with the passion to destroy, to simplify, *to make riddance of*. His hands trembled. He tried to reason. This excrescence in the heart of Kush was not lava, it was an artifact, a plurality of arti-facts, that had been called here by money. Where money exists, there must have been pillage: Marx proves this much. There must be capital, exploitation, transmutation of raw materials. In a word, industry. Where there is industry, there is machin-ery, delicately poised and precariously adjusted. This poise, this adjustment, can be destroyed, and the whole devilish fabric with it. There was a blue-collar stink to this town. Franchise had been cleaner, with its breezy lake, its ivied sanctuary. Many of the men on this street wore oily coveralls, and some affected aluminum hardhats.

Ellelloû bid Mtesa stop the Mercedes before the entryway to an Army and Navy store, which, he discovered within, ca-tered principally to the proletarian fads of youth, and was so far, here in the Ippi Rift, from the centers of distribution that its stock, especially for a man of Ellelloû's precise and wiry stat-ure, was absurdly limited. In exchange for his khaki uniform —the Galla trader behind the counter was happy to have it, for the sheen and softness acquired during natural wear cannot be machine-imitated, and is much prized by the young—and several thousand *lu* Ellelloû obtained a pair, not of the greasy gray coveralls conspicuous on the streets but of blue bib over-alls stiff with newness and double-stitching, an antique pith helmet in lieu of a hardhat, and a lemon-yellow T-shirt upon which were stencilled the words *Left Handers Are Easy to Love*. Thus attired, the dictator commenced, as was his way, to mingle with his people, leaving Mtesa and Opuku illegally parked in a loading zone.

The Saharan sun beat down dryly upon the twinkling conveniences of this doomed suburb of nothingness. Ellelloû felt this doom blazing within him. Thirsty, he entered a corner drugstore. It was cool within. Tall phials of colored water symbolized the healing magic of pharmaceutics. A rack of sunglasses stood dim with dust, untouched. The commercial contents of the shelves were a mere scattered shadow of the merchandise of the drugstore in Franchise. Lest the reader imagine that the disembodied head's facile diagnosis of the dictator's supposed psychotic condition was here being borne out by an hallucinatory echo of Franchise, Wisconsin, he should understand that this city was in every respect inferior to that prosperous lakeside paper-town; it was a Third-World stab at an industrial settlement, scarcely a block deep on either side of the main "drag," thin of soil and devoid of history and shade trees, its citizens transparently African, its commercialism sketchy and even, one could say, humorously halfhearted. Franchise was to this place as a fondly pruned and deeply rooted hydrangea bush would be to a tumbleweed.

The druggist, a tall black Hassouna in the traditional high-buttoned antiseptic jacket, glanced at the disguised tyrant's pith helmet with amusement. "Allah is good," he said. "How can I serve you, sir?"

"I am thirsty," Ellelloû explained. "Do you have a soda fountain?"

"Such frills went out of modern use years ago," the druggist explained, "when the minimum wage for soda jerks went sky-high. You are living in the past, it seems. A machine that vends cans of soft drinks purrs in the rear of the store, next to the rack of plastic eggs holding gossamer panty hose. Take care, my friend, not to drop the pull-tab, once removed, back into the can. Several customers of mine have choked to death in that manner. We call it the Death of the Last Drop."

"I also, effendi, need advice," Ellelloû told him, less timorous now that he had caught something of the man's accent and style. For all its brave show of consumer-goods, the shop seemed infrequently visited, and its keeper had not lost the desert love of conversation. Words will bloom where nothing else does. Ellellou confided, "I am looking for useful work."

The druggist lifted his elbows and polished the top of his case with his hands, which were long and limp as rags. "What sort of work might the gentleman be able to perform?"

The dictator was at a sudden loss. Fakir, digger, orange-peddler—his costume corresponded to none of his priorly assumed professions. He thought of Mr. Cunningham, his patchy florid face, his starched white shirts. He said, "I am in the insurance racket. I am a claims adjuster."

"I have heard of such men," the druggist admitted. He straightened up with startling briskness, as if suddenly awakened to the possibility that this stranger might be a hold-up man. His voice took on a solemn hollow threatening tone. "Well, sir, around here, the only work is to be had at the wells. Without the wells, and the toubab know-how, this would still be wilderness. You have heard, I dare say, of the wells?"

"Of course," Ellellou lied.

"A tremendous natural resource," the other solemnly affirmed, having relaxed again, and replaced his tattered elbows upon the glass case, which his dusting had revealed to contain packets of candy-colored condoms and a fan of cream-colored vibrators, like smooth flashlights searching in all directions. "Hydrocarbons," the druggist intoned. "That is the future in a word, sir. The path away from poverty, the redemption of the nation. Gross national product, balance of trade, you know all these terms, I am sure. They might well have need for a man of your experience, sir. I have heard tell of accidents amid the machinery, of near-explosions. I recommend that you apply, and my *baraka* go with you. Would you like to freshen up on your way to the personnel offices? Some deodorant, a swig of mouthwash? Personal hygiene counts for a lot with these infidels. God sees the soul; men smell the flesh."

A wearisome fellow, really. A nation of shopkeepers is a morass of pleasantries. Woe to the economy that puts its goods on the rack of petty mark-ups. *Nationalize*, Ellellou thought furiously. *Nationalize*. He asked, "How do I find these wells?"

"You follow your nose, man. Where have you been living, beneath the ground?"

"I have come from the Balak," the traveller apologized. "I have been a long time tracking down a claim. Permit me one more question, of a simplicity that may astonish you. Pray, what is the name of this town in which I find myself?"

The druggist indeed looked astonished. "Ellelloû," he said. He straightened again to his height before the banked Latinate myriads of his medicine-shelves, his dried herbs, his poisons distilled from convolute carnivorous flowers, his love-potions, sleeping-potions, antihistamines, and diuretics. "*Ellelloû*," he boomed, with the volume of a muezzin calling. "Our national independence leader, a god descended to us to fight for our freedom, a great man whose iron will is matched by his penis of steel." The druggist leaned far over the counter and whispered, "I trust you are not among those who with the archtraitor Michaelis Ezana conspired against the purposes and teachings of our inspired head."

"I am a simple apolitical professional man," the disguised dictator replied, with dignity, "seeking employment in the midst of a drought."

"No drought here, my good man. Our peerless leader, whose enemies foreign and domestic gnash their teeth in vain, perceived that the Rift, in its geological contradictions, would trap all life-enhancing fluids—water and petroleum, to name the foremost two."

Ellelloû had the irritating impression, from the discontinuous vigor with which the druggist adopted one manner after another, of a systematic insincerity that might relate (it occurred to him) to his failure to make a purchase. Still thirsty, but embarrassed and anxious to be off, he said in farewell, "God is good."

"God is great," was the disappointed answer.

Outside, the Saharan sun pounded down upon the faded awnings, unlit neon signs, and brick false fronts of the Avenue, a sign proclaimed, of the End of Woe. Ellelloû entered a luncheonette, narrow as a running man's stride and every surface of it coated with a film of wiped-away thumbprints and spillings. He ordered a lime phosphate, which he drank up with a single long lunge through the straw. The short-skirted waitress read his T-shirt and giggled. Her face was ugly—her teeth stuck straight out—but her legs were firm and smooth and the color of good healthy shit. He ordered a second lime phosphate and took it to a booth. Each booth had a mock-ivory selector for the jukebox at the back of the luncheonette, and he was surprised, flipping its yellowed leaves, to recognize some of the songs: "Sixteen Tons," by Tennessee Ernie Ford; "The Rock and Roll Waltz," by Kay Starr; "Blueberry Hill," by Fats Domino; "My Prayer," by the Platters. This last he could almost hum, as green fields and silver silos skimmed by. He began to feel bloated with flavored carbonation. And the Formica tabletop depressed him, its oft-wiped smoothness too much like the blankness of the sky. Ellelloû got up, paid, tipped the waitress a *lu*, and left. As he went out the door, the jukebox began to play, very scratchily, "Love Letters in the Sand."

A siesta emptiness possessed the streets. At the intersection where the Avenue of the End of Woe met another, an oblong traffic island held a statue of himself in bronze—even his sunglasses and bootlaces in oversize bronze, his face deep in shadow, his *képi* and epaulettes whitened by guano—within a fountain, whose rhythmic surges of water tossed upwards veils and ghosts of spray that evaporated before the droplets could fall back into the stone bowl from which these patient explosions were fed. Around the rim of this great bowl the nation's twelve languages spelled their word for Freedom. In Wanj there was no word, all of life was a form of slavery, and this gap in the circle of words children had worn smooth, clambering to frolic in the water. There were no children now. They were captive in school, he imagined, thinking of how aptly this fountain symbolized the universe, that so dazzlingly and continuously pours forth something into nothing. Sinuous green growth of a Venezuelan density flourished in the lee of the fountain, whose wafted breath licked him like a tongue as he crossed the shimmering intersection. Alone on the pavements with his sharp small shadow, helmeted and baggy, Ellelloû followed his nose. The shopping district thinned to barbershops and grimy-windowed printing emporia with cases of their alphabets gathering dust beside the quiet presses. Low cafés and *pombe* bars awaited the after-hours wave of worker clientele. Single-bladed ceiling fans desultorily turned within; there was sawdust on the floors, and big green bottles keeping cool under soaked burlap. An odor met his nostrils as sulphuric even, as caustic and complex, as the scent of the lakeside paper mills in Franchise. There, too, there had been, along the approaches to the industrial heart of the place, its satanic *raison d'être*, this multiplication of trailer-homes with bravely set-out window-boxes and birdbaths, ever more overwhelmingly mingled with low cinder-block buildings enigmatically named or in naked anonymity serving the central complex, which was enclosed in apparent miles of link fence hung with scarlet signs warning of high voltage, explosive materials, and steep fines for even loitering on the fringes.

Ellelloû approached this fence and looked in. Across a large margin of macadamized desert that made absolute dimensions difficult to grasp, a dark heap of slant-roofed sheds, inscrutable chutes, black-windowed barracks, tapered chimneys, towers with flaming tips, and rigs for pounding pumps belched forth a many-faceted clatter and the oceanic chemical stench of hydrocarbon refining. The ball-topped fractionating towers, the squat storage tanks were linked to their underworld source of supply by a silver spaghetti of parallel piping. Little pennants of burn-off flame adorned the construct like a castle. Though Ellelloû's eyes spotted few human figures, which perhaps in this uncertain scale would have been invisible, the whole monstrous thing was delicately in motion, eating something from the soil and digesting it into a layered excrement palatable to the white devils worlds away. Beyond and above the stinking, smoking, churning, throbbing emissary of consumerism, the lavender western wall of the Rift, too precipitous for any road, too barren for any life, hung like a diaphanous curtain behind which waited like a neglected concubine the idea of Kush. But Ellelloû could not smell the desert. Everything in the land his heart knew had been erased, save the blank sky, its blue so intense it verged on purple, overhead.

He moved along the fence, through the litter of drained cans and discarded brown pay-envelopes, until he came to a guard post, a plywood shack no wider than a telephone booth, and asked the man slumped in there for admission.

"Show me your pass."

"I have no pass, but I have business inside."

"Those at the main gate will determine that. What sort of business? You are dressed like a fool."

"I have a claim to adjust. I am a claims adjuster. There has been an accident inside."

This guard, a long limp Moundang in an unclean burnoose, studied him suspiciously. "There's been no accident here."

"From my mother I inherited the gift of foresight, maybe the accident is soon to occur," Ellellou replied, and was about to improvise an ingratiating fable when he recognized the other man. "Wadal!" he cried. "Wadal the well-digger—have you forgotten your servant? We met north of the Hulūl, in Ramadan, and together we repelled the American infiltration."

From within the hood of his burnoose Wadal studied me with deepened suspicion, and placed his hand on the rifle in the sentry box. "I remember much confusion and smoke," he said. "And my Kutunda being taken from me."

"Kutunda for whom you had no use, and whom you had taken from another, and who in turn has been taken from me, by one who will not keep her long. You exploited her because you have been exploited. Let me in, Wadal, and we will bring these desecrators and exploiters of the poor to justice. There is fuel for much smoke here."

He was still trying to fix me in his mind, as, emerging from the shadows of his tent, a traveller squints to distinguish mirage from mountain. "You claimed to be Ellellou," he said, "and were clumsy with a shovel."

"I was clumsy because you chose unworthy places to dig. But now your nose has led you nobly. How did you come to this place? How long has it been here? How is it capitalized, and who provides the expertise? Who is its manager, its president?"

"We never see him, and we never ask," Wadal said, still unfriendly, the gun brought in close to his body. Through a rent in his burnoose I glimpsed his penis, languid. "He feeds us and pays us, and that is enough. He generates employment and boosts the gross national product. A few more wells, and we will be another Libya, another Oman."

"Another Bayonne, another Galveston," Ellellou replied. He commanded, "Admit me to this inferno."

Instead of obeying, Wadal lifted his rifle as if to strike with the butt. A happy spark, the prospect of righting an old imagined wrong, lit his morose face from within; but at that moment a gray Mercedes in the silence of its perfect workings slid by on the crackling, littered gravel alley that ran beside the fence, and Wadal lowered his weapon. Ellelloû waved the car on, and turned his back upon the guard, having formed a more visionary plan than brute coercion wherewith to secure admission.

He went back through the streets of this new world named for him, into the barbershops and drugstores, the economy furniture outlets and the *cinq et dix* stores, the *pombe* bars and real-estate offices, the dens where men labored to repair electrical appliances engineered to be irreparable and the cinemas where numb heads pondered giant pink genitals laboring to symphonic music, and Ellelloû asked the citizens of Kush he found in these places, "Are you happy?" When their embarrassment produced a silence, or a grunted "What's it to you?" or a defiant "Yes" or an equally defiant "No" or an evasive measured response, he pursued the issue, saying, "Those who are not perfectly happy, follow me." And some did, though many did not, and some others were drawn along with the crowd, attracted by its promise of excitement, its air of destination, for they led lives of relative prosperity yet were kept by the very nature of the economy, its need to justify production by exciting consumption, in a low fever of dissatisfaction and ill-defined hopefulness. This little brown man, with his attractively fanatic military bearing in his crisp and absurd costume, fed that hopefulness, as does a comet, a mass murderer, a state lottery, an albino camel, or any other such remission from the hunger pains of the ordinary. With a mob at his back Ellelloû demanded admission at the main gate.

Wadal must have alerted his employers of impending trouble, for a number of armed, uniformed guards were assembled behind the padlocked pipe-and-wire gates, and a toubab had been produced from within the insidious alchemy of the oil works. He was short and pink and flustered; he wore a button-down shirt with rolled-up sleeves and had several pens clipped to the pocket. In the past, some had leaked, leaving blue spots. This was a mere desk-worker, a timid engineer, an agent of agencies in distant cities of glass. He was no taller than I, and his eyes peered levelly into mine through his rimless spectacles and the electrified mesh. "You want work?" he asked.

"I want justice. We want reparations."

"Uh—think you've come to the wrong place. Hasn't he?" He made this inquiry of a tall black Nuer who had appeared beside him, clad in a three-piece checked suit of some slithery synthetic summer stuff, his shoulders wide as a buzzard's wings, a clipboard in his hand.

"You bet the punk has," this black man said, and told me, "I'm in P-R here. What's the story, buddy?" His brow bore the Nuer scars but his American English was smooth.

"I am Ellelloû," I told him.

"Sure, and I'm O. J. Simpson. You don't look so easy to love to me."

"The shirt is not my message. My message is, Justice, or Destruction."

"How about that? What sort of justice you have in mind? Big justice, little justice, or justice of the peace?"

"Justice for all. These citizens of Kush behind me claim to be imperfectly happy."

"So that's news? They sure as hell busted their asses to get here. Look, I don't know how well you know the local situation, but it's not exactly a hotbed of alternatives. We don't ask 'em to come to us, we fight 'em off. This is a pilot project, we're trying to keep it low-profile."

Ellelloû wearied of looking upwards at this slangy front man; he spoke to the plump white devil. "By whose authority was this project established?"

"Everybody's, as I understand it. We deal with the Ministry of the Interior, mostly. The President's a canny type who's lent his name but keeps his distance otherwise. The initial contacts were finalized before my time; they only keep us here a year, it's considered hardship duty. My company's cut of this operation is peanuts, but the top brass back in Texas has a soft spot for the Third World. The chairman of the board came up from a turnip farm."

"This isn't business," the P-R man interposed, a bit stiffly, in unspoken rebuke of his superior's garrulity, "this is phil*an*thropy."

Ellelloû asked the toubab, "You are yourself not top brass? What is your title?"

"Engineer's my title; recovery's my racket. A new strike like this is an oddball at this late date, better recovery in the established fields is the name of the game. Hydraulics and fluids have been my life. It's a miracle, what you can squeeze out of a rock if you know where to pinch it. There's enough water down there in domes to flood the Hulūl."

"And the oil? Is it O.K.?"

"Beautiful," said the engineer, chattery with the relief these infidels feel when discussing their work in avoidance of emotional or ideological issues. "It comes up so sweet you could gargle it. Prettiest sludge I've seen outside of Oklahoma. You know oil? When you crack most crude by the Burton process—"

The P-R man interrupted. "You are wasting your time with this man. He is a terrorist. He has no interest in real information."

"Anyway," the toubab lamely concluded, reluctant to leave his specialty, "your Mr. Ezana, he's pleased as punch, and he's got reason to be."

The crowd, bored by a technical conversation they could not hear, was beginning to chant, "Ellelloû, Ellelloû. . . ." The P-R man with his winglike shoulders and Nuer brow scars correctly scented danger in the situation, though he pretended not to recognize his President. At his command a small army of harried, bearded boys had appeared bearing a tangle of wires and an assortment of electronic boxes— loudspeakers, transformers, tuners. This system was set up on the parched earth. When the connections had all been made, he took up a hand mike of the phallic type, with a glans of soft black rubber, *whoofed* into it experimentally, and, satisfied, spoke:

"Ladies and gentlemen, workers and independent tradesmen, all citizens of Kush irregardless of tribe and tint: return to your homes and places of business. This madman, no doubt inspired by religious impulses he deems genuine, has misled you with a vision of unreal happiness. Your hopes of real happiness, that is to say, a relative absence of tension and deprivation, lie not with absolutists and charismatics but with an orderly balance of capitalist incentives and socialist mediations. Joy-ously allow foreign capital and expertise to combine with your native resources and ingrained cultural patterns." He consulted his clipboard, and continued: "The African humanism of your forefathers, as over against the antlike societies of Asia and the neurotic sublimations of the Christian West, urges upon you the ideals of patient cheerful labor, intuitive common sense, and a many-stranded web of kinship ties that reinforces rather than dilutes individuality. Do not, ladies and gentlemen, yield your priceless personhood to destructive gestures by alleged saviors. There is no God, though you are free to worship as you wish, as you are free to indulge in bizarre sexual practices with another consenting adult."

The speech went on too long, not so much for the crowd, which, ceasing to chant "Ellelloû," had fallen under the spell exerted by oratory in our still predominantly oral culture, as for the American, who, natively impatient, of short attention span, and anxious to make an impression of himself as a genial and forceful fellow not prone to "stand on ceremony" and per-meated with a sense of "fair play," took the microphone from his eloquent assistant and awkwardly boomed into it:

"Open the gates, we're not afraid of these good folks. Indus-try's been a fine friend to this oasis, and by golly we intend to continue to be!"

The gates were swung open, the mob laughingly pushed through. The young technical crew hastily relocated their equipment and unsnarled the wires, and in the confusion Ellelloû—gently, as if lifting a little burden from the pink hand, a flower or libation proffered in homage—took up the micro-phone himself. It was as if he had seized a gun; he became potent; the crowd halted, conceding him a little stage of bare earth. His heart was pounding; his hand, holding the instru-ment, looked to his own eyes small and magically withered. He was beset by variable mental winds. The thought of Sheba re-turned to him—her dull betrayed eyes sought his from within a crush of cloth and coral—and with it a weary soft awareness of his lack of a woman, a woman who would lull him out of anger and put him to bed. But then he began to talk, and the breath of his throat as it leaped the inch between his lips and the spongy tip of the microphone was in his ears taken up by an amplified echo that seemed to blanket the world and impose a hush upon all its multitudinous contraindications, and his heart was at peace in the center of the storm of his voice:

"Citizens of Kush! You have been grievously betrayed! You have been led by the atmospheric machinations of Roul the desert devil, in league with the dead hand of Edumu the Fourth and the living perfidy of Michaelis Ezana, to dwell in this pestilential hellhole called Ellelloû! *I* am Ellelloû! *I* am freedom!" He took off his pith helmet, to show his visage. The cheering was less than he expected. The P-R man had made a move to grab the mike, but now stood idly by, close, checking the integrity of his manicure, whistling through his teeth in an impudent attempt at distraction.

"What is freedom?" Ellelloû went on. "Can you put it on with chains, can you hold it within stone walls, behind steel doors, in the circumference of electrified fences?"

"The fences are electrified for the safety of juveniles and stray dogs," the P-R man swiftly whispered.

Ellelloû spurned the clarification, urging into the amplifying system the swollen self-answer, "*No.* These heavy material things do not bestow freedom, they bestow its opposite, bondage. Freedom is spirit. Freedom is peace within the skull. Freedom is righteous disdain of that world which Allah has cast forth as a vapor, a dream. The Koran says, *The mountains, for all their firmness, will pass away like clouds.* The Koran asks, *Have you heard of the Event, which will overwhelm Mankind?* Freedom is foreknowledge of that Event, whose blazing light is the only true light, whose fire melts our chains and evaporates the walls of our impoverished lives!"

The P-R man muttered at his side, "Make your pitch. We can give you five more minutes."

Ellelloû said, and the microphone turned his words into clouds, scudding above the choppy black sea of the faces of the crowd, "You see at my side a bought black man, dressed in a white man's suit and taught to mouth the white man's glib tricknology. You see at my left an authentic pink devil, as apparently mild as the first suck of milk a baby lamb takes from its mother in the misted dawn pasture, but in truth as poisonous as the sting the scorpion saves for the adder. You see at my back a monstrous pyramid, foul in its smell and foul in its purpose, a parasite upon the soil of Kush and a corrupter of its people. As your President I command you, as your servant I beg you, to destroy this unclean interloper. A few well-aimed bullets should do it. The conflagration will lighten your hearts forever, and become the subject of a song you can sing your grandchildren!"

"He's advocating violence," the white man said, behind El-lelloû's back.

"He's got to be kidding," the P-R man reassured him. He held up three fingers where Ellelloû could see them, to indicate to the orator that, by some arcane rigor of technology, only three minutes were left to him.

"The beast behind me, drinking the sacred black blood of our earth, belching smoke and blue flame, and defecating the green by-products of petroleum," Ellelloû enunciated into the microphone, "is a mortal creature like any other, and I advise that my soldiers direct their first bullets into its jugular vein —that is, the exposed conduit removing the volatile gasoline vapors from the top of the fractionating tower, below the con-denser ball." He wondered at himself, that he could spout all this; it was like holding live coals in the mouth, all it took was saliva and faith.

Yet the soldiers did not shoot. They stood in their green uni-forms within the motley crowd, innocent bemused boys from herders' tents and grass huts, waiting for an apparition they could take an order from.

Ellelloû strove to become that apparition, with only his voice and two more minutes of electricity to lift him above the mass. The crowd, in its still good-humored bafflement and wishing perhaps to touch the fabulous electronic equipment, which in flaking gilt bore the name of a now-dismantled, drugs-scuttled rock group called Le Fuzz, crowded closer, menacingly close. As he tried to gather his inner forces to speak, he was aware at his back of the P-R man and the white engineer scratch-ing quick memos—contingency plans, "scenarios"—to one another and also of, high in his nasal passages, an incongru-ous odor overriding the chemical stenches of industry. The smell had a penetrating sweetness, it carried with it woolen clothes and falling leaves and rosy Caucasian cheeks, it was, yes, the fresh glazed doughnuts the Off-Campus Luncheonette

peddled to students as they sought a refuge from the sub-zero
Wisconsin cold on mornings between classes. The doughnuts
were laid out on waxpaper, still warm from the baking, their
dough so cunningly fluffed it melted to a sugary nothing in
the mouth, leaving flakes of glaze on the lips—how could that
scent, forerunner of the taste, be present here, so vividly that
Ellelloû, in this pause of his oration, salivated? No snack-cart
for the workers was visible; yet the scent lived in his nostrils.
And in his ears the scratching pencils of his enemies. These
distractions joggled the fragile chalice holding the distillate of
his message, his cosmic indignation, and prevented, perhaps,
from being as good as it should have been this, the last speech
of his public career.

He returned, in a low-pitched, factual voice, to the theme of
petroleum by-products. "What does the capitalist infidel make,
you may ask, of the priceless black blood of Kush? He extracts
from it, of course, a fuel that propels him and his overweight,
quarrelsome family—so full of sugar and starch their faces
fester—back and forth on purposeless errands and ungratefully
received visits. Rather than live as we do in the same village
with our kin and our labor, the Americans have flung themselves wide across the land, which they have buried under tar
and stone. They consume our blood also in their factories and
skyscrapers, which are ablaze with light throughout the night
and as hot as noon in the Depression of Hulûl! My people: in
my travels, undertaken only for love of you, that I may better
bear your burdens, I have visited this country of devils and can
report that they make from your sacred blood slippery green
bags in which they place their garbage and even the leaves that
fall from their trees! They make of petroleum toys that break
in their children's hands, and hair curlers in which their obese
brides fatuously think to beautify themselves while they parade
in supermarkets buying food wrapped in transparent petroleum
and grown from fertilizers based upon your blood! Of your
blood they make deodorants to mask their God-given body
scents and wax for the matches to ignite their death-dealing
cigarettes and more wax to shine their shoes while the people
of Kush tread upon the burning sands barefoot!"

A new scent, also sweet but astringent, had arisen; he groped
to identify it, while returning to larger, more spiritual themes:

"Such are the follies of a race that scorns both Marx and Allah. The world groans beneath the voracious vulgarity of these unbelievers. They suck dry vast delicate nations in the service of the superfluous and the perverse. The earth, misconstrued as a provider of petty comforts and artificial excitements, cannot but collapse into a cinder, into a gnawed bone whirling in space. Hasten that Day of Disaster, blessed soldiers of our patriotic army, and shoot the giant slave of grease mercifully in the throat, and restore this ancient Rift to its pristine desolation, beloved of Allah, the wise and all-knowing!"

Ellelloû identified the odor that had intruded: it was of the pink, "sanitizing" cake of soaplike substance that reposed within the bottom lip of urinals in the men's "rest" rooms of some American service stations and restaurants, and which had puzzled young Félix until he had been acclimated enough to understand it intuitively.

"You may say these wells have brought water. I say the Almighty could have made a river flow in this Rift. You say grass grows here now, where sheep can feed, and date palms, and orange trees, and what cannot be grown is purchased. I say, the Sahara once was altogether green, and the Merciful bestowed upon it a superior beauty, the beauty of the minimal, the changeless, the unpolluted, the necessary. The battle now in the world lies between the armies of necessity and those of superfluity. Join that battle. God has placed in your hands today the power to pulverize and incinerate this evil visitation, this malodorous eruption!"

But had he, intuitively or otherwise, understood its essence? The pink cake of strange substance, no doubt petroleum-derived, had sat across the porcelain slots meant to carry urine away; what purpose did this obstruction serve? A spiritual purpose, that of a talisman, a *juju*, an offering to the idea of purity.

"You say," he called into the microphone, which now seemed the narrow neck of a great echoing calabash trumpet, "that life here is hard and the drought has made it harder. I say, the unclouded sky mirrors the unclouded heart of Kush, the heart released from the tyranny of matter. *Magnify your Lord, cleanse your garments, and keep away from all pollution.*"

The devils behind him were still consulting. The crowd, whose depths and reaches he could not see, felt to his sense like a sail on far-off Lake Timmebago, at that instant when either the wind would catch, bellying the sail out taut, or else, the wind's drift having been misjudged, the sail would luff.

"My people: your President has carried our drought in his heart heavily, it has nearly dragged me down, until I made this recognition: the drought is a form of the Manifest Radiance, and our unhappiness within it is blasphemy. The Book accuses: *Your hearts are taken up with worldly gain from the cradle to the grave.* The Book promises: *You shall before long come to know. Indeed, if you know the truth with certainty, you would see the fire of Hell: you would see it with your very eyes.* Come, my people, let us build a great pyre. The white devils and their machinery have entered by the gate of our weakness, our wandering and unsteady dedication to the ideals of Islamic Marxism, the beauty of L'Émergence, the glory of Kush that was the envy of the Pharaohs and anathema to the Christians of Axum! Redeem your wandering, my people! Destroy this vile temple to Mammon! Soldiers, shoot! Ellelloû orders you to shoot!!"

In the answering, teetering silence, the P-R man's voice muttered, "O.K., that's plenty." The microphone was pulled from the dictator's hand. The P-R man said into it, "The management has a question I'm sure everybody here would like to hear your response to. The question is, What makes you think you're Colonel Ellelloû?"

"It shall now be proven," he said serenely, and waited for the crowd to give way before the irresistible certification, the Presidential Mercedes.

But the crowd failed to move as a single thing, as a sea pushed aside; instead, each head oscillated expectantly, amusedly, while the minute yielded no unifying phenomenon. Ellelloû stood on tiptoe, then attempted to jump himself higher by placing a hand on the P-R man's winglike shoulder. He saw neither Mtesa nor Opuku—no, on the third leap, there was Opuku, standing as a passive spectator just outside the fence with, the fourth jump revealed, the gum-chewing girl in the apricot halter. Of Mtesa and his Mercedes there was no sign, except possibly the scarlet letters, quickly faded to salmon in the Sahara sunshine, atop a ramp-riddled concrete structure, spelling PARK.

Beyond this sign, the sky was blank.

The crowd, as no omen materialized, began to rumble, cheated. The white engineer—his face glazed with perspiration and the parallel harrow-marks of a comb fresh in his thin pale hair, hair the color of the dung of a sick goat—said into the indispensable microphone, "Whaddeya think, good people? I think we've given this fella his chance. Any of you folks thirsty, you can have one free beer each at the commissary, to the right of the front door as you enter. Don't push, there's plenty for everybody."

"This is treason," Ellell: managed to shout, his last official utterance, before the crowd with murderous jubilation rolled over him. He became a beanbag, a toy. The wells continued to pump, and on the other side of town the lawn sprinklers continued to twirl. A little cloud covered the sun.

VII

*The struggle between man and fate is a totally alien concept
to Arab culture.*

—SAHAIR EL-CALAMAWY, *1976*

I LIVE. Perhaps the white devil's offer of free beer saved my
life, for the crowd was in too much of a thirsty hurry to
halt and pummel me with the annihilatory zeal my address
had attempted to instill. One cracked rib, a fat lip, the removal
of my shoes, the bestowal of a quantity of derisive spittle, and
they were through with my body. The life of a charismatic
national leader cannot be all roses. My wallet, with its rainbow
of *lu*, its snapshots of my four wives clothed and my mistress
Kutunda in the nude, its credit cards and plastic perpetual calendar and embossed national air alert codes and Brezhnev's
unlisted telephone number, had also been lifted, and no doubt
this semeiotic treasure-lode enriches the arcana of some light-
fingered ex-nomad secure in his niche in the burgeoning oil
industry. A little picturesque behanding would set the rascal
straight, I think—but then my judicial opinion is no longer
solicited.

To be barefoot and walletless in Kush, in even this modern-
ized pocket of it, is to be at no very striking disadvantage. A
few days and nights of soggy mendicancy, while the monsoon
rains pattered down with their pre-Émergence verve, and
during which I was kicked from more than one melting doorway by the property-proud burghers of Ellelloû, served to adjust me to the fact that I had indeed been abandoned by my
bodyguard among the masses with whom it had once pleased
me whimsically to mingle. After the loss of Sheba, such a fall
followed as one segment of a telescope brings with it another,
slightly smaller. No one to blow me, no one to bow to me.
Takbīr! I was driven to look for work and shelter amid the
happy mud. In my student need across the seas I had held a
variety of lowly jobs—"nigger work," in the friendly phrase of
the lily-white elite of Franchise.

The very luncheonette where, in the twilit last hours of my Presidency, I had treated myself to not one but two lime phosphates, hired me as a counterman, once I had demonstrated sufficient mastery of the junk cuisine with which the iron-stomached Satans of North America are poisoning the world. Cheeseburgers, baconburgers, pepperburgers; fried eggs in all their slangy permutations of ups and downs and overs; hash browns, onion rings, and hot pastrami were all within my repertoire at the sizzling, curdling grill. Egg rolls and pizza arrived frozen from the poles of Marco Polo's travels, needing only to be warmed. "Hero" sandwiches were cannibalized by my customers, who still believed, primitively, we become what we eat. From six to two, or from two to ten, I chopped, flipped, served. I juggled the orders in a rolling sea of music, for if the customers did not feed the ivory tune-selectors, Rose, as the toothy leggy waitress was called, did. She was a maddening hummer-along, and yet disappointingly uncooperative in other respects: my attempts to seduce her fell on barren soil—her hard-packed determination to achieve, with her husband Bud, upward mobility. They lived in an aluminum box on the edge of town, equipped with a chemical toilet and a fold-away kitchen sink. Once this domicile was mortgage-free they planned to sell and move onwards to a two-and-a-half-bedroom ranch house, with one-and-a-half children. The next stage of escalation would be a two-and-a-half-story fake-beam mock-Tudor overlooking the sixth green of the golf course, while Bud squirmed upwards through the greased tubing of the refinery. Such progress in husbanded half-steps was freedom to Rose, and my sidling attempts to drag her off the bandwagon into my anarchic arms were as idle as an attempt to seduce a locomotive from its tracks. No virtue as iron as that forged on the edge of poverty. When he came into the luncheonette, Bud, a big Moubi with arms that could have hurled a spear seventy meters, sat with those mighty arms meekly folded on the godless Formica as he stared up into the spectral works of a hierarchical machine, his lips pinched in unconscious imitation of the white man's scolding visage. They shared, as she slaved, one dream. Her only straying was in her head, as the lukewarm melodies bathed our ears in their moony ache day after day. Kush was the last stop on a long descent through levels of national development; these records, their grooves scoured of all but hoarse ghosts of song, had taken twenty years to reach the Ippi Rift from their source in the America of the Fifties. Over and over, hearty, hollowly healthy voices blended with violins toward an uplifted climax of pre-rock wail, a ululant submission to the patriotic, economic call to sublimate. "Love Me Tender," the youthful Presley requested; "Cry Me a River," Johnny Ray begged; "Qué Será, Será," Doris Day philosophized, her voice snagging each time on some thorn in my soul. The regal voices of Grace Kelly and Bing Crosby lightly entwined in the drifting waltz of "True Love," and Debbie Reynolds as delicately lisped of her clinging attachment to "Tammy." There was, too, in counterpoint to these feminine trailings-off, a choral, masculine voice: "The Yellow Rose of Texas," "The Happy Wanderer": when these rousing tunes surged from the well of time, Rose and I slapped the plates down harder and shuffled more swiftly behind the counter (never failing, it seemed to me, to brush hips tantalizingly—was this altogether my doing?). "A Whole Lotta Shakin' Goin' On," Jerry Lee Lewis assured us, ecstatic as a dervish. Even the grill grew hotter, the fast food came faster. And when the whistling section of "The River Kwai March" penetrated us, we knew, knew in our bones, that we would win the Cold War. Freedom, like music, rolled straight through the heart. Oh Rose, my Secret Love and Queen of the Hop, my Sugarfoot Standing on the Corner amid Autumn Leaves, my Naughty Lady of Shady Lane, in this chronicle too crowded with vexed women yours is the unique aura of happiness, of the bubbling, deep-fat aroma of productive, contented labor, as hoped for by Adam Smith.

Ellelloû, known to his co-workers only as Flapjack, served as a short-order cook for three months, before grease burns compelled him to take employment as a parking attendant in the city's one multi-level garage. It was here, he imagined, that Mtesa had hidden the Mercedes at a crucial hour; but the car and the driver were gone, and the oil spots on cement were indistinguishable clues, and the girl in the apricot halter had vanished with Opuku. Yet one day, in a concrete nook at a turning of the third-tier ramp, he found, wrapped in a *tag-ilmust* like a baby in bunting, Sheba's *anzad*. The gift seemed a gentle enough irony. He smiled; like any believer, he was not affronted by the notion that he was being watched. He, who had always been chauffeured, became ruthlessly deft in the reverse-gear rearrangement of automobiles, mostly old chrome-heavy guzzlers from Detroit's Happy Times, well into the second revolution of their odometers and their dents beyond counting.

Meanwhile, through the two months of Jumādā, in this season the Tuareg term Akasa, rain continued to fall upon Kush, rain enough even for a namesake of Noah's grandson. Sweet grass grew tall in the vacant lots of Ellelloû and in the millions of hectares around; the cattle of the pastoralists fed so handsomely their weakened legs snapped, and the herdsmen toppled to the earth with excess of festival dancing and millet beer. The very bones strewn parched upon the sands put on flesh and gave milk; seeds dormant several millennia hurled toward the serried nimbus giant blossoms and bulbous fruit absent from even the most encyclopedic botanic handbooks. All this, Ellelloû thought sadly, I achieved by ceasing to exist. *I* was the curse upon the land.

National news was hard to come by in the Rift; the local paper was boastfully devoted to parochial concerns: oil prices, OPEC conferences, the end of the embargo, new shopping centers in the area, zoning regulations to control the housing boom. No report of any coup was heard in Ellelloû, where all civic projects, all literacy programs and health clinics, all paving, sewering, and dedication of parkland were carried forward in the name of the national leader who, with the grand elisions of historical myth, had singlehandedly and as it were simultaneously crushed the French, the king, and counter-revolutionary elements within SCRME. Events widely separated in time and causation, and some of them set in motion when I was a mere foot soldier and foreign student—the *loi-cadre* proclamation, de Gaulle's imperious withdrawal from *la France, d'Outre-mer*, the constitutional-monarchial interval, the revolt led by General Soba, the expulsion of the neo-*colons*, the incineration of Gibbs, the execution of the king—had been lumped and smoothed into one triumphant sequence whose signature was the green flag, whose climax was the green grass swaying like an ocean beneath the benevolent gray sky. Allah was mighty, immovable, and undiscernible; so was President Ellellou; praise him.

Anonymous within the bustling *polis* that had absorbed my name, I searched the papers for news of myself. Page two sometimes carried bulletins from the capital—as far away, remember, as Rome from Amsterdam, as the Crater Copernicus from the Lacus Somniorum. They referred always to a vague "People's Government" as it issued a vigorous barrage of new wage incentives, tax holidays for foreign investors, relaxations of import tariffs and tourist visas, official welcomes extended to Israeli experts in drip irrigation and USAID malnutritionists, preliminary plans for a cantilevered Braille Library to be imposed on the center of Istiqlal, and other such political promiscuities savoring much of the trusting nature and unholy energy of Michaelis Ezana. Toward the end of my tenure as burger chef, beneath an item hailing the arrival of a team of Dutch specialists in flood control (I imagined them with whitened, waterlogged thumbs), a snippet of fine print said,

> Colonel Ellellou, President-for-Life and Supreme Teacher, has been away from the capital on a fact-finding mission.

And so in a sense I was. Working by day, strolling the streets by night, I spent much time contemplating my fellow-Kushites, as they had developed in this isolated oasis of plenty. They had lost, make no mistake, the attractive muscular lightness of alert predators, the leanness that balanced them upon the land as airily as our maidens balance bundles of tamarisk faggots upon their heads. People no longer looked carved, as they had in the village, in the army, and even in those early days of independence and monarchy in Istiqlal. These bodies sauntering along the Avenue of the End of Woe, clothed in a decaled denim that did for holidays as well as labor days, had been less whittled than patted into shape. A loss of tension, of handsome savagery, was declared also in their accents, which had yielded the glottal explosiveness of their aboriginal tongues to a gliding language of genial implication and sly nonchalance. There was no longer, with plenty, the need to thrust one's personality into the face of the person opposite. Eye contact was hard to make along the damp sidewalks of Ellelloû, where puddles took tints from neon signs. The little hard-cornered challenges—to honor, courage, manliness, womanliness—by which our lives had been in poverty shaped were melting away, like our clay shambas and mosques, rounded into an inner reserve secret as a bank account; intercourse in Ellelloû moved to a music of disavowal that new arrivals, prickly and hungry from the bush, mistook for weakness but that was in fact the luxurious demur of strength. The business of oil, of the businesses that clustered around the business of oil, pre-empted the mental spaces formerly devoted to battle and ritual, to death and God, so that these last two came to loom (I suspected) as not only strangers but monsters, unthinkables, like the abstruse formulae of science whereby oil was lifted from its porous matrix and its tangled molecules sorted into saleable essences. The volume of mysteries upon which men float had been displaced, but the shimmer of small amusements and daily poetries, the sly willingness of people to be pleased, appeared perennial. I, submerged in posthumous glory, immersed in the future I had pitted all my will against, relaxed at last. Often I arose early, conveying my frame with its clinging dreams to the luncheonette or to the concrete spiral of the parking garage; on my way I witnessed the droll earnest children being herded to school by the educational imperatives of the industrial state, dangling their schoolbags and clutching their books, solemn in their confidence that a grave thing was being asked of them, and that by obediently responding they were creating a nation. Their figures, uniformed, some of them, in green—our Kushite green, no longer an arid remembrance of Green Sahara but here, all around us, in the flourishing grass—seemed mute in the early morning, little figures silent as in a painting, collecting in clots at the bus stops. One does not know what it is to love a country until one has seen its children going off to school.

I was accumulating my earnings and assembling my shattered poise toward the inevitable return to Istiqlal. In the second month of my employment at the parking garage, when I had been promoted to the man who takes the ticket and the *lu* and releases the striped wooden arm at the bottom of the ramp, an idle task that leaves much time for reading, another item appeared on page two of the daily *Rift Report*:

> The Government today acknowledged official fears that Colonel Ellelloû, Chairman of SCRME, while seeking to negotiate the phasing-out of Soviet Russian missile sites within the Hulūl Depression, has been abducted by leftward-leaning terrorists.

So the ground for his official extinction was being prepared. The President decided the moment had come for his return. As he hitchhiked south with Sheba's *anzad* strapped to his back, the sky brightened, as if blanching in dread of his return to power. A truck carrying bales of last year's Parisian fashions—shantung hip-huggers, see-through jumpsuits —from Algeria to the *souks* and boutiques of Istiqlal picked him up. The driver was a young Belgian seeking a better quality of life. The cab radio interrupted its playing of *La Plus Haute Quarantaine* to repeat a bulletin that the President, long missing, had been presumed dead, and the Acting President with reluctance and sorrow had taken up the reins of government. To formalize his succession of Ellelloû, which of course is the Berber word for "freedom," the new leader had assumed the name Dorfû, an expressive Salu term with the double meaning of "solidarity" and "consolidation." The national anthem was played, followed by the theme song from *2001*, by Richard Strauss.

Actually, the Salu *dorfû* has the root meaning of "crocodile-torpid-on-the-riverbank-but-far-from-dead," as distinguished from *durfo*, "crocodile-thrashing-around-with-prey."

Michaelis Ezana and Angelica Gibbs were having dinner with Candy and Mr. Klipspringer. Candy had unwrapped herself and, out of purdah, looked, in a sensible yet snug gray wool knit dress with a single strand of cultured pearls, much what she was: an attractive woman nearing forty who had survived an unfortunate first marriage. Mrs. Gibbs, on the other hand, was resplendent in a crimson and mauve *boubou*, and she had hidden her brass-blond hair in a matching headcloth. Her tan, acquired at the poolside of the reopened Club Sahare, where the punctilious ghosts of colonial officers made way for basking

Dutch hydrologists and the brawny steelworkers assembling the adventurous skeleton of the Braille Library, would never be mistaken for the complexion of an African, though she now imitated the slit-eyed, careful, sidelong expression of native women. She was squatting on a packing crate of self-help books and asking Candy, "How can you bear to leave? The smells! The pace! For the first time in my life, I'm one with my blood. God, how I hated America, now that I think about it. Do this, do that. Turn right on red only. Rush, rush. Those dreadful slushy winters—they'll kill you."

"I'm only afraid when I see my first snowfall I'll die of bliss."

"Say, hasn't this rain been something?" Klipspringer exclaimed, rubbing his thighs to emphasize his enthusiasm, his tirelessness, his unflappability. "Right into August, wow!" The party was in farewell of him too. He had done his job here: established rapport, contacts, and a basis for expanded relations. His Arabic was now fluent, his Sara acceptable. He was wearing a dashiki purchased in Georgetown, D.C.

Ezana tilted his head, so his round cheeks gleamed in the light of Candy's candles, the sole illumination remaining in her stripped, fixtureless villa. "And yet," he said, "it has not rained for a week. I think it an uneasy omen, this return of the sun."

"Everything's mildewing," Candy said. "I tried to burn my furniture and it stank up the neighborhood."

"All the flowering shrubs the French planted have come back into bloom," Ezana said. "It is as when I was a boy, and the Jesuits taught us Pascal and his calculus."

Angelica laid a slender freckled hand on his tightly trousered thigh. "It's a beautiful city, dear," she said.

"Everything changes, everything heals," Klipspringer abruptly observed. He lifted a glass of *kaikai*. "Here's to 'er, Mother Change. A tough old bitch, but we love 'er."

The other three responded, Angelica with a glass of Perrier water; she was taking instruction in the Koran, and had already learned how to pound millet. Michaelis Ezana frowned down at her touch; in her African garb she seemed less giddying, less a radiant wind from Paradise. An awkward baggage rather, her infatuation with him a heaviness. The present Mrs. Ezana was horrible—a bare-breasted Amazon, a bluestocking—but with a horror totally familiar; he had grown pleasantly deaf in the range of her squawks, and could conduct his side of their quarrels in perfect absent-mindedness. Like dark planets, their relationship was exquisitely inertial. She gave him space. Her repulsiveness boosted him aloft. Ezana's lips parted thought-fully and his gold tooth gleamed like a cufflink as he turned to Klipspringer and began to discuss his favorite subjects, irriga-tion, electricity, and indebtedness.

"The thing about indebtedness," Klipspringer told him, "is it's the best insurance policy you can buy. The deeper in debt the debtor gets, the more the creditor will invest to keep him from going under. You guys were taking an incredible risk, not owing us a thing all those years."

"Our Great Teacher," Ezana admitted, "was perhaps too in-spired for our imperfect world."

"I don't feel I *know* you," Mrs. Gibbs impatiently blurted on his other side. She tugged at his hand with that fretful, propri-etorial impatience of her wolvish race. "Michael, even in bed I feel it. Some secret you're withholding."

"Don't bug him," Candy advised her. "They love their se-crets, they really can't help it. The African man hates to have his photograph taken. My husband of sixteen years, he was supposed to be the father of our country and nobody knew what he looked like."

"Sorry I never got to meet him," Klipspringer said. "He sounds like quite a character."

Sounds: amid the rustling of palm fronds on the roof, the rats scurrying in the empty rooms, and the late-night patter of their conversation, rustling their blood in hopeful torrents, the knock at the door was muffled.

"The male secret, of course," Ezana gallantly offered the la-dies, "is our weakness, our need. But such a secret, like the symmetrically evolved ability of the female to nurture and soothe this need, becomes in exposure boring, monotonous, too—is this the word?—sempiternal. Life is like an overlong drama through which we sit being nagged by vague memories of having read the reviews."

Candace's big Songhai maid came into the room and said there was a beggar at the door. She had told him to go away, and he said he had oranges to sell. When she said they needed no oranges, he offered to dig a well or to sing a song. There was something autocratic about him, beyond her control, and would the mistress like to deal with him now?

The beggar, an *anzad* strapped to his back, had shadowed the maid into the room. "Holy Christ, look who it isn't," Candy said. The intruder, wearing tattered blue jeans and a T-shirt from which the stencilled legend had faded, looked small, pathetically frail, on the edge of their candlelight. Angelica and Klipspringer were politely puzzled, sensing an extraordinary impertinence and tension. Michaelis Ezana perched forward to study the stranger and, touching a reassuring hardness near his left armpit, sat back, returning his face to shadow. "You have your fucking nerve," Candy was continuing, and Ezana thought, Would that change, so bumptiously saluted by our American emissary, were all there were to the world. As well, there is a deadly sameness. The infant cries for suck; the mother heeds; the child grows; the man dies.

In his high-pitched nervous beggar's whine the interloper announced, "I have come not to disturb your feast, but to beguile it with a song." He removed the *anzad* from his back and with his bow of bent goa wood produced a wheedling of melody. He sang through his nose:

"*A land without a conscience is an empty land,*
a blasted land, a desert land
where the children have red hair and bloated bellies,
where the adults have covetous smiles and cruel laughs.

A conscience is more central to a land
than oil wells, foreign loans, and peanut co-operatives;
a conscience puts erectitude into the posture of the young men
and soft fire into the glances of the ladyfolk.

But nowhere in the bureaucracy of Kush
amid so many posts for stamp-lickers and boot-lickers
is there regular employment for such a presence.
I ask you, should not a national conscience have a pension?"

The musician gave himself over to a partially fumbled riff in minor thirds, and rested the bow at his side. His hostess said, "Oh my God, Happy. Don't you realize you can be shot now? They've gone on without you."

Ezana had taken an interest in the song and asked, "Is it not the essence of a conscience, that it be invisible and ignorable?"

The intruder nodded. "Visible only in its benign effects. As with Allah, to be nakedly present would be to institute tyranny."

"Then," Ezana ventured, "I would think a pension might be arranged, if the conscience in the past had performed services to the state. Unfortunately, I am in no official position to do more than speculate; for in the Dorfû administration Michaelis Ezana holds an emeritus position only. Which, however, is a promotion from his incarceration under the previous administration."

There comes a time in a man's life, the beggar thought, when he thinks of himself in the third person.

Angelica Gibbs, who had not yet mastered the African woman's sublime though deceptive attitude of subservience, asked irritably, "Who is this joker? Darling, why are we letting him ruin our party?"

"Kinda fun, *I* think," Klipspringer interposed tactfully, his smile doubled by the up-tilting two gray thorns of his fine mustache. "This is their style here, they just let things happen. I think it's great."

The beggar addressed the widow directly. "I bring you good news of the murderer of your husband. He like his victim is vanished in smoke. In time the two will become indistinguishable. Together their sacrifices have opened the sluices to American aid, whose triumph is signified by these twin jinn of the pragmatic, your lover and your escort. The Book says, *Each soul shall come attended by one who will testify against it and another who will drive it on.* Thus black and white, dry and wet, exert their rhythms. Your own pendulum, Madame, is swinging; I salute your costume, pure in its native authenticity. My own, I know, is a shabby mishmash. But you have long been in my mind's eye, and it rewards a life of wandering, that this beggar may gaze upon thee."

The lady was affronted. "Where did he pick up his English?" she asked Ezana and, with a quick switch of her vexed face, "What did he mean, about Don's murderer?"

"Our self-appointed conscience hopes to affirm," Ezana said, "for no doubt conscientious reasons of his own, that your husband willed his own passing, from which, however, much good has arisen."

"I think the fella's making a plea," Klipspringer amplified, "for continuity and orderly transition in government. I'm with him there, one hundred and ten per cent. If your people can't find it in their hearts to grant him this pension he's angling for, I wonder if the USIS couldn't rummage him up a travelling fellowship. Hey, here's an idea. Make him a Donald—what was his middle initial?"

"I've forgotten," Angelica said.

"Make him a Donald X. Gibbs Travelling Fellow," Klipspringer concluded, rubbing his thighs with brisk satisfaction. "We can free up a grant somewhere."

"I've forgotten a lot about Don," Mrs. Gibbs continued to confess. "I actually didn't see that much of him, he was always trying to help people. But he only liked to help people he didn't know. It kept us moving. I wonder if I hated him."

"Such selflessness," Ezana reassured her, "you will not find here in Africa. Here, ego and id are still yoked to pull the oxcart of simple survival."

Something sad in his tone, his assurance of an infinite Africa stretching before her, frightened the young widow, and she looked toward the other American woman for help; but Candy was leaving, not only Africa but leaving the room. With trembling hand she had taken the beggar aside, and moved him toward the front hall, suffused with the scent of *Petrea volubilis* come again into bloom.

Her trembling touched him, this wifely pulse beneath her skin, an amorous agitation superficially like anger, a sense of multiple percussions of blood chiming with his old impression of her as pouncing, as a predator that knows itself as a prey. "You really must get out of Kush," she told him sharply. "This new crowd in power doesn't have any of your irony. They're grim."

"Would you like to take me back with you, to the land of milk and honey?"

Her trembling increased. She gave him a little shove, as she had given the rack of sunglasses a shove. "No. I'm getting a divorce, Happy. This hasn't worked, and it would work even worse there. You *did* hate the States, you know, though you tend to remember the idyllic things. That's how Kush will be for me, I know, once I get out of it. But it's boring back home

now. The Cold War is over, Nixon's over. All that's left is picking up the pieces and things like kissing OPEC's ass. You'd be
depressed. It turns out the Fifties were when all the fun was,
though nobody knew it at the time."

"I could become a professor of Black Studies. I could go
into partnership with your father, and re-open the Chicago
office, since I am a soul brother. They are looking now for to-
kens, are they not—your Establishment? We could create children, of a harmonious color. You could teach me to ice-skate."

"Happy, no. That could have been once, maybe; but not
now. We'd just embarrass each other, like we always did. I
know it's hard for you to believe, but we're through. Honest."

She was right, it is hard for a man to believe that his sexual
power over a woman, however abused in its exercise, has diminished: as if we imagine that these our mysterious attractions
travel in a frictionless ether, forever, instead of as they do, upon
the rocky and obstructed ground of other human lives. The
beggar said, "My best to your Dad," and, both of her white
hands squeezed in one of his, whispered in the hollow hall,
"*Tallaqtukī. Tallaqtukī. Tallaqtukī.*"

Kadongolimi had said, "In this house you will be welcome
when everything else crumbles." But as Ellelloû approached
the villa in Les Jardins that had been transformed into a smoky,
fragrant village compound, he saw that her other prophecy had
already been fulfilled: weeds had sprung up. In the long rains
rot had advanced through the thatch of the outbuildings and
pulpy, hollow-stemmed vegetation had sprung up faster than
footsteps could beat the ground bare. Without a word Ellelloû
was recognized through his disguise of jeans and sunglasses.
The drunken bony man again met him; the naked girl again
took his hand, but she led him to a grave. In the center of the
courtyard where the flagstones had been pried up to make baking ovens, fresh earth, already adorned with a maidenhair of
bright green grass, formed a mound of prodigious dimension.
Kadongolimi then had sunk beneath her weight of flesh to displace this mass of forgetful earth. "Her heart was smothered,
in the end she cried out for space, for the open skies," the girl
told Ellelloû, and he looked at her with surprise, hearing in her

voice his first wife's dancing accent, seeing in this slim body the continuum of women asserted, the form reborn he had taken, once, into his arms. I the lion, she the gazelle.

"Did she cry out for Bini?" I asked.

"For him among many. But there were many to attend her. Our touches were all one. She lived to see the ground watered again, and told us that our father had succeeded."

"I was going to ask her to take me back. Now I must ask you."

"We are being moved. Dorfù has his own blood-ties, his own people. Already, you can see, the huts are empty, the yam plots are overgrown. White men have come and bought our tools and *jujus* for their museums. Anu and I are staying until the earth settles a little more upon our mother, and there is nothing left to desecrate." Anu had also been my evil uncle's name; the thread of his lechery and menace had descended, tangled with the thread of beauty that had come into my hand, through the skein of blood-ties that was, after all, the one robe in which I would always be clothed, even in death, as long as the *griots* could sing my ancestry. The compound around me was returning to nature. The narrowest of footpaths, like the paths rabbits trace in the savanna, led diagonally across patios where the stringy bronzed wives of French administrators had laid aside their Bain-de-Soleil-spotted copies of de Beauvoir and loudly clapped for their servants to bring more *citron pressé*, more Campari-and-soda, more love disguised as servitude. Kadongolimi had lain on one of their abandoned chaise longues and then it had collapsed, heaving up this monstrous splash of earth at my feet. A miniature mountain, whereupon rain had begun to work erosion between the little weeds.

I asked the girl, "Will you go back to the village?"

"The village site is no longer ours. The land, they say, is zoned for agribusiness, subsidized by the new government. The government has plans, many plans."

"Do you hate the new government?"

"No," the girl said solemnly, in the dead tone of prudent words. "They are an aftermath, they are men with flat heads, who cannot be blamed. Kadongolimi talked with them, of our eviction, and was much amused. She forgave them. She told them there had been too much magic in Kush, that after a while magicians become evil men. She did not mind their flat heads. They offered her a pension."

Ellelloû was interested. "And did she accept it? Where is it? Did she fill out forms?"

"My mother refused. She said her youth had been sweet, and she had tasted it fully, and now she wished to taste unsweetened the bitterness of dying. She said her world was dying, her life had performed its circle; she asked them for a month undisturbed, that her body could be weighted to sink. For me she asked a scholarship. I think I will become an agronomist, or a pediatrician. Do I have your blessing?"

"Why ask? You have no need of it. The government proceeds without Ellelloû, his craziness got in the way, technology rules instead of craziness, man has resigned himself to being the animal of animals, the champ. Go farm your wombs, or whatever other microscopic deviltry the toubabs urge upon you. Their knowledge is nothing but Hell; they know this now, still they thrust it upon us, they drag us along, that were standing by the side of the march, they take from us all hope of Paradise. They look into the microscope and tell us there is no spirit. There is no way to imagine the next thousand years upon Earth without imagining Hell, life under one big microscope."

The girl said, "My mother told me you were my father and would not refuse a blessing. Even in the snake, each new skin is caressed by the old as it leaves." The words were no doubt Kadongolimi's, but pronounced softer, with no hint of teasing, of what in Salu we call having-it-both-ways.

"Where will your scholarship take you?"

"Some say Cairo. Some say Florida. It is a United State. Our government, with their oil revenues, are establishing a program there."

"I have heard the climate is oppressive. Be sure to take malaria pills. And your Uncle Anu—what will be happening to him?"

"I believe he has been hired by the Postal Department, as a sorter. He has merely to sit on a stool and toss envelopes into bags. The bags then are thrown into the Grionde. Since our ties with the revolutionary government in America have been strengthened, there has been a great influx of third-class mail. I have not heard your blessing."

"Why bless the unavoidable?"

"It is just that," she said, "which needs to be blessed. The impossible is self-sufficient."

I turned away. I thought if I listened, I could hear Kadongolimi speak, out of this mound of earth that was so little different from her last manifestation to me. What we most miss, of those that slip from us, is their wit, the wit that attends those who know us—lovers, grandmothers, children. The sparks in their eyes are kindled just once by our passing. The girl waited with me for Kadongolimi to speak, until we realized together that these flourishing weeds, and these rivulets of erosion on the heaped mud, were her words. There came now, from the dilapidated thatch of the compounds, a scent reminiscent of the stocked peanut fodder that served, for the young of the village in their years of license, as cave and bed both; in my mind the shadows of the foraging giraffes loped away, incredible orb-eyed marauders fleeing, floating stiff-legged away from the clacking of mortars and pestles brandished by overexcited small boys. Kadongolimi had taken these shadows into the earth with her, leaving me now no shelter save that which I could fabricate. Rain had started up again, pecking at the grave, twitching the ticking leaves. The naked girl beside me shivered. I put both hands on her head, its hair set out in tight braided rows, and pronounced, in the disappearing accent of the Amazeg, my blessing.

Kutunda was not easy to glimpse, let alone confront. She still lived, with the simplicity the powerful sometimes affect, to cloak their power, in the narrow slum building in Hurriyah where she, an illiterate doxy, had been established by Ellelloû upon their return from the Sahel border in the Mercedes. Now this same Mercedes, driven still by Mtesa, whose mustache had flourished, carried her back and forth along the steep sandy alleys between her apartment and the Palais de l'Administration des Noirs; but the windows had been replaced by a murky bulletproof glass through which only the little tipped smudge of a profile could be glimpsed. Photographs of her, by

Dorfû's side at this or that public ceremony, were frequently in the now-official pages of *Nouvelles en noire et blanc*; but the Kushite printing hands had not yet mastered the newly imported American offset presses, and Kutunda's image was mottled or smeared beyond recognition. (Before it had gone underground in 1968, as a subversive counter-revolutionary sheet, having degenerated under the king's constitutional reign into a scandalous tabloid dealing in the pornography of thalidomide freaks and the astrology of the starlets, *Nouvelles* had been handsomely produced on a flatbed letterpress by Frenchmen who, working with Didot fonts and scorning all pictography, had printed the same hermetically inclusive and symmetrical regulations over and over, along with meditations upon Négritude from the latest masterpieces of Gide, Sartre, and Genet.)

The basket shop beneath Kutunda's rooms still operated, and the hollow-cheeked young addicts still emerged clutching their contraband wrapped in raffia, but the place now was clearly manned by government bodyguards. Indeed more than once Ellelloû spotted Opuku, his bald head masked by a narrow-brimmed fedora and his great shoulders clothed in an FBIish gray suit, running a security check on this outpost of the internal police. The Mercedes came early in the morning and brought Kutunda back rarely earlier than midnight. By then, a single dull green light in the basket shop showed the presence of a drowsy lone plainclothesman, and the agile beggar skulking in the archway of the Koran school down the alley dared move with his *anzad* to a position beneath her narrow slatted window, which the slope of the hill here put so close above his head he hardly had to lift his voice, singing,

> "*Round and firm as the breasts of one's beloved's younger sister,*
> *she who exposes her gums when she laughs,*
> *and spies from her pallet wondering when her time will come,*
>
> *one final orange floats in the mind like a moon*
> *that has wrested itself free of the horizon*
> *but still is entangled in the branches of the baobab tree . . .*"

Kutunda's voice, at conversational pitch, said sharply, "Come up." A heavy tangle of keys was slithered through the slats and fell like a star at the beggar's feet. It was not easy, by moonlight, to distinguish the key that disconnected the alarm from the key that opened the door at the foot of the narrow stairs, and again to decipher, while the narrow pisé walls seemed to be leaning in, listening, the four keys needed for the two double locks on the two steel doors where once there had been a single great plank of mpafu he could open by tapping out the syllables of his name. Ellellôu manipulated the keys clumsily, taking the longest possible route: the first lock was opened by the fourth key he tried; of the three remaining, the third opened the second lock and the second of the two unused keys opened the third; then, in the last lock, the fourth key failed to turn! He tried the others, in reverse order, and found at last that the first key worked. This second door, reinforced with a lattice of riveted ribbing, bore a tiny brass plaque engraved in a script that would have been invisible but for the faint traces of brass polish left within the intaglio. He made out the inscription

Minister of the Interior
Protector of Female Rights

A space of clean brass below awaited further titles. As delicately as Ezana some months before had touched open his old office door, Ellellôu touched this one. The door swung open upon a cube of light whose center held a shadow, a dim human core. His eyes, habituated to alley darkness, smarted.

She wore a silk bathrobe of queenly length and her eyes, once brown and flecked, were solid blue. Her posture, too, had changed; the heavy-haunched, cautious stoop of the woman as servant, reluctantly daring to lift herself from the earth, had become the slim erectitude of one who gives orders. At a light indication of her hand, he closed the door behind him. The intimate room he remembered had been expanded upwards, so that where there had been twisted rafters and falling plaster tufted with camel hair a hung dome held a grid of little round dressing-mirror bulbs adjustable to provide (he surmised) appropriate illumination for every situation, however confidential. For this occasion Kutunda had set the rheostat at full cold blaze. Her eyes unnaturally flashed. She wore contact lenses.

"You have run out of masks," she told him. "That was not a good song."

"It entranced my mistress once," the beggar said, hunched against the glare of her apartment, of her authority. Where the walls had been crowded with filing cabinets an executive bareness reigned, relieved only by silver abstractions ordered, he imagined, from Georg Jensen or the Franklin Mint. Her overstuffed armoires had vanished, her wardrobe and beautification equipment fled to another room—for this entire building and its neighbor, the hash shop downstairs reduced to a mere front, had been hollowed out to house Kutunda. Where her pot had been, a spiral iron staircase painted ivory led to the second floor of a bachelor-girl duplex. The dirty pallet from which her lover would contemplate the blank side, glowing rose at dawn, of the Palais de l'Administration des Noirs, had become a waterbed heaped with brocaded pillows, and her steel desk a rosewood escritoire exquisite in its fleur-de-lis pulls. Here, papers of state slipped from their pigeonholes and were, he imagined, initialled. She had vaulted from illiteracy into that altitude of power where reading and writing are a condescension.

"Sit down," she said, indicating a chair that was molded plastic as in an airport waiting-room, taking for herself an oval-backed, satin-covered Louis XVI armchair. "Tell me what you've been doing since the coup."

"I worked in that oil town in the Rift—"

"We call it Ellelloû," she said. "For lack of a better name."

"—and when I had a little stake I hitched back to Istiqlal."

"Have you seen the new library?"

"I've watched them pouring endless cement. I wonder if those wings suspended on the cables won't crack when the harmattan blows. Gravity, as you know, is a little extra near the equator. Or do you still doubt that the earth is round?"

She replied pompously, "We have experts to worry about that."

"When I was in power, I found that experts can't be trusted. For this simple reason: unlike tyrants, they are under no delusion that a country, a people, is their body. Under this delusion a tyrant takes everything personally. An expert takes nothing personally. Nothing is ever precisely his fault. If a bridge collapses, or a war miscarries, he has already walked away. He

still has his expertise. Also, about the library, but applicable
to many ventures—am I boring you? you, who told tales so
amusingly in a ditch?—people imagine that because a thing is
big, it has had a great deal of intelligent thought given to it.
This is not true. A big idea is even more apt to be wrong than
a small one, because the scale is inorganic. The Great Wall, for
instance, is extremely stupid. The two biggest phenomena in
the world right now are Maoism and American television, and
both are extremely stupid."

"Then you will be pleased to know that the Braille Library
is no longer to be named after your patron King Edumu. Michaelis Ezana has asked that the building be designated the
Donald X. Gibbs Center for Trans-Visual Koranic Studies, as
a wedding present to his new wife, Gibbs's rapidly acclimated
widow."

The beggar said, "A beautiful gift, to crown a coupling so
ill-fated. And a suitable monument for that insipid devil who
in his racist blindness attempted to dump chemical pap and
sorghum for cattle into the stomachs of our children."

"The gift she asked for, and has been refused, was your
head in a basket. She wished to have you named as public
enemy, found, and prosecuted. We have held back from that.
We wish instead that your name be venerated, especially by
schoolchildren."

"But there exists a venerable tradition of the criminal-king,
from Nero to the sultans, from Ivan the Terrible to our own
mischievous Edumu. A nation comes to take perverse pride in
the evil it could support, the misgovernment it has survived.
You scrupled too much, dear Kutunda, who for all your shimmering robes of high office retain the shifty-eyed timidity of a
polluted, detribalized wench. Speaking of eyes, how have yours
changed color?"

"Contact lenses, if you must know. They've been in sixteen
hours, and they hurt."

"Take them out," he commmand. "And tell my successor, I
forget his pseudonym, that in the annals of history moderation
is invisible ink."

"I am not sure," she said, pausing to pry with the fingers of
one hand her lids apart so that the lens fell into the cupped
palm of the other, and then gazing at him bichromatically,

"you should be talking to me like this." Picassoesque imbalances, he felt, radiated outwards through the room like the shatter of a windshield from the central asymmetry of her eyes. She bowed her head and removed the other lens, and gropingly removed from a pocket of her robe the curious capsule that held, one on each convex end, the lenses as hard to find, if dropped, as the obsolete Kushite coinage of mirrors.

Ellelloû asked, "Why have you made your eyes blue? Their beauty was brown."

"Dorfû has a penchant for Tuareg women, though the Tuareg are anachronistic, and will soon be settled, under government plans, in communities practicing a profitable mix of peanut cultivation and light industry."

"Dorfû. Are you aware that the word, in Salu, also signifies the torpor suffered by a reptile when it has swallowed too big a meal? Mothers putting their babies to sleep murmur *dorfû, dorfû . . .*"

Kutunda blinked away her tears and resumed the hauteur befitting a cabinet member. "It is true, he wastes no motion, unlike his predecessor. How have you enjoyed these months of vagabondage since your resignation?"

"I have been," Ellelloû told her, "indescribably happy. The wet weather delights me as it does every patriotic citizen of Kush. But beyond that I found, in that town of Ellelloûville, a middling happiness foreign, I fear, to both the mighty and the helpless of our continent. And in Istiqlal, to my surprise, I find that happiness intensified; indeed I now think that the natural condition of men is one of happiness, and that cities, being concentrations of men, are the happier in direct proportion to their size, and that the Koran was right to de-emphasize the tragic, except as it applies to non-believers, who are vermin and shadows in any case."

"If you are happy, why have you sought me out, risking death? My guards are trained to shoot to kill; that is the only technique for fanatic terrorists. Ordinary selfish criminals can be reasoned with, and merely maimed. Opuku's brother heads the new Ministry of Discipline. He has revived, from the days of the Foreign Legion, the *crapaudine*."

Her unreal blue lenses shed, Kutunda's face had softened—the sable irises flecked with gold or sand, the wide flat Sara face broadest across the jawbones, the mouth whose lips seemed the pod for many little white peas, the cinnamon freckles on her dusky cheeks, the wet-looking hair that wandered across her cheeks for all her crisp tailoring of power, her lovable look of being *besmirched*. I thought of her thighs and her buttocks wobbling with weight beneath the quicksilver folds of her queenly robe; my loins sweetened. I had too long been chaste. I said, "My dear Minister of the Interior and Protector of Female Rights, let me present three petitions. One, would you like, now, to marry me? Several vacancies have opened up in my sanctioned quartet of wives."

"This petition comes too late. I am betrothed to the state, and to the ideals of Islamic Marxism, stripped of irresponsible adventurism and romantic individualism. Dorfû has lovingly explained to me that we must never, he and I, marry. Thus we will each stand separate but equal, living exemplars to the men and women of Kush. We will be like the frontal heroic statues in limestone of the Pharaoh and his sister-bride, rather than one muddled image, as in Rodin's *The Kiss*."

"Or in the manner of Hitler and his Eva, rather than the amorously intertwined Roosevelts."

"My President's especial admiration, among statesmen of that period, is for Canada's Mackenzie King, who conferred with his mother in the hereafter. 'The Canada of Africa' is the motto we intend to put on our license plates." She yawned, my freckled foundling, her open mouth a cave of bliss pillowed by her powerful tongue. "My appointments at the Palais begin at nine a.m. sharp," she said. "What was your second petition?"

"For a pension, Madame. I am entitled to one, and with it I will leave the country forever, leaving it forever conscienceless. You will be free to do what you can with this hopeless, beautiful land."

"We feel free now, Dorfû and I."

"But you are not. You are now the actuality of Kush. Actuality breeds discontent, and if I were to reappear, as did Napoleon after Elba, the counter-counter-revolution would be launched. Already, my guess is, Michaelis Ezana chafes at the unofficial limbo in which he must operate, and he has acquired this toubab wife as a possible counter in the game you must, through your rash estrangement of my friends the Soviets, play with the Americans. Where their libraries come, Coca-Cola follows; as our thirst for Coca-Cola grows, our well of debt deepens, and the circle of sky above"—I drew one with my hands, beneath her dome of harsh lights—"is filled with Klipspringer's smile. The oil revenues will bring you dollars good for nothing but to buy what the makers of dollars also make."

Kutunda asked, "Why pay you to leave, when a bullet costs less than a *lu*?"

"The people know I am alive. I pass among them, and they do not need to name me. If I die, the dream of your rule will cease; it is built upon my safe sleep. Dorfù knows this, though you, who rashly advised me to kill the king, do not. Were the king still alive, attracting all blame to himself, I would still be President."

Her words were both clipped and bored. "Pensions are not my department."

Yawn as she would, her known warmth in this pillowed room, some olfactional echo of her tangy, short-legged, downward-tugged *volupté*, had deeply stirred me. My sitting position and loose beggar's robes concealed a club that had grown like a fungus in the dark of my lap.

"What was this third petition?" she asked.

I rose and presented it, my dusty old lust reborn like the desert and so swollen that those of my teeth less than perfectly sound ached at their roots. "Or tell me one of your stories," I begged. "Tell me a vile tale as you used to in the ditch, coming to me under the moon still moist from Wadal and the dwarf."

Kutunda too stood, her silk robe falling straight as armor from the tips of her breasts. "No. The time of fables is over for Africa. We must live among stern realities. You are arrested, as a traitor, an exhibitionist, and an indigent."

The men that came into the room, one through the double door and the other down the resounding iron spiral stairs, from a listening post wherein no doubt all our noises had been taped, including my scratchy struggles with the two double locks and Kutunda's sexy yawns, were not Opuku and Mtesa, they were Opuku and Mtesa's spiritual descendants. Along with their handcuffs and mandatory arm-twisting they brought the something detached (like energetic young actors going through the motions of a play composed by an old homosexual fogey whose off-stage blandishments they have resisted and whose political-religious opinions they despise) and chillingly gentle that is their generation's contribution to the evolution of humanity.

The king's cell had been only perfunctorily cleaned up. His rubble of royalty—the broken stool, *les joujous*, the rags once soaked in the blood of some poor shrieking sacrifice of poultry or livestock and now caked the dullest brown of earth—had been swept toward one corner, but the sweeper had wandered away, perhaps to answer the call to prayer, and had not returned. Michaelis Ezana's all-too-brief (in my book) tenure had added a slippery drift of magazines—*Paris-Match*, *Der Spiegel*, *Tel Quel*, *The Economist*, the Italian edition of *Playboy*. Also filter-stubs of low-tar-content cigarettes, empty Ovaltine tins, and bedroom slippers of the softness of human genitals, the wool of unborn karakul lambs within and, without, the stitched hides of Greek lizards snared while sunning on the marbles of the Acropolis. Foreign imports, I thought, the Third World's ruination. Christendom and whoredom, two for the price of one. Still, such were no longer my problems; these had shrunk to the dimensions of my own imperilled hide.

I dropped the slippers out the window, so they followed at an interval of time that barefoot descent of Ezana which my mind's eye has previously in these pages so vividly projected. The slippers plopped some seconds later, not quite simultaneously, refuting Galileo, in the courtyard below. This was the little dank Cour de Justice; in the courtyard beyond, over the tile roof of a kitchen passageway, I could see the schoolgirls of the Anti-Christian High School forming the circles and parallelograms of some after-school games. Their cries came like the calls of blue-uniformed birds feasting on grasshoppers stirred up whirring by the passing of a herd of wildebeests. Light from the clay-colored sun slanted horizontally into the cell; the call to *salāt al-'asr* was sprung, with a twang, from the minaret of the Mosque of the Day of Disaster, and weakly echoed from the Mosque of the Clots of Blood. The supper smell of scorched feathers arose in the corridor, with the rustle and twitter of the soldiers' women. The brown shadows

in the corners of my room turned blue; a pink blush seeped
upwards into the sky, a delicate dye repelled, as by a dropping
of wax, by a shadow-eyed three-quarters moon. The sun had
set. The *salāt al-maghrib* was intoned. A meal was brought
to me, of *fool* and boiled goat's knuckles. I leafed around in
Paris–Match, which had devoted its issue to American porn
queens and West German terrorists, the daughters of clergy-
men and *Wirtschaftswunderarchitekten*. Both groups of young
women looked drained by fatigue, the vampire shadow of the
camera flash stark behind them on the empty walls. The rooms
these photographs were taken in, and wherein these interviews
were taped, appeared replications of the same room, a room
hidden from the world yet, in effect, the world itself. Rooms, I
thought—the world had become a ball of rooms, a hive, where
once it had been a vast out-of-doors lightly dented by pockets
of shelter. Our skulls are rooms, closeting each brain with its
claustrophobic terror, and all Istiqlal, a mass of mud boxes,
comprised a mosaic of inescapable privacies. The concealed
cellars and apartments where the young celebrities of these
wrinkled pages hatched their escapades and platitudes with an
identical soul-dead fervor implied a fearful space beyond, and
the word *room* seemed to contain some riddle without whose
solution the world's sliding could not be halted, its sorrow
capped. As night filled all the corners I waited for the spirit
of the dead king to repossess his room and with rustling and
tapping revive his dead toys and terrify me; but nothing happened save the curious chemical capture and release of sleep. I
awoke to hear a soft rain steadily falling. The city was melting,
the wet lights of the distant airfield glimmered, enlarged. My
life hung in the balance, but I was utterly relaxed. Thus have I
seen a leopard dangle all its four limbs from a high branch of
a swaying acacia, murderous dreams now and then twitching
its front paws.

Days passed in this rhythm; then at last Dorfù came to visit
me, in the late afternoon, toward the end of the wet season. I
was struck again by his beauty beyond gender, like that of polished wood, or of a supple vine whose graceful, gripping ascent
into the light makes no mistakes. His smile within my cell was
like the dab of sun that finds its way to the forest floor. His fez,

his signature, was of a glossier plum, and his uniform, the color of a scrubbed winestain, harmonized without ostentation. In tailoring at least, Kush had found a leader to surpass Ellelloû. He had that fine Fula skin, that seems always freshly oiled. Tall, he moved with a certain stiff economy of motion, refuting any presumption that his administration would be frivolous. A toubab might have marvelled at Dorfû's regal ease, he having been so recently a lowly police spy; but we Africans have little difficulty in adjusting upwards to luxury and power. Indeed it may be true for all the sons of Adam that no good fortune, however extravagant, seems out of keeping with our proper, Edenic inheritance. He spoke in a courtly mix of English and Arabic. He carried a book bound in gold cloth.

"I believe," Dorfû smiled, "in some lands political prisoners are subjected to what is called re-education. Here, we prefer to think of it as entertainment. I thought I would read to you, as I once did to the pious Edumu." He settled cross-legged on his green cushion, opened the Koran with curved thumb, and read, where he had left off nearly a year before, ". . . *and adorned with bracelets of silver. Their Lord will give them a pure beverage to drink.*" He looked up and asked, "What purer beverage than freedom?"

"None purer," answered Ellelloû. "I thirst for it."

Dorfû continued to read. "*The unbelievers love this fleeting life too well, and thus prepare for themselves a heavy day of doom. We created them, and endowed their limbs and joints with strength; but if We please We can replace them by other men.*"

Dorfû and Allah both, Ellelloû noticed, preferred to say *We*. A trick of leadership he himself had failed to master.

Dorfû concluded the sura. "*He is merciful to whom He will: but for the wrongdoers He has prepared a grievous punishment.*" The President lifted his eyes benignly from the glowing page. "A peculiar problem of African government," he said, "is the disposal of the bodies of the deposed. In Togo, the clever Sylvanus Olympio was inelegantly gunned down by the hand of his successor, Colonel Eyadema. In Mali and Niger, the ex-Presidents Keita and Diori are rather awkwardly incarcerated, awaiting their natural deaths. In this nation, our friend Edumu was manfully slain, but his body became a haunting marionette.

Now you have suggested, in a taped interview with our sister Kutunda, that you be not only pardoned but assigned a pension in exile. A proposal as impudent as your ill-timed and obscene assault upon her chastity."

Ellellou felt in his throat an odd constriction, overruling even thirst. "Like every citizen of Kush," he said, "I entrust myself to your mercy."

Dorfu's smile broadened. "You make a virtue of a necessity; that is the art of living. I have not forgotten who elevated me, albeit in haste, even with some scorn of my potential, to the rank of interim Minister. And I thought your reasoning, as expressed to Kutunda, not without all merit. She, I should inform you, has advised for you a variety of ingenious tortures, climaxed by cremation, that your lewdness no longer pollute the purity of Kush. I would hesitate to disregard her usually sound advice, but in this instance certain international and media considerations prevail. You died, as President, in the city that bears your name. Now the honor of the *Presidency* must be safeguarded. We must show our friends the Americans that we too value the office above the man."

"I do not wish to survive thanks to some American superstition."

"There is also the indigenous consideration that, on a continent where materialism has yet to cast its full spell, a live man far away is less of a presence than a dead man underfoot."

The constriction in Ellellou's throat eased. "I would defer gladly to scruples authentically native. How much will my pension be, and when may I secure it?"

"We have decided that a colonel's pension would be appropriate, added to by half again as much for each wife who accompanies you, and a third again for each dependent child. Enough will be advanced for your passage abroad; when you have an address, the checks will arrive monthly. All this contingent, of course, upon your anonymity and silence."

"You will get off cheap. No wife will come with me."

"There is one, our intelligence-gathering arm reports, that you have not asked. But that is your *affaire*, as the French say." He bowed his head and read again the verses, "*Let him that will, take the right path to the Lord. Yet you cannot will except by the will of Allah.*" Dorfû closed the Koran yet seemed in no hurry to go. Something lingered in the cell, with its jumbled relics and orange slant of late-afternoon sun, congenial to both men.

"Strange," Dorfû said. "You took the name Freedom, and have been captive, until now, of your demons. Our capital is called Independence, yet our polity is an interweave of dependencies. Even the purity of water is a paradox; for unless it be chemically impure, it cannot be drunk. To be free of hunger, men gave up something of themselves to the tribe. To fight against oppression, men must band in an army and become less free, some might say, than before. Freedom is like a blanket which, pulled up to the chin, uncovers the feet."

"You are saying, perhaps," ventured the prisoner, "that freedom is like all things directional. One of the magazines that Ezana abandoned, *Les Méchaniques Populaires* I believe, assures its credulous readers that all things move swiftly in some direction or other; even the universe by which we measure the separate motions of the earth and the sun itself moves, through some unimaginable medium, toward some unimaginable destination. How delicious it is, my President, to pause in movement, and to feel that divine momentum hurtling one forward!"

"It must have been the rushing of your blood you heard. The wind does not feel the wind. To be within the will of Allah is to know utter peace. Once, in the course of my training as a member of the coercive branch of government, I parachuted, expecting tumult; instead there was peace beyond understanding as the earth lifted beneath me, offering as on a platter its treetops, the branching patterns of its dried riverbeds, the star-like dots of its herds, and the thatched rooftops from whose cooking-fires smoke drifted as I did. This was near Sobaville, and I noticed how perilously slender the road between the barracks and the capital appeared. One of my first acts, as Acting Minister of the Interior, was to have this highway made four-lane. In our infant governments, the connection between the head and the coercive arm must be close. Your wanderings as President perhaps should have included more visits to Sobaville."

"I had some taste for battle," Ellell*û* allowed, "but none for the forced *camaraderie*, the latrine humor, of peacetime barracks. Men together generate unhealthy vapors. Am I free to leave, and, if so, when, Mr. President?"

With a little pragmatic shrug Dorfû lifted his hands from where they gracefully rested, wrists on knees. "When you are free within yourself, to terminate."

"I'd like to try it right now," I said. The main obstacle was my sensation that he needed me, and this, I saw, was a delusion.

Dorfû smiled. "Do not forget Sheba's *anzad*." He added, "You should write some of your songs down."

"The pension—is it to be paid in *lu*, or a less chimerical currency?"

"On the strength of the projected peanut harvest, we are thinking of making the *lu* convertible and letting it float. However, if you would rather be paid in dollars—"

"Dollars!" Ellell*û* cried, flaring up as when an evening breeze makes dark coals glow again. "That green scum which sits on the stagnant pond of capitalism, that graven pilfering of our sacred eagles and brooding pyramids, that paper bile the octopus spews forth! Pay me *en franc*."

Dorfû nodded; the round top of his fez winked violet, floating like a momentary UFO in the horizontal, ebbing light. The four-color photograph Edumu had once upon a time framed, of a little girl and a presumed black man frozen in mid-tap on a make-believe staircase, had been removed from its sumptuous frame, the frame stolen for its gold but the paper image reverently tacked back up. It fluttered, as the evening call to prayer entered in at the green-silled window.

Sittina's villa was one vast flower, all overgrown by the oleander, bottlebrush, hibiscus, and plumbago that flourished in our hospitable climate. She herself was not at home, though the sounds of her children squabbling and playing nostalgia-rock records arose from within. I looked through a window. Her *Well-Tempered Clavier* gathered dust on the harpsichord, its pages open to a fugue whose five sharps had stymied her. Our Chagall still hung on the far wall. The Ife mask looked tatty and askew. As I turned to leave, Sittina came along loping through the morning mists, through the shade of the fully leafed chestnut trees, clad in a blue jogging suit, her hair no longer held back by fish spines but cut close as a cap to her head. As she ran, she looked bow-legged in the manner of runners, the shins incurved so the resilient feet can keep pace on an invisible straight line. "Félix," she said to me, scarcely panting, and continuing to jog up and down as she talked, "why —are you wearing—a three-piece business suit?"

"It's what they give you when you leave prison," I told her. "Also a beggar's disguise gets you arrested. Begging has been declared non-existent by the government. Long life to Dorfù! Death to extremists of both rightist and leftist tendencies!"

"Don't make me—laugh," she said, "it throws—my breathing off. It's ecstasy—once you hit—your stride. I've lost—five pounds. Unfortunately—it's all come off my ass—instead of my belly."

"That's middle age," I told her.

"I thought—you were—evaporated."

"Demoted," I said. "Can't we go inside? I'm getting a headache watching you jiggle."

"I've been offered a job—calisthenicist for the work teams —being organized in the refugee camps—over at Al-Abid."

"You want the job?"

"No. You know me. I hate being—tied down. But I need the *lu*—since you blew the dictatorship."

In addition to cropping her hair, she had minimized her wind-resistance by substituting for her great hoop earrings little sleepers of agate. Her narrow Tutsi skull offered to the air as compliant an edge as the prow of a yacht to the waves, as the profile of Nefertiti to the oceans of time. Sittina showed me this profile, saying over her shoulder, "Come on in"; she swept back a shaggy branch of feathery bamboo and tugged open her swollen front door. "The house's a mess," she apologized. "The last *au pair* I had took a cushy government job, in the Bureau of Detribalization. The Tuareg are all busy being house-guards for the people who got rich during the famine, and the government's trying to retrain the slum-dwellers to become nomadic herdsmen, because the nomads are good for the ecology. Mind if I take a quick shower? Otherwise the leg muscles cramp."

Her children had gathered around me curiously, solemn

appraisers of a line of lovers. One child had orange hair—
a sign, it relieved me to see, not of kwashiorkor but of Celtic
sperm. "What is your name?" I asked him.

"Ellelloû."

"Do you know what that means?"

"It means solidarity."

"No, that is wrong. It means freedom."

"I don't *care*," the child told me, and turned on his heel to
hide a trembling lip. He was gleefully pounced upon by his
siblings as he sought to control his humiliated sobbing. They
jostled and tumbled him like hyaenas at a hamstrung impala;
but when they let him up, he was laughing. It was right, that
I had not intervened. In the skirmish I had counted six heads,
which totalled up, in welfare's new arithmetic, to two full pensions. My vest hugged my belly with premonitions of bourgeois comfort. A child slightly larger than the frizzy redhead, a
girl in a Gucci pinafore, with a Nilotic slant to her eyes, asked
me, "You love my mommy?"

"I admire her speed," I said.

"You going to take care of us?"

Before I could frame another evasion, Sittina raced through
the living-room wet and nude. Her long tapered thighs, her
bean-shaped buttocks. "Damn towels are in the dryer," she
called over her shoulder. "Tell the kids it's time for the bus."

One of her children had been watching through a window,
where the crowding flowers permitted a peephole; when he
shouted, the others scrambled for their books, their slates,
their hand-computers, their spiral-bound notebooks and
supplementary cassettes. I helped them through the door,
through the tangle of their rubber boots and clinging pet patas
monkeys. The bus, imported yellow but overpainted with the
national green, lurched to the shady corner and held its stop
long enough to receive their noisy, needful bodies. Even the
three-year-old was enrolled in a Montessori beadwork group.
I breathed, in amplification of the *salāt as-subh* with which I
had ceremonialized the dawn, a silent prayer of thanks for free
public education, the cornerstone of participatory democracy
and domestic bliss.

Sittina had returned to the living-room still naked. Her sharp
small breasts, her high central pocket of soft curls. "Weren't in

the dryer either," she said. "I remember I put them out on the line to save electricity. But nothing dries outdoors anymore. I'd go see, but some lousy American tourist'd take my picture. Really, they're *so* awful. The women in the *souk*, with those long red fingernails and blue hair in bandanas and those cracked whiskey voices. The West Germans are worse—all straps and fat and hiking boots. Remember how I used to complain about the Albanians? I'm sorry, you were right. I was wrong. We should have stayed isolationist. There are nice things in the shops now but who can afford them except the tourists? The boutiques up under the Gibbs Center are chic but they're always full of lepers." Noticing my eyes upon her body, she spun, in that room of incompleted curves, and asked, "What do you think? Don't tell me. I know. My ass is too skinny."

As usual, she had raced on ahead of me. Later, when, with trembling legs, I went to the bathroom, there were plenty of towels there, fluffily clean and shockingly white, white as new snow, as raw salt. She, scenting the eschatological drift of my call, had chosen to sustain her side of our exchange in elemental, traditional costume. "Not too skinny," I answered numbly. "Just right." The numbness—Livingstone's in the mouth of the lion, the pious man's in the grip of his fate—I had experienced before in the course of this narrative, at most of its crucial turns.

"Still?" Sittina asked flirtatiously, in profile, the long round brow of the Tutsi royal line as erotic, as meek and glistening, as the twin bulges of her taut buttocks. Her nipples were long and blue.

"Still," Ellelloû said, adding, "I must go away."

"To the Balak with Sheba again?"

"No."

"Back to the Bulub with Kutunda?"

"I think not."

"Down to the underworld with Kadongolimi?"

"This is a cruel litany."

"Off to the States with Candy?"

"She's left already. We're divorced. None of our friends was surprised; mixed marriages have a lot of extra stresses."

"Any marriage is mixed. Where will you go now, poor Félix, and who with?"

"With you? It's just a scenario. We could go somewhere where you could paint more seriously."

"Not sure seriously's my style," she said, striding on long legs into her long living-room, with harassed-looking waves of both arms indicating the fibrous brown masks and musty Somali camel saddles that overlooked like a baffled animal chorus her twinkling furniture of smudged glass and scratched aluminum. Among the Africana she had hung or propped canvases more or less eagerly begun but left with blank corners and unfilled outlines. "I can't bear to finish things, beyond a certain point they get heavy. There's something so dead about a finished painting. Or a finished anything, in this climate. Maybe it's palm trees and clay houses. You slave away, and what do you have in the end? A picture postcard from Timbuctoo."

"The South of France," Ellelloû said, "has very paintable trees." He had taken a step after her, she had grown so slender with distance, and Sittina answered his step by striding back to him, brown between her brown walls, and draping her long arms lightly on his shoulders. Tufts of armpit hair, still wet from the shower. Mustache traces above the corners of her smile, at the level of his eyes. "You smell like you want something," she said.

"I want to consolidate," Ellelloû confessed.

"Then we ought to try *us*, as a starter."

She did still coo, when she spread her legs. The mats on the floor, once they cleared away the children's toys, seemed in their marital haste soft enough. Beds are for toubabs, whose skins Mr. Yacub bred to lack the resilient top layer. Ellelloû was excited by the five-petalled faces of the audience of oleander at the windows. He in her—his pelvis cradled in her elegant thighs, his hand cupping the firm ellipses beneath—Sittina rolled her eyes in wild Watusi display of the bloodshot whites, taking in the furniture and wall ornaments upside-down. She moaned, "My God, think of the packing! And the children's dental appointments!!"

The good citizens of France no longer look up at the sight of *noirs* strolling down their avenues. Their African empire, which a passion for abstraction led them to carve from the most vacant sector of the continent, backed up on them a bit, like those other cartographic reservoirs for a century flooded with ink of European tints, and doused the home country with a sprinkling of dark diplomats, students, menial laborers, and political exiles. Even in Nice, along La Promenade des Anglais, which becomes Le Quai des États-Unis, amid the singing of the beach pebbles and the signing of autographs by topless young leftovers from the Cannes Film Festival, an ebony family, decently attired, draws only that flickering glance with which a Frenchman files another *aperçu* in the passionate cabinets of his *esprit*. Africa has been legitimized here by art. Delacroix skimmed the Maghrib and Picasso imported cubism from Gabon. Josephine Baker, Sidney Bechet . . . *noire est belle.*

The woman is extremely chic: tall as a model, with a little haughtily tipped head and a stride that swings the folds of her rainbow-dyed culottes. The man with her is relatively unprepossessing, insignificant even, shorter than she, half his face masked in NoIR sunglasses. He does not appear to be the father of the variegated children who march at their sides. From his carriage he might have been a soldier. The boys from their look of well-fed felicity will never be soldiers, or will make bad ones. The girls, the girls will be many wonderful things— dancers, mothers, strumpets, surgeons, stewardesses, acrobats, agronomists, magicians' assistants, mistresses, *causes célèbres,* sunbathers, fading photographs in mental albums, goddesses glimpsed like cool black swans amid the glitter of an opera house, caped in chinchilla, one gloved hand resting on the gilded balcony rail as they turn to go. The pagans pray to females. It gladdens the writer's heart, to contemplate the future of his girls. The boys, he worries about. He fears they may fall, civilian casualties in the war of muchness that is certain to overtake the planet.

The family lives, apparitions from a rumored continent, beyond Carabacel, where the streets become steep and the tile-topped garden walls bear a profusion of bougainvillea and a forgotten rusting pair of scissors, in the Rue de Ste.-Clément. Behind their walls they are assiduous, economical, conjugal, temperate, optimistic, dynamic, middling, and modern. The woman, it is rumored, paints. The children, the neighbors attest, take violin, *anzad,* clarinet, *kakaki,* piano, and *sanza* lessons. The small black man can be seen sitting at round white tables along the Quai, or a few blocks inland from the distracting, sail-speckled Mediterranean, at open-air cafés beside the river of traffic along the Esplanade de Général de Gaulle. He has always a drink at his elbow, a Fanta, Campari-and-soda, or *citron pressé* with a dash of anisette; he seems to be an eternally thirsty man. His other elbow pins down a sheaf of papers. He is writing something, dreaming behind his sunglasses, among the clouds of Vespa exhaust, trying to remember, to relive.

Little news of Kush comes here. France has become what China once was—an island of perfect civilization, self-satisfying, decaying, deaf. What does it care for the smoothly continuing coups in sandy lands where once its second sons in cerulean pill-box hats chased blue-skinned Tuareg deeper and deeper into the dunes? At an OPEC conference in Geneva, among the oil ministers taken hostage and harangued by an Austrian divinity-school dropout and his emaciated girl friend, was named one Michael Azena [misprint] of Couche. He survived the episode, though the revolutionaries smashed his wristwatch. Otherwise, Kush comes as a dusky whiff reminiscent of peanut fodder, or a green band of sunset sky toward Biot, or the taste of orange in a sip of Cointreau, or the shade of the Cinzano *ombrelle* over-head, faintly suggestive, when the sea breeze flaps its fringed edges, of the shade of a tent, the most erotic shelter in the world. Kush is around us in these hints, these airy coded bulletins, but the crush of present reality—the oblique temperate sun, the sensational proximity of the sea—renders these clues no more than fragile scraps of wreckage that float to the surface, fewer and fewer as the waves continue to break, to hiss, to slide, to percolate through the pebbles. All yesterdays are thus submerged, continental chunks sunk from sight that once were under our feet. How did he come here? the pink passersby perhaps ask, insulted by the *nègre*'s air of preoccupation, amid the beauties of their city, his face downcast to the *cahiers* in which he pens long tendrils like the tendrilous chains of contingency that have delivered us, each, to where we sit now on the skin of the world, water-lilies concealing our masses of root. *Those who have gone before them also plotted, but Allah is the master of every plot: He knows the deserts of every soul.* The man is happy, hidden. The sea breeze blows, the waiters ignore him. He is writing his memoirs. No, I should put it more precisely: Colonel Ellelloû is rumored to be working on his memoirs.

RABBIT IS RICH

"At night he lights up a good cigar, and climbs into the little old 'bus, and maybe cusses the carburetor, and shoots out home. He mows the lawn, or sneaks in some practice putting, and then he's ready for dinner."

—George Babbitt, of the Ideal Citizen

The difficulty to think at the end of day,
When the shapeless shadow covers the sun
And nothing is left except light on your fur . . .

—Wallace Stevens, "A Rabbit as King of the Ghosts"

I

RUNNING OUT of gas, Rabbit Angstrom thinks as he stands behind the summer-dusty windows of the Springer Motors display room watching the traffic go by on Route 111, traffic somehow thin and scared compared to what it used to be. The fucking world is running out of gas. But they won't catch him, not yet, because there isn't a piece of junk on the road gets better mileage than his Toyotas, with lower service costs. Read *Consumer Reports*, April issue. That's all he has to tell the people when they come in. And come in they do, the people out there are getting frantic, they know the great American ride is ending. Gas lines at ninety-nine point nine cents a gallon and ninety per cent of the stations to be closed for the weekend. The governor of the Commonwealth of Pennsylvania calling for five-dollar minimum sales to stop the panicky topping-up. And truckers who can't get diesel shooting at their own trucks, there was an incident right in Diamond County, along the Pottsville Pike. People are going wild, their dollars are going rotten, they shell out like there's no tomorrow. He tells them, when they buy a Toyota, they're turning their dollars into yen. And they believe him. A hundred twelve units new and used moved in the first five months of 1979, with eight Corollas, five Coronas including a Luxury Edition Wagon, and that Celica that Charlie said looked like a Pimpmobile unloaded in these first three weeks of June already, at an average gross mark-up of eight hundred dollars per sale. Rabbit is rich.

He owns Springer Motors, one of the two Toyota agencies in the Brewer area. Or rather he co-owns a half-interest with his wife Janice, her mother Bessie sitting on the other half inherited when old man Springer died five years back. But Rabbit feels as though he owns it all, showing up at the showroom day after day, riding herd on the paperwork and the payroll, swinging in his clean suit in and out of Service and Parts where the men work filmed with oil and look up white-eyed from the bulb-lit engines as in a kind of underworld while he makes contact with the public, the community, the star and spearpoint of all these two dozen employees and hundred thousand square feet of working space, which seem a wide shadow behind him as he stands there up front. The wall of imitation boards, really sheets of random-grooved Masonite, around the door into his office is hung with framed old clippings and team portraits, including two all-county tens, from his days as a basketball hero twenty years ago—no, more than twenty-five years now. Even under glass, the clippings keep yellowing, something in the chemistry of the paper apart from the air, something like the deepening taint of sin people used to try to scare you with. ANGSTROM HITS FOR 42. *"Rabbit" Leads Mt. Judge Into Semi-Finals.* Resurrected from the attic where his dead parents had long kept them, in scrapbooks whose mucilage had dried so they came loose like snakeskins, these clippings thus displayed were Fred Springer's idea, along with that phrase about an agency's reputation being the shadow of the man up front. Knowing he was dying long before he did, Fred was getting Harry ready to be the man up front. When you think of the dead, you got to be grateful.

Ten years ago when Rabbit got laid off as a Linotyper and reconciled with Janice, her father took him on as salesman and when the time was ripe five years later had the kindness to die. Who would have thought such a little tense busy bird of a man could get it up for a massive coronary? Hypertense: his diastolic had been up around one-twenty for years. Loved salt. Loved to talk Republican, too, and when Nixon left him nothing to say he had kind of burst. Actually, he had lasted a year into Ford, but the skin of his face was getting tighter and the red spots where the cheek and jaw bones pressed from underneath redder. When Harry looked down at him rouged in the coffin he saw it had been coming, dead Fred hadn't much changed. From the way Janice and her mother carried on you would have thought a mixture of Prince Valiant and Moses had bit the dust. Maybe having already buried both his own parents made Harry hard. He looked down, noticed that Fred's hair had been parted wrong, and felt nothing. The great thing about the dead, they make space.

While old man Springer was still prancing around, life at the lot was hard. He kept long hours, held the showroom open on winter nights when there wasn't a snowplow moving along

Route 111, was always grinding away in that little high-pitched grinder of a voice about performance guidelines and washout profits and customer servicing and whether or not a mechanic had left a thumbprint on some heap's steering wheel or a cigarette butt in the ashtray. When he was around the lot it was like they were all trying to fill some big skin that Springer spent all his time and energy imagining, the ideal Springer Motors. When he died that skin became Harry's own, to stand around in loosely. Now that he is king of the lot he likes it here, the acre of asphalt, the new-car smell present even in the pamphlets and pep talks Toyota mails from California, the shampooed carpet wall to wall, the yellowing basketball feats up on the walls along with the plaques saying Kiwanis and Rotary and C of C and the trophies on a high shelf won by the Little League teams the company sponsors, the ample square peace of this masculine place spiced by the girls in billing and reception that come and go under old Mildred Kroust, and the little cards printed with HAROLD C. ANGSTROM on them and CHIEF SALES REPRESENTATIVE. The man up front. A center of sorts, where he had been a forward. There is an airiness to it for Harry, standing there in his own skin, casting a shadow. The cars sell themselves, is his philosophy. The Toyota commercials on television are out there all the time, preying on people's minds. He likes being part of all that; he likes the nod he gets from the community, that had overlooked him like dirt ever since high school. The other men in Rotary and Chamber turn out to be the guys he played ball with back then, or their ugly younger brothers. He likes having money to float in, a big bland good guy is how he sees himself, six three and around two fifteen by now, with a forty-two waist the suit salesman at Kroll's tried to tell him until he sucked his gut in and the man's thumb grudgingly inched the tape tighter. He avoids mirrors, when he used to love them. The face far in his past, crew-cut and thin-jawed with sleepy predatory teen-age eyes in the glossy team portraits, exists in his present face like the chrome bones of a grille within the full front view of a car and its fenders. His nose is still small and straight, his eyes maybe less sleepy. An ample blown-dry-looking businessman's haircut masks his eartips and fills in where his temples are receding. He didn't much like the counterculture with all its drugs and draft-dodging but he does like being allowed within limits to let your hair grow longer than those old Marine cuts and to have it naturally fluff out. In the shaving mirror a chaos of wattles and slack cords blooms beneath his chin in a way that doesn't bear study. Still, life is sweet. That's what old people used to say and when he was young he wondered how they could mean it.

Last night it hailed in Brewer and its suburbs. Stones the size of marbles leaped up from the slant little front yards and drummed on the tin signs supporting flickering neon downtown; then came a downpour whose puddles reflected a dawn gray as stone. But the day has turned breezy and golden and the patched and white-striped asphalt of the lot is dry, late in the afternoon of this longest Saturday in June and the first of calendar summer. Usually on a Saturday Route 111 is buzzing with shoppers pillaging the malls hacked from the former fields of corn, rye, tomatoes, cabbages, and strawberries. Across the highway, the four concrete lanes and the median divider of aluminum battered by many forgotten accidents, stands a low building faced in dark clinker brick that in the years since Harry watched its shell being slapped together of plywood has been a succession of unsuccessful restaurants and now serves as the Chuck Wagon, specializing in barbecued take-outs. The Chuck Wagon too seems quiet today. Beyond its lot littered with flattened take-out cartons a lone tree, a dusty maple, drinks from a stream that has become a mere ditch. Beneath its branches a picnic table rots unused, too close to the overflowing dumpster the restaurant keeps by its kitchen door. The ditch marks the bound of a piece of farmland sold off but still awaiting its development. This shapely old maple from its distance seems always to be making to Harry an appeal he must ignore.

He turns from the dusty window and says to Charlie Stavros, "They're running scared out there."

Charlie looks up from the desk where he is doing paperwork, the bill of sale and NV-1 on a '74 Barracuda 8 they finally moved for twenty-eight hundred yesterday. Nobody wants these old guzzlers, though you got to take them on trade-in. Charlie handles the used cars. Though he has been with Springer Motors twice as long as Harry, his desk is in a corner of the showroom, out in the open, and the title on his card is SENIOR SALES REPRESENTATIVE. Yet he bears no grudge. He sets down his pen even with the edge of his papers and in response to his boss asks, "Did you see in the paper the other day where some station owner and his wife somewhere in the middle of the state were pumping gas for a line and one of the cars slips its clutch and crushes the wife against the car next in line, broke her hip I think I read, and while the husband was holding her and begging for help the people in the cars instead of giving him any help took over the pumps and gave themselves free gas?"

"Yeah," Harry says, "I guess I heard that on the radio, though it's hard to believe. Also about some guy in Pittsburgh who takes a couple of two-by-fours with him and drives his back wheels up on them so as to get a few more cents' worth of gas in his tank. That's fanatical."

Charlie emits a sardonic, single-syllabled laugh, and explains, "The little man is acting like the oil companies now. I'll get mine, and screw you."

"I don't blame the oil companies," Harry says tranquilly. "It's too big for them too. Mother Earth is drying up, is all."

"Shit, champ, you never blame anybody," Stavros tells the taller man. "Skylab could fall on your head right now and you'd go down saying the government had done its best."

Harry tries to picture this happening and agrees, "Maybe so. They're strapped these days like everybody else. About all the feds can do these days is meet their own payroll."

"That they're guaranteed to do, the greedy bastards. Listen, Harry. You know damn well Carter and the oil companies have rigged this whole mess. What does Big Oil want? Bigger profits. What does Carter want? Less oil imports, less depreciation of the dollar. He's too chicken to ration, so he's hoping higher prices will do it for him. We'll have dollar-fifty no-lead before the year is out."

"And people'll pay it," Harry says, serene in his middle years. The two men fall silent, as if arrived at a truce, while the scared traffic kicks up dust along the business strip of Route 111 and the unbought Toyotas in the showroom exude new-car smell. Ten years ago Stavros had an affair with Harry's wife Janice. Harry thinks of Charlie's prick inside Janice and his feeling is hostile and cozy in almost equal proportions, coziness getting the edge. At the time he took his son-in-law on, old man Springer asked him if he could stomach working with him, Charlie. Rabbit didn't see why not. Sensing he was being asked to bargain, he said he'd work with him, not under him. *No question of that, you'd be under me only, as long as I'm among the living,* Springer had promised: *you two'll work side by side.* Side by side then they had waited for customers in all weathers and bemoaned their boss's finickiness and considered monthly which of the used cars on inventory would never move and should be wholesaled to cut carrying costs. Side by side they had suffered with Springer Motors as the Datsun franchise came into the Brewer area, and then those years when everyone was buying VWs and Volvos, and now the Hondas and Le Car presenting themselves as the newest thing in cute economy. In these nine years Harry added thirty pounds to his frame while Charlie went from being a chunky Greek who when he put on his shades and a checked suit looked like an enforcer for the local numbers racket to a shrivelled little tipster-type. Stavros had always had a tricky ticker, from rheumatic fever when he was a boy. Janice had been moved by this, this weakness hidden within him, his squarish chest. Now like a flaw ramifying to the surface of a crystal his infirmity has given him that dehydrated prissy look of a reformed rummy, of a body preserved day to day by taking thought. His eyebrows that used to go straight across like an iron bar have dwindled in to be two dark clumps, disconnected, almost like the charcoal dabs clowns wear. His sideburns have gone white so the top of his tightly wavy hair looks dyed in a broad stripe. Each morning at work Charlie changes his lavender-tinted black hornrims for ones with amber lenses the instant he's indoors, and walks through the day's business like a grizzled old delicate ram who doesn't want to slip on a crag and fall. *Side by side, I promise you.* When old man Springer promised that, when he turned his full earnestness on anything, the pink patches in his face glowed red and his lips tightened back from his teeth so you thought all the more of his skull. Dirty yellow teeth loaded with gum-line fillings, and his sand-colored mustache never looked quite even, or quite clean.

The dead, Jesus. They were multiplying, and they look up begging you to join them, promising it is all right, it is very soft down here. Pop, Mom, old man Springer, Jill, the baby called Becky for her little time, Tothero. Even John Wayne, the other day. The obituary page every day shows another stalk of a harvest endlessly rich, the faces of old teachers, customers, local celebrities like himself flashing for a moment and then going down. For the first time since childhood Rabbit is happy, simply, to be alive. He tells Charlie, "I figure the oil's going to run out about the same time I do, the year two thousand. Seems funny to say it, but I'm glad I lived when I did. These kids coming up, they'll be living on table scraps. We had the meal."

"You've been sold a bill of goods," Charlie tells him. "You and a lot of others. Big Oil has enough reserves located right now to last five hundred years, but they want to ooze it out. In the Delaware Bay right now I heard there's seventeen supertankers, seventeen, at anchor waiting for the prices to go up enough for them to come into the South Philly refineries and unload. Meanwhile you get murdered in gas lines."

"Stop driving. Run," Rabbit tells him. "I've begun this jogging thing and it feels great. I want to lose thirty pounds." Actually his resolve to run before breakfast every day, in the dew of the dawn, lasted less than a week. Now he contents himself with trotting around the block after supper sometimes to get away from his wife and her mother while they crab at each other.

He has touched a sore point. Charlie confides as if to the NV-1 form, "Doctor tells me if I try any exercise he washes his hands."

Rabbit is abashed, slightly. "Really? That's not what that Doctor Whatsisname used to say. White. Paul Dudley White."

"He died. Exercise freaks are dropping down dead in the parks like flies. It doesn't get into the papers because the fitness industry has become big bucks. Remember all those little health-food stores hippies used to run? You know who runs 'em now? General Mills."

Harry doesn't always know how seriously to take Charlie. He does know, in relation to his old rival, that he is hearty and huge, indisputably preferred by God in this chance matter of animal health. If Janice had run off with Charlie like she wanted to she'd be nothing but a nursemaid now. As is, she plays tennis three, four times a week and has never looked sharper. Harry keeps wanting to downplay himself around Charlie, protecting the more fragile man from the weight of his own good fortune. He keeps silent, while Charlie's mind works its way back from the shame and shadow of his doctor washing his hands, back into memory's reserves of energy. "Gasoline," he suddenly says, giving it that Greek cackle, almost a wheeze. "Didn't we used to burn it up? I had an Imperial once with twin carburetors and when you took off the filter and looked down through the butterfly valve when the thing was idling it looked like a toilet being flushed."

Harry laughs, wanting to ride along. "Cruising," he says, "after high school got out, there was nothing to do but cruise. Back and forth along Central, back and forth. Those old V-8s, what do you think they got to the gallon? Ten, twelve miles? Nobody ever thought to keep track."

"My uncles still won't drive a little car. Say they don't want to get crumpled if they meet a truck."

"Remember Chicken? Funny more kids weren't killed than were."

"Cadillacs. If one of his brothers got a Buick with fins, my father had to have a Cadillac with bigger fins. You couldn't count the taillights, it looked like a carton of red eggs."

"There was one guy at Mt. Judge High, Don Eberhardt, 'd get out on the running board of his Dad's Dodge when it was going down the hill behind the box factory and steer from out there. All the way down the hill."

"First car I bought for myself, it was a '48 Studebaker, with that nose that looked like an airplane. Had about sixty-five thousand miles on it, it was the summer of '53. The dig-out on that baby! After a stoplight you could feel the front wheels start to lift, just like an airplane."

"Here's a story. One time when we were pretty newly married I got sore at Janice for something, just being herself probably, and drove to West Virginia and back in one night. Crazy. You couldn't do that now without going to the savings bank first."

"Yeah," Charlie says slowly, saddened. Rabbit hadn't wanted to sadden him. He could never figure out, exactly, how much the man had loved Janice. "She described that. You did a lot of roaming around then."

"A little. I brought the car back though. When she left me, she took the car and kept it. As you remember."

"Do I?"

He has never married, and that says something flattering, to Janice and therefore to Harry, the way it's worked out. A man fucks your wife, it puts a new value on her, within limits. Harry wants to restore the conversation to the cheerful plane of dwindling energy. He tells Stavros, "Saw a kind of funny joke in the paper the other day. It said, You can't beat Christopher Columbus for mileage. Look how far he got on three galleons." He pronounces the crucial word carefully, in three syllables; but Charlie doesn't act as if he gets it, only smiles a one-sided twitch of a smile that could be in response to pain.

"The oil companies made us do it," Charlie says. "They said, Go ahead, burn it up like madmen, all these highways, the shopping malls, everything. People won't believe it in a hundred years, the sloppy way we lived."

"It's like wood," Harry says, groping back through history, which is a tinted fog to him, marked off in centuries like a football field, with a few dates—1066, 1776—pinpointed and a few faces—George Washington, Hitler—hanging along the sidelines, not cheering. "Or coal. As a kid I can remember the anthracite rattling down the old coal chute, with these red dots they used to put on it. I couldn't imagine how they did it, I thought it was something that happened in the ground. Little elves with red brushes. Now there isn't any anthracite. That stuff they strip-mine now just crumbles in your hand." It gives him pleasure, makes Rabbit feel rich, to contemplate the world's wasting, to know that the earth is mortal too.

"Well," Charlie sighs. "At least it's going to keep those chinks from ever having an industrial revolution."

That seems to wrap it up, though Harry feels they have let something momentous, something alive under the heading of energy, escape. But a lot of topics, he has noticed lately, in private conversation and even on television where they're paid to talk it up, run dry, exhaust themselves, as if everything's been said in this hemisphere. In his inner life too Rabbit dodges among more blanks than there used to be, patches of burnt-out gray cells where there used to be lust and keen dreaming and wide-eyed dread; he falls asleep, for instance, at the drop of a hat. He never used to understand the phrase. But then he never used to wear a hat and now, at the first breath of cold weather, he does. His roof wearing thin, starlight showing through.

YOU ASKED FOR IT, WE GOT IT, the big paper banner on the showroom window cries, in tune with the current Toyota television campaign. The sign cuts a slice from the afternoon sun and gives the showroom a muted aquarium air, or that of a wide sunken ship wherein the two Coronas and the acid-green Corolla SR-5 liftback wait to be bought and hoisted into the air on the other side of the glass and set down safe on the surface of the lot and Route 111 and the world of asphalt beyond.

A car swings in from this world: a fat tired '71 or '2 Country Squire wagon soft on its shocks, with one dented fender hammered out semi-smooth but the ruddy rustproofing underpaint left to do for a finish. A young couple steps out, the girl milky-pale and bare-legged and blinking in the sunshine but the boy roughened and reddened by the sun, his jeans dirt-stiffened by actual work done in the red mud of the county. A kind of crate of rough green boards has been built into the Squire's chrome roof rack and from where Rabbit is standing, a soft wedge shot away, he can see how the upholstery and inner padding have been mangled by the station wagon's use as a farm truck. "Hicks," Charlie says from his desk. The pair comes in shyly, like elongated animals, sniffing the air-conditioned air.

Feeling protective, God knows why, Charlie's snipe ringing in his ears, Harry walks toward them, glancing at the girl's hand to see if she wears a wedding ring. She does not, but such things mean less than they used to. Kids shack up. Her age he puts at nineteen or twenty, the boy a bit older—the age of his own son. "Can I help you folks?"

The boy brushes back his hair, showing a low white forehead. His broad baked face gives him a look of smiling even when he isn't. "We chust came in for some information." His accent bespeaks the south of the county, less aggressively Dutch than the north, where the brick churches get spiky and the houses and barns are built of limestone instead of sandstone. Harry figures them for leaving some farm to come into the city, with no more need to haul fenceposts and hay bales and pumpkins and whatever else this poor heap was made to haul. Shack up, get city jobs, and spin around in a little Corolla. We got it. But the boy could be just scouting out prices for his father, and the girlfriend be riding along, or not even be a girlfriend, but a sister, or a hitchhiker. A little touch of the hooker about her looks. The way her soft body wants to spill from these small clothes, the faded denim shorts and purple Paisley halter. The shining faintly freckled flesh of her shoulders and top arms and the busy wanton abundance of her browny-red many-colored hair, carelessly bundled. A buried bell rings. She has blue eyes in deep sockets and the silence of a girl from the country used to letting men talk while she holds a sweet-and-sour secret in her mouth, sucking it. An incongruous disco touch in her shoes, with their high cork heels and ankle straps. Pink toes, painted nails. This girl will not stick with this boy. Rabbit wants this to be so; he imagines he feels an unwitting swimming of her spirit upward toward his, while her manner is all stillness. He feels she wants to hide from him, but is too big and white, too suddenly womanly, too nearly naked. Her shoes accent the length of her legs; she is taller than average, and not quite fat, though tending toward chunky, especially around the chest. Her upper lip closes over the lower with a puffy bruised look. She is bruisable, he wants to protect her; he relieves her of the pressure of his gaze, too long by a second, and turns to the boy.

"This is a Corolla," Harry says, slapping orange tin. "The two-door model begins at thirty-nine hundred and will give you highway mileage up to forty a gallon and twenty to twenty-five city driving. I know some other makes advertise more but believe me you can't get a better buy in America to-day than this jalopy right here. Read *Consumer Reports*, April issue. Much better than average on maintenance and repairs through the first four years. Who in this day and age keeps a car much longer than four years? In four years we may all be pushing bicycles the way things are going. This particular car has four-speed synchromesh transmission, fully transistorized ignition system, power-assisted front disc brakes, vinyl reclin-ing bucket seats, a locking gas cap. That last feature's getting to be pretty important. Have you noticed lately how all the auto-supply stores are selling out of their siphons? You can't buy a siphon in Brewer today for love nor money, guess why. My mother-in-law's old Chrysler over in Mt. Judge was drained dry the other day in front of the hairdresser's, she hardly ever takes the buggy out except to go to church. People are getting rough. Did you notice in the paper this morning where Carter is taking gas from the farmers and going to give it to the truckers? Shows the power of a gun, doesn't it?"

"I didn't see the paper," the boy says.

He is standing there so stolidly Harry has to move around him with a quick shuffle-step, dodging a cardboard cutout of a happy customer with her dog and packages, to slap acid-green. "Now if you want to replace your big old wagon, that's some antique, with another wagon that gives you almost just as much space for half the running expense, this SR-5 has some beautiful features—a *five*-speed transmission with an overdrive that really saves fuel on a long trip, and a fold-down split rear seat that enables you to carry one passenger back there and still have the long space on the other side for golf clubs or fenceposts or whatever. I don't know why Detroit never thought it, that split seat. Here we're supposed to be Automobile Heaven and the foreigners come up with all the ideas. If you ask me Detroit's let us all down, two hundred million of us. I'd much rather handle native American cars but between the three of us they're junk. They're cardboard. They're pretend."

"Now what are those over there?" the boy asks.

"That's the Corona, if you want to move toward the top of the line. Bigger engine—twenty-two hundred ccs. Instead of sixteen. More of a European look. I drive one and love it. I get about thirty miles to the gallon on the highway, eighteen or so in Brewer. Depends on how you drive, of course. How heavy a foot you have. Those testers for *Consumer Reports*, they must really give it the gun, their mileage figures are the one place they seem off to me. This liftback here is priced at sixty-eight five, but remember you're buying yen for dollars, and when trade-in time comes you get your yen back."

The girl smiles at "yen." The boy, gaining confidence, says, "And this one here now." The young farmer has touched the Celica's suave black hood. Harry is running out of enthusiasm. Interested in that, the kid wasn't very interested in buying.

"You've just put your hand on one super machine," Harry tells him. "The Celica GT Sport Coupe, a car that'll ride with a

Porsche or an MG any day. Steel-belted radials, quartz crystal clock, AM/FM stereo—all standard. *Standard.* You can imagine what the extras are. This one has power steering and a sun roof. Frankly, it's pricey, pretty near five figures, but like I say, it's an investment. That's how people buy cars now, more and more. That old Kleenex mentality of trade it in every two years is gone with the wind. Buy a good solid car now, you'll have something for a long while, while the dollars if you keep 'em will go straight to Hell. Buy good goods, that's my advice to any young man starting up right now."

He must be getting too impassioned, for the boy says, "We're chust looking around, more or less."

"I understand that," Rabbit says quickly, pivoting to face the silent girl. "You're under absolutely no pressure from me. Picking a car is like picking a mate—you want to take your time." The girl blushes and looks away. Generous paternal talkativeness keeps bubbling up in Harry. "It's still a free country, the Commies haven't gotten any further than Cambodia. No way I can make you folks buy until you're good and ready. It's all the same to me, this product sells itself. Actually you're lucky there's such a selection on the floor, a shipment came in two weeks ago and we won't have another until August. Japan can't make enough of these cars to keep the world happy. Toyota is number-one import all over the globe." He can't take his eyes off this girl. Those chunky eye-sockets reminding him of somebody. The milky flecked shoulders, the dent of flesh where the halter strap digs. Squeeze her and you'd leave thumbprints, she's that fresh from the oven. "Tell me," he says, "which size're you thinking of? You planning to cart a family around, or just yourselves?"

The girl's blush deepens. Don't marry this chump, Harry thinks. His brats will drag you down. The boy says, "We don't need another wagon. My dad has a Chevy pick-up, and he let me take the Squire over when I got out of high school."

"A great junk car," Rabbit concedes. "You can hurt it but you can't kill it. Even in '71 they were putting more metal in than they do now. Detroit is giving up the ghost." He feels he is floating—on their youth, on his money, on the brightness of this June afternoon and its promise that tomorrow, a Sunday, will be fair for his golf game. "But for people planning to tie the knot and get serious you need something more than a nostalgia item, you need something more like this." He slaps orange tin again and reads irritation in the cool pallor of the girl's eyes as they lift to his. Forgive me, baby, you get so fucking bored standing around in here, when the time comes you tend to run off at the mouth.

Stavros, forgotten, calls from his desk, across the showroom space awash in sun shafts slowly approaching the horizontal, "Maybe they'd like to take a spin." He wants peace and quiet for his paperwork.

"Want to test drive?" Harry asks the couple.

"It's pretty late," the boy points out.

"It'll take a minute. You only pass this way once. Live it up. I'll get some keys and a plate. Charlie, are the keys to the blue Corolla outside hanging on the pegboard or in your desk?"

"I'll get 'em," Charlie grunts. He pushes up from his desk and, still bent, goes into the corridor behind the waist-high partition of frosted glass—a tacky improvement ordered by Fred Springer toward the end of his life. Behind it, three hollow flush doors in a wall of fake-walnut pressboard open into the offices of Mildred Kroust and the billing girl, whoever she is that month, with the office of the Chief Sales Representative between them. The doors are usually ajar and the girl and Mildred keep crossing back and forth to consult. Harry prefers to stand out here on the floor. In the old days there were just three steel desks and a strip of carpet; the one closed door marked the company toilet with its dispenser of powdered soap you turned upside down to get any out of. Reception now is off in another separate cubicle, adjoining the waiting room where few customers ever wait. The keys Charlie needs hang, among many others, some no longer unlocking anything in this world, on a pegboard darkened by the touch of greasy fingertips beside the door on the way to Parts: Parts, that tunnel of loaded steel shelves whose sliding window overlooks the clangorous cavern of Service. No reason for Charlie to go except he knows where things are and you don't want to leave customers alone for a moment and feeling foolish, they're apt to sneak away. More timid than deer, customers. With nothing to say between them, the boy, the girl, and Harry can hear the faint strained wheeze of Charlie's breathing as he comes back with the demonstrator Corolla keys and the dealer's plate on its rusty spring clip. "Want me to take these youngsters out?" he asks.

"No, you sit and rest," Harry tells him, adding, "You might start locking up in back." Their sign claims they are open Saturdays to six but on this ominous June day of gas drought quarter of should be close enough. "Back in a minute."

The boy asks the girl, "Want to come or stay here?"

"Oh, *come*," she says, impatience lighting up her mild face as she turns and names him. "Jamie, Mother expects me *back*."

Harry reassures her, "It'll just take a minute." Mother. He wishes he could ask her to describe Mother.

Out on the lot, bright wind is bringing summer in. The spots of grass around the asphalt sport buttery dabs of dandelion. He clips the plate to the back of the Corolla and hands the boy the keys. He holds the seat on the passenger side forward so the girl can get into the rear; as she does so the denim of her shorts permits a peek of cheek of ass. Rabbit squeezes into the death seat and explains to Jamie the trinkets of the dashboard, including the space where a tape deck could go. They are, all three passengers, on the tall side, and the small car feels stuffed. Yet with imported spunk the Toyota tugs them into rapid motion and finds its place in the passing lane of Route 111. Like riding on the back of a big bumblebee; you feel on top of the buzzing engine. "Peppy," Jamie acknowledges.

"And smooth, considering," Harry adds, trying not to brake on the bare floor. To the girl he calls backwards, "You O.K.? Shall I slide my seat forward to give more room?" The way the shorts are so short now you wonder if the crotches don't hurt. The stitching, pinching up.

"No I'm all right, I'll sit sideways."

He wants to turn and look at her but at his age turning his head is not so easy and indeed some days he wakes with pains all through the neck and shoulders from no more cause than his dead weight on the bed all night. He tells Jamie, "This is the sixteen hundred cc., they make a twelve hundred base model but we don't like to handle it, I'd hate to have it on my conscience that somebody was killed because he didn't have enough pick-up to get around a truck or something on these American roads. Also we believe in carrying a pretty full complement of options; without 'em you'll find yourself short-changed on the trade-in when the time comes." He manages to work his body around to look at the girl. "These Japanese for all their good qualities have pretty short legs," he tells her. The way she has to sit, her ass is nearly on the floor and her knees are up in the air, these young luminous knees inches from his face.

Unself-consciously she is pulling a few long hairs away from her mouth where they have blown and gazing through the side window at this commercial stretch of greater Brewer. Fast-food huts in eye-catching shapes and retail outlets of every-thing from bridal outfits to plaster birdbaths have widened the aspect of this, the old Weisertown Pike, with their parking lots, leaving the odd surviving house and its stump of a front lawn sticking out painfully. Competitors—Pike Porsche and Renault, Diefendorfer Volkswagen, Old Red Barn Mazda and BMW, Diamond County Automotive Imports—flicker their FUEL ECONOMY banners while the gasoline stations intermixed with their beckoning have shrouded pumps and tow trucks parked across the lanes where automobiles once glided in, were filled, and glided on. An effect of hostile barricade, late in the day. Where did the shrouds come from? Some of them quite smartly tailored, in squared-off crimson canvas. A new industry, gas pump shrouds. Among vacant lakes of asphalt a few small stands offer strawberries and early peas. A tall sign gestures to a cement-block building well off the road; Rabbit can remember when this was a giant Mister Peanut pointing toward a low shop where salted nuts were arrayed in glass cases, Brazil nuts and hazelnuts and whole cashews and for a lesser price broken ones, Diamond County a great area for nuts but not that great, the shop failed. Its shell was broken and doubled in size and made into a nightclub and the sign repainted, keeping the top hat but Mister Peanut becoming a human reveller in white tie and tails. Now after many mutilations this sign has been turned into an ill-fitted female figure, a black silhouette with no bumps indicating clothing, her head thrown back and the large letters D I S C O falling in bubbles as if plucked one by one from her cut throat. Beyond such advertisements the worn green hills hold a haze of vapor and pale fields bake as their rows of corn thicken. The inside of the Corolla is warming with a mingled human smell. Harry thinks of the girl's long thigh as she stretched her way into the back seat and imagines he smells vanilla. Cunt would be a good flavor of ice cream, Sealtest ought to work on it.

The silence from the young people troubles him. He prods it. He says, "Some storm last night. I heard on the radio this morning the underpass at Eisenhower and Seventh was flooded for over an hour."

Then he says, "You know it seems gruesome to me, all these gas stations closed up like somebody has died."

Then he says, "Did you see in the paper where the Hershey company has had to lay off nine hundred people because of the truckers' strike? Next thing we'll be in lines for Hershey bars."

The boy is intently passing a Freihofer's Bakery truck and Harry responds for him: "The downtown stores are all pulling out. Nothing left in the middle of the city now but the banks and the post office. They put that crazy stand of trees in to make a mall but it won't do any good, the people are still scared to go downtown."

The boy is staying in the fast lane, and in third gear, either for the pep or because he's forgotten there is a fourth. Harry asks him, "Getting the feel of it, Jamie? If you want to turn around, there's an intersection coming up."

The girl understands. "Jamie, we better turn around. The man wants to get home for supper."

As Jamie slows to ease right at the intersection, a Pacer— silliest car on the road, looks like a glass bathtub upside-down —swings left without looking. The driver is a fat spic in a Hawaiian shirt. The boy slaps the steering wheel in vain search for the horn. Toyota indeed has put the horn in a funny place, on two little arcs a thumb's reach inside the steering-wheel rim; Harry reaches over quick and toots for him. The Pacer swerves back into its lane, with a dark look back above the Hawaiian shirt. Harry directs, "Jamie, I want you to take a left at the next light and go across the highway and take the next left you can and that'll bring us back." To the girl he explains, "Prettier this way." He thinks aloud, "What can I tell you about the car I haven't? It has a lot of locks. Those Japanese, they live on top of each other and are crazy about locks. Don't kid yourselves, we're coming to it, I won't be here to see it, but you will. When I was a kid nobody ever thought to lock their house and now everybody does, except my crazy wife. If she locked the door she'd lose the key. One of the reasons I'd like to go to Japan —Toyota asks some of their dealers but you got to have a bigger gross than I do—is to see how you lock up a paper house. At any rate. You can't get the key out of the ignition without releasing this catch down here. The trunk in back releases from this lever. The locking gas cap you already know about. Did either of you hear about the woman somewhere around Ardmore this week who cut into a gas line and the guy behind her got so mad he sneaked his own locking gas cap onto her tank so when she got to the pump the attendant couldn't remove it? They had to tow her away. Serve the bitch right, if you ask me."

They have taken their two lefts and are winding along a road where fields come to the edge so you can see the clumps of red earth still shiny from where the plow turned them, and where what businesses there are—LAWNMOWERS SHARPENED, PA. DUTCH QUILTS—seem to stem from an earlier decade than those along Route III, which runs parallel. On the banks of the road, between mailboxes some of which are painted with a heart or hex design, crown vetch is in violet flower. At a crest the elephant-colored gas tanks of Brewer lift into view, and the brick-red rows as they climb Mt. Judge and smudge its side. Rabbit dares ask the girl, "You from around here?"

"More toward Galilee. My mother has a farm."

And is your mother's name Ruth? Harry wants to ask, but doesn't, lest he frighten her, and destroy for himself the vibration of excitement, of possibility untested. He tries to steal another peek at her, to see if her white skin is a mirror, and if the innocent blue in her eyes is his own, but his bulk restrains him, and the tightness of the car. He asks the boy, "You follow the Phillies, Jamie? How about that seven-zip loss last night? You don't see Bowa commit an error that often."

"Is Bowa the one with the big salary?"

Harry will feel better when he gets the Toyota out of this moron's hands. Every turn, he can feel the tires pull and the sudden secret widen within him, circle upon circle, it's like seed: seed that goes into the ground invisible and if it takes hold cannot be stopped, it fulfills the shape it was programmed for, its destiny, sure as our death, and shapely. "I think you mean Rose," he answers. "He's not been that much help, either. They're not going anywhere this year, Pittsburgh's the team. Pirates or Steelers, they always win. Take this left, at the yellow blinker. That'll take you right across One Eleven and then you swing into the lot from the back. What's your verdict?"

From the side the boy has an Oriental look—a big stretch of skin between his red ear and red nose, puffy eyes whose glitter gives away nothing. People who gouge a living out of the dirt are just naturally mean, Harry has always thought. Jamie says, "Like I said we were looking around. This car seems pretty small but maybe that's chust what you're used to."

"Want to give the Corona a whirl? That interior feels like a palace after you've been in one of these, you wouldn't think it would, it's only about two centimeters wider and five longer." He marvels at himself, how centimeters trip off his tongue. Another five years with these cars and he'll be talking Japanese. "But you better get used," he tells Jamie, "to a little scaling down. The big old boats have had it. People trade 'em in and we can't give 'em away. Wholesale half of 'em, and the wholesalers turn 'em into windowboxes. The five hundred trade-in I'd allow you on yours is just a courtesy, believe me. We like to help young people out. I think it's a helluva world we're coming to, where a young couple like yourselves can't afford to buy a car or own a home. If you can't get your foot on even the bottom rung of a society geared like this, people are going to lose faith in the system. The Sixties were a lark in the park compared to what we're going to see if things don't straighten out."

Loose stones in the back section of the lot crackle. They pull into the space the Corolla came from and the boy can't find the button to release the key until Harry shows him again. The girl leans forward, anxious to escape, and her breath stirs the colorless hairs on Harry's wrist. His shirt is stuck to his shoulder blades, he discovers standing to his height in the air. All three of them straighten slowly. The sun is still bright but horsetails

high in the sky cast doubt upon the weather for tomorrow's
golf game after all. "Good driving," he says to Jamie, having
given up on any sale. "Come back in for a minute and I'll give
you some literature." Inside the showroom the sun strikes the
paper banner and makes the letters TI TOƆ ꟼW show through.
Stavros is nowhere to be seen. Harry hands the boy his CHIEF
card and asks him to sign the customer register.

"Like I said—" the boy begins.

Harry has lost patience with this escapade. "It doesn't com-
mit you to a blessed thing," he says. "Toyota'll send you a
Christmas card is all it means. I'll do it for you. First name
James—?"

"Nunemacher," the boy says warily, and spells it. "R. D.
number two, Galilee."

Harry's handwriting has deteriorated over the years, gained a
twitch at the end of his long arm, which yet is not long enough
for him to see clearly what he writes. He owns reading glasses
but it is his vanity never to wear them in public. "Done," he
says, and all too casually turns to the girl. "O.K. young lady,
how about you? Same name?"

"No way," she says, and giggles. "You don't want me."

A boldness sparks in the cool flat eyes. In that way of women
she has gone all circles, silly, elusive. When her gaze levels there
is something sexy in the fit of her lower lids, and the shadow
of insufficient sleep below them. Her nose is slightly snub. "Jamie's our neighbor, I just came along for the ride. I was going
to look for a sundress at Kroll's if there was time."

Something buried far back glints toward the light. Today's
slant of sun has reached the shelf where the trophies Springer
Motors sponsors wait to be awarded; oval embossments on
their weightless white-metal surfaces shine. Keep your name,
you little cunt, it's still a free country. But he has given her
his. She has taken his card from Jamie's broad red hand and
her eyes, childishly alight, slip from its lettering to his face to
the section of far wall where his old headlines hang yellowing,
toasted brown by time. She asks him, "Were you ever a famous
basketball player?"

The question is not so easy to answer, it was so long ago.
He tells her, "In the dark ages. Why do you ask, you've heard
the name?"

"Oh no," this visitant from lost time gaily lies. "You just have that look."

When they have gone, the Country Squire swaying off on its soupy shocks, Harry uses the toilet down past Mildred Kroust's door along the corridor half of frosted glass and meets Charlie coming back from locking up. Still, there is pilferage, mysterious discrepancies eating into the percentages. Money is like water in a leaky bucket: no sooner there, it begins to drip. "Whajja think of the girl?" Harry asks the other man, back in the showroom.

"With these eyes, I don't see the girls anymore. If I saw 'em, with my condition I couldn't do anything about it. She looked big and dumb. A lot of leg."

"Not so dumb as that hick she was with," Harry says. "God when you see what some girls are getting into it makes you want to cry."

Stavros's dark dabs of eyebrows lift. "Yeah? Some could say it was the other way around." He sits down to business at his desk. "Manny get to talk to you about that Torino you took on trade?"

Manny is head of Service, a short stooping man with black pores on his nose, as if with that nose he burrows through each day's dirty work. Of course he resents Harry, who thanks to his marriage to Springer's daughter skates around in the sun of the showroom and accepts clunky Torinos on trade-in. "He told me the front end's out of alignment."

"Now he thinks in good conscience it should have a valve job. He also thinks the owner turned back the odometer."

"What could I do, the guy had the book right in his hand, I couldn't give him less than book value. If I don't give 'em book value Diefendorfer or Pike Porsche sure as hell will."

"You should have let Manny check it out, he could have told at a glance it had been in a collision. And if he spotted the odometer monkey business put the jerk on the defensive."

"Can't he weight the front wheels enough to hide the shimmy?"

Stavros squares his hands patiently on the olive-green top of his desk. "It's a question of good will. The customer you unload that Torino on will never be back, I promise you."

"Then what's your advice?"

Charlie says, "Discount it over to Ford in Pottsville. You had a cushion of nine hundred on that sale and can afford to give away two rather than get Manny's back up. He has to mark up his parts to protect his own department and when they're Ford parts you're carrying a mark-up already. Pottsville'll put a coat of wax on it and make some kid happy for the summer."

"Sounds good." Rabbit wants to be outdoors, moving through the evening air, dreaming of his daughter. "If I had my way," he tells Charlie, "we'd wholesale the American makes out of here as fast as they come in. Nobody wants 'em except the blacks and the spics, and even they got to wake up some day."

Charlie doesn't agree. "You can still do well in used, if you pick your spots. Fred used to say every car has a buyer somewhere, but you shouldn't allow more on any trade-in than you'd pay cash for that car. It *is* cash, you know. Numbers are cash, even if you don't handle any lettuce." He tips back his chair, letting his palms screech with friction on the desktop. "When I first went to work for Fred Springer in '63 we sold nothing but second-hand American models, you never saw a foreign car this far in from the coast. The cars would come in off the street and we'd paint 'em and give 'em a tune-up and no manufacturer told us what price to attach, we'd put the price on the windshield in shaving cream and wipe it off and try another if it didn't move inside a week. No import duty, no currency devaluation; it was good clean dog eat dog."

Reminiscence. Sad to see it rotting Charlie's brain. Harry waits respectfully for the mood to subside, then asks as if out of the blue, "Charlie, if I had a daughter, what d'you think she'd look like?"

"Ugly," Stavros says. "She'd look like Bugs Bunny."

"It'd be fun to have a daughter, wouldn't it?"

"Doubt it." Charlie lifts his palms so the legs of his chair slap to the floor. "What d'you hear from Nelson?"

Harry turns vehement. "Nothing much, thank God," he says. "The kid never writes. Last we heard he was spending the summer out in Colorado with this girl he's picked up." Nelson attends college at Kent State, in Ohio, off and on, and has a year's worth of credits still to go before he graduates, though the boy was twenty-two last October.

"What kind of girl?"

"Lordy knows, I can't keep track. Each one is weirder than the last. One had been a teen-age alcoholic. Another told fortunes from playing cards. I think that same one was a vegetarian, but it may have been somebody else. I think he picks 'em to frustrate me."

"Don't give up on the kid. He's all you've got."

"Jesus, what a thought."

"You just go ahead. I want to finish up here. I'll lock up."

"O.K., I'll go see what Janice has burned for supper. Want to come take pot luck? She'd be tickled to see you."

"Thanks, but *Manna mou* expects me." His mother, getting decrepit herself, lives with Charlie now, in his place on Eisenhower Avenue, and this is another bond between them, since Harry lives with his mother-in-law.

"O.K. Take care, Charlie. See you in Monday's wash."

"Take care, champ."

The day is still golden outside, old gold now in Harry's lengthening life. He has seen summer come and go until its fading is one in his heart with its coming, though he cannot yet name the weeds that flower each in its turn through the season, or the insects that also in ordained sequence appear, eat, and perish. He knows that in June school ends and the playgrounds open, and the grass needs cutting again and again if one is a man, and if one is a child games can be played outdoors while the supper dishes tinkle in the mellow parental kitchens, and the moon is discovered looking over your shoulder out of a sky still blue, and a silver blob of milkweed spittle has appeared mysteriously on your knee. Good luck. Car sales peak in June: for a three-hundred-car-a-year dealer like Harry this means upwards of twenty-five units, with twenty-one accounted for already and six selling days to go. Average eight hundred gross profit times twenty-five equals twenty grand minus the twenty-five per cent they estimate for salesmen's compensation both salary and incentives leaves fifteen grand minus between eight and ten for other salaries those cute little cunts come and go in billing one called Cissy a Polack a few years ago they got as far

as rubbing fannies easing by in that corridor and the rent that
Springer Motors pays itself old man Springer didn't believe in
owning anything the banks could own but even he had to pay
off the mortgage eventually boy the rates now must kill anybody starting up and the financing double-digit interest Brewer
Trust been doing it for years and against the twelve per cent
you got to figure the two or three per cent that comes back as
loss reserves nobody likes to call it kick-back and the IRS calls
it taxable earnings and the upkeep the electricity that Sun 2001
Diagnostic Computer Manny wants would use a lot of juice
and the power tools they can't even turn a nut on a wheel anymore it has to be pneumatic *rrrrrt* and the heat thank God a
few months' reprieve from that the fucking Arabs are killing us
and the men won't wear sweaters under the coveralls the young
mechanics are the worst they say they lose feeling in their fingertips and health insurance there's another killer up and up
the hospitals keeping people alive that are really dead like some
game they're playing at Medicaid's expense and the advertising
he often wonders how much good it does a rule of thumb he
read somewhere is one and a half per cent of gross sales but if
you look at the Auto Sales page of the Sunday paper you never
saw such a jumble just the quiet listing of the prices and the
shadow of the dealer like old man Springer said the man he
gets known to be at Rotary and in the downtown restaurants
and the country club really he should be allowed to take all
that off as business expenses the four seventy-five a week he
pays himself doesn't take into account the suits to make himself
presentable he has to buy three or four a year and not at Kroll's
anymore he doesn't like that salesman who measured his fat
waist Webb Murkett knows of a little shop on Pine Street that's
as good as hand tailoring and then the property taxes and the
kids keep throwing stones or shooting BBs at the glass signs
outside we ought to go back to wood grouted wood but national Toyota has its specifications, where was he, let's say nine
total monthly expenses variable and invariable that leaves four
net profit and deduct another thousand from that for inflation
and pilferage and the unpredictable that's always there you still
have three, fifteen hundred for Ma Springer and fifteen hundred for Janice and him plus the two thousand salary when his
poor dead dad used to go off to the print shop at quarter after

seven every morning for forty dollars a week and that wasn't considered bad money then. Harry wonders what his father would think if he could only see him now, rich.

His 1978 Luxury Edition liftback five-door Corona is parked in its space. Called Red Metallic, it is a color more toward brown, like tired tomato soup. If the Japanese have a weakness it is their color sense: their Copper Metallic to Harry's eyes is a creosote brown, the Mint Green Metallic something like what he imagines cyanide to be, and what they called Beige a plain lemon yellow. In the war there used to be all these cartoons showing the Japanese wearing thick glasses and he wonders if it can be true, they don't see too well, all their colors falling in between the stripes of the rainbow. Still, his Corona is a snug machine. Solid big-car feel, padded tilt steering wheel, lumbar support lever for adjustable driver comfort, factory-installed AM/FM/MPX four-speaker radio. The radio is what he enjoys, gliding through Brewer with the windows up and locked and the power-boosted ventilation flowing through and the four corners of the car dinging out disco music as from the four corners of the mind's ballroom. Peppy and gentle, the music reminds Rabbit of the music played on radios when he was in high school, "How High the Moon" with the clarinet breaking away, the licorice stick they used to call it, "Puttin' on the Ritz": city music, not like that country music of the Sixties that tried to take us back and make us better than we are. Black girls with tinny chiming voices chant nonsense words above a throbbing electrified beat and he likes that, the thought of those black girls out of Detroit probably, their boyfriends goofing off on the assembly line, in shimmery tinsel dresses throbbing one color after another as the disco lights spin. He and Janice ought to visit at least the place down Route 111 D I S C O he noticed today for the hundredth time, never dared go in. In his mind he tries to put Janice and the colored girls and the spinning lights all together and they fly apart. He thinks of Skeeter. Ten years ago this small black man came and lived with him and Nelson for a crazy destructive time. Now Skeeter is dead, he learned just this April. Someone anonymous sent him, in a long stamped envelope such as anybody can buy at the post office, addressed in neat block ballpoint printing such as an accountant or a schoolteacher might use, a clipping in the familiar type of the Brewer *Vat*, where Harry had been a Linotyper until Linotyping became obsolete:

FORMER RESIDENT
SLAIN IN PHILLY

Hubert Johnson, formerly of Brewer, died of gunshot wounds in General Municipal Hospital, Philadelphia, after an alleged shoot-out with police officers.

Johnson was purported to have fired the first shots without provocation upon officers investigating reported violations of sanitation and housing laws in a religious commune supposedly headed by Johnson, whose Messiah Now Freedom Family included a number of black families and young persons.

Numerous complaints had been occasioned among neighbors by their late singing and abrasive behavior. The Messiah Now Freedom Family was located on Columbia Avenue.

Johnson Wanted

Johnson, last of Plum Street, city, was remembered locally as "Skeeter" and also went under the name of Farnsworth. He was wanted here under several complaints, local officials confirmed.

Philadelphia police lieutenant Roman Surpitski informed reporters that he and his men had no choice but to return fire upon Johnson. Fortunately, no officers and no other "commune" members suffered wounds in the exchange.

The office of outgoing Mayor
Frank Rizzo declined to comment upon the incident. "We
don't come up against as many of
these crazies as we used to," Lieutenant Surpitski volunteered.

The clipping had been accompanied by no note. Yet the
sender must have known him, known something of his past,
and be watching him, as the dead supposedly do. Creepy.
Skeeter dead, a certain light was withdrawn from the world,
a daring, a promise that all would be overturned. Skeeter had
foretold this, his death young. Harry last had seen him heading across a field of corn stubble, among crows gleaning. But
that had been so long ago the paper in his hand this last April
felt little different from any other news item or from those
sports clippings hanging framed in his showroom, about himself. Your selves die too. That part of him subject to Skeeter's
spell had shrivelled and been overlaid. In his life he had known
up close no other black people and in truth had been beyond
all fear and discomfort flattered by the attentions of this hostile
stranger descended like an angel; Harry felt he was seen by this
furious man anew, as with X-rays. Yet he was surely a madman
and his demands inordinate and endless and with him dead
Rabbit feels safer.

As he sits snug in his sealed and well-assembled car the venerable city of Brewer unrolls like a silent sideways movie past
his closed windows. He follows 111 along the river to West
Brewer, where once he lived with Skeeter, and then cuts over
the Weiser Street Bridge renamed after some dead mayor
whose name nobody ever uses and then, to avoid the pedestrian mall with fountains and birch trees the city planners put
in the broadest two blocks of Weiser to renew the downtown
supposedly (the joke was, they planted twice as many trees as
they needed, figuring half would die, but in fact almost all of
them thrived, so they have a kind of forest in the center of
town, where a number of muggings have taken place and the
winos and junkies sleep it off), Harry cuts left on Third Street
and through some semi-residential blocks of mostly ophthalmologists' offices to the diagonal main drag called Eisenhower,
through the sector of old factories and railroad yards. Railroads

and coal made Brewer. Everywhere in this city, once the fifth
largest in Pennsylvania but now slipped to seventh, structures
speak of expended energy. Great shapely stacks that have not
issued smoke for half a century. Scrolling cast-iron light stan-
chions not lit since World War II. The lower blocks of Weiser
given over to the sale of the cut-rate and the X-rated and the
only new emporium a big windowless enlargement in white
brick of Schoenbaum Funeral Directors. The old textile plants
given over to discount clothing outlets teeming with a gimcrack cheer of banners FACTORY FAIR and slogans *Where the
Dollar Is Still a Dollar*. These acres of dead railroad track and
car shops and stockpiled wheels and empty boxcars stick in the
heart of the city like a great rusting dagger. All this had been
cast up in the last century by what now seem giants, in an explosion of iron and brick still preserved intact in this city where
the sole new buildings are funeral parlors and government offices, Unemployment and Join the Army.

Beyond the car yards and the underpass at Seventh that had
been flooded last night, Eisenhower Avenue climbs steeply
through tight-built neighborhoods of row houses built solid
by German workingmen's savings and loans associations, only
the fanlights of stained glass immune to the later layers of aluminum awning and Permastone siding, the Polacks and Ital-
ians being squeezed out by the blacks and Hispanics that in
Harry's youth were held to the low blocks down by the river.
Dark youths thinking in languages of their own stare from the
triangular stone porches of the old corner grocery stores.

The vanished white giants as they filled Brewer into its grid
named these higher streets that Eisenhower crosses for fruits
and the seasons of the year: Winter, Spring, Summer, but no
Fall Street. For three months twenty years ago Rabbit lived on
Summer with a woman, Ruth Leonard. There he fathered the
girl he saw today, if that was his daughter. There is no getting
away; our sins, our seed, coil back. The disco music shifts to
the Bee Gees, white men who have done this wonderful thing
of making themselves sound like black women. "Stayin' Alive"
comes on with all that amplified throbbleo and a strange nasal
whining underneath: the John Travolta theme song. Rabbit
still thinks of him as one of the Sweathogs from Mr. Kotter's
class but for a while back there last summer the U.S.A. was one

hundred per cent his, every twat under fifteen wanting to be humped by a former Sweathog in the back seat of a car parked in Brooklyn. He thinks of his own daughter getting into the back seat of the Corolla, bare leg up to her ass. He wonders if her pubic hair is ginger in color like her mother's was. That curve where a tender entire woman seems an inch away around a kind of corner, where no ugly penis hangs like sausage on the rack, blue-veined. Her eyes his blue: wonderful to think that he has been turned into cunt, a secret message carried by genes all that way through all these comings and goings all these years, the bloody tunnel of growing and living, of staying alive. He better stop thinking about it, it fills him too full of pointless excitement. Some music does that.

Some car with double headlights, a yellow LeMans with that big vertical bar in the middle of the grille, is riding his tail so close he eases over behind a parked car and lets the bastard by: a young blonde with a tipped-up tiny profile is driving. How often that seems to be the case these days, some pushy road-hog you hate turns out to be a little girl at the wheel, who must be somebody's daughter and from the lackadaisical glassy look on her face has no idea of being rude, just wants to get there. When Rabbit first began to drive the road was full of old fogeys going too slow and now it seems nothing but kids in a hell of a hurry, pushing. Let 'em by, is his motto. Maybe they'll kill themselves on a telephone pole in the next mile. He hopes so.

His route takes him up into the area of the stately Brewer High School, called the Castle, built in 1933, the year of his birth is how he remembers. They wouldn't build it now, no faith in education, indeed they say with zero growth rate approaching there aren't enough students to fill the schools now, they are closing a lot of the elementary schools down. Up this high the city builders had run out of seasons and went to tree names. Locust Boulevard east of the Castle is lined with houses with lawns all around, though the strips between are narrow and dark and rhododendrons die for lack of sun. The better-off live up here, the bone surgeons and legal eagles and middle management of the plants that never had the wit to go south or have come in since. When Locust begins to curve through the municipal park its name changes to Cityview Drive, though with all the trees that have grown up in time there isn't much view left; Brewer can be seen all spread out really only from the Pinnacle Hotel, now a site of vandalism and terror where once there had been dancing and necking. Something about spics they don't like to see white kids making out, they surround the car and smash the windshield with rocks and slit the clothes off the girl while roughing up the boy. What a world to grow up in, especially for a girl. He and Ruth walked up to the Pinnacle once or twice. The railroad tie steps probably rotted now. She took off her shoes because the high heels dug into the gravel between the railroad ties, he remembers her city-pale feet lifting ahead of him under his eyes, naked just for him it seemed. People satisfied with less then. In the park a World War II tank, made into a monument, points its guns at tennis courts where the nets, even the ones made of playground fencing, keep getting ripped away. The strength these kids use, just to destroy. Was he that way at that age? You want to make a mark. The world seems indestructible and won't let you out. Let 'em by.

There is a stoplight and, turning left, Harry passes between houses gabled and turreted the way they did early in the century when men wore straw hats and made ice cream by hand and rode bicycles, and then there is a shopping center, where a four-theater movie complex advertises on its sign high up where vandals can't reach it to steal letters ALIEN MOONRAKER MAIN EVENT ESCAPE FROM ALCATRAZ. None of them does he want to see though he likes the way Streisand's hair frizzes up and that Jewish nose, not just the nose, there is Jewishness in the thrust of her voice that thrills him, must have to do with being the chosen people, they do seem more at home here on Earth, the few he knows, more full of bounce. Funny about Streisand, if she isn't matched up with an Egyptian like Sharif it's with a super Waspy-looking type like Ryan O'Neal; same thing with Woody Allen, nothing Jewish about Diane Keaton, though her hair does frizz come to think of it.

The music stops, the news comes on. A young female voice reads it, with a twang like she knows she's wasting our time. Fuel, truckers. Three Mile Island investigations continue. Date for Skylab fall has been revised. Somoza in trouble too. Stay of execution of convicted Florida killer denied. Former leader of Great Britain's Liberal Party acquitted of charges of conspiring to murder his former homosexual lover. This annoys Rabbit, but his indignation at this pompous pansy's getting off scot-free dissolves in his curiosity about the next criminal case on the news, this of a Baltimore physician who was charged with murdering a Canada goose with a golf club. The defendant claims, the disinterested female voice twangs on, that he had accidentally struck the goose with a golf ball and then had dispatched the wounded creature with a club to end its misery. The voice concludes, "A mercy killing, or murder most foul?" He laughs aloud, in the car, alone. He'll have to try to remember that, to tell the gang at the club tomorrow. Tomorrow will be a sunny day, the woman reassures him, giving the weather. "And now, the Number One Hit coast to coast, 'Hot Stuff,' by the Queen of Disco, Donna Summer!"

> *Sittin' here eatin' my heart out waitin'*
> *Waitin' for some lover to call. . . .*

Rabbit likes the chorus where the girls in the background chime in, you can picture them standing around some steamy city corner chewing gum and who knows what else:

> *Hot stuff*
> *I need hot stuff*
> *I want some hot stuff*
> *I need hot stuuuuuff!*

Still he liked Donna Summer best in the days when she was doing those records of a woman breathing and panting and sighing like she was coming. Maybe it wasn't her, just some other slim black chick. But he thinks it was her.

The road takes on a number, 422, and curves around the shoulders of Mt. Judge, with a steep drop on the right side and a view of the viaduct that once brought water to the city from the north of the county across the black breadth of the Running Horse River. Two gas stations mark the beginning of the borough of Mt. Judge; instead of keeping on 422 toward Philadelphia Harry steers his Corona off the highway onto Central by the granite Baptist church and then obliquely up Jackson Street and after three blocks right onto Joseph. If he stays on Jackson two more blocks he will pass his old house, one number in from the corner of Maple, but since Pop passed on, after holding on without Mom for a couple of years, doing all the yardwork and vacuuming and meals by himself until his emphysema just got too bad and you'd find him sitting in a chair all curled over like a hand sheltering a guttering candle-flame from the wind, Rabbit rarely drives by: the people he and Mim had sold it to had painted the wood trim an awful grape color and hung an ultraviolet plant light in the big front window. Like these young couples in Brewer who think anything goes on a row house, however cute, and they're doing the world a favor by taking it on. Harry hadn't liked the guy's accent, haircut, or leisure suit; he had liked the price he had paid, though: fifty-eight thousand for a place that had cost Mom and Pop forty-two hundred in 1935. It made a nice bundle even with Mim taking her half with her back out to Nevada and the real-estate agents' and lawyers' fees, they just step in everywhere where money's changing hands. He had begged Janice at the time to use the twenty grand to buy a new house, just for them, maybe over in Penn Park in West Brewer, five minutes from the lot. But no, Janice didn't think they should desert Mother: the Springers had taken them in when they had no house, their own house had burned, and their marriage had hit rock bottom and what with Harry being promised to head up new car sales at about the time Pop died and Nelson having had so many shocks already in his life and so many bad aftereffects still smoldering at that end of Brewer, the inquest for Jill and a police investigation and her parents thinking of suing all the way from Connecticut and the insurance company taking forever to come through with the claim because there were suspicious circumstances and poor Peggy Fosnacht having to swear Harry had been with her and so couldn't have set it himself, what with all this it seemed better to lie low, to hide behind the Springer name in the big stucco house, and the weeks had become months and the months years without the young Angstroms going into another place of their own, and then with Fred dying so suddenly and Nelson going off to college there seemed more room and less reason than ever to move. The house, 89 Joseph, always reminds Harry under its spreading trees with its thready lawn all around of the witch's house made out of candy, penuche for the walls and licorice Necco wafers for the thick slate roof. Though the place looks big outside the downstairs is crammed with furniture come down through Ma Springer's people the Koerners and the shades are always half drawn; except for the screened-in back porch and the little up-stairs room that had been Janice's when she was a girl and then Nelson's for those five years before he went away to Kent, there isn't a corner of the Springer house where Harry feels able to breathe absolutely his own air.

He circles around into the alley of bluestone grit and puts the Corona into the garage beside the '74 navy-blue Chrysler Newport that Fred got the old lady for her birthday the year before he died and that she drives around town with both hands tight on the wheel, with the look on her face as if a bomb might go off under the hood. Janice always keeps her Mustang convertible parked out front by the curb, where the maple drippings can ruin the top faster. When the weather gets warm she leaves the top down for nights at a time so the seats are always sticky. Rabbit swings down the overhead garage door and carries up the cement walk through the back yard like twin car headlights into a tunnel his strange consciousness of having not one child now but two.

Janice greets him in the kitchen. Something's up. She is wearing a crisp frock with pepperminty stripes but her hair is still scraggly and damp from an afternoon of swimming at the club pool. Nearly every day she has a tennis date with some of her girlfriends at the club they belong to, the Flying Eagle Tee and Racquet, a newish organization laid out on the lower slopes of Mt. Judge's woodsy brother mountain with the Indian name, Mt. Pemaquid, and then kills the rest of the afternoon lying at poolside gossiping or playing cards and getting slowly spaced on Spritzers or vodka-and-tonics. Harry likes having a wife who can be at the club so much. Janice is thickening through the middle at the age of forty-three but her legs are still hard and neat. And brown. She was always dark-complected and with July not even here she has the tan of a savage, legs and arms almost black like some little Polynesian in an old Jon Hall movie. Her lower lip bears a trace of zinc oxide, which is sexy, even though he never loved that stubborn slotlike set her mouth gets. Her still-wet hair pulled back reveals a high forehead somewhat mottled, like brown paper where water has been dropped and dried. He can tell by the kind of heat she is giving off that she and her mother have been fighting. "What's up now?" he asks.

"It's been wild," Janice says. "She's in her room and says we should eat without her."

"Yeah well, she'll be down. But what's to eat? I don't see anything cooking." The digital clock built into the stove says 6:32.

"Harry. Honest to God I was going to shop as soon as I came back and changed out of tennis things but then this post-card was here and Mother and I have been at it ever since. Anyway it's summer, you don't want to eat too much. Doris Kaufmann, I'd give anything to have her serve, she says she never has more than a glass of iced tea for lunch, even in the middle of winter. I thought maybe soup and those cold cuts I bought that you and Mother refuse to touch, they have to be eaten sometime. And the lettuce is coming on in the garden now so fast we must start having salads before it gets all leggy." She had planted a little vegetable garden in the part of the back yard where Nelson's swing set used to be, getting a man from down the block to turn the earth with his Rototiller, the earth miraculously soft and pungent beneath the crust of winter and Janice out there enthusiastic with her string and rake in the gauzy shadows of the budding trees; but now that summer is here and the leafed-out trees keep the garden in the shade and the games at the club have begun she has let the plot go to weeds.

Still, he cannot dislike this brown-eyed woman who has been his indifferent wife for twenty-three years this past March. He is rich because of her inheritance and this mutual knowledge rests adhesively between them like a form of sex, comfortable and sly. "Salad and baloney, my favorite meal," he says, re-signed. "Lemme have a drink first. Some window-shoppers came in to the lot today just as I was leaving. Tell me what postcard."

As he stands by the refrigerator making a gin-and-bitter-lemon, knowing these sugary mixers add to the calories in the alcohol and help to keep him overweight but figuring that this Saturday evening meal in its skimpiness will compensate and maybe he'll jog a little afterwards, Janice goes in through the

dark dining room into the musty front parlor where the shades
are drawn and Ma Springer's sulking spirit reigns, and brings
back a postcard. It shows a white slope of snow under a stark
blue wedge of sky; two small dark hunched figures are tracing linked S's on the slanted snow, skiing. GREETINGS FROM
COLORADO red cartoon letters say across the sky that looks
like blue paint. On the opposite side a familiar scrawled hand,
scrunched as if something in the boy had been squeezed too
tight while his handwriting was coming to birth, spells out:

> Hi Mom & Dad & Grandmom:
>   These mts. make Mt. Judge
> look sick! No snow tho,
> just plenty of grass (joke).
> Been learning to hang glide.
> Job didn't work out, guy was
> a bum. Penna. beckons.
> OK if I bring Melanie
> home too? She could get
> job and be no troble. Love,
>   Nelson

"Melanie?" Harry asks.

"That's what Mother and I have been fighting about. She
doesn't want the girl staying here."

"Is this the same girl he went out there with two weeks ago?"

"I was wondering," Janice says. "She had a name more like
Sue or Jo or something."

"Where would she sleep?"

"Well, either in that front sewing room or Nelson's room."

"*With* the kid?"

"Well really, Harry, I wouldn't be utterly surprised. He *is*
twenty-two. When have you gotten so Puritanical?"

"I'm not being Puritanical, just practical. It's one thing to
have these kids go off into the blue and go hang gliding or
whatever else and another to have them bring all their dope
and little tootsies back to the nest. This house is awkward upstairs, you know that. There's too much hall space and you
can't sneeze or fart or fuck without everybody else hearing; it's
been bliss, frankly, with just us and Ma. Remember the kid's
radio all through high school to two in the morning, how he'd

fall asleep to it? That bed of his is a little single, what are we supposed to do, buy him and Melody a double bed?"

"Melanie. I don't know, she can sleep on the floor. They all have sleeping bags. You can try putting her in the sewing room but I know she won't stay there. We wouldn't have." Her blurred dark eyes gaze beyond him into time. "We spent all our energy sneaking down hallways and squirming around in the back seats of cars and I thought we could spare our children that."

"We have a child, not children," he says coldly, as the gin expands his inner space. They had children once, but their infant daughter Becky died. It was his wife's fault. The entire squeezed and cut-down shape of his life is her fault; at every turn she has been a wall to his freedom. "Listen," he says to her, "I've been trying to get out of this fucking depressing house for years and I don't want this shiftless arrogant goof-off we've raised coming back and pinning me in. These kids seem to think the world exists to serve them but I'm sick of just standing around waiting to be of service."

Janice stands up to him scarcely flinching, armored in her country-club tan. "He is our son, Harry, and we're not going to turn away a guest of his because she is female in sex. If it was a boyfriend of Nelson's you wouldn't be at all this excited, it's the fact that it's a *girl*friend of Nelson's that's upsetting you, a girlfriend of *Nelson*'s. If it was a girlfriend of *yours*, the upstairs wouldn't be too crowded for you to fart in. This is my son and I want him here if he wants to be here."

"I don't have any girlfriends," he protests. It sounds pitiful. Is Janice saying he should have? Women, once sex gets out in the open, they become monsters. You're a creep if you fuck them and a creep if you don't. Harry strides into the dining room, making the glass panes of the antique breakfront shudder, and calls up the dark stained stairs that are opposite the breakfront, "Hey Bessie, come on down! I'm on your side!"

There is a silence as from God above and then the creak of a bed being relieved of a weight, and reluctant footsteps slither across the ceiling toward the head of the stairs. Mrs. Springer on her painful dropsical legs comes down talking: "This house is legally mine and that girl is not spending one night under a roof Janice's father slaved all his days to keep over our heads."

The breakfront quivers again; Janice has come into the dining room. She says in a voice tightened to match her mother's, "Mother, you wouldn't be keeping this enormous roof over your head if it weren't for Harry and me sharing the upkeep. It's a great sacrifice on Harry's part, a man of his income not having a house he can call his own, and you have no right to forbid Nelson to come home when he wants to, *no* right, Mother."

The plump old lady groans her way down to the landing three steps shy of the dining-room floor and hesitates there saying, in a voice tears have stained, "Nellie I'm happy to see whenever he deems fit, I love that boy with all my soul even though he hasn't turned out the way his grandfather and I had hoped."

Janice says, angrier in proportion as the old lady makes herself look pathetic, "You're always bringing Daddy in when he can't speak for himself but as long as he was alive he was *very* hospitable and tolerant of Nelson and his friends. I remember that cookout Nelson had in the back yard for his high-school graduation when Daddy had had his first stroke already, I went upstairs to see if it was getting too rowdy for him and he said with his wry little smile"—tears now stain her own voice too —"'The sound of young voices does my old heart good.'"

That slippery-quick salesman's smile of his, Rabbit can see it still. Like a switchblade without the click.

"A cookout in the back yard is one thing," Mrs. Springer says, thumping herself in her dirty aqua sneakers down the last three steps of the stairs and looking her daughter level in the eye. "A slut in the boy's bed is another."

Harry thinks this is pretty jazzy for an old lady and laughs aloud. Janice and her mother are both short women; like two doll's heads mounted on the same set of levers they turn identically chocolate-eyed, slot-mouthed faces to glare at his laugh. "We don't know the girl is a slut," Harry apologizes. "All we know is her name is Melanie instead of Sue."

"You said you were on my side," Mrs. Springer says.

"I am, Ma, I am. I don't see why the kid has to come storming home; we gave him enough money to get him started out there, I'd like to see him get some kind of grip on the world. He's not going to get it hanging around here all summer."

"Oh, money," Janice says. "That's all you ever think about. And what have *you* ever done except hang around here? Your father got you one job and my father got you another, I don't call that any great adventure."

"That's not all I think about," he begins lamely, of money, before his mother-in-law interrupts.

"Harry doesn't want a home of his own," Ma Springer tells her daughter. When she gets excited and fearful of not making herself understood her face puffs up and goes mottled. "He has such disagreeable associations from the last time you two went out on your own."

Janice is firm, younger, in control. "Mother, you know nothing about it. You know nothing about life period. You sit in this house and watch idiotic game shows and talk on the phone to what friends you have that are still alive and then sit in judgment on Harry and me. You know *nothing* of life now. You have no *idea*."

"As if playing games at a country club with the nickel rich and coming home tiddled every night is enough to make you wise," the old lady comes back, holding on with one hand to the knob of the newel post as if to ease the pain in her ankles. "You come home," she goes on, "too silly to make your husband a decent supper and then want to bring this tramp into a house where I do all the housekeeping, even if I can scarcely stand to stand. I'm the one that would be here with them, you'd be off in that convertible. What will the neighbors make of it? What about the people in the church?"

"I don't care even if they care, which I dare say they won't," Janice says. "And to bring the church into it is ridiculous. The last minister at St. John's ran off with Mrs. Eckenroth and this one now is so gay I wouldn't let my boy go to his Sunday school, if I had a boy that age."

"Nellie didn't go that much anyway," Harry recalls. "He said it gave him headaches." He wants to lower the heat between the two women before it boils over into grief. He sees he must break this up, get a house of his own, before he runs out of gas. Stone outside, exposed beams inside, and a sunken living room: that is his dream.

"Melanie," his mother-in-law is saying, "what kind of name is that? It sounds colored."

"Oh Mother, don't drag out all your prejudices. You sit and giggle at the Jeffersons as if you're one of them and Harry and Charlie unload all their old gas-hogs on the blacks and if we take their money we can take what else they have to offer too."

Can Melanie actually be black? Harry is asking himself, thrilled. Little cocoa babies. Skeeter would be so pleased.

"Anyway," Janice is going on, looking frazzled suddenly, "nobody's said the girl is black, all we know is she hang glides."

"Or is that the other one?" Harry asks.

"If she comes, I go," Bessie Springer says. "Grace Stuhl has all those empty rooms now that Ralph's passed on and she's more than once said we should team up."

"Mother, I find that hum*il*iating, that you've been begging Grace Stuhl to take you in."

"I haven't been begging, the thought just naturally occurred to the both of us. I'd expect to be bought out here, though, and the values in the neighborhood have been going way up since they banned the through truck traffic."

"Mother. Harry *hates* this house."

He says, still hoping to calm these waters, "I don't hate it, exactly; I just think the space upstairs—"

"Harry," Janice says. "Why don't you go out and pick some lettuce from the garden like we said? Then we'll eat."

Gladly. He is glad to escape the house, the pinch of the women, their heat. Crazy the way they flog at each other with these ghosts of men, Daddy dead, Nelson gone, and even Harry himself a kind of ghost in the way they talk of him as if he wasn't standing right there. Day after day, mother and daughter sharing that same house, it's not natural. Like water blood must run or grow a scum. Old lady Springer always plump with that sausage look to her wrists and ankles but now her face puffy as well like those movie stars whose cheeks they stuff cotton up into to show them getting older. Her face not just plumper but wider as if a screw turning inside is spreading the sides of her skull apart, her eyes getting smaller, Janice heading the same way though she tries to keep trim, there's no stopping heredity. Rabbit notices now his own father talking in his own brain sometimes when he gets tired.

Bitter lemon fading in his mouth, an aluminum colander pleasantly light in his hand, he goes down the brick back steps into grateful space. He feels the neighborhood filter through to him and the voices in his brain grow still. Dark green around him is damp with coming evening, though this long day's lingering brightness surprises his eye above the shadowy masses of the trees. Rooftops and dormers notch the blue as it begins to blush brown; here also electric wires and television aerials mar with their scratches the soft beyond, a few swallows dipping as they do at day's end in the middle range of air above the merged back yards, where little more than a wire fence or a line of hollyhocks marks the divisions of property. When he listens he can hear the sounds of cooking clatter or late play, alive in this common realm with a dog's bark, a bird's *weep weep*, the rhythmic far tapping of a hammer. A crew of butch women has moved in a few houses down and they're always out in steel-toed boots and overalls with ladders and hammers fixing things, they can do it all, from rain gutters to cellar doors: terrific. He sometimes waves to them when he jogs by in twilight but they don't have much to say to him, a creature of another species.

Rabbit swings open the imperfect little gate he constructed two springs ago and enters the fenced rectangle of silent vegetable presences. The lettuce flourishes between a row of bean plants whose leaves are badly bug-eaten and whose stems collapse at a touch and a row of feathery carrot tops all but lost in an invasion of plantain and chickweed and purslane and a pulpy weed with white-and-yellow flowers that grows inches every night. It is easy to pull, its roots let go docilely, but there are so many he wearies within minutes of pulling and shaking the moist earth free from the roots and laying bundles of the weed along the chicken-wire fence as mulch and as barrier to the invading grasses. Grass that won't grow in the lawn where you plant it comes in here wild to multiply. Seed, so disgustingly much of it, Nature such a cruel smotherer. He thinks again of the dead he has known, the growingly many, and of the live child, if not his then some other father's, who visited him today with her long white legs propped up on cork heels, and of the other child, undoubtedly his, the genes show even in that quick scared way he looks at you, who has threatened to return. Rabbit pinches off the bigger lettuce leaves (but not the ones at the base so big as to be tough and bitter) and looks into his heart for welcome, welcoming love for his son. He finds instead a rumple of apprehensiveness in form and texture like a towel tumbled too soon from the dryer. He finds a hundred memories, some vivid as photographs and meaningless, snapped by the mind for reasons of its own, and others mere facts, things he knows are true but has no snapshot for. Our lives fade behind us before we die. He changed the boy's diapers in the sad apartment high on Wilbur Street, he lived with him for some wild months in an apple-green ranch house called 26 Vista Crescent in Penn Villas, and here at 89 Joseph he watched him become a high-school student with a wispy mustache that showed when he stood in the light, and a headband like an Indian's instead of getting a haircut, and a fortune in rock records kept in the sunny room whose drawn shades are above Harry's head now. He and Nelson have been through enough years together to turn a cedar post to rot and yet his son is less real to Harry than these crinkled leaves of lettuce he touches and plucks. Sad. Who says? The calm eyes of the girl who showed up at the lot today haunt the growing shadows, a mystery arrived at this time of his own numb life, death taking his measure with the invisible tapping of that neighborhood hammer: each day he is a little less afraid to die. He spots a Japanese beetle on a bean plant leaf and with a snap of his fingernail—big fingernails, with conspicuous cuticle moons—snaps the iridescent creature off. Die.

Back in the house, Janice exclaims, "You've picked enough for six of us!"

"Where'd Ma go?"

"She's in the front hall, on the telephone to Grace Stuhl. Really, she's impossible. I really think senility is setting in. Harry, what shall we *do*?"

"Ride with the punches?"

"Oh, great."

"Well honey it *is* her house, not ours and Nelson's."

"Oh, drop dead. You're no help." An illumination rises sluggishly within her sable, gin-blurred eyes. "You don't want to be any help," she announces. "You just like to see us fight."

The evening passes in a stale crackle of television and suppressed resentment. *Waitin' for some lover to call.* . . . Ma

Springer, having condescended to share with them at the kitchen table some lumpy mushroom soup Janice has warmed and the cold cuts slightly sweaty from waiting too long in the refrigerator and all that salad he picked, stalks upstairs to her own room and shuts the door with a firmness that must carry out into the neighborhood as far as the butch women's house. A few cars, looking for hot stuff, prowl by on Joseph Street, with that wet-tire sound that makes Harry and Janice feel alone as on an island. For supper they opened a half-gallon of Gallo Chablis and Janice keeps drifting into the kitchen to top herself up, so that by ten o'clock she is lurching in that way he hates. He doesn't blame people for many sins but he does hate uncoördination, the root of all evil as he feels it, for without coördination there can be no order, no connecting. In this state she bumps against doorframes coming through and sets her glass on the sofa arm so a big translucent lip of contents slops up and over into the fuzzy gray fabric. Together they sit through *Battlestar Galactica* and enough of *The Love Boat* to know it's not one of the good cruises. When she gets up to fill her glass yet again he switches to the Phillies game. The Phillies are being held to one hit by the Expos, he can't believe it, all that power. On the news, there is rioting in Levittown over gasoline, people are throwing beer bottles full of gasoline; they explode, it looks like old films of Vietnam or Budapest but it is Levittown right down the road, north of Philadelphia. A striking trucker is shown holding up a sign saying To HELL WITH SHELL. And Three Mile Island leaking radioactive neutrons just down the road in the other direction. The weather for tomorrow looks good, as a massive high continues to dominate from the Rocky Mountain region eastward all the way to Maine. Time for bed.

Harry knows in his bones, it has been borne in on him over the years, that on the nights of the days when Janice has fought with her mother and drunk too much she will want to make love. The first decade of their marriage, it was hard to get her to put out, there were a lot of things she wouldn't do and didn't even know were done and these seemed to be the things most on Rabbit's mind, but then with the affair with Charlie Stavros opening her up at about the time of the moon shot, and the style of the times proclaiming no holds barred, and for that matter death eating enough into her body for her to realize it wasn't such a precious vessel and there wasn't any superman to keep saving it for, Harry has no complaints. Indeed what complaints there might be in this line would come from her about him. Somewhere early in the Carter administration his interest, that had been pretty faithful, began to wobble and by now there is a real crisis of confidence. He blames it on money, on having enough at last, which has made him satisfied all over; also the money itself, relaxed in the bank, gets smaller in real value all the time, and this is on his mind, what to do about it, along with everything else: the Phils, and the dead, and golf. He has taken the game up with a passion since they joined the Flying Eagle, without getting much better at it, or at least without giving himself any happier impression of an absolute purity and power hidden within the coiling of his muscles than some lucky shots in those first casual games he played once did. It is like life itself in that its performance cannot be forced and its underlying principle shies from being permanently named. *Arms like ropes,* he tells himself sometimes, with considerable success, and then, when that goes bad, *Shift the weight.* Or, *Don't chicken-wing it,* or, *Keep the angle,* meaning the angle between club and arms when wrists are cocked. Sometimes he thinks it's all in the hands, and then in the shoulders, and even in the knees. When it's in the knees he can't control it. Basketball was somehow more instinctive. If you thought about merely walking down the street the way you think about golf you'd wind up falling off the curb. Yet a good straight drive or a soft chip stiff to the pin gives him the bliss that used to come thinking of some woman, imagining if only you and she were alone on a warm island.

Naked, Janice bumps against the doorframe from their bathroom back into their bedroom. Naked, she lurches onto the bed where he is trying to read the July issue of *Consumer Reports* and thrusts her tongue into his mouth. He tastes Gallo, baloney, and toothpaste while his mind is still trying to sort out the virtues and failings of the great range of can openers put to the test over five close pages of print. The Sunbeam units were most successful at opening rectangular and dented cans and yet pierced coffee cans with such force that grains of coffee spewed out onto the counter. Elsewhere, slivers of metal were dangerously produced, magnets gripped so strongly that the contents of the cans tended to spatter, blades failed to reach deep lips, and one small plastic insert so quickly wore away that the model (Ekco C865K) was judged Not Acceptable. Amid these fine discriminations Janice's tongue like an eyeless eager eel intrudes and angers him. Ever since in her late thirties she had her tubes burned to avoid any more bad side effects from the Pill, a demon of loss (never any more children never ever) has given her sexuality a false animation, a thrust somehow awry. Her eyes as her face backs off from the kiss he has resisted, squirming, have in them no essential recognition of him, only a glaze of liquor and blank unfriendly wanting. By the light by which he had been trying to read he sees the hateful aged flesh at the base of her throat, reddish and tense as if healed from a burn. He wouldn't see it so clearly if he didn't have his reading glasses on. "Jesus," he says, "at least let's wait till I turn out the light."

"I like it on." Her insistence is slurred. "I like to see all the gray hair on your chest."

This interests him. "Is there much?" He tries to see, past his chin. "It's not gray, it's just blond, isn't it?"

Janice pulls the bedsheet down to his waist and crouches to examine him hair by hair. Her breasts hang down so her nipples, bumply in texture like hamburger, sway an inch above his belly. "You do here, and here." She pulls each gray hair.

"Ouch. Damn you, Janice. *Stop*." He pushes his stomach up so her nipples vanish and her breasts are squashed against her own frail ribs. Gripping the hair of her head in one fist in his rage at being invaded, the other hand still holding the magazine in which he was trying to read about magnets gripping, he arches his spine so she is thrown from his body to her side of the bed. In her boozy haze mistaking this for love play, Janice tugs the sheet down still lower on him and takes his prick in a fumbling, twittering grip. Her touch is cold from having just washed her hands in the bathroom. The next page of *Consumer Reports* is printed on blue and asks, *Summer cooling, 1979: air-conditioner or fan?* He tries to skim the list of advantages and disadvantages peculiar to each (*Bulky and heavy to install* as opposed to *Light and portable*, *Expensive to run* as against *Inexpensive to run*, the fan seems to be scoring all the points) but can't quite disassociate himself from the commotion below his waist, where Janice's anxious fingers seem to be asking the same question over and over, without getting the answer they want. Furious, he throws the magazine against the wall behind which Ma Springer sleeps. More carefully, he removes his reading glasses and puts them in his bedside table drawer and switches off the bedside lamp.

His wife's importunate flesh must then compete with the sudden call to sleep that darkness brings. It has been a long day. He was awake at six-thirty and got up at seven. His eyelids have grown too thin to tolerate the early light. Even now near midnight he feels tomorrow's early dawn rotating toward him. He recalls again the blue-eyed apparition who seemed to be his and Ruth's genes mixed; he is reminded then from so long ago of that Ruth whom he fucked upwards the first time, saying "Hey" in his surprise at her beauty, her body one long underbelly erect in light from the streetlamp outside on Summer Street, his prick erect in her ripe, ripe loveliness above him, *Hey*, it seems a melancholy falling that an act so glorious has been dwindled to this blurred burrowing of two old bodies, one drowsy and one drunk. Janice's rummaging at his prick has become hostile now as it fails to rise; her attention burns upon it like solar rays focused by a magnifying glass upon a scrap of silk, kids used to kill ants that way. Harry watched but never participated. We are cruel enough without meaning to be. He resents that in her eagerness for some dilution of her sense of being forsaken, having quarrelled with her mother, and perhaps also afraid of their son's return, Janice gives him no space of secrecy in which blood can gather as it did behind his fly in ninth-grade algebra sitting beside Lotty Bingaman who in raising her hand to show she had the answers showed him wisps of armpit hair and pressed the thin cotton of her blouse tighter against the elastic trusswork of her bra, so its salmon color strained through. Then the fear was the bell would ring and he would have to stand with this hard-on.

He resolves to suck Janice's tits, to give himself a chance to pull himself together, this is embarrassing. A pause at the top, you need a pause at the top to generate momentum. His spit glimmers within her dark shape above him; the headboard of their bed is placed between two windows shaded from the light of sun and moon alike by a great copper beech whose leaves yet allow a little streetlight through.

"That feels nice." He wishes she wouldn't say this. Nice isn't enough. Without some shadow of assault or outrage it becomes another task, another duty. To think, all along, that Lotty was sitting there itching to be fucked. It wasn't just him. She was holding a dirty yearning between her legs just like the lavatory walls said, those drawings and words put there by the same kids who magnified the ants to death, that little sticky pop they died with, you could hear it, did girls too make a little sticky noise when they opened up? The thought of her *knowing* when she raised her hand that her blouse was tugged into wrinkles all pointing to the tip of her tit and that an edge of bra peeped out through the cotton armhole with those little curly virgin hairs and that he was watching for it all to happen does make blood gather. In the fumbly worried dark, with Ma Springer sleeping off her sulk a thickness of plaster away, Harry as if casually presents his stiffened prick to Janice's hand. *Hot stuuuuff.*

But wanderings within her own brain have blunted her ardor and her touch conveys this, it is too heavy, so in a desperate mood of self-rescue he hisses "Suck" in her ear, "Suck." Which she does, turning her back, her head heavy on his belly. Diagonal on the bed he stretches one arm as if preparing to fly and caresses her ass, these lower globes of hers less spherical than once they were, and the fur between more findable by his fingers. She learned to blow when she went away with Stavros but doesn't really get her head into it, nibbles more, the top inch or two. To keep himself excited he tries to remember Ruth, that exalted "Hey" and the way she swallowed it once, but the effort brings back with such details the guilt of their months together and, betrayal betrayed, his desertion and the final sour sorrow of it all.

Janice lets him slide from her mouth and asks, "What are you thinking about?"

"Work," he lies. "Charlie worries me. He's taking such good care of himself you hate to ask him to do anything. I seem to handle most of the customers now."

"Well why not? You give yourself twice the salary he gets and he's been there forever."

"Yeah, but I married the boss's daughter. He could have, but didn't."

"Marriage wasn't our thing," Janice says.

"What was?"

"Never mind."

Absentmindedly he strokes her long hair, soft from all that swimming, as it flows on his abdomen. "Pair of kids came into the lot late today," he begins to tell her, then thinks better of it. Now that her sexual push is past, his prick has hardened, the competing muscles of anxiety having at last relaxed. But she, she is relaxed all over, asleep with his prick in her face. "Want me inside?" he asks softly, getting no answer. He moves her off his chest and works her inert body around so they lie side by side and he can fuck her from behind. She wakes enough to cry "Oh" when he penetrates. Slickly admitted, he pumps slowly, pulling the sheet up over them both. Not hot enough yet for the fan versus air-conditioner decision, both are tucked around the attic somewhere, back under the dusty eaves, strain your back lifting it out, he has never liked the chill of air-conditioning even when it was only to be had at the movies and thought to be a great treat drawing you in right off the hot sidewalk, the word COOL in blue-green with icicles on the marquee, always seemed to him healthier to live in the air God gave however lousy and let your body adjust, Nature can adjust to anything. Still, some of these nights, sticky, and the cars passing below with that wet-tire sound, the kids with their windows open or tops down and radios blaring just at the moment of dropping off to sleep, your skin prickling wherever it touched cloth and a single mosquito alive in the room. His prick is stiff as stone inside a sleeping woman. He strokes her ass, the crease where it nestles against his belly, must start jogging again, the crease between its halves and that place within the crease, opposite of a nipple, dawned on him gradually over these years that she had no objection to being touched there, seemed to like it when she was under him his hand beneath her bottom. He touches himself too now and then to test if he is holding hard; he is, thick as a tree where it comes up out of the grass, the ridges of the roots, her twin dark moons swallowing and letting go, a little sticky sound. The long slack oily curve of her side, ribs to hip bone, floats under his fingertips idle as a gull's glide. Love has lulled her, liquor has carried her off. Bless that dope. "Jan?" he whispers. "You awake?" He is not displeased to be thus stranded, another consciousness in bed is a responsibility, a snag in the flow of his thoughts. Further on in that issue an article *How to shop for a car loan* he ought to look at for professional reasons though it's not the sort of thing that interests him, he can't get it out of his head how they noticed those coffee grounds that jump out of the can when punctured. Janice snores: a single rasp of breath taken underwater, at some deep level where her nose becomes a harp. Big as the night her ass unconscious wraps him all around in this room where dabs of streetlight sifted by the beech shuffle on the ceiling. He decides to fuck her, the stiffness in his cock is killing him. His hard-on was her idea anyway. The Japanese beetle he flicked away comes into his mind as a model of delicacy. Hold tight, dream girl. He sets three fingers on her flank, the pinky lifted as in a counting game. He is stealthy so as not to wake her but single in his purpose, quick, and pure. The climax freezes his scalp and stops his heart, all stealthy; he hasn't come with such a thump in months. So who says he's running out of gas?

"I hit the ball O.K.," Rabbit says next afternoon, "but damned if I could score." He is sitting in green bathing trunks at a white outdoor table at the Flying Eagle Tee and Racquet Club with the partners of his round and their wives and, in the case of Buddy Inglefinger, girlfriend. Buddy had once had a wife too but she left him for a telephone lineman down near West Chester. You could see how that might happen because Buddy's girlfriends are sure a sorry lot.

"When did you *ever* score?" Ronnie Harrison asks him so loudly heads in the swimming pool turn around. Rabbit has known Ronnie for thirty years and never liked him, one of those locker-room show-offs always soaping himself for everybody to see and giving the JVs redbellies and out on the basketball court barging around all sweat and elbows trying to make up in muscle what he lacked in style. Yet when Harry and Janice joined Flying Eagle there old Ronnie was, with a respectable job at Schuylkill Mutual and this nice proper wife who taught third grade for years and must be great in bed, because that's all Ronnie ever used to talk about, he was like frantic on the subject, in the locker room. His kinky brass-colored hair, that began to thin right after high school, is pretty thoroughly worn through on top now, and the years and respectability have drained some pink out of him; the skin from his temples to the corners of his eyes is papery and bluish, and Rabbit doesn't remember that his eyelashes were white. He likes playing golf with Ronnie because he loves beating him, which isn't too hard: he has one of those herky-jerky punch swings short stocky guys gravitate toward and when he gets excited he tends to roundhouse a big banana right into the woods.

"I heard Harry was a big scorer," Ronnie's wife Thelma says softly. She has a narrow forgettable face and still wears that quaint old-fashioned kind of one-piece bathing suit with a little pleated skirt. Often she has a towel across her shoulders or around her ankles as if to protect her skin from the sun; except for her sunburnt nose she is the same sallow color all over. Her wavy mousy hair is going gray strand by strand. Rabbit can never look at her without wondering what she must do to keep Harrison happy. He senses intelligence in her but intelligence in women has never much interested him.

"I set the B-league county scoring record in 1951," he says, to defend himself, and to defend himself further adds, "Big deal."

"It's been broken long since," Ronnie feels he has to explain. "By blacks."

"Every record has," Webb Murkett interposes, being tactful. "I don't know, it seems like the miles these kids run now have shrunk. In swimming they can't keep the record books up to date." Webb is the oldest man of their regular foursome, fifty and then some—a lean thoughtful gentleman in roofing and siding contracting and supply with a calming gravel voice, his long face broken into longitudinal strips by creases and his hazel eyes almost lost under an amber tangle of eyebrows. He is the steadiest golfer, too. The one unsteady thing about him, he is on his third wife; this is Cindy, a plump brown-backed honey still smelling of high school, though they have two little ones, a boy and a girl, ages five and three. Her hair is cut short

and lies wet in one direction, as if surfacing from a dive, and
when she smiles her teeth look unnaturally even and white in
her tan face, with pink spots of peeling on the roundest part
of her cheeks; she has an exciting sexually neutral look, though
her boobs slosh and shiver in the triangular little hammocks of
her bra. The suit is one of those minimal black ones with only
a string or two between the nape of her neck and where her
ass begins to divide, a cleft more or less visible depending on
the sag of her black diaper. Harry admires Webb. Webb always
swings within himself, and gets good roll.

"Better nutrition, don't you think that's it?" Buddy Inglefinger's girl pipes up, in a little-girl reedy voice that doesn't
go with her pushed-in face. She is some kind of physical ther-
apist, though her own shape isn't too great. The girls Buddy
brings around are a good lesson to Harry in the limits of being
single—hard little secretaries and restaurant hostesses, witchy-
looking former flower children with grizzled ponytails and flat
chests full of Navajo jewelry, overweight assistant heads of personnel in one of those grim new windowless office buildings
a block back from Weiser where they spend all day putting
computer print-outs in the wastebasket. Women pickled in
limbo, their legs chalky and their faces slightly twisted, as if
they had been knocked into their thirties by a sideways blow.
They remind Harry somehow of pirates, jaunty and maimed,
though without the eye patches. What the hell was this one's
name? She had been introduced around not a half hour ago,
but when everybody was still drunk on golf.

Buddy brought her, so he can't let her two cents hang up
there while the silence gets painful. He fills in, "My guess is it's
mostly in the training. Coaches at even the secondary level have
all these techniques that in the old days only the outstanding
athlete would discover, you know, pragmatically. Nowadays the
outstanding isn't that outstanding, there's a dozen right behind
him. Or her." He glances at each of the women in a kind of dutiful tag. Feminism won't catch him off guard, he's traded jabs
in too many singles bars. "And in countries like East Germany
or China they're pumping these athletes full of steroids, like
beef cattle, they're hardly human." Buddy wears steel-rimmed
glasses of a style that only lathe operators used to employ, to
keep shavings out of their eyes. Buddy does something with

electronics and has a mind like that, too precise. He goes on, to bring it home, "Even golf. Palmer and now Nicklaus have been trampled out of sight by these kids nobody has heard of, the colleges down south clone 'em, you can't keep their names straight from one tournament to the next."

Harry always tries to take an overview. "The records fall because they're there," he says. "Aaron shouldn't have been playing, they kept him in there just so he could break Ruth's record. I can remember when a five-minute mile in high school was a miracle. Now girls are doing it."

"It is amazing," Buddy's girl puts in, this being her conversation, "what the human body can do. Any one of us women here could go out now and pick up a car by the front bumper, if we were motivated. If say there was a child of ours under the tires. You read about incidents like that all the time, and at the hospital where I trained the doctors could lay the statistics of it right out on paper. We don't use half the muscle-power we have."

Webb Murkett kids, "Hear that, Cin? Gas stations all closed down, you can carry the Audi home. Seriously, though. I've always marvelled at these men who know a dozen languages. If the brain is a computer think of all the gray cells this entails. There seems to be lots more room in there, though."

His young wife silently lifts her hands to twist some water from her hair, that is almost too short to grab. This action gently lifts her tits in their sopping black small slings and reveals the shape of each erect nipple. A white towel is laid across her lap as if to relieve Harry from having to think about her crotch. What turns him off about Buddy's girl, he realizes, is not only does she have pimples on her chin and forehead but on her thighs, high on the inside, like something venereal. Georgene? Geraldine? She is going on in that reedy too-eager voice, "Or the way these yogas can lift themselves off the ground or go back in time for thousands of years. Edgar Cayce has example after example. It's nothing supernatural, I can't believe in God, there's too much suffering, they're just using human powers we all have and never develop. You should all read the Tibetan Book of the Dead."

"Really?" Thelma Harrison says dryly. "Who's the author?"

Now silence does invade their group. A greenish reflective

wobble from the pool washes ghostly and uneasy across their faces and a child gasping as he swims can be heard. Then Webb kindly says, "Closer to home now, we've had a spooky experience lately. I bought one of these Polaroid SX-70 Land Cameras as kind of a novelty, to give the kids a charge, and all of us can't stop being fascinated, it is super*na*tural, to watch that image develop right under your eyes."

"The kind," Cindy says, "that spits it out at you like this." She makes a cross-eyed face and thrusts out her tongue with a *thrrupp*ing noise. All the men laugh, and laugh.

"*Consumer Reports* had something on it," Harry says.

"It's magical," Cindy tells them. "Webb gets really turned on." When she grins her teeth look stubby, the healthy gums come so babyishly low.

"Why is my glass empty?" Janice asks.

"Losers buy," Harry virtually shouts. Such loudness years ago would have been special to male groups but now both sexes have watched enough beer commercials on television to know that this is how to act, jolly and loud, on weekends, in the bar, beside the barbecue grill, on beaches and sundecks and mountainsides. "Winners bought the first round," he calls needlessly, as if among strangers or men without memories, while several arms flail for the waitress.

Harry's team lost the Nassau, but he feels it was his partner's fault. Buddy is such a flub artist, even when he hits two good shots he skulls the chip and takes three putts to get down. Whereas Harry as he has said hit the ball well, if not always straight: arms like ropes, start down slow, and *look at the ball* until it seems to swell. He ended with a birdie, on the long par-five that winds in around the brook with its watercress and sandy orange bottom almost to the clubhouse lawn; and that triumph—the wooden gobbling sound the cup makes when a long putt falls!—eclipses many double bogeys and suffuses with a limpid certainty of his own omnipotence and immortality the sight of the scintillating chlorinated water, the sunstruck faces and torsos of his companions, and the undulant shadow-pitted flank of Mt. Pemaquid where its forest begins above the shaven bright stripes of the fairways. He feels brother to this mountain in the day's declining sunlight. Mt. Pemaquid has only been recently tamed; for the two centuries while Mt. Judge presided above the metropolitan burgeoning of Brewer, the mountain nearby yet remained if not quite a wilderness a strange and forbidding place, where resort hotels failed and burned down and only hikers and lovers and escaping criminals ventured. The developers of the Flying Eagle (its name plucked from a bird, probably a sparrow hawk, the first surveyor spotted and took as an omen) bought three hundred acres of the lower slopes cheap; as the bulldozers ground the second-growth ash, poplar, hickory, and dogwood into muddy troughs that would become fairways and terraced tennis courts, people said the club would fail, the county already had the Brewer Country Club south of the city for the doctors and the Jews and ten miles north the Tulpehocken Club behind its fieldstone walls and tall wrought-iron fencing for the old mill-owning families and their lawyers and for the peasantry several nine-hole public courses tucked around in the farmland. But there was a class of the young middle-aged that had arisen in the retail businesses and service industries and software end of the new technology and that did not expect liveried barmen and secluded card-rooms, that did not mind the pre-fab clubhouse and sweep-it-yourself tennis courts of the Flying Eagle; to them the polyester wall-to-wall carpeting of the locker rooms seemed a luxury, and a Coke machine in a cement corridor a friendly sight. They were happy to play winter rules all summer long on the immature, patchy fairways and to pay for all their privileges the five hundred, now risen to six-fifty, in annual dues, plus a small fortune in chits. Fred Springer for years had angled for admission to the Brewer C.C.—the Tulpehocken was as out of reach as the College of Cardinals, he knew that—and had failed; now his daughter Janice wears whites and signs chits just like the heiresses of Sunflower Beer and Frankhauser Steel. Just like a du Pont. At the Flying Eagle Harry feels exercised, cleansed, cherished; the biggest man at the table, he lifts his hand and a girl in the restaurant uniform of solid green blouse and checked skirt of white and green comes and takes his order for more drinks on this Sunday of widespread gas dearth. She doesn't ask his name; the people here know it. Her own name is stitched *Sandra* on her blouse pocket; she has milky skin like his daughter but is shorter, and the weary woman she will be is already moving into her face.

"Do you believe in astrology?" Buddy's girl abruptly asks Cindy Murkett. Maybe she's a Lesbian, is why Harry can't remember her name. It was a name soft around the edges, not Gertrude.

"I don't know," Cindy says, the widened eyes of her surprise showing very white in her mask of tan. "I look at the horoscope in the papers sometimes. Some of the things they say ring so true, but isn't there a trick to that?"

"It's no trick, it's ancient science. It's the most ancient science there is."

This assault on Cindy's repose agitates Harry so he turns to Webb and asks if he watched the Phillies game last night.

"The Phillies are dead," Ronnie Harrison butts in.

Buddy comes up with the statistic that they've lost twenty-three of their last thirty-four games.

"I was brought up a Catholic," Cindy is saying to Buddy's girl in a voice so lowered Harry has to strain to hear. "And the priests said such things are the work of the Devil." She fingers as she confides this the small crucifix she wears about her throat on a chain so fine it has left no trace in her tan.

"Bowa's being out has hurt them quite a lot," Webb says judiciously, and pokes another cigarette into his creased face, lifting his rubbery upper lip automatically like a camel. He shot an 84 this afternoon, with a number of three-putt greens.

Janice is asking Thelma where she bought that lovely bathing suit. She must be drunk. "You can't find that kind at all in Kroll's anymore," Rabbit hears her say. Janice is wearing an old sort of Op-pattern blue two-piece, with a white cardigan bought to go with her tennis whites hung capelike over her shoulders. She holds a cigarette in her hand and Webb Murkett leans over to light it with his turquoise propane lighter. She's not so bad, Harry thinks, remembering how he fucked her in her sleep. Or was it, for she seemed to moan and stop snoring afterwards. Compared to Thelma's passive sallow body Janice's figure has energy, edge, the bones of the knees pressing their shape against the skin as she leans forward to accept his light. She does this with a certain accustomed grace. Webb respects her, as Fred Springer's daughter.

Harry wonders where his own daughter is this afternoon, out in the country. Doing some supper chore, having come back from feeding chickens or whatever. Sundays in the sticks aren't so different, animals don't know about holidays. Would she have gone to church this morning? Ruth had no use for that. He can't picture Ruth in the country at all. For him, she was city, those solid red brick rows of Brewer that take what comes. The drinks come. Grateful cries, like on the beer commercials, and Cindy Murkett decides to earn hers by going for another swim. When she stands, the backs of her thighs are printed in squares and her skimpy black bathing suit bottom, still soaked, clings in two thin arcs well below two dimples symmetrically set in her fat like little whirlpools; the sight dizzies Harry. Didn't he used to take Ruth to the public pool in West Brewer? Memorial Day. There was the smell of grass pressed under your damp towel spread out in the shade of the trees away from the tile pool. Now you sit in chairs of enamelled wire that unless you have a cushion print a waffle pattern on the backs of your thighs. The mountain is drawing closer. Sun reddening beyond the city dusts with gold the tips of trees high like a mane on the crest of Pemaquid and deepens the pockets of dark between each tree in the undulating forest that covers like deep-piled carpet the acreage between crest and course. Along the far eleventh fairway men are still picking their way, insect-sized. As his eyes are given to these distances Cindy flat-dives and a few drops of the splash prick Harry's naked chest, that feels broad as the basking mountain. He frames in his mind the words, *I heard a funny story on the radio yesterday driving home. . . .*

". . . if I had your nice legs," Ronnie's plain wife is concluding to Janice.

"Oh but you still have a waist. Creeping middle-itis, that's what I've got. Harry says I'm shaped like a pickle." Giggle. First she giggles, then she begins to lurch.

"He looks asleep."

He opens his eyes and announces to the air, "I heard a funny story on the radio yesterday driving home."

"Fire Ozark," Ronnie is insisting loudly. "He's lost their respect, he's demoralizing. Until they can Ozark and trade Rose away, the Phillies are D, E, A, D, dead."

"I'm listening," Buddy's awful girlfriend tells Harry, so he has to go on.

"Oh just some doctor down in Baltimore, the radio announcer said he was hauled into court for killing a goose on the course with a golf club."

"Course on the golf with a goose club," Janice giggles. Some day what would give him great pleasure would be to take a large round rock and crush her skull in with it.

"Where'd you hear this, Harry?" Webb Murkett asks him, coming in late but politely tilting his long head, one eye shut against the smoke of his cigarette.

"On the radio yesterday, driving home," Harry answers, sorry he has begun.

"Speaking of yesterday," Buddy has to interrupt, "I saw a gas line five blocks long. That Sunoco at the corner of Ash and Fourth, it went down Fourth to Buttonwood, Buttonwood to Fifth, Fifth back to Ash, and then a new line beginning the other side of Ash. They had guys directing and everything. I couldn't believe it, and cars were still getting into it. Five fucking blocks long."

"Big heating-oil dealer who's one of our clients," Ronnie says, "says they have plenty of crude, it's just they've decided to put the squeeze on gasoline and make more heating oil out of it. The crude. In their books winter's already here. I asked the guy what was going to happen to the average motorist and he looked at me funny and said, 'He can go screw himself instead of driving every weekend to the Jersey Shore.'"

"Ronnie, Harry's trying to tell a story," Thelma says.

"It hardly seems worth it," he says, enjoying now the prolonged focus on him, the comedy of delay. Sunshine on the mountain. The second gin is percolating through his system and elevating his spirits. He loves this crowd, his crowd, and the crowds at the other tables too, that are free to send delegates over and mingle with theirs, everybody knowing everybody else, and the kids in the pool, that somebody would save even if that caramel-colored lifeguard-girl popping bubble gum weren't on duty, and loves the fact that this is all on credit, the club not taking its bite until the tenth of every month.

Now they coax him. "Come on, Harry, don't be a prick," Buddy's girl says. She's using his name now, he has to find hers. Gretchen. Ginger. Maybe those aren't actually pimples on her thighs, just a rash from chocolate or poison oak. She looks allergic, that pushed-in face, like she'd have trouble breathing. Defects come in clumps.

"So this doctor," he concedes, "is hauled into court for killing a goose on the course with a golf club."

"What club?" Ronnie asks.

"I knew you'd ask that," Harry says. "If not you, some other jerk."

"I'd think a sand wedge," Buddy says, "right at the throat. It'd clip the head right off."

"Too short in the handle, you couldn't get close enough," Ronnie argues. He squints as if to judge a distance. "I'd say a five or even an easy four would be the right stick. Hey Harry, how about that five-iron I put within a gimme on the fifteenth from way out on the other side of the sand trap? In deep rough yet."

"You nudged it," Harry says.

"Heh?"

"I saw you nudge the ball up to give yourself a lie."

"Let's get this straight. You're saying I cheated."

"Something like that."

"Let's hear the story, Harry," Webb Murkett says, lighting another cigarette to dramatize his patience.

Ginger was in the ballpark. Thelma Harrison is staring at him with her big brown sunglasses and that is distracting too. "So the doctor's defense evidently was that he had hit the goose with a golf ball and injured it badly enough he had to put it out of its misery. Then this announcer said, it seemed cute at the time, she was a female announcer—"

"Wait a minute sweetie, I don't understand," Janice says. "You mean he threw a golf ball at this goose?"

"Oh my God," Rabbit says, "am I ever sorry I got started on this. Let's go home."

"No *tell* me," Janice says, looking panicked.

"He didn't *throw* the ball, the goose was on the fairway probably by some pond and the guy's drive or whatever it was—"

"Could have been his second shot and he shanked it," Buddy offers.

His nameless girlfriend looks around and in that fake little-girl voice asks, "Are geese allowed on golf courses? I mean, that may be stupid, Buddy's the first golfer I've gone out with—"

"You call *that* a golfer?" Ronnie interrupts.

Buddy tells them, "I've read somewhere about a course in Alaska where these caribou wander. Maybe it's Sweden."

"I've heard of moose on courses in Maine," Webb Murkett says. Lowering sun flames in his twisted eyebrows. He seems sad. Maybe he's feeling the liquor too, for he rambles on, "Wonder why you never hear of a Swedish golfer. You hear of Bjorn Borg, and this skier Stenmark."

Rabbit decides to ride it through. "So the announcer says, 'A mercy killing, or murder most foul?'"

"Ouch," someone says.

Ronnie is pretending to ruminate, "Maybe you'd be better off with a four-wood, and play the goose off your left foot."

"Nobody heard the punch line," Harry protests.

"I heard it," Thelma Harrison says.

"We all heard it," Buddy says. "It's just very distressing to me," he goes on, and looks very severe in his steel-rimmed glasses, so the women at first take him seriously, "that nobody here, I mean *no*body, has shown any sympathy for the goose."

"Somebody sympathized enough to bring the man to court," Webb Murkett points out.

"I discover myself," Buddy complains sternly, "in the midst of a crowd of people who while pretending to be liberal and tolerant are really anti-goose."

"Who, me?" Ronnie says, making his voice high as if goosed. Rabbit hates this kind of humor, but the others seem to enjoy it, including the women.

Cindy has returned glistening from her swim. Standing there with her bathing suit slightly awry, she tugs it straight and blushes in the face of their laughter. "Are you talking about me?" The little cross glints beneath the hollow of her throat. Her feet look pale on the poolside flagstones. Funny, how pale the tops of feet stay.

Webb gives his wife's wide hips a sideways hug. "No, honey. Harry was telling us a shaggy goose story."

"Tell me, Harry."

"Not now. Nobody liked it. Webb will tell you."

Sandra in her green and white uniform comes up to them. "Mrs. Angstrom."

The words shock Harry, as if his mother has been resurrected. "Yes," Janice answers matter-of-factly.

"Your mother is on the phone."

"Oh Lordie, what now?" Janice stands, lurches slightly, composes herself. She takes her beach towel from the back of her chair and wraps it around her hips rather than walk in merely a bathing suit past dozens of people into the clubhouse. "What do you think it is?" she asks Harry.

He shrugs. "Maybe she wants to know what kind of baloney we're having tonight."

A dig in that, delivered openly. The awful girlfriend titters. Harry is ashamed of himself, thinking in contrast of Webb's sideways hug of Cindy's hips. This kind of crowd will do a marriage in if you let it. He doesn't want to get sloppy.

In defiance Janice asks, "Honey, could you order me another vod-and-ton while I'm gone?"

"No." He softens this to, "I'll think about it," but the chill has been put on the party.

The Murketts consult and conclude it may be time to go, they have a thirteen-year-old babysitter, a neighbor's child. The same sunlight that ignited Webb's eyebrows lights the halo of fine hairs standing up from the goosebumps on Cindy's thighs. Not bothering with any towel around her, she saunters to the ladies' locker room to change, her pale feet leaving wet prints on the gray flagstones. Wait, wait, the Sunday, the weekend cannot be by, a golden sip remains in the glass. On the transparent tabletop among the wire chairs drinks have left a ghostly clockwork of rings refracted into visibility by the declining light. What can Janice's mother want? She has called out to them from a darker older world he remembers but wants to stay buried, a world of constant clothing and airless front parlors, of coal bins and narrow houses with spitefully drawn shades, where the farmer's drudgery and the millworker's ruled land and city. Here, clean children shivering with their sudden emergence into the thinner element are handed towels by their mothers. Cindy's towel hangs on her empty chair. To be Cindy's towel and to be sat upon by her: the thought dries Rabbit's mouth. To stick your tongue in just as far as it would go while her pussy tickles your nose. No acne in that crotch.

Heaven. He looks up and sees the shaggy mountain shouldering into the sun still, though the chairs are making long shadows, lozenge checkerboards. Buddy Inglefinger is saying to Webb Murkett in a low voice whose vehemence is not ironical, "Ask yourself sometime who benefits from inflation. The people in debt benefit, society's losers. The government benefits because it collects more in taxes without raising the rates. Who doesn't benefit? The man with money in his pocket, the man who's paid his bills. That's why"—Buddy's voice drops to a conspiratorial hiss—"that man is vanishing like the red Indian. Why should I work," he asks Webb, "when the money is taken right out of my pocket for the benefit of those who don't?"

Harry is thinking his way along the mountain ridge, where clouds are lifting like a form of steam. As if in driven motion Mt. Pemaquid cleaves the summer sky and sun, though poolside is in shadow now. Thelma is saying cheerfully to the girlfriend, "Astrology, palm-reading, psychiatry—I'm for all of it. Anything that helps get you through." Harry is thinking of his own parents. They should have belonged to a club. Living embattled, Mom feuding with the neighbors, Pop and his union hating the men who owned the printing plant where he worked his life away, both of them scorning the few kin that tried to keep in touch, the four of them, Pop and Mom and Hassy and Mim, against the world and a certain guilt attaching to any reaching up and outside for a friend. *Don't trust anybody: Andy Mellon doesn't, and I don't.* Dear Pop. He never got out from under. Rabbit basks above that old remembered world, rich, at rest.

Buddy's voice nags on, aggrieved. "Money that goes out of one pocket goes into somebody else's, it doesn't just evaporate. The big boys are getting rich out of this."

A chair scrapes and Rabbit feels Webb stand. His voice comes from a height, gravelly, humorously placating. "Become a big boy yourself I guess is the only answer."

"Oh sure," Buddy says, knowing he is being put off.

A tiny speck, a bird, the fabled eagle it might be, no, from the motionlessness of its wings a buzzard, is flirting in flight with the ragged golden-green edge of the mountain, now above it like a speck on a Kodak slide, now below it out of sight, while a blue-bellied cloud unscrolls, endlessly, powerfully. Another chair is scraped on the flagstones. His name, "Harry," is sharply called, in Janice's voice.

He lowers his gaze at last out of glory and as his eyes adjust his forehead momentarily hurts, a small arterial pain; perhaps with such a negligible unexplained ache do men begin their deaths, some slow as being tumbled by a cat and some fast as being struck by a hawk. Cancer, coronary. "What did Bessie want?"

Janice's tone is breathless, faintly stricken. "She says Nelson's come. With this girl."

"Melanie," Harry says, pleased to have remembered. And his remembering brings along with it Buddy's girlfriend's name. Joanne. "It was nice to have met you, Joanne," he says in parting, shaking her hand. Making a good impression. Casting his shadow.

As Harry drives them home in Janice's Mustang convertible with the top down, air pours over them and lends an illusion of urgent and dangerous speed. Their words are snatched from their mouths. "What the fuck are we going to do with the kid?" he asks her.

"How do you mean?" With her dark hair being blown back, Janice looks like a different person. Eyes asquint against the rush of wind and her upper lip lifted, a hand held near her ear to keep her rippling silk head scarf from flying away. Liz Taylor in *A Place in the Sun*. Even the little crow's-feet at the corner of her eye look glamorous. She is wearing her tennis dress and the white cashmere cardigan.

"I mean is he going to get a job or what?"

"Well Harry. He's still in college."

"He doesn't act like it." He feels he has to shout. "I wasn't so fucking fortunate as to get to college and the guys that did didn't goof off in Colorado hang gliding and God knows what until their father's money ran out."

"You don't know what they did. Anyway times are different. Now you be nice to Nelson. After the things you put him through—"

"Not just me."

"—after what he went through you should be grateful he *wants* to come home. Ever."

"I don't know."

"You don't know *what?*"

"This doesn't feel good to me. I've been too happy lately."

"Don't be irrational," Janice says.

She is not, this implies. But one of their bonds has always been that her confusion keeps pace with his. As the wind pours past he feels a scared swift love for something that has no name. Her? His life? The world? Coming from the Mt. Pemaquid direction, you see the hillside borough of Mt. Judge from a spread-out angle altogether different from what you see coming home from the Brewer direction: the old box factory a long lean-windowed slab down low by the dried-up falls, sent underground to make electricity, and the new supertall Exxon and Mobil signs on their tapered aluminum poles along Route 422 as eerie as antennae arrived out of space. The town's stacked windows burn orange in the sun that streams level up the valley, and from this angle great prominence gathers to the sandstone spire of the Lutheran church where Rabbit went to Sunday school under crusty old Fritz Kruppenbach, who pounded in the lesson that life has no terrors for those with faith but for those without faith there can be no salvation and no peace. *No* peace. A sign says THICKLY SETTLED. As the Mustang slows, Harry is moved to confess to Janice, "I started to tell you last night, this young couple came into the lot yesterday and the girl reminded me of Ruth. She would be about the right age too. Slimmer, and not much like her in her way of talking, but there was, I don't know, something."

"Your imagination is what it was. Did you get the girl's name?"

"I asked, but she wouldn't give it. She was cute about it, too. Kind of flirty, without anything you could put your finger on."

"And you think that girl was your daughter."

From her tone he knows he shouldn't have confessed. "I didn't say that exactly."

"Then what did you say? You're telling me you're still thinking of this bag you fucked twenty years ago and now you and she have a darling little *baby*." He glances over and Janice no longer suggests Elizabeth Taylor, her lips all hard and crinkled as if baked in her fury. Ida Lupino. Where did they go, all the great Hollywood bitches? In town for years there had been just a Stop sign at the corner where Jackson slants down into Central but the other year after the burgess's own son smashed up a car running the sign the borough put in a light, that is mostly on blink, yellow this way and red the other. He touches the brake and takes the left turn. Janice leans with the turn to keep her mouth close to his ear. "You are crazy," she shouts. "You *al*ways want what you don't have instead of what you *do*. Getting all cute and smiley in the face thinking about this *girl* that doesn't exist while your *real* son, that you had with your *wife*, is waiting at home right now and you saying you wished he'd stay in Colo*ra*do."

"I do wish that," Harry says—anything to change the subject even slightly. "You're wrong about my wanting what I don't have. I pretty much like what I have. The trouble with that is, then you get afraid somebody will take it from you."

"Well it's not going to be Nelson, he wants nothing from you except a little love and he doesn't get that. I don't know *why* you're such an unnatural father."

So they can finish their argument before they reach Ma Springer's he has slowed their speed up Jackson, under the shady interlock of maples and horsechestnuts, that makes the hour feel later than it is. "The kid has it in for me," he says mildly, to see what this will bring on.

It re-excites her. "You keep saying that but it's not *true*. He *loves* you. Or did." Where the sky shows through the mingled tree tops there is still a difference of light, a flickering that beats upon their faces and hands mothlike. In a sullen semi-mollified tone she says, "One thing definite, I don't want to hear any more about your darling illegitimate daughter. It's a disgusting idea."

"I know. I don't know why I mentioned it." He had mistaken the two of them for one and entrusted to her this ghost of his alone. A mistake married people make.

"Dis*gus*ting!" Janice cries.

"I'll never mention it again," he promises.

They ease into Joseph, at the corner where the fire hydrant still wears, faded, the red-white-and-blue clown outfit that schoolchildren three Junes ago painted on for the Bicentennial.

Polite in his freshened dislike of her, he asks, "Shall I put the car in the garage?"

"Leave it out front, Nelson may want it."

As they walk up the front steps his feet feel heavy, as if the world has taken on new gravity. He and the kid years ago went through something for which Rabbit has forgiven himself but which he knows the kid never has. A girl called Jill died when Harry's house burned down, a girl Nelson had come to love like a sister. At least like a sister. But the years have piled on, the surviving have patched things up, and so many more have joined the dead, undone by diseases for which only God is to blame, that it no longer seems so bad, it seems more as if Jill just moved to another town, where the population is growing. Jill would be twenty-eight now. Nelson is twenty-two. Think of all the blame God has to shoulder.

Ma's front door sticks and yields with a shove. The living room is dark and duffel bags have been added to its clutter of padded furniture. A shabby plaid suitcase, not Nelson's, sits on the stair landing. The voices come from the sunporch. These voices lessen Harry's gravity, seem to refute the world's rumors of universal death. He moves toward the voices, through the dining room and then the kitchen, into the porch area conscious of himself as slightly too drunk to be cautious enough, overweight and soft and a broad target.

Copper-beech leaves crowd at the porch screen. Faces and bodies rise from the aluminum and nylon furniture like the cloud of an explosion with the sound turned down on TV. More and more in middle age the world comes upon him like images on a set with one thing wrong with it, like those images the mind entertains before we go to sleep, that make sense until we look at them closely, which wakes us up with a shock. It is the girl who has risen most promptly, a curly-headed rather sturdy girl with shining brown eyes halfway out of her head and a ruby-red dimpling smile lifted from a turn-of-the-century valentine. She has on jeans that have been through everything and a Hindu sort of embroidered shirt that has lost some sequins. Her handshake surprises him by being damp, nervous.

Nelson slouches to his feet. His usual troubled expression wears a mountaineer's tan, and he seems thinner, broader in the shoulders. Less of a puppy, more of a mean dog. At some point in Colorado or at Kent he has had his hair, which in high school used to fall to his shoulders, cut short, to give a punk look. "Dad, this is my friend Melanie. My father. And my mother. Mom, this is Melanie."

"Pleased to meet you both," the girl says, keeping the merry red smile as if even these plain words are prelude to a joke, to a little circus act. That is what she reminds Harry of, those somehow unreal but visibly brave women who hang by their teeth in circuses, or ride one-footed the velvet rope up to fly through the spangled air, though she is dressed in that raggy look girls hide in now. A strange wall or glare has instantly fallen between himself and this girl, a disinterest that he takes to be a gesture toward his son.

Nelson and Janice are embracing. *Those little Springer hands*, Harry remembers his mother saying, as he sees them press into the back of Janice's tennis dress. Tricky little paws, something about the curve of the stubby curved fingers that hints of sneaky strength. No visible moons to the fingernails and the ends look nibbled. A habit of sullen grievance and blank stubbornness has descended to Nelson from Janice. The poor in spirit.

Yet when Janice steps aside to greet Melanie, and father and son are face to face, and Nelson says, "Hey, Dad," and like his father Harry wonders whether to shake hands or hug or touch in any way, love floods clumsily the hesitant space.

"You look fit," Harry says.

"I feel beat."

"How'd you get here so soon?"

"Hitched, except for a stretch after Kansas City where we took a bus as far as Indianapolis." Places where Rabbit has never been, restless though his blood is. The boy tells him, "The night before last we spent in some field in western Ohio, I don't know, after Toledo. It was weird. We'd gotten stoned with the guy who picked us up in this van all painted with designs, and when he dumped us off Melanie and I were really disoriented, we had to keep talking to each other so we wouldn't panic. The ground was colder than you'd think, too. We woke up frozen but at least the trees had stopped looking like octopuses."

"Nelson," Janice cries, "something dreadful could have happened to you! To the two of you."

"Who cares?" the boy asks. To his grandmother, Bessie sitting in her private cloud in the darkest corner of the porch, he says, "You wouldn't care, would you Mom-mom, if I dropped out of the picture?"

"Indeed I would," is her stout response. "You were the apple of your granddad's eye."

Melanie reassures Janice, "People are basically very nice." Her voice is strange, gurgling as if she has just recovered from a fit of laughter, with a suspended singing undertone. Her mind seems focused on some faraway cause for joy. "You only meet the difficult ones now and then, and they're usually all right as long as you don't show fear."

"What does your mother think of your hitchhiking?" Janice asks her.

"She hates it," Melanie says, and laughs outright, her curls shaking. "But she lives in California." She turns serious, her eyes shining on Janice steadily as lamps. "Really though, it's ecologically sound, it saves all that gas. More people should do it, but everybody's afraid."

A gorgeous frog, is what she looks like to Harry, though her body from what you can tell in those flopsy-mopsy clothes is human enough, and even exemplary. He tells Nelson, "If you'd budgeted your allowance better you'd've been able to take the bus all the way."

"Buses are boring, Dad, and full of creeps. You don't *learn* anything on a bus."

"It's true," Melanie chimes in. "I've heard terrible stories from girlfriends of mine, that happened to them on buses. The drivers can't do anything, they just drive, and if you look at all, you know, what they think of as hippie, they egg the guys on it seems."

"The world is no longer a safe place," Ma Springer announces from her dark corner.

Harry decides to act the father. "I'm glad you made it," he tells Nelson. "I'm proud of you, getting around the way you do. If I'd seen a little more of the United States when I was your age, I'd be a better citizen now. The only free ride I ever got was when Uncle sent me to Texas. Lubbock, Texas. They'd let us out," he tells Melanie, "Saturday nights, in the middle of a tremendous cow pasture. Fort Larson, it was called." He is overacting, talking too much.

"Dad," Nelson says impatiently, "the country's the same now wherever you go. The same supermarkets, the same plastic shit for sale. There's nothing to see."

"Colorado was a disappointment to Nelson," Melanie tells them, with her merry undertone.

"I liked the state, I just didn't care for the skunks who live in it." That aggrieved stunted look on his face. Harry knows he will never find out what happened in Colorado, to drive the kid back to him. Like those stories kids bring back from school where it was never them who started the fight.

"Have these children had any supper?" Janice asks, working up her mother act. You get out of practice quickly.

Ma Springer with unexpected complacence announces, "Melanie made the most delicious salad out of what she could find in the refrigerator and outside."

"I love your garden," Melanie tells Harry. "The little gate. Things grow so beautifully around here." He can't get over the way she warbles everything, all the while staring at his face as if fearful he will miss some point.

"Yeah," he says. "It's depressing, in a way. Was there any baloney left?"

Nelson says, "Melanie's veggy, Dad."

"Veggy?"

"Vege*tar*ian," the boy explains in his put-on whine.

"Oh. Well, no law against that."

The boy yawns. "Maybe we should hit the hay. Melanie and I got about an hour's sleep last night."

Janice and Harry go tense, and eye Melanie and Ma Springer. Janice says, "I better make up Nellie's bed."

"I've already done it," her mother tells her. "And the bed in the old sewing room too. I've had a lot of time by myself today, it seems you two are at the club more and more."

"How was church?" Harry asks her.

Ma Springer says unwillingly, "It was not very inspiring. For the collection music they had brought out from St. Mary's in Brewer one of those men who can sing in a high voice like a woman."

Melanie smiles. "A countertenor. My brother was once a countertenor."

"Then what happened?" Harry asks, yawning himself. He suggests, "His voice changed."

Her eyes are solemn. "Oh no. He took up polo playing."

"He sounds like a real sport."

"He's really my half-brother. My father was married before."

Nelson tells Harry, "Mom-mom and I ate what was left of the baloney, Dad. We ain't no veggies."

Harry asks Janice, "What's there left for me? Night after night, I starve around here."

Janice waves away his complaint with a queenly gesture she wouldn't have possessed ten years ago. "I don't know, I was thinking we'd get a bite at the club, then Mother called."

"I'm not sleepy," Melanie tells Nelson.

"Maybe she ought to see a little of the area," Harry offers. "And you could pick up a pizza while you're out."

"In the West," Nelson says, "they hardly have pizzas, everything is this awful Mexican crap, tacos and chili. Yuk."

"I'll phone up Giordano's, remember where that is? A block beyond the courthouse, on Seventh?"

"Dad, I've lived my whole life in this lousy county."

"You and me both. How does everybody feel about pepperoni? Let's get a couple, I bet Melanie's still hungry. One pepperoni and one combination."

"Jesus, Dad. We keep telling you, Melanie's a vegetarian."

"Oops. I'll order one plain. You don't have any bad feelings about cheese, do you Melanie? Or mushrooms. How about with mushrooms?"

"I'm full," the girl beams, her voice slowed it seems by its very burden of delight. "But I'd love to go with Nelson for the ride, I really like this area. It's so lush, and the houses are all kept so neat."

Janice takes this opening, touching the girl's arm, another gesture she might not have dared in the past. "Have you seen the upstairs?" she asks. "What we normally use for a guest room is across the hall from Mother's room, you'd share a bathroom with her."

"Oh, I didn't expect a room at all. I had thought just a

sleeping bag on the sofa. Wasn't there a nice big sofa in the room where we first came in?"

Harry assures her, "You don't want to sleep on that sofa, it's so full of dust you'll sneeze to death. The room upstairs is nice, honest; if you don't mind sharing with a dressmaker's dummy."

"Oh no," the girl responds. "I really just want a tiny corner where I won't be in the way, I want to go out and get a job as a waitress."

The old lady fidgets, moving her coffee cup from her lap to the folding tray table beside her chair. "I made all my dresses for years but once I had to go to the bifocals I couldn't even sew Fred's buttons on," she says.

"By that time you were rich anyway," Harry tells her, jocular in his relief at the bed business seeming to work out so smoothly. Old lady Springer, when you cross her there's no end to it, she never forgets. Harry was a little hard on Janice early in the marriage and you can still see resentment in the set of Bessie's mouth. He dodges out of the sunporch to the phone in the kitchen. While Giordano's is ringing, Nelson comes up behind him and rummages in his pockets. "Hey," Harry says, "what're ya robbing me for?"

"Car keys. Mom says take the car out front."

Harry braces the receiver between his shoulder and ear and fishes the keys from his left pocket and, handing them over, for the first time looks Nelson squarely in the face. He sees nothing of himself there except the small straight nose and a cowlick in one eyebrow that sends a little fan of hairs the wrong way and seems to express a doubt. Amazing, genes. So precise in all that coiled coding they can pick up a tiny cowlick like that. That girl had had Ruth's tilt, exactly: a little forward push of the upper lip and thighs, soft-tough, comforting.

"Thanks, Pops."

"Don't dawdle. Nothing worse than cold pizza."

"What was that?" a tough voice at the other end of the line asks, having at last picked up the phone.

"Nothing, sorry," Harry says, and orders three pizzas—one pepperoni, one combination, and one plain in case Melanie changes her mind. He gives Nelson a ten-dollar bill. "We ought to talk sometime, Nellie, when you get some rest." The remark goes with the money, somehow. Nelson makes no answer, taking the bill.

When the young people are gone, Harry returns to the sunporch and says to the women, "Now that wasn't so bad, was it? She seemed happy to sleep in the sewing room."

"Seems isn't being," Ma Springer darkly says.

"Hey that's right," Harry says. "Whaddid you think of her anyway? The girlfriend."

"Does she feel like a girlfriend to you?" Janice asks him. She has at last sat down, and has a small glass in her hand. The liquid in the glass he can't identify by its color, a sickly but intense red like old-fashioned cream soda or the fluid in thermometers.

"Whaddeya mean? They spent last night in a field together. God knows how they shacked up in Colorado. Maybe in a cave."

"I'm not sure that follows anymore. They try to be friends in a way we couldn't when we were young. Boys and girls."

"Nelson does not look contented," Ma Springer announces heavily.

"When did he ever?" Harry asks.

"As a little boy he seemed very hopeful," his grandmother says.

"Bessie, what's your analysis of what brought him back here?"

The old lady sighs. "Some disappointment. Some thing that got too big for him. I'll tell you this though. If that girl doesn't behave herself under our roof, I'm moving out. I talked to Grace Stuhl about it after church and she's more than willing, poor soul, to have me move in. She thinks it might prolong her life."

"Mother," Janice asks, "aren't you missing *All in the Family*?"

"It was to be a show I've seen before, the one where this old girlfriend of Archie's comes back to ask for money. Now that it's summer it's all reruns. I did hope to look at *The Jeffersons* though, at nine-thirty, before this hour on Moses, if I can stay awake. Maybe I'll go upstairs to rest my legs. When I was making up Nellie's little bed, a corner hit a vein and it won't stop throbbing." She stands, wincing.

"Mother," Janice says impatiently, "I would have made up

those beds if you'd just waited. Let me go up with you and look at the guest room."

Harry follows them out of the sunporch (it's getting too tragic in there, the copper beech black as ink, captive moths beating their wings to a frazzle on the screens) and into the dining room. He likes the upward glimpse of Janice's legs in the tennis dress as she goes upstairs to help her mother make things fit and proper. Ought to try fucking her some night when they're both awake. He could go upstairs and give her a hand now but he is attracted instead to the exotic white face of the woman on the cover of the July *Consumer Reports*, that he brought downstairs this morning to read in the pleasant hour between when Ma went off to church and he and Janice went off to the club. The magazine still rests on the arm of the Barcalounger, that used to be old man Springer's evening throne. You couldn't dislodge him, and when he went off to the bathroom or into the kitchen for his Diet Pepsi the chair stayed empty. Harry settles into it. The girl on the cover is wearing a white bowler hat on her white-painted face above the lapels of a fully white tuxedo; she is made up in red, white, and blue like a clown and in her uplifted hand has a dab of gooey white face cleaner. Jism, models are prostitutes, the girls in blue movies rub their faces in jism. *Broadway tests face cleansers* it says beneath her, for face cleansers are one of the commodities this month's issue is testing, along with cottage cheese (how unclean is it? it is rather unclean), air-conditioners, compact stereos, and can openers (why do people make rectangular cans anyway?). He turns to finish with the air-conditioners and reads that if you live in a high-humidity area (and he supposes he does, at least compared to Arizona) almost all models tend to drip, some enough *to make them doubtful choices for installation over a patio or walkway.* It would be nice to have a patio, along with a sunken living room like Webb Murkett does. Webb and that cute little cunt Cindy, always looking hosed down. Still, Rabbit is content. This is what he likes, domestic peace. Women circling with dutiful footsteps above him and the summer night like a lake lapping at the windows. He has time to read about compact stereos and even try the piece on car loans before Nelson and Melanie come back out of this night with three stained boxes of pizza. Quickly Harry snatches off his reading glasses, for he feels strangely naked in them.

The boy's face has brightened and might even be called cheerful. "Boy," he tells his father, "Mom's Mustang really can dig when you ask it to. Some jungle bunny in about a '69 Caddy kept racing his motor and I left him standing. Then he tailgated me all the way to the Running Horse Bridge. It was scary."

"You came around that way? Jesus, no wonder it took so long."

"Nelson was showing me the city," Melanie explains, with her musical smile, that leaves trace of the hum in the air as she moves with the flat cardboard boxes toward the kitchen. Already she has that nice upright walk of a waitress.

He calls after her, "It's a city that's seen better days."

"I think it's beauti-ful," her answer floats back. "The people paint their houses in these different colors, like something you'd see in the Mediterranean."

"The spics do that," Harry says. "The spics and the wops."

"Dad you're really prejudiced. You should travel more."

"Naa, it's all in fun. I love everybody, especially with my car windows locked." He adds, "Toyota was going to pay for me and your mother to go to Atlanta, but then some agency toward Harrisburg beat our sales total and they got the trip instead. It was a regional thing. It bothered me because I've always been curious about the South: love hot weather."

"Don't be so chintzy, Dad. Go for your vacation and pay your way."

"Vacations, we're pretty well stuck with that camp up in the Poconos." Old man Springer's pride and joy.

"I took this course in sociology at Kent. The reason you're so tight with your money, you got the habit of poverty when you were a child, in the Depression. You were traumatized."

"We weren't that bad off. Pop got decent money, printers were never laid off like some of the professions. Anyway who says I'm tight with my money?"

"You owe Melanie three dollars already. I had to borrow from her."

"You mean those three pizzas cost thirteen dollars?"

"We got a couple of sixpacks to go with them."

"You and Melanie can pay for your own beer. We never drink it around here. Too fattening."

"Where's Mom?"

"Upstairs. And another thing. Don't leave your mother's car out front with the top down. Even if it doesn't rain, the maples drop something sticky on the seats."

"I thought we might go out again."

"You're kidding. I thought you said you got only an hour's sleep last night."

"Dad, lay off the crap. I'm going on twenty-three."

"Twenty-three, and no sense. Give me the keys. I'll put the Mustang out back in the garage."

"*Mo-om,*" the boy shouts upwards. "Dad won't let me drive your car!"

Janice is coming down. She has put on her peppermint dress and looks tired. Harry tells her, "All I asked was for him to put it in the garage. The maple sap gets the seats sticky. He says he wants to go out again. Christ, it's nearly ten o'clock."

"The maples are through dripping for the year," Janice says. To Nelson she merely says, "If you don't want to go out again maybe you should put the top up. We had a terrible thunderstorm two nights ago. It hailed, even."

"Why do you think," Rabbit asks her, "your top is all black and spotty? The sap or whatever it is drips down on the canvas and can't be cleaned off."

"Harry, it's not your car," Janice tells him.

"Piz-za," Melanie calls from the kitchen, her tone bright and pearly. "*Mangiamo, prego!*"

"Dad's really into cars, isn't he?" Nelson asks his mother. "Like they're magical, now that he sells them."

Harry asks her, "How about Ma? She want to eat again?"

"Mother says she feels sick."

"Oh great. One of her spells."

"Today was an exciting day for her."

"Today was an exciting day for me too. I was told I'm a tightwad and think cars are magical." This is no way to be, spiteful. "Also, Nelson, I birdied the eighteenth, you know that long dogleg? A drive that just cleared the creek and kept bending right, and then I hit an easy five-iron and then wedged it up to about twelve feet and sank the damn putt! Still have your clubs? We ought to play." He puts a paternal hand on the boy's back.

"I sold them to a guy at Kent." Nelson takes an extra-fast step, to get out from under his father's touch. "I think it's the stupidest game ever invented."

"You must tell us about hang gliding," his mother says.

"It's neat. It's very quiet. You're in the wind and don't feel a thing. Some of the people get stoned beforehand but then there's the danger you'll think you can really fly."

Melanie has sweetly set out plates and transferred the pizzas from their boxes to cookie sheets. Janice asks, "Melanie, do you hang glide?"

"Oh no," says the girl. "I'd be terrified." Her giggling does not somehow interrupt her lustrous, caramel-colored stare. "Pru used to do it with Nelson. I never would."

"Who's Pru?" Harry asks.

"You don't know her," Nelson tells him.

"I know I don't. I know I don't know her. If I knew her I wouldn't have to ask."

"I think we're all cross and irritable," Janice says, lifting a piece of pepperoni loose and laying it on a plate.

Nelson assumes that plate is for him. "Tell Dad to quit leaning on me," he complains, settling to the table as if he has tumbled from a motorcycle and is sore all over.

In bed, Harry asks Janice, "What's eating the kid, do you think?"

"I don't know."

"Something is."

"Yes."

As they think this over they can hear Ma Springer's television going, chewing away at Moses from the Biblical sound of the voices, shouting, rumbling, with crescendos of music between. The old lady falls asleep with it on and sometimes it crackles all night, if Janice doesn't tiptoe in and turn it off. Melanie had gone to bed in her room with the dressmaker's dummy. Nelson came upstairs to watch *The Jeffersons* with his grandmother and by the time his parents came upstairs had gone to bed in his old room, without saying goodnight. Sore all over. Rabbit wonders if the young couple from the country will come into the lot tomorrow. The girl's pale round face and the television screen floating unwatched in Ma Springer's room become confused in his mind as the exalted music soars. Janice is asking, "How do you like the girl?"

"Melanie baby. Spooky. Are they all that way, of that generation, like a rock just fell on their heads and it was the nicest experience in the world?"

"I think she's trying to ingratiate herself. It must be a difficult thing, to go into a boyfriend's home and make a place for yourself. I wouldn't have lasted ten minutes with your mother."

Little she knows, the poison Mom talked about her. "Mom was like me," Harry says. "She didn't like being crowded." New people at either end of the house and old man Springer's ghost sitting downstairs on his Barcalounger. "They don't act very lovey," he says. "Or is that how people are now? Hands off."

"I think they don't want to shock us. They know they must get around Mother."

"Join the crowd."

Janice ponders this. The bed creaks and heavy footsteps slither on the other side of the wall, and the excited cries of the television set are silenced with a click. Burt Lancaster just getting warmed up. Those teeth: can they be his own? All the stars have them crowned. Even Harry, he used to have a lot of trouble with his molars and now they're snug, safe and painless, in little jackets of gold alloy costing four hundred fifty each.

"She's still up," Janice says. "She won't sleep. She's stewing." In the positive way she pronounces her *s*'s she sounds more and more like her mother. We carry our heredity concealed for a while and then it pushes through. Out of those narrow DNA coils.

In a stir of wind as before a sudden rain the shadows of the copper-beech leaves surge and fling their ragged interstices of streetlight back and forth across the surfaces where the ceiling meets the far wall. Three cars pass, one after the other, and Harry's sense of the active world outside sliding by as he lies here safe wells up within him to merge with the bed's nebulous ease. He is in his bed, his molars are in their crowns. "She's a pretty good old sport," he says. "She rolls with the punches."

"She's waiting and watching," Janice says in an ominous voice that shows she is more awake than he. She asks, "When do I get my turn?"

"Turn?" The bed is gently turning, Stavros is waiting for him by the great display window that brims with dusty morning light. *You asked for it.*

"You came last night, from the state I was in this morning. Me and the sheet."

The wind stirs again. Damn. The convertible is still out there with the top down. "Honey, it's been a long day." Running out of gas. "Sorry."

"You're forgiven," Janice says. "Just." She has to add, "I might think I don't turn you on much anymore."

"No, actually, over at the club today I was thinking how much sassier you look than most of those broads, old Thelma in her little skirt and the awful girlfriend of Buddy's."

"And Cindy?"

"Not my type. Too pudgy."

"Liar."

You got it. He is dead tired yet something holds him from the black surface of sleep, and in that half-state just before or after he sinks he imagines he hears lighter, younger footsteps slither outside in the hall, going somewhere in a hurry.

Melanie is as good as her word, she gets a job waitressing at a new restaurant downtown right on Weiser Street, an old restaurant with a new name, The Crêpe House. Before that it was the Café Barcelona, painted tiles and paella, iron grillwork and gazpacho; Harry ate lunch there once in a while but in the evening it had attracted the wrong element, hippies and Hispanic families from the south side instead of the white-collar types from West Brewer and the heights along Locust Boulevard, that you need to make a restaurant go in this city. Brewer never has been much for Latin touches, not since Carmen Miranda and all those Walt Disney Saludos Amigos movies. Rabbit remembers there used to be a Club Castanet over on Warren Avenue but the only thing Spanish had been the name and the frills on the waitresses' uniforms, which had been orange. Before the Crêpe House had been the Barcelona it had been for many years Johnny Frye's Chophouse, good solid food day and night for the big old-fashioned German eaters, who have eaten themselves pretty well into the grave by now, taking with them tons of pork chops and sauerkraut and a river of Sunflower Beer. Under its newest name, Johnny Frye's is a success; the lean new race of downtown office workers comes out of the banks and the federal offices and the deserted department stores and makes its way at noon through the woods the city planners have inflicted on Weiser Square and sits at the little tile tables left over from the Café Barcelona and dabbles at glorified pancakes wrapped around minced whatever. Even driving through after a movie at one of the malls you can see them in there by candlelight, two by two, bending toward each other over the crêpes earnest as hell, on the make, the guys in leisure suits with flared open collars and the girls in slinky dresses that cling to their bodies as if by static electricity, and a dozen more just like them standing in the foyer waiting to be seated. It has to do with diet, Harry figures—people now want to feel they're eating less, and a crêpe sounds like hardly a snack whereas if they called it a pancake they would have scared everybody away but kids and two-ton Katrinkas. Harry marvels that this new tribe of customers exists, on the make, and with money. The world keeps ending but new people too dumb to know it keep showing up as if the fun's just started. The Crêpe House is such a hit they've bought the decrepit brick building next door and expanded into the storerooms, leaving the old cigar store, that still has a little gas pilot to light up by by the cash register, intact and doing business. To staff their new space the Crêpe House needed more waitresses. Melanie works some days the lunch shift from ten to six and other days she goes from five to near one in the morning. One day Harry took Charlie over to lunch for him to see this new woman in the Angstrom life, but it didn't work out very well: having Nelson's father show up as a customer with a strange man put roses of embarrassment in Melanie's cheeks as she served them in the midst of the lunchtime mob.

"Not a bad looker," Charlie said on that awkward occasion, gazing after the young woman as she flounced away. The Crêpe House dresses its waitresses in a kind of purple colonial mini, with a big bow in back that switches as they walk.

"You can see that?" Harry said. "I can't. It bothers me,

actually. That I'm not turned on. The kid's been living with us two weeks now and I should be climbing the walls."

"A little old for wall-climbing, aren't you, chief? Anyway there are some women that don't do it for some men. That's why they turn out so many models."

"As you say she has all the equipment. Big knockers, if you look."

"I looked."

"The funny thing is, she doesn't seem to turn Nelson on either, that I can see. They're buddies all right; when she's home they spend hours in his room together playing his old records and talking about God knows what, sometimes they come out of there it looks like he's been crying, but as far as Jan and I can tell she sleeps in the front room, where we put her as a sop to old lady Springer that first night, never thinking it would stick. Actually Bessie's kind of taken with her by now, she helps with the housework more than Janice does for one thing; so at this point wherever Melanie sleeps I think she'd look the other way."

"They've *got* to be fucking," Stavros insisted, setting his hands on the table in that defining, faintly menacing way he has: palms facing, thumbs up.

"You'd think so," Rabbit agreed. "But these kids now are spooky. These letters in long white envelopes keep arriving from Colorado and they spend a lot of time answering. The postmark's Colorado but the return address printed on is some dean's office at Kent. Maybe he's flunked out."

Charlie scarcely listened. "Maybe I should give her a buzz, if Nelson's not ringing her bell."

"Come on, Charlie. I didn't say he's not, I just don't get that vibe around the house. I don't think they do it in the back of the Mustang, the seats are vinyl and these kids today are too spoiled." He sipped his Margarita and wiped the salt from his lips. The bartender here was left over from the Barcelona days, they must have a cellarful of tequila. "To tell you the truth I can't imagine Nelson screwing anybody, he's such a sourpussed little punk."

"Got his grandfather's frame. Fred was sexy, don't kid yourself. Couldn't keep his hands off the clerical help, that's why so many of them left. Where'd you say she's from?"

"California. Her father sounds like a bum, he lives in Oregon after being a lawyer. Her parents split a time ago."

"So she's a long way from home. Probably needs a friend, along more mature lines."

"Well I'm right there across the hall from her."

"You're family, champ. That doesn't count. Also you don't appreciate this chick and no doubt she twigs to that. Women do."

"Charlie, you're old enough to be her father."

"Aah. These Mediterranean types, they like to see a little gray hair on the chest. The old *mastoras*."

"What about your lousy ticker?"

Charlie smiled and put his spoon into the cold spinach soup that Melanie had brought. "Good a way to go as any."

"Charlie, you're crazy," Rabbit said admiringly, admiring yet once again in their long relationship what he fancies as the other man's superior grip upon the basic elements of life, elements that Harry can never settle in his mind.

"Being crazy's what keeps us alive," Charlie said, and sipped, closing his eyes behind his tinted glasses to taste the soup better. "Too much nutmeg. Maybe Janice'd like to have me over, it's been a while. So I can feel things out."

"Listen, I can't have you over so you can seduce my son's girlfriend."

"You said she wasn't a girlfriend."

"I said they didn't act like it, but then what do I know?"

"You have a pretty good nose. I trust you, champ." He changed the subject slightly. "How come Nelson keeps showing up at the lot?"

"I don't know, with Melanie off at work he doesn't have much to do, hanging around the house with Bessie, going over to the club with Janice swimming till his eyes get pink from the chlorine. He shopped around town a little for a job but no luck. I don't think he tried too hard."

"Maybe we could fit him in at the lot."

"I don't want that. Things are cozy enough around here for him already."

"He going back to college?"

"I don't know. I'm scared to ask."

Stavros put down his soup spoon carefully. "Scared to ask,"

he repeated. "And you're paying the bills. If my father had ever said to anybody he was scared of anything to do with me, I think the roof would have come off the house."

"Maybe scared isn't the word."

"Scared is the word you used." He looked up squinting in what seemed to be pain through his thick glasses to perceive Melanie more clearly as, in a flurry of purple colonial flounces, she set before Harry a *Crêpe con Zucchini* and before Charlie a *Crêpe aux Champignons et Oignons*. The scent of their vegetable steam remained like a cloud of perfume she had released from the frills of her costume before flying away. "Nice," Charlie said, not of the food. "Very nice." Rabbit still couldn't see it. He thought of her body without the frills and got nothing in the way of feeling except a certain fear, as if seeing a weapon unsheathed, or gazing upon an inflexible machine with which his soft body should not become involved.

But he feels obliged one night to say to Janice, "We haven't had Charlie over for a while."

She looks at him curiously. "You want to? Don't you see enough of him at the lot?"

"Yeah but you don't see him there."

"Charlie and I had our time, of seeing each other."

"Look, the guy lives with his mother who's getting to be more and more of a drag, he's never married, he's always talking about his nieces and nephews but I don't think they give him shit actually—"

"All right, you don't have to sell it. I *like* seeing Charlie. I must say I think it's creepy that you encourage it."

"Why shouldn't I? Because of that old business? I don't hold a grudge. It made you a better person."

"Thanks," Janice says dryly. Guiltily he tries to count up how many nights since he's given her an orgasm. These July nights, you get thirsty for one more beer as the Phillies struggle and then in bed feel a terrific weariness, a bliss of inactivity that leads you to understand how men can die willingly, gladly, into an eternal release from the hell of having to perform. When Janice hasn't been fucked for a while, her gestures speed up, and the thought of Charlie's coming intensifies this agitation. "What night?" she asks.

"Whenever. What's Melanie's schedule this week?"

"What does that have to do with it?"

"He might as well meet her properly. I took him over to the crêpe place for lunch and though she tried to be pleasant she was rushed and it didn't really work out."

"What would 'work out' mean, if it did?"

"Don't give me a hard time, it's too fucking humid. I've been thinking of asking Ma to go halves with us on a new air-conditioner, I read where a make called Friedrich is best. I mean 'work out' just as ordinary human interchange. He kept asking me embarrassing questions about Nelson."

"Like what? What's so embarrassing about Nelson?"

"Like whether or not he was going to go back to college and why he kept showing up at the lot."

"Why shouldn't he show up at the lot? It was his grand-father's. And Nelson's always loved cars."

"Loves to bounce 'em around, at least. The Mustang has a whole new set of rattles, have you noticed?"

"I hadn't noticed," Janice says primly, pouring herself more Campari. In an attempt to cut down her alcohol intake, to slow down creeping middle-itis, she has appointed Campari-and-soda her summer drink; but keeps forgetting to put in the soda. She adds, "He's used to those flat Ohio roads."

Out at Kent Nelson had bought some graduating senior's old Thunderbird and then when he decided to go to Colo-rado sold it for half what he paid. Remembering this adds to Rabbit's suffocating sensation of being put upon. He tells her, "They have the fifty-five-mile-an-hour speed limit out there too. The poor country is trying to save gas before the Arabs turn our dollars into zinc pennies and that baby boy of yours does fifty-five in second gear."

Janice knows he is trying to get her goat now, and turns her back with that electric swiftness, as of speeded-up film, and heads toward the dining-room phone. "I'll ask him for next week," she says. "If that'll make you less bitchy."

Charlie always brings flowers, in a stapled green cone of pa-per, that he hands to Ma Springer. After all those years of kiss-ing Springer's ass he knows his way around the widow. Bessie takes them without much of a smile; her maiden name was Koerner and she never wholly approved of Fred's taking on a

Greek, and then her foreboding came true when Charlie had an affair with Janice with such disastrous consequences, around the time of the moon landing. Well, nobody is going to the moon much these days.

The flowers, unwrapped, are roses the color of a palomino horse. Janice puts them in a vase, cooing. She has dolled up in a perky daisy-patterned sundress for the occasion, that shows off her brown shoulders, and wears her long hair up in the heat, to remind them all of her slender neck and to display the gold necklace of tiny overlapping fish scales that Harry gave her for their twentieth wedding anniversary three years ago. Paid nine hundred dollars for it then, and it must be worth fifteen hundred now, gold going crazy the way it is. She leans forward to give Charlie a kiss, on the mouth and not the cheek, thus effortlessly reminding those who watch of how these two bodies have travelled within one another. "Charlie, you look too thin," Janice says. "Don't you know how to feed yourself?"

"I pack it in, Jan, but it doesn't stick to the ribs anymore. You look terrific, on the other hand."

"Melanie's got us all on a health kick. Isn't that right, Mother? Wheat germ and alfalfa sprouts and I don't know what all. Yogurt."

"I feel better, honest to God," Bessie pronounces. "I don't know though if it's the diet or just having a little more life around the house."

Charlie's square fingertips are still resting on Janice's brown arm. Rabbit sees the phenomenon as he would something else in nature—a Japanese beetle on a leaf, or two limbs of a tree rubbing together in the wind. Then he remembers, descending into the molecules, what love feels like: huge, skin on skin, planets impinging.

"We all eat too much sugar and sodium," Melanie says, in that happy uplifted voice of hers, that seems unconnected to what is below, like a blessing no one has asked for. Charlie's hand has snapped away from Janice's skin; he is all warrior attention; his profile in the gloom of this front room through which all visitors to this household must pass shines, low-browed and jut-jawed, the muscles around the hollow of his jaw pulsing. He looks younger than at the lot, maybe because the light is poorer.

"Melanie," Harry says, "you remember Charlie from lunch the other day, doncha?"

"Of course. He had the mushrooms and capers."

"Onions," Charlie says, his hand still poised to take hers.

"Charlie's my right-hand man over there, or I'm his is I guess how he'd put it. He's been moving cars for Springer Motors since—" He can't think of a joke.

"Since they were called horseless buggies," Charlie says, and takes her hand in his. Watching, Harry marvels at her young hand's narrowness. We broaden all over. Old ladies' feet: they look like little veiny loaves of bread, rising. Away from her spacey stare Melanie is knit as tight together as a new sock. Charlie is moving in on her. "How are you, Melanie? How're you liking these parts?"

"They're nice," she smiles. "Quaint, almost."

"Harry tells me you're a West Coast baby."

Her eyes lift, so the whites beneath the irises show, as she looks toward her distant origins. "Oh yes. I was born in Marin County. My mother lives now in a place called Carmel. That's to the south."

"I've heard of it," Charlie says. "You've got some rock stars there."

"Not really, I don't think. . . . Joan Baez, but she's more what you'd call traditional. We live in what used to be our summer place."

"How'd that happen?"

Startled, she tells him. "My father used to work in San Francisco as a corporation lawyer. Then he and my mother broke up and we had to sell the house on Pacific Avenue. Now he's in Oregon learning to be a forester."

"That's a sad story, you could say," Harry says.

"Daddy doesn't think so," Melanie tells him. "He's living with a lovely girl who's part Yakima Indian."

"Back to Nature," Charlie says.

"It's the only way to go," Rabbit says. "Have some soybeans." This is a joke, for he is passing them Planter's dry-roasted cashews in a breakfast bowl, nuts that he bought on impulse at the grocery next to the state liquor store fifteen minutes ago, running out in the rattling Mustang to stoke up for tonight's company. He had been almost scared off by the price on the

jar, $2.89, up 30¢ from the last time he'd noticed, and reached
for the dry-roasted peanuts instead. Even these, though, were
over a dollar, $1.09, peanuts that you used to buy a big sack
of unshelled for a quarter when he was a boy, so he thought,
What the hell's the point of being rich, and took the cashews
after all.

He is offended when Charlie glances down and holds up
a fastidious palm, not taking any. "No salt," Harry urges.
"Loaded with protein."

"Never touch junk," Charlie says. "Doc says it's a no-no."

"Junk!" he begins to argue.

But Charlie is keeping the pressure on Melanie. "Every winter, I head down to Florida for a month. Sarasota, on the Gulf
side."

"What's that got to do with California?" Janice asks, cutting in.

"Same type of Paradise," Charlie says, turning a shoulder so
as to keep speaking directly to Melanie. "It's my meat. Sand in
your shoes, that's the feeling, wearing the same ragged cut-offs
day after day. This is over on the Gulf side. I hate the Miami
side. The only way you'd get me over on the Miami side would
be inside an alligator. They have 'em, too: come up out of these
canals right onto your lawn and eat your pet dog. It happens
a lot."

"I've never been to Florida," Melanie says, looking a little
glazed, even for her.

"You should give it a try," Charlie says. "It's where the real
people are."

"You mean we're *not* real people?" Rabbit asks, egging
him on, helping Janice out. This must hurt her. He takes a
cashew between his molars and delicately cracks it, prolonging
the bliss. That first fracture, in there with tongue and spit and
teeth. He loves nuts. Clean eating, not like meat. In the Garden of Eden they ate nuts and fruit. Dry-roasted, the cashew
burns a little. He prefers them salted, soaked in sodium, but
got this kind in deference to Melanie; he's being brainwashed
about chemicals. Still, some chemical must have entered into
this dry-roasting too, there's nothing you can eat won't hurt
you down here on earth. Janice must just hate this.

"It's not just all old people either," Charlie is telling Melanie.

"You see plenty of young people down there too, just living in their skins. Gorgeous."

"Janice," Mrs. Springer says, pronouncing it *Chaniss*. "We should go on the porch and you should offer people drinks." To Charlie she says, "Melanie made a lovely fruit punch."

"How much gin can it absorb?" Charlie asks.

Harry loves this guy, even if he is putting the make on Melanie in front of Janice. On the porch, when they've settled on the aluminum furniture with their drinks and Janice is in the kitchen stirring at the dinner, he asks him, to show him off, "How'd you like Carter's energy speech?"

Charlie cocks his head toward the rosy-cheeked girl and says, "I thought it was pathetic. The man was right. I'm suffering from a crisis in confidence. In him."

Nobody laughs, except Harry. Charlie passes the ball. "What did you think of it, Mrs. Springer?"

The old lady, called onto the stage, smooths the cloth of her lap and looks down as if for crumbs. "He seems a well-intentioned Christian man, though Fred always used to say the Democrats were just a tool for the unions. Still and all. Some businessman in there might have a better idea what to do with the inflation."

"He *is* a businessman, Bessie," Harry says. "He grows peanuts. His warehouse down there grosses more than we do."

"I thought it was sad," Melanie unexpectedly says, leaning forward so her loose gypsyish blouse reveals cleavage, a tube of air between her braless breasts, "the way he said people for the first time think things are going to get worse instead of better."

"Sad if you're a chick like you," Charlie says. "For old crocks like us, things are going to get worse in any case."

"You believe that?" Harry asks, genuinely surprised. He sees his life as just beginning, on clear ground at last, now that he has a margin of resources, and the stifled terror that always made him restless has dulled down. He wants less. Freedom, that he always thought was outward motion, turns out to be this inner dwindling.

"I believe it, sure," Charlie says, "but what does this nice girl here believe? That the show's over? How *can* she?"

"I believe," Melanie begins. "Oh, I don't know—Bessie, help me."

Harry didn't know she calls the old lady by her first name. Took him years of living with her to work up to feeling easy about that, and it wasn't really until after one day he had accidentally walked in on her in her bathroom, Janice hogging theirs.

"Say what's on your mind," the old woman advises the younger. "Everybody else is."

The luminous orbs of Melanie's eyes scout their faces in a sweep that ends in an upward roll such as you see in images of saints. "I believe the things we're running out of we can learn to do without. I don't need electric carving knives and all that. I'm more upset about the snail darters and the whales than about iron ore and oil." She lingers on this last word, giving it two syllables, and stares at Harry. As if he's especially into oil. He decides what he resents about her is she seems always to be trying to hypnotize him. "I mean," she goes on, "as long as there are growing things, there's still a world with endless possibilities."

The hum beneath her words hangs in the darkening space of the porch. Alien. Moonraker.

"One big weed patch," Harry says. "Where the hell is Nelson, anyway?" He is irked, he figures, because this girl is out of this world and that makes his world feel small. He feels sexier even toward fat old Bessie. At least her voice has a lot of the county, a lot of his life, in it. That time he blundered into the bathroom he didn't see much; she shouted, sitting on the toilet with her skirt around her knees, and he heard her shout and hardly saw a thing, just a patch of flank as white as a butcher's marble counter.

Bessie answers him dolefully, "I believe he went out for a reason. Janice would know."

Janice comes to the doorway of the porch, looking snappy in her daisies and an orange apron. "He went off around six with Billy Fosnacht. They should have been back by now."

"Which car'd they take?"

"They had to take the Corona. You were at the liquor store with the Mustang."

"Oh great. What's Billy Fosnacht doing around anyway? Why isn't he in the volunteer army?" He feels like making a show, for Charlie and Melanie, of authority.

There is authority, too, in the way Janice is holding a wooden stirring spoon. She says, to the company in general, "They say he's doing very well. He's in his first year of dental school up somewhere in New England. He wants to be a, what do they call it—?"

"Ophthalmologist," Rabbit says.

"Endodontist."

"My God," is all Harry can say. Ten years ago, the night his house had burned, Billy had called his mother a bitch. He had seen Billy often since, all the years Nelson was at Mt. Judge High, but had never forgotten that, how Peggy had then slapped him, this little boy just thirteen years old, the marks of her fingers leaping up pink on the child's delicate cheek. Then he had called her a whore, Harry's jism warm inside her. Later that night Nelson had vowed to kill his father. *You fucking ass-hole, you've let her die. I'll kill you. I'll kill you*. Harry had put up his hands to fight. The misery of life. It has carried him away from the faces on the porch. In the silence he hears from afar a neighbor woman's hammer knocking. "How are Ollie and Peggy?" he asks, his voice rough even after clearing it. Billy's parents have dropped from his sight, as the Toyota business lifted him higher in the social scale.

"About the same," Janice says. "Ollie's still at the music store. They say Peggy's gotten into causes." She turns back to her stirring.

Charlie tells Melanie, "You should book yourself on a flight to Florida when you get fed up around here."

"What's with you and Florida?" Harry asks him loudly. "She says she comes from California and you keep pushing Florida at her. There's no connection."

Charlie pulls at his spiked pink punch and looks like a pathetic old guy, the skin pegged ever tighter to the planes of his skull. "We can make a connection."

Melanie calls toward the kitchen, "Janice, can I be of any help?"

"No dear, thanks; it's all but done. Is everybody starving? Does anybody else want their drink freshened?"

"Why not?" Harry asks, feeling reckless. This bunch isn't going to be fun, he'll have to make his fun inside. "How about you, Charlie?"

"Forget it, champ. One's my limit. The doctors tell me even that should be a no-no, in my condition." Of Melanie he asks, "How's your Kool-Aid holding up?"

"Don't call it Kool-Aid, that's rude," Harry says, pretending to joust. "I admire anybody of this generation who isn't polluting their system with pills and booze. Ever since Nelson got back, the sixpacks come and go in the fridge like, like coal down a chute." He feels he has said this before, recently.

"I'll get you some more," Melanie sings, and takes Charlie's glass, and Harry's too. She has no name for him, he notices. Nelson's father. Over the hill. Out of this world.

"Make mine weak," he tells her. "A g-and-t."

Ma Springer has been sitting there with thoughts of her own. She says to Stavros, "Nelson has been asking me all these questions about how the lot works, how much sales help there is, and how the salesmen are paid, and so on."

Charlie shifts his weight in his chair. "This gas crunch's got to affect car sales. People won't buy cows they can't feed. Even if so far Toyota's come along smelling pretty good."

Harry intervenes. "Bessie, there's no way we can make room for Nelson on sales without hurting Jake and Rudy. They're married men trying to feed babies on their commissions. If you want I could talk to Manny and see if he can use another kid on clean-up—"

"He doesn't want to work on clean-up," Janice calls sharply from the kitchen.

Ma Springer confirms, "Yes, he told me he'd like to see what he could do with sales, you know he always admired Fred so, idolized him you might say—"

"Oh come *on*," Harry says. "He never gave a damn about either of his grandfathers once he hit about tenth grade. Once he got onto girls and rock he thought everybody over twenty was a sap. All he wanted was to get the hell out of Brewer, and I said, O.K., here's the ticket, go to it. So what's he pussy-footing around whispering to his mother and grandmother now for?"

Melanie brings in the two men's drinks. Waitressly erect, she holds a triangulated paper napkin around the dewy base of each. Rabbit sips his and finds it strong when he asked for it weak. A love message, of sorts?

Ma Springer puts one hand on each of her thighs and points her elbows out, elbows all in folds like little pug dog faces. "Now Harry—"

"I know what you're going to say. You own half the company. Good for you, Bessie, I'm glad. If it'd been me instead of Fred I'd've left it all to you." He quickly turns to Melanie and says, "What they really should do with this gas crisis is bring back the trolley cars. You're too young to remember. They ran on tracks but the power came from electric wires overhead. Very clean. They went everywhere when I was a kid."

"Oh, I know. They still have them in San Francisco."

"Harry, what I wanted to say—"

"But you're *not* running it," he continues to his mother-in-law, "and never have, and as long as I am, Nelson, if he wants a start there, can hose down cars for Manny. I don't want him in the sales room. He has none of the right attitudes. He can't even straighten up and smile."

"I thought those were cable cars," Charlie says to Melanie.

"Oh they just have those on a few hills. Everybody keeps saying how dangerous they are, the cables snap. But the tourists expect them."

"Harry. Dinner," Janice says. She is stern. "We won't wait for Nelson any more, it's after eight."

"Sorry if I sound hard," he says to the group as they rise to go eat. "But look, even now, the kid's too rude to come home in time for dinner."

"Your own son," Janice says.

"Melanie, what do you think? What's his plan? Isn't he heading back to finish college?"

Her smile remains fixed but seems flaky, painted-on. "Nelson may feel," she says carefully, "that he's spent enough time at college."

"But where's his degree?" He hears his own voice in his head as shrill, sounding trapped. "Where's his degree?" Harry repeats, hearing no answer.

Janice has lit candles on the dining table, though the July day is still so light they look wan. She had wanted this to be nice for Charlie. Dear old Jan. As Harry walks to the table behind her he rests his eyes on what he rarely sees, the pale bared nape of her neck. In the shuffle as they take places he brushes

Melanie's arm, bare also, and darts a look down the ripe slopes loosely concealed by the gypsy blouse. Firm. He mutters to her, "Sorry, didn't mean to put you on the spot just now. I just can't figure out what Nelson's game is."

"Oh you didn't," she answers crooningly. Ringlets fall and tremble; her cheeks flame within. As Ma Springer plods to her place at the head of the table, the girl peeks up at Harry with a glint he reads as sly and adds, "I think one factor, you know, is Nelson's becoming more security-minded."

He can't quite follow. Sounds like the kid is going to enter the Secret Service.

Chairs scrape. They wait while a dim tribal memory of grace flits overhead. Then Janice dips her spoon into her soup, tomato, the color of Harry's Corona. Where is it? Out in the night, with the kid at the wheel making every joint rattle. They rarely sit in this room—even with the five of them now they eat around the kitchen table—and Harry is newly aware of, propped on the sideboard where the family silver is stored, tinted photos of Janice as a high-school senior with her hair brushed and rolled under in a page-boy to her shoulders, of Nelson as an infant propped with his favorite teddy bear (that had one eye) on a stagy sunbathed window seat of this very house, and then Nelson as himself a high-school senior, his hair almost as long as Janice's, but less brushed, looking greasy, and his grin for the cameraman lopsided, half-defiant. In a gold frame broader than his daughter and grandson got, Fred Springer, misty-eyed and wrinkle-free courtesy of the portrait studio's darkroom magic, stares in studied three-quarters profile at whatever it is the dead see.

Charlie asks the table, "Did you see where Nixon gave a big party at San Clemente in honor of the moon-landing anniversary? They should keep that guy around forever, as an example of what sheer gall can do."

"He did some good things," Ma Springer says, in that voice of hers that shows hurt, tight and dried-out, somehow. Harry is sensitive to it after all these years.

He tries to help her, to apologize if he had been rough with her over who ran the company. "He opened up China," he says.

"And what a can of worms that's turned out to be," Stavros says. "At least all those years they were hating our guts they didn't cost us a nickel. This party of his wasn't cheap either. Everybody was there—Red Skelton, Buzz Aldrin."

"You know I think it broke Fred's heart," Ma Springer pronounces. "Watergate. He followed it right to the end, when he could hardly lift his head from the pillows, and he used to say to me, 'Bessie, there's never been a President who hasn't done worse. They just have it in for him because he isn't a glamour boy. If that had been Roosevelt or one of the Kennedys,' he'd say, 'you would never have heard "boo" about Watergate.' He believed it, too."

Harry glances at the gold-framed photograph and imagines it nodded. "I believe it," he says. "Old man Springer never steered me wrong." Bessie glances at him to see if this is sarcasm. He keeps his face motionless as a photograph.

"Speaking of Kennedys," Charlie puts in—he really is talking too much, on that one Kool-Aid—"the papers are sure giving Chappaquiddick another go-around. You wonder, how much more can they say about a guy on his way to neck who drives off a bridge instead?"

Bessie may have had a touch of sherry, too, for she is working herself up to tears. "Fred," she says, "would never settle on its being that simple. 'Look at the result,' he said to me more than once. 'Look at the result, and work backwards from that.'" Her berry-dark eyes challenge them to do so, mysteriously. "What was the result?" This seems to be in her own voice. "The result was, a poor girl from up in the coal regions was killed."

"Oh Mother," Janice says. "Daddy just had it in for Democrats. I loved him dearly, but he was absolutely hipped on that."

Charlie says, "I don't know, Jan. The worst things I ever heard your father say about Roosevelt was that he tricked us into war and died with his mistress, and it turns out both are true." He looks in the candlelight after saying this like a cardsharp who has snapped down an ace. "And what they tell us now about how Jack Kennedy carried on in the White House with racketeers' molls and girls right off the street Fred Springer in his wildest dreams would never have come up with." Another ace. He looks, Harry thinks, like old man Springer in a way: that hollow-templed, well-combed look. Even the little dabs of eyebrows sticking out like toy artillery.

Harry says, "I never understood what was so bad about Chappaquiddick. He *tried* to get her out." Water, flames, the tongues of God: a man is helpless.

"What was bad about it," Bessie says, "was he put her in."

"What do you think about all this, Melanie?" Harry asks, playing cozy to get Charlie's goat. "Which party do you back?"

"Oh the parties," she exclaims in a trance. "I think they're both evil." *Ev-il*: a word in the air. "But on Chappaquiddick a friend of mine spends every summer on the island and she says she wonders why more people don't drive off that bridge, there are no guard rails or anything. This is lovely soup," she adds to Janice.

"That spinach soup the other day was terrific," Charlie tells Melanie. "Maybe a little heavy on the nutmeg."

Janice has been smoking a cigarette and listening for a car door to slam. "Harry, could you help me clear? You might want to carve in the kitchen."

The kitchen is suffused with the strong, repugnant smell of roasting lamb. Harry doesn't like to be reminded that these are living things, with eyes and hearts, that we eat; he likes salted nuts, hamburger, Chinese food, mince pie. "You know I can't carve lamb," he says. "Nobody can. You're just having it because you think it's what Greeks eat, showing off for your old lover boy."

She hands him the carving set with the bumpy bone handles. "You've done it a hundred times. Just cut parallel slices perpendicular to the bone."

"Sounds easy. You do it if it's so fucking easy." He is thinking, stabbing someone is probably harder than the movies make it look, cutting underdone meat there's plenty of resistance, rubbery and tough. He'd rather hit her on the head with a rock, if it came to that, or that green glass egg Ma has as a knickknack in the living room.

"Listen," Janice hisses. A car door has slammed on the street. Footsteps pound on a porch, their porch, and the reluctant front door pops open with a bang. A chorus of voices around the table greet Nelson. But he keeps coming, searching for his parents, and finds them in the kitchen. "Nelson," Janice says. "We were getting worried."

The boy is panting, not with exertion but the shallow-lunged panting of fear. He looks small but muscular in his grape-colored tie-dyed T-shirt: a burglar dressed to shinny in a window. But caught, here, in the bright kitchen light. He avoids looking Harry in the eye. "Dad. There's been a bit of a mishap."

"The car. I knew it."

"Yeah. The Toyota got a scrape."

"My Corona. Whaddeya mean, a scrape?"

"Nobody was hurt, don't get carried away."

"Any other car involved?"

"No, so don't worry, nobody's going to *sue*." The assurance is contemptuous.

"Don't get smart with *me*."

"O.K., O.K., Jesus."

"You drove it home?"

The boy nods.

Harry hands the knife back to Janice and leaves the kitchen to address the candlelit group left at the table—Ma at the head, Melanie bright-eyed next to her, Charlie on Melanie's other side, his square cufflink reflecting a bit of flame. "Everybody keep calm. Just a mishap, Nelson says. Charlie, you want to come carve some lamb for me? I got to look at this."

He wants to put his hands on the boy, whether to give him a push or comfort he doesn't know; the actual touch might demonstrate which, but Nelson stays just ahead of his father's fingertips, dodging into the summer night. The streetlights have come on, and the Corona's tomato color looks evil by the poisonous sodium glow—a hollow shade of black, its metallic lustre leeched away. Nelson in his haste has parked it illegally, the driver's side along the curb. Harry says, "This side looks fine."

"It's the *other* side, Dad." Nelson explains: "See Billy and I were coming back from Allenville where his girlfriend lives by this windy back road and because I knew I was getting late for supper I may have been going a little fast, I don't know, you can't go too fast on those back roads anyway, they wind too much. And this woodchuck or whatever it was comes out in front of me and in trying to avoid it I get off the road a little and the back end slides into this telephone pole. It happened so fast, I couldn't believe it."

Rabbit has moved to the other side and by lurid light views the damage. The scrape had begun in the middle of the rear door and deepened over the little gas-cap door; by the time the pole reached the tail signal and the small rectangular side-light, it had no trouble ripping them right out, the translucent plastic torn and shed like Christmas wrapping, and inches of pretty color-coded wiring exposed. The urethane bumper, so black and mat and trim, that gave Harry a small sensuous sensation whenever he touched the car home against the concrete parking-space divider at the place on the lot stencilled ANGSTROM, was pulled out from the frame. The dent even carried up into the liftback door, which would never seat exactly right again.

Nelson is chattering, "Billy knows this kid who works in a body shop over near the bridge to West Brewer and he says you should get some real expensive rip-off place to do the estimate and then when you get the check from the insurance company give it to him and he can do it for less. That way there'll be a profit everybody can split."

"A profit," Harry repeats numbly.

Nails or rivets in the pole have left parallel longitudinal gashes the length of the impact depression. The chrome-and-rubber stripping has been wrenched loose at an angle, and behind the wheel socket on this side—hooded with a slightly protruding flare like an eyebrow, one of the many snug Japanese details he has cherished—a segment of side strip has vanished entirely, leaving a chorus of tiny holes. Even the many-ribbed hubcap is dented and besmirched. He feels his own side has taken a wound. He feels he is witnessing in evil light a crime in which he has collaborated.

"Oh come *on*, Dad," Nelson is saying. "Don't make such a big deal of it. It'll cost the insurance company, not you, to get it fixed, and anyway you can get a new one for almost nothing, don't they give you a terrific discount?"

"Terrific," Rabbit says. "You just went out and smashed it up. My Corona."

"I didn't *mean* to, it was an *ac*cident, shit. What do you want me to do, piss blood? Get down on my knees and cry?"

"Don't bother."

"Dad, it's just a *thing*; you're looking like you lost your best friend."

A breeze, too high to touch them, ruffles the treetops and makes the streetlight shudder on the deformed metal. Harry sighs. "Well. How'd the woodchuck do?"

II

O NCE THAT first weekend of riots and rumors is over, the
summer isn't so bad; the gas lines never get so long again.
Stavros says the oil companies have the price hike they wanted
for now, and the government has told them to cool it or face
an excess profits tax. Melanie says the world will turn to the
bicycle, as Red China has already done; she has bought herself
a twelve-speed Fuji with her waitress's wages, and on fair days
pedals around the mountain and down, her chestnut curls flying, through Cityview Park into Brewer. Toward the end of
July comes a week of record heat; the papers are full of thermal
statistics and fuzzy photographs of the time at the turn of the
century when the trolley tracks warped in Weiser Square, it was
so hot. Such heat presses out from within, against our clothes;
we want to break out, to find another self beside the sea or in
the mountains. Not until August will Harry and Janice go to
the Poconos, where the Springers have a cottage they rent to
other people for July. All over Brewer, air-conditioners drip
onto patios and into alleyways.

On an afternoon of such hot weather, with his Corona still
having bodywork done, Harry borrows a Caprice trade-in
from the lot and drives southwest toward Galilee. On curving
roads he passes houses of sandstone, fields of corn, a cement
factory, a billboard pointing to a natural cave (didn't natural
caves go out of style a while ago?), and another billboard with
a great cutout of a bearded Amishman advertising "Authentic
Dutch Smörgåsbord." Galilee is what they call a string town,
a hilly row of houses with a feed store at one end and a tractor
agency at the other. In the middle stands an old wooden inn
with a deep porch all along the second story and a renovated
restaurant on the first with a window full of credit card stickers
to catch the busloads of tourists that come up from Baltimore,
blacks most of them, God knows what they hope to see out
here in the sticks. A knot of young locals is hanging around in
front of the Rexall's, you never used to see that in farm country, they'd be too busy with the chores. There is an old stone
trough, a black-lacquered row of hitching posts, a glossy new

bank, a traffic island with a monument Harry cannot make out the meaning of, and a small brick post office with its bright silver letters GALILEE up a side street that in a block dead-ends at the edge of a field. The woman in the post office tells Harry where the Nunemacher farm is, along R. D. 2. By the landmarks she gives him—a vegetable stand, a pond rimmed with willows, a double silo close to the road—he feels his way through the tummocks and swales of red earth crowded with shimmering green growth, merciless vegetation that allows not even the crusty eroded road embankments to rest barren but makes them bear tufts and mats of vetch and honeysuckle vines and fills the stagnant hot air with the haze of exhaled vapor. The Caprice windows are wide open and the Brewer disco station fades and returns in twists of static as the land and electrical wires obtrude. NUNEMACHER is a faded name on a battered tin mailbox. The house and barn are well back from the road, down a long dirt lane, brown stones buried in pink dust.

Rabbit's heart rises in his chest. He cruises the road, surveying the neighboring mailboxes; but Ruth gave him, when he once met her by accident in downtown Brewer a dozen years ago, no clue to her new name, and the girl a month ago refused to write hers in his showroom ledger. All he has to go by, other than Nunemacher's being his daughter's neighbor, if she is his daughter, is Ruth's mentioning that her husband besides being a farmer ran a fleet of school buses. He was older than she and should be dead now, Harry figures. The school buses would be gone. The mailboxes along this length of road say BLANKENBILLER, MUTH, and BYER. It is not easy to match the names with the places, as glimpsed in their hollows, amid their trees, at the end of their lanes of grass and dirt. He feels conspicuous, gliding along in a magenta Caprice, though no other soul emerges from the wide landscape to observe him. The thick-walled houses hold their inhabitants in, this hazy mid-afternoon too hot for work. Harry drives down a lane at random and stops and backs around in the beaten, rutted space between the buildings while some pigs he passed in their pen set up a commotion of snorting and a fat woman in an apron comes out of a door of the house. She is shorter than Ruth and younger than Ruth would be now, with black hair pulled tight beneath a Mennonite cap. He waves and keeps going. This was the Blankenbillers, he sees by the mailbox as he pulls onto the road again.

The other two places are nearer the road and he thinks he might get closer on foot. He parks on a widened stretch of shoulder, packed earth scored by the herringbone of tractor tire treads. When he gets out of the car, the powerful sweetish stench of the Blankenbillers' pigsty greets him from a distance, and what had seemed to be silence settles into his ear as a steady dry hum of insects, an undercoat to the landscape. The flowering weeds of mid-summer, daisies and Queen Anne's lace and chicory, thrive at the side of the road and tap his pants legs as he hops up onto the bank. In his beige summerweight salesman's suit he prowls behind a hedgerow of sumac and black gum and wild cherry overgrown with poison ivy, shining leaves of it big as valentines and its vines having climbed to the tips of strangled trees. The roughly shaped sandstones of a tumbled old wall lie within this hedgerow, hardly one upon another. At a gap where wheeled vehicles have been driven through he stands surveying the cluster of buildings below him—barn and house, asbestos-sided chicken house and slat-sided corn crib, both disused, and a newish building of cement-block with a roof of corrugated overlapped Fiberglas. Some kind of garage, it looks like. On the house roof has been mounted a copper lightning rod oxidized green and an H-shaped television aerial, very tall to catch the signals out here. Harry means only to survey, to relate this layout to the Nunemacher spread across the next shaggy rise, but a soft clinking arising from somewhere amid the buildings, and the ripples a little runnel makes pouring itself into a small pond perhaps once for ducks, and an innocent clutter of old tractor seats and axles and a rusted iron trough in a neglected patch between the woodpile and the mowed yard lure him downward like a species of music while he churns in his head the story he will tell if approached and challenged. This soft dishevelled farm feels like a woman's farm, in need of help. An unreasonable expectancy brings his heart up to the pitch of the surrounding insect-hum.

Then he sees it, behind the barn, where the woods are encroaching upon what had once been a cleared space, sumac and cedar in the lead: the tilted yellow shell of a school bus. Its wheels and windows are gone and the snub hood of its cab has been torn away to reveal a hollow space where an engine was cannibalized; but like a sunken galleon it testifies to an empire, a fleet of buses whose proprietor has died, his widow left with an illegitimate daughter to raise. The land under Rabbit seems to move, with the addition of yet another citizen to the sub-terrain of the dead.

Harry stands in what once had been an orchard, where even now lopsided apple and pear trees send up sprays of new shoots from their gutted trunks. Though the sun burns, wetness at the root of the orchard grass has soaked his suede shoes. If he ventures a few steps farther he will be in the open and li-able to be spotted from the house windows. There are voices within the house he can hear now, though they have the dim steady rumble that belongs to voices on radio or television. A few steps farther, he could distinguish these voices. A few steps farther still, he will be on the lawn, beside a plaster bird-bath balanced off-center on a pillar of blue-tinted fluting, and then he will be committed to stride up bravely, put his foot on the low cement porch, and knock. The front door, set deep in its socket of stone, needs its green paint refreshed. From the tattered composition shingles of its roof to the dreary roller shades that hang in its windows the house exhales the tired breath of poverty.

What would he say to Ruth if she answered his knock?

Hi. You may not remember me . . .

Jesus. I wish I didn't.

No, wait. Don't close it. Maybe I can help you.

How the hell would you ever help me? Get out. Honest to God, Rabbit, just looking at you makes me sick.

I have money now.

I don't want it. I don't want anything that stinks of you. When I did need you, you ran.

O.K., O.K. But let's look at the present situation. There's this girl of ours—

Girl, she's a woman. Isn't she lovely? I'm so proud.

Me too. We should have had lots. Great genes.

Don't be so fucking cute. I've been here for twenty years, where have you been?

It's true, he could have tried to look her up, he even knew she lived around Galilee. But he hadn't. He hadn't wanted to face her, the complicated and accusing reality of her. He wanted to hold her in his mind as just fucked and satisfied, lifting white and naked above him on an elbow. Before he drifted off to sleep she got him a drink of water. He does not know if he loved her or not, but with her he had known love, had experienced that cloudy inflation of self which makes us infants again and tips each moment with a plain excited purpose, as these wands of grass about his knees are tipped with packets of their own fine seeds.

A door down below slams, not on the sides of the house he can see. A voice sounds the high note we use in speaking to pets. Rabbit retreats behind an apple sapling too small to hide him. In his avidity to see, to draw closer to that mysterious branch of his past that has flourished without him, and where lost energy and lost meaning still flow, he has betrayed his big body, made it a target. He crowds so close to the little tree that his lips touch the bark of its crotch, bark smooth as glass save where darker ridges of roughness at intervals ring its gray. The miracle of it: how things grow, always remembering to be themselves. His lips have flinched back from the unintended kiss. Living microscopic red things—mites, aphids, he can see them—will get inside him and multiply.

"Hey!" a voice calls. A woman's voice, young on the air, frightened and light. Could Ruth's voice be so young after so many years?

Rather than face who it is, he runs. Up through the heavy orchard grass, dodging among the old fruit trees, breaking through as if a sure lay-up waits on the other side of the ragged hedgerow, onto the red tractor path and back to the Caprice, checking to see if he tore his suit as he trots along, feeling his age. He is panting; the back of his hand is scratched, by raspberries or wild rose. His heart is pounding so wildly he cannot fit the ignition key into the lock. When it does click in, the motor grinds for a few revolutions before catching, overheated from waiting in the sun. The female voice calling "Hey" so lightly hangs in his inner ear as the motor settles to its purr and he listens for pursuing shouts and even the sound of a rifle. These farmers all have guns and think nothing of using them, the years he worked as a typesetter for the *Vat* hardly a week went by without some rural murder all mixed in with sex and booze and incest.

But the haze of the country around Galilee hangs silent above the sound of his engine. He wonders if his figure had been distinct enough to be recognized, by Ruth who hadn't seen him since he'd put on all this weight or by the daughter who has seen him once, a month ago. They report this to the police and use his name it'll get back to Janice and she'll raise hell to hear he's been snooping after this girl. Won't wash so good at Rotary either. Back. He must get back. Afraid of getting lost the other way, he dares back around and head back the way he came, past the mailboxes. He decides the mailbox that goes with the farm he spied on down in its little tousled valley with the duck pond is the blue one saying BYER. Fresh sky blue, painted this summer, with a decal flower, the sort of decoration a young woman might apply.

Byer. Ruth Byer. His daughter's first name Jamie Nunemacher never pronounced, that Rabbit can recall.

He asks Nelson one night, "Where's Melanie? I thought she was working days this week."

"She is. She's gone out with somebody."

"Really? You mean on a date?"

The Phillies have been rained out tonight and while Janice and her mother are upstairs watching a *Waltons* rerun he and the kid find themselves in the living room, Harry leafing through the August *Consumer Reports* that has just come (*"Are hair dyes safe?" "Road tests: 6 pickup trucks" "An alternative to the $2000 funeral"*) while the boy is looking into a copy of a book he has stolen from Fred Springer's old office at the lot, which has become Harry's. He doesn't look up. "You could call it a date. She just said she was going out."

"But *with* somebody."

"Sure."

"That's O.K. with you? Her going out with somebody?"

"Sure. Dad, I'm trying to read."

The same rain that has postponed the Phils against the Pirates at Three Rivers Stadium has swept east across the Commonwealth and beats on the windows here at 89 Joseph Street, into the low-spreading branches of the copper beech that is the pride of the grounds, and at times thunderously upon the roof and spouting of the front porch roof. "Lemme see the book," Harry begs, and from within the Barcalounger holds out a long arm. Nelson irritably tosses over the volume, a squat green handbook on automobile dealership written by some crony of old man Springer's who had an agency in Paoli. Harry has looked into it once or twice: mostly hot air, hotshot stuff geared to the greater volume you can expect in the Philly area. "This tells you," he tells Nelson, "more than you need to know."

"I'm trying to understand," Nelson says, "about the financing."

"It's very simple. The bank owns the new cars, the dealer owns the used cars. The bank pays Mid-Atlantic Toyota when the car leaves Maryland; also there's something called holdback that the manufacturer keeps in case the dealer defaults on parts purchases, but that he rebates annually, and that to be frank about it has the effect of reducing the dealer's apparent profit in case he gets one of these wiseass customers who takes a great interest in the numbers and figures he can jew you down. Toyota insists we sell everything at their list so there's not much room for finagling, and that saves you a lot of headaches in my opinion. If they don't like the price they can come back a month later and find it three hundred bucks higher, the way the yen is going. Another wrinkle about financing, though, is when the customer takes out his loan where we send him—Brewer Trust generally, and though this magazine right here had an article just last month about how you ought to shop around for loans instead of going where the agency recommends it's a hell of a hassle actually to buck the system, just to save maybe a half of a per cent—the bank keeps back a percentage for our account, supposedly to cover the losses of selling repossessed vehicles, but in fact it amounts to a kickback. Follow me? Why do you care?"

"Just interested."

"You should have been interested when your granddad Springer was around to be talked to. He ate this crap up. By the time he had sold a car to a customer the poor bozo thought he was robbing old Fred blind when the fact is the deal had angles to it like a spider web. When he wanted Toyota to give him the franchise, he claimed sixty thousand feet of extra service space that was just a patch of weeds, and then got a contractor who owed him a favor to throw down a slab and put up an uninsulated shell. That shop is still impossible to heat in the winter, you should hear Manny bitch."

Nelson asks, "Did they used to ever chop the clock?"

"Where'd you learn that phrase?"

"From the book."

"Well. . . ." This isn't so bad, Harry thinks, talking to the kid sensibly while the rain drums down. He doesn't know why it makes him nervous to see the kid read. Like he's plotting something. They say you should encourage it, reading, but they never say why. "You know chopping the clock is a felony. But maybe in the old days sometimes a mechanic, up in the dashboard anyway, kind of had his screwdriver slip on the odometer. People who buy a used car know it's a gamble anyway. A car might go twenty thousand miles without trouble or pop a cylinder tomorrow. Who's to say? I've seen some amazing wear on cars that were running like new. Those VW bugs, you couldn't kill 'em. The body so rotten with rust the driver can see the road under his feet but the engine still ticking away." He tosses the chunky green book back. Nelson fumbles the catch. Harry asks him, "How do you feel, about your girlfriend's going out with somebody else?"

"I've told you before, Dad, she's not my girlfriend, she's my friend. Can't you have a friend of the opposite sex?"

"You can try it. How come she settled on moving back here with you then?"

Nelson's patience is being tried but Harry figures he might as well keep pushing, he's not learning anything playing the silent game. Nelson says, "She needed to blow the scene in Colorado and I was coming east and told her my grandmother's house had a lot of empty rooms. She's not been any trouble, has she?"

"No, she's charmed old Bessie right out of her sneakers. What was the matter with the scene in Colorado, that she needed to blow it?"

"Oh, you know. The wrong guy was putting a move on her, and she wanted to get her head together."

The rain restates its theme, hard, against the thin windows. Rabbit has always loved that feeling, of being inside when it rains. Shingles in the attic, pieces of glass no thicker than cardboard keeping him dry. Things that touch and yet not.

Delicately Harry asks, "You *know* the guy she's out with?"

"Yes, Dad, and so do you."

"Billy Fosnacht?"

"Guess again. Think older. Think Greek."

"Oh my God. You're kidding. That old crock?"

Nelson watches him with an alertness, a stillness of malice. He is not laughing, though the opportunity has been given. He explains, "He called up the Crêpe House and asked her, and she thought Why not? It gets pretty boring around here, you have to admit. Just for a meal. She didn't promise to go to bed with him. The trouble with your generation, Dad, you can only think along certain lines."

"Charlie Stavros," Harry says, trying to get a handle on it. The kid seems in a pretty open mood. Rabbit dares go on, "You remember he saw your mother for a while."

"I remember. But everybody else around here seems to have forgotten. You all seem so cozy now."

"Times change. You don't think we should be? Cozy."

Nelson sneers, sinking lower into the depths of the old sofa. "I don't give that much of a damn. It's not my life."

"It was," Harry says. "You were right there. I felt sorry for you, Nelson, but I couldn't think what else to do. That poor girl Jill—"

"Dad—"

"Skeeter's dead, you know. Killed in a Philadelphia shootout. Somebody sent me a clipping."

"Mom wrote me that. I'm not surprised. He was crazy."

"Yeah, and then not. You know he said he'd be dead in ten years. He really did have a certain—"

"Dad. Let's cool this conversation."

"O.K. Suits me. Sure."

Rain. So sweet, so solid. In the garden the smallest scabs of earth, beneath the lettuce and lopsided bean leaves perforated by Japanese beetles, are darkening, soaking, the leaves above them glistening, dripping, in the widespread vegetable sharing of this secret of the rain. Rabbit returns his eyes to his magazine from studying Nelson's stubborn clouded face. The best type of four-slice toaster, he reads, is the one that has separate controls for each pair of toast slots. Stavros and Melanie, can you believe? Charlie had kept saying he had liked her style.

As if in apology for having cut his father off when the rain was making him reminiscent, Nelson breaks the silence. "What's Charlie's title over there, anyway?"

"Senior Sales Rep. He's in charge of the used cars and I take care of the new. That's more or less. In practice, we overlap. Along with Jake and Rudy, of course." He wants to keep reminding the kid of Jake and Rudy. No rich men's sons, they give a good day's work for their dollar.

"Are you satisfied with the job Charlie does for you?"

"Absolutely. He knows the ropes better than I do. He knows half the county."

"Yeah, but his health. How much energy you think he has?"

The question has a certain collegiate tilt to it. He hasn't asked Nelson enough about college, maybe that's the way through to him. All these women around, it's too easy for Nelson to hide. "Energy? He has to watch himself and take it easy, but he gets the job done. People don't *like* to be hustled these days, there was too much of that, the way the car business used to be. I think a salesman who's a little—what's the word?— laid back, people trust more. I don't mind Charlie's style." He wonders if Melanie does. Where are they, in some restaurant? He pictures her face, bright-eyed almost like a thyroid bulge and her cheeks that look always rouged, rosy with exertion even before she bought the Fuji, her young face dense and smooth as she smiles and keeps smiling opposite old Charlie's classic con-man's profile, as he puts his move on her. And then later that business down below, his thick cock that blue-brown of Mediterranean types and, he wonders if her hair there is as curly as the hair on her head, in and out, he can't believe it will happen, while the rest of them sit here listening to the rain.

Nelson is saying, "I was wondering if something couldn't be done with convertibles." A heavy shamed diffidence thickens his words so they seem to drop one by one from his face, downturned where he sits in the tired gray sofa with his muskrat cut.

"Convertibles? How?"

"You know, Dad, don't make me say it. Buy 'em and sell 'em. Detroit doesn't make 'em anymore, so the old ones are more and more valuable. You could get more than you paid for Mom's Mustang."

"If you don't wreck it first."

This reminder has the effect Rabbit wants. "Shit," the boy exclaims, defenseless, darting looks at every corner of the ceiling looking for the escape hatch, "I didn't wreck your damn precious Corona, I just gave it a little dent."

"It's still in the shop. Some dent."

"I didn't do it on purpose, Christ, Dad, you act like it was some divine chariot or something. You've gotten so uptight in your old age."

"Have I?" He asks sincerely, thinking this might be information.

"Yes. All you think about is money and *things.*"

"That's not good, is it?"

"No."

"You're right. Let's forget about the car. Tell me about college."

"It's yukky," is the prompt response. "It's Dullsville. People think because of that shooting ten years ago it's some great radical place but the fact is most of the kids are Ohio locals whose idea of a terrific time is drinking beer till they throw up and having shaving cream fights in the dorms. Most of 'em are going to go into their father's business anyway, they don't care."

Harry ignores this, asking, "You ever have reason to go over to the big Firestone plant? I keep reading in the paper where they kept making those steel-belted radial five hundreds even after they kept blowing up on everybody."

"Typical," the boy tells him. "All the products you buy are like that. All the American products."

"We used to be the best," Harry says, staring into the distance as if toward a land where he and Nelson can perfectly agree.

"So I'm told." The boy looks downward into his book.

"Nelson, about work. I told your mother we'd make a summer job for you over there on wash-up and maintenance. You'd learn a lot, just watching Manny and the boys."

"Dad, I'm too old for wash-up. And maybe I need more than a summer job."

"Are you trying to tell me you'd drop out of college with one lousy year to go?"

His voice has grown loud and the boy looks alarmed. He stares at his father open-mouthed, the dark ajar spot making with his two eyesockets three holes, in a hollow face. The rain drums on the porch roof spout. Janice and her mother come down from *The Waltons* weeping. Janice wipes at her eyes with her fingers and laughs. "It's so stupid, to get carried away. It was in *People* how all the actors couldn't stand each other, that's what broke up the show."

"Well, they have lots of reruns," Ma Springer says, dropping onto the gray sofa beside Nelson, as if this little trip downstairs has been all her legs can bear. "I'd seen that one before, but still they get to you."

Harry announces, "The kid here says he may not go back to Kent."

Janice had been about to walk into the kitchen for a touch of Campari but freezes, standing. She is wearing just her short see-through nightie over underpants in the heat. "You knew that, Harry," she says.

Red bikini underpants, he notices, that show through as dusty pink. At the height of the heat wave last week she got her hair cut in Brewer by a man Doris Kaufmann goes to. He exposed the back of her neck and gave her bangs; Harry isn't used to them yet, it's as if a strange woman was slouching around here nearly naked. He almost shouts, "The hell I did. After all the money we've put into his education?"

"Well," Janice says, swinging so her body taps the nightie from within, "maybe he's got what he can out of it."

"I don't get all this. There's something fishy going on. The kid comes home with no explanation and his girlfriend goes out with Charlie Stavros while he sits here hinting to me I should can Charlie so I can hire him instead."

"Well," Ma Springer pronounces peacefully, "Nelson's of an age. Fred made space for you, Harry, and I know if he was here he'd make space for Nelson."

In on the dining-room sideboard, dead Fred Springer listens to the rain, misty-eyed.

"Not at the top he wouldn't," Harry says. "Not to somebody who quits college a few lousy credits short of graduating."

"Well Harry," Ma Springer says, as calm and mellow as if the TV show had been a pipe of pot, "some would have said you weren't so promising when Fred took you on. More than one person advised him against it."

Out in the country, under the ground, old Farmer Byer mourns his fleet of school buses, rotting in the rain.

"I was a forty-year-old man who'd lost his job through no fault of his own. I sat and did Linotype as long as there was Linotype."

"You worked at your father's trade," Janice tells him, "and that's what Nelson's asking to do."

"Sure, *sure*," Harry shouts, "when he gets out of college if that's what he wants. Though frankly I'd hoped he'd want more. But what is the *rush*? What'd he come home for anyway? If I'd ever been so lucky at his age to get to a state like Colorado I'd sure as hell have stayed at least the summer."

Sexier than she can know, Janice drags on a cigarette. "Why don't you want your own son home?"

"He's too *big* to be home! What's he running from?" From the look on their faces he may have hit on something, he doesn't know what. He's not sure he wants to know what. In the silence that answers him he listens again to the downpour, an incessant presence at the edge of their lamplight domain, gentle, insistent, unstoppable, a million small missiles striking home and running in rivulets from the face of things. Skeeter, Jill, and the Kent State Four are out there somewhere, bone dry.

"Forget it," Nelson says, standing up. "I don't want any job with this creep."

"What's he so hostile for?" Harry beseeches the women. "All I've said was I don't see why we should fire Charlie so the kid can peddle convertibles. In time, sure. In 1980, even. Take over, young America. Eat me up. But one thing at a time, Jesus. There's tons of time."

"Is there?" Janice asks strangely. She does know something. Cunts always know something.

He turns to her directly. "You. I'd think *you'd* be loyal to Charlie at least."

"More than to my own son?"

"I'll tell you this. I'll tell you all this. If Charlie goes, I go." He struggles to stand, but the Barcalounger has a sticky grip.

"Hip, hip hooray," Nelson says, yanking his denim jacket from the clothes tree inside the front door and shrugging it on. He looks humpbacked and mean, a rat going out to be drowned.

"Now he's going out to wreck the Mustang." Harry struggles to his feet and stands, taller than them all.

Ma Springer slaps her knees with open palms. "Well this discussion has ruined my mood. I'm going to heat up water for a cup of tea, the damp has put the devil in my joints."

Janice says, "Harry, say goodnight to Nelson nicely."

He protests, "He hasn't said goodnight nicely to me. I was down here trying to talk nicely to him about college and it was like pulling teeth. What's everything such a secret for? I don't even know what he's majoring in now. First it was pre-med but the chemistry was too hard, then it was anthropology but there was too much to memorize, last I heard he'd switched to social science but it was too much bullshit."

"I'm majoring in geography," Nelson admits, nervous by the door, tense to scuttle.

"Geography! That's something they teach in the third grade! I never heard of a grownup studying geography."

"Apparently it's a great specialty out there," Janice says.

"Whadde they do all day, color maps?"

"Mom, I got to split. Where's your car keys?"

"Look in my raincoat pocket."

Harry can't stop getting after him. "Now remember the roads around here are slippery when wet," he says. "If you get lost just call up your geography professor."

"Charlie's taking Melanie out really bugs you, doesn't it?" Nelson says to him.

"Not at all. What bugs me is why it doesn't bug you."

"I'm queer," Nelson tells him.

"Janice, what have I done to this kid to deserve this?"

She sighs. "Oh, I expect you know."

He is sick of these allusions to his tainted past. "I took care of him, didn't I? While you were off screwing around who was it put his breakfast cereal on the table and got him off to school?"

"My daddy did," Nelson says in a bitter mincing voice.

Janice intervenes. "Nellie, why don't you go now if you're going to go? Did you find the keys?"

The child dangles them.

"You're committing automotive suicide," Rabbit tells her. "This kid is a car killer."

"It was just a fucking *dent*," Nelson cries to the ceiling, "and he's going to make me suffer and *suf*fer." The door slams, having admitted a sharp gust of the aroma of the rain.

"Now who else would like some tea?" Ma Springer calls from the kitchen. They go in to her. Moving from the stuffy overfurnished living room to the kitchen with its clean enamelled surfaces provides a brighter perspective on the world. "Harry, you shouldn't be so hard on the boy," his mother-in-law advises. "He has a lot on his mind."

"Like what?" he asks sharply.

"Oh," Ma says, still mellow, setting out plates of comfort, Walton-style, "the things young people do."

Janice has on underpants beneath her nightie but no bra and in the bright light her nipples show inside the cloth with their own pink color, darker, more toward wine. She is saying, "It's a hard age. They seem to have so many choices and yet they don't. They've been taught by television all their lives to want this and that and yet when they get to be twenty they find money isn't so easy to come by after all. They don't have the opportunities even we had."

This doesn't sound like her. "Who have *you* been talking to?" Harry asks scornfully.

Janice is harder to put down than formerly; she tidies her bangs with a fiddling raking motion of her fingers and answers, "Some of the girls at the club, their children have come home too and don't know what to do with themselves. It even has a name now, the back-to-the-nest something."

"Syndrome," he says; he is being brought round. He and Pop and Mom sometimes after Mim had been put to bed would settle like this around the kitchen table, with cereal or cocoa if not tea. He feels safe enough to sound plaintive. "If he'd just *ask* for help," he says, "I'd try to give it. But he doesn't ask. He wants to take without asking."

"And isn't that just human nature," Ma Springer says, in a

spruced-up voice. The tea tastes to her satisfaction and she adds as if to conclude, "There's a lot of sweetness in Nelson, I think he's just a little overwhelmed for now."

"Who isn't?" Harry asks.

In bed, perhaps it's the rain that sexes him up, he insists they make love, though at first Janice is reluctant. "I would have taken a bath," she says, but she smells great, deep jungle smell, of precious rotting mulch going down and down beneath the ferns. When he won't stop, crazy to lose his face in this essence, the cool stern fury of it takes hold of her and combatively she comes, thrusting her hips up to grind her clitoris against his face and then letting him finish inside her beneath him. Lying spent and adrift he listens again to the rain's sound, which now and then quickens to a metallic rhythm on the window glass, quicker than the throbbing in the iron gutter, where ropes of water twist.

"I like having Nelson in the house," Harry says to his wife. "It's great to have an enemy. Sharpens your senses."

Murmurously beyond their windows, yet so close they might be in the cloud of it, the beech accepts, leaf upon leaf, shelves and stairs of continuous dripping, the rain.

"Nelson's not your enemy. He's your boy and needs you more now than ever though he can't say it."

Rain, the last proof left to him that God exists. "I feel," he says, "there's something I don't know."

Janice admits, "There is."

"What is it?" Receiving no answer, he asks then, "How do you know it?"

"Mother and Melanie talk."

"How bad is it? Drugs?"

"Oh Harry no." She has to hug him, his ignorance must make him seem so vulnerable. "Nothing like that. Nelson's like you are, underneath. He likes to keep himself pure."

"Then what the fuck's up? Why can't I be told?"

She hugs him again, and lightly laughs. "Because you're not a Springer."

Long after she has fallen into the steady soft rasping of sleep he lies awake listening to the rain, not willing to let it go, this sound of life. You don't have to be a Springer to have secrets. Blue eyes so pale in the light coming into the back seat of that

Corolla. Janice's taste is still on his lips and he thinks maybe
it wouldn't be such a good idea for Sealtest. Twice as he lies
awake a car stops outside and the front door opens: the first
time from the quietness of the motor and the lightness of the
steps on the porch boards, Stavros dropping off Melanie; the
next time, not many minutes later, the motor brutally raced
before cut-off and the footsteps loud and defiant, must be Nelson, having had more beers than was good for him. From the
acoustical quality surrounding the sounds of this second car
Rabbit gathers that the rain is letting up. He listens for the
young footsteps to come upstairs but one set seems to trap the
other in the kitchen, Melanie having a snack. The thing about
vegetarians, they seem always hungry. You eat and eat and
it's never the right food. Who told him that, once? Tothero,
he seemed so old there at the end but how much older than
Harry is now was he? Nelson and Melanie stay in the kitchen
talking until the eavesdropper wearies and surrenders. In his
dream, Harry is screaming at the boy over the telephone at the
lot, but though his mouth is open so wide he can see all his
own teeth spread open like in those dental charts they marked
your cavities on that looked like a scream, no sound comes out;
his jaws and eyes feel frozen open and when he awakes it seems
it has been the morning sun, pouring in hungrily after the rain,
that he has been aping.

The display windows at Springer Motors have been recently washed and Harry stands staring through them with
not a fleck of dust to show him he is not standing outdoors,
in an air-conditioned outdoors, the world left rinsed and pud-
dled by last night's rain, with yet a touch of weariness in the
green of the tree across Route 111 behind the Chuck Wagon, a
dead or yellow leaf here and there, at the tips of the crowded
branches that are dying. The traffic this weekday flourishes.
Carter keeps talking about a windfall tax on the oil companies'
enormous profits but that won't happen, Harry feels. Carter
is smart as a whip and prays a great deal but his gift seems to
be the old Eisenhower one of keeping much from happening,
just a little daily seepage.

Charlie is with a young black couple wrapping up the sale
of a trade-in, unloading a '73 Buick eight-cylinder two-tone

for three K on good folks too far behind in the rat race to know times have changed, we're running out of gas, the smart money is into foreign imports with sewing-machine motors. They even got dressed up for the occasion, the wife wears a lavender suit with the skirt old-fashionedly short, her calves hard and high up on her skinny bow legs. They really aren't shaped like we are; Skeeter used to say they were the latest design. Her ass is high and hard along the same lines as her calves as she revolves gleefully around the garish old Buick, in the drench of sunshine, on the asphalt still wet and gleaming. A pretty sight, out of the past. Still it does not dispel the sour unease in Harry's stomach after his short night's sleep. Charlie says something that doubles them both up laughing and then they drive the clunker off. Charlie comes back to his desk in a corner of the cool showroom and Harry approaches him there.

"How'd you dig Melanie last night?" He tries to keep the smirk out of his voice.

"Nice girl." Charlie keeps his pencil moving. "Very straight."

Harry's voice rises indignantly. "What's straight about her? She's kooky as a bluebird, for all I can see."

"Not so, champ. Very level head. She's one of those women you worry about, that they see it all so clearly they'll never let themselves go."

"You're telling me she didn't let herself go with you."

"I didn't expect her to. At my age—who needs it?"

"You're younger than I am."

"Not at heart. You're still learning."

It is as when he was a boy in grade school, and there seemed to be a secret everywhere, flickering up and down the aisles, bouncing around like the playground ball at recess, and he could not get his hands on it, the girls were keeping it from him, they were too quick. "She mention Nelson?"

"A fair amount."

"Whatcha think is going on between them?"

"I think they're just buddies."

"You don't think anymore they got to be fucking?"

Charlie gives up, slapping his desk and pushing back from his paperwork. "Hell, I don't know how these kids have it organized. In our day if you weren't fucking you'd move on. With them it may be different. They don't want to be killers like we were. If they *are* fucking, from the way she talks about him it has about the charge of cuddling a teddy bear before you go to sleep."

"She sees him that way, huh? Childish."

"Vulnerable is the way she'd put it."

Harry offers, "There's some piece missing here. Janice was dropping hints last night."

Stavros delicately shrugs. "Maybe it's back in Colorado. The piece."

"Did she say anything specific?"

Stavros ponders before answering, pushing up his amber glasses with a forefinger and then resting that finger on the bridge of his nose. "No."

Harry tries outright grievance. "I can't figure out what the kid *wants*."

"He wants to get started at the real world. I think he wants in around here."

"I *know* he wants in, and I don't *want* him in. He makes me uncomfortable. With that sorehead look of his he couldn't sell—"

"Coke in the Sahara," Charlie finishes for him. "Be that as it may, he's Fred Springer's grandson. He's *engonaki*."

"Yeah, both Janice and Bessie are pushing, you saw that the other night. They're driving me wild. We have a nice symmetrical arrangement here, and how many cars'd we move in July?"

Stavros checks a sheet of paper under his elbow. "Twenty-nine, would you believe. Thirteen used, sixteen new. Including three of those Celica GTs for ten grand each. I didn't think it would go, not against all the little sports coming out of Detroit at half the price. Those Nips, they know their market research."

"So to hell with Nelson. There's only one month left in the summer anyway. Why screw Jake and Rudy out of sales commission just to accommodate a kid too spoiled to take a job in the shop? He wouldn't even have had to dirty his hands, we could have put him in Parts."

Stavros says, "You could put him on straight salary here on the floor. I'd take him under my wing."

Charlie doesn't seem to realize he is the one to get pushed out. You try to defend somebody and he undermines you while you're doing it. But Charlie sees the problem after all;

he expresses it: "Look. You're the son-in-law, you can't be touched. But me, the old lady is my connection here, and it's sentimental at that, she likes me because I remind her of Fred, of the old days. Sentiment doesn't beat out blood. I'm in no position to hang tough. If you can't beat 'em, join 'em. Furthermore I think I can talk to the kid, do something for him. Don't worry, he'll never stick in this business, he's too twitchy. He's too much like his old man."

"I see no resemblance," Harry says, though pleased.

"You wouldn't. I don't know, it seems to be hard these days, being a father. When I was a kid it seemed simple. Tell the kid what to do and if he doesn't do it sock him one. Here's my thought. When you and Jan and the old lady are taking your weeks in the Poconos, has Nelson been planning to come along?"

"They've asked him, but he didn't seem too enthusiastic. As a kid he was always lonely up there. Jesus, it'd be hell, in that little space. Even around the house every time you come into a room it seems he's sitting there with a beer."

"Right. Well how about buying him a suit and tie and letting him come in here? Give him the minimum wage, no commission and no draw. He wouldn't be getting on your nerves, or you on his."

"How could I be getting on his nerves? He walks all over me. He takes the car all the time and tries to make me feel guilty besides."

Charlie doesn't dignify this with an answer; he knows too much of the story.

Harry admits, "Well, it's an idea. Then he'd be going back to college?"

Charlie shrugs. "Let's hope. Maybe you can make that part of the bargain."

Looking down upon the top of Charlie's fragile wavy-haired skull, Rabbit cannot avoid awareness of his own belly, an extensive, suit-straining slope; he has become a person and a half, where the same years have pared Charlie's shape, once stocky, bit by bit. He asks him, "You really want to do this for Nelson?"

"I like the kid. To me, he's just another basket case. At his age now they're all basket cases."

A couple has parked out in the glare and is heading for the showroom doors, a well-dressed Penn Park sort of pair that will probably collect the literature and sneak off to buy a Mercedes, as an investment. "Well, it's your funeral," Harry tells Charlie. Actually it might be nice all around. Melanie wouldn't be left alone in that big house all by herself. And it occurs to him that this all may be Melanie's idea, and Charlie's way of keeping his move on her alive.

In bed Melanie asks Nelson, "What are you learning?"

"Oh, stuff." They have decided upon her bed in the front room for these weeks when the old people are in the Poconos. Melanie in the month and more of her tenancy here has gradually moved the headless dress dummy to a corner and hidden some of the Springers' other ugly possessions—slid some rolled-up hall carpeting beneath the bed, tucked a trunkful of old curtains and a broken foot-pedalled Singer into the back of the closet, already crammed with outgrown and outmoded clothes in polyethylene cleaner bags. She has Scotch-taped a few Peter Max posters to the walls and made the room her own. They have used Nelson's room up to now, but his childhood bed is single and in truth he feels inhibited there. They had not intended to sleep together at all in this house but out of their long and necessary conversations it had been inevitable they sink into it. Melanie's breasts are indeed, as Charlie had noticed at a glance, large; their laden warm sway sometimes sickens Nelson, reminding him of a more shallow-breasted other, whom he has abandoned. He elaborates: "Lots of things. There's all these pressures that don't show, like between the agency and the manufacturer. You got to buy sets of their special tools, for thousands of dollars, and they keep loading their base models with what used to be extras, where the dealer used to make a lot of his profit. Charlie told me a radio used to cost the dealer about thirty-five dollars and he'd add about one-eighty on to the sales price. See then by the manufacturer getting greedy and taking these options away from the dealer the dealers have to think up more gimmicks. Like undercoating. And rustproofing. There's even a treatment they'll give the vinyl upholstery to keep it from wearing supposedly. All that stuff. It's all cutthroat but kind of jolly at the same time, all these little pep talks people keep giving each other. My grand-father used to have a performance board but Dad's let it drop. You can tell Charlie thinks Dad's really lazy and sloppy the way he runs things."

She pushes herself more upright in the bed, her breasts slug-gish and luminous in the half-light the maples filter from the sodium lamps on Joseph Street. There is that something heavy and maternal and mystical in her he cannot escape. "Charlie's asked me out on another date," she says.

"Go," Nelson advises, enjoying the altered feeling of the bed, Melanie's lifting her torso above him deepening the rum-pled trough in which he lies. When he was a little child and Mom and Dad were living in that apartment high on Wilbur Street and they would come visit here he would be put to bed in this very room, his grandmother's hair all black then but the patterns of light carved on the ceiling by the window mul-lions just the same as they are now. Mom-mom would sing him songs, he remembers, but he can't remember what they were. In Pennsylvania Dutch, some of them. *Reide, reide, Geile.* . . .

Melanie pulls a hairpin from the back of her head and fishes with it in the ashtray for a dead roach that may have a hit or two left in it. She holds it to her red lips and lights it; the pa-per flares. When she lifted her arm to pull the hairpin, the hair in her armpit, unshaved, has flared in Nelson's field of vision. Despite himself, to no purpose, his prick with little knocks of blood begins to harden down in the trough of childish warmth. "I don't know," Melanie says. "I think with them away, he's psyched to score."

"How do you feel about that?"

"Not so great."

"He's a pretty nice guy," Nelson says, snuggling deeper be-side her abstracted body, enjoying the furtive growth of his erection. "Even if he did screw Mom."

"Suppose it kills him, how would I feel then? I mean, one of the reasons for my coming with you was to clean my head of all this father-figure shit."

"You came along because Pru told you to." Saying the oth-er's name is delicious, a cool stab in the warmth. "So I wouldn't get away."

"Well, yeah, but I wouldn't have if I hadn't had reasons of

my own. I'm glad I came. I like it here. It's like America used to be. All these brick houses built so solid, one against the other."

"I hate it. Everything's so humid and stuffy and, so *closed*."

"You really feel that Nelson?" He likes it when she kind of purrs his name. "I thought you acted frightened, in Colorado. There was too much space. Or maybe it was the situation."

Nelson loses Colorado in awareness of his erection, like a piece of round-ended ridged ivory down there, and of the womanly thick cords in her throat swelling as she sucks one last hit from the tiny butt held tight against her painted lips. Melanie always wears makeup, lipstick and touches of red to her cheeks to make her complexion less olive, where Pru never wore any, her lips pale as her brow, and everything about her face precise and dry as a photograph. Pru: the thought of her is a gnawing in his stomach, like somebody rolling a marble around over grits of sand. He says, "Maybe what I mind about around here is Dad." At the thought of Dad the abrasion intensifies. "I can't stand him, the way he sits there in the living room hogging the Barcalounger. He"—he can hardly find words, the discomfort is so great—"just sits there in the middle of the whole fucking world, taking and taking. He doesn't know anything the way Charlie does. What did he ever do, to build up the lot? My granddad was grubbing his way up while my father wasn't doing anything but being a lousy husband to my mother. That's all he's done to deserve all this money: be too lazy and shiftless to leave my mother like he wanted to. I think he's queer. You should have seen him with this black guy I told you about."

"You loved your granddad, didn't you Nelson?" When she's high on pot her voice gets husky and kind of trancy, like one of these oracles sitting over her tripod they talked about in anthro at Kent. Kent: more sand rubbing in his stomach.

"He liked *me*," Nelson insists, writhing a little and noticing with his hand that his erection has slightly wilted, possessing no longer the purity of ivory but the compromised texture of flesh and blood. "He wasn't always criticizing me because I wasn't some great shakes athlete and ten feet tall."

"I've never heard your father criticize you," she says, "except when you cracked up his car."

"Goddam it I *did*n't crack it up, I just dented the bastard and he's going through this whole big deal, weeks in the body shop while I'm supposed to feel guilty or inept or something. And there *was* an animal in the road, some little thing I don't know what it was, a woodchuck, I would have seen the stripes if it had been a skunk, I don't know why they don't make these dumb animals with longer legs, it *waddled.* Right into the headlights. I wish I'd killed it. I wish I'd smashed up all Dad's cars, the whole fucking inventory."

"This is really crazy talk Nelson," Melanie says from within her amiable trance. "You need your father. We all need fathers. At least yours is where you can find him. He's not a bad man."

"He *is* bad, really bad. He doesn't know what's up, and he doesn't *care*, and he thinks he's so great. That's what gets me, his *hap*piness. He is so fucking *hap*py." Nelson almost sobs. "You think of all the misery he's caused. My little sister dead because of him and then this Jill he let die."

Melanie knows these stories. She says in a patient singsong, "You mustn't forget the circumstances. Your father's not God." Her hand follows down inside the bedsheet where his has been exploring. She smiles. Her teeth are perfect. She's had orthodontia, and poor Pru never did, her people were too poor, so she hates to smile, though the irregularity isn't really that noticeable, just a dog tooth slightly overlapping on one side. "You're feeling frustrated right now," Melanie tells him, "because of your situation. But your situation is not your father's fault."

"It *is*," Nelson insists. "Everything's his fault, it's his fault I'm so fucked up, and he en*joys* it, the way he looks at me sometimes, you can tell he's really eating it up, that I'm fucked up. And then the way Mom waits on him, like he's actually *done* something for her, instead of the other way around."

"Come on Nelson, let it go," Melanie croons. "Forget everything for now. I'll help you." She flips down the sheet and turns her back. "Here's my ass. I love being fucked from behind when I have a buzz on. It's like I'm occupying two planes of being."

Melanie hardly ever tries to come when they make love, takes it for granted she is serving the baby male and not herself. With Pru, though, the woman was always trying, breathing "Wait"

in his ear and squirming around with her pelvis for the right
contact, and even when he couldn't wait and failed, this was
somehow more flattering. Remembering Pru this way he feels
the nibble of guilt in the depths of his stomach take a sharper
bite, like the moment in *Jaws* when the girl gets pulled under.

Water. Rabbit distrusts the element though the little brown
hourglass-shaped lake that laps the gritty beach in front of the
Springers' old cottage in the Poconos seems friendly and tame,
and he swims in it every day, taking a dip before breakfast, before Janice is awake, and while Ma Springer in her quilty bathrobe fusses at the old oil stove to make the morning coffee. On
weekdays when there aren't so many people around he walks
down across the coarse imported sand wrapped in a beach towel
and, after a glance right and left at the cottages that flank theirs
back in the pines, slips into the lake naked. What luxury! A chill
silver embrace down and through his groin. Gnats circling near
the surface shatter and reassemble as he splashes through them,
cleaving the plane of liquid stillness, sending ripples right and
left toward muddy rooty banks city blocks away. A film of mist
sits visible on the skin of the lake if the hour is early enough.
He was never an early-to-rise freak but sees the point of it now,
you get *into* the day at the start, before it gets rolling, and roll
with it. The film of mist tastes of evening chill, of unpolluted
freshness in a world waking with him. As a kid Rabbit never
went to summer camps, maybe Nelson is right they were too
poor, it never occurred to them. The hot cracked sidewalks and
dusty playground of Mt. Judge were summer enough, and the
few trips to the Jersey Shore his parents organized stick up in
his remembrance as almost torture, the hours on poky roads
in the old Model A and then the mud-brown Chevy, his sister
and mother adding to the heat the vapors of female exasperation, Pop dogged at the wheel, the back of his neck sweaty and
scrawny and freckled while the flat little towns of New Jersey
threw back at Harry distorted echoes of his own town, his own
life, for which he was homesick after an hour. Town after town
numbingly demonstrated to him that his life was a paltry thing,
roughly duplicated by the millions in settings where houses
and porches and trees mocking those in Mt. Judge fed the
illusions of other little boys that their souls were central and

important and invisibly cherished. He would look at the little girls on the sidewalks they drove alongside wondering which of them he would marry, for his idea of destiny was to move away and marry a girl from another town. The traffic as they neared the Shore became thicker, savage, metropolitan. Cars, he has always found cars, their glitter, their exhalations, cruel. Then at last arriving in a burst of indignities—the parking lot full, the bathhouse attendant rude—they would enter upon a few stilted hours on the alien beach whose dry sand burned the feet and scratched in the crotch and whose wet ribs where the sea had receded had a deadly bottomless smell, a smell of vast death. Every found shell had this frightening faint stink. His parents in bathing suits alarmed him. His mother didn't look obscenely fat like some of the other mothers but bony and long and hard, and as she stood to call him or little Mim back from the suspect crowds of strangers or the dangerous rumor of undertow her arms seemed to be flapping like featherless wings. Not Rabbit then, he would be called as "Hassy! Hassy!" And his father's skin where the workclothes always covered it seemed so tenderly white. He loved his father for having such whiteness upon him, secretly, a kind of treasure; in the bathhouse he and Pop changed together rapidly, not looking at one another, and at the end of the day changed again. The ride back to Diamond County was always long enough for the sunburn to start hurting. He and Mim would start slapping each other just to hear the other yell and to relieve the boredom of this wasted day that could have been spent among the fertile intrigues and perfected connections of the Mt. Judge playground.

In his memory of these outings they always seem to be climbing toward the ocean as toward a huge blue mountain. Sometimes at night before falling to sleep he hears his mother say with a hiss, "Hassy." He sees now that he is rich that these were the outings of the poor, ending in sunburn and stomach upset. Pop liked crabcakes and baked oysters but could never eat them without throwing up. When the Model A was tucked into the garage and little Mim tucked into bed Harry could hear his father vomiting in a far corner of the yard. He never complained about vomiting or about work, they were just things you had to do, one more regularly than the other.

So as a stranger to summer places Rabbit had come to this
cottage Fred Springer had bought rather late in his life, after the Toyota franchise had made him more than a used-car
dealer, after his one child was married and grown. Harry and
Janice used to come for just visits of a week. The space was too
small, the tensions would begin to rub through, with Nelson
bored and bug-eaten after the first day or so. You can only go
visit Bushkill Falls so often, climbing up and down those steps
admiring the ferns.

When old man Springer died Harry became the man of the
place and at last understood that Nature isn't just something
that pushes up through the sidewalk cracks and keeps the farmers trapped in the sticks but is an elixir, a luxury that can be
bought and fenced off and kept pure for the more fortunate,
in an impure age. Not that this five-room, dark-shingled cottage, which Ma Springer rents for all but these three weeks of
August, taking the Labor Day gravy and renting into hunting
season if she can, was in any league with the gabled estates
and lodges and resort hotels that are all around them tumbling down or being broken up by developers; but it has two
acres of woods behind it and a dock and rowboat of its own,
and holds out to Harry the possibility that life can be lived
selectively, as one chooses from a menu, or picks a polished
fruit from a bowl. Here in the Poconos food, exercise, and
sleep, no longer squeezed into the margins of the day, swell
to a sumptuous importance. The smell of fresh coffee drifting
to greet him as he walks still wet back from his swim; the kiss
of morning fog through a rusted window screen; the sight of
Janice with bare brown feet wearing the same tennis shorts
and kid's black T-shirt day after day; the blue jay switching
stances on the porch rail; the smooth rose-veined rock holding
shut the upstairs door that has lost its latch; the very texture of
root-riddled mud and reeds where the fresh cedar dock pilings
have been driven: he feels love for each phenomenon and not
for the first time in his life seeks to bring himself into harmony
with the intertwining simplicities that uphold him, that were
woven into him at birth. There must be a good way to live.

He eases off on the gin and snacks. He swims and listens
to Ma Springer reminisce over the morning coffee and goes
down into the village with Janice each day to shop. At night

they play three-handed pinochle by the harsh light of bridge lamps, the light feeling harsh because when he had first come to this place they lit kerosene lamps, with fragile interior cones of glowing ash, and went to bed soon after dark, the crickets throbbing. He does not like to fish, nor does he much like playing tennis with Janice against one of the other couples that have access to the lake community's shared court, an old rectangle of clay in the pines, the edges coated with brown needles and the chicken-wire fencing drooping like wet wash. Janice plays every day at the Flying Eagle, and beside her efficient grace he feels cumbersome and out of it. The ball hops at him with a speed his racket cannot match. Her black T-shirt has on it in faded 3-D script the word *Phillies*; it is a shirt he bought Nelson on one of their excursions to Veterans Stadium, and the boy left it behind when he went away to Kent, and Janice in her middle-aged friskiness found it and made it hers. Typical of the way things have gone, that the kid's growing up should seem a threat and a tragedy to him and to her an excuse to steal a T-shirt. Not that it would fit Nelson anymore. It fits her fine; he feels her beside him in the corner of his eye nimbler and freer than he in her swarthy thick-middled old girl's shape with her short hair and bouncing bangs. The ball arcs back steadily from her racket while he hits it too hard or else, trying to "stroke" it like she tells him, pops it weakly into the net. "Harry, don't try to *steer* it," she says. "Keep your knees bent. Point your hip toward the net." She has had a lot of lessons. The decade past has taught her more than it has taught him.

What has he done, he wonders as he waits to receive the serve, with this life of his more than half over? He was a good boy to his mother and then a good boy to the crowds at the basketball games, a good boy to Tothero his old coach, who saw in Rabbit something special. And Ruth saw in him something special too, though she saw it winking out. For a while Harry had kicked against death, then he gave in and went to work. Now the dead are so many he feels for the living around him the camaraderie of survivors. He loves these people with him, penned in among the lines of the tennis court. Ed and Loretta: he's an electrical contractor from Easton specializing in computer installations. Harry loves the treetops above their heads, and the August blue above these. What does he know?

He never reads a book, just the newspaper to have something to say to people, and then mostly human interest stories, like where the Shah is heading next and how sick he really is, and that Baltimore doctor. He loves Nature, though he can name almost nothing in it. Are these pines, or spruces, or firs? He loves money, though he doesn't understand how it flows to him, or how it leaks away. He loves men, uncomplaining with their pot bellies and cross-hatched red necks, embarrassed for what to talk about when the game is over, whatever the game is. What a threadbare thing we make of life! Yet what a marvellous thing the mind is, they can't make a machine like it, though some of these computers Ed was telling about fill rooms; and the body can do a thousand things there isn't a factory in the world can duplicate the motion. He used to love screwing, though more and more he's willing just to think about it and let the younger people mess with it, meeting in their bars and cars, amazing how many of them there are now, just walking down the street or getting into a movie line he often seems to be the oldest guy in sight. At night when he's with Janice, she needing a touch of cock to lead her into sleep, he tries to picture what will turn him on, and he's running out of pictures; the last that works is of a woman on all fours being fucked by one man while she blows another. And it's not clear in the picture if Harry is doing the fucking or is the man being blown, he is looking at all three from the outside, as if up on a screen at one of these movie theaters on upper Weiser with titles like *Harem Girls* and *All the Way*, and the woman's sensations seem nearer to him than the man's, the prick in your mouth like a small wet zucchini, plus the other elsewhere, in and out, in and out, a kind of penance at your root. Sometimes he prays a few words at night but a stony truce seems to prevail between himself and God.

He begins to run. In the woods, along the old logging roads and bridle trails, he ponderously speeds in tennis shoes first, orange with clay dust, and then in gold-and-blue Nikes bought at a sporting goods shop in Stroudsburg especially for this, running shoes with tipped-up soles at toe and heel, soles whose resilient circlets like flattened cleats lift him powerfully as, growing lighter and quicker and quieter, he runs. At first he feels his weight like some murderous burden swaddled about his heart and lungs and his thigh muscles ache in the morning so that he staggers in leaving the bed and laughs aloud in surprise. But as over the days, running after supper in the cool of the early evening while all the light has not ebbed from the woods, he accustoms his body to this new demand, his legs tighten, his weight seems less, his chest holds more air, the twigs fly past his ears as if winged on their own, and he extends the distance he jogs, eventually managing the mile and a half to the waist of the hourglass, where the gates of an old estate bar the way. Carbon Castle the locals call the estate, built by a coal baron from Scranton and now little utilized by his scattered and dwindled descendants, the swimming pool drained, the tennis courts overgrown, energy gone. The glass eyes of the stuffed deer heads in the hunting lodge stare through cobwebs; the great main house with its precipitous slate roofs and diamond-paned windows is boarded up, though ten years ago one of the grandsons tried to make of it a commune, the villagers say. The young people vandalized the place, the story runs, and sold off everything they could move, including the two bronze brontosaurs that guarded the main entrance, emblems of the Coal Age. The heavy iron gates to Carbon Castle are double-chained and padlocked; Rabbit touches the forbidding metal, takes a breath for a still second while the world feels still to be rushing on, pouring through the tremble of his legs, then turns and jogs back, casting his mind wide, so as to become unconscious of his heaving body. There is along the way an open space, once a meadow, now spiked with cedars and tassle-headed weeds, where swallows dip and careen, snapping up insects revived in the evening damp. Like these swallows Rabbit, the blue and gold of his new shoes flickering, skims, above the earth, above the dead. The dead stare upwards. Mom and Pop are lying together again as for so many years on that sway-backed bed they'd bought second-hand during the Depression and never got around to replacing though it squeaked like a tricycle left out in the rain and was so short Pop's feet stuck out of the covers. Papery-white feet that got mottled and marbled with veins finally: if he'd ever have exercised he might have lived longer. Tothero down there is all eyes, eyes big as saucers staring out of his lopsided head while his swollen tongue hunts for a word. Fred Springer, who put Harry where he is, eggs him on, hunched over and grimacing like a man with a poker hand so good it hurts. Skeeter, who that newspaper clipping claimed had fired upon the Philly cops first even though there were twenty of them in the yard and hallways and only some pregnant mothers and children on the commune premises, Skeeter black as the earth turns his face away. The meadow ends and Harry enters a tunnel, getting dark now, the needles a carpet, he makes no sound, Indians moved without sound through trees without end where a single twig snapping meant death, his legs in his fatigue cannot be exactly controlled but flail against the cushioned path like arms of a loose machine whose gears and joints have been bevelled by wear. Becky, a mere seed laid to rest, and Jill, a pale seedling held from the sun, hang in the earth, he imagines, like stars, and beyond them there are myriads, whole races like the Cambodians, that have drifted into death. He is treading on them all, they are resilient, they are cheering him on, his lungs are burning, his heart hurts, he is a membrane removed from the hosts below, their filaments caress his ankles, he loves the earth, he will never make their mistake and die.

The last hundred feet, up their path to the tilting front porch, Rabbit sprints. He opens the front screen door and feels the punky floorboards bounce under him. The milk-glass shades of the old kerosene lamps, increasingly valuable as antiques, tremble, like the panes in the breakfront back on Joseph Street. Janice emerges barefoot from the kitchen and says, "Harry, you're all red in the face."

"I'm. All. Right."

"Sit down. For heaven's sakes. What are you training for?"

"The big bout," he pants. "It feels great. To press against. Your own limitations."

"You're pressing too hard if you ask me. Mother and I thought you got lost. We want to play pinochle."

"I got to take. A shower. The trouble with running is. You get all sweaty."

"I still don't know what you're trying to prove." With that Phillies shirt on she looks like Nelson, before he needed to shave.

"It's now or never," he tells her, the blood of fantasy rushing through his brain. "There's people out to get me. I can lie down now. Or fight."

"*Who's* out to get you?"

"You should know. You hatched him."

The hot water here runs off a little electric unit and is scalding for a few minutes and then cools with lightning speed. Harry thinks, A good way to kill somebody would be to turn off the cold water while they're in the shower. He dances out before the hot expires totally, admires the wet prints of his big feet on the bare pine floors of this attic-shaped upstairs, and thinks of his daughter, her feet in those cork-soled platforms. With her leggy pallor and calm round face she glows like a ghost but unlike the dead shares the skin of this planet with him, breathes air, immerses herself in water, moves from element to element, and grows. He goes into the bedroom he and Janice have here and dresses himself in Jockey shorts, an alligator shirt, and soft Levis all washed and tumble-dried at the laundromat behind the little Acme in the village. Each crisp item seems another tile of his well-being he is fitting into place. As he sits on the bed to put on fresh socks a red ray of late sun slices through a gap in the pines and falls knifelike across his toes, the orangish corns and the little hairs between the joints and the nails translucent like the thin sheets in furnace peepholes. There are feet that have done worse than his, on a lot of women's in summer sandals you notice how the little toes have been bent under by years of pointy high-heeled shoes, and the big toes pushed over so the joint sticks out like a broken bone; thank God since he is a man that has never had to happen to him. Nor to Cindy Murkett either, come to think of it: toes side by side like candies in a box. Suck. That lucky stiff Webb. Still. It's good to be alive. Harry goes downstairs and adds the fourth element to his happiness; he lights a fire. Ma Springer, riding shrewdly with the times, has bought a new wood stove. Its bright black flue pipe fits snugly into the smudged old fireplace of ugly fieldstones. Old man Springer had installed baseboard electric heat when the cottage was connected for electricity, but his widow begrudges the expense of turning it on, even though by August the nights bring in a chill from the lake. The stove comes from Taiwan and is clean as a skillet, installed just this summer. Harry lays some rough sticks found around the cottage on top of a crumpled Sports page from the Philadelphia *Bulletin* and watches them catch, watches the words EAGLES READY ignite and blacken, the letters turning white on the crinkling ash; then he adds some crescent-shaped scraps of planed fruitwood a local furniture-maker sells by the bushel outside his factory. This fire greets the dark as Janice and her mother, the dishes done, come in and get out the pinochle deck.

As she deals, Ma Springer says, the words parcelled out in rhythm with the cards, "Janice and I were saying, really we don't think it's so wise, for you to be running like this, at your age."

"My age is the age to do it. Now's the time to start taking care of myself, I've had a free ride up to now."

"Mother says you should have your heart checked first," Janice says. She has put on a sweater and jeans but her feet are still bare. He glances at them under the card table. Pretty straight, the toes are. Not too much damage, considering. Bony and brown and boyish. He likes it, that up here in the Poconos she looks so often like a boy. His playmate. As when a child he would stay over at a playmate's house.

"Your father, you know," Ma Springer is telling him, "was taken off by his heart."

"He'd been suffering for years," Harry says, "with a lot of things. He was seventy. He was ready to go."

"You may not think so when your time comes."

"I've been thinking about all the dead people I know lately," Harry says, looking at his cards. Ace, ten, king, and jack of spades, but no queen. No pinochle either therefore. No runs. No four of anything. A raft of low clubs. "I pass."

"Pass," Janice says.

"I'll take it at twenty-one," Ma Springer sighs, and lays down a run in diamonds, and the nine, and a queen of spades to go with the jack.

"Wow," Harry tells her. "What power."

"Which dead, Harry?" Janice asks.

She is afraid he means Becky. But he really rarely thinks of their dead infant, and then pleasantly, as of a brief winter day's sun on last night's snowfall, though her name was June. "Oh,

Pop and Mom mostly. Wondering if they're watching. You do so much to get your parents' attention for so much of your life, it seems weird to be going on without them. I mean, who cares now?"

"A lot of people care," Janice says, clumsily earnest.

"You don't know what it feels like," he tells her. "You still have your mother."

"For just a little while yet," Bessie says, playing an ace of clubs. Gathering in the trick with a deft rounding motion of her hand, she pronounces, "Your father now was a good worker, who never gave himself airs, but your mother I must confess I never could abide. A sharp tongue, in a plain body."

"Mother. Harry loved his mother."

Bessie snaps down the ace of hearts. "Well that's right and proper I guess, at least they say it is, for a boy to like his mother. But I used to feel sorry for him when she was alive. She drove him to have an uncommon high opinion of himself and yet could give him nothing to grab a hold of, the way Fred and I could you."

She talks of Harry as if he too is dead. "I'm still here, you know," he says, flipping on the lowest heart he has.

Bessie's mouth pinches in and her face slightly bloats as her black eyes stare down at her cards. "I know you're still here, I'm not saying anything I won't say to your face. Your mother was an unfortunate woman who caused a lot of devilment. You and Janice when you were starting out would never have had such a time of it if it hadn't been for Mary Angstrom, and that goes for ten years ago too. She thought too much of herself for what she was." Ma has that fanatic tight look about the cheeks women get when they hate one another. Mom didn't think that much of Bessie Springer either—*little upstart married to that crook, a woman without enough brains to grease a saucepan living in that big house over on Joseph Street looking down her nose. The Koerners were dirt farmers and not even the good dirt, they farmed the hills.*

"Mother, Harry's mother was bedridden all through that time the house burned down. She was dying."

"Not so dying she didn't stir up a lot of mischief before she went. If she'd have let you two work out your relations with these others there would never have been a separation and all the grief. She was envious of the Koerners and had been since Day One. I knew her when she was Mary Renninger two classes ahead of me in the old Thad Stevens School before they built the new high school where the Morris farm used to be, and she thought too much of herself then. The Renningers weren't country people, you see, they came right out of Brewer and had that slum mentality, that cockiness. Too tall for her sex and too big for her britches. Your sister, Harry, got all her looks from your father's side. Your father's father they say was one of those very fair Swedes, a plasterer." With a thump of her thumb she lays down the ace of diamonds.

"You can't lead trump until after the third trick," Harry reminds her.

"Oh, foolish." She takes the ace back and stares at her cards through the unbecoming though fashionable eyeglasses she bought recently—heavy blue shell frames hinged low to S-shaped temples and with a kind of continuous false eyebrow of silvery inlay. They aren't even comfortable, she has to keep touching the bridge to push them up on her little round nose.

Her agony is so great pondering the cards, Harry reminds her, "You only need one point to make your bid. You've already made it."

"Yes, well . . . make all you can while you can, Fred used to say." She fans her cards a little wider. "Ah. I thought I had another one of those." She lays down a second ace of clubs.

But Janice trumps it. She pulls in the trick and says, "Sorry, Mother. I only had a singleton of clubs, how could you know?"

"I had a feeling as soon as I put down that ace. I had a premonition."

Harry laughs; you have to love the old lady. Cabined with these two women, he has grown soft and confiding, as when he was a little boy and asked Mom where ladies went wee-wee. "I used to sometimes wonder," he confides to Bessie, "if Mom had ever, you know, been false to Pop."

"I wouldn't have put it past her," she says, grim-lipped as Janice leads out her own aces. Her eyes flash at Harry. "See, if you'd have let me play that diamond she wouldn't have gotten in."

"Ma," he says, "you can't take every trick, don't be so greedy. I know Mom must have been sexy, because look at Mim."

"What do you hear from your sister?" Ma asks to be polite,

staring down at her cards again. The shadows thrown by her ornate spectacle frames score her cheeks and make her look old, dragged down, where there is no anger to swell the folds of her face.

"Mim's fine. She's running this beauty parlor in Las Vegas. She's getting rich."

"I never believed half of what people said about her," Ma utters absently.

Now Janice has run through her aces and plays a king of spades to the ace she figures Harry must have. Since she joined up with that bridge-and-tennis bunch of witches over at the Flying Eagle, Janice isn't as dumb at cards as she used to be. Harry plays the expected ace and, momentarily in command, asks Ma Springer, "How much of my mother do you see in Nelson?"

"Not a scrap," she says with satisfaction, whackingly trumping his ten of spades. "Not a whit."

"What can I do for the kid?" he asks aloud. It is as if another has spoken, through him. Fog blowing through a window screen.

"Be patient," Ma answers, triumphantly beginning to run out the trumps.

"Be loving," Janice adds.

"Thank God he's going back to college next month."

Their silence fills the cottage like cool lake air. Crickets.

He accuses, "You both know stuff I don't."

They do not deny it.

He gropes. "What do you both think of Melanie, really? I think she depresses the kid."

"I dare say the rest are mine," Ma Springer announces, laying down a raft of little diamonds.

"Harry," Janice tells him. "Melanie's not the problem."

"If you ask me," Ma Springer says, so firmly they both know she wants the subject changed, "Melanie is making herself altogether too much at home."

On television Charlie's Angels are chasing the heroin smugglers in a great array of expensive automobiles that slide and screech, that plunge through fruit carts and large panes of glass and finally collide one with another, and then another, tucking into opposing fenders and grilles in a great slow-motion climax of bent metal and arrested motion and final justice. The Angel who has replaced Farrah Fawcett-Majors gets out of her crumpled Malibu and tosses her hair: this becomes a freeze-frame. Nelson laughs in empathetic triumph over all those totalled Hollywood cars. Then the more urgent tempo and subtly louder volume of the commercial floods the room; a fresh palette of reflected light paints the faces, chubby and clownish side by side, of Melanie and Nelson as they sit on the old sofa of gray nappy stuff cut into a pattern and gaze at the television set where they have placed it in the rearranged living room, where the Barcalounger used to be. Beer bottles glint on the floor beneath their propped-up feet; hanging drifts of sweetish smoke flicker in polychrome as if the ghosts of Charlie's Angels are rising to the ceiling. "Great smash-up," Nelson pronounces, with difficulty rising and fumbling the television off.

"I thought it was stupid," Melanie says in her voice of muffled singing.

"Oh shit, you think everything is stupid except what's his name, Kerchief."

"G. I. Gurdjieff." She has a prim mode of withdrawal, into mental regions where she knows he cannot reach. At Kent it became clear there were realms real for others not real to him—not just languages he didn't know, or theorems he couldn't grasp, but drifting areas of unprofitable knowledge where nevertheless profits of a sort were being made. Melanie was mystical, she ate no meat and felt no fear, the tangled weedy gods of Asia spelled a harmony to her. She lacked that fury against limits that had been part of Nelson since he had known he would never be taller than five nine though his father was six three, or perhaps before that since he had found himself helpless to keep his father and mother together and to save Jill from the ruin she wanted, or perhaps before that since he had watched grownups in dark suits and dresses assembling around a small white coffin, with silvery handles and something sparkly in the paint, that they told him held what had been his baby sister, born and then allowed to die without anybody asking *him*; nobody ever asked him, the grownup world was like that, it just ground on, and Melanie was part of that world, smugly smiling out at him from within that bubble where the mystery resided that amounted to power.

It would be nice, as long as he was standing, to take up one of the beer bottles and smash it down into the curly hair of Melanie's skull and then to take the broken half still in his hand and rotate it into the smiling plumpnesses of her face, the great brown eyes and cherry lips, the mocking implacable Buddha calm. "I don't care what the fuck his dumb name is, it's all bullshit," he tells her instead.

"You should read him," she says. "He's wonderful."

"Yeah, what does he say?"

Melanie thinks, unsmiling. "It's not easy to sum up. He says there's a Fourth Way. Besides the way of the yogi, the monk, and the fakir."

"Oh, great."

"And if you go this way you'll be what he calls awake."

"Instead of asleep?"

"He was very interested in somehow grasping the world as it is. He believed we all have plural identities."

"I want to go out," he tells her.

"Nelson, it's ten o'clock at night."

"I promised I might meet Billy Fosnacht and some of the guys down at the Laid-Back." The Laid-Back is a new bar in Brewer, at the corner of Weiser and Pine, catering to the young. It used to be called the Phoenix. He accuses her, "You go out all the time with Stavros leaving me here with nothing to do."

"You could read Gurdjieff," she says, and giggles. "Anyway I haven't gone out with Charlie more than four or five times."

"Yeah, you work all the other nights."

"It isn't as if we ever *do* anything, Nelson. The last time we sat and watched television with his mother. You ought to see her. She looks younger than he does. All black hair." She touches her own dark, vital, springy hair. "She was wonderful."

Nelson is putting on his denim jacket, bought at a shop in Boulder specializing in the worn-out clothes of ranch hands and sheep herders. It had cost twice what a new one would have cost. "I'm working on a deal with Billy. One of the other guys is going to be there. I gotta go."

"Can I come along?"

"You're working tomorrow, aren't you?"

"You know I don't care about sleep. Sleep is giving in to the body."

"I won't be late. Read one of your books." He imitates her giggle.

Melanie asks him, "When have you last written to Pru? You haven't answered any of her recent letters."

His rage returns; his tight jacket and the very wallpaper of this room seem to be squeezing him smaller and smaller. "How can I, she writes twice every fucking day, it's worse than a newspaper. Christ, she tells me her temperature, what she's eaten, when she's taken a crap practically—"

The letters are typewritten, on stolen Kent stationery, page after page, flawlessly.

"She thinks you're interested," Melanie says in reproach. "She's lonely and apprehensive."

Nelson gets louder. "*She's* apprehensive! What does she have to be apprehensive about? Here I am, good as gold, with you such a goddam watchdog I can't even go into town for a beer."

"Go."

He is stabbed by guilt. "Honest, I did promise Billy; he's going to bring this kid whose sister owns a '76 TR convertible with only fifty-five thousand miles on it."

"Just go," Melanie says quietly. "I'll write to Pru and explain how you're too busy."

"Too busy, too busy. Who the hell am I doing all this for except for fucking silly-ass Pru?"

"I don't know, Nelson. I honestly don't know what you're doing or who you're doing it for. I do know that I found a job, according to our plan, whereas you did nothing except finally bully your poor father into making up a job for you."

"My *poor* father! *Poor* father! Listen who do you think put him where he is? Who do you think owns the company, my mother and grandmother own it, my father is just their front man and doing a damn lousy job of it too. Now that Charlie's run out of moxie there's nobody over there with any drive or creativity at all. Rudy and Jake are stooges. My father's running that outfit into the ground; it's sad."

"You can say all that, Nelson, and that Charlie's run out of moxie which I think I'm in a better position than you to know, but you haven't shown me much capacity for responsibility."

He hears, though frustrated and guilty to the point of tears, a deliberate escalation in her "capacity for responsibility" in answer to his mention of "creativity." Against the Melanies of the world he will always come in tongue-tied. "Bullshit" is all he can say.

"You have a lot of *feel*ings, Nelson," she tells him. "But feelings aren't actions." She stares at him as if to hypnotize him, batting her eyes once.

"Oh Christ. I'm doing exactly what you and Pru wanted me to do."

"You see, that's how your mind works, putting everything off on others. We didn't *want* you to *do* anything specific, we just wanted you to cope like an adult. You couldn't seem to do it out there so you came back here to put yourself in phase with reality. I don't see that you've done it." When she bats her eyelids like that, her head becomes a doll's, all hollow inside. Fun to smash. "Charlie says," Melanie says, "you're overanxious as a salesman; when the people come in, they're scared away."

"They're scared away by the lousy tinny Japanese cars that cost a fortune because of the shit-eating yen. I wouldn't buy one, I don't see why anybody else should buy one. It's Detroit. Detroit has let everybody down, millions of people depending for jobs on Detroit's coming up with some decent car design and the assholes won't do it."

"Don't swear so much, Nelson. It doesn't impress me." As she gazes steadily up at him her eyeballs show plenty of white; he pictures the also plentiful white orbs of her breasts and he doesn't want this quarrel to progress so far she won't comfort him in bed. She hasn't ever sucked him off but he bets she does it for Charlie, that's the only way these old guys can get it up. Smiling that hollow-headed Buddha smile, Melanie says, "You go off and play with the other little boys, I'll stay here and write Pru and won't tell her you said her ass is silly. But I'm getting very tired, Nelson, of covering for you."

"Well who asked you to? You're getting something out of it too." In Colorado she had been sleeping with a married man who was also the partner of the crumb Nelson was supposed to spend the summer working for, putting up condominiums in ski country. The man's wife was beginning to make loud noises though she had been around herself and the other guy Melanie was seeing had visions of himself as a cocaine supplier to the beautiful people at Aspen and yet lacked the cool and the contacts, and seemed headed for jail or an early grave depending on which foot he tripped over first. Roger the guy's name was and Nelson had liked him, the way he sidled along like a lanky yellow hound who knows he's going to be kicked. It had been Roger who had gotten them into hang gliding, Melanie too prudent but Pru surprisingly willing to try, joking about how this would be one way to solve all their problems. Her face so slender in the great white crash helmet they rented you at the Highlands base, up on the Golden Horn, in the second before the launch into astonishing, utterly quiet space she would give him that same wry sharp estimating look sideways he had seen the first time she had decided to sleep with him, in her little studio apartment in that factorylike high-rise over in Stow, her picture window above a parking lot. He had met Melanie first, in a course they both took called the Geography of Religions: Shintō, shamanism, the Jains, all sorts of antique superstitions thriving, according to the maps, in overlapping patches, like splotches of disease, and in some cases even spreading, the world was in such a desperate state. Pru was not a student but a typist for the Registrar's office over in Rockwell Hall; Melanie had gotten to know her during a campaign by the Students' League for a Democratic Kent to create discontent among the university employees, especially the secretaries. Most of such friendships withered when the next cause came along but Pru had stuck. She wanted something. Nelson had been drawn to her grudging crooked smile, as if she too had trouble spinning herself out for display, not like these glib kids who had gone from watching TV straight to the classroom with never a piece of the world's real weather to halt their tongues. And also her typist's hard long hands, like the hands of his grandmother Angstrom. She had taken her portable Remington west with her in hopes of finding some free-lance work out of Denver, so she typed her letters telling him when she went to sleep and when she woke up and when she felt like vomiting, whereas he has to respond in his handwriting that he hates, it is such a childish-looking scrawl. The fluent perfection of her torrent of letters overwhelms him, he couldn't have known she would be the source of such a stream. Girls write easier than boys some-how: he remembers the notes in green ink Jill used to leave around the house in Penn Villas. And he remembers, sud-denly, more of the words of the song Mom-mom used to sing: "*Reide, reide, Geile / Alle Schtunn en Meili / Geht's iwwer der*

Schtumbe / Fallt's Bubbli nunner!" with the last word, where Baby falls down, *nunner*, not sung but spoken, in a voice so solemn he always laughed.

"What am I getting out of it, Nelson?" Melanie asks with that maddening insistent singingness.

"Kicks," he tells her. "Safe kicks, too, the kind you like. Controlling me, more or less. Charming the old folks."

Her voice relaxes and she sounds sad. "I think that's wearing thin. Maybe I've talked too much to your grandmother."

"Could be." As he stands there he feels some advantage return to him. This is his house, his town, his inheritance. Melanie is an outsider here.

"Well, I *liked* her," she says, strangely using the past tense. "I'm always drawn to older people."

"She makes more sense at least than Mom and Dad."

"What do you want me to tell Pru if I write?"

"I don't *know*." His shoulders shiver in his jacket as if the taut little coat is an electric contact; he feels his face cloud, even his breath grow hot. Those white envelopes, the white of the crash helmet she put on, the white of her belly. Space would open up immensely under you after you launched but was not menacing somehow, the harness holding you tight and the trees falling away smaller along the grassy ski trails and tilted meadows below and the great nylon wing responsive to every tug on the control bar. "Tell her to hold on."

Melanie says, "She's *been* holding on, Nelson, she can't keep holding on forever. I mean, it *shows*. And I can't stay on here much longer either. I have to visit my mother before I go back to Kent."

Everything seems to complicate, physically, in front of his mouth, so he is conscious of the effort of breathing. "And *I* gotta get to the Laid-Back before everybody leaves."

"Oh, go. Just go. But tomorrow I want you to help me start tidying up. They'll be back Sunday and you haven't once weeded the garden or mowed the lawn."

Driving Ma Springer's cushy old Newport up Jackson to where Joseph Street intersects, the first thing Harry sees is his tomato-red Corona parked in front, looking spandy-new and just washed besides. They had got it fixed at last. It was cute

of the kid to have had it washed. Loving, even. A surge of remorse for all the ill will he has been bearing Nelson gives a
quickening countercurrent to the happiness he feels at being
back in Mt. Judge, on a sparkling Sunday noon late in August
with the dry-grass smell of football in the air and the maples
thinking of turning gold. The front lawn, even that awkward
little section up by the azalea bushes and the strip between the
sidewalk and the curb where roots are coming to the surface
and hand-clippers have to be used, has been mowed. Harry
knows how those hand-clippers begin to chafe in the palm.
When the boy comes out on the porch and down to the street
to help with the bags, Harry shakes Nelson's hand. He thinks of
kissing him but the start of a frown scares him off; his impulse
to be extra friendly flounders and drowns amidst the clutter of
greetings. Janice embraces Nelson and, more lightly, Melanie.
Ma Springer, overheated from the car ride, allows herself to be
kissed on the cheek by both young people. Both are dressed up,
Melanie in a peach-colored linen suit Harry didn't know she
owned and Nelson in a gray sharkskin he knows the boy didn't
have before. A new suit to be a salesman in. The effect is touchingly trimmer; in the tilt of the child's combed head his father
is startled to see a touch of the dead Fred Springer, con artist.

Melanie looks taller than he remembers: high heels. In her
pleased croon of a voice she explains, "We went to church,"
turning toward Ma Springer. "You had said over the phone
you might try to make the service and we thought we'd surprise you in case you did."

"Melanie, I couldn't get them up in time," Bessie says. "They
were just a pair of lovebirds up there."

"The mountain air, nothing personal," Rabbit says, handing
Nelson a duffel bag full of dirty sheets. "It was supposed to be
a vacation and I wasn't going to get up at dawn the last day we
were there just so Ma could come make cow eyes at that fag."

"He didn't seem that faggy, Dad. That's just how ministers
talk."

"To me he seemed pretty radical," Melanie says. "He went
on about how the rich have to go through a camel's eye." To
Harry she says, "You look *thin*ner."

"He's been running, like an idiot," Janice says.

"Also not having to eat lunch at a restaurant every day," he says. "They give you too much. It's a racket."

"Mother, be careful of the curb," Janice says sharply. "Do you want an arm?"

"I've been managing this curb for thirty years, you don't need to tell me it's here."

"Nelson, help Mother up the steps," Janice nevertheless says.

"The Corona looks great," Harry tells the boy. "Better than new." He suspects, though, that that annoying bias in the steering will still be there.

"I really got on 'em about it, Dad. Manny kept giving it bottom priority because it was yours and you weren't here. I told him by the time you *were* here I wanted that car *done*, period."

"Take care of the paying customers first," Harry says, vaguely obliged to defend his service chief.

"Manny's a jerk," the boy calls over his shoulder as he steers his grandmother and the duffel bag through the front door, under the stained-glass fanlight that holds among leaded foliate shapes the number 89.

Toting suitcases, Harry follows them in. This house had faded in his mind. "Oh boy," he breathes. "Like an old shoe."

Ma is dutifully admiring the neatness, the flowers from the border beds arranged in vases on the sideboard and dining-room table, the vacuumed rugs and the laundered antimacassars on the nappy gray sofa and matching easy chair. She touches the tufted chenille. "These pieces haven't looked so good since Fred fought with the cleaning woman, old Elsie Lord, and we had to let her go."

Melanie explains, "If you use a damp brush, with just a dab of rug cleaner—"

"Melanie, you know how to do a job," Harry says. "The only trouble with you, you should have been a man." This comes out rougher than he had intended, but a sudden small vexation had thrown him off balance when he stepped into the house. His house, yet not his. These stairs, those knickknacks. He lives here like a boarder, a rummy old boarder in his undershirt, too fuddled to move. Even Ruth has her space. He wonders how his round-faced girl is doing, out in that overgrown terrain, in her sandstone house with its scabby green door.

Ma Springer is sniffing the air. "Something smells sweet," she says. "It must be the rug cleaner you used."

Nelson is at Harry's elbow, closer than he usually gets. "Dad, speaking of jobs, I have something I want to show you."

"Don't show me anything till I get these bags upstairs. It's amazing how much crap you need just to walk around in sneakers in the Poconos."

Janice bangs the kitchen door, coming in from the outside. "Harry, you should see the garden, it's all beautifully weeded! The lettuce comes up to my knees, the kohlrabi has gotten *enor*mous!"

Harry says to the young people, "You should have eaten some, the kohlrabi gets pulpy if you let it grow too big."

"It *never* has any taste, Dad," Nelson says.

"Yeah. I guess nobody much likes it except me." He likes to nibble, is one reason he's fat. While growing up he had many sensitive cavities and now that he has his molars crowned eating has become perhaps too much of a pleasure. No more twinges, just everlasting gold.

"Kohlrabi," Melanie is saying dreamily, "I wondered what it was, Nelson kept telling me turnips. Kohlrabi is rich in vitamin C."

"How're the crêpes cooking these days?" Harry asks her, trying to make up for having told the girl she should have been a man. He may have hit on something, though; in her a man's normal bossiness has had to turn too sweet.

"Fine. I've given them my notice and the other waitresses are going to give me a party."

Nelson says, "She's turned into a real party girl, Dad. I hardly ever saw her when we were here together. Your pal Charlie Stavros keeps taking her out, he's even coming for her this afternoon."

You poor little shnook, Rabbit thinks. Why is the kid standing so close? He can hear the boy's worried breath.

"He's taking me to Valley Forge," Melanie explains, bright-eyed, those bright eyes concealing what mischief, Rabbit may never know now. The girl is pulling out. "I'm about to leave Pennsylvania and I really haven't seen any of the sights, so Charlie's being nice enough to take me to some of the places. Last weekend we went into Amish country and saw all the buggies."

"Depressing damn things, aren't they?" Harry says, going on, "Those Amish are mean bastards—mean to their kids, to their animals, to each other."

"Dad—"

"If you're going as far as Valley Forge you might as well go look at the Liberty Bell, see if it still has a crack in it."

"We weren't sure it was open Sundays."

"Philly in August is a sight to see anyhow. One big swamp of miserable humanity. They cut your throat for a laugh down there."

"Melanie, I'm so sorry to hear you're leaving," Janice intervenes smoothly. It sometimes startles Harry, how smooth Janice can be in her middle age. Looking back, he and Jan were pretty rough customers—kids with a grudge, and not much style. No style, in fact. A little dough does wonders.

"Yeah," the guest of their summer says, "I should visit my family. My mother and sisters, I mean, in Carmel. I don't know if I'll go up to see my father or not, he's gotten so *strange*. And then back to college. It's been wonderful staying here, you were all so kind. I mean, considering that you didn't even *know* me."

"No problem," Harry says, wondering about her sisters, if they all have such eyes and ruby lips. "You did it yourself; you paid your way." Lame, lame. Never could talk to her.

"I know Mother will really miss your company," Janice says, and calls over, "Isn't that right, Mother?"

But Ma Springer is examining the china in her breakfront, to see if anything has been stolen, and doesn't seem to hear.

Harry asks Nelson abruptly, "So what did you want to show me in such a hurry?"

"It's over at the lot," the boy says. "I thought we could drive over when you came back."

"Can't I even have lunch first? I hardly had any breakfast, with all this talk of making church. Just a couple of Pecan Sandies that the ants hadn't gotten to." His stomach hurts to think of it.

"I don't think there is that much for lunch," Janice says.

Melanie offers, "There's some wheat germ and yogurt in the fridge, and some Chinese vegetables in the freezer."

"I have no appetite," Ma Springer announces. "And I want

to try my own bed. Without exaggerating I don't believe I had more than three hours' sleep in a row all that time up there. I kept hearing the raccoons."

"She's just sore about missing church," Rabbit tells the others. He feels trapped by all this fuss of return. There is a tension here that wasn't here before. You never return to the same place. Think of the dead coming back on Resurrection Day. He goes out through the kitchen into his garden and eats a kohlrabi raw, tearing off the leaves with his hands and stripping the skin from the bland crisp bulb with his front teeth. The butch women up the street are still hammering away—what can they be building? How did that poem used to go? *Build thee more stately something O my soul.* Lotty Bingaman would have known, waving her hand in the air. The air feels nice. A flatter noon than earlier, the summer settling to its dust. The trees have dulled down from the liquid green of June and the undertone of insect hum has deepened to a constant dry rasp, if you listen. The lettuce is tall and seedy, the beans are by, a carrot he pulls up is stubby as a fat man's prick, all its push gone upwards into greens. Back in the kitchen Janice has found some salami not too dried-out to eat and has made sandwiches for him and Nelson. This excursion to the lot seems bound to happen, when Harry had hoped to get over to the club this afternoon and see if the gang has missed him. He can see them gathered by the shuddering bright pool of chlorinated aqua, laughing, Buddy and his dog of the month, the Harrisons, foxy old Webb and his little Cindy. Little Cindy Blackbottom Babytoes. Real sunlight people, not these shadows in the corners of Ma's glum house. Charlie honks out front but doesn't come in. Embarrassed, and he should be, the babysnatcher. Harry looks at Janice to see how she takes it when the front door slams. Not a flicker. Women are tough. He asks her, "So what're *you* going to do this afternoon?"

"I was going to tidy up the house, but Melanie seems to have done it all. Maybe I'll go over to the club and see if I can get into a game. At least I could swim." She swam at Hourglass Lake, and in truth does look more supple through the middle, longer from hips to breasts. Not a bad little bride, he sometimes thinks, surprised by their connivance in this murky world of old blood and dark strangers.

"How'd you like that, about Charlie and Melanie?" he asks.

She shrugs, imitating Charlie. "I like it fine, why not? More power to him. You only live once. They say."

"Whyn't you go over and Nellie and I'll come join you after I look at this thing of his, whatever it is?"

Nelson comes into the kitchen, mouth ajar, eyes suspicious.

Janice says, "Or I could come with you and Nelson to the lot and then we all three could go to the club together and save gas by using only the one car."

"Mom, it's *business*," Nelson protests, and from the way his face clouds both parents see that they had better let him have his way. His gray suit makes him seem extra vulnerable, in the way of children placed in unaccustomed clothes for ceremonies they don't understand.

So Nelson and Harry, behind the wheel of his Corona for the first time in a month, drive through the Sunday traffic the route they both know better than the lines in their palms, down Joseph to Jackson to Central and around the side of the mountain. Harry says, "Car feels a little different, doesn't it?" This is a bad start; he tries to patch it with, "Guess a car never feels the same after it's been banged up."

Nelson bridles. "It was just a dent, it didn't have anything to do with the front end, that's where you'd feel the difference if there was any."

Harry holds his breath and then concedes, "Probably imagining it."

They pass the view of the viaduct and then the shopping center where the four-theater complex advertises AGATHA MANHATTAN MEATBALLS AMITYVILLE HORROR. Nelson asks, "Did you read the book, Dad?"

"What book?"

"*Amityville Horror*. The kids at Kent were all passing it around."

Kids at Kent. Lucky stiffs. What he could have done with an education. Been a college coach somewhere. "It's about a haunted house, isn't it?"

"Dad, it's about Satanism. The idea is some previous occupant of the house had conjured up the Devil and then he wouldn't go away. Just an ordinary-looking house on Long Island."

"You believe this stuff?"

"Well—there's evidence that's pretty hard to get around."

Rabbit grunts. Spineless generation, no grit, nothing solid to tell a fact from a spook with. Satanism, pot, drugs, vegetarianism. Pathetic. Everything handed to them on a platter, think life's one big TV, full of ghosts.

Nelson reads his thoughts and accuses: "Well *you* believe all that stuff they say in church and that's really sick. You should have seen it, they were giving out communion today and it was incredible, all these people sort of patting their mouths and looking serious when they come back from the altar rail. It was like something out of anthropology."

"At least," Harry says, "it makes people like your grandmother feel better. Who does this Amityville horror make feel better?"

"It's not sup*posed* to, it's just something that *hap*pened. The people in the house didn't want it to happen either, it just *did*." From the pitch of his voice the kid is feeling more in a corner than Rabbit had intended. He doesn't want to think about the invisible anyway; every time in his life he's made a move toward it somebody has gotten killed.

In silence father and son wind along Cityview Drive, with its glimpses through trees grown too tall of the flowerpot-colored city that German workers built on a grid laid out by an English surveyor and where now the Polacks and spics and blacks sit crammed in listening to each other's television sets jabber through the walls, and each other's babies cry, and each other's Saturday nights turn ugly. Tricky to drive now, all these bicycles and mopeds and worst of all the roller skaters in jogging shorts with earphones on their heads, looking like boxers, all doped up, roller-skating as though they owned the street. The Corona coasts along Locust, where the doctors and lawyers hole up in their long brick single-family dwellings, set back and shady, with retaining walls and plantings of juniper fighting the slope of the ground, and passes on the right Brewer High, that he thought of as a kid as a castle, the multiple gyms and rows of lockers you wouldn't believe, receding to infinity it seemed, the few times he went there, the times the Mt. Judge varsity played the Brewer JV squad, more or less for laughs (theirs). He thinks of telling Nelson about this, but knows the kid hates to have him reminisce about his sporting days. Brewer kids, Rabbit remembers in silence, were mean, with something dirty-looking about their mouths, as if they'd all just sucked raspberry popsicles. The girls fucked and some of the really vicious types smoked things called reefers in those days. Now even Presidents' kids, that Ford son and who knows about Chip, fuck and smoke reefers. Progress. In a way, he sees now, he grew up in a safe pocket of the world, like Melanie said, like one of those places you see in a stream where the twigs float backward and accumulate along the mud.

As they swing down into the steep part of Eisenhower, Nelson breaks the silence and asks, "Didn't you used to live up on one of these cross streets?"

"Yeah. Summer. For a couple of months, ages ago. Your mother and I were having some problems. What makes you ask?"

"I just remembered. Like when you feel you've been some-place before, only it must have been in a dream. When I'd miss you real bad Mom used to put me in the car and we'd drive over here and look at some house hoping you'd come out. It was in a row that all looked alike to me."

"And did I? Come out."

"Not that I can ever remember. But I don't remember much about it, just being there in the car, and Mom having brought some cookies along to keep me entertained, and her starting to cry."

"Jesus, I'm sorry. I never knew about this before, that she drove you over."

"Maybe it just happened once. But it feels like more than once. I remember her being so big."

Eisenhower flattens out and they pass without comment number 1204, where Janice years later had fled to Charlie Stavros, and where Nelson used to come on his bicycle and look up at the window. The kid had been desperate for a mini-bike at the time, and Mim had finally gotten him one, but he hadn't used it much, a sadness had attached to it, it was a piece of junk somewhere now. Funny about feelings, they seem to come and go in a flash yet outlast metal.

Down over the abandoned car yards they go, through the factory outlet district, and left on Third, then right on lower

Weiser, past white windowless Schoenbaum Funeral Directors, and then over the bridge. The traffic is mostly composed of old ladies poking back from their restaurant lunch they owed themselves after church and of carloads of kids already beered-up heading for the ballgame in the stadium north of Brewer where the Blasts play. Left on Route III. D I S C O. FUEL ECONOMY. They have forgotten to turn on the radio, so distracting has the tension between them been. Harry clears his throat and says, "So Melanie's getting set to go back to college. You must be too."

Silence. The subject of college is hot, too hot to touch. He should have been asking the kid what he's been learning at the lot. SPRINGER MOTORS. They pull in. Three weeks since Harry's seen it, and as with the house there's been a pollution. That Caprice he sometimes drove when the Corona was out of action isn't there, must have been sold. Six new Corollas are lined up next to the highway in their sweet and sour colors. Harry can never quite get over how small their wheels look, almost like tricycle wheels compared to the American cars he grew up with. Still, they're the guts of the line: buy cheap, most people are still poor, face it. You don't get something for nothing but hope springs eternal. Like a little sea of melting candy his cars bake in the sun. Since it's Sunday Harry parks right next to the hedge that struggles up front around the entrance and that collects at its roots all the stray wrappers and napkins that blow across III from the Chuck Wagon. The display windows need washing again. A paper banner bearing the slogan of the new TV campaign, OH WHAT A FEELING, fills the top half of the lefthand pane. The showroom has two new Celicas, one black with a yellow side stripe and one blue with a white one. Under the OH WHAT A FEELING poster, featuring some laughing cunt in a bathing suit splashing around in some turquoise pool with an Alp or Rocky in the background, lurks something different, a little low roachlike car that is no Toyota. Harry has no key; Nelson lets them in the double glass door with his. The strange car is a TR-6 convertible, polished up for sale but unmistakably worn, the windshield dull with the multiplied scratches of great mileage, the fender showing that slight ripple where metal has been bruised and healed. "What the hell is this?" Harry asks, lifted to a great height by the comparative lowness of this intruding automobile.

"Dad, that's my idea we talked about, to sell convertibles. Honest, hardly anybody makes 'em anymore, even Jaguar has quit, they're bound to go up and up. We're asking fifty-five hundred and already a couple of guys have almost bought it."

"Why'd the owner get rid of it if it was worth so much? What'd you give him on the trade?"

"Well, it wasn't a trade-in exactly—"

"What was it, exactly?"

"We bought it—"

"You *bought* it!"

"A friend of Billy Fosnacht's has this sister who's marrying some guy who's moving to Alaska. It's in great shape, Manny went all over it."

"Manny and Charlie let you go ahead with this?"

"Why wouldn't they? Charlie's been telling me how he and old man Springer used to do all these crazy things, they'd give away stuffed animals and crates of oranges and have these auctions with girls in evening gowns where the highest bid got the car even if it was only five dollars—guys from car rodeos used to come—"

"That was the good old days. These are the bad new days. People come in here looking for Toyotas, they don't want some fucking British sports car—"

"But they will, once we have the name."

"We *have* a name. Springer Motors, Toyota and used. That's what we're known for and that's what people come in here for." He hears his voice straining, feels that good excited roll of anger building in him, like in a basketball game when you're down ten points and less than five minutes left on the clock and you've just taken one too many elbows in the ribs, and all the muscles go loose suddenly and something begins lifting you and you know nothing is impossible, with faith. He tries to hold himself back, this is a fragile kid and his son. Still, this has been his lot. "I don't remember discussing any convertibles with you."

"One night, Dad, we were sitting in the living room just the two of us, only you got sore about the Corona and changed the subject."

"And Charlie really gave you the green light?"

"Sure; he kind of shrugged. With you gone he had the new cars to manage, and this whole shipment came in early—"

"Yeah. I saw. That close to the road they'll pick up all the dust."

"—and anyway Charlie's not my boss. We're equals. I told him Mom-mom had thought it was a good idea."

"Oh. You talked to Ma Springer about this?"

"Well not exactly at the time, she was off with you and Mom, but I know she wants me to plug into the lot, so it'll be three generations and all that stuff."

Harry nods. Bessie will back the kid, they're both black-eyed Springers. "O.K., I guess no harm done. How much you pay for this crate?"

"He wanted forty-nine hundred but I jewed him down to forty-two."

"Jesus. That's way over book. Did you look at the book? Do you know what the book is?"

"Dad of course I know what the fucking book is, the point is convertibles don't go by the book, they're like antiques, there's only so many and there won't be any more. They're what they call collectibles."

"You paid forty-two for a '76 TR that cost six new. How many miles on it?"

"A girl drove it, they don't drive a car hard."

"Depends on the girl. Some of these tootsies I see on the road are really pushing. How many miles did you say?"

"Well, it's kind of hard to say; this guy who went to Alaska was trying to fix something under the dashboard and I guess he didn't know which—"

"Oh boy. O.K., let's see if we can unload it for wholesale and chalk it up to experience. I'll call Hornberger in town tomorrow, he still handles TR and MG, maybe he'll take it off our hands as a favor."

Harry realizes why Nelson's short haircut troubles him: it reminds him of how the boy looked back in grade school, before all that late Sixties business soured everything. He didn't know how short he was going to be then, and wanted to become a baseball pitcher like Jim Bunning, and wore a cap all summer that pressed his hair in even tighter to his skull, that bony freckled unsmiling face. Now his necktie and suit seem like that baseball cap to be the costume of doomed hopes. Nelson's eyes brighten as if at the approach of tears. "Take it off our hands for cost? Dad, I *know* we can sell it, and clear a thousand. And there's two more."

"Two more TRs?"

"Two more convertibles, out back." By now the kid is scared, white in the face so his eyelids and eartips look pink. Rabbit is scared too, he doesn't want any more of this, but things are rolling, the kid has to show him, and he has to react. They walk back along the corridor past the parts department, Nelson leading the way and picking a set of car keys off the pegboard fastened next to the metal doorframe, and then they let themselves into the great hollow space of the garage, so silent on Sunday, a bare-girdered ballroom with its good warm stink of grease and acetylene. Nelson switches off the burglar alarm and pushes against the crash bar of the back door. Air again. Brewer far across the river, the tip of the tall courthouse with its eagle in concrete relief peeking above the forest of weeds, thistle and poke, at the lot's unvisited edge. This back area is bigger than it should be and always makes Rabbit think somehow of Paraguay. Making a little island of their own on the asphalt, two extinct American convertibles sit: a '72 Mercury Cougar, its top a tattered cream and its body that intense pale scum-color they called Nile Green, and a '74 Olds Delta 88 Royale, in color the purply-red women wore as nail polish in the days of spy movies. They were gallant old boats, Harry has to admit to himself, all that stretched tin and aerodynamical razzmatazz, headed down Main Street straight for a harvest moon with the old accelerator floored. He says, "These are here on spec, or what? I mean, you haven't paid for them yet." He senses that even this is the wrong thing to say.

"They're bought, Dad. They're ours."

"They're mine?"

"They're not yours, they're the *com*pany's."

"How the hell'd you work it?"

"What do you mean, how the hell? I just asked Mildred Kroust to write the checks and Charlie told her it was O.K."

"Charlie said it was O.K.?"

"He thought we'd all *agreed*. Dad, cut it out. It's not such a big deal. That's the idea here, isn't it—buy cars and sell 'em at a profit?"

"Not those crazy cars. How much were they?"

"I bet we make six, seven hundred on the Merc and more on the Olds. Dad, you're too uptight. It's only money. Was I supposed to have any responsibility while you were away, or not?"

"How much?"

"I forget exactly. The Cougar was about two thousand and the Royale, some dealer toward Pottsville that Billy knows had it but I thought we should be able to offer, you know, a selection, it came to I think around two-five."

"Two thousand five hundred dollars."

Just repeating the numbers slowly makes him feel good, in a bad kind of way. Any debt he ever owed Nelson is being paid back now. He goes at it again. "Two thousand five hundred good American—"

The child almost screams. "We'll get it back, I promise! It's like antiques, it's like gold! You can't lose, Dad."

Harry can't stop adding. "Forty-two hundred for the little chop-clock TR, four thousand five hundred—"

The boy is begging. "Leave me alone, I'll do it myself. I've already put an ad in the paper, they'll be gone in two weeks. I promise."

"You promise. You'll be back in college in two weeks."

"Dad. I won't."

"You won't?"

"I want to quit Kent and stay here and work." This little face all frightened and fierce, so pale his freckles seem to be coming forward and floating on the surface, like flecks in a mirror.

"Jesus, that is all I need," Harry sighs.

Nelson looks at him shocked. He holds up the car keys. His eyes blur, his lower lip is unsteady. "I was going to let you drive the Royale for fun."

Harry says, "Fun. You know how much gas these old hot rods burn? You think people today with gas a dollar a gallon are going to want these eight-cylinder inefficient guzzlers just to feel the wind in their hair? Kid, you're living in a dream world."

"They don't *care*, Dad. People don't *care* that much about money anymore, it's all shit anyway. Money is shit."

"Maybe to you but not to me I'll tell you that now. Let's keep calm. Think of the parts. These things sure as hell need some work, the years they've been around. You know what six-, seven-year-old parts cost these days, when you can get 'em at all? This isn't some fancy place dealing in antiques, we sell Toyotas. Toyotas."

The child shrinks beneath his thunder. "Dad, I won't buy any more, I promise, until these sell. These'll sell, I promise."

"You'll promise me nothing. You'll promise me to keep your nose out of my car business and get your ass back to Ohio. I hate to be the one telling you this, Nelson, but you're a disaster. You've gotta get yourself straightened out and it isn't going to happen here."

He hates what he's saying to the kid, though it's what he feels. He hates it so much he turns his back and tries to get back into the door they came out of but it has locked behind them, as it's supposed to do. He's locked out of his own garage and Nelson has the keys. Rabbit rattles the knob and thumps the metal door with the heel of his hand and even as in a blind scrimmage knees it; the pain balloons and coats the world in red so that though he hears a car motor start up not far away he doesn't connect it to himself until a squeak of rubber and a roar of speed slam metal into metal. That black gnashing cuts through the red. Rabbit turns around and sees Nelson backing off for a second go. Small parts are still settling, tinkling in the sunshine. He thinks the boy might now aim to crush him against the door where he is paralyzed but that is not the case. The Royale rams again into the side of the Mercury, which lifts up on two wheels. The pale green fender collapses enough to explode the headlight; the lens rim flies free.

Seeing the collision coming, Harry expected it to happen in slow motion, like on television, but instead it happened comically fast, like two dogs tangling and then thinking better of it. The Royale's motor dies. Through the windshield's granular fracture Nelson's face looks distorted, twisted by tears, twisted small. Rabbit feels a wooden sort of choked hilarity rising within him as he contemplates the damage. Pieces of glass finer than pebbles, bright grit, on the asphalt. Shadows on the broad skins of metal where shadows were not designed to be. The boy's short haircut looking like a round brush as he bends his face to the wheel sobbing. The whisper of Sunday traffic continuing from the other side of the building. These strange awkward blobs of joy bobbing in Harry's chest. Oh what a feeling.

Within a week, at the club, it has become a story he tells on himself. "Five thousand bucks' worth of metal, *crunch*. I had this terrible impulse to laugh, but the kid was in there crying, they were *his* cars after all, the way he saw it. The only thing I could think of to do was go stand by the Olds with my arms out like *this*." He spreads his arms wide, under the benign curve of the mountain. "If the kid'd come out swinging my gut would've been wide open. But sure enough he stumbles out all blubbery and I take him into my arms." He demonstrates the folding, consoling motion. "I haven't felt so close to Nelson since he was about two. What makes me really feel rotten, he was right. His ad for the convertibles ran that same Sunday and we must have had twenty calls. The TR was gone by Wednesday, for fifty-five Cs. People aren't counting their pennies anymore, they're throwin' 'em out the window."

"Like the Arabs," Webb Murkett says.

"Jesus, those Arabs," Buddy Inglefinger says. "Wouldn't it be bliss just to nuke 'em all?"

"Did you see what gold did last week?" Webb smiles. "That's the Arabs dumping their dollars in Europe. They smell a rat."

Buddy asks, "D'you see in today's paper where some investigation out of Washington showed that absolutely the government rigged the whole gas shortage last June?"

"We knew it at the time, didn't we?" Webb asks back, the red hairs that arc out of his eyebrows glinting.

Today is the Sunday before Labor Day, the day of the members-only fourball. Their foursome has a late starting time and they are having a drink by the pool waiting, with their wives. With some of their wives: Buddy Inglefinger has no wife, just that same dumb pimply Joanne he's been dragging around all summer, and Janice this morning said she'd go with her mother to church and show up at the club around drink time, for the after-the-fourball banquet. This is strange. Janice loves the Flying Eagle even more than he does. But ever since

Melanie left the house this last Wednesday something is cooking. Charlie has taken two weeks off now that Harry is back from the Poconos, and with Nelson being persona non grata around the lot the Chief Sales Representative has his hands full. There is always a little uptick at the end of summer, what with the fall models being advertised and raised prices already in the wind and the standing inventory beginning to look like a bargain, what with inflation worse and worse. There always comes in September a parched brightness to the air that hits Rabbit two ways, smelling of apples and blackboard dust and marking the return to school and work in earnest, but then again reminding him he's suffered another promotion, taken another step up the stairs that has darkness at the head.

Cindy Murkett hoists herself out of the pool. Dry sun catches in every drop beaded on her brown shoulders, so tan the skin bears a flicker of iridescence. Her boyishly cut hair is plastered in a fringe of accidental feathers halfway down the back of her skull. Standing on the flagstones, she tilts her head to twist water from this hair. Hair high inside her thigh merges with the black triangle of her string bikini. Walking over to their group, Cindy leaves plump wet footprints, heel and sole pad and tiny round toes. Little circular darkdab sucky toes.

"You think gold is still a good thing to buy?" Harry asks Webb, but the man has turned his narrow creased face to gaze up at his young wife. The fat eaves of her body drip onto his lap, the checks of his golf pants, darkening their lime green by drops. From the length of those eyebrow hairs of Webb's that curve out it's a wonder some don't stab him in the eye. He hugs her hips sideways; the Murketts look framed as for an ad against the green sweep of Mt. Pemaquid. Behind them a diver knifes supply into the chlorine. Harry's eyes sting.

Thelma Harrison has been listening to his story, its sad undertone. "Nelson must have been desolated by what he'd done," she says.

He likes the word "desolated," so old-fashioned, coming from this mousy sallow woman who somehow keeps the lid on that jerk Harrison. "Not so's you'd notice," he says. "We had that moment right after it happened, but he's been mean as hell to everybody since, especially since I made the mistake of telling him his ad had produced some results. He wants to keep coming to the lot but I told him to stay the hell away. You know what he did borders on crazy."

Thelma offers, "Maybe there's more on his mind than he can tell you." The sun must be right behind his head from the way she shields her eyes to look up at him, even though she has on her sunglasses, big rounded brown ones that darken at the top like windshields. They hide the top half of her face so her lips seem to move with a strange precise independence; though thin, they have a dozen little curves that might fit sweetly around Harrison's thick prick, if you try to think what her hold on him might be, though this is hard to imagine. She's such a schoolteacher with her little pleated skirt and studied way of holding herself and pronouncing words. For all of her lotions her nose is pink and the pinkness spreads into the area below her eyes, that her sunglasses all but hide.

In his floating wifeless state beside the pool, near the bottom of his g-and-t with its wilted sprig of mint, waiting for his four-ball to start, he finds Thelma's solemn staring mottled look a bit befuddling. "Yeah," he says, eyes on the sprig. "Janice keeps suggesting that. But she won't tell me what it might be."

"Maybe she can't," Thelma says, pressing her legs together tighter and tugging the skirt of her bathing suit down over an inch of thigh. She has these little purple veins women her age get but Harry can't see why she'd be self-conscious with an old pot-bellied pal like him.

He tells her, "He doesn't seem to want to go back to college so maybe he's flunked out and never told us. But wouldn't we have gotten a letter from the dean or something? These letters from Colorado, boy, we see plenty of them."

"You know Harry," Thelma tells him, "a lot of fathers Ronnie and I know complain how the boys don't *want* to come into the family business. They have these businesses and no one to carry them on. It's a tragedy. You should be glad Nelson does care about cars."

"All he cares about is smashing 'em up," Harry says. "It's his revenge." He lowers his voice to confide, "I think one of the troubles between me and the kid is every time I had a little, you know, slip-up, he was there to see it. That's one of the reasons I don't like to have him around. The little twerp knows it, too."

Ronnie Harrison, trying to put some kind of a move on poor old Joanne, looks up and shouts across to his wife, "What's the old hotshot trying to sell ya, hon? Don't let him do a number on ya."

Thelma ignores her husband with a dim smile and tells Harry matter-of-factly, "I think that's more in you than in Nelson. I'm wondering, could he be having girl trouble? Nelson."

Harry is wondering if another g-and-t might erase a little headache that's beginning. Drinking in the middle of the day always does that to him. "Well I can't see how. These kids, they just drift in and out of each other's beds like a bunch of gerbils. This girl he brought with him, Melanie, they didn't seem to have any contact really, in fact were getting pretty short with each other toward the end. She took some kind of a crazy shine to Charlie Stavros, of all people."

"Why 'of all people'?" Her smile is less dim, its thin curves declare that she knows Charlie had been Janice's lover, in the time before this club existed.

"Well he's old enough to be her father for one thing and he has one foot in the grave for another. He had rheumatic fever as a kid and it left him with a bum ticker. You ought to see him toddle around the lot now, it's pathetic."

"Having an ailment doesn't mean you want to give up living," she says. "You know I have what they call lupus; that's why I try to protect myself against the sun and can't get nice and tan like Cindy."

"Oh. Really?" Why is she telling him this?

Thelma from a wryness in her smile sees that she's presumed. "Some men with heart murmurs live forever," she says. "And now the girl and Charlie are out of the county together."

This is a new thought also. "Yeah, but in totally different directions. Charlie goes to Florida and Melanie's visiting her family on the West Coast." But he remembers Charlie talking up Florida to her at the dinner table and he finds the possibility that they are together depressing. You can't trust anybody not to fuck. He turns his head to let the sun strike the skin of his face; his eyes close, the lids glowing red. He should be practicing chipping for the fourball instead of lying here drowning in these voices. He heard on the radio driving over that a hurricane is approaching Florida.

Ronnie Harrison's voice, close at hand, shouts, "What's that hon, you say I'm going to live forever? You bet your sweet bippy I am!"

Rabbit opens his eyes and sees that Ronnie has changed the position of his chair to make room for Cindy Murkett, who is at home enough now among them all not to fuss covering her lap with the towel the way she did earlier in the summer; she just sits there on the wire grid of her poolside chair naked but for a few black strings and the little triangles they hold in place, letting her boobs wobble the way they will as she pushes back the wet hair from her ears and temples, not once but several times, self-conscious at that. In her happiness with Webb she is letting her weight slip up, there is almost too much baby fat; when she stands, Harry knows, the pattern of the chair bottom will be printed in the backs of her thighs like a waffle iron releasing two warm slabs of dark dough. Still, that wobble: to lick and suck and let them fall first one and then the other into your eyesockets. He closes his eyes. Ronnie Harrison is trying to entrance Joanne and Cindy simultaneously with a story that involves a lot of deep-pitched growling as the hero-self talks back to the villain-other. What a conceited shit.

Webb Murkett leans forward to tell Harry, "In answer to your question, yes, I think gold is an excellent buy. It's up over sixty per cent in less than a year and I see no reason for it not to appreciate at the same rate as long as the world energy situation holds. The dollar is bound to keep leaking, Harry, until they figure out how to get gasoline cheap out of grain alcohol, which'll put us back in the driver's seat. Grain we've got."

From the other side of the group, Buddy Inglefinger calls over, "Nuke 'em, I say; let's take their oil from the Arabs the same way we took it from the Eskimos." Joanne gives this an obligatory giggle, Ronnie's story having been overridden for a minute. Buddy sees Harry as his straight man and calls, "Hey Harry, did you see in *Time* where people stuck with their big old American cars are giving 'em to charity and taking a deduction or leaving 'em on the street to be stolen so they can collect the insurance? It said some dealer somewhere is giving you a free Chevette if you buy a Cadillac Eldorado."

"We don't get *Time*," Harry tells him coolly. Looked at a certain way, the world is full of twerps. Oh but to close your eyes and just flicker out with your tongue for Cindy's nipples as she swung them back and forth, back and forth, teasing.

Joanne tries to join in: "Meanwhile the President is floating down the Mississippi."

"What else can the poor schmuck do?" Harry asks her, himself feeling floating and lazy and depressed.

"Hey Rabbit," Harrison calls, "whaddidya think when he was attacked by that killer rabbit?"

This gets enough of a laugh so they stop teasing him. Thelma speaks softly at his side. "Children are hard. Ron and I have been lucky with Alex, once we gave him an old television set he could take apart he's known what he's wanted to do, electronics. But now our other boy Georgie sounds a lot like your Nelson, though he's a few years younger. He thinks what his father does is gruesome, betting against people that they're going to die, and Ron can't make him understand how life insurance is really such a small part of the whole business."

"They're disillusioned," Webb Murkett asserts in that wise voice of tumbling gravel. "They've seen the world go crazy since they were age two, from JFK's assassination right through Vietnam to the oil mess now. And here the other day for no good reason they blow up this old gent Mountbatten."

"Huh," Rabbit grunts, doubting. According to Skeeter the world was never a pleasant place.

Thelma intervenes, saying, "Harry was saying about how Nelson wants to come into the car business with him, and his negative feelings about it."

"Be the very worst thing you could do for him," Webb says. "I've had five kids, not counting the two tykes Cindy has given me, bless her for it, and when any of them mentioned the roofing business to me I'd say, 'Go get a job with another roofer, you'll never learn a thing staying with me.' I couldn't give 'em an order, and if I did they wouldn't obey it anyway. When those kids turned twenty-one, boy or girl, I told each one of them, 'It's been nice knowing you, but you're on your own now.' And not one has ever sent me a letter asking for money, or advice, or anything. I get a Christmas card at Christmastime if I'm lucky. One once said to me, Marty the oldest, he said, 'Dad, thanks for being such a bastard. It's made me fit for life.'"

Harry contemplates his empty glass. "Webb, whaddeya

think? Should I have another drink or not? It's fourball, you can carry the team."

"Don't do it, Harry, we need you. You're the long knocker. Stay sober."

He obeys, but can't shake his depression, thinking of Nelson. Thanks for being such a bastard. He misses Janice. With her around, his paternity is diluted, something the two of them did together, conniving, half by accident, and can laugh together about. When he contemplates it by himself, bringing a person into the world seems as terrible as pushing somebody into a furnace. By the time they finally get out onto the golf course, green seems a shade of black. Every blade of grass at his feet is an individual life that will die, that has flourished to no purpose. The fairway springy beneath his feet blankets the dead, is the roof of a kingdom where his mother stands at a cloudy sink, her hands red and wearing sleeves of soap bubbles when she lifts them out to give him some sort of warning. Between her thumb and knobby forefinger, the hands not yet badly warped by Parkinson's, a bubble pops. Mountbatten. And this same week their old mailman has died, Mr. Abendroth, a cheerful overweight man with his white hair cut in a whiffle, dead of a thrombosis at sixty-two. Ma Springer had heard about it from the neighbors, he'd been bringing the neighborhood their bills and magazines ever since Harry and Janice had moved in; it had been Mr. Abendroth who had delivered last April that anonymous envelope containing the news that Skeeter was dead. As he held that clipping that day the letters of type like these blades of grass drew Harry's eyes down, down into a blackness between them, as the ribs of a grate reveal the unseen black river rushing in the sewer. The earth is hollow, the dead roam through caverns beneath its thin green skin. A cloud covers the sun, giving the grass a silver sheen. Harry takes out a seven-iron and stands above his ball. Hit *down*. One of the weaknesses of Harry's game is he cannot make himself take a divot, he tries with misapplied tenderness to skim it off the turf, and hits it thin. This time he hits the ball fat, into a sand bunker this side of the tenth green. Must have rocked forward onto his toes, another fault. His practice swing is always smooth and long but when the pressure is on anxiety and hurry enter in. "You dummy," Ronnie Harrison shouts over at him. "What'd you do that for?"

"To annoy you, you creep," Rabbit tells him. In a fourball one of the foursome must do well on every hole or the aggregate suffers. Harry here had the longest drive. Now look at him. He wriggles his feet to root himself in the sand, keeping his weight back on his heels, and makes himself swing through with the wedge, pick it up and swing it *through*, blind faith, usually he picks it clean in his timidity and flies it over the green but in this instance with his fury at Ronnie and his glum indifference it all works out: the ball floats up on its cushioning spray of sand, bites, and crawls so close to the pin the three others of his foursome cackle and cheer. He sinks the putt to save his par. Still, the game seems long today, maybe it's the gin at noon or the end-of-summer doldrums, but he can't stop seeing the fairways as chutes to nowhere or feeling he should be somewhere else, that something has happened, *is* happening, that he's late, that an appointment has been made for him that he's forgotten. He wonders if Skeeter had this feeling in the pit of his stomach that moment when he decided to pull his gun out and get blasted, if he had that feeling when he woke on the morning of that day. Tired flowers, goldenrod and wild carrot, hang in the rough. The millions of grass blades shine, ready to die. This is what it all comes to, a piece of paper that itself turns yellow, a news item you cut out and mail to another with no note. File to forget. History carves these caverns with a steady drip-drip. Dead Skeeter roams below, cackling. Time seeps up through the blades of grass like a colorless poison. He is tired, Harry, of summer, of golf, of the sun. When he was younger and just taking up the game twenty years ago and even when he took it up again eight years or so ago there were shots that seemed a miracle, straight as an edge of glass and longer than any power purely his could have produced, and it was for the sake of collaboration with this power that he kept playing, but as he improved and his handicap dwindled from sky's-the-limit to a sane sixteen, these super shots became rarer, even the best of his drives had a little tail or were struck with a little scuff, and a shade off line one way or another, and the whole thing became more like work, pleasant work but work, a matter of approximations in the realm of the imperfect, with nothing breaking through but normal healthy happiness. In pursuit of such happiness Harry feels guilty, out on the course as the shadows lengthen, in the company of these three men, who away from their women loom as boring as they must appear to God.

Janice is not waiting for him in the lounge or beside the pool when at last around 5:45 they come in from playing the par-5 eighteenth. Instead one of the girls in their green and white uniforms comes over and tells him that his wife wants him to call home. He doesn't recognize this girl, she isn't Sandra, but she knows his name. Everybody knows Harry at the Flying Eagle. He goes into the lounge, his hand lifted in continuous salute to the members there, and puts the same dime he's been using as a ball marker on the greens into the pay phone and dials. Janice answers after a single ring.

"Hey come on over," he begs. "We miss you. I played pretty good, the second nine, once I worked a g-and-t out of my system. With our handicap strokes Webb figures our best ball to be a sixty-one, which ought to be good for an alligator shirt at least. You should have seen my sand shot on the third."

"I'd like to come over," Janice says, her voice sounding so careful and far away the idea crosses his mind she's being held for ransom and so must be careful what she says, "but I can't. There's somebody here."

"Who?"

"Somebody you haven't met yet."

"Important?"

She laughs. "I believe so."

"Why are you being so fucking mysterious?"

"Harry, just come."

"But there's going to be the banquet, and the prizes. I can't desert my foursome."

"If you won any prize Webb can give it to you later. I can't keep talking forever."

"This better be good," he warns her, hanging up. What can it be? Another accident for Nelson, the police have come for him. The kid has a criminal slouch. Harry goes back to the pool and tells the others, "Crazy Janice says I have to come home but she won't say why."

The women's faces show concern but the men are on their second round of drinks now and feeling no pain. "Hey Harry," Buddy Inglefinger shouts. "Before you go, here's one you might not have heard up in the Poconos. Why did the Russian ballet dancer defect to the U.S.A.?"

"I don't know, why?"

"Because Communism wasn't Goodunov."

The obliging laughter of the three women, as they all gaze upward in the reddening slant sun toward Harry's face, is like some fruit, three different ripenesses on the same branch, still hanging there when he turns his back. Cindy has put on over her bare shoulders a peach-colored silken shirt and in the V of its throat her little gold cross twinkles; he hadn't noticed it when she was nearly naked. He changes out of his golf shoes in the locker room and instead of showering just takes the hanger holding the sports coat and slacks he was going to put on for the banquet out to the parking lot on his arm. The Corona still doesn't feel right. He hears on the radio the Phillies have eked out a victory in Atlanta, 2–1. The gang never mentions the Phillies anymore, they're in fifth place, out of it. Get out of it in this society and you're as good as dead, an embarrassment. Not Goodunov. Keep Our City Clean. The radio announcer is not that wiseass woman but a young man with a voice like bubbles of fat in water, every syllable. Hurricane David has already left six hundred dead in the Caribbean region, he says, and, finally, life may exist, some scientists are coming to believe, on Titan, Saturn's largest moon. Harry passes the old box factory and enjoys yet once again the long view of the town of Mt. Judge you get coming in the Route 422 way. The row houses ascending the slope of the mountain like stairs, their windows golden with setting sun like holes in a Hallowe'en pumpkin. Suppose he had been born on Titan instead, how different would he feel down deep? He thinks of those cindery lunar surfaces, the chunky men in their white suits hopping, the footprints they left in the dust there forever. He remembers how when they'd come visiting the Springers or after the fire the first years they lived here he and Nelson used to watch *Lost in Space* together on the gray sofa, how they'd squirm and groan when Doctor Smith did some dumb imperilling egotistical thing, and only that manly-voiced robot and the little boy Will with enough sense to pull the thing off, the spaceship fighting free of man-eating plants or whatever the week's villains were. He wonders now if Nelson saw himself as Will, saving the grownups from themselves, and he wonders where the boy actor is now, what he is, Rabbit hopes not a junkie the way so many of these child stars seem to end up. That was good solid space they were lost in, not this soupy psychedelic space they have on TV now, all tricks with music and lights, tricks he associates with the movie *2001*, an unpleasant association since that was the time Janice ran off with Charlie and all hell broke loose on the home front. The problem is, even if there is a Heaven how can there be one we can stand forever? On Earth, when you look up from being bored, things have changed, you're that much closer to the grave, and that's exciting. Imagine climbing up and up into that great tree of night sky. Dizzying. Terrible. Rabbit didn't even like to get too high into these little Norway maples around town, though with the other kids as witnesses he pushed himself up, gripping tighter and tighter as the branches got smaller. From a certain angle the most terrifying thing in the world is your own life, the fact that it's yours and nobody else's. A loop is rising in his chest as in a rope when you keep twisting. Whatever can have happened bad enough to make Janice miss the fourball banquet?

He accelerates along Jackson as the streetlights come on, earlier each day now. Janice's Mustang is out along the curb with the top down, she must have gone somewhere after church, she wouldn't take Bessie to church with the top down. Inside the front door, a wealth of duffel bags and suitcases has been deposited in the living room as by a small army. In the kitchen there is laughter and light. The party comes to meet him halfway, in the shadowy no-man's land between the staircase and the breakfront. Ma Springer and Janice are overtopped by a new female, taller, with a smoothly parted head of hair from which the kitchen light strikes an arc of carrot color, where Melanie's hair would have caught in its curls a straggly halo. He had grown used to Melanie. It is Nelson who speaks. "Dad, this here is Pru," the "this here" a little scared joke.

"Nelson's fiancée," Janice amplifies in a voice tense but plump, firmly making the best of it.

"Is that a fact?" Harry hears himself ask. The young woman saunters forward, a slender slouching shape, and he takes the bony hand she extends. In the lingering daylight that the dining-room windows admit she stands plain, a young redhead past girlhood, with arms too long and hips too wide for the boniness of her face, an awkward beauty, her body helplessly not only hers but somehow theirs, overcommitted, with a look about her of wry, slightly twisted resignation, of having been battered by life young as she is, but the battering having not yet reached her eyes, which are clear green, though guarded. As she entrusts her hand to his her smile is a fraction slow, as if inside she must make certain there is something to smile at, but then comes forth eagerly enough, with a crimp in one corner. She wears a baggy brown sweater and the new looser style of jeans, bleach spattered across the thighs. Her hair, swept back behind her ears to form a single fanning sheaf down her back, looks ironed, it is so straight, and dyed, it is so vivid a pallid red.

"I wouldn't say fiancée exactly," Pru says, directly to Harry. "There's no ring, look." She holds up a naked trembling hand.

Harry in his need to get a fix on this new creature glances from Nelson right through Janice, whom he can grill later in bed, to Ma Springer. Her mouth is clamped shut; if you tapped her she'd ring like a gong, rigid in her purple church dress. Nelson's mouth is ajar. He is a sick man fascinated by the ministration of doctors around him, his illness at last confessed and laid open to cure. In Pru's presence he looks years younger than when Melanie was about, a nervous toughness melted all away. It occurs to Harry that this girl is older than the boy, and another, deeper, instinctive revelation pounds in upon him even as he hears himself saying, as humorous paternal host, "Well in any case it's nice to meet you, Pru. Any friend of Nelson's, we put up with around here." This maybe falls flat, so he adds, "I bet you're the girl's been sending all those letters."

Her eyes glance down, the demure plane of her cheek reddened as if he's slapped her. "Too many I suppose," she says.

"No bother to me," he assures her, "I'm not the mailman. He recently upped and died, by the way. Not your fault, though."

She lifts her eyes, a flourishing green.

Pru is pregnant. One of the few advantages of not having been born yesterday is that a man acquires, like a notion of tomorrow's weather from the taste of the evening air, some sense of the opposite sex's physiology, its climate. She has less waist than a woman so young should, and that uncanny green clarity of her eyes and a soft slowed something in her motions as she turns away from Harry's joke to take a cue from Nelson bespeak a burden beyond disturbing, a swell beneath the waves. In her third or fourth month, Rabbit guesses. And with this guess a backwards roll of light illumines the months past. And the walls of this house, papered with patterns sunk into them like stains, change meaning, containing this seed between them. The fuzzy gray sofa and the chair that matches and the Barcalounger and the TV set (an Admiral) and Ma Springer's pompous lamps of painted porcelain and tarnished brass and the old framed watercolors sunk to the tint of dust from never being looked at, the table runners Ma once crocheted and her collection of brittle bright knickknacks stored on treble corner shelves nicked and sanded to suggest antique wood but stemming from an era of basement carpentry in Fred Springer's long married life: all these souvenirs of the dead bristle with new point, with fresh mission, if as Harry imagines this intruder's secret is a child to come.

He feels swollen. His guess has been like a fist into him. As was not the case with Melanie he feels kinship with this girl, is touched by her, turned on: *he* wants to be giving her this baby.

In bed he asks Janice, "How long have you known?"

"Oh," she says, "about a month. Melanie let some of the cat out of the bag and then I confronted Nelson with it. He was relieved to talk, he cried even. He just didn't want *you* to know."

"Why not?" He is hurt. He is the boy's father.

Janice hesitates. "I don't know, I guess he was afraid you'd be mad. Or laugh at him."

"Why would I laugh at him? The same thing happened to me."

"He doesn't know that, Harry."

"How could he not? His birthday keeps coming around seven months after our anniversary."

"Well, yes." In her impatience she sounds much like her mother, setting the heel of her voice into each word. The bed creaks as she flounces in emphasis. "Children don't *want* to know these things, and by the time they're old enough to care it's all so long ago."

"When did he knock the girl up, does he remember that much?"

"Weren't you funny, guessing so quickly she was in a family way? We weren't going to tell you for a while."

"Thanks. It was the first thing that hit me. That baggy sweater. That, and that she's taller than Nelson."

"Harry, she isn't. He's an inch taller, he's told me himself, it's just that his posture is so poor."

"And how much older is she? You can see she's older."

"Well, a year or less. She was a secretary in the Registrar's office—"

"Yeah and why wasn't he fucking another student? What does he have to get mixed up in the secretarial pool for?"

"Harry, you should talk to *them* if you want to know every in and out of it all. You know though how he used to say how phony these college girls were, he never felt comfortable in that atmosphere. He's from business people on my side and working people on yours and there hasn't been much college in his background."

"Or in his future from the way it looks."

"It's not such a bad thing the girl can do a job. You heard her say at supper she'd like him to go back to Kent and finish, and she could take in typing in their apartment."

"Yeah and I heard the little snot say he wanted no part of it."

"You won't get him to go back by shouting at him."

"I didn't shout."

"You got a look on your face."

"Well, Jesus. Because the kid gets a girl pregnant he thinks he's entitled to run Springer Motors."

"Harry, he doesn't want to run it, he just wants a place in it."

"You can't give him a place without taking a place from somebody else."

"Mother and I think he should have a place," Janice says, so definitely it seems her mother has spoken, out of the dark air of this bedroom where the old lady's presence was always felt as a rumble of television or a series of snores coming through the wall.

He reverts to his question, "When did he get her pregnant?"

"Oh, when these things happen, in the spring. She missed her first period in May, but they waited till they got to Colorado to do the urine test. It was positive and Pru told him she wasn't going to get an abortion, she didn't believe in them and too many of her friends had had their insides messed up."

"In this day and age, she said all that."

"Also I believe there's Catholicism in her background, on her mother's side."

"Still, she looks like she has some common sense."

"Maybe it was common sense talking. If she goes ahead and has the baby then Nelson has to do something."

"Poor little devil. How come she got pregnant in the first place? Don't they all have the Pill, and loops, and God knows what else now? I was reading in *Consumer Reports* about these temporary polyurethane tube ties."

"Some of these new things are getting a bad name in the papers. They give you cancer."

"Not at her age they wouldn't. So then she sat out there in the Rocky Mountains hatching this thing while Melanie kept him on a short leash around here."

Janice is growing sleepy, whereas Harry fears he will be awake forever, with this big redhead out of the blue across the hall. Ma Springer had made it clear she expected Pru to sleep in Melanie's old room and had stomped upstairs to watch *The Jeffersons*. The old crow had just sat there pretty silent all evening, looking like a boiler with too much pressure inside. She plays her cards tight. Harry nudges Janice's sleepy soft side to get her talking again.

She says, "Melanie said Nelson became very hard to manage, once the test came back positive—running around with a bad crowd out there, making Pru take up hang gliding. Then when he saw she wouldn't change her mind all he wanted to do was run back here. They couldn't talk him out of it, he went and quit this good job he had with a man building condominiums. Melanie I guess had some reasons of her own to get away so she invited herself along. Nelson didn't want her to but I guess the alternative was Pru letting her parents and us know what the situation was and instead of that he begged for time, trying to get some kind of nest ready for her here and maybe still hoping it would all go away, I don't know."

"Poor little Nelson," Harry says. Sorrow for the child bleeds upward to the ceiling with its blotches of streetlight shuffling through the beech. "This has been Hell for him."

"Well Melanie's theory was not Hell enough; she didn't like the way he kept going out with Billy Fosnacht and his crowd instead of facing us with the facts and telling us why he really wanted to go to work at the lot."

Harry sighs. "So when's the wedding?"

"As soon as it can be arranged. I mean, it's her fifth month. Even you spotted it."

Even you, he resents this, but doesn't want to tell Janice of the instinctive bond he has with this girl. Pru is like his mother, awkward and bony, with big hands, but less plain.

"One of the reasons I took Mother to church this morning was so we could have a word with Reverend Campbell."

"That fag? Lordy-O."

"Harry you know nothing about him. He's been uncommonly sweet to Mother and he's really done a lot for the parish."

"The little boys' choir especially, I bet."

"You are so un-open. Mother with all her limitations is more open than you." She turns her face away and says into her pillow, "Harry, I'm very tired. All this upsets me too. Was there anything else you wanted to ask?"

He asks, "Does he love the girl, do you think?"

"You've seen her. She's striking."

"I can see that, but can Nelson? You know they say history repeats but it never does, exactly. When we got married everybody was doing it but now when these kids hang back and just live together it must be a bigger deal. I mean, marriage must be more frightening."

Janice turns her head back again and offers, "I think it's good, that she's a little older."

"Why?"

"Well, Nelson needs steadying."

"A girl who gets herself knocked up and then pulls this right-to-life act isn't my idea of steady. What kind of parents does she come from anyway?"

"They're just average people in Ohio. I think the father works as a steamfitter."

"A-*ha*," he says. "Blue collar. She's not marrying Nelson, she's marrying Springer Motors."

"Just like you did," Janice says.

He should resent this but he likes it, her new sense of herself as a prize. He lays his hand in that soft place where her waist dips. "Listen," he says, "when I married you you were selling salted nuts at Kroll's and my parents thought your dad was a shifty character who was going to wind up in jail."

But he didn't, he wound up in Heaven. Fred Springer made that long climb into the tree of the stars. Lost in space. Now Janice is following, his touch tipping her into sleep just as he feels below his waist a pulsing that might signal a successful erection. Nothing like the thought of fucking money. He doesn't fuck her enough, his poor dumb moneybags. She has fallen asleep naked. When they were newly married and for years thereafter she wore cotton nighties that made her look like that old-fashioned Time to Retire ad, but sometime in the Seventies she began to come to bed in just her skin, her little still-tidy snake-smooth body brown wherever the tennis dress didn't cover, with a fainter brown belly where that Op-pattern two-piece bathing suit exposed her middle. How quickly Cindy's footprints dried on the flagstones behind her today! The strange thing is he can never exactly picture fucking her, it is like looking into the sun. He turns on his back, frustrated yet relieved to be alone in the quiet night where his mind can revolve all that is new. In middle age you are carrying the world in a sense and yet it seems out of control more than ever, the self that you had as a boy all scattered and distributed like those pieces of bread in the miracle. He had been struck in Kruppenbach's Sunday School by the verse that tells of the clean-up, twelve baskets full of the fragments. Keep Your City Clean. He listens for the sound of footsteps slithering out of Melanie's—no, Pru's—room, she'd come a long way today and had met a lot of new faces, what a hard thing for her this evening must have been. While Ma and Janice had scraped together supper, another miracle of sorts, the girl had sat there in the bamboo basket chair brought in from the porch and they all eased around her like cars easing past an accident on the highway. Harry could hardly take his eyes from this grown woman sitting there so demure and alien and perceptibly misshapen. She breathed that air he'd forgotten, of high-school loveliness, come uninvited to bloom in the shadow of railroad overpasses, alongside telephone poles, within earshot of highways with battered aluminum center strips, out of mothers gone to lard and fathers ground down by gray days of work and more work, in an America littered with bottlecaps and pull-tabs and pieces of broken muffler. Rabbit remembered such beauty, seeing it caught here in Pru, in her long downy arms and skinny bangled wrists and the shining casual fall of her hair, caught as a stick snags the flow of a stream with a dimpled swirl. Janice sighs in her sleep. A car swishes by, the radio trailing disco through the open window. Labor Day Eve, the end of something. He feels the house swell beneath him, invading presences crowding the downstairs, the dead awakened. Skeeter, Pop, Mom, Mr. Abendroth. The photograph of Fred Springer fading on the sideboard fills with the flush of hectic color Fred carried on his cheeks and where the bridge of his nose pressed. Harry buries his mind in the girls of Mt. Judge High as they were in the Forties, the fuzzy sweaters and dimestore pearls, the white blouses that let the beige shadow of the bra show through, the skirts, always skirts, long as gowns when the New Look was new, swinging in the locker-lined halls, and then out along the pipe rail that guarded the long cement wells that let light into the basement windows of the shop and home ec. and music rooms, the long skirts in rows, the saddle shoes and short white socks in rows, the girls exhaling winter breath like cigarette smoke, their pea jackets, nobody wore parkas then, the dark lipstick of those girls, looking all like Rita Hayworth in the old yearbooks. The teasing of their skirts, open above their socks, come find me if you can, the wild fact of pubic hair, the thighs timidly parted in the narrow space of cars, the damp strip of underpants, Mary Ann his first girl, her underpants down around her saddle shoes like an animal trap, the motor running to keep the heater on in Pop's new blue Plymouth, that they let him borrow one night a week in spite of all Mim's complaining and sarcasm. Mim a flat-chested brat until about seventeen when she began to have her own secrets. Between Mary Ann's legs a locker-room humidity and flesh smell turned delicate, entrusted to him. Married another while he was in the Army. Invited another into that secret space of hers, he couldn't believe it. Lost days, buried at the back of his brain, deep inside, gray cells of which millions die every day he has read somewhere, taking his life with them into blackout, his only life, trillions of electric bits they say, makes even the biggest computer look sick: having found and entered again that space he notices his prick has stayed hard and grown harder, the process there all along, little sacs of blood waiting for the right deep part of the brain to come alive again. Left-handedly, on his back so as not to disturb Janice, he masturbates, remembering Ruth. Her room on Summer. The first night, him having run, all that sad craziness with dead Tothero, then the privacy of this room. This island, their four walls, her room. Her fat white body out of her clothes and her poking fun of his Jockey underpants. Her arms seemed thin, thin, pulling him down and rising above him, one long underbelly erect in light.

Hey.

Hey.

You're pretty.

Come on. Work.

He shoves up and comes, the ceiling close above him, his body feeling curved as if tied to a globe that is growing, growing as his seed bucks up against the sheet. More intense than pumping down into darkness. Weird behavior for an old guy. He stealthily slides from the bed and gropes after a handkerchief in a drawer, not wanting the scrape to wake Janice or Ma Springer or this Pru, cunts all around him. Back in bed, having done his best, though it's always queer where the wet is, maybe it doesn't come out when you feel it does, he composes himself for sleep by thinking of his daughter, her pale round face floating in what appeared to be a milky serene disposition. A voice hisses, *Hassy.*

The Reverend Archie Campbell comes visiting a few nights later, by appointment. He is short and slight, but his voice compensates by being deep and mellow; he enunciates with such casual smiling sonorousness that his sentences seem to keep travelling around a corner after they are pronounced. His head is too big for his body. His lashes are long and conspicuous and he sometimes shuts his eyes as if to display the tremor in his closed lids. He wears his backwards collar with a flimsy black buttonless shirt and a seersucker coat. When he smiles, thick lips like Carter's reveal small even teeth, like seeds in a row, stained by nicotine.

Ma Springer offers him a cup of coffee but he says, "Dear me, no thank you, Bessie. This is my third call this evening and any more caffeine intake will positively give me the shakes." The sentence travels around a corner and disappears up Joseph Street.

Harry says to him, "A real drink then, Reverend. Scotch? A g-and-t? It's still summer officially."

Campbell glances around for their reaction—Nelson and Pru side by side on the gray sofa, Janice perched on a straight chair brought in from the dining room, Ma Springer uneasy on her legs, her offer of coffee spurned. "Well as a matter of fact yes," the minister drawls. "A touch of the sauce might be sheer bliss. Harry, do you have vodka, perchance?"

Janice intervenes, "Way in the back of the corner cupboard, Harry, the bottle with the silver label."

He nods. "Anybody else?" He looks at Pru especially, since in these few days of living with them she's shown herself to be no stranger to the sauce. She likes liqueurs; she and Nelson the other day brought back from a shopping expedition along with the beer sixpacks Kahlúa, Cointreau, and Amaretto di Saronno, chunky little bottles, there must have been between twenty and thirty dollars invested in that stuff. Also they have found in the corner cupboard some crème de menthe left over from a dinner party Harry and Janice gave for the Murketts and Harrisons last February and a little bright green gleam of it appears by Pru's elbow at surprising times, even in the morning, as she and Ma watch *Edge of Night*. Nelson says he wouldn't turn down a beer. Ma Springer says she's going to have coffee anyway, she even has decaffeinated if the rector would prefer. But Archie sticks to his guns, with a perky little bow of thanks to her and a wink all around. The guy is something of a card, Rabbit can see that. Probably the best way to play it, at this late date A.D. They had figured him for the gray easy chair that matches the sofa, but he foxes them by pulling out the lopsided old Syrian hassock from behind the combination lamp and table, where Ma keeps some of her knickknacks, and squatting down. Thus situated, the minister grins up at them all and, nimble as a monkey, fishes a pipe from his front coat pocket and stuffs its bowl with a brown forefinger.

Janice gets up and goes with Harry into the kitchen while he makes the drinks. "That's some little pastor you've got there," he tells her softly.

"Don't be snide."

"What's snide about that?"

"Everything." She pours herself some Campari in an orange-juice glass and without comment fills with crème de menthe one of the set of eight little cylindrical liqueur glasses that came as a set with a decanter she had bought at Kroll's years ago, about the same time they joined the Flying Eagle. They hardly ever have used them. When Harry returns to the living room with Campbell's vodka-and-tonic and Nelson's beer and his own g-and-t Janice follows him in and sets this cylinder of gaudy green on the end table next to Pru's elbow. Pru gives no sign of noticing.

Reverend Campbell has persuaded Ma Springer to take the Barcalounger, where Harry had anticipated sitting, and to raise up its padded extension for her legs. "I must say," she says, "that does wonders for the pressure in my ankles."

Thus laid back the old lady looks vulnerable, and absurdly reduced in importance within the family circle. Janice, seeing her mother stretched out helpless, volunteers, "Mother, I'll fetch you your coffee."

"And that plate of chocolate-chip cookies I set out. Though I don't suppose anybody with liquor wants cookies too."

"I do, Mom-mom," Nelson says. He wears a different expression since Pru arrived—the surly clotted look has relaxed into an expectant emptiness, a wide-eyed docility that Harry finds just as irritating.

Since the minister declined to take the gray easy chair, Harry must. As he sinks into it his legs stretch out, and Campbell without rising jumps the hassock and himself together a few feet to one side, like a bullfrog hopping, pad and all, to avoid being touched by Harry's big suede shoes. Grinning at his own agility, the little man resonantly announces, "Well now. I understand somebody here wants to get married."

"Not me, I'm married already," Rabbit says quickly, as a joke of his own. He has the funny fear that Campbell, one of whose little hands (they look grubby, like his teeth) rests on the edge of the hassock inches from the tips of Harry's shoes, will suddenly reach down and undo the laces. He moves his feet over, some more inches away.

Pru had smiled sadly at his joke, gazing down, her green-filled glass as yet untouched. Seated beside her, Nelson stares forward, solemnly unaware of the dabs of beer on his upper lip. A baby eating: Rabbit remembers how Nelson used to batter with the spoon, held left-handed in his fist though they tried to get him to take it in his right, on the tray of the high chair in the old apartment on Wilbur Street, high above the town. He was never one of the messier babies, though—always wanting to be good. Harry wants to cry, gazing at the innocently ignored mustache of foam on the kid's face. They're selling him down the river. Pru touches her glass furtively, without giving it a glance.

Ma Springer's voice sounds weary, rising from the Barcalounger. "Yes they'd like to have it be in the church, but it won't be one of your dressy weddings. Just family. And as soon as convenient, even next week we were thinking." Her feet in their dirty aqua sneakers, with rounded toes and scuffed rims of white rubber, look childish and small off the floor, up on the padded extension.

Janice's voice sounds hard, cutting in. "Mother there's no need for such a rush. Pru's parents will need time to make arrangements to come from Ohio."

Her mother says, with a flip of her tired hand toward Pru, "She says her folks may not be bothering to come."

The girl blushes, and tightens her touch on the glass, as if to pick it up when attention has moved past her. "We're not as close as this family is," she says. She lifts her eyes, with their translucent green, to the face of the minister, to explain, "I'm one of seven. Four of my sisters are married already, and two of those marriages are on the rocks. My father's sour about it."

Ma Springer explains, "She was raised Catholic."

The minister smiles broadly. "Prudence seems such a Protestant name."

The blush, as if quickened by a fitful wind, deepens again. "I was baptized Teresa. My friends in high school used to think I was prudish, that's where Pru came from."

Campbell giggles. "*Really!* That's *fas*cinating!" The hair on the top of his head, Rabbit sees, is getting thin, young as he is. Thank God that's one aspect of aging Harry doesn't have to worry about: good lasting heads of hair on both sides of his family, though Pop's toward the end had gone through gray to yellow, finer than cornsilk, and too dry to comb. They say the mother's genes determine. One of the things he never liked about Janice was her high forehead, like she might start to go bald. Nelson's too young to tell yet. Old man Springer used to slick his hair back so he always looked like a guy in a shirt collar ad, even on Saturday mornings, and in the coffin they got the parting all wrong; the newspaper obituary had reversed the photo in doing the halftone and the mortician had worked from that. With Mim, one of the first signs of her rebellion as he remembers was she bleached stripes into her hair, "Protestant rat" she used to call the natural color, in tenth grade, and Mom would get after her saying, "Better that than look like a skunk." It was true, with those blond pieces Mim did look tough, suddenly—besmirched. That's life, besmirching yourself. The young clergyman's voice is sliding from syllable to syllable smoothly, his surprising high giggle resettled in the back of his throat. "Bessie, before we firm up particulars like the date and the guest list, I think we should investigate some basics. Nelson and Teresa: do you love one another, and are you both prepared to make the eternal commitment that the church understands to exist at the heart of Christian marriage?"

The question is a stunner. Pru says "Yes" in a whisper and takes the first sip from her glass of crème de menthe.

Nelson looks so glazed his mother prompts, "Nelson."

He wipes his mouth and whines, "I *said* I'd do it, didn't I? I've been here all summer trying to work things out. I'm not going back to school, I'll never graduate now, because of this. What more do you people want?"

All flinch into silence but Harry, who says, "I thought you didn't like Kent."

"I didn't, much. But I'd put in my time and would just as soon have gotten the degree, for what it's worth, which isn't much. All summer, Dad, you kept bugging me about college and I wanted to say, O.K., O.K., you're right, but you didn't know the story, you didn't know about *Pru*."

"Don't marry me then," Pru says quickly, quietly.

The boy looks sideways at her on the sofa and sinks lower into the cushions. "I'd just as soon," he says. "It's time I got serious."

"We can get married and still go back for a year and have you finish." Pru has transferred her hands to her lap and with them the little glass of green; she gazes down into it and speaks steadily, as if she is drawing up out of its tiny well words often rehearsed, her responses to Nelson's complaints.

"Naa," Nelson says, shamed. "That seems silly. If I'm gonna be married, let's really do it, with a job and clunky old station wagon and a crummy ranch house and all that drill. There's nothing I can get at Kent'll make me better at pushing Dad's little Japanese kiddy cars off on people. If Mom and Mom-mom can twist his arm so he'll take me in."

"Jesus, how you distort!" Harry cries. "We'll all take you in, how can we help but? But you'd be worth a helluva lot more to the company and what's more to your*self* if you'd finish up at college. Because I keep saying this I'm treated around here like a monster." He turns to Archie Campbell, forgetting how low the man is sitting and saying over his head, "Sorry about all this chitchat, it's hardly up your alley."

"No," the young man mellifluously disagrees, "it's part of the picture." Of Pru he asks, "What would be *your* preference, of where to live for the coming year? The first year of married life, all the little books say, sets the tone for all the rest."

With one hand Pru brushes back her long hair from her shoulders as if angry. "I don't have such happy associations with Kent," she allows. "I'd be happy to begin in a fresh place."

Campbell's pipe is filling the room with a sweetish tweedy perfume. Probably less than thirty and there's nothing they can throw at him that he hasn't fielded before. A pro: Rabbit can respect that. But how did he let himself get queer?

Ma Springer says in a spiteful voice, "You may wonder now why they don't wait that year."

The small man's big head turns and he beams. "No, I hadn't wondered at that."

"She's got herself in a family way," the old lady declares, needlessly.

"With Nelson's help, of course," the minister smiles.

Janice tries to intervene: "Mother, these things happen."

Ma snaps back, "Don't tell me. I haven't forgotten it happened to you."

"*Mother.*"

"This is horrible," Nelson announces from the sofa. "What'd we drag this poor guy in here for anyway? Pru and I didn't ask to be married in a church, I don't believe any of that stuff anyway."

"You don't?" Harry is shocked, hurt.

"No, Dad. When you're dead, you're dead."

"You are?"

"Come off it, you know you are, everybody knows it down deep."

"Nobody knows for sure," Pru points out in a quiet voice.

Nelson asks her furiously, "How many dead people have you seen?"

Even as a child, Harry remembers, Nelson's face would get white around the gills when he was angry. He would get nervous stomach aches, and clutch at the edge of the banister on his way upstairs to get his books. They would send him off to school anyway. Harry still had his job at Verity and Janice was working part-time at the lot and they had no babysitter. School was the babysitter.

Reverend Campbell, puffing unruffled on his aromatic pipe, asks Pru another question. "How do your parents feel about your being married outside of the Roman faith?"

That tender blush returns, deepening the green of her eyes. "Only my mother was a Catholic actually, and I think by the time I came along she had pretty much given up. I was baptized but never confirmed, though there was this confirmation dress my sisters had worn. Daddy had beaten it out of her I guess you could say. He didn't like having all the children to feed."

"What was his denomination?"

"He was a nothing."

Harry remembers out loud, "Nelson's grandfather came from a Catholic background. *His* mother was Irish. My dad's side, I'm talking about. Hell, what I think about religion is—"

All eyes are upon him.

"—is without a little of it, you'll sink."

Saying this, he gazes toward Nelson, mostly because the child's vivid pale-gilled face falls at the center of his field of vision. That muskrat haircut: it suggests to Harry a convict's shaved head that has grown out. The boy sneers. "Well don't sink, Dad, whatever you do."

Janice leans forward to speak to Pru in that mannerly mature woman's bosomy voice she can produce now. "I *wish* you could persuade your parents to come to the wedding."

Ma Springer says, trying a more placating tone, since she has got the minister here and the conference is not delivering for her, "Around here the Episcopalians are thought the next thing to the Catholics anyway."

Pru shakes her head, her red hair flicking, a creature at bay. She says, "My parents and I don't talk much. They didn't approve of something I did before I met Nelson, and they wouldn't approve of this, the way I am now."

"What did you do?" Harry asks.

She doesn't seem to have heard, saying as if to herself, "I've learned to take care of myself without them."

"I'll say this," Campbell says pleasantly, his pipe having gone dead and its relighting having occupied his attention for the last minute. "I'm experiencing some difficulty wrapping my mind around"—the phrase brings out his mischievous grin, stretched like that guy's on *Mad*—"performing a church ceremony for two persons one of whom belongs to the Church of Rome and the other, he has just told us, is an atheist." He gives a nod to Nelson. "Now the bishop gives us more latitude in these matters than we used to have. The other day I married a divorced Japanese man, but with an Episcopal background, to a young woman who originally wanted the words 'Universal Mother' substituted for 'God' in the service. We talked her out of that. But in this case, good people, I really don't see much indication that Nelson and his *very* charming fiancée are at all prepared for, or desirous of, what you might call our brand of magic." He releases a great cloud of smoke and closes his lips in that prissy satisfied way of pipe-smokers, waiting to be contradicted.

Ma Springer is struggling as if to rise from the Barcalounger. "Well no grandson of Fred Springer is going to get married in a Roman Catholic church!" Her head falls back on the padded headrest. Her gills look purple.

"Oh," Archie Campbell says cheerfully. "I don't think my dear friend Father McGahern could handle them either. The young lady was never even confirmed. You know," he adds, knitting his hands at one knee and gazing into space, "a lot of wonderful, dynamic marriages have been made in City Hall. Or a Unitarian-Universalist service. My friend Jim Hancock of the fellowship in Maiden Springs has more than once taken some of our problem betrothals."

Rabbit jumps up. Something awful is being done here, he doesn't know exactly what, or to whom. "Anybody besides me for another drink?"

Without looking at Harry, Campbell holds out a glass which has become empty, as has Pru's little glass of crème de menthe. The green of it has all gone into her eyes. The minister is telling her, and Nelson, "Truly, under some circumstances, even for the most devout it can be the appropriate recourse. At a later date, the wedding can be consecrated in a church; we see a number now of these reaffirmations of wedding vows."

"Why don't they just keep living in sin right here?" Harry asks. "We don't mind."

"We do indeed," Ma says, sounding smothered.

"Hey Dad," Nelson calls, "could you bring me another beer?"

"Get it yourself. My hands are full." Yet he stops in front of Pru and takes up the little liqueur glass. "Sure it's good for the baby?"

She looks up with unexpected coldness. He was feeling so fatherly and fond and from her eyes he is a dumb traffic cop. "Oh yes," she tells him. "It's the beer and wine that are bad; they bloat you."

By the time Rabbit returns from the kitchen, Campbell is allowing himself to be brought around. He has what they want:

a church wedding, a service acceptable in the eyes of the Grace Stuhls of this world. Knowing this, he is in no hurry. Beneath the girlish lashes his eyes are as dark as Janice's and Ma's, the Koerner eyes. Ma Springer is holding forth, the little rounded toes of her aqua sneakers bouncing. "You must take what the boy says with a grain of salt. At his age I didn't know what I believed myself, I thought the government was foolish and the gangsters had the right idea. This was back in Prohibition days."

Nelson looks at her with his own dark eyes, sullen. "Mommom, if it matters so much to you, I don't care that much, one way or another."

"What does Pru think?" Harry asks, giving her her poison. He wonders if the girl's frozen stiffness of manner, and those little waits while her smile gets unstuck, aren't simply fear: it is she who is growing another life within her body, and nobody else.

"I think," she responds slowly, so quietly the room goes motionless to hear, "it would be nicer in a church."

Nelson says, "I know I sure don't want to go down to that awful new concrete City Hall they've built behind where the Bijou used to be, some guy I know was telling me the contractor raked off a million and there's cracks in the cement already."

Janice in her relief says, "Harry, I could use some more Campari."

Campbell lifts his replenished glass from his low place on the hassock. "Cheers, good people." He states his terms: "The customary procedure consists of at least three sessions of counseling and Christian instruction after the initial interview. This I suppose we can consider the interview." As he addresses Nelson particularly, Harry hears a seductive note enrich the great mellow voice. "Nelson, the church does not expect that every couple it marries be a pair of Christian saints. It does ask that the participants have some understanding of what they are undertaking. *I* don't take the vows; you and Teresa do. Marriage is not merely a rite; it is a sacrament, an invitation from God to participate in the divine. And the invitation is not for one moment only. Every day you share is meant to be sacramental. Can you feel a meaning in that? There were wonderful words in the old prayer book; they said that marriage was not 'to be entered into unadvisedly or lightly; but reverently, discreetly, advisedly, soberly, and in the fear of God.'" He grins, having intoned this, and adds, "The new prayer book omits the fear of God."

Nelson whines, "I *said*, I'd go along."

Janice asks, a little prim, "How long would these sessions of instructions take?" It is like she is sitting, in that straight-backed dining-room chair, on an egg that might hatch too soon.

"Oh," Campbell says, rolling his eyes toward the ceiling, "I should think, considering the various factors, we could get three of them in in two weeks. I just happen, the officious clergyman said, to have my appointment book here." Before reaching into the breast pocket of the seersucker coat, Campbell taps out the bowl of his pipe with a finicky calm that conveys to Harry the advantages of being queer: the world is just a gag to this guy. He walks on water; the mud of women and making babies never dirties his shoes. You got to take off your hat: nothing touches him. That's real religion.

Some rebellious wish to give him a poke, to protest the smooth bargain that has been struck, prompts Harry to say, "Yeah, we want to get 'em in before the baby comes. He'll be here by Christmas."

"God willing," Campbell smiles, adding, "He or she."

"January," Pru says in a whisper, after putting down her glass. Harry can't tell if she is pleased or displeased by the gallant way he keeps mentioning the baby that everybody else wants to ignore. While the appointments are being set up she and Nelson sit on that sofa like a pair of big limp Muppets, with invisible arms coming up through the cushions into their torsos and heads.

"Fred had his birthday in January," Ma Springer announces, grunting as she tries to get out of the Barcalounger, to see the minister off.

"Oh Mother," Janice says. "One twelfth of the world has January birthdays."

"*I* was born in January," Archie Campbell says, rising. He grins to show his seedy teeth. "In my case, after much prayerful effort. My parents were *an*cient. It's a wonder I'm here at all."

The next day a warm rain is beginning to batter the yellowing leaves down from the trees in the park along Cityview Drive as Harry and Nelson drive through Brewer to the lot. The kid is still persona non grata but he's asked to check on the two convertibles he crunched, one of which, the Royale, Manny is repairing. The '72 Mercury, hit twice from the side, was more severely damaged, and parts are harder to get. Rabbit's idea had been when the kid went off to school to sell it for junk and write off the loss. But he didn't have the heart not to let the boy look at the wrecks at least. Then Nelson is going to borrow the Corona and visit Billy Fosnacht before he goes back to Boston to become an endodontist. Harry had a root canal job once; it felt like they were tickling the underside of his eyeball. What a hellish way to make a living. Maybe there's no entirely good way. The Toyota's windshield wipers keep up a steady rubbery singsong as the Brewer traffic slows, brake lights burning red all along Locust Boulevard. The Castle has started up again and yellow school buses loom ahead in the jam. Harry switches the wipers from Fast to Intermittent and wishes he still smoked cigarettes. He wants to talk to the kid.

"Nelson."

"Unhh?"

"How do you feel?"

"O.K. I woke up with a soreness in my throat but I took two of those five-hundred-milligram vitamin Cs Melanie talked Bessie into getting."

"She was really a health nut, wasn't she? Melanie. We still have all that Granola in the kitchen."

"Yeah, well. It was part of her act. You know, mystical gypsy. She was always reading this guru, I forget his name. It sounded like a sneeze."

"You miss her?"

"Melanie? No, why would I?"

"Weren't you kind of close?"

Nelson avoids the implied question. "She was getting pretty grouchy toward the end."

"You think she and Charlie went off together?"

"Beats me," the boy says.

The wipers, now on Intermittent, startle Rabbit each time they switch across, as if someone other than he is making decisions in this car. A ghost. Like in that movie about Encounters of the Third Kind the way the truck with Richard Dreyfuss in it begins to shake all over and the headlights behind rise up in the air instead of pulling off to one side. He readjusts the knob from Intermittent to Slow. "I didn't mean your physical health, exactly. I meant more your state of mind. After last night."

"You mean about that sappy minister? I don't mind going over to listen to his garbage a couple times if it'll satisfy the Springer honor or whatever."

"I guess I mean more about the marriage in general. Nellie, I don't want to see you railroaded into anything."

The boy sits up a little in the side of Harry's vision; the yellow buses ahead pull into the Brewer High driveway and the line of cars begins to move again, slowly, beside a line of parked cars whose rooftops are spattered with leaves the rain has brought down. "Who says I'm being railroaded?"

"Nobody says it. Pru seems a fine girl, if you're ready for marriage."

"You don't think I'm ready. You don't think I'm ready for anything."

He lets the hostility pass, trying to talk meditatively, like Webb Murkett. "You know, Nelson, I'm not sure any man is ever a hundred per cent ready for marriage. I sure as hell know I wasn't, from the way I acted toward your mother."

"Yeah, well," the boy says, in a voice a little crumbled, from his father's not taking the bait. "She got her own back."

"I never could hold that against her. Or Charlie either. You ought to understand. After we got back together that time, we've both been pretty straight. We've even had a fair amount of fun together, in our dotage. I'm just sorry we had so much working out to do, with you still on the scene."

"Yeah, well." Nelson's voice sounds breathy and tight, and he keeps looking at his knees, even when Harry hangs that tricky left turn onto Eisenhower Avenue. The boy clears his throat and volunteers, "It's the times, I guess. A lot of the kids I got to know at Kent, they had horror stories worse than any of mine."

"Except that thing with Jill. They couldn't top that, I bet." He doesn't quite chuckle. Jill is a sacred name to the boy; he will never talk about it. Harry goes on clumsily, as the car gains momentum downhill and the spic and black kids strolling up-hill to school insolently flirt with danger, daring him to hit them, his fenders brushing their bodies, "There's something that doesn't feel right to me in this new development. The girl gets knocked up, O.K., it takes two to tango, you have some responsibility there, nobody can deny it. But then as I under-stand it she flat out refuses to get the abortion, when one of the good things that's come along in twenty years along with a lot that's not so good is you can go have an abortion now right out in the open, in a hospital, safe and clean as having your appendix out."

"So?"

"So why didn't she?"

The boy makes a gesture that Rabbit fears might be an attempt to grab the wheel; his grip tightens. But Nelson is merely waving to indicate a breadth of possibilities. "She had a lot of reasons. I forget what all they were."

"I'd like to hear them."

"Well for one thing she said she knew of women who had their insides all screwed up by abortions, so they could *never* have a baby. You say it's easy as an appendix but you've never had it done. She didn't *believe* in it."

"I thought she wasn't that much of a Catholic."

"She wasn't, she isn't, but still. She said it wasn't natural."

"What's natural? In this day and age with all these contra-ceptives getting knocked up like that isn't natural."

"Well she's *shy*, Dad. They don't call her Pru for nothing. Going to a doctor like that, and having him scrape you out, she just didn't want to do it."

"You bet she didn't. Shy. She wanted to have a baby, and she wasn't too shy to manage that. How much younger're you than she?"

"A year. A little more. What does it matter? It wasn't just a baby she wanted to have, it was *my* baby. Or so she said."

"That's sweet. I guess. What did you think about it?"

"I thought it was O.K., probably. It was her body. That's what they all tell you now, it's their body. I didn't see much I could do about it."

"Then it's sort of her funeral, isn't it?"

"How do you mean?"

"I mean," Harry says, in his indignation honking at some kids at the intersection of Plum Street who saunter right out toward him, this early in the school year the crossing guards aren't organized yet, "so she decides to keep pregnant till there's no correcting it while this other girl babysits for you, and your mother and grandmother and now this nance of a minister all decide when and how you're going to marry the poor broad. I mean, where do you come in? Nelson Angstrom. I mean, what do *you* want? Do you know?" In his frustration he hits the rim of the steering wheel with the heel of his hand, as the avenue dips down beneath the blackened nineteenth-century stones of the underpass at Eisenhower and Seventh, that in a bad rainstorm is flooded but not today. The arch of this underpass, built without a keystone, by masons all long dead, is famous, and from his earliest childhood has reminded Rabbit of a crypt, of death. They emerge among the drooping wet pennants of low-cost factory outlets.

"Well, I want—"

Fearing the kid is going to say he wants a job at Springer Motors, Harry interrupts: "You look scared, is all I see. Scared to say No to any of these women. I've never been that great at saying No either, but just because it runs in the family doesn't mean you have to get stuck. You don't necessarily have to lead my life, I guess is what I want to say."

"Your life seems pretty comfy to me, frankly." They turn down Weiser, the forest of the inner-city mall a fogged green smear in the rearview mirror.

"Yeah, well," Harry says, "it's taken me a fair amount of time to get there. And by the time you get there you're pooped. The world," he tells his son, "is full of people who never knew what hit 'em, their lives are over before they wake up."

"Dad, you keep talking about yourself but I don't see what it has to do with *me*. What *can* I do with Pru except marry her? She's not so bad, I mean I've known enough girls to know they all have their limits. But she's a person, she's a friend. It's as if you want to deny her to me, as if you're jealous or something. The way you keep mentioning her baby."

This kid should have been spanked at some point. "I'm not jealous, Nelson. Just the opposite. I feel sorry for you."

"Don't feel sorry for me. Don't waste your feelings on me."

They pass Schoenbaum Funeral Directors. Nobody out front in this rain. Harry swallows and asks, "Don't you want out, if we could rig it somehow?"

"How could we rig it? She's in her fifth month."

"She could go ahead have the baby without you marrying her. These adoption agencies are crying for white babies, you'd be doing somebody else a favor."

"Pru would never consent."

"Don't be too sure. We could ease the pain. She's one of seven, she knows the value of a dollar."

"Dad, this is crazy talk. You're forgetting this baby is a person. An Angstrom!"

"Jesus, how could I forget that?"

The light at the foot of Weiser, before the bridge, is red. Harry looks over at his son and gets an impression of something freshly hatched, wet and not quite unfolded. The light turns green. A bronze plaque on a pillar of pebbled concrete names the mayor for whom the bridge was named but it is raining too hard to read it.

He starts up again, "Or you could just, I don't know, not make any decision, just disappear for a while. I'd give you the money for that."

"Money, you're always offering me money to stay away."

"Maybe because when I was your age I wanted to get away and I couldn't. I didn't have the money. I didn't have the sense. We tried to send you away to get some sense and you've thumbed your nose at it."

"I haven't thumbed my nose, it's just that there's not that much out there. It isn't what you think, Dad. College is a rip-off, the professors are teaching you stuff because they're getting paid to do it, not because it does you any good. They don't give a fuck about geography or whatever any more than you do. It's all phony, they're there because parents don't want their kids around the house past a certain age and sending them to college makes them look good. 'My little Johnny's at Haavahd.' 'My little Nellie's at Kent.'"

"Really, that's how you see it? In my day kids *wanted* to get out in the world. We were scared but not so scared we kept running back to Mama. And Grandmama. What're you going to do when you run out of women to tell you what to do?"

"Same thing you'll do. Drop dead."

D I S C O. DATSUN. FUEL ECONOMY. Route III has a certain beauty in the rain, the colors and the banners and the bluish asphalt of the parking lots all run together through the swish of traffic, the beat of wipers. Rubbery hands flailing, *Help, help.* Rabbit has always liked rain, it puts a roof on the world. "I just don't like seeing you *caught*," he blurts out to Nelson. "You're too much *me*."

Nelson gets loud. "I'm not you! I'm not caught!"

"Nellie, you're caught. They've got you and you didn't even squeak. I hate to see it, is all. All I'm trying to say is, as far as I'm concerned you don't have to go through with it. If you want to get out of it, I'll help you."

"I don't want to be helped that way! I *like* Pru. I like the way she looks. She's great in bed. She needs me, she thinks I'm neat. She doesn't think I'm a baby. You say I'm caught but I don't feel caught, I feel like I'm becoming a man!"

Help, help.

"Good," Harry says then. "Good luck."

"Where I want your help, Dad, you won't give it."

"Where's that?"

"Here. Stop making it so hard for me to fit in at the lot."

They turn into the lot. The tires of the Corona splash in the gutter water rushing toward its grate along the highway curb. Stonily Rabbit says nothing.

III

A NEW SHOP has opened on Weiser Street in one of those
scruffy blocks between the bridge and the mall, opposite the enduring old variety store that sells out-of-town newspapers, warm unshelled peanuts, and dirty magazines for
queers as well as straights. From the look of it the new store
too might be peddling smut, for its showcase front window is
thoroughly masked by long thin blond Venetian blinds, and
the lettering on its windows is strikingly discreet. Gold letters
rimmed in black and very small simply say FISCAL ALTERNA-
TIVES and below that, smaller yet, *Old Coins, Silver and Gold
Bought and Sold.* Harry passes the place by car every day, and
one day, there being two empty metered spaces he can slide
into without holding up traffic, he parks and goes in. The next
day, after some business at his bank, the Brewer Trust two
blocks away, he comes out of Fiscal Alternatives with thirty
Krugerrands purchased for $377.14 each, including commis-
sion and sales tax, coming to $11,314.20. These figures had
been run off inside by a girl with platinum hair; her long scarlet fingernails didn't seem to hamper her touch on the hand
computer. She was the only person visible, at her long glass-
topped desk, with beige sides and swivel chair to match. But
there were voices and monitoring presences in other rooms,
back rooms into which she vanished and from which she
emerged with his gold. The coins came in cunning plastic cylinders of fifteen each, with round blue-tinted lids that suggested dollhouse toilet seats; indeed, bits of what seemed toilet
paper were stuffed into the hole of this lid to make the fit tight
and to conceal even a glimmer of the sacred metal. So heavy,
the cylinders threaten to tear the pockets off his coat as Harry
hops up Ma Springer's front steps to face his family. Inside the
front door, Pru sits knitting on the gray sofa and Ma Springer
has taken over the Barcalounger to keep her legs up while
some quick-lipped high yellow from Philly is giving her the
six-o'clock news. Mayor Frank Rizzo has once again denied
charges of police brutality, he says, in a rapid dry voice that
pulls the rug out from every word. Used to be Philadelphia

was a distant place where no one dared visit, but television has pulled it closer, put its muggy murders and politics right next door. "Where's Janice?" Harry asks.

Ma Springer says, "Shh."

Pru says, "Janice took Nelson over to the club, to fill in with some ladies' doubles, and then I think they were going to go shopping for a suit."

"I thought he bought a new suit this summer."

"That was a business suit. They think he needs a three-piece suit for the wedding."

"Jesus, the wedding. How're you liking your sessions with what's-his-name?"

"I don't mind them. Nelson hates them."

"He says that just to get his grandmother going," Ma Springer calls, twisting to push her voice around the headrest. "I think they're really doing him good." Neither woman notices the hang of his coat, though it feels like a bull's balls tugging at his pockets. It's Janice he wants. He goes upstairs and snuggles the two dense, immaculate cylinders into the back of his bedside table, in the drawer where he keeps a spare pair of reading glasses and the rubber tip on a plastic handle he is supposed to massage his gums with to keep out of the hands of the periodontist and the pink wax earplugs he stuffs in sometimes when he has the jitters and can't tune out the house noise. In this same drawer he used to keep condoms, in that interval between when Janice decided the Pill was bad for her and when she went and had her tubes burned, but that was a long while ago and he threw them all away, the whole tidy tin box of them, after an indication, the lid not quite closed, perhaps he imagined it, that Nelson or somebody had been into the box and filched a couple. From about that time on he began to feel crowded, living with the kid. As long as Nelson was socked into baseball statistics or that guitar or even the rock records that threaded their sound through all the fibers of the house, his occupation of the room down the hall was no more uncomfortable than the persistence of Rabbit's own childhood in an annex of his brain; but when the stuff with hormones and girls and cars and beers began, Harry wanted out of fatherhood. Two glimpses mark the limits of his comfort in this matter of men descending from men. When he was about twelve or thirteen he walked into his parents' bedroom in the half-house on Jackson Road not expecting his father to be there, and the old man was standing in front of his bureau in just socks and an undershirt, innocently fishing in a drawer for his undershorts, that boxer style that always looked sad and dreary to Harry anyway, and here was his father's bare behind, such white buttocks, limp and hairless, mute and helpless flesh that squeezed out shit once a day and otherwise hung there in the world like linen that hadn't been ironed; and then when Nelson was about the same age, a year older he must have been for they were living in this house already and they moved when the kid was thirteen, Harry had wandered into the bathroom not realizing Nelson would be stepping out of the shower and had seen the child frontally: he had pubic hair and, though his body was still slim and pint-sized, a man-sized prick, heavy and oval, unlike Rabbit's circumcised and perhaps because of this looking brutal, and big. Big. This was years before the condoms were stolen. The drawer rattles, stuck, and Harry tries to ease it in, hearing that Janice and Nelson have come into the house, making the downstairs resound with news of tennis and clothing stores and of the outer world. Harry wants to save his news for Janice. To knock her out with it. The drawer suddenly eases shut and he smiles, anticipating her astonished reception of his precious, lustrous, lead-heavy secret.

As with many anticipated joys it does not come exactly as envisioned. By the time they climb the stairs together it is later than it should be, and they feel unsettled and high. Dinner had to be early because Nelson and Pru were going over to Soupy, as they both call Campbell, for their third session of counseling. They returned around nine-thirty with Nelson in such a rage they had to break out the dinner wine again while with a beer can in hand he did an imitation of the young minister urging the church's way into the intimate space between these two. "He keeps talking about the church being the be-riide of Ke-riist. I kept wanting to ask him, Whose little bride are you?"

"Nelson," Janice said, glancing toward the kitchen, where her mother was making herself Ovaltine.

"I mean, it's ob*scene*," Nelson insisted. "What does He do, fuck the church up the ass?"

Pru laughed, Harry noticed. Did Nelson do that to her? It was about the last thing left a little out of the ordinary for these kids, blowing all over the magazines these days, giving head they call it, there was that movie *Shampoo* where Julie Christie who you associate with costume dramas all decked out in bonnets announced right on the screen she wanted to blow Warren Beatty, actually said it, and it wasn't even an X, it was a simple R, with all these teen-age dating couples sitting there holding hands as sweetly as if it was a return of *Showboat* with Kathryn Grayson and Howard Keel, the girls laughing along with the boys. Pru's long-boned mute body does not declare what it does, nor her pale lips, that in repose have a dry, pursed look, an expression maybe you learn in secretarial school. *Great in bed*, Nelson had said.

"I'm sorry, Mom, but he really pisses me off. He gets me to say these things I don't believe and then he grins and acts jolly like it's all some kind of crappy joke. Mom-mom, how can you and those other old ladies stand him?"

Bessie had come in from the kitchen, her mug of Ovaltine steaming as she stared it steady and her hair pinned tight up against her skull with a net over it all, for bed. "Oh," she said, "he's higher than some, and lower than others. At least he doesn't choke us on all the incense like the one that became a Greek Orthodox priest finally. And he did a good job of getting the diehards to accept the new form. My tongue still sticks at some of the responses."

Pru offered, "Soupy seemed quite proud that the new service doesn't have 'obey.'"

"People never did obey, I guess they might as well leave it out," Ma said.

Janice seemed determined to have a go at Nelson herself. "Really you shouldn't put up such resistance, Nelson. The man is leaning over backwards to give us a church service, and I think from the way he acts he sincerely likes you. He really does have a feel for young people."

"Does he ever," Nelson said, soft enough for Ma Springer not to hear, then mimicking loudly, "Dear Mater and Pater were *ain*cient. It's such a *whun*der I got here at all. In case you *whun*der why I have this *toad*stool look."

"You shouldn't mind people's physical appearance," Janice said.

"Oh but Mater, one simply *does*." For some while they went on in this way, it was as good as television, Nelson imitating Soupy's mellow voice, Janice pleading for reason and charity, Ma Springer drifting in some world of her own where the Episcopal Church has presided since Creation; but Harry felt above them all, a golden man waiting to take his wife upstairs and show her their treasure. When the joking died, and a rerun of *M**A*S*H came on that Nelson wanted to see, the young couple looked tired and harried suddenly, sitting there on the sofa, being beaten into one. Already each took an accustomed place, Pru over on the end with the little cherry side table for her crème de menthe and her knitting, and Nelson on the middle cushion with his feet in their button-soled Adidas up on the reproduction cobbler's bench. Now that he didn't go to the lot he didn't bother to shave every day, and the whiskers came in as reddish bristle on his chin and upper lip but his cheeks were still downy. To hell with this scruffy kid. Rabbit has decided to live for himself, selfishly at last.

When Janice comes back from the bathroom naked and damp inside her terrycloth robe, he has locked their bedroom door and arranged himself in his underpants on the bed. He calls in a husky and insinuating voice, "Hey. Janice. Look. I bought us something today."

Her dark eyes are glazed from all that drinking and parenting downstairs; she took the shower to help clear her head. Slowly her eyes focus on his face, which must show an intensity of pleasure that puzzles her.

He tugs open the sticky drawer and is himself startled to see the two tinted cylinders sliding toward him, still upright, still there. He would have thought something so dense with preciousness would broadcast signals bringing burglars like dogs to a bitch in heat. He lifts one roll out and places it in Janice's hand; her arm dips with the unexpected weight, and her robe, untied, falls open. Her thin brown used body is more alluring in this lapsed sheath of rough bright cloth than a girl's; he wants to reach in, to where the shadows keep the damp fresh.

"What is it, Harry?" she asks, her eyes widening.

"Open it," he tells her, and when she fumbles too long at the transparent tape holding on the toilet-seat-shaped little lid he pries it off for her with his big fingernails. He removes the wad of tissue paper and spills out upon the quilted bedspread the fifteen Krugerrands. Their color is redder than gold in his mind had been. "Gold," he whispers, holding up close to her face, paired in his palm, two coins, showing the two sides, the profile of some old Boer on one and a kind of antelope on the other. "Each of these is worth about three hundred sixty dollars," he tells her. "Don't tell your mother or Nelson or anybody."

She does seem bewitched, taking one into her fingers. Her nails scratch his palm as she lifts the coin off. Her brown eyes pick up flecks of yellow. "Is it all right?" Janice asks. "Where on earth did you get them?"

"A new place on Weiser across from the peanut store that sells precious metals, buys and sells. It was simple. All you got to do is produce a certified check within twenty-four hours after they quote you a price. They guarantee to buy them back at the going rate any time, so all you lose is their six per cent commission and the sales tax, which at the rate gold is going up I'll have made back by next week. Here. I bought two stacks. Look." He takes the other thrillingly hefty cylinder from the drawer and undoes the lid and spills those fifteen antelopes slippingly upon the bedspread, thus doubling the riches displayed. The spread is a lightweight Pennsylvania Dutch quilt, small rectangular patches sewed together by patient biddies, graded from pale to dark to form a kind of dimensional effect, of four large boxes having a lighter and darker side. He lies down upon its illusion and places a Krugerrand each in the sockets of his eyes. Through the chill red pressure of the gold he hears Janice say, "My God. I thought only the government could have gold. Don't you need a license or anything?"

"Just the bucks. Just the fucking bucks, Wonder Woman." Blind, he feels amid the pure strangeness of the gold his prick firming up and stretching the fabric of his jockey shorts.

"Harry. How much did you spend?"

He wills her to lift down the elastic of his underpants and suck, suck until she gags. When she fails to read his mind and do this, he removes the coins and gazes up at her, a dead man reborn and staring. No coffin dark greets his open eyes, just his wife's out-of-focus face, framed in dark hair damp and stringy from the shower and fringy across the forehead so that Mamie Eisenhower comes to mind. "Eleven thousand five hundred more or less," he answers. "Honey, it was just sitting in the savings account drawing a lousy six per cent. At only six per cent these days you're losing money, inflation's running about twelve. The beauty of gold is, it loves bad news. As the dollar sinks, gold goes up. All the Arabs are turning their dollars into gold. Webb Murkett told me all about it, the day you wouldn't come to the club."

She is still examining the coin, stroking its subtle relief, when he wants her attention to turn to him. He hasn't had a hard-on just blossom in his pants since he can't remember when. Lotty Bingaman days. "It's pretty," Janice admits. "Should you be supporting the South Africans though?"

"Why not, they're making jobs for the blacks, mining the stuff. The advantage of the Krugerrand, the girl at this fiscal alternatives place explained, is it weighs one troy ounce exactly and is easier to deal with. You can buy Mexican pesos if you want, or there's a little Canadian maple leaf, though there she said it's so fine the gold dust comes off on your hands. Also I liked the look of that deer on the back. Don't you?"

"I do. It's exciting," Janice confesses, at last looking at him, where he lies tumescent amid scattered gold. "Where are you going to keep them?" she asks. Her tongue sneaks forward in thought, and rests on her lower lip. He loves her when she tries to think.

"In your great big cunt," he says, and pulls her down by the lapels of her rough robe. Out of deference to those around them in the house—Ma Springer just a wall's thickness away, her television a dim rumble, the Korean War turned into a joke—Janice tries to suppress her cries as he strips the terry-cloth from her willing body and the coins on the bedspread come in contact with her skin. The cords of her throat tighten; her face darkens as she strains in the grip of indignation and glee. His underwear off, the overhead light still on, his prick up like a jutting piece of pink wreckage, he calms her into lying motionless and places a Krugerrand on each nipple, one on her navel, and a number on her pussy, enough to mask the hair with a triangle of unsteady coins overlapping like snake scales. If she laughs and her belly moves the whole construction will collapse. Kneeling at her hips, Harry holds a Krugerrand by the edge as if to insert it in a slot. "*No!*" Janice protests, loud enough to twitch Ma Springer awake through the wall, loud enough to jar loose the coins so some do spill between her legs. He hushes her mouth with his and then moves his mouth south, across the desert, oasis to oasis, until he comes to the ferny jungle, which his wife lays open to him with a humoring toss of her thighs. A kind of interest compounds as, seeing red, spilled gold pressing on his forehead, he hunts with his tongue for her clitoris. He finds what he thinks is the right rhythm but doesn't feel it take; he thinks the bright overhead light might be distracting her and risks losing his hard-on in hopping from the bed to switch it off over by the door. Turning then in the half-dark he sees she has turned also, gotten up onto her knees and elbows, a four-legged moonchild of his, her soft cleft ass held high to him in the gloom as her face peeks around one shoulder. He fucks her in this position gently, groaning in the effort of keeping his jism in, letting his thoughts fly far. The pennant race, the recent hike in the factory base price of Corollas. He fondles her underside's defenseless slack flesh, his own belly massive and bearing down. Her back looks so breakable and brave and narrow—the long dent of its spine, the cross-bar of pallor left by her bathing-suit bra. Behind him his bare feet release a faraway sad odor. Coins jingle, slithering in toward their knees, into the depressions their interlocked weights make in the mattress. He taps her ass and asks, "Want to turn over?"

"Uh-huh." As an afterthought: "Want me to sit on you first?"

"Uh-huh." As an afterthought: "Don't make me come."

Harry's skin is bitten as by ice when he lies on his back. The coins: worse than toast crumbs. So wet he feels almost nothing, Janice straddles him, vast and globular in the patchy light that filters from the streetlight through the big copper beech. She picks up a stray coin and places it glinting in her eye, as a monocle. Lording it over him, holding him captive, she grinds her wet halves around him; self to self, bivalve and tuber, this is what it comes to. "Don't come," she says, alarmed enough so that her mock-monocle drops to his tense abdomen with a thud. "Better get underneath," he grunts. Her body then seems thin and black, silhouetted by the scattered circles, reflecting according to their tilt. Gods bedded among stars, he gasps in her ear, then she in his.

After this payoff, regaining their breaths, they can count in the semi-dark only twenty-nine Krugerrands on the rumpled bedspread, its landscape of ridged green patches. He turns on the overhead light. It hurts their eyes. By its harshness their naked skins seem also rumpled. Panic encrusts Harry's drained body; he does not rest until, naked on his knees on the rug, a late strand of spunk looping from his reddened glans, he finds, caught in the crack between the mattress and the bed side-rail, the precious thirtieth.

He stands with Charlie gazing out at the bleak September light. The tree over beyond the Chuck Wagon parking lot has gone thin and yellow at its top; above its stripped twigs the sky holds some diagonal cirrus, bands of fat in bacon, promising rain tomorrow. "Poor old Carter," Harry says. "D'ya see where he nearly killed himself running up some mountain in Maryland?"

"He's pushing," Charlie says. "Kennedy's on his tail." Charlie has returned from his two weeks' vacation with a kiss of Florida tan undermined by a weak heart and the days intervening. He did not come from Florida directly. Simultaneously with his return Monday a card sent from Ohio arrived at Springer Motors, saying in his sharply slanted book-keeper's hand,

> Hi Gang—
> Detoured on way
> back from Fla. thru Gt.
> Smokies. Southern belles,
> mile after mile. Now near
> Akron, exploded radial
> capital of the world. Fuel
> economy a no-no out here,
> big fins & V-8s still reign.
> Miss you all lots.   Chas.

The joke especially for Harry was on the other side: a picture of a big flat-roofed building like a quarter of a pie, identified as KENT STATE STUDENT COMPLEX, *embracing the largest open-stack library in northeastern Ohio.*

"Sort of pushing yourself these days, aren't you?" Harry asks him. "How was Melanie all that while?"

"Who says I was with Melanie?"

"You did. With that card. Jesus, Charlie, a young kid like that grinding your balls could kill you."

"What a way to go, huh champ? You know as well as I do it's not the chicks that grind your balls, it's these middle-aged broads time is running out on."

Rabbit remembers his bout with Janice amid their gold, yet still remains jealous. "Whajja do in Florida with her?"

"We moved around. Sarasota, Venice, St. Pete's. I couldn't talk her out of the Atlantic side so we drove over from Naples on 75, old Alligator Alley, and did the shmeer—Coral Gables, Ocean Boulevard, up to Boca and West Palm. We were going to take in Cape Canaveral but ran out of time. The bimbo didn't even bring a bathing suit, the one we bought her was one of these new ones with the sides wide open. Great figure. Don't know why you didn't appreciate her."

"I *could*n't appreciate her, it was Nelson brought her into the house. It'd be like screwing your own daughter."

Charlie has a toothpick left over from lunch downtown, a persimmon-colored one, and he dents his lower lip with it as he gazes out the tired window. "There's worse things," he offers bleakly. "How's Nelson and the bride-to-be?"

"Pru." Harry sees that Charlie is set to guard the details of his trip, to make him pull them out one by one. Miles of Southern belles. Fuck this guy. Rabbit has secrets too. But, thinking this, he can picture only a farm, its buildings set down low in a hollow.

"Melanie had a lot to say about Pru."

"Like what?"

"Like she thinks she's weird. Her impression is that shy as she seems she's a tough kid up from a really rocky upbringing and isn't too steady on her feet, emotionally speaking."

"Yeah well, some might say a girl who gets her kicks screwing an old crow like you is pretty weird herself."

Charlie looks away from the window straight up into his eyes, his own eyes behind their tinted spectacles looking watery. "You shouldn't say things like that to me, Harry. Both of us getting on, two guys just hanging in there ought to be nice to each other."

Harry wonders from this if Charlie knows how threatened his position is, Nelson on his tail.

Charlie continues, "Ask me whatever you want about Melanie. Like I said, she's a good kid. Solid, emotionally. The trouble with you, champ, is you have screwing on the brain. My biggest kick was showing this young woman something of the world she hadn't seen before. She ate it up—the cypresses, that tower with the chimes. She said she'd still take California though. Florida's too flat. She said if this Christmas I could get my ass out to Carmel she'd be happy to show me around. Meet her mother and whoever else is around. Nothing heavy."

"How much—how much future you think you two have?"

"Harry, I don't have much future with anybody." His voice is whispery, barely audible. Harry would like to take it and wire-brush it clean.

"You never know," he reassures the smaller man.

"You *know*," Stavros insists. "You know when your time is running out. If life offers you something, take it."

"O.K., O.K. I will. I do. What'd your poor old *Manna mou* do, while you were bombing around with Bimbo in the Everglades?"

"Well," he says, "funny thing there. A female cousin of mine, five or so years younger, I guess has been running around pretty bad, and her husband kicked her out this summer, and kept the kids. They lived in Norristown. So Gloria's been living in an apartment by herself out on Youngquist a couple blocks away and was happy to babysit for the old lady while I was off and says she'll do it again any time. So I have some freedom now I didn't used to have." Everywhere, it seems to Harry, families are breaking up and different pieces coming together like survivors in one great big lifeboat, while he and Janice keep sitting over there in Ma Springer's shadow, behind the times.

"Nothing like freedom," he tells his friend. "Don't abuse it now. You asked about Nelson. The wedding's this Saturday. Immediate family only. Sorry."

"Wow. Poor little Nellie. Signed, sealed, and delivered."

Harry hurries by this. "From what Janice and Bessie let drop the mother will probably show up. The father's too sore."

"You should see Akron," Charlie tells him. "I'd be sore too if I had to live there."

"Isn't there a golf course out there where Nicklaus holds a tournament every year?"

"What I saw wasn't any golf course."

Charlie has come back from his experiences tenderized, nostalgic it seems for his life even as he lives it. So aged and philosophical he seems, Harry dares ask him, "What'd Melanie think of me, did she say?"

A very fat couple are prowling the lot, looking at the little cars, testing by their bodies, sitting down on air beside the driver's doors, which models might be big enough for them. Charlie watches this couple move among the glittering roofs and hoods a minute before answering. "She thought you were neat, except the women pushed you around. She thought about you and her balling but got the impression you and Janice were very solid."

"You disillusion her?"

"Couldn't. The kid was right."

"Yeah how about ten years ago?"

"That was just cement."

Harry loves the way he ticks this off, Janice's seducer; he loves this savvy Greek, dainty of heart beneath his coat of summer checks. The couple have wearied of trying on cars for size and get into their old car, a '77 Pontiac Grand Prix with cream hardtop, and drive away. Harry asks suddenly, "How do you feel about it? Think we can live with Nelson over here?"

Charlie shrugs, a minimal brittle motion. "Can he live with me? He wants to be a cut above Jake and Rudy, and there aren't that many cuts in an outfit like this."

"I've told them, Charlie, if you go I go."

"You can't go, Chief. You're family. Me, I'm old times. I can go."

"You know this business cold, that's what counts with me."

"Ah, this isn't selling. It's like supermarkets now: it's shelf-stacking, and ringing it out at the register. When it was all used, we used to try to fit a car to every customer. Now it's take it or leave it. With this seller's market there's no room to improvise. Your boy had the right idea: go with convertibles, antiques, something with a little amusement value. I can't take these Jap bugs seriously. This new thing called the Tercel we're supposed to start pushing next month, have you seen the stats? One point five liter engine, twenty-inch tires. It's like those little cars they used to have on merry-go-rounds for the kids who were too scared to ride the horses."

"Forty-three m.p.g. on the highway, that's the stat people care about, the way the world's winding."

Charlie says, "You don't see too many bugs down in Florida. The old folks are still driving the big old hogs, the Continentals, the Toronados, they paint 'em white and float around. Of course the roads, there isn't a hill in the state and never any frost. I've been thinking about the Sun Belt. Go down there and thumb my nose at the heating-oil bills. Then they get you on the air-conditioning. You can't escape."

Harry says, "Sodium wafers, that's the answer. Electricity straight from sunlight. It's about five years off, that's what *Consumer Reports* was saying. Then we can tell those Arabs to take their fucking oil and grease their camels with it."

Charlie says, "Traffic fatalities are up. You want to know why they're up? Two reasons. One, the kids are pretty much off drugs now and back into alcohol. Two, everybody's gone to compacts and they crumple like paper bags."

He chuckles and twirls the flavored toothpick against his lower lip as the two men gaze out the window at the river of dirty tin. An old low-slung station wagon pulls into the lot but it has no wooden rack on top; though Harry's heart skips, it is not his daughter. The station wagon noses around and heads out into III again, just casing. Burglaries are up. Harry asks Charlie, "Melanie really thought about"—he balks at "balling," it is not his generation's word—"going to bed with me?"

"That's what the lady said. But you know these kids, they come right out with everything we used to keep to ourselves. Doesn't mean there's more of it. Probably less as a matter of fact. By the time they're twenty-five they're burnt out."

"I was never attracted to her, to tell you the truth. Now this new girl of Nelson's—"

"I don't want to hear about it," Charlie says, pivoting to go back to his desk. "They're about to get married, for Chrissake."

Running. Harry has continued the running he began up in the Poconos, as a way of getting his body back from those sodden years when he never thought about it, just ate and did what he wanted, restaurant lunches downtown in Brewer plus the Rotary every Thursday, it begins to pack on. The town he runs through is dark, full of slanty alleys and sidewalks cracked and tipped from underneath, whole cement slabs lifted up by roots like crypt lids in a horror movie, the dead reach up, they catch at his heels. He keeps moving, pacing himself, overriding the protest of his lungs and fashioning of his stiff muscles and tired blood a kind of machine that goes where the brain directs, uphill past the wide-eaved almost Chinese-looking house where the butch women hammer, their front windows never lit, must watch a lot of television or else snuggle into whatever it is they do early or else saving electricity, women won't get paid the same as men until ERA passes, at least having a nest of them moving into the neighborhood not like blacks or Puerto Ricans, they don't breed.

Norway maples shade these streets. Not much taller than when he was a boy. Grab a low branch and hoist yourself up into a hornets' nest. Split the seeds and stick them to your nose to make yourself a rhinoceros. Panting, he cuts through their shadow. A slim pain cuts through his high left side. Hold on, heart. Old Fred Springer popped off in a blaze of red, anyway Rabbit has always imagined the last thing you'd see in a heart attack would be a bright flash of red. Amazing, how dark these American houses are, at nine o'clock at night. A kind of ghost town, nobody else on the sidewalk, all the chickens in their coop, only a brownish bit of glow showing through a window crack here and there, night light in a child's room. His mind strides on into a bottomless sorrow, thinking of children. Little Nellie in his room newly moved into Vista Crescent, his teddies stacked in a row beside him, his eyes like theirs unable to close, scared of dying while asleep, thinking of baby Becky who did fall through, who did die. A volume of water still stood in the tub many hours later, dust on the unstirring gray surface, just a little rubber stopper to lift and God in all His strength did nothing. Dry leaves scrape and break underfoot, the sound of fall, excitement in the air. The Pope is coming, and the wedding is Saturday. Janice asks him why is his heart so hard toward Nelson. Because Nelson has swallowed up the boy that was and substituted one more pushy man in the world, hairy wrists, big prick. Not enough room in the world. People came north from the sun belt in Egypt and lived in heated houses and now the heat is being used up, just the oil for the showroom and offices and garage has doubled since '74 when he first saw the Springer Motors books and will double in the next year or two again and when you try to cut it down to where the President says, the men in the garage complain, they have to work with their bare hands, working on a concrete slab they can wear thick socks and heavy soles, he thought at one point he should get them all that kind of golf glove that leaves the fingertips bare but it would have been hard to find ones for the right hand, guys under thirty now just will not work without comfort and all the perks, a whole new ethic, soft, socialism, heat tends to rise in a big space like that and hang up there amid the crossbraces, if they built it now they'd put in twenty inches of insulation. If the Pope is so crazy about babies why doesn't *he* try to keep them warm?

He is running along Potter Avenue now, still uphill, saving the downhill for the homeward leg, along the gutter where the water from the ice plant used to run, an edge of green slime, life tries to get a grip anywhere, on earth that is, not on the moon, that's another thing he doesn't like about the thought of climbing through the stars. Once clowning on the way to school along the gutter that now is dry he slipped on the slime and fell in, got his knickers soaked, those corduroy knickers they used to make you wear, *swish swish*, and the long socks, incredible how far back he goes now, he can remember girls in first grade still wearing high-button shoes: Margaret Schoelkopf, she was so full of life her nose would start to bleed for no reason. When he fell in the gutter of ice-plant water his knickers were so wet he had to run home crying and change, he hated being late for school. Or for anywhere, it was something Mom drummed into him, she didn't so much care where he went but he had to be home on time, and for most of his life this sensation would overtake him, anywhere, in the locker room, on a 16A bus, in the middle of a fuck, that he was late for somewhere and he was in terrible dark trouble, a kind of tunnel would open in his mind with Mom at the end of it with a switch. *Do you want a switching Hassy?* she would ask him as if asking if he wanted dessert, the switches came off the base of the little pear tree in the narrow back yard on Jackson Road; angry yellowjackets would hover over the fallen rotting fruit. Lately he no longer ever feels he is late for somewhere, a strange sort of peace at his time of life: a thrown ball at the top of its arc is for a second still. His gold is rising in value, ten dollars an ounce or so in the papers every day, ten times thirty is three hundred smackers without his lifting a finger, you think how Pop slaved. Janice putting that monocle on was a surprise, the only trouble with her in bed is she still doesn't like to blow, something mean about her mouth and always was, Melanie had those funny saucy stubborn cherry lips, a wonder Charlie didn't pop his aorta in some motel down there in the sands, how lovely it is when a woman forgets herself and opens her mouth to laugh or exclaim so wide you see the whole round cavern the ribbed pink roof and the tongue like a rug in a hall and the butterfly-shaped blackness in the back that goes down into the throat, Pru did that the other day in the kitchen at something Ma Springer said, her smile usually wider on one side than the other and a bit cautious like she might get burned, but all the girls coming up now blew, it was part of the culture, taken for granted, fuck-and-suck movies they call them, right out in the open, you take your date, ADULT FILMS NEW EACH FRIDAY in the old Baghdad on upper Weiser where in Rabbit's day they used to go see Ronald Reagan being co-pilot against the Japs. Lucky Nelson, in a way. Still he can't envy him. A worn-out world to find his way in. Funny about mouths, they must do so much, and don't tell what went into them, even a minute later. One thing he does hate is seeing bits of food, rice or cereal or whatever, hanging in the little hairs of a face during a meal. Poor Mom in those last years.

His knees are jarring. His big gut jounces. Each night he tries to extend his run among the silent dark houses, through the cones of the streetlights, under the ice-cold lopsided moon, that the other night driving home in the Corona he happened to see through the tinted upper part of the windshield and for a second thought, My God, it *is* green. Tonight he pushes himself as far as Kegerise Street, a kind of alley that turns downhill again, past black-sided small factories bearing mysterious new names like Lynnex and Data Development and an old stone farmhouse that all the years he was growing up had boarded windows and a yard full of tumbledown weeds milkweed and thistle and a fence of broken slats but now was all fixed up with a little neat sign outside saying *Albrecht Stamm Homestead* and inside all sorts of authentic hand-made furniture and quaint kitchen equipment to show what a farmhouse was like around 1825 and in cases in the hall photographs of the early buildings of Mt. Judge before the turn of the century but not anything of the fields when the area of the town was in large part Stamm's farm, they didn't have cameras that far back or if they did didn't point them at empty fields. Old man Springer had been on the board of the Mt. Judge Historical Society and helped raise the funds for the restoration, after he died Janice and Bessie thought Harry might be elected to take his place on the board but it didn't happen, his checkered past haunting him. Even though a young hippie couple lives upstairs and leads the visitors through, to Harry the old Stamm place is full of ghosts, those old farmers lived weird lives, locking their crazy sisters in the attic and strangling the pregnant hired girl in a fit of demon rum and hiding the body in the potato bin so that fifty years later the skeleton comes to light. Next door the Sunshine Athletic Association used to be, that Harry as a boy had thought was full of athletes, so he hoped he could some day belong, but when twenty years ago he did get inside it smelled of cigar butts and beer gone flat in the bottom of the glass. Then through the Sixties it fell into dilapidation and disrepute, the guys who drank and played cards in there getting older and fewer and more morose. So when the building came up for sale the Historical Society bought it and tore it down and made where it was into a parking lot for the visitors who came by to the Stamm Homestead on their way to Lancaster to look at the Amish or on their way to Philadelphia to look at the Liberty Bell. You wouldn't think people could find it tucked away on what used to be Kegerise Alley but an amazing number do, white-haired most of them. History. The more of it you have the more you have to live it. After a little while there gets to be too much of it to memorize and maybe that's when empires start to decline.

Now he is really rolling, the alley slants down past the body shop and a chicken house turned into a little leather-working plant, these ex-hippies are everywhere, trying to hang on, they missed the boat but had their fun, he has pushed through the first wave of fatigue, when you think you can't drag your body another stride, your thighs pure pain. Then second wind comes and you break free into a state where your body does it by itself, a machine being ridden, your brain like the astronaut in the tip of the rocket, your thoughts just flying. If only Nelson would get married and go away and come back rich twenty years from now. Why can't these kids get out on their own instead of crawling back? Too crowded out there. The Pope, Jesus, you have to hope he isn't shot, just like America to have some nut take a shot to get his name in the papers, that Squeaky Fromme who used to lay the old cowboys for the Manson ranch, all the ass that Manson had you'd think it would have made him nicer since it's being sexually frustrated that causes war, he read somewhere. He knows how the Pope feels about contraception though, he could never stand rubbers, even when they gave them to you free in the Army, this month's *Consumer Reports* has an article on them, page after page, all this testing, some people apparently prefer bright-colored ones with ribs and little nubbins to give the woman an added tickle inside, did the staffers on the magazine all ask the secretaries to screw or what, some people even liked ones made out of sheep intestine, the very thought of it makes him crawl down there, with names like Horizon Nuda and Klingtie Naturalamb, Harry couldn't read to the end of the article, he was so turned off. He wonders about his daughter, what she uses, country methods they used to kid about in school, squat on a cornstalk, she looked pretty virginal in that one glimpse of her and who wouldn't be, surrounded by rubes? Ruth would set her straight, what pigs men are. And that barking dog would be a discouragement too.

There is a longer way home, down Jackson to Joseph and

over, but tonight he takes the shortcut, diagonally across the lawn of the big stone Baptist church, he likes the turf under his feet for a minute, the church façade so dark, to the concrete steps that take you down onto Myrtle, and on past the red, white, and blue post office trucks parked in a row at the back platform, the American flag hanging limp and bright over the fake gable out front, used to be you shouldn't fly the flag at night but now all the towns do it with a spotlight, waste of electricity, soaking up the last dribble of energy flying the flag. Myrtle leads into Joseph from the other end. They will be sitting around waiting for him, watching the boob tube or going on about the wedding, getting silly about it now that it's so close and Soupy has declared all systems go, they've invited Charlie Stavros after all and Grace Stuhl and a batch of other biddies and a few friends from the Flying Eagle and it turns out Pru or Teresa as they call her in the announcement they want to send out has an aunt and uncle in Binghamton, New York, who will come down even if the father is some sorehead who wants to strangle his daughter and put her in the potato bin. In he will come and Janice will make her usual crack about him killing himself with a heart attack, it's true he does get very red in his white face, he can see in the mirror in the foyer, with his blue eyes, Santa Claus without the whiskers, and has to bend over the back of a chair gasping for a while to get his breath, but that's part of the fun, giving her a scare, poor mutt what would she do without him, have to give up the Flying Eagle and everything, go back to selling nuts in Kroll's. In he will come and there Pru will be sitting on the sofa right next to Nelson like the police officer who takes the criminal from one jail to another on the train without letting the handcuffs show, the one thing Harry is fearful of now that Pru is in the family is stinking up the room with his sweat. Tothero had it that time in the Sunshine, an old man's sour sad body smell, and getting out of bed in the morning sometimes Harry surprises it on himself, this faraway odor like a corpse just beginning to sweeten. Middle age is a wonderful country, all the things you thought would never happen are happening. When he was fifteen, forty-six would have seemed the end of the rainbow, he'd never get there, if a meaning of life was to show up you'd think it would have by now.

Yet at moments it seems it has, there are just no words for it, it is not something you dig for but sits on the top of the table like an unopened dewy beer can. Not only is the Pope coming but the Dalai Lama they bounced out of Tibet twenty years ago is going around the U.S.A. talking to divinity schools and appearing on TV talk shows, Harry has always been curious about what it would feel like to *be* the Dalai Lama. A ball at the top of its arc, a leaf on the skin of a pond. A water strider in a way is what the mind is like, those dimples at the end of their legs where they don't break the skin of the water quite. When Harry was little God used to spread in the dark above his bed like that and then when the bed became strange and the girl in the next aisle grew armpit hair He entered into the blood and muscle and nerve as an odd command and now He had withdrawn, giving Harry the respect due from one well-off gentleman to another, but for a calling card left in the pit of the stomach, a bit of lead true as a plumb bob pulling Harry down toward all those leaden dead in the hollow earth below.

The front lights of Ma Springer's big shadowy stucco house blaze, they are all excited by the wedding, Pru now has a constant blush and Janice hasn't played tennis for days and Bessie evidently gets up in the middle of the night and goes downstairs to watch on the bigger TV the old Hollywood comedies, men in big-brimmed hats and little mustaches, women with shoulders broader than their hips swapping wisecracks in newspaper offices and deluxe hotel suites, Ma must have seen these movies first when she had all black hair and the Brewer downtown was a great white way. Harry jogs in place to let a car pass, one of those crazy Mazdas with the Wankel engine like a squirrel wheel, Manny says they'll never get the seal tight enough, crosses from curb to curb under the streetlight, notices Janice's Mustang isn't parked out front, sprints down the brick walk and up the porch steps, and at last on the porch, under the number 89, stops running. His momentum is such that the world for a second or two streams on, seeming to fling all its trees and housetops outward against star-spangled space.

In bed Janice says, "Harry."

"What?" After you run your muscles have a whole new pulled, sheathed feel and sleep comes easy.

"I have a little confession to make."

"You're screwing Stavros again."

"Don't be so rude. No, did you notice the Mustang wasn't left out front as usual?"

"I did. I thought, 'How nice.'"

"It was Nelson who put it out back, in the alley. We really ought to clean out that space in the garage some day, all these old bicycles nobody uses. Melanie's Fuji is still in there."

"O.K., good. Good for Nelson. Hey, are you going to talk all night, or what? I'm beat."

"He put it there because he didn't want you to see the front fender."

"Oh no. That son of a bitch. That little son of a bitch."

"It wasn't his fault exactly, this other man just kept coming, though I guess the Stop sign was on Nelson's street."

"Oh Christ."

"Luckily both hit their brakes, so it really was just the smallest possible bump."

"The other guy hurt?"

"Well, he said something about whiplash, but then that's what people are trained to say now, until they can talk to their lawyer."

"And the fender is mashed?"

"Well, it's tipped in. The headlight doesn't focus the same place the other does. But it's fine in the daytime. It's really hardly more than a scratch."

"Five hundred bucks' worth. At least. The masked fender-bender strikes again."

"He really was terrified to tell you. He made me promise I wouldn't, so you can't say anything to him."

"I can't? Then why are you telling me? How can I go to sleep now? My head's pounding. It's like he has it in a vise."

"Because I didn't want you noticing by yourself and making a scene. Please, Harry. Just until after the wedding. He's really very embarrassed about it."

"The fuck he is, he loves it. He has my head in a vise and he just keeps turning the screw. That he'd do it to *your* car, after you've been knocking yourself out for him, that's really gratitude."

"Harry, he's about to get married, he's in a state."

"Well, shit, now I'm in a state. Where're some clothes? I got to go outside and see the damage. That flashlight in the kitchen, did it ever get new batteries?"

"I'm sorry I told you. Nelson was right. He said you wouldn't be able to handle it."

"Oh did he say that? Our own Mr. Cool."

"So just settle down. I'll take care of the insurance forms and everything."

"And who do you think pays for the increase in our insurance rates?"

"We do," she says. "The two of us."

St. John's Episcopal Church in Mt. Judge is a small church that never had to enlarge, built in 1912 in the traditional low-sided steep-roofed style, of a dark gray stone hauled from the north of the county, whereas the Lutheran church was built of local red sandstone, and the Reformed, next to the fire station, of brick. Ivy has been encouraged to grow around St. John's pointed windows. Inside, it is dark, with knobby walnut pews and dados and, on the walls between stained-glass windows of Jesus in violet robes making various gestures, marble plaques in memory of the dead gentry who contributed heavily here, in the days when Mt. Judge was a fashionable suburb. WHITELAW. STOVER. LEGGETT. English names in a German county, gone to give tone to the realms of the departed after thirty years as wardens and vestrymen. Old man Springer had done his bit but the spaces between the windows were used up by then.

Though the wedding is small and the bride an Ohio workingman's daughter, yet in the eyes of passersby the gathering would make a bright brave flurry before the church's rust-red doors, on the verge of four o'clock this September the twenty-second. A person or persons driving past this Saturday afternoon on the way to the MinitMart or the hardware store would have a pang of wanting to be among the guests. The organist with his red robe over his arm is ducking into the side door. He has a goatee. A little grubby guy in green coveralls like a troll is waiting for Harry to show up so he can get paid for the flowers, Ma said it was only decent to decorate the altar at least, Fred would have died to see Nellie married in St. John's with a bare altar. Two bouquets of white mums and baby's breath come to $38.50, Rabbit pays him with two twenties, it was a bad sign when the banks started paying out in twenties instead of tens, and yet the two-dollar bill still isn't catching on. People are superstitious. This wasn't supposed to be a big wedding but in fact it's costing plenty. They've had to take three rooms over at the Four Seasons Motel on Route 422: one for the mother of the bride, Mrs. Lubell, a small scared soul who looks like she thinks they'll all stick forks into her if she drops her little smile for a second; and another for Melanie, who came across the Commonwealth with Mrs. Lubell from Akron in a bus, and for Pru, who has been displaced from her room—Melanie's old room and before that the sewing dummy's—by the arrival from Nevada of Mim, whom Bessie and Janice didn't want in the house at all but Harry insisted, she's his only sister and the only aunt Nelson has got; and the third room for this couple from Binghamton, Pru's aunt and uncle, who were driving down today but hadn't checked in by three-thirty, when the shuttle service Harry has been running in the Corona picked up the two girls and the mother to bring them to the church. His head is pounding. This mother bothers him, her smile has been on her face so long it's as dry as a pressed flower, she doesn't seem to belong to his generation at all, she's like an old newspaper somebody has used as a drawer liner and then in cleaning house you lift out and try to read; Pru's looks must have all come from the father's side. At the motel the woman kept worrying that the messages they were leaving at the front desk for her tardy brother and sister-in-law weren't clear enough, and began to cry, so her smile got damp and ruined. A case of Mumm's second-best champagne waits back in the Joseph Street kitchen for the little get-together afterwards that nobody would call a reception; Janice and her mother decided they should have the sandwiches catered by a grandson of Grace Stuhl's who would bring along this girlfriend in a serving uniform. And then they ordered a cake from some wop over on Eleventh Street who was charging one hundred and eighty-five American dollars for a cake, a *cake*—Harry couldn't believe it. Every time Nelson turns around, it costs his father a bundle.

Harry stands for a minute in the tall ribbed space of the empty church, reading the plaques, hearing Soupy's giggle greet the three dolled-up women off in a side room, one of those out-of-sight chambers churches have where the choir puts itself into robes and the deacons count the collection plates and the communion wine is stored where the acolytes won't drink it and the whole strange show is made ready. Billy Fosnacht was supposed to be best man but he's up at Tufts so a friend of theirs from the Laid-Back called Slim is standing around with a carnation in his lapel waiting to usher. Uncomfortable from the way this young man's slanted eyes brush across him, Rabbit goes outside to stand by the church doors, whose rust-red paint in the September sun gives back heat so as to remind him of standing in his fresh tan uniform on a winter day in Texas at the side of the barracks away from the wind, that incessant wind that used to pour from that great thin sky across the treeless land like the whine of homesickness through this soldier who had never before been away from Pennsylvania.

Standing there thus for a breath of air, in this pocket of peace, he is trapped in the position of a greeter, as the guests suddenly begin to arrive. Ma Springer's stately dark-blue Chrysler pulls up, grinding its tires on the curb, and the three old ladies within claw at the door handles for release. Grace Stuhl has a translucent wart off-center on her chin but she hasn't forgotten how to dimple. "I bet but for Bessie I'm the only one here went to your wedding too," she tells Harry on the church porch.

"Not sure I was there myself," he says. "How did I act?"

"Very dignified. Such a tall husband for Janice, we all said."

"And he's kept his looks," adds Amy Gehringer, the squattest of these three biddies. Her face is enlivened with rouge and a flaking substance the color of Russian salad dressing. She pokes him in the stomach, hard. "Even added to them some," the old lady wisecracks.

"I'm trying to take it off," he says, as if he owes her something. "I go jogging most every night. Don't I, Bessie?"

"Oh it frightens me," Bessie says. "After what happened to Fred. And you know there wasn't an ounce extra on him."

"Take it easy, Harry," Webb Murkett says, coming up behind with Cindy. "They say you can injure the walls of your intestines, jogging. The blood all rushes to the lungs."

"Hey Webb," Harry says, flustered. "You know my mother-in-law."

"My pleasure," he says, introducing himself and Cindy all around. She is wearing a black silk dress that makes her look like a young widow. Would that she were, Jesus. Her hair has been fluffed up by a blow-dryer so it doesn't have that little-headed wet-otter look that he loves. The top of her dress is held together with a pin shaped like a bumblebee at the lowest point of a plunging V-shaped scoop.

And Bessie's friends are staring at gallant Webb with such enchantment Harry reminds them, "Go right in, there's a guy there leading people to their seats."

"I want to go right up front," Amy Gehringer says, "so I can get a good look at this young minister Bessie raves so about."

"'Fraid this screwed up golf for today," Harry apologizes to Webb.

"Oh," Cindy says, "Webb got his eighteen in already, he was over there by eight-thirty."

"Who'd you get to take my place?" Harry asks, jealous and unable to trust his eyes not to rest on Cindy's tan décolletage. The tops of tits are almost the best part, nipples can be repulsive. Just above the bumblebee a white spot that even her bikini bra hides from the sun shows. The little cross is up higher, just under the sexy hollow between her collarbones. What a package.

"The young assistant pro went around with us," Webb confides. "A seventy-three, Harry. A seventy-*three*, with a ball into the pond on the fifteenth, he hits it so far."

Harry is hurt but he has to greet the Fosnachts, who are pushing behind. Janice didn't want to invite them, especially after they decided not to invite the Harrisons, to keep it all small. But since Nelson wanted Billy as best man Harry thought they had no choice, and also even though Peggy has let herself slide there is that aura about a woman who's once upon a time taken off all her clothes for you however poorly it turned out. What the hell, it's a wedding, so he bends down and kisses Peggy to one side of the big wet hungry mouth he remembers. She is startled, her face broader than he remembers. Her eyes swim up at him in the wake of the kiss, but since one of them is a walleye he never knows which to search for expression.

Ollie's handshake is limp, sinewy, and mean: a mean-spirited little loser, with ears that stick out and hair like dirty straw. Harry crunches his knuckles together a little, squeezing. "How's the music racket, Ollie? Still tootling?" Ollie is one of these reedy types, common around Brewer, who can pick out a tune on anything but never manage to make it pay. He works in a music store, Chords 'n' Records, renamed Fidelity Audio, on Weiser Street near the old Baghdad, where the adult movies show now.

Peggy, her voice defensive from the kiss, says, "He sits in on synthesizer sometimes with a group of Billy's friends."

"Keep at it, Ollie, you'll be the Elton John of the Eighties. Seriously, how've you both been? Jan and I keep saying, we got to have you two over." Over Janice's dead body. Funny, just that one innocent forlorn screw, and Janice holds a grudge, where he's forgiving as hell of Charlie, just about his best friend in the world in fact.

And here is Charlie. "Welcome to the merger," Harry kids.

Charlie chuckles, his shrug small and brief. He knows the tide is running against him, with this marriage. Still, he has some reserve within him, some squared-off piece of philosophy that keeps him from panicking.

"You seen the bridesmaid?" Harry asks him. Melanie.

"Not yet."

"The three of 'em went over into Brewer last night and got drunk as skunks, to judge from Nelson. How's that for a way to act on the night before your wedding?"

Charlie's head ticks slowly sideways in obliging disbelief. This elderly gesture is jarred, however, when Mim, dressed in some crinkly pants outfit in chartreuse, with ruffles, grabs him from behind around the chest and won't let go. Charlie's face tenses in fright, and to keep him from guessing who it is Mim presses her face against his back so that Harry fears all her makeup will rub off on Charlie's checks. Mim comes on now any hour of the day or night made up like a showgirl, every tint and curl exactly the way she wants it; but really all the creams and paints in a world of jars won't counterfeit a flexible skin, and rimming your eyes in charcoal may be O.K. for these apple-green babies that go to the disco but at forty it makes a woman look merely haunted, staring, the eyes lassoed. Her

teeth are bared as she hangs on, wrestling Charlie from behind
like an eleven-year-old with Band-Aids on her knees. "Jesus,"
Charlie grunts, seeing the hands at his chest with their purple
nails long as grasshoppers, but slow to think back through all
the women he has known who this might be.

Embarrassed for her, worried for him, Harry begs, "C'mon,
Mim."

She won't let go, her long-nosed tarted-up face mussed and
distorted as she maintains the pressure of her grip. "Gotcha,"
she says. "The Greek heartbreaker. Wanted for transporting a
minor across state lines and for misrepresenting used cars. Put
the handcuffs on him, Harry."

Instead Harry puts his hands on her wrists, encountering
bracelets he doesn't want to bend, thousands of dollars' worth
of gold on her bones, and pulls them apart, having set his own
body into the jostle for leverage, while Charlie, looking grim-
mer every second, holds himself upright, cupping his fragile
heart within. Mim is wiry, always was. Pried loose at last, she
touches herself rapidly here and there, putting each hair and
ruffle back into place.

"Thought the boogyboo had gotten you, didn't you Charlie?" she jeers.

"Pre-owned," Charlie tells her, pulling his coat sleeves taut
to restore his dignity. "Nobody calls them used cars anymore."

"Out west we call them shitboxes."

"Shh," Harry urges. "They can hear you inside. They're
about to get started." Still exhilarated by her tussle with Charlie, and amused by the disapproving conscientious man her
brother has become, Mim wraps her arms around Harry's neck
and hugs him hard. The frills and pleats of her fancy outfit
crackle, crushing against his chest. "Once a bratty little sister,"
she says in his ear, "always a bratty little sister."

Charlie has slipped into the church. Mim's eyelids, shut,
shine in the sunlight like smears left by some collision of
greased vehicles—often on the highways Harry notices the
dark swerves of rubber, the gouges of crippled metal left to
mark where something unthinkable had suddenly happened to
someone. Though it happened the day's traffic continues. *Hold
me, Harry*, she used to cry out, little Mim in her hood between
his knees as their sled hit the cinders spread at the bottom of

Jackson Road, and orange sparks flew. Years before, a child had died under a milk truck sledding here and all the children were aware of this: that child's blank face leaned toward them out of each snowstorm. Now Harry sees a glisten in Mim's eyelids as in the backs of the Japanese beetles that used to cluster on the large dull leaves of the Bolgers' grape arbor out back. Also he sees how her earlobes have been elongated under the pull of jewelry and how her ruffles shudder as she pants, out of breath after her foolery. She is sinking through all her sins and late nights toward being a pathetic hag, he sees, one of those women you didn't believe could ever have been loved, with only Mom's strong bones in her face to save her. He hesitates, before going in. The town falls away from this church like a wide flight of stairs shuffled together of roofs and walls, a kind of wreck wherein many Americans have died.

He hears the side door where the organist hurried in open, and peeks around the corner, thinking it might be Janice needing him. But it is Nelson who steps out, Nelson in his cream-colored three-piece marrying suit with pinched waist and wide lapels, that looks too big for him, perhaps because the flared pants almost cover the heels of his shoes. Three hundred dollars, and when will he ever wear it again?

As always when he sees his son unexpectedly Harry feels shame. His upper lip lifts to call out in recognition, but the boy doesn't look his way, just appears to sniff the air, looking around at the grass and down toward the houses of Mt. Judge and then up the other way at the sky at the edge of the mountain. *Run*, Harry wants to call out, but nothing comes, just a stronger scent of Mim's perfume at the intake of breath. Softly the child closes the door again behind him, ignorant that he has been seen.

Behind the ajar rust-red portal the church is gathering in silence toward its eternal deed. The world then will be cloven between those few gathered in a Sunday atmosphere and all the sprawling fortunate Saturday remainder, the weekday world going on about its play. From childhood on Rabbit has resented ceremonies. He touches Mim on the arm to take her in, and over the spun glass of her hairdo sees a low-slung dirty old Ford station wagon with the chrome roof rack heightened by rough green boards crawl by on the street. He isn't quick enough to see the passengers, only gets a glimpse of a fat angry face staring from a back window. A fat mannish face yet a woman's.

"What's the matter?" Mim asks.

"I don't know. Nothing."

"You look like you've seen a ghost."

"I'm worrying about the kid. How do *you* feel about all this?"

"Me. Aunt Mim? It seems all right. The chick will take charge."

"That's good?"

"For a while. You must let go, Harry. The boy's life is his, you live your own."

"That's what I've been telling myself. But it feels like a cop-out."

They go in. A pathetic little collection of heads juts up far down front. This mysterious slant-eyed Slim, smoothly as if he were a professional usher, escorts Mim down the aisle to the second pew and indicates with a graceful sly gesture where Harry should settle in the first, next to Janice. The space has been waiting. On Janice's other side sits the other mother. Mrs. Lubell's profile is pale; like her daughter she is a redhead but her hair has been rinsed to colorless little curls, and she never could have had Pru's height and nice rangy bearing. She looks, Harry can't help thinking it, like a cleaning lady. She gives over to him her desiccated but oddly perfect smile, a smile such as flickered from the old black-and-white movie screens, coy and certain, a smile like a thread of pure melody, that when she was young must have seemed likely to lift her life far above where it eventually settled. Janice has pulled back her head to whisper with her mother in the booth behind. Mim has wound up in the same pew as Ma Springer and her biddies. Stavros sits with the Murketts in the third pew, he has Cindy's neckline to look down when he gets bored, let him see what country-club tits look like after all those stuffed grape leaves. In willful awkwardness the Fosnachts were seated or seated themselves across the aisle, on what would have been the bride's side if there had been enough to make a side, and are quarrelling in whispers between themselves: much hissed emphasis from Peggy and stoic forward-gazing mutter from Ollie. The organist is doodling through the ups and downs of some fugue to give everybody a chance to cough and recross their legs. The tip of his little ruddy goatee dips about an inch above the keyboard during the quiet parts. The way he slaps and tugs at the stops reminds Harry of the old Linotype he used to operate, the space adjuster and how the lead jumped out hot, all done with computer tapes now. To the left of the altar one of the big wall panels with rounded tops opens, it is a secret door like in a horror movie, and out of it steps Archie Campbell in a black cassock and white surplice and stole. He flashes his *What? Me worry?* grin, those sudden seedy teeth.

Nelson follows him out, head down, looking at nobody.

Slim slides up the aisle, light as a cat, to stand beside him. He must be a burglar in his spare time. He stands a good five inches taller than Nelson. Both have these short punk haircuts. Nelson's hair makes a whorl in back that Harry knows so well his throat goes dry, something caught in it.

Peggy Fosnacht's last angry whisper dies. The organ has been silent this while. With both plump hands lifted, Soupy bids them all stand. To the music of their rustle Melanie leads in Pru, from another side room, along the altar rail. The secret knowledge shared by all that she is pregnant enriches her beauty. She wears an ankle-length crêpey dress that Ma Springer calls oatmeal in color and Janice and Melanie call champagne, with a brown sash they decided to leave off her waist lest they have to tie it too high. It must have been Melanie who wove the little wreath of field flowers, already touched by wilt, that the bride wears as a crown. There is no train or veil save an invisible aura of victory. Pru's face, downcast and purse-lipped, is flushed, her carroty hair brushed slick down her back and tucked behind her ears to reveal their crimped soft shell shapes hung with tiny hoops of gold. Harry could halt her with his arm as she paces by but she does not look at him. Melanie gives all the old folks a merry eye; Pru's long red-knuckled fingers communicate a tremble to her little bouquet of baby's breath. Now her bearing as she faces the minister is grave with that gorgeous slowed composure of women carrying more than themselves.

Soupy calls them Dearly Beloved. The voice welling up out of this little man is terrific, Harry had noticed it at the house, but here, in the nearly empty church, echoing off the walnut knobs and memorial plaques and high arched rafters, beneath the tall central window of Jesus taking off into the sky with a pack of pastel apostles for a launching pad, the timbre is doubled, enriched by a rounded sorrowful something Rabbit hadn't noticed hitherto, gathering and pressing the straggle of guests into a congregation, subduing any fear that this ceremony might be a farce. Laugh at ministers all you want, they have the words we need to hear, the ones the dead have spoken. *The union of husband and wife,* he announces in his great considerate organ tones, *is intended by God for their mutual joy,* and like layers of a wide concealing dust the syllables descend, *prosperity, adversity, procreation, nurture.* Soupy bats his eyelids between phrases, is his only flaw. Harry hears a faint groan behind him: Ma Springer standing on her legs too long. Mrs. Lubell over past Janice has removed a grubby-looking handkerchief from her purse and dabs at her face with it. Janice is smiling. There is a dark dent at the corner of her lips. With a little white hat on her head like a flower she looks Polynesian.

Ringingly Soupy addresses the rafters: "If any of you can show just cause why they may not lawfully be married, speak now; or else for ever hold your peace."

Peace. A pew creaks. The couple from Binghamton. Dead Fred Springer. Ruth. Rabbit fights down a crazy impulse to shout out. His throat feels raw.

The minister now speaks to the couple direct. Nelson, from hanging lamely over on the side, his eyes murky in their sockets and the carnation crooked in his lapel, moves closer to the center, toward Pru. He is her height. The back of his neck looks so thin and bare above his collar. That whorl.

Pru has been asked a question. In an exceedingly small voice she says she will.

Now Nelson is being questioned and his father's itch to shout out, to play the disruptive clown, has become something else, a prickling at the bridge of his nose, a pressure in the two small ducts there.

Woman, wife, covenant, love her, comfort her, honor and keep her, sickness, health, forsaking all others as long as you both shall live?

Nelson in a voice midway in size between Soupy's and Pru's says he will.

And the burning in his tear ducts and the rawness scraping at the back of his throat have become irresistible, all the forsaken poor ailing paltry witnesses to this marriage at Harry's back roll forward in hoops of terrible knowing, an impalpable suddenly sensed mass of human sadness concentrated burningly upon the nape of Nelson's neck as he and the girl stand there mute while the rest of them grope and fumble in their thick red new prayer books after the name and number of a psalm announced; Soupy booms angelically above their scattered responses, *wife, a fruitful vine*, to which Rabbit cannot contribute, *the man who fears the Lord*, because he is weeping, weeping, washing out the words, the page, which has become as white and blank as the nape of Nelson's poor mute frail neck. Janice looks up at him in jaunty surprise under her white hat and Mrs. Lubell with that wistful cleaning-lady smile passes over her grubby handkerchief. He shakes his head No, he is too big, he will overwhelm the cloth with his effluvia; then takes it anyway, and tries to blot this disruptive tide. There is this place the tears have unlocked that is endlessly rich, a spring.

"May you live to see your children's children," Soupy intones in his huge mellow encompassing fairy's voice. "May peace be upon Israel," he adds.

And outside, when it is done, the ring given, the vows taken in the shaky young voices under the towering Easter-colored window of Christ's space shot and the Lord's Prayer mumbled through and the pale couple turned from the requisite kiss (poor Nellie, couldn't he be just another inch taller?) to face as now legally and mystically one the little throng of their blood, their tribe, outside in the sickly afternoon, clouds having come with the breeze that flows toward evening, the ridiculous tears dried in long stains on Harry's face, then Mim comes into his arms again, a sisterly embrace, all sorts of family grief since the days he held her little hand implied, the future has come upon them darkly, his sole seed married, marriage that daily doom which she may never know; lean and crinkly in his arms she is getting to be a spinster, even a hooker can be a spinster, think of all she's had to swallow all these years, his baby sister, crying in imitation of his own tears, out here where the air quickly dries them, and the after-church smiles of the others flicker about them like butterflies born to live a day.

Oh this day, this holiday they have made just for themselves from a mundane Saturday, this last day of summer. What a great waste of gas it seems as they drive in procession to Ma Springer's house through the slanted streets of the town. Harry and Janice in the Corona follow Bessie's blue Chrysler in case the old dame plows into something, with Mim bringing Mrs. Lubell in Janice's Mustang, its headlight still twisted, behind. "What made you cry so much?" Janice asks him. She has taken off her hat and fiddled her bangs even in the rearview mirror.

"I don't know. Everything. The way Nellie looked from the back. The way the backs of kids' heads *trust* you. I mean they really *liked* that, this little dumb crowd of us gathered to watch."

He looks sideways at her silence. The tip of her little tongue rests on her lower lip, not wanting to say the wrong thing. She says, "If you're so full of tears you might try being less mean about him and the lot."

"I'm not mean about him and the lot. He doesn't give a fuck about the lot, he just wants to hang around having you and your mother support him and the easiest way to put a face on that is to go through some sort of motions over at the lot. You know how much that caper of his with the convertibles cost the firm? Guess."

"He says you got him so frustrated he went crazy. He says you knew you were doing it, too."

"Forty-five hundred bucks, that was what those shitboxes cost. Plus now all the parts Manny's had to order and the garage time to fix 'em, you can add another grand."

"Nelson said the TR sold right off."

"That was a fluke. They don't make TRs anymore."

"He says Toyotas have had their run at the market, Datsun and Honda are outselling them all over the East."

"See, that's why Charlie and me don't want the kid over at the lot. He's full of negative thinking."

"Has Charlie said he doesn't want Nelson over at the lot?"

"Not in so many words. He's too much of a nice guy."

"I never noticed he was such a nice guy. Nice in that way. I'll ask him over at the house."

"Now don't go lighting into poor Charlie, just because he's

moved on to Melanie. I don't know what he's ever said about Nelson."

"Moved *on*! Harry, it's been ten years. You *must* stop living in the past. If Charlie wants to make a fool of himself chasing after some twenty-year-old it couldn't matter to me less. Once you've achieved closure with somebody, all you have is good feelings for them."

"What's this achieving closure? You've been looking at too many talk shows."

"It's a phrase people use."

"Those hussies you hang out with over at the club. Doris Kaufmann. Fuck her." It stung him, that she thinks he lives in the past. Why should he be the one to cry at the wedding? Mr. Nice Guy. Mr. Tame Guy. To Hell with them. "Well at least Charlie's avoiding marriage so that makes him less of a fool than Nelson," he says, and switches on the radio to shut off their conversation. The four-thirty news: earthquake in Hawaii, kidnapping of two American businessmen in El Salvador, Soviet tanks patrolling the streets of Kabul in the wake of last Sunday's mysterious change of leadership in Afghanistan. In Mexico, a natural-gas pact with the United States signals possible long-term relief for the energy crisis. In California, ten days of brush fire have destroyed more acres than any such fire since 1970. In Philadelphia, publishing magnate Walter Annenberg has donated fifty thousand dollars to the Catholic Archdiocese to help defray costs of the controversial platform from which Pope John Paul the Second is scheduled to celebrate Mass on October the third. Annenberg, the announcer gravely concludes, is a Jew.

"Why did they tell us that?" Janice asks.

God, she is dumb still. The realization comforts him. He tells her, "To make us alleged Christians feel lousy we've all been such cheapskates about the Pope's platform."

"I must say," Janice says, "it does seem extravagant, to build such a thing you're only going to use once."

"That's life," Harry says, pulling up to the curb along Joseph Street. There are so many cars in front of number 89 he has to park halfway up the block, in front of the house where the butch ladies live. One of them, a hefty youngish woman wearing an Army surplus fatigue jacket, is lugging a big pink roll of foil-backed insulation up onto the front porch.

"My son got married today," Harry calls out to her, on impulse.

His butch neighbor blinks and then calls back, "Good luck to her."

"Him."

"I meant the bride."

"O.K., I'll tell her."

The expression on the woman's face, slit-eyed like a cigar-store Indian, softens a little; she sees Janice getting out of the car on the other side, and calls to her, in a shouting mood now, "Jan, how do *you* feel about it?"

Janice is so slow to answer Harry answers for her, "She feels great. Why wouldn't she?" What he can't figure out about these butch ladies is not why they don't like him but why he wants them to, why just the distant sound of their hammering has the power to hurt him, to make him feel excluded.

Somehow, this Slim person, driving a canary-yellow Le Car with its name printed a foot high on the side, has made it from the church with bride, groom, and Melanie ahead of Harry and Janice; and Ollie and Peggy too, in their cinnamon-brown '73 Dodge Dart with a Fiberglas-patched fender; and even Soupy has beat their time, because his snappy little black Opel Manta with vanity plate STJOHN is also parked by the curb this side of the maple that Ma Springer has been seeing from her front bedroom for over thirty years. These guests already crowd the living room, while this flustered little fat girl in a stab at a wait-ress uniform tries to carry around those hors d'oeuvres that are costing a fortune, muddled things that look like cheese melted on Taco Chips with a sprig of parsley added; Harry dodges through, elbows lifted out of old basketball habit in case some-body tries to put a move on him, to get the champagne in the kitchen. Bottles of Mumm's at twelve dollars apiece even at case price fill the whole second shelf of the fridge, stacked 69-style, foil heads by heavy hollow butts, beautiful. CHAMPAGNE PRO-VIDED AT SHOTGUN WEDDING, he thinks. *Angstrom Foots Bill.* Grace Stuhl's grandson turns out to be a big beefy kid, can't weigh less than two hundred fifty, with a bushy pirate's beard,

and he has teeny weenies frying in a pan on the stove and
something wrapped in bacon in the oven. Also a beer he took
from the fridge open on the counter. The noise in the living
room keeps growing, and the front door keeps opening, Stavros and the Murketts following Mim and Ma's brood in, and all
the fools come gabbling when the first cork pops. Boy, it's like
coming, it can't stop, the plastic hollow-stemmed champagne
glasses Janice found at the Acme are on the round Chinese
tray on the counter behind Grace Stuhl's grandson's beer, too
far away for Harry to reach without some of the tawny foam
spilling onto the linoleum. The glasses as he fills them remind
him of the gold coins, precious down through the ages, and a
latch inside him lifts to let his sorrow out. What the hell, we're
all going down the chute together. Back in the living room, in
front of the breakfront, Ma Springer proposes a nervous little
toast she's worked up, ending with the Pennsylvania Dutch,
"*Dir seid nur eins: halt es selle weg.*"

"What does that mean, Mom-mom?" Nelson asks, afraid
something's being put over on him, such a child beside the
blushing full-grown woman he's crazily gone and married.

"I was going to say," Bessie says irritably. "You are now one:
keep it that way."

Everybody cheers, and drinks, if they haven't already.

Grace Stuhl glides a step forward, into the circle of space
cleared by the breakfront, maybe she was a great dancer fifty
years ago, a certain type of old lady keeps her ankles and her
feet small, and she is one. "Or as they always used to say," she
proposes, "*Bussie waiirt ows, kocha dut net.* Kissing wears out,
cooking don't."

The cheers are louder. Harry pops another bottle and settles
on getting drunk. Those melted Taco Chips aren't so bad, if
you can get them to your mouth before they break in your fingers, and the little fat girlfriend has an amazing bosom. All this
ass, at least there's no shortage of that, it just keeps arriving. It
seems an age since he lay awake disturbed by the entrance into
this house of Pru Lubell, now Teresa Angstrom. Harry finds
himself standing next to her mother. He asks her, "Have you
ever been to this part of the world before?"

"Just passing through from time to time," she says, in a wisp
of a voice he has to bend over to hear, as at a deathbed. How

softly Pru had spoken her vows at the ceremony! "My people are from Chicago, originally."

"Well, your daughter does you proud," he tells her. "We love her already." He sounds to himself, saying this, like an impersonator; life, just as we first thought, is playing grownup.

"Teresa tries to do the right thing," her mother says. "But it's never been easy for her."

"It hasn't?"

"She takes after her father's people. You know, always going to extremes."

"Really?"

"Oh yes. Stubborn. You daren't go against them."

Her eyes widen. He feels with this woman as if he and she have been set to making a paper chain together, with inadequate glue, and the links keep coming unstuck. It is not easy to hear in this room. Soupy and that Slim are giggling now together.

"I'm sorry your husband can't be here," Harry says.

"You wouldn't be if you knew him," Mrs. Lubell replies serenely, and waggles her plastic glass as if to indicate how empty it is.

"Lemme get you some more." Rabbit realizes with a shock that she is his proper date: old as she seems this woman is about his age and instead of naked in dreamland with stacked chicks like Cindy Murkett and Grace Stuhl's grandson's girlfriend he should be in mental bed with the likes of Mrs. Lubell. He retreats into the kitchen to look after the champagne supply and finds Nelson and Melanie busy at the bottles. The countertop is strewn with those little wire cages each cork comes trapped in.

"Dad, there may not be *enough*," Nelson whines.

These two. "Why don't you kids switch to milk?" he suggests, taking a bottle from the boy. Heavy and green and cold, like money. The label engraved. His own poor dead dad never drank such bubbly in his life. Seventy years of beer and rusty water. To Melanie he says, "That expensive bike of yours is still in the garage."

"Oh I know," she says, innocently staring. "If I took it back to Kent someone would steal it." Her bulging brown eyes show no awareness that he has been curt, feeling betrayed by her.

He tells her, "You ought to go out and say hello to Charlie."

"Oh, we've *said* hello." Did she leave the motel room he was paying for to go shack up with Charlie? Harry can't follow it all. As if to make things right Melanie says, "I'll tell Pru she can use the bike if she wants. It's wonderful exercise for those muscles."

What muscles? Back in the living room, nobody has been kind enough to take his place beside the mother of the bride. As he refills her readily proffered glass he says to her, "Thanks for the handkerchief. Back in the church."

"It must be hard," she says, looking up at him more cozily now, "when there's only one."

There's not only one, he wants to tell her, drunker than he intended. There's a dead little sister lying buried in the hill above us, and a long-legged girl roaming the farmland south of Galilee. Who does she remind him of, Mrs. Lubell, when she flirts her head like that, looking up? Thelma Harrison, beside the pool. The Harrisons maybe should have been invited, but then you get into things like Buddy Inglefinger's feelings being hurt. And Ronnie would have been gross. The organist with the goatee (who invited *him?*) has joined Soupy and Slim now and something in the gaiety there leads the minister to remember his duty to others. He comes and joins Harry and the mother, a Christian act.

"Well," Harry blurts to him. "What's done is done, huh?"

Becky a skeleton by now, strange to think. The nightie they buried her in turned to cobwebs. Her little toenails and fingernails bits of confetti scattered on the satin.

Reverend Campbell's many small tobacco-darkened teeth display themselves in a complacent smile. "The bride looked lovely," he tells Mrs. Lubell.

"She gets her height from her father's people," she says. "And her straight hair. Mine just curls naturally, where Frank's sticks up all over his head, he can never get it to lay down. Teresa's isn't quite that stubborn, since she's a girl."

"Just lovely," Soupy says, his smile getting a glaze.

Harry asks the man, "How does that Opel of yours do for mileage?"

He takes out his pipe to address the question. "Up and down on these hills isn't exactly optimum, is it? I'd say twenty-five, twenty-six at best. I do a lot of stopping and starting and with nothing but short trips the carbon builds up."

Harry tells him, "You know the Japanese make these cars even though Buick sells 'em. I heard they may not be importing any after the 1980 model. That's going to put a squeeze on parts."

Soupy is amused, his twinkling eyes tell Mrs. Lubell. Toward Harry he slides these eyes with mock severity and asks, "Are you trying to sell me a Toyota?"

Mom getting to be a skeleton too, come to think of it. Those big bones in the earth like dinosaur bones.

"Well," Harry says, "we have a new little front-wheel drive called the Tercel, don't know where they get these names from but never mind, it gets over forty m.p.g. on the highway and is plenty of car for a single man."

Waiting for the Resurrection. Suppose it never comes?

"But suppose I get *mar*ried," the small man protests, "and have an *enor*mous brood!"

"And indeed you should," Mrs. Lubell unexpectedly pipes up. "The priests are leaving the church in droves because they've got the itch. All this sex, in the movies, books, everywhere, even on the television if you stay up late enough, no wonder they can't resist. Be grateful you don't have that conflict."

"I have often thought," Soupy tells her in a muted return of his great marrying voice, "I might have made an excellent priest. I a*dore* structure."

Rabbit says, "Just now in the car we heard that Annenberg down in Philadelphia gave the Catholics fifty thousand so they could put up this platform for the Pope without all this squawking from the civil liberties people."

Soupy sniffs. "Do you know how much publicity that fifty thousand is going to get him? It's a bargain."

Slim and the organist seem to be discussing clothes, fingering each other's shirts. If he has to talk to the organist Harry can ask why he didn't play "Here Comes the Bride."

Mrs. Lubell says, "They wanted the Pope to come to Cleveland but I guess he had to draw the line somewhere."

"I hear he's going to some farm way out in nowhere," Harry says.

Soupy touches the mother of the bride on the wrist and tips his head so as to show to Harry the beginnings of his bald spot. "Mr. Annenberg is our former ambassador to the Court of St. James in England. The story goes that when presenting his credentials to the Queen she held out her hand to be kissed and he shook it instead and said, 'How're ya doin', Queen?'"

His growl is good. Mrs. Lubell laughs outright, a titter jumps from her to her shame, for she quickly covers her mouth with her knuckles. Soupy loves it, giving her back a deep laugh as from a barrel-chested old fart. If that's the way they're going to carry on Rabbit figures he can leave them to it, and using Soupy as a pick makes his move away. He scouts over the gathered heads looking for an opening. It's always slightly dark in the living room, no matter how many lights are on or what the time of day; the trees and the porch cut down the sun. He'd like a house some day with lots of light, splashing in across smart square surfaces. Why bury yourself alive?

Ma Springer has Charlie locked in a one-on-one over by the breakfront, her face puffy and purplish like a grape with the force of the unheard words she is urging into his ear; he politely bows his tidy head, once broad like a ram's but now whittled to an old goat's, nodding almost greedily, like a chicken pecking up grains of corn. Up front, silhouetted against the picture window, the Murketts are holding forth with the Fosnachts, old Ollie no doubt letting these new folks know what a clever musical fellow he is and Peggy gushing, backing him up, holding within herself the knowledge of what a shiftless rat he amounts to domestically. The Murketts belong to the new circle in Harry's life and the Fosnachts to the old and he hates to see them overlap; even if Peggy was a pretty good lay that time he doesn't want those dismal old high-school tagalongs creeping into his country-club set, yet he can see flattery is doing it, flattery and champagne, Ollie ogling Cindy (don't you wish) and Peggy making cow-eyed moos all over Murkett, she'll flop for anybody, Ollie must be very unsatisfying, one of those very thin reedy pricks probably. Harry wonders if he'd better not go over there and break it up, but foresees a wall of razzing he feels too delicate to push through, after all those tears in church, and remembering Becky and Pop and Mom and even old Fred who aren't here. Mim is on the sofa with

Grace Stuhl and that other old biddy Amy, and Christ if they aren't having a quiet little ball, the two of them recalling Mim as a child to herself, the Diamond County accent and manner of expressing things making her laugh every minute, and she reminding them, all painted and done up in flowerpot foil, of the floozies they sit and watch all day and night on television, the old souls don't even know they are floozies, these celebrity women playing *Beat the Clock* or *Hollywood Squares* or giving Merv or Mike or Phil the wink sitting in those talk show soft chairs with their knees sticking up naked, they all got there on their backs, nobody cares anymore, the times have caught up with Mim and put her on the gray sofa with the church folk. Nelson and Melanie and Grace Stuhl's lout of a grandson are still in the kitchen and the girlfriend, after going around with the teeny weenies under her tits in a tricky little warmer with a ketchup dip, seems to have given up and joined them; they have in there the little portable Sony Janice sometimes watches the Carol Burnett reruns on as she makes supper, and from the sound of it—cheers, band music—these useless drunken kids have turned on the Penn State–Nebraska game. Meanwhile there's Pru in her champagne-colored wedding dress, the little wreath off her head now, standing alone over by the three-way lamp examining that heavy green glass bauble of Ma Springer's, with the teardrop of air sealed inside, turning it over and over under the wan light with her long pink hands, where a wedding ring now gleams. Laughter explodes from the Fosnacht-Murkett group, which Janice has joined. Webb pushes past Harry toward the kitchen, his fingers full of plastic glasses. "How about that crazy Rose?" he says, going by, to say something.

Pete Rose has been hitting over .600 lately and only needs four more hits to be the first player ever to get two hundred hits in ten major league seasons. But it doesn't mean that much, the Phillies are twelve and a half games out. "What a showboat," Rabbit says, what they used to say about him, nearly thirty years ago.

Perhaps in her conspicuous pregnancy Pru is shy of pushing through the crowd to join the others of her generation in the kitchen. Harry goes to her side and stoops down to kiss her demure warm cheek before she is aware; champagne makes it easy. "Aren't you supposed to kiss the bride?" he asks her.

She turns her head and gives him that smile that hesitates and then suddenly spreads, one corner tucked awry. Her eyes have taken green from contemplating the glass, that strange glossy egg Harry has more than once thought would be good to pound into Janice's skull. "Of course," she says. Held against her belly the bauble throws from its central teardrop a pale blade of light. He senses that she had been aware of his approaching in the side of her vision but had held still like a deer in danger. Among these strange people, her fate sealed by a ceremony, of course she is afraid. Rabbit tries to comfort his daughter-in-law: "I bet you're beat. Don't you get sleepy as hell? As I remember it Janice did."

"You feel clumsy," Pru allows, and with both hands replaces the green glass orb on the round table that is like a wooden leaf all around the stem of the standing lamp. Abruptly she asks, "Do you think I'll make Nelson happy?"

"Oh sure. The kid and I had a good long talk about it once. He thinks the world of you."

"He doesn't feel trapped?"

"Well, frankly, that's what I was curious about, 'cause in his position I might. But honest to God, Teresa, it doesn't seem to bother him. From little on up he's always had this sense of fairness and in this case he seems to feel fair is fair. Listen. Don't you worry yourself. The only thing bothering Nelson these days is his old man."

"He thinks the world of you," she says, her voice very small, in case this echo is too impudent.

Harry snorts; he loves it when women sass him, and any sign of life from this one is gratefully received. "It'll all work out," he promises, though Teresa's aura of fright remains intense and threatens to spread to him. When the girl dares a full smile you see her teeth needed braces and didn't get them. The taste of champagne keeps reminding him of poor Pop. Beer and rusty water and canned mushroom soup.

"Try to have some fun," he tells Pru, and cuts across the jammed room, around the boisterous Murkett-Fosnacht-Janice crowd, to the sofa where Mim sits between the two old ladies. "Are you being a bad influence on my little sister?" he asks Amy Gehringer.

While Grace Stuhl laughs at this Amy struggles to get to her feet. "Don't get up on my account," Rabbit tells her. "I just came over to see if I could get any of you anything."

"What I need," Amy grunts, still floundering, so he pulls her up, "I must get for myself."

"What's that?" he asks.

She looks at him a little glassily, like Melanie when he told her to drink milk. "A call of nature," Amy answers, "you could say."

Grace Stuhl holds up a hand that when he takes it, to pull her up, feels like a set of worn stones in a sack of the finest driest paper, strangely warm. "I better say goodbye to Becky," she says.

"She's over there talking the ear off Charlie Stavros," Harry tells her.

"Yes, and probably saying too much by now." She seems to know the subject; or does he imagine that? He drops down onto the sofa beside Mim wearily.

"So," she says.

"Next I gotta marry you off," he says.

"I've been asked, actually, now and then."

"And whajja say?"

"At my age it seemed like too much trouble."

"Your health good?"

"I make it good. No more smoking, notice?"

"How about those crazy hours you keep, staying up to watch Ol' Blue Eyes? I knew he was called Ol' Blue Eyes, by the way. I just didn't know *which* Ol' Blue Eyes, I thought a new one might have come along." When he had called her long-distance to invite her to the wedding she said she had a date with a very dear friend to see Ol' Blue Eyes and he had asked, *Who's Ol' Blue Eyes?* She said *Sinatra, ya dummy, where've you been all your life?* and he answered, *You know where I've been, right here* and she said, *Yeah, it shows.* God, he loves Mim; in the end there's nothing to understand you like your own blood.

Mim says, "You sleep it off during the day. Anyway I'm out of the fast lane now, I'm a businesswoman." She gestures toward the other side of the room. "What's Bessie trying to do, keep me from talking to Charlie? She's been at him an hour."

"I don't know what's going on."

"You never did. We all love you for it."

"Drop dead. Hey how do you like the new Janice?"

"What's new about her?"

"Don't you see it? More confident. More of a woman, some-how."

"Hard as a nut, Harry, and always will be. You were always feeling sorry for her. It was a wasted effort."

"I miss Pop," he suddenly says.

"You're getting more and more like him. Especially from the side."

"He never got a gut like mine."

"He didn't have the teeth for all those munchies you like."

"You notice how this Pru looks like him a little? And Mom's big red hands. I mean, she seems more of an Angstrom than Nelson."

"You guys like tough ladies. She's pulled off a trick I didn't think could be pulled off anymore."

He nods, imagining through her eyes his father's toothless profile closing in upon his own. "She's running scared."

"And how about you?" Mim asks. "What're *you* doing these days, to feed the inner man?"

"I play golf."

"And still fuck Janice?"

"Sometimes."

"You two. Mother and I didn't give it six months, the way she trapped you."

"Maybe I trapped myself. And what's up with you? How does money work, out in Vegas? You really own a beauty parlor, or you just a front for the big guys?"

"I own thirty-five per cent. That's what I got for being a front for the big guys."

He nods again. "Sounds familiar."

"You fucking anybody else? You can tell me, I'll be on that plane tomorrow. How about the broad bottom over there with the Chinesey eyes?"

He shakes his head. "Nope. Not since Jill. That shook me up."

"O.K., but ten years, that's not normal, Harry. You're letting them turn you into a patsy."

"Remember," he asks, "how we used to go sledding on Jackson Road? I often think about it."

"That happened maybe once or twice, it never *snows* around here, for Cry-eye. Come out to Lake Tahoe; now there's *snow*. We'll go over to Alta or Taos; you should see me ski. Come on out by yourself, we'll fix you up with somebody really nice. Blonde, brunette, redhead, you name it. Good clean small-town girl too; nothing crude."

"Mim," he says, blushing, "you're the limit," and thinks of telling her how much he loves her, but there is a commotion at the front door.

Slim and the organist are leaving together and they encounter there a dowdy couple who have been ringing the disconnected doorbell for some time. From the look of them they are selling encyclopaedias, except that people don't do that in pairs, or going door-to-door for the Jehovah's Witnesses, except that instead of *The Watchtower* they are holding on to a big silver-wrapped wedding present. This is the couple from Binghamton. They took the wrong turn off the Northeast Extension and found themselves lost in West Philadelphia. The woman sheds tears of relief and exhaustion once inside the foyer. "Blocks and blocks of blacks," the man says, telling their story, still staggered by the wonder of it.

"*Oh*," Pru cries from across the room, "Uncle Rob!" and throws herself into his arms, home at last.

Ma Springer has made the Poconos place available to the young couple for a honeymoon in these golden last weeks of warm weather—the birches beginning to turn, the floats and canoes pulled in from the lake. All of it wasted on the kid, they'll be lucky if he doesn't burn the cottage down frying his brain and his genes with pot. But it's not Harry's funeral. Now that Nelson is married it's like a door has been shut in his mind, a debt has been finally paid, and his thoughts are turning again to that farm south of here where another child of his may be walking, walking and waiting for her life to begin.

One evening when nothing she likes is on television Ma calls a little conference in the living room, easing her legs wrapped around with flesh-colored bandages (a new thing her doctor has prescribed; when Harry tries to visualize an entire creature made out of the flesh the bandage manufacturers are matching, it would make the Hulk look healthy) up on the hassock and letting the man of the house have the Barcalounger. Janice sits on the sofa with a post-dinner nip of some white creamy poison fermented from coconut milk the kids have brought into the house, looking girlish beside her mother, with her legs tucked up under her. Nice taut legs. She's kept those and he has to take his hat off to her, tiddly half the time or not. What more can you ask of a wife in a way than that she stick around and see with you what happens next?

Ma Springer announces, "We must settle now what to do with Nelson."

"Send him back to college," Harry says. "She had an apartment out there, they can both move into one."

"He doesn't want to go," Janice tells them, not for the first time.

"And why the hell not?" Harry asks, the question still exciting to him, though he knows he's beaten.

"Oh Harry," Janice says wearily, "nobody knows. You didn't go to college, why should he?"

"That's the reason. Look at me. I don't want him to live my life. I'm living it and that's enough."

"Darling, I said that from his point of view, not to argue with you. Of course Mother and I would have preferred he had graduated from Kent and not got so involved with this secretary. But that's not the way it is."

"He can't go back to college with a wife as if nothing happened," Bessie states. "They knew her out there as one of the employees and I think he'd be embarrassed. He needs a job."

"Great," Harry says, enjoying being perverse, letting the women do the constructive thinking. "Maybe his father-in-law can get him a job out in Akron."

"You saw the mother," Ma Springer says. "There's no help there."

"Uncle Rob was a real swinger, though. What does he do up in the shoe factory? Punch the holes for the laces?"

Janice imitates her mother's flat, decided rhythm. "Harry. Nelson must come to work at the lot."

"Oh Christ. Why? *Why?* This is a huge country. It has old factories, new factories, farms, stores, why can't the lazy brat get a job at one of *them*? All those summers he was back from

Kent he never got a job. He hasn't had a job since that paper route when he was fourteen and needed to buy Beatles records."

Janice says, "Going up to the Poconos a month every summer meant he couldn't get anything too serious, he used to complain about it. Besides, he did do some things. He babysat for a time there, and he helped that high-school teacher who was building his own home, with the solar panels and the cellar full of rocks that stored heat."

"Why doesn't he go into something like that? That's where the future is, not selling cars. Cars have had it. The party's over. It's going to be all public transportation twenty years from now. Ten years from now, even. Why doesn't he take a night course and learn how to program a computer? If you look at the want ads, that's all there is, computer programmers and electronic engineers. Remember when Nelson rigged up all those hi-fi components and even had speakers hooked up on the sunporch? He could do all that, what happened?"

"What happened is, he grew up," Janice says, finishing off the coconut liqueur, tilting her head back so far her throat shows the pale rings that when her head is held normally are wrinkles. Her tongue probes the bottom of the glass. With Nelson and Pru part of the household, Janice drinks more freely; they sit around getting silly and waiting up for Johnny Carson or *Saturday Night Live*, her smoking has gotten back up to over a pack a day in spite of Harry's nagging to get her to quit. Now in this discussion she's acting as if he is some natural disturbance they must let boringly run its course.

He is getting madder. "I *of*fered to take him on in Service, there's the department they can always use an extra man, Manny'd have him trained as a full-fledged mechanic in no time. You know what mechanics pull down an hour now? Seven bucks, and it costs me over eight to pay 'em that what with all this fringe stuff. And once they can work faster than the flat rate they get bonuses. Our top men take home over fifteen thousand a year and a couple of them aren't much older than Nelson."

"Nelson doesn't want," Janice says, "to be a grease monkey any more than you do."

"Happiest days of my life," he lies, "were spent working with my hands."

"It isn't easy," Ma Springer decides to tell them, "being old, and a widow. In everything I do, after I pray about it, I try to ask myself, 'Now what would Fred want?' And I know with absolute certainty in this instance he would want little Nellie to come work on the lot if that's what the boy desired. A lot of these young men now wouldn't want such a job, they don't have the thick skins a salesman has to have, and it's not so glamorous, unless you began by following the hind end of a horse around all day the way the people of my generation did."

Rabbit bristles, impatient. "Bessie, every generation has its problems, we all start behind the eight ball. Face the facts. How much you gonna pay Nelson? How much salary, how much commission? You know what a dealer's profit margin is. Three per cent, three lousy little per cent, and that's being cut down to nothing by a lot of new overhead you can't pass on the customer with these fixed prices Toyota has. Oil going up takes everything up with it; in the five years I've been in charge heating costs have doubled, electricity is way up, delivery costs are up, plus all these social security hikes and unemployment to pay so the bums in this country won't have to give up their yacht or whatever, half the young people in the country go to work just enough to collect unemployment, and now the interest on the inventory is going out of sight. It's just like the Weimar thing, people's savings are being washed right down the tube, everybody agrees there's a recession coming to curl your hair. The economy is *shot*, Ma, we can't hack it, we don't have the discipline the Japs and Germans do, and on top of this you want me to hire a piece of dead weight who happens to be my son."

"In answer to your question," Ma says, grunting a little as she shifts the sorer leg on the hassock, "the minimum wage is going to be three-ten an hour so if he works forty hours a week you'll have to give him a hundred twenty-five a week, and then the bonuses you'd have to figure on the usual formula, isn't it now something like twenty percent of the gross profit on the sale, and then going to twenty-five over a certain minimum? I know it used to be a flat five per cent of the net amount of the sale, but Fred said you couldn't do that with foreign cars for some reason."

"Bessie, with all respect, and I love you, but you are crazy. You pay Nelson five hundred a month to start with and set commissions on top of that he's going to be taking home a thousand a month for bringing in the company only twenty-five hundred. To pay Nelson that amount it should mean he sells, depending on the proportion of new to used, between seven to ten cars a month for an agency that doesn't move twenty-five a month overall!"

"Well, maybe with Nelson there you'll move more," Ma says.

"*Dreamer*," Harry says to her. "Detroit's getting tooled up finally to turn out subcompacts a dime a dozen, and there's going to be stiffer import taxes any day now. Twenty-five a month is optimum, honest to God."

"The people remember Fred will like to see Nelson there," she insists.

Janice says, "Nelson says the mark-up on the new Toyotas is at least a thousand dollars."

"That's a loaded model, with all the extras. The people who buy Toyotas aren't into extras. Basic Corollas are what we sell mostly, four to one. And even on the bigger models the carrying costs amount to a couple hundred per unit with money going to Hell the way it is."

She is obstinate and dumb. "A thousand a car," she says, "means he has to sell only five a month, the way you figure it."

"What about Jake and Rudy!" he cries. "How could the kid sell even five without cutting into Jake and Rudy? Listen, if you two want to know who your loyal employees are, it's Jake and Rudy. They work all the shit hours you ask 'em to, on the floor nights and weekends, they moonlight to make up for all the low hours you tell 'em to stay away, Rudy runs a little bike repair shop out of his garage, in this day and age, everybody else begging for handouts, they're still taking a seventy-five base and a one-fifty draw. You can't turn guys like that out in the cold."

"I wasn't thinking so much of Jake and Rudy," Ma Springer says, with a frown resting one ankle on top of the other. "How much now does Charlie make?"

"Oh no you don't. We've been through this. Charlie goes, I go."

"Just for my information."

"Well, Charlie pulls down around three-fifty a week—rounds out to over twenty thousand a year with the bonuses."

"Well, then," Ma Springer pronounces, easing the ankle back to where it was, "you'd actually save money, taking Nelson on instead. He has this interest in the used cars, and that's Charlie's department, hasn't it been?"

"Bessie, I can't believe this. Janice, talk to her about Charlie."

"We've talked, Harry. You're making too much of it. Mother has talked to me and I thought it might do Charlie good to make a change. She also talked to Charlie and he agreed."

Harry is disbelieving. "*When* did you talk to Charlie?"

"At the reception," Ma Springer admits. "I saw you looking over at us."

"Well my God, whajja say?"

This is some old lady, Rabbit thinks, sneakers, Ace bandages, cotton dress up over her knees, puffy throat, funny silver-browed eyeglasses, and all. Once in a while, in the winters since old Fred cashed in, she has visited the lot wearing the mink coat he gave her for their twenty-fifth wedding anniversary, and there was a glitter on that fur like needles of steel, like a signal crackling out of mission control. She says, "I asked him how his health was."

"The way we worry about Charlie's health you'd think he was in a wheelchair."

"Janice has told me, even ten years ago he was taking nitro-glycerine. For a man only in his thirties then, that's not good."

"Well what did *he* say, how his health was?"

"Fair," Ma Springer answers, giving it the local two syllables, *Fai-ir*. "Janice herself claims you complain he doesn't do his share anymore, just sits huddled at the desk playing with paperwork he should leave for Mildred to do."

"Did I say all that?" He looks at Janice, his betrayer. He has always thought of her darkness as a Springer trait but of course old man Springer was fair, thin-skinned pink; it is her mother's blood, the Koerners', that has determined her coloring.

She flicks her cigarette at the ashtray impatiently. "More than once," she says.

"Well I didn't mean your mother should go fire the guy."

"Fire was never used as a word," Ma Springer says. "Fred would never have fired Charlie, unless his personal life got all out of hand."

"You got to go pretty far to get out of hand these days," Harry says, resenting that this is the case. He had tried to have fun too early.

Ma Springer rolls her weight uncomfortably on the sofa. "Well I must say, this chasing that girl out to Ohio—"

"He took her to Florida, too," Harry says, so quickly both women stare at him with their button-black eyes. It's true, it galls him more than it should, since he could never warm to Melanie himself and had nowhere to take her anyhow.

"We talked about Florida," Ma Springer says. "I asked him if now that winter's coming he mightn't be better off down there. Amy Gehringer's son-in-law, that used to work in an asbestos plant in New Jersey until they got that big scare, has retired down there on the compensation, and he's under fifty. She says he tells her there are a lot of young people coming down there now, to get away from the oil crisis, it's not just the old people like in all the jokes, and of course there are jobs to be had there too. Charlie's clever. Fred recognized that from the start."

"He has this mother, Ma. An old Greek lady who can't speak English and who's never been out of Brewer hardly."

"Well maybe it's time she was. You know people think we old people are such sticks in the mud but Grace Stuhl's sister, older than she is, mind you, and buried two husbands right in the county, went out to visit her son in Phoenix and loved it so she's bought her own little condominium and even, Grace was telling me, her burial plot, that's how much she pulled up her roots."

"Charlie's not like you, Harry," Janice explains. "He's not scared of change."

He could take that green glass egg and in one stride be at the sofa and pound it down into her dense skull. Instead he ignores her, saying to Ma, "I still haven't heard exactly what you said to Charlie, and he said to you."

"Oh, we reminisced. We talked about the old days with Fred and we agreed that Fred would want Nellie to have a place at the lot. He was always one for family, Fred, even when family let him down."

That must mean him, Rabbit thinks. Letting that shifty little wheeler-dealer down is about the last thing on his conscience.

"Charlie understands family," Janice interposes, in that smooth matronly voice she can do now, imitating her mother. "All the time I was, you know, seeing him, he was absolutely ready to stand aside and have me go back."

Bragging about her affair to her own mother. The world is falling apart fast.

"And so," Ma Springer sighs—she is wearying of this, her legs hurt and aren't improving, old people need their privacy —"we tried to come to an understanding of what Fred would want and came up with this idea of a leave for Charlie, for six months with half pay, and then at the end we'd see how Nellie was working out. In the meantime if the offer of another job comes Charlie's way he's to be free to take it, and then we'll settle at that point with two months' pay as a bonus, plus whatever his Christmas bonus would be for all of 1979. This wasn't just worked out at the party, I was over there today while you were playing golf."

He had been carrying an 83 into the last hole and then hooked into the creek and took an 8. It seems he'll never break 90 there, unless he does it in his sleep. Webb Murkett's relaxed swing is getting on his nerves. "Sneaky," he says. "I thought you didn't trust yourself to drive the Chrysler in Brewer traffic anymore."

"Janice drove me over."

"Aha." He asks his wife, "How did Charlie like seeing you there on this mission of mercy?"

"He was sweet. This has all been between him and Mother. But he knows Nelson is our son. Which is more than you seem to."

"No, no, I know he is, that's the trouble," Harry tells her. To old lady Springer he says, "So you're paying Charlie thousands to hand Nelson a job he probably can't do. Where's the savings for the firm in that? And you're going to lose sales without Charlie, I don't have half the contacts around town he does. Not just Greeks, either. Being single he's been in a lot of bars, that's where you win people's trust around here."

"Well, it may be." Ma Springer gets herself to her feet and stamps each one softly on the carpet, testing if either is asleep. "It may all be a mistake, but in this life you can't always be afraid of mistakes. I never liked that about Charlie, that he was unwilling to get married. It bothered Fred too, I know. Now I must get myself upstairs and see my Angels. Though it's not been the same since Farrah left."

"Don't I get a vote?" Harry asks, almost yelling, strapped as he feels into the Barcalounger. "I vote against it. I don't *want* to be bothered with Nelson over there."

"Well," Ma says, and in her long pause he has time to appreciate how big she is, how broad from certain angles, like a tree trunk seen suddenly in terms of all the toothpicks it would make, all those meals and days gone into this bulk, the stiff heavy seesaw of her hips, the speckled suet of her arms, "as I understand Fred's will, he left the lot to me and Janice, and I think we're of a mind."

"Two against three, Harry, in any case," Janice says, with a winning smile.

"Oh screw you," he says. "Screw Springer Motors. I suppose if I don't play dead doggie you two'll vote to can me too."

They don't deny it. While Ma's steps labor up the staircase, Janice, beginning to wear that smudged look she gets when the day's intake catches up with her, gets to her feet and tells him confidentially, "Mother thought you'd take it worse than you did. Want anything from the kitchen? This CocoRibe is really addictive."

October first falls on a Monday. Autumn is starting to show its underside: out of low clouds like a row of torn mattresses a gray rain is knocking the leaves one by one off the trees. That lonely old maple behind the Chuck Wagon across Route 111 is bare now down to its lower branches, which hang on like a monk's fringe. Not a day for customers: Harry and Charlie gaze together through the plate-glass windows where the posters now say COMING, ALL NEW COROLLAS • *New 1.8-liter engine* • *New aerodynamic styling* • *Aluminum wheels on SR5 models* • *Removable sunroof/moonroof* • *Best selling car in the world!* Another paper banner proclaims THE COROLLA TERCEL • *First Front-Wheel Drive Toyota* • *Toyota's Lowest Price &*

Highest Mileage • 33 Est. MPG • 43 EPA Estimated Highway MPG. "Well," Harry says, after clearing his throat, "the Phillies went out with a bang." By shutting out the Montreal Expos on the last day of the season, 2–0, they enabled Pittsburgh to win the championship of the National League East.

"I was rooting for the Expos," Charlie says.

"Yeah, you hate to see Pittsburgh win again. They're so fucking jivey. All that Family crap."

Stavros shrugs. "Well, a team of blacks like that, you need a slogan. They all grew up on television commercials, the box was the only mother they had. That's the tragedy of blacks these days."

It relieves Harry, to hear Charlie talk. He came in half expecting to find him crushed. "At least the Eagles screwed the Steelers," he says. "That felt good."

"They were lucky. That fumble going into the end zone. Bradshaw you can expect to throw some interceptions, but you don't expect Franco Harris to fumble going into the end zone."

Harry laughs aloud, in remembered delight. "How about that barefoot rookie kicker the Eagles got? Wasn't that beautiful?"

Charlie says, "Kicking isn't football."

"A forty-eight-yard field goal barefoot! That guy must have a big toe like a rock."

"For my money they can ship all these old soccer players back to Argentina. The contact in the line, that's football. The Pit. That's where the Steelers will get you in the end. I'm not worried about the Steelers."

Harry sniffs anger here and changes the subject, looking out at the weather. Drops on the glass enlarge and then abruptly dart down, dodgingly, leaving trails. The way he wept. Ever since earliest childhood, his consciousness dawning by the radiators in the old half-house on Jackson Road, it has been exciting for Harry to stand near a window during a rain, his face inches from the glass and dry, where a few inches away everything is wet. "Wonder if it's going to rain on the Pope." The Pope is flying into Boston that afternoon.

"Never. He'll just wave his arms and the sky'll be full of bluebirds. Bluebirds and horseshit."

Though no Catholic, Harry feels this is a bit rude; no doubt about it, Charlie is prickly this morning. "Ja see those crowds on television? The Irish went wild. One crowd was over a million, they said."

"Micks are dumb," Charlie says, and starts to turn away. "I gotta get hot on some NV-1s."

Harry can't let him go. He says, "And they gave the old Canal back last night."

"Yeah. I get sick of the news. This country is sad, everybody can push us around."

"You were the guy wanted to get out of Vietnam."

"That was sad too."

"Hey."

"Yeah?"

"I hear you had a talk with Ma Springer."

"The last of a long series. She's not so sad. She's tough."

"Any thoughts about where you're going to be going?" Nelson and Pru are due back from the Poconos Friday.

"Nowhere, for a while. See a few movies. Hit a few bars."

"How about Florida, you're always talking about Florida."

"Come on. I can't ask the old lady to move down there. What would she do, play shuffleboard?"

"I thought you said you had a cousin taking care of her now."

"Gloria. I don't know, something's cooking there. She and her husband may be getting back together. He doesn't like scrambling his own eggs in the morning."

"Oh. Sorry." Harry pauses. "Sorry about everything."

Charlie shrugs. "What can *you* do?"

This is what he wants to hear; relief bathes him like a kind of light. When you feel better, you see better; he sees all the papers, wrappers and take-out cup lids that have blown across the highway from the Chuck Wagon, lying in the bushes just outside the window, getting soaked. He says, "I could quit myself."

"That's crazy, champ. What would you do? Me, I can sell anywhere, that's no worry. Already I've had some feelers. News travels fast in this business. It's a hustling business."

"I told her, 'Ma, Charlie's the heart of Springer Motors. Half the clients come in because of him. More than half.'"

"I appreciate your putting in a word. But you know, there comes a time."

"I guess." But not for Harry Angstrom. Never, never.

"How about Jan? What'd *she* have to say about giving me the gate?"

A tough question. "Not much, that I heard. You know she can't stand up to the old lady; never could."

"If you want to know what I think cooked my goose, it was that trip with Melanie. That cooled it with both the Springer girls."

"You think Janice still cares that much?"

"You don't stop caring, champ. You still care about that little girl whose underpants you saw in kindergarten. Once you care, you always care. That's how stupid we are."

A rock in space, is the image these words bring to Rabbit's mind. He is interested in space, and scans the paper every day for more word on these titanic quasars on the edge of everything, and in the Sunday section studies the new up-close photos of Jupiter, expecting to spot a clue that all those scientists have missed; God might have a few words to say yet. In the vacuum of the heart love falls forever. Janice jealous of Charlie, we get these ideas and can't let go, it's been twenty years since he slept with Ruth but whenever in some store downtown or along Weiser he sees from behind a woman with gingery hair bundled up carelessly with a few loops flying loose, his heart bumps up. And Nelson, he was young at the time but you're never too young to fall, he loved Jill and come to think of it Pru has some of the hippie style, long hair flat down the back and that numb look daring you to hurt her, though Jill of course was of a better class, she was no Akron steamfitter's daughter. Harry says to Charlie, "Well at least now you can run out to Ohio from time to time."

Charlie says, "There's nothing out there for me. Melanie's more like a daughter. She's smart, you know. You ought to hear her go on about transcendental meditation and this crazy Russian philosopher. She wants to go on and get a Ph.D. if she can worm the money out of her father. He's out there on the West Coast fucking Indian maidens."

Coast to coast, Rabbit thinks, we're one big funhouse. It's

done with mirrors. "Still," he tells Charlie, "I wish I had some of your freedom."

"You got freedom you don't even use. How come you and Jan keep living in that shabby old barn with her mother? It's not doing Jan any good, it's keeping her childish."

Shabby? Harry had never thought of the Springer place as shabby: old-fashioned maybe but with big rooms full of the latest and best goods, just the way he saw it the first time, when he began to take Janice out, the summer they were both working at Kroll's. Everything looked new and smelled so clean, and in the side room off the living room a long wrought-iron table held a host of tropical plants, a jungle of their own that seemed the height of luxury. Now the table stands there hollow and you can see where it's stained the hardwood floor with rusty drippings. And he thinks of the gray sofa and the wallpaper and watercolors that haven't changed since the days he used to pick Jan up for a night of heavy petting in the back of the old Nash he bought in the Army and maybe it is shabby. Ma doesn't have the energy she did and what she does with all her money nobody knows. Not buy new furniture. And now that it's fall the copper beech outside their bedroom window is dropping its nuts, the little triangular seedpods explode and with all the rustling and crackling it's not so easy to sleep. That room has never been ideal. "Childish, huh?"

"Speaking of which," Charlie says, "remember those two kids who came in at the beginning of the summer, the girl that turned you on? The boy came back Saturday, while you were out on the golf course, I can't think of his name."

"Nunemacher."

"Right. He bought that orange Corolla liftback with standard transmission out on the lot. No trade-in, and these new models coming in, I quoted him two hundred off the list. I thought you'd want me to be nice to him."

"Right. Was the girl with him?"

"Not that I could see."

"And he didn't trade in that Country Squire?"

"You know these farmers, they like to keep junk in their yards. Probably hitch it up to a band saw."

"My God," Harry says. "Jamie bought the orange Corolla."

"Well come on, it's not that much of a miracle. I asked him why he waited so long and he said he thought if he waited to fall the '79s would be down in price a little. And the dollar would be worth less. The yen too as it turns out."

"When's he taking delivery?"

"He said around noon tomorrow. That's one of the NV-1s I gotta do."

"Shit. That's when I have Rotary."

"The girl wasn't with him, what do you care? You talk about me; she was younger than Melanie. That girl might have been as young as sixteen, seventeen."

"Nineteen is what she'd be," Rabbit says. "But you're right. I don't care." Rain all around them leads his heart upward by threads; he as well as Charlie has his options.

Tuesday after Rotary with the drinks still working in him Harry goes back to the lot and sees the orange Corolla gone and can hardly focus with happiness, God has kissed him out of space. Around four-thirty, with Rudy on the floor and Charlie over in Allenville trying to wrap up a used-car package with a dealer there to clear the books a little before Nelson takes over, he eases out of his office and down the corridor and out through the shop where Manny's men are still whacking metal but their voices getting louder as the bliss of quitting time approaches and out the back door, taking care not to dirty his shirt cuffs on the crash bar, and out into air. Paraguay. On this nether portion of the asphalt the Mercury with its mashed-in left side and fender and grille still waits upon a decision. It turns out Charlie was able to unload the repaired Royale for thirty-six hundred to a young doctor from Royersford, he wasn't even a regular doctor but one of these homeopathic or holistic doctors as they call it now who looks at your measles and tells you to eat carrots or just hum at a certain pitch for three hours a day, he must be doing all right because he snapped up that old Olds, said a guy he admired at college had driven one like it and he'd always wanted one just that color, evidently—that purply-red nail-polish color. Harry squeezes himself into his Corona the color of tired tomato soup and slides out of the lot softly and heads down III the way away from Brewer, toward Galilee. Springer Motors well behind him, he turns on the radio and that heavy electrified disco beat threatens to pop the stereo speakers. Tinny sounds, wiffling sounds, sounds like a kazoo being played over the telephone come at him from the four corners of the vinyl-upholstered interior, setting that hopeful center inside his ribs to jingling. He thinks back to the Rotary luncheon and Eddie Pastorelli of Pastorelli Realty with his barrel chest and stiff little bow legs now, that used to do the 440 in less than fifty seconds, giving them a slide show on the proposed planned development of the upper blocks of Weiser, which were mostly parking lots and bars these days, and little businesses like vacuum-cleaner repair and pet supplies that hadn't had the capital to move out to the malls, Eddie trying to tell them that some big glass boxes and a corkscrew-ramped concrete parking garage are going to bring the shoppers back in spite of all the spic kids roaming around with transistors glued to their ears and knives up their wrists. Harry has to laugh, he remembers Eddie when he was a second-string guard for Hemmigtown High, a meaner greaseball never stayed out of reform school. Donna Summer comes on singing, *Dim all the lights sweet darling* . . . When you see pictures of her she's much less black than you imagine, a thin-cheeked yellow staring out at you like what are you going to do about it. The thing about those Rotarians, if you knew them as kids you can't stop seeing the kid in them, dressed up in fat and baldness and money like a cardboard tuxedo in a play for high-school assembly. How can you respect the world when you see it's being run by a bunch of kids turned old? That's the joke Rabbit always enjoys at Rotary. With a few martinis inside him Eddie can be funny as hell, when he told that joke about the five men in the airplane the tip of his nose bent down like it was on a little string and his laugh came out as an old woman's wheeze. *Knapsack! hee hee hee.* Rabbit must try to remember and try it out on the gang at the Flying Eagle. Five men: a hippie, a priest, a policeman, and Henry Kissinger, the smartest man in the world. But who was the fifth? Donna Summer says to turn her brown body white, at least that's what he thinks she's said, you can't be sure with all this disco *wowowow*, some doped-up sound engineer wiggling the knobs to give that sound, the words don't matter, it's that beat pushed between your ribs like a knife, making the soul jingle.

Houses of sandstone. A billboard pointing to a natural cave. He wonders who goes there anymore, natural caves a thing of the past, like waterfalls. Men in straw hats. Women with not even their ankles showing. Natural wonders. That smart-ass young female announcer—he hasn't heard her for a while, he thought maybe the station had fired her, too sassy or got pregnant—comes on and says that the Pope has addressed the UN and is stopping in Harlem on his way to Yankee Stadium. Harry saw the cocky little guy on television last night, getting soaked in Boston in his white robes, you had to admire his English, about his seventh language, and who was the deadpan guy standing there holding the umbrella over him? Some Vatican bigwig, but Pru didn't seem to know any more than he did, what's the good of being raised a Catholic? In Europe, gold rose today to a new high of four hundred forty-four dollars an ounce while the dollar slipped to new lows. The station fades and returns as the road twists among the hilly fields. Harry calculates, up eighty dollars in less than three weeks, thirty times eighty is two thousand four hundred, when you're rich you get richer, just like Pop used to say. In some of the fields the corn stands tall, others are stubble. He glides through the ugly string town of Galilee, on the lookout for the orange Corolla. No need to ask at the post office this time. The vegetable stand is closed for the season. The pond has some geese on it, he doesn't remember those, migrating already, the green little turds they leave all over the fairways, maybe that was the reason that doctor . . . He turns off the radio. BLANKENBILLER. MUTH. BYER. He parks on the same widened spot of red dirt road shoulder. His heart is pounding, his hands feel swollen and numb, resting on the steering wheel. He turns off the ignition, digging himself in deeper. It's not as if he's doing anything illegal. When he gets out of the car, the pigsty whiff isn't in the air, the wind is from the other direction, and there is no insect hum. They have died, millions. Across the silence cuts the far-off whine and snarl of a chain saw. The new national anthem. *Oho say can you saw* . . . The woods are a half-mile off and can't be part of the Byer farm. He begins to trespass. The hedgerow that has swallowed the stone wall is less leafy, he is less hidden. A cool small wind slips through the tangled black gum and wild cherry and licks his hands. Poison

ivy leaves have turned, a Mercurochrome red, some of them half-dyed as if dipped. As he ventures down through the old orchard, a step at a time, he treads on fallen apples lying thick in the grass grown to hay. Mustn't turn an ankle, lie up here and rot as well. Poor trees, putting out all this wormy fruit for nothing. Perhaps not nothing from their point of view, when men didn't exist they were doing the same. Strange thought. Harry looks down upon the farmhouse now, the green door, the birdbath on its pale blue pillar. Smoke is rising from the chimney; the nostalgic smell of burning wood comes to him. So close, he gets behind a dying apple tree with a convenient fork at the height of his head. Ants are active in the velvety light brown rot inside the trunk, touching noses, telling the news, hurrying on. The tree trunk is split open like an unbut-toned overcoat but still carries life up through its rough skin to the small round leaves that tremble where the twigs are young and smooth. Space feels to drop away not only in front of him but on all sides, even through the solid earth, and he won-ders what he is doing here in his good beige suit, his backside exposed to any farmer with a shotgun who might be walking along in the field behind him and his face posed in this fork like a tin can up for target practice were anybody to look up from the buildings below, he who has an office with his name on the door and CHIEF SALES REPRESENTATIVE on his business cards and who a few hours back was entertaining other men in suits with the expense and complications of his son's wedding, the organist going off with this Slim and the couple turning up so late he thought they were Jehovah's Witnesses; and for some seconds of panic cannot answer himself why, except that out here, in the air, nameless, he feels purely alive. Then he remembers: he hopes to glimpse his daughter. And what if he were to gather all his nerve and go down and knock at the green door in its deep socket of wall and she were to answer? She would be in jeans this time of year, and a sweatshirt or sweater. Her hair would be less loose and damp than in its summer do, maybe pulled back and held by a rubber band. Her eyes, widely spaced, would be pale blue little mirrors.
    Hi. You don't remember me—
    Sure I do. You're the car dealer.
    I'm more than that, I think.

Like what?

Is your mother's name by any chance Ruth Byer?

Well . . . yes.

And has she ever talked to you about your father?

My father's dead. He used to run the school buses for the township.

That wasn't your father. I'm your father.

And that broad pale face in which he saw his own would stare at him furious, disbelieving, fearful. And if he did at last make her believe, she would be angry at him for taking from her the life she had lived and substituting for it one she could never live now. He sees that these fields where his seed may have taken hold hold nothing of harvest for him but, if he seizes it, the space at his back to escape in. Yet he stands, in his tired summer suit—time to have it cleaned and stored in the big plastic clothes bag until next April—transfixed by the motionlessness of the scene below, but for the rising smoke. His heart races in steady alarm at his having strayed so far off track. You have a life and there are these volumes on either side that go unvisited; some day soon as the world winds he will lie beneath what he now stands on, dead as those insects whose sound he no longer hears, and the grass will go on growing, wild and blind.

His idling heart jumps at a rustle close behind him in the orchard. He has lifted his arms and framed the first words of his self-explanation before he sees that the other presence is not a person but a dog, an old-looking collie with one red eye and its coat loaded with burrs. Rabbit is uncomfortable with dogs anyway and knows collies to be especially nervous and prone to attack, Lassie to the contrary. This dog is blacker than Lassie. It stands the length of a long putt away, head cocked, the hair behind its ears electric, set to bark.

"Hi," Harry says, his voice a hoarse shade above a whisper, lest it carry down to the house.

The collie cocks its narrow head at a sharper tilt, as if to favor the sore eye, and the long white hair around its throat like a bib riffles where the breeze flattens it.

"You a good doggie?" Harry asks. He envisions the distance to the car, sees himself running, the dog at his legs in two seconds, the tearing of cloth, the pointed yellowish canines, the way dogs lift that black split upper lip to bare the little front teeth in hate; he feels his ankle pinned as if between two grinding cogwheels, his fall, his arms up in a futile attempt to save his face.

But the dog makes a decision in its narrow skull. Its dropped tail cautiously wags, and it lopes forward with that horrible silent lightness of four-footed animals through the orchard grass. It sniffs at Harry's knees and then leans against his legs, allowing its neck to be scratched as Harry keeps up a whispered patter. "Nice boy, good girl, where'd you get all these burrs, *baaad* burrs." Don't let them smell your terror. You sure know you're out in the country when you meet dogs running around without collars just like bears.

Distantly, a car door slams. The sound echoes off the barn wall so that at first he looks in the wrong spot. Then he sees through the fork of the apple tree, about a six-iron away allowing for the slope, the orange Corolla in the big bare spot between the house and the garage, which has the yellow shell of the school bus behind it.

So a wild hope is confirmed, but most of his mind stays with the opaque bundle of muscle and teeth at his knees, how to keep it from barking, how to keep it from biting. Tiny brains, change in a second, a collie belonging to old Mrs. Zug down Jackson Road lived in a barrel, snapped one time when nobody expected it, Harry still has the faint white scar on two middle fingers, pulling them loose felt like skinning a carrot, he can still feel it.

The dog too hears the car door slam and, flattening its ears, rockets down through the orchard. Around the Corolla it sets up a barking that is frantic but remote, delayed by echo and space. Harry seizes the moment to scurry back to a tree farther away. From there he sees the car's driver step out, lanky Jamie, no longer wearing dirty dungarees but pinkish bell-bottoms and a red turtleneck shirt. The collie jumps up and down, greeting, apologizing for barking at the unfamiliar car. The boy's drawl drifts up through the orchard, doing singsong dog talk, the words indistinct. Rabbit drops his eyes a moment to the earth, where two yellowjackets are burrowing into a rotten apple. When he looks again, a girl, his girl, her round white face unmistakable, her hair shorter than in June, steps out of the Corolla's passenger side and hunkers down to the dog, mingling herself with its flurry. She turns her face away from a thrust of the dog's muzzle and stares upwards at the exact spot from which Harry, frozen, watches. He sees when she stands that she is dressed trimly, in dark brown skirt and russet sweater, a little plaid jacket squaring up her shoulders so she looks sharp, collegiate, a city girl. Still there is that certain languor of her legs as she takes a stride or two toward the house. Her voice lifts in calling. Both their young faces have turned to the house, so Rabbit takes the opportunity to retreat to yet a farther tree, slimmer than the one previous. But he is close to the tangled hedgerow now and perhaps against this invisible in his light brown suit, camouflaged among pieces of sky.

Down below, echoing off the stucco and cinder-block walls, the cries of greeting and pleasure have a melancholy, drifting sound. From out of the house, following a thin slam of its door, a fat elderly woman has emerged, moving under the burden of her own weight so cautiously that the collie, herding, nudges her forward, encircling her legs. This might be the woman he glimpsed in the old station wagon when it went by the church on the day of the wedding, but it cannot be Ruth, for her hair, that had been a kind of soft and various wiry fire, is an iron cap of gray fitted to her head, and her body is enormous, so big her clothes from this distance seem wide as a sail. In pants and shirt this person advances plodding to admire the new car. There is no exchange of kisses, but from the way they all rotate and slide one past another these three are well acquainted. Their voices drift to Harry unintelligibly.

The boy demonstrates the liftback. The girl taps the old woman, as if to say, *Go on*; she is being teased. Then they fish from the car's interior two tall brown paper bags, groceries, and the collie dog, bored with these proceedings, lifts its head and points its nose in the direction where Harry, his heart thunderous, is holding as still as the man concealed in the tangled lines of those puzzle drawings that used to be in Sunday papers.

The dog begins to bark and races up into the orchard toward him; Harry has no choice but to turn and run. Perhaps he makes it through the hedgerow before the people look up and see him. They call out for the dog—"Fritzie! Fritzie!"—in two female voices. Twigs scratch his hands; the loose stones of the old wall nearly trip him, and scuff one shoe. Now he flies. The red earth marred by tractor treads skims underfoot. Yet the dog, he sees glancing behind, will overtake him before he can reach the car; already the creature, its hair and ears swept flat by its speed, has broken through the hedgerow and is streaming along beside the corn stubble. Oh Christ. Rabbit stops, wraps his arms around his face, and waits. The house is out of sight below the rise of land; he is all alone with this. He hears the dog's claws rattle past him in momentum and a bark dies to a growl in its throat. He feels his legs being nosed through his trousers, then leaned on. The dog doesn't want to bring him down but to gather him in, to herd him also.

"Nice Fritzie," Harry says. "Good Fritzie. Let's go to my car. Let's trot along." Foot by careful foot he consumes the little distance to the shoulder of the road, the dog bumping and sniffing him all the way. The cries from the house, invisible, persist raggedly; the collie's tail, uncertainly wagging, pats Harry's calves while the long skull inquires upward with its sick red eye. Harry pulls his hands up to the level of his lapels. Dirty yellow drooly teeth would skin his fingers like a carrot grater. He tells Fritzie, "You're a beautiful girl, a wonderful girl," and eases around the back of the Corona. The chain saw is still zipping along. He opens the driver's door and slides in. Slams it. The collie stands on the overgrown banking of red earth looking puzzled, her shepherding come to an end. Harry finds the car key in his pocket, the engine starts. His heart is still pounding. He leans over toward the passenger's window and scrabbles his fingers on the glass. "Hey Fritzie!" he shouts and keeps up the scrabbling until the dog starts to bark again. *Bark. Bark bark bark.* Laughing, Rabbit pops the clutch and digs out, the thing inside his chest feeling fragile and iridescent like a big soap bubble. Let it pop. He hasn't felt so close to breaking out of his rut since Nelson smashed those convertibles.

Webb Murkett is handy about the house; he has a cellar full of expensive power tools and subscribes to magazines with titles like *Fine Woodworking* and *Homecraft*. In every corner of the garrison colonial he and Cindy have shared for the seven years of their marriage there are hand-made refinements of rounded, stained, and varnished wood—shelves, cabinets, built-in lazy susans with as many compartments as a seashell —expressing the patience and homelovingness of the house's master. There is a way of working with rotten wood, and making it as solid as marble, and like marble swirled and many-shaded; this art is on display in the base of several lamps and in a small bowl holding an untouched spiral of cigarettes on the butler's-tray table, which Webb has also fashioned, down to its gleaming copper hinges shaped like butterflies. Some of these objects must have come from the homes of Webb's previous marriages, and Harry wonders what these phantom women have kept, that so much remains. Webb's previous marriages are represented in his great long sunken living room only by color photographs, in ensemble frames of unusual proportion that Webb himself has cut and grooved and cemented together of Lucite, of children too old to be his and Cindy's, caught in a moment of sunshine on the flagstone stoop of another suburban house, or in a sailboat against the blue of a lake that the Kodak chemicals are permitting to fade to yellow, or at a moment of marriage or graduation—for some of these children were now adult, older than Nelson, and infants of a third generation stare out unsmiling, propped on a pillow or held in firm young arms, from among the many smiles of these family groups. Harry has several times in Webb's house slyly searched these photos for the sight of a former wife; but though there are women beheaded or sliced to a splinter by the edge of a frame or another picture, and here and there an unidentifiable mature hand and forearm intrudes behind a set of children's heads, no face seems preserved of the vanished mistresses of all this fleeting family happiness.

When Webb and Cindy entertain, built-in speakers bathe the downstairs rooms in a continuous sweetness of string music and spineless arrangements, of old show tunes or mollified rock classics, voiceless and seamless and with nagging dental associations for Harry. Behind a mahogany bar that Webb salvaged from the tavern of a farmer's hotel being demolished in Brewer and then transported with its brass rail to a corner of his living room, he has constructed a kind of altar to booze, two high doors with rounded tops that meet in a point and shelves that come forward on a lazy-tongs principle with not only the basic whisky, gin, and vodka but exotic drinks like rum and tequila and sake and all the extras you could want from bitters to powdered Old-fashioned mix in little envelopes. And the bar has its own small refrigerator, built in. Much as he admires Webb, Harry thinks when he gets his own dream house he will do without the piped music and such elaborate housing for the liquor.

The bathroom, though, enchants him, with its little enamelled dishes of rosebud-shaped soap, its furry blue toilet seat cover, and its dazzling mirror rimmed with naked light bulbs like actors have in their dressing rooms. Everything in here that doesn't shine is tinted and scented. The toilet paper, very dulcet, is printed with old comic strips, each piece a panel. Poor Popeye, eating shit instead of spinach. And the towels have W and M and L for Lucinda intertwined in such a crusty big monogram he hates to think what it would do to Cindy's sweet underparts if she forgot and rubbed herself hard. But Harry wonders if this downstairs bathroom is ever used by the Murketts and their rather pasty-looking little kids or is set up primarily for guests. Certain mysterious artifacts in it—a big sort of sugar bowl, white, with a knobbed lid painted with two women dressed in filmy gowns sitting on clouds or a sofa that fades into nothing, and their feet in pink ballerina shoes and their ankles crossed and the toes of one woman touching the other's and one bare arm of each interwined above the knob, yet when the lid is lifted utterly empty, so empty you feel nothing has ever been put inside; and a pink plastic hand on a stick, meant maybe for a comic backscratcher; and an egg-shaped jar a third full of lavender crystalline salts; and a kind of tiny milkman's carrier of what he takes to be bath oils; and a flexible plastic cylinder holding a pastel rainbow of powder puffs like a stack of pancakes—all seem put there, on the set of open shelves hung on two black dowels between the bathtub and the toilet, for exhibit more than use. To think of little Cindy though, pouring that oil into her bath and then just soaking there, playing with herself with the backscratcher, her nipples poking through the blanket of soapsuds. Harry feels sexy. In the mirror that makes things too vivid his eyes stare with a pallor almost white, like the little frost-flowers that appear on the skin of a car in the morning, and his lips look bluish. He is drunk. He has had two tequila fizzes before dinner, as much Gallo Chablis as he could grab during the meal, and a brandy and a half afterwards. In the middle of the second brandy the need to urinate came upon him like yet another pressure of happiness, added to his health and prosperity and the privilege of being there sitting across a coffee table from Cindy watching her body rotate within the strange coarse cloth of the exotic Arab-looking thing she is wearing, her wrists and her feet, bare but for sandals, as exciting in this outfit as the insides of her thighs in a bikini. Besides himself and Janice the Murketts have invited the Harrisons and for a new thrill the moronic Fosnachts, whom they just met at Nelson's wedding two weeks ago. Harry doesn't suppose the Murketts know he and Peggy had a fling years back when Ollie had done one of his copouts, but maybe they do, people know more than you ever think they do, and it turns out it doesn't much matter. Look at what you read every week in *People* magazine, and you still keep watching television, the actors all dope addicts and adulterers. He has an urge to peek into the medicine cabinet framed by the rim of showbiz bulbs and waits until a gale of laughter from the drunken bunch in the living room arises to drown out any possible *click* of him opening the mirror-door. *Click*. The cabinet has more in it than he would have supposed: thick milk-glass jars of skin cream and flesh-tint squeeze bottles of lotion and brown tubes of suntan lotion, Parepectolin for diarrhea, Debrox for ear wax control, menthol Chloraseptic, that mouthwash called Cēpacol, several kinds of aspirin, both Bayer and Anacin, and Tylenol that doesn't make your stomach burn, and a large chalky bottle of liquid Maalox. He wonders which of the Murketts needs Maalox, they both always look so relaxed and at peace. The pink poison ivy goo would be down-stairs handy for the kids, and the Band-Aids, but how about the little flat yellow box of Preparation H for hemorrhoids? Carter of course has hemorrhoids, that grim over-motivated type who wants to do everything on schedule ready or not, pushing, pushing, but old Webb Murkett with that gravelly voice and easy swing, like the swing you see crooners use at celebrity tour-naments, unwrapping one of those little wax bullets and poking it up his own asshole? You have to go into a squat and the place is not easy to find, Rabbit remembers from his own experience, years ago, when he was sitting all day at the Linotype on that hard steel bench, under tension, the matrices rattling down in response to the touch of his fingertips, every slip a ruined slug, everybody around him unhappy, the kid still small, his own life closed in to a size his soul had not yet shrunk to fit. And what of these amber pill bottles with *Lucinda R. Murkett* typed in pale blue script face on the prescription labels? White pills, lethally small. He should have brought his reading glasses. Harry is tempted to lift one of these containers off its shelf in hopes of deciphering what illness might have ever found its way into that plump and supple and delectable body, but a superstitious fear of fingerprints restrains him. Medicine cabinets are tragic, he sees by this hard light, and closes the door so gently no one will hear the click. He returns to the living room.

They are discussing the Pope's visit, loudly. "Did you *see*," Peggy Fosnacht is shouting, "what he said in Chicago yesterday about *sex*!" The years since Harry knew her have freed her to stop wearing dark glasses to hide her walleye and to be sloppy in her person and opinions both; she's become the kind of woman who looks permanently out of press, as a protest of sorts. "He said everything outside marriage was *wrong*. Not just if you're married, but *before* you're married too. What does that man *know*? He doesn't know anything about *life*, life as she is lived."

Webb Murkett offers in a soft voice, trying to calm his guest down, "I liked what Earl Butz said some years ago. 'He no play-a the game, he no make-a the rules.'" Webb is wearing a maroon turtleneck under a coarse yarny gray sweater that has something to do, Rabbit thinks, with Scandinavian fishermen. The way the neck is cut. Harry and Ronnie came in suits; Ollie was with-it enough to know you don't wear suits out even on a Saturday night anymore. He came in tight faded jeans and an embroidered shirt that made him look like a cowboy too runty to be on the range.

"No play-a the game!" Peggy Fosnacht yells. "See if you're a pregnant slum mother and can't get an abortion legally if you think it's such a game."

Rabbit says to her, "Webb's agreeing with you," but she doesn't hear him, babbling on headlong, face flushed by wine and the exciting class of company, her hairdo coming uncurled like taffy softening in the sun.

"Did any of you watch except me—I can't stop watching, I get so furious—the performance he put on in Philly where he said absolutely No to women priests? And he kept smiling, what really got my goat, he kept smiling while spouting all this sexist crap about only men in the priesthood and how it was the conviction of the church and God's decision and all that, so solly. He's so *smooth* about it, I think is what gets to me, at least somebody like Nixon or Hitler had the decency to be frantic."

"He is one smooth old Polack," Ollie says, uneasy at this outburst by his wife. He is into cool, you can see. Music, dope. Just on the fringes, but enough to give you the pitch.

"He sure can kiss those nigger babies," Ronnie Harrison comes in with, maybe trying to help. It's fascinating to Rabbit how long those strands of hair are Ronnie is combing over his bald spot these days, if you pulled one the other way it would go below his ear. In this day and age why fight it? There's a bald look, go for it. Blank and pink and curved, like an ass. Everybody loves an ass. Those wax bullets in the yellow box—could they have been for Cindy? Sore there from, but would Webb? Harry has read somewhere that male homosexuals have a lot of trouble with hemorrhoids. Amazing the things they try to put up—fists, light bulbs. He squirms on his cushion.

"I think he's very sexy," Thelma Harrison states. Everything she says sounds like a schoolteacher, enunciated. He looks at her through the enhancing lens of liquor: thin lips and that unhealthy yellowy color. Harry can hardly ever look at her without seeing Ronnie's prick, flat like a board on the upper side it's so thick. "He is a beautiful man," Thelma insists. Her eyes are half-shut. She's had a glass or two too many herself. Her throat rises absolutely straight, like a person trying not to hiccup. He has to look down the front of her dress, velvet that mousy blue of old movie seats, the way she's holding herself. Nothing much there. That little stocky guy in white with all those gold buttons and different funny hats, to see him as sexy you'd have to be a nun. Ronnie is stocky like that, actually. She likes thick men. He looks down the front of her dress again. Maybe more there than you'd think.

Janice is saying, she has known Peggy for ages and is trying to save her from herself, "What I liked today, I don't know if you were watching, Peggy, was when he came out on the balcony of that cathedral in Washington, before he went to the White House, to this crowd that was shouting, 'We want the Pope, we want the Pope,' and he came out on the balcony waving and shouted, 'John Paul Two, he wants you!' Actually."

"Actually" because the men had laughed, it was news to them. Three of them had been out on the Flying Eagle course today, summer had made one last loop back to Diamond County, bringing out fat buds on the magnolias by the sixth tee. Their fourth had been the young assistant pro, the same kid who had shot a 73 the day Nelson got married. He hits a long ball, Webb was right, but Harry doesn't like his swing: too wristy. Give him a few years around his waist he'll be hooking everything. Buddy Inglefinger had been dropped, lately; his golf was a drag and the wives didn't like his tarty girlfriends. But Ollie Fosnacht is no substitute. The only thing he plays is the synthesizer, and his sloppy wife won't stop blabbering.

"I'd *like* to find it amusing," Peggy says, hoisting her voice above the laughter, "but to me the issues he's trampling on are too damn serious."

Cindy Murkett unexpectedly speaks. "He's been a priest in a Communist country; he's used to taking a stand. What is it that offends you, Peggy, if you're not a Catholic and don't have to listen?"

A hush has surrounded her words because they all except the Fosnachts know that she was Catholic until she married Webb. Peggy senses this now but like a white sad heifer having charged in one direction cannot turn herself around. "You're Catholic?" she bluntly asks.

Cindy tips her chin up, not used to this kind of spotlight, the baby of their group. "I was raised as one," she says.

"So was my daughter-in-law, it turns out," Harry volunteers. He is amused by the idea of his having a daughter-in-law at all, a new branch of his wealth. And he hopes to be distracting. He hates to see women fight, he'd be happy to get these two off the spot. Cindy comes up from that swimming pool like a wet dream, and Peggy was kind enough to lay him when he was down.

But no one is distracted. "When I married a divorced man," Cindy explains levelly to the other woman, "I couldn't take communion anymore. But I still go to Mass sometimes. I still believe." Her voice softens saying this, for she is the hostess, younger though she is.

"And do you use birth control?" Peggy asks.

Back to nowhere, Fosnachts. Harry is just as pleased; he liked his little crowd the way it was.

Cindy hesitates. She can go all girlish and slide and giggle away from the question, or she can sit still and get dignified. With just the smallest of dignified smiles she says, "I'm not sure that's any of your business."

"Nor the Pope's either, that's my point!" Peggy sounds triumphant, but even she must be feeling the battle slipping away. She will not be invited here again.

Webb, always the gentleman, perches on the arm of the easy chair in which cumbersome Peggy has set herself up as anti-Pope and leans down a deft inch to say to his guest alone, "I think Cindy's point, as I understand it, is that John Paul is addressing the doctrinal issues for his fellow Catholics while bringing good will to every American."

"He can keep his good will along with the doctrine as far as I'm concerned," Peggy says, trying to shut up but unable. Rabbit remembers how her nipples had felt like gumdrops and how sad her having gotten good at screwing since Ollie left her had seemed to him at the time, ten years ago.

Cindy attacks a little now, "But he sees the trouble the church has got into since Vatican Two. The priests—"

"The church is in trouble because it's a monument to a lie, run by a bunch of antiquated chauvinists who don't know *any*-thing. I'm sorry," Peggy says, "I'm talking too much."

"Well, this is America," Harry says, coming to her rescue, somewhat. "Let's all sock it to each other. Today I said good-bye to the only friend I've ever had, Charlie Stavros."

Janice says, "Oh, Harry," but nobody else takes him up on it. The men were supposed to say *they* were his friends.

Webb Murkett tilts his head, his eyebrows working toward Ronnie and Ollie. "Did either of you see in the paper today where Nixon finally bought a house in Manhattan? Right next to David Rockefeller. I'm no great admirer of tricky Dick's, but

I must say the way he's been excluded from apartment houses in a great city is a disgrace to the Constitution."

"If he'd been a spade," Ronnie begins, "every civil rights—"

"Well how would *you* like," Peggy Fosnacht has to say, "a lot of secret service men checking your handbag every time you came back from the store?"

The chair Peggy sits in is squared-off ponderous modern with a pale fabric thick as plywood; it matches another chair and a long sofa set around that kind of table with no overhang to the top they call a Parsons table, which is put together in alternating blocks of light and dark wood with a curly knotty grain such as they make golf club heads of. The entire deep space of the room, which Webb added on when he and Cindy acquired this house in the pace-setting development of Brewer Heights, gently brims with appointments chosen all to harmonize. Its tawny wallpaper has vertical threads of texture in it like the vertical folds of the slightly darker pull drapes, and reproductions of Wyeth watercolors lit by spots on track lighting overhead echo with scratchy strokes the same tints, and the same lighting reveals little sparkles, like mica on a beach, in the overlapping arcs of the rough-plastered ceiling. When Harry moves his head these sparkles in the ceiling change location, wave upon wave of hidden silver. He announces, "I heard a kind of funny story at Rotary the other day involving Kissinger. Webb, I don't think you were there. There were these five guys in an airplane that was about to crash—a priest, a hippie, a policeman, somebody else, and Henry Kissinger. And only four parachutes."

Ronnie says, "And at the end the hippie turns to the priest and says, 'Don't worry, Father. The Smartest Man in the World just jumped out with my knapsack.' We've all heard it. Speaking of which, Thel and I were wondering if you'd seen this." He hands him a newspaper clipping, from an Ann Landers column printed in the Brewer *Standard*, the respectable paper, not the *Vat*. The second paragraph is marked in tidy ballpoint. "Read it aloud," Ronnie demands.

He doesn't like being given orders by sweaty skinheads like Harrison when he's come out for a pleasant low-key time with the Murketts, but all eyes are on him and at least it gets them off the Pope. He explains, more to the Fosnachts than the others, since the Murketts seem to be in on the joke already, "It's a letter to Ann Landers from somebody. The first paragraph tells about a news story about some guy whose pet python bit him in the stomach and wouldn't let go, and when the paramedics came he yelled at them to get out of his apartment if they're going to hurt his snake." There is a little laughter at that and the Fosnachts, puzzled, try to join in. The next paragraph goes:

> The other news story was about a Washington, D.C., physician who beat a Canadian goose to death with his putter on the 16th green of a country club. (The goose honked just as he was about to sink one.) The reason for printing those letters was to demonstrate that truth is stranger than fiction.

Having read this aloud, he explains to the Fosnachts, "The reason they're razzing me with this is last summer I heard about the same incident on the radio and when I tried to tell them about it at the club they wouldn't listen, nobody believed me. Now here's proof it happened."

"You chump, *that's* not the point," Ronnie Harrison says.

"The point is, Harry," Thelma says, "it's so *different*. You said he was from Baltimore and this says he was from Washington. You said the ball hit the goose accidentally and the doctor put him out of his misery."

Webb says, "Remember—'A mercy killing, or murder most foul?' That really broke me up."

"You didn't show it at the time," Harry says, pleased however.

"According to Ann Landers, then, it *was* murder most foul," Thelma says.

"Who cares?" Ronnie says, getting ugly. This clipping was clearly her idea. Her touch on the ballpoint too.

Janice has been listening with that glazed dark look she gets when deep enough into the booze. She and Webb have been trying some new imported Irish liqueur called Greensleeves. "Well not if the goose honked," she says.

Ollie Fosnacht says, "I can't believe a goose honking would make that much difference on a putt."

All the golfers there assure him it would.

"Shit," he says, "in music, you do your best work at two in

the morning, stoned half out of your mind and a lot of drunks acting up besides."

His mention of music reminds them all that in the background Webb's hidden speakers are incessantly performing; a Hawaiian melody at the moment, with Vibra-Harp.

"Maybe it wasn't a goose," Harry says. "Maybe it was a very little caddy with feathers."

"That's music," Ronnie sneers, of Ollie's observation. "Hey Webb, how come there isn't any beer in this place?"

"There's beer, there's beer. Miller Lite and Heineken's. What can I get everybody?"

Webb acts a little jumpy, and Rabbit worries that the party is in danger of flattening out. He misses, whom he never thought he would, Buddy Inglefinger, and tries to say the kind of thing Buddy would if he were here. "Speaking of dead geese," he says, "I noticed in the paper the other day where some anthropologist or something says about a fourth of the animal species on earth right now will be extinct by the year 2000."

"Oh *don't*," Peggy Fosnacht protests loudly, shaking herself ostentatiously, so the fat on her upper arms jiggles. She is wearing a short-sleeved dress, out of season. "Don't mention the year 2000, just the thought of it gives me the *creeps*."

Nobody asks her why.

Rabbit at last says, "Why? You'll still be alive."

"No I won't," she says flatly, wanting to make an argument even of that.

The heated flush the papal argument roused in Cindy still warms her throat and upper chest, that with its tiny gold cross sits half-exposed by the unbuttoned two top buttons or stringlatches of the Arab-style robe, her tapering forearms looking childishly fragile within its wide sleeves, her feet bare but for the thinnest golden sandals below the embroidered hem. In the commotion as Webb takes drink orders and Janice wobbles up to go to the john, Harry goes over and sits on a straight chair beside their young hostess. "Hey," he says, "I think the Pope's pretty great. He really knows how to use TV."

Cindy says, with a sharp quick shake of her face as if stung, "I don't like a lot of what he says either, but he's got to draw the line somewhere. That's his job."

"He's running scared," Rabbit offers. "Like everybody else."

She looks at him, her eyes a bit Chinesey like Mim said, the fatty pouches of her lower lids giving her a kind of squint, as if she's been beaten or is suffering from ragweed, so she twinkles even as she's being serious, her pupils large in this shadowy center of the room away from the track lighting. "Oh, I can't think of him that way, though you're probably right. I've still too much parochial school in me." The ring of brown around her pupils is smooth chocolate, without flecks or fire. "Webb's so gentle, he never pushes me. After Betsey was born, and we agreed he's been father enough, Webb, I couldn't make myself use a diaphragm, it seemed so evil, and he didn't want me on the Pill, what he'd read about it, so he offered to get himself fixed, you know, like the men are paid to do in India, what do they call it, a vasectomy. Rather than have him do that and do God knows what to his psyche, I went impulsively one day and got myself fitted for the diaphragm, I still don't know if I'm putting it in right when I do it, but poor Webb. You know he had five other children by his other wives, and they're both after his money *con*stantly. Neither has married though they're living with men, that's what I would call immoral, to keep bleeding him that way."

This is more than Harry had bargained for. He tries to confess back at her. "Janice had her tubes cauterized the other year, and I must say, it's great not to have to worry about it, whenever you want it, night or day, no creams or crap or anything. Still, sometimes she starts crying, for no reason. At being sterile at forty-three."

"Well of course, Harry. I would too." Cindy's lips are long and in their lipstick lie together with a wised-up closeness of fit, a downward tug at the end of sentences, he has never noticed before tonight.

"But you're a baby," he tells her.

Cindy gives him a wise slanting look and almost toughly says, "I'm getting there, Harry. I'll be thirty this April."

Twenty-nine, she must have been twenty-two when Webb started fucking her, what a sly goat, he pictures her body all brown with its little silken slopes and rolls of slight excess inside the rough loose garment, shadowy spaces you could put your hand in, for the body to breathe in that desert heat, it goes with the gold threads on her feet and the bangles around her wrists, still small and round as a child's, veinless. The vehemence of his lust dries his mouth. He stands to go after his brandy but loses his balance so his knee knocks against Peggy Fosnacht's ponderous square chair. She is not in it, she is standing at the top of the two steps that lead upward out of the living room, with the out-of-date dull plaid coat she came in draped around her shoulders. She looks down at them like one placed above and beyond, driven away.

Ollie, though, is seated around the Parsons table waiting for Webb to bring the beer and oblivious of his wife's withdrawal. Ronnie Harrison, so drunk his lips are wet and the long hair he brushes across his bald spot stands up in a loop, asks Ollie, "How goes the music racket these days? I hear the guitar craze is over now there's no more revolution."

"They're into flutes now, it's weird. Not just the girls, but guys too, who want to play jazz. A lot of spades. A spade came in the other day wanted to buy a platinum flute for his daughter's eighteenth birthday, he said he read about some Frenchman who had one. I said, 'Man, you're crazy. I can't begin to guess what a flute like that would cost.' He said, 'I don't give a flying fuck, man,' and showed me this roll of bills, there must have been an inch of hundred-dollar bills in it. At least those on top were hundreds."

Any more feeling-out with Cindy would be too much for now; Harry sits down heavily on the sofa and joins the male conversation. "Like those gold-headed putters a few years ago. Boy I bet *they've* gone up in value."

Like Peggy, he is ignored. Harrison is boring in. These insurance salesmen: they have that way of putting down their heads and just boring in until it's either scream or say, sure, you'll take out another fifty thousand of renewable life.

Ronnie says to Ollie, "How about electric stuff? You see this guy on television even has an electric violin. That stuff must cost."

"An arm and a leg," Ollie says, looking up gratefully as Webb sets a Heineken's on a light square of the table in front of him. "Just the amplifiers take you into the thousands," he says, pleased to be talking, pleased to sound rich. Poor sap, when most of his business is selling thirteen-year-old dumplings records to make them wet their pants. What did Nelson used to call it? Lollipop music. Nelson used to be serious about the guitar, that one he saved from the fire and then the one they got him with a big pearl plate on the face, but the chords stopped coming from his room after school when he got his driver's license.

Ronnie has tilted his head to bore in at a different angle. "You know I'm in client service at Schuylkill Mutual and my boss told me the other day, 'Ron, you cost this company eight thousand seven hundred last year.' That's not salary, that's benefits. Retirement, health insurance, participation options. How do you handle that in your operation? If you don't have employer-financed insurance and retirement in this day and age, you're in the soup. People expect it and without it they won't perform."

Ollie says, "Well, I'm my own employer in a way. Me and my partners—"

"How about Keogh? You gotta have Keogh."

"We try to keep it simple. When we started out—"

"You gotta be kidding, Ollie. You're just robbing yourself. Schuylkill Mutual offers a terrific deal on Keogh, and we could plug you in, in fact we advise plugging you in, on the corporate end so not a nickel comes out of your personal pocket, it comes out of the corporate pocket and there's that much less for Uncle to tax. These poor saps carrying their own premiums with no company input are living in the dark ages. There's nothing shady about rigging it this way, we're just using the laws the government has put there. They *want* people to take advantage, it all works to up the gross national product. You know what I mean by Keogh, don't you? You're looking kind of blank."

"It's something like social security."

"A thousand times better. Social security's just a rip-off to benefit the freeloaders now; you'll never see a penny of what you put in. In the Keogh plan, up to seventy-five hundred goes untaxed, every year; you just set it aside, with our help. Our usual suggestion is, depending on circumstances—how many dependents you got?—"

"Two, if you count the wife. My son Billy's out of college and up in Massachusetts studying specialized dentistry."

Ronnie whistles. "Boy, you were smart. Limiting yourself to one offspring. I saddled myself with three and only these last few years am I feeling out of the woods. The older boy, Alex, has taken to electronics but the middle boy, Georgie, needed special schools from the start. Dyslexia. I'd never heard of it, but I'll tell you I've heard of it now. Couldn't make any goddam sense at all out of anything written, and you'd never know it from his conversation. He could outtalk me at this job, that's for certain, but he can't see it. He wants to be an artist, Jesus. There's no money there, Ollie, you know that better than I do. But even with just the one kid, you don't want him to starve if you were suddenly out of the picture, or the good woman either. Any man in this day and age carrying less than a hundred, a hundred fifty thousand dollars straight life just isn't being realistic. A decent funeral alone costs four, five grand."

"Yeah, well—"

"Lemme get back to the Keogh a minute. We generally recommend a forty-sixty split, take the forty per cent of seventy-five hundred in straight life premiums, which generally comes to close to the hundred thou, assuming you pass the exam that is. You smoke?"

"Off and on."

"Uh-oh. Well, lemme give you the name of a doctor who gives an exam everybody can live with."

Ollie says, "I think my wife wants to go."

"You're kidding, Foster."

"Fosnacht."

"You're kidding. This is Saturday night, man. You got a gig or something?"

"No, my wife—she needs to go to some anti-nuclear meeting tomorrow morning at some Universalist church."

"No wonder she's down on the Pope then. I hear the Vatican and Three Mile Island are hand-in-glove, just ask friend Harry here. Ollie, here's my card. Could I have one of yours please?"

"Uh—"

"That's O.K. I know where you are. Up there next to the fuck movies. I'll come by. No bullshit, you really owe it to yourself to listen to some of these opportunities. People keep saying the economy is shot but it isn't shot at all from where I sit, it's booming. People are begging for shelters."

Harry says, "Come on, Ron. Ollie wants to go."

"Well, I don't exactly but Peggy—"

"Go. Go in peace, man." Ronnie stands and makes a ham-handed blessing gesture. "Gott pless Ameri-ca," he pronounces in a thick slow foreign accent, loud, so that Peggy, who has been conferring with the Murketts, patching things up, turns her back. She too went to high school with Ronnie and knows him for the obnoxious jerk he is.

"Jesus, Ronnie," Rabbit says to him when the Fosnachts have gone. "What a snow job."

"Ahh," Ronnie says. "I wanted to see how much garbage he could eat."

"I've never been that crazy about him either," Harry confesses. "He treats old Peggy like dirt."

Janice, who has been consulting with Thelma Harrison about something, God knows what, their lousy children, over-hears this and turns and tells Ronnie, "Harry screwed her years ago, that's why he minds Ollie." Nothing like a little booze to freshen up old sore points.

Ronnie laughs to attract attention and slaps Harry's knee. "You screwed that big pig, funny eyes and all?"

Rabbit pictures that heavy glass egg with the interior tear-drop of air back in Ma Springer's living room, its smooth heft in his hand, and imagines himself making the pivot from pounding it into Janice's stubborn dumb face to finishing up with a one-handed stuff straight down into Harrison's pink brainpan. "It seemed a good idea at the time," he has to admit, uncross-ing his legs and stretching them in preparation for an extended night. The Fosnachts' leaving is felt as a relief throughout the room. Cindy is tittering to Webb, clings briefly to his coarse gray sweater in her rough loose Arab thing, like a loving pair advertising vacations abroad. "Janice had run off at the time with this disgusting Greek smoothie Charlie Stavros," Harry explains to anybody who will listen.

"O.K. O.K.," Ronnie says, "you don't need to tell us. We've all heard the story, it's ancient history."

"What isn't so ancient, you twerpy skinhead, is I had to kiss

Charlie goodbye today because Janice and her mother got him canned from Springer Motors."

"Harry likes to say that," Janice said, "but it was as much Charlie's idea as anybody's."

Ronnie is not so potted he misses the point. He tips his head and looks at Janice with a gaze that from Harry's angle is mostly furry white eyelashes. "You got your old boyfriend fired?" he asks her.

Harry amplifies, "All so my shiftless son who won't even finish college with only one year to go can take over this job he's no more qualified for than, than——"

"Than Harry was," Janice finishes for him—in the old days she would never have been quick with sass like that—and giggles. Harry has to laugh too, even before Ronnie does. His cock isn't the only thick thing about Harrison.

"This is what I like," Webb Murkett says in his gravelly voice above them. "Old friends." He and Cindy side by side stand presiding above their circle as the hour settles toward midnight. "What can I get anybody? More beer? How about a light highball? Scotch? Irish? A CC and seven?" Cindy's tits jut out in that caftan or burnoose or whatever like the angle of a tent. Desert silence. Crescent moon. Put the camel to bed. "We-ell," Webb exhales with such pleasure he must be feeling that Greensleeves, "and what did we think of the Fosnachts?"

"They won't do," Thelma says. Harry is startled to hear her speak, she has been so silent. If you close your eyes and pretend you're blind, Thelma has the nicest voice. He feels melancholy and mellow, now that the invasion from the pathetic world beyond the Flying Eagle has been repelled.

"Ollie's been a sap from Day One," he says, "but she didn't used to be such a blabbermouth. Did she, Janice?"

Janice is cautious, defending her old friend. "She always had a tendency," she says. "Peggy never thought of herself as attractive, and that was a problem."

"You did, huh?" Harry accuses.

She stares at him, having not followed, her face moistened as by a fine spray.

"Of *course* she did," Webb gallantly intervenes, "Jan is mighty attractive, at least to this old party," and goes around behind her chair and puts his hands on her shoulders, close to her neck so that her shoulders hunch.

Cindy says, "She was a lot pleasanter just chatting with me and Webb at the door. She said she sometimes just gets carried away."

Ronnie says, "Harry and Janice I guess see a lot of 'em. I'll have a brew as long as you're up, Webb."

"We don't at all. Nelson's best friend is their obnoxious son Billy, is how they got to the wedding. Webb, could you make that two?"

Thelma asks Harry, her voice softly pitched for him alone, "How *is* Nelson? Have you heard from him in his married state?"

"A postcard. Janice has talked to them on the phone a couple times. She thinks they're bored."

Janice interrupts, "I don't think, Harry. He *told* me they're bored."

Ronnie offers, "If you've done all your fucking before marriage, I guess a honeymoon can be a drag. Thanks, Webb."

Janice says, "He said it's been chilly in the cabin."

"Too lazy no doubt to carry the wood in from the stack outside," Harry says. "Yeah, thanks." The *pffft* of opening a can isn't near as satisfying since they put that safety tab on to keep idiots from choking themselves.

"Harry, he told us they've been having a fire in the wood stove all day long."

"Burning it all up so somebody else can chop. He's his mamma's boy."

Thelma, tired perhaps of the tone the Angstroms keep setting, lifts her voice and bends her face far back, exposing a startling length of sallow throat. "Speaking of the cold, Webb. Are you and Cindy going away at all this winter?" They usually go to an island in the Caribbean. The Harrisons once went with them, years ago. Harry and Janice have never been.

Webb has been circling behind Thelma getting a highball for someone. "We've talked about it," he tells Thelma. Through the haze of beer laid over brandy there seems an enchanting conspiracy between her bent-back throat and Webb's arched and lowered voice. Old friends, Harry thinks. Fit like pieces of a puzzle. Webb bends down and reaches over her shoulder to put a tall weak Scotch-and-soda on a dark square in front of her. "I'd like to go," he is going on, "where they have a golf course. You can get a pretty fair deal, if you shop around for a package."

"Let's all go," Harry announces. "The kid's taking over the lot Monday, let's get the hell out of here."

"Harry," Janice says, "he's not taking over the lot, you're being irrational about this. Webb and Ronnie are shocked, to hear you talk about your son this way."

"They're not shocked. *Their* kids are eating 'em alive too. I want to go to the Caribbean and play golf this winter. Let's bust out. Let's ask Buddy Inglefinger to be the fourth. I hate the winter around here—there's no snow, you can't ice-skate, it's just boring and raw, month after month. When I was a kid, there was snow all the time, what ever happened to it?"

"We had a ton of snow in '78," Webb observes.

"Harry, maybe it's time to go home," Janice tells him. Her mouth has turned to a slot, her forehead under her bangs is shiny.

"I don't want to go home. I want to go to the Caribbean. But first I want to go to the bathroom. Bathroom, home, Caribbean, in that order." He wonders if a wife like that ever dies of natural causes. Never, those dark wiry types, look at her mother, still running the show. Buried poor old Fred and never looked back.

Cindy says, "Harry, the downstairs john is plugged, Webb just noticed. Somebody must have used too much toilet paper."

"Peggy Gring, that's who," Harry says, standing and wondering why the wall-to-wall carpeting has a curve to it, like the deck of a ship falling away on all sides. "First she attacks the Pope, then she abuses the plumbing."

"Use the one in our bedroom," Webb says to him. "At the head of the stairs, turn left, past the two closet doors with the slats."

". . . wiping away her tears . . . ," Rabbit hears Thelma Harrison saying dryly as he leaves. Up the two carpeted steps, his head floating far above his feet. Then down a hall and up stairs in different-colored carpeting, a dirty lime, more wear, older part of the house. Someone else's upstairs always has that hush. Tired nights, a couple talking softly to themselves.

The voices below him fade. Turn left, Webb had said. Slatted doors. He stops and peeks in. Female clothes, strips of many colors, fragrant of Cindy. Get her down there in that sand, who can say, talking to him about her diaphragm already. He finds the bathroom. Every light in it is lit. What a waste of energy. Going down with all her lights blazing, the great ship America. This bathroom is smaller than the one downstairs, and of a deeper tint, wall tiles and wallpaper and shag carpeting and towels and tinted porcelain all brown, with touches of tangerine. He undoes his fly and in a stream of blissful relief fills one of this room's bright bowls with gold. His bubbles multiply like coins. He and Janice took their Krugerrands from the bedside table drawer and together went downtown and into the Brewer Trust with them and nestled them in their little cylinders like blue-tinted dollhouse toilets into their stout long safe-deposit box and in celebration had drinks with their lunch at the Crêpe House before he went back to the lot. Because he was never circumcised he tends to retain a drop or two, and pats his tip with a piece of lemon-yellow toilet paper, plain, the comic strips were to amuse guests. Who was Thelma saying would wipe away her tears? The shocking flash of long white throat, muscular, the swallowing muscles developed, she must have something, to hold Harrison. Maybe she meant Peggy using toilet paper to wipe away her tears had clogged the toilet. Cindy's eyes had had a glisten, too shy to like arguing like that with poor Peggy, telling him instead about her diaphragm, Jesus, inviting him to think about it, her sweet red dark deep, could she mean it? *Getting there, Harry*: her voice more wised-up and throaty than he ever noticed before, her eyes pouchy, sexy when women's lower lids are like that, up a little like eggcups, his daughter's lids he noticed that day did that. All around in here are surfaces that have seen Cindy stark naked. Harry looks at his face in this less dazzling mirror, fluorescent tubes on either side, and his lips look less blue, he is sobering up for the drive home. Oh but blue still the spaces in his eyes, encircling the little black dot through which the world flows, a blue with white and gray mixed in from the frost of his ancestors, those beefy blonds in horned helmets pounding to a pulp with clubs the hairy mammoth and the slant-eyed Finns amid snows so pure and widespread their whiteness would have made eyes less pale hurt. Eyes and hair and skin, the dead live in us though their brains are dust and their eyesockets of bone empty. His pupils enlarge as he leans closer to the mirror, making a shadow, seeking to see if there truly is a soul. That's what he used to think ophthalmologists were looking at when they pressed that little hot periscope of a flashlight tight against your eye. What they saw, they never told him. He sees nothing but black, out of focus, because his eyes are aging.

He washes his hands. The faucet is one of those single-handed Lavomaster mixers with a knob on the end of the handle like a clown's nose or big pimple, he can never remember which way is hot and which cold, what was wrong with the old two faucets that said H and C? The basin, though, is good, with a wide lip of several ledges to hold soap without its riding off, these little ridges most basins have now don't hold anything, dinky cheap pseudo-marble, he supposes if you're in the roofing industry you know plumbing suppliers who can still provide the good stuff, even though there's not much market for it. The curved lavender bar he has right in his hands must have lost its lettering making lather for Cindy's suntanned skin, suds in her crotch, her hair must be jet black there, her eyebrows are: you should look at a woman's eyebrows not the hair on her head for the color of her pussy. This bathroom has not been so cleaned up for guests as the downstairs one, *Popular Mechanics* on the straw hamper next to the toilet, the towels slung crooked on the plastic towel holders and a touch of damp to them, the Murketts showering just a few hours ago for this party. Harry considers opening this bathroom cabinet as he did the other one but thinking of fingerprints notices the chrome rim and refrains. Nor does he dry his hands, for fear of touching the towel Webb used. He has seen that long yellow body in the Flying Eagle locker room. The man has moles all across his back and shoulders that probably aren't contagious but still.

He can't return downstairs with wet hands. That shit Harrison would make some crack. *Ya still got scum on your hands, ya jerkoff.* Rabbit stands a moment in the hall, listening to the noise of the party rise, a wordless clatter of voices happy without him, the women's the most distinct, a kind of throbbing in it like the melody you sometimes hear in a ragged engine

idling, a song so distinct you expect to hear words. The hall is
carpeted here not in lime but in a hushed plum, and he moves
to follow its color to the threshold of the Murketts' bedroom.
Here it happens. It hollows out Harry's stomach, makes him
faintly sick, to think what a lucky stiff Webb is. The bed is low
in modern style, a kind of tray with sides of reddish wood, and
the covers had been pulled up hastily rather than made. Had
it just happened? Just before the showers before the party that
left the towels in the bathroom damp? In mid-air above the
low bed he imagines in afterimage her damp and perfect toes,
those sucky little dabtoes whose print he has often spied on the
Flying Eagle flagstones, here lifted high to lay her cunt open,
their baby dots mingling with the moles on Webb's back. It
hurts, it isn't *fair* for Webb to be so lucky, not only to have a
young wife but no old lady Springer on the other side of the
walls. Where do the Murketts put their kids? Harry twists his
head to see a closed white door at the far other end of the plum
carpet. There. Asleep. He is safe. The carpet absorbs his footsteps as, silent as a ghost, he follows its color into the bedroom.
A cavernous space, forbidden. Another shadowy presence jars
his heart: a man in blue suit trousers and rumpled white shirt
with cuffs folded back and a loosened necktie, looking overweight and dangerous, is watching him. Jesus. It is himself, his
own full-length reflection in a large mirror placed between two
matching bureaus of wood bleached so that the grain shows
through as through powder. The mirror faces the foot of the
bed. Hey. These two. It hasn't been just his imagination. They
fuck in front of a mirror. Harry rarely sees himself head to toe
except when he's buying a suit at Kroll's or that little tailor on
Pine Street. Even there you stand close in to the three-way
mirrors and there's not this weird surround of space, so he's
meeting himself halfway across the room. He looks mussed
and criminal, a burglar too overweight for this line of work.

Doubled in the mirror, the calm room holds few traces of
the Murketts' living warmth. No little lacy bits of underwear
lying around smelling of Cindy-cunt. The curtains are a thick
red striped material like a giant clown's pants ballooning, and
they have window shades of that room-darkening kind that
he keeps asking Janice to get; now that the leaves are letting
go the light barrels through the copper beech right into his

face at seven in the morning, he's making nearly fifty thousand a year and this is how he has to live, he and Janice will never get themselves organized. The far window here with its shade drawn for a nap must overlook the pool and the stand of woods everybody has up here in this development between the houses, but Harry doesn't want to get himself that deep into the room, already he's betraying hospitality. His hands have dried, he should go down. He is standing near a corner of the bed, its mute plane lower than his knees, the satiny peach bedspread tugged smooth in haste, and he impulsively, remembering the condoms he used to keep in a parallel place, steps to the curly maple bedside table and ever so stealthily pulls out the small drawer. It was open an inch anyway. No diaphragm, that would be in the bathroom. A ballpoint pen, an unlabelled box of pills, some match folders, a few receipts tossed in, a little yellow memo pad with the roofing company logo on it and a diagonally scrawled phone number, a nail clippers, some paper clips and golf tees, and—his thumping heart drowns out the mumble of the party beneath his feet. At the back of the drawer are tucked some black-backed Polaroid instant photos. That SX-70 Webb was bragging about. Harry lifts the little stack out delicately, turns it over, and studies the photos one by one. Shit. He should have brought his reading glasses, they're downstairs in his coat pocket, he must get over pretending he doesn't need them.

The top photo, flashlit in this same room, on this same satiny bedspread, shows Cindy naked, lying legs spread. Her pubic hair is even darker than he imagined, the shape of it from this angle a kind of T, the upright of the T infolded upon a redness as if sore, the underside of her untanned ass making a pale blob on either side. At arm's length he holds the glazed picture closer to the bedside light; his eyes water with the effort to see everything, every crease, every hair. Cindy's face, out of focus beyond her breasts, which droop more to either side than Harry would have hoped, smiles with nervous indulgence at the camera. Her chin is doubled, looking so sharply down. Her feet look enormous. In the next shot, she has turned over, showing a relaxed pair of buttocks, fish-white with an eyelike widening staring from the crack. For the next couple of photos the camera has switched hands, and old Webb, stringy and sheepish, stands as Harry has often seen him after a shower, except without the hard-on, which he is helping with his hand. Not a great hard-on, pointing to ten o'clock, not even ten but more like a little after nine, but then you can't expect a guy over fifty to go for high noon, leave that to the pimply teen-agers: when Rabbit was fourteen in soc sci class, a spot of sun, the shadow of Lotty Bingaman's armpit as she raised her hand with a pencil in it, that sweet strain of cloth and zipper against thick blood. Webb has length but not much bulk at the base; still, there he is, game and even with the pot belly and gnarled skinny legs and shit-eating expression somehow debonair, not a hair on his wavy head out of place. The next shots were in the nature of experiments, by natural light, the shades must have all been up, bold to the day: slabby shapes and shelves of flesh interlocked and tipped toward violet by the spectrum of underexposure. Harry deciphers one bulge as Cindy's cheek, and then the puzzle fits, she is blowing him, that purply stalk is his prick rooted in her stretched lips and the fuzzy foreground is Webb's chest hair as he takes the picture. In the next one he has improved the angle and light and the focus is perfect on the row of one eye's black lashes. Beyond the shiny tan tip of her nose, her fingers, boneless and blue-knuckled, with stubby nails, hold the veined thing in its place, her little finger lifted as on a flute. What was Ollie saying about flutes? For the next shot Webb had the idea of using the mirror; he is standing sideways with the camera squarely where his face ought to be and Cindy's own dear face impaled, as she kneels naked, on this ten-o'clock hook of his. Her profile is snub-nosed and her nipples jut out stiff. The old bastard's tricks have turned the little bitch on. But her head seems so small and round and brave, stuck on his prick like a candy apple. Harry wants in the next picture to see come like toothpaste all over her face like in the fuck movies, but Webb has turned her around and is fucking her from behind, his prick vanished in the fish-white curve of her ass and his free hand steadying her with his thumb sunk where her asshole would be; her tits hang down pear-shaped in their weight and her legs next to Webb's appear stocky. She's getting there. She will get fatter. She will turn ugly. She is looking into the mirror and laughing. Perhaps in the difficulty of keeping her balance while Webb's one hand operates the camera, Cindy laughed at that moment a big red laugh like a girl on a poster, with this yellow prick in her from behind. The light in the room must have been dying that day for the flesh of both the Murketts appears golden and the furniture reflected in the mirror is dim in blue shadow as if underwater. This is the last picture; there were eight and a camera like this takes ten. *Consumer Reports* had a lot to say a while ago about the SX-70 Land Camera but never did explain what the SX stood for. Now Harry knows. His eyes burn.

The party noise below is lessening, perhaps they are listening for a sound from upstairs, wondering what has happened to him. He slips the Polaroids back into the drawer, face down, black backs up, and tries to slide shut the drawer to the exact inch it was open by. The room otherwise is untouched; the mirror will erase his image instantly. The only clue remaining, he has given himself an aching great erection. He can't go downstairs like this: he tries to tear his mind loose from that image of her open mouth laughing at the sight of herself being fucked, who would have thought sweet Cindy could be so dirty? It takes some doing to realize that other boys are like you are, that dirty, and then to realize that girls can go right along with it takes more than one lifetime to assimilate. Rabbit tries to fling away that laugh, out of his mind, but it has no more carry to it than a handkerchief. He tries to displace what he has just seen with his other secrets. His daughter. His gold. His son coming down from the Poconos tomorrow to claim his place at the lot. That does it, the thing is wilting. Holding gloomy Nelson firmly in his mind, Harry goes into the bathroom and turns on the faucet as if washing his hands in case somebody down below is listening while he undoes his belt and tucks himself properly into his underpants. What is killing, he has seen her laugh that same laugh at poolside, at something he or Buddy Inglefinger or even some joker from outside their group altogether has just said. She'd go down on anybody.

As he descends the stairs his head still feels to be floating on a six-foot string attached to his big shoes. The gang in the long living room has realigned itself in a tighter circle about the Parsons table. There seems to be no place for him. Ronnie Harrison looks up. "My God, whatcha been doin', jacking off?"

"I'm not feeling so great," Rabbit says, with dignity.

"Your eyes look red," Janice says. "Have you been crying again?"

They are too excited by the topic among themselves to tease him long. Cindy doesn't even turn around. The nape of her neck is thick and brown, soft and impervious. Treading to them on spongy steps across the endless pale carpeting, he pauses by the fireplace mantel to notice what he had failed to notice before, two Polaroid snaps propped up, one each of the Murketts' little children, the five-year-old boy with an outsize fielder's mitt standing sadly on the bricks of their patio, and the three-year-old girl on this same hazily bright summer afternoon, before the parents took a nap, squinting with an obedient and foolish half-smile up toward some light-source that dazzles her. Betsey is wearing both pieces of a play-muddied little bikini and Webb's shadow, arms lifted to his head as if to scare her with horns, fills one corner of the exposed square of film. These are the missing two shots from that pack of ten.

"Hey, Harry, how about the second week of January?" Ronnie hoots at him.

They have all been discussing a shared trip to the Caribbean, and the women are as excited about it as the men.

It is after one when he and Janice drive home. Brewer Heights is a development of two-acre lots off the highway to Maiden Springs, a good twenty minutes from Mt. Judge. The road sweeps down in stylish curves; the developer left trees, and six hours ago when they drove up this road each house was lit in its bower of unbulldozed woods like displays in the façade of a long gray department store. Now the houses, all but the Murketts', are dark. Dead leaves swirl in the headlights, pour from the trees in the fall wind as if from bushel baskets. The seasons catch up to you. The sky gets streaky, the trees begin to be bare. Harry can think of little to say, intent upon steering on these winding streets called drives and boulevards. The stars flickering through the naked swaying treetops of Brewer Heights yield to the lamp-lit straightaway of the Maiden Springs Pike. Janice drags on a cigarette; the glow expands in the side of his vision, and falls away. She clears her throat and says, "I suppose I should have stuck up more for

Peggy, she being an old friend and all. But she did talk out of turn, I thought."

"Too much women's lib."

"Too much Ollie maybe. I know she keeps thinking of leaving him."

"Aren't you glad we have all that behind us?"

He says it mischievously, to hear her grapple with whether they did or didn't, but she answers simply, "Yes."

He says nothing. His tongue feels trapped. Even now, Webb is undressing Cindy. Or she him. And kneeling. Harry's tongue seems stuck to the floor of his mouth like those poor kids every winter who insist on touching their tongues to iron railings.

Janice tells him, "Your idea of taking this trip in a bunch sure took hold."

"It'll be fun."

"For you men playing golf. What'll *we* do all day?"

"Lie in the sun. There'll be things. They'll have tennis courts." This trip is precious to him, he speaks of it gingerly.

Janice drags again. "They keep saying now how sunbathing leads to cancer."

"No faster than smoking."

"Thelma has this condition where she shouldn't be in the sun at all, it could kill her she's told me. I'm surprised she's so keen on going."

"Maybe she won't be in the morning on second thought. I don't see how Harrison can afford it, with that kid of theirs in defective school."

"Can we I wonder? Afford it. On top of the gold."

"Honey, of course. The gold's already gone up more than the trip will cost. We're so pokey, we should have taken up travelling years ago."

"You never wanted to go anywhere, with just me."

"Of course I did. We were running scared. We had the Poconos to go to."

"I was wondering, it might mean leaving Nelson and Pru just at the time."

"Forget it. The way she hung on to Nelson, she'll hang on to this baby till the end of January. Till Valentine's Day."

"It seems mean," she says. "And then leaving Nelson at the lot alone with too much responsibility."

"It's what he wanted, now he's got it. What can happen? Jake and Rudy'll be around. Manny'll run his end."

Her cigarette glows once more, and then with that clumsy scrabbling motion that always annoys him she stubs it out. He hates having the Corona ashtray dirty, it smells for days even after you've emptied it. She sighs. "I wish in a way it was just us going, if we must go."

"We don't know the ropes. Webb does. He's been there before, I think he's been going since long before Cindy, with his other wives."

"You can't mind Webb," she admits. "He's nice. But to tell the truth I could do without the Harrisons."

"I thought you had a soft spot for Ronnie."

"That's you."

"I hate him," Rabbit says.

"You like him, all that vulgarity. He reminds you of basket-ball days. Anyway it's not just him. Thelma worries me."

"How can she? She's a mouse."

"I think she's very fond of you."

"I never noticed. How can she be?" Stay off Cindy, he'll let it all out. He tries to see those photographs again, hair by hair in his mind's eye, and already they are fading. The way their bodies looked golden at the end, like gods.

Janice says with a sudden surprising stiffness, "Well, I don't know what you think's going to happen down there but we're not going to have any funny stuff. We're too *old*, Harry."

A pick-up truck with its high beams glaring tailgates him blindingly and then roars around him, kids' voices jeering.

"The drunks are out," he says, to change the subject.

"What were you *doing* up there in the bathroom so long anyway?" she asks.

He answers primly, "Waiting for something to happen that didn't."

"Oh. Were you sick?"

"Heading toward it, I thought. That brandy. That's why I switched to beer."

Cindy is so much on his mind he cannot understand why Janice fails to mention her, it must be deliberate. All that blow-ing, Lord. There's birth control. White gobs of it pumping in, being swallowed; those little round teeth and the healthy low baby gums that show when she laughs. Webb on front and him from behind, or the other way around, Harry doesn't care. Ronnie operating the camera. His prick has reawaked, high noon once more in his life, and the steering wheel as they turn into Central Street caresses its swollen tip through the cloth. Janice should appreciate this: if he can get it up to their room intact.

But her mind has wandered far from sex, for as they head down through the cones of limb-raddled light along Wilbur she says aloud, "Poor Nelson. He seemed so young, didn't he, going off with his bride?"

This town they know so well, every curb, every hydrant, where every mailbox is. It gives way before them like a veil, its houses dark, their headlights low. "Yeah," he agrees. "You sometimes wonder," he hears himself go on, "how badly you yourself fucked up a kid like that."

"We did what we could," Janice says, firm again, sounding like her mother. "We're not God."

"Nobody is," Rabbit says, scaring himself.

IV

THE HOSTAGES have been taken. Nelson has been working at Springer Motors for five weeks. Teresa is seven months pregnant and big as a house, a house within a house as she slops around Mom-mom's in those maternity slacks with Spandex in front and some old shirts of Dad's he let her have. When she walks down the upstairs hall from the bathroom she blocks out all the light, and when she tries to help in the kitchen she drops a dish. Because there are five of them now they have had to dip into the good china Mom-mom keeps in the breakfront and the dish Pru dropped was a good one. Though Mom-mom doesn't say much you can see by the way her throat gets mottled it's a deal for her, the kind of thing that is a big deal for old ladies, going on about those dishes that she and Fred bought fifty years ago together at Kroll's when the trolley cars ran all up and down Weiser every seven minutes and Brewer was a hot shit kind of place.

What Nelson can't stand about Pru, she farts. And lying on her back in bed because she can't sleep on her stomach, she snores. A light but raspy little rhythmic noise he can't ignore, lying there in the front room with the streetlights eating away at the windowshades and the cars roaring by on the street below. He misses his quiet old room at the back of the house. He wonders if Pru has what they call a deviated septum. Until he married her, he didn't notice that her nostrils aren't exactly the same size: one is more narrow than the other, as if her thin pointy hooked nose with its freckles had been given a sideways tweak when it was still soft back there in Akron. And then she keeps wanting to go to bed early at just the hour after dinner when the traffic outside picks up and he is dying to go out, over to the Laid-Back for a brew or two or even just down to the Superette on Route 422 to check out some new faces after the claustrophobia of hanging around the lot all day trying to deal around Dad and then coming home and having to deal around him some more, his big head grazing the ceiling and his silly lazy voice laying down the law on everything, if you listen, putting Nelson down, looking at him so nervously, with that sad-eyed little laugh, *Did I say that?*, when he thinks he's said something funny. The trouble with Dad is he's lived in a harem too long, Mom and Mom-mom doing everything for him. Any other man around except Charlie who was dying in front of your eyes and those goons he plays golf with, he gets nasty. Nobody except Nelson in the world seems to realize how nasty Harry C. Angstrom is and the pressure of it sometimes makes Nelson want to scream, his father comes into the room all big and fuzzy and sly when he's a killer, a body-count of two to his credit and his own son next if he can figure out how to do it without looking bad. Dad doesn't like to look bad anymore, that was one thing about him in the old days you could admire, that he didn't care that much how he looked from the outside, what the neighbors thought when he took Skeeter in for instance, he had this crazy dim faith in himself left over from basketball or growing up as everybody's pet or whatever so he could say Fuck You to people now and then. That spark is gone, leaving a big dead man on Nelson's chest. He tries to explain it to Pru and she listens but she doesn't understand.

At Kent she was slender and erect and quick in her way of walking, her terrific long carrotty hair up in a sleek twist when it wasn't let flat down her back looking ironed. Going to meet her up at the new part of Rockwell around five, a student out of water, he would feel enlarged to be taking this working woman a year older than he away from the typewriters and files and cool bright light; the administration offices seemed a piece of the sky of the world's real business that hung above the tunnels of the classes he wormed through every day. Pru had none of that false savvy, she knew none of the names to drop, the fancy dead, and could talk only about what was alive now, movies and records and what was on TV and the scandals day to day at work, who burst into tears and who had been propositioned by one of the deans. One of the other secretaries at work was fucking the man she worked for without much liking him but out of a kind of flip indifference to her own life and body and it thrilled Nelson to think how that could be Pru just as well, there was a tightness to lives in Pennsylvania that loosened out here and let people drift where they would. It thrilled him how casually tough she was, with that who-cares? way of walking beside him, smelling of perfume, and a softer scent attached to

her clothes, beneath all those trees they kept bragging about at
Kent, that and all those gyms in the Student Center Complex
and having the biggest campus bus system in the world, all that
bullshit heaped on to try to make people forget the only claim
to fame Kent State would ever have, which was May 4, 1970,
when the Guardsmen fired from Blanket Hill. As far as Nelson
was concerned they could have shot all those jerks. When in
'77 there was all that fuss about Tent City Nelson stayed in his
dorm. He didn't know Pru then. At one of the bars along Water Street she would get into the third White Russian and tell
him horror stories of her own growing up, beatings and rages
and unexplained long absences on her father's part and then
the tangled doings of her sisters as they matured sexually and
began to kick the house down. His tales seemed pale in comparison. Pru made him feel better about being himself. With
so many of the students he knew, including Melanie, he felt
mocked, outsmarted by them at some game he didn't want
to play, but with Pru Lubell, this secretary, he did not feel
mocked. They agreed about things, basic things. They knew
that at bottom the world was brutal, no father protected you,
you were left alone in a way not appreciated by these kids horsing around on jock teams or playing at being radicals or doing
the rah-rah thing or their own thing or whatever. That Nelson
saw it was all bullshit gave him for Pru a certain seriousness.
Across the plywood booth tables of the workingman's-type bar
in north Akron they used to go to in her car—she had a car
of her own, a salt-rotted old Plymouth Valiant, its front fender
flapping like a flag, and this was another thing he liked about
her, her being willing to drive such an ugly old clunker, and
having worked for the money to pay for it—Nelson could tell
he looked pretty good. In terms of the society she knew he
was a step up. And so was she, in terms of this environment,
the local geography. Not only a car but an apartment, small
but all her own, with a stove she cooked her own dinners on,
and liquor she would pour for him after putting on a record.
From their very first date, not counting the times they were
messing around with Melanie and her freaky SLDK friends,
Pru had taken him back to her apartment house in this town
called Stow, assuming without making any big deal of it that
fucking was what they were both after. She came with firm

quick thrusts that clipped him tight and secure into his own coming. He had fucked other girls before but hadn't been sure if they had come. With Pru he was sure. She would cry out and even flip a little, like a fish that flashes to the surface of a gloomy lake. And afterwards cooking him up something to eat she would walk around naked, her hair hanging down her back to about the sixth bump on her spine, even though there were a lot of windows across the apartment courtyard she could be seen from. Who cares? She liked being looked at, actually, in the dancing spots they went to some nights, and in private let him look at her from every angle, her big smooth body like that of a doll whose arms and legs and head stayed where you set them. His intense gratitude for all this, where another might have casually accepted, added to his value in her eyes until he was locked in, too precious to let go of, ever.

Now she sits all day watching the afternoon soaps with Mom-mom and sometimes Mom, *Search for Tomorrow* on Channel 10 and then *Days of Our Lives* on 3 and back to 10 for *As the World Turns* and over to 6 for *One Life to Live* and then 10 again for *The Guiding Light*, Nelson knows the routine from all those days before they let him work at the lot. Now Pru farts because of some way the baby is displacing her insides and drops things and says she thinks his father is perfectly nice.

He has told her about Becky. He told her about Jill. Pru's response is, "But that was long ago."

"Not to me. It is to him. He's forgotten, the silly shit, just to look at him you can see he's forgotten. He's forgotten every-thing he ever did to us. The stuff he did to Mom, incredible, and I don't know the half of it probably. He's so smug and *sat*-isfied, is what gets me. If I could *just once* make him see himself for the shit he is, I maybe could let it go."

"What good would it do, Nelson? I mean, your father's not perfect, but who is? At least he stays home nights, which is more than mine ever did."

"He's gutless, that's why he stays home. Don't you think he wouldn't like to be out chasing pussy every night? Just the way he used to look at Melanie. It isn't any great love of Mom that holds him back, I tell you that. It's the lot. Mom has the whip hand now, no thanks to herself."

"Why, honey. I think from what I've seen your parents are

quite fond of each other. Couples that have stayed together that long, they must have something."

To dip his mind into this possibility disgusts Nelson. The wallpaper, its tangled pattern of things moving in and out of things, looks evil. As a child he was afraid of this front room where now they sleep, across the hall from the mumble of Mom-mom's television. Cars passing on Joseph Street, underneath the bare maple limbs, wheel sharp-edged panels around the walls, bright shapes rapidly altering like in those computer games that are everywhere now. When a car brakes at the corner, a patch of red shudders across the wallpaper and a pale framed print of a goateed farmer with a wooden bucket at some stone well: this fading print has always hung here. The farmer too had seemed evil to the child's eyes, a leering devil. Now Nelson can see the figure as merely foolish, sentimental. Still, the taint of malevolence remains, caught somewhere in the transparency of the glass. The red shudders, and winks away; a motor guns, and tires dig out. Go: the fury of this unseen car, escaping, becoming a mere buzz in the distance, gratifies Nelson vicariously.

He and Pru are lying in the old swaybacked bed he used to share with Melanie. He thinks of Melanie, unpregnant, free, having a ball at Kent, riding the campus buses, taking courses in Oriental religion. Pru is dead sleepy, lying there in an old shirt of Dad's buttoned at the breasts and unbuttoned over her belly. He had offered her some shirts of his, now that he has this job he has had to buy shirts, and she said they were too small and pinched. The room is hot. The furnace is directly under it and heat rises, there's nothing they can do about it, here it is the middle of November and they still sleep under a sheet. He is wide awake and will be for hours, agitated by his day. Those friends of Billy's are after him to buy some more convertibles and though the Olds Delta 88 Royale did sell for $3600 to that doctor Dad says and says Manny backs him up on this that by the time you figure in the deductible on the insurance and the carrying costs there really wasn't any profit.

And now the Mercury is in the shop though the insurance man wanted to declare it totalled, he said that would be simplest with a virtual antique like this, parts at a premium and the front end screwed up like somebody had done it deliberately;

Manny estimates that the repair costs are going to come in four to five hundred above the settlement check, they can't give you more than car book value, and when he asked Manny if some of the mechanics couldn't do it in their spare time he said, looking so solemn, his brow all furrowed and the black pores in his nose jumping out at you, *Kid, there is no spare time, these men come in here for their bread and butter*, implying he didn't, a rich man's son. Not that Dad backs him up in any of this, he takes the attitude the kid's being taught a lesson, and enjoys it. The only lesson Nelson's being taught is that everybody is out for their own little pile of dollars and nobody can look up to have any vision. He'll show them when he sells that Mercury for forty-five hundred or so, he knows a lot of guys at the Laid-Back money like that is nothing to. This Iranian thing is going to scare gas prices even higher but it'll blow over, they won't dare keep them long, the hostages. Dad keeps telling him how it costs three to five dollars a day every day to carry a car in inventory but he can't see why, if it's just sitting there on a lot you already own, the company even pays rent to itself, he's discovered, to gyp the government.

Pru beside him starts to snore, her head propped up on two pillows, her belly shiny like one of those puffballs you find in the woods attached to a rotten stump. Downstairs Mom and Dad are laughing about something, they've been high as kites lately, worse than kids, going out a lot more with that crummy crowd of theirs, at least kids have the excuse there isn't much else to do. He thinks of those hostages in Tehran and it's like a pill caught in his throat, one of those big dry vitamins Melanie was always pushing on him, when it won't go down or come up. Take a single big black helicopter in there on a moon-less night, commandos with blackened faces, a little piano wire around the throats of those freaky radical Arabs, *uuglh, arg*, you'd have to whisper, women and children first, and lift them all away. Drop a little tactical A-bomb on a minaret as a calling card. Or else a tunnel or some sort of boring machine like James Bond would have. That fantastic scene in *Moonraker* when he's dumped from the plane without a parachute and free-falls into one of the bad guys and steals his, can't be much worse than hang gliding. By the moonlight Pru's belly-button is casting a tiny shadow, it's been popped like inside out, he never knew a pregnant woman naked before, he had no idea it was that bad. Like a cannonball, that hit from behind and stuck.

Once in a while they get out. They have friends. Billy Fosnacht has gone back to Tufts but the crowd at the Laid-Back still gathers, guys and these scumbags from around Brewer still hanging around, with jobs in the new electronics plants or some government boondoggle or what's left of the downtown stores; you go into Kroll's these days, where Mom met Dad in prehistoric days, you go in through that forest where Weiser Square used to be and it's like the deserted deck of a battleship just after the Japs bombed Pearl Harbor, a few scared salesladies standing around cut off at the waist by the On Sale tables. Mom used to work at the salted nut and candy section but they don't have one anymore, probably figured out after thirty years and six people died of worms it wasn't sanitary. But if there hadn't been a nut counter Nelson wouldn't exist, or would exist as somebody else, which doesn't make sense. He and Pru don't know all their friends' first names, they have first names like Cayce and Pam and Jason and Scott and Dody and Lyle and Derek and Slim, and if you show up at the Laid-Back enough you get asked along to some of their parties. They live in places like those new condos with stained rough-planking walls and steep-pitched roofs like a row of ski lodges thrown up on the side of Mt. Pemaquid out near the Flying Eagle, or like those city mansions of brick and slate with lots of ironwork and chimneys that the old mill money built along the north end of Youngquist or out beyond the car yards and now are broken up into apartments, where they haven't been made into nursing homes or office buildings for cutesy outfits like handcrafted-leather shops and do-it-yourself framers and young architects specializing in solar panels and energy saving and young lawyers with fluffy hair and bandit mustaches along with their business suits, that charge their young clients a flat fee of three hundred dollars whether it's for a divorce or beating a possession rap. In these neighborhoods healthfood stores have sprung up, and little long restaurants in halfbasements serving vegetarian or macrobiotic or Israeli cuisine, and bookstores with names like Karma Paperbacks, and little shops heavy on macramé and batik and Mexican wedding shirts and Indian silk and those drifter hats that make everybody look like the part of his head with the brain in it has been cut off. Old machine shops with cinder-block sides now sell pieces of unpainted furniture you put together yourselves, for these apartments where everybody shares.

The apartment Slim shares with Jason and Pam is on the third floor of a tall old house on the high side of Locust, blocks beyond the high school, in the direction of Maiden Springs. A big bay of three four-paned windows overlooks the deadened heart of the city: where once the neon outlines of a boot, a peanut, a top hat, and a great sunflower formed a garland of advertisement above Weiser Square now only the Brewer Trust's beacons trained on its own granite façade mark the center of the downtown: four great pillars like four white fingers stuck in a rich black pie, the dark patch made by the planted trees of the so-called shopping mall. From this downtown the standard sodium-yellow lamps of the city streets spread outward, a rectilinear web receding down toward the curving river and on into suburbs whose glow flattens to a horizon swallowed by hills that merge with the clouds of night. Slim's front bay windows have in their upper panes the stained-glass transom lights, those simplified flowers of pieces of purple and amber and milky green, that are along with pretzels Brewer's pride. But the old floors of parqueted oak have been covered wall-to-wall with cheap shag carpeting speckled like pimento, and hasty plasterboard partitions have divided up the generous original rooms. The high ceilings have been lowered, to save heat, and reconstituted in soft white panels of something like pegboard. Nelson sits on the floor, his head tipped back, a can of beer cold between his ankles; he has shared two joints with Pru and the little holes in the ceiling are trying to tell him something, an area of them seems sharp and vivid and aggressive, like the blackheads on Manny's nose the other day, and then this look fades and another area takes it up, as if a jellyfish of intensity is moving transparently across the ceiling. Behind him on the wall is a large grimacing poster of Ilie Nastase. Slim belongs to a tennis club out next to the Hemmigtown Mall and loves Ilie Nastase. Nastase is beaded with sweat, his legs thick as posts. Hairy, knotty posts. The stereo is playing Donna Summer, something about a telephone, very loud. Out in the center of the room between Nelson and some potted ferns and broad-leaved plants like Mom-mom used to have in that side room off the living room (he remembers sitting with his father looking at them some day when an awful thing had happened, a thing enormous and hollow under them while the leaves of the plants drank the sunlight as these bigger plants too must do when the sun comes slanting in the tall bay windows) there is a space and in this space Slim is dancing like a snake on a string with another skinny boy with a short haircut called Lyle. Lyle has a narrow skull with hollows at the back and wears tight jeans and some long-sleeved shirt like a soccer shirt with a broad green stripe down the middle. Slim is queer and though Nelson isn't supposed to mind that he does. He also minds that there are a couple of slick blacks making it at the party and that one little white girl with that grayish kind of sharp-chinned Polack face from the south side of Brewer took off her shirt while dancing even though she has no tits to speak of and now sits in the kitchen with still bare tits getting herself sick on Southern Comfort and Pepsi. At these parties someone is always in the bathroom being sick or giving themselves a hit or a snort and Nelson minds this too. He doesn't mind any of it very much, he's just tired of being young. There's so much wasted energy to it. He sees on the ceiling that the jellyfish intensity flitting across the holes is energy such as flows through the binary bits of computers but he can't take it any further than that. At Kent he was curious about computer science but in just the introductory course Math 10061 in Merrill Hall the math got to be too much for him, all those Jewish kids and Koreans with faces flat as platters just breezing along like it was plain as day, what a function was, it didn't seem to be anything you could actually point to, just the general idea somehow of the equation, another jellyfish, but how to extract it out? It beat him. So he figured he might as well come home and share the wealth. His father was holding him on his lap that day, the sensation of a big warm sad-smelling body all around and under his has stayed with him along with a memory of a beam of sunlight eating into the crescent edge of a furry leaf in that iron table of green plants, it must have been around when Becky died. Mom-mom can't last forever and when she kicks the bucket that leaves him and Mom in charge of the lot, with Dad up front like one of those life-size cardboard cutouts you used to see in car showrooms before cardboard became too expensive. Those blacks mooching around so superior, that decided cool way they have of saying hello, daring you to outstare them, not taking responsibility for anything though, makes him itch with anger, though the joints should be working him around toward mellow by now. Maybe another beer. Then he remembers the beer between his knees, it's cold and heavy because it's full and fresh from Slim's fridge, and takes a sip. Nelson studies his hand carefully because it feels holding the can as though he has a mitten on.

Why doesn't Dad just die? People that age get diseases. Then he and Mom. He knows he can manage Mom.

He's not that young, he's turned twenty-three, and what makes him feel foolish among these people, he's married. Nobody else here looks married. There is sure nobody else pregnant, that it shows. It makes him feel put on display, as a guy who didn't know better. To be fair to her Pru didn't want to come out, she was willing to sit over there like one of these green plants basking in the light of the television set, watching *The Love Boat* and then *Fantasy Island* with poor old Mom-mom, she's been fading lately, Dad and Mom used to sit home with her but now like tonight they're out somewhere with that Flying Eagle crowd, incredible how irresponsible grownups so-called get when they think they're ahead of the game, Mom has told him all about their crazy gold, maybe he should have offered to stay home, him and Pru with Mom-mom, she's the one with all the cards after all, but by that time Pru had gotten herself dolled up thinking she owed Nelson a little social life because he was working so hard and always housebound with her—families, doing everything for each other out of imagined obligation and always getting in each other's way, what a tangle. Then once Pru got here and got a buzz on, the madwoman of Akron took over, she decided to play to the hilt the token pregnant woman, throwing her weight around, dancing in shoes she really shouldn't even be walking in, thick-soled wedgy platforms held on by thin green plastic strapping like that gimp the playground supervisors at the Mt. Judge Rec Field used to have you braid lanyards for a whistle out of, there was even he remembers a way of weaving called butterflies, you could make a keyholder this way as if kids ever had keys to hold. Maybe she's doing it out of spite. But he has undergone an abandonment of his own and enjoys watching her from a distance of his own, through the smoke. She has flash, Pru, flash and glitter in this electric-green beltless dress she bought herself at a new shop over on Locust where the old retired people are being forced out by gentrification, the middle class returning to the cities. Sleeves wide as wings lift when she whirls and that cannonball of a stomach sticks out tugging up her dress in front to show more of the orange elastic stockings the doctor told her to wear to save her young veins. Her shiny platforms can barely shuffle on the shag carpeting but she leaves them on, showing she can do it, more spite at him; her body as if skewered through a spot between her shoulder blades writhes to the music while her arms lift shimmery green and her fantastic long hair snaps in a circle, again and again.

Nelson cannot dance, which is to say he will not, for all dancing is now is standing in place and letting the devil of the music enter you, which takes more faith than he's got. He doesn't want to appear a fool. Now Dad, Dad would do it if he were here, just like when Jill was there he gave himself to Skeeter and never looked back even when all the worst had happened, such a fool he really believes there is a God he is the apple of the eye of. The dots on the ceiling don't let Nelson take this glimpse higher than this and he returns his eyes to Pru, painfully bright in the dazzle dress, its flow like a jewel turned liquid, her face asleep in the music above her belly, which is solid and not hers alone but also his, so he is dancing too. He hates for a second that in himself which cannot do it, just as he could not join in the flickering mind play of computer science and college generally and could not be the floating easy athlete his father had been. The dark second passes, dissolved by the certainty that some day he will have his revenge on them all.

Pru's partner for some of the dancing has been one of the sassy Brewer blacks, the bigger one, in bib overalls and cowboy boots, and then Slim comes out of a twirl over by the potted plants with Lyle and swings into orbit with Pru, who keeps at it whether or not anybody is there, up and down, little flips of her hands, and a head toss. Her face does look asleep. That hooked nose of hers sharp in profile. People keep touching her belly, as if for luck: in spinning and snapping their fingers their loose fingers trail across the sacred bulge where something that belongs to him too is lodged. But how to fend off their touches, how to protect her and keep her clean? She is too big, he would look like a fool, she likes the dirt, she came out of it. Once she drove him past her old home in Akron, she never took him in, what a sad row, houses with wooden porches with old refrigerators on them. Melanie would have been better, her brother played polo. At least Pru should take off her shoes. He sees himself rising up to tell her but in truth feels too stoned to move, obliged to sit here and mellow between the fluffy worms of the carpet and the worm holes of the ceiling. The music has gas bubbles in it, popping in the speakers, and Donna Summer's zombie voice slides in and out of itself, doubling, taking all parts. *Stuck on you, stuck like glue.* The fairy that Slim stopped dancing with offers Pru a toke and she sucks the wet tip of the joint and holds it down deep without losing a beat of the music, belly and feet keeping that twitch. Nelson sees that to an Akron slum kid like this Brewer is a city of hicks and she's showing them all something.

A girl he noticed before, she came here with some big red-faced clod who actually wore a coat and tie to this brawl, comes and sits on the floor beside Nelson under Ilie Nastase and takes the beer from between his ankles to sip from it. Her smiling pale round face looks a little lost here but willing to please. "Where do *you* live?" she asks, as if picking up with him a conversation begun with someone else.

"In Mt. Judge?" He thinks that's the answer.

"In an apartment?"

"With my parents and my grandmother."

"Why is that?" Her face shines amiably with sweat. She has been drinking too. But there is a calm about her he is grateful for. Her legs stretch out beside his in white pants that look radiant where that jellyfish of strangeness moves across them.

"It's cheaper." He softens this. "We thought no point in looking for a place until the baby comes."

"You have a wife?"

"There she is." He gestures toward Pru.

The girl drinks her in. "She's terrific."

"You could say that."

"What does *that* tone of voice mean?"

"It means she's bugging the shit out of me."

"Should she be bouncing like that? I mean, the baby."

"Well, they say exercise. Where do *you* live?"

"Not far. On Youngquist. Our apartment isn't near as grand as this, we're on the first floor back, overlooking a little yard where all the cats come. They say our building might be going condo."

"That good or bad?"

"Good if you have the money, bad if you don't I guess. We just started working in town and my—my man wants to go to college when we get our stake."

"Tell him, Forget it. I've been to college and it's absolute horse poop." She has a pleasant puffy look to her upper lip and he's sorry to see, from the way she holds her mouth, that he's left her nothing to say. "What do you work at?" he asks her.

"I'm a nurses' aide in an old people's home. I doubt if you know it, Sunnyside out toward the old fairgrounds."

"Isn't it depressing?"

"People say that but I don't mind it. They talk to me, that's mostly what people want, company."

"You and this man aren't married?"

"Not yet. He wants to get further along in life. I think it's good. We might want to change our minds."

"Smart. That chick in green out there got herself knocked up and I had no choice." Not much answer to this either. Yet the girl doesn't show boredom, like so many people do with him. At the lot he watches Jake and Rudy prattle away and he envies how they do it without feeling idiotic. This strange face hangs opposite his calmly, mildly attentive, the eyes a blue paler than you almost ever see and her skin milky and her nose slightly tipped up and her gingery hair loosely bundled to the back. Her ears are exposed and pierced but unadorned. In his stoned condition the squarish white folds of these ears seem very vivid. "You say you just moved to town," Nelson says. "Where'd you move from?"

"Near Galilee. Know where that is?"

"More or less. When I was a kid we went down there to the drag race strip a couple times."

"You can hear the engines from our place, on a quiet night. My room is on the side and I used to always hear them."

"Where we live there's always traffic going by. My room used to be out in back but now it's up front." Dear little ears, small like his, though nothing else about her is small, especially. Her thighs really fill those bright white pants. "What does your father do, he a farmer?"

"My father's dead."

"Oh. Sorry."

"No, it was hard, but he was getting along. He was a farmer, you're right, and he had the school bus contract for the township."

"Still, that's too bad."

"I have a wonderful mother though."

"What's wonderful about her?"

In his stupidity he keeps sounding combative. But she doesn't seem to mind. "Oh. She's just very understanding. And can be very funny. I have these two brothers—"

"You do?"

"Yes, and she's never tried to make me feel I should back down or anything because I'm a girl."

"Well why would she?" He feels jealous.

"Some mothers would. They think girls should be quiet and smart. Mine says women get more out of life. With men, it's if you don't win every time, you're nothing."

"Some momma. She has it all figured."

"And she's fatter than I am and I love her for that."

You're not fat, you're just nice, he wants to tell her. Instead he says, "Finish up the beer. I'll get us another."

"No thanks—what's your name?"

"Nelson." He should ask her hers but the words stick.

"Nelson. No thanks, I just wanted a sip. I should go see what Jamie's doing. He's in the kitchen with some girl—"

"Who's showing her tits."

"That's right."

"My theory on that is, those that got real tits to show don't." He glances down. The vertical ribs of her russet knit sweater are pushed slightly apart as they pass over the soft ample shelf there. Below that the white cloth of her slacks, taut in wrinkles where belly meets thighs in a triangle, has a radiance that manifests the diagonal run of the threads, the way the cloth was woven and cut. Below that her feet are bare, with a pinkness along the outer edge of each big toe fresh from the pressure of her discarded shoes.

The girl has been made to blush by this survey of her body. "What do you do since college, Nelson?"

"I just veg out. No, actually, I sell cars. Not your ordinary tacky cars but special old convertibles, that nobody makes anymore. Their value is going to go up and up, it *has* to."

"Sounds exciting."

"It is. Jesus, the other day in the middle of town I saw this white Thunderbird parked, with red leather seats, the guy still had the top down though it's getting pretty cold, and I nearly flipped. It looked like a yacht. When they turned out those things there wasn't all this penny-pinching."

"Jamie and I just bought a Corolla. It's in his name but I'm the one that uses it, there isn't any bus that goes out to the fairgrounds anymore and Jamie has a job he can walk to, in this place that makes bug-killers, you know, those electric grids with a purple light that people put outdoors by their pools or barbecues."

"Sounds groovy. Must be a slack season for him though."

"You'd think so but it's not, they're busy making them for next year, and they ship all over the South."

"Huh." Maybe they've had enough of this conversation. He doesn't want to hear any more about Jamie's bug-killers.

But the girl keeps going, she's relaxed with him now, and so young everything is new to her. Nelson guesses she's three or four years younger than he is. Pru is over a year older, and that irritates him right now, along with her defiant dancing and her pregnancy and all these blacks and queers she's not afraid of. "So I really should put in my half," she is explaining, "even though he makes twice what I do. His parents and my mother loaned us the down payment equally though I know she couldn't afford it. Next year if I can get a part-time job somewhere I want to begin nurse's training. Those RNs make a fortune doing just what I'm doing now, except they're allowed to give injections."

"Jesus, you want to spend your whole life around sick people?"

"I like taking care of things. On the farm until my father died there were always chickens and animals. I used to shear my own sheep even."

"Huh." Nelson has always been allergic to animals.

"Do you dance, Nelson?" she asks him.

"No. I sit and drink beer and feel sorry for myself." Pru is bouncing around now with a Puerto Rican or something. Manny has a couple of them working for him in the shop now. He doesn't know what disease they get as kids, but their cheeks have worse than pocks—like little hollow cuts all over.

"Jamie won't dance either."

"Ask one of the fairies. Or just go do it by yourself, somebody'll pick you up."

"I love to dance. Why do you feel sorry for yourself?"

"Oh . . . my father's a prick." He doesn't know why this popped out of his mouth. Something about the goody-goody way in which the girl speaks of her own parents. But in thinking of his father, what strikes Nelson about the large bland face that appears to his inner eye is a mournful helplessness. His father's face bloats like an out-of-focus close-up in some war movie in the scramble of battle before floating away. Big and white and vague as on that day when he held him on his lap, when the world was too much for the two of them.

"You shouldn't say that," the girl says, and stands. Luminous long legs. Her thighs make a kind of lap even when she stands. Her pink-rimmed bare feet sunk in the shag rug so close nearly kill him, they are so sexy. What did she say that for? Making him feel guilty and scolded. Her own father is dead. She makes him feel he's killed his. She can go fuck. She goes and dances, standing shy along the wall for a minute and then moving in, loosening. He doesn't want to watch and get envious; he heaves himself up, to get another beer and steal another look at the girl in the kitchen. Sad, tits by themselves, on a woman sitting up. Little half-filled purses. This Jamie's face and hands are broad and scraped-looking and he has loosened his tie to let his bull neck breathe. Another girl is reading his palm; they are all sitting around a little porcelain kitchen table, with spots worn black where place settings were, which reminds Nelson of something. What? A poster in here is of Marlon Brando in the black-leather get-up of *The Wild One*.

Another shows Alice Cooper with his green eyelids and long fingernails. The refrigerator with its cool shelves of yogurt in paper cups and beer in sharply lettered sixpacks seems an island of decent order amid all this. Nelson is reminded of the lot, its rows of new Toyotas, and his stomach sinks. Sometimes at the lot, standing in the showroom with no customers in sight, he feels return to him from childhood that old fear of being in the wrong place, of life being run by rules nobody would share with him. He returns to the big front room with its fake ceiling and thinks that Pru looks ridiculously older than the other dancers: a little frizzy-haired girl called Dody Weinstein interning in teen fashions at Kroll's and Slim and this Lyle in the soccer shirt back together again and Pam their hostess in a big floppy muu-muu her body is having fits within, while the wan lights of Brewer fall away beyond the bay window, and the girl without a name waits in her white pants to be picked up while she stands to one side shivering from side to side in time to the music. *One night in a lifetime, one life in a night.* She looks a little self-conscious but happy to be here, out of the sticks. The black bubbles in the speakers pop faster and faster, and his wife with her cannonball gut is about to fall flat on her face. He goes to Pru and pulls her by her wrist away. Her spic thug of a partner dead-pan writhes to the girl in white pants and picks her up. *Babe it's gotta be tonight, babe it's gotta be to-night.* Nelson is squeezing Pru's wrist to hurt. She is unsteady, pulled out of the music, and this further angers him, his wife getting tipsy. Defective equipment breaking down on purpose just to show him up. Her brittle imbalance makes him want to smash her completely.

"You're *hurt*ing me," she says. Her voice arrives, tiny and dry, from a little box suspended in air behind his ear. As she tries to pull her wrist away her bangles pinch his fingers, and this is infuriating.

He wants to get her somewhere out of this. He pulls her across a hallway looking for a wall to prop her up against. He finds one, in a small side room; the light-switch plate beside her shoulder has been painted like an open-mouthed face with an off-on tongue. He puts his own face up against Pru's and hisses, "Listen. You shape up for Chrissake. You're going to hurt yourself if you don't shape up. And the baby. What're you tryin' to do, shake him loose? Now you calm down."

"I am calm. You're the one that's not calm, Nelson." Their eyes are so close her eyes threaten to swallow his with their blurred green. "And who says it's going to be a him?" Pru gives him her lopsided smirk. Her lips are painted vampire red in the new style and it's not becoming, it emphasizes her hatchet face, her dead calm bloodless look. That blank defiance of the poor: you can't scare them enough.

He pleads, "You shouldn't be drinking and smoking pot at all, you'll cause genetic damage. You know that."

She forms her words in response slowly. "Nelson. You don't give a shit about genetic damage."

"You silly bitch. I do. Of course I do. It's my kid. Or is it? You Akron kids'll fuck anybody."

They are in a strange room. Flamingos surround them. Whoever lives in this side room with its view of the brick wall across two narrow sideyards has collected flamingos as a kind of joke. A glossy pink stuffed satin one drapes its ridiculous long black legs over the back of the sofabed, and hollow plastic ones with stick legs are propped along the walls on shelves. There are flamingos worked into ashtrays and coffee mugs and there are little 3-D tableaux of the painted pink birds with lakes and palms and sunsets, souvenirs of Florida. For one souvenir a trio of them were gathered in knickers and Scots caps on a felt putting green. Some of the bigger ones wear on their hollow drooping beaks those limp candylike sunglasses you can get in five and dimes. There are hundreds, other gays must give them to him, it has to be Slim who lives in here, that sofabed wouldn't be enough for Jason and Pam.

"It is," Pru promises. "You know it is."

"I don't know. You're acting awfully whorey tonight."

"I didn't want to come, remember? You're the one always wants to go out."

He begins to cry: something about Pru's face, that toughness out of Akron closed against him, her belly bumping his, that big doll-like body he used to love so much, that she might just as easily have entrusted to another, its clefts, its tufts, and might just as easily take from him now, he is nothing to her.

All their tender times, picking her up on the hill and walking under the trees, and the bars along Water Street, and his going ahead and letting her out there in Colorado make such a sucker of him while he stewed in Diamond County, nothing. He is nothing to her like he was nothing to Jill, a brat, a bug to be humored, and look what happened. Love feels riddled through all his body like rot, down clear to his knees spongy as punk. "You'll do damage to yourself," he sobs; tears add their glitter to the green of her dress at the shoulder, yet his own crumpled face hangs as clear in the back of his brain as a face on a TV screen.

"You're strange," Pru tells him, her voice breathier now, a whispery rag stuffed in his ear.

"Let's get out of this creepy place."

"That girl you were talking to, what did she say?"

"Nothing. Her boyfriend makes bug-killers."

"You talked together a long time."

"She wanted to dance."

"I could see you pointing and looking at me. You're ashamed of my being pregnant."

"I'm not. I'm proud."

"The fuck you are, Nelson. You're embarrassed."

"Don't be so hard. Come on, let's split."

"See, you are embarrassed. That's all this baby is to you, an embarrassment."

"Please come. What're you trying to do, make me get down on my knees?"

"Listen, Nelson. I was having a perfectly good time dancing and you come out and pull this big macho act. My wrist still hurts. Maybe you broke it."

He tries to lift her wrist to kiss it but she stiffly resists: at times she seems to him, body and soul, a board, flat, with that same abrasive grain. And then the fear comes upon him that this flatness is her, that she is not withholding depths within but there are no depths, this is what there is. She gets on a track sometimes and it seems she can't stop. His pulling at her wrist again, only to kiss it but she doesn't want to see that, has made her altogether mad, her face all pink and pointy and rigid. "You know what you are?" She tells him, "You're a little Napoleon. You're a *twerp*, Nelson."

"Hey don't."

The space around her vampire lips is tight and her voice is a dead level engine that won't stop. "I didn't really know you. I've been watching how you act with your family and you're very spoiled. You're spoiled and you're a bully, Nelson."

"Shut up." He mustn't cry again. "I was never spoiled, just the opposite. You don't know what my family did to me."

"I've heard about it a thousand times and to me it never sounded like any big deal. You expect your mother and poor old grandmother to take care of you no matter what you do. You're horrid about your father when all he wants is to love you, to have a halfway normal son."

"He didn't want me to work at the lot."

"He didn't think you were ready and you weren't. You aren't. You aren't ready to be a father either but that's my mistake."

"Oh, even you make mistakes." The green she is wearing is a hateful color, shimmery electric arsenic like a big fat black hooker would wear to get attention on the street. He turns his eyes away and sees over on a bureau top some bendable toy flamingos have been arranged in a copulating position, one on top of the other's back, and another pair in what he supposes is a blow job, but the droopy beaks spoil the effect.

"I make plenty," Pru is going on, "why wouldn't I, nobody has ever taught me anything. But I'll tell you one thing Nelson Angstrom I'm going to have this baby no matter what you do. You can go to Hell."

"I can, huh?"

"Yes." She has to weaken it. Her very belly seems to soften against his, nestling. "I don't want you to but you can. I can't stop you and you can't stop me, we're two people even if we did get married. You never wanted to marry me and I shouldn't have let you, it turns out."

"I did though, I did," he says, fearful that confessing this will make his face crumple again.

"Then stop being a bully. You bullied me to come here and now you're bullying me to go. I like these people. They have better senses of humor than the people in Ohio."

"Let's stay then." There are things other than flamingos in the room—hideous things, he sees. A plaster cast of Elvis Presley with votive candles in red cups at its base. An aquarium without fish in it but full of Barbie dolls and polyplike plastic things he thinks are called French ticklers. Tacked-up postcards of women in tinsel triangles somersaulting, mooning, holding giant breasts in their silver-gloved hands, postcards from Germany printed on those tiny ridges that hold two views, one coy and one obscene, depending on how you move your head. The room all over has the distinctness and variousness of vomit that still holds whole green peas and orange carrot dice from the dinner of an hour ago. He can't stop looking.

As he moves from one horror to the next Pru slips away, giving his hand a squeeze that may be apologetic for all they've said. What have they said? In the kitchen the girl with bare tits has put on a T-shirt saying ERA, Jamie has taken off his coat and his necktie. Nelson feels very tall, so tall he can't hear what he himself is saying, but it doesn't matter, and they all laugh. In a dark bedroom off the kitchen someone is watching the eleven-thirty special report from Iran, time slips by in that rapid spasmodic skid of party time. When Pru returns to him asking to go she is dead pale, a ghost with the lipstick on her face like movie blood and worn in the center where her lips meet. Things are being dyed blue by something in his head and her teeth look crooked as she tells him almost inaudibly that she has taken off her shoes like he wanted her to and now she can't find them. She plops down on a kitchen chair and stretches her orange legs out so her belly thrusts up like a prick and laughs with all those around her. What pigs. Nelson in searching for her shoes finds instead in the side room of horrible tinsel and flamingos the girl in white pants asleep on the sofabed. With her face slack she looks even younger than before. Her hand curls beside her snub nose pale palm up. The calm and mildly freckled bulge of her forehead sleeps without a crease. Only her hair holds that deep force of a woman, unbundled from its pins and many-colored in the caves and ridges of its tangle. He wants to cover her up but sees no blanket, just the French ticklers and Barbie dolls brilliant in their aquarium. A sliver of milky bare skin peeps where her russet knit sweater has ridden up from the waist of her slacks. Nelson looks down and wonders, Why can't a woman just be your friend, even with the sex? Why do you have to keep dealing with all this ego, giving back hurt just to defend yourself? Gazing down at that milky bit of skin, he forgets what he came in here to find. He needs to urinate, he realizes.

And in the bathroom after his bladder has emptied in those unsteady dribbles that mean it's been allowed to get too full he becomes fascinated by a big slick book sitting on the hamper, belonging to Slim most likely, an album printed of photographs and posters from the Nazi days in Germany, beautiful blond boys in rows singing and a handsome fat man in a white uniform loaded with medals and Hitler looking young and lean and gallant, gazing toward some Alps. Having this here is some kind of swish thing like those tinselled cards showing women as so ugly and there seems no protection against all the ugliness that is in the world, no protection for that girl asleep or for him. Pru has found her horrible green platform shoes and in the kitchen is sitting in a straight chair while that Puerto Rican she picked up with like little knife cuts all over his face kneels at her feet doing up the little buckles on the straps like gimp. When she stands she acts rocky, what have they been giving her? She lets herself be slipped into that velvet jacket she used to wear in fall and spring at Kent, red so with the bright green dress she looks like Christmas six weeks early, all wrapped up. Jason is dancing in that front room where now Jamie and the girl with ERA across her pathetic tits are trying it out too, so they say their goodbyes to Pam and Slim, Pam giving Pru a kiss on the cheek woman to woman as if whispering the code word in her ear and Slim putting his hands together in front of his chest and bowing Buddha-style. That slanty look to his eyes, Nelson wonders if it's natural or comes with doing perverted things. The jellyfish of intensity crawls across Slim's lips. Last little waves and smiles and the door closes on the party noise.

The door to the apartment is an old-fashioned heavy one of yellow oak. He and Pru on this third-floor landing are sealed into something like silence. Rain is tapping on the black skylight of chicken-wire glass above their heads.

"Still think I'm a twerp?" he asks.

"Nelson, why don't you grow up?"

The solid wooden banister on the right does a dizzying double loop down the two flights to the first floor. Looking down, Nelson can see the tops of two plastic garbage cans set in the

basement far below. Impatiently Pru passes him on the left, fed
up with him and anxious to be out in the air, and afterwards
he remembers her broad hip bumping into his and his anger at
what seemed her willful clumsiness, but not if he gives her a bit
of hip back, a little vengeful shove. On the left of the stairwell
there is no banister, and the plaster wall here is marred by ragged nail holes where the renovators stripped away what must
have been panelling. So when Pru in those wedgy platforms
turns her ankle, there is nothing for her to hold on to; she
gives a little grunt but her pale face is impassive as in the old
days of hang gliding, at the moment of launch. Nelson grabs
for her velvet jacket but she is flying beyond his reach, her legs
no longer under her; he sees her face skid past these nail holes
as she twists toward the wall, clawing for support there, where
there is none. She topples then twisting sideways, headfirst, the
metal-edged treads ripping at her belly. It is all so fast yet his
brain has time to process a number of sensations—the touch
of her velvet humming in his fingertips, the scolding bump
her hip gave him, his indignation at her clunky shoes and the
people who stripped the staircase of its banister, all precisely
layered in his mind. Distinctly he sees the patch of darker orange reinforcing at the crotch of her tights like the center of a
flagrant green flower as her dress is flung wide with her legs by
first impact. Her arms keep trying to brace her slithering body
and one arm ends at an angle when she stops, about halfway
down the steep flight, a shoe torn loose on a string of gimp,
her head hidden beneath the splayed mass of her beautiful hair
and all her long form still.

Fallt's Bubbli nunner!

In soft sweeps the rain patters on the skylight. Music leaks
through the walls from the party. The noise of her fall must
have been huge, for the yellow oak door pops open at once and
people thunder all around, but the only sound Nelson heard
was a squeak Pru gave when she first hit like one of those plastic floating bath toys suddenly accidentally stepped on.

Soupy is in fine form at the hospital, kidding the nurses and
staff and moving through this white world in his black clothes
like a happy germ, an exception to all the rules. He comes
forward as if to embrace Ma Springer but at the last second

holds back and gives her instead a somewhat jaunty swat on the shoulder. To Janice and Harry he gives his mischievous small-toothed grin; to Nelson he turns a graver, but still bright-eyed, face. "She looks just dandy, except for the cast on her arm. Even there she was fortunate. It's the left arm."

"She's left-handed," Nelson tells him. The boy is grouchy and stoops with lack of sleep. He was with her at the hospital from one to three and now at nine-thirty is back again. He called the house around one-fifteen and nobody answered and that has been added to his twenty years of grievances. Mom-mom had been in the house but had been too old and dopey to hear the phone through her dreams and his parents had been out with the Murketts and Harrisons at the new strip joint along Route 422 beyond the Four Seasons toward Pottstown and then had gone back to the Murketts' for a nightcap. So the family didn't hear the news until Nelson, who had crawled into his empty bed at three-thirty, awoke at nine. On the ride over to the hospital in his mother's Mustang he claimed he hadn't fallen asleep until the birds began to chirp.

"What birds?" Harry said. "They've all gone south."

"Dad, don't bug me, there are these black sort of birds right outside the window."

"Starlings," Janice offered, peacemaking.

"They don't chirp, they scrawk," Harry insisted. "*Scrawk, scrawk.*"

"Doesn't it stay dark late now?" Ma Springer interposed. It's aging her, this constant tension between her son-in-law and her grandson.

Nelson sitting there all red-eyed and snuffly and stinking of last night's vapors did annoy Harry, short of sleep and hung-over himself. He fought down the impulse to say *Scrawk* again. At the hospital, he asks Soupy, "How'd you get here so soon?" genuinely admiring. Snicker all you want, the guy *is* magical somehow.

"The lady herself," the clergyman gaily announces, doing a little side-step that knocks a magazine to the floor from a low table where too many are stacked. *Woman's Day. Field and Stream.* A hospital of course wouldn't get *Consumer Reports.* A killing article in there a while ago about medical costs and the fantastic mark-up on things like aspirin and cold pills. Soupy stoops to retrieve the magazine and comes up slightly breathless. He tells them, "Evidently, after they calmed the dear girl down and set her arm and reassured her that the fetus appeared unaffected she still felt such concern that she woke up at seven a.m. and knew Nelson would be asleep and didn't know who to call. So she thought of *me*." Soupy beams. "I of course was still wrapped in the arms of Morpheus but got my act together and told her I'd rush over between Holy Communion and the ten o'clock service and, behold, here I am. *Ecce homo.* She wanted to pray with me to keep the baby, she'd been praying *con*stantly, and at least to this point in time as they used to say it seems to have *worked*!" His black eyes click from one to another face, up and down and across. "The doctor who received her went off duty at eight but the nurse in attendance *sol*emnly swore to me that for all of the mother's bruises that little heartbeat in there is just as strong as ever, and *no* signs of vaginal bleeding or anything nasty like that. That Mother Nature, she is one tough old turkey." He has chosen Ma Springer to tell this to. "Now I *must* run, or the hungry sheep will look up and be not fed. Visiting hours here don't really begin until one p.m., but I'm *sure* the authorities wouldn't object if you took a quick peek. Tell them I gave you my blessing." And his hand reflexively lifts, as if to give them a blessing. But instead he lays the hand on the sleeve of Ma Springer's glistening fur coat. "If you *can't* make the service," he entreats, "*do* come for the meeting afterwards. It's the meeting to advise the vestry on the new tracker organ, and a lot of pennypinchers are coming out of the woods. They put a dollar a week into the plate all year, and their vote is as good as mine or thine." He flies away, scattering the V-for-peace sign down the hall.

Boy, these boys do love misery, Harry thinks. Well, it's a turf nobody else wants. St. Joseph's Hospital is in the tatty north-central part of Brewer where the old Y.M.C.A. was before they tore it down for yet another drive-in bank and where the old wooden railroad bridge has been rebuilt in concrete that started to crack immediately. They used to talk about burying the tracks along through here in a tunnel but then the trains pretty much stopped running and that solved that. Janice had had Rebecca June here when the nurses were all nuns, they may still be nuns but now there's no way of telling. The receptionist for this floor wears a salmon-colored pants suit. Her swollen bottom and slumping shoulders lead the way. Half-open doors reveal people lying emaciated under white sheets staring at the white ceiling, ghosts already. Pru is in a four-bed room and two women in gauzy hospital johnnies scatter back into their beds, ambushed by early visitors. In the fourth bed an ancient black woman sleeps. Pru herself is all but asleep. She still wears flecks of last night's mascara but the rest of her looks virginal, especially the fresh white cast from elbow to wrist. Nelson kisses her lightly on the lips and then, sitting in the one bedside chair while his elders stand, sockets his face in the space on the bed edge next to the curve of Pru's hip. What a baby, Harry thinks.

"Nelson was wonderful," Pru is telling them. "So caring." Her voice is more musical and throaty than Harry has ever heard it. He wonders if just lying down does that to a woman: changes the angle of her voice box.

"Yeah, he felt sick about it," Harry says. "We didn't hear the story till this morning."

Nelson lifts his head. "They were at a *strip* joint, can you imagine?"

"Jesus," Harry says to Janice. "Who's in charge here? What does he want us to do, sit around the house all the time aging gracefully?"

Ma Springer says, "Now we can only stay a minute, I want to get to church. It wouldn't look right I think just to go to the meeting like Reverend Campbell said."

"Go to that meeting, Ma," Harry points out, "they'll hit you up for a fortune. Tracker organs don't grow on trees."

Janice says to Pru, "You poor sweetie. How bad is the arm?"

"Oh, I wasn't paying that much attention to what the doctor said." Her voice floats, she must be full of tranquilizers. "There's a bone on the outside, with a funny name—"

"Femur," Harry suggests. Something about all this has jazzed him up, made him feel nerved-up and defiant. Those strippers last night, some of them young enough to be his daughter. The Gold Cherry, the place was called.

Nelson lifts his head again from burrowing in Pru's side. "That's in the *thigh*, Dad. She means the humerus."

"Ha ha," Harry says.

Pru seems to moan. "Ulna," she supplies. "He said it was just a simple fracture."

"How long's it gonna be on?" Harry asks.

"He said six weeks if I do what he says."

"Off by Christmas," Harry says. Christmas is a big thing in his mind this year, for beyond it, and the mop-up of New Year's, they're going to take their trip, they have the hotel, the plane reservations, they were discussing it all last night again, after the excitement of the strippers.

"You poor sweetie," Janice repeats.

Pru begins to sing, without music. But the words come out as if sung. "Oh my God, I don't mind, I'm glad for it, I deserve to be punished somehow. I honestly believe"—she keeps looking straight at Janice, with an authority they haven't seen from her before—"it's God telling me this is the price He asks for my not losing the baby. I'm glad to pay it, I'd be glad if every bone in my body was broken, I really wouldn't care. Oh my God, when I felt my feet weren't under me and I knew there wasn't anything for me to do but fall down those horrible stairs, the thoughts that ran through my head! You must know."

Meaning Janice must know what it's like to lose a baby. Janice kind of yelps and falls on the bedridden girl so hard Harry winces, and plucks at her back to pull her off. Feeling the rock of plaster against her breasts, Janice arches her spine under his hands; through the cloth her skin feels taut as a drum, and hot. But Pru shows no pain, smiling her crooked careful smile and keeping her eyelids with their traces of last night's blue closed serenely, accepting the older woman's weight upon her. The hand not captured in a cast Pru sneaks around to pat Janice's back; her fingers come close to Harry's own. Pat, they go, pat pat. He thinks of Cindy Murkett's round fingers and marvels how much more childish and grublike they look than these, bony though young and reddened at the knuckles: his mother's hands had that tough scrubbed look. Janice can't stop sobbing, Pru can't stop patting, the two other women patients awake in the room can't stop glancing over. Moments this complicated rub Harry the wrong way. He feels rebuked, since the official family version is that the baby's dying at Janice's hands was all his fault. Yet now the truth seems declared that he was just a bystander. Nelson, pushed to one side by his mother's assault of grief, sits up and stares, poor frazzled kid. These damn women so intent on communing should leave us out of it entirely. At last Janice rights herself, having snuffled so hard her upper lip is wet with snot.

Harry hands her his handkerchief.

"I'm so happy," she says with a big runny sniff, "for Pru."

"Come on, shape up," he mutters, taking back the handkerchief.

Ma Springer soothes the waters with, "It does seem a miracle, all the way down those stairs and nothing worse. Up that high in those old Brewer houses the stairs were just for the servants."

"I didn't go all the way down," Pru says. "That's how I broke my arm, stopping myself. I don't remember any pain."

"Yeah," Harry offers. "Nelson said you were feeling no pain."

"Oh no, no." Her hair spread out across the pillow by Janice's embrace makes her look like she is falling through white space, singing. "I'd hardly had anything, the doctors all say you shouldn't, it was those terrible tall platforms they're making us all wear. Isn't that the dumbest style? I'm going to burn them up, absolutely, as soon as I get back."

"When will that be now?" Ma asks, shifting her black purse to the other hand. She has been dressed for church since before Nelson woke up and the fuss began. She's a slave to that church, God knows what she gets out of it.

"Up to a week, he said," Pru says. "To keep me quiet and, you know, to make sure. The baby. I woke up this morning with what I thought were contractions and they scared me so I called Soupy. He was wonderful."

"Yes, well," Ma says.

Harry hates the way they all keep calling it the baby. More like a piglet or a wobbly big frog at this stage, as he pictures it. What if she had lost it, wouldn't it have lived? They keep five-month preemies alive now and pretty soon you'll have life in a test tube start to finish. "We gotta get Ma to church," he announces. "Nelson, you want to wake up and come or stay here and sleep?" The boy's head had gone back down onto the hospital mattress again. He used to fall asleep at the kitchen table that way.

"Harry," Janice says. "Don't be so rough on everybody."

"He thinks we're all silly about the baby," Pru says dreamily, dimly teasing.

"No, hey: I think it's great about the baby." He bends over to kiss her goodbye for now and wants to whisper in her ear about all the babies he has had, dead and alive, visible and invisible. Instead he tells her, straightening, "Keep cool. We'll be back after this when we can stay longer."

"Don't not play golf," she says.

"Golf's shot. They don't like you to walk on the greens after a certain point."

Nelson is asking her, "What do you want me to do, go or stay?"

"Go, Nelson, for heaven's sake. Let me get some sleep."

"You know, I'm sorry last night if I said anything. I was skunked. When they told me last night they didn't think you'd lose the baby I was so relieved I cried. Honest." He would cry again but his face clouds with embarrassed awareness that the others have listened. That's why we love disaster, Harry sees, it puts us back in touch with guilt and sends us crawling back to God. Without a sense of being in the wrong we're no better than animals. Suppose the baby had aborted at the very moment he was watching that olive chick with the rolling tongue tug down her tinsel underpants to her knees and peek at the audience from behind her shoulder while tickling her asshole with that ostrich feather: he'd feel terrible.

Pru waves her husband's quavery words and all their worried faces away. "I'm *fine*. I love all of you so much." Her hair streams outward as she waits to sink into sleep, into more wild prayer, into the dreaming fluids of her own bruised belly. Her stumpy wing of snow-white plaster lifts a few inches from her chest in farewell. They leave her to the company of ex-nuns and shuffle back through the hospital corridors, their footsteps clamorous amid their silent determination to save their quarrels for the car.

"A week!" Harry says, as soon as they're rolling in the Mustang. "Does anybody have any idea how much a week in a hospital costs these days?"

"Dad, how can you keep thinking about money all the time?"

"Somebody has to. A week is a thousand dollars minimum. *Min*imum."

"You *have* Blue Cross."

"Not for daughter-in-laws I don't. Not for you either, once you're over nineteen."

"Well I don't know," Nelson says, "but I don't like her being in a ward with all those other women barfing and moaning all night. One of 'em was even black, did you notice?"

"How did you get so prejudiced? Not from me. Anyway that's not a ward, that's what you call a semi-private," Harry says.

"I want my wife to have a private room," Nelson says.

"Is that a fact? You want, you want. And who's going to foot the bill, big shot? Not you."

Ma Springer says, "I know when I had my diverticulitis, Fred wouldn't hear of anything but a private room for me. And it was a corner room at that. A wonderful view of the arboretum, the magnolias just in bloom."

Janice asks, "How about at the lot, isn't he under the group insurance there?"

Harry tells her, "Maternity benefits don't start till you've worked for Springer Motors nine months."

"A broken arm isn't what I'd call maternity," Nelson says.

"Yeah but if it weren't for her maternity she'd be out walking around with it."

"Maybe Mildred could look into it," Janice suggests.

"O.K.," he concedes, with ill grace. "I don't know what our exact policy is."

Nelson should let it go at that. Instead he says, leaning forward from the back seat so his voice presses on Harry's ear, "Without Mildred and Charlie there isn't much you do know exactly. I mean—"

"I know what you mean and I know a lot more about the car business than you ever will at the rate you're going, if you don't stop futzing around with these old Detroit hotrods that lose us a bundle and start focusing on the line we carry."

"I wouldn't mind if they were Datsuns or Hondas, but frankly Dad, Toyotas—"

"The Toyota franchise is what old Fred Springer landed

and Toyotas are what we sell. Bessie, why doncha slap the kid around a little? I can't reach him."

His mother-in-law's voice comes from the back seat after a pause. "I was wondering if I should go to church after all. I know his heart's set on a big drive for the organ and there aren't too many that enthusiastic. If I show up I might get made a committee head and I'm too old for that."

"Didn't Teresa seem sweet?" Janice asks aloud. "It seemed like she'd grown up overnight."

"Yeah," Harry says, "and if she'd fallen down all two flights she'd be older than we are."

"Jesus, Dad," Nelson says. "Who *do* you like?"

"I like everybody," Harry says. "I just don't like getting boxed in."

The way from St. Joseph's to Mt. Judge is to keep going straight over the railroad tracks and then continue right on Locust past Brewer High and on through Cityview Park and then left past the shopping mall as usual. On a Sunday morning the people out in cars are mostly the older American type, the women with hair tinted blue or pink like the feathers of those Easter chicks before they outlawed it and the men gripping the steering wheel with two hands like the thing might start to buck and bray: with no-lead up to a dollar thirteen at some city stations thanks to the old Ayatollah they have to try to squeeze value out of every drop. Actually, people's philosophy seems to be they'll burn it while it's here and when it's fourth down and twenty-seven Carter can punt. The four features at the mall cinema are BREAKING AWAY STARTING OVER RUNNING and "*10*." He'd like to see "*10*," he knows from the ads this Swedish-looking girl has her hair in corn rows like a black chick out of Zaire. One world: everybody fucks everybody. When he thinks of all the fucking there's been in the world and all the fucking there's going to be, and none of it for him, here he sits in this stuffy car dying, his heart just sinks. He'll never fuck anybody again in his lifetime except poor Janice Springer, he sees this possibility ahead of him straight and grim as the known road. His stomach, sour from last night's fun, binds as it used to when he was running to school late. He says suddenly to Nelson, "How the hell could you let her fall, why didn't you keep ahold of her? What were you *doing* out so late anyway? When your mother was pregnant with you we never went *any*where."

"Together at least," the boy says. "You went a lot of places by yourself the way I heard it."

"Not when she was pregnant with *you*, we sat there night after night with the boob tube, *I Love Lucy* and all that family comedy, didn't we Bessie? And we weren't snorting any dope, either."

"You don't snort dope, you smoke it. Coke is what you snort."

Ma Springer responds slowly to his question. "Oh I don't know how you and Janice managed exactly," she says wearily, in a voice that is looking out the window. "The young people are different now."

"I'll say they are. You fire somebody to give 'em a job and they knock the product."

"It's an O.K. product if all you want is to get from here to there," Nelson begins.

Harry interrupts furiously, thinking of poor Pru lying there with a snivelling baby burying his head in her side instead of a husband, of Melanie slaving away at the Crêpe House for all those creeps from the banks that lunch downtown, of his own sweet hopeful daughter stuck with that big red-faced Jamie, of poor little Cindy having to put on a grin at being fucked from behind so old Webb can have his kicks with his SX-70, of Mim going down on all those wop thugs out there all those years, of Mom plunging her old arms in gray suds and crying the kitchen blues until Parkinson's at last took mercy and got her upstairs for a rest, of all the women put upon and wasted in the world as far as he can see so little punks like this can come along. "Let me tell you something about Toyotas," he calls back at Nelson. "They're put together by little yellow guys in white smocks that work in one plant cradle to grave and go crazy if there's a fleck of dust in the fuel injector system and those jalopies Detroit puts out are slapped together by jiga-boos wearing headphones pumping music into their ears and so zonked on drugs they don't know a slothead screw from a lug nut and furthermore are taught by the NAACP to hate the company. Half the cars come through the Ford assembly line are deliberately sabotaged, I forget where I read all this, it wasn't *Consumer Reports*."

"Dad, you're so prejudiced. What would Skeeter say?"

Skeeter. In quite another voice Harry says, "Skeeter was killed in Philly last April, did I tell ya?"

"You *keep* telling me."

"I'm not blaming the blacks on the assembly line, I'm just saying it sure makes for lousy cars."

Nelson is on the attack, frazzled and feeling rotten, poor kid. "And who are you to criticize me and Pru for going out to see some friends when you were off with yours seeing those ridiculous exotic dancers? How could you stand it, Mom?"

Janice says, "It wasn't as bad as I'd thought. They keep it within bounds. It really wasn't any worse than it used to be at the old fairgrounds."

"Don't answer him," Harry tells her. "Who's he to criticize?"

"The funny thing," Janice goes on, "is how Cindy and Thelma and I could agree which girl was the best and the men had picked some girl entirely different. We all liked this tall Oriental who was very graceful and artistic and *they* liked, Mother, the men liked some little chinless blonde who couldn't even dance."

"She had that look about her," Harry explains. "I mean, she meant it."

"And then that tubby dark one that turned you on. With the feather."

"Olive-complected. She was nice too. The feather I could have done without."

"Mom-mom doesn't want to hear all this disgusting stuff," Nelson says from the back seat.

"Mom-mom doesn't mind," Harry tells him. "Nothing fazes Bessie Springer. Mom-mom loves life."

"Oh I don't know," the old lady says with a sigh. "We didn't have such things when we might have been up to it. Fred I remember used to bring home the *Playboy* sometimes, but to me it seemed more pathetic than not, these eighteen-year-old girls that are really just children except for their bodies."

"Well who isn't?" Harry asks.

"Speak for yourself, Dad," Nelson says.

"No now, I meant," Ma insists, "you wonder what their

parents raised them for, seeing them all naked just the way they were born. And what the parents must think." She sighs. "It's a different world."

Janice says, "I guess at this same place Monday nights they have ladies' night with male strippers. And they say really the young men become frightened, Doris Kaufmann was telling me, the women grab for them and try to get up on the stage after them. The women over forty they say are the worst."

"That's so sick," Nelson says.

"Watch your mouth," Harry tells him. "Your mother's over forty."

"*Dad.*"

"Well I wouldn't behave like that," she says, "but I can see how some might. I suppose a lot of it depends on how satisfying the husband you have is."

"*Mo-om,*" the boy protests.

They have swung around the mountain and turned up Central and by the electric clock in the dry cleaner's window it is three of ten. Harry calls back, "Looks like we'll make it, Bessie!"

The town hall has its flag at half-mast because of the hostages. At the church the people in holiday clothes are still filing in, beneath the canopy of bells calling with their iron tongues, beneath the wind-torn gray clouds of this November sky with its scattered silver. Letting Ma out of the Mustang, Harry says, "Now don't pledge the lot away, just for Soupy's organ."

Nelson asks, "How will you get home, Mom-mom?"

"Oh, I guess I can get a ride with Grace Stuhl's grandson, he generally comes for her. Otherwise it won't kill me to walk."

"Oh Mother," Janice says. "You could never walk it. Call us at the house when the meeting's over if you haven't a ride. We'll be home." The club is down to minimal staff now; they serve only packaged sandwiches and half the tennis court nets are down and already they have relocated the pins to temporary greens. A sadness in all this plucks at Rabbit. Driving home with just Janice and Nelson he remembers the way they used to be, just the three of them, living together, younger. The kid and Janice still have it between them. He's lost it. He says aloud, "So you don't like Toyotas."

"It's not a question of like, Dad, there isn't that much about 'em to like or dislike. I was talking to some girl at the party last night who'd just bought a Corolla, and all we could talk about was the old American cars, how great they were. It's like Volvos, they don't have it anymore either, it's not something anybody can con*trol*. It's like, you know, time of life."

The boy is trying to be conversational and patch things up; Harry keeps quiet, thinking, Time of life, the crazy way you're going, zigzagging around and all those drugs, you'll be lucky to get to my time of life.

"Mazdas," Nelson says. "That's what I'd want to have an agency in. That rotary engine is *so* much more efficient than the four-cycle piston, you could run this country on half the gas, once they get the seal perfected."

"Go over and ask Abe Chafetz for a job then. I heard he was going broke, the Mazdas have so many bugs. Manny says they'll never get the seal right."

Janice says, placating, "I think the Toyota ads on television are very clever and glamorous."

"Oh the *ads* have charisma," Nelson says. "The ads are terrific. It's the cars I'm talking about."

"Don't you love," Harry asks, "that new one with Scrooge, the way he cackles and goes off into the distance?" He cackles, and Janice and Nelson laugh, and for the last block home, down Joseph Street beneath the bare maples, their three heads entertain common happy memories, of Toyota commercials, of men and women leaping, average men and women, their clothes lifted in cascading slow-motion folds like angels' robes, like some intimate violence of chemical mating or humming-bird wing magnified and laid bare in its process, leaping and falling, grinning and then in freeze-frame hanging there, defying gravity.

"We got to get out of here," Harry says hoarsely to Janice in their bedroom some days later, on the eve of Pru's return from her week of grace in the hospital. It is night; the copper beech, stripped of its leaves and clamorous pods, admits more streetlight into their room than in summer. One or two of the panes in the window on the side nearer the street, the side where Rabbit sleeps, hold imperfections, patches of waviness or elongated bubbles, scarcely visible to the eye of day but which at night hurl onto the far wall, with its mothlike shadows of medallion pattern, dramatic amplifications, the tint of each pane also heightened in the enlargement, so that an effect of stained glass haunts the area above Janice's jumbled mahogany dresser descended from the Koerners, beside the four-panelled door that locks out the world. Ten years of habitancy, in the minutes or hours between when the bedside lamps are extinguished and sleep is achieved, have borne these luminous rectangles into Harry's brain as precious entities, diffuse jewels pressed from the air, presences whose company he will miss if he leaves this room. He must leave it. Intermixed with the abstract patterns the imperfect panes project are the unquiet shadows of the beech branches as they shudder and sway in the cold outside.

"Where would we go?" Janice asks.

"We'd buy a house like everybody else," he says, speaking in a low hoarse voice as if Ma Springer might overhear this breath of treachery through the wall and the mumble and soft roar of her television set as a crisis in her program is reached, then a commercial bursts forth, and another crisis begins to build. "On the other side of Brewer, closer to the lot. That drive through the middle of town every day is driving me crazy. Wastes gas, too."

"Not Penn Villas," she says. "You'll never get me back into Penn Villas."

"Me neither. What about Penn Park though? With all those nice divorce lawyers and dermatologists? I've always kind of dreamed, ever since we used to play them in basketball, of living over there somewhere. Some house with at least stone facing on the front, and maybe a sunken living room, so we can entertain the Murketts in decent style. It's awkward having anybody back here, Ma goes upstairs after dinner but the place is so damn gloomy, and now we're going to be stuck with Nelson and his crew."

"He was saying, they plan to get an apartment when things work out."

"Things aren't going to work out, with his attitude. You know that. The ride is free here and with him around we wouldn't feel so rotten leaving your mother. This is our chance." His hand has crept well up into her nightie; in his wish to have his

vision shared he grips her breasts, familiar handfuls, a bit limp
like balloons deflating with her age; but still thanks to all that
tennis and swimming and old Fred Springer's stingy lean genes
her body is holding up better than most. Her nipples stiffen,
and his prick with no great attention paid to it is hardening
on the sly. "Or maybe," he pursues, his voice still hoarse, "one
of those mock-Tudor jobbies that look like piecrust and have
those steep pitched roofs like witches' houses. Jesus, wouldn't
Pop be proud, seeing me in one of those?"

"Could we afford it," Janice asks, "with the mortgage rates
up around thirteen per cent now?"

He shifts his hand down the silvery slick undulations of her
belly to the patch of her hair, that seems to bristle at his touch.
He ought to eat her sometime. Bed her down on her back with
her legs hanging over the side and just kneel and chew her cunt
until she came. He used to when they were courting in that
apartment of the other girl's with its view of the old gray gas
tanks by the river, kneel and just graze in her ferny meadow
for hours, nose, eyelids rubbing up against the wonder of it.
Any woman, they deserve to be eaten once in a while, they
don't come so your mouth is full like with an oyster, how do
whores stand it, cock after cock, cuts down on VD, but having to swallow, must amount to pints in the course of a week.
Ruth hated it that time, but some cunts now if you read the sex
tapes in *Oui* lap it up, one said it tasted to her like champagne.
Maybe it wouldn't be the living room that would be sunken,
it could be the den, just somewhere where there's a carpeted
step down or two, so you know you're in a modern home.
"That's the beauty of inflation," he says seductively to Janice.
"The more you owe, the better you do. Ask Webb. You pay
off in shrunken dollars, and the interest Uncle Sam picks up as
an income tax deduction. Even after buying the Krugerrands
and paying the September taxes we have too much money in
the bank, money in the bank is for dummies now. Sock it into
the down payment for a house, we'd be letting the bank worry
about the dollar going down and have the house appreciat-
ing ten, twenty per cent a year at the same time." Her cunt is
moistening, its lips growing loose.

"It seems hard on Mother," Janice says in that weak voice

she gets, lovemaking. "She'll be leaving us this place some day and I know she expects we'd stay in it with her till then."

"She'll live for another twenty years," Harry says, sinking his middle finger in. "In twenty years you'll be well over sixty."

"And wouldn't it seem strange to Nelson?"

"Why? It's what he wants, me out of the way. I depress the kid."

"Harry, I'm not so sure it's you that's doing it. I think he's just scared."

"What's he got to be scared of?"

"The same thing you were scared of at his age. Life."

Life. Too much of it, and not enough. The fear that it will end some day, and the fear that tomorrow will be the same as yesterday. "Well he shouldn't have come home if that's the way he was going to feel," Harry says. He's losing his erection.

"He didn't know," Janice says. He can feel, his finger still in her, that her mind too is drifting away from their flesh, into sad realms of family. "He didn't know you'd be so hard on him. Why are you?"

Fucking kid not thirteen years old and tried to take Jill from him, back in Penn Villas after Janice had gone. "He's hard on me," Harry says. He has ceased to whisper. Ma Springer's television set, when he listens, is still on—a rumbling, woofing, surging noise less like human voices than a noise Nature would make in the trees or along the ocean shore. She has become a fan of the ABC eleven-thirty special report on the hostages and every morning tells them the latest version of nothing happening. Khomeini and Carter both trapped by a pack of kids who need a shave and don't know shit, they talk about old men sending young men off to war, if you could get the idiotic kids out of the world it might settle down to being a sensible place. "He gets a disgruntled look on his face every time I open my mouth to talk. Everything I try to tell him at the lot he goes and does the opposite. Some guy comes in to buy this Mercury that was the other one of the convertibles the kid wrecked that time and offers a snowmobile on the trade-in. I thought it was a joke until the other day I go in and the Mercury's gone and this little yellow Kawasaki snowmobile is sitting up in the front row with the new Tercels. I hit the roof and Nelson tells me to stop being so uptight, he allowed the guy four hundred on it and it'll give us more publicity than twice that in ads, the crazy lot that took a snowmobile on trade-in."

Janice makes a soft noise that were she less tired would be laughter. "That's the kind of thing Daddy used to do."

"And then behind my back he's taken on about ten grand's worth of old convertibles that get about ten miles to the gallon nobody'll want and this caper with Pru is running up a fucking fortune. There's no *bene*fits covering her."

"Shh. Mother can hear."

"I *want* her to hear, she's the one giving the kid all his high and mighty ideas. Last night, you hear them cooking up how he's going to have his own car for him and Pru, when that old Newport of hers just sits in the garage six days out of seven?" A muffled sound of chanting comes through the papered wall, Iranians outside the Embassy demonstrating for the benefit of the TV cameras. Rabbit's throat constricts with frustration. "I got to get out, honey."

"Tell me about the house," Janice says, taking his hand in hers and returning it to her pussy. "How many rooms would it have?"

He begins to massage, dragging his fingers along the crease on one side, then the other, of the triangle, and then bisecting with a thoughtful stroke, looking for the fulcrum, the nub, of it. Cindy's hair had looked darker than Janice's, less curly, alive maybe with needles of light like the fur of Ma Springer's old coat. "We wouldn't need a lot of bedrooms," he tells Janice, "just a big one for us, with a big mirror you can see from the bed—"

"A mirror! Where'd you get the idea of a mirror?"

"Everybody has mirrors now. You watch yourself making love in them."

"Oh, Harry. I couldn't."

"I think you could. And then at least another bedroom, in case your mother has to come live with us, or we have guests, but not next to ours, with at least a bathroom between so we don't hear her television, and downstairs a kitchen with all new equipment including a Cuisinart—"

"I'm scared of them. Doris Kaufmann says for the first three weeks she had hers everything came out mush. One night it was pink mush and the next night green mush was the only difference."

"You'll learn," he croons, drawing circles on her front, circles that widen to graze her breasts and beaver and then diminish to feather into her navel like the asshole of that olive bitch along 422, "there are instruction books, and a refrigerator with an automatic ice-maker, and one of those wall ovens that's at the height of your face so you don't have to bend over, and I don't know about all this microwave, I was reading somewhere how they fry your brains even if you're in the next room . . ." Moist, she is so moist her cunt startles him, touching it, like a slug underneath a leaf in the garden. His prick undergoes such a bulbous throb it hurts. ". . . and this big sunken living room with lights along the side where we can give parties."

"Who would we give these parties for?" Her voice is sinking into the pillow like the dust of a mummy's face, so weak.

"Oh . . ." His hand continues to glide, around and around, carrying the touch of wetness up to her nipples and adorning first one then the other with it like tinsel on the tips of a Christmas tree. ". . . everybody. Doris Kaufmann and all those other tennis Lesbians at the Flying Eagle, Cindy Murkett and her trusty sidekick Buddy Inglefinger, all the nice girls who work their pretty asses off for a better America down at the Gold Cherry, all the great macho guys in the service and parts department of Springer Motors—"

Janice giggles, and simultaneously the front door downstairs slams. After visiting Pru, Nelson has been going to that bar that used to be the Phoenix and bumming around with that creepy crowd that kills time there. It oppresses Harry, this freedom: if the kid has been excused from evening floor duty to visit Pru for the week then he has no business going out getting stewed on the time. If the kid was so shook up when she took her tumble he ought to be doing something better than this out of gratitude or penance or whatever. His footsteps below sound drunken, one plunked down on top of the other, bump, bump, across the living room between the sofa and the Barcalounger and past the foot of the stairs, making the china in the sideboard tingle, on into the kitchen for one more beer. Harry's breath comes quick and short, thinking of that surly puzzled face sucking the foam out of one more can: drinking and eating up the world, and out of sheer spite at that. He feels the boy's mother at his side listening to the footsteps and puts her hand on his prick; in expert reflex her fingers pump the loose skin of the sides. Simultaneous with Nelson's footsteps below as he treads back into the living room toward the Barcalounger, Harry thrusts as hard as if into the olive chick's ass into the socket Janice's wifely hand makes and speeds up his hypnotic tracing of rapid smooth circles upon the concave expectancy of her belly, assuring her hoarsely, of the house he wants, "You'll love it. You'll love it."

Nelson says to Pru, as they drive together into Brewer in Ma Springer's stately old navy-blue Chrysler, "Now guess what. He's talked Mom into them getting a house. They've looked at about six so far, she told me. They all seem too big to her but Dad says she should learn to think big. I think he's flipping out."

Pru says, quietly, "I wonder how much it has to do with us moving in." She had wanted them to find an apartment of their own, in the same general neighborhood as Slim and Jason and Pam, and couldn't understand Nelson's need to live with his grandmother.

A defensive fury begins to warm him. "I don't see why, any decent father would be glad to have us around. There's plenty of room, Mom-mom shouldn't live by herself."

"I think maybe it's natural," his wife offers, "in a couple that age, to want your own space."

"What's natural, to leave old ladies to die all alone?"

"Well, we're in the house now."

"Just temporarily."

"That's what I thought at first, Nelson, but now I don't believe you want us to have a place of our own. I'd be too much for you, just the two of us, you and me."

"I hate ticky-tacky apartments and condos."

"It's all right, I'm not complaining. I'm at home there now. I like your grandmother."

"I hate crummy old inner-city blocks getting all revitalized with swish little stores catering to queers and stoned interracial couples. It all reminds me of Kent. I came back here to get away from all that phony stuff. Somebody like Slim acts so counterculture sniffing coke and taking mesc and all that, you know what he does for a living? He's a biller for Diamond County Light and Power, he stuffs envelopes and is going to be Head Stuffer if he keeps at it for ten more years, how's that for Establishment?"

"He doesn't pretend to be a revolutionary, he just likes nice clothes and other boys."

"People ought to be con*si*stent," Nelson says, "it isn't *fair* to milk the society and then sneer at it at the same time. One of the reasons I liked you better than Melanie was she was so sold on all this radical stuff and I didn't think you were."

"I didn't know," Pru says, even more quietly, "that Melanie and I were competing for you. How much sexual *was* there between you two this summer?"

Nelson stares ahead, sorry his confiding has led to this. The Christmas lights are up in Brewer already, red and green and shivering tinsel looking dry and wilted above the snowless streets, the display a shadow of the seasonal glory he remembers as a boy, when there was abundant energy and little vandalism. Then each lamppost wore a giant wreath of authentic evergreen cut in the local hills and a lifelike laughing Santa in a white-and-silver sleigh and a line of eight glassy-eyed reindeer coated in what seemed real fur were suspended along cables stretched from the second story of Kroll's to the roof of the cigar-store building that used to be opposite. The downtown windows from below Fourth up to Seventh were immense with painted wooden soldiers and camels and Magi and golden organ pipes intertwined with clouds of spun glass and at night the sidewalks were drenched with shoppers and carols overflowing from the heated stores into air that prickled like a Christmas tree and it was impossible not to believe that somewhere, in the dark beyond the city, baby Jesus was being born. Now, it was pathetic. City budget had been cut way back and half the downtown stores were shells.

Pru insists, "Tell me. I know there was some."

"How do you know?"

"I know."

He decides to attack: let these young wives get the upper hand now they'll absolutely take over. "You don't know anything," he tells her, "the only thing you know is how to hang on to that damn thing inside you, *that* you're really good at. Boy."

Now she stares ahead, the sling on her arm a white blur in the corner of his vision. His eyes are stung by perforations of festive light in the December darkness. Let her play the martyr all she wants. You try to speak the truth and all you get is grief.

Mom-mom's old car feels silky but sluggish under him: all that metal they used to put in, even the glove compartment is lined with metal. When Pru goes silent like this, a kind of taste builds up in his throat, the taste of injustice. He didn't ask her to conceive this baby, nobody did, and now that he's married her she has the nerve to complain he isn't getting her an apartment of her own, give them one thing they instantly want the next. Women. They are holes, you put one thing in after another and it's never enough, you stuff your entire life in there and they smile that crooked little sad smile and are sorry you couldn't have done better, when all is said and done. He's gotten in plenty deep already and she's not getting him in any deeper. Sometimes when he looks at her from behind he can't believe how big she has grown, hips wide as a barn getting set to hatch not some little pink being but a horny-hided white rhinoceros no more in scale with Nelson than the mottled man in the moon, that's what cunts do to you when Nature takes over: go out of control.

The build-up of the taste in his throat is too great; he has to speak. "Speaking of fucking," he says, "what about *us*?"

"I don't think we're supposed to this late. Anyway I feel so ugly."

"Ugly or not, you're mine. You're my old lady."

"I get so sleepy, you can't imagine. But you're right. Let's do something tonight. Let's go home early. If somebody asks us back from the Laid-Back to their place let's not go."

"See if we had an apartment like you're so crazy for *we'd* have to ask people back. At least at Mom-mom's you're safe from that."

"I do feel safe there," she says, sighing. Meaning what? Meaning he shouldn't be bringing her out at night: he's married now, he works, he's not supposed to have any fun. Nelson dreads work, he wakes every workday morning with a gnawing in his stomach like he's the one with something inside him, that white rhinoceros. Those convertibles staring at him un-bought every day and the way Jake and Rudy can't get over his taking that little Kawasaki, as if it's some great joke he's deliberately played on Dad, when he hadn't meant it that way at all, the guy had been so pleading and Nelson was anxious to get the Mercury off the lot, it reminded him every time he saw it of that time Dad had been so scoffing, wouldn't even listen, it wasn't *fair*, he had had to ram the two cars together to wipe that you've-got-to-be-kidding smirk off his face.

On that showroom floor it's like a stage where he hasn't quite learned the lines yet. Maybe it's the stuff he's been taking, too much coke burns the septum out and now they say pot really does rot your brain cells, the THC gets tucked in the fatty tissue and makes you stupid for months, all these teen-age boys coming through with breasts now because something was suppressed when they were turning on at age thirteen, Nelson has these visions lately though he's standing upright with his eyes open, people with holes where their noses should be because of too much coke, or Pru lying there in the hospital with this pink-eyed baby rhinoceros, maybe it has to do with that cast on her arm, dirty and crumbling at the edges now, the gauze underneath the plaster fraying through. And Dad. He's getting bigger and bigger, never jogs anymore, his skin glows like his pores are absorbing food out of the air.

One of the books Nelson had as a child, with those stiff shiny cartoon covers and a black spine like electrical tape, had a picture in it of a giant, his face all bumpy and green with hairs coming out of it here and there, and smiling—that made it worse, that the giant was grinning, looking in, with those blubbery lips and separated teeth giants have, looking into some cave where two children, a boy and a girl, brother and sister probably, who were the heroes of the story are crouching, silhouettes in shadow, you see only the backs of their heads, they are *you*, looking out, hunted, too scared to move a muscle or breathe a breath as the great bumpy gleeful face fills the sunny mouth of the cave. That's how he sees Dad these days: he Nelson is in a tunnel and his father's face fills the far end where he might get out into the sun. The old man doesn't even know he's doing it, it comes on with that little nibbly sorry smile, a flick of dismissal as he pivots away, disappointed, that's it, he's

disappointed his father, he should be something other than
he is, and now at the lot all the men, not just Jake and Rudy
but Manny and his mechanics all grimy with grease, only the
skin around their eyes white, staring, see that too: he is not his
father, lacks that height, that tossing off that Harry Angstrom
can do. And no witness but Nelson stands in the universe to
proclaim that his father is guilty, a cheat and coward and murderer, and when he tries to proclaim it nothing comes out, the
world laughs as he stands there with open mouth silent. The
giant looks in and smiles and Nelson sinks back deeper into
the tunnel. He likes that about the Laid-Back, the tunnel snugness of it, and the smoke and the booze and the joints passed
from hand to hand under the tables, and the acceptance, the
being all in the smoky tunnel together, rats, losers, who cares,
you didn't have to listen to what anybody said because nobody
was going to buy a Toyota or insurance policy or anything
anyway. Why don't they make a society where people are given
what they need and do what they want to do? Dad would say
that's fantastic but it's how animals live all the time.

"I still think you fucked Melanie," Pru says, in her dried-up
slum cat's flat voice. One track and that's it.

Without braking Nelson swings the big Chrysler around the
corner where that shaggy park blocks the way down Weiser
Street. Pine Street has been made one way and he has to approach it from around the block so Pru doesn't have too far to
walk. "Oh, what if I did?" he says. "You and I weren't married,
what does it matter now?"

"It doesn't matter because of *you*, we all know you'll grab
anything you can get you're so greedy, it matters because she
was my *friend*. I trusted her. I trusted you both."

"For Chrissake, don't snivel."

"I'm not snivelling." But he foresees how she will sit there
beside him in the booth sulking and not saying anything, not
listening to anything but that kicking in her belly, her broken
arm making her look even more ridiculous, belly and sling and
all, and picturing it that way makes him feel a little sorry for
her, until he tells himself it's his way of taking care of her,
bringing her along when a lot of guys wouldn't.

"Hey," he says gruffly. "Love you."

"Love you, Nelson," she responds, lifting the hand not in a

sling from her lap as he lifts one of his from the wheel to give hers a squeeze. Funny, the fatter the middle of her is getting the thinner and drier her hands and face seem.

"We'll leave after two beers," he promises. Maybe the girl in white pants will be there. She sometimes comes in with that big dumb Jamie and Nelson can tell it is she who gets them here; she digs the scene and he doesn't.

The Laid-Back under this new name is such a success that parking along Pine is hard to find; he wants to spare Pru at least a long walk in the cold, though the doctor says exercise is good. He hates the cold. When he was little he had loved December because it had Christmas in it toward the end and he was so excited by all the things there were to get in the world that he never noticed how the dark and cold closed in, tighter and tighter. And now Dad is taking Mom off for this fancy holiday on some island with these putrid other couples, to lie there and bask while Nelson freezes and holds the fort at the lot; it's not fair. The girl doesn't always wear white slacks, the last time he saw her she had on one of that new style of skirt with the big slit down the side. There is a space in front of the long low brick building that used to be the Verity Press, between an old two-tone Fairlane and a bronze Honda station wagon, that looks big enough, just. The trick of tight parking is to swing your back bumper square into the other guy's headlights and don't leave yourself too far out from the curb or you'll be forever jockeying in. And don't be afraid to cut it tight on the left, you always have more room than you think. He pulls so close to the Fairlane Pru speaks up sharply, "Nelson."

He says, "I see him, I *see* him, shut up and let me concentrate." He intends, with that heavy Chrysler's veloured steering wheel—a ratio on the power steering you could turn a cruise ship with—to snap the car into its slot slick as a skater stopping on ice. God, figure skaters' costumes are sexy, the way their little skirts flip up when they skate ass-backwards, and he remembers, straining to see the Honda's rather low little headlights, how that girl's slit skirt fell away to show a whole long load of shining thigh before she arranged herself on the barstool, having given Nelson a brief shy smile of recognition. Mom-mom's ponderous Chrysler slips into reverse and his anticipation of ideal liquid motion is so strong he does not hear the subtle grinding of metal on metal until it has proceeded half the car's length and Pru is yelping, Jesus, like she's having the baby now.

Webb Murkett says gold has gone about as far as it can go for now: the little man in America has caught the fever and when the little man climbs on the bandwagon the smart money gets off. Silver, now that's another story: the Hunt brothers down in Texas are buying up silver futures at the rate of millions a day, and big boys like that must know something. Harry decides to change his gold into silver.

Janice was going to come downtown anyway to do some Christmas shopping, so he meets her at the Crêpe House (which she still calls Johnny Frye's) for lunch, and then they can go to the Brewer Trust with the safe-deposit key and take out the thirty Krugerrands Harry bought for $11,314.20 three months before. In the cubicle the bank lets you commune with your safe-deposit box in, he fishes out from behind the insurance policies and U.S. Savings Bonds the two blue-tinted cylinders like dollhouse toilets, and passes them into Janice's hands, one into each, and smiles when her face acknowledges with renewed surprise the heft, the weight of the gold. Solid citizens by this extra degree, then, the two of them walk out between the great granite pillars of the Brewer Trust into the frail December sunlight and cross through the forest, where the fountains are dry and the concrete park benches are spray-painted full of young people's names, and on down the east side of Weiser past two blocks of stores doing scattered Christmas business. Underfed little Puerto Rican women are the only ones scuttling in and out of the cut-rate entranceways, and kids who ought to be in school, and bleary retirees in dirty padded parkas and hunter's hats, with whiskery loose jaws; the mills have used these old guys up and spit them out.

The tinsel of the wreaths hung on the aluminum lampposts tingles, audibly shivering, as Harry passes each post. Gold, gold, his heart sings, feeling the weight balanced in the two deep pockets of his overcoat and swinging in time with his strides. Janice hurries beside him with shorter steps, a tidy dense woman warm in a sheepskin coat that comes down to her boots, clutching several packages whose paper rattles in this same wind that stirs the tinsel. He sees them together

in the flecked scarred mirror next to a shoestore entrance:
him tall and unbowed and white of face, her short and dark
and trotting beside him in boots of oxblood leather zippered
tight to her ankles, with high heels, so they thrust from her
swinging coat with a smartness of silhouette advertising as
clear as his nappy black overcoat and Irish bog hat that he
is all set, that they are all set, that their smiles as they walk
along can afford to discard the bitter blank glances that flicker
toward them on the street, then fall away.

Fiscal Alternatives with its long thin Venetian blinds is in
the next block, a block that once had the name of disreputable
but with the general sinking of the downtown is now no worse
than the next. Inside, the girl with platinum hair and long fingernails smiles in recognition of him, and pulls a plastic chair
over from the waiting area for Janice. After a telephone call to
some far-off trading floor, she runs some figures through her
little computer and tells them, as they sit bulky in their coats
at the corner of her desk, that the price of gold per ounce
had nearly touched five hundred earlier this morning but now
she can offer them no more than $488.75 per coin, which will
come to—her fingers dance unhampered by her nails; the gray
display slot of the computer staggers forth with its bland magnetic answer—$14,662.50. Harry calculates inwardly that he
has made a thousand a month on his gold and asks her how
much silver he can buy for that now. The young woman slides
out from under her eyelashes a glance as if she is a manicurist
deciding whether or not to admit that she does, in the back
room, also give massages. At his side Janice has lit a cigarette,
and her smoke pours across the desk and pollutes the relationship this metallic temptress and Harry have established.

The girl explains, "We don't deal in silver bullion. We only
handle silver in the form of pre-'65 silver dollars, which we sell
under melt value."

"Melt value?" Harry asks. He had pictured a tidy ingot that
would slip into the safe-deposit box snug as a gun into a holster.

The salesgirl is patient, with something sultry about her dis-
passion. Some of the silky weightiness of precious metals has
rubbed off onto her. "You know, the old-fashioned cartwheel"
—she makes an illustrative circle with daggerlike forefinger and
thumb—"the U.S. Mint put out until fifteen years ago. Each

one contains point seventy-five troy ounces of silver. Silver this noon was going for"—she consults a slip on her desk, next to the vanilla push-dial telephone—"$23.55 a troy ounce, which would make each coin, irrespective of collector value, worth" —the calculator again—"$17.66. But there's some wear on some of the coins, so were you and your wife to decide to buy now I could give you a quote under that."

"These are old coins?" Janice asks, that Ma Springer edge in her voice.

"Some are, some aren't," the girl answers coolly. "We buy them by weight from collectors who have sifted through them for collector value."

This isn't what Harry had pictured, but Webb had sworn that silver was where the smart money was. He asks, "How many could we buy with the gold money?"

A flurry of computation follows; $14,662.50 would convert to the magical number of 888. Eight hundred eighty-eight silver dollars priced at $16.50 each, including commission and Pennsylvania sales tax. To Rabbit eight hundred eighty-eight seems like a lot of anything, even matchsticks. He looks at Janice. "Sweetie. Whaddeya think?"

"Harry, I don't know what to think. It's your investment."

"But it's our money."

"You don't want to just keep the gold."

"Webb says silver could double, if they don't return the hostages."

Janice turns to the girl. "I was just wondering, if we found a house we wanted to put a down payment on, how liquid is this silver?"

The blonde speaks to Janice with new respect, at a softer pitch, woman to woman. "It's very liquid. Much more so than collectibles or land. Fiscal Alternatives guarantees to buy back whatever it sells. These coins today, if you brought them in, we'd pay"—she consults the papers on her desk again— "thirteen fifty each."

"So we'd be out three dollars times eight hundred eighty-eight," Harry says. His palms have started to sweat, maybe it's the overcoat. Make a little profit in this world and right away the world starts scheming to take it from you. He wishes he had the gold back. It was so pretty, that little delicate deer on the reverse side.

"Oh, but the way silver's been going," the girl says, pausing to scratch at some fleck of imperfection adjacent to the corner of her lips, "you could make that up in a week. I think you're doing the smart thing."

"Yeah, but as you say, suppose the Iran thing gets settled," Harry worries. "Won't the whole bubble burst?"

"Precious metals aren't a bubble. Precious metals are the ultimate security. I myself think what's brought the Arab money into gold was not so much Iran as the occupation of the Great Mosque. When the Saudis are in trouble, then it's *really* a new ballgame."

A new ballgame, hey. "O.K.," he says, "let's do it. We'll buy the silver."

Platinum-hair seems a bit surprised, for all of her smooth sales talk, and there is a long hassle over the phone locating so many coins. At last some boy she calls Lyle brings in a gray cloth sack like you would carry some leftover mail in; he is swaying with the effort and grunts right out, lifting the sack up onto her desk, but then he has a slender build, with something faggy about him, maybe his short haircut. Funny how that's swung completely around: the squares let their hair grow now and the fags and punks are the ones with butches. Harry wonders what they're doing in the Marines, probably down to their shoulders. This Lyle goes off, after giving Harry a suspicious squint like he's bought not only the massage but the black-leather-and-whip trick too.

At first Harry and Janice think that only the girl with the platinum hair and all but perfect skin may touch the coins. She pushes her papers to one side of her desk and struggles to lift a corner of the bag. Dollars spill out. "Damn." She sucks at a fingernail. "You can help count if you would." They take off their coats and dig in, counting into stacks of ten. Silver is all over the desk, hundreds of Miss Libertys, some thinned by wear, some as chunky as if virgin from the mint. Handling such a palpable luxury of profiles and slogans and eagles makes Janice titter, and Harry knows what she means: playing in the mud. The muchness. The stacks proliferate and are arranged in ranks of ten times ten. The bag at last yields its final coin, with a smidgeon of lint the girl flicks away. Unsmiling, she waves her red-tipped hand across her stacks. "I have three hundred and ninety."

Harry taps his stacks and reports, "Two forty."

Janice says of hers, "Two hundred fifty-eight." She beat him. He is proud of her. She can become a teller if he suddenly dies.

The calculator is consulted: 888. "Exactly right," the girl says, as surprised as they. She performs the paperwork, and gives Harry back two quarters and a ten-dollar bill in change. He wonders if he should hand it back to her, as a tip. The coins fit into three cardboard boxes the size of fat bricks. Harry puts them one on top of another, and when he tries to lift all three Janice and the girl both laugh aloud at the expression on his face.

"My God," he says. "What do they weigh?"

The platinum-headed girl fiddles at her computer. "If you take each one to be a troy ounce at least, it comes to seventy-four pounds. There are only twelve ounces troy measure in a pound."

He turns to Janice. "You carry one."

She lifts one and it's his turn to laugh, at the look on her face, her eyelids stretched wide. "I can't," she says.

"You must," he says. "It's only up to the bank. Come on, I gotta get back to the lot. Whajja play all that tennis for if you don't have any muscles?"

He is proud of that tennis; he is performing for the blond girl now, acting the role of eccentric Penn Park nob. She suggests, "Maybe Lyle could walk up with you."

Rabbit doesn't want to be seen on the street with that fag. "We can manage." To Janice he says, "Just imagine you're pregnant. Come on. Let's go." To the girl he says, "She'll be back for her packages." He picks up two of the boxes and pushes the door open with his shoulder, forcing Janice to follow. Out in the cold sunlight and shimmering wind of Weiser Street he tries not to grimace, or to return the stares of those who glance wonderingly at the two small boxes clutched so fiercely in his two hands at the level of his fly.

A black man in a blue watch cap, with bloodshot eyes like marbles dropped in orange juice, halts on the pavement and stumbles a step toward Harry. "Hey buddy you wanna hep out a fren'—" Something about these blacks they really zero in on Rabbit. He pivots to shield the silver with his body, and its swung weight tips him so he has to take a step. In moving off, he doesn't dare look behind him to see if Janice is following. But standing on the curb next to a bent parking meter he hears her breathing and feels her struggle to his side.

"This coat is so heavy too," she pants.

"Let's cross," he says.

"In the middle of the block?"

"Don't argue," he mutters, feeling the puzzled black man at his back. He pushes off the curb, causing a bus halfway down the block to hiss with its brakes. In the middle of the street, where the double white line has wobbled in summer's soft tar, he waits for Janice to catch up. The girl has given her the mail sack to carry the third box of silver in, but rather than sling it over her shoulder Janice carries it cradled in her left arm like a baby. "How're you doing?" he asks her.

"I'll manage. Keep moving, Harry."

They reach the far curb. The peanut store now not only has porno magazines inside but has put an array of them on a rack outside. Young muscular oiled boys pose singly or in pairs under titles such as DRUMMER and SKIN. A Japanese in a three-piece pinstripe suit and gray bowler hat steps smartly out of the door, folding a *New York Times* and a *Wall Street Journal* together under his arm. How did the Japanese ever get to Brewer? As the door eases shut, the old circus smell of warm roasted peanuts drifts out to the cold sidewalk. Harry says to Janice, "We could put all three boxes in the bag and I could lug it over my shoulder. You know, like Santa Claus. Ho ho."

A small crowd of pocked dark street kids mixed with shaggy rummies in their winter layered look threatens to collect around them as they confer. Harry tightens his grip on his two boxes. Janice hugs her third and says, "Let's push on this way. The bank's only a block more." Her face is flushed and bitten by the cold, her eyes squinting and watering and her mouth a determined slot.

"A good block and a half," he corrects.

Past then the Brewer Wallpaper Company with its display rolls stiffening in the dusty windows like shrouds, past

Blimline's Sandwiches and Manderbach Wholesale Office Supplies and a narrow place jammed with flat boxes called Hobby Heaven, past the cigar store with its giant rusting Y-B sign and the ornately iron-barred windows of the old Conrad Weiser Oyster House that now promises *Live Entertainment* in desperate red letters on its dark doors, across Fourth Street when the light at last turns green, past the long glass-block-inlaid façade of the Acme they say is going out of business at the end of the year, past Hollywood Beauty Supplies and Imperial Floor Coverings and Zenith Auto Parts and Accessories with its sweetish baked smell of fresh tires and window of chrome tailpipes they go, man and wife, as the wind intensifies and the sparkling sidewalk squares grow in size.

The squared-off weight in Harry's hands has become a hostile thing, burning his palms, knocking against his crotch. Now when he would almost welcome being robbed he feels that the others on this west side of the street are shying from them, as somehow menacing, distorted into struggling shapes by the force-fields of their dense boxes. He keeps having to wait for Janice to catch up, while his own burden, double hers, pulls at his arms. The tinsel wound around the aluminum lampposts vibrates furiously. He is sweating across his back beneath his expensive overcoat and his shirt collar keeps drying to a clammy cold edge. During these waits he stares up Weiser toward the mauve and brown bulk of Mt. Judge; in his eyes as a child God had reposed on the slopes of that mountain, and now he can imagine how through God's eyes from that vantage he and Janice might look below: two ants trying to make it up the sides of a bathroom basin.

They pass a camera store advertising Agfa film, the Hexerei Boutique with its mannequins flaunting their nippleless boobs through transparent blouses and vests of gold mail, a Rexall's with pastel vibrators among the suggested Christmas gifts in the windows festooned with cotton and angel hair, the Crêpe House with its lunching couples, the locally famous cigar store saved as an act of historical preservation, and a new store called PedalEase specializing in male and female footwear for jogging and tennis and even racquetball and squash, that young couples or pairs of young singles do together these days, to judge from the big cardboard blow-ups in the window. The

Dacron-clad girl's honey-colored hair lifts like air made liquid as she laughingly strokes a ball on easy feet. Next, at last,
the first of the four great granite columns of the Brewer Trust
looms. Harry leans his aching back against its Roman breadth
while waiting for Janice to catch up. If she's robbed in this gap
between them it will cost them a third of $14,652 or nearly
$5000 but at this point the risk doesn't seem so real. Some
distance away he sees spray-painted on the back of one of the
concrete benches in the mall of trees a slogan SKEETER LIVES.
If he could go closer he could be sure that's what it says. But
he cannot move. Janice arrives beside his shoulder. Red-faced,
she looks like her mother. "Let's not stand here," she pants.
Even the circumference of the pillar seems a lengthy distance
as she leads him around it and pushes ahead of him through
the revolving doors.

Christmas carols are pealing within the great vaulted interior. The high groined ceiling is painted blue here in every
season, with evenly spaced stars of gold. When Harry sets
his two boxes down on one of the shelves where you write
checks, his relieved body seems to rise toward this false sky.
The teller, a lady in an orchid pants suit, smiles to be re-
admitting them to their safe-deposit box so soon. Their box is
a four by four—narrower, they discover, than the boxes of silver dollars three rows abreast. Hearts still laboring, their hands
still hurting, Harry and Janice are slow to grasp the disparity,
once the frosted glass door has sealed them into the cubicle.
Harry several times measures the width of one paper lid against
the breadth of tin before concluding, "We need a bigger box."
Janice is delegated to go back out into the bank and request
one. Her father had been a good friend of the manager. When
she returns, it is with the news that there has been a run lately
on safe-deposit boxes, that the best the bank could do was put
the Angstroms on a list. The manager that Daddy knew has
retired. The present one seemed to Janice very young, though
he wasn't exactly rude.

Harry laughs. "Well we can't sell 'em back to Blondie down
there, it'd cost us a fortune. Could we dump everything back
in the bag and stuff it in?"

Crowded together in the cubicle, he and Janice keep bumping into each other, and he scents rising from her for the first

time a doubt that he has led them well in this new inflated
world; or perhaps the doubt he scents arises from him. But
there can be no turning back. They transfer silver dollars from
the boxes to the bag. When the silver clinks loudly, Janice
winces and says, "*Shh.*"

"Why? Who'll hear?"

"The people out there. The tellers."

"What do they care?"

"I care," Janice says. "It's stifling in here." She takes off
her sheepskin coat and in the absence of a hook to hang it
on drops it folded to the floor. He takes off his black overcoat and drops it on top. Sweat of exertion has made her
hair springier; her bangs have curled back to reveal that high
glossy forehead that is so much her, now and twenty years
ago, that he kisses it, tasting salt. He wonders if people have
ever screwed in these cubicles and imagines that a vault would
be a nice place, one of those primped-up young tellers and a
lecherous old mortgage officer, put the time-lock on to dawn
and ball away. Janice feeds stacks of coins into the coarse gray
pouch furtively, suppressing the clink. "This is so embarrassing," she says, "suppose one of those ladies comes in," as if the
silver is naked flesh; and not for the first time in twenty-three
years he feels a furtive rush of loving her, caught with him as
she is in the tight places life affords. He takes one of the silver
dollars and slips it down the neck of her linen blouse into her
bra. As he foresaw, she squeals at the chill and tries to suppress the squeal. He loves her more, seeing her unbutton her
blouse a button and frowningly dig into her bra for the coin;
old as he is it still excites him to watch women fiddle with
their underwear. Make our own coat hook in here.

After a while she announces, "It simply will *not* go in." Stuff
and adjust as they will, hardly half of the bagged coins can
be made to fit. Their insurance policies and Savings Bonds,
Nelson's birth certificate and the never-discarded mortgage
papers for the house in Penn Villas that burned down—all the
scraps of paper preserved as evidence of their passage through
an economy and a certain legal time—are lifted out and reshuffled to no avail. The thick cloth of the bag, the tendency of
loose coins to bunch in a clump, the long slender shape of the
gray tin box frustrate them as side by side they tug and push,

surgeons at a hopeless case. The eight hundred eighty-eight coins keep escaping the mouth of the sack and falling onto the floor and rolling into corners. When they have pressed the absolute maximum into the box, so its tin sides bulge, they are still left with three hundred silver dollars, which Harry distributes among the pockets of his overcoat.

When they emerge from the cubicle, the friendly teller in her orchid outfit offers to take the loaded box off his hands. "Pretty heavy," he warns her. "Better let me do it." Her eyebrows arch; she backs off and leads him into the vault. They go through a great door, its terraced edges gleaming, into a space walled with small burnished rectangles and floored in waxy white. Not a good place to fuck, he was wrong about that. She lets him slide his long box into the empty rectangle. R.I.P. Harry is in a sweat, bent over with effort. He straightens up and apologizes, "Sorry we loaded it up with so much crap."

"Oh no," the orchid lady says. "A lot of people nowadays . . . all this burglary."

"What happens if the burglars get in here?" he jokes.

This is not funny. "Oh . . . they *can't*."

Outside the bank, the afternoon has progressed, and shadows from the buildings darken the glitter of tinsel. Janice taps one of his pockets playfully, to hear him jingle. "What are you going to do with all these?"

"Give 'em away to the poor. That bitch down the street, that's the last time I buy anything from her." Cold cakes his face as his sweat dries. Several guys he knows from Rotary come out of the Crêpe House looking punchy on lunch and he gives them the high sign, while striding on. God knows what's happening over on the lot without him, the kid may be accepting roller skates for trade-in.

"You could use the safe at the lot," Janice suggests. "They could go into one of these." She hands him one of the empty cardboard boxes.

"Nelson will steal 'em," he says. "He knows the combination now too."

"Harry. What a thing to say."

"You know how much that scrape he gave your mother's Chrysler is going to cost? Eight hundred fucking bucks minimum. He must have been out of his head. You could see poor

Pru was humiliated, I wonder how long she'll let things cook before she gets smart and asks for a divorce. That'll cost us, too." His overcoat, so weighted, drags his shoulders down. He feels, as if the sidewalk now is a downslanted plane, the whole year dropping away under him, loss after loss. His silver is scattered, tinsel. His box will break, the janitor will sweep up the coins. It's all dirt anyway. The great sad lie told to children that is Christmas stains Weiser end to end, and through the murk he glimpses the truth that to be rich is to be robbed, to be rich is to be poor.

Janice recalls him to reality, saying, "Harry, please. Stop looking so tragic. Pru loves Nelson, and he loves her. They won't get a divorce."

"I wasn't thinking about that. I was thinking about how silver's going to go down."

"Oh, what do we care if it does? Everything's just a gamble anyway."

Bless that dope, still trying. The daughter of old Fred Springer, local high roller. Rolled himself into a satin-lined coffin. In the old days they used to bury the silver and put the corpses in slots in the wall.

"I'll walk down to the car with you," Janice says, worried-wifely. "I have to get my packages back from that bitch as you call her. How much did you want to go to bed with her by the way?" Trying to find a topic he'll enjoy.

"Hardly at all," he confesses. "It's terrifying in fact, how little. Did you get a look at her fingernails? Sccr-*ratch*."

The week between the holidays is a low one for car sales: people feel strapped after Christmas, and with winter coming, ice and salt on the road and fenderbenders likely, they are inclined to stick with the heap they have. Ride it out to spring is the motto. At least the snowmobile's been moved around to the back where nobody can see it, instead of its sitting there like some kind of cousin of those new little front-wheel-drive Tercels. Where do they get their names? Sounds like an Edsel. Even Toyota, it has too many *o*'s, makes people think of "toy." Datsun and Honda, you don't know where they're coming from. Datsun could be German from the sound of it, data, rat-tat-tat, rising sun. The Chuck Wagon across Route lll isn't doing much of a business either, now that it's too cold to eat outdoors or in the car, unless you leave the motor running, people die doing that every winter, trying to screw. The build-up is terrific though of hoagie wrappers and milkshake cartons blowing around in the lot, with the dust. Different kind of dust in December, grayer and grittier than summer dust, maybe the colder air, less lift in it, like cold air holds less water, that's why the insides of the storm windows now when you wake up in the morning have all that dew. Think of all the problems. Rust. Dry rot. Engines that don't start in the morning unless you take off the distributor cap and wipe the wires. Without condensation the world might last forever. On the moon, for example, there's no problem. Or on Mars either it turns out. New Year's, Buddy Inglefinger is throwing the blast this year, guess he was afraid of dropping out of sight with the old gang, getting the wind up about the trip to the islands they're taking without inviting him. Wonder who his hostess is going to be, that flat-chested sourpuss with straight black hair running some kind of crazy shop in Brewer or that girl before her, with the rash on the inside of her thighs and even between her breasts you could see in a bathing suit, what *was* her name? Ginger. Georgene. He and Janice just want to make an appearance to be polite, you get to a certain age you know nothing much is going to happen at parties, and leave right after midnight. Then ten more days and, *powie*, the islands. Just the six of them. Little Cindy down there in all that sand. He needs a rest, things are getting him down. Sell less than a car a day in this business not counting Sundays and you're in trouble. All this tin getting dusty and rusty, the chrome developing pimples. Metal corrodes. Silver dropped two dollars an ounce the minute he bought it from that bitch.

Nelson, who has been in the shop with Manny fussing over the repairs to the Chrysler, the kid wanting a break on the full $18.50 customer rate and Manny explaining over and over like to a moron how if you shave the rate for agency employees it shows up in the books and affects everybody's end-of-the-month incentive bonus, comes over and stands by his father at the window.

Harry can't get used to the kid in a suit, it makes him seem even shorter somehow, like one of those midget emcees in a tuxedo, and with his hair shaped longer now and fluffed up by Pru's blow-drier after every shower Nellie seems a little mean-eyed dude Harry never knew. Janice used to say when the boy was little how he had Harry's ears with that crimp in the fold at the tip like one of the old-fashioned train conductors had taken his punch, but the tips of Nelson's are neatly covered by soft shingles of hair and Harry hasn't bothered to study his own since at about the age of forty he came out of that adolescent who-am-I vanity trip. He just shaves as quick as he can now and gets away from the mirror. Ruth had sweetly small tightly folded ears, he remembers. Janice's get so tan on top an arch of tiny dark spots comes out. Her father's lobes got long as a Chinaman's before he died. Nelson has a hot-looking pimple almost due to pop in the crease above his nostril, Harry notices in the light flooding through the showroom window. The slant of sun makes all the dust on the plate glass look thick as gold leaf this time of year, the arc of each day is so low. The kid is trying to be friendly. Come on. Unbend.

Harry asks him, "You stay up to watch the 76ers finish?"

"Naa."

"That Gervin for San Antonio was something, wasn't he? I heard on the radio this morning he finished with forty-six points."

"Basketball is all goons, if you ask me."

"It's changed a lot since my day," Rabbit admits. "The refs used to call travelling once in a while at least; now, Christ, they eat up half the floor going in for a lay-up."

"I like hockey," Nelson says.

"I know you do. When you have the damn Flyers on there's nowhere in the house you can go to get away from the yelling. All those apes in the crowd go for is to see a fight break out and someone's teeth get knocked out. Blood on the ice, that's the drawing card." This isn't going right; he tries another topic. "What do you think about those Russkis in Afghanistan? They sure gave themselves a Christmas present."

"It's stupid," Nelson says. "I mean, Carter's getting all up-set. It's no worse than what we did in Vietnam, it's not even as bad because at least it's right next door and they've had a puppet government there for years."

"Puppet governments are O.K., huh?"

"Well *ev*erybody has 'em. All of South America is our puppet governments."

"I bet that'd be news to the spics."

"At least the Russians, Dad, *do* it when they're going to do it. We *try* to do it and then everything gets all bogged down in politics. We can't do *any*thing anymore."

"Well not with young people talking like you we can't," Harry says to his son. "How would you feel about going over and fighting in Afghanistan?"

The boy chuckles. "Dad, I'm a married man. And way past draft age besides."

Can this be? Harry doesn't feel too old to fight, and he's going to be forty-seven in February. He's always been sort of sorry they didn't send him to Korea when they had him in the Army, though at the time he was happy enough to hunker down in Texas. They had a funny straight-on way of looking at the world out there: money, booze, and broads, and that was it. Down to the bones. What is it Mim likes to say? God didn't go west, He died on the trail. To Nelson he says, "You mean you got married to stay out of the next war?"

"There won't be any next war, Carter will make a lot of noise but wind up letting them have it, just like he's letting Iran have the hostages. Actually, Billy Fosnacht was saying the only way we'll get the hostages back is if Russia invades Iran. Then they'd give us the hostages and sell us the oil because they need our wheat."

"Billy Fosnacht—that jerk around again?"

"Just for vacation."

"No offense, Nelson, but how can you stand that pill?"

"He's my friend. But I know why you can't stand him."

"Why can't I?" Harry asks, his heart rising to what has become a confrontation.

Turning full toward his father beside the gold-dusted pane, the boy's face seems to shrink with hate, hate and fear of being hit for what he is saying. "Because Billy was there the night you were screwing his mother while Skeeter was burning up Jill in the house we should have been in, protecting her."

That night. Ten years ago, and still cooking in the kid's head, alive like a maggot affecting his growth. "That still bugs you, doesn't it?" Rabbit says mildly.

The boy doesn't hear, his eyes lost in those sockets sunk as if thumbs had gripped too deep in clay, trying to pick up a lump. "You let Jill die."

"I didn't, and Skeeter didn't. We don't know who burnt the house down but it wasn't us. It was the neighbors, their idea of a Welcome Wagon. You got to let it go, kid. Your mother and me have let it go."

"I know you have." The sound of Mildred Kroust's electric typewriter rattles muffled in the distance, a couple in maroon parkas is stalking around in the lot checking the price stickers taped inside the windows, the boy stares as if stunned by the sound of his father's voice trying to reach him.

"The past is the past," Harry goes on, "you got to live in the present. Jill was headed that way no matter what the rest of us did. The first time I saw her, she had the kiss of death on her face."

"I know that's what you want to think."

"It's the only way to think. When you're my age you'll see it. At my age if you carried all the misery you've seen on your back you'd never get up in the morning." A flicker of something, a split second when he feels the boy actually listening, encourages Harry to urge his voice deeper, more warmly. "Once that baby of yours shows up," he tells the boy, "you'll have your hands full. You'll have a better perspective."

"You want to know something?" Nelson asks in a rapid dead voice, looking through him with lifted eyes the slant light has stolen color from.

"What?" Rabbit's heart skips.

"When Pru fell down those stairs. I'm not sure if I gave her a push or not. I can't remember."

Harry laughs, scared. "Of course you didn't push her. Why would you push her?"

"Because I'm as crazy as you."

"We're not crazy, either of us. Just frustrated, sometimes."

"Really?" This seems information the kid is grateful for.

"Sure. Anyway, everybody survived. When is he due? He or she." Fear rolls off this kid so thick Harry doesn't want to keep talking to him. The way his eyes looked transparent that instant, all the brown lifted out.

Nelson lowers his eyes, surly again. "They think about three more weeks."

"That's great. We'll be back in plenty of time. Look, Nelson. Maybe I haven't done everything right in my life. I know I haven't. But I haven't committed the greatest sin. I haven't laid down and died."

"Who says that's the greatest sin?"

"Everybody says it. The church, the government. It's against Nature, to give up, you've got to keep moving. That's the thing about you. You're not moving. You don't want to be here, selling old man Springer's jalopies. You want to be out *there*, learning something." He gestures toward the west, beyond West Brewer. "How to hang glide, or run a computer, or whatever."

He has talked too much and closed up the space that opened in Nelson's resistance for a second. Nelson accuses: "You don't want me here."

"I want you where you're happy and that's not here. Now I didn't want to say anything but I've been going over the figures with Mildred and they're not that hot. Since you came here and Charlie left, gross sales are down about eleven per cent over last year, this same period, November–December."

The boy's eyes water. "I *try*, Dad. I try to be friendly and semi-aggressive and all that when the people come in."

"I know you do, Nelson. I know you do."

"I can't go out and *drag* 'em in out of the cold."

"You're right. Forget what I said. The thing about Charlie was, he had connections. I've lived in this county all my life except those two years in the Army and I don't have that kind of connections."

"I know a *lot* of people my age," Nelson protests.

"Yeah," Harry says, "you know the kind of people who sell you their used-up convertibles for a fancy price. But Charlie knows the kind of people who actually come in and buy a car. He expects 'em to; he's not surprised, they're not surprised. Maybe it's being Greek, I don't know. No matter what they say about you and me, kid, we're not Greek."

This joking doesn't help; the boy has been wounded, deeper than Harry wanted. "I don't think it's me," Nelson says. "It's the economy."

The traffic on Route III is picking up; people are heading home in the gloom. Harry too can go; Nelson is on the floor till eight. Climb into the Corona and turn on the four-speaker radio and hear how silver is doing. Hi ho, Silver. Harry says, in a voice that sounds sage in his own ears, almost like Webb Murkett's, "Yeah, well, that has its wrinkles. This oil thing is hurting the Japanese worse than it is us, and what hurts them should be doing us good. The yen is down, these cars cost less in real dollars than they did last year, and it ought to be reflected in our sales." That look on Cindy's face in the photograph, Harry can't get it out of his mind: an anxious startled kind of joy, as if she was floating away in a balloon and had just felt the earth lurch free. "Numbers," he tells Nelson in stern conclusion. "Numbers don't lie, and they don't forgive."

New Year's Day was when Harry and Janice had decided to go to Ma Springer with their news, which they had been keeping to themselves for nearly a week. Dread of how the old lady might react had prompted the postponement, plus a groping after ceremony, a wish to show respect for the sacred bonds of family by announcing the break on a significant day, the first of a new decade. Yet now that the day is here, they feel hungover and depleted from having stayed at Buddy Inglefinger's until three in the morning. Their tardy departure had been further prolonged by an uproarious commotion over cars in the driveway—a car that wouldn't start, belonging to Thelma Harrison's Maryland cousin, who was visiting. There was a lot of boozy shouting and falling-down helpfulness in the headlights as jump cables were found and Ronnie's Volvo was jockeyed nose to nose with the cousin's Nova, everybody poking their flashlight in to make sure Ronnie was connecting positive to positive and not going to blow out the batteries. Harry has seen jump cables actually melt in circumstances like this. Some woman he hardly knew had a mouth big enough to put the head of a flashlight in it, so her cheeks glowed like a lampshade. Buddy and his new girl, a frantic skinny six-footer with frizzed-out hair and three children from a broken marriage, had made some kind of punch of pineapple juice and rum and brandy, and the taste of pineapple still at noon keeps returning. On top of Harry's headache Nelson and Pru, who stayed home with Mom-mom last night watching on television straight from Times Square Guy Lombardo's brother now that Guy Lombardo is dead, are hogging the living room watching the Cotton Bowl Festival Parade from Texas, so he and Janice have to take Ma Springer into the kitchen to get some privacy. A deadly staleness flavors the new decade. As they sit down at the kitchen table for their interview, it seems to him that they have already done this, and are sitting down to a rerun.

Janice, her eyes ringed by weariness, turns to him in his daze and says, "Harry, you begin."

"Me?"

"My goodness, what can this be?" Ma asks, pretending to be cross but pleased by the formality, the two of them touching her elbows and steering her in here. "You're acting like Janice is pregnant but I know she had her tubes tied."

"Cauterized," Janice says softly, pained.

Harry begins. "Bessie, you know we've been looking at houses."

Playfulness snaps out of the old lady's face as if pulled by a rubber band. The skin at the corners of her set lips is crossed and recrossed, Harry suddenly sees, by fine dry wrinkles. In his mind his mother-in-law has stayed as when he first met her, packed into her skin; but unnoticed by him Bessie's hide has loosened and cracked like putty in a cellar window, has developed the complexity of paper crumpled and then smoothed again. He tastes pineapple. A small black spot of nausea appears and grows as if rapidly approaching down the great parched space of her severe, expectant silence.

"Now," he must go on, swallowing, "we think we've found one we like. A little stone two-story over in Penn Park. The realtor thinks it might have been a gardener's cottage that somebody sold off when the estates were broken up and then was enlarged to fit a better kitchen in. It's on a little turnaround off Franklin Drive behind the bigger houses; the privacy is great."

"It's only twenty minutes away, Mother."

Harry can't stop studying, in the cold kitchen light, the old woman's skin. The dark life of veins underneath that gave her her flushed swarthy look that Janice inherited has been overlaid with a kind of dust of fine gray threads, wrinkles etched on the lightstruck flat of the cheek nearest him like rows and rows of indecipherable writing scratched on a far clay cliff. He feels himself towering, giddy, and all of his poor ashamed words strike across a great distance, a terrible widening as Ma listens motionless to her doom. "Virtually next door," he says to her, "and with three bedrooms upstairs, I mean there's a little room that the kids who lived there had used as a kind of clubhouse, two bedrooms though absolutely, and we'd be happy to put you up any time if it came to that, for as long as needs be." He feels he is blundering: already he has the old lady living with them again, her TV set muttering on the other side of the wall.

Janice breaks in: "Really, Mother, it makes much more sense for Harry and me at this point of our lives."

"But I had to talk her into it, Ma; it was my idea. When you and Fred very kindly took us in after we got back together I never thought of it as for forever. I thought of it as more of a stop-gap thing, until we got our feet back under us."

What he had liked about it, he sees now, was that it would have made it easy for him to leave Janice: just walk out under the streetlights and leave her with her parents. But he hadn't left her, and now cannot. She is his fortune.

She is trying to soften her mother's silence. "Also as an investment, Mother. Every couple we know owns their own house, even this bachelor we were with last night, and a lot of the men earn less than Harry. Property's the only place to put money if you have any, what with inflation and all."

Ma Springer at last does speak, in a voice that keeps rising in spite of herself. "You'll have this place when I'm gone, if you could just wait. Why can't you wait a little yet?"

"Mother, that's ghoulish when you talk like that. We don't want to wait for *your* house; Harry and I want our house *now*." Janice lights a cigarette, and has to press her elbow onto the tabletop to hold the match steady.

Harry assures the old lady, "Bessie, you're going to live forever." But having seen what's happening to her skin he knows this isn't true.

Wide-eyed suddenly, she asks, "What's going to happen to this house then?"

Rabbit nearly laughs, the old lady's expression is so childlike, taken with the pitch of her voice. "It'll be fine," he tells her. "When they built places like this they built 'em to last. Not like the shacks they slap up now."

"Fred always wanted Janice to have this house," Ma Springer states, staring with eyes narrowed again at a place just between Harry's and Janice's heads. "For her security."

Janice laughs now. "Mother, I have plenty of security. We told you about the gold and silver."

"Playing with money like that is a good way to lose it," Ma says. "I don't want to leave this house to be auctioned off to some Brewer Jew. They're heading out this way, you know, now that the blacks and Puerto Ricans are trickling into the north side of town."

"Come on, Bessie," Harry says, "what do you care? Like I said, you got a lot of life ahead of you, but when you're gone, you're gone. Let go, you got to let some things go for other people to worry about. The Bible tells you that, it says it on every page. Let go; the Lord knows best."

Janice from her twitchy manner thinks he is saying too much. "Mother, we might come back to the house—"

"When the old crow is dead. Why didn't you and Harry tell me my presence was such a burden? I tried to stay in my room as much as I could. I went into the kitchen only when it looked like nobody else was going to make the meal—"

"Mother, stop it. You've been lovely. We both love you."

"Grace Stuhl would have taken me in, many's the times she offered. Though her house isn't half the size of this and has all those front steps." She sniffs, so loudly it seems a cry for help.

Nelson shouts in from the living room, "Mom-mom, when's lunch?"

Janice says urgently, "See, Mother. You're forgetting Nelson. He'll be here, with his *family*."

The old lady sniffs again, less tragically, and replies with pinched lips and a level red-rimmed gaze, "He may be or he may not be. The young can't be depended on."

Harry tells her, "You're right about that all right. They won't fight and they won't learn, just sit on their asses and get stoned."

Nelson comes into the kitchen holding a newspaper, today's Brewer *Standard*. He looks cheerful for once, on his good night's sleep. He has folded the paper to a quiz on Seventies trivia and asks them all, "How many of these people can you identify? Renée Richards, Steven Weed, Megan Marshack, Marjoe Gortner, Greta Rideout, Spider Sabich, D. B. Cooper. I got six out of seven, Pru got only four."

"Renée Richards was Patty Hearst's boyfriend," Rabbit begins.

Nelson sees the state his grandmother's face is in and asks, "What's happening here?"

Janice says, "We'll explain later, sweetie."

Harry tells him, "Your mother and I have found a house we're going to move to."

Nelson stares from one to the other of his parents and it seems he might scream, the way he goes white around the gills. But instead he pronounces quietly, "What a copout. What a fucking pair of copout artists. Well screw you both. Mom, Dad. Screw you."

And he returns to the living room where the rumble of drums and trombones merges with the mumble of unheard words as he and Pru confer within the tunnel of their young marriage. The kid had felt frightened. He felt left. Things are getting too big for him. Rabbit knows the feeling. For all that is wrong between them there are moments when his heart and Nelson's might be opposite ends of a single short steel bar, he knows so exactly what the kid is feeling. Still, just because people are frightened of being alone doesn't mean he has to sit still and be everybody's big fat patsy like Mim said.

Janice and her mother are holding hands, tears blurring both faces. When Janice cries, her face loses shape, dissolves to the ugly child she was. Her mother is saying, moaning as if to herself, "Oh I knew you were looking but I guess I didn't believe you'd actually go ahead and buy one when you have this free. Isn't there any adjustment we could make here so you could change your minds or at least let me get adjusted first? I'm too old, is the thing, too old to take on responsibility. The boy means well in his way but he's all *ferhuddled* for now, and the girl, I don't know. She wants to do it all but I'm not sure she can. To be honest, I've been dreading the baby, I've been trying to remember how it was with you and Nelson, and for the life of me I can't. I remember the milk didn't come the way they thought it should, and the doctor was so rude to you about it Fred had to step in and have a word."

Janice is nodding, nodding, tears making the side of her nose shine, the cords on her throat jumping out with every sob. "Maybe we could wait, though we said we'd pass papers, if you feel that way at least wait until the baby comes."

There is a rhythm the two of them are rocking to, hands clasped on the table, heads touching. "Do what you must, for your own happiness," Ma Springer is saying, "the ones left behind will manage. It can't do worse than kill me, and that might be a blessing."

She is turning Janice into a mess: face blubbery and melting, the pockets beneath her eyes liverish with guilt, Janice is leaning hard into her mother, giving in on the house, begging for forgiveness, "Mother we thought, Harry was certain, you'd feel less alone, with—"

"With a worry like Nelson in the house?"

Tough old turkey. Harry better step in before Janice gives it all away. His throat hardens. "Listen, Bessie. You asked for him, you got him."

Free! Macadam falls away beneath the wheels, a tawny old fort can be glimpsed as they lift off the runway beneath the rounded riveted edge of one great wing, the gas tanks of South Philadelphia are reduced to a set of white checkers. The wheels thump, retracted, and cruel photons glitter on the aluminum motionless beside the window. The swift ascent of the plane makes their blood weighty; Janice's hand sweats in his. She had wanted him to have the window seat, so she wouldn't have to look. There is marsh below, withered tan and blue with salt-water. Harry marvels at the industrial buildings beyond the Delaware: flat gravel roofs vast as parking lots and parking lots all inlaid with glittering automobile roofs like bathroom floors tiled with jewels. And in junkyards of cars the effect is almost as brilliant. The NO SMOKING sign goes off. Behind the Angstroms the voices of the Murketts and the Harrisons begin to chatter. They all had a drink at an airport bar, though the hour was eleven in the morning. Harry has flown before, but to Texas with the Army and dealers' conferences in Cleveland and Albany: never aloft on vacation like this, due east into the sun.

How quickly, how silently, the 747 eats up the toy miles below! Sun glare travels with the plane across lakes and rivers in a second's glinting. The winter has been eerily mild thus far, to spite the Ayatollah; on golf courses the greens show as living discs and ovals amid the white beans of the traps and on the fairways he can spot moving specks, men playing. Composition tennis courts are dominoes from this height, drive-in movies have the shape of a fan, baseball diamonds seem a species of tattered money. Cars move very slowly and with an odd perfection, as if the roads hold tracks. The houses of the Camden area scatter, relenting to disclose a plowed field or an estate with its prickly mansion and its eye of a swimming pool tucked into mist-colored woods; and then within another minute, still climbing, Harry is above the dark carpet of the Jersey Pines, scored with yellow roads and patches of scraping but much of it still unmarred, veins of paler unleafed trees following the slope of land and flow of water among the darker evergreens, the tints of competition on earth made clear to the eye so hugely lifted. Janice lets go of his hand and gives signs of having swallowed her terror.

"What do you see?" she asks.

"The Shore."

It is true, in another silent stride the engines had inched them to the edge of the ocean of trees and placed underneath them a sandy strip, separated from the mainland by a band of flashing water and filled to a precarious fullness with linear summer cities, etched there by builders who could not see, as Harry can, how easily the great shining shoulder of the ocean could shrug and immerse and erase all traces of men. Where the sea impinges on the white sand a frill of surf slowly waves, a lacy snake pinned in place. Then this flight heads over the Atlantic at an altitude from which no whitecaps can be detected in the bluish hemisphere below, and immensity becomes nothingness. The plane, its earnest droning without and its party mutter and tinkle within, becomes all of the world there is.

An enamelled stewardess brings them lunch, sealed on a tray of blond plastic. Though her makeup is thickly applied Harry thinks he detects beneath it, as she bends close with a smile to ask what beverage he would prefer, shadowy traces of a hectic night. They fuck on every layover, he has read in *Club* or *Oui*, a separate boyfriend in every city, twenty or thirty men, these women the fabulous horny sailors of our time. Ever since the airport he has been amazed by other people: the carpeted corridors seemed thronged with freaks, people in crazy sizes and clothes, girls with dead-white complexions and giant eyeglasses and hair frizzed out to fill a bushel basket, black men swaggering along in long fur coats and hip-hugging velvet suits, a tall pale boy in a turban and a down vest, a dwarf in a plaid tam-o'-shanter, a woman so obese she couldn't sit in the molded plastic chairs of the waiting areas and had to stand propping herself on a three-legged aluminum cane. Life outside Brewer was gaudy, wild. Everyone was a clown in costume. Rabbit and his five companions were in costume too, flimsy summer clothes under winter overcoats. Cindy Murkett is wearing high-heeled slides on naked ankles; Thelma Harrison pads along in woolly socks and tennis sneakers. They all keep laughing among themselves, in that betraying Diamond County way. Harry doesn't mind getting a little high, but he doesn't want to sacrifice awareness of the colors around him, of the revelation that outside Brewer there is a planet without ruts worn into it. In such moments of adventure he is impatient with his body, that its five windows aren't enough, he can't get the world all in. Joy makes his heart pound. God, having shrunk in Harry's middle years to the size of a raisin lost under the car seat, is suddenly great again, everywhere like a radiant wind. Free: the dead and the living alike have been left five miles below in the haze that has annulled the earth like breath on a mirror.

Harry turns from the little double-paned airplane window of some tinted soft substance that has been scratched again and again horizontally as by a hail of meteorites. Janice is leafing through the airline magazine. He asks her, "How do you think they'll do?"

"Who?"

"Your mother and Nelson and Pru, who else?"

She flips a glossy page. Her mother is in that set of the lips, as if they have just pronounced a mournful truth and will not take it back. "I expect better than when we're there."

"They say anything to you about the house?"

Harry and Janice passed papers two days ago, a Tuesday. The day before, Monday the seventh, they had sold their silver back to Fiscal Alternatives. The metal, its value driven up by panic buying in the wake of Afghanistan by heavy holders

of petrodollars, stood at $36.70 that day, making each of the
silver dollars, bought for $16.50 including sales tax, worth
$23.37, according to the calculations of the platinum-haired
young woman. Janice, who had not worked all these years off
and on at her father's lot for nothing, slid the hand computer
toward herself and after some punching politely pointed out
that if silver stood at $36.70 a troy ounce, then seventy-five
per cent of that would give a melt value of $27.52. Well, the
young woman pointed out, you couldn't expect Fiscal Alternatives to sell at less than melt value and not buy back for less
too. She was less soignée than formerly; the tiny imperfection
at one corner of her lips had bloomed into something that
needed to be covered with a little circular Band-Aid. But after
a phone call to some office deeper than hers, hidden by more
than a sheet of thin Venetian blinds, she conceded that they
could go to $24 even. Times 888 came to $21,312, or a profit
in less than a month of $6,660. Harry wanted to keep eight
of the handsome old cartwheels as souvenirs and this reduced
the check to $21,120, a more magical number anyway. From
the Brewer Trust safe-deposit box and the safe at Springer
Motors they retrieved their cumbersome riches, taking care
this time to minimize portage by double-parking the Corona
on Weiser Street. The next day, while silver was dropping to
$31.75 an ounce, they signed, at this same Brewer Trust, a
twenty-year mortgage for $62,400 at 13½ per cent, 1½ per
cent below the current prime rate, with a one-point fee of
$624 and a three-year renegotiation proviso. The little stone
house, once a gardener's cottage, in Penn Park cost $78,000.
Janice wanted to put down $25,000, but Harry pointed out
to her that in inflationary times debt is a good thing to have,
that mortgage interest is tax-deductible, and that six-month
$10,000-minimum money market certificates are paying close
to 12 per cent these days. So they opted for the 20 per cent
minimum of equity, or $15,600, which the bank, consider-
ing the excellent credit standing in the community of Mr.
Angstrom and his family, was pleased to allow. Stepping out
between the monumental pillars into the winter daylight
blinking, Janice and Harry owned a house, and the day after
tomorrow would fly into summer. For years nothing happens;

then everything happens. Water boils, the cactus blooms, cancer declares itself.

Janice replies, "Mother seems resigned. She told me a long story about how her parents, who were better regarded, you know, in the county than the Springers, offered to have her and Daddy come stay with them while he was still studying accountancy and he said, No, if he couldn't put a roof over a wife he shouldn't have taken a wife."

"She should tell that story to Nelson."

"I wouldn't push at Nelson too hard these days. Something's working at him from inside."

"I don't push at him, he's pushing me. He's pushed me right out of the house."

"It may be our going off has frightened him. Made it more real, that he has these responsibilities."

"About time the kid woke up. What do you think poor Pru makes of all this?"

Janice sighs, a sound lost in the giant whispering that upholds them. Little dull nozzles above their heads hiss oxygen. Harry wants to hear that Pru hates Nelson, that she is sorry she has married him, that the father has made the son look sick. "Oh, I don't think she knows what to make," Janice says. "We have these talks sometimes and she knows Nelson is unhappy but still has this faith in him. The fact of it is Teresa was so anxious to get away from her own people in Ohio she can't afford to be too picky about the people she's gotten in with."

"She still keeps putting away that crème de menthe."

"She's a little heedless but that's how you are at that age. You think whatever happens, you can manage; the Devil won't touch you."

He nudges her elbow with his comfortingly, to show he remembers. The Devil touched her twenty years ago. The guilt they share rests in their laps like these safety belts, holding them fast, chafing only when they try to move.

"Hey you two lovebirds." Ronnie Harrison's loud shallow voice breaks upon them from above; he is looking down with his boozy breath from the backs of their seats. "Deal us in, you can neck at home." For the rest of the flight's three droning hours they party with the other four, swapping seats, standing

in the aisle, moving around in the 747's wide body as if it were
Webb Murkett's long living room. They stoke themselves with
drinks and reminisce about times they have already shared as
if, were silence and forgetfulness once to enter, the bubble of
this venture together would pop and all six would go tumbling into the void that surrounds and upholds the shuddering
skin of the plane. Cindy seems, in this confusion, amiable but
remote, a younger sister, or another passenger swept up into
their holiday mood. She perches forward on the edge of her
reclined window seat to catch each gust of jocularity; it is hard
to believe that her outer form, clothed in a prim black suit with
a floppy white cravat that reminds Harry of George Washington, has secret places, of folds and fur and moist membranes,
where a diaphragm can go, and that entry into these places is
the purpose of his trip and his certain destination.

The plane drops; his stomach clenches; the pilot's omnipo-
tent Texas voice comes on and tells them to return to their seats
and prepare for arrival. Harry asks Janice now that she's loose
on booze if she wouldn't like the window seat but she says No,
she doesn't dare to look until they land. Through his patch of
scratched Plexiglas he sees a milky turquoise sea mottled with
purple-green shadows cast from underneath, islands beneath
the surface. A single sailboat. Then a ragged arm of rocky land
in a sleeve of white beach. Small houses with red corrugated
roofs rise toward him. The wheels of the plane groan and unwind down and lock in place. They are skimming a swamp. He
thinks to pray but his thoughts scatter; Janice is grinding the
bones of his fingers together. A house with a wind sock, an
unmanned bulldozer, branchless trees that are palms flash by;
there is a thud, a small swerve, a loud hiss, and a roar straining
backwards, a screaming straining. It stops, they slow, they are
on the ground, and a low pink air terminal is wheeled into view
as the 747 taxis close. The passengers move, suddenly sweating,
clutching their winter coats and groping for sunglasses, toward
the exits. At the head of the silver stairs down to the macadam,
the tropical air, so warm, moist, and forgiving, composed all of
tiny little circles, strikes Rabbit's face as if gusted from an at-
omizer; but Ronnie Harrison ruins the moment by exclaiming
distinctly, behind his ear, "Oh boy. That's better than a blow
job." And, worse even than Ronnie's smearing his voice across

so precious a moment of first encounter with a new world, the women laugh, having been meant to overhear. Janice laughs, the dumb mutt. And the stewardess, her enamel gone dewy in the warmth by the door where she poses saying goodbye, goodbye, promiscuously smiles.

Cindy's laugh skips girlishly above the others and is quickly followed by her drawled word, "Ronnie." Rabbit is excited amid his disgust, remembering those Polaroids tucked in a drawer.

As the days of the vacation pass, Cindy turns the same mahogany brown she wears in the summer, by the pool at the Flying Eagle, and comes up dripping from the beryl Caribbean in the same bikini of black strings, only with salt-glisten on her skin. Thelma Harrison burns badly the first day, and has some pain connected with that quiet ailment of hers. She spends the whole second day in their bungalow, while Ronnie bounces in and out of the water and supervises the fetching of drinks from the bar built on the sand entirely of straw. Old black ladies move up and down the beach offering beads and shells and sunclothes for sale, and on the morning of the third day Thelma buys from one of them a wide-brimmed straw hat and a pink ankle-length wrapper with long sleeves, and thus entirely covered, with sun block on her face and a towel across the tops of her feet, she sits reading in the shade of the sea-grape trees. Her face in the shade of her hat seems sallow and thin and mischievous, when she glances toward Harry as he lies in the sun. Next to her, he tans least easily, but he is determined to keep up with the crowd. The ache of a sunburn reminds him nostalgically of the muscle aches after athletic exertion. In the sea, he doggy-paddles, secretly afraid of sharks.

The men spend each morning on the golf course that adjoins the resort, riding in canopied carts down sere fairways laid out between brambly jungles from which there is no recovery; indeed, in looking for lost balls there is a danger of stepping into a deep hole. The substance of the island is coral, pitted with caves. At night, there is entertainment, set in a rigid weekly cycle. They arrived on a Thursday, the evening of the crab races, and on the next night witnessed a limbo dance, and on the next, a Saturday, themselves danced to a steel band. Every night there is music to dance to, beside the Olympic-length

pool under stars that seem closer down here, and that hang in
the sky with a certain menace, fragments of a frozen explosion.
Some of the constellations are strange; Webb Murkett, who
knows stars from his years in the Navy—he enlisted in '45,
when he was eighteen, and crossed the Pacific on an aircraft
carrier as the war was ending—points out the Southern Cross,
and a ghostly blur in the sky he says is another galaxy altogether; and they can all see that the Big Dipper stands on its
handle here in a way never seen in southeastern Pennsylvania.

Oh, that little Cindy, browner at every dinnertime, just begging for love. You can see it in her teeth, they are getting so
white, and the way she picks an oleander blossom from the
bush outside their bungalow every night to wear in her hair
all fluffy from swimming so much, and the swarthiness of her
toes that makes the nails look pale as petals also. She wears on
her dark skin white dresses that shine from far across the swimming pool—lit from underneath at night as if it has swallowed
the moon—when she is coming back from the ladies' room
beyond the bamboo bar. She claims she is getting fatter, too:
those piña coladas and banana Daiquiris and rum punches, all
those calories, shameless. Yet she never turns a drink down,
none of them do; from the Bloody Marys that fortify the golfers for their morning on the course to the last round of Stingers after midnight, they keep a gentle collective buzz on. Janice
wonders, "Harry, what's the final tab going to look like? You
keep signing for everybody."

He tells her, "Relax. Might as well spend it as have it eaten
up by inflation. Did you hear Webb saying that the dollar now
is worth exactly half what it was ten years ago in 1970? So
these are fifty-cent dollars; relax." The expense in his mind is
part of a worthy campaign, to sleep with Cindy before their
seven days are over. He feels it coming, coming upon all of
them, the walls between them are wearing thin, he knows exactly when Webb will clear his throat or how he will light his
cigarette, eye-glance and easy silence are hour by hour eroding
constraint, under sun and under stars they stretch out their
six bodies on the folding chaises, with vinyl strapping, that
are everywhere. Their hands touch passing drinks and matches
and suntan lotion, they barge in and out of one another's bungalows; indeed Rabbit has seen Thelma Harrison bare-assed

by accident returning their Solarcaine one afternoon. She had been lying on the bed letting her burned skin breathe and hustled into the bathroom at the sound of his voice at the door, but not quick enough. He saw the crease between her cheeks, the whole lean sallow length of her fleeing, and handed the Solarcaine to Ronnie, himself naked, without comment or apology, they were half-naked with each other all the day long, but for Thelma huddled under the sea-grape: Janice rubbing Coppertone into the criss-crossing creases of Webb's red neck, Ronnie's heavy cock bulging the front of his obscene little European-style trunks, sweet Cindy untying a black string to give her back an even tan and showing the full nippled silhouette of one boob when she reached up for her Planter's Punch from the tray of them the boy had brought. These blacks down here are silkier than American blacks, blacker, their bodies moving to a gentler beat. Toward four o'clock, the shadows of the sea-grape coming forward like knobby fingers onto the sand, the men's faces baked red despite the canopies on the golf carts, they move their act from the beach (the rustling of palm trees gets on Harry's nerves; at night he keeps thinking it's raining, and it never is) to the shaded area beside the Olympic pool, where young island men in white steward's jackets circle among them taking drink orders and the hard white pellet of the sun slowly lowers toward the horizon of the sea, which it meets promptly at six, in a perfunctory splash of purples and pinks. Stupefied, aching with pleasure, Harry stares at the way, when Cindy rolls her body into a new position on the chaise, the straps have bitten laterally into her delicious fat, like tire treads in mud. Thelma sits among them swaddled and watchful, Webb drones on, Ronnie is making some new friends at the bamboo bar. It's the salesman in him, he has to keep trying his pitch. His voice balloons above the rippling as a single fair child, waterlogged and bored, dives and paddles away the time to dinner. Janice, much as he loves her now and then, down here is a piece of static, getting between Harry and what signals Cindy may be sending; luckily Webb keeps her entertained, talking to her as one member of the lesser Brewer gentry to another, about that tireless subject of money. "You think fourteen per cent is catastrophic, in Israel they live with a hundred eleven per cent, a color television set costs eighteen hundred dollars. In Argentina it's a hundred fifty per cent per year, believe me I kid you not. In Tokyo a pound of steak costs twenty dollars and in Saudi Arabia a pack of cigarettes goes for a fin. Five dollars a pack. You may think we're hurting but the U.S. consumer still gets the best deal to be had in any industrialized nation." Janice hangs on his words and bums his cigarettes. Her hair since summer has grown long enough to pull back in a little stubby ponytail; she sits by his feet, dabbling her legs in the pool. The hair on Webb's long skinny legs spirals around like the stripes on a barber pole, and his face with its wise creases has tanned the color of lightly varnished pine. It occurs to Harry that she used to listen to her father bullshit this way, and likes it.

By Sunday night they are bored with the routine around the resort and hire a taxi to take them across the island to the casino. In the dark they pass through villages where black children are invisible until their eye-whites gleam beside the road. A herd of goats trotting with dragging rope halters materializes in the headlights of the taxi. Shuttered cabins up on cinder blocks reveal by an open door that they are taverns, with bottle-crammed shelves and a sheaf of standing customers. An old stone church flings candlelight from its pointed windows, which have no glass, and the moan of one phrase of a hymn, that is swiftly left behind. The taxi, a '69 Pontiac with a lot of voodoo dolls on the dashboard, drives ruthlessly, on the wrong side of the road, for this was an English colony. The truncated cone-shapes of abandoned sugar mills against the sky full of stars remember the past, all those dead slaves, while Janice and Thelma and Cindy chatter in the surging dark about people left behind in Brewer, about Buddy Inglefinger's newest awful girlfriend with all that height and all those children, Buddy's such a victim-type, and about impossible Peggy Fosnacht, whom rumor has reported to be very hurt that she and Ollie weren't asked along on this trip to the Caribbean, even though everybody knows they could never afford it.

The casino is attached to another beach resort, grander than theirs. Boardwalks extend out over the illuminated coral shelf. There are worlds within worlds, Harry thinks. Creatures like broken bags of noodles wave upward from within the golden-green slipslop. He has come out here to clear his head. He got hooked on blackjack and in an attempt to recoup his losses by doubling and redoubling his bets cashed three hundred in Traveller's Checks and, while his friends marvelled, lost it all. Well, that's less than half the profit on the sale of one Tercel, less than three per cent of what Nelson's pranks have cost. Still, Harry's head throbs and he feels shaky and humiliated. The black dealer didn't even glance up when, cleaned out, he pushed away from the garish felt of the table. He walks along the boards toward the black horizon, as the tropical air soothes his hot face with microscopic circular kisses. He imagines he could walk to South America, that has Paraguay in it; he thinks fondly of that area of tall weeds behind the asphalt of the lot, and of that farm he has always approached as a spy, through the hedgerow that grew up over the tumbled sandstone wall. The grass in the orchard will be flattened and bleached by winter now, smoke rising from the lonely house below. Another world.

Cindy is beside him suddenly, breathing in rhythm with the slipslop of the sea. He fears their moment has come, when he is far from ready; but she says in a dry commiserating voice, "Webb says you should always set a limit for yourself before you sit down, so you won't get carried away."

"I wasn't carried away," Harry tells her. "I had a theory." Perhaps she figures that his losses have earned a compensation and she is it. Her brown arms are set off by a crocheted white shawl; with the flower behind her ear she looks flirty. What would it be like, to press his own high heavy face down into those apple-hard roundnesses of hers, cheeks and brow and nose-tip, and her alert little life-giving slits, long-lipped mouth and dark eyes glimmering with mischief like a child's? Slipslop. Will their faces fit? Her eyes glance upward toward his and he gazes away, at the tropical moon lying on its side at an angle you never see in Pennsylvania. As if accidentally, while gazing out to sea, he brushes his fingertips against her arm. An electric warmth seems to linger from her Sunday in the sun. Kelp slaps the pilings of the catwalk, a wave collapses its way along the beach, his moment to pounce is here. Something too firm in the protuberances of her face holds him off, though she is lightly smiling, and tips her face up, as if to make it easier for him to slip his mouth beneath her nose.

But footsteps rumble toward them and Webb and Janice, almost running, their hands in the confused mingled lights of moon and subaqueous spots and blazing casino beyond seeming linked, then released, come up to this angle of the boardwalk and announce excitedly that Ronnie Harrison is burning up the crap table inside. "Come and see, Harry," Janice says. "He's at least eight hundred ahead."

"That Ronnie," Cindy says, in a tone of girlish dry reproach, and the casino lights glow through her long skirt as she hurries toward these lights, her legs silhouetted beneath her dark wide ass.

They get back to their own resort after two. Ronnie stayed too long at the crap table and wound up only a few bucks better than even. He and Janice fall asleep on the long ride back, while Thelma sits tensely in Rabbit's lap and Webb and Cindy sit up front with the driver, Webb asking questions about the island that the man answers in a reluctant, bubbling language that is barely English. At the gate to their resort a uniformed guard lets them in. Everything down here is guarded, theft is rampant, thieves and even murderers pour outward from the island's dark heart to feed on its rim of rich visitors. Guest bungalows are approached along paths of green-painted concrete laid down on the sand, under muttering palm trees, between bushes of papery flowers that attract hummingbirds in the morning. While the men confer as to what hour tomorrow's golf should be postponed to, the three women whisper at a little distance, at the point in the concrete walk where the paths to their separate bungalows diverge. Janice, Cindy, and Thelma are tittering and sending glances this way, glances flickering birdlike in the moon-glazed warm night. Cindy's shawl glimmers like a splotch of foam on surging water. But in the end, making the hushed grove of palms ring with cries of "'Night. 'Night," each wife walks to her own bungalow with her husband. Rabbit fucks Janice out of general irritation and falls asleep hoping that morning will be indefinitely postponed.

But it comes on schedule, in the form of bars of sunlight the window louvers cast on to the floor of hexagonal tiles, while the little yellow birds they have that song about down here follow the passage of clinking breakfast trays along the concrete paths. It is not so bad, once he stands up. The body was evolved for adversity. As has become his custom he takes a short, cautious swim off the deserted beach, where last night's plastic glasses are still propped in the sand. It is the one moment of the day or night when Harry is by himself, not counting the old couples, with the wives needing an arm to make their way down across the sand, who also like an early swim. The sea between soft breakers seems the color of a honeydew melon, that pale a green. Floating on his back he can see, on the roads along the scraggly steep hills that flank the bay, those to whom this island is no vacation, blacks in scraps of bright cloth, strolling to work, some of the women toting bundles and even buckets on their heads. They really do that. Their voices carry on fresh morning air, along with the slap and swoosh and fizz of warm saltwater sliding and receding at his feet. The white sand is spongy, and full of holes where crabs breathe. He has never seen sand this white, minced coral fine as sugar. The early sun sits lightly on his sensitive shoulders. This is it, health. Then the girl with the breakfast tray comes to their door—their bungalow number is 9—and Janice in her terrycloth bathrobe opens the louvered door and calls *"Har*ry" out across the beach where an old black rummy in khaki pants is already sweeping up seaweed and plastic glasses, and the party, the hunt, is on again.

He plays golf badly today; when he is tired he tends to overswing, and to flip his hands instead of letting the arms ride through. Keep the wrist-cock, don't waste it up at the top. Don't sway onto your toes, imagine your nose pressed against a pane of glass. Think railroad tracks. Follow through. These tips are small help today; it seems a long morning's slog between hungry wings of coral jungle, up to greens as bumpy as quilts, though he supposes it's a miracle of sorts to have greens at all under this sun. He hates Webb Murkett, who is sinking everything inside of twenty feet today. Why should this stringy old bullshitter hog that fantastic little cunt and take the Nassau besides? Harry misses Buddy Inglefinger, to feel superior to. Ronnie's sparse scalp and naked high forehead look like a peeling pink egg when he stoops to his shot. Swings like an ape, all the hair off his head gone into his arms, how can Thelma stand him? Women, they'll put up with anything for the sake of a big prick evidently. Harry can't stop thinking of that three hundred dollars he blew last night, that his father would have slaved six weeks for. Poor Pop, he didn't live to see money get unreal.

But things look up in the afternoon, after a couple of piña coladas and a crabmeat-salad sandwich. They all decide to rent three Sunfishes, and they pair up so that he and Cindy go out together. He has never sailed, so she stands up to her tits in the water fussing with the rudder while he sits high and dry holding the ropes that pull this striped three-cornered sail, that doesn't look to him firmly attached enough, flapping this way and that while one aluminum pipe rubs against another. The whole thing feels shaky. They have you wear a kind of black rubber pad around your middle and in hers Cindy looks pretty cute with that short otter haircut, butch, like one of those female cops on TV or a frogwoman. He has never before noticed how dark and thick her eyebrows are; they knit toward each other and almost touch until the rudder catch clicks in finally. Then she gives a grunt and up she jumps, flat on her front so her tits squeeze out sideways, the untanned parts of them white as Maalox, her legs kicking in the water to bring her ass all black and shiny aboard, she is too much woman for this little boat, it is tilting like crazy. He pulls her by the arm and the aluminum pole at the bottom of the sail swings and hits him on the back of the head. Hard. He is stunned. She has grabbed the rope from him while still holding on to the rudder handle and keeps shouting, "The centerboard, the centerboard," until he figures out what she means. This splintery long wood fin under his leg should go in that slot. He gets it out from under him and shoves it in. Instead of congratulating him, Cindy says, "Shit." The little Fiberglas shell is parallel to the beach, where an arc of bathers has gathered to watch, and each wave is slopping them closer in. Then the wind catches the sail and flattens it taut, so the aluminum mast creaks, and they slowly bob out over the breaking waves toward the point of land on the right where the bay ends.

Once you get going you don't feel how fast you're moving, the water having no landmarks. Harry is toward the front, crouching way over in case the boom swings at his head again. Sitting yoga-style in her stout rubber gasket, the center strip of her bikini barely covering her opened-up crotch, Cindy tends the tiller and for the first time smiles. "Harry, you don't have to keep holding on to the top of the centerboard, it doesn't have to be pulled until we hit the beach." The beach, the palms, the bungalows have been reduced to the size of a postcard.

"Should we be this far out?"

She smiles again. "We're not far out." The sailing gear tugs at her hands, the boat tips. The water out here is no longer the pale green of a honeydew melon but a green like bile, black in the troughs.

"We're not," he repeats.

"Look over there." A sail scarcely bigger than the flash of a wave. "That's Webb and Thelma. They're much further out than we are."

"Are you sure that's them?"

Cindy takes pity. "We'll come about when we're closer to those rocks. You know what come about means, Harry?"

"Not exactly."

"We'll change direction. The boom will swing, so watch your head."

"Do you think there are any sharks?" Still, he tells himself, there is an intimacy to it, just the two of them, the same spray hitting his skin and hers, the wind and water sounds that drown out all others, the curve of her shoulder shining like metal in the light of that hard white sun that makes the sun he grew up under seem orange and bloated in memory.

"Did you see *Jaws II*?" she asks back.

"D'you ever get the feeling everything these days is sequels?" he asks in turn. "Like people are running out of ideas." He feels so full of fatigue and long-held lust as to be careless of his life, amid this tugging violence of elements. Even the sunsparkle on the water feels cruel, a malevolence straight from Heaven, like those photons beating on the wings of the airplane flying down.

"Coming about," Cindy says. "Hard alee."

He crouches, and the boom misses. He sees another sail out here with them, Ronnie and Janice, headed for the horizon. She seems to be at the back, steering. When did she learn? Some summer camp. You have to be rich from the start to get the full benefits. Cindy says, "Now Harry, you take over. It's simple. That little strip of cloth at the top of the mast is called a telltale. It tells what direction the wind is coming from. Also,

look at the waves. You want to keep the sail at an angle to the
wind. What you don't want is to see the front edge of the sail
flapping. That's called luffing. It means you're headed directly
into the wind, and then you must head off. You push the tiller
away from you, away from the sail. You'll feel it, I promise.
The tension between the tiller and the line—it's like a scissors,
sort of. It's fun. Come on, Harry, nothing can happen. Change
places with me." They manage the maneuver, while the boat
swings like a hammock beneath their bulks. A little cloud covers the sun, dyeing the water dark, then releasing it back into
sunshine with a pang. Harry takes hold of the tiller and gropes
until the wind takes hold with him. Then, as she says, it's fun:
the sail and tiller tugging, the invisible sea breeze pushing, the
distances not nearly so great and hopeless once you have control. "You're doing fine," Cindy tells him, and from the way she
sits with legs crossed facing ahead he can see the underside of
all five toes of one bare foot, the thin blue skin here wrinkled,
the littlest dear toe bent into the toe next to it as if trying to
hide. She trusts him. She loves him. Now that he has the hang
of it he dares to heel, pulling the mainsheet tighter and tighter,
so the waves spank and his palm burns. The land is leaping
closer, they are almost safe when, in adjusting his aim toward
the spot on the beach where Janice and Ronnie have already
dragged their Sunfish up, he lets out the sail a touch and the
wind catches it full from behind; the prow goes under abruptly
in a furious surging film; heavily the whole shell slews around
and tips; he and Cindy have no choice but to slide off together,
entangled with line. A veined translucence closes over his head.
Air he thinks wildly and comes up in sudden shade, the boat
looming on edge above them. Cindy is beside him in the water.
Gasping, wanting to apologize, he clings briefly to her. She
feels like a shark, slimy and abrasive. Their two foam-rubber
belts bump underwater. Each hair in her eyebrows gleams in
the strange light here, amid shadowed waves and the silence of
stilled wind, only a gentle slipslap against the hollow hull. With
a grimace she pushes him off, takes a deep breath, and disappears beneath the boat. He tries to follow but his belt roughly
buoys him back. He hears her grunting and splashing on the
other side of the upright keel, first pulling at, then standing on
the centerboard until the Sunfish comes upright, great pearls

of water exploding from it as the striped sail sweeps past the sun. Harry heaves himself on and deftly she takes the boat in to shore.

The episode is inglorious, but they all laugh about it on the beach, and in his self-forgiving mind their underwater embrace has rapidly dried to something tender and promising. The slither of two skins, her legs fluttering between his. The few black hairs where her eyebrows almost meet. The hairs of her crotch she boldly displayed sitting yoga-style. It all adds up.

Lunch at the resort is served by the pool or brought by tray to the beach, but dinner is a formal affair within a vast pavilion whose rafters drip feathery fronds yards long and at whose rear, beside the doors leading into the kitchen, a great open barbecue pit sends flames roaring high, so that shadows twitch against the background design of thatch and carved masks, and highlights spark in the sweating black faces of the assistant chefs. The head chef is a scrawny Belgian always seen sitting at the bar between meals, looking sick, or else conferring in accents of grievance with one of the prim educated native women who run the front desk. Monday night is the barbecue buffet, with a calypso singer during the meal and dancing to electrified marimbas afterward; but all six of the holidayers from Diamond County agree they are exhausted from the night at the casino and will go to bed early. Harry after nearly drowning in Cindy's arms fell asleep on the beach and then went inside for a nap. While he was sleeping, a sudden sharp tropical rainstorm drummed for ten minutes on his tin roof. When he awoke, the rain had passed, and the sun was setting in a band of orange at the mouth of the bay, and his pals had been yukking it up in the bar ever since the shower an hour ago. Something is cooking. They seem, the three women, very soft-faced by the light of the candle set on the table in a little red netted hurricane lamp, amid papery flowers that will be wilted before the meal is over. They keep touching one another, their sisterhood strengthened and excited down here. Cindy is wearing a yellow hibiscus in her hair tonight, and that Arab thing, unbuttoned halfway down. She more than once reaches past Webb's drink and stringy brown hands as they pose on the tablecloth to touch Janice on a wrist, remembering "that fresh colored boy behind the bar today, I told him I was down here with my husband and he shrugged like it made no difference whatsoever!" Webb looks sage, letting the currents pass around him, and Ronnie sleepy and puffy but still full of beans, in that grim play-maker way of his. Harry and Ronnie were on the Mt. Judge basketball varsity together and more than once Rabbit had to suppress a sensation that though he was the star the coach, Marty Tothero, liked Ronnie better, because he never quit trying and was more "physical" around the backboards. The world runs on push. Rabbit's feeling about things has been that if it doesn't happen by itself it's not worth making happen. Still, that Cindy. A man could kill for a piece of that. Pump it in, and die like a male spider. The calypso singer comes to their table and sings a long dirty song about the Big Bamboo. Harry doesn't understand all the allusions but the wives titter after every verse. The singer smiles and the song smiles but his bloody eyes glitter like those of a lizard frozen on the wall and his skull when bent over the guitar shows gray wool. An old act. A dying art. Harry doesn't know if they are supposed to tip him or just applaud. They applaud and quick as a lizard's tongue his hand flickers out to take the bill that Webb, leaning back, has offered. The old singer moves on to the next table and begins that one about Back to back, and Belly to belly. Cindy giggles, touches Janice on the forearm, and says, "I bet all the people back in Brewer will think we've swapped down here."

"Maybe we should then," Ronnie says, unable to suppress a belch of fatigue.

Janice, in that throaty mature woman's voice cigarettes and age have given her but that Harry is always surprised to hear she has, asks Webb, who sits beside her, gently, "How do you feel about that sort of thing, Webb?"

The old fox knows he has the treasure to barter and takes his time, pulling himself up in his chair to release an edge of coat he's sitting on, a kind of dark blue captain's jacket with spoked brass buttons, and takes his pack of Marlboro Lights from his side pocket. Rabbit's heart races so hard he stares down at the table, where the bloody bones, ribs and vertebrae, of their barbecue wait to be cleared away. Webb drawls, "Well, after two marriages that I'd guess you'd have to say were not fully successful, and some of the things I've seen and done before, after, and between, I must admit a little sharing among friends doesn't seem to me so bad, if it's done with affection and respect. Respect is the key term here. Every party involved, and I mean every party, has to be willing, and it should be clearly understood that whatever happens will go no further than that particular occasion. Secret affairs, that's what does a marriage in. When people get romantic."

Nothing romantic about him, the king of the Polaroid pricks. Harry's face feels hot. Maybe it's the spices in the barbecue settling, or the length of Webb's sermon, or a blush of gratitude to the Murketts, for arranging all this. He imagines his face between Cindy's thighs, tries to picture that black pussy like a curved snug mass of eyebrow hairs, flattened and warmed to fragrance from being in underpants and framed by the white margins the bikini bottom had to cover to be decent. He will follow her slit down with his tongue, her legs parting with that same weightless slither he felt under water today, down and in, and around the corner next to his nose will be that whole great sweet ass he has a thousand times watched jiggle as she dried herself from swimming in the pool at the Flying Eagle, under the nappy green shadow of Mt. Pemaquid. And her tits, the fall of them forward when she obediently bends over. Something is happening in his pants, like the stamen of one of these floppy flowers on the tablecloth jerking with shadow as the candle-flame flickers.

"Down the way," the singer sings at yet another table, "where the nights are gay, and the sun shines daily on the moun-tain-top." Black hands come and smoothly clear away the dark bones and distribute dessert menus. There is a walnut cake they offer here that Harry especially likes, though there's nothing especially Caribbean about it, it's probably flown in from Fort Lauderdale.

Thelma, who is wearing a sort of filmy top you can see her cocoa-colored bra through, is gazing into middle distance like a schoolteacher talking above the heads of her class and saying, ". . . simple female curiosity. It's something you hardly ever see discussed in all these articles on female sexuality, but I think it's what's behind these male strippers rather than any real desire on the part of the women to go to bed with the boys. They're just curious about the penises, what they look like. They *do* look a lot different from each other, I guess."

"That how you feel?" Harry asks Janice. "Curious?"

She lowers her eyes to the guttering hurricane lamp. She murmurs, "Of course."

"Oh I'm not," Cindy says, "not the shape. I don't think I am. I really am not."

"You're very young," Thelma says.

"I'm thirty," she protests. "Isn't that supposed to be my sexual prime?"

As if rejoining her in the water, Harry tries to take her side. "They're ugly as hell. Most of the pricks I've seen are."

"You don't see them erect," Thelma lightly points out.

"Thank God for that," he says, appalled, as he sometimes is, by this coarse crowd he's in—by human coarseness in general.

"And yet he loves his own," Janice says, keeping that light and cool and as it were scientific tone that has descended upon them, in the hushed dining pavilion. The singer has ceased. People at other tables are leaving, moving to the smaller tables at the edge of the dance floor by the pool.

"I don't love it," he protests in a whisper. "I'm stuck with it."

"It's you," Cindy quietly tells him.

"Not just the pricks," Thelma clarifies, "it has to be the whole man who turns you on. The way he carries himself. His voice, the way he laughs. But it all refers to that, I guess."

Pricks. Can it be? They let the delicate subject rest, as dessert and coffee come. Revitalized by food and their talk, they decide after all to sit with Stingers and watch the dancing a while, under the stars that on this night seem to Harry jewels of a clock that moves with maddening slowness, measuring out the minutes until he sinks himself in Cindy as if a star were to fall and sizzle into this Olympic-sized pool. Once, on some far lost summer field of childhood, someone, his mother it must have been though he cannot hear her voice, told him that if you stare up at the night sky while you count to one hundred you are bound to see a shooting star, they are in fact so common. But though he now leans back from the Stinger and the glass table and the consolatory, conspiratory murmur of his friends until his neck begins to ache, all the stars above him hang unbudging in their sockets. Webb Murkett's gravelly voice growls, "Well, kiddies. As the oldest person here, I claim the privilege of announcing that I'm tired and want to go to bed." And as Harry turns his face from the heavens there it is, in a corner of his vision, vivid and brief as a scratched match, a falling star, doused in the ocean of ink. The women rise and gather their skirts about them; the marimbas, after a consultation of fluttering, fading notes, break into "Send in the Clowns." This plaintive pealing is lost behind them as they move along the pool, and past the front desk where the haggard, alcoholic resort manager is trying to get through long-distance to New York, and across the hotel's traffic circle with its curbs of whitewashed coral, down into the shadowy realm of concrete paths between bushes of sleeping flowers. The palms above them grow noisy as the music fades. The *shoosh* of surf draws nearer. At the moonlit point where the paths diverge into three, goodnights are nervously exchanged but no one moves; then a woman's hand reaches out softly and takes the wrist of a man not her husband. The others follow suit, with no person looking at another, a downcast and wordless tugging serving to separate the partners out and to draw them down the respective paths to each woman's bungalow. Harry hears Cindy giggle, at a distance, for it is not her hand with such gentle determination pulling him along, but Thelma's.

She has felt him pull back, and tightens her grip, silently. On the beach, he sees, a group has brought down a hurricane lamp, with their drinks; the lamp and their cigarettes glow red in the shadows, while the sea beyond stretches pale as milk beyond the black silhouette of a big sailboat anchored in the bay, under the half-moon tilted onto its back. Thelma lets go of his arm to fish in her sequinned purse for the bungalow key. "You can have Cindy tomorrow night," she whispers. "We discussed it."

"O.K., great," he says lamely, he hopes not insultingly. He is figuring, this means that Cindy wanted that pig Harrison, and Janice got Webb. He had been figuring Janice would have to take Ronnie, and felt sorry for her, except from the look of him he'd fall asleep soon, and Webb and Thelma would go together, both of them yellowy stringy types. Thelma closes the bungalow door behind them and switches on a straw globe light above the bed. He asks her, "Well, are tonight's men the first choice for you ladies or're you just getting the second choice out of the way?"

"Don't be so competitive, Harry. This is meant to be a loving sharing sort of thing, you heard Webb. One thing we absolutely agreed on, we're not going to carry any of it back to Brewer. This is all the monkey business there's going to be, even if it kills us." She stands there in the center of her straw rug rather defiantly, a thin-faced sallow woman he scarcely knows. Not only her nose is pink in the wake of her sunburn but patches below her eyes as well: a kind of butterfly is on her face. Harry supposes he should kiss her, but his forward step is balked by her continuing firmly, "I'll tell you one thing though, Harry Angstrom. You're *my* first choice."

"I am?"

"Of course. I adore you. *Adore* you."

"Me?"

"Haven't you ever sensed it?"

Rather than admit he hasn't, he hangs there foolishly.

"Shit," Thelma says. "Janice did. Why else do you think we weren't invited to Nelson's wedding?" She turns her back, and starts undoing her earring before the mirror, that just like the one in his and Janice's bungalow is framed in woven strips of bamboo. The batik hanging in here is of a tropical sunset with a palm in the foreground instead of the black-mammy fruit-seller he and Janice have, but the batik manufacturer is the same. The suitcases are the Harrisons', and the clothes hanging on the painted pipe that does for a closet. Thelma asks, "You mind using Ronnie's toothbrush? I'll be a while in there, you better take the bathroom first."

In the bathroom Harry sees that Ronnie uses shaving cream, Gillette Foamy, out of a pressure can, the kind that's eating up the ozone so our children will fry. And that new kind of razor with the narrow single-edge blade that snaps in and out with a click on the television commercials. Harry can't see the point, it's just more waste, he still uses a rusty old two-edge safety razor he bought for $1.99 about seven years ago, and lathers himself with an old imitation badger-bristle on whatever bar of soap is handy. He shaved before dinner after his nap so no need now. Also the Harrisons use chlorophyll Crest in one of those giant tubes that always buckles and springs a leak when he and Janice try to save a couple pennies and buy one. He wonders whatever happened to Ipana and what was it *Consumer Reports* had to say about toothpastes a few issues back, probably came out in favor of baking soda, that's what he and Mim used to have to use, some theory Mom had about the artificial flavoring in toothpaste contributing to tartar. The trouble with consumerism is, the guy next door always seems to be doing better at it than you are. Just the Harrisons' bathroom supplies make him envious. Plain as she is, Thelma carries a hefty medicine kit, and beauty aids, plus a sun block called Eclipse, and Solarcaine. Vaseline, too, for some reason. Tampax, in a bigger box than Janice ever buys. And a lot of painkiller, aspirin in several shapes and Darvon and more pills in little prescription bottles than he would have expected. People are always a little sicker than you know. Harry debates whether he should take his leak sitting down to spare Thelma the sound of its gross splashing and rejects the idea, since she's the one wants to fuck him. It streams noisily into the bowl it seems forever, embarrassingly, all those drinks at dinner. Then he sits down on the seat anyway, to let out a little air. Too much shellfish. He imagines he can smell yesterday's crabmeat and when he stands he tests with a finger down there to see if he stinks. He decides he does. Better use a washcloth. He debates which washcloth is Ronnie's, the blue or the brown. He settles on the brown and scrubs all his undercarriage, everything that counts. Getting ready for the ball. He erases his scent by giving the cloth a good rinsing no matter whose it is.

When he steps back into the room Thelma is down to her underwear, cocoa bra and black panties. He didn't expect this, nor to be so stirred by it. Breasts are strange: some look bigger in clothes than they are and some look smaller. Thelma's are the second kind; her bra is smartly filled. Her whole body, into her forties, has kept that trim neutral serviceability nurses and grade-school teachers surprise you with, beneath their straight faces. She laughs, and holds out her arms like a fan dancer. "Here I am. You look shocked. You're such a sweet prude, Harry—that's one of the things I adore. I'll be out in five minutes. Try not to fall asleep."

Clever of her. What with the sleep debt they're all running down here and the constant booze and the trauma in the water today—his head went under and a bottomless bile-green volume sucked at his legs—he was weary. He begins to undress and doesn't know where to stop. There are a lot of details a husband and wife work out over the years that with a strange woman pop up all over again. Would Thelma like to find him naked in the bed? Or on it? For him to be less naked than she when she comes out of the bathroom would be rude. At the same time, with this straw-shaded light swaying above the bed on so bright, he doesn't want her to think seeing him lying there on display that he thinks he's a *Playgirl* centerfold. He knows he could lose thirty pounds and still have a gut. In his underpants he crosses to the bamboo-trimmed bureau in the room and switches on the lamp there whose cheap wooden base is encrusted with baby seashells glued on. He takes off his underpants. The elastic waistband has lost its snap, the only brand of this type to buy is Jockey, but those cut-rate stores in Brewer don't like to carry it, quality is being driven out everywhere. He switches off the light over the bed and in shadow stretches himself out, all of him, on top of the bedspread, as he is, as he was, as he will be before the undertakers dress him for the last time, not even a wedding ring to relieve his nakedness; when he and Janice got married men weren't expected to wear wedding rings. He closes his eyes to rest them for a second in the red blankness there, beneath his lids. He has to get through this, maybe all she wants to do is talk, and then somehow be really rested for tomorrow night. Getting there. . . . That slither underwater. . . .

Thelma with what breaks upon him like the clatter of an earthquake has come out of the bathroom. She is holding her underclothes in front of her, and with her back to him she sorts the underpants into the dirty pile the Harrisons keep beside the bureau, behind the straw wastebasket, and the bra, clean enough, back into the drawer, folded. This is the second time in this trip, he thinks drowsily, that he has seen her ass. Her body as she turns eclipses the bureau lamp and the front of her gathers shadow to itself; she advances timidly, as if wading into water. Her breasts sway forward as she bends to turn the light he switched off back on. She sits down on the edge of the bed.

His prick is still sleepy. She takes it into her hand. "You're not circumcised."

"No, they somehow weren't doing it at the hospital that day. Or maybe my mother had a theory, I don't know. I never asked. Sorry."

"It's lovely. Like a little bonnet." Sitting on the edge of the bed, more supple naked than he remembers her seeming with clothes on, Thelma bends and takes his prick in her mouth. Her body in the lamplight is a pale patchwork of faint tan and peeling pink and the natural yellowy tint of her skin. Her belly puckers into flat folds like stacked newspapers and the back of her hand as it holds the base of his prick with two fingers shows a dim lightning of blue veins. But her breath is warm and wet and the way that in lamplight individual white hairs snake as if singed through the mass of dull brown makes him want to reach out and stroke her head, or touch the rhythmic hollow in her jaw. He fears, though, interrupting the sensations she is giving him. She lifts a hand quickly to tuck back a piece of her hair, as if to let him better see.

He murmurs, "Beautiful." He is growing thick and long but still she forces her lips each time down to her fingers as they encircle him at his base. To give herself ease she spreads her legs; between her legs, one of them lying aslant across the bed edge, he sees emerging from a pubic bush more delicate and reddish than he would have dreamed a short white string. Unlike Janice's or Cindy's as he imagined it, Thelma's pussy is not opaque; it is a fuzz transparent upon the bruise-colored labia that with their tongue of white string look so lacking and defenseless Harry could cry. She too is near tears, perhaps from the effort of not gagging. She backs off and stares at the staring eye of his glans, swollen free of his foreskin. She pulls up the bonnet again and says crooningly, teasingly, "Such a serious little face." She kisses it lightly, once, twice, flicking her tongue, then bobs again, until it seems she must come up for air. "God," she sighs. "I've wanted to do that for so long. Come. Come, Harry. Come in my mouth. Come in my mouth and all over my face." Her voice sounds husky and mad saying this and all through her words Thelma does not stop gazing at the little slit of his where a single cloudy tear has now appeared. She licks it off.

"Have you really," he asks timidly, "liked me for a while?"

"Years," she says. "Years. And you never noticed. You shit. Always under Janice's thumb and mooning after silly Cindy. Well you know where Cindy is now. She's being screwed by my husband. He didn't want to, he said he'd rather go to bed with me." She snorts, in some grief of self-disgust, and plunges her mouth down again, and in the pinchy rush of sensation as he feels forced against the opening of her throat he wonders if he should accept her invitation.

"Wait," Harry says. "Shouldn't I do something for you first? If I come, it's all over."

"If you come, then you come again."

"Not at my age. I don't think."

"Your age. Always talking about your age." Thelma rests her face on his belly and gazes up at him, for the first time playful, her eyes at right angles to his disconcertingly. He has never noticed their color before: that indeterminate color called hazel but in the strong light overhead, and brightened by all her deep-throating, given a tawny pallor, an unthinking animal translucence. "I'm too excited to come," she tells him. "Anyway, Harry, I'm having my period and they're really bloody, every other month. I'm scared to find out why. In the months in between, these terrible cramps and hardly any show."

"See a doctor," he suggests.

"I see doctors all the time, they're useless. I'm dying, you know that, don't you?"

"Dying?"

"Well, maybe that's too dramatic a way of putting it. Nobody knows how long it'll take, and a lot of it depends upon me. The one thing I'm absolutely supposed not to do is go out in the sun. I was crazy to come down here, Ronnie tried to talk me out of it."

"Why did you?"

"Guess. I tell you, I'm crazy, Harry. I got to get you out of my system." And it seems she might make that sob of disgusted grief again, but she has reared up her head to look at his prick. All this talk of death has put it half to sleep again.

"This is this lupus?" he asks.

"Mmm," Thelma says. "Look. See the rash?" She pulls back her hair on both sides. "Isn't it pretty? That's from being so stupid in the sun Friday. I just wanted so badly to be like the rest of you, not to be an invalid. It was terrible Saturday. Your joints ache, your insides don't work. Ronnie offered to take me home for a shot of cortisone."

"He's very nice to you."

"He loves me."

His prick has stiffened again and she bends to it. "Thelma." He has not used her name before, this night. "Let me do something to you. I mean, equal rights and all that."

"You're not going down into all that blood."

"Let me suck these sweet things then." Her nipples are not bumply like Janice's but perfect as a baby's thumb-tips. Since it is his treat now he feels free to reach up and switch off the light over the bed. In the dark her rashes disappear and he can see her smile as she arranges herself to be served. She sits cross-legged, like Cindy did on the boat, women the flexible sex, and puts a pillow in her lap for his head. She puts a finger in his mouth and plays with her nipple and his tongue together. There is a tremble running through her like a radio not quite turned off. His hand finds her ass, its warm dents; there is a kind of glassy texture to Thelma's skin where Janice's has a touch of fine, fine sandpaper. His prick, lightly teased by her fingernails, has come back nicely. "Harry." Her voice presses into his ear. "I want to do something for you so you won't forget me, something you've never had with anybody else. I suppose other women have sucked you off?"

He shakes his head yes, which tugs the flesh of her breast.

"How many have you fucked up the ass?"

He lets her nipple slip from his mouth. "None. Never."

"You and Janice?"

"Oh God no. It never occurred to us."

"Harry. You're not fooling me?"

How dear that was, her old-fashioned "fooling." From talking to all those third-graders. "No, honestly. I thought only queers . . . Do you and Ronnie?"

"All the time. Well, a lot of the time. He loves it."

"And you?"

"It has its charms."

"Doesn't it hurt? I mean, he's big."

"At first. You use Vaseline. I'll get ours."

"Thelma, wait. Am I up to this?"

She laughs a syllable. "You're up." She slides away into the bathroom and while she is gone he stays enormous. She returns and anoints him thoroughly, with an icy expert touch. Harry shudders. Thelma lies down beside him with her back turned, curls forward as if to be shot from a cannon, and reaches behind to guide him. "Gently."

It seems it won't go, but suddenly it does. The medicinal odor of displaced Vaseline reaches his nostrils. The grip is tight at the base but beyond, where a cunt is all velvety suction and caress, there is no sensation: a void, a pure black box, a casket of perfect nothingness. He is in that void, past her tight ring of muscle. He asks, "May I come?"

"Please do." Her voice sounds faint and broken. Her spine and shoulder blades are taut.

It takes only a few thrusts, while he rubs her scalp with one hand and clamps her hip steady with the other. Where will his come go? Nowhere but mix with her shit. With sweet Thelma's sweet shit. They lie wordless and still together until his prick's slow shrivelling withdraws it. "O.K.," he says. "Thank you. That I won't forget."

"Promise?"

"I feel embarrassed. What does it do for you?"

"Makes me feel full of you. Makes me feel fucked up the ass. By lovely Harry Angstrom."

"Thelma," he admits, "I can't believe you're so fond of me. What have I done to deserve it?"

"Just existed. Just shed your light. Haven't you ever noticed, at parties or at the club, how I'm always at your side?"

"Well, not really. There aren't that many sides. I mean, we see you and Ronnie—"

"Janice and Cindy noticed. They knew you were who I'd want."

"Uh—not to, you know, milk this, but what is it about me that turns you on?"

"Oh darling. Everything. Your height and the way you move, as if you're still a skinny twenty-five. The way you never sit down anywhere without making sure there's a way out. Your little provisional smile, like a little boy at some party where the bullies might get him the next minute. Your good humor. You *believe* in people so—Webb, you hang on his words where nobody else pays any attention, and Janice, you're so proud of her it's pathetic. It's not as if she can *do* anything. Even her tennis, Doris Kaufmann was telling us, really—"

"Well it's nice to see her have fun at something, she's had a kind of dreary life."

"See? You're just terribly generous. You're so grateful to be anywhere, you think that tacky club and that hideous house of Cindy's are heaven. It's wonderful. You're so glad to be alive."

"Well, I mean, considering the alternative—"

"It kills me. I love you *so much* for it. And your hands. I've always loved your hands." Having sat up on the edge of the bed, she takes his left hand, lying idle, and kisses the big white moons of each fingernail. "And now your prick, with its little bonnet. Oh Harry I don't care if this kills me, coming down here, tonight is worth it."

That void, inside her. He can't take his mind from what he's discovered, that nothingness seen by his single eye. In the shadows, while humid blue moonlight and the rustle of palms seep through the louvers by the bed, he trusts himself to her as if speaking in prayer, talks to her about himself as he has talked to none other: about Nelson and the grudge he bears the kid and the grudge the boy bears him, and about his daughter, the daughter he thinks he has, grown and ignorant of him. He dares confide to Thelma, because she has let him fuck her up the ass in proof of love, his sense of miracle at being himself, himself instead of somebody else, and his old inkling, now fading in the energy crunch, that there was something that wanted him to find it, that he was here on earth on a kind of assignment.

"How lovely to think that," Thelma says. "It makes you"— the word is hard for her to find—"radiant. And sad." She gives him advice on some points. She thinks he should seek out Ruth and ask her point-blank if that is his daughter, and if so is there anything he can do to help? On the subject of Nelson, she thinks the child's problem may be an extension of Harry's; if he himself did not feel guilty about Jill's death and before that Rebecca's, he would feel less threatened by Nelson and more comfortable and kindly with him. "Remember," she says, "he's just a young man like you once were, looking for his path."

"But he's not like me!" Harry protests, having come at last into a presence where the full horror of this truth, the great falling-off, will be understood. "He's a goddam little Springer, through and through."

Thelma thinks he's more like Harry than he knows. Wanting to learn to hang glide—didn't he recognize himself in that? And the thing with two girls at once. Wasn't he, possibly, a bit jealous of Nelson?

"But I never had the impulse to screw Melanie," he confesses. "Or Pru either, much. They're both out of this world, somehow."

Of course, Thelma says. "You shouldn't want to fuck them. They're your daughters. Or Cindy either. You should want to fuck *me*. I'm your generation, Harry. I can *see* you. To those girls you're just an empty heap of years and money."

And, as they drift in talk away from the constellations of his life, she describes her marriage with Ronnie, his insecurities and worries beneath that braggart manner that she knows annoys Harry. "He was never a star like you, he never had that for a moment." She met him fairly well along in her twenties, when she was wondering if she'd die a spinster schoolteacher. Being old as she was, with some experience of men, and with a certain gift for letting go, she was amused by the things he thought of. For their honeymoon breakfast he jerked off into the scrambled eggs and they ate his fried jism with the rest. If you go along with everything on that side of Ronnie, he's wonderfully loyal, and docile, you could say. He has no interest in other women, she knows this for a fact, a curious fact even, given the nature of men. He's been a perfect father. When he was lower down on the totem pole at Schuylkill Mutual, he lost twenty pounds, staying awake nights worrying. Only in these last few years has the weight come back. When the first diagnosis of her lupus came through, he took it worse than she did, in a way. "For a woman past forty, Harry, when you've had children. . . . If some Nazi or somebody came to me and they'd take either me or little Georgie, say—he's the one that's needed most help, so he comes to mind—it wouldn't be a hard choice. For Ronnie I think it might be. To lose me. He thinks what I do for him not every woman would. I suspect he's wrong but there it is." And she admits she likes his cock. But what Harry might not appreciate, being a man, is that a big one like Ronnie's doesn't change size that much when it's hard, just the angle changes. It doesn't go from being a little bonneted sleeping baby to a tall fierce soldier like this. She has worked him up again, idly toying as she talks, while the night outside their louvered window has grown utterly still, the last drunken shout and snatch of music long died, nothing astir but the incessant sighing of the sea and the piping of some high-pitched cricket they have down here. Courteously he offers to fuck her through her blood, and she refuses with an almost virginal fright, so that he wonders if on the excuse of her flow she is not holding this part of herself back from him, aloof from her love and shamelessness, pure for her marriage. She has explained, "When I realized I was falling in love with you, I was so *mad* at myself, I mean it couldn't contribute to *any*thing. But then I came to see that something must be missing between me and Ronnie, or maybe in any life, so I tried to accept it, and even quietly enjoy it, just watching you. My little hairshirt." He has not kissed her yet on the mouth, but now having guessed at her guilty withholding of herself from being simply fucked he does. Guilt he can relate to. Her lips feel cool and dry, considering. Since she will not admit him to her cunt, as compromise he masturbates her while sitting on her face, glad he thought of washing where he did. Her tongue probes there and her fingers, as cool on top of his as if still filmed with Vaseline, guide his own as they find and then lose and find again the hooded little center that is *her*. She comes with a smothered cry and arches her back so this darkness at the center of her pale and smooth and unfamiliar form rises hungrily under his eyes, a cloud with a mouth, a fish lunging upwards out of water. Getting her breath, she returns the kindness and with him watches the white liquid lift and collapse in glutinous strings across her hand. She rubs his jism on her face, where it shines like sun lotion. The stillness outside is beginning to brighten, each leaf sharp in the soft air. Drunk on fatigue and self-exposure, he begs her to tell him something that he can do to her that Ronnie has never done. She gets into the bathtub and has him urinate on her. "It's hot!" she exclaims, her sallow skin drummed upon in

designs such as men and boys drill in the snow. They reverse
the experience, Thelma awkwardly straddling, and having to
laugh at her own impotence, looking for the right release
in the maze of her womanly insides. Above him as he waits
her bush has a masculine jut, but when her stream comes, it
dribbles sideways; women cannot *aim*, he sees. And her claim
of heat seems to him exaggerated; it is more like coffee or
tea one lets cool too long at the edge of the desk and then
must drink in a few gulps, this side of tepid. Having tried together to shower the ammoniac scent of urine off their skins,
Thelma and Harry fall asleep among the stripes of dawn now
welling through the louvers, they sleep as if not a few more
stolen hours but an entire married life of sanctioned intimacy
stretches unto death before them.

A savage rattling at the door. "Thelma. Harry. It's *us*."
Thelma puts on a robe to answer the knocking while Rabbit
hides beneath the sheet and peeks. Webb and Ronnie stand
there in the incandescence of another day. Webb is resplendent
in grape-colored alligator shirt and powder-blue plaid golf
pants. Ronnie wears last night's dinner clothes and needs to
get inside. Thelma shuts the door and hides in the bathroom
while Harry dresses in last night's rumpled suit, not bothering to knot the necktie. He still smells of urine, he thinks. He
runs to his own bungalow to change into a golf outfit. Black
girls, humming, pursued by yellow birds, are carrying tinkling
breakfast trays along the cement paths. Janice is in the bathroom, running a tub.

He shouts out, "You O.K.?"

She shouts back, "As O.K. as you are," and doesn't emerge.

On the way out, Harry stuffs an unbuttered croissant and
some scalding sips of coffee into his mouth. The papery orange and magenta flowers beside the door hurt his head. Webb
and Ronnie are waiting for him where the green cement paths
meet. Among the three men, as they push through their golf,
there is much banter and good humor, but little eye-contact.
When they return from the course around one o'clock, Janice
is sitting by the Olympic pool in the same off-white linen suit
she wore down in the airplane. Linen wrinkles terribly. "Harry,
Mother phoned. We have to go back."

"You're kidding. Why?" He is groggy, and had pictured a long afternoon nap, to be in shape for tonight. Also his foreskin was tender after last night's workout and slightly chafed every time he swung, thinking of Cindy, hoping her vagina would be nonfrictional. His golf, threaded through vivid afterimages of Thelma's underside and a ticklish awareness of his two businesslike partners as silently freighted with mental pictures of their own, was mysteriously good, his swing as it were emptied of impurities, until fatigue caught him on the fifteenth hole with three balls sliced along the identical skyey groove into the lost-ball terrain of cactus and coral and scrub growth. "What's happened? The baby?"

"No," Janice says, and by the easy way she cries he knows she's been crying off and on all morning, here in the sun. "It's *Nel*son. He's run off."

"He has? I better sit down." To the black waiter who comes to their glass table under its fringed umbrella he says, "Piña colada, Jeff. Better make that two. Janice?" She blearily nods, though there is an empty glass already before her. Harry looks around at the faces of their friends. "Jeff, maybe you should make that six." He has come to know the ropes in this place. The other people sitting around the pool look pale, newly pulled from the airplane.

Cindy has just come out of the pool, her shoulders blueblack, the diaper-shape of her bikini bottom wetly adhering. She tugs the cloth to cover the pale margin of skin above, below. She is getting fatter, day by day. Better hurry, he tells himself. But it is too late. Her face when she turns, towelling her back with a contortion that nearly pops one tit out of its triangular sling, is solemn. She and Thelma have heard Janice's story already. Thelma is sitting at the table in that ankle-length wrapper, the same dusty-pink as her nose, that she bought down here along with the wide straw hat. The big brown sunglasses she brought from home, tinted darker at the top, render her expressionless. Harry takes the chair at the table next to her. His knee accidentally touches one of hers; she pulls it away at once.

Janice is telling him, through tears, "He and Pru had a fight Saturday night, he wanted to go into Brewer for a party with that Slim person and Pru said she was too pregnant and couldn't face those stairs again, and he went by himself." She swallows. "And he didn't come back." Her voice is all roughened from swallowing the saltwater of the tears. With scrapings that hurt Harry's head Webb and Ronnie pull chairs to their table in its tight circle of shade. When Jeff brings their round of drinks Janice halts her terrible tale and Ronnie negotiates for lunch menus. He, like his wife, wears sunglasses. Webb wears none, trusting to his bushy brows and the crinkles of his flinty eyes, which gaze at Janice like those of some encouraging old fart of a father.

Her cheeks are drenched with the slime of distress and Harry has to love her for her ugliness. "I told you the kid was a rat," he tells her. He feels vindicated. And relieved, actually.

"He didn't come back," Janice all but cries, looking only at him, not at Webb, with that smeared lost balked expression he remembers so well from their earliest days, before she got cocky. "But Mother didn't want to b-bother us on our vacation and P-Pru thought he just needed to blow off steam and pretended not to be worried. But Sunday after going to church with Mother she called this Slim and Nelson had never showed up!"

"Did he have a car?" Harry asks.

"Your Corona."

"Oh boy."

"I think just scrambled eggs for me," Ronnie tells the waitress who has come. "Loose. You understand? Not too well done."

This time Rabbit deliberately seeks to touch Thelma's knee with his under the table but her knee is not there for him. Like Janice down here she has become a piece of static. The waitress is at his shoulder and he is wondering if he might dare another crabmeat-salad sandwich or should play it safe with a BLT. Janice's face, which the movement of the sun overhead is hoisting out of shadow, goes wide in eyes and mouth as she might shriek. "Harry you *can't* have lunch, you *must* get dressed and out of here! I packed for you, everything but the gray suit. The woman at the front desk was on the phone for me nearly an hour, trying to get us back to Philadelphia but it's impossible this time of year. There's not even anything to New York. She got us two seats on a little plane to San Juan and a room at the hotel airport so we can get a flight to the mainland first thing in the morning. Atlanta and then Philadelphia."

"Why not just use our regular reservations Thursday? What good's an extra day going to do?"

"I cancelled them. Harry, you didn't talk to Mother. She's wild, I've never heard her like this, you know how she always makes sense. I called back to tell her the plane on Wednesday and she didn't think she could drive the Philadelphia traffic to meet us, she burst into tears and said she was too old."

"Cancelled." It is sinking in. "You mean we can't stay here tonight because of something Nelson has done?"

"Finish your story, Jan," Webb urges. Jan, is it now? Harry suddenly hates people who seem to *know*; they would keep us blind to the fact that there is nothing to know. We are each of us filled with a perfect blackness.

Janice gulps again, and snuffles, calmed by Webb's voice. "There's nothing to finish. He didn't come back Sunday or Monday and none of these friends they have in Brewer had seen him and Mother finally couldn't stand it anymore and called this morning, even though Pru kept telling her not to bother us, it was her husband and she took the responsibility."

"Poor kid. Like you said, she thought she could work miracles." He tells her, "I don't *want* to leave before tonight."

"Stay here then," Janice says. "I'm going."

Harry looks over at Webb for some kind of help, and gets instead a sage and useless not-my-funeral grimace. He looks at Cindy but she is gazing down into her piña colada, her eyelashes in sharp focus. "I still don't understand the rush," he says. "Nobody's died."

"Not yet," Janice says. "Is that what you need?"

A rope inside his chest twists to make a kink. "Son of a fucking bitch," he says, and stands, bumping his head on the fringed edge of the umbrella. "When'd you say this plane to San Juan is?"

Janice snuffles, guilty now. "Not until three."

"O.K." He sighs. In a way this is a relief. "I'll go change and bring the suitcases. Could one of you guys at least order me a hamburger? Cindy. Thel. See you around." The two ladies let themselves be kissed, Thelma primly on the lips, Cindy on her apple-firm cheek, toasty from the sun.

Throughout their twenty-four-hour trip home Janice keeps crying. The taxi ride past the old sugar mills, through the goat herds and the straggling black towns and the air that seems to be blowing them kisses; the forty-minute hop in a swaying two-engine prop plane to Puerto Rico, over mild green water beneath whose sparkling film lurk buried reefs and schools of sharks; the stopover in San Juan where everybody is a real spic; the long stunned night of porous sleep in a hotel very like that motel on Route 422 where Mrs. Lubell stayed so long ago; and in the morning two seats on a jet to Atlanta and then Philly: through all this Janice is beside him with her cheeks glazed, eyes staring ahead, her eyelashes tipped with tiny balls of dew. It is as if all the grief that swept through him at Nelson's wedding now at last has reached Janice's zone, and he is calm and emptied and as cold as the void suspended beneath the airplane's shuddering flight. He asks her, "Is it just Nelson?"

She shakes her head so violently the fringe of bangs bobs. "*Ev*erything," she blurts, so loud he fears the heads just glimpsable in the seats ahead might turn around.

"The swapping?" he pursues softly.

She nods, not so violently, pinching her lower lip in a kind of turtle mouth her mother sometimes makes.

"How *was* Webb?"

"Nice. He's always been nice to me. He respected Daddy." This sets the tears to flowing again. She takes a deep breath to steady herself. "I felt so sorry for you, having Thelma when you wanted Cindy so much." With that there is no stopping her crying.

He pats her hands, which are loosely fisted together in her lap around a damp Kleenex. "Listen, I'm sure Nelson's all right, wherever he is."

"He"—she seems to be choking, a stewardess glances down as she strides by, this is embarrassing—"*hates* himself, Harry."

He tries to ponder if this is true. He snickers. "Well he sure screwed me. Last night was my dream date."

Janice sniffs and rubs each nostril with the Kleenex. "Webb says she's not as wonderful as she looks. He talked a lot about his first two wives."

Beneath them, through the scratched oval of Plexiglas, there is the South, irregular fields and dry brown woods, more woods than he would have expected. Once he had dreamed of going south, of resting his harried heart amid all that cotton, and now there it is under him, like the patchwork slope of one big hill they are slowly climbing, fields and woods and cities at the bends and mouths of rivers, streets eating into green, America disgraced and barren, mourning her hostages. They are flying too high for him to spot golf courses. They play all winter down here, swinging easy. The giant motors he is riding whine. He falls asleep. The last thing he sees is Janice staring ahead, wide awake, the bulge of tears compounding the bulge of her cornea. He dreams of Pru, who bursts while he is trying to manipulate her limbs, so there is too much water, he begins to panic. He is changing weight and this wakes him up. They are descending. He thinks back to his night with Thelma, and it seems in texture no different from the dream. Only Janice is real, the somehow catastrophic creases in her linen sleeve and the muddy line of her jaw, her head slumped as from a broken neck. She fell asleep, the same magazine open in her lap that she read on the way down. They are descending over Maryland and Delaware, where horses run and the du Ponts are king. Rich women with little birdy breasts and wearing tall black boots in from the hunt. Walking past the butler into long halls past marble tables they flick with their whips. Women he will never fuck. He has risen as high as he can, the possibility of such women is falling from him, falling with so many other possibilities as he descends. No snow dusts the dry earth below, rooftops and fields and roads where cars are nosing along like windup toys in invisible grooves. Yet from within those cars they are speeding, and feel free. The river flashes its sheet of steel, the plane tilts alarmingly, the air nozzles hissing above him may be the last thing he hears, Janice is awake and bolt upright. *Forgive me.* Fort Mifflin hulks just under their wheels, their speed is titanic. *Please, God.* Janice is saying something into his ear but the thump of the wheels drowns it out. They are down, and taxiing. He gives a squeeze to Janice's damp hand, that he didn't realize he was holding. "What did you say?" he asks her.

"That I love you."

"Oh, really? Well, same here. That trip was fun. I feel satisfied."

In the long slow trundle to their gate, she asks him shyly, "Was Thelma better than me?"

He is too grateful to be down to lie. "In ways. How about Webb?"

She nods and nods, as if to spill the last tears from her eyes.

He answers for her, "The bastard was great."

She leans her head against his shoulder. "Why do you think I've been crying?"

Shocked, he admits, "I thought about Nelson."

Janice sniffs once more, so loudly that one man already on his feet, arranging a Russian-style fur cap upon his sunburned bald head, briefly stares. She concedes, "It was, mostly," and she and Harry clasp hands once more, conspirators.

At the end of miles of airport corridor Ma Springer is standing apart from the cluster of other greeters. In the futuristic perspectives of this terminal she looks shrunken and bent, wearing her second-best coat, not the mink but a black cloth trimmed with silver fox, and a little cherry-red brimless hat with folded-back net that might get by in Brewer but appears quaint here, among the cowboys and the slim kids of indeterminate sex with their cropped hair dyed punk-style in pastel feathers and the black chicks whose hair is frizzed up in structures like three-dimensional Mickey Mouse ears. Hugging her, Rabbit feels how small the old lady, once the terror of his young manhood, has become. Her former look of having been stuffed tight with Koerner pride and potential indignation has fled, leaving her skin collapsed in random folds and bloodless. Deep liverish gouges underscore her eyes, and her wattled throat seems an atrocious wreck of flesh.

She can hardly wait to speak, backing a step away to give her voice room to make its impact. "The baby came last night. A girl, seven pounds and some. I couldn't sleep a wink, after getting her to the hospital and then waiting for the doctor to call." Her voice is shaky with blame. The airport Muzak, a tune being plucked on the strings of many coördinated violins, accompanies her announcement in such triumphant rhythm that Harry and Janice have to suppress smiles, not even daring to step closer in the jostle and shuffle, the old lady is so childishly, precariously intent on the message she means to deliver. "And then all the way down on the Turnpike, trucks kept tooting their horns at me, tooting these big foghorns they have. As if there were someplace else I could go; I couldn't drive the Chrysler off the *road*," Bessie says. "And after Conshohocken, on the Expressway, it's really a wonder I wasn't killed. I never saw so much traffic, though I thought at noon it would be letting up, and you know the signs, they aren't at all clear even if you have good eyes. All the way along the river I kept praying to Fred and I honestly believe it was him that got me here, I couldn't have done it alone."

And, her manner plainly implies, she will never attempt anything like it again; Janice and Harry find her at the terminus of the last great effort of her life. Henceforth, she is in their hands.

V

YET MA Springer wasn't so totally thrown by events that she didn't have the wit to call up Charlie Stavros and have him come back to the lot. His own mother took a turn for the worse in December—her whole left side feels numb, so even with a cane it frightens her to walk—and as Charlie predicted his cousin Gloria went back to Norristown and her husband, though Charlie wouldn't give it a year; so he has been pretty well tied down. This time it's Harry who's come back with a tan. He gives Charlie a two-handed handclasp, he's so happy to see him at Springer Motors again. The Greek sales rep doesn't look that hot, however: those trips to Florida were like a paint job. He looks pale. He looks as if you pricked his skin he'd bleed gray. He stands hunched over protecting his chest like he'd smoked three packs a day all his life, though Charlie like most Mediterranean types has never really had the self-destructive habits you see in northern Europeans and Negroes. Harry wouldn't have given him such an all-out handshake this way a week ago, but since fucking Thelma up the ass he's felt freer, more in love with the world again.

"The old *mastoras*. You look great," he exuberantly lies to Charlie.

"I've felt better," Charlie tells him. "Thank God it hasn't been any kind of a winter so far." Harry can see, through the plate-glass window, a snowless, leafless landscape, the dust of all seasons swirling and drifting, intermixed with the paper refuse from the Chuck Wagon that has blown across Route 111. A new banner is up: THE ERA OF COROLLA. *Toyota = Total Economy.* Charlie volunteers, "It's pretty damn depressing, watching *Manna mou* head straight downhill. She gets out of bed just to go to the bathroom and keeps telling me I ought to get married."

"Good advice, maybe."

"Well, I made a little move on Gloria in that direction, and it may be what scared her back to her husband. That guy, what a shit. She'll be back."

"Wasn't she a cousin?"

632

"All the better. Peppy type. About four eleven, little heavy in the rumble seat, not quite classy enough for you, champ. But cute. You should see her dance. I hadn't been to those Hellenic Society Saturday nights for years, she talked me into it. I loved to watch her sweat."

"You say she'll be back."

"Yeah but not for me. I've missed that boat." He adds, "I've missed a lot of boats."

"Who hasn't?"

Charlie rolls a toothpick in the center of his lower lip. Harry doesn't like to look at him closely; he's become one of those old Brewer geezers who go into cigar stores to put ten dollars on the numbers and hang around the magazine racks waiting for a conversation. "You've caught a few," he ventures to tell Harry.

"No, listen. Charlie. I'm in rotten shape. A kid who's disappeared and a new house with no furniture in it." Yet these facts, species of emptiness and new possibility, excite and please him more than not.

"The kid'll turn up," Charlie says. "He's just letting off steam."

"That's what Pru says. You never saw anybody so calm, considering. We went up to the hospital last night after getting in from the islands and, Jesus, is she happy about that baby. You'd think she was the first woman in the history of the world to pull this off. I guess she was worried about the kid being normal, after that fall she took a while ago."

"Worried about herself, more likely. Girl like that who's been knocked around a lot by life, having a baby's the one way they can prove to themselves they're human. What're they thinking of calling it?"

"She doesn't want to call it after her mother, she wants to name it after Ma. Rebecca. But she wants to wait to hear from Nelson, because, you know, that was his sister's name. The infant that, you know, didn't make it."

"Yeah." Charlie understands. Inviting bad luck. The sound of Mildred Kroust's typewriter bridges their silence. In the shop one of Manny's men is pounding an uncoöperative piece of metal. Charlie asks, "What're you going to do about the house?"

"Move in, Janice says. She surprised me, the way she talked to her mother. Right in the car driving home. She told her she was welcome to move in with us but she didn't see why she couldn't have a house of her own like other women her age and since Pru and the baby were obviously going to have to stay she doesn't want her to feel crowded in her own home. Bessie, that is."

"Huh. About time Jan stood on her own two feet. Wonder who she's been talking to?"

Webb Murkett, it occurs to Harry, through a tropical night of love; but things always work best between him and Charlie when they don't go too deep into Janice. He says, "The trouble with having the house is we have no furniture of our own. And everything costs a fucking fortune. A simple mattress and box spring and steel frame to set it on for six hundred dollars; if you add a headboard that's another six hundred. Carpets! Three, four thousand for a little Oriental, and they all come out of Iran and Afghanistan. The salesman was telling me they're a better investment than gold."

"Gold's doing pretty well," Charlie says.

"Better than we are, huh? Have you had a chance to look at the books?"

"They've looked better," Charlie admits. "But nothing a little more inflation won't cure. Young couple came in here Tuesday, the first day I got the call from Bessie, and bought a Corvette convertible Nelson had laid in. Said they wanted a convertible and thought the dead of winter would be a good time to buy one. No trade-in, weren't interested in financing, paid for it with a check, a regular checking account. Where do they get the money? Neither one of 'em could have been more than twenty-five. Next day, yesterday, kid came in here in a GMC pick-up and said he'd heard we had a snowmobile for sale. It took us a while to find it out back but when we did he got that light in his eyes so I began by asking twelve hundred and we settled at nine seventy-five. I said to him, There isn't any snow, and he said, That's all right, he was moving up to Vermont, to wait out the nuclear holocaust. Said Three Mile Island really blew his mind. D'y'ever notice how Carter can't say 'nuclear'? He says 'nookier.'"

"You really got rid of that snowmobile? I can't believe it."

"People don't care about economizing anymore. Big Oil has sold capitalism down the river. What the czar did for the Russians, Big Oil is doing for us."

Harry can't take the time to talk economics today. He apologizes, "Charlie, I'm still on vacation in theory, to the end of the week, and Janice is meeting me downtown, we got a thousand things to do in connection with this damn house of hers."

Charlie nods. "Amscray. I got some sorting out to do myself. One thing nobody could accuse Nelson of is being a neatness freak." He shouts after Harry as he goes into the corridor for his hat and coat, "Say hello to Grandma for me!"

Meaning Janice, Harry slowly realizes.

He ducks into his office, where the new 1980 company calendar with its photo of Fujiyama hangs on the wall. He makes a mental note to himself, not for the first time, to do something about those old clippings that hang outside on the pressedboard partition, they're getting too yellow, there's a process he's heard about where they photograph old halftones so they look white as new, and can be blown up to any size. Might as well blow them up big, it's a business expense. He takes from old man Springer's heavy oak coat-rack with its four little bow legs the sheepskin overcoat Janice got him for Christmas and the little narrow-brim suede hat that goes with it. At his age you wear a hat. He went all through last winter without a cold, because he had taken to wearing a hat. And vitamin C helps. Next it'll be Geritol. He hopes he didn't cut Charlie short but he found talking to him today a little depressing, the guy is at a dead end and turning cranky. Big Oil doesn't know any more what's up than Little Oil. But then from Harry's altitude at this moment anyone might look small and cranky. He has taken off; he is flying high, on his way to an island in his life. He takes a tube of Life Savers (Butter Rum) from his top lefthand desk drawer, to sweeten his breath in case he's kissed, and lets himself out through the back of the shop. He is careful with the crash bar: a touch of grease on this sheepskin and there's no getting it off.

Nelson having stolen his Corona, Harry has allocated to himself a grape-blue Celica Supra, the "ultimate Toyota," with padded dash, electric tachometer, state-of-the-art four-speaker solid-state AM/FM/MPX stereo, quartz-accurate digital clock, automatic overdrive transmission, cruise control, computer-tuned suspension, ten-inch disc brakes on all four wheels, and quartz halogen hi-beam headlights. He loves this smooth machine. The Corona for all its dependable qualities was a stodgy little bug, whereas this blue buzzard has charisma. The blacks along lower Weiser really stared yesterday afternoon when he drove it home. After Janice and he had brought Ma back to 89 Joseph in the Chrysler (which in fact even Harry found not so easy to steer, after a week of being driven in taxis on the wrong side of the road), they put her to bed and came into town in the Mustang, Janice all hyper after her standing up for herself about the house, to Schaechner Furniture, where they looked at beds and ugly easy chairs and Parsons tables like the Murketts had, only not so nice as theirs, the wood grain not checkerboarded. They couldn't make any decisions; when the store was about to close she drove him over to the lot so he could have a car too. He picked this model priced in five digits. Blacks stared out from under the neon Signs, JIM-BO's *Friendly* LOUNGE and LIVE ENTERTAINMENT and ADULT ADULT ADULT, as he slid by in virgin blue grapeskin; he was afraid some of them lounging in the cold might come running out at a stoplight and scratch his hood with a screwdriver or smash his windshield with a hammer, taking vengeance for their lives. On a number of walls now in this part of town you can see spray-painted SKEETER LIVES, but they don't say where.

He has lied to Charlie. He doesn't have to meet Janice until one-thirty and it is now only 11:17 by the Supra's quartz clock. He is driving to Galilee. He turns on the radio and its sound is even punkier, richer, more many-leaved and many-layered, than that of the radio in the old Corona. Though he moves the dial from left to right and back again he can't find Donna Summer, she went out with the Seventies. Instead there is a guy singing hymns, squeezing the word "Jesus" until it drips. And that kind of mellow mixed-voice backup he remembers from the records when he was in high school: the jukeboxes where you could see the record fall and that waxy rustling cloth, organdy or whatever, the girls went to dances in, wearing the corsage you gave them. The corsage would get crushed as the dancing got closer and the girls' perfumes would be released from between their powdery breasts as their bodies were warmed and pressed by partner after partner, in the violet light of the darkened gym, crêpe-paper streamers drooping overhead and the basketball hoops wreathed with paper flowers, all those warm bodies softly bumping in anticipation of the cold air stored in cars outside, the little glowing dashboard lights, the body heat misting the inside of the windshield, the organdy tugged and mussed, chilly fingers fumbling through coats and pants and underpants, clothes become a series of tunnels, Mary Ann's body nestling toward his hands, the space between her legs so different and mild and fragrant and safe, a world apart. And now, the news, on the half hour. That wise-voiced young woman is long gone from this local station, Harry wonders where she is by now, doing go-go or assistant vice-president at Sunflower Beer. The new announcer sounds like Billy Fosnacht, fat-lipped. President Carter has revealed that he personally favors a boycott of the 1980 Moscow Olympics. Reaction from athletes is mixed. Indian Prime Minister Indira Gandhi has backed off from yesterday's apparently pro-Soviet stance on Afghanistan. On the crowded campaign trail, U.S. Representative Philip Crane of Illinois has labelled as "foolish" Massachusetts Senator Edward Kennedy's proposal that the Seabrook, New Hampshire, proposed nuclear plant be converted to coal. In Japan, former Beatle Paul McCartney was jailed on charges of possessing eight ounces of marijuana. In Switzerland, scientists have succeeded in programming bacteria to manufacture the scarce human protein interferon, an anti-viral agent whose artificial production may usher in an era as beneficial to mankind as the discovery of penicillin. Meanwhile, if the fillings in your teeth cost more, it's because the price of gold hit eight hundred dollars an ounce in New York City today. Fuck. He sold too soon. Eight hundred times thirty equals twenty-four thousand, that's up nearly ten grand from fourteen six, if he'd just held on, damn that Webb Murkett and his silver. And the 76ers continue their winning ways, 121 to 110 over the Portland Trail Blazers at the Spectrum last night. Poor old Eagles out of their misery, Jaworski went down flinging. And now, to continue our program of Nice Music for Nice Folks, the traditional melody "Savior, Keep a Watch Over Me." Harry turns it off, driving to the purr of the Supra.

He knows the way now. Past the giant Amishman pointing to the natural cave, through the narrow town with its Purina feedstore sign and old inn and new bank and hitching posts and tractor agency. The corn stubble of the fields sticks up pale, all the gold bleached from it. The duck pond has frozen edges but a wide center of black water, so mild has the winter been. He slows past the Blankenbiller and Muth mailboxes, and turns down the driveway where the box says BYER. His nerves are stretched so nothing escapes his vision, the jutting stones of the two beaten reddish tracks that make the old road, the fringe of dried weeds each still bearing the form its green life assumed in the vanished summer, the peeling pumpkin-colored school bus husk, a rusting harrow, a small springhouse whitewashed years ago, and then the shabby farm buildings, corn crib and barn and stone house, approached from a new angle, for the first time from the front. He drives the Celica into the space of packed dirt where he once saw the Corolla pull in; in turning off the engine and stepping from the car he sees the ridge from which he spied, a far scratchy line of black cherry and gum trees scarcely visible through the apple trees of the orchard, farther away than it had felt, the odds were no one had ever seen him. This is crazy. Run.

But, as with dying, there is a moment that must be pushed through, a slice of time more transparent than plate glass; it is in front of him and he takes the step, drawing heart from that loving void Thelma had confided to him. In his sheepskin coat and silly small elf hat and three-piece suit of pinstriped wool bought just this November at that tailor of Webb's on Pine Street, he walks across the earth where silted-over flat sandstones once formed a walk. It is cold, a day that might bring snow, a day that feels hollow. Though it is near noon no sun shows through, not even a silver patch betrays its place in the sky, one long ribbed underbelly of low gray clouds. A drab tall thatch of winter woods rears up on his right. In the other direction, beyond the horizon, a chain saw sounds stuck. Even before, removing one glove, he raps with a bare hand on the door, where paint a poisonous green is coming loose in long curving flakes, the dog inside the house hears his footsteps scrape stone and sets up a commotion of barking.

Harry hopes the dog is alone, its owner out. There is no car or pick-up truck in the open, but one might be parked in the barn or the newish garage of cement blocks with a roof of corrugated overlapped Fiberglas. Inside the house no light burns that he can see, but then it is near noon, though the day is dull and growing darker. He peers in the door and sees himself reflected with his pale hat in another door, much like this one, with two tall panes of glass, the thickness of a stone wall away. Beyond the old panes a hallway with a tattered striped runner recedes into unlit depths. As his eyes strain to see deeper his nose and ungloved hand sting with the cold. He is about to turn away and return to the warm car when a shape materializes within the house and rushes, puffed up with rage, toward him. The black-haired collie leaps and leaps again against the inner door, frantic, trying to bite the glass, those ugly little front teeth a dog has, inhuman, and the split black lip and lavender gums, unclean. Harry is paralyzed with fascination; he does not see the great shape materialize behind Fritzie until a hand clatters on the inner door latch.

The fat woman's other hand holds the dog by the collar; Harry helps by opening the green outer door himself. Fritzie recognizes his scent and stops barking. And Rabbit recognizes, buried under the wrinkles and fat but with those known eyes blazing out alive, Ruth. So amid a tumult of wagging and the whimpers of that desperate doggy need to reclaim a friend, the two old lovers confront one another. Twenty years ago he had lived with this woman, March to June. He saw her for a minute in Kroll's eight years later, and she had spared him a few bitter words, and now a dozen years have poured across them both, doing their damage. Her hair that used to be a kind of dirty fiery gingery color is flattened now to an iron gray and pulled back in a bun like the Mennonites wear. She wears wide denim dungarees and a man's red lumberjack shirt beneath a black sweater with unravelled elbows and dog hairs and wood chips caught in the greasy weave. Yet this is Ruth. Her upper lip still pushes out a little, as if with an incipient blister, and her flat

blue eyes in their square sockets still gaze at him with a hostility that tickles him. "What do you want?" she asks. Her voice
sounds thickened, as by a cold.

"I'm Harry Angstrom."

"I can see that. What do you want here?"

"I was wondering, could we talk a little? There's something
I need to ask you."

"No, we can't talk a little. Go away."

But she has released the dog's collar, and Fritzie sniffs at
his ankles and his crotch and writhes in her urge to jump up,
to impart the scarcely bearable joy locked in her narrow skull,
behind her bulging eyes. Her bad eye still looks sore. "Good
Fritzie," Harry says. "Down. Down."

Ruth has to laugh, that quick ringing laugh of hers, like
change tossed onto a counter. "Rabbit, you're cute. Where'd
you learn her name?"

"I heard you all calling her once. A couple times I've been
here, up behind those trees, but I couldn't get up my nerve to
come any closer. Stupid, huh?"

She laughs again, a touch less ringingly, as if she is truly
amused. Though her voice has roughened and her bulk has
doubled and there is a down including a few dark hairs along
her cheeks and above the corners of her mouth, this is really
Ruth, a cloud his life had passed through, solid again. She is
still tall, compared to Janice, compared to any of the women of
his life but Mim and his mother. She always had a weight about
her; she joked the first night when he lifted her that this would
put him out of action, a weight that pushed him off, along with
something that held him fast, an air of being willing to play,
in the little space they had, and though the time they had was
short. "So you were scared of us," she says. She bends slightly,
to address the dog. "Fritzie, shall we let him in for a minute?"
The dog's liking him, a dim spark of dog memory setting her
tail wagging, has tipped the balance.

The hall inside smells decidedly of the past, the way these
old farm houses do. Apples in the cellar, cinnamon in the cooking, a melding of the old plaster and wallpaper paste, he doesn't
know. Muddy boots stand in a corner of the hall, on newspapers spread there, and he notices that Ruth is in stocking
feet—thick gray men's work socks, but sexy nonetheless, the

silence of her steps, though she is huge. She leads him to the right, into a small front parlor with an oval rug of braided rags on the floor and a folding wooden lawn chair mixed in with the other furniture. The only modern piece is the television set, its overbearing rectangular eye dead for the moment. A small wood fire smolders in a sandstone fireplace. Harry checks his shoes before stepping onto the rag rug, to make sure he is not tracking in dirt. He removes his fancy little sheepskin hat.

As if regretting this already, Ruth sits on the very edge of her chair, a cane-bottomed rocker, tipping it forward so her knees nearly touch the floor and her arm can reach down easily to scratch Fritzie's neck and keep her calm. Harry guesses he is supposed to sit opposite, on a cracked black leather settee beneath two depressing sepia studio portraits, a century old at least they must be, in matching carved frames, of a bearded type and his buttoned-up wife, both long turned to dust in their coffins. But before sitting down he sees across the room, by the light of a window whose deep sill teems with potted African violets and those broad-leafed plants people give for Mother's Days, a more contemporary set of photographs, color snapshots that line one shelf of a bookcase holding rows of the paperback mysteries and romances Ruth used to read and apparently still does. That used to hurt him about her in those months, how she would withdraw into one of those trashy thrillers set in England or Los Angeles though he was right there, in the flesh, a living lover. He crosses to the bookcase and sees her, younger but already stout, standing before a corner of this house within the arm of a man older, taller, and stouter than she: this must have been Byer. A big sheepish farmer in awkward Sunday clothes, squinting against the sunlight with an expression like that of the large old portraits, his mouth wistful in its attempt to satisfy the camera. Ruth looks amused, her hair up in a bouffant do and still gingery, amused that for this sheltering man she is a prize. Rabbit feels, for an instant as short and bright as the click of a shutter, jealous of these lives that others led: this stout plain country couple posing by a chipped corner of brown stucco, on earth that from the greening state of the grass suggests March or April. Nature's old tricks. There are other photographs, color prints of combed and smiling adolescents, in those cardboard frames high-school pictures come in. Before he can examine them, Ruth says sharply, "Who said you could look at those? Stop it."

"It's your family."

"You bet it is. Mine and not yours."

But he cannot tear himself away from the images in flashlit color of these children. They gaze not at him but past his right ear, each posed identically by the photographer as he worked his school circuit May after May. A boy and the girl at about the same age—the senior photo—and then in smaller format a younger boy with darker hair, cut longer and parted on the other side of his head from his brother. All have blue eyes. "Two boys and a girl," Harry says. "Who's the oldest?"

"What the hell do you care? God, I'd forgotten what a pushy obnoxious bastard you are. Stuck on yourself from cradle to grave."

"My guess is, the girl is the oldest. When did you have her, and when did you marry this old guy? How can you stand it, by the way, out here in the boondocks?"

"I stand it fine. It's more than anybody else ever offered me."

"I didn't have much to offer anybody in those days."

"But you've done fine since. You're dressed up like a pansy."

"And you're dressed up like a ditchdigger."

"I've been cutting wood."

"You operate one of those chain saws? Jesus, aren't you afraid you'll cut off a finger?"

"No, I'm not. The car you sold Jamie works fine, if that's what you came to ask."

"How long have you known I've been at Springer Motors?"

"Oh, always. And then it was in the papers when Springer died."

"Was that you drove past in the old station wagon the day Nelson got married?"

"It might have been," Ruth says, sitting back in her rocking chair, so it tips the other way. Fritzie has stretched out to sleep. The wood fire spits. "We pass through Mt. Judge from time to time. It's a free country still, isn't it?"

"Why would you do a crazy thing like that?" She loves him.

"I'm not saying I did anything. How would I know Nelson was getting married at that moment?"

"You saw it in the papers." He sees she means to torment

him. "Ruth, the girl. She's mine. She's the baby you said you couldn't stand to have the abortion for. So you had it and then found this old chump of a farmer who was glad to get a piece of young ass and had these other two kids by him before he kicked the bucket."

"Don't talk so rude. You're not proving anything to me except what a sad case I must have been ever to take you in. You are Mr. Bad News, honest to God. You're nothing but me, me and gimme, gimme. When I *had* something to give you I gave it even though I knew I'd never get anything back. Now thank God I have nothing to give." She limply gestures to indicate the raggedly furnished little room. Her voice in these years has gained that country slowness, that stubborn calm with which the country withholds what the city wants.

"Tell me the truth," he begs.

"I just did."

"About the girl."

"She's younger than the older boy. Scott, Annabelle, and then Morris in '66. He was the afterthought. June 6, 1966. Four sixes."

"Don't stall, Ruth, I got to get back to Brewer. And don't lie. Your eyes get all watery when you lie."

"My eyes are watery because they can't stand looking at you. A regular Brewer sharpie. A dealer. The kind of person you used to hate, remember? And fat. At least when I knew you you had a body."

He laughs, enjoying the push of this; his night with Thelma has made his body harder to insult. "*You*," he says, "are calling *me* fat?"

"I am. And how did you get so red in the face?"

"That's my tan. We just got back from the islands."

"Oh Christ, the islands. I thought you were about to have stroke."

"When did your old guy pack it in? Whajja do, screw him to death?"

She stares at him a time. "You better go."

"Soon," he promises.

"Frank passed away in August of '76, of cancer. Of the colon. He hadn't even reached retirement age. When I met him was younger than we are now."

"O.K., sorry. Listen, stop making me be such a prick. Tell me about our girl."

"She's *not* our girl, Harry. I *did* have the abortion. My parents arranged it with a doctor in Pottsville. He did it right in his office and about a year later a girl died afterwards of complications and they put him in jail. Now the girls just walk into the hospital."

"And expect the taxpayer to pay," Harry says.

"Then I got a job as the day cook in a restaurant over toward Stogey's Quarry to the east of here and Frank's cousin was the hostess for that time and one thing led to another pretty fast. We had Scott in late 1960, he just turned nineteen last month, one of these Christmas babies that always get cheated on presents."

"Then the girl when? Annabelle."

"The next year. He was in a hurry for a family. His mother had never let him marry while she was alive, or anyway he blamed her."

"You're lying. I've seen the girl; she's older than you say."

"She's eighteen. Do you want to see birth certificates?"

This must be a bluff. But he says, "No."

Her voice softens. "Why're you so hepped on the girl anyway? Why don't you pretend the boy's yours?"

"I have one boy. He's enough"—the phrase just comes—"bad news." He asks, brusquely, "And where *are* they? Your boys."

"What's it to you?"

"Nothing much. I was just wondering how come they're no around, helping you with this place."

"Morris is at school, he gets home on the bus after three Scott has a job in Maryland, working in a plant nursery. I tol both him and Annie, Get out. This was a good place for me t come to and hide, but there's nothing here for young peopl When she and Jamie Nunemacher got this scheme of goin and living together in Brewer, I couldn't say No, though h people were dead set against it. We had a big conference, told them that's how young people do now, they live togethe and aren't they smart? They know I'm an old whore anywa I don't give a fuck what they think. The neighbors always l us alone and we let them alone. Frank and old Blankenbill

hadn't talked for fifteen years, since he began to take me out."
She sees she has wandered, and says, "Annabelle won't be with
the boy forever. He's nice enough, but . . ."

"I agree," Rabbit says, as if consulted. Ruth is lonely, he sees,
and willing to talk, and this makes him uneasy. He shifts his
weight on the old black sofa. Its springs creak. A shift in the
air outside has created a downdraft that sends smoke from the
damp fire curling into the room.

She glances to the dead couple in their frames like carved
coffins above his head and confides, "Even when Frank was
healthy, he had to have the buses to make ends meet. Now I
rent the big fields and just try to keep the bushes down. The
bushes and the oil bills." And it is true, this room is so cold he
has not thought of taking his heavy coat off.

"Yes well," he sighs. "It's hard." Fritzie, wakened by some
turn in the dream that had been twitching the ends of her
paws, stands and skulks over to him as if to bark, and instead
drops down to the rug again, coiling herself trustfully at his
feet. With his long arm Harry reaches to the bookcase and lifts
out the photograph of the daughter. Ruth does not protest.
He studies the pale illumined face in its frame of maroon cardboard: backed by a strange background of streaked blue like an
imitation sky, the girl gazes beyond him. Round and polished
like a fruit by the slick silk finish of the print, the head, instead of revealing its secret, becomes more enigmatic, a shape
as strange as those forms of sea life spotlit beneath the casino
boardwalk. The mouth is Ruth's, that upper lip he noticed at
the lot. And around the eyes, that squared-off look, though her
brow is rounder than Ruth's and her hair, brushed to a photo-
genic gloss, less stubborn. He looks at the ear, for a nick in
the edge like Nelson has; her hair would have to be lifted. Her
nose is so delicate and small, the nostrils displayed by a slight
upturn of the tip, that the lower half of her face seems heavy,
still babyish. There is a candor to her skin and a frosty light to
the eyes that could go back to those Swedes in their world of
snow; he glimpsed it in the Murketts' bathroom mirror. His
blood. Harry finds himself reliving with Annabelle that moment when her turn came in the unruly school line to enter
the curtained corner of the gym and, suddenly blinded, to pose
for posterity, for the yearbook, for boyfriend and mother, for

time itself as it wheels on unheeding by: the opportunity come to press your face up against blankness and, by thinking right thoughts, to become a star. "She looks like me."

Ruth laughs now. "You're seeing things."

"No kidding. When she came to the lot that first time, something hit me—her legs, maybe, I don't know. Those aren't your legs." Which had been thick, twisting like white flame as she moved naked about their room.

"Well, Frank had legs too. Until he let himself get out of shape, he was on the lanky side. Over six foot, when he straightened up, I'm a sucker for the big ones I guess. Then neither of the boys inherited his height."

"Yeah, Nelson didn't get mine, either. A shrimp just like his mother."

"You're still with Janice. You used to call her a mutt," Ruth reminds him. She has settled into this situation comfortably now, leaning back in the rocker and rocking, her stocking feet going up on tiptoe, then down on the heels, then back on tiptoe. "Why am I telling you all about my life when you don't say a thing about yours?"

"It's pretty standard," he says. "Don't be sore at me because I stayed with Janice."

"Oh Christ no. I just feel sorry for her."

"A sister," he says, smiling. Women are all sisters, they tell us now.

Fat has been added to Ruth's face not in smooth scoops but in lumps, so when she lifts her head her eye sockets seem built of bony welts. A certain forgiving mischief has lifted her armored glance. "Annie was fascinated by you," she volunteers. "She several times asked me if I'd ever heard of you, this basketball hero. I said we went to different high schools. She was disappointed when you weren't there when she and Jamie went back to pick up the car finally. Jamie had been leaning to a Fiesta."

"So you don't think Jamie is the answer for her?"

"For now. But you've seen him. He's common."

"I hope she doesn't—"

"Go my way? No, it'll be all right. There aren't whores anymore, just healthy young women. I've raised her very innocent. I always felt *I* was very innocent, actually."

"We all are, Ruth."

She likes his saying her name, he should be careful about saying it. He puts the photograph back and studies it in place, Annabelle between her brothers. "How about money?" he asks, trying to keep it light. "Would some help her? I could give it to you so it, you know, wouldn't come out of the blue or anything. If she wants an education, for instance." He is blushing, and Ruth's silence doesn't help. The rocker has stopped rocking.

At last she says, "I guess this is what they call deferred payments."

"It's not for you, it would be for her. I can't give a lot. I mean, I'm not that rich. But if a couple thousand would make a difference—"

He lets the sentence hang, expecting to be interrupted. He can't look at her, that strange expanded face. Her voice when it comes has the contemptuous confident huskiness he heard from her ages ago, in bed. "Relax. You don't have to worry, I'm not going to take you up on it. If I ever get really hard up here I can sell off a piece of road frontage, five thousand an acre is what they've been getting locally. Anyway, Rabbit. Believe me. She's not yours."

"O.K., Ruth. If you say so." In his surge of relief he stands.

She stands too, and having risen together their ghosts feel their inflated flesh fall away; the young man and woman who lived illicitly together one flight up on Summer Street, across from a big limestone church, stand close again, sequestered from the world, and as before the room is hers. "Listen," she hisses up at him, radiantly is his impression, her distorted face gleaming. "I wouldn't give you the satisfaction of that girl being yours if there was a million dollars at stake. I raised her. She and I put in a lot of time together here and where the fuck were you? You saw me in Kroll's that time and there was no follow-up, I've known where you were all these years and you didn't give a simple shit what had happened to me, or my kid, or *any*thing."

"You were married," he says mildly. *My kid*: something odd here.

"You bet I was," she rushes on. "To a better man than you'll ever be, sneer all you want. The kids have had a wonderful

father and they know it. When he died we just carried on as
if he was still around, he was that strong. Now I don't know
what the hell is going on with you in your little life up there in
Mt. Judge—"

"We're moving," he tells her. "To Penn Park."

"Swell. That's just where you belong, with those phonies.
You should have left that mutt of yours twenty years ago for
her good as well as your own, but you didn't and now you can
stew in it; stew in it but *leave my Annie alone*. It's *creepy*, Harry.
When I think of you thinking she's your daughter it's like rubbing her all over with shit."

He sighs through his nose. "You still have a sweet tongue,"
he says.

She is embarrassed; her iron hair has gone straggly and she
presses it flat with the heels of her hands as if trying to crush
something inside her skull. "I shouldn't say something like that
but it's *fright*ening, having you show up in your fancy clothes
wanting to claim my daughter. You make me think, if I hadn't
had the abortion, if I hadn't let my parents have their way, it
might have all worked out differently, and we could *have* a
daughter now. But you—"

"I know. You did the right thing." He feels her fighting the
impulse to touch him, to cling to him, to let herself be crushed
into his clumsy arms as once. He looks for a last topic. Awkwardly he asks, "What're you going to do, when Morris grows
up and leaves home?" He remembers his hat and picks it up,
pinching the soft new crown in three fingers.

"I don't know. Hang on a little more. Whatever happens,
land won't go down. Every year I last it out here is money in
the bank."

He sighs through his nose again. "O.K., if that's how it is.
I'll run then. Really no soap on the girl?"

"Of course not. Think it through. Suppose she *was* yours. At
this stage it'd just confuse her."

He blinks. Is this an admission? He says, "I never was too
good at thinking things through."

Ruth smiles at the floor. The squarish dent above her cheekbone, seen this way from above, was one of the first things he
noticed about her. Chunky and tough but kindly, somehow.
Another human heart, telling him he was a big bunny, out by

the parking meters in the neon light, the first time they met. Trains still ran through the center of Brewer then. "Men don't have to be," she says. "They don't get pregnant."

The dog became agitated when they both stood and Ruth's voice became louder and angry, and now Fritzie leads them from the room and waits, tail inquisitively wagging, with her nose at the crack of the door leading outside. Ruth opens it and the storm door wide enough for the dog to pass through but not Harry. "Want a cup of coffee?" she asks.

He told Janice one o'clock at Schaechner's. "Oh Jesus, thanks, but I ought to get back to work."

"You came here just about Annabelle? You don't want to hear about me?"

"I *have* heard about you, haven't I?"

"Whether I have a boyfriend or not, whether I ever thought about you?"

"Yeah, well, I'm sure that'd be interesting. From the sound of it you've done terrifically. Frank and Morris and, who's the other one?"

"Scott."

"Right. And you have all this land. Sorry, you know, to have left you in such a mess way back then."

"Well," Ruth says, with a considering slowness in which he imagines he can hear her late husband speaking. "I guess we make our own messes."

She seems now not merely fat and gray but baffled: straw on her sweater, hair on her cheeks. A shaggy monster, lonely. He longs to be out that double door into the winter air, where nothing is growing. Once he escaped by telling her, *I'll be right back*, but now there is not even that to say. Both know, what people should never know, that they will not meet again. He notices on the hand of hers that grips the doorknob a thin gold ring all but lost in the flesh of one finger. His heart races, trapped.

She has mercy on him. "Take care, Rabbit," she says. "I was just kidding about the outfit, you look good." Harry ducks his head as if to kiss her cheek but she says, "No." By the time he has taken a step off the concrete porch, her shadow has vanished from the double door's black glass. The gray of the day has intensified, releasing a few dry flakes of snow that will not amount to anything, that float sideways like flecks of ash. Fritzie trots beside him to the glossy grape-blue Celica, and has to be discouraged from jumping into the back seat.

Once on his way, out the driveway and past the mailboxes that say BLANKENBILLER and MUTH, Harry pops a Life Saver into his mouth and wonders if he should have called her bluff on the birth certificates. Or suppose Frank had had another wife, and Scott was his child by that marriage? If the girl was as young as Ruth said, wouldn't she still be in high school? But no. Let go. Let it go. God doesn't want him to have a daughter.

Waiting in the overheated front room of Schaechner's surrounded by plush new furniture, Janice looks petite and prosperous and, with her Caribbean tan, younger than forty-three. When he kisses her, on the lips, she says, "Mmm. Butter Rum. What are you hiding?"

"Onions for lunch."

She dips her nose close to his lapel. "You smell of smoke."

"Uh, Manny gave me a cigar."

She hardly listens to his lies, she is breathy and electric with news of her own. "Harry, Melanie called Mother from Ohio. Nelson is with her. Everything's all right."

As Janice continues, he can see her mouth move, her bangs tremble, her eyes widen and narrow, and her fingers tug in excitement at the pearl strand the lapels of her coat disclose, but Rabbit is distracted from the exact sense of what she is saying by remembering, when he bent his face close to old Ruth's in the light of the door, a glitter there, on the tired skin beneath her eyes, and by the idiotic thought, which it seems he should bottle and sell, that our tears are always young, the saltwater stays the same from cradle, as she said, to grave.

The little stone house that Harry and Janice bought for $78,000, with $15,600 down, sits on a quarter-acre of bushy land tucked in off a macadamized dead end behind two larger examples of what is locally known as Penn Park Pretentious: a tall mock-Tudor with gables like spires and red-tiled roofs and clinker bricks sticking out at crazy melted angles, and a sort of neo-plantation manse of serene thin bricks the pale yellow of lemonade, with a glassed-in sunporch and on the other side a row of Palladian windows, where Harry guesses the dining room is. He has been out surveying his property, looking for a sunny patch where a garden might be dug in this spring. The spot behind Ma Springer's house on Joseph Street had been too shady. He finds a corner that might do, with some cutting back of oak limbs that belong to his neighbor. The earth generally in this overgrown, mature suburb is well-shaded; his lawn is half moss, which this mild winter has dried but left exposed and resilient still. He also finds a little cement fish pond with a blue-painted bottom, dry and drifted with pine needles. Someone had once sunk seashells in the wet cement of the slanting rim. The things you buy when you buy a house. Doorknobs, windowsills, radiators. All his. If he were a fish he could swim in this pond, come spring. He tries to picture that moment when whoever it was, man, woman, or child or all three, had set these shells here, in the summer shade of trees a little less tall than these above him now. The weak winter light falls everywhere in his yard, webbed by the shadows from leafless twigs. He senses standing here a silt of caring that has fallen from purchaser to purchaser. The house was built in that depressed but scrupulous decade when Harry was born. Suave gray limestone had been hauled from the quarries in the far north of Diamond County and dressed and fitted by men who took the time to do it right. At a later date, after the war, some owner broke through the wall facing away from the curb and built an addition of clapboards and white-blotched brick. Paint is peeling from the clapboards beneath the Andersen windows of what is now Janice's kitchen. Harry makes a mental note to trim back the branches that brush against the house, to cut down the dampness. Indeed there are several trees here that might be turned altogether into firewood, but until they leaf out in the spring he can't be sure which should go. The house has two fireplaces, one in the big long living room and the other, off the same flue, in the little room behind, that Harry thinks of as a den. His den.

He and Janice moved in yesterday, a Saturday. Pru was coming home from the hospital with the baby and if they were not there she could take their Joseph Street bedroom, with its own bathroom, away from the street. Also they thought the confusion might mask for Janice's mother the pain of their escape. Webb Murkett and the others got back from the Caribbean Thursday night as planned, and Saturday morning Webb brought one of his roofer's trucks with extension ladders roped to both sides and helped them move. Ronnie Harrison, that fink, said he had to go into the office to tackle the backlog of paperwork that had built up during his vacation; he had worked Friday night to midnight. But Buddy Inglefinger came over with Webb, and it didn't take the three men more than two hours to move the Angstroms. There wasn't much furniture they could call their own, mostly clothes, and Janice's mahogany bureau, and some cardboard boxes of kitchen equipment that had been salvaged when the previous house they could call their own had burned down in 1969. All of Nelson's stuff, they left. One of the butch women came out onto her porch and waved goodbye; so news travels in a neighborhood, even when the people aren't friendly. Harry had always meant to ask them what it was like, and why. He can see not liking men, he doesn't like them much himself, but why would you like women any better, if you were one? Especially women who hammer all the time, just like men.

From Schaechner's on Thursday afternoon he and Janice had bought, and got them to deliver on Friday, a new color Sony TV (Rabbit hates to put any more money into Japanese pockets but he knows from *Consumer Reports* that in this particular line they can't be touched for quality) and a pair of big padded silvery-pink wing chairs (he has always wanted a wing chair, he hates drafts on his neck, people have died from drafts on their necks) and a Queen-size mattress and box springs on a metal frame, without headboard. This bed he and Webb and Buddy carry upstairs to the room at the back, with a partially slanted ceiling but space for a mirror if they want it on the blank wall next to the closet door, and the chairs and TV go not into the living room, which is too big to think about furnishing at first, but into the much cozier room just off it, the den. Always he has wanted a den, a room where people would have trouble getting at him. What he especially loves about this little room, besides the fireplace and the built-in shelves where you could keep either books or Ma's knickknacks and china when she dies, with liquor in the cabinets below, and even room for a little refrigerator when they get around to it, are the wall-to-wall carpeting of a kind of green-and-orange mix that reminds him of cheerleaders' tassels and the little high windows whose sashes crank open and shut and are composed of leaded lozenge-panes such as you see in books of fairy tales. He thinks in this room he might begin to read books, instead of just magazines and newspapers, and begin to learn about history, say. You have to step down into the den, one step down from the hardwood floor of the living room, and this small difference in plane hints to him of many reforms and consolidations now possible in his life, like new shoots on a tree cropped back.

Franklin Drive is the elegant street their dead-end spur cuts off of; 14½ Franklin Drive is their postal address, and the spur itself has no street name, they should call it Angstrom Way. Webb suggested Angstrom Alley, but Harry has had enough of alleys in his Mt. Judge years, and resents Webb's saying this. First he tells you to sell gold too soon, then he fucks your wife, and now he puts your house down. Harry has never lived at so low a number as 14½ before. But the mailman in his little red, white, and blue jeep knows where they are. Already they've received mail here: flyers to RESIDENT collected while they were in the Caribbean, and Saturday around one-thirty, after Webb and Buddy were gone, while Janice and Harry in the kitchen were arranging spoons and pans they'd forgotten they owned, the letter slot clacked and a postcard and a white envelope lay on the front hall's bare floor. The envelope, one of the long plain stamped ones you buy at the post office, had no return address and was postmarked Brewer. It was addressed to just MR. HARRY ANGSTROM in the same slanting block printing that had sent him last April the clipping about Skeeter. Inside this new envelope the clipping was very small, and the same precise hand that had addressed it had schoolteacherishly inscribed in ballpoint along the top edge, *From "Golf Magazine" Annual "Roundup."* The item read:

A COSTLY BIRDIE

Dr. Sherman Thomas cooked his own goose when he killed one of the Canadian variety at Congressional CC. The court levied a $500 fine for the act.

Janice forced a laugh, reading at his side, there in the echoing bare hallway, that led through a white arch into the long living room.

He looked over at her guiltily and agreed with her unspoken thought. "Thelma."

Her color had risen. A minute before, they had been in sentimental raptures over an old Mixmaster that, plugged in again after ten years in Ma Springer's attic, had whirred. Now she blurted, "She'll never let us alone. Never."

"Thelma? Of course she will, that was the deal. She was very definite about it. Weren't you, with Webb?"

"Oh of course, but words don't mean anything to a woman in love."

"Who? You with Webb?"

"No, you goon. Thelma. With you."

"She told me, she loves Ronnie. Though I don't see how she can."

"He's her bread and butter. You're her dream man. You really turn her on."

"You sound amazed," he said accusingly.

"Oh, you don't *not* turn me on, I can see what she sees, it's just . . ." She turned away to hide her tears. Everywhere he looked, women were crying. ". . . . the in*tru*sion. To know that that was her that sent that other thing way back then, to think of her watching us all the time, waiting to pounce . . . They're evil people, Harry. I don't want to see any of them anymore."

"Oh come on." He had to hug her, there in the hollow hall. He likes it now when she gets all flustered and frowny, her breath hot and somehow narrow with grief; she seems most his then, the keystone of his wealth. Once when she got like this, her fear contaminated him and he ran; but in these middle years it is so clear to him that he will never run that he can laugh at her, his stubborn prize. "They're just like us. That was a holiday. In real life they're very square."

Janice was vehement. "I'm *furious* with her, doing such a flirtatious thing, so soon after. They'll never let us alone, never, now that we have a house. As long as we were at Mother's we were protected."

And it was true, the Harrisons and the Murketts and Buddy

Inglefinger and the tall new girlfriend with her frizzy hair now up in corn rows and juju beads like the woman in "*10*" did come over last night, the Angstroms' first night in their new house, bearing bottles of champagne and brandy, and stayed until two, so Sunday feels sour and guilty. Harry has no habits yet in this house; without habits and Ma Springer's old furniture to cushion him, his life stretches emptily on all sides, and it seems that moving in any direction he's bound to take a fall.

The other piece of mail that came Saturday, the postcard, was from Nelson.

> Hi Mom & Dad—
> Spring Semester begins the 28th so am in good shape. Need certified check for $1087 (397 instrucional fee, 90 general fee, 600 surcharge for non Ohio students) plus living expenses. $2000–2500 shd. be enuff. Will call when you have phone. Melanie says Hi. Love, Nelson

On the other side of the card was a modern brick building topped by big slatted things like hot air vents, identified as *Business Administration Building, Kent State University.* Harry asked, "What about Pru? The kid's a father and doesn't seem to know it."

"He knows it. He just can't do everything at once. He's told Pru over the phone he'll drive back as soon as he's registered and look at the baby and leave us the car he took. Though maybe, Harry, we could just let him use it for now."

"That's *my* Corona!"

"He's doing what you wanted him to do, go back to college. Pru understands."

"She understands she's linked up with a hopeless loser," Harry said, but his heart wasn't in it. The kid was no threat to him for now. Harry was king of the castle.

And today is Super Sunday. Janice tries to get him up for church, she is driving Mother, but he is far too hungover and wants to return to the warm pocket of a dream he had been having, a dream involving a girl, a young woman, he has never met before, with darkish hair, they have met somehow at a party and are in a little bathroom together, not speaking but with a rapport, as if just having had sex or about to have sex, between them, sex very certain and casual between them but not exactly happening, the floor of many small square tiles at an angle beneath them, the small space of the bathroom cupped around them like the little chrome bowl around the flame of the perpetual cigar lighter at the old tobacco store downtown, the bliss of a new relationship, he wants it to go on and on but is awake and can't get back. This bedroom, its bright slanted ceiling, is strange. They must get curtains soon. Is Janice up to this? Poor mutt, she's never had to do much. He makes what breakfast he can of a single orange in the nearly empty refrigerator, plus some salted nuts left over from the party last night, plus a cup of instant coffee dissolved with hot water straight from the tap. This house too, like Webb's, has those single-lever faucets shaped like a slender prick stung on the tip by a bee. The refrigerator went with the place and, one of the things that sold him, has an automatic ice-maker that turns out crescent-shaped cubes by the bushel. Even though the old Mixmaster works he hasn't forgotten his promise to Janice to buy her a Cuisinart. Maybe the trouble she has getting meals on the table related to its being Ma Springer's old-fashioned kitchen. He roams through his house warily exulting in the cast-iron radiators, the brass window catches, the classy little octagonal bathroom tiles, and the doors with key-lock knobs; these details of what he has bought shine out in the absence of furniture and will soon sink from view as the days here clutter them over. Now they are naked and pristine.

Upstairs, in a slanting closet off of what once must have been a boys' bedroom—its walls pricked with dozens of thumbtack holes and marred with ends of Scotch tape used to hold posters —he finds stacks of *Playboys* and *Penthouses* from the early Seventies. He fetches from out beside the kitchen steps, under the slowly revolving electric meter, one of the big green plastic trash barrels he and Janice bought yesterday at Shur Valu; but before disposing of each magazine Rabbit leafs through it, searching out the center spreads month after month, year after year, as the airbrushing recedes and the pubic hair first peeks and then froths boldly forth and these young women perfect as automobile bodies let their negligees fall open frontally and revolve upon their couches of leopard skin so subscribers' eyes at last can feast upon their full shame and treasure. An invisible force month after month through each year's seasons forces gently wider open their flawless thighs until somewhere around the bicentennial issues the Constitutional triumph of open beaver is attained, and the buxom boldly gazing girls from Texas and Hawaii and South Dakota yield up to the lights and lens a vertical rosy aperture that seems to stare back, out of a blood-flushed nether world, scarcely pretty, an ultimate of disclosure which yet acts as a barrier to some secret beyond, within, still undisclosed as the winter light diminishes at the silent window. Outside, a squirrel is watching, its gray back arched, its black eye alert. Nature, Harry sees, is everywhere. This tree that comes so close to the house he thinks is a cherry, its bark in rings. The squirrel, itself spied, scurries on. The full load of magazines makes the trash barrel almost too heavy to lift. A ton of cunt. He lugs it downstairs. Janice comes back after two, having had lunch with her mother and Pru and the baby.

"Everybody seemed cheerful," she reports, "including Baby."

"Baby have a name yet?"

"Pru asked Nelson about Rebecca and he said absolutely not. Now she's thinking of Judith. That's her mother's name. I told them to forget Janice, I never much liked it for myself."

"I thought she hated her mother."

"She doesn't hate her, she doesn't much respect her. It's her father she hates. But he's been on the phone to her a couple of times and been very, what's the word, conciliatory."

"Oh great. Maybe he can come and help run the lot. He can do our steam fitting. How does Pru feel about Nelson's running off, just on the eve?"

Janice takes off her hat, a fuzzy violet loose-knit beret she wears in winter and that makes her look with the sheepskin coat like some brown-faced boy of a little soldier off to the wars. Her hair stands up with static electricity. In the empty living room she has nowhere to drop her hat, and throws it onto a white windowsill. "Well," she says, "she's interesting about it. For just now she says she's just as glad he isn't around, it would be one more thing to cope with. In general she feels it's something he had to do, to get his shit together—that's her expression. I think she knows she pushed him. Once he gets his degree, she thinks, he'll be much more comfortable with himself. She doesn't seem at all worried about losing him for good or anything."

"Huh. Whaddeya have to do to get blamed for something these days?"

"They're very tolerant of each other," Janice says, "and I think that's nice." She heads upstairs, and Harry follows her up, closely, afraid of losing her in the vast newness of their house.

He asks, "She gonna go out there and live with him in an apartment or what?"

"She thinks her going out there with the baby would panic him right now. And of course for Mother it'd be much nicer if she stayed."

"Isn't Pru at all miffed about Melanie?"

"No, she says Melanie will watch after him for her. They don't have this jealousy thing the way we do, if you can believe them."

"If."

"Speaking of which." Janice drops her coat on the bed and bends over, ass high, to unzip her boots. "Thelma had left a message with Mother about whether or not you and I wanted to come over to their house for a light supper and watch the Super Bowl. I guess the Murketts will be there."

"And you said?"

"I said No. Don't worry, I was quite sweet. I said we were having Mother and Pru over here to watch the game on our brand-new Sony. It's true. I invited them." In stocking feet she stands and puts her hands on the hips of her black church suit as if daring him to admit he would rather go out and be with that racy crowd than stay home with his family.

"Fine," he says. "I haven't really seen—"

"Oh, and quite a sad thing. Mother got it from Grace Stuhl, who's good friends apparently with Peggy Fosnacht's aunt. While we were down there Peggy went into her doctor's for a check-up and by nighttime he had her in the hospital and a breast taken off."

"My God." Breast he had sucked. Poor old Peggy. Flicked away by God's fingernail. Life is too big for us, in the end.

"They of course said they got it all but then they always say that."

"She seemed lately headed for something unfortunate."

"She's been grotesque. I should call her, but not today."

Janice is changing into dungarees to do housecleaning. She says the people have left the place filthy but he can't see it, except for the *Playboy*s. She has never been much of a neatness freak wherever they have lived before. Uncurtained winter light bouncing off the bare floors and blank walls turns her underwear to silver and gives her shoulders and arms a quick life as of darting fish before they disappear into an old shirt of his and a moth-eaten sweater. Behind her their new bed, unmade, hasn't been fucked on yet, they were too drunk and exhausted last night. In fact they haven't since that night on the island. He asks her irritably what about *his* lunch.

Janice asks, "Oh, didn't you find something in the fridge?"

"There was one orange. I ate it for breakfast."

"I know I bought eggs and sliced ham but I guess Buddy and what's-her-name—"

"Valerie."

"Wasn't her hair wild? do you think she takes drugs?—ate it all up in that omelette they made after midnight. Isn't that a sign of drugs, an abnormal appetite for food? I know there's some cheese left, Harry. Couldn't you make do with cheese and crackers until I go out and buy something for Mother later? I don't know what's open Sundays around here, I can't keep running back to the Mt. Judge Superette and using up gas."

"No," he agrees, and makes do with cheese and crackers and a Schlitz that is left over from the three sixpacks Ronnie and Thelma brought over. Webb and Cindy brought the brandy and champagne. All afternoon he helps Janice clean, Windexing windows and wiping woodwork while she mops floors and even scours the kitchen and bathroom sinks. They have a downstairs bathroom here but he doesn't know where to buy toilet paper printed with comic strips. Janice has brought her mother's waxing machine in the Mustang along with some Butcher's paste and he wipes the wax on the long

blond living-room floor, each whorl of wood grain and slightly
popped-up nail and old scuff of a rubber heel his, his house.
As he lays the wax on with circular swipes Rabbit keeps chasing the same few thoughts in his brain, stupid as brains are
when you do physical work. Last night he kept wondering if
the other two couples had gone ahead and swapped, Ronnie
and Cindy doing it the second time, after he and Janice had left
and they *did* act cozy, as if the four of them made the innermost circle of the party and the Angstroms and poor Buddy
and that hungry Valerie were second echelon or third worlders
somehow. Thelma got pretty drunk for her, her sallow skin
gleaming to remind him of Vaseline, though when he thanked
her for sending the clipping about the goose she stared at him
and then sideways at Ronnie and then back at him as if he had
rocks in his head. He guesses it'll all come out, what happened
down there afterwards, people can't keep a good secret, but
it pains him to think that Thelma would let Webb do to her
everything the two of them did or that Cindy really wanted to
go with Ronnie again and would lift up her heavy breast with
a motherly hand so that loud-mouthed jerk could suck and tell
about it, with his scalp bare like that he's such a baby, Harrison.
No point in keeping secrets, we'll all be dead soon enough,
already we're survivors, the kids are everywhere, making the
music, giving the news. Ever since that encounter with Ruth
he's felt amputated, a whole world half-seen in the corner of
his eye snuffed out. Janice and the waxing machine are whining and knocking behind him and the way his brain is going
on reminds him of some article he read last year in the paper
or *Time* about some professor at Princeton's theory that in ancient times the gods spoke to people directly through the left
or was it the right half of their brains, they were like robots
with radios in their heads telling them everything to do, and
then somehow around the time of the ancient Greeks or As-
syrians the system broke up, the batteries too weak to hear the
orders, though there are glimmers still and that is why we go to
church, and what with all these jigaboos and fags roller-skating
around with transistorized earmuffs on their heads we're getting back to it. How at night just before drifting off he hears
Mom's voice clear as a whisper from the corner of the room
saying *Hassy*, a name as dead as the boy that was called that

is dead. Maybe the dead are gods, there's certainly something kind about them, the way they give you room. What you lose as you age is witnesses, the ones that watched from early on and cared, like your own little grandstand. Mom, Pop, old man Springer, baby Becky, good old Jill (maybe that dream had to do with the time he took her in so suddenly, except her hair wasn't dark, it was so intense, the dream, there's nothing like a new relationship), Skeeter, Mr. Abendroth, Frank Byer, Mamie Eisenhower just recently, John Wayne, LBJ, JFK, Skylab, the goose. With Charlie's mother and Peggy Fosnacht cooking. And his daughter Annabelle Byer snuffed out with that whole world he was watching in the corner of his eye like those entire planets obliterated in *Star Wars*. The more dead you know it seems the more living there are you don't know. Ruth's tears, when he was leaving: maybe God is in the universe the way salt is in the ocean, giving it a taste. He could never understand why people can't drink saltwater, it can't be any worse than mixing Coke and potato chips.

Behind him he hears Janice knocking her waxer clumsily against the baseboards at every sweep and it comes to him why they're being so busy, they're trying not to panic here in this house, where they shouldn't be at all, so far from Joseph Street. Lost in space. Like what souls must feel when they awaken in a baby's body so far from Heaven: not only scared so they cry but guilty, guilty. A huge hole to fill up. The money it'll take to fill these rooms with furniture when they had it all free before: he's ruined himself. And the mortgage payments: $62,400 at 13½ per cent comes to nearly $8500 interest alone, $700 a month over twenty years nibbling away at the principal until he's sixty-six. What did Ruth say about her youngest, 6/6/66? Funny about numbers, they don't lie but do play tricks. Three score and ten, all the things he'll never get to do now: to have Cindy arrange herself in the pose of one of those *Penthouse* sluts on a leopard skin and get down in front of her on all fours and just eat and eat and eat.

Last night Buddy turned to him so drunk his silver-rimmed eyeglasses were steamed and said he knew it was crazy, he knew what people would say about her being too tall and having three children and all, but Valerie really did it for him. She is the one, Harry. With tears in his eyes he said that. The big news from over at the Flying Eagle was Doris Kaufmann's planning to get married again. To a guy Rabbit used to know slightly, Don Eberhardt, who had gotten rich buying up inner-city real estate when nobody wanted it, before the gas crunch. Life is sweet, that's what they say.

Light still lingers in the windows, along the white window-sills, at five when they finish, the days this time of year lengthening against the grain. The planets keep their courses no matter what we do. In the freshly waxed hall by the foot of the stairs he touches Janice underneath her chin where the flesh is soft but not really repulsive and suggests a little nap upstairs, but she gives him a kiss warm and competent, the competence cancelling out the warmth, and tells him, "Oh Harry, that's a sweet idea but I have no idea when they might be coming, it's all mixed up with a lie-down Mother was going to have, she really does seem frailer, and the baby's feeding time, and I haven't even shopped yet. Isn't the Super Bowl on?"

"Not till six, it's on the West Coast. There's a pre-game thing on at four-thirty but it's all hoopla, you can only take so much. I wanted to watch the Phoenix Open at two-thirty, but you were so damn frantic to clean up just because your mother's coming over."

"You should have said something. I could have done it myself."

While she goes off in the Mustang he goes upstairs, because there isn't any place downstairs to lie down. He hopes to see the squirrel again, but the animal is gone. He thought squirrels hibernated, but maybe this winter is too mild. He holds his hands over a radiator, his, and with pride and satisfaction feels it breathing heat. He lies down on their new bed with the Amish quilt they brought from Mt. Judge and almost without transition falls asleep. In his dream he and Charlie are in trouble at the agency, some crucial papers with numbers on them are lost, and where the new cars should be in the showroom there are just ragged craters, carefully painted with stripes and stars, in the concrete floor. He awakes realizing he is running scared. There has been another explosion, muffled: Janice closing the door downstairs. It is after six. "I had to drive out almost to the ballpark before I found this MinitMart that was open. They didn't have fresh anything of course, but I got four frozen Chinese dinners that the pictures of on the box looked good."

"Isn't crap like that loaded with chemicals? You don't want to poison Pru's milk."

"And I bought you lots of baloney and eggs and cheese and crackers so stop your complaining."

The nap, that at first waking had felt as if somebody had slugged him in the face with a ball of wet clothes, begins to sink into his bones and cheer him up. Darkness has erased the staring depth of day; the windows might be black photographic plates in their frames. Thelma and Nelson are out there circling, waiting to move in. Janice bought thirty dollars' worth at the MinitMart and as she fills the bright refrigerator he sees in a corner there are two more beers that escaped the vultures last night. She even brought him a jar of salted peanuts for all of $1.29 to watch the game with. The first half sways back and forth. He is rooting for the Steelers to lose, he hates what they did to the Eagles and in any case doesn't like overdogs; he pulls for the Rams the way he does for the Afghan rebels against the Soviet military machine.

At half-time a lot of girls in colored dresses and guys that look like fags in striped jerseys dance while about a thousand pieces of California brass imitate the old Big Bands with an off-key blare; these kids try to jitterbug but they don't have the swing, that one-beat wait back on your heels and then the twirl. They do a lot of disco wiggling instead. Then some little piece of sunshine with an Andrews-sisters pageboy sings "Sentimental Journey" but it doesn't have that Doris Day wartime Forties soul, how could it? No war. These kids were all born, can you believe it, around 1960 at the earliest and, worse yet, are sexually mature. On the "a-all aboard" they snake together in what is supposed to be the Chattanooga Choo-choo and then produce, out there in cloudless California, flashing sheets like tinfoil that are supposed to be solar panels. "Energy is people," they sing. "People are en-er-gy!" Who needs Khomeini and his oil? Who needs Afghanistan? Fuck the Russkis. Fuck the Japs, for that matter. We'll go it alone, from sea to shining sea.

Tired of sitting in his den alone with a hundred million other boobs watching, Harry goes into the kitchen for that second beer, Janice sits at a card table her mother parted with as a loan grudgingly, even though she never plays cards except in the Poconos. "Where are our guests?" he asks.

Janice is sitting there helping the Chinese dinners warm up in the oven and reading a copy of *House Beautiful* she must have bought at the MinitMart. "They must have fallen asleep. They're up a good deal of the night, in a way it's a mercy, Harry, we're not there anymore."

He trims his lips in upon a bitter taste in the beer. Grain gone bad. Men love their poison. "Well I guess living in this house with just you is the way for me to lose weight. I never get fed."

"You'll get fed," she says, turning a slick page.

Jealous of the magazine, of the love for this house he feels growing in her, he complains, "It's like waiting for a shoe to drop."

She darts a dark, not quite hostile look up at him. "I'd think you've had enough shoes drop lately to last ten years."

From her tone he supposes she means something about Thelma but that had been far from his mind, for now.

Their guests don't arrive until early in the fourth quarter, just after Bradshaw, getting desperate, has thrown a bomb to Stallworth; receiver and defender go up together and the lucky stiff makes a circus catch. Rabbit still feels the Rams are going to win it. Janice calls that Ma and Pru are here. Ma Springer is all chattery in the front hall, taking off her mink, about the drive through Brewer, where hardly any cars were moving because she supposes of the game. She is teaching Pru to drive the Chrysler and Pru did very well once they figured out how to move the seat back: she hadn't realized what long legs Pru has. Pru, pressing a pink-wrapped bundle tight to her chest out of the cold, looks worn and thin in the face but more aligned, like a bed tugged smooth. "We would have been here earlier but I was typing a letter to Nelson and wanted to finish," she apologizes.

"It worries me," Ma is going on, "they used to say it brought bad luck to take a baby out visiting before it was baptized."

"Oh Mother," Janice says; she is eager to show her mother the cleaned-up house and leads her upstairs, even though the only lights are some 40-watt neo-colonial wall sconces in which the previous owners had let many of the bulbs die.

As Harry resettles himself in one of his silvery-pink wing chairs in front of the game, he can hear the old lady clumping on her painful legs directly above his head, inspecting, searching out the room where she might some day have to come and stay. He assumes Pru is with them, but the footsteps mingling on the ceiling are not that many, and Teresa comes softly down the one step into his den and deposits into his lap what he has been waiting for. Oblong cocooned little visitor, the baby shows her profile blindly in the shuddering flashes of color jerking from the Sony, the tiny stitchless seam of the closed eyelid aslant, lips bubbled forward beneath the whorled nose as if in delicate disdain, she knows she's good. You can feel in the curve of the cranium she's feminine, that shows from the first day. Through all this she has pushed to be here, in his lap, his hands, a real presence hardly weighing anything but alive. Fortune's hostage, heart's desire, a granddaughter. His. Another nail in his coffin. His.

THE WITCHES OF EASTWICK

Chapters

I. The Coven 671

II. Maleficia 774

III. Guilt 854

I.

The Coven

"He was a meikle blak roch man, werie cold."

—*Isobel Gowdie, in 1662*

"Now efter that the deuell had endit his admonitions, he cam down out of the pulpit, and caused all the company to com and kiss his ers, quhilk they said was cauld lyk yce; his body was hard lyk yrn, as they thocht that handled him."

—*Agnes Sampson, in 1590*

"AND OH yes," Jane Smart said in her hasty yet purposeful way; each *s* seemed the black tip of a just-extinguished match held in playful hurt, as children do, against the skin. "Sukie said a man has bought the Lenox mansion."

"A man?" Alexandra Spofford asked, feeling off-center, her peaceful aura that morning splayed by the assertive word.

"From New York," Jane hurried on, the last syllable almost barked, its *r* dropped in Massachusetts style. "No wife and family, evidently."

"Oh. One of those." Hearing Jane's northern voice bring her this rumor of a homosexual come up from Manhattan to invade them, Alexandra felt intersected where she was, in this mysterious crabbed state of Rhode Island. She had been born in the West, where white and violet mountains lift in pursuit of the delicate tall clouds, and tumbleweed rolls in pursuit of the horizon.

"Sukie wasn't so sure," Jane said swiftly, her *s*'s chastening. "He appeared quite burly. She was struck by how hairy the backs of his hands were. He told the people at Perley Realty he needed all that space because he was an inventor with a lab. And he owns a number of pianos."

Alexandra giggled; the noise, little changed since her Colorado girlhood, seemed produced not out of her throat but by a birdlike familiar perched on her shoulder. In fact the telephone was aching at her ear. And her forearm tingled, going numb. "How many pianos can a man have?"

This seemed to offend Jane. Her voice bristled like a black cat's fur, iridescent. She said defensively, "Well Sukie's only going by what Marge Perley told her at last night's meeting of the Horse Trough Committee." This committee supervised the planting and, after vandalism, the replanting of a big blue marble trough for watering horses that historically stood at the center of Eastwick, where the two main streets met; the town was shaped like an L, fitted around its ragged bit of Narragansett Bay. Dock Street held the downtown businesses, and Oak Street at right angles to it was where the lovely big old homes were. Marge Perley, whose horrid canary-yellow For Sale signs leaped up and down on trees and fences as on the tides of economics and fashion (Eastwick had for decades been semi-depressed and semi-fashionable) people moved in and out of the town, was a heavily made-up, go-getting woman who, if one at all, was a witch on a different wavelength from Jane, Alexandra, and Sukie. There was a husband, a tiny fussy Homer Perley always trimming their forsythia hedge back to stubble, and this made a difference. "The papers were passed in Providence," Jane explained, pressing the *nce* hard into Alexandra's ear.

"And with hairy backs to his hands," Alexandra mused. Near her face floated the faintly scratched and flecked and often repainted blankness of a wooden kitchen-cabinet door; she was conscious of the atomic fury spinning and skidding beneath such a surface, like an eddy of weary eyesight. As if in a crystal ball she saw that she would meet and fall in love with this man and that little good would come of it. "Didn't he have a name?" she asked.

"That's the stupidest thing," Jane Smart said. "Marge told Sukie and Sukie told me but something's scared it right out of my head. One of those names with a 'van' or a 'von' or a 'de' in it."

"How very swell," Alexandra answered, already dilating, diffusing herself to be invaded. A tall dark European, ousted from

his ancient heraldic inheritance, travelling under a curse . . .
"When is he supposed to move in?"

"She said he said soon. He could be in there now!" Jane
sounded alarmed. Alexandra pictured the other woman's
rather too full (for the rest of her pinched face) eyebrows lifting to make half-circles above her dark resentful eyes, whose
brown was always a shade paler than one's memory of it. If
Alexandra was the large, drifting style of witch, always spreading herself thin to invite impressions and merge with the landscape, and in her heart rather lazy and entropically cool, Jane
was hot, short, concentrated like a pencil point, and Sukie
Rougemont, busy downtown all day long gathering news and
smiling hello, had an oscillating essence. So Alexandra reflected, hanging up. Things fall into threes. And magic occurs
all around us as nature seeks and finds the inevitable forms,
things crystalline and organic falling together at angles of sixty
degrees, the equilateral triangle being the mother of structure.

She returned to putting up Mason jars of spaghetti sauce,
sauce for more spaghetti than she and her children could consume even if bewitched for a hundred years in an Italian fairy
tale, jar upon jar lifted steaming from the white-speckled blue
boiler on the trembling, singing round wire rack. It was, she
dimly perceived, some kind of ridiculous tribute to her present lover, a plumber of Italian ancestry. Her recipe called for
no onions, two cloves of garlic minced and sautéed for three
minutes (no more, no less; that was the magic) in heated oil,
plenty of sugar to counteract acidity, a single grated carrot,
more pepper than salt; but the teaspoon of crumbled basil is
what catered to virility, and the dash of belladonna provided
the release without which virility is merely a murderous congestion. All this must be added to her own tomatoes, picked
and stored on every window sill these weeks past and now
sliced and fed to the blender: ever since, two summers ago,
Joe Marino had begun to come into her bed, a preposterous
fecundity had overtaken the staked plants, out in the side garden where the southwestern sun slanted in through the line
of willows each long afternoon. The crooked little tomato
branches, pulpy and pale as if made of cheap green paper,
broke under the weight of so much fruit; there was something
frantic in such fertility, a crying-out like that of children frantic

to please. Of plants tomatoes seemed the most human, eager and fragile and prone to rot. Picking the watery orange-red orbs, Alexandra felt she was cupping a giant lover's testicles in her hand. She recognized as she labored in her kitchen the something sadly menstrual in all this, the bloodlike sauce to be ladled upon the white spaghetti. The fat white strings would become her own white fat. This female struggle of hers against her own weight: at the age of thirty-eight she found it increasingly unnatural. In order to attract love must she deny her own body, like a neurotic saint of old? Nature is the index and context of all health and if we have an appetite it is there to be satisfied, satisfying thereby the cosmic order. Yet she sometimes despised herself as lazy, in taking a lover of a race so notoriously tolerant of corpulence.

Alexandra's lovers in the handful of years since her divorce had tended to be odd husbands let stray by the women who owned them. Her own former husband, Oswald Spofford, rested on a high kitchen shelf in a jar, reduced to multi-colored dust, the cap screwed on tight. Thus she had reduced him as her powers unfolded after their move to Eastwick from Norwich, Connecticut. Ozzie had known all about chrome and had transferred from a fixture factory in that hilly city with its too many peeling white churches to a rival manufacturer in a half-mile-long cinder-block plant south of Providence, amid the strange industrial vastness of this small state. They had moved seven years ago. Here in Rhode Island her powers had expanded like gas in a vacuum and she had reduced dear Ozzie as he made his daily trek to work and back along Route 4 first to the size of a mere man, the armor of patriarchal protector falling from him in the corrosive salt air of Eastwick's maternal beauty, and then to the size of a child as his chronic needs and equally chronic acceptance of her solutions to them made him appear pitiful, manipulable. He quite lost touch with the expanding universe within her. He had become much involved with their sons' Little League activities, and with the fixture company's bowling team. As Alexandra accepted first one and then several lovers, her cuckolded husband shrank to the dimensions and dryness of a doll, lying beside her in her great wide receptive bed at night like a painted log picked up at a roadside stand, or a stuffed baby alligator. By the time of their actual divorce her former lord and master had become mere dirt—matter in the wrong place, as her mother had briskly defined it long ago—some polychrome dust she swept up and kept in a jar as a souvenir.

The other witches had experienced similar transformations in their marriages; Jane Smart's ex, Sam, hung in the cellar of her ranch house among the dried herbs and simples and was occasionally sprinkled, a pinch at a time, into a philtre, for piquancy; and Sukie Rougemont had permanized hers in plastic and used him as a place mat. This last had happened rather recently; Alexandra could still picture Monty standing at cocktail parties in his Madras jacket and parsley-green slacks, braying out the details of the day's golf round and inveighing against the slow feminine foursome that had held them up all day and never invited them to play through. He had hated uppity women—female governors, hysterical war protesters, "lady" doctors, Lady Bird Johnson, even Lynda Bird and Luci Baines. He had thought them all butch. Monty had had wonderful teeth when he brayed, long and very even but not false, and, undressed, rather touching, thin bluish legs, much less muscular than his brown golfer's forearms. And with that puckered droop to his buttocks common to the softening flesh of middle-aged women. He had been one of Alexandra's first lovers. Now, it felt queer and queerly satisfying to set a mug of Sukie's tarry coffee upon a glossy plastic Madras, leaving a gritty ring.

This air of Eastwick empowered women. Alexandra had never tasted anything like it, except perhaps a corner of Wyoming she had driven through with her parents when she was about eleven. They had let her out of the car to pee beside some sagebrush and she had thought, seeing the altitudinous dry earth for the moment dampened in a dark splotch, *It doesn't matter. It will evaporate.* Nature absorbs all. This girlhood perception had stayed forever with her, along with the sweet sage taste of that roadside moment. Eastwick in its turn was at every moment kissed by the sea. Dock Street, its trendy shops with their perfumed candles and stained-glass shadepulls aimed at the summer tourists and its old-style aluminum diner next to a bakery and its barber's next to a framer's and its little clattering newspaper office and long dark hardware store run by Armenians, was intertwined with saltwater as it slipped and slapped and slopped against the culverts and pilings the street in part was built upon, so that an unsteady veiny aqua sea-glare shimmered and shuddered on the faces of the local matrons as they carried orange juice and low-fat milk, luncheon meat and whole-wheat bread and filtered cigarettes out of the Bay Superette. The real supermarket, where one did a week's shopping, lay inland, in the part of Eastwick that had been farmland; here, in the eighteenth century, aristocratic planters, rich in slaves and cattle, had paid social calls on horseback, a slave galloping ahead of them to open the fence gates one after the other. Now, above the asphalted acres of the shopping-mall parking lot, exhaust fumes dyed with leaden vapors air within memory oxygenated by fields of cabbages and potatoes. Where corn, that remarkable agricultural artifact of the Indians, had flourished for generations, windowless little plants with names like Dataprobe and Computech manufactured mysteries, components so fine the workers wore plastic caps to keep dandruff from falling into the tiny electro-mechanical works.

Rhode Island, though famously the smallest of the fifty states, yet contains odd American vastnesses, tracts scarcely explored amid industrial sprawl, abandoned homesteads and forsaken mansions, vacant hinterlands hastily traversed by straight black roads, heathlike marshes and desolate shores on either side of the Bay, that great wedge of water driven like a stake clean to the state's heart, its trustfully named capital. "The fag end of creation" and "the sewer of New England," Cotton Mather called the region. Never meant to be a separate polity, settled by outcasts like the bewitching, soon-to-die Anne Hutchinson, this land holds manifold warps and wrinkles. Its favorite road sign is a pair of arrows pointing either way. Swampy poor in spots, elsewhere it became a playground of the exceedingly rich. Refuge of Quakers and antinomians, those final distillates of Puritanism, it is run by Catholics, whose ruddy Victorian churches loom like freighters in the sea of bastard architecture. There is a kind of metallic green stain, bitten deep into Depression-era shingles, that exists nowhere else. Once you cross the state line, whether at Pawtucket or Westerly, a subtle change occurs, a cheerful dishevelment, a contempt for appearances, a chimerical uncaring. Beyond the clapboard slums yawn lunar stretches where only an abandoned roadside stand offering the ghost of last summer's CUKES betrays the yearning, disruptive presence of man.

Through such a stretch Alexandra now drove to steal a new look at the old Lenox mansion. She took with her, in her pumpkin-colored Subaru station wagon, her black Labrador, Coal. She had left the last of the sterilized jars of sauce to cool on the kitchen counter and with a magnet shaped like Snoopy had pinned a note to the refrigerator door for her four children to find: MILK IN FRIG, OREOS IN BREADBOX, BACK IN ONE HOUR, LOVE.

The Lenox family in the days when Roger Williams was still alive had cozened the sachems of the Narragansett tribe out of land enough to form a European barony, and though a certain Major Lenox had heroically fallen in the Great Swamp Fight in King Philip's War, and his great-great-great-grandson Emory had eloquently urged New England's secession from the Union at the Hartford Convention of 1815, the family had taken a generally downward trend. By the time of Alexandra's arrival in Eastwick there was not a Lenox left in South County save one old widow, Abigail, in the stagnant quaint village of Old Wick; she went about the lanes muttering and cringing from the pebbles thrown at her by children who, called to account by the local constable, claimed they were defending themselves against her evil eye. The vast Lenox lands had long been broken up. The last of the effective male Lenoxes had caused to be built on an island the family still owned, in the tracts of salt marsh behind East Beach, a brick mansion in diminished but locally striking imitation of the palatial summer "cottages" being erected in Newport during this gilded age. Though a causeway had been constructed and repeatedly raised by fresh importation of gravel, the mansion always suffered the inconvenience of being cut off when the tide was high, and had been occupied fitfully by a succession of owners since 1920, and had been allowed by them to slide into disrepair. The great roof slates, some reddish and some a bluish gray, came crashing unobserved in the winter storms and lay like nameless tombstones in summer's lank tangle of uncut grass; the cunningly fashioned copper gutters and flashing turned green and rotten; the ornate octagonal cupola with a view to all points of the compass developed a list to the west; the massive end chimneys, articulated like bundles of organ pipes or thickly muscled throats, needed mortar and were dropping bricks. Yet the silhouette the mansion presented from afar was still rather chasteningly grand, Alexandra thought. She had parked on the shoulder of the beach road to gaze across the quarter-mile of marsh.

This was September, season of full tides; the marsh between here and the island this afternoon was a sheet of skyey water flecked by the tips of salt hay turning golden. It would be an hour or two before the causeway in and out became passable. The time now was after four; there was a stillness, and a clothy weight to the sky that hid the sun. Once the mansion would have been masked by an *allée* of elms continuing the causeway upward toward the front entrance, but the elms had died of Dutch elm disease and remained as tall stumps lopped of their wide-arching branches, standing like men in shrouds, leaning like that armless statue of Balzac by Rodin. The house had a forbidding, symmetrical face, with many windows that seemed slightly small—especially the third-story row, which went straight across beneath the roof without variation: the servants' floor. Alexandra had been in the building years ago, when, still trying to do the right wifely things, she had gone with Ozzie to a benefit concert held in its ballroom. She could remember little but room after room, scantly furnished and smelling of salt air and mildew and vanished pleasures. The slates of its neglected roof merged in tint with a darkness gathering in the north—no, more than clouds troubled the atmosphere. Thin white smoke was lifting from the left-hand chimney. Someone was inside.

That man with hairy backs to his hands.

Alexandra's future lover.

More likely, she decided, a workman or watchman he had hired. Her eyes smarted from trying to see so far, so intensely. Her insides like the sky had gathered to a certain darkness, a sense of herself as a pathetic onlooker. Female yearning was in all the papers and magazines now; the sexual equation had become reversed as girls of good family flung themselves toward brutish rock stars, callow unshaven guitarists from the slums of Liverpool or Memphis somehow granted indecent power, dark suns turning these children of sheltered upbringing into suicidal orgiasts. Alexandra thought of her tomatoes, the juice of violence beneath the plump complacent skin. She thought of her own older daughter, alone in her room with those Monkees and Beatles . . . one thing for Marcy, another for her mother to be mooning so, straining her eyes.

She shut her eyes tight, trying to snap out of it. She got back into the car with Coal and drove the half-mile of straight black road to the beach.

After season, if no one was about, you could walk with a dog unleashed. But the day was warm, and old cars and VW vans with curtained windows and psychedelic stripes filled the narrow parking lot; beyond the bathhouses and the pizza shack many young people wearing bathing suits lay supine on the sand with their radios as if summer and youth would never end. Alexandra kept a length of clothesline on the back-seat floor in deference to beach regulations. Coal shivered in distaste as she passed the loop through his studded collar. All muscle and eagerness, he pulled her along through the resisting sand. She halted to tug off her beige espadrilles and the dog gagged; she dropped the shoes behind a tuft of beach grass near the end of the boardwalk. The boardwalk had been scattered into its six-foot segments by a recent high tide, which had also left above the flat sand beside the sea a wrack of Clorox bottles and tampon sleeves and beer cans so long afloat their painted labels had been eaten away; these unlabelled cans looked frightening —blank like the bombs terrorists make and then leave in public places to bring the system down and thus halt the war. Coal pulled her on, past a heap of barnacled square-cut rocks that had been part of a jetty built when this beach was the toy of rich men and not an overused public playground. The rocks were a black-freckled pale granite and one of the largest held a bolted bracket rusted by the years to the fragility of a Giacometti. The emissions of the young people's radios, rock of an airier sort, washed around her as she walked along, conscious of her heaviness, of the witchy figure she must cut with her bare feet and men's baggy denims and worn-out green brocaded jacket, something from Algeria she and Ozzie had bought in Paris on their honeymoon seventeen years ago. Though she turned a gypsyish olive in summer, Alexandra was of northern blood;

her maiden name had been Sorensen. Her mother had recited to her the superstition about changing your initial when you marry, but Alexandra had been a scoffer at magic then and on fire to make babies. Marcy had been conceived in Paris, on an iron bed.

Alexandra wore her hair in a single thick braid down her back; sometimes she pinned the braid up like a kind of spine to the back of her head. Her hair had never been a true clarion Viking blond but of a muddy pallor now further dirtied by gray. Most of the gray hair had sprouted in front; the nape was still as finespun as those of the girls that lay here basking. The smooth young legs she walked past were caramel in color, with white fuzz, and aligned as if in solidarity. One girl's bikini bottom gleamed, taut and simple as a drum in the flat light.

Coal plunged on, snorting, imagining some scent, some dissolving animal vein within the kelpy scent of the ocean-side. The beach population thinned. A young couple lay intertwined in a space they had hollowed in the pocked sand; the boy murmured into the base of the girl's throat as if into a microphone. An overmuscled male trio, their long hair flinging as they grunted and lunged, were playing Frisbee, and only when Alexandra purposefully let the powerful black Labrador pull her through this game's wide triangle did they halt their insolent tossing and yelping. She thought she heard the word "hag" or "bag" at her back after she had passed through, but it might have been an acoustic trick, a mistaken syllable of sea-slap. She was drawing near to where a wall of eroded concrete topped by a helix of rusted barbed wire marked the end of public beach; still there were knots of youth and seekers of youth and she did not feel free to set loose poor Coal, though he repeatedly gagged at the restraint of his collar. His desire to run burned the rope in her hand. The sea seemed unnaturally still—tranced, marked by milky streaks far out, where a single small launch buzzed on the sounding board of its level surface. On Alexandra's other side, nearer to hand, beach pea and woolly hudsonia crept down from the dunes; the beach narrowed here and became intimate, as you could see from the nests of cans and bottles and burnt driftwood and the bits of shattered Styrofoam cooler and the condoms like small dried jellyfish corpses. The cement wall had been spray-painted with linked names. Everywhere, desecration had set its hand and only footsteps were eased away by the ocean.

The dunes at one point were low enough to permit a glimpse of the Lenox mansion, from another angle and farther away; its two end chimneys stuck up like hunched buzzard's wings on either side of the cupola. Alexandra felt irritated and vengeful. Her insides felt bruised; she resented the overheard insult "hag" and the general vast insult of all this heedless youth prohibiting her from letting her dog, her friend and familiar, run free. She decided to clear the beach for herself and Coal by willing a thunderstorm. One's inner weather always bore a relation to the outer; it was simply a question of reversing the current, which occurred rather easily once power had been assigned to the primary pole, oneself as a woman. So many of Alexandra's remarkable powers had flowed from this mere reappropriation of her assigned self, achieved not until midlife. Not until midlife did she truly believe that she had a right to exist, that the forces of nature had created her not as an afterthought and companion—a bent rib, as the infamous *Malleus Maleficarum* had it—but as the mainstay of the continuing Creation, as the daughter of a daughter and a woman whose daughters in turn would bear daughters. Alexandra closed her eyes while Coal shivered and whimpered in fright and she willed this vast interior of herself—this continuum reaching back through the generations of humanity and the parenting primates and beyond them through the lizards and the fish to the algae that cooked up the raw planet's first DNA in their microscopic tepid innards, a continuum that in the other direction arched to the end of all life, through form after form, pulsing, bleeding, adapting to the cold, to the ultraviolet rays, to the bloating, weakening sun—she willed these so pregnant depths of herself to darken, to condense, to generate an interface of lightning between tall walls of air. And the sky in the north did rumble, so faintly only Coal could hear. His ears stiffened and swivelled, their roots in his scalp come alive. *Mertalia, Musalia, Dophalia*: in loud unspoken syllables she invoked the forbidden names. *Onemalia, Zitanseia, Goldaphaira, Dedulsaira*. Invisibly Alexandra grew huge, in a kind of maternal wrath gathering all the sheaves of this becalmed September world to herself, and the lids of her eyes flew open as if at a command. A blast of cold air hit from the north, the approach of a front that whipped the desultory pennants on the distant bathhouse straight out from their staffs. Down at that end, where the youthful naked crowd was thickest, a collective sigh of surprise arose, and then titters of excitement as the wind stiffened, and the sky toward Providence stood revealed as possessing the density of some translucent, empurpled rock. *Gheminaiea, Gegropheira, Cedani, Gilthar, Godieb.* At the base of this cliff of atmosphere cumulus clouds, moments ago as innocuous as flowers afloat in a pond, had begun to boil, their edges brilliant as marble against the blackening air. The very medium of seeing was altered, so that the seaside grasses and creeping glassworts near Alexandra's fat bare toes, corned and bent by years in shoes shaped by men's desires and cruel notions of beauty, seemed traced in negative upon the sand, whose tracked and pitted surface, suddenly tinted lavender, appeared to rise like the skin of a bladder being inflated under the stress of the atmospheric change. The offending youths had seen their Frisbee sail away from their hands like a kite and were hurrying to gather up their portable radios and their six-packs, their sneakers and jeans and tie-dyed tank tops. Of the couple who had made a hollow for themselves, the girl could not be comforted; she was sobbing while the boy with fumbling haste tried to relatch the hooks of her loosened bikini bra. Coal barked at nothing, in one direction and then the other, as the drop in barometric pressure maddened his ears.

Now the immense and impervious ocean, so recently tranquil all the way to Block Island, sensed the change. Its surface rippled and corrugated where sweeping cloud shadows touched it—these patches shrivelling, almost, like something burned. The motor of the launch buzzed more sharply. The sails at sea had melted and the air vibrated with the merged roar of auxiliary engines churning toward harbor. A hush caught in the throat of the wind, and then the rain began, great icy drops that hurt like hailstones. Footsteps pounded past Alexandra as honey-colored lovers raced toward cars parked at the far end, by the bathhouses. Thunder rumbled, at the top of the cliff of dark air, along whose face small scuds of paler gray, in the shape of geese, of gesticulating orators, of unravelling skeins of yarn, were travelling rapidly. The large hurtful drops broke up into a finer, thicker rain, which whitened in streaks where the wind like a harpist's fingers strummed it. Alexandra stood still while cold water glazed her; she recited in her inner spaces, *Ezoill, Musil, Puri, Tamen.* Coal at her feet whimpered; he had wrapped her legs around with clothesline. His body, its hair licked flat against the muscles, glistened and trembled. Through veils of rain she saw that the beach was empty. She undid the rope leash and set the dog free.

But Coal stayed huddled by her ankles, alarmed as lightning flashed once, and then again, double. Alexandra counted the seconds until thunder: five. By rough rule this made the storm she had conjured up two miles in diameter, if these strokes were at the heart. Blunderingly thunder rumbled and cursed. Tiny speckled sand crabs were emerging now from their holes by the dozen and scurrying sideways toward the frothing sea. The color of their shells was so sandy they appeared transparent. Alexandra steeled herself and crunched one beneath the sole of her bare foot. Sacrifice. There must always be sacrifice. It was one of nature's rules. She danced from crab to crab, crushing them. Her face from hairline to chin streamed and all the colors of the rainbow were in this liquid film, because of the agitation of her aura. Lightning kept taking her photograph. She had a cleft in her chin and a smaller, scarcely perceptible one in the tip of her nose; her handsomeness derived from the candor of her broad brow beneath the gray-edged wings of hair swept symmetrically back to form her braid, and from the clairvoyance of her slightly protuberant eyes, the gun-metal gray of whose irises was pushed to the rims as if each utterly black pupil were an anti-magnet. Her mouth had a grave plumpness and deep corners that lent the appearance of a smile. She had attained her height of five-eight by the age of fourteen and had weighed one-twenty at the age of twenty; she was somewhere around one hundred sixty pounds now. One of the liberations of becoming a witch had been that she had ceased constantly weighing herself.

As the little sand crabs were transparent on the speckled sand, so Alexandra, wet through and through, felt transparent to the rain, one with it, its temperature and that of her blood brought into concord. The sky over the sea had now composed itself into horizontal fuzzy strips; the thunder was subsiding to a mutter and the rain to a warm drizzle. This downpour would never make the weather maps. The crab she had first crushed was still moving its claws, like tiny pale feathers touched by a breeze. Coal, his terror slipped at last, ran in circles, wider and wider, adding the quadruple gouges of his claws to the triangular designs of gull feet, the daintier scratches of the sandpipers, and the dotted lines of crab scrabble. These clues to other realms of being—to be a crab, moving sideways on tiptoe with eyes on stems! to be a barnacle, standing on your head in a little folding bucket kicking food toward your mouth!—had been cratered over by raindrops. The sand was soaked to the color of cement. Her clothes even to her underwear had been plastered against her skin so that she felt to herself like a statue by Segal, pure white, all the sinuous tubes and bones of her licked by a kind of mist. Alexandra strode to the end of the purged public beach, to the wire-topped wall, and back. She reached the parking lot and picked up her sodden espadrilles where she had left them, behind a tuft of *Ammophila breviligulata*. Its long arrowlike blades glistened, having relaxed their edges in the rain.

She opened the door of her Subaru and turned to call loudly for Coal, who had vanished into the dunes. "Come, doggie!" this stately plump woman sang out. "Come, baby! Come, angel!" To the eyes of the young people huddled with their sodden gritty towels and ignominious goosebumps inside the gray-shingled bathhouse and underneath the pizza shack's awning (striped the colors of tomato and cheese), Alexandra appeared miraculously dry, not a hair of her massive braid out of place, not a patch of her brocaded green jacket damp. It was such unverifiable impressions that spread among us in Eastwick the rumor of witchcraft.

Alexandra was an artist. Using few tools other than toothpicks and a stainless-steel butter knife, she pinched and pressed into shape little lying or sitting figurines, always of women in gaudy costumes painted over naked contours; they sold for fifteen or twenty dollars in two local boutiques called the Yapping Fox and the Hungry Sheep. Alexandra had no clear idea of who bought them, or why, or exactly why she made them, or who was directing her hand. The gift of sculpture had descended with her other powers, in the period when Ozzie turned into colored dust. The impulse had visited her one morning as she sat at the kitchen table, the children off at school, the dishes done. That first morning, she had used one of her children's Play-Doh, but she came to depend for clay upon an extraordinarily pure kaolin she dug herself from a little pit near Coventry, a slippery exposed bank of greasy white earth in an old widow's back yard, behind the mossy wreck of an outhouse and the chassis of a prewar Buick just like, by uncanny coincidence, one that Alexandra's father used to drive, to Salt Lake City and Denver and Albuquerque and the lonely towns between. He had sold work clothes, overalls and blue jeans before they became fashionable—before they became the world's garb, the costume that sheds the past. You took your own burlap sacks to Coventry, and you paid the widow twelve dollars a bag. If the sacks were too heavy she helped you lift them; like Alexandra she was strong. Though at least sixty-five, she dyed her hair a glittering brass color and wore pants suits of turquoise or magenta so tight the flesh below her belt was bunched in sausagey rolls. This was nice. Alexandra read a message for herself here: Getting old could be jolly, if you stayed strong. The widow sported a high horselaugh and big gold loop earrings her brassy hair was always pulled back to display. A rooster or two performed its hesitant, preening walk in the tall grass of this unkempt yard; the back of the woman's lean clapboard house had peeled down to the bare gray wood, though the front was painted white. Alexandra, with the back of her Subaru sagging under the weight of the widow's clay, always returned from these trips heartened and exhilarated, full of the belief that a conspiracy of women upholds the world.

Her figurines were in a sense primitive. Sukie or was it Jane had dubbed them her "bubbies"—chunky female bodies four or five inches long, often faceless and without feet, coiled or bent in recumbent positions and heavier than expected when held in the hand. People seemed to find them comforting and took them away from the shops, in a steady, sneaking trickle that intensified in the summer but was there even in January. Alexandra sculpted their naked forms, stabbing with the tooth-pick for a navel and never failing to provide a nicked hint of the vulval cleft, in protest against the false smoothness there of the dolls she had played with as a girl; then she painted clothes on them, sometimes pastel bathing suits, sometimes impossibly clinging gowns patterned in polka dots or asterisks or wavy cartoon-ocean stripes. No two were quite alike, though all were sisters. Her procedure was dictated by the feeling that as clothes were put on each morning over our nakedness, so they should be painted upon rather than carved onto these primal bodies of rounded soft clay. She baked them two dozen at a time in a little electric Swedish kiln kept in a workroom off her kitchen, an unfinished room but with a wood floor, unlike the next room, a dirt-floored storage space where old flowerpots and lawn rakes, hoes and Wellington boots and pruning shears were kept. Self-taught, Alexandra had been at sculpture for five years—since before the divorce, to which it, like most manifestations of her blossoming selfhood, had contributed. Her children, especially Marcy, but Ben and little Eric too, hated the bubbies, thought them indecent, and once in their agony of embarrassment had shattered a batch that was cooling; but now they were reconciled, as if to defective siblings. Children are of a clay that to an extent remains soft, though irremediable twists show up in their mouths and a glaze of avoidance hardens in their eyes.

Jane Smart, too, was artistically inclined—a musician. She gave piano lessons to make ends meet, and substituted as choir director in local churches sometimes, but her love was the cello; its vibratory melancholy tones, pregnant with the sadness of wood grain and the shadowy largeness of trees, would at odd moonlit hours on warm nights come sweeping out of the screened windows of her low little ranch house where it huddled amid many like it on the curved roads of the Fifties development called Cove Homes. Her neighbors on their quarter-acre lots, husband and wife, child and dog, would move about, awakened, and discuss whether or not to call the police. They rarely did, abashed and, it may be, intimidated by the something naked, a splendor and grief, in Jane's playing. It seemed easier to fall back to sleep, lulled by the double-stopped scales, first in thirds, then in sixths, of Popper's études, or, over and over, the four measures of tied sixteenth-notes (where the cello speaks almost alone) of the second andante of Beethoven's Quartet No. 15, in A Minor. Jane was no gardener, and the neglected tangle of rhododendron, hydrangea, arbor-vitae, barberry, and box around her foundations helped muffle the outpour from her windows. This was an era of many pro-claimed rights, and of blatant public music, when every super-market played its Muzak version of "Satisfaction" and "I Got You, Babe" and wherever two or three teen-agers gathered to-gether the spirit of Woodstock was proclaimed. Not the volume but the timbre of Jane's passion, the notes often fumbled at but resumed at the same somber and undivertible pitch, caught at the attention bothersomely. Alexandra associated the dark notes with Jane's dark eyebrows, and with that burning insis-tence in her voice that an answer be provided forthwith, that a formula be produced with which to wedge life into place, to nail its secret down, rather than drifting as Alexandra did in the faith that the secret was ubiquitous, an aromaless element in the air that the birds and blowing weeds fed upon.

Sukie had nothing of what she would call an artistic talent but she loved social existence and had been driven by the reduced circumstances that attend divorce to write for the local weekly, the Eastwick *Word*. As she marched with her bright lithe stride up and down Dock Street listening for gossip and speculating upon the fortunes of the shops, Alexandra's gaudy figurines in the window of the Yapping Fox, or a poster in the window of the Armenians' hardware store advertising a chamber-music concert to be held in the Unitarian Church and including *Jane Smart, cello* thrilled her like a glint of beach glass in the sand or a quarter found shining on the dirty sidewalk—a bit of code buried in the garble of daily experience, a stab of communi-cation between the inner and outer world. She loved her two friends, and they her. Today, after typing up her account of last night's meetings at Town Hall of the Board of Assessors (dull: the same old land-poor widows begging for an abate-ment) and the Planning Board (no quorum: Herbie Prinz was in Bermuda), Sukie looked forward hungrily to Alexandra's and Jane's coming over to her house for a drink. They usually convened Thursdays, in one of their three houses. Sukie lived in the middle of town, which was convenient for her work, though the house, a virtually miniature 1760 saltbox on a kind of curved little alley off Oak called Hemlock Lane, was a great step down from the sprawling farmhouse—six bedrooms,

thirty acres, a station wagon, a sports car, a Jeep, four dogs
—that she and Monty had shared. But her girlfriends made it
seem fun, a kind of pretense or interlude of enchantment; they
usually affected some odd and colorful bit of costume for their
gatherings. In a gold-threaded Parsi shawl Alexandra entered,
stooping, at the side door to the kitchen; in her hands, like
dumbbells or bloody evidence, were two jars of her peppery,
basil-flavored tomato sauce.

The witches kissed, cheek to cheek. "Here sweetie, I know
you like nutty dry things best *but*," Alexandra said, in that
thrilling contralto that dipped deep into her throat like a Russian woman saying "*byelo*." Sukie took the twin gifts into her
own, more slender hands, their papery backs stippled with fading freckles. "The tomatoes came on like a plague this year for
some reason," Alexandra continued. "I put about a hundred
jars of this up and then the other night I went out in the garden in the dark and shouted, 'Fuck you, the rest of you can all
rot!'"

"I remember one year with the zucchini," Sukie responded,
setting the jars dutifully on a cupboard shelf from which she
would never take them down. As Alexandra said, Sukie loved
dry nutty things—celery, cashews, pilaf, pretzel sticks, tiny little
nibbles such as kept her monkey ancestors going in the trees.
When alone, she never sat down to eat, just dipped into some
yoghurt with a Wheat Thin while standing at the kitchen sink
or carrying a 79¢ bag of onion-flavored crinkle chips into her
TV den with a stiff bourbon. "I did *ev*erything," she said to Alexandra, relishing exaggeration, her active hands flickering in
the edges of her own vision. "Zucchini bread, zucchini soup,
salad, frittata, zucchini stuffed with hamburger and baked, cut
into slices and fried, cut into sticks to use with a dip, it was
wild. I even threw a lot into the blender and told the children
to put it on their bread instead of peanut butter. Monty was
desperate; he said even his shit smelled of zucchini."

Though this reminiscence had referred, implicitly and plea-
surably, to her married days and their plenty, mention of an old
husband was a slight breach of decorum and snatched away
Alexandra's intention to laugh. Sukie was the most recently
divorced and the youngest of the three. She was a slender
redhead, her hair down her back in a sheaf trimmed straight

across and her long arms laden with these freckles the cedar color of pencil shavings. She wore copper bracelets and a pentagram on a cheap thin chain around her throat. What Alexandra, with her heavily Hellenic, twice-cleft features, loved about Sukie's looks was the cheerful simian thrust: Sukie's big teeth pushed her profile below the brief nose out in a curve, a protrusion especially of her upper lip, which was longer and more complex in shape than her lower, with a plumpness on either side of the center that made even her silences seem puckish, as if she were tasting amusement all the time. Her eyes were hazel and round and rather close together. Sukie moved nimbly in her little comedown of a kitchen, everything crowded together and the sink stained and miniature, and beneath it a smell of poverty lingering from all the Eastwick generations who had lived here and had imposed their patchy renovations in the centuries when old hand-hewn houses like this were not considered charming. Sukie pulled a can of Planter's Beer Nuts, wickedly sugary, from a cupboard shelf with one hand and with the other took from the rubber-coated wire drainer on the sink a little paisley-patterned brass-rimmed dish to hold them. Boxes crackling, she strewed an array of crackers on a platter around a wedge of red-coated Gouda cheese and some supermarket pâté still in the flat tin showing a laughing goose. The platter was coarse tan earthenware gouged and glazed with the semblance of a crab. Cancer. Alexandra feared it, and saw its emblem everywhere in nature—in clusters of blueberries in the neglected places by rocks and bogs, in the grapes ripening on the sagging rotten arbor outside her kitchen windows, in the ants bringing up conical granular hills in the cracks in her asphalt driveway, in all blind and irresistible multiplications. "Your usual?" Sukie asked, a shade tenderly, for Alexandra, as if older than she was, had with a sigh dropped her body, without removing her shawl, into the kitchen's one welcoming concavity, an old blue easy chair too disgraceful to have elsewhere; it was losing stuffing at its seams and at the corners of its arms a polished gray stain had been left where many wrists had rubbed.

"I guess it's still tonic time," Alexandra decided, for the coolness that had come in with the thunderstorm some days ago had stayed. "How's your vodka supply?" Someone had once told her that not only was vodka less fattening but it irritated the lining of your stomach less than gin. Irritation, psychic as well as physical, was the source of cancer. Those get it who leave themselves open to the idea of it; all it takes is one single cell gone crazy. Nature is always waiting, watching for you to lose faith so she can insert her fatal stitch.

Sukie smiled, broader. "I knew you were coming." She displayed a brand-new Gordon's bottle, with its severed boar's head staring with a round orange eye and its red tongue caught between teeth and a curling tusk.

Alexandra smiled to see this friendly monster. "Plenty of tonic, puh-*leese*. The calories!"

The tonic bottle fizzed in Sukie's fingers as if scolding. Perhaps cancer cells were more like bubbles of carbonation, percolating through the bloodstream, Alexandra thought. She must stop thinking about it. "Where's Jane?" she asked.

"She said she'd be a little late. She's rehearsing for that concert at the Unitarians'."

"With that awful Neff," Alexandra said.

"With that awful Neff," Sukie echoed, licking quinine water from her fingers and looking in her bare refrigerator for a lime. Raymond Neff taught music at the high school, a pudgy effeminate man who yet had fathered five children upon his slovenly, sallow, steel-bespectacled, German-born wife. Like most good schoolteachers he was a tyrant, unctuous and insistent; in his dank way he wanted to sleep with everybody. Jane was sleeping with him these days. Alexandra had succumbed a few times in the past but the episode had moved her so little Sukie was perhaps unaware of its vibrations, its afterimage. Sukie herself appeared to be chaste vis-à-vis Neff, but then she had been available least long. Being a divorcee in a small town is a little like playing Monopoly; eventually you land on all the properties. The two friends wanted to rescue Jane, who in a kind of indignant hurry was always selling herself short. It was the hideous wife, with her strawy dull hair cut short as if with grass clippers and her carefully pronounced malapropisms and her goggle-eyed intent way of listening to every word, whom they disapproved of. When you sleep with a married man you in a sense sleep with the wife as well, so she should not be an utter embarrassment.

"Jane has such *beaut*iful possibilities," Sukie said a bit automatically, as she scrabbled with a furious monkey-motion in the refrigerator's icemaker to loosen some more cubes. A witch can freeze water at a glance but sometimes unfreezing it is the problem. Of the four dogs she and Monty had supported in their heyday, two had been loping silvery-brown Weimaraners, and she had kept one, called Hank; he was now leaning on her legs in the hope that she was struggling in the refrigerator on his behalf.

"But she *wastes* herself," Alexandra said, completing the sentence. "Wastes in the old-fashioned sense," she added, since this was during the Vietnam War and the war had given the word an awkward new meaning. "If she's serious about her music she should go somewhere serious with it, a city. It's a terrible waste, a conservatory graduate playing fiddle for a bunch of deaf old biddies in a dilapidated church."

"She feels safe here," Sukie said, as if they didn't.

"She doesn't even wash herself, have you ever noticed her smell?" Alexandra asked, not about Jane but about Greta Neff, by a train of association Sukie had no trouble following, their hearts were so aligned on one wavelength.

"And those granny glasses!" Sukie agreed. "She looks like John Lennon." She made a kind of solemn sad-eyed thin-lipped John Lennon face. "I sink sen we can drink ouur —*sprechen Sie wass?*—bev-er-aitches neeoauu." There was an awful un-American diphthong that came out of Greta Neff's mouth, a kind of twisting of the vowel up against her palate.

Cackling, they took their drinks into the "den," a little room with peeling wallpaper in a splashy faded pattern of vines and fruit baskets and a bellied plaster ceiling at a strange sharp slant because the room was half tucked under the stairs that went up to the atticlike second floor. The room's one window, too high for a woman not standing on a stool to peer out of, had lozenge panes of leaded glass, thick glass bubbled and warped like bottle bottoms.

"A cabbagy smell," Alexandra amplified, lowering herself and her tall silvery drink onto a love seat covered in a crewelwork of flamboyant tattered swirls, stylized vines unravelling. "He carries it on his clothes," she said, thinking simultaneously that this was a little like Monty and the zucchini and that she was evidently inviting Sukie with this intimate detail to guess that she had slept with Neff. Why? It was nothing to brag about. And yet, it was. How he had sweated! For that matter she had slept with Monty, too; and had never smelled zucchini. One fascinating aspect of sleeping with husbands was the angle they gave you on their wives: they saw them as nobody else did. Neff saw poor dreadful Greta as a kind of quaint beribboned Heidi, a sweet bit of edelweiss he had fetched from a perilous romantic height (they had met in a Frankfurt beer hall while he was stationed in West Germany instead of fighting in Korea), and Monty . . . Alexandra squinted at Sukie, trying to remember what Monty had said of her. He had said little, being such a would-be gentleman. But once he had let slip, having come to Alexandra's bed from some awkward consultation at the bank, and being still preoccupied, the words "She's a lovely girl, but bad luck, somehow. Bad luck for others, I mean. I think she's fairly good luck for herself." And it was true, Monty had lost a great deal of his family's money while married to Sukie, which everyone had blamed simply on his own calm stupidity. *He* had never sweated. He had suffered from that hormonal deficiency of the wellborn, an inability to relate himself to the possibility of hard labor. His body had been almost hairless, with that feminine soft bottom.

"Greta must be great in the sack," Sukie was saying. "All those *Kinder. Fünf,* yet."

Neff had allowed to Alexandra that Greta was ardent but strenuous, very slow to come but determined to do so. She would make a grim witch: those murderous Germans. "We must be nice to her," Alexandra said, back to the subject of Jane. "Speaking to her on the phone yesterday, I was struck by how angry she sounded. That lady is burning up."

Sukie glanced over at her friend, since this seemed a slightly false note. Some intrigue had begun for Alexandra, some new man. In the split-second of Sukie's glance, Hank with his lolling gray Weimaraner tongue swept two Wheat Thins off the crab platter, which she had set down on a much-marred pine sea chest refinished by an antique dealer to be used as a coffee table. Sukie loved her shabby old things; there was a kind of blazonry in them, a costume of rags affected by the soprano in the second act of the opera. Hank's tongue was coming back for the cheese when Sukie caught the motion in the corner of her eye and slapped his muzzle; it was rubbery, in the hard way of automobile tires, so the slap hurt her own fingers. "Ow, you bastard," she said to the dog, and to her friend, "Angrier than anybody else?," meaning themselves. She took a rasping sip of neat bourbon. She drank whiskey summer and winter and the reason, which she had forgotten, was that a boyfriend at Cornell had once told her that it brought out the gold flecks in her green eyes. For the same vain reason she tended to dress in shades of brown and in suede with its animal shimmer.

"Oh yes. We're in lovely shape," the bigger, older woman answered, her mind drifting from this irony toward the subject of that conversation with Jane—the new man in town, in the Lenox mansion. But even as it drifted, her mind, like a passenger in an airplane who amidst the life-imperilling sensations of lifting off looks down to marvel at the enamelled precision and glory of the Earth (the houses with their roofs and chimneys so sharp, so finely made, and the lakes truly mirrors as in the Christmas yards our parents had arranged while we were sleeping; it was all true, and even maps are true!), took note of how lovely Sukie was, bad luck or not, with her vivid hair dishevelled and even her eyelashes looking a little mussed after her hard day of typing and looking for the right word under the harsh lights, her figure in its milky-green sweater and dark suede skirt so erect and trim, her stomach flat and her breasts perky and high and her bottom firm, and that big broad-lipped mouth on her monkeyish face so mischievous and giving and brave.

"Oh I *know* about him!" she exclaimed, having read Alexandra's mind. "I have such *tons* to tell, but I wanted to wait until Jane got here."

"I can wait," Alexandra said, suddenly resenting now, as if suddenly feeling a cool draft, this man and his place in her mind. "Is that a new skirt?" She wanted to touch it, to stroke it, its doelike texture, the firm lean thigh underneath.

"Resurrected for the fall," Sukie said. "It's really too long, the way skirts are going."

The kitchen doorbell rang: a tittering, ragged sound. "That connection's going to burn the house down some day," Sukie prophesied, darting from the den. Jane had let herself in already. She looked pale, her pinched hot-eyed face overburdened by a floppy furry tam-o'-shanter whose loud plaid fussily matched that of her scarf. Also she was wearing ribbed kneesocks. Jane was not physically radiant like Sukie and was afflicted all over her body with small patches of asymmetry, yet an appeal shone from her as light from a twisted filament. Her hair was dark and her mouth small, prim, and certain. She came from Boston originally and that gave her something there was no unknowing.

"That Neff is such a bitch," she began, clearing a frog from her throat. "He had us do the Haydn over and over. He said my intonation was prissy. *Prissy.* I burst into tears and told him he was a disgusting male chauv." She heard herself and couldn't resist a pun. "I should have told him to chauv it."

"They can't help it," Sukie said lightly. "It's just their way of asking for more love. Lexa's having her usual diet drink, a v-and-t. *Moi,* I'm ever deeper into the bourbon."

"I shouldn't be doing this, but I'm so fucking hurt I'm going to be a bad girl for once and ask for a martini."

"Oh, baby. I don't think I have any dry vermouth."

"No sweat, pet. Just put the gin on the rocks in a wine glass. You don't by any chance have a bit of lemon peel?"

Sukie's refrigerator, rich in ice, yoghurt, and celery, was barren of much else. She had her lunches at Nemo's Diner downtown, three doors away from the newspaper offices, past the framer's and the barber's and the Christian Science reading room, and had taken to having her evening meals there too, because of the gossip she heard in Nemo's, the mutter of Eastwick life all around her. The old-timers congregated there, the police and the highway crew, the out-of-season fishermen and the momentarily bankrupt businessmen. "Don't seem to have any oranges either," she said, tugging at the two produce drawers of sticky green metal. "I did buy some peaches at that roadside stand over on 4."

"Do I dare to eat a peach?" Jane quoted. "I shall wear white flannel trousers, and walk upon the beach." Sukie winced, watching the other woman's agitated hands—one tendony and long, from fingering the strings, and the other squarish and slack, from holding the bow—dig with a rusty dull carrot grater into the blushing cheek, the rosiest part, of the yellow pulpy peach. Jane dropped the rosy sliver in; a sacred hush, the spell of any recipe, amplified the tiny *plip*. "I can't start drinking utterly raw gin this early in life," Jane announced with puritanical satisfaction, looking nevertheless haggard and impatient. She moved toward the den with that rapid stiff walk of hers.

Alexandra guiltily reached over and snapped off the TV, where the President, a lugubrious gray-jawed man with pained dishonest eyes, had been making an announcement of great importance to the nation.

"Hi there, you gorgeous creature," Jane called, a bit loudly in this small slant space. "Don't get up, I can see you're all settled. Tell me, though—was that thunderstorm the other day yours?"

The peach skin in the inverted cone of her drink looked like a bit of brightly diseased flesh preserved in alcohol.

"I went to the beach," Alexandra confessed, "after talking to you. I wanted to see if this man was in the Lenox place yet."

"I *thought* I'd upset you, poor chicken," said Jane. "And was he?"

"There was smoke from the chimney. I didn't drive up."

"You should have driven up and said you were from the Wetlands Commission," Sukie told her. "The noise around town is that he wants to build a dock and fill in enough on the back of the island there to have a tennis court."

"That'll never get by," Alexandra told Sukie lazily. "That's where the snowy egrets nest."

"Don't be too sure" was the answer. "That property hasn't paid any taxes to the town for ten years. For somebody who'll put it back on the rolls the selectmen can evict a lot of egrets."

"Oh, isn't this *cozy*!" Jane exclaimed, rather desperately, feeling ignored. Their four eyes upon her then, she had to improvise. "Greta came into the church," she said, "right after he called my Haydn prissy, and laughed."

Sukie did a German laugh: "Hö hö hö."

"Do they still fuck, I wonder?" asked Alexandra idly, amid this ease with her friends letting her mind wander and gather images from nature. "How could he stand it? It must be like excited sauerkraut."

"No," Jane said firmly. "It's like—what's that pale white stuff they like so?—sauerbraten."

"They marinate it," Alexandra said. "In vinegar, with garlic, onions, and bay leaves. And I think peppercorns."

"Is that what he tells you?" Sukie asked Jane mischievously.

"We never talk about it, even at our most intimate," Jane prissily said. "All he ever confided on the subject was that she had to have it once a week or she began to throw things."

"A poltergeist," Sukie said, delighted. "A polterfrau."

"Really," Jane said, not seeing the humor of it, "you're right. She is an impossibly awful woman. So pedantic; so smug; such a *Nazi*. Ray's the only one who doesn't see it, poor soul."

"I wonder how much she guesses," Alexandra mused.

"She doesn't *want* to guess," Jane said, pressing home the assertion so the last word hissed. "If she guessed she might have to do something about it."

"Like turn him loose," Sukie supplied.

"Then we'd all have to cope with him," Alexandra said, envisioning this plump dank man as a tornado, a voracious natural reservoir, of desire. Desire did come in containers out of all proportion.

"Hang on, Greta!" Jane chimed in, seeing the humor at last. All three cackled.

The side door solemnly slammed, and footsteps slowly marched upstairs. It was not a poltergeist but one of Sukie's children, home from school, where extracurricular activities had kept him or her late. The upstairs television came on with its comforting humanoid rumble.

Greedily Sukie had crammed too big a handful of salted nuts into her mouth; she flattened her palm against her chin to keep morsels from falling. Still laughing, she sputtered crumbs. "Doesn't *any*body want to hear about this new man?"

"Not especially," Alexandra said. "Men aren't the answer, isn't that what we've decided?"

She was different, a little difficult, when Jane was present, Sukie had often noticed. Alone with Sukie she had not tried to conceal her interest in this new man. The two women had in common a certain happiness in their bodies, which had often been called beautiful, and Alexandra was enough older (six years) to establish when just they were gathered, a certain maternal fit: Sukie frisky and chatty, Lexa lazy and sybilline. Alexandra tended to dominate, when the three were together, by being somewhat sullen and inert, making the other two come to her.

"They're not the answer," Jane Smart said. "But maybe they're the question." Her gin was two-thirds gone. The bit of peach skin was a baby waiting to be thrust out dry into the world. Beyond the graying lozenge panes blackbirds were noisily packing the day away, into its travelling bag of dusk.

Sukie stood to make her announcement. "He's rich," she said, "and forty-two. Never married, and from New York, one of the old Dutch families. He was evidently a child prodigy at the piano, and invents things besides. The whole big room in the east wing, where the billiard table still is, and the laundry area under it are to be his laboratory, with all these stainless-steel sinks and distilling tubes and everything, and on the west side, where the Lenoxes had this greenhousy whatchama-callum, a conservatory, he wants to install a big sunken tub, with the walls wired for stereo." Her round eyes, quite green in the late light, shone with the madness of it. "Joe Marino has the plumbing contract and was talking about it last night after they couldn't get a quorum because Herbie Prinz went to Bermuda without telling anybody. Joe was really freaked out: no estimate asked for, everything the best, price be damned. A *teak* tub eight feet in diameter, and the man doesn't like the feel of tile under his feet so the whole floor is going to be some special fine-grained slate you have to order from Tennessee."

"He sounds pompous," Jane told them.

"Does this big spender have a name?" Alexandra asked, thinking what a romantic Sukie was as well as a gossip colum-nist and wondering if a second vodka-and-tonic would give her a headache later, when she was home alone in her ram-bling former farmhouse with only the steady breathing of her sleeping children and Coal's restless scratching and the baleful staring of the moon to keep her stark-awake spirit company. In the West a coyote would howl in the lavender distance and even farther away a transcontinental train would pull its slithering miles of cars and these sounds would lead her spirit out of the window and dissolve its wakefulness in the delicate star-blanched night. Here, in the crabbed, waterlogged East, everything was so close; night-sounds surrounded her house like a bristling thicket. Even these women, in Sukie's cozy little cubbyhole, loomed close, so that each dark hair of Jane's faint mustache and the upright amber down, sensitive to static, of Sukie's long forearms made Alexandra's eyes itch. She was jealous of this man, that the very shadow of him should so excite her two friends, who on other Thursdays were excited simply by her, her regally lazy powers stretching there like a cat's power to cease purring and kill. On those Thursdays the three friends would conjure up the spectres of Eastwick's little lives and set them buzzing and circling in the darkening air. In the right mood and into their third drinks they could erect a cone of power above them like a tent to the zenith, and know at the base of their bellies who was sick, who was sinking into debt, who was loved, who was frantic, who was burning, who was asleep in a remission of life's bad luck; but this wouldn't happen today. They were disturbed.

"Isn't that funny about his name?" Sukie was saying, staring up at the day's light ebbing from the leaded window. She could not see through the high wobbly lozenge panes, but in her mind's eye clearly stood her back yard's only tree, a slender young pear tree overburdened with pears, heavy yellow suspended shapes like costume jewels hung on a child. Each day now was redolent of hay and ripeness, the little pale late asters glowing by the side of the roads like litter. "They were all saying his name last night, and I heard it before from Marge Perley, it's on the tip of my tongue. . . ."

"Mine too," Jane said. "*Damn*. It has one of those little words in it."

"De, da, du," Alexandra prompted hopelessly.

The three witches fell silent, realizing that, tongue-tied, they were themselves under a spell, of a greater.

Darryl Van Horne came to the chamber-music concert in the Unitarian Church on Sunday night, a bearish dark man with greasy curly hair half-hiding his ears and clumped at the back so that his head from the side looked like a beer mug with a monstrously thick handle. He wore gray flannels bagged at the backs of his knees somehow and an elbow-patched jacket of Harris Tweed in a curious busy pattern of green and black. A pink Oxford button-down shirt of the type fashionable in the Fifties and, on his feet, incongruously small and pointy black loafers completed the costume. He was out to make an impression.

"So you're our local sculptress," he told Alexandra at the reception afterwards, which was held in the church parlor, for the players and their friends, and centered about an unspiked punch the color of antifreeze. The church was a pretty enough little Greek Revival, with a shallow Doric-columned porch and a squat octagonal tower, on Cocumscussoc Way, off of Elm behind Oak, which the Congregationalists had put up in 1823 but which a generation later had gone under to the Unitarian tide of the 1840s. In this hazy late age of declining doctrine its interior was decorated here and there with crosses anyway, and the social parlor bore on one wall a large felt banner, concocted by the Sunday school, of the Egyptian tau cross, the hieroglyph for "life," surrounded by the four triangular alchemic signs for the elements. The category of "players and their friends" included everyone except Van Horne, who pushed into the parlor anyway. People knew who he was; it added to the excitement. When he spoke, his voice resounded in a way that did not quite go with the movements of his mouth and jaw, and this impression of an artificial element somewhere in his speech apparatus was reinforced by the strange slipping, patched-together impression his features made and by the excess of spittle he produced when he talked, so that he occasionally paused to wipe his coat sleeve roughly across the corners of his mouth. Yet he had the confidence of the cultured and well-to-do, stooping low to achieve intimacy with Alexandra.

"They're just little things," Alexandra said, feeling abruptly petite and demure, confronted by this brooding dark bulk. It was that time of the month when she was especially sensitive to auras. This thrilling stranger's was the shiny black-brown of a wet beaver pelt and stood up stiff behind his head. "My friends call them my bubbies," she said, and fought a blush. Fighting it made her feel slightly faint, in this crowd. Crowds and new men were not what she was used to.

"Little things," Van Horne echoed. "But so *po*tent," he said, wiping his lips. "So full of psychic juice, you know, when you pick one up. They knocked me out. I bought all they had at, what's that place?—the Noisy Sheep—"

"The Yapping Fox," she said, "or the Hungry Sheep, two

doors the other side of the little barbershop, if you ever get a haircut."

"Never if I can help it. Saps my strength. My mother used to call me Samson. But yeah, one of those. I bought all they had to show to a pal of mine, a really relaxed terrific guy who runs a gallery in New York, right there on Fifty-seventh Street. It's not for me to promise you anything, Alexandra—O.K. if I call you that?—but if you could bring yourself to create on a bigger scale, I bet we could get you a show. Maybe you'll never be Marisol but you could sure as hell be another Niki de Saint-Phalle. You know, those 'Nanas.' Now *those* have scale. I mean, she's *real*ly let go, she's not just futzin' around."

With some relief Alexandra decided she quite disliked this man. He was pushy, coarse, and a blabbermouth. His buying her out at the Hungry Sheep felt like a rape, and she would have to run another batch through the kiln now earlier than she had planned. The pressure his personality set up had intensified her cramps, which she had woken with that morning, days ahead of schedule; that was one of the signs of cancer, irregularities in your cycle. Also, she had brought with her from the West a regrettable trace of the regional prejudice against Indians and Chicanos, and to her eyes Darryl Van Horne didn't look *washed*. You could almost see little specks of black in his skin, as if he were a halftone reproduction. He wiped his lips with the hairy back of a hand, and his lips twitched with impatience while she searched her heart for an honest but polite response. Dealing with men was work, a chore she had become lazy at. "I don't *want* to be another Niki de Saint-Phalle," she said. "I want to be me. The potency, as you put it, comes from their being small enough to hold in the hand." Hastening blood made the capillaries in her face burn; she smiled at herself for being excited, when intellectually she had decided the man was a fraud, an apparition. Except for his money; that had to be real.

His eyes were small and watery, and looked rubbed. "Yeah, Alexandra, but what *is* you? Think small, you'll wind up small. You're not giving you a chance, with this old-giftie-shoppie mentality. I couldn't believe how little they were charging—a lousy twenty bucks, when you should be thinking five figures."

He was New York vulgar, she perceived, and felt sorry for

him, landed in this subtle province. She remembered the wisp of smoke, how fragile and brave it had looked. She asked him forgivingly, "How do you like your new house? Are you pretty well settled in?"

With enthusiasm, he said, "It's hell. I work late, my ideas come to me at night, and every morning around seven-fifteen these fucking workmen show up! With their fucking radios! Pardon my Latin."

He seemed aware of his need for forgiveness; the need surrounded him, and rippled out from every clumsy, too-urgent gesture.

"You *gotta* come over and see the place," he said. "I need advice all over the lot. All my life I've lived in apartments where they decide everything for you, and the plumber I've got's an asshole."

"Joe?"

"You know him?"

"Everybody knows him," Alexandra said; this stranger should be told that insulting local people was not the way to win friends in Eastwick.

But his loose tongue and mouth tumbled on unabashed. "Little funny hat all the time?"

She had to nod, but perhaps not to smile. She sometimes hallucinated that Joe was still wearing his hat while making love to her.

"He's out to lunch every meal of the day," Van Horne said. "All he wants to talk about is how the Red Sox pitching collapsed again and how the Pats still don't have any pass defense. Not that the old guy doing the floor is any wizard either; this priceless slate, practically marble, up from Tennessee, and he lays it half with the rough side up, where you can see the marks of the quarry saw. These butchers you call workmen up here wouldn't last one day on a union job in Manhattan. No offense, I can see you're thinking, 'What a snob,' and I guess the hicks don't get much practice, putting up chicken coops; but no wonder it's such a weird-looking state. Hey, Alexandra, between us: I'm crazy about that huffy frozen look you get on your face when you get defensive and can't think what to say. And the tip of your nose is cute." Astonishingly, he reached out and touched it, the little cleft tip she was sensitive about, a touch so quick and improper she wouldn't have believed it happened but for the chilly tingle it left.

She didn't just dislike him, she hated him; yet still she stood there smiling, feeling trapped and faint and wondering what her irregular insides were trying to tell her.

Jane Smart came up to them. For the performance she had had to spread her legs and therefore was the only woman at the gathering in a full-length gown, a shimmering concoction of aqua silk and lace trim perhaps a touch too bridal. "Ah, *la artiste*," Van Horne exclaimed, and he seized her hand not in a handshake but like a manicurist inspecting, taking her hand upon his wide palm and then rejecting it, since it was the left he wanted, the tendony fingering hand with its glazed calluses where she pressed the strings. The man made a tender sandwich of it between his own hairy two. "What intonation," he said. "What vibrato and stretch. Really. You think I'm an obnoxious madman but I do know music. It's the one thing makes me humble."

Jane's dark eyes lightened, indeed glowed. "Not prissy, you think," she said. "Our leader keeps saying my intonation is prissy."

"What an asshole," pronounced Van Horne, wiping spit from the corners of his mouth. "You have precision but that's not prissy necessarily; precision is where passion begins. Without precision, *beaucoup de rien*, huh? Even your thumb, on your thumb position: you really keep that pressure on, where a lot of men crump out, it hurts too much." He pulled her left hand closer to his face and caressed the side of her thumb. "See that?" he said to Alexandra, brandishing Jane's hand as if it were detached, a dead thing to be admired. "That is one beautiful callus."

Jane tugged her hand back, feeling eyes gathering upon them. The Unitarian minister, Ed Parsley, was taking notice of the scene. Van Horne perhaps relished an audience, for he dramatically let Jane's left hand drop and seized the unguarded right, as it hung at Jane's side, to shake it in her own astonished face. "It's *this* hand," he almost shouted. "It's this hand's the fly in the ointment. Your *bow*ing. God! Your *spiccato* sounds like *marcato*, your *legato* like *détaché*. Honey, *string* those phrases together, you're not playing just notes, one after the other, biddledy um-um-um, you're playing *phrases*, you're playing human *out*cries!"

As if in silent outcry Jane's prim thin mouth dropped open and Alexandra saw tears form second lenses upon her eyes, whose brown was always a little lighter in color than you remembered, a tortoiseshell color.

Reverend Parsley joined them. He was a youngish man with a slippery air of doom about him; his face was like a handsome face distorted in a slightly warped mirror—too long from sideburn to nostril, as if perpetually being tugged forward, and the too full and expressive lips caught in the relentless smile of one who knows he is in the wrong place, on the wrong platform of the bus station in a country where no known language is spoken. Though just into his thirties, he was too old to be a window-trashing LSD-imbibing soldier in the Movement and this added to his sense of displacement and inadequacy, though he was always organizing peace marches and vigils and read-ins and proposing to his parish of dryasdust dutiful souls that they let their pretty old church become a sanctuary, with cots and hot plates and chemical toilet facilities, for the hordes of draft evaders. Instead, tasteful cultural events were sheltered here, where the acoustics were accidentally marvellous; those old builders perhaps did have secrets. But Alexandra, having been raised in the stark land mined for a thousand cowboy movies, was inclined to think that the past is often romanticized, that when it was the present it had that same curious hollowness we all feel now.

Ed looked up—he was not tall; this was another of his disappointments—at Darryl Van Horne quizzically. Then he addressed Jane Smart with a sharp shouldering-aside note in his voice: "Beautiful, Jane. Just a damn beautiful job all four of you did. As I was saying to Clyde Gabriel just now, I wish there had been a better way to advertise, to get more of the Newport crowd over here, though I know his paper did all it could, he took it that I was criticizing; he seems a lot on edge lately." Sukie was sleeping with Ed, Alexandra knew, and perhaps Jane had slept with him in the past. There was a quality men's voices had when you had slept with them, even years ago: the grain came up, like that of unpainted wood left out in the weather. Ed's aura—Alexandra couldn't stop seeing auras, it went with menstrual cramps—emanated in sickly chartreuse waves of anxiety and narcissism from his hair, which was combed away from an inflexible part and was somehow colorless without being gray. Jane was still fighting back tears and in the awkwardness Alexandra had become the introducer, this strange outsider's sponsor.

"Reverend Parsley—"

"Come on, Alexandra. We're better friends than that. The name's Ed, *please*." Sukie must talk about her a little while sleeping with him, so he felt this familiarity. Everywhere you turn people know you better than you know them; there is all this human spying. Alexandra could not make herself say "Ed," his aura of doom was so repulsive to her.

"—this is Mr. Van Horne, who's just moved into the Lenox place, you've probably heard."

"Indeed I have heard, and it's a delightful surprise to have you here, sir. Nobody had said you were a music-lover."

"In a half-ass way, you could say that. My pleasure, Reverend." They shook hands and the minister flinched.

"No 'Reverend,' please. Everybody, friend or foe, calls me Ed."

"Ed, this is a swell old building you have here. It must cost you a bundle in fire insurance."

"The Lord is our carrier," Ed Parsley joked, and his sickly aura widened in pleasure at this blasphemy. "To be serious, you can't rebuild this kind of plant, and the older members complain about all the steps. We've had people drop out of the choir because they can't make it up into the loft. Also, to my mind, an opulent building like this, with all its traditional associations, gets in the way of the message the modern-day Unitarian-Universalists are trying to bring. What I'd like to see is us open a storefront church right down there on Dock Street; that's where the young people gather, that's where business and commerce do their dirty work."

"What's dirty about it?"

"I'm sorry, I didn't catch your first name."

"Darryl."

"Darryl, I see you like to pull people's legs. You're a man of sophistication and know as well as I do that the connection between the present atrocities in Southeast Asia and that new little drive-in branch Old Stone Bank has next to the Superette is direct and immediate; I don't need to belabor the point."

"You're right, fella, you don't," Van Horne said.

"When Mammon talks, Uncle Sam jumps."

"Amen," said Van Horne.

How nice it was, Alexandra thought, when men talked to one another. All that aggression: the clash of shirt fronts. Eavesdropping, she felt herself thrilled as when on a walk in the Cove woods she came upon traces in some sandy patch of a flurry of claws, and a feather or two, signifying a murderous encounter. Ed Parsley had sized Van Horne up as a banker type, an implementer of the System, and was fighting dismissal in the bigger man's eyes as a shrill and ineffectual liberal, the feckless agent of a nonexistent God. Ed wanted to be the agent of another System, equally fierce and far-flung. As if to torment himself he wore a clergyman's collar, in which his neck looked both babyish and scrawny; for his denomination such a collar was so unusual as to be, in its way, a protest.

"Did I hear," he said now, his voice gravelly in its insinuating sonority, "you offering a critique of Jane's cello-playing?"

"Just her bowing," Van Horne said, suddenly a bashful shambles, his jaw slipping and drooling. "I said the rest of it was great, her bowing just seemed a little choppy. Christ, you have to watch yourself around here, stepping on everybody's toes. I mentioned to sweet old Alexandra here about my plumbing contractor being none too swift and it turns out he's her best friend."

"Not best friend, just a friend," she felt obliged to intercede. The man, Alexandra saw even amid the confusions of this encounter, had the brute gift of bringing a woman out, of getting her to say more than she had intended. Here he had insulted Jane and she was gazing up at him with the moist mute fascination of a whipped dog.

"The Beethoven was especially splendid, don't you agree?" Parsley was still after Van Horne, to wring some concession out of him, the start of a pact, a basis they could meet on next time.

"Beethoven," the big man said with bored authority, "sold his soul to write those last quartets; he was stone deaf. All those nineteenth-century types sold their souls. Liszt. Paganini. What they did wasn't human."

Jane found her voice. "I practiced till my fingers bled," she said, gazing straight up at Van Horne's lips, which he had just rubbed with his sleeve. "All those terrible sixteenth-notes in the second andante."

"You keep practicing, little Jane. It's five-sixths muscle memory, as you know. When muscle memory takes over, the heart can start to sing its song. Until then, you're stymied. You're just going through the motions. Listen. Whyncha come over some time to my place and we'll fool around with a bit of old Ludwig's piano and cello stuff? That Sonata in A is an absolute honey, if you don't panic on the legato. Or that E Minor of Brahms: *fabuloso. Quel schmaltz!* I think it's still in the old fingers." He wiggled them, his fingers, at all of their faces. Van Horne's hands were eerily white-skinned beneath the hair, like tight surgical gloves.

Ed Parsley coped with his unease by turning to Alexandra and saying in sickly conspiracy, "Your friend appears to know whereof he speaks."

"Don't look at me, I just met the gentleman," Alexandra said.

"He was a child *pro*digy," Jane Smart told them, become somehow angry and defensive. Her aura, usually a rather dull mauve, had undergone a streaked orchid surge, betokening arousal, though by which man was not clear. The whole parlor to Alexandra's eyes was clouded by merged and pulsating auras, sickening as cigarette smoke. She felt dizzy, disenchanted; she longed to be home with Coal and her quietly ticking kiln and the expectant cold wet plasticity of clay in its burlap sacks hauled from Coventry. She closed her eyes and wished that this particular nexus around her—of arousal, dislike, radical insecurity, and a sinister will to dominate emanating not only from the dark stranger—would dissolve.

Several elderly parishioners were nudging forward for their share of Reverend Parsley's attention, and he turned to flatter them. The white hair of the women was touched in the caves of the curls of their perms with the tenderest golds and blues. Raymond Neff, profusely sweating and aglow with the triumph of the concert, came up to them all and, enduring in the deafness of celebrity their simultaneous compliments, jollily bore away Jane, his mistress and comrade in musical battle. She, too, had been glazed, shoulders and neck, by the exertions of the performance. Alexandra noticed this and was touched. What did Jane see in Raymond Neff? For that matter what did Sukie see in Ed Parsley? The smells of the two men when they had stood close had been, to Alexandra's nostrils, rank—whereas Joe Marino's skin had a certain sweet sourness, like the stale-milk aroma that arises from a baby's pate when you settle your cheek against its fuzzy bony warmth. Suddenly she was alone with Van Horne again, and feared she would have to bear again upon her breast the imploring inchoate weight of his conversation; but Sukie, who feared nothing, all russet and crisp and glimmering in her reportorial role, edged through the crowd and conducted an interview.

"What brings you to this concert, Mr. Van Horne?" she asked, after Alexandra had shyly performed introductions.

"My TV set's on the blink" was his sullen answer. Alexandra saw that he preferred to make the approaches himself; but there was no denying Sukie in her interrogating mood, her little pushy monkey-face bright as a new penny.

"And what has brought you to this part of the world?" was her next question.

"Seems time I got out of Gotham," he said. "Too much mugging, rent going sky-high. The price up here seemed right. This going into some paper?"

Sukie licked her lips and admitted, "I might put a mention in a column I write for the *Word* called 'Eastwick Eyes and Ears.'"

"Jesus, don't do that," the big man said, in his baggy tweed coat. "I came up here to cool the publicity."

"What kind of publicity were you receiving, may I ask?"

"If I told you, that'd be more publicity, wouldn't it?"

"Could be."

Alexandra marvelled at her friend, so cheerfully bold. Sukie's brazen ochre aura merged with the sheen of her hair. She asked, as Van Horne made as if to turn away, "People are saying you're an inventor. What sort of thing do you invent?"

"Toots, even if I took all night to explain it to ya ya wouldn't understand. It mostly deals with chemicals."

"Try me," Sukie urged. "See if I understand."

"Put it in your 'Eyes and Ears' and I might as well write a circular letter to my competition."

"Nobody who doesn't live in Eastwick reads the *Word*, I promise. Even in Eastwick nobody reads it, they just look at the ads and for their own names."

"Listen, Miss—"

"Rougemont. Ms. I was married."

"What was he, a French Canuck?"

"Monty always said his ancestors were Swiss. He acted Swiss. Don't the Swiss have square heads, supposedly?"

"Beats me. I thought that was the Manchurians. They have skulls like cement blocks, that's how Genghis Khan could stack 'em up so neatly."

"Do you feel we've wandered rather far from the subject?"

"About the inventions, listen, I can't talk. I am *watched*."

"How exciting! For all of us," Sukie said, and she let her smile push her upper lip, creasing deliciously, up so far her nose wrinkled and a band of healthy gum showed. "How about for my eyes and ears only? And Lexa's here. Isn't she gorgeous?"

Van Horne turned his big head stiffly as if to check; Alexandra saw herself through his bloodshot blinking eyes as if at the end of a reversed telescope, a figure frighteningly small, cleft here and there and with wisps of gray hair. He decided to answer Sukie's earlier question: "I've been doing a fair amount lately with protective coatings—a floor finish you can't scratch with even a steak knife after it hardens, a coating you can spray on the red-hot steel as it's cooling so it bonds with the carbon molecules; your car body'll get metal fatigue before oxidization sets in. Synthetic polymers—that's the name of your brave new world, honeybunch, and it's just getting rolling. Bakelite was invented around 1907, synthetic rubber in 1910, nylon around 1930. Better check those dates if you use any of this. The point is, this century's just the infancy; synthetic polymers're going to be with us to the year one million or until we blow ourselves up, whichever comes sooner, and the beauty of it is, you can *grow* the raw materials, and when you run out of land you can grow 'em in the ocean. Move over, Mother Nature, we've got you beat. Also I'm working on the Big Interface."

"What interface is that?" Sukie was not ashamed to ask. Alexandra would just have nodded as if she knew; she had a lot still to learn about overcoming acculturated female recessiveness.

"The interface between solar energy and electrical energy," Van Horne told Sukie. "There *has* to be one, and once we find the combination you can run every appliance in your house right off the roof and have enough left over to recharge your electric car in the night. Clean, abundant, and *free*. It's coming, honeybunch, it's coming!"

"Those panels look so ugly," Sukie said. "There's a hippie in town who's done over an old garage so he can heat his water, I have no idea why, he never takes a bath."

"I'm not talking about collectors," Van Horne said. "That's Model T stuff." He looked about him; his head turned like a barrel being rolled on its edge. "I'm talking about a *paint*."

"A paint?" Alexandra said, feeling she should make a contribution. At least this man was giving her something new to think about, beyond tomato sauce.

"A paint," he solemnly assured her. "A simple paint you brush on with a brush and that turns the entire epidermis of your lovely home into an enormous low-voltaic cell."

"There's only one word for that," Sukie said.

"Yeah, what's that?"

"Electrifying."

Van Horne aped being offended. "Shit, if I'd known that's the kind of flirtatious featherheaded thing you like to say I wouldn't have wasted my time spilling my guts. You play tennis?"

Sukie stood up a little taller. Alexandra experienced a wish to stroke that long flat stretch from the other woman's breasts to below her waist, the way one longs to dart out a hand and stroke the belly a cat on its back elongates in stretching, the toes of its hind paws a-tremble in this moment of muscular ecstasy. Sukie was just so nicely *made*. "A bit," she said, her tongue peeking through her smile and adhering for a moment to her upper lip.

"You gotta come over in a couple weeks or so, I'm having a court put in."

Alexandra interrupted. "You can't fill wetlands," she said.

This big stranger wiped his lips and repulsively eyed her. "Once they're filled," he said in his imperfectly synchronized, slightly slurring voice, "they're not wet."

"The snowy egrets like to nest there, in the dead elms out back."

"T, O, U, F, F," Van Horne said. "Tough."

From the sudden stariness of his eyes she wondered if he was wearing contact lenses. His conversation did seem distracted by a constant slipshod effort to keep himself together. "Oh," she said, and what Alexandra noticed now gave her, already slightly dizzy, the sensation of looking down a deep hole. His aura was gone. He had absolutely none, like a dead man or a wooden idol, above his head of greasy hair.

Sukie laughed, pealingly; her dainty round belly pumped under the waistband of her suede skirt in sympathy with her diaphragm. "I love that. May I quote you, Mr. Van Horne? Filled Wetlands No Longer Wet, Declares Intriguing New Citizen."

Disgusted by this mating dance, Alexandra turned away. The auras of all the others at the party were blinding now, like the peripheral lights along a highway as raindrops collect on the windshield. And very stupidly she felt within herself the obscuring moisture of an unwanted infatuation condensing. The big man was a bundle of needs; he was a chasm that sucked her heart out of her chest.

Old Mrs. Lovecraft, her aura the tawdry magenta of those who are well pleased with their lives and fully expect to go to Heaven, came up to Alexandra bleating, "Sandy dear, we *miss* you at the Garden Club. You *must*n't keep so to yourself."

"*Do* I keep to myself? I *feel* busy. I've been putting up tomatoes, it's just incredible the way they kept coming this fall."

"I *know* you've been gardening; Horace and I admire your house every time we drive down Orchard Road: that *cun*ning little bed you have by your doorway, chock-a-block full of button mums. I've several times said to him, 'Let's *do* drop in,' but then I think, No, she might be making her little *things*, and we don't want to dis*turb* her inspiration."

Making her little things or love with Joe Marino, Alexandra thought: that was what Franny Lovecraft was implying. In a town like Eastwick there were no secrets, just areas of avoidance. When she and Oz were still together and new in town they had spent a number of evenings in the company of sweet old bores like the Lovecrafts; now Alexandra felt infinitely fallen from the world of decent and dreary amusements they represented.

"I'll come to some meetings this winter, when there's nothing else to do," Alexandra said, relenting. "When I'm homesick for nature," she added, though knowing she would never go, she was far beyond such tame delights. "I like the slide shows on English gardens; are you having any of them?"

"You *must* come next Thursday," Franny Lovecraft insisted, overplaying her hand as people of minor distinction—vice-presidents of savings banks, granddaughters of clipper-ship captains—will. "Daisy Robeson's son Warwick has *just* got back from three years in Iran, where he and his lovely little family had *such* a nice time, he was working as an adviser there, it somehow has all to do with oil, he says the Shah is performing *mir*acles, all this splendid modern architecture right in their capital city—oh, what *is* its name, I want to say New Delhi. . . ."

Alexandra offered no help though she knew the name Tehran; the devil was getting into her.

"At *any* rate, Wicky is going to give a slide show on Oriental rugs. You see, Sandy dear, in the Arab mind, the rug *is* a garden, it's an indoor garden in their tents and palaces in the middle of all that desert, and there's all manner of real flowers in the design, that to casual eyes looks so abstract. Now *does*n't that sound fascinating?"

"It does," Alexandra said. Mrs. Lovecraft had adorned her wrinkled throat, collapsed upon itself in folds and gulleys like those of an eroded roadside embankment, with a strand of artificial pearls of which the centerpiece was an antique mother-of-pearl egg in which a tiny gold cross had been tediously inlaid. With an irritated psychic effort, Alexandra willed the frayed old string to break; fake pearls slipped down the old lady's sunken front and cascaded in constellations to the floor.

The floor of the church parlor was covered with industrial carpeting the dull green of goose scat; it muffled the patter of pearls. The crowd was slow to detect the disaster, and at first only those in the immediate vicinity stooped to collect them. Mrs. Lovecraft, her face blanched with shock beneath the patches of rouge, was herself too arthritic and brittle to stoop. Alexandra, while kneeling at the old lady's dropsical feet, wickedly willed the narrow strained straps of her once-fashionable lizardskin shoes to come undone. Wickedness was like food: once you got started it was hard to stop; the gut expanded to take in more and more. Alexandra straightened up and set a half-dozen retrieved pearls in her victim's trembling, blue-knuckled, greedily cupped hand. Then she backed away, through the widening circle of squatting searchers. These bodies squatting seemed grotesque giant cabbages of muscle and avidity and cloth; their auras were all confused like watercolors running together to make gray. Her way to the door was blocked by Reverend Parsley, his handsome waxy face with that Peer Gynt tweak of doom to it. Like many a man who shaves in the morning, he sported a visible stubble by nighttime.

"*Al*exandra," he began, his voice deliberately forced into its most searching, low-pitched register. "I was *so* much hoping to see you here tonight." He wanted her. He was tired of fucking Sukie. In the nervousness of his overture he reached up to scratch his quaintly combed head, and his intended victim took the opportunity to snap the cheap expansion band of his important-looking gold-plated watch, an Omega. He felt it release and grabbed the expensive accessory where it was entangled in his shirt cuff before it had time to drop. This gave Alexandra a second to slip past the smear of his startled face —a pathetic smear, as she was to remember it guiltily; as if by sleeping with him she could have saved him—into the open air, the grateful black air.

The night was moonless. The crickets stridulated their everlasting monotonous meaningful note. Car headlights swept by on Cocumscussoc Way, and the bushes by the church door, nearly stripped of leaves, sprang up sharp in the illumination like the complicated mandibles and jointed feelers and legs of insects magnified. The air smelled faintly of apples making cider by themselves, in their own skins where these apples fell uncollected and rotting in the neglected orchards that backed up onto the church property, empty land waiting for its developer. The sheltering humped shapes of cars waited in the gravel parking lot. Her own little Subaru figured in her mind as a pumpkin-colored tunnel at whose far end glowed the silence of her rustic kitchen, Coal's tail-thumping welcome, the breathing of her children as they lay asleep or feigning in their rooms, having turned off television the instant her headlights glared at the windows. She would check them, their bodies each in its room and bed, and then take twenty of her baked bubbies, cunningly stacked so that no two had touched and married, out of the Swedish kiln, which would still be ticking, cooling, talking to her as of the events in the house in the time in which she had been away—for time flowed everywhere, not just in the rivulet of the delta in which we have been drifting. Then, duty done to her bubbies, and to her bladder, and to her teeth, she would enter upon the spacious queendom of her bed, a kingdom without a king, all hers. Alexandra was reading an endless novel by a woman with three names and an air-brushed photograph of herself on the shiny jacket; a few pages of its interminable woolly adventures among cliffs and castles served each night to smooth the border-crossing into unconsciousness. In her dreams she ranged far and wide, above the housetops, visiting rooms carved confusedly from the jumble of her past but seemingly solid as her oneiric self stood in each one, a ghost brimming with obscure mourning as she picked up an apple-shaped pincushion from her mother's sewing basket or waited while staring out at the snow-capped mountains for a playmate long dead to telephone. In her dreams omens cavorted around her as gaudily as papier-mâché advertisements beckoning innocents this way and that at an amusement park. Yet we never look forward to dreams, any more than to the fabled adventures that follow death.

Gravel crackled at her back. A dark man touched the soft flesh above her elbow; his touch was icy, or perhaps she was feverish. She jumped, frightened. He was chuckling. "The damnedest thing happened back in there just now. The old dame whose pearls let loose a minute ago tripped over her own shoes in her excitement and everybody's scared she broke her hip."

"How sad," Alexandra said, sincerely but absent-mindedly, her spirit drifting, her heart still thumping from the scare he gave her.

Darryl Van Horne leaned close and thrust words into her ear. "Don't forget, sweetheart. Think bigger. I'll check into that gallery. We'll be in touch. Nitey-nite."

"You actually *went?*" Alexandra asked Jane with a dull thrill of pleasure, over the phone.

"Why not?" Jane said firmly. "He really did have the music for the Brahms Sonata in E Minor, and plays amazingly. Like Liberace, only without all that smiling. You wouldn't think it; his hands don't look like they could do anything, somehow."

"You were alone? I keep picturing that perfume ad." The one which showed a young male violinist seducing his accompanist in her low-cut gown.

"Don't be vulgar, Alexandra. He feels quite asexual to me. And there are all these workmen around, including your friend Joe Marino, all dressed up in his little checked hat with a feather in it. And there's this constant rumbling from the backhoes moving boulders for the tennis court. Evidently they've had to do a lot of blasting."

"How can he get away with that, it's wetlands."

"I don't know, sweet, but he has the permit tacked up right on a tree."

"The poor egrets."

"Oh Lexa, they have all the rest of Rhode Island to nest in. What's nature for if it's not adaptable?"

"It's adaptable up to a point. Then it gets hurt feelings."

October's crinkled gold hung in her kitchen window; the big ragged leaves on her grape arbor were turning brown, from the edges in. Off to the left, toward her bog, a little stand of birches released in a shiver of wind a handful as of bright spear-points, twinkling as they fell to the lawn. "How long did you stay?"

"Oh," Jane drawled, lying. "About an hour. Maybe an hour and a half. He really *does* have some feeling for music and his manner when you're alone with him isn't as clownish as it may have seemed at the concert. He said being in a church, even a Unitarian one, gave him the creeps. I think behind all that bluffing he's really rather shy."

"Darling. You never give up, do you?"

Alexandra felt Jane Smart's lips move an inch back from the mouthpiece in indignation. Bakelite, the first of the synthetic polymers, that man had said. Jane was saying hissingly, "I don't see it's a question of giving up or not, it's a question of doing your thing. You do your thing moping around in your garden in men's pants and then cooking up your little figurines, but to make music you *must* have people. *Oth*er people."

"They're not figurines and I don't mope around."

Jane was going on, "You and Sukie are always poking fun of my being with Ray Neff ever and yet until this other man has shown up the only music I could make in town was with Ray."

Alexandra was going on, "They're *sculp*tures, just because they're not on a big scale like a Calder or Moore, you sound as vulgar as Whatsisname did, insinuating I should do something bigger so some expensive New York gallery can take fifty percent, even if they *were* to sell, which I very much doubt. Everything now is so trendy and violent."

"Is that what he said? So he had a proposition for you too."

"I wouldn't call it a proposition, just typical New York pushiness, sticking your nose in where it doesn't belong. They all have to be in on the action, any action."

"He's fascinated by us," Jane Smart asserted. "Why we all live up here wasting our sweetness on the desert air."

"Tell him Narragansett Bay has always taken oddballs in and what's he doing up here himself?"

"I wonder." In her flat Massachusetts Bay style Jane slighted the *r*. "He almost gives the impression that things got too hot for him where he was. And he does love all the space in the big house. He owns three pianos, honestly, though one of them is an upright that he keeps in his library; he has all these beautiful old books, with leather bindings and titles in Latin."

"Did he give you anything to drink?"

"Just tea. This manservant he has, that he talks Spanish to, brought it on a huge tray with a lot of liqueurs in funny old bottles that had that air, you know, of coming out of a cellar full of cobwebs."

"I thought you said you just had tea."

"Well really, Lexa, maybe I did have a sip of blackberry cordial or something Fidel was very enthusiastic about called mescal; if I'd known I was going to have to make such a complete report I'd have written the name down. You're worse than the CIA."

"I'm sorry, Jane. I'm very jealous, I suppose. And my *per*iod. It's lasted five days now, ever since the concert, and the ovary on the left side *hurts*. Do you think it could be menopause?"

"At thirty-eight? Honey, really."

"Well then it must be cancer."

"It couldn't be cancer."

"Why couldn't it be?"

"Because you're you. You have too much magic to have cancer."

"Some days I don't feel like I have any magic. Anyway, other people have magic too." She was thinking of Gina, Joe's wife. Gina must hate her. The Italian word for witch was *strega*. All over Sicily, Joe had told her, they give each other the evil eye. "Some days my insides feel all tied in knots."

"See Doc Pat, if you're seriously worried," said Jane, not quite unsympathetically. Dr. Henry Paterson, a plump pink man their age, with wounded wide watery eyes and a beautiful gentle firm touch when he palpated. His wife had left him years ago. He had never grasped why or remarried.

"He makes me feel strange," Alexandra said. "The way he drapes you with a sheet and does everything under that."

"The poor man, what is he supposed to do?"

"Not be so sly. I have a body. He knows it. I know it. Why do we have to pretend with this sheet?"

"They all get sued," Jane said, "if there isn't any nurse in the room." Her voice had a double to it, like a television signal when a truck goes by. This wasn't what she had called to talk about. Something else was on her mind.

"What else did you learn at Van Horne's?" Alexandra asked.

"*Well*—promise you won't tell anybody."

"Not even Sukie?"

"*Es*pecially not Sukie. It's about her. Darryl is really rather remarkable, he picks everything up. He stayed at the reception later than we did, I went off to have a beer with the rest of the quartet at the Bronze Barrel—"

"Greta along?"

"Oh God yes. She told us all about Hitler, how her parents couldn't stand him because his German was so uncouth. Apparently on the radio he didn't always end his sentences with the verb."

"How awful for them."

"—and I guess you faded into the night after playing that dreadful trick with poor Franny Lovecraft's pearls—"

"What pearls?"

"Don't pretend, Lexa. You were naughty. I know your style. And then the shoes, she's been in bed ever since but I guess she didn't break anything; they were worried about her hip. Do you know a woman's bones shrink to about half by the time she gets old? That's why everything snaps. She was lucky: just contusions."

"I don't know, looking at her made me wonder if I was going to be so sweet and boring and bullying when I got to be that age, if I *do* get to be, which I doubt. It was like looking into a mirror at my own dreary future, and I'm sorry, it drove me *wild*."

"All *right*, sweetie; it's no skin off my nose. As I was trying to say, Darryl hung around to help clean up and noticed while Brenda Parsley was in the church kitchen putting the plastic cups and paper plates into the Trashmaster Ed and Sukie had both disappeared! Leaving poor Brenda to put the best face on it she could—but imagine, the humiliation!"

"They really should be more discreet."

Jane paused, waiting for Alexandra to say something more; there was a point here she was supposed to grasp and express, but her mind was off, entertaining images of cancer spreading within her like the clouds of galaxies whirling softly out into the blackness, setting a deadly star here, there. . . .

"He's such a wimp," Jane at last supplied, lamely, of Ed. "And why is she always implying to us that she's given him up?"

Now Alexandra's mind pursued the lovers into the night, Sukie's slim body like a twig stripped of bark, but with pliant and muscular bumps; she was one of those women just this side of boyishness, of maleness, but vibrant, so close to this edge, the femininity somehow steeped in the guiltless energy men have, their lives consecrated like arrows, flying in slender storms at the enemy, taught from their cruel boyhoods onward how to die. Why don't they teach women? Because it isn't true that if you have daughters you will never die. "Maybe a clinic," she said aloud, having rejected Doc Pat, "where they don't know me."

"Well I would think *some*thing," Jane said, "rather than going on tormenting yourself. And being rather boring, if I do say so."

"I think part of Ed's appeal to Sukie," Alexandra offered, trying to get back on Jane's wavelength, "may be her professional need to feel in the local swim. At any rate what's interesting is not so much her still seeing him as this Van Horne character's bothering to notice so avidly, when he's just come to town. It's flattering, I suppose we're meant to think."

"Darling Alexandra, in some ways you're still awfully unliberated. A man can be just a person too, you know."

"I know that's the theory, but I've never met one who thought he was. They all turn out to be men, even the faggots."

"Remember when we were wondering if he was one? Now he's after all of us!"

"I thought he wasn't after you, you were both after Brahms."

"We were. We are. Really, Alexandra. Relax. You *are* sounding *aw*fully crampy."

"I'm a mess. I'll be better tomorrow. It's my turn to have it, remember."

"Oh my God yes. I nearly forgot. That's the other thing I was calling about. I can't make it."

"Can't make a Thursday? What's happening?"

"Well, you'll sniff. But it's Darryl again. He has some lovely little Webern bagatelles he wants to try me on, and when I suggested Friday he said he has some roving Japanese investors coming by to look at his undercoating. I was thinking of swinging by Orchard Road this afternoon if you'd like, one of the boys wanted me to go watch him play soccer after school but I could just produce my face for a minute on the sidelines—"

"No thanks dear," Alexandra said. "I have a guest coming."

"Oh." Jane's voice was ice, dark ice with ash in it such as freezes in the winter driveway.

"Possibly," Alexandra softened it to. "He or she wasn't sure they could make it."

"Darling, I quite understand. No need to say any more."

It made Alexandra angry, to be put on the defensive, when she was the one being snubbed. She told her friend, "I thought Thursdays were sacred."

"They are, usually," Jane began.

"But I suppose in a world where nothing else is there's no reason for Thursdays to be." Why was she so hurt? Her weekly rhythm depended on the infrangible triangle, the cone of power. But she mustn't let her voice drag on, betraying her this way.

Jane was apologizing, "Just this one time—"

"It's *fine*, sweetie. All the more devilled eggs for me." Jane Smart loved devilled eggs, chalky and sharp with paprika and a pinch of dry mustard, garnished with chopped chives or an anchovy laid across each stuffed white like the tongue of a toad.

"Were you really going to the trouble of devilled eggs?" she asked plaintively.

"Of course not, dear," Alexandra said. "Just the same old soggy Saltines and stale Velveeta. I must hang up."

An hour later, gazing abstracted past the furry bare shoulder (with its touching sour-sweet smell like a baby's pate) of Joe Marino as he with more rigor than inspiration pumped away at her, while her bed groaned and swayed beneath the unaccustomed double weight, Alexandra had a vision. She saw the Lenox mansion in her mind's eye, clear as a piece of calendar art, with the one wisp of smoke that she had observed that day, its pathetic strand of vapor confused with the poignance of Jane's describing Van Horne as shy and hence clownish. Disoriented, had been more Alexandra's impression: like a man peering through a mask, or listening with wool in his ears. "Focus, for Chrissake," Joe snarled in her own ear, and came, helplessly, excited by his own anger, his bare furry body—the work-hardened muscles gone slightly punky with prosperity— heaving once, twice, and the third time, ending in a little shiver like a car with carbon build-up shuddering after the ignition has been turned off. She tried to catch up but the contact was gone.

"Sorry," he growled. "I thought we were doing great but you wandered off." He had been generous, too, in forgiving her the tag end of her period, though there was hardly any blood.

"My fault," Alexandra said. "Absolutely. You were lovely. I was lousy." *Plays amazingly*, Jane had said.

The ceiling in the wake of her vision wore a sudden clarity, as if seen for the first time: its impassive dead square stretch, certain small flaws in its surface scarcely distinguishable from the specks in the vitreous humor of her eyes, except that when she moved her focus these latter drifted like animalcules in a pond, like cancer cells in our lymph. Joe's rounded shoulder and the side of his neck were as indifferent and pale as the ceiling, and as smoothly traversed by these optical impurities, which were not usually part of her universe but when they did intrude were hard to shake, hard not to see. A sign of old age. Like snowballs rolling downhill we accumulate grit.

She felt her front, breasts and belly, swimming in Joe's sweat and by this circuitous route her mind was returning to enjoyment of his body, its spongy texture and weight and confiding male aroma and rather miraculous, in a world of minor miracles, thereness. He was usually not there. Usually he was with Gina. He rolled off Alexandra with a wounded sigh. She had wounded his Mediterranean vanity. He was tan and bald on top, his shiny skull somewhat rippled, like the pages of a book we have left out in the dew, and it was part of his vanity to put back on, first thing, his hat. He said he felt cold without it. Hat in place, he showed a youngish profile, with the sharply hooked nose we see in Bellini portraits and with liverish deep dents beneath his eyes. She had been attracted to that sluggish debauched look, that hint of the leaden-eyed *barone* or doge or Mafioso who deals life and death with a contemptuous snick of his tongue and teeth. But Joe, whom she had seduced when he came to repair a toilet that murmured all night, proved to be toothless in this sense, a devout bourgeois honest down to the last brass washer, an infatuated father of five children under eleven, and an in-law to half the state. Gina's family had packed this coast from New Bedford to Bridgeport with kin. Joe was a glutton for loyalties; his heart belonged to more sports teams —Celtics, Bruins, Whalers, Red Sox, Pawtucket Sox, Pats, Teamen, Lobsters, Minutemen—than she had dreamed existed. Once a week he came and pumped away at her with much that same faithfulness. Adultery had been a step toward damnation for him, and he was honoring one more obligation, a satanic one. Also, it was something of a contraceptive measure; his fertility had begun to be frightening to him, and the more seed of his that Alexandra with her IUD absorbed, the less there was for Gina to work with. The affair was in its third summer and Alexandra should be ending it, but she liked Joe's taste —salty-sugary, like nougat—and the way the air shimmered about an inch above the gentle ridges of his skull. His aura had no malice or bad color to it; his thoughts, like his plumber's hands, were always seeking a certain fittingness. Fate had passed her from a maker of chrome fixtures to their installer.

To see the Lenox mansion as it had been in her vision, distinct in its bricks, its granite sills and quoins and Arguslike windows, so frontally, one would have to be hovering in midair above the marsh, flying. Rapidly the vision had diminished in size, as if receding in space, beckoning her. It became the size of a postage stamp and had she not closed her eyes it might have vanished like a pea down the drain. It was when her eyes were closed that he had come. Now she felt dazed, and splayed, as if the orgasm had been partly hers.

"Maybe I should cash it in with Gina and start up fresh somewhere with you," Joe was saying.

"Don't be silly. You don't want to do anything of the kind," Alexandra told him. High unseen in the windy day above her ceiling, geese in a V straggled south, honking to reassure one another: *I'm here, you're here.* "You're a good Roman Catholic with five *bambini* and a thriving business."

"Yeah, what am I doing here then?"

"You're bewitched. It's easy. I tore your picture out of the Eastwick *Word* when you'd been to a Planning Board meeting and smeared my menstrual fluid all over it."

"Jesus, you can be disgusting."

"You like that, don't you? Gina is never disgusting. Gina is as sweet as Our Lady. If you were any kind of a gentleman you'd finish me off with your tongue. There isn't much blood, it's the tag end."

Joe grimaced. "How's about I give you a rain check on that?" he said, and looked around for clothes to put on under his hat. Though growing pudgy, his body had a neatness; he had been a schoolboy athlete, deft with every ball, though too short to star. His buttocks were taut, even if his abdomen had developed a swag. A big butterfly of fine black hair rested on his back, the top edge of its wings along his shoulders and its feet feathering into the dimples flanking the low part of his spine. "I gotta check in at that Van Horne job," he said, tucking in a pink slice of testicle that had peeped through one leg-hole of his elasticized shorts. They were bikini-style and tinted purple, a new thing, to go with the new androgyny. Among Joe's loyalties was one to changes of male fashion. He had been one of the first men around Eastwick to wear a denim leisure suit, and to sense that hats were making a comeback.

"How's that going, by the way?" Alexandra asked lazily, not

wanting him to go. A desolation had descended to her from the ceiling.

"We're still waiting on this silver-plated faucet unit that had to be ordered from West Germany, and I had to send up to Cranston for a copper sheet big enough to fit under the tub and not have a seam. I'll be glad when it's done. There's something not right about that set-up. The guy sleeps past noon usually, and sometimes you go and there's nobody there at all, just this long-haired cat rubbing around. I hate cats."

"They're disgusting," Alexandra said. "Like me."

"No, listen, Al. You're *mia vacca. Mia vacca bianca.* You're my big plate of ice cream. What else can a poor guy say? Every attempt I make to get serious you turn me off."

"Seriousness scares me," she said seriously. "Anyway in your case I know it's just a tease."

But it was she who teased him, by making the laces of his shoes, oxblood cordovans like college men wear, come loose as fast as he tied them in bows; finally Joe had to shuffle out, defeated in his vanity and tidiness, with the laces dragging. His steps diminished on the stairs, one within the other, smaller and smaller, and the slam of the door was like the solid little nub, a mere peg of painted wood, innermost in a set of nested Russian dolls. Starling song scraped at the windows toward the yard; wild blackberries drew them to the bog by the hundreds. Abandoned and unsatisfied in the middle of a bed suddenly huge again, Alexandra tried to recapture, by staring at the blank ceiling, that strangely sharp and architectural vision of the Lenox place; but she could only produce a ghostly afterimage, a rectangle of extra pallor as on an envelope so long stored in the attic that the stamp has flaked off without being touched.

Inventor, Musician, Art Fancier
Busy Renovating Old Lenox Manse

BY SUZANNE ROUGEMONT

Courtly, deep-voiced, handsome in a casual, bearish way, Mr. Darryl Van Horne, recently of Manhattan and now a contented Eastwick taxpayer, welcomed your reporter to his island.

Yes, his island, for the famous "Lenox Manse" that this newcomer has purchased sits surrounded by marsh and at high tide by sheer sheets of water!

Constructed circa 1895 in a brick English style, with a symmetrical façade and massive chimneys at either end, the new proprietor hopes to convert his acquisition to multiple usages—as laboratory for his fabulous experiments with chemistry and solar energy, as a concert hall containing no less than three pianos (which he plays expertly, believe me), and as a large gallery upon whose walls hang startling works by such contemporary masters as Robert Rauschenburg, Claes Oldenburg, Bob Indiana, and James Van Dine.

An elaborate solarium-cum-greenhouse, a Japanese bath that will be a luxurious vision of exposed copper piping and polished teakwood, and an AsPhlex composition tennis court are all under construction as the privately owned island rings with the sound of hammer and saw and the beautiful pale herons who customarily nest in the lee of the property seek temporary refuge elsewhere.

Progress has its price!

Van Horne, though a genial host, is modest about his many enterprises and hopes to enjoy seclusion and opportunity for meditation in his new residence.

"I was attracted," he told your inquiring reporter, "to Rhode Island by the kind of space and beauty it affords, rare along the Eastern Seaboard in these troubled and overpopulated times. I feel at home here already.

"This is one heck of a spot!" he added informally, standing with your reporter on the ruins of the old Lenox dock and gazing out upon the vista of marsh, drumlin, channel, low-lying shrubland, and distant ocean horizon visible from the second floor.

The house with its vast stretches of parqueted maple floor and high ceiling bearing chandelier rosettes of molded plaster plus dentil molding along the sides felt chilly on the day of our fall visit, with much of the new "master's" equipment and furniture still in its sturdy packing cases, but he assured your reporter that the coming winter held no terrors for our resourceful host.

Van Horne plans to install a number of solar panels over the slates of the great roof and furthermore feels close to the eventual perfection of a closely guarded process that will render consumption of fossil fuels needless in the near future. Speed the day!

The grounds now abandoned to sumac, ailanthus, chokecherry and other weed trees the new proprietor envisions as a semi-tropical paradise brimming with exotic vegetation sheltered for the winter in the Lenox mansion's elaborate solarium-cum-greenhouse. The period statuary adorning the once-Versailles-like mall, now unfortunately so eroded by years of weather that many figures lack noses and hands, the proud owner plans to restore indoors, substituting Fiberglas replicas along the stately mall (well remembered in its glory by elderly citizens of this area) in the manner of the celebrated caryatids at the Parthenon in Athens, Greece.

The causeway, Van Horne said with an expansive gesture so characteristic of the man, could be improved by the addition of anchored aluminum pontoon sections at the lowest portions.

"A dock would be a lot of fun," he volunteered in a possibly humorous vein. "You could run a Hovercraft over to Newport or up to Providence."

Van Horne shares his extensive residence with no more company than an assistant-cum-butler, Mr. Fidel Malaguer, and an adorable fluffy Angora kitten whimsically yclept Thumbkin, because the animal has extra thumbs on several paws.

A man of impressive vision and warmth, your reporter welcomed the newcomer to this fabled region of South County confident that she spoke on behalf of many neighbors.

The Lenox Manse has again become a place to keep an eye on!

"You went there!" Alexandra jealously accused Sukie, over the phone, having read the article in the *Word*.

"Sweetie, it was an assignment."

"And whose idea was the assignment?"

"Mine," Sukie admitted. "Clyde wasn't sure it was news. And sometimes in cases like this when you talk about what a lovely home et cetera the person gets robbed the next week and sues the newspaper." Clyde Gabriel, a stringy weary man with a disagreeable do-gooding wife, edited the *Word*. Apologetically Sukie asked, "What did you think of the piece?"

"Well, honey, it had color, but you *do* run on a bit and honestly—now don't be offended—you *must* watch your participles. They dangle all over the place."

"If it's less than five paragraphs you don't get a byline. And he got me drunk. First it was rum in the tea and then it was rum without the tea. That creepy spic kept bringing it on this enormous silver tray. I never saw such a big tray: it was like a tabletop, all engraved and chased or whatever."

"What about *him*? How did he act? Darryl Van Horne."

"Well he talked a blue streak I must say. Giving me a saliva bath half the time. It was hard to know how seriously to take some of the things—the pontoon bridge, for instance. He said the canisters if that's what they are could be painted green and would blend right in with the marsh grass. The tennis court is going to be green, even the fencing. It's almost done and he wants us all to come play while the weather isn't too bad yet."

"All of who?"

"All of *us*, you and me and Jane. He seemed very interested, and I told him a little bit, just the part everybody knows, about our divorces and finding ourselves and so on. And what a comfort especially you are. I don't find Jane all that comforting lately, I think she's looking for a husband behind our backs. And I don't mean awful Neff, either. Greta has him too socked in with those children. God, don't children get in the way? I keep having the most terrible fights with mine. They say I'm never home and I try to explain to the little shits that I'm *earn*ing a *liv*ing."

Alexandra would not be distracted from the encounter she wanted to envision, between Sukie and this Van Horne man. "You told him the dirt about us?"

"Is there dirt? I just don't let gossip get to me, Lexa, frankly. Hold your head up and keep thinking, *Fuck you*: that's how I get down Dock Street every day. No, of course I didn't. I was very discreet as always. But he did seem so curious. I think it might be you he loves."

"Well I don't love him. I hate complexions that dark. And I can't stand New York chutzpah. And his face doesn't fit his mouth, or his voice, or something."

"I found that rather appealing," Sukie said. "His clumsiness."

"What did he do clumsy, spill rum all over your lap?"

"And then lick it up, no. Just the way he lurched from one thing to another, showing me his crazy paintings—there must be a fortune on those walls—and then his lab and playing the piano a little, 'Mood Indigo,' I think it was, done to waltz time as sort of a joke. Then he went running around outdoors so one of the backhoes nearly knocked him into a pit, and wanted to know if I wanted to see the view from the cupola."

"You *did*n't go into the cupola with him! Not on your first date."

"Baby, you make me keep *say*ing, It wasn't a date, it was an as*sign*ment. No. I thought I had enough and I knew I was drunk and had this deadline." She paused. Last night there had been a high wind and this morning, Alexandra saw through her kitchen window, the birches and the grape arbor had been stripped of so many leaves that a new kind of light was in the air, that naked gray short-lived light of winter that shows us the lay of the land and how close the houses of our neighbors sit. "He *did* seem," Sukie was saying, "I don't know, almost too eager for publicity. I mean, it's just a little local paper. It's as if—"

"Go on," said Alexandra, touching the chill windowpane with her forehead as if to let her thirsty brain drink the fresh wide light.

"I just wonder if this business of his is really doing so well, or is it just whistling in the dark? If he's really making these things, shouldn't there be a factory?"

"Good questions. What sort of questions did he ask about us? Or, rather, what sort of things did you choose to tell him?"

"I don't know why you sound so huffy about it."

"I don't either. I mean, I really don't."

"I mean, I don't have to tell you any of this."

"You're right. I'm being awful. Please don't stop." Alexandra did not want her ill humor to close the window on the outside world that Sukie's gossip gave her.

"Oh," Sukie answered tantalizingly. "How cozy we are. How much we've discovered we prefer women to men, and so on."

"Did that offend him?"

"No, he said he preferred women to men too. They were much the superior mechanism."

"He said 'mechanism.'"

"Some word like that. Listen, angel, I must run, honest. I'm supposed to be interviewing the committee heads about the Harvest Festival."

"Which church?"

In the pause, Alexandra shut her eyes and saw an irides-cent zigzag, as if a diamond on an unseen hand were etching darkness in electric parallel with Sukie's darting thoughts. "You know, the Unitarian. All the others think it's too pagan."

"May I ask, how are you feeling toward Ed Parsley these days?"

"Oh, the usual. Benign but distant. Brenda is *such* an impossible prig."

"What is she being impossibly priggish about, does he say?"

A certain reserve concerning sexual specifics obtained among the witches, but Sukie, by way of making up, moved against this constraint and broke into confession: "She doesn't do *any*-thing for him, Lexa. And before he went to divinity school he knocked about quite a bit, so he knows what he's missing. He keeps wanting to run away and join the Movement."

"He's too old. He's over thirty. The Movement doesn't want him."

"He *knows* that. He de*spis*es himself. I *can't* be rejecting to him every time, he's too pa*thet*ic," Sukie cried out in protest.

Healing belonged to their natures, and if the world accused them of coming between men and wives, of tying the disruptive ligature, of knotting the *aiguillette* that places the kink of impotence or emotional coldness in the entrails of a marriage seemingly secure in its snugly roofed and darkened house, and if the world not merely accused but burned them alive in the tongues of indignant opinion, that was the price they must pay. It was fundamental and instinctive, it was womanly, to want to heal—to apply the poultice of acquiescent flesh to the wound of a man's desire, to give his closeted spirit the exaltation of seeing a witch slip out of her clothes and go skyclad in a room of tawdry motel furniture. Alexandra released Sukie with no more implied rebuke of the younger woman's continuing to minister to Ed Parsley.

In the silence of her house, childless for two more hours, Alexandra battled depression, moving beneath its weight like a fish sluggish and misshapen at the bottom of the sea. She felt suffocated by her uselessness and the containing uselessness of this house, a mid-nineteenth-century farmhouse with musty small rooms and a smell of linoleum. She thought of eating, to cheer herself up. All things, even giant sea slugs, feed; feeding is their essence, and teeth and hoofs and wings have all evolved from the millions of years of small bloody struggles. She made herself a sandwich of sliced turkey breast and lettuce on diet whole-wheat bread, all hauled from the Bay Superette this morning, with Comet and Calgonite and this week's issue of the *Word*. The many laborious steps lunch involved nearly overwhelmed her—taking the meat from the refrigerator and undoing its taped jacket of butcher paper, locating the mayonnaise on the shelf where it hid amid jars of jelly and salad oil, clawing loose from the head of lettuce its clinging crinkling skin of plastic wrap, arranging these ingredients on the counter with a plate, getting a knife from the drawer to spread the mayonnaise, finding a fork to fish a long spear of pickle from the squat jar where seeds clouded a thin green juice, and then making herself coffee to wash the taste of turkey and pickle away. Every time she returned to its place in the drawer the little plastic dip that measured the coffee grounds into the percolator, a few more grains of coffee accumulated there, in the cracks, out of reach: if she lived forever these grains would become a mountain, a range of dark brown Alps. All around her in this home was an inexorable silting of dirt: beneath the beds, behind the books, between the spines of the radiators. She put away all the ingredients and equipment her hunger had called forth. She went through some motions of housekeeping. Why was there nothing to sleep in but beds that had to be remade, nothing to eat from but dishes that had to be washed? Inca women had had it no worse. She was indeed as Van Horne had said a mechanism, a robot cruelly conscious of every chronic motion.

She had been a cherished daughter, in that high western town, with its main street like a wide and dusty football field, the drugstore and the tack shop and the Woolworth's and the barbershop scattered over the space like creosote bushes that poison the earth around them. She had been the life of her family, a marvel of amusing grace flanked by dull brothers, boys yoked to the clattering cart of maleness, their lives one team after another. Her father, returning from his trips selling Levi's, had looked upon the growing Alexandra as upon a plant that grew in little leaps, displaying new petals and shoots at each reunion. As she grew, little Sandy stole health and power from her fading mother, as she had once sucked milk from her breasts. She rode horses and broke her hymen. She learned to ride on the long saddle-shaped seats of motorcycles, clinging so tightly her cheek took the imprint of the studs on the back of the boy's jacket. Her mother died and her father sent her east to college; her high-school guidance counselor had fastened on something with the safe-sounding name of Connecticut College for Women. There in New London, as field-hockey captain and fine-arts major, she moved through the many brisk costumes of the East's four picture-postcard seasons and in the June of her junior year found herself one day all in white and the next with the many uniforms of wife lined up limp in her wardrobe. She had met Oz on a sailing day on Long Island that others had arranged; holding drink after drink steady in a fragile plastic glass, he had seemed neither sick nor alarmed, when she had been both, and this had impressed her. Ozzie had delighted in her too—her full figure and her western, mannish way of walking. The wind shifted, the sail flapped, the boat yawed, his grin flashed reassuringly in the sun-scorched gin-fed pink of his face; he had a one-sided sheepish smile a little like her father's. It was a fall into his arms, but by such fallings she dimly understood life to rise, from strength to strength. She shouldered motherhood, the garden club, car pools, and cocktail parties. She shared morning coffee with the cleaning lady and midnight cognac with her husband, mistaking drunken lust for reconciliation. Around her the world was growing—child after child leaped from between her legs, they built an addition onto the house, Oz's raises kept pace with inflation—and somehow she was feeding the world but no longer fed by it. Her depressions grew worse. Her doctor prescribed Tofranil, her psychotherapist analysis, her clergyman *Either/Or*. She and Oz lived at that time, in Norwich, within sound of church bells and as winter afternoon darkened and before school returned her children to her Alexandra would lie in her bed beaten flatter by every stroke, feeling as shapeless and ill-smelling as an old galosh or the pelt of a squirrel killed days before on the highway. As a girl she would lie on the bed in their innocent mountain town excited by her body, a visitor of sorts who had come out of nowhere to enclose her spirit; she had studied herself in the mirror, saw the cleft in her chin and the curious dent at the end of her nose, stood back to appraise the sloping wide shoulders and gourd-like breasts and the belly like a shallow inverted bowl glowing above the demure triangular bush and solid oval thighs, and decided to be friends with her body; she could have been dealt a worse. Lying on the bed, she would marvel at her own ankle, turning it in the window light—the taut glimmer of its bones and sinews, the veins of palest blue with their magical traffic of oxygen—or stroke her own forearms, downy and plump and tapered. Then in mid-marriage her own body disgusted her, and Ozzie's attempts to make love to it seemed an unkind gibe. It was the body outside, beyond the windows, that light-struck, water-riddled, foliate flesh of that other self the world to which beauty still clung; when divorce came it was as if she had flown through that window. The morning after the decree, she was up at four, pulling up dead pea plants and singing by moonlight, singing by the light of that hard white stone with the tilted sad unisex face—a celestial presence, and dawn in the east the gray of a cat. This other body too had a spirit.

Now the world poured through her, wasted, down the drain. A woman is a hole, Alexandra had once read in the memoirs of a prostitute. In truth it felt less like being a hole than being a sponge, a heavy squishy thing on this bed soaking out of the air all the futility and misery there is: wars nobody wins, diseases conquered so we can all die of cancer. Her children would be clamoring home, so awkward and needy, plucking, clinging, looking to her for nurture, and they would find not a mother but only a frightened fat child no longer cute, no longer amazing to a father whose ashes two years ago had been scattered from a crop-duster over his favorite mountain meadow, where the family used to go gathering wildflowers —alpine phlox and sky pilot with its skunky-smelling leaves, monkshood and shooting stars and avalanche lily that blooms in the moist places left as the snow line retreats. Her father had carried a flower guide; little Sandra would bring him fresh-plucked offerings to name, delicate blooms with shy pale petals and stems chilly, it seemed to the child, from being out all night in the mountainous cold.

The chintz curtains that Alexandra and Mavis Jessup, the decorator divorcee from the Yapping Fox, had hung at the bedroom windows bore a big splashy pattern of pink and white peonies. The folds of the draperies as they hung produced out of this pattern a distinct clown's face, an evil pink-and-white clown's face with a little slit of a mouth: the more Alexandra looked, the more such sinister clowns' faces there were, a chorus of them amid the superimpositions of the peonies. They were devils. They encouraged her depression. She thought of her little bubbies waiting to be conjured out of the clay and they were images of her—sodden, amorphous. A drink, a pill, might uplift and glaze her, but she knew the price: she would feel worse two hours later. Her wandering thoughts were drawn as if by the glamorous shuttle and syncopated clatter of machinery toward the old Lenox place and its resident, that dark prince who had taken her two sisters in as if in calculated insult to her. Even in his insult and vileness there was something to push against and give her spirit exercise. She yearned for rain, the relief of its stir beyond the blankness of the ceiling, but when she turned her eyes to the window, there was no change in the cruelly brilliant weather outside. The maple against her window coated the panes with gold, the last flare of outlived leaves. Alexandra lay on her bed helpless, weighed down by all the incessant uselessness there is in the world.

Good Coal came in to her, scenting her sorrow. His lustrous long body, glittering in its loose sack of dogskin, loped across the oval rug of braided rags and heaved without effort up onto her swaying bed. He licked her face in worry, and her hands, and nuzzled where for comfort she had loosened the waist of her dirt-hardened Levi's. She tugged up her blouse to expose more of her milk-white belly and he found the supernumerary pap there, a hand's-breadth from her navel, a small pink rubbery bud that had appeared a few years ago and that Doc Pat had assured her was benign and not cancerous. He had offered to remove it but she was frightened of the knife. The pap had no feeling, but the flesh around it tingled while Coal nuzzled and lapped as at a teat. The dog's body radiated warmth and a faint perfume of carrion. Earth has in her all these shades of decay and excrement and Alexandra found them not offensive but in their way handsome, decomposition's deep-woven plaid.

Abruptly Coal was exhausted by his suckling. He collapsed into the curve her grief-drugged body made on the bed. The big dog, sleeping, snored with a noise like moisture in a straw. Alexandra stared at the ceiling, waiting for something to happen. The watery skins of her eyes felt hot, and dry as cactus skins. Her pupils were two black thorns turned inwards.

Sukie turned in her story of the Harvest Festival ("Rummage Sale, Duck-the-Clown / Part of Unitarian Plans") to Clyde Gabriel in his narrow office and discovered him, disconcertingly, slumped at his desk with his head in his arms. He heard the sheets of her copy rustle in his wire basket and looked up. His eyes were red-rimmed but whether from crying or sleep or hangover or last night's sleeplessness she could not tell. She knew from rumor that he not only was a drinker but owned a telescope he would sometimes sit at for hours on his back porch, examining the stars. His oak-pale hair, thin on top, was mussed; he had puffy blue welts below his eyes and the rest of his face was faintly gray like newsprint. "Sorry," she said, "I thought you'd want to pop this in."

Without much raising his head off the desk he squinted at her pages. "Pop, schnop," he said, embarrassed by being found slumped over. "This item doesn't deserve a two-line head. How about 'Peacenik Parson Plans Poppycock'?"

"I didn't talk to Ed; it was his committee chairpersons."

"Oops, pardon me. I forgot you think Parsley's a great man."

"That isn't altogether what I think," Sukie said, standing extra erect. These unhappy or unlucky men it was her fate to be attracted to were not above pulling you down with them if you allowed it and didn't stand tall. His nasty sardonic side, which made some others of the staff cringe and which had soured his reputation around town, Sukie saw as a masked apology, a plea turned upside down. At a point earlier in his life he must have been beautiful with promise, but his handsomeness—high square forehead, broad could-be passionate mouth, and eyes a most delicate icy blue and framed by starry long lashes—was caving in; he was getting that dried-out starving look of the persistent drinker.

Clyde was a little over fifty. On the pegboard wall behind his desk, along with a sampler of headline sizes and some framed citations awarded to the *Word* under earlier managements, he had hung photographs of his daughter and son but none of his wife, though he was not divorced. The daughter, pretty in an innocent, moon-faced way, was an unmarried X-ray technician at Michael Reese Hospital in Chicago, on her way perhaps to becoming what Monty would have laughingly called a "lady doctor." The Gabriel son, a college dropout interested in the-atre, had spent the summer on the fringes of summer stock in Connecticut, and had his father's pale eyes and the pouty good looks of an archaic Greek statue. Felicia Gabriel, the wife left off the wall, must have been a perky bright handful once but had developed into a sharp-featured little woman who could not stop talking. She was in this day and age outraged by ev-erything: by the government and by the protesters, by the war, by the drugs, by dirty songs played on WPRO, by *Playboy*'s being sold openly at the local drugstores, by the lethargic town government and its crowd of downtown loafers, by the sum-mer people scandalous in both costume and deed, by noth-ing's being quite as it would be if she were running everything. "Felicia was just on the phone," Clyde volunteered, in oblique apology for the sad posture in which Sukie had found him, "furious about this Van Horne man's violation of the wetlands regulations. Also she says your story about him was altogether too flattering; she says she's heard rumors about his past in New York that are pretty unsavory."

"Who'd she hear them from?"

"She won't say. She's protecting her sources. Maybe she got the poop straight from J. Edgar Hoover." Such antiwifely irony added little animation to his face, he had been ironical at Feli-cia's expense so often before. Something had died behind those long-lashed eyes. The two adult children pictured on his wall had his ghostliness, Sukie had often thought: the daughter's round features like an empty outline in their perfection and the boy also eerily passive, with his fleshy lips and curly hair and silvery long face. This colorlessness in Clyde's instance was stained by the brown aromas of morning whiskey and cigarette tobacco and a strange caustic whiff the back of his neck gave off. Sukie had never slept with Clyde. But she had this moth-ering sense that she could give him health. He seemed to be sinking, clutching his steel desk like an overturned rowboat.

"You look exhausted," she was forward enough to tell him.

"I am. Suzanne, I really am. Felicia gets on the phone every night to one or another of her causes and leaves me to drink too much. I used to go use the telescope but I really need a stronger power, it barely brings the rings of Saturn in."

"Take her to the movies," Sukie suggested.

"I did, some perfectly harmless thing with Barbra Streisand —God, what a voice that woman has, it goes through you like a knife!—and she got so sore at the violence in one of the previews she went back and spent half the movie complaining to the manager. Then she came back for the last half and got sore because she thought they showed too much of Streisand's tits when she bent over, in one of these turn-of-the-century gowns. I mean, this wasn't even a PG movie, it was a G! It was all people singing on old trolley cars!" Clyde tried to laugh but his lips had lost the habit and the resultant crimped hole in his face was pathetic to look at. Sukie had an impulse to peel up her cocoa-brown wool sweater and unfasten her bra and give this dying man her perky breasts to suck; but she already had Ed Parsley in her life and one wry intelligent sufferer at a time was enough. Every night she was shrinking Ed Parsley in her mind, so that when the call came she could travel sufficiently lightened across the flooded marsh to Darryl Van Horne's island. That's where the action was, not here in town, where oil-streaked harbor water lapped the pilings and placed a shudder of reflected light upon the haggard faces of the citizens of Eastwick as they plodded through their civic and Christian duties.

Still, Sukie's nipples had gone erect beneath her sweater in awareness of her healing powers, of being for any man a garden stocked with antidotes and palliatives. Her areolas tingled, as when once babies needed her milk or as when she and Jane and Lexa raised the cone of power and a chilly thrill, a kind of alarm going off, moved through her bones, even her finger and toe bones, as if they were slender pipes conveying streams of icy water. Clyde Gabriel bent his head to a piece of editing; touchingly, his colorless scalp showed between the long loose strands of oak-pale hair, an angle he never saw.

Sukie left the *Word* offices and stepped out onto Dock Street and walked to Nemo's for lunch; the perspective of sidewalks and glaring shopfronts pulled tight as a drawstring around her upright figure. The masts of sailboats moored beyond the pilings like a forest of slender varnished trees had thinned. At the south end of the street, at Landing Square, the huge old beeches around the little granite war memorial formed a fragile towering wall of yellow, losing leaves to every zephyr. The water as it turned toward winter cold became a steelier blue, against which the white clapboards of houses on the Bay side of the street looked dazzlingly chalky, every nail hole vivid. *Such beauty!* Sukie thought, and felt frightened that her own beauty and vitality would not always be part of it, that some day she would be gone like a lost odd-shaped piece from the center of a picture puzzle.

Jane Smart was practicing Bach's Second Suite for unaccompanied cello, in D Minor, the little black sixteenth-notes of the prelude going up and down and then up again with the sharps and flats like a man slightly raising his voice in conversation, old Bach setting his infallible tonal suspense engine in operation again, and abruptly Jane began to resent it, these notes, so black and certain and masculine, the fingering getting trickier with each sliding transposition of the theme and he not caring, this dead square-faced old Lutheran with his wig and his Lord and his genius and two wives and seventeen children, not caring how the tips of her fingers hurt, or how her obedient spirit was pushed back and forth, up and down, by these military notes just to give him a voice after death, a bully's immortality; abruptly she rebelled, put down the bow, poured herself a little dry vermouth, and went to the phone. Sukie would be back from work by now, throwing some peanut butter and jelly at her poor children before heading out to the evening's idiotic civic meeting.

"We *must* do something about getting Alexandra over to Darryl's place" was the burden of Jane's call. "I swung by late Wednesday even though she had told me not to because she seemed so hurt about our Thursday not working out, she has gotten much too dependent on Thursdays, and she looked just terribly down, *sick* with jealousy, first me and the Brahms and then your article, I must say your prose did somehow rub it in, and I couldn't get her to say a word about it and I didn't dare press the topic myself, why she hasn't been invited."

"But darling, she *has* been, as much as you and I were. When he was showing me his art works for the article he even pulled out an expensive-looking catalogue for a show this Niki Whatever had had in Paris and said he was saving it for Lexa to see."

"Well she won't go now until she's formally asked and I can tell it's eating the poor thing alive. I thought maybe you could say something."

"Sweetie, why me? You're the one who knows him better, you're over there all the time now with all this music."

"I've been there twice," Jane said, hissing the last word most positively. "You just have that way about you, you can get away with saying things to a man. I'm too definite somehow; it would come out as meaning too much."

"I'm not sure he even liked the article," Sukie fended. "He never called me about it."

"Why wouldn't he have liked it? It was lovely, and made him seem very romantic and dashing and impressive. Marge Perley has it up on her bulletin board and tells all her prospective clients that this was her sale."

At Sukie's end of the line a crying female child came up to her; her older brother, this child managed to explain between sobs while Jane's voice crackled on like static, wouldn't let her watch an educational special about lions mating instead of a rerun of *Hogan's Heroes* on a UHF channel that *he* wanted to see. Peanut butter and jelly flecked this little girl's lips; her fine hair was an uncombed tangle. Sukie wanted to slap the repulsive child's dirty face and knock a little sense into those TV-glazed eyes. Greed, that was all TV taught, turning our minds to total pap. Darryl Van Horne had explained to her how TV was responsible for all the riots and war resistance; the commercial interruptions and the constant switching back and forth between channels had broken down in young people's brains the synapses that make logical connections, so that Make Love Not War seemed to them an actual idea.

"I'll think about it," she promised Jane hastily, and hung up. She had to go out to an emergency session of the Highway Department; last February's unexpected blizzards had used up all this year's snow-removal and road-salting budget and the chairman, Ike Arsenault, was threatening to resign. Sukie hoped to be able to leave early for a tryst with Ed Parsley at Point Judith.

First she had to settle the squabble in the TV den. The children had their own set upstairs but to be perverse preferred to use hers; the noise filled the tiny house, and their glasses of milk and cocoa cups left rings on the sea chest refinished as a coffee table, and she would find bread crusts turning green between the love-seat cushions. She flounced in a fury and assigned the rudest brat to put the supper dishes into the dishwasher. "And be sure to rinse the peanut-butter knife, rinse and *wipe* it; if you just throw it in the heat bakes the peanut butter so you can *never* get it off." Before leaving the kitchen Sukie chopped up an Alpo can of blood-colored horsemeat and set it on the floor, in the plastic dog dish a child with a Magic Marker had lettered HANK, for the ravenous Weimaraner to gobble. She crammed half a fistful of salted Spanish peanuts into her own mouth; bits of red skin stuck to her sumptuous lips.

She went upstairs. To get to Sukie's bedroom, you went up the narrow stair and turned left into a narrow slanted hall of unadorned boards and then right, through an authentic eighteenth-century door studded in a double X pattern of squarish cut nails. She shut this door and with a wrought-iron latch shaped like a claw locked herself in. The room was papered in an old pattern of vines growing straight up like bean plants on poles, and the cobwebbed ceiling sagged like the underside of a hammock. Large washers bolted at the worst cracks kept the plaster from falling down. A single geranium was dying on the sill of the room's one small window. Sukie slept in a sway-backed double bed that wore a threadbare coverlet of dotted Swiss. She had remembered there was a copy of last week's *Word* by her bedside; with a pair of curved nail scissors she carefully cut out her "Inventor, Musician, Art Fancier" article, breathing warmly upon it as her nearsighted eyes strained not to include a single adjacent letter of any item that did not concern Darryl Van Horne. This done, she wrapped the article face inwards around a heavy-hipped, tiny-footed naked bubby Alexandra had given Sukie for her thirtieth birthday two years ago but which for the purposes of magic would represent the creatrix herself. With a special string Sukie kept in a narrow cupboard beside the walled-in fireplace, a furry pale green jute such as gardeners used to tie up plants and whose properties included therefore that of encouraging growth, she tightly wound the package around until not a glint of the crackling print-filled paper showed. She tied it with a bow, then another, and a third, for magic. The fetish weighed pleasantly in the hand, a phallic oblong with the texture of a closely woven basket. Uncertain what the proper spell might be, she touched it lightly to her forehead, her two breasts, her navel that was a single link in the infinite chain of women, and, lifting her skirt but keeping her underpants on, her pudendum. For good measure she gave the thing a kiss. "Have fun, you two," she said, and, remembering a word of her schoolgirl Latin, chanted in a whisper, "*Copula, copula, copula.*" Then she kneeled and put this hairy green charm underneath her bed, where she spotted about a dozen dust mice and a pair of lost pantyhose she was in too much of a hurry to retrieve. Already her nipples had stiffened, foreseeing Ed Parsley, his dark parked car, the sweeping accusatory beam of the Point Judith lighthouse, the crummy dank motel room he would have already paid eighteen dollars for, and the storms of his guilt she would have to endure once he was sexually satisfied.

On this afternoon of cold low silver sky Alexandra thought East Beach might be too windy and raw so she stopped the Subaru on a shoulder of the beach road not far from the Lenox causeway. Here was a wide stretch of marsh, the grass now bleached and pressed flat in patches by the action of the tides, where Coal could have a run. Between the speckled boulders that were the causeway's huge bones the sea deposited dead gulls and empty crab shells the dog loved to sniff and rummage among. Here also stood what was left of an entrance gate: two brick pillars capped by cement bowls of fruit and holding the rusting pivot pins for an iron gate that had vanished. While she stood gazing in the direction of the glowering symmetrical house, its owner pulled up behind her silently in his Mercedes. The car was an off-white that looked dirty; one front fender had been dented and the other repaired and repainted in an ivory that did not quite match. Alexandra was wearing a red bandanna against the wind, so when she turned she saw her face in the smiling dark man's eye as a startled oval, framed in red against the silver streaks over the sea, her hair covered like a nun's.

His car window had slid smoothly down on a motor. "You've come at last," he called, less with that prying clownish edge of the post-concert party than as a simple factual declaration by a busy man. His seamed face grinned. Beside him on the front seat sat a shadowy conical shape—a collie, but one in whose tricolor hair the black was unusually dominant. This creature yapped mercilessly when loyal Coal rallied from his far-ranging carrion-sniffing to his mistress's side.

She gripped her pet's collar to restrain him as he bristled and gagged, and lifted her voice to make it heard above the dogs' din. "I was just parking here, I wasn't . . ." Her voice came out frailer and younger than her own; she had been caught.

"I know, I know," Van Horne said impatiently. "Come on over anyway and have a drink. You haven't had your tour yet."

"I have to get back in a minute. The children will be coming home from school." But even as she said it Alexandra was dragging Coal, suspicious and resisting, toward her car. His run wasn't over, he wanted to say.

"Better hop in my jalopy with me," the man shouted. "The tide's coming in and you don't want to get stranded."

I don't? she wondered, obeying like an automaton, betraying her best friend by shutting Coal alone in the Subaru. He had expected her to join him and drive home. She cranked the driver's window down an inch, for air, and punched the locks on the doors. The dog's black face rumpled with incredulity. His ears were thrust out as far from his skull as their crimped inner folds would bear their floppy weight. These velvety pink folds she had often fondled by the fireside, examining them for ticks. She turned away. "Really just a minute," she stammered to Van Horne, torn, awkward, years fallen from her with their poise and powers.

The collie, whom Sukie's article had not mentioned, shed all ferocity and slunk gracefully into the back seat as she opened the Mercedes door. The car's interior was red leather; the front seats had been dressed in sheep hides, woolly side up. With an expensive punky sound the door closed at her side.

"Say howdy-do, Needlenose," Van Horne said, twisting his big head, like an ill-fitting helmet, toward the back seat. The dog did indeed have a very pointed nose, which he pushed into Alexandra's palm when she offered it. Pointed, moist, and shocking—the tip of an icicle. She pulled her hand back quickly.

"The tide won't be in for hours," she said, trying to return her voice to its womanly register. The causeway was dry and full of potholes. His renovations had not extended this far.

"The bastard can fool you," he said. "How the hell've you been, anyway? You look depressed."

"I do? How can you tell?"

"I can tell. Some people find fall depressing, others hate spring. I've always been a spring person myself. All that growth, you can feel Nature groaning, the old bitch; she doesn't want to do it, not again, no, anything but *that*, but she *has* to. It's a fucking torture rack, all that budding and pushing, the sap up the tree trunks, the weeds and the insects getting set to fight it out once again, the seeds trying to remember how the hell the DNA is supposed to go, all that compe*tit*ion for a little bit of nitrogen; Christ, it's cruel. Maybe I'm too sensitive. I bet you revel in it. Women aren't that sensitive to things like that."

She nodded, hypnotized by the bumpy road diminishing under her, growing at her back. Brick pillars twin to those at the far end stood at the entrance to the island, and these still had their gate, its iron wings flung wide for years and the rusted scrolls become a lattice for wild grapevines and poison ivy and even interpenetrated by young trees, swamp maples, their little leaves turning the tenderest red, almost a rose. One of the pillars had lost its crown of mock fruit.

"Women take pain in their stride pretty much," Van Horne was going on. "Me, I can't stand it. I can't even bring myself to swat a housefly. The poor thing'll be dead in a couple days anyway."

Alexandra shuddered, remembering houseflies landing on her lips as she slept, their feathery tiny feet, the electric touch of their energy, like touching a frayed cord while ironing. "I like May," she admitted lamely. "Except every year it does feel, as you say, more of an effort. For gardeners, anyway."

Joe Marino's green truck, to her relief, was not parked anywhere out front of the mansion. The heavy work on the tennis court seemed to have been done; instead of the golden earthmovers Sukie had described, a few shirtless young men were with dainty pinging noises fastening wide swatches of green plastic-coated fencing to upright metal posts all around what at the distance, as she looked down from a curve of the drive-way to where the snowy egrets used to nest in the dead elms, seemed a big playing card in two flat colors imitating grass and earth; the grid of white lines looked sharp with signification, as compulsively precise as a Wiccan diagram. Van Horne had stopped the car so she could admire. "I looked into that Har-True and even if you see your way past the initial expense the maintenance of any kind of clay is one hell of a headache. With this AsPhlex composition all you need do is sweep the leaves off it now and then and with any luck you can play right into December. Couple of days more it'll be ready to baptize; my thought was with you and your two buddies we might have a foursome."

"My goodness, are we up to such an honor? I'm really in no shape—" she began, meaning her game. Ozzie and she for a time had played a lot of doubles with other couples, but in the years since, though Sukie once or twice a summer got her out for some Saturday singles on the battered public courts toward Southwick, she had really played hardly at all.

"Then *get* in shape," Van Horne said, misunderstanding, spitting in his enthusiasm. "Move around, get rid of that flub. Hell, thirty-eight is *young*."

He knows my age, Alexandra thought, more relieved than offended. It was nice to have yourself known by a man; it was getting to be known that was embarrassing: all that self-conscious verbalization over too many drinks, and then the bodies revealed with the hidden marks and sags like disap-pointing presents at Christmastime. But how much of love, when you thought about it, was not of the other but of yourself naked in his eyes: of that rush, that little flight, of shedding your clothes, and being you at last. With this over-bearing strange man she felt known, essentially, already. His being awful rather helped.

He put the car into motion and coasted around the crack-ling driveway circle and halted at the front door. Two steps led up to a paved, pillared porch holding in tesserae of green mar-ble the inlaid initial *L.* The door itself, freshly painted black, was so massive Alexandra feared it would pull its hinges loose when the owner swung it open. Inside the foyer, a sulphurous chemical smell greeted her; Van Horne seemed oblivious of it, it was his element. He ushered her in, past a stuffed hollow elephant foot full of knobbed and curved canes and one umbrella. He was not wearing baggy tweed today but a dark three-piece suit as if he had been somewhere on business. He gestured right and left with excited stiff arms that returned to his sides like collapsed levers. "Lab's over there, past the pianos, used to be the ballroom, nothing in there but a ton of equipment half of it still in crates, we've hardly begun to roll yet, but when we do, boy, we're going to make dynamite look like firecrackers. Here on the other side, let's call it the study, half my books still in cartons in the basement, some of the old sets I don't want to put out in the light till I can get an air-control unit set up, these old bindings, you know, and even the threads hold 'em together turn into dust like mummies when you lift the lid . . . cute room, though, isn't it? The antlers were here, and the heads. I'm no hunter myself, get up at four in the morning go out and blast some big-eyed doe never did anybody any harm in the world in the face with a shotgun, crazy. People are crazy. People are really wicked, you have to believe it. Here's the dining room. The table's mahogany, six leaves if I want to give a banquet, myself I prefer dinners on the intimate side, four, six people, give everybody a chance to shine, strut their stuff. You invite a mob and mob psychology takes over, a few leaders and a lot of sheep. I have some super candelabra still packed, eighteenth-century, expert I know says positively from the workshop of Robert Joseph Auguste though it doesn't have the hallmark, the French were never into hallmarks like the English, the de*tail* on it you wouldn't believe, imitation grapevines down to the tiniest little curlicue tendril, you can even see a little bug or two on 'em, you can even see where insects chewed the leaves, everything done two-thirds scale; I hate to get it up here in plain view until I have a foolproof burglar alarm installed, though burglars generally don't like to tackle a place like this, only one way in and out, they like to have an escape hatch. Not that that's any insurance policy, they're getting bolder, the drugs make the bastards desperate, the drugs and the general breakdown in respect for any damn thing at all; I've heard of people gone for only half an hour and cleaned out, they keep track of your routines, your every move, you're watched, that's one thing you can be sure of in this society, baby: you are *watched*."

Of Alexandra's responses to this outpouring she had no consciousness: polite noises, no doubt, as she held herself a distance behind him in fear of being accidentally struck as the big man wheeled and gestured. She was aware of, beyond his excited dark shape as he lavishly bragged, a certain penetrating bareness: a shabbiness of empty corners and rugless scratched floors, of ceilings whose cracks and buckled patches had gone untouched for decades, of woodwork whose once-white paint had yellowed and chipped and of elegant hand-printed panoramic wallpapers drooping loose in the corners and along the dried-out seams; vanished paintings and mirrors were remembered by rectangular and oval ghosts of lesser discoloration. For all his talk of glories still to be unpacked, the rooms were badly underfurnished; Van Horne had the robust instincts of a creator but with only, it seemed, half the needed raw materials. Alexandra found this touching and saw in him something of herself, her monumental statues that could be held in the hand.

"*Now*," he announced, booming as if to drown out these thoughts in her head, "here's the room I wanted you to see. *La chambre de résistance*." It was a long living room, with a portentous fireplace pillared like the façade of a temple—leafy Ionic pillars carved to support a mantel above which a great bevelled mirror gave back the room a speckled version of its lordly space. She looked at her own image and removed the bandanna, shaking down her hair, not fixed in a braid today but with a sticky twistiness still in it. As her voice had come out of her startled mouth younger than she was, so she looked younger in this antique, forgiving mirror. It was slightly tipped; she looked up into it, pleased that the flesh beneath her chin did not show. In the bathroom mirror at home she looked terrible, a hag with cracked lips and a dented nose and with broken veins in her septum, and when, driving in the Subaru, she stole a peek at herself in the rearview mirror, she looked worse yet, corpselike in color, the eyes quite wild and a single stray lash laid like a beetle leg across one lower lid. As a tiny girl Alexandra had imagined that behind every mirror a different person waited to peek back out, a different soul. Like so much of what we fear as a child, it turned out to be in a sense true.

Van Horne had put around the fireplace some boxy modern stuffed chairs and a curved four-cushioned sofa, refugees from a New York apartment obviously, and well worn; but the room was mostly furnished with works of art, including several that took up floor space. A giant hamburger of violently colored, semi-inflated vinyl. A white plaster woman at a real ironing board, with an actual dead cat from a taxidermist's rubbing at her ankles. A vertical stack of Brillo cartons that close inspection revealed to be not airy stamped cardboard but meticulously silk-screened sheets mounted on great cubes of something substantial and immovable. A neon rainbow, unplugged and needing a dusting.

The man slapped an especially ugly assemblage, a naked woman on her back with legs spread; she had been concocted of chicken wire, flattened beer cans, an old porcelain chamber pot for her belly, pieces of chrome car bumper, items of underwear stiffened with lacquer and glue. Her face, staring straight up at the sky or ceiling, was that of a plaster doll such as Alexandra used to play with, with china-blue eyes and cherubic pink cheeks, cut off and fixed to a block of wood that had been crayoned to represent hair. "Here's the genius of the bunch for my money," Van Horne said, wiping the corners of his mouth dry with a two-finger pinching motion. "Kienholz. A Marisol with guts. You know, the tac*til*ity; there's nothing monotonous or pre-ordained about it. That's the kind of thing *you* should be setting your sights toward. The richness, the *Vielfältigkeit*, the, you know, the ambi*gu*ity. No offense, friend Lexa, but you're a Johnny-one-note with those little poppets of yours."

"They're not poppets, and this statue is rude, a joke against women," she said languidly, feeling splayed and out of focus, in tune with the moment—a gliding sensation, the world passing through her or she moving the world, a cosmic confusion such as when the train silently tugs away from the station and it seems the platform is sliding backwards. "My little bubbies aren't jokes, they're meant affectionately." Yet her hand wandered on the assemblage and found there the glossy yet resistant texture of life. On the walls of this long room, once perhaps hung with Lenox family portraits from eighteenth-century Newport, there now hung or protruded or dangled gaudy travesties of the ordinary—giant pay telephones in limp canvas, American flags duplicated in impasto, oversize dollar bills rendered with deadpan fidelity, plaster eyeglasses with not eyes but parted lips behind the lenses, relentless enlargements of our comic strips and advertising insignia, our movie stars and bottle caps, our candies and newspapers and traffic signs. All that we wish to use and discard with scarcely a glance was here held up bloated and bright: permanized garbage. Van Horne gloated, snorted, and repeatedly wiped his lips as he led Alexandra through his collection, down one wall and back the other; and in truth she saw that he had acquired of this mocking art specimens of good quality. He had money and needed a woman to help him spend it. Across his dark vest curved the gold chain of an antique watch fob; he was an inheritor, though ill at ease with his inheritance. A wife could put him at ease.

The tea with rum came, but formed a more sedate ceremony than she had imagined from Sukie's description. Fidel materialized with that ideal silence of servants, a tidy scar placed so flatteringly beneath one cheekbone it seemed appliquéd to his mocha skin, a deliberate fillip to his small slanting features. The long-haired cat called Thumbkin, with the deformed paws mentioned in the *Word*, leaped onto Alexandra's lap just as she lifted her cup to sip; its liquid content scarcely swayed. The horizon of sea visible through the Palladian windows from where she sat stayed level also: the world was in part a gently shuffled deck of horizontal liquids, it occurred to her, thinking of the cold dense stratum of the sea where only giant eyeless slugs moved beneath the pressure, and then of mist licking the autumnal surface of a woodland pond, and of the spheres of ever-thinner gas that our astronauts pierce without puncturing, so the sky's blue does not leak away. She felt at peace here, which she had not expected, here in these rooms virtually empty but for their overload of sardonic art, rooms eloquent of a bachelor's lacks. Her host seemed pleasanter too. The manner of a man who wants to sleep with you is slicing and aggressive, testing, foreshadowing his eventual anger if he succeeds, and there seemed little of that in Van Horne's manner today. He looked tired, slumped in his tatty boxy armchair covered in a mushroom-colored corduroy. She fantasized that the business appointment for which he had put on his solemn three-piece suit had been a disappointment, perhaps a petition for a bank loan that had been refused. With plain need he poured extra rum into his tea from the bottle of Mount Gay his butler had set at his elbow, on a Queen Anne piecrust table. "How did you come to acquire such a large and wonderful collection?" Alexandra asked him.

"My investment adviser" was his disappointing answer. "Smartest thing financially you can ever do except strike oil in your back yard is buy a name artist before he has the name. Think of those two Russkis who picked up all that Picasso and Matisse cheap in Paris just before the war and now it sits over there in Leningrad where nobody can lay their eyes on it. Think of the lucky fools who took an early Pollock off his hands for the price of a bottle of Scotch. Even hit or miss you'll average out better than the stock market. One Jasper Johns makes up for an awful lot of junk. Anyway, I love the junk."

"I see you do," Alexandra said, trying to help him. How could she ever rouse this heavy rambling man to fall in love with her? He was like a house with too many rooms, and the rooms with too many doors.

He did lurch forward in his chair, spilling tea. He had done it so often, evidently, that by reflex he spread his legs and the tan liquid flipped between them to the carpet. "Greatest thing about Orientals," he said. "They don't show your sins." With the sole of one little pointy black shoe—his feet were almost monstrously small for his bulk—he rubbed the tea stain in. "I *hated*," he volunteered, "that abstract stuff they were trying to sell us in the Fifties; Christ, it all reminded me of Eisenhower, a big blah. I want art to *show* me something, to tell me where I'm at, even if it's Hell, right?"

"I guess so. I'm really very dilettantish," Alexandra said, less comfortable now that he did seem to be rousing. What underwear had she put on? When had she last had a bath?

"So when this Pop came along, I thought, Jesus, this is the stuff for me. So fucking cheerful, you know—going down but going down with a smile. Like the late Romans in a way. 'Djou ever read Petronius? *Fun*ny. Funny, God, you can look at that goat Rauschenberg put in the rubber tire and laugh until sundown. I was in this gallery years ago on Fifty-seventh Street —that's where I'd like to see you, as I guess I've been saying to the point where it's boring—and the dealer, this faggot called Mischa, they used to call him Mischa the Muff, hell of a knowledgeable guy though, showed me these two beer cans by Johns —Ballantine ale, actually—in bronze, but painted up so sweet, with that ever-so-exact but slightly free way Johns has, and one with a triangle in the top where a beer opener had been and the other virgin, unopened. Mischa says to me, 'Pick that one up.' 'Which one?' I say. 'Any one,' he says. I pick up the virgin one. It's heavy. 'Pick up the other one,' he says. 'Really?' I ask. 'Go ahead,' he says. I do. It's lighter! The beer had been drunk!! In terms of the art, that is. I nearly came in my pants, that was such a turn-on when I saw the light."

He had sensed that Alexandra did not mind his talking dirty. She in fact rather liked it; it had a secret sweetness, like the scent of carrion on Coal's coat. She must go. Her dog's big heart would break in that little locked car.

"I asked him what the price was for these beer cans and Mischa told me and I said, 'No way.' There are limits. How much cash can you tie up in two fake beer cans? Alexandra, no kidding, if I'd taken the plunge I would have quintupled my money by now, and that wasn't so many years ago. Those cans are worth more than their weight in pure gold. I honestly believe, when future ages look back on us, when you and I are just a pair of skeletons lying in those idiotic expensive boxes they make you buy, our hair and bones and fingernails pillowed on all this ridiculous satin these fat-cat funeral directors rip you off for, Jesus I'm getting carried away, they can just take my *corpus* and dump it on the dump would suit me fine, when you and I are dead is all I mean to say, those beer cans, ale cans I should be saying, are going to be our Mona Lisa. We were talking about Kienholz; you know there's this entire sawed-off Dodge car he did, with a couple inside fucking. The car sits on a mat of artificial turf and a little ways away from it he put a little other patch of Astroturf or whatever he used, about the size of a checkerboard, with a single empty beer bottle on it! To show they'd been drinking and chucked it out. To give the lovers' lane ambience. That's genius. The little extra piece of mat, the apartness. Somebody else would have just put the beer bottle on the main mat. But having it separate is what makes it art. Maybe *that's* our Mona Lisa, that empty of

Kienholz's. I mean, I was out there in L.A. looking at this crazy sawed-off Dodge and tears came to my eyes. I'm not shitting you, Sandy. Tears." And he held his unnaturally white, waxy-looking hands in front of his eyes as if to pluck these watery reddish orbs from his skull.

"You travel," she said.

"Less than I used to. I'm just as glad. You go everywhere but it's always you unpacks the bag. Same bag, same you. You girls up here have the right idea. Find a Nowheresville and make your own space. All the junk comes after you anyway, with the TV and the global village and all." He slumped in his mushroom chair, empty at last of phrases. Needlenose trotted into the room and curled at his master's feet, tucking his long nose under his tail.

"Speaking of travel," Alexandra said. "I must run. I locked my poor doggie in the car, and my children will be home from school by now." She set down her teacup—monogrammed with *N*, strangely, instead of any of Van Horne's initials—on his scratched and chipped Mies van der Rohe glass table and stood to her height. She was wearing her brocaded Algerian jacket over a silver-gray cotton turtleneck, with her slacks of forest-green serge. A pang of relief at her waist as she stood reminded her of how uncomfortably tight these slacks had become. She had vowed to lose weight; but winter was the worst time for it, one nibbled to keep warm, to keep the early dark at bay, and anyway in this bulky man's eyes, turned upwards appraising the jut of her breasts, she read no demand to change her shape. Joe called her in their privacy his cow, his woman-and-a-half. Ozzie used to say she was better at night than two more blankets. Sukie and Jane called her gorgeous. She brushed from the serge tightly covering her pelvis several long white hairs Thumbkin had deposited there. She retrieved her bandanna with a scarlet flick from the arm of the curved sofa.

"But you haven't seen the lab!" Van Horne protested. "Or the hot-tub room, we *fin*ally got the mother finished, all but some accessory wiring. Or the upstairs. My big Rauschenberg lithographs are all upstairs."

"Perhaps there will be another time," Alexandra said, her voice quite settled now into her womanly contralto. She was enjoying leaving. Seeing him frantic, she was confident again of her powers.

"You ought at least to see my bedroom," Van Horne pleaded, leaping up and barking his shin on a corner of the glass table so that pain slipped his features awry. "It's all in black, even the sheets," he told her; "it's damn hard to buy good black sheets, what they call black is really navy blue. And in the hall I've just got some very subtly raunchy oils by a newish painter called John Wesley, no relation to the crazy Methodist, he does what look like illustrations to children's animal books until you realize what they're showing. Squirrels fucking and stuff like that."

"Sounds fun," Alexandra said, and moved briskly in a wide arc, an old hockey-player's move, so the chair blocked him for a moment and he could only loudly follow as she sailed out of the room with its ugly art, on through the library, past the music room, into the hall with the elephant's foot, where the rotten-egg smell was strongest but the breath of the out-of-doors could be scented too. The black door had been left its natural two-toned oak on this side.

Fidel had appeared from nowhere to position himself with a hand on the great brass latch. To Alexandra he seemed to be looking past her face toward his master; they were going to trap her here. In her fantasy she would count to five and start to scream; but there must have been a nod, for the latch clicked on the count of three.

Van Horne said behind her, "I'd offer to give you a ride back to the road but the tide may be up too far." He sounded out of breath: emphysema from too many cigarettes or inhaling those Manhattan bus fumes. He did need a wife's care.

"But you promised it wouldn't be!"

"Listen, what the hell do I know? I'm more of a stranger here than you are. Let's walk down and have a gander."

Whereas the driveway curved around, the grass mall, lined with limestone statues the weather and vandals had robbed of hands and noses, led directly down to where the causeway met the edge of the island. An untidy shore of weeds—seaside goldenrod, beach clotbur with its huge loose leaves—and gravel and a rubble of old asphalt paving spread behind the vine-entangled gate. The weeds trembled in a chill wind off the flooded marsh. The sky had lowered its bacon stripes of gray; the most luminous thing in sight was a great egret, not a snowy, loitering in the direction of the beach road, its yellow bill close to the color of her abandoned Subaru. Between here and there a tarnished glare of water had overswept the causeway. The scratch of tears arose in Alexandra's throat. "How *could* this have happened, we haven't been an hour!"

"When you're having fun . . ." he murmured.

"It wasn't *that* much fun! I can't get back!"

"Listen," Van Horne said close to her ear, and lightly closed his fingers on her upper arm, so she just felt his touch through the cloth. "Come on back and phone your kids and we'll have Fidel whip up a light supper. He does a terrific chili."

"It's not the *kids*, it's the *dog*," she cried. "Coal will be frantic. How deep is it?"

"I don't know. A foot, maybe two toward the middle. I could try to splash through with the car but get stuck out there it's bye-bye to a lot of fine old German machinery. Get saltwater in your brakes and differential, a car never drives the same. Like having your cherry popped."

"I'll wade," Alexandra said, and shook her arm free of his fingers, but not before, as if he had read her mind, he gave her a sharp quick pinch.

"Your pants'll get soaked," he said. "That water's brutal this time of year."

"I'll take my slacks off," she said, leaning on him to pull off her sneakers and socks. The spot where he had pinched her burned but she refused to acknowledge this presumptuous injury. After he had seemed so boyish and befuddled, spilling his tea and confiding his love of art. He was in truth a monster. Gravel prodded her bare feet. If she was going to do this she mustn't hesitate. "Here goes," she said. "Don't look."

She undid the side zipper of her slacks and pushed down at the waistband and her thighs joined the egret for brightness in this scene of rust and gray. Afraid she might topple on the unsteady stones, she bent over and pushed the shiny green serge past her pink ankles and blue-veined feet, and stepped out. Startled air lapped her naked legs. She made a bundle of sneakers and slacks and walked away from Van Horne down the causeway. Not looking back, she felt his eyes on her, her heavy thighs, their vulnerable ripple and jiggle. No doubt he had been watching with his hot tired eyes when she bent over. Alexandra had forgotten what underpants she had put on this morning and was relieved, glancing down, to discover them a plain beige, not ridiculously flowered or indecently cut like most you had to buy in the stores these days, designed for slim young hippies or groupies, half your ass hanging out behind and the crotch narrow as a rope. The air, endlessly tall, was cool on her skin. She enjoyed her own nakedness usually, especially in the open, taking a sunbath after lunch in her back yard on a blanket those first warm days of April and May before the bugs come. And under the full moon, gathering herbs skyclad.

So little used these years since the Lenoxes left, the causeway had grown grassy; barefoot she trod the center mane like the top of a soft broad wall. Color had drained from its wands of *Spartina patens* and the stretches of marsh on either side had turned sere. Where water first overcrept the surface of the road the matted grass gently swung in the transparent inches. The tide, infiltrating, made chuckling, hissing noises. Behind her, Darryl Van Horne was shouting something, encouragement or warning or apology, but Alexandra was too intent on the shock of her toes' first immersion to hear. How serious, how stark, the cold of this water was! Another element, where her blood was an alien. Brown pebbles stared up at her refracted and meaninglessly vivid, like the letters of an alphabet one doesn't know. The marsh grass had become seaweed, indolent and adrift, streaming leftwards with the rising water. Her own feet looked small, refracted like the pebbles. She must wade through quickly, while still numb. The tide covered her ankles now, and the distance to dry road was great, farther than she could have thrown a pebble. A dozen more shocking strides, and the water was up to her knees, and she could feel the sideways suck of its mindless flow. The coldest thing about this pull was that it would be here whether she was or not. It had been here before she was born and would be here when she was dead. She did not think it could knock her down, but she felt herself leaning against its force. And her ankles had begun to cry out, the numbness eaten through, the ache unendurable except that it must be endured.

Alexandra could no longer see her own feet, and the nodding tips of marsh grass no longer kept her company. She began to try to run, splashing; the splashing drowned out the sound of her host still shouting gibberish at her back. The intensity of her gaze enlarged the Subaru. She could see Coal's hopeful silhouette in the driver's seat, his ears lifted as high as they would go as he sensed rescue approaching. The icy pull came high on her thighs and her underpants were getting splashed. Foolish, so foolish, so vain and falsely girlish, she deserved this for leaving her only friend, her true and uncomplicated friend. Dogs perch on the edge of understanding, their bright eyes polished by the yearning to comprehend; an hour no worse than a minute to them, they live in a world without time, without accusation, without acceptance because there was no foresight. The water with its deathgrip rose to her crotch; a noise was forced from her throat. She was close enough to alarm the egret, who with a halt uncertain motion, like that of an old man tentatively reaching to brace himself on the arms of his chair, beat the air with the inverted W of his wings and rose, dragging his black stick feet behind him. Him? Her? Turning her own head with its bedraggled hair, Alexandra did see in the opposite direction, toward the ashen sand-hills of the beach, another white hole in the day's gray, another great egret, this one's mate though acres separated them under this dirty striped sky.

At the first bird's lift-off, the murderous clamps of the ocean had loosened a little on her thighs, sliding down as she waded on upwards, breathless, weeping with the shock and comedy of it, to the dry stretch of causeway that led to her car. Where the tide had been deepest there had been a kind of exultation, and now this ebbed. Alexandra shivered like a dog and laughed at her own folly, in seeking love, in getting stranded. The spirit needs folly as the body needs food; she felt healthier for this. Visions of herself as drowned, tinted greenish and locked stiff in the twist of last agony like those two embracing women in that amazing painting *Undertow* by Winslow Homer, had not come true. Drying, her feet hurt as if stung by a hundred wasps.

Manners demanded that she turn and wave in derisive flirtatious triumph toward Van Horne. He, a little black Y between the brick uprights of his crumbling gate, waved back with both arms held straight out. He applauded, beating his hands together to make a noise that arrived across the intervening plane of water a fraction of a second delayed. He shouted something of which she only heard the words "You *can* fly!" She dried her beaded, goosebumped legs with the red bandanna and pulled herself into her slacks while Coal woofed and pounded his tail on the vinyl within the Subaru. His happiness was infectious. She smiled to herself, wondering whom she should call first to tell about this, Sukie or Jane. At last she too had been initiated. Where he had pinched, her upper arm still burned.

The little trees, the sapling sugar maples and the baby red oaks squatting close to the ground, were the first to turn, as if green were a feat of strength, and the smallest weaken first. Early in October the Virginia creeper had suddenly drenched in alizarin crimson the tumbled boulder wall at the back of her property, where the bog began; the drooping parallel daggers of the sumac then showed a red suffused with orange. Like the slow sound of a great gong, yellow overspread the woods, from the tan of beech and ash to the hickory's spotty gold and the flat butter color of the mitten-shaped leaves of the sassafras, mittens that can have a thumb or two or none. Alexandra had often noticed how adjacent trees of the same species, sprung from two seeds spinning down together the same windy day, yet have leaves notched in different rhythms, and one turns as if bleached, from dull to duller, while the other looks as if each leaf were hand-painted by a Fauvist in clashing patches of red and green. The ferns underfoot in fading declared an extravagant variety of forms. Each cried out, *I am, I was.* There was thus in fall a rebirth of identity out of summer's mob of verdure. The breadth of the event, from the beach plums and bayberries along Block Island Sound to the sycamores and horse-chestnut trees lining the venerable streets (Benefit, Benevolent) on Providence's College Hill, answered to something diffuse and gentle within Alexandra, her sense of merge, her passive ability to contemplate a tree and feel herself a rigid trunk with many arms running to their tips with sap, to become the oblong cloud oddly alone in the sky or the toad hopping from the mower's path into deeper damper grass—

a wobbly bubble on leathery long legs, a spark of fear behind a warty broad forehead. She was that toad, and as well the cruel battered black blades attached to the motor's poisonous explosions. The panoramic ebb of chlorophyll from the swamps and hills of the Ocean State lifted Alexandra up like smoke, like the eye above a map. Even the exotic imports of the Newport rich—the English walnut, the Chinese smoke tree, the *Acer japonicum*—were swept into this mass movement of surrender. A natural principle was being demonstrated, that of divestment. We must lighten ourselves to survive. We must not cling. Safety lies in lessening, in becoming random and thin enough for the new to enter. Only folly dares those leaps that give life. This dark man on his island was possibility. He was the new, the magnetic, and she relived their stilted teatime together moment by moment, as a geologist lovingly pulverizes a rock.

Some shapely young maples with the sun behind them became blazing torches, a skeleton of shadow within an incandescent halo. The gray of naked branches more and more tinged the woods beside the roads. The sullen conical evergreens lorded where other substance had dissolved. October did its work of undoing day by day and came to its last day still fair, fair enough for outdoor tennis.

Jane Smart in her pristine whites tossed up the tennis ball. It became in midair a bat, its wings circled in small circumference at first and, next instant, snapped open like an umbrella as the creature flicked away with its pink blind face. Jane shrieked, dropped her racket, and called across the net, "That was not funny." The other witches laughed, and Van Horne, who was their fourth, belatedly, halfheartedly enjoyed the joke. He had powerful, educated strokes but did seem to have trouble seeing the ball, in the slant late-afternoon sun that beamed in rays through the sheltering stand of larches here at the back end of his island; the larches were dropping their needles and these had to be swept from the court. Jane's own eyes were excellent, preternaturally sharp. Bats' faces looked to her like flattened miniature versions of children pressing their noses against a candy-store window, and Van Horne, who played incongruously dressed in basketball sneakers and a Malcolm X T-shirt and the trousers of an old dark suit, had something of this same childish greed on his bewildered, glassy-eyed face. He coveted their wombs, was Jane's belief. She prepared to toss and serve again, but even as she weighed the ball in her hand it took on a liquid heft and a squirming wartiness. Another transformation had been wrought. With a theatrical sigh of patience, she set the toad down on the blood-red composition surface over by the bright green fence and watched it wriggle through. Van Horne's feeble-minded and wrynecked collie, Needlenose, raced around the outside of the fence to inspect; but he lost the toad in the tumble of earth and blasted rocks the bulldozers had left here.

"Once more and I quit," Jane called across the net. She and Alexandra had been pitted against Sukie and their host. "The three of you can play Canadian doubles," she threatened. With the bespectacled gesturing face on Van Horne's T-shirt it seemed there were five of them present anyway. The next tennis ball in her hand went through some rapid textural changes, first slimy like a gizzard then prickly like a sea urchin, but she resolutely refused to look at it, to cede it that reality, and when it appeared against the blue sky above her head it was a fuzzy yellow Wilson, which, following instruction books she had read, she imagined as a clockface to be struck at two o'clock. She brought the strings smartly through this phantom and felt from the surge of follow-through that the serve would be good. The ball kicked toward Sukie's throat and she awkwardly defended her breasts with the racket held in the backhand position. As if the strings had become noodles, the ball plopped at her feet and rolled to the sideline.

"Super," Alexandra muttered to Jane. Jane knew her partner loved, in different erotic keys, both their opponents, and their partnering, which Sukie had arranged at the outset of the match with a suspect twirl of her racket, must give Alexandra some jealous pain. The other two were a mesmerizing team, Sukie with her coppery hair tied in a bouncing ponytail and her slender freckled limbs swinging from a little peach tennis dress, and Van Horne with his machinelike swiftness, animated as when playing the piano by a kind of demon. His effectiveness was only limited by moments of dim-sighted uncoördination in which he missed the ball entirely. Also, his demon tended to play at a constant *forte* that sent some of his shots, when a subtle chop into a vacant space would have won the point, skimming out just past the base line.

As Jane prepared to serve to him, Sukie called gaily, "Foot fault!" Jane looked down to see not her sneaker toe across the line but the line itself, though a painted one, across the front of her sneaker and holding it fast like a bear trap. She shook off the illusion and served to Darryl Van Horne, who returned the ball with a sharp forehand that Alexandra alertly poached, directing the ball at Sukie's feet; Sukie managed to scoop it on the short hop into a lob that Jane, having come to the net at her partner's adroit and aggressive poach, just reached in time to turn it into another lob, which Van Horne, eyes flashing fire, set himself to smash with a grunting overhead and which he would have smashed, had not a magical small sparkling storm, what they call in many parts of the world a dust devil, arisen and caused him to snap a sheltering right hand to his brow with a curse. He was left-handed and wore contact lenses. The ball remained suspended at the level of his waist while he blinked away the pain; then he stroked it with a forehand so firm the orb changed color from optical yellow to a chameleon green that Jane could hardly see against the background of green court and green fence. She swung where she sensed the ball to be and the contact felt sweet; Sukie had to scramble to make a weak return, which Alexandra volleyed down into the opponents' forecourt so vehemently it bounced impossibly high, higher than the setting sun. But Van Horne skittered back quicker than a crab underwater and tossed his metal racket toward the stratosphere, slowly twirling, silvery. The disembodied racket returned the ball without power but within the base lines, and the point continued, the players interlacing, round and round, now clockwise, now widdershins, the music of it all enthralling, Jane Smart felt: the counterpoint of their four bodies, eight eyes, and sixteen extended limbs scored upon the now nearly horizontal bars of sunset red filtered through the larches, whose falling needles pattered like distant applause. When the rally and with it the match was at last over, Sukie complained, "My racket kept feeling dead."

"You should use catgut instead of nylon," Alexandra suggested benignly, her side having won.

"It felt absolutely leaden; I kept having shooting pains in my forearm trying to lift it. Which one of you hussies was doing that? Absolutely no fair."

Van Horne also pleaded in defeat. "Damn contact lenses," he said. "Get even a speck of dust behind them it's like a fucking razor blade."

"It was lovely tennis," Jane pronounced with finality. Often she was cast, it seemed to her, in this role of peacemaking parent, of maiden aunt devoid of passion, when in fact she was seething.

The end of Daylight Savings Time had been declared and darkness came swiftly as they filed up the path to the many lit windows of the house. Inside, the three women sat in a row on the curved sofa in Van Horne's long, art-filled, yet somehow barren living room, drinking the potions he brought them. Their host was a master of exotic drinks, drinks alchemically concocted of tequila and grenadine and crème de cassis and Triple Sec and Seltzer water and cranberry juice and apple brandy and additives even more arcane, all kept in a tall seventeenth-century Dutch cabinet topped by two startled angel's heads, their faces split, right through the blank eyeballs, by the aging of the wood. The sea seen through his Palladian windows was turning the color of wine, of dogwood leaves before they fall. Between the Ionic pillars of his fireplace, beneath the ponderous mantel, stretched a ceramic frieze of fauns and nymphs, naked figures white on blue. Fidel brought hors d'oeuvres, pastes and dips of crushed sea creatures, *empanadillas, calamares en su tinta* that were consumed with squeals of disgust, with fingers that turned the same muddy sepia as the blood of these succulent baby squids. Now and then one of the witches would exclaim that she *must* do something about the children, either go home to make their suppers or at least phone the house to put the oldest daughter officially in charge. Tonight was already deranged: it was the night of trick-or-treat, and some of the children would be at parties and others out begging on the shadowy crooked streets of downtown Eastwick. Toddling in rustling groups along the fences and hedges would be little pirates and Cinderellas wearing masks with fixed grimaces and live moist eyes darting in papery eyeholes; there would be ghosts in pillow cases carrying shopping bags rattling with M & M's and Hershey Kisses. Doorbells would be constantly ringing. A few days ago Alexandra had gone shopping with her baby, little Linda, in the Woolworth's at the mall, the lights of this trashy place brave against the darkness outside, the elderly overweight clerks weary amid their child-tempting gimcracks at the end of the day, and for a moment Alexandra had felt the old magic, seeing through this nine-year-old child's wide gaze the symbolic majesty of the cut-rate spectres, the authenticity of the packaged goblin—mask, costume, and plastic trick-or-treat sack all for $3.98. America teaches its children that every passion can be transmuted into an occasion to buy. Alexandra in a moment of empathy became her own child wandering aisles whose purchasable wonders were at eye level and scented each with its own potent essence of ink or rubber or sugary dough. But such motherly moments came to her ever more rarely as she took possession of her own self, a demigoddess greater and sterner than any of the uses others might have for her. Sukie next to her on the sofa arched her back inward, stretching in her scant peach dress so that her white frilled panties showed, and said with a yawn, "I really should go home. The poor darlings. That house right in the middle of town, it must be besieged."

Van Horne was sitting opposite her in his corduroy armchair; he had been perspiring glowingly and had put on an Irish knit sweater, of natural wool still smelling oilily of sheep, over the stencilled image of gesticulating, buck-toothed Malcolm X. "Don't go, my friend," he said. "Stay and have a bath. That's what I'm going to do. I stink."

"Bath?" Sukie said. "I can take one at home."

"Not in an eight-foot teak hot tub you can't," the man said, twisting his big head with such violent roguishness that bushy Thumbkin, alarmed, jumped off his lap. "While we're all having a good long soak Fidel can cook up some paella or tamales or something."

"Tamale and tamale and tamale," Jane Smart said compulsively. She was sitting on the end of the sofa, beyond Sukie, and her profile had an angry precision, Alexandra thought. The smallest of them physically, she got the most drunk, trying to keep up. Jane sensed she was being thought about; her hot eyes locked onto Alexandra's. "What about you, Lexa? What's your thought?"

"Well," was the drifting answer, "I *do* feel dirty, and I ache. Three sets is too much for this old lady."

"You'll feel like a million after this experience," Van Horne assured her. "Tell you what," he said to Sukie. "Run on home, check on your brats, and come back here soon as you can."

"Swing by my house and check on mine too, could you sweetie?" in chimed Jane Smart.

"Well I'll see," Sukie said, stretching again. Her long freckled legs displayed at their tips dainty sneakerless feet in little tasselled Peds like lucky rabbit's-feet. "I may not be back at all. Clyde was hoping I could do a little Halloween color piece—just go downtown, interview a couple trick-or-treaters on Oak Street, ask at the police station if there's been any destruction of property, maybe get some of the old-timers hanging around Nemo's to talking about the bad old days when they used to soap windows and put buggies on the roof and things."

Van Horne exploded. "Why're you always mothering that sad-ass Clyde Gabriel? He scares me. The guy is sick."

"That's why," Sukie said, very quickly.

Alexandra perceived that Sukie and Ed Parsley were at last breaking up.

Van Horne picked up on it too. "Maybe I should invite him over here some time."

Sukie stood and pushed her hair back from her face haughtily. She said, "Don't do it on my account, I see him all day at work." There was no telling, from the way she snatched up her racket and flung her fawn sweater around her neck, whether she would return or not. They all heard her car, a pale gray Corvair convertible with front-wheel drive and her ex-husband's vanity plate ROUGE still on the back (the engine also, oddly, was in the rear), start up and spin out and crackle away down the drive. The tide was low tonight, low under a new moon, so low ancient anchors and rotten dory ribs jutted into starlight where saltwater covered them for all but a few hours of each month.

Sukie's departure left the three remaining more comfortable with themselves, at ease in their relatively imperfect skins. Still in their sweaty tennis clothes, their fingers dyed by squid ink, their throats and stomachs invigorated by the peppery sauces of Fidel's tamales and enchiladas, they walked with fresh drinks into the music room, where the two musicians showed Alexandra how far they had proceeded with the Brahms E Minor. How the man's ten fingers did thunder on the help-less keys! As if he were playing with hands more than human, stronger, and wide as hay rakes, and never fumbling, folding trills and arpeggios into the rhythm, gobbling them up. Only his softer passages lacked something of expressiveness, as if there were no notch in his system low enough for the tender touch necessary. Dear stubby Jane, brows knitted, struggled to keep up, her face turning paler and paler as concentration drained it, the pain in her bowing arm evident, her other hand scuttling up and down, pressing the strings as if they were too hot to pause upon. It was Alexandra's motherly duty to ap-plaud when the tense and tumultuous performance was over.

"It's not my cello, of course," Jane explained, unsticking black hair from her brow.

"Just an old Strad I had lying around," Van Horne joked and then, seeing that Alexandra would believe him—for there was coming to be in her lovelorn state nothing she did not believe within his powers and possessions—amended this to: "Actually, it's a Ceruti. He was Cremona too, but later. Still, an O.K. old fiddlemaker. Ask the man who owns one." Suddenly he shouted as loudly as he had made the harp of the piano resound, so that the thin black windowpanes in their seats of cracked putty vibrated in sympathy. "Fidel!" he called into the emptiness of the vast house. "Margaritas! ¡Tres! Bring them into the bath! ¡Tráigalas al baño! ¡Rápidamente!!"

So the moment of divestment was at hand. To embolden Jane, Alexandra rose and followed Van Horne at once; but per-haps Jane needed no emboldening after her private musical sessions in this house. It was the ambiguous essence of Alexan-dra's relation with Jane and Sukie that she was the leader, the profoundest witch of the three, and yet also the slowest, a bit in the dark, a bit—yes—innocent. The other two were younger and therefore slightly more modern and less beholden to na-ture with its massive patience, its infinite care and imperious cruelty, its ancient implication of a slow-grinding, anthropo-centric order.

The procession of three passed through the long room of dusty modern art and then a small chamber hastily crammed with stacked lawn furniture and unopened cardboard boxes. New double doors, the inner side padded with black vinyl quilting, sealed off the heat and damp of the rooms Van Horne had added where the old copper-roofed conservatory used to be. The bathing space was floored in Tennessee slate and lit by overhead lights sunk in the ceiling, itself a dark pegboardy substance. "Rheostatted," Van Horne explained in his hollow, rasping voice. He twisted a luminous knob inside the double doors so these upside-down ribbed cups brimmed into a brightness photographs could have been taken by and then ebbed back to the dimness of a developing room. These lights were sunk above not in rows but scattered at random like stars. He left them at dim, in deference perhaps to their puckers and blemishes and the telltale false teats that mark a witch. Beyond this darkness, behind a wall of plate glass, vegetation was underlit green by buried bulbs and lit from above by violet growing lamps that fed spiky, exotic shapes—plants from afar, selected and harbored for their poisons. A row of dressing cubicles and two shower stalls, all black like the boxes in a Nevelson sculpture, occupied another wall of the space, which was dominated as by a massive musky sleeping animal by the pool itself, a circle of water with burnished teak rim, an element opposite from that icy tide Alexandra had braved some weeks ago: this water was so warm the very air in here started sweat on her face. A small squat console with burning red eyes at the tub's near edge contained, she supposed, the controls.

"Take a shower first if you feel so dirty," Van Horne told her, but himself made no move in that direction. Instead he went to a cabinet on another wall, a wall like a Mondrian but devoid of color, cut up in doors and panels that must all conceal a secret, and took out a white box, not a box but a long white skull, perhaps a goat's or a deer's, with a hinged silver lid. Out of this he produced some shredded something and a packet of old-fashioned cigarette papers at which he began clumsily fiddling like a bear worrying a fragment of beehive.

Alexandra's eyes were adjusting to the gloom. She went into a cubicle and slipped out of her gritty clothes and, wrapping herself in a purple towel she found folded there, ducked into the shower. Tennis sweat, guilt about the children, a misplaced bridal timidity—all sluiced from her. She held her face up into the spray as if to wash it away, that face given to you at birth like a fingerprint or Social Security number. Her head felt luxuriously heavier as her hair got wet. Her heart felt light like a small motor skimming on an aluminum track toward its inevitable connection with her rough strange host. Drying herself, she noticed that the monogram stitched into the nap of the towel seemed to be an *M*, but perhaps it was *V* and *H* merged. She stepped back into the shadowy room with the towel wrapped around her. The slate presented a fine reptilian roughness to the soles of her feet. The caustic pungence of marijuana scraped her nose like a friendly fur. Van Horne and Jane Smart, shoulders gleaming, were already in the tub, sharing the joint. Alexandra walked to the tub edge, saw the water was about four feet deep, let her towel drop, and slipped in. Hot. Scalding. In the old days, before burning her completely at the stake they would pull pieces of flesh from a witch's flesh with red-hot tongs; this was a window into that, that furnace of suffering.

"Too hot?" Van Horne asked, his voice even hollower, more mock-manly, amid these sequestered, steamy acoustics.

"I'll get used," she said grimly, seeing that Jane had. Jane looked furious that Alexandra was here at all, making waves, gently though she had tried to lower herself into the agonizing water. Alexandra felt her breasts tug upwards, buoyant. She had slipped in up to her neck and so had no dry hand to accept the joint; Van Horne placed it between her lips. She drew deep and held in the smoke. Her submerged trachea burned. The water's temperature was becoming one with her skin and, looking down, she saw how they had all been dwindled, Jane's body distorted with wedge-shaped wavering legs and Van Horne's penis floating like a pale torpedo, uncircumcised and curiously smooth, like one of those vanilla plastic vibrators that have appeared in city drugstore display windows now that the revolution is on and the sky is the limit.

Alexandra reached up and behind her to the towel she had dropped and dried her hands and wrists enough to accept in her turn the little reefer, fragile as a chrysalis, as it was passed among the three of them. She had had pot before; her older boy, Ben, in fact grew it in their back yard, in a patch past the tomato plants, which it superficially resembled. But it had never been part of their Thursdays: alcohol, calorie-rich goodies, and gossip had been transporting enough. After several deep tokes amid this steam Alexandra imagined she felt herself changing, growing weightless in the water and in the tub of her skull. As when a sock comes through the wash turned inside out and needs to be briskly reached into and pulled, so the universe; she had been looking at it as at the back side of a tapestry. This dark room with its just barely discernible seams and wires was the other side of the tapestry, the consoling reverse to nature's sunny fierce weave. She felt clean of worry. Jane's face still expressed worry, but her mannish brows and that smudge of insistence in her voice no longer intimidated Alexandra, seeing their source in the thick black pubic bush which beneath the water seemed to sway back and forth almost like a penis.

"God," Darryl Van Horne announced aloud, "I'd love to be a woman."

"For heaven's sake, why?" Jane sensibly asked.

"Think what a female body can do—make a baby and then make milk to feed it."

"Well think of your own body," Jane said, "the way it can turn food into shit."

"*Jane*," Alexandra scolded, shocked by the analogy, which seemed despairing, though shit too was a kind of miracle if you thought about it. To Van Horne she confirmed, "It *is* wonderful. At the moment of birth there's nothing left of your ego, you're just a channel for this effort that comes from beyond."

"Must be," he said, dragging, "a fantastic high."

"You're so drugged you don't notice," the other woman said, sourly.

"Jane, that isn't true. It wasn't true for me. Ozzie and I did the whole natural-childbirth thing, with him in the room giving me ice chips to suck, I got so dehydrated, and helping me breathe. With the last two babies we didn't even have a doctor, we had a monitrice."

"Do you know," Van Horne stated, going into that pedantic, ponderous squint that Lexa instinctively loved, as a glimpse of the shy clumsy boy he must have been, "the whole witchcraft scare was an attempt—successful, as it turned out—on the part of the newly arising male-dominated medical profession, beginning in the fourteenth century, to get the childbirth business out of the hands of midwives. That's what a lot of the women burned were—midwives. They had the ergot, and atropine, and probably a lot of right instincts even without germ theory. When the male doctors took over they worked blind, with a sheet around their necks, and brought all the diseases from the rest of their practice with them. The poor cunts died in droves."

"Typical," said Jane abrasively. She had evidently decided that being nasty would keep her in the forefront of Van Horne's attention. "If there's one thing that infuriates me more than male chauvs," she told him now, "it's creeps who take up feminism just to work their way into women's underpants."

But her voice, it seemed to Alexandra, was slowing, softening, as the water worked upon them from without and the cannabis from within. "But baby you're not even wearing underpants," Alexandra pointed out. It seemed an illumination of some merit. The room was growing brighter, with nobody touching a dial.

"I'm not kidding," Van Horne pursued, that myopic little boy-scholar still in him, worming to understand. His face was set on the water's surface as on a platter; his hair was long as John the Baptist's and merged with the curls licked flat on his shoulders. "It comes from the heart, can't you girls tell? I love women. My mother was a brick, smart and pretty, Christ. I used to watch her slave around the house all day and around six-thirty in wanders this little guy in a business suit and I think to myself, 'What's this wimp butting in for?' My old dad, the hard-working wimp. Tell me honest, how does it feel when the milk flows?"

"How does it feel," Jane asked irritably, "when you come?"

"Hey come on, let's not get ugly."

Alexandra perceived genuine alarm on the man's heavy, seamed face; for some reason coming was a tender area in his mind.

"I don't see what's ugly," Jane was saying. "You want to talk physiology, I'm just offering a physiological sensation that women can't have. I mean, we don't come that way. Quite. Don't you love that word they have for the clitoris, 'homologous'?"

Alexandra offered, apropos of giving milk, "It feels like when you have to go pee and can't and then suddenly you can."

"That's what I love about women," Van Horne said. "Their homely similes. There's no such word as 'ugly' in your vocabulary. Men, Christ, they're so squeamish about everything —blood, spiders, blow jobs. You know, in a lot of species the bitch or sow or whatever eats the afterbirth?"

"I don't think you realize," Jane said, striving for a dry tone, "what a chauvinistic thing that is to say." But her dryness took a strange turn as she stood on tiptoe in the tub, so her breasts lifted silvery from the water; one was a little higher and smaller than the other. She held them in her two hands and explained to a point in space between the man and the other woman, as if to the invisible witness of her life, a witness we all carry with us and seldom address aloud, "I always wanted my breasts to be bigger. Like Lexa's. She has lovely big boobs. Show him, sweet."

"Jane, *please*. You're making me blush. I don't think it's the size that matters so much to men, it's the, it's the *tilt*, and the way they go with the whole body. And what you yourself think of them. If you're pleased, others will be. Am I right or wrong?" she asked Van Horne.

But he would not be held to the role of male spokesman. He too stood up out of the water and cupped his hairy-backed palms over his vestigial male nipples, tiny warts surrounded by wet black snakes. "Think of e*volv*ing all that," he beseeched. "The machinery, all that plumbing, of the body of one sex to make food, food more exactly suited to the baby than any formula you can cook up in a lab. Think of evolving sexual pleasure. Do squids have it? What about plankton? With them, they don't have to think, but we, we think. To keep us in the game, what a bait they had to rig up! There's more built into it than one of these crazy reconnaissance planes that costs the taxpayers a zillion before it gets shot down. Suppose they left it out, nobody would fuck anybody and the species would stop dead with everybody admiring sunsets and the Pythagorean theorem."

Alexandra liked the way his mind worked; she had no trouble following it. "I adore this room," she announced dreamily. "At first I didn't think I would. All the black, except for the nice copper tubing Joe put in. Joe can be sweet, when he takes off his hat."

"Who's Joe?" Van Horne asked.

"This conversation," Jane said, so the *s*'s in her words slightly burned, "seems to have descended to a rather primitive level."

"I could put on some music," Van Horne said, touchingly anxious that they not be bored. "We're all wired up for four-track stereo."

"*Shh*," Jane said. "I heard a car on the driveway."

"Trick-or-treaters," Van Horne suggested. "Fidel'll give 'em some razor-blade apples we've been cooking up."

"Maybe Sukie's come back," Alexandra said. "I love you, Jane; you have such good ears."

"Aren't they nice?" the other woman agreed. "I *do* have pretty ears, even my father always said. Look." She held her hair back from one and then, turning her head, the other. "The only trouble is, one's a little higher than the other, so any glasses I wear sit cockeyed on my nose."

"They're rather square," Alexandra said.

Taking it as a compliment, Jane added, "And nice and flat to the skull. Sukie's are cupped out like a monkey's, have you ever noticed?"

"Often."

"Her eyes are too close together, too, and her overbite should have been corrected when she was young. And her nose, just a little blob really. I honestly don't know how she makes it all work as well as she does."

"I don't think Sukie will be coming back," Van Horne said. "She's too tied up with these neurotic creeps that run this town."

"She is and she isn't," someone said; Alexandra thought it had to be Jane but it sounded like her own voice.

"Isn't this cozy and nice?" she said, to test her own voice. It sounded deep, a man's voice.

"Our home away from home," Jane said, sarcastically, Alexandra supposed. It was really by no means easy to attain etheric harmony with Jane.

The sound Jane had heard was not Sukie, it was Fidel, bringing margaritas, on the enormous engraved silver tray Sukie had once mentioned to Alexandra admiringly, each broad wineglass on its thin stem rimmed with chunky sea-salt. It looked odd to Alexandra, so at home in her nudity had she already become, that Fidel was not naked too, but wearing a pajamalike uniform the color of army chinos.

"Dig this, ladies," Van Horne called, boyish in his boasting and also in the look of his white behind, for he had gotten out of the water and was fiddling with some dials at the far black wall. There was a greased rumble and, overhead, the ceiling, not perforated here but of dull corrugated metal as in a tool shed, rolled back to disclose the inky sky and its thin splash of stars. Alexandra recognized the sticky web of the Pleiades and giant red Aldebaran. These preposterously far bodies and the unseasonably warm but still sharp autumn air and the Nevelson intricacies of the black walls and the surreal Arp shapes of her own bulbous body all fitted around her sensory self exactly, as tangible as the steaming bath and the chilled glass stem pinched between her fingertips, so that she was as it were interlocked with a multitude of ethereal bodies. These stars condensed as tears and cupped her warm eyes. Idly she turned the stem in her hand to the stem of a fat yellow rose and inhaled its aroma. It smelled of lime juice. Her lips came away loaded with salt crystals fat as dewdrops. A thorn in the stem had pricked one finger and she watched a single drop of blood well up at the center of the whorl of a fingerprint. Darryl Van Horne was bending over to fuss at some more of his controls and his white bottom glowingly seemed the one part of him that was not hairy or repellently sheathed by a kind of exoskeleton but authentically his self, as we take in most people the head to be their true self. She wanted to kiss it, his glossy innocent unseeing ass. Jane passed her something burning which she obediently put to her lips. The burning inside Alexandra's trachea mingled with the hot angry look of Jane's stare as under the water her friend's hand fishlike nibbled and slid across her belly, around those buoyant breasts she had said she coveted.

"Hey don't leave me out," Van Horne begged, and splashed back into the water, shattering the moment, for Jane's little hand, with its callused fingertips like fish teeth, floated away.

They resumed their conversing, but the words drifted free of meaning, the talk was like touching, and time fell in lazy loops through the holes in Alexandra's caressed consciousness until Sukie did come back, bringing time back with her.

In she hurried with autumn caught in the suede skirt with its frontal ties of rawhide and her tweed jacket nipped at the waist and double-pleated at the back like a huntswoman's, her peach tennis dress left at home in a hamper. "Your kids are fine," she informed Jane Smart, and did not seem nonplussed to find them all in the tub, as if she knew this room already, with its slates, its bright serpents of copper, the jagged piece of illumined green jungle beyond, and the ceiling with its cold rectangle of sky and stars. With her wonderful matter-of-fact quickness, first setting down a leather pocketbook big as a saddlebag on a chair Alexandra had not noticed before— there was furniture in the room, chairs and mattresses, black so they blended in—Sukie undressed, first slipping off her low-heeled square-toed shoes, and then removing the hunting jacket, and then pushing the untied suede skirt down over her hips, and then unbuttoning the silk blouse of palest beige, the tint of an engraved invitation, and pushing down her half-slip, the pink-brown of a tea rose, and her white panties with it, and lastly uncoupling her bra and leaning forward with extended arms so the two emptied cups fell down her arms and into her hands, lightly; her exposed breasts swayed outward with this motion. Sukie's breasts were small enough to keep firm in air, rounded cones whose tips had been dipped in a deeper pink without there being any aggressive jut of button-like nipple. Her body seemed a flame, a flame of soft white fire to Alexandra, who watched as Sukie calmly stooped to pick her underthings up from the floor and drop them onto the chair that was like a shadow materialized and then matter-of-factly rummaged in her big loose-flapped pocketbook for some pins to put up her hair of that pale yet plangent color called red but that lies between apricot and the blush at the heart of yew wood. Her hair was this color wherever it was, and her pinning gesture bared the two tufts, double in shape like two moths alighted sideways, in her armpits. This was progressive of her; Alexandra and Jane had not yet broken with the patriarchal command to shave laid upon them when they were young and learning to be women. In the Biblical desert women had been made to scrape their armpits with flint; female hair challenged men, and Sukie as the youngest of the witches felt least obliged to trim and temper her natural flourishing. Her slim body, freckled the length of her forearms and shins, was yet ample enough for her outline to undulate as she walked toward them, into the sallow floor lights that guarded the rim of the tub, out of the black background of this place, its artificial dark monotone like that of a recording studio; the edge of the apparition of her naked beauty undulated as when in a movie a series of stills are successively imposed upon the viewer to give an effect of fluttering motion, disturbing and spectral, in silence. Then Sukie was close to them and restored to three dimensions, her so lovely long bare side marred endearingly by a pink wart and a livid bruise (Ed Parsley in a fit of radical guilt?) and not only her limbs freckled but her forehead too, and a band across her nose, and even, a distinct constellation, on the flat of her chin, a little triangular chin crinkled in determination as she sat on the tub edge and, taking a breath, with arched back and tensed buttocks eased herself into the smoking, healing water. "Holy Mo," Sukie said.

"You'll get used," Alexandra reassured her. "It's heavenly once you make your mind up."

"You kids think this is hot?" Darryl Van Horne bragged anxiously. "I set the thermostat twenty degrees higher when it's just me. For a hangover it's great. All those poisons, they bake right out."

"What were they doing?" Jane Smart asked. Her head and throat looked shrivelled, Alexandra's eyes having dwelt so long and fondly on Sukie.

"Oh," Sukie answered her, "the usual. Watching old movies on Channel Fifty-six and getting themselves sick on the candy they'd begged."

"You didn't by any chance swing by my house?" Alexandra asked, feeling shy, Sukie was so lovely and now beside her in the water; waves she made laved Alexandra's skin.

"Baby, Marcy is seventeen," Sukie said. "She's a big girl. She can cope. Wake up." And she touched Alexandra on the shoulder, a playful push. Reaching the little distance to give the push lifted one of Sukie's rose-tipped breasts out of the water; Alexandra wanted to suck it, even more than she had wanted to kiss Van Horne's bottom. She suffered a prevision of the experience, her face laid sideways in the water, her hair streaming loose and drifting into her lips as they shaped their receptive O. Her left cheek felt hot, and Sukie's green glance showed she was reading Alexandra's mind. The auras of the three witches merged beneath the skylight, pink and violet and tawny, with Van Horne's stiff brown collapsible thing over his head like a clumsy wooden halo on a saint in an impoverished Mexican church.

The girl Sukie had spoken of, Marcy, had been born when Alexandra was only twenty-one, having dropped out of college at Oz's entreaties to be his wife, and she was reminded now of her four babies, how as they came one by one it was the female infants suckling that tugged at her insides more poignantly, the boys already a bit like men, that aggressive vacuum, the hurt of the sudden suction, the oblong blue skulls bulging and bullying above the clusters of frowning muscles where their masculine eyebrows would some day sprout. The girls were daintier, even those first days, such hopeful thirsty sweet clinging sugar-sacks destined to become beauties and slaves. Babies: their dear rubbery bowlegs as if they were riding tiny horses in their sleep, the lovable swaddled crotch the diaper makes, their flexible violet feet, their skin everywhere fine as the skin of a penis, their grave indigo stares and their curly mouths so forthrightly drooling. The way they ride your left hip, clinging lightly as vines to a wall to your side, the side where your heart is. The ammonia of their diapers. Alexandra began to cry, thinking of her lost babies, babies swallowed by the children they had become, babies sliced into bits and fed to the days, the years. Tears slid warm and then by contrast to her hot face cool down the sides of her nose, finding the wrinkles hinged at her nostril wings, salting the corners of her mouth and dribbling down her chin, making a runnel of the little cleft there. Amid all these thoughts Jane's hands had never left her; Jane intensified her caresses, massaging now the back of Alexandra's neck, then the *musculus trapezius* and on to the deltoids and the pectorals, oh, that did ease sorrow, Jane's strong hand, that pressure now above, now below the water, below even the

waist, the little red eyes of the thermal controls keeping poolside watch, the margarita and marijuana mixing their absolving
poisons in the sensitive hungry black realm beneath her skin,
her poor neglected children sacrificed so she could have her
powers, her silly powers, and only Jane understanding, Jane
and Sukie, Sukie lithe and young next to her, touching her,
being touched, her body woven not of aching muscle but of a
kind of osier, supple and gently speckled, the nape beneath her
pinned-up hair of a whiteness that never sees the sun, a piece
of pliant alabaster beneath the amber wisps. As Jane was doing
to Alexandra Alexandra did to Sukie, caressed her. Sukie's body
in her hands seemed silk, seemed heavy slick fruit, Alexandra
so dissolved in melancholy triumphant affectionate feelings
there was no telling the difference between caresses given and
caresses received; shoulders and arms and breasts emergent,
the three women drew closer to form, like graces in a print, a
knot, while their hairy swarthy host, out of the water, scrabbled through his black cabinets. Sukie in a strange practical
voice that Alexandra heard as if relayed from a great distance
into this recording studio was discussing with this Van Horne
man what music to put on his expensive and steam-resistant
stereo system. He was naked and his swinging gabbling pallid
genitals had the sweetness of a dog's tail curled tight above the
harmless button of its anus.

Our town of Eastwick was to gossip that winter—for here as
in Washington and Saigon there were leaks; Fidel made friends
with a woman in town, a waitress at Nemo's, a sly black woman
from Antigua called Rebecca—about the evil doings at the old
Lenox place, but what struck Alexandra this first night and ever
after was the amiable human awkwardness of it all, controlled
as it was by the awkwardness of their eager and subtly ill-made
host, who not only fed them and gave them shelter and music
and darkly suitable furniture but provided the blessing without
which courage of our contemporary sort fails and trickles away
into ditches others have dug, those old ministers and naysayers
and proponents of heroic constipation who sent lovely Anne
Hutchinson, a woman ministering to women, off into the wilderness to be scalped by redmen in their way as fanatic and
unforgiving as Puritan divines. Like all men Van Horne demanded the women call him king, but his system of taxation at

least dealt in assets—bodies, personal liveliness—they did have and not in spiritual goods laid up in some nonexistent Heaven. It was Van Horne's kindness to subsume their love for one another into a kind of love for himself. There was something a little abstract about his love for them and something therefore formal and merely courteous in the obeisances and favors they granted him—wearing the oddments of costume he provided, the catskin gloves and green leather garters, or binding him with the *cingulum*, the nine-foot cord of plaited red wool. He stood, often, as at that first night, above and beyond them, adjusting his elaborate and (his proud claims notwithstanding) moisture-sensitive equipment.

He pressed a button and the corrugated roof rumbled back across the section of night sky. He put on records—first Joplin, yelling and squawking herself hoarse on "Piece of My Heart" and "Get It While You Can" and "Summertime" and "Down on Me," the very voice of joyful defiant female despair, and then Tiny Tim, tiptoeing through the tulips with a thrilling androgynous warbling that Van Horne couldn't get enough of, returning the needle to the beginning grooves over and over, until the witches clamorously demanded Joplin again. On his acoustical system the music surrounded them, arising in all four corners of the room; they danced, the four clad in only their auras and hair, with shy and minimal motions, keeping within the music, often turning their backs, letting the titanic ghostly presences of the singers soak them through and through. When Joplin croaked "Summertime" at that broken tempo, remembering the words in impassioned spasms as if repeatedly getting up off the canvas in some internal drug-hazed prizefight, Sukie and Alexandra swayed in each other's arms without their feet moving, their fallen hair stringy and tangled with tears, their breasts touching, nuzzling, fumbling in pale pillow fight lubricated by drops of sweat worn on their chests like the broad bead necklaces of ancient Egypt. And when Joplin with that deceptively light-voiced opening drifted into the whirlpool of "Me and Bobby McGee," Van Horne, his empurpled penis rendered hideously erect by a service Jane had performed for him on her knees, pantomimed with his uncanny hands—encased it seemed in white rubber gloves with wigs of hair and wide at the tips like the digits of a tree toad or lemur

—in the dark above her bobbing head the tumultuous solo provided by the inspired pianist of the Full Tilt Boogie band.

On the black velour mattresses Van Horne had provided, the three women played with him together, using the parts of his body as a vocabulary with which to speak to one another; he showed supernatural control, and when he did come his semen, all agreed later, was marvellously cold. Dressing after midnight, in the first hour of November, Alexandra felt as if she were filling her clothes—she played tennis in slacks, to hide somewhat her heavy legs—with a weightless gas, her flesh had been so rarefied by its long immersion and assimilated poisons. Driving home in her Subaru, whose interior smelled of dog, she saw the full moon with its blotchy mournful face in the top of her tinted windshield and irrationally thought for a second that astronauts had landed and in an act of imperial atrocity had spray-painted that vast sere surface green.

II.

Maleficia

"I will not be other than I am; I find too much content in my condition; I am always caressed."

—*a young French witch, c. 1660*

"HE HAS?" Alexandra asked over the phone. At her kitchen windows the Puritan hues of November prevailed, the arbor a tangle of peeling vines, the birdfeeder hung up and filled now that the first frosts had shrivelled the berries of the woods and bog.

"That's what Sukie says," said Jane, her *s*'s burning. "She says she saw it long coming but didn't want to say anything to betray him. Not that telling just us would be betraying anybody, if you ask me."

"But how long has Ed known the girl?" A row of Alexandra's teacups, hung on brass hooks beneath a pantry shelf, swayed as if an invisible hand had caressed them in the manner of a harpist.

"Some months. Sukie thought he seemed different with her. He just wanted mostly to talk, to use her as a sounding board. She's glad: think of the venereal diseases she might have gotten. All these flower children have crabs at the least, you know."

The Reverend Ed Parsley had run off with a local teen-ager, was the long and short of it. "Have I ever seen this girl?" Alexandra asked.

"Oh certainly," Jane said. "She was always in that gang in front of the Superette after about eight at night, waiting for a drug pusher I suppose. A pale smudgy face wider than it was high, somehow, with dirty flaxen hair just hanging down any old how, and dressed like a little female lumberjack."

"No love beads?"

Jane answered seriously. "Well, no doubt she owned some,

to wear when she wanted to go to a debutante party. Can't you picture her? She was one of those picketing the town meeting last March and threw sheep's blood they got at the slaughterhouse all over the war memorial."

"I can't, honey, maybe because I don't want to. These kids in front of the Superette always frighten me, I just hustle out between them without looking to the right or the left."

"You shouldn't be frightened, they're not even seeing you. To them you're just part of the landscape, like a tree."

"Poor Ed. He did look so harassed lately. When I saw him at the concert, he even seemed to want to cling to *me*. I thought that was being disloyal to Sukie, so I shook him off."

"The girl isn't even from Eastwick, she was always hanging around here but she lived up in Coddington Junction, some perfectly awful broken home in a trailer there, living with her common-law stepfather because her mother was always on the road doing something in a carnival, they call it acrobatics."

Jane sounded so prim, you would think she was a virgin spinster if you hadn't seen her functioning with Darryl Van Horne. "Her name is Dawn Polanski," Jane was going on. "I don't know if her parents called her Dawn or she called herself that, people like that do give themselves names now, like Lotus Blossom and Heavenly Avatar or whatever."

Her toughened little hands had been incredibly busy, and when the cold semen had spurted out, it was Jane who had appropriated most of it. Other women's sexual styles are something you are left mostly to guess at and perhaps wisely, for it can be *too* fascinating. Alexandra tried to blink the pictures out of her mind and asked, "But what are they going to *do*?"

"I daresay they have no idea, after they go to some motel and screw till they're sick of it. Really, it *is* pathetic." It was Jane who had stroked her first, not Sukie. Picturing Sukie, the soft white flame her body had been, posing on the slates, opened a little hollow space in Alexandra's abdomen, near her left ovary. Her poor insides: she was sure one day she'd have an operation, and they'd open it all too late, just crawling with black cancer cells. Except they probably weren't black but a brighter red, and shiny, like cauliflower of a bloody sort. "Then I suppose," Jane was saying, "they'll head for some big city and try to join the Movement. I think Ed thinks it's like joining the army: you find a recruitment center and they give you a physical and if you pass they take you in."

"It seems so deluded, doesn't it? He's too old. As long as he stayed around here he seemed rather young and dashing, or at least *in*teresting, and he had his church, it gave him a forum of sorts. . . ."

"He hated being respectable," Jane broke in sharply. "He thought it was a sellout."

"Oh my, what a world," Alexandra sighed, watching a gray squirrel make his stop-and-start wary way across the tumbled stone wall at the edge of her yard. A batch of her bubbies was baking in the ticking kiln in the room off the kitchen; she had tried to make them bigger, but as she did so the crudities of her self-taught technique, her ignorance of anatomy, seemed to matter more. "What about Brenda, how is she taking it?"

"About as you'd expect. Hysterically. She was virtually openly condoning Ed's carrying on on the side but she never thought he'd leave her. It's going to be a problem for the church, too. All she and the kids have is the parsonage and it's not theirs, of course. They'll have to be kicked out eventually." The calm crackle of malice in Jane's voice took Alexandra a bit aback. "She'll have to get a job. She'll find out what it's like, being on your own."

"Maybe we . . ." *Should befriend her*, was the unfinished thought.

"*Never*," telepathic Jane responded. "She was just too fucking smug, if you ask me, being Mrs. Minister, sitting there like Greer Garson behind the coffee urn, snuggling up to all the old ladies, you should have seen her breeze in and out of that church during our rehearsals. I know," she said, "I shouldn't take such satisfaction in another woman's comeuppance, but I do. You think I'm wrong. You think I'm wicked."

"Oh no," Alexandra said, insincerely. But who is to say what wicked is? Poor Franny Lovecraft could have broken her hip that night and be on a walker till she stepped into her grave. Alexandra had come to the phone holding a wooden stirring spoon and idly, as she waited for Jane to be milked of all her malice, she bent the thing with her mind waves so that its handle curled back like a dog's tail and rested in the carved bowl of the spoon. Then she bade the snakelike circle coil slowly up her arm. The abrasive caress of the wood set her teeth on edge. "And how about Sukie?" Alexandra asked. "Isn't she sort of left too?"

"She's delighted. She en*cour*aged him, she told me, to find what he could with this Dawn creature. I think she'd had her little ride with Ed."

"But does that mean she's going to go after Darryl now?" The spoon had draped itself around her neck and was touching its bowl end to her lips. It tasted of salad oil. She flickered her tongue against its wood and her tongue felt feathery, forked. Coal was nuzzling against her legs, worriedly, smelling magic, which had a tiny burnt odor like a gas jet when first turned on.

"I daresay," Jane was saying, "she has other plans. She's not as attracted to Darryl as you are. Or as I am, for that matter. Sukie likes men to be *down*. Keep your eye on Clyde Gabriel, is my advice."

"Oh that awful wife," Alexandra exclaimed. "She should be put out of her misery." She was scarcely minding what she was saying, for to tease Coal she had put the writhing spoon on the floor and the hair on his withers had bristled; the spoon lifted its head, and Coal's lips tugged up from his teeth, and his eyes kindled to attack.

"Let's do it," Jane Smart briskly replied.

Distracted by this sharp new wickedness in Jane, and a bit frightened by it, Alexandra let the spoon unbend; it dropped its head and clattered flat on the linoleum. "Oh I don't think it's for us to do," she protested, mildly.

"I always did despise him and am not in the least surprised," Felicia Gabriel announced in her flat self-satisfied manner, as if addressing a small crowd of friends who unanimously thought she was wonderful, though in fact she was speaking to her husband, Clyde. He had been trying to comprehend through his drunken post-supper fog a *Scientific American* article on the newer anomalies of astronomy. She stood with a nagging expectant tension in the doorway of the shelf-lined room he tried to use as a study now that Jenny and Chris were no longer around to pollute it with electronic noises, with Joan Baez and the Beach Boys.

Felicia had never outgrown the presumingness of a pretty and vivacious high-school girl. She and Clyde had gone through the public schools of Warwick together, and what a fetching live-wire she had been, in on every extracurricular activity from student council to girls' volleyball and a straight A average to boot, not to mention being the first female captain ever of the debating team. A thrilling voice that would lift out above all the others in the impossibly high part of "The Star-Spangled Banner": it cut right through him like a knife. She had had dozens of boyfriends; she had been a real catch. He kept reminding himself of this. At night, when she fell asleep beside him with that depressing promptitude of the virtuous and hyperactive, leaving him to wrestle for hours alone with the demons of insomnia an evening's worth of liquor had planted in his system, he would examine her still features by moonlight, and the shadowed fit of her shut lids in their sockets and of her lips buttoned over some unspoken utterance of dream debate would disclose to his inspection an old perfection of nicely whittled bones. Felicia seemed frail when unconscious. He would lie propped up on one elbow and gaze at her, and the form of the peppy teen-ager he had loved would be restored to him, in her fuzzy pastel sweaters and her long plaid skirts swinging down the halls lined with tall green metal lockers, along with a sensation of being again his gangling "brainy" teen-aged self; a giant insubstantial column of lost and wasted time would arise from the bedroom walls so that they seemed to be lying like two crumpled bodies at the base of an airshaft. But now she stood erect before him, unignorable, dressed in the black skirt and white sweater in which she had chaired the evening's meeting of the Wetlands Watchdog Committee, where she had heard the news about Ed Parsley, from Mavis Jessup.

"He was *weak*," she stated, "a weak man somebody had once told he was handsome. He never looked handsome to me, with that pseudo-aristocratic nose and those slidy eyes. He never should have entered the ministry, he had no call, he thought he could charm God just as he charmed the old ladies into overlooking that he was a hollow man. To me—Clyde, *look* at me when I'm talking—he utterly failed to project the qualities of a man of God."

"I'm not sure the Unitarians care that much about God," he mildly answered, still hoping to read. Quasars, pulsars, stars emitting every millisecond jets of more matter than is contained in all the planets: perhaps in such cosmic madness he himself was looking for the old-fashioned heavenly God. Back in those innocent days when he had been "brainy" he had written for special credit in biology a long paper called "The Supposed Conflict Between Science and Religion," concluding that there was none. Though the paper had been given an A+, thirty-five years ago, by pie-faced, effeminate Mr. Thurmann, Clyde saw now that he had lied. The conflict was open and implacable and science was winning.

"Whatever they care about it's more than staying young forever, which is what drove Ed Parsley into the arms of that pathetic little tramp," Felicia announced. "He must have taken a good look one day at that perfectly deplorable Sukie Rougemont you're so fond of and realized that she was over thirty and he better find a younger mistress or he'd be dragged into growing up himself. That saint Brenda Parsley, why she put up with it I have no idea."

"Why? Why not? What options did she have?" Clyde hated to hear her rant yet he could not resist replying now and then.

"Well, she'll kill him. This new one will absolutely kill him. He'll be dead inside of a year in some hovel where she's led him, his arms full of needle marks, and Ed Parsley will get none of my sympathy. I'll spit on his grave. Clyde, you must stop reading that magazine. What did I just say?"

"You'll thspit on his grave."

Semiconsciously he had imitated a slight strangeness in her diction. He looked up in time to see her remove a piece of tinted fuzz from between her lips. She rolled the fuzz into a tight pellet with rapid nervous fingers at her side while she talked on. "Brenda Parsley was telling Marge Perley it might have been that your friend Sukie gave him a push so she could give this Van Horne creature her undivided attention, though from what I hear around town his attention is divided . . . three ways every . . . Thursday night."

The uncharacteristic hesitation in her phrasing led him to look up from the jagged graphs of pulsar flashes; she had removed something else from her mouth and was making another pellet, staring him down as if daring him to notice. When she had been a high-school girl she had had shining round eyes, but now her face, without growing fat, with every year was pressing in upon these lamps of her soul; her eyes had become piggy, with a vengeful piggy glitter.

"Sukie's not a friend," he said mildly, determined not to fight. *Just this once, not a fight*, he Godlessly prayed. "She's an employee. We have no friends."

"You better *tell* her she's an employee because from the way she acts down there she's the veritable queen of the place. Walks up and down Dock Street as if she owns it, swinging her hips and in all that junk jewelry, everybody laughing at her behind her back. Leaving her was the smartest thing Monty ever did, about the *only* smart thing he ever did, I don't know why those women bother to go on living, whores to half the town and not even getting paid. And those poor neglected children of theirs, it's a positive crime."

At a certain point, which she invariably pressed through to reach, he couldn't bear it any more: the mellowing anaesthetic effect of the Scotch was abruptly catalyzed into rage. "And the reason we have no friends," he growled, letting the magazine with its monstrous celestial news drop to the carpet, "is you talk too Goddamn much."

"Whores and neurotics and a disgrace to the community. And *you*, when the *Word* is supposed to give some voice to the community and its legitimate concerns, instead give employment to this, this *per*son who can't even write a decent English sentence, and allow her space to drip her ridiculous poison into everybody's ears and let her have that much of a hold over the people of the town, the few good people that are left, frightened as they are into the corners by all this vice and shamelessness everywhere."

"Divorced women have to work," Clyde said, sighing, slowing his breathing, fighting to keep reasonable, though there was no reasoning with Felicia when her indignation started to flow, it was like a chemical, a kind of chemical reaction. Her eyes shrank to diamond points, her face became frozen, paler and paler, and her invisible audience grew larger, so she had to raise her voice. "Married women," he explained to her, "don't have to do anything and can fart around with liberal causes."

She didn't seem to hear him. "That dreadful man," she called to the multitudes, "building a tennis court right into the wetlandth, they thay"—she swallowed—"they say he uses the island to smuggle drugs, they row it in in dorieth when the tide ith high—"

This time there was no hiding it; she pulled a small feather, striped blue as from a blue jay, out of her mouth, and quickly made a fist around it at her side.

Clyde stood up, his feelings quite changed. Anger and the sense of entrapment fell from him; her old pet name emerged from his mouth. "Lishy, what on earth . . . ?" He doubted his eyes; saturated with galactic strangeness, they might be playing tricks. He pried open her unresisting fist. A bent wet feather lay upon her palm.

Felicia's tense pallor relaxed into a blush. She was embarrassed. "It's been happening lately," she told him. "I have no idea why. This scummy taste, and then these *things*. Some mornings I feel as if I'm choking, and pieces like straw, dirty straw, come out when I'm brushing my teeth. But I know I've not eaten anything. My breath is terrible. Clyde! I don't know what's *hap*pening to me!"

As this cry escaped her, Felicia's body was given an anxious twist, a look of being about to fly off somewhere, that reminded Clyde of Sukie: both women had fair dry skin and an ectomorphic frame. In high school Felicia had been drenched in freckles and her "pep" had been something like his favorite reporter's nimble, impudent carriage. Yet one woman was heaven and the other hell. He took his wife into his arms. She sobbed. It was true; her breath smelled like the bottom of a chicken coop. "Maybe we should get you to a doctor," he suggested. This flash of husbandly emotion, in which he enfolded her frightened soul in a cape of concern, burned away much of the alcohol clouding his mind.

But after her moment of wifely surrender Felicia stiffened and struggled. "*No.* They'll make out I'm crazy and tell you to put me away. Don't think I don't know your thoughts. You wish I was dead. You bastard, you *do*. You're just like Ed Parsley. You're all bastards. Pitiful, corrupt . . . all you care about ith awful women. . . ." She writhed out of his arms; in the corner of his eye her hand snatched at her mouth. She tried to hide this hand behind her but, furious above all at the way that truth, for which men die, was mixed in with her frantic irrelevant self-satisfaction, he gripped her wrist and forced her clenched fingers open. Her skin felt cold, clammy. In her unclenched palm lay curled a wet pinfeather, as from a chick, but an Easter chick, for the little soft feather had been dyed lavender.

"He sends me letters," Sukie told Darryl Van Horne, "with no return address, saying he's gone underground. They've let him and Dawn into a group that's learning how to make bombs out of alarm clocks and cordite. The System doesn't stand a chance." She grinned monkeyishly.

"How does that make you feel?" the big man smoothly asked, in a hollow psychiatric voice. They were having lunch at a restaurant in Newport, where no one else from Eastwick was likely to be. Elderly waitresses in starchy brown miniskirts, with taffeta aprons tied behind in big bows evocative of Playboy bunny tails, brought them large menus, printed brown on beige, full of low-cal things on toast. Her weight was not among Sukie's worries: all that nervous energy, it burned everything up.

She squinted into space, trying to be honest, for she sensed that this man offered her a chance to be herself. Nothing would shock or hurt him. "It makes me feel relieved," she said. "That he's off my hands. I mean, what he wanted wasn't something a woman could give him. He wanted power. A woman can give a man power over herself in a way, but she can't put him in the Pentagon. That's what excited Ed about the Movement as he imagined it, that it was going to replace the Pentagon with an army of its own and have the same, you know, kind of thing— uniforms and speeches and board rooms with big maps and all. That really turned me off, when he started raving about that. I like *gentle* men. My father was gentle, a veterinarian in this little town in the Finger Lakes region, and he loved to read. He had all first editions of Thornton Wilder and Carl Van Vechten, with these plastic covers to protect the jackets. Monty used to be pretty gentle too, except when he'd get his shotgun down and go out with the boys and blast all these poor birds and furry things. He'd bring home these rabbits he had blasted up the ass, because of course they were trying to run away. Who wouldn't? But that only happened once a year—around now, as a matter of fact, is what must have made me think of it. That hunting smell is in the air. Small game season." Her smile was marred by the paste of cracker and bean spread that clung in dark spots between her teeth; the waitress had brought this free hors d'oeuvre to the table and Sukie had stuffed her face.

"How about old Clyde Gabriel? He gentle enough for you?" Van Horne lowered his big woolly barrel of a head when he was burrowing into a woman's secret life. His eyes had the hot swarming half-hidden look of children's when they put on Halloween masks.

"He might have been once, but he's pretty far gone. Felicia has done bad things to him. Sometimes at the paper, when some little layout girl just beginning the job has, I don't know, put a favored advertiser in a lower-left corner, he goes, really, wild. The girl has nothing to do but burst into tears. A lot of them have quit."

"But not you."

"He's easy on me for some reason." Sukie lowered her eyes —a lovely sight, with her reddish arched brows and her lids just touched with lavender make up and her sleek shimmering apricot hair demurely backswept and held in place on both sides by barrettes whose copper backs were echoed by a necklace close to her throat of linked copper crescents.

Her eyes lifted and flashed their green. "But then I'm a good reporter. I really am. Those baggy old men in Town Hall who make all the decisions—Herbie Prinz, Ike Arsenault—they really like me, and tell me what's up."

While Sukie consumed the crackers and bean spread, Van Horne puffed on a cigarette, doing it awkwardly, in the Continental manner, the burning tip cupped near the palm. "What's with you and these married types?"

"Well, the advantage of a wife is she saves you from making any decisions. That's what was beginning to frighten me about Brenda Parsley: she really had ceased to be any check on Ed, they were so far gone as a couple. We used to spend whole nights in these awful fleabags together. And it wasn't as if we were making love, after the first half-hour; he was going on about the wickedness of the corporate power structure's sending our boys to Vietnam for the benefit of their stock-holders, not that I ever understood how it was benefiting them exactly, or got much impression that Ed really cared about those boys, the actual soldiers were just white and black trash as far as he was concerned. . . ." Her eyes had dropped and lifted again; Van Horne felt a surge of possessive pride in her beauty, her vital spirit. His. His toy. It was lovely how in a pensive pause her upper lip dominated her lower. "Then *I*," she said, "had to get up and go home and make breakfast for the kids, who were terrified because I'd been gone all night, and stagger right off to the paper—*he* could sleep all day. Nobody knows what a minister is supposed to be doing, just give his silly sermon on Sundays, it's really such a ripoff."

"People don't terrifically mind," Darryl said sagely, "being ripped off, is something I've discovered over the years." The waitress with her varicose legs exposed to mid-thigh brought Van Horne skinned shrimp tails on decrusted triangles of bread, and Sukie chicken à la king, cubed white meat and sliced mushrooms oozing in their cream over a scalloped flaky patty shell, and also brought him a Bloody Mary and her a Chablis spritzer paler than lemonade, because Sukie had to go back and write up the latest wrinkle in the Eastwick High-way Department's budget embarrassments as winter with its blizzards drew ever closer. Dock Street had been battered this summer by an unusually heavy influx of tourists and eight-axle trucks, so the slabs of mesh-reinforced concrete over the culverts there by the Superette were disintegrating; you could look right down into the tidal creek through the potholes. "So you think Felicia's an evil woman," Van Horne pursued, apropos of wives.

"I wouldn't say evil, exactly . . . yes I would. She really is. She's like Ed in a way, all causes and no respect for actual people around her. Poor Clyde sinking right in front of her eyes, and she's on the phone with this petition to restore a dress code at the high school. Coat and ties for the boys and nothing but skirts for the girls, no jeans or hotpants. They talk about fascists a lot now but she really is one. She got the news store to put *Playboy* behind the counter and then had a fit be-cause some photography annual had a little tit and pussy in it, the models on some Caribbean beach, you know, with the sun sparkling all over them through a Polaroid filter. She actually wants poor Gus Stevens put in jail for having this magazine on his rack that his suppliers just brought him, they didn't ask. She wants *you* put in jail, for that matter, for unauthorized landfill. She wants everybody put in jail and the person she really *has* put in jail is her own husband."

"Well." Van Horne smiled, his red lips redder from the tomato juice in his Bloody Mary. "And you want to give him a parole."

"It's not just that; I'm at*trac*ted," Sukie confessed, suddenly close to tears, this whole matter of attraction so senseless, and silly. "He's so grateful for just the . . . the minimum."

"Coming from you, minimum is pretty max," Van Horne said gallantly. "You're a winner, tiger."

"But I'm not," Sukie protested. "People have these fantasies about redheads, we're supposed to be hot I suppose, like those little cinnamony candy hearts, but really we're just people, and though I bustle around a lot and try, you know, to look smart, at least by Eastwick standards, I don't think of myself as having the *real* whatever it is—power, mystery, womanliness—that Alexandra has, or even Jane in her kind of lumpy way, you know what I mean?" With other men also Sukie had noticed this urge of hers to talk about the two other witches, to seek coziness conversationally in evoking the three of them, this triune body under its cone of power being the closest approach to a mother she had ever had; Sukie's own mother—a busy little birdy woman physically like, come to think of it, Felicia Gabriel, and like her fascinated by doing good—was always out of the house or on the phone to one of her church groups or committees or boards; she was always taking orphans or refugees in, little lost Koreans were the things in those years, and then abandoning them along with Sukie and her brothers in the big brick house with its back yard sloping down to the lake. Other men, Sukie felt, minded when her thoughts and tongue gravitated to the coven and its coziness and mischief, but not Van Horne; it was his meat somehow, he was like a woman in his steady kindness, though of course terribly masculine in form: when he fucked you it hurt.

"They're dogs," he said now, simply. "They don't have your nifty knockers."

"Am I wrong?" she asked, feeling she could say anything to Van Horne, throw any morsel of herself into that dark cauldron of a simmering, smiling man. "With Clyde. I mean, I know all the books say you should *never*, with an employer, you lose your job then afterwards, and Clyde's so desperately unhappy there's something dangerous about it in any case. The whites of his eyeballs are yellow; what's that a sign of?"

"Those whites of his eyeballs were marinating," Van Horne assured her, "when you were still playing with Barbie dolls. You go to it, girl. Easy on the guilt trip. We didn't deal the deck down here, we just play the cards."

Thinking that if they talked about it any more, her affair with Clyde would be as much Darryl's as hers, Sukie steered the conversation away from herself; for the rest of the luncheon Van Horne talked about himself, his hopes of finding a loophole in the second law of thermodynamics. "There *has* to be one," he said, beginning to sweat and wipe his lips in excitement, "and it's the same fucking loophole whereby everything crossed over from nonbeing. It's the singularity at the bottom of the Big Bang. Yeah, and what a*bout* gravity? These smug scientists everybody thinks are so sacred talk as if we've all understood it ever since Newton rigged those formulas but the fact is it's a *hell*uva mystery; Einstein says it's like a screwy graph paper that's getting bent all the time but, Sukie baby, don't drift off, it's a *force*. It lifts the tides; step out of an airplane it'll suck you right down, and what kind of a force is it that operates across space instantly and has nothing to do with the electromagnetic field?" He was forgetting to eat; flecks of spit were appearing on the lacquered tabletop. "There's a formula out there, there's gotta be, and it's going to be as elegant as good old $E = mc^2$. The sword from the stone, you know what I mean?" His big hands, disturbing like the leaves of those tropical house plants that look plastic though we know they're natural, made a decisive sword-pulling motion. Then, with salt and pepper and a ceramic ashtray bearing a prim pink image of Newport's historical Old Colony House, Van Horne tried to illustrate subatomic particles and his faith that a combination could be found to generate electricity without further energy input. "It's like ju-jitsu: you toss the guy over your shoulder with more force than he came at you with. Levering. You gotta *swing* those electrons." His repulsive hands showed how. "You think just mechanically or chemically on this, you're licked; the old second law's got you every time. You know what Cooper pairs are? No? You're kidding. You a journalist or not? The news isn't all who's screwing who, you know. They're pairs of loosely bound electrons that make up the heart of superconductors. Know anything about superconductors? No? O.K., their resistance is zero. I don't mean it's very small, I mean it's *zero*. Well, suppose we found some Cooper *trip*lets. You'd have resistance of *less* than zero. There's gotta be an element, like selenium was for the Xerox process. Those assholes up in Rochester didn't have a thing until they hit upon selenium, out of the blue, they just fell into it. Well, once we get our equivalent of selenium, there's no stopping us, Sukie babes. You get down there under the chemical skin, every roof in the world can become a generator with just a coat of paint. This photovoltaic cell they use in the satellites is just a sandwich, really. What you need isn't ham, cheese, and lettuce—translate that silicon, arsenic, and boron—what you need is ham salad, where the macro arrangement isn't an issue. All *I* have to do is figure out the fucking mayonnaise."

Sukie laughed and, still hungry, took a breadstick from a miniature beanpot on the table and unwrapped it and began to nibble. To her it all sounded like fantastical presumption. There were all these men in Rochester and Schenectady, she had grown up with the type, science majors with little straight mouths and receding hairlines and those plastic liners in their shirt pockets in case their pens leaked, working away systematically at these problems, with government funds and nice little wives and children to go home to at night. But then she recognized this thought as sheer prejudice left over from her old life, before sheer womanhood had exploded within her and she realized that the world men had systematically made was all dreary poison, good for nothing really but battlefields and waste sites. Why couldn't a wild man like Darryl blunder into one of the universe's secrets? Think of Thomas Edison, deaf because as a boy he had been lifted into a cart by his ears. Think of that Scotsman, what was his name, watching the steam lift the lid of the kettle and then cooking up railroads. It was on the tip of her tongue to tell Van Horne how for fun she and

Jane Smart had been casting spells on Clyde's awful wife; using a Book of Common Prayer Jane had stolen from the Episcopalian church where she sometimes pinch-hit as choir director, they had solemnly baptized a cookie jar Felicia and would toss things into it—feathers, pins, sweepings from Sukie's incredibly ancient little house on Hemlock Lane.

There, not ten hours after her lunch with Darryl Van Horne, she entertained Clyde Gabriel. The children were asleep. Felicia had gone off in a caravan of buses from Boston, Worcester, Hartford, and Providence to protest something in Washington: they were going to chain themselves to pillars in the Capitol and clog everything, human grit in the wheels of government. Clyde could stay the night, if he arose before the first child awoke. He made a touching mock-husband, with his bifocals and flannel pajamas and a little partial denture that he discreetly wrapped in a Kleenex and tucked into a pocket of his suit coat when he thought Sukie wasn't watching.

But she was, for the bathroom door didn't altogether close, due to the old frame of the house settling over the centuries, and she had to sit on the toilet some minutes waiting for the pee to come. Men, they were able to conjure it up immediately, that was one of their powers, that thunderous splashing as they stood lordly above the bowl. Everything about them was more direct, their insides weren't the maze women's were, for the pee to find its way through. Sukie, waiting, peeked out; Clyde, with an elderly tilt to his head and that bump on the back of his skull studious men have, crossed the vertical slit that she could see of her bedroom. From the angle of his arms she saw he was taking a thing out of his mouth. There was a brief pink glint of false gum and then he was slipping his little packet of folded Kleenex into the side pocket of his coat where he would not forget it when he groped out of her room at dawn. Sukie sat with her lovely oval knees together and her breath held: since girlhood she had liked to spy on men, this other race interwoven with hers, so full of bravado and dirty tough talk but such babies really, as they proved whenever you gave them your breasts to suck or opened your crotch for them to go down on, the way they burrowed there and wanted to crawl back in. She liked to sit just as she was, only on a chair, and spread her legs so her bush felt all big and the curls of it glittery and let them just lap and kiss and eat. Hair pie, a boy she used to know in New York State called it.

The pee at last came. She turned off the bathroom light and went into the bedroom, where the only illumination arose from the street lamp up at the corner of Hemlock Lane and Oak Street. She and Clyde had never spent a night together before, though lately they had taken to driving into the Cove woods at lunchtime (she walking along Dock Street as far as the war monument and he picking her up in his Volvo there); the other day she had grown bored with kissing his sad dry face with its long nostril hairs and tobaccoey breath and, to amuse herself and him, had unzipped his fly and swiftly, sweetly (she herself felt) jerked him off, coolly watching. These comic jets of semen, like the cries of a baby animal in the claws of a hawk. He had been flabbergasted by her witch's trick; when he laughed his lips pulled back strangely, exposing back rows of jagged teeth with pockets of blackened silver. That had been a little frightening, corrosion and pain and time all bared. She felt timid again, stepping unseeing into her own room with this man in it, her eyes not yet adjusted from the bathroom. Where Clyde sat in the corner his pajamas glowed like a fluorescent bulb that has just been switched off. A red cigarette tip glowed near his head. She could see herself, her white flanks and nervous ribbed sides, more clearly than she saw him, for several mirrors—gilt-framed, ancient, inherited from an Ithaca aunt—hung on her walls. These mirrors were mottled with age; the damp plaster walls of old stone houses had eaten the mercury off their backs. Sukie preferred such mirrors to perfect ones; they gave her back her beauty with less cavil. Clyde's voice growled, "Not sure I'm up to this."

"If not you, who?" Sukie asked the shadows.

"Oh, I can think of a number," he said, nevertheless standing and beginning to unbutton his pajama top. The glowing cigarette had been transferred to his mouth and its red tip bounced as he spoke.

Sukie felt a chill. She had expected to be folded instantly into his arms, with long, starved, bad-breath kisses such as they had shared in the car. Her prompt nakedness put her at a disadvantage; she had devalued herself. These frightful fluctuations a woman must endure on the stock exchange of male minds, up and down from minute to minute, as their ids and superegos haggle. She had half a mind to turn and closet herself again in the bright bathroom, and damn him. He had not moved. His dehydrated once-handsome face, taut at the cheekbones, was scrunched wiseguy-style around the cigarette, one eye held shut against the smoke. That was how he would sit editing copy, his soft pencil scurrying and slashing, his jaundiced eyes sheltered under a green eyeshade, his cigarette smoke loosing drifting galactic shapes in the cone of his desk light, his own cone of power. Clyde loved to cut, to find an entire superfluous paragraph that could be disposed of without a seam; though lately he had grown tender with her own prose, correcting only the misspellings. "How big a number?" she asked. He thought she was a whore. Felicia must keep telling him that. The chill Sukie had felt: was it the cold of the room, or the thrilling sight of her own white flesh simultaneously haunting the three mirrors?

Clyde killed his cigarette and finished undoing his pajamas. Now he was naked too. The amount of pallor in the mirrors doubled. His penis was impressive, lank like him, dangling in that helpless heavy-headed way penises have, this most precarious piece of flesh. His skin slithered anxiously against hers as he at last attempted an embrace; he was bony but surprisingly warm.

"Not too big," he answered. "Just enough to make me jealous. God, you're lovely. I could cry."

She led him into bed, trying to suppress any movements that might wake the children. Under the covers his head with its sharp angles and scratchy whiskers rested heavily on her breast; his cheekbone grated on her clavicle. "This shouldn't make you cry," she said soothingly, easing bone off bone. "It's supposed to be a happy thing." As Sukie said this, Alexandra's broad face swam into her mind: broad, a bit sun-browned even in winter from her walks outdoors, the gentle clefts at her chin and the tip of her nose giving her an impassive goddesslike strangeness, the blankness of one who holds to a creed: Alexandra believed that nature, the physical world, was a happy thing. This huddling man, this dogskin of warm bones, did not believe that. The world for him had been rendered tasteless as paper, composed as it was of inconsequent messy events that flickered across his desk on their way to the moldering back files. Everything for him had become secondary and sour. Sukie wondered about her own strength, how long she could hold these grieving, doubting men on her own chest and not be contaminated.

"If I could have you every night, it might be a happy thing," Clyde Gabriel conceded.

"Well, then," Sukie said, in a mother's tone, staring frightened at the ceiling, trying to launch herself into the agreed-upon surrender, that flight into sex her body promised others. This man's body out of its half-century released a complex masculine odor that included the rotted scent of whiskey—a taint she had often noticed, bending over him at the desk as his pencil jabbed at her typewritten copy. It was part of him, something woven in. She stroked the hair on his skull with its long bump of intelligence. His hair was thinning: how fine it was! As if every hair truly had been numbered. His tongue began to flick at her nipple, rosy and erect. She caressed the other, rolling it between thumb and forefinger, to arouse herself. His sadness had been cast into her, and she could not quite shake it. His climax, though he was slow to come in that delicious way of older men, left her own demon unsatisfied. She needed more of him, though now he wanted to sleep. Sukie asked, "Do you feel guilty toward Felicia, being with me this way?" It was an unworthy, flirtatious thing to say, but sometimes after being fucked she felt a desperate sliding, a devaluation too steep.

The room's single window held stony moonlight. Bald November reigned outside. Lawn chairs had been taken in, the lawns were dead and flat as floors, the outdoors was bare as a house after the movers had come. The little pear tree bejewelled with fruit had become a set of sticks. A dead geranium stood in a pot on the windowsill. The narrow cupboard beside the cold fireplace held green string. A charm slept beneath the bed. Clyde fetched his answer up from a depth near dreams. "No guilt," he said. "Just rage. That bitch has gabbled and prattled my life away. I'm usually numb. Your being so lovely wakes me up a little, and that's not good. It shows me what I've missed, what that self-righteous boring bitch has made me miss."

"I think," Sukie said, still flirtatious, "I'm supposed to be a little extra, I'm not supposed to make you *an*gry." Meaning, too, that she was not the one to take him on and get him out from under, he was too sad and poisoned; though she did feel wifely stirrings, still, viewing such men in their dailiness—that stoop their shoulders have when they got up from a chair, the shamefaced awkward way they step in and out of their trousers, how docilely they scrape their whiskers off their faces every day and go out in the world looking for money.

"It makes me dizzy, what you show me," Clyde said, lightly stroking her firm breasts, her flat long abdomen. "You're like a cliff. I want to jump."

"Please don't jump," Sukie said. She heard a child, her youngest, turning in her bed. The house was so small, they were all in one another's arms at night, through the papered odd-shaped walls.

Clyde fell asleep with his hand on her belly, so she had to lift his heavy arm—the soft rasp of his snoring stopped, then resumed—to slide herself from the sway-backed bed. She tried to pee again and failed, took her nightie and bathrobe from the back of the bathroom door, and checked on the restless child, whose covers had all been kicked in the agitation of some nightmare to the floor. Back in bed Sukie lulled herself by flying in her mind to the old Lenox place—the tennis games they could play all winter now that Darryl extravagantly had installed a great canvas bubble-top held up by warm air, and the drinks Fidel would serve them afterwards with their added color-spots of lime and cherry and mint and pimiento, and the way their eyes and giggles and gossip would interlace like the wet circles their glasses left on the glass table in Darryl's huge room where Pop Art was gathering dust. Here, the women were free, on holiday from the stale-smelling life that snored at their sides. When Sukie slept, she dreamed of yet another woman, Felicia Gabriel, her tense triangular face, talking, talking, angrier and angrier, her face coming closer, the tip of her tongue the color of a bit of pimiento, wagging in relentless level indignation behind her teeth, now flickering between her teeth, touching Sukie here, there, maybe we shouldn't, but it does feel, who's to say what's natural, whatever exists has to be natural, and nobody's watching anyway, nobody, oh, such a hard rapid little red tip, so considerate really, so good. Sukie briefly awoke to realize that the climax Clyde had failed to give her the apparition of Felicia had sought to. Sukie finished the effort with her own left hand, out of rhythm with Clyde's snores. The tiny staggering shadow of a bat passed in front of the moon and this too Sukie found consoling, the thought of something awake besides her mind, as when a late-night trolley car screeched around a distant unseen corner in the night when she was a girl in New York State, in that little brick city like a fingernail at the end of a long icy lake.

Being in love with Sukie made Clyde drink more; drunk, he could sink more relaxedly into the muck of longing. There was now an animal inside him whose gnawing was companionable, a kind of conversation. That he had once longed for Felicia this way made his situation seem all the more satisfactorily hopeless. It was his misfortune to see through everything. He had not believed in God since he was seven, in patriotism since he was ten, in art since the age of fourteen, when he realized he would never be a Beethoven, a Picasso, or a Shakespeare. His favorite authors were the great seers-through—Nietzsche, Hume, Gibbon, the ruthless jubilant lucid minds. More and more he blacked out somewhere between the third and fourth Scotches, unable to remember next morning what book he had been holding in his lap, what meetings Felicia had returned from, when he had gone to bed, how he had moved through the rooms of the house that felt like a vast and fragile husk now that Jennifer and Christopher were gone. Traffic shuddered on Lodowick Street outside like the senseless pumping of Clyde's heart and blood. In his solitary daze of booze and longing he had pulled down from a high dusty shelf his college Lucretius, scribbled throughout with the interlinear translations of his studious, hopeful college self. *Nil igitur mors est ad nos neque pertinet hilum, quandoquidem natura animi mortalis habetur.* He leafed through the delicate little book, its Oxford-blue spine worn white where his youthful moist hands had held it over and over. He looked in vain for that passage where the swerve of atoms is described, that accidental undetermined swerve whereby matter complicates, and all things are thus, through accumulating collisions, including men in their miraculous freedom, brought into being; for without this swerve all atoms would fall ever downwards through the *inane profundum* like drops of rain.

It had been his habit for years to step out into the relative quiet of the back yard before going up to bed and to gaze for a minute at the implausible spatter of stars; it was a knife edge of possibility, he knew, that allowed these fiery bodies to be in the sky, for had the primeval fireball been a shade more homogeneous no galaxies could have formed and had it been a shade less the galaxies would have billions of years ago consumed themselves in a heterogeneity too rash. He would stand by the corroding portable barbecue grill, never used now that the kids were gone, and remind himself to wheel it into the garage now that winter was in the air, and never manage to do it, night after night, lifting his face thirstily to that enigmatic miracle arching overhead. Light sank into his eyes that had started on its way when cave men prowled the vast world in little bands like ants on a pool table. Cygnus, its unfinished cross, and Andromeda, its flying V with, clinging near the second star, the bit of fuzz that—his neglected telescope had often made clear—is a spiral galaxy beyond the Milky Way. Night after night the heavens were the same; Clyde was like a photographic plate exposed again and again; the stars had bored themselves into him like bullet holes in a tin roof.

Tonight his old college *De Rerum Natura* folded its youthfully annotated pages and slipped between his knees. He was thinking of going out for his ritual stargaze when Felicia barged into his study. Though of course it was not his study but theirs, as every room in the house was theirs, and every flaking clapboard and bit of crumbling insulation on the old single-strand copper wiring was theirs, and the rusting barbecue and above the front doorway the wooden eagle plaque with its red, white, and blue weathered in the rain of atoms to rose, yellow, and black.

Felicia unwound striped wool scarves from around her head and throat and stamped her booted feet in indignation. "There are *such* stupid people running this town; they actually voted to change the name of Landing Square to Kazmierczak Square, in honor of that idiotic boy who went off and got himself killed in Vietnam." She pulled off her boots.

"Well," Clyde said, determined to be tactful. Since Sukie's flesh and fur and musk had flooded those cells of his brain set aside for a mate, Felicia seemed diaphanous, an image of a woman painted on tissue paper that might blow away. "That area hasn't really been a boat landing for eighty years. It got all silted in the blizzard of '88." He was innocently proud to be specific; along with astronomy, Clyde, in the days when his head was clear, used to be interested in terrestrial disasters: Krakatoa blowing its top and shrouding the Earth in dust, the Chinese flood of 1931 that killed nearly four million, the Lisbon earthquake of 1755 that struck when all the faithful were in church.

"But it was so *pleas*ant," Felicia said, giving that irrelevant quick smile which showed she thought her words inarguable, "up there at the end of Dock Street, with the benches for the old people, and that old granite obelisk that didn't look like a war memorial at all."

"It might still be pleasant," he offered, wondering if one more inch of Scotch would mercifully knock him out.

"No it won't," Felicia said definitely. She stripped off her coat. She was wearing a broad copper bracelet that Clyde had never seen before. It reminded him of Sukie, who sometimes left her jewelry on but nothing else and walked in nakedness glinting, in the shadowy rooms where they made love. "Next thing they'll want to be naming Dock Street and then Oak Street and then Eastwick itself after some lower-class dropout who couldn't think of anything better to do than go over there and napalm villages."

"Kazmierczak was a pretty good kid, actually. Remember, a few years back, he was their quarterback, and on the honor roll at the same time? That's why people took it so hard when he got killed last summer."

"Well *I* didn't take it hard," Felicia said, smiling as if her point had been clinched. She came near the fire he had built in the grating, to warm her hands now that her mittens were off. She half-turned her back and fiddled with her mouth, as if disentangling a hair from her lips. Clyde didn't know why this by now familiar gesture angered him, since of all the unattractive traits that had come upon her with age this one affliction could not be construed as her fault. In the morning he would see feathers, straw, pennies still slick with saliva stuck to her pillow and want to shake her awake, his own head thundering. "It's not ath if," she insisted, "he was even born and bred in Eastwick. His family moved here about five years ago, and his father refuthes to get a job, just works on the highway crew long enough to get another six months of unemployment. He was at the meeting tonight, wearing a black tie with egg stains all over it. Poor Mrs. K., she tried to dress up so as not to look like a tart but I'm afraid she failed."

Felicia had a considerable love for the underprivileged in the abstract but when actual cases got close to her she tended to hold her nose. There was a fascinating spin to Felicia and Clyde couldn't always resist giving a poke to keep her going. "I don't think Kazmierczak Square has such a bad ring to it," he said.

Felicia's beady furious eyes flashed. "No you wouldn't. You wouldn't think Shithouse Square had such a bad ring to it either. You don't give a damn about the world we pass on to our children or the wars we inflict on the innocent or whether or not we poison ourselves to death, you're poisoning yourself to death right now tho what do you care, drag the whole globe down with you ith the way you look at it." The diction of her tirade had become thick and she carefully lifted from her tongue a small straight pin and what looked like part of an art-gum eraser.

"Our children," he sneered. "I don't see them around to receive the world in whatever shape we pass it on." He drained the glass of Scotch—a taste of smoke and heather amid the cubes of fluoridated water. Ice rattled against his upper lip; he thought of Sukie's lips, their cushiony expression of pleasure even when she was trying to be solemn and sad. He made her sad, was one of his sorrows. Her lipstick tasted ever so faintly of cherry and sometimes left a line across her two front teeth. He stood to replenish his glass, and staggered. Bits of Sukie—her plump parallel toes tipped with scarlet, her copper necklace of crescents, the pale orange tufts in her armpits—fluttered about him unsteadily. The bottle lived on a lower shelf, beneath a long uniform set of Balzac like so many miniature brown coffins.

"Yes, that's another thing you can't stand, the way Jenny and Chris have gone off, as if you can keep children home forever, as if the world doesn't have to *change* and *grow*. Wake up, Clyde. You thought life was going to be just like those children's books Mommy and Daddy kept piling on your bed every time you were sick, all those Wee Astronomers and Children's Classics and coloring books with safe little outlines and nice pointy crayons in their snug little boxes, when the fact is it's an *or*ganism, Clyde—the world is an organism, it's vital, it's sensitive, it's moving *on*, Clyde, while you sit over there playing with that silly little paper of yours as if you were still Mommy's pet sick in bed. Your so-called reporter Sukie Rougemont was there tonight at the meeting, her piggy little nose in the air, giving me that I-know-something-you-don't-know-look."

Language, he was thinking, perhaps *is* the curse, that took us out of Eden. And here we are trying to teach it to these poor good-natured chimpanzees and grinning dolphins. The Johnnie Walker bottle chortled obligingly in its tilted throat.

"Don't you think, *ooh*," Felicia was going on, exclaiming as the vortex of fury gripped her, "don't you think I don't know about you and that minx, I can read you like a book and don't you forget it, how you'd like to fuck her if you had the guts but you don't, you don't."

The picture of Sukie as she was, blurred and gentle and with a sort of distended amazement in her expression beneath him, when she was being fucked, came into his mind and the strong honey of it paralyzed his tongue, which had wanted to protest, *But I do.*

"You sit here," Felicia was going on, with a chemical viciousness that had become independent of her body, a possession controlling her mouth, her eyes, "you sit here mooning about Jenny and Chris who've at least had the guts and the sense to kiss this Godforsaken town good-bye forever and try to make careers for themselves where things are *hap*pening, you sit here mooning but you know what they used to say to me about you? You really want to know, Clyde? They would say, 'Hey, Mom, wouldn't it be great if Dad would leave us? But, you know,' they would have to add, 'he just doesn't have the guts.'" Scornfully, as if still in the voice of others: "'He just doesn't —have—the guts.'"

The polish, Clyde thought, the polish of her rhetoric was what made it truly insufferable: the artful pauses and repetitions, the way she had picked up the word "guts" and turned it into a musical theme, the way she was making her orotund points before a huge mental audience rapt to the uttermost tier of the bleachers. A crowd of thumbtacks had come up from her gullet during the climax of her peroration, but not even this had stopped her. Felicia spat them swiftly into her hand and tossed them into the log fire he had built. They faintly sizzled; their colored heads blackened. "No gutth at all," she said, extracting one last tack and flicking it through the gap between the bricks and the fire screen, "but he wants to turn the entire town into a memorial for this horrible war. It must all fit, it must be, what do they call it, a syndrome. A drunken weakling wants the entire world to go down with him. Hitler, that's who you remind me of, Clyde. Another weak man the world didn't stand up to. Well, it's not going to happen this time." Now the imaginary crowd had gotten behind her—troops she was leading. " *We're standing up to evil,*" she called, her eyes focused above and beyond his head.

And she stood with legs braced as if he might try to knock her down. But he had taken a step her way because the fire, under its mouthful of wet tacks, seemed to be dying. He pulled back the screen and gave the spread logs a poke with the brass-handled poker. The logs snuggled closer, with sparks. He was reminded of himself and Sukie: a curious benison attendant upon sex with Sukie was how sleepy her proximity made him; at the slithering touch of her skin a blissful languor would steal upon him, after a life of insomnia. Before and after sex her naked body rode so lightly at his side he seemed to have found his spot in space at last. Just thinking of this peace the red-haired divorcee bestowed drew a merciful blankness across his brain.

Perhaps minutes passed. Felicia was vehemently talking. His children's vigorous contempt for him had become involved with his criminal willingness to sit in a chair while unjust wars, fascist governments, and profit-greedy exploiters ravaged the world. The poker's smooth heft was still in his hand. In its chemical indignation her face had gone white as a skull; her eyes burned like the tiny flames of votive candles deep in the waxy pockets they have hollowed. Her hair seemed to be standing up in a ragged, skimpy halo. Most horribly, things kept coming out of her mouth—parrot feathers, dead wasps, bits of eggshell all mixed in an unstoppable thin gruel she kept wiping from her chin in a rhythmic gesture like cocking a gun. He saw these extrusions as a sign; this woman was possessed, she bore no relation to the woman he in good faith had married. "Hey come on, Lishy," Clyde begged, "let's cool it. Let's call it a day." The chemical and mechanical action that had replaced her soul surged on; in her trance of indignation she had ceased to see and hear. Her voice would wake the neighbors. Her voice was growing louder, fed inexhaustibly from within. His drink was in his left hand; he lifted the poker in his right and slashed it down across her head, just to interrupt the flow of energy for a moment, to plug the hole through which too much was pouring. The bone of her skull gave off a surprising high-pitched noise, as if two blocks of wood had been playfully knocked together. Her eyeballs rolled upward, displaying their whites, and her lips parted involuntarily, showing on her tongue an impossibly blue small feather. He knew he was making a mistake but the silence felt heaven-sent. His own chemicals took over; he hit her head with the poker again and again, pursuing it in its slow fall to the floor, until the sound the blows made was more liquid than that of wood knocking wood. He had plugged this hole in cosmic peace forever.

An immense sheath of relief slid upward from Clyde Gabriel, a film slipping from his sweat-coated body like a polyethylene protecting bag being pulled from a clean suit. He sipped on the Scotch and avoided looking at the floor. He thought of the stars outside and of the impervious pattern they would be making on this night of his life as on every other in the aeons since the galaxy condensed. Though he still had a lot to do, and some of it very difficult, a miraculously refreshed perspective gave each of his actions a squared-off clarity, as if indeed he had been returned to those illustrated children's books Felicia had scornfully conjured up. How curious of her to do so: she had been right, he had loved those days of staying home from school sick. She knew him too well. Marriage is like two people locked up with one lesson to read, over and over, until the words become madness. He thought she whimpered from the floor but decided it was only the fire digesting a tiny vein of sap.

As a conscientious, neatness-loving child Clyde had relished architectural drawings—ones that showed every molding and lintel and ledge and made manifest the triangular diminishments of perspective. With ruler and blue pencil he used to extend the diminishing lines of drawings in magazines and comic books to the vanishing point, even when the point lay well off the page. That such a point existed was a pleasing concept to him, and perhaps his first glimpse into adult fraudulence was the discovery that in many flashy-looking drawings the artists had cheated: there was no exact vanishing point. Now Clyde in person had arrived at this place of final perspective, and everything was ideally lucid and crisp around him. Vast problematical areas—next Wednesday's issue of the *Word*, the arrangement of his next tryst with Sukie, that perpetual struggle of lovers to find privacy and a bed that did not feel tawdry, the recurrent pain of putting back on his underclothes and leaving her, the necessity to consult with Joe Marino about the no-longer-overlookable decrepitude of this house's old furnace and deteriorating pipes and radiators, the not dissimilar condition of his liver and stomach lining, the periodic blood tests and consultations with Doc Pat and all the insincere resolutions his deplorable condition warranted, and now no end of complication with the police and the law courts—were swept away, leaving only the outlines of this room, the lines of its carpentry clean as laser beams.

He tossed down the last of his drink. It scraped his guts. Felicia had been wrong to say he didn't have any. In setting the tumbler on the fireplace mantel he could not avoid the peripheral vision of her stocking feet, fallen awkwardly apart as if in mid-step of an intricate dance. She had in truth been a nimble jitterbugger at Warwick High. That wonderful pumping, wah-wahing big-band sound even little local bands could fabricate in those days. The tip of her girlish tongue would show between her teeth as she set herself to be twirled. He stooped and picked up the Lucretius from the floor and returned it to its place on the shelf. He went down into the cellar to look for a rope. The disgraceful old furnace was chewing its fuel with a strained whine; its brittle rusty carapace leaked so much heat the basement was the coziest part of the house. There was an old laundry room where the previous owners had left an antique Bendix with wringers and an old-fashioned smell of naphtha and even a basket of clothespins on the round tin lid of its tub. The games he used to play with clothespins, crayoning them into little long-legged men wearing round hats somewhat like sailor hats. Clothesline, nobody uses clothesline any more. But here was a coil, neatly looped and tucked behind the old washer in a world of cobwebs. The transparent hand of Providence, Clyde suddenly realized, was guiding him. With his own, opaque hands—veiny, gnarled, an old man's claws, hideous—he gave the rope a sharp yank and inspected six or eight feet of it for frayed spots that might give way. A rusty pair of metal shears lay handy and he cut off the needed length.

As when climbing a mountain, take one step at a time and don't look too far ahead up the path: this resolve carried him smoothly back up the stairs, holding the dusty rope. He turned left into the kitchen and looked up. The ceiling here had been lowered in renovation and presented a flimsy surface of textured cellulose tiles held in a grid of aluminum strapping. The house had nine-foot plaster ceilings in the other downstairs rooms; the ornate chandelier canopies, none of which still held a chandelier, might not take his weight even if he climbed a stepladder and found a protuberance to knot the clothesline around.

He went back into his library to pour one more drink. The fire was burning a bit less merrily and could do with another log; but such an attention lay on that vast sheet of concerns no longer relevant, no longer his. It took some getting used to, how hugely much no longer mattered. He sipped the drink and felt the smoky amber swallow descend toward a digestion that was also off the board, in the dark, not to occur. He thought of the cozy basement and wondered whether, if he promised just to live there in one of the old coal bins and never go outdoors, all might be forgiven and smoothed over. But this cringing thought polluted the purity he had created in his mind minutes ago. Think again.

Perhaps the rope was the problem. He had been a newspaperman for thirty years and knew of the rich variety of methods whereby people take their own lives. Suicide by automobile was actually one of the commonest; automotive suicides were buried every day by satisfied priests and unaffronted loved ones. But the method was uncertain and messily public and at this vanishing point all the aesthetic prejudices Clyde had suppressed in living seemed to be welling up along with images from his childhood. Some people, given the blaze in the fireplace, the awful evidence on the floor, and the thoroughly wooden house, might have made a pyre for themselves. But this would leave Jenny and Chris with no inheritance and Clyde was *not* one of those like Hitler who wanted to take the world with him; Felicia had been crazy in this comparison. Further, how could he trust himself not to save his scorched skin and flee to the lawn? He was no Buddhist monk, trained in discipline of that craven beast the body and able to sit in calm protest until the charred flesh toppled. Gas was held to be painless but then he was no mechanic either, to find the masking tape and string putty to seal off the many windows of the kitchen whose roominess and sunniness had been one of the factors in Felicia's and his decision to buy the house thirteen years ago this December. All of this year's December, it occurred to him with a guilty joy, December with its short dark tinselly days and ghastly herd buying and wooden homage to a dead religion (the dime-store carols, the pathetic crèche at Landing—Kazmierczak—Square, the Christmas tree erected at the other end of Dock Street in that great round marble urn called the Horse Trough), all of December was among the many things now off Clyde's sublimely simplified calendar. Nor would he have to pay next month's oil bill. Or gas bill. But he disdained the awkward wait gas would require, and he did not want his last view of reality to be the inside of a gas oven as he held his head in it on all fours in the servile position of a dog about to be fed. He rejected the messiness with knives and razor blades and bathtubs. Pills were painless and tidy but one of Felicia's causes had been a faddish militance against the pharmaceutical companies and what she said was their attempt to create a stoned America, a nation of drug-dependent zombies. Clyde smiled, the deep crease in his cheek leaping up. Some of what the old girl said had made sense. She hadn't been entirely babble. But he did not think she was right about Jennifer and Chris; he had never expected or desired them to stay home forever, he was offended only by Chris's going into such a flaky profession as the stage and Jenny's moving so far away, to Chicago no less, and letting herself be bombarded by X-rays, her ovaries exposed so she might never bear him any grandchildren. They too were off the map, grandchildren. Having children is something we think we ought to do because our parents did it, but when it is over the children are just other members of the human race, rather disappointingly. Jenny and Chris had been good quiet children and there had been something a bit disappointing in that too; by being good they had been evading Felicia, who when younger and not so plugged into altruism had had a terrible temper (sexual frustration no doubt at the root of it, but how can any husband keep a woman protected and excited at the same time?), and in the process the children had evaded him also. Jenny when about nine used to worry about death and once asked him why he didn't say prayers with her like the other daddies and though he didn't have much of an answer that was the closest together they had ever drawn. He had always been trying to read and her coming to him had been an interruption. With a better pair of parents Jenny could have grown to be a saint, such light pale clear eyes, a face as smooth as a photographed face after the retoucher is done with it. Until he had had a girl baby Clyde had never really seen female genitals, so sweet and puffy like twin little pale buns off a pastry tray.

The town had grown very silent around them, around him: not a car was stirring on Lodowick Street. His stomach hurt. It usually did, this time of night: an incipient ulcer. Doc Pat had told him, If you *must* keep drinking, at least eat. One of the unfortunate side effects of his affair with Sukie was skipping lunch in order to fuck. She sometimes brought a jar of cashews but with his bad teeth he wasn't that fond of nuts any more; the crumbs got under the appliance and cut his gums.

Amazing, women, the way loving never fills them up. If you do a good job they want more the next minute, as bad as getting out a newspaper. Even Felicia, for all she said she hated him. This time of night he would be having one more nip by the dying fire, giving her time to get herself into bed and fall asleep waiting for him. Having talked herself out, she toppled in a minute into the oblivion of the just. He wondered now if she had been hypoglycemic: in the mornings she had been clearheaded and the ghostly audience she gave her speeches to had dispersed. She had never seemed to grasp how much she infuriated him. Some mornings, on a Saturday or Sunday, she would keep her nightie on as provocation, by way of making up. You would think a man and woman living together so many hours of their lives would find a moment to make up in. Missed opportunities. If tonight he had just ridden it out and let her get safely upstairs . . . But that possibility, too, along with his grandchildren and the healing of his liquor-pitted stomach and his troubles with his little denture, was off the map.

Clyde had the sensation of there being several of him, like ghost images on TV. This time of night he, in a parade of such ghost images, would mount the stairs. The stairs. The limp dry old rope still dangled in his hand. Its cobwebs had come off on his corduroy trousers. Lord give me strength.

The staircase was a rather grand Victorian construction that doubled back after a midway landing with a view of the back yard and its garden, once elaborate but rather let go in recent years. A rope tied to the base of one of the upstairs balusters should provide enough swing room over the stairs below, which could serve as a kind of gallows platform. He carried the rope upstairs to the second-floor landing. He worked rapidly, fearing the alcohol might overtake him with a blackout. A square knot was right over left, then left over right. Or was it? His first attempt produced a granny. It was hard to move his hands through the narrow spaces between the squared baluster bases; his knuckles got skinned. His hands seemed to be a great distance from his eyes, and to have become luminous, as though plunged into an ethereal water. It took prodigies of calculation to figure where the loop in the rope should come (not more than six or eight inches under the narrow facing board with its touchingly fine Victorian molding, or his feet might touch the stairs and that blind animal his body would struggle to keep alive) and how big the loop for his head should be. Too big, he would fall through; too snug, he might merely strangle. The hangman's art: the neck should break, he had read more than once in his life, thanks to a sudden sharp pressure on the cervical vertebrae. Prisoners in jail used their belts with blue-faced results. Chris had been in Boy Scouts but that had been years ago and there had been a scandal with the scoutmaster that had broken up the den. Clyde finally produced a messy kind of compound slip knot and let the noose hang over the side. Viewed from above, by leaning over the banister, the perspective was sickening; the rope lightly swayed and kept swaying, turned into a pendulum by some waft of air that moved uninvited through this drafty house.

Clyde's heart was no longer in it but with the methodical determination that had put ten thousand papers to bed he went into the warm cellar (the old furnace chewing, chewing fuel) and fetched the aluminum stepladder. It felt feather-light; the might of angels was descending upon him. He also carried up some lumber scraps and with these set the ladder on the carpeted stairs so that, one pair of plastic feet resting three risers lower than the other on pieces of wood, the stepless cross-braced rails were vertical and the entire tilted *A*-shape would topple over at a nudge. The last thing he would see, he estimated, would be the front doorway and the leaded fanlight of stained glass, its vaguely sunriselike symmetrical pattern lit up by the sodium glow of a distant street lamp. By light nearer to hand, scratches on the aluminum seemed traces left by the swerving flight of atoms in a bubble chamber. Everything was touched with transparency; the many tapering, interlocked lines of the staircase were as the architect had dreamed them; it came to Clyde Gabriel, rapturously, that there was nothing to fear, of course our spirits passed through matter like the sparks of divinity they were, of course there would be an afterlife of infinite opportunities, in which he could patch things up with Felicia, and have Sukie too, not once but an infinity of times, just as Nietzsche had conjectured. A lifelong fog was lifting; it was all as clear as rectified type, the meaning that the stars had been singing out to him, *candida sidera*, tingeing with light his sluggish spirit sunk in its proud muck.

The aluminum ladder shivered slightly, like a highstrung youthful steed, as he trusted his weight to it. One step, two, then the third. The rope nestled dryly around his neck; the ladder trembled as he reached up and behind to slip the knot tighter, snug against what seemed the correct spot. Now the ladder was swinging violently from side to side; the agitated blood of its jockey was flailing it toward the hurdle, where it lifted, as he had foreseen, at the most delicate urging, and fell away. Clyde heard the clatter and thump. What he had not expected was the burning, as though a hot rasp were being pulled up through his esophagus, and the way the angles of wood and carpet and wallpaper whirled, whirled so widely it seemed for a second he had sprouted eyes in the back of his head. Then a redness in his overstuffed skull was followed by blackness, giving way, with the change of a single letter, to blankness.

"Oh baby, how horrible for you," Jane Smart said to Sukie, over the phone.

"Well it's not as if I'd had to see any of it myself. But the guys down at the police station were plenty vivid. Apparently she didn't have any face *left*." Sukie was not crying but her voice had that wrinkled quality of paper that has been damp and though dry will never lie flat again.

"Well she was a *vile* woman," Jane said firmly, comforting, though her head with its eyes and ears was still back in the suite of Bach unaccompanieds—the exhilarating, somehow malevolently onrushing Fourth, in E-flat Major. "So boring, so self-righteous," she hissed. Her eyes rested on the bare floor of her living room, splintered by repeated heedless socketing of her cello's pointed steel foot.

Sukie's voice faded in and out, as though she were letting the telephone drop away from her chin. "I've never known a man," she said, a bit huskily, "gentler than Clyde."

"Men are violent," Jane said, her patience wearing thin. "Even the mildest of them. It's biological. They're full of rage because they're just accessories to reproduction."

"He hated even to correct anybody at work," Sukie went on, as the sublime music—its diabolical rhythms, its wonderfully cruel demands upon her dexterity—slowly faded from Jane's mind, and the sting from the side of her left thumb, where she had been ardently pressing the strings. "Though once in a while he would blow up at some proofreader who had let just *oo*dles of things slip through."

"Well darling, it's obvious. That's why. He was keeping it all inside. When he blew up at Felicia he had thirty years' worth of rage, no wonder he took off her head."

"It's not fair to say he took off her head," Sukie said. "He just kind of—what's that phrase everybody's using these days? —*was*ted it."

"And then wasted himself," prompted Jane, hoping by such efficient summary to hasten this conversation along so she could return to her music; she liked to practice two hours in the mornings, from ten to noon, and then give herself a tidy lunch of cottage cheese or tuna salad spooned into a single large curved lettuce leaf. This afternoon she had set up a matinee with Darryl Van Horne at one-thirty. They would work for an hour on one of the two Brahmses or an amusing little Kodály Darryl had unearthed in a music shop tucked in the basement of a granite building on Weybosset Street just beyond the Arcade, and then have, their custom was, Asti Spumante, or some tequila milk Fidel would do in the blender, and a bath. Jane still ached, at both ends of her perineum, from their last time together. But most of the good things that come to a woman come through pain and she had been flattered that he would want her without an audience, unless you counted Fidel and Rebecca padding in and out with trays and towels; there was something precarious about Darryl's lust that was flattered and soothed by the three of them being there together and that needed the most extravagant encouragements when Jane was with him by herself. She added to Sukie irritably, "That he was clear-minded enough to carry it through is what I find surprising."

Sukie defended Clyde. "Liquor never made him confused unusually, he really drank as a kind of medicine. I think a lot of his depression must have been metabolic; he once told me his blood pressure was one-ten over seventy, which in a man his age was really wonderful."

Jane snapped, "I'm sure a lot of things about him were wonderful for a man of his age. I certainly preferred him to that deplorable Ed Parsley."

"Oh, Jane, I know you're dying to get me off the phone, but speaking of Ed . . ."

"Yess?"

"Have you been noticing how close Brenda has grown to the Neffs?"

"I've rather lost track of the Neffs, frankly."

"I know you have, and good for you," Sukie said. "Lexa and I always thought he abused you and you were much too gifted for his little group; it really was just jealousy, his saying your bowing or whatever he said was prissy."

"Thank you, sweet."

"Anyway, the two of them and Brenda are apparently thick as thieves now, they eat out at the Bronze Barrel or that new French place over toward Pettaquamscutt all the time and evidently Ray and Greta have encouraged her to put in for Ed's position at the church and become the new Unitarian minister. Apparently the Lovecrafts are all for it too and Horace you know is on the church board."

"But she's not ordained. Don't you have to be ordained? The Episcopalians where I fill in are very strict about things like that; you can't even join as a member unless a bishop has put his hands somewhere, I think on your head."

"No, but she *is* in the parsonage with those brats of theirs —abso*lu*tely undisciplined, neither Ed or Brenda believed in ever saying No—and making her the new minister might be more graceful than getting her to leave. Maybe there's a course or something you can take by mail."

"But can she preach? You *do* have to preach."

"Oh I don't think that would be any real problem. Brenda has wonderful posture. She was studying to be a modern dancer when she met Ed at an Adlai Stevenson rally; she was in one of the warm-up acts and he was to ask the blessing. He told me about it more than once, I used to wonder if he wasn't still in love with her after all."

"She is a ridiculous vapid woman," Jane said.

"Oh Jane, don't."

"Don't what?"

"Don't sound like that. That's the way we used to talk about Felicia, and look what happened."

Sukie had become very small and curled over at her end of the line, like a lettuce leaf wilting. "Are you blaming *us*?" Jane asked her briskly. "Her sad sot of a husband I would think instead should be blamed."

"On the surface, sure, but we *did* cast that spell, and put those things in the cookie jar when we got tiddly, and things did keep coming out of her mouth, Clyde mentioned it to me so innocently, he tried to get her to go to a doctor but she said medicine ought to be entirely nationalized in this country the way it is in England and Sweden. She hated the drug companies, too."

"She was full of hate, darling. It was the hate coming out of her mouth that did her in, not a few harmless feathers and pins. She had lost touch with her womanhood. She needed pain to remind her she was a woman. She needed to get down on her knees and drink some horrible man's nice cold come. She needed to be beaten, Clyde was right about that, he just went at it too hard."

"Please, Jane. You frighten me when you talk like that, the things you say."

"Why *not* say them? Really, Sukie, you sound infantile." Sukie was a weak sister, Jane thought. They put up with her for the gossip she gathered and that kid-sister shine she used to bring to their Thursdays but she really was just a conceited immature girl, she couldn't please Van Horne the way that Jane did, that burning stretching; even Greta Neff, washed-out old bag as she was with her granny glasses and pathetic pedantic accent, was more of a woman in this sense, a woman who could hold whole kingdoms of night within her, burning. "Words are just words," she added.

"They're not: they make things *hap*pen!" Sukie wailed, her voice shrivelled to a pathetic wheedle. "Now two people are dead and two children are orphans because of us!"

"I don't think you can be an orphan after a certain age," Jane said. "Stop talking nonsense." Her *s*'s hissed like spit on a stove top. "People stew in their own juice."

"If I hadn't slept with Clyde he wouldn't have gone so crazy, I'm sure of it. He loved me so, Jane. He used to just hold my foot in his two hands and kiss between each pair of toes."

"Of course he did. That's the kind of thing men are supposed to do. They're supposed to adore us. They're shits, try to keep that in mind. Men are absolutely shits, but we get them in the end because we can suffer better. A woman can outsuffer a man every time." Jane felt huge in her impatience; the black notes she had swallowed that morning bristled within her, alive. Who would have thought the old Lutheran had so much jism? "There will always be men for you, sweetie," she told Sukie. "Don't bother your head about Clyde any more. You gave him what he asked for, it's not your fault he couldn't handle it. Listen, truly. I must run." Jane Smart lied, "I have a lesson coming in at eleven."

In fact her lesson was not until four. She would rush back from the old Lenox place aching and steamy-clean and the sight of those grubby little hands on her pure ivory keys mangling some priceless simplified melody of Mozart's or Mendelssohn's would make her want to take the metronome and with its heavy base mash those chubby fingers as if she were grinding beans in a pestle. Since Van Horne had come into her life Jane was more passionate than she had ever been about music, that golden high-arched exit from this pit of pain and ignominy.

"She sounded so harsh and strange," Sukie said to Alexandra over the phone a few days later. "It's as if she thinks she has the inside track with Darryl and is fighting to protect it."

"That's one of his diabolical arts, to give each of us that impression. I'm really quite sure it's me he loves," said Alexandra, laughing with cheerful hopelessness. "He has me doing these bigger pieces of sculpture now, varnished papier-mâché is what this Saint-Phalle woman uses, I don't know how she does it, the glue gets all over your fingers, into your hair, *yukk*. I get one side of a figure looking right and then the other side has no shape at all, just a bunch of loose ends and lumps."

"Yes he was saying to me when I lose my job at the *Word* I should try a novel. I can't imagine sitting down day after day to the same story. And the people's names—people just don't *exist* without their real names."

"Well," Alexandra sighed, "he's challenging us. He's stretching us."

Over the phone she did sound stretched—more diffuse and distant every second, sinking into a translucent quicksand of estrangement. Sukie had come back to her house after the Gabriels' funeral, and no child was home from school yet, yet the little old house was sighing and muttering to itself, full of memories and mice. There were no nuts or munchies in the kitchen and as the next best consolation she had reached for the phone. "I miss our Thursdays," she abruptly confessed, childlike.

"I know, baby, but we have our tennis parties instead. Our baths."

"They frighten me sometimes. They're not as cozy as we used to be by ourselves."

"*Are* you going to lose your job? What's happening with that?"

"Oh I don't know, there are so many rumors. They say the owner rather than find a new editor is going to sell out to a chain of small-town weeklies the gangsters operate out of Providence. Everything is printed in Pawtucket and the only local news is what a correspondent phones in from her home and the rest is statewide feature articles and things they buy from a syndicate and they give them away to everybody like supermarket fliers."

"Nothing is as cozy as it used to be, is it?"

"*No*," Sukie blurted, but could not quite, like a child, cry.

A pause occurred, where in the old days they could hardly stop talking. Now each woman had her share, her third, of Van Horne to be secretive about, their solitary undiscussed visits to the island which in stark soft gray December had become more beautiful than ever; the ocean's silver-tinged horizon was visible now from those upstairs Arguslike windows behind which Van Horne had his black-walled bedroom, visible through the leafless beeches and oaks and swaying larches surrounding the elephantine canvas bubble that held the tennis court, where the snowy egrets used to nest. "How was the funeral?" Alexandra at last asked.

"Well, you know how they are. Sad and gauche at the same time. They were cremated, and it seemed so strange, burying these little rounded boxes like Styrofoam coolers, only brown, and smaller. Brenda Parsley said the prayer at the undertaker's, because they haven't found a replacement for Ed yet, and the Gabriels weren't anything really, though Felicia was always going on about everybody else's Godlessness. But the daughter wanted I guess some kind of religious touch. Very few people came, actually, considering all the publicity. Mostly *Word* employees putting in an appearance hoping to keep their jobs, and a few people who had been on committees with Felicia, but she had quarrelled you know with almost everybody. The people at Town Hall are delighted to have her off their backs, they all called her a witch."

"Did you speak to Brenda?"

"Just a bit, out at the cemetery. There were so few of us."

"How did she act toward you?"

"Oh, very polished and cool. She owes me one and she knows it. She wore a navy-blue suit with a ruffled silk blouse that did look sort of wonderfully ministerial. And her hair done in a different way, swept back quite severely and without those bangs like the woman in Peter, Paul, and Mary that used to make her look, you know, puppyish. An improvement, really. It was Ed used to make her wear those mini-skirts, so he'd feel more like a hippie, which was really rather humiliating, if you have Brenda's piano legs. She spoke quite well, especially at the graveside. This lovely fluting voice floating out over the headstones. She talked about how much into community service both the deceased were and tried to make some connection between their deaths and Vietnam, the moral confusion of our times, I couldn't quite follow it."

"Did you ask her if she hears from Ed?"

"Oh I wouldn't dare. Anyway I doubt it, since *I* never do any more. But she did bring him up. Afterwards, when the men were tugging the plastic grass around, she looked me very levelly in the eye and said his leaving was the best thing ever happened to her."

"Well, what else can she say? What else can any of us say?"

"Lexa sweet, whatever do you mean? You sound as though you're weakening."

"Well, one does get weary. Carrying everything alone. The bed is so cold this time of year."

"You should get an electric blanket."

"I have one. But I don't like the feeling of electricity on top of me. Suppose Felicia's ghost comes in and pours a bucket of cold water all over the bed, I'd be electrocuted."

"Alexandra, don't. Don't scare me by sounding so depressed. We all look to you for whatever it is. Mother-strength."

"Yes, and that's depressing too."

"Don't you believe in any of it any more?"

In freedom, in witchcraft. Their powers, their ecstasy.

"Of course I do, poops. Were the children there? What do they look like?"

"Well," Sukie said, her voice regaining animation, giving the news, "rather remarkable. They both look like Greek statues in a way, very stately and pale and perfect. And they stick together like twins even though the girl is a good bit older. Jennifer, her name is, is in her late twenties and the boy is college-age, though he's not in college; he wants to be something in show business and spends all his time getting rides back and forth between Los Angeles and New York. He was a stagehand at a summer-theatre place in Connecticut and the girl flew in from Chicago where she's taken a leave from her job as an X-ray technician. Marge Perley says they're going to stay here in the house a while to get the estate settled; I was thinking maybe we should do something with them. They seem such babes in the woods, I hate to think of their falling into Brenda's clutches."

"Baby, they've surely heard all about you and Clyde and blame you for everything."

"Really? How could they? I was being nothing but kind."

"You upset his internal balances. His ecology."

Sukie confessed, "I don't like feeling guilty."

"Who does? How do you think I feel, poor dear quite unsuitable Joe keeps offering to leave Gina and that swarm of fat children for me."

"But he never will. He's too Mediterranean. Catholics never get conflicted like us poor lapsed Protestants do."

"Lapsed," Alexandra said. "Is that how you think of yourself? I'm not sure I ever had anything to lapse from."

There entered into Sukie's mind, broadcast from Alexandra's, a picture of a western wooden church with a squat weather-beaten steeple, high in the mountains and unvisited. "Monty was very religious," Sukie said. "He was always talking about his ancestors." And on the same wavelength the image of Monty's drooping milk-smooth buttocks came to her and she knew at last for certain that he and Alexandra had had an affair. She yawned, and said, "I think I'll go over to Darryl's and unwind. Fidel is developing some wonderful new concoction he calls a Rum Mystique."

"Are you sure it isn't Jane's day?"

"I think she was having her day the day I talked to her. Her talk was really excited."

"It burns."

"Exactly. Oh, Lexa, you really should see Jennifer Gabriel, she's delicious. She makes me look like a tired old hag. This pale round face and these pale blue eyes like Clyde had and a pointy chin like Felicia had and the most delicate little nose, with a fine straight edge like something you would sculpture with a butter knife but slightly dented into her face, like a cat's if you can picture it. And such skin!"

"Delicious," Alexandra echoed, driftingly. Alexandra used to love her, Sukie knew. That first night at Darryl's, dancing to Joplin, they had clung together and wept at the curse of heterosexuality that held them apart as if each were a rose in a plastic tube. Now there was a detachment in Alexandra's voice. Sukie remembered that charm she made, with its magical triple bow, and reminded herself to take it out from under her bed. Spells go bad, lose efficacy, within about a month, if no human blood is involved.

And a few more days later Sukie met the female Gabriel orphan walking without her brother along Dock Street: on that wintry, slightly crooked sidewalk, half the shops shuttered for the winter and the others devoted to scented tinted candles and Austrian-style Christmas ornaments imported from Korea, these two stars shone to each other from afar and tensely let gravitational attraction bring them together, while the windows of the travel agency and the Superette, of the Yapping Fox with its cable-knit sweaters and sensible plaid skirts and of the Hungry Sheep with its slightly slinkier wear, of Perley Realty with its faded snapshots of Cape-and-a-halfs and great dilapidating Victorian gems along Oak Street waiting for an enterprising young couple to take them over and make the third floor into apartments, of the bakery and the barbershop and the Christian Science reading room all stared. The Eastwick branch of the Old Stone Bank had installed against much civic objection a drive-in window, and Sukie and Jennifer had to wait as if on opposite banks of a stream while several cars nosed in and out of the slanted accesses carved into the sidewalk. The downtown was much too cramped and historic, the objectors, led by the late Felicia Gabriel, had pointed out in vain, for such a further complication of traffic.

Sukie at last made it to the younger woman's side, around the giant fins of a crimson Cadillac being guardedly steered by fussy, dim-sighted Horace Lovecraft. Jennifer wore a dirty old buff parka wherein the down had flattened and one of Felicia's scarves, a loose-knit purple one, wrapped several times around her throat and chin. Several inches shorter than Sukie, she seemed an under-nurtured waif, her eyes watery and nostrils pink. The thermometer that day stood near zero.

"How's it going?" Sukie asked, with forced cheer.

In size and age this girl was to Sukie as Sukie was to Alexandra; though Jennifer was wary, she had to yield to superior powers. "Not so bad," she responded, in a small voice whittled smaller by the cold. She had acquired in Chicago a touch of Midwestern nasality in her pronunciation. She studied Sukie's face and took a little plunge, adding confidingly, "There's so much stuff; Chris and I are overwhelmed. We've both been living like gypsies, and Mommy and Daddy kept *every*thing— drawings we both did in kindergarten, our grade-school report cards, boxes and boxes of old photographs. . . ."

"It must be sad."

"Well, that, and *frus*trating. They should have made some of these decisions themselves. And you can see how things were let slide these last years; Mrs. Perley said we'd be cheating ourselves if we didn't wait to sell it until after we can get it painted in the spring. It would cost maybe two thousand and add ten to the value of the place."

"Look. You look frozen." Sukie herself was snug and imperial-looking in a long sheepskin coat, and a hat of red fox fur that picked up the copper glint of her own. "Let's go over to Nemo's and I'll buy you a cup of coffee."

"Well . . ." The girl wavered, looking for a way out, but tempted by the idea of warmth.

Sukie pressed her offensive. "Maybe you hate me, from things you've heard. If so, it might do you good to talk it out."

"Mrs. Rougemont, why would I hate you? It's just Chris is at the garage with the car, the Volvo—even the car they left us was way overdue for its checkup."

"Whatever's wrong with it will take longer to fix than they said," Sukie said authoritatively, "and I'm sure Chris is happy. Men love garages. All that banging. We can sit at a table in the front so you can see him go by if he does. Please. I want to say how sorry I am about your parents. He was a kind boss and I'm in trouble too, now that he's gone."

A badly rusted '59 Chevrolet, its trunk shaped like gull wings, nearly brushed them with its chrome protuberances as it lumbered up over the curb toward the browny-green drive-in window; Sukie touched the girl's arm to safeguard her. Then, not letting go, she urged her across the street to Nemo's. Dock Street had been widened more than once as motor traffic increased in this century; its crooked sidewalks had been pared in places to the width of a single pedestrian and some of the older buildings jutted out at odd angles. Nemo's Diner was a long aluminum box with rounded corners and a broad red stripe along its sides. In mid-morning it held only the counter crowd—underemployed or retired men several of whom with casual handlift or nod greeted Sukie, but less gladly, it seemed to her, than before Clyde Gabriel had let horror into the town.

The little tables at the front were empty, and the picture window that overlooked the street here sweated and trickled with condensation. As Jennifer squinted against the light, small creases leaped up at the corners of her ice-pale eyes and Sukie saw that she was not quite so young as she had seemed on the street, swaddled in rags. Her dirty parka, patched with iron-on rectangles of tan vinyl, she laid a bit ceremoniously across the chair beside her, and coiled the long purple skein of scarf upon it. Underneath, she wore a simple gray skirt and white lamb's-wool sweater. She had a tidy plump figure; and there was a roundness to her that seemed too simple—her arms and breasts and cheeks and throat all defined with the same neat circular strokes.

Rebecca, the slatternly Antiguan Fidel was known to keep company with, came with crooked hips and her heavy gray lips twisted wryly shut on all she knew. "Now what you ladies be liking?"

"Two coffees," Sukie asked her, and on impulse also ordered johnnycakes. She had a weakness for them; they were so crumby and buttery and today would warm her insides.

"Why did you say I might hate you?" the other woman asked, with surprising directness, yet in a mild slight voice.

"Because." Sukie decided to get it over with. "I was your father's—whatever. You know. Lover. But not for long, only since summer. I didn't mean to mess anybody up, I just wanted to give him something, and I'm all I have. And he *was* lovable, as you know."

The girl showed no surprise but became more thoughtful, lowering her eyes. "I know he was," she said. "But not much recently, I think. Even when we were little, he seemed distracted and sad. And then smelled funny at night. Once I knocked some big book out of his lap trying to cuddle and he started to spank me and couldn't seem to stop." Her eyes lifted as her mouth shut on further confession; there was a curious vanity, the vanity of the meek, in the way her nicely formed, unpainted lips sealed so tidily one against the other. Her upper lip lifted a bit in faint distaste. "*You* tell me about him. My father."

"What about him?"

"What he was like."

Sukie shrugged. "Tender. Grateful. Shy. He drank too much but when he knew he was going to see me he would try not to, so he wouldn't be—stupid. You know. Sluggish."

"Did he have a lot of girlfriends?"

"Oh no. I don't think so." Sukie was offended. "Just me, was my conceited impression. He loved your mother, you know. At least until she became so—obsessed."

"Obsessed with what?"

"I'm sure you know better than I. With making the world a perfect place."

"That's rather nice, isn't it, that she wanted it to be?"

"I suppose." Sukie had never thought of it as nice, Felicia's public nagging: a spiteful ego trip, rather, with more than an added pinch of hysteria. Sukie did not appreciate being put on the defensive by this bland little ice maiden, who from the sound of her voice might be getting a cold. Sukie volunteered, "You know, if you're single in a town like this you pretty much have to take what you can find."

"No I don't know," said Jennifer, but softly. "But then I guess I don't know much about that sort of thing altogether."

Meaning what? That she was a virgin? It was hard to know if the girl was empty or if her strange stillness manifested an exceptionally complete inner poise. "Tell me about you," Sukie said. "You're going to become a doctor? Clyde was so proud of that."

"Oh, but it's a fraud. I keep running out of money and flunking anatomy. It was the chemistry I liked. The technician job is really as far as I'm ever going to go. I'm stuck."

Sukie told her, "You should meet Darryl Van Horne. He's trying to get us all *un*stuck."

Jennifer unexpectedly smiled, her little flat nose whitening with the tension. Her front teeth were round as a child's. "What a grand name," she said. "It sounds made up. Who is he?"

But she must, Sukie thought, have heard about our sabbats. The girl was difficult to see through; patches of an unnatural innocence, as though she had been skipped by life, blocked telepathy as lead blocks X-rays. "Oh, a sort of eccentric young-ish middle-aged man who's bought the old Lenox place. You know, the big brick mansion toward the beach."

"The haunted plantation, we used to call that. I was fifteen when my parents moved here and really never got to know the area terribly well. There's an enormous amount to it, though it looks like nothing on the map."

Insolent tropical Rebecca brought their coffee in Nemo's heavy white mugs, and the golden johnnycakes; along with the pronounced warm fragrances of these there carried across the glazed table a spicy sour smell that Sukie linked to the waitress herself, her broad pelvis and heavy coffee-colored breasts, as she leaned over to set the mugs and plates in place. "Is there anything wanting now of you ladies' happi-ness?" the waitress asked, looking down upon them from the great slopes of herself. Her head looked rather small and sinewy—her black hair done in corn rows of tight braids—upon the mass of her flesh.

"Is there any cream, Becca?" Sukie asked.

"I get you de one." Putting down the little aluminum pitcher, she told them, "You can say 'cream' if you likes, milk is what de boss puts in every mornin'."

"Thank you, darling, I *meant* milk." But for a little joke Sukie quickly said to herself the white spell *Sator arepo tenet opera rotas*, and the milk poured thick and yellow, cream. Curdled flecks rotated on the circular surface of her coffee. Johnnycake turned to buttery fragments in her mouth. Indian ghosts of cornmeal slipped through the forest of her tastebuds. She swallowed and said, of Van Horne, "He's nice. You'd like him, once you got over his manner."

"What's wrong with his manner?"

Sukie wiped crumbs from her smiling lips. "He comes on rough, but it's a put-on really. He's really no threat, anybody can manage Darryl. A couple of my girlfriends and I play tennis with him in this fantastic big canvas bubble he's put up. Do you play?"

Jennifer's round shoulders shrugged. "A little. Mostly at summer camp. And a bunch of us used to go use the U. of C. courts occasionally."

"How long are you going to be around, before you go back to Chicago?"

Jennifer was watching the curds swirl in her own coffee. "A while. It may take until summer to sell the house, and Chris has nothing much to do as it turns out and we get along easily; we always have. Maybe I won't go back. As I said, it wasn't working out that great at Michael Reese."

"Were you having man trouble?"

"Oh *no*." Her eyes lifted, displaying below her pale irises arcs of pure youthful white. "Men don't seem all that interested in me."

"But why not? If I may say so, you're lovely."

The girl lowered her eyes. "Isn't this funny milk? So thick and sweet. I wonder if it's gone bad."

"No, I think you'll find it very fresh. You haven't eaten your johnnycake."

"I nibbled at it. I never was that crazy about them, they're just fried dough."

"That's why we Rhode Islanders like them. They come as they are. I'll finish yours if you don't want it."

"I must do something wrong that men sense. I used to talk about it with my friends sometimes. *My* girlfriends."

"A woman needs woman friends," Sukie said complacently.

"I didn't have that many of those either. Chicago is a tough town. These birdlike little ethnic women studying all night and full of all the answers. If you ask them anything personal, though, like what you're doing wrong with these men you have to meet, they clam right up."

"It's hard to be right with men, actually," Sukie told her. "They're very angry with us because we can have babies and they can't. They're terribly jealous, poor dears: Darryl tells us that. I don't really know whether or not to believe him; as I say, a lot of him is pure put-on. At lunch the other day he was trying to describe his theories to me, they all have to do with some chemical whose name begins with 'silly.'"

"Selenium. It's a magical element. It's the secret of those doors in airports that open automatically in front of you. Also it takes the green color out of glass that iron gives it. Selenic acid can dissolve gold."

"Well, my goodness, you do know a thing or two. If you're that into chemistry, maybe you could be Darryl's assistant."

"Chris keeps saying I should just hang out in our house with him a while, at least until we sell it. He's fed up with New York, *it's* too tough. He says the gays control all the fields he's interested in—window dressing, stage design."

"I think you should."

"Should what?"

"Hang around. Eastwick's amusing." Rather impatiently— the morning was wasting—Sukie brushed all the johnnycake crumbs from the front of her sweater. "This is *not* a tough town. This is a *sweet*ie-pie town." She washed down the crumbs in her mouth with a last sip of coffee and stood.

"I feel that," the other woman said, getting the signal and beginning to gather up her scarf, her pathetic patched parka. Dressed and on her feet, Jenny performed a surprising, thrilling mannish action: she took Sukie's hand in a firm grip. "Thank you," she said, "for talking to me. The only other person who has taken any interest in us, except for the lawyers of course, is that nice lady minister, Brenda Parsley."

"She's a minister's wife, not a minister, and I'm not sure she's so nice either."

"Her husband behaved horribly to her, everybody tells me."

"Or she to him."

"I *knew* you'd say something like that," Jennifer said, and smiled, not unpleasantly; but it made Sukie feel naked, she could be seen right through, with no lead vest of innocence to protect her. Her life was lived in full view of the town; even this little stranger knew a thing or two.

Before Jennifer flicked the scarf into place Sukie noticed that around her neck hung a thin gold chain of the type that for some people supports a cross. But at the base of the girl's slender soft white throat hung the Egyptian tau cross, its loop at the top like the head of a tiny man—an ankh, symbol of life and death both, an ancient sign of mysteries come newly into vogue.

Seeing Sukie's eyes linger there, Jennifer looked oppositely at the other's necklace of copper moons and said, "My mother was wearing copper. A broad plain bracelet I'd never seen before. As if—"

"As if what, dear?"

"As if she were trying to ward something off."

"Aren't we all?" said Sukie cheerily. "I'll be in touch about tennis."

The space inside Van Horne's great bubble was acoustically and atmospherically weird: the sounds of shouts and of balls being hit seemed smothered even as they rang out, and a faint prickly sensation of pressure weighed on Sukie's freckled brow and forearms. The amber hair of these forearms stood up as if electrified. Beneath the overarching firmament of dun canvas everything seemed in slightly slow motion; the players moved through an aura of compression, though in fact the limp dome stayed inflated because the air within it, pumped by a tireless fan through a boxy plastic mouth sealed by duct tape low in one corner, was warmer than the winter air outside. Today was the shortest day of the year. An earth hard as iron lay locked beneath a sky whose mottled clouds spit snow like ashes sucked up a chimney and then dispersed with the smoke. Thin powdery lines appeared next to brick edges and exposed tree roots but melted in the wan noon sun; there was no accumulation, though every shop and bank with its seasonal pealing and cotton mimicry was inviting Christmas to be white. Dock Street, as early darkness overtook the muffled shoppers, looked harried, its gala lights a forestallment of sleep, a desperate hollow-eyed attempt to live up to some

promise in the bitter black air. Playing tennis in their tights
and leg warmers and ski sweaters and double pairs of socks
stuffed into their sneakers, the young divorced mothers of
Eastwick were taking a holiday from the holiday.

Sukie feared guiltily that she might have spoiled it for the
others by bringing Jennifer Gabriel along. Not that Darryl
Van Horne had objected to her suggestion over the phone; it
was his nature to welcome new recruits and perhaps their little
circle of four was becoming narrow for him. Like most men,
especially wealthy men, especially wealthy men from New York
City, he was easily bored. But Jennifer had taken the liberty of
bringing her brother along, and Darryl would surely be appalled by the entry into his home of this boy, who was in the
newest fashion of youth inarticulate and sullen, with glazed
eyes, a slack fuzzy jaw, and tangled curly hair so dirty as to be
scarcely blond. Instead of tennis sneakers he had worn beat-up
rubber-cleated running shoes that even in the chill vastness of
the bubble gave off a stale foul smell of male sweat. Sukie wondered how pristine Jennifer could stand a housemate so slovenly. Monty for all his faults had been fastidious, always taking
showers and rinsing out coffee cups she had abandoned on an
end table after a phone conversation. The boy had borrowed a
racket and shown no ability to hit the ball over the net, and no
embarrassment at his inability, only a sluggish petulance. Ever
the courteous host and seeming gentleman, Darryl, though
all suited up to play, in an outfit of maroon jogging pants and
purple down vest that made him look like a macaw, had suggested that the four females enjoy a set of ladies' doubles while
he took Christopher away for a tour of the library, the lab, the
little conservatory of poisonous tropical plants. The boy followed with languid ingratitude as Darryl gestured and spouted
words; through the walls of the bubble they could hear him
exclaiming all the way up the path to the house. Sukie did feel
guilty.

She took Jenny as her partner in case the girl proved inept, though in warming up she had shown a firm stroke from
both sides; in play she showed herself to be a spunky sound-
enough player, though without much range—which may
have been partly deference to Sukie's leggy, reaching style. At
about the age of eleven, Sukie, learning the game on an old,

rhododendron-screened macadam court a friend of her family's had on his lakeside estate, had been complimented by her father for a spectacular, lunging "get"; and ever after she had been a "fetching" style of player, even lagging in one corner and then the other to make her returns seem spectacular. It was the ball right in on her fists Sukie sometimes couldn't handle. She and Jenny quickly went up four games to one on Alexandra and Jane, and then the tricks began. Though the object coming into Sukie's forehand was an optic-yellow Wilson, what she got her racket on—knees bent, head down, power flowing forward and up for a topspin return—was a gob of putty; the weight of it took a chip out of her elbow, it felt like. What dribbled up to the net between Jennifer's feet was inarguably, again, a tennis ball. On the next point the serve came to her backhand and, braced against another lump of putty, she felt something lighter than a sparrow fly from her strings; it disappeared into the shadowy vault of the dome, beyond the ring of clear plastic portholes that admitted light, and fell far out of bounds in the form of an optic-yellow Wilson.

"Play fair, you two fiends," Sukie shouted across the net.

Jane Smart called back flutingly, "Keep your eye on the ball, sugar, and bad things won't happen."

"The hell you say, Jane Pain. I put perfect swings into both those shots." Sukie was angry because it wasn't *fair*, when her partner was an innocent. Jennifer, who had been poised on the half-court line, had seen only the outcome of these shots and turned now to show Sukie a forgiving, encouraging face, heart-shaped and flushed a bright pink. On the next exchange, the girl darted to the net after a weak return from Jane, and Sukie willed Alexandra to freeze; Jenny's sharp volley thudded against the big woman's immobilized flesh. Released from the spell in a twinkling, Alexandra rubbed the stung spot on her thigh.

Reproachfully she told Sukie, "That would have really hurt if I weren't wearing woolies under my tights."

A welt would arise there, though, and Sukie apologetically pleaded, "Come on, let's just play real tennis." But both opponents were sore now. A grinding pain seized Sukie's joints as she stretched to volley an easy shot coming over the center of the net; pulled up short, she helplessly watched the blurred ball bounce on the center stripe. But she heard Jenny's feet drum behind her and saw the ball, miraculously returned, drop between Jane and Alexandra, who had thought they had the point won. This brought the game back to deuce, and Sukie, still staggered by that sudden ache injected into her joints but determined to protect her partner from all this *maleficia*, said the blasphemous backwards words *Retson Retap* three times rapidly to herself and created an air pocket, a fault in the crystal of space, above their opponents' forecourt, so that Jane double-faulted twice, the ball diving in mid-trajectory as from a table edge.

That made the game score five to one and brought the serve to Jenny. When she tossed the ball up, it became an egg and spattered all over her upturned face, through the gut strings. Sukie threw down her racket in disgust and it became a snake, that then had nowhere to slither to, the great bubble being sealed all along the edge; frantically the creature, damned at the dawn of creation, whipped its S's and zetas of motion back and forth across the blood-colored AsPhlex that framed the green court, its diagrammed baselines and boundaries. "All right," Sukie announced. "That does it. The game's over." Little Jenny with an inadequate feminine handkerchief was trying to wipe away from around her eyes the webby watery albumen and the yolk with its fleck of blood. The egg had been fertilized. Sukie took the hanky from her and dabbed. "I'm sorry, so sorry," she said. "They just can't stand to lose, they are terrible women."

"At least," Alexandra called across the net apologetically, "it wasn't a *rot*ten egg."

"It's all right," Jennifer said, a little breathless but her voice still level. "I knew you all have these powers. Brenda Parsley told me."

"That idiotic blabbermouth," Jane Smart said. The other two witches had come around the net to help wipe Jennifer's face. "We don't have any powers she doesn't, now that she's been left."

"Is that what does it, being left?" Jenny asked.

"Or doing the leaving," Alexandra said. "The strange thing is it doesn't make any difference. You'd think it would. Anyway, I'm sorry about the egg. But my thigh's going to be black and blue tomorrow because Sukie wouldn't let me move; it wasn't really playing the game."

Sukie said, "It was as much playing the game as what you were doing to me."

"You mis-hit those shots plain and simple," Jane Smart called over; she had gone to the edge of the court to look for something.

"I thought too," said Jennifer softly, courting the others, "your head came up, at least on the backhand."

"You weren't watching."

"I was. And you have a tendency to straighten your knees at impact."

"I *don't*. You're supposed to be my *part*ner. You're supposed to en*cour*age me."

"You were wonderful," the girl said obediently.

Jane returned holding in her cupped palm a little heap of black sand she had scraped up with her fingernails at the side of the court. "Close your eyes," she ordered Jennifer, and threw the sand directly into her face. Magically, the glutinous remains of egg evaporated, leaving, however, the grit, which gave the smooth upturned features a startled barbaric look, as if wearing a speckled mask.

"Maybe it's time for our bath," Alexandra remarked, gazing maternally at Jennifer's gritty face.

Sukie wondered how they could have their usual bath with these strangers among them and blamed herself, for having been too forthcoming in inviting them. It was her mother's fault; back home in New York State there had always been extra people at the dinner table, people in off the street, possible angels in disguise to her mother's way of thinking. Aloud Sukie protested, "But Darryl hasn't played yet! Or Christopher," she added, though the boy had been lackadaisical and arrogantly inept.

"They don't seem to be coming back," Jane Smart observed.

"Well we better go do something or we'll all catch cold," Alexandra said. She had borrowed Jenny's damp handkerchief (monogrammed *J*) and with an intricately folded corner of it was removing, grain by grain, the sand from the girl's docile round face, tilted up toward this attention like a pink flower to the sun.

Sukie felt a pang of jealousy. She swung her arms and said, "Let's go up to the house," though her muscles still had lots of tennis in them. "Unless somebody wants to play singles."

Jane said, "Maybe Darryl."

"Oh he's too marvellous, he'd slaughter me."

"I don't think so," Jenny said softly, having observed their host warm up and as yet unable to see, fully, the wonder of him. "You have much better form. He's quite wild, isn't he?"

Jane Smart said coldly, "Darryl Van Horne is quite the most civilized person I know. And the most tolerant." Irritably she went on, "Lexa dear, do stop fussing with that. It'll all come off in the bath."

"I didn't bring a bathing suit," said Jennifer, her eyes wide and questing from face to face.

"It's quite dark in there, nobody can see anything," Sukie told her. "Or if you'd rather you can go home."

"Oh, no. It's too depressing. I keep imagining Daddy's body hanging in midair and that makes me too scared to go up and start sorting the things in the attic."

And it occurred to Sukie that whereas the three of them all had children they should be tending to, Jennifer and Christopher *were* children, tending to themselves. She suffered a sad vision of Clyde's prick, a father's, which could have been her own father's and in truth *had* seemed a relic of sorts, with a jaundiced tinge on its underside when erect and enormously long gray hairs, like hairs from an old woman's head, snaking down from the testicles. No wonder he had overreacted when she spread her legs. Sukie led the other women out of the tennis bubble, whose oval door unzipped from either side and had to be used quickly, to keep warm air from escaping.

The dying December day nipped at their faces, their sneakered feet. Coal, that loathsome Labrador of Alexandra's, and Darryl's blotchy nervous collie, Needlenose, who had together trapped and torn apart some furry creature in the island's little woods, came and romped around them, their black muzzles bloody. The earth of the once gently bellied lawn leading up to the house had been torn by bulldozers to build the court this fall and the clumps of sod and clay, frozen hard, made a moonscape treacherous to tread. Tears of cold in Sukie's eyes gave her companions a rainbow aura and it hurt her cheeks to talk. On the firmness of the driveway she broke into a sprint; at her back the others followed like a single clumsy beast on the gravel. The great oak door yielded to her push as if sensate, and in the marble-floored foyer, with its hollow elephant's foot, a sulphurous pillow of heat hit her in the face. Fidel was nowhere in sight. Following a mutter of voices, the women found Darryl and Christopher sitting on opposite sides of the round leather-topped table in the library. Old comic books and a tea tray were arranged on the table between them. Above them hung the melancholy stuffed moose and deer heads that had been left by the sporting Lenoxes: mournful glass eyes that did not blink though burdened with dust. "Who won?" Van Horne asked. "The good or the wicked?"

"Which witch is which?" Jane Smart asked, flinging herself down on a crimson beanbag chair under a cliff of bound arcana, pale-spined giant volumes identified in spidery Latin. "The fresh blood won," she said, "as it usually does." Fluffy, malformed Thumbkin had been standing still as a statuette on the hearth tiles, so close to the fire the tips of her whiskers seemed to spark; now with great dignity she stalked over to Jane's ankles and, as if Jane's white athletic socks were scratching posts, sunk the arcs of her claws deeply in, her tail at the same time shivering bolt upright as though she were blissfully urinating. Jane yowled and with the toe of one sneakered foot hoisted the animal high into space. Thumbkin spun like a great snowflake before noiselessly landing on her double paws over near where the brass-handled poker, tongs, and ash shovel glittered in their stand. The offended cat's eyes blinked and then joined their brass glitter; the vertical pupils narrowed in their yellow irises, contemplating the gathering.

"They began to use dirty tricks," Sukie tattled. "I feel gypped."

"That's how you tell a real woman," joked Darryl Van Horne in his throaty, faraway voice. "She always feels gypped."

"Darryl, don't be dreary and epigrammatical," Alexandra said. "Chris, does that tea taste as good as it looks?"

"'TsO.K.," the boy managed to get out, sneering and not meeting anyone's eye.

Fidel had materialized. His khaki jacket looked more mussed than usual. Had he been with Rebecca in the kitchen?

"*Té para las señoras y la señorita, por favor*," Darryl told him. Fidel's English was excellent and increasingly idiomatic, but it was part of their master-servant relationship that they spoke Spanish as long as Van Horne knew the words.

"*Sí, señor.*"

"*Rápidamente*," Van Horne pronounced.

"*Sí, sí.*" Away he went.

"Oh isn't this cozy!" Jane Smart exclaimed, but in truth something about it dissatisfied Sukie and made her sad: the whole house was like a stage set, stunning from one angle but from others full of gaps and unresolved shabbiness. It was an imitation of a real house somewhere else.

Sukie pouted, "I didn't get the tennis out of my system. Darryl: come down and play singles with me. Just until the light goes. You're all suited up for it and everything."

He said gravely, "What about young Chris here? He hasn't played either."

"He doesn't want to I'm sure," Jennifer interjected in a sisterly voice.

"I stink," the boy agreed. He really was blah, Sukie thought. A girl his age would be so amusing, so alert and socially sensitive, gathering in impressions, turning them into flirtation and sympathy, making the room her web, her nest, her theatre. Sukie felt herself quite frantic, standing and tossing her hair, verging on rudeness and exhibitionism, and she didn't quite know what to blame, except that she was embarrassed at having brought the Gabriels here—never again!—and hadn't had sex with a man since Clyde committed suicide two weeks ago. She had found herself lately at night thinking of Ed, wondering what he was doing off in the underground with that little low-class smudge Dawn Polanski.

Darryl, intuitive and kind for all his coarse manner, rose in his red jogging pants and put his purple down vest back on, plus a Day-Glo orange hunting cap with a bill and earflaps that he sometimes wore for a joke, and took up his racket, an aluminum Head. "One quick set," he warned, "with a seven-point tie breaker, if it goes to six-six. First ball turns into a toad, you forfeit. Anybody want to come watch?" Nobody did, they were waiting for their *té*. Lonely as a married couple then, the two of them went out into the dimming gray afternoon—the silent woods and bushes lavender and the sky an enamelled green in the east—down to the dome with its graveyard closeness and quiet.

The tennis was grand; not only did Darryl play like a robot, clumsy-looking but infallible, but he drew forth from Sukie amazing shots, impossible gets turned into singing winners, the segmented breadths and widths of the court miniaturized by her unnatural speed and adroitness. The ball hung like a moon as she raced for it; her body became an instrument of thought, present wherever she willed it. She even brought off a few backhand overheads. She felt herself stretch at the top of her serves like a bow releasing an arrow. She was Diana, Isis, Astarte. She was female grace and strength shed, for this silver moment, of its rough garb of servitude. Gloom gathered in the corners of the dun bubble; the portholes of sky hovered overhead like a mammoth crown of aquamarines; her eyes could no longer see the dark opponent scrambling and thumping and heaving on the far side of the net. The ball kept coming back, and with pace, springing up at her face like a predator repeatedly reborn from the painted asphalt. Hit, hit, she kept hitting, and the ball got smaller and smaller—the size of a golf ball, the size of a golden pea, and at last there was no bounce on the inky far side of the net, just a leathery swallowing sound, and the game was over. "That was bliss," Sukie announced, to whoever was there.

Van Horne's voice scraped and rumbled forward, saying, "I was a pal to you, how's about being a pal to me?"

"O.K.," Sukie said. "What do I do?"

"Kiss my ass," he said huskily. He offered it to her over the net. It was hairy, or downy, depending on how you felt about men. Left, right . . .

"And in the middle," he demanded.

The smell seemed to be a message he must deliver, a word brought from afar, not entirely unsweet, a whiff of camel essence coming through the flaps of the silken tents of the Dragon Throne's encampment in the Gobi Desert.

"Thanks," Van Horne said, pulling up his pants. In the dark he sounded like a New York taxi driver, raspy. "Seems silly to you, I know, but it gives me a helluva boost."

They walked together up the hill, Sukie's sweat caking on her skin. She wondered how they would manage the hot tub with Jennifer Gabriel there and showing no disposition to leave. Back in the house, the loutish brother was alone in the library, reading a big blue volume that Sukie in a glance over his shoulder saw to be bound comic books. A caped man in a blue hood with pointed ears: Batman. "The complete fucking set," Van Horne boasted. "It cost me a bundle, some of those old ones, going back to the war, that if I'd had the sense to save as a kid I could have made a fortune on. Christ I wasted my childhood waiting for next month's issue. Loved The Joker. Loved The Penguin. Loved the Batmobile in its underground garage. You're both too young to have gotten the bug."

The boy uttered a complete sentence. "They used to be on TV."

"Yeah, but they camped it up. They didn't have to do that. They made it all a joke, that was damn poor taste. The old comic books, there's real evil there. That white face used to haunt my dreams, I'm not kidding. How do you feel about Captain Marvel?" Van Horne pulled from the shelves a volume from another set, bound in red rather than blue, and with a comic fervor boomed, "Sha-ZAM!" To Sukie's surprise he settled himself in a wing chair and began to leaf through, his big face skidding with pleasure.

Sukie followed the faint sound of female voices through the long room of moldering Pop Art, the small room of unpacked boxes, and the double doors leading to the slate-lined bath. The lights in their round ribbed wells had been rheostatted to low. The stereo's red eye was watching over the gentle successions of a Schubert sonata. Three heads of pinned-up hair were disposed upon the surface of steaming water. The voices murmured on, and no head turned to watch Sukie undress. She slid from her many stiff layers of tennis clothes and walked through the humid air naked, sat on the stone edge, and arched her back to give herself to the water, at first too fiery to bear but then not, not. Oh. Slowly she became a new self. Water like sleep sucks our natural heaviness away. Alexandra's and Jane's familiar bodies bobbed about her; their waves and hers merged in one healing agitation. Jennifer Gabriel's round head and round shoulders rested in the center of her vision; the girl's round breasts floated just beneath the surface of the transparent black

water and in it her hips and feet were foreshortened like a mis-
begotten fetus's. "Isn't this lovely?" Sukie asked her.

"It is."

"He has all these controls," Sukie explained.

"Is he going to come in with us?" Jennifer asked, afraid.

"I think not," Jane Smart said, "this time."

"Out of deference to you, dear," Alexandra added.

"I feel so safe. Should I?"

"Why not?" one of the witches asked.

"Feel safe while you can," another advised.

"The lights are like stars, aren't they? Random, I mean."

"Watch this." They all knew the controls now. At the push
of a finger the roof rumbled back. The first pale piercings—
planets, red giants—showed early evening's mothering turquoise dome to be an illusion, a nothing. There were spheres
beyond spheres, each transparent or opaque as the day and
year turned.

"My goodness. The outdoors."

"Yess."

"Yet I don't feel cold."

"Heat rises."

"How much money do you think he put into all this?"

"Thousands."

"But why? For what purpose?"

"For us."

"He loves us."

"Only us?"

"We don't really know."

"It's not a useful question."

"Aren't you content?"

"Yes."

"Yess."

"But I'm thinking Chris and I should be getting back. The
pets should be fed."

"What pets?"

"Felicia Gabriel used to say we shouldn't waste protein on
pets when everybody in Asia was starving."

"I didn't know Clyde and Felicia had pets."

"They didn't. But shortly after we got here somebody put

a puppy in the Volvo one night. And a cat came to the door a little later."

"Think of us. We have children."

"Poor neglected little scruffy things," Jane Smart said in a mocking tone that indicated she was imitating another voice, a voice "out there" raised in hostile gossip against them.

"Well I was raised very protectively," Sukie offered, "and it got to be oppressive. Looking back on it I don't think my parents were doing me any favors, they were working out some problems of their own."

"You can't live others' lives for them," said Alexandra driftingly.

"Women must stop serving everybody and then getting even psychologically. That's been our politics up to now."

"Oh. That does feel good," Jenny said.

"It's therapy."

"Close the roof again. I want to feel *cozy*."

"And shut off the fucking Schubert."

"Suppose Darryl comes in."

"With that hideous kid."

"Christopher."

"Let them."

"Mm. You're strong."

"My art, it giffs me muskles efen ünter me fingernails, like."

"Lexa. How much tequila was in your tea?"

"How late does the supermarket toward Old Wick stay open?"

"I have no idea, I absolutely have stopped going there. If the Superette downtown doesn't have it, we don't eat it."

"But they have hardly any fresh vegetables and no fresh meat."

"Nobody notices. All they want are those frozen dinners so they don't have to come to the table and interrupt TV, and hero sandwiches. The onions they slop in! I think it's what made me stop kissing the brats good night."

"My oldest, it's incredible, nothing but crinkle chips and Pecan Sandies since he was twelve and still he's six foot two, and not a cavity. The dentist says he's never seen such a beautiful mouth."

"It's the fluoride."

"I *like* Schubert. He isn't always *af*ter you like Beethoven is."

"Or Mahler."

"Oh my God, Mahler."

"He really is monstrously too much."

"My turn."

"*My* turn."

"Ooh, lovely. You've found the spot."

"What does it mean when your neck always hurts, and up near your armpits?"

"That's lymph. Cancer."

"Please, don't even joke."

"Try menopause."

"I wouldn't care about that."

"I look forward to it."

"You do wonder, sometimes, if being fertile isn't overrated."

"You hear terrible things about IUDs now."

"The best subs, funnily enough, are from that supertacky-looking pizza shack at East Beach. But they close October to August. I hear the man and his wife go to Florida and live with the millionaires in Fort Lauderdale, that's how well they do."

"That one-eyed man who cooks in a tie-dyed undershirt?"

"I've never been sure if it's really one eye or is he always winking?"

"It's his wife does the pizzas. I wish I knew how she keeps the crusts from getting soggy."

"I have all this tomato sauce and my children have gone on strike against spaghetti."

"Give it to Joe to take home."

"He takes enough home."

"Well, he leaves you something, too."

"Don't be coarse."

"*What* does he take home?"

"Smells."

"Memories."

"Oh. My goodness."

"Just let yourself float."

"We're all here."

"We're right with you."

"I feel that," Jenny said in a voice even smaller and softer than her usual one.

"How very lovely you are."

"Wouldn't it be funny to be that young again?"

"I can't believe I ever was. It must have been somebody else."

"Close your eyes. One last nasty piece of grit right here in the corner. There."

"Wet hair is really the problem, this time of year."

"The other day my breath froze my scarf right to my face."

"I'm thinking of getting mine layered. They say the new barber on the other side of Landing Square, in that little long building where they used to sharpen saws, does a wonderful job."

"On women?"

"They have to, men have stopped getting them. They've upped the price, though. Seven fifty, that's without any wave or wash or anything."

"The last thing I did for my father was wheel him into the barber for a haircut. He knew it was his last, too. He announced it to everybody, all these men sitting around. 'This is my daughter, who's bringing me in for the last haircut I'll have in my life.'"

"Kazmierczak Square. Have you seen the new sign?"

"Horrible. I can't believe it'll last."

"People forget. The schoolchildren now, World War Two to them is just a myth."

"Don't you wish you still had skin like this? Not a scar, not a mole."

"Actually, there is a little pink thing I noticed the other day, up high. Higher."

"Oh yess. That hurt?"

"No."

"Good."

"Did you ever notice, once you start investigating yourself for lumps like they say you should, they seem to be everywhere? The body is just *ter*ribly complicated."

"Please don't even make me think about it."

"In the new dictionary they got at the paper there are these transparencies bound in with regular pages at the entry 'Man,' only a woman's body is there too. Veins, muscles, bones, each on a sheet of their own, it's incredible. How it all fits."

"I don't think it's really complicated, it's just our thinking about it makes it complicated. Like a lot of things."

"How wonderfully round they are. Perfect semicircles."

"Hemispheres."

"That sounds so political."

"Hemispheres of influence."

"That *is* one of the unjoys. Erogenous-zone sag. I looked at my bottom in the mirror the other day and here were these definite undeniable puckers. Maybe that's why I have a stiff neck."

"Nemo's makes a pretty good sausage sub."

"Too many hot red peppers. Fidel is getting to Rebecca. He's flavoring her."

"What color do you think their babies would be?"

"Beige."

"Mocha."

"Does that feel too intrusive?"

"Not exactly."

"How well she speaks!"

"Oh God: the trouble with being young and beautiful is nobody helps you really appreciate it. When I was twenty-two and at my peak I guess all I did was worry about pleasing my mother-in-law and if I was as good in bed as these whores Monty knew in college."

"It's like being rich. You know you have something and you get uptight about being taken advantage of."

"Darryl doesn't seem to let it worry him."

"How rich *is* he, really?"

"He still hasn't paid Joe's bill, I know."

"That's how the rich are. They hold their money and collect the interest."

"Pay attention, love."

"How can I not?"

"My fingertips are all shrivelled."

"Maybe it's time we see if amphibians can lay their eggs on land."

"Okey-dokey."

"Here we go."

Splashing, they emerged cumbersomely: silver born in a chemical tumult from lead. They groped for towels.

"Where *is* he?"

"Asleep? I gave him a pretty strenuous game, if I do say so."

"They say, unless you use oil afterwards, water isn't good for your skin past a certain age."

"We have ointments."

"We have buckets of ointments."

"Just stretch out. Are you still relaxed?"

"Oh yes. I really am."

"Here's another, just under your pretty little boob. Like a tiny pink snout." Dark as the room was, it did not seem strange that this could be seen, for the pupils of the four of them had expanded as if to overflow their gray, hazel, brown, and blue irises. One witch pinched Jennifer's false teat and asked, "Feel anything?"

"No."

"Good."

"Feel any shame?" another asked.

"No."

"Good," pronounced the third.

"*Isn't* she good?"

"She is."

"Just think, 'Float.'"

"I feel I'm flying."

"So do we."

"All the time."

"We're right with you."

"It's killing."

"I love being a woman, really," Sukie said.

"You might as well," Jane Smart said dryly.

"I mean, it's not just propaganda," Sukie insisted.

"My baby," Alexandra was saying.

"Oh" escaped Jenny's lips.

"Gently. Gentler."

"This is paradise."

"Well, *I* thought," Jane Smart said over the phone emphatically, as if certain of being contradicted, "she was a bit *too* ingratiating. Too demure and Alice-in-Wonderlandish. I think she's up to something."

"But what would that be? We're all poor as church mice

and a town scandal besides." Alexandra's mind was still in her workroom, with the half-fleshed-out armatures of two floating, lightly interlocked women, wondering, as she patted handfuls of paste-impregnated shredded paper here and there, why she couldn't muster the confidence she used to bring to her little clay figurines, her little hefty bubbies meant to rest so securely on end tables and rumpus-room mantels.

"Think of the situation," Jane directed. "Suddenly she's an orphan. Obviously she was making a mess of things out in Chicago. The house is too big to heat and pay taxes on. But she has nowhere else to go."

Lately Jane seemed intent on poisoning every pot. Outside the window, the sparrow-brown twigs of an as yet snowless winter moved in a cold breeze, and the swaying birdfeeder needed refilling. The Spofford children were home for Christmas vacation but had gone ice-skating, giving Alexandra an hour to work in; it shouldn't be wasted. "I thought Jennifer was a nice addition," she said to Jane. "We mustn't get ingrown."

"We mustn't ever leave Eastwick either," Jane surprisingly said. "Isn't it horrible about Ed Parsley?"

"What about him? Has he come back to Brenda?"

"In pieces he'll come back" was the cruel reply. "He and Dawn Polanski blew themselves up in a row house in New Jersey trying to make bombs." Alexandra remembered his ghostly face the night of the concert, her last glimpse of Ed, his aura tinged with sickly green and the tip of his long vain nose seeming to be pulled so that his face was slipping sideways like a rubber mask. She could have said then that he was doomed. Jane's harsh image of coming back in pieces sliced Alexandra, her crooked arm and hand floating away with the telephone and Jane's voice in it, while her eyes and body let the window mullions pass through them like the parallel wires of an egg slicer. "He was identified by the fingerprints of a hand they found in the rubble," Jane was saying. "Just this hand by itself. It was all over television this morning, I'm surprised Sukie hasn't called you."

"Sukie's been a little huffy with me, maybe she felt upstaged by Jennifer the other night. Poor Ed," Alexandra said, feeling herself drift away as in a slow explosion. "She must be devastated."

"Not so it showed when I talked to her a half-hour ago. She sounded mostly worried about how much of a story the new management at the *Word* would want; there's this boy in Clyde's office now younger than we are, he's been sent by the owners, who everybody thinks are front men for the Mafia that hangs out, you know, on Federal Hill. He's just out of Brown and knows nothing about editing."

"Does she blame herself?"

"No, why would she? She never urged Ed to leave Brenda and run off with that ridiculous little slut, she was doing what she could to hold the marriage together. Sukie told me she told him to stick with Brenda and the ministry at least until he had looked into public relations. That's what these ministers and priests who leave the church go into, public relations."

"I don't know, general involvement," Alexandra weakly said. "Did they find Dawn's hands too?"

"I don't know what they found of Dawn's but I don't see how she could have escaped unless . . ." *Unless she were a witch* was the unspoken thought.

"Even that wouldn't do much against cordite, or whatever they call it. Darryl would know."

"Darryl thinks I'm ready for some Hindemith."

"Sweetie, that's wonderful. I wish he'd tell me I'm ready to go back to my bubbies. I miss the money, for one thing."

"Alexandra S. Spofford," Jane Smart chastised. "Darryl's trying to do something wonderful for you. Those New York dealers get ten thousand dollars for just a doodle."

"Not my doodles," she said, and hung up depressed. She didn't want to be a mere ingredient in Jane's poison pot, part of the daily local stew, she wanted to look out of her window and see miles and miles of empty golden land, dotted with sage, and the tips of the distant mountains a white as vaporous as that of clouds, only coming to a point.

Sukie must have forgiven Alexandra for being too taken with Jenny, for she called after Ed's memorial service to give an account. Snow had fallen in the meantime: one does forget that annual marvel, the width of it all, the air given presence, the diagonal strokes of the streaming flakes laid across everything like an etcher's hatching, the tilted big beret the birdbath wears next morning, the deepening in color of the dry brown oak leaves that have hung on and the hemlocks with their drooping deep green boughs and the clear blue of the sky like a bowl that has been decisively emptied, the excitement that vibrates off the walls within the house, the suddenly supercharged life of the wallpaper, the mysteriously urgent intimacy the potted amaryllis on the window enjoys with its pale phallic shadow. "Brenda spoke," Sukie said. "And some sinister fat man from the Revolution, in a beard and ponytail. Said Ed and Dawn were martyrs to pig tyranny, or something. He became quite excited, and there was a gang with him in Castro outfits that I was afraid would start beating us up if anybody muttered or got out of line somehow. But Brenda was quite brave, really. She's gotten rather wonderful."

"She has?" A sheen, was how Alexandra remembered Brenda: a sleekly blond head of hair done up in a tight twist, turning away at the concert party amid the peacock confusion of auras. From other encounters her mind's eye could supply a long, rather chalky face, with complacent lips more brightly painted than one quite expected, with that vehement gloss of a rose about to drop its petals.

"She has her outfit down to a T now—dark suits with padded shoulders, and a silk necktie in front so broad it looks like a napkin she forgot to take out after eating lobster. She spoke for about ten minutes, about what a caring minister Ed had been, *so* interested in Eastwick and its delicate ecology and its conflicted young people and all that, until his conscience— and here, on the word 'conscience,' Brenda got her voice to break, you would have loved it, she dabbed with her hanky at her eyes, just one tear from each eye, ex*act*ly enough—until his conscience, she said, demanded he take his energies away from the confines of this town, where they were so much appreciated"—Sukie's powers of mimicry were in full gear now; Alexandra could see her upper lip crinkling and protruding drolly—"and devote them, these wonderful energies, to trying to correct the *dread*ful, my dear, malaise that is poisoning the heartblood of our nation. She said our nation is laboring under a malignant spell and looked me right in the eye."

"What did you do?"

"Smiled. It wasn't *me* who got him down there in New Jersey with the bomb squad, it was Dawn. Very little mention of her, by the way, when the fat man got done. Like none. Apparently they never found any pieces of her, just bits of clothing that could have come out of a closet. She was such a scruffy little thing maybe she sailed out through the roof. The Polanskis or whatever their name is, the stepfather and the mother, showed up, though, dressed like something out of a Thirties movie. I guess they don't get out of their trailer that often. I kept looking at the mother wondering about these acrobatics she does for the circus, I must say she's kept her figure; but her *face*. Frightening. So tough it was growing things all over it like you have on your heel from bad shoes. Nobody knew what to say to them, since the girl was just Ed's floozie and not even officially dead at that. Even Brenda didn't quite know how to handle it at the door, since the family was at the root of her troubles in a way, but I must say, she was magnificent—very courteous and *grande dame*, gave them her sympathy with a glistening eye. Brenda's not our sort, I know, but I really do admire the way she's picked herself up and made something of her situation. Speaking of situations . . ."

"Yes?" Alexandra asked on cue. The pause had been a probe to see if she was still paying attention. Alexandra had been idly making dots with her fingertips on the fogged patches in the lower panes of her kitchen window—semiconscious conjurings of snow, or Sukie's freckles, or the holes in the telephone mouthpiece, or the paint dabs with which Niki de Saint-Phalle decorated her internationally successful "Nanas." Alexandra was glad Sukie was talking to her again; she sometimes feared that if it were not for Sukie she would lose all contact with the world of daily events and go off sailing into the stratosphere just like little Dawn blown out of that house in New Jersey.

"I've been fired," Sukie said.

"Baby! You haven't! How could they, you're the only undreary thing about that paper now."

"Well, maybe you could say I quit. The boy who's taken Clyde's place, with some Jewish name I can't remember, Bernstein, Birnbaum, I don't even *want* to remember it, cut my obituary of Ed from a column and a half to two little dumb paragraphs; he said they had a space problem this week because another poor local has been killed in Vietnam but I know it's because everybody's told him Ed had been my lover and he's afraid of my going overboard in print and people tittering. A long time ago Ed had given me these poems he wrote in the style of Bob Dylan and I *had* put a couple of them in but wouldn't have complained if they'd come and asked me to cut those; but they even took out how he founded the Fair Housing Group and was in the top third of his class at Harvard Divinity School. I said to the boy, 'You've just come to Eastwick and I don't think you realize what a beloved figure Reverend Parsley was,' and this brat from Brown smiled and said, 'I've heard about his being beloved,' and I said, 'I quit. I work hard on my copy and Mr. Gabriel almost never cut a word.' That made this insufferable child smile all the more and there was nothing to do but walk out. Actually, before I walked out I took the pencil out of his hand and broke it right in front of his eyes."

Alexandra laughed, grateful to have such a spirited friend, a friend in three dimensions unlike those evil clown faces in her bedroom. "Oh Sukie, you honestly did?"

"Yes, and I even said, 'Go break a leg,' and threw the two pieces on his desk. The smug little kike. But now what do I do? All I have is about seven hundred dollars in the bank."

"Maybe Darryl . . ." Alexandra's thoughts did fly to Darryl Van Horne at all hours: his overeager face with its flecks of spit, and certain dusty corners of his home awaiting a woman's touch, and such moments as the frozen one after he had laughed his harsh brittle bark, when his jaw snapped shut and the world as it were had to come unstuck from a momentary spell. These images did not visit Alexandra's brain by invitation or with a purpose but as one radio station overlaps another as we travel a winding road. Whereas Sukie and Jane seemed to have gathered fresh strength and vehemence from their rites on the island, Alexandra found her independent existence had gone from clay to paper in substance and her sustaining ties with nature had slackened. She had let her roses head into winter unmulched; she had not composted the leaves as in other Novembers; she kept forgetting to fill the birdfeeder and no longer bothered to rap on the window to drive the greedy gray squirrels away. She dragged herself about with a lassitude that even Joe Marino noticed, and that discouraged him. Boredom in a wife is part of the social contract, but boredom in a mistress undermines a man. All Alexandra wanted was to soak her bones in the teak hot tub and lean her head on Van Horne's hairy matted torso while Tiny Tim warbled over the stereo, "Livin' in the sunlight, lovin' in the moonlight, havin' a wonderful time!"

"Darryl has his hands full," Sukie told her. "The town is about to shut off his water for nonpayment of his bill and he's, at my suggestion I guess, hired Jenny Gabriel to be his lab assistant."

"At your suggestion?"

"Well, she *was* this technician out in Chicago, and now here she is pretty much all alone. . . ."

"Sukie, your darling guilt. Aren't you sly?"

"I thought I owed her a *lit*tle something, and she does look awfully cute and serious in this little white coat over there. A bunch of us were over there yesterday."

"There was a party over there yesterday and nobody told me?"

"Not a real party. Nobody got undressed."

She must get hold of herself, Alexandra told herself. She must find a new center to her life.

"It was for less than an hour, baby, honest. It just happened. The man from town water was there too, with a court order or whatever they have to have. Then he couldn't find the turn-off and accepted a drink and we all tried on his hardhat. You know Darryl loves you best."

"He doesn't. I'm not as pretty as you are and I don't do all the things for him that Jane does."

"But you're his body type," Sukie reassured her. "You look good together. Sweetie, I really ought to run. I heard that Perley Realty might take on a new trainee in anticipation of the spring rush."

"You're going to sell real estate?"

"I might have to. I have to do something, I'm spending millions on orthodontia, and I can't imagine why; Monty had beautiful teeth, and mine aren't bad, just that slight overbite."

"But is Marge—what did you say about Brenda?—our sort?"

"If she gives me a job she is."

"I thought Darryl wanted you to write a novel."

"Darryl wants, Darryl wants," Sukie said. "If Darryl'll pay my bills he can have what he wants."

Cracks were appearing, it seemed to Alexandra after Sukie hung up, in what had for a time appeared perfect. She was behind the times, she realized. She wanted things never to change, or, rather, to repeat always in the same way, as nature does. The same tangle of poison ivy and Virginia creeper on the tumbled wall at the edge of the marsh, the same glinting mineral mix in the pebbles of the road. How magnificent and abysmal pebbles are! They lie all around us billions of years old, not only rounded smooth by centuries of the sea's tumbling but their very matter churned and remixed by the rising of mountains and their chronic eroding, not once but often in the vast receding cone of aeons, snow-capped mountains arisen where Rhode Island and New Jersey now have their marshes, while oceans spawned diatoms where now the Rockies rise, fossils of trilobites embedded in their cliffs. Museums had dazed Alexandra as a girl with their mineral exhibits, interlocked crystalline prisms in colors vulgar save that they came straight from nature, lepidolite and chrysoberyl and tourmaline with their regal names, all struck off like giant frozen sparks in the churning of the earth, the very granite outcrops around us fluid, the continents bobbing in basalt. At times she felt dizzy, tied to all this massive incremental shifting, her consciousness a fleck of mica. The sensation persisted that she was not merely riding the universe but a partner to it, herself enormous within, capable of extracting medicine from the seethe of weeds and projecting rainstorms out of her thought. She and the seethe were one.

In winter, when the leaves fell, forgotten ponds moved closer, iced-over and brilliant, through the woods, and the summer-cloaked lights of the town loomed neighborly, and placed a whole new population of shadows and luminous rectangles upon the wallpaper of the rooms her merciless insomnia set her to wandering through. Her powers afflicted her most at night. The clown faces created by the overlapping peonies of her chintz curtains thronged the shadows and chased her from the bedroom. The sound of the children's breathing pumped through the house, as did the groans of the furnace. By moonlight, with a curt confident gesture of plump hands just beginning to show on their backs the mottling of liver spots, she would bid the curly-maple sideboard (which had been Oz's grandmother's) move five inches to the left; or she would direct a lamp with a base like a Chinese vase—its cord waggling and waving behind it in midair like the preposterous tail plumage of a lyrebird—to change places with a brass-candlestick lamp on the other side of the living room. One night a dog's barking in the yard of one of the neighbors beyond the line of willows at the edge of her yard irritated her exceptionally; without sufficient reflection she willed it dead. It had been a puppy, unused to being tied, and she thought too late that she might as easily have untied the unseen leash, for witches are above all adepts of the knot, the *aiguillette*, with which they promote enamorments and alliances, barrenness in women or cattle, impotence in men, and discontent within marriages. With knots they torment the innocent and entangle the future. The puppy had been known to her children and next morning the youngest of them, baby Linda, came home in tears. The owners were sufficiently incensed to have the vet perform an autopsy. He found no poison or sign of disease. It was a mystery.

The winter passed. In the darkroom of overnight blizzards, New England picture postcards were developed; the morning's sunshine displayed them in color. The not-quite-straight sidewalks of Dock Street, shovelled in patches, manifested patterns of compressed bootprints, like dirty white cookies with treads. A jagged wilderness of greenish ice cakes swung in and out with the tides, pressing on the bearded, barnacled pilings that underlay the Bay Superette. The new young editor of the *Word*, Toby Bergman, slipped on a frozen slick outside the barber shop and broke his leg. Ice backup during the owners' winter vacation on Sea Island, Georgia, forced gallons of water to seep by capillary action between the shingles of the Yapping Fox gift shop and to pour down the front inside wall, ruining a fortune in Raggedy Ann dolls and découpage by the handicapped.

The town in winter, deprived of tourists, settled more compactly upon itself, like a log fire burning late into the evening. A dwindled band of teen-agers hung out in front of the

Superette, waiting for the psychedelic-painted VW van the drug dealer from south Providence drove. On the coldest days they stood inside and, until chased by the choleric manager (a moonlighting tax accountant who got by on four hours sleep a night), clustered in the warmth to one side of the electric eye, beside the Kiwanis gumball machine and the other that for a nickel released a handful of stale pistachios in shells dyed a psychedelic pink. Martyrs of a sort they were, these children, along with the town drunk, in his basketball sneakers and buttonless overcoat, draining blackberry brandy from a paper bag as he sat on his bench in Kazmierczak Square, risking nightly death by exposure; martyrs too of a sort were the men and women hastening to adulterous trysts, risking disgrace and divorce for their fix of motel love—all sacrificing the outer world to the inner, proclaiming with this priority that everything solid-seeming and substantial is in fact a dream, of less account than a merciful rush of feeling.

The crowd inside Nemo's—the cop on duty, the postman taking a breather, the three or four burly types collecting unemployment against the spring rebirth of construction and fishing —became as winter wore on so well known to one another and the waitresses that even ritual remarks about the weather and the war dried up, and Rebecca filled their orders without asking, knowing what they wanted. Sukie Rougemont, no longer needing gossip to fuel her column "Eastwick Eyes and Ears" in the *Word*, preferred to take her clients and prospective buyers into the more refined and feminine atmosphere of the Bakery Coffee Nook a few doors away, between the framer's shop run by two fags originally from Stonington and the hardware store run by a seemingly endless family of Armenians; different Armenians, in different sizes but all with intelligent liquid eyes and kinky hair glistening low on their foreheads, waited on you each time. Alma Sifton, the proprietress of the Bakery Coffee Nook, had begun in what had been an old clam shack, with simply a coffee urn and two tables where shoppers who didn't want to run the gauntlet of stares in Nemo's might have a pastry and rest their feet; then more tables were added, and a line of sandwiches, mostly salad spreads (egg, ham, chicken), easily dished up. By her second summer Alma had to build an addition to the Nook twice the size of the original and put in a griddle and microwave oven; the Nemo's kind of greasy spoon was becoming a thing of the past.

Sukie loved her new job: getting into other people's houses, even the attics and cellars and laundry rooms and back halls, was like sleeping with men, a succession of subtly different flavors. No two homes had quite the same style or smell. The energetic bustling in and out of doors and up and down stairs and saying hello and good-bye constantly to people who were themselves on the move, and the gamble of it all appealed to the adventuress in her, and challenged her charm. Her sitting hunched over at a typewriter inhaling other people's cigarette smoke all day had not been healthy. She took a night course in Westerly and passed her exam and got her real-estate license by March.

Jane Smart continued to give lessons and fill in on the organ at South County churches and to practice her cello. There were certain of the Bach unaccompanied suites—the Third, with its lovely bourrée, and the Fourth, with that opening page of octaves and descending thirds which becomes a whirling, inconsolable outcry, and even the almost impossible Sixth, composed for an instrument with five strings—where she felt for measures at a time utterly *with* Bach, his mind exactly coterminous with hers, his vanished passion, lesser even than dust dispersed, stretching her fingers and flooding her cerebral lobes with triumph, his insistent questioning of the harmonics an operation of her own perilous soul. So this was the immortality men had built their pyramids and rendered their blood sacrifices for, this rebirth of a drudging old wife-fucking Lutheran *Kapellmeister* in the nervous system of a late-twentieth-century bachelor girl past her prime. Small comfort it must bring to his bones. But the music did talk, in its syntax of variation and reprise, reprise and variation; the mechanical procedures accumulated to form a spirit, a breath that rippled the rapid mathematics of it all like those footsteps wind makes on still, black water. It was communion. Jane did not see much of the Neffs, now that they were involved in the circle Brenda Parsley had gathered around her, and would have been endlessly solitary but for the crowd at Darryl Van Horne's.

Where once there had been three and then four, now there were six, and sometimes eight, when Fidel and Rebecca were enlisted in the fun—in the game of touch football, for instance, that they played with a beanbag in the echoing length of the big living room, the giant vinyl hamburger and silk-screened Brillo boxes and neon rainbow all pushed to one side, jumbled beneath the paintings like junk in an attic. A certain contempt for the physical world, a voracious appetite for immaterial souls, prevented Van Horne from being an adequate caretaker of his possessions. The parqueted floor of the music room, which he had had sanded and polyurethaned at significant expense, already held a number of pits gouged by the endpin of Jane Smart's cello. The stereo equipment in the hot-tub room had been soaked so often there were pops and crackles in every record played. Most spectacularly, a puncture had mysteriously deflated the tennis-court dome one icy night, and the gray canvas lay sprawled there in the cold and snow like the hide of a butchered brontosaurus, waiting for spring to come, since Darryl saw no point in bothering with it until the court could be used as an outdoor court again. In the touch-football games, he was always one of the quarterbacks, his nearsighted bloodshot eyes rolling as he faded back to pass, the corners of his mouth flecked with a foam of concentration. He kept crying out, "The pocket, the pocket!" —begging for protection, wanting Sukie and Alexandra, say, to block out Rebecca and Jenny moving in for the tag, while Fidel circled out for the bomb and Jane Smart cut back for the escape-hatch buttonhook. The women laughed and bumbled at the game, unable to take it seriously. Chris Gabriel languidly went through the motions, like a disbelieving angel, misplaced in all this adult foolishness. Yet he usually came along, having made no friends his own age; the small towns of America are generally empty of people his age, at college as they are, or in the armed forces, or beginning their careers amid the temptations and hardships of a city. Jennifer worked many afternoons with Van Horne in his lab, measuring out grams and deciliters of colored powders and liquids, deploying large copper sheets coated with this or that doped compound under batteries of overhead sunlamps while tiny wires led to meters monitoring electrical current. One sharp jump of the needle, Alexandra was led to understand, and more than the riches of the Orient would pour in upon Van Horne; in the meantime, there was an acrid and desolate chemical stink dragged up from the dungeons of the universe, and a mess of unscrubbed aluminum sinks and spilled and scattered elements, and plastic siphons clouded and melted as if by sulphurous combustion, and glass beakers and alembics with hardened black sediments crusted to the bottoms and sides. Jenny Gabriel, in a stained white smock and the clunky big sunglasses she and Van Horne wore in the perpetual blue glare, moved through this hopeful chaos with a curious authority, sure-fingered and quietly decisive. Here, as in their orgies, the girl—more than a girl, of course; indeed, only ten years younger than Alexandra—moved uncontaminable and in a sense untouched and yet among them, seeing, submitting, amused, unjudging, as if nothing were quite new to her, though her previous life seemed to have been one of exceptional innocence, the very barbarity of the times serving, in Chicago, to keep her within her citadel. Sukie had told the others how the girl had all but confided, in Nemo's, that she was still a virgin. Yet the girl disclosed her body to them with a certain shameless simplicity during the baths and the dances and submitted to their caresses not insensitively, and not without reciprocating. The touch of her hands, neither brusquely powerful like that of Jane's callused tips nor rapid and insinuating as with Sukie, had a penetration of its own, a gentle lingering as if in farewell, a forgiving slithering inquisitive something, ever less tentative, that pushed through to the bone. Alexandra loved being oiled by Jennifer, oiled while lying stretched on the black cushions or on several thicknesses of towels spread on the slates, the dampness of the bath enfolded and lifted up amid essences of aloe and coconut and almond, of sodium lactate and valerian extract, of aconite and cannabis indica. In the misted mirrors that Van Horne had installed on the outside of the shower doors, folds and waves of flesh glistened, and the younger woman, pale and perfect as a china figurine, could be seen kneeling in those angled deep distances mirrors create. The women developed a game called Serve Me, a sort of charade, though nothing like the charades Van Horne tried to organize in his living room when they were drunk but which collapsed beneath their detonations of mental telepathy and the clumsy fervor of his own mimicry, which disdained word-by-word enactments but sought to concentrate in one ferocious facial expression such full titles as *The History of the Decline and Fall of the Roman Empire* and *The Sorrows of Young Werther* and *The Origin of Species. Serve me,* the thirsty skins and spirits clamored, and patiently Jennifer oiled each witch, easing the transforming oils into the frowning creases, across the spots, around the bulges, rubbing against the grain of time, dropping small birdlike coos of sympathy and extollation.

"You have a lovely neck."

"I've always thought it was too short. Stubby. I've always hated my neck."

"Oh, you shouldn't have. Long necks are grotesque, except on black people."

"Brenda Parsley has an Adam's apple."

"Let's not be unkind. Let's think serene-making thoughts."

"Do me. Do me next, Jenny," Sukie nagged in a piping child's voice; she reverted quite dramatically, and while stoned was not above sucking her thumb.

Alexandra groaned. "What indecent bliss. I feel like a big sow rolling around."

"Thank God you don't smell that way," Jane Smart said. "Or does she, Jenny?"

"She smells very sweet and clean," Jenny primly said. From within that transparent bell of innocence or unknowing her slightly nasal voice came from as if far away, though distinctly; in the mirrors she was, kneeling, the shape and size and luster of one of those hollow porcelain birds, with holes at either end, from which children produce a few whistled notes.

"Jenny, the backs of my thighs," Sukie begged. "Just slowly along the backs, incredibly slowly. And use your fingernails. Don't be afraid of the insides of the thighs. The backs of the knees are wonderful. *Won*derful. Oh my God." Her thumb slid into her mouth.

"We're going to wear Jenny out," Alexandra warned in a considerate, drifting, indifferent voice.

"No, I like it," the girl said. "You're all so appreciative."

"We'll do you," Alexandra promised. "As soon as we get over this drugged feeling."

"I don't really care about being rubbed that much," Jenny confessed. "I'd rather do it than have it done to me, isn't that perverse?"

"It works out very well for us," Jane said, hissing the last word.

"Yes it does," Jenny agreed politely.

Van Horne, out of respect perhaps for the delicate initiate, seldom bathed with them now, or if he did he left the room swiftly, his hairy body wrapped from waist to knees in a towel, to keep Chris entertained with a game of chess or backgammon in the library. He made himself available afterwards, however, wearing clothes of increasing foppishness—a silk paisley strawberry-colored bathrobe, for instance, with bellbottom slacks of a fine green vertical stripe protruding below, and a mauve foulard stuffed about his throat—and affecting an ever-more-preening manner of magisterial benevolence, to preside over tea or drinks or a quick supper of Dominican *sancocho* or Cuban *mondongo*, of Mexican *pollo picado con tocino* or Colombian *soufflé de sesos*. Van Horne watched his female guests gobble these spicy delicacies rather ruefully, puffing tinted cigarettes through a curious twisted horn holder he lately brandished; he had himself lost weight and seemed feverish with hopes for his selenium-based solution to the problem of energy. Away from this topic, he often fell apathetically silent, and sometimes left the room abruptly. In retrospect, Alexandra and Sukie and Jane Smart might have concluded that he was bored with them; but they were themselves so far from bored with him that boredom did not enter their imaginations. His vast home, which they had nicknamed Toad Hall, expanded their meagre domiciles; in Van Horne's realm they left their children behind and became children themselves.

Jane came faithfully for her sessions of Hindemith and Brahms and, most recently attempted, Dvořák's swirling, dizzying Concerto for cello in B Minor. Sukie as that winter slowly melted away began to trip back and forth with notes and diagrams for her novel, which she and her mentor believed could be preplanned and engineered, a simple verbal machine for the arousal and then the relief of tension. And Alexandra timidly invited Van Horne to come view the large, weightless, enamelled statues of floating women she had patted together with gluey hands and putty knives and wooden salad spoons. She felt shy, having him to her house, which needed fresh paint in all the downstairs rooms and new linoleum on the kitchen floor; and between her walls he did seem diminished and aged, his jaw blue and the collar of his button-down Oxford frayed, as if shabbiness were infectious. He was wearing that baggy green-and-black tweed jacket with leather elbow-patches in which she had first met him, and he seemed so much an unemployed professor, or one of those sad men who as eternal graduate students haunt every university town, that she wondered how she had ever read into him so much magic and power. But he praised her work: "Baby, I think you've found your *shtik*! That sort of corny carny quality Lindner has, but with you there's not that metallic hardness, more of a Miró feeling, and sexy—sex-*ee*, hoo boy!" With an alarming speed and clumsiness, he loaded three of her papier-mâché figures into the back seat of his Mercedes, where they looked to Alexandra like gaudy little hitchhikers, corky bright limbs tangled and the wires that would suspend them from a ceiling snarled. "I'm driving to New York day after tomorrow more or less, and I'll show these to my guy on Fifty-seventh Street. He'll nibble, I'll bet my bottom buck; you've really caught something in the cultural works now, a sort of end-of-the-party feel. That unreality. Even the clips of the war on TV look unreal, we've all seen too many war movies."

Out in the open air, next to her car, dressed in a sheepskin coat with grimy cuffs and elbows, the matching sheepskin hat too small for his bushy head, he looked to Alexandra beyond capture, a lost cause; but, with an unpredictable lurch, he yielded to the bend of her mind and came back into the house with her and, breathing wheezily, up to her bedroom, to the bed she had lately denied to Joe Marino. Gina was pregnant again and that made it just too heavy. Darryl's potency had something infallible and unfeeling about it, and his cold penis hurt, as if it were covered with tiny little scales; but today, his taking her poor creations so readily with him to sell, and his stitched-together, slightly withered appearance, and the grotesque peaked sheepskin hat on his head, all had melted her heart and turned her vulva super-receptive. She could have mated with an elephant, thinking of becoming the next Niki de Saint-Phalle.

The three women, meeting downtown on Dock Street, checking in with one another by telephone, silently shared the sorority of pain that went with being the dark man's lover. Whether Jenny too carried this pain her aura did not reveal. When discovered by an afternoon visitor in the house, she always was wearing her lab coat and a frontal, formal attitude of efficiency. Van Horne used her, in part, because she was opaque, with her slightly brittle, deferential manner, her trait of letting certain vibrations and insinuations pass right through her, the somehow schematic roundness to her body. Within a group each member falls into a slot of special usefulness, and Jenny's was to be condescended to, to be "brought along," to be treasured as a version of each mature, divorced, disillusioned, empowered woman's younger self, though none had been quite like Jenny, or had lived alone with her younger brother in a house where her parents had met violent deaths. They loved her on their own terms, and, in fairness, she never indicated what terms she would have preferred. The most painful aspect of the afterimage the girl left, at least in Alexandra's mind, was the impression that she had trusted them, had confided herself to them as a woman usually first confides herself to a man, risking destruction in the determination to *know*. She had knelt among them like a docile slave and let her white round body shed the glow of its perfection upon their darkened imperfect forms sprawled wet on black cushions, under a roof that never slid back after, one icebound night, Van Horne had pushed the button and a flash made a glove of blue fire around his hairy hand.

Insofar as they were witches, they were phantoms in the communal mind. One smiled, as a citizen, to greet Sukie's cheerful pert face as it breezed along the crooked sidewalk; one saluted a certain grandeur in Alexandra as in her sandy riding boots and old green brocaded jacket she stood chatting with the proprietress of the Yapping Fox—Mavis Jessup, herself divorced, and hectic in complexion, and her dyed red hair hanging loose in Medusa ringlets. One credited to Jane Smart's angry dark brow, as she slammed herself into her old moss-green Plymouth Valiant, with its worn door latch, a certain distinction, an inner boiling such as had in other cloistral towns produced Emily Dickinson's verses and Emily Brontë's inspired novel. The women returned hellos, paid bills, and in the Armenians' hardware store tried, like everybody else, to describe with finger sketches in the air the peculiar thingamajiggy needed to repair a decaying home, to combat entropy; but we all knew there was something else about them, something as monstrous and obscene as what went on in the bedroom of even the assistant high-school principal and his wife, who both looked so blinky and tame as they sat in the bleachers chaperoning a record hop with its bloodcurdling throbbing.

We all dream, and we all stand aghast at the mouth of the caves of our deaths; and this is our way in. Into the nether world. Before plumbing, in the old outhouses, in winter, the accreted shit of the family would mount up in a spiky frozen stalagmite, and such phenomena help us to believe that there is more to life than the airbrushed ads at the front of magazines, the Platonic forms of perfume bottles and nylon nightgowns and Rolls-Royce fenders. Perhaps in the passageways of our dreams we meet, more than we know: one white lamplit face astonished by another. Certainly the fact of witchcraft hung in the consciousness of Eastwick; a lump, a cloudy density generated by a thousand translucent overlays, a sort of heavenly body, it was rarely breathed of and, though dreadful, offered the consolation of completeness, of rounding out the picture, like the gas mains underneath Oak Street and the television aerials scraping *Kojak* and Pepsi commercials out of the sky. It had the uncertain outlines of something seen through a shower door and was viscid, slow to evaporate: for years after the events gropingly and even reluctantly related here, the rumor of witchcraft stained this corner of Rhode Island, so that a prickliness of embarrassment and unease entered the atmosphere with the most innocent mention of Eastwick.

III.

Guilt

Recall the famous witch trials: the most acute and humane judges were in no doubt as to the guilt of the accused; the "witches" *themselves did not doubt it*—and yet there was no guilt.

—*Friedrich Nietzsche, 1887*

"You have?" Alexandra asked Sukie, over the phone. It was April; spring made Alexandra feel dopey and damp, slow to grasp even the simplest thing through the omnipresent daze of sap running again, of organic filaments warming themselves once again to crack the mineral earth and make it yield yet more life. She had turned thirty-nine in March and there was a weight to this too. But Sukie sounded more energetic than ever, breathless with her triumph. She had sold the Gabriel place.

"Yes, a lovely serious rather elderly couple called Hallybread. He teaches physics over at the University in Kingston and she I think counsels people, at least she kept asking me what *I* thought, which I guess is part of the technique they learn. They had a house in Kingston for twenty years but he wants to be nearer the sea now that he's retired and have a sailboat. They don't mind the house's not being painted yet, they'd rather pick the color themselves, and they have grandchildren and step-grandchildren that come and visit so they can use those rather dreary rooms on the third floor where Clyde kept all his old magazines, it's a wonder the weight didn't break the beams."

"What about the emanations, will that bother them?" For some of the other prospects who had looked at the house this winter had read of the murder and suicide and were scared off. People are still superstitious, even with all of modern science.

"Oh yes, they had read about it when it happened. It made a big splash in every paper in the state except the *Word*. They were amazed when somebody, not me, told them this had been the house. Professor Hallybread looked at the staircase and said Clyde must have been a clever man to make the rope just long enough so his feet didn't hit the stairs. I said, Yes, Mr. Gabriel had been very clever, always reading Latin and these abstruse astrological things, and I guess I began to look teary, thinking of Clyde, because Mrs. Hallybread put her arm around me and began to act, you know, like a counsellor. I think it may have helped sell the house actually, it put us on this footing where they could hardly say no."

"What are their names?" Alexandra asked, wondering if the can of clam chowder she was warming on the stove would boil over. Sukie's voice through the telephone wire was seeking painfully to infuse her with vernal vitality. Alexandra tried to respond and take an interest in these people she had never met, but her brain cells were already so littered with people she had met and grown to know and got excited by and even loved and then had forgotten. That cruise on the *Coronia* to Europe twenty years ago with Oz had by itself generated enough acquaintances to populate a lifetime—their mates at the table with the edge that came up in rough weather, the people in blankets beside them on the deck having bouillon at elevenses, the couples they met in the bar at midnight, the stewards, the captain with his square-cut ginger beard, everyone so friendly and interesting because they were young, young; youth is a kind of money, it makes people fawn. Plus the people she had gone to high school and Conn. College with. The boys with motorcycles, the pseudo-cowboys. Plus a million faces on city streets, mustached men carrying umbrellas, curvaceous women pausing to straighten a stocking in the doorway of a shoe store, cars like cartons of faces like eggs driving constantly by—all real, all with names, all with souls they used to say, now compacted in her mind like dead gray coral.

"Kind of cute names," Sukie was saying. "Arthur and Rose. I don't know if you'd like them or not, they seemed practical more than artistic."

One of the reasons for Alexandra's depression was that Darryl had some weeks ago returned from New York with the word that the manager of the gallery on Fifty-seventh Street had thought her sculptures were too much like those of Niki de Saint-Phalle. Furthermore, two of the three had returned damaged; Van Horne had taken Chris Gabriel along to help with the driving (Darryl became hysterical on the Connecticut Turnpike: the trucks tailgating him, hissing and knocking on all sides of him, these repulsive obese drivers glaring down at his Mercedes from their high dirty cabs) and on the way home they had picked up a hitchhiker in the Bronx, so the pseudo-Nanas riding in the back were shoved over to make room. When Alexandra had pointed out to Van Horne the bent limbs, the creases in the fragile papier-mâché, and the one totally torn-off thumb, his face had gone into its patchy look, his eyes and mouth too disparate to focus, the glassy left eye drifting outward toward his ear and saliva escaping the corners of his lips. "Well Christ," he had said, "the poor kid was standing out there on the Deegan a couple blocks from the worst slum in the fucking country, he coulda got mugged and killed if we hadn't picked him up." He thought like a taxi driver, Alexandra realized. Later he asked her, "Why don'tcha try working in wood at least? You think Michelangelo ever wasted his time with gluey old newspapers?"

"But where will Chris and Jenny go?" she mustered the wit to ask. Also on her mind uncomfortably was Joe Marino, who even while admitting that Gina was in a family way again was increasingly tender and husbandly toward his former mistress, coming by at odd hours and tossing sticks at her windows and talking in all seriousness down in her kitchen (she wouldn't let him into the bedroom any more) about his leaving Gina and their setting themselves up with Alexandra's four children in a house somewhere in the vicinity but out of Eastwick, perhaps in Coddington Junction. He was a shy decent man with no thought of finding another mistress; that would have been disloyal to the team he had assembled. Alexandra kept biting back the truth that she would rather be single than a plumber's wife; it had been bad enough with Oz and his chrome. But just thinking a thought so snobbish and unkind made her feel guilty enough to relent and take Joe upstairs to her bed. She had put on seven pounds during the winter and that little extra layer of fat may have been making it harder for her to have an orgasm; Joe's naked body felt like an incubus and when she opened her eyes it seemed his hat was still on his head, that absurd checked wool hat with the tiny brim and little iridescent brown feather.

Or it may have been that somewhere someone had tied an *aiguillette* attached to Alexandra's sexuality.

"Who knows?" Sukie asked in turn. "I don't think they know. They don't want to go back where they came from, I know that. Jenny is so sure Darryl's close to making a breakthrough in the lab she wants to put all her share of the house money into his project."

This did shock Alexandra, and drew her full attention, either because any talk of money is magical, or because it had not occurred to her that Darryl Van Horne needed money. That *they* all needed money—the child-support checks ever later and later, and dividends down because of the war and the overheated economy, and the parents resisting even a dollar raise in the price of a half-hour's piano lesson by Jane Smart, and Alexandra's new sculptures worth less than the newspapers shredded to make them, and Sukie having to stretch her smile over the weeks between commissions—was assumed, and gave a threadbare gallantry to their little festivities, the extravagance of a fresh bottle of Wild Turkey or a jar of whole cashews or a tin of anchovies. And in these times of national riot, with an entire generation given over to the marketing and consumption of drugs, ever more rarely came the furtive wife knocking on the back door for a gram of dried orchis to stir into an aphrodisiac broth for her flagging husband, or the bird-loving widow wanting henbane with which to poison her neighbor's cat, or the timid teen-ager hoping to deal for an ounce of distilled moonwort or woadwaxen so as to work his will upon a world still huge in possibilities and packed like a honeycomb with untasted treasure. Nightclad and giggling, in the innocent days when, freshly liberated from the wraps of housewifery, the witches used to sally out beneath the crescent moon to gather such herbs where they nestled at the rare and delicate starlit junction of suitable soil and moisture and shade. The market for all their magic was drying up, so common and multiform had sorcery become; but if they were poor, Van Horne was rich, and his wealth theirs to enjoy for their dark hours of holiday from their shabby sunlit days. That Jenny Gabriel might offer him money of her own, and he accept, was a transaction Alexandra had never envisioned. "Did you talk to *her* about this?"

"I told her I thought it would be crazy. Arthur Hallybread teaches physics and he says there is absolutely no foundation in electromagnetic reality for what Darryl is trying to do."

"Isn't that the sort of thing professors always say, to anybody with an idea?"

"Don't be so defensive, darling. I didn't know you cared."

"I don't care, really," Alexandra said, "what Jenny does with her money. Except she *is* another woman. How did she react when you said this to her?"

"Oh, you know. Her eyes got bigger and stared and her chin turned a little more pointy and it was as if she hadn't heard me. She has this stubborn streak underneath all the docility. She's too good for this world."

"Yes, that is the message she gives off, I suppose," Alexandra said slowly, sorry to feel that they were turning on her, their own fair creature, their *ingénue*.

Jane Smart called a week or so later, furious. "Couldn't you have *guessed*? Alexandra, you *do* seem abstracted these days." Her *s*'s hurt, stinging like match tips. "She's moving in! He's invited her and that foul little brother to move in!"

"Into Toad Hall?"

"Into the old *Len*ox place," Jane said, discarding the pet name they had once given it as if Alexandra were stupidly babbling. "It's what she's been angling for all along, if we'd just opened our foolish eyes. We were so *nice* to that vapid girl, taking her in, doing our thing, though she always *did* hold back as if really she were above it all and time would tell, like some smug little Cinderella squatting in the ashes knowing there was this glass slipper in her future—oh, the *priss*iness of her now is what gets me, swishing about in her cute little white lab coat and getting *paid* for it, when he owes everybody in town and the bank is thinking of foreclosing but it doesn't want to get stuck with the property, the upkeep is a *night*mare. Do you know what a new slate roof for that pile would run to?"

"Baby," Alexandra said, "you sound so financial. Where did you learn all this?"

The fat yellow lilac buds had released their first small bursts of heart-shaped leaves and the arched wands of forsythia, past bloom, had turned chartreuse like miniature willows. The gray squirrels had stopped coming to the feeder, too busy mating to eat, and the grapevines, which look so dead all winter, were beginning to shade the arbor again. Alexandra felt less sodden this week, as spring muddiness dried to green; she had returned to making her little clay bubbies, getting ready for the summer trade, and they were slightly bigger, with subtler anatomies and a deliberately Pop intensity to their coloring: she had learned something over the winter, by her artistic misadventure. So in this mood of rejuvenation she had trouble quickly sharing Jane's outrage; the pain of the Gabriel children's moving into a house that had felt fractionally hers sank in slowly. She had always held to the conceited fantasy that in spite of Sukie's superior beauty and liveliness and Jane's greater intensity and commitment to witchiness, she, Alexandra, was Darryl's favorite—in size and in a certain psychic breadth most nearly his match, and destined, somehow, to *reign* with him. It had been a lazy assumption.

Jane was saying, "Bob Osgood told me." He was the president of the Old Stone Bank downtown: stocky, the same physical type as Raymond Neff, but without a teacher's softness and that perspiring bullying manner teachers get; solid and confident, rather, from association with money Bob Osgood was, and utterly, beautifully bald, with a freshly minted shine to his skull and a skinned pinkness catching at his ears and his eyelids and nostrils, even his tapering quick fingers, as if he had stepped fresh from a steam room.

"You *see* Bob Osgood?"

Jane paused, registering distaste at the direct question as much as uncertainty how to answer. "His daughter Deborah is the last lesson on Tuesdays, and picking her up he's stayed once or twice for a beer. You know what an impossible bore Harriet Osgood is; poor Bob can't get it up to go home to her."

"Get it up" was one of those phrases the young had made current; it sounded a bit false and harsh in Jane's mouth. But then Jane *was* harsh, as people from Massachusetts tend to be.

Puritanism had landed smack on that rock and after regaining its strength at the expense of the soft-hearted Indians had thrown its steeples and stone walls all across Connecticut, leaving Rhode Island to the Quakers and Jews and antinomians and women.

"Whatever happened to you and those nice Neffs?" Alexandra asked maliciously.

Harshly Jane laughed, as it were hawked into the mouthpiece of the telephone. "*He* can't get it up at all these days; Greta has reached the point where she tells anybody in town who'll listen, and she practically asked the boy doing checkout at the Superette to come back to the house and fuck her."

The *aiguillette* had been tied; but who had tied it? Witchcraft, once engendered in a community, has a way of running wild, out of control of those who have called it into being, running so freely as to confound victim and victimizer.

"Poor Greta," Alexandra heard herself mumble. Little devils were gnawing at her stomach; she felt uneasy, she wanted to get back to her bubbies and then, once they were snug in the Swedish kiln, to raking the winter-fallen twigs out of her lawn, and attacking the thatch with a pitchfork.

But Jane was on her own attack. "Don't give me that pitying earth-mother crap," she said, shockingly. "What are we going to *do* about Jennifer's moving in?"

"But sweetest, what can we do? Except show how hurt we are and have everybody laughing at us. Don't you think the town won't be amused enough anyway? Joe tells me some of the things people whisper. Gina calls us the *streghe* and is afraid we're going to turn the baby in her tummy into a little pig or a thalidomide case or something."

"Now you're talking," Jane Smart said.

Alexandra read her mind. "Some sort of spell. But what difference would it make? Jenny's there, you say. She has *his* protection."

"Oh it will make a difference believe you me," Jane Smart pronounced in one long shaking utterance of warning like a tremulous phrase drawn from a single swoop of her bow.

"What does Sukie think?"

"Sukie thinks just as I do. That it's an outrage. That we've been betrayed. We've nursed a viper, my dear, in our bos*ooms*. And I don't mean the vindow viper."

This allusion did make Alexandra nostalgic for the nights, which in truth had become rarer as winter wore on, when they would all listen, nude and soaking and languid with pot and California Chablis, to Tiny Tim's many voices surrounding them in the stereophonic darkness, warbling and booming and massaging their interiors; the stereophonic vibrations brought into relief their hearts and lungs and livers, slippery fatty presences within that purple inner space for which the dim-lit tub room with its asymmetrical cushions was a kind of amplification. "I would think things will go on much as before," she reassured Jane. "He loves *us*, after all. And it's not as if Jenny does half the things we do for him; it was us she liked to cater to. The way that upstairs rambles, it's not as if they'll all be sharing quarters or anything."

"Oh Lexa," Jane sighed, fond in despair. "It's really *you* who're the innocent."

Having hung up, Alexandra found herself less than reassured. The hope that the dark stranger would eventually claim her cowered in its corner of her imagining; could it be that her queenly patience would earn itself no more reward than being used and discarded? The October day when he had driven her up to the front door as to something they mutually possessed, and when she had to wade away through the tide as if the very elements were begging her to stay: could such treasured auguries be empty? How short life is, how quickly its signs exhaust their meaning. She caressed the underside of her left breast and seemed to detect a small lump there. Vexed, frightened, she met the bright beady gaze of a gray squirrel that had stolen into the feeder to rummage amid the sunflower-seed husks. He was a plump little gentleman in a gray suit with white shirt-front, come bright-eyed to dine. The effrontery, the greed. His tiny gray hands, mindless and dry as bird feet, were arrested halfway to his chest by sudden awareness of her gaze, her psyche's impingement; his eyes were set sideways in the oval skull so as to seem in their convexity opaque turrets, slanted and gleaming. The spark of life inside the tiny skull wanted to flee, to twitch away to safety, but Alexandra's sudden focus froze the spark even through glass. A dim little spirit, programmed for feeding and evasion and seasonal copulation, was meeting a greater. *Morte, morte, morte,* Alexandra said firmly in her mind, and the squirrel dropped like an instantly emptied sack. One last spasm of his limbs flipped a few husks over the edge of the plastic feeder tray, and the luxuriant frosty plume of a tail flickered back and forth a few more seconds; then the animal was still, the dead weight making the feeder with its conical green plastic roof swing on the wire strung between two posts of an arbor. The program was cancelled.

Alexandra felt no remorse; it was a delicious power she had. But now she would have to put on her Wellingtons and go outside and with her own hand lift the verminous body by its tail and walk to the edge of her yard and throw it into the bushes over the stone wall, where the bog began. There was so much dirt in life, so many eraser crumbs and stray coffee grounds and dead wasps trapped inside the storm windows, that it seemed all of a person's time—all of a woman's time, at any rate—was spent in reallocation, taking things from one place to another, dirt being as her mother had said simply matter in the wrong place.

Comfortingly, that very night, while the children were lurking around Alexandra demanding, depending upon their ages, the car, help with their homework, or to be put to bed, Van Horne called her, which was unusual, since his sabbats usually arose as if spontaneously, without the deigning of his personal invitation, but through a telepathic, or telephonic, merge of the desires of his devotees. They would find themselves there without quite knowing how they came to be there. Their cars —Alexandra's pumpkin-colored Subaru, Sukie's gray Corvair, Jane's moss-green Valiant—would take them, pulled by a tide of psychic forces. "Come on over Sunday night," Darryl growled, in that New York taxi-driver rasp of his. "It's a helluva depressing day, and I got some stuff I want to try out on the gang."

"It's not easy," Alexandra said, "to get a sitter on a Sunday night. They've got to get up for school in the morning and want to stay home and watch Archie Bunker." In her unprecedented resistance she heard resentment, an anger that Jane

Smart had planted but whose growth was being fed now with her own veins.

"Ah come on. Those kids of yours are ancient, how come they still need sitters?"

"I can't saddle Marcy with the three younger, they don't accept her discipline. Also she may want to drive over to a friend's house and I don't want her not to be able to; it's not fair to burden a child with your own responsibilities."

"What gender friend the kid seeing?"

"It's none of your business. A girlfriend, as it happens."

"Christ, don't snap at *me*, it wasn't me conned you into having those little twerps."

"They're *not* twerps, Darryl. And I do neglect them."

Interestingly, he did not seem to mind being talked back to, which she had not done before: perhaps it was the way to his heart. "Who's to say," he responded mildly, "what's neglect? If my mother had neglected me a little more I might be a better all-round guy."

"You're an O.K. guy." It felt forced from her, but she liked it that he had bothered to seek reassurance.

"Thanks a fuck of a lot," he answered with a jolting coarseness. "We'll see you when you get here."

"Don't be huffy."

"Who's huffy? Take it or leave it. Sunday around seven. Dress informal."

She wondered why next Sunday should be depressing to him. She looked at the kitchen calendar. The numerals were interlaced with lilies.

Easter evening turned out to be a warm spring night with a south wind pulling the moon backwards through wild, blanched clouds. The tide had left silver puddles on the causeway. New green marsh grass was starting up in the spaces between the rocks; Alexandra's headlights swung shadows among the boulders and across the tree-intertwined entrance gate. The driveway curved past where the egrets used to nest and now the collapsed tennis-court bubble lay creased and hardened like a lava flow; then her car climbed, circling the mall lined by noseless statues. As the stately silhouette of the house loomed, the grid of its windows all alight, her heart lifted into its holiday flutter; always, coming here, night or day, she expected to meet the momentous someone who was, she realized, herself, herself unadorned and untrammelled, forgiven and nude, erect and perfect in weight and open to any courteous offer: the beautiful stranger, her secret self. Not all the next day's weariness could cure her of the exalted expectation that the Lenox place aroused. Your cares evaporated in the entry hall, where the sulphurous scents greeted you, and an apparent elephant's-foot umbrella stand holding a cluster of old-fashioned knobs and handles on second glance turned out to be a single painted casting, even to the little strap and snap button holding the umbrella furled—one more mocking work of art.

Fidel took her jacket, a man's zippered windbreaker. More and more Alexandra found men's clothes comfortable; first she began to buy their shoes and gloves, then corduroy and chino trousers that weren't so nipped at the waist as women's slacks were, and lately the nice, roomy, efficient jackets men hunt and work in. Why should they have all the comfort while we martyr ourselves with spike heels and all the rest of the slave-fashions sadistic fags wish upon us?

"*Buenas noches, señora,*" Fidel said. "*Es muy agradable tenerla nuevamente en esta casa.*"

"The mister have all sort of gay party planned," Rebecca said behind him. "Oh there big changes afoot."

Jane and Sukie were already in the music room, where some oval-backed chairs with a flaking silvery finish had been set out; Chris Gabriel slouched in a corner near a lamp, reading *Rolling Stone*. The rest of the room was candlelit; candles in all the colors of jellybeans had been found for the cobwebbed sconces along the wall, each draft-tormented little flame doubled by a tin mirror. The aura of the flames was an acrid complementary color: green eating into the orange glow yet constantly repelled, like the viscid contention amid unmixing chemicals. Darryl, wearing a tuxedo of an old-fashioned double-breasted cut, its black dull as soot but for the broad lapels, came up and gave her his cold kiss. Even his spit on her cheek was cold. Jane's aura was slightly muddy with anger and Sukie's rosy and amused, as usual. They had all, in their sweaters and dungarees, evidently underdressed for the occasion.

The tuxedo did give Darryl a less patchy and shambling air than usual. He cleared his froggy throat and announced,

"Howzabout a little concert? I've been working up some ideas here and I want to get you girls' feedback. The first number is entitled"—he froze in mid-gesture, his sharp little greenish teeth gleaming, his spectacles for the night so small that the pale-plastic frames seemed to have his eyes trapped—"'The A Nightingale Sang in Berkeley Square Boogie.'"

Masses of notes were struck off as if more than two hands were playing, the left hand setting up a deep cloudy stride rhythm, airy but dark like a thunderhead growing closer above the treetops, and then the right hand picking out, in halting broken phrases so that the tune only gradually emerged, the rainbow of the melody. You could see it, the misty English park, the pearly London sky, the dancing cheek-to-cheek, and at the same time feel the American rumble, the good gritty whorehouse tinkling only this continent could have cooked up, in the tasselled brothels of a southern river town. The melody drew closer to the bass, the bass moved up and swallowed the nightingale, a wonderfully complicated flurry ensued while Van Horne's pasty seamed face dripped sweat onto the keyboard and his grunts of effort smudged the music; Alexandra pictured his hands as white waxy machines, the phalanges and flexor tendons tugging and flattening and directly connected to the rods and felts and strings of the piano, this immense plangent voice one hyperdeveloped fingernail. The themes drew apart, the rainbow reappeared, the thunderhead faded into harmless air, the melody was restated in an odd high minor key reached through an askew series of six descending, fading chords struck across the collapsing syncopation.

Silence, but for the hum of the piano's pounded harp.

"Fantastic," Jane Smart said dryly.

"Really, baby," Sukie urged upon their host, exposed and blinking now that his exertion was over. "I've never heard anything like it."

"I could cry," Alexandra said sincerely. He had stirred such memories within her, and such inklings of her future; music lights up with its pulsing lamp the cave of our being.

Darryl seemed disconcerted by their praise, as if he might be dissolved in it. He shook his shaggy head like a dog drying itself, and then seemed to press his jaw back into place with the same two fingers that wiped the corners of his mouth. "That one mixed pretty well," he admitted. "O.K., let's try this one now. It's called 'The How High the Moon March.'" This mix went less well, though the same wizardry was in operation. A wizardry, Alexandra thought, of theft and transformation, with nothing of guileless creative engendering about it, only a boldness of monstrous combination. The third offering was the Beatles' tender "Yesterday," broken into the stutter-rhythms of a samba; it made them all laugh, which hadn't been the effect of the first and which wasn't perhaps the intention. "So," Van Horne said, rising from the bench. "That's the idea. If I could work up a dozen or so of these a friend of mine in New York says he has an in with a recording executive and maybe we can raise a modicum of moolah to keep this establishment afloat. So what's your input?"

"It may be a bit . . . special," Sukie offered, her plump upper lip closing upon her lower in a solemn way that looked nevertheless amused.

"What's special?" Van Horne asked, pain showing, his face about to fly apart. "Tiny Tim was special. Liberace was special. Lee Harvey Oswald was special. To get any attention at all in this day and age you got to be way out."

"This establishment needs moolah?" Jane Smart asked sharply.

"So I'm told, toots."

"Honey, by whom?" Sukie asked.

"Oh," he said, embarrassed, squinting out through the candlelight as if he could see nothing but reflections, "a bunch of people. Banker types. Prospective partners." Abruptly, in tune perhaps with the old tuxedo, he ducked into horror-movie clowning, bobbing in his black outfit as if crippled, his legs hinged the wrong way. "That's enough business," he said. "Let's go into the living room. Let's get *smashed*."

Something was up. Alexandra felt a sliding start within her; an immense slick slope of depression was revealed as if by the sliding upwards of an automatic garage door, the door activated by a kind of electric eye of her own internal sensing and giving on a wide underground ramp whose downward trend there was no reversing, not by pills or sunshine or a good night's sleep. Her life had been built on sand and she knew that everything she saw tonight was going to strike her as sad.

The dusty ugly works of Pop Art in the living room were

sad, and the way several fluorescent tubes in the track lighting overhead were out or flickered, buzzing. The great long room needed more people to fill it with the revelry it had been designed for; it seemed to Alexandra suddenly an ill-attended church, like those that Colorado pioneers had built along the mountain roads and where no one came any more, an ebbing more than a renunciation, everybody too busy changing the plugs in their pickup truck or recovering from Saturday night, the parking places outside gone over to grass, the pews with their racks still stocked with hymnals visible inside. "Where's Jenny?" she asked aloud.

"The lady still cleaning up in de labora*tory*," Rebecca said. "She work so hard, I worry sickness take her."

"How's it all going?" Sukie asked Darryl. "When can I paint my roof with kilowatts? People still stop me on the street and ask about that because of the story I wrote on you."

"Yeah," he snarled, ventriloquistically, so the voice emerged from well beside his head, "and those old fogies you sold the Gabriel dump to bad-mouthing the whole idea, I hear. Fuck 'em. They laughed at Leonardo. They laughed at Leibniz. They laughed at the guy who invented the zipper, what the hell was his name? One of invention's unsung greats. Actually, I've been wondering if microörganisms aren't the way to go—use a mechanism that's already set in place and self-replicates. Biogas technology: you know who's way ahead in that department? The Chinese, can you believe it?"

"Couldn't we just use less electricity?" Sukie asked, interviewing out of habit. "And use our bodies more? Nobody needs an electric carving knife."

"You need one if your neighbor has one," Van Horne said. "And then you need another to replace the one you get. And another. And another. Fidel! *Deseo beber!*"

The servant in his khaki pajamas, abjectly shapeless and yet also with a whisper of military menace, brought drinks, and a tray of *huevos picantes* and palm hearts. Without Jenny here, surprisingly, conversation lagged; they had grown used to her, as someone to display themselves to, to amuse and shock and instruct. Her wide-eyed silence was missed. Alexandra, hoping that art, any art, might staunch the internal bleeding of her melancholy, moved among the giant hamburgers and ceramic dartboards as if she had never seen them before; and indeed some of them she hadn't. On a four-foot plinth of plywood painted black, beneath a plastic pastry bell, rested an ironically realistic replica—a three-dimensional Wayne Thiebaud—of a white-frosted wedding cake. Instead of the conventional bride and groom, however, two nude figures stood on the topmost tier, the female pink and blond and rounded and the black-haired man a darker pink, but for the dead-white centimeter of his semi-erect penis. Alexandra wondered what the material of this fabrication was: the cake lacked the scoring of cast bronze and also the glaze of enamelled ceramic. Acrylicked plaster was her guess. Seeing that no one but Rebecca, passing a tray of tiny crabs stuffed with *xu-xu* paste, was observing her, Alexandra lifted the bell and touched the frostinglike rim of the object. A tender dab of it came away on her finger. She put the finger in her mouth. Sugar. It was real frosting, a real cake, and fresh.

Darryl, with wide splaying gestures, was outlining another energy approach to Sukie and Jane. "With geothermal, once you get the shaft dug—and why the hell not? they make tunnels twenty miles long over in the Alps every day of the week —your only problem is keeping the energy from burning up the converter. Metal will melt like lead soldiers on Venus. You know what the answer is? Unbelievably simple. Stone. You got to make all your machinery, all the gearing and turbines, out of stone. They can do it! They can chisel granite now as fine as they can mill steel. They can make springs out of poured cement, would you believe?—particle size is what it all boils down to. Metal has had it, just like flint when the Bronze Age came in."

Another work of art Alexandra hadn't noticed before was a glossy female nude, a mannequin without the usual matte skin and the hinged limbs, a Kienholz in its assaultiveness but smooth and minimally defined in the manner of Tom Wesselmann, crouching as if to be fucked from behind, her face blank and bland, her back flat enough to be a tabletop. The indentation of her spine was straight as the groove for blood in a butcher's block. The buttocks suggested two white motorcycle helmets welded together. The statue stirred Alexandra with its blasphemous simplification of her own, female form.

She took another margarita from Fidel's tray, savored the salt (it is a myth and absurd slander that witches abhor salt; salt-peter and cod liver oil, both associated with Christian virtue, are what they cannot abide), and sauntered up to their host. "I feel sexy and sad," she said. "I want to take my bath and smoke my joint and get home. I swore to the babysitter I'd be home by ten-thirty; she was the fifth girl I tried and I could hear her mother shouting at her in the background. These parents don't want them to come near us."

"You're breaking my heart," Van Horne said, looking sweaty and confused after his gaze into the geothermal furnace. "Don't rush things. I don't feel smashed yet. There's a schedule here. Jenny's about to come down."

Alexandra saw a new light in Van Horne's glassy bloodshot eyes; he looked scared. But what could scare *him?*

Jenny's tread was silent on the carpeted curved front stair-case; she came into the long room with her hair pulled back like Eva Perón's and wearing a powder-blue bathrobe that swept the floor. Above each of her breasts the robe bore as dec-oration three embroidered cuts like large buttonholes, which reminded Alexandra of military chevrons. Jenny's face, with its wide round brow and firm triangular chin, was shiny-clean and devoid of make-up; nor did a smile adorn it. "Darryl, don't get drunk," she said. "You make even less sense when you're drunk than when you're sober."

"But he gets in*spi*red," Sukie said with her practiced sauci-ness, feeling her way with this new woman, in residence and somehow in charge.

Jenny ignored her, looking around, past their heads. "Where's dear Chris?"

From the corner Rebecca said, "Young man in de liberry reading his magazines."

Jenny took two steps forward and said, "Alexandra. Look." She untied her cloth belt and spread the robe's wings wide, revealing her white body with its roundnesses, its rings of baby fat, its cloud of soft hair smaller than a man's hand. She asked Alexandra to look at that translucent wart under her breast. "Do you think it's getting bigger or am I imagining it? And up here," she said, guiding the other woman's fingers into her armpit. "Do you feel a little lump?"

"It's hard to say," Alexandra said, flustered, for such touching occurred in the steamy dark of the tub room but not in the bald fluorescent light here. "We're all so full of little lumps just naturally. I don't feel anything."

"You aren't *con*centrating," Jenny said, and with a gesture that in another context would have seemed loving took Alexandra's wrist in her fingers and led her right hand to the other armpit. "There's sort of the same thing there too. Please, Lexa. Concentrate."

A faint bristle of shaven hair. A silkiness of applied powder. Underneath, lumps, veins, glands, nodules. Nothing in nature is quite homogeneous; the universe was tossed off freehand. "Hurt?" she asked.

"I'm not sure. I feel *some*thing."

"I don't think it's anything," Alexandra pronounced.

"Could it be connected with this somehow?" Jenny lifted her firm conical breast to further expose her transparent wart, a tiny cauliflower or pug face of pink flesh gone awry.

"I don't think so. We all get those."

Suddenly impatient, Jenny closed her bathrobe and pulled the belt tight. She turned to Van Horne. "Have you told them?"

"My dear, my dear," he said, wiping the corners of his smiling mouth with a trembling thumb and finger. "We must make a ceremony of it."

"The fumes today have given me a headache and I think we've all had enough ceremonies. Fidel, just bring me a glass of soda water, *aqua gaseosa, o horchata, por favor. Pronto, gracias.*"

"The wedding cake," exclaimed Alexandra, with an icy thrill of clairvoyance.

"Now you're cooking, little Sandy," Van Horne said. "You've got it. I saw you poke and lick that finger," he teased.

"It wasn't that so much as Jenny's manner. Still, I can't believe it. I know it but I can't believe it."

"You better believe it, ladies. The kid here and I were married as of yesterday afternoon at three-thirty p.m. The craziest little justice of the peace up in Apponaug. He stuttered. I never thought you could have a stutter and still get the license. D-d-d-do you, D-D-D-D-D—"

"Oh Darryl, you didn't!" Sukie cried, her lips pulled so far back in a mirthless grin that the hollows at the top of her upper gums showed.

Jane Smart hissed at Alexandra's side.

"How could you two do that to us?" Sukie asked.

The word "us" surprised Alexandra, who felt this announcement as a sudden sore place in her abdomen alone.

"So sneakily," Sukie went on, her cheerful party manner slightly stiff on her face. "We would at least have given her a shower."

"Or some casserole dishes," Alexandra said bravely.

"She did it," Jane was saying seemingly to herself but of course for Alexandra and the others to overhear. "She actually managed to pull it off."

Jenny defended herself; the color in her cheeks was high. "It wasn't so much managing, it just came to seem natural, me here all the time anyway, and naturally . . ."

"Naturally nature took its nasty natural course," Jane spit out.

"Darryl, what's in it for you?" Sukie asked him, in her frank and manly reporter's voice.

"Oh, you know," he said sheepishly. "The standard stuff. Settle down. Security. Look at her. She's beautiful."

"Bullshit," Jane Smart said slowly, the word simmering.

"With all respect, Darryl, and I *am* fond of our little Jenny," Sukie said, "she *is* a bit of a blah."

"Come on, cut it out, what sort of reception is this?" the big man said helplessly, while his robed bride beside him didn't flinch, taking shelter as she always had behind the brittle shield of innocence, the snobbery of ignorance. It was not that her brain was less efficient than theirs, within its limits it was more so; but it was like the keyboard of an adding machine as opposed to that of typewriters. Van Horne was trying to collect his dignity. "Listen, you bitches," he said. "What's this attitude that I owe you anything? I took you in, I gave you eats and a little relief from your lousy lives—"

"Who made them lousy?" Jane Smart swiftly asked.

"Not me. I'm new in town."

Fidel brought in a tray of long-stemmed glasses of champagne. Alexandra took one and tossed its contents at Van

Horne's face; the rarefied liquid fell short, wetting only the area of his fly and one pants leg. All she had achieved was to make him seem the victim and not herself. She threw the glass vehemently at the sculpture of intertwined automobile bumpers; here her aim was better, but the glass in mid-flight turned into a barn swallow, and flicked itself away. Thumbkin, who had been licking herself on the satin love seat, worrying with avid tongue the tiny pink gap in her raiment of long white fur, perked up and gave chase; with that comical deadly solemnity of cats, green eyes flattened across the top, she stalked along the back of the curved four-cushion sofa and batted in frustration at the air when she reached the edge. The bird took shelter by perching upon a hanging Styrofoam cloud by Marjorie Strider.

"Hey, this isn't at all the way I pictured it," Van Horne complained.

"How *did* you picture it, Darryl?" Sukie asked.

"As a blast. We thought you'd be pleased as hell. You brought us together. You're like Cupids. You're like the maids of honor."

"I *never* thought they'd be pleased," Jenny corrected. "I just didn't think they'd be quite so ill-mannered."

"Why *would*n't they be pleased?" Van Horne held his rubbery strange hands open in a supplicatory fashion, arguing with Jenny, and they did look the very tableau of a married couple. "We'd be pleased for *them*," he said, "if some schnook came along and took 'em off the market. I mean, what's this jealousy bag, with the whole damn world going up in napalm? How fucking bourgeois can you get?"

Sukie was the first to soften. Perhaps she just wanted to nibble something. "All right," she said. "Let's eat the cake. It better have hash in it."

"The best. Orinoco beige."

Alexandra had to laugh, Darryl was so funny and hopeful and discombobulated. "There is no such thing."

"Sure there is, if you know the right people. Rebecca knows the guys who drive that crazy-painted van down from south Providence. *La crème de la crooks*, honest. You'll fly out of here. Wonder what the tide's doing?"

So he did remember: her braving the ice-cold tide that day, and him standing on the far shore shouting "You *can* fly!"

The cake was set on the tablelike back of the crouching nude. The marzipan figures were removed and broken and passed around for them to eat in a circle. Alexandra got the prick—tribute of a sort. Darryl mumbled "*Hoc est enim corpus meum*" as he did the distribution; over the champagne he intoned, "*Hic est enim calix sanguinis mei.*" Across from Alexandra, Jenny's face had turned a radiant pink; she was allowing her joy to show, she was dyed clear through by the blood of triumph. Alexandra's heart went out to her, as if to a younger self. They all fed cake to one another with their fingers; soon its tiered cylinders looked eviscerated by jackals. Then they linked dirty hands and, their backs to the crouching statue, upon whose left buttock Sukie with lipstick and frosting had painted a grinning snaggle-toothed face, they danced in a ring, chanting in the ancient fashion, "*Emen hetan, Emen hetan*" and "*Har, har, diable, diable, saute ici, saute là, joue ici, joue là!*"

Jane, by now the drunkest of them, tried to sing all the stanzas to that unspeakable Jacobean song of songs, "Tinkletum Tankletum," until laughter and alcohol broke her memory down. Van Horne juggled first three, then four, then five tangerines, his hands a frantic blur. Christopher Gabriel stuck his head out of the library to see what all the hilarity was about. Fidel had been holding back some marinated capybara balls, which now he served forth. The night was becoming a success; but when Sukie proposed that they all go have a bath now, Jenny announced with a certain firmness, "The tub's been drained. It had gotten all scummy, and we're waiting for a man from Narragansett Pool Hygiene to come and give the teak a course of fungicide."

So Alexandra got home earlier than expected and surprised the babysitter intertwined with her boyfriend on the sofa downstairs. She backed out of the room and reëntered ten minutes later and paid the embarrassed sitter. The girl was an Arsenault and lived downtown; her friend would drive her home, she said. Alexandra's next action was to go upstairs and tiptoe into Marcy's room and verify that her daughter, seventeen and a woman's size, was virginally asleep. But for hours into the night the vision of the pallid undersides of the Arsenault girl's thighs clamped around the nameless boy's furry buttocks, his jeans pulled down just enough to give his genitals freedom while she had been stripped of all her clothes, burned in Alexandra's brow like the moon sailing backwards through tattered, troubled clouds.

They met, the three of them, somewhat like old times, in Jane Smart's house, the ranch house in the Cove development that had been such a comedown, really, for Jane after the lovely thirteen-room Victorian, with its servants' passageways and ornamental ball-and-stick work and Tiffany-glass chandeliers, that she and Sam in their glory days had owned on Vane Street, one block back from Oak, away from the water. Her present house was a split-level ranch standing on the standard quarter-acre, its shingled parts painted an acid blue. The previous owner, an underemployed mechanical engineer who had finally gone to Texas in pursuit of work, had spent his abundant spare time "antiquing" the little house, putting up pine cabinets and false boxed beams, and knotty wainscoting with induced chisel scars, and even installing light switches in the form of wooden pump handles and a toilet bowl sheathed in oaken barrel staves. Some walls were hung with old carpentry tools, plow planes and frame saws and drawknives; and a small spinning wheel had been cunningly incorporated into the banister at the landing where the split in levels occurred. Jane had inherited this fussy overlay of Puritania without overt protest; but her contempt and that of her children had slowly eroded the precious effect. Whittled light switches were snapped in rough haste. Once one stave had been broken by a kick, the whole set of them collapsed around the toilet bowl. The cute boxy toilet-paper holder had come apart too. Jane gave her piano lessons at the far end of the long open living room, up six steps from the kitchen-dinette-den level, and the uncarpeted living-room floor showed the ravages of an apparently malign fury; the pin of her cello had gouged a hole wherever she had decided to set her stand and chair. And she had roamed the area fairly widely, rather than play in one settled place. Nor did the damage end there; everywhere in the newish little house, built of green pine and cheap material in a set pattern like a series of dances enacted by the construction crews, were marks of its fragility, scars in the paint and holes in the plasterboard and missing tiles on the kitchen floor. Jane's awful Doberman pinscher, Randolph, had chewed chair rungs and had clawed at doors until troughs were worn in the wood. Jane really did live, Alexandra told herself in extenuation, in some unsolid world part music, part spite.

"So what shall we do about it?" Jane asked now, drinks distributed and the first flurry of gossip dispersed—for there could be only one topic today, Darryl Van Horne's astounding, insulting marriage.

"How smug and 'at home' she was in that big blue bathrobe," Sukie said. "I hate her. To think it was me that brought her to tennis that time. I hate myself." She crammed her mouth with a handful of salted pepita seeds.

"And she was quite competitive, remember?" Alexandra said. "That bruise on my thigh didn't go away for weeks."

"That should have told us something," Sukie said, picking a green husk from her lower lip. "That she wasn't the helpless little doll she appeared. It's just I felt so guilty about Clyde and Felicia."

"Oh *stop* it," Jane insisted. "You *did*n't feel guilty, how *could* you feel guilty? It wasn't your screwing Clyde rotted his brain, it wasn't you who made Felicia such a horror."

"They had a symbiosis," Alexandra said consideringly. "Sukie's being so lovely for Clyde upset it. I have the same problem with Joe except I'm pulling out. Gently. To defuse the situation. People," she mused. "People *are* explosive."

"Don't you just *hate* her?" Sukie asked Alexandra. "I mean, we all understood he was to be yours if he was to be anybody's, among the three of us, once the novelty and everything wore off. Isn't that so, Jane?"

"It is not so" was the definite response. "Darryl and I are both musical. And we're dirty."

"Who says Lexa and I aren't dirty?" Sukie protested.

"You work at it," Jane said. "But you have other tendencies too. You both have goody-goody sides. You haven't committed yourselves the way I have. For me, there is nobody except Darryl."

"I thought you said you were seeing Bob Osgood," Alexandra said.

"I said I was giving his daughter Deborah piano lessons," Jane responded.

Sukie laughed. "You should see how uppity you look, saying that. Like Jenny when she called us all ill-mannered."

"And didn't she boss him around, in her chilly little way," Alexandra said. "I knew they were married just from the way she stepped into the room, making a late entrance. And he was different. Less outrageous, more tentative. It was sad."

"We *are* committed, sweetie," Sukie said to Jane. "But what can we do, except snub them and go back to being our old cozy selves? I think it may be nicer now. I feel closer to the two of you than for months. And all those hot hors d'oeuvres Fidel made us eat were getting to my stomach."

"What can we *do*?" Jane asked rhetorically. Her black hair, brushed from a central part in two severe wings, fell forward, eclipsing her face, and was swiftly brushed back. "It's obvious. We can *hex* her."

The word, like a shooting star suddenly making its scratch on the sky, commanded silence.

"You can hex her yourself if you feel that vehement," Alexandra said. "You don't need us."

"I do. It needs the three of us. This mustn't be a little hex, so she'll just get hives and a headache for a week."

Sukie asked after a pause, "What *will* she get?"

Jane's thin lips clamped shut upon a bad-luck word, the Latin for "crab." "I think it's obvious, from the other night, where her anxieties lie. When a person has a fear like that it takes just the teeniest-weeniest psychokinetic push to make it come true."

"Oh, the poor child," Alexandra involuntarily exclaimed, having the same terror herself.

"Poor child nothing," said Jane. "She is"—and her thin face put on additional hauteur—"Mrs. Darryl Van Horne."

After another pause Sukie asked, "How would the hex work?"

"Perfectly straightforwardly. Alexandra makes a wax figure of her and we stick pins in it under our cone of power."

"Why must *I* make it?" Alexandra asked.

"Simple, my darling. You're the sculptress, we're not. And

you're still in touch with the larger forces. My spells lately tend to go off at about a forty-five degree angle. I tried to kill Greta Neff's pet cat about six months ago when I was still seeing Ray, and from what he let drop I gather I killed all the rodents in the house instead. The walls stank for weeks but the cat stayed disgustingly healthy."

Alexandra asked, "Jane, don't you ever get scared?"

"Not since I accepted myself for what I am. A fair cellist, a dreadful mother, and a boring lay."

Both the other women protested this last, gallantly, but Jane was firm: "I give good enough head, but when the man is on top and in me something resentful takes over."

"Just try imagining it's your own hand," Sukie suggested. "That's what I do sometimes."

"Or think of it that *you're* fucking *him*," Alexandra said. "That he's just something you're toying with."

"It's too late for all that. I like what I am by now. If I were happier I'd be less effective. Here's what I've done for a start. When Darryl was passing the marzipan figures around I bit off the head of the one representing Jenny but didn't swallow it, and spit it out when I could in my handkerchief. Here." She went to her piano bench, lifted the lid, and brought out a crumpled handkerchief; gloatingly she unfolded the handkerchief for their eyes.

The little smooth candy head, further smoothed by those solvent seconds in Jane's mouth, did have a relation to Jenny's round face—the washed-out blue eyes with their steady gaze, the blond hair so fine it lay flat on her head like paint, a certain blankness of expression that had something faintly challenging and defiant and, yes, galling about it.

"That's good," Alexandra said, "but you also need something more intimate. Blood is best. The old recipes used to call for *sang de menstrues*. And hair, of course. Fingernail clippings."

"Belly-button lint," chimed in Sukie, silly on two bourbons.

"Excrement," Alexandra solemnly continued, "though if you're not in Africa or China that's hard to come by."

"Hold on. Don't go away," Jane said, and left the room.

Sukie laughed. "I should write a story for the Providence *Journal-Bulletin*, 'The Flush Toilet and the Demise of Witch-craft.' They said I could submit features as a free-lancer to them if I wanted to get back into writing." She had kicked off her shoes and curled her legs under her as she leaned on one arm of Jane's acid-green sofa. In this era even women well into middle age wore miniskirts, and Sukie's kittenish posture exposed almost all the thigh she had, plus her freckled, gleaming knees, perfect as eggs. She was in a wool pullover dress scarcely longer than a sweater, sharp orange in color; this color made with the sofa's vile green the arresting clash one finds everywhere in Cézanne's landscapes and that would be ugly were it not so oddly, boldly beautiful. Sukie's face wore that tipsy slurred look—eyes too moist and sparkling, lipstick rubbed away but for the rims by too much smiling and chattering—that Alexandra found sexy. She even found sexy Sukie's least successful feature, her short, fat, and rather unchiselled nose. There was no doubt, Alexandra thought to herself dispassionately, that since Van Horne's marriage her heart had slipped its moorings, and that away from the shared unhappiness of these two friends there was little but desolation. She could pay no attention to her children; she could see their mouths move but the sounds that came out were jabber in a foreign language.

"Aren't you still doing real estate?" she asked Sukie.

"Oh I am, honey. But it's *such* thin pickings. There are these hundreds of other divorcees running around in the mud showing houses."

"You made that sale to the Hallybreads."

"I know I did, but that just about brought me even with my debts. Now I'm slipping back into the red again and I'm getting desperate." Sukie smiled broadly, her lips spreading like cushions sat on. She patted the empty place beside her. "Gorgeous, come over and sit by me. I feel I'm shouting. The acoustics in this hideous little house, I don't know how she can stand hearing herself."

Jane had gone up the little half-flight of stairs to where the bedrooms were in this split-level, and now returned with a linen hand towel folded to hold some delicate treasure. Her aura was the incandescent purple of Siberian iris, and pulsed in excitement. "Last night," she said, "I was so upset and angry about all this I couldn't sleep and finally got up and rubbed myself all over with aconite and Noxema hand cream, with just a little bit of that fine gray ash you get after you put the oven on automatic cleaner, and flew to the Lenox place. It was wonderful! The spring peepers are all out, and the higher you get in the air the better you can hear them for some reason. At Darryl's, they were all still downstairs, though it was after midnight. There was this kind of Caribbean music that they make on oil drums pouring full blast out of the stereo, and some cars in the driveway I didn't recognize. I found a bedroom window open a couple of inches and slid it up, ever so carefully—"

"Janie, this is so thrilling!" Sukie cried. "Suppose Needlenose had smelled you! Or Thumbkin!"

For Thumbkin, Van Horne had solemnly assured them, beneath her fluffy shape was the incarnate soul of an eighteenth-century Newport barrister who had embezzled from his firm to feed his opium habit (he had been hooked during spells of the terrible toothaches and abscesses common to all ages before ours) and, to save himself from prison and his family from disgrace, had pledged his spirit after death to the dark powers. The little cat could assume at will the form of a panther, a ferret, or a hippogriff.

"A dab of Ivory detergent in the ointment quite kills the scent, I find," Jane said, displeased by the interruption.

"Go on, go on," Sukie begged. "You opened the window —do you think they sleep in the same bed? How can she stand it? That body so cold and clammy under the fur. He was like opening the door of a refrigerator with something spoiling in it."

"Let Jane tell her story," Alexandra said, a mother to them both. The last time she had attempted flight, her astral body had lifted off and her material body had been left behind in the bed, looking so small and pathetic she had felt a terrible rush of shame in midair, and had fled back into her heavy shell.

"I could hear the party downstairs," Jane said. "I think I heard Ray Neff's voice, trying to lead some singing. I found a bathroom, the one that *she* uses."

"How could you be sure?" Sukie asked.

"I know her style by now. Prim on the outside, messy on the inside. Lipsticky Kleenexes everywhere, one of those cardboard circles that hold the Pill so you don't forget the right day lying around all punched out, combs full of long hair. She dyes it, by the way. A whole bottle of pale Clairol right there on the sink. And pancake make-up and blusher, things I'd *die* before ever using. I'm a hag and I know it and a hag is what I want to look like."

"Baby, you're beautiful," Sukie told her. "You have raven hair. And naturally tortoiseshell eyes. And you take a tan. I wish I did. Nobody can take a freckled person quite seriously, for some reason. People think I'm being funny even when I feel lousy."

"What did you bring back in that sweetly folded towel?" Alexandra asked Jane.

"That's *his* towel. I stole it," Jane told them. Yet the delicate script monogram seemed to be a *P* or a *Q*. "Look. I went through the wastebasket under the bathroom sink." Carefully Jane unfolded the rose-colored hand towel upon a spidery jumble of discarded intimate matter: long hairs pulled in billowing snarls from a comb, a Kleenex bearing a tawny stain in its crumpled center, a square of toilet paper holding the vulval image of freshly lipsticked lips being blotted, a tail of cotton from a pill bottle, the scarlet pull thread of a Band-Aid, strands of used dental floss. "Best of all," Jane said, "these little specks —can you see them? Look close. Those were in the bathtub, on the bottom and stuck in the ring—she doesn't even have the decency to wash out a tub when she uses it. I dampened the towel and wiped them up. They're leg hairs. She shaved her legs in the bath."

"Oh that's nice," Sukie said. "You're scary, Jane. You've taught me now to always wash out the tub."

"Do you think this is enough?" Jane asked Alexandra. The eyes that Sukie had called tortoiseshell in truth looked paler, with the unsteady glow of embers.

"Enough for what?" But Alexandra already knew, she had read Jane's mind; knowing chafed that sore place in Alexandra's abdomen, the sore place that had begun the other night, with too much reality to digest.

"Enough to make the charm," Jane answered.

"Why ask me? Make the charm yourself and see how it goes."

"Oh no, dearie. I've already said. We don't have your—how can I put it?—access. To the deep currents. Sukie and I are like pins and needles, we can prick and scratch and that's about it."

Alexandra turned to Sukie. "Where do you stand on this?"

Sukie tried, high on whiskey as she was, to make a thoughtful mouth; her upper lip bunched adorably over her slightly protruding teeth. "Jane and I have talked about it on the phone, a little. We *do* want you to do it with us. We do. It should be unanimous, like a vote. You know, by myself last fall I cast a little spell to bring you and Darryl together, and it worked up to a point. But only up to a point. To be honest, honey, I think my powers are lessening all the time. Everything seems drab. I looked at Darryl the other night and he looked all slapped together somehow—I think he's running scared."

"Then why not let Jenny have him?"

"*No*," Jane interposed. "She mustn't. She stole him. She made fools of us." Her *s*'s lingered like a smoky odor in the long ugly scarred room. Beyond the little flights of stairs that went down to the kitchen area and up to the bedrooms, a distant, sizzling, murmuring sound signified that Jane's children were engrossed in television. There had been another assassination, somewhere. The President was giving speeches only at military installations. The body count was up but so was enemy infiltration.

Alexandra still turned to Sukie, hoping to be relieved of this looming necessity. "You cast a spell to bring me and Darryl together that day of the high tide? He wasn't attracted to me by himself?"

"Oh I'm sure he was, baby," Sukie said, but shruggingly. "Anyway who can tell? I used that green gardener's twine to tie the two of you together and I checked under the bed the other day and rats or something had nibbled it through, maybe for the salt that rubbed off from my hands."

"That wasn't very nice," Jane told Sukie, "when you knew I wanted him myself."

This was the moment for Sukie to tell Jane that she liked Alexandra better; instead she said, "We *all* wanted him, but I figured you could get what you wanted by yourself. And you did. You were over there all the time, fiddling away, if that's what you want to call it."

Alexandra's vanity had been stung. She said, "Oh hell. Let's do it." It seemed simplest, a way of cleaning up another tiny pocket of the world's endless dirt.

Taking care not to touch any of it with their hands, lest their own essences—the salt and oil from their skins, their multitudinous personal bacteria—become involved, the three of them shook the Kleenexes and the long blond hairs and the red Band-Aid thread and, most important, the fine specks of leg bristle, that jumped in the weave of the towel like live mites, into a ceramic ashtray Jane had stolen from the Bronze Barrel in the days when she would go there after rehearsal with the Neffs. She added the staring sugar head she had saved in her mouth and lit the little pyre with a paper match. The Kleenexes blazed orange, the hairs crackled blue and emitted the stink of singeing, the marzipan reduced itself to a bubbling black curdle. The smoke lifted to the ceiling and hung like a cobweb on the artificial surface, papery plasterboard roughed with a coat of sand-impregnated paint to feign real plaster.

"Now," Alexandra said to Jane Smart. "Do you have an old candle stump? Or some birthday candles in a drawer? The ashes must be crushed and mixed into about a half-cup of melted wax. Use a saucepan and butter it thoroughly first, bottom and sides; if any wax sticks, the spell is flawed."

While Jane carried out this order in the kitchen, Sukie laid a hand on the other woman's forearm. "Sweetie, I know you don't want to do this," she said.

Caressing the delicate tendony offered hand, Alexandra noticed how the freckles, thickly strewn on the back and the first knuckles, thinned toward the fingernails, as if this mixture had been insufficiently stirred. "Oh but I do," she said. "It gives me a lot of pleasure. It's artistry. And I love the way you two believe in me so." And without forethought she leaned and kissed Sukie on the complicated cushions of her lips.

Sukie stared. Her pupils contracted as the shadow of Alexandra's head moved off her green irises. "But you had liked Jenny."

"Only her body. The way I liked my children's bodies. Remember how they smelled as babies?"

"Oh Lexa: do you think any of us will ever have any more babies?"

It was Alexandra's turn to shrug. The question seemed sentimental, unhelpful. She asked Sukie, "You know what witches used to make candles out of? Baby fat!" She stood, not altogether steadily. She had been drinking vodka, which does not stain the breath or transport too many calories but which also does not pass like a stream of neutrinos through the system altogether without effect. "We must go help Jane in the kitchen."

Jane had found an old box of birthday candles at the back of a drawer, pink and blue mixed. Melted together in the buttered saucepan, and the ashes from their tiny pyre stirred in with an egg whisk, the wax came out a pearly, flecked lavender-gray.

"Now what do you have for a mold?" Alexandra asked. They rummaged for cookie cutters, rejected a pâté mold as much too big, considered demitasse cups and liqueur glasses, and settled on the underside of an old-fashioned heavy glass orange-juice squeezer, the kind shaped like a sombrero with a spout on the rim. Alexandra turned it upside down and deftly poured; the hot wax sizzled within the ridged cone but the glass didn't crack. She held the top side under running cold water and tapped on the edge of the sink until the convex cone of wax, still warm, fell into her hand. She gave it a squeeze to make it oblong. The incipient human form gazed up at her from her palm, dented four times by her fingers. "Damn," she said. "We should have saved out a few strands of her hair."

Jane said, "I'll check to see if any is still clinging to the towel."

"And do you have any orangesticks by any chance?" Alexandra asked her. "Or a long nail file. To carve with. I could even make do with a hairpin." Off Jane flew. She was used to taking orders—from Bach, from Popper, from a host of dead men. In her absence Alexandra explained to Sukie, "The trick is not to take away more than you must. Every crumb has some magic in it now."

She selected from the knives hanging on a magnetic bar a dull paring knife with a wooden handle bleached and softened by many trips through the dishwasher. She whittled in to make a neck, a waist. The crumbs fell on a ScotTowel spread on the Formica countertop. Balancing the crumbs on the tip of the knife, and with the other hand holding a lighted match under this tip, she dripped the wax back onto the emerging figurine to form breasts. The subtler convexities of belly and thighs Alexandra also built up in this way. The legs she pared down to tiny feet in her style. The crumbs left over from this became—heated, dripped, and smoothed—the buttocks. All the time she held in her mind the image of the girl, how she had glowed at their baths. The arms were unimportant and were sculpted in low relief at the sides. The sex she firmly indicated with the tip of the knife held inverted and vertical. Other creases and contours she refined with the bevelled oval edge of the orangestick Jane had fetched. Jane had found one more long hair clinging to the threads of the towel. She held it up to the window light and, though a single hair scarcely has color, it appeared neither black nor red in the tint of its filament, and paler, finer, purer than a strand from Alexandra's head would have been. "I'm quite certain it's Jenny's," she said.

"It better be," Alexandra said, her voice grown husky through concentration upon the figure she was making. With the edge of the soft fragrant stick that pushed cuticles she pressed the single hair into the yielding lavender scalp.

"She has a head but no face," Jane complained over her shoulder. Her voice jarred the sacred cone of concentration.

"We provide the face" was Alexandra's whispered answer. "We know who it is and project it."

"It feels like Jenny to me already," said Sukie, who had attended so closely to the manufacture that Alexandra had felt the other woman's breath flitting across her hands.

"Smoother," Alexandra crooned to herself, using the rounded underside of a teaspoon. "Jenny is smooooth."

Jane criticized again: "It won't stand up."

"Her little women never do," Sukie intervened.

"Shhh," Alexandra said, protecting her incantatory tone. "She must take this lying down. That's how we ladies do it. We take our medicine lying down."

With the magic knife, the *Athame*, she incised grooves in imitation of Jenny's prim new Eva Perón hairdo on the little simulacrum's head. Jane's complaint about the face nagged, so with the edge of the orangestick she attempted the curved dents of eye sockets. The effect, of sudden sight out of the gray lump, was alarming. The hollow in Alexandra's abdomen turned leaden. In attempting creation we take on creation's burden of guilt, of murder and irreversibility. With the tine of a fork she pricked a navel into the figure's glossy abdomen:

born, not made; tied like all of us to mother Eve. "Enough," Alexandra announced, dropping her tools with a clatter into the sink. "Quickly, while the wax has a little warmth in it still. Sukie. Do you believe this is Jenny?"

"Why . . . sure, Alexandra, if you say so."

"It's important that *you* believe. Hold her in your hands. Both hands."

She did. Her thin freckled hands were trembling.

"Say to it—don't smile—say to it, 'You are Jenny. You must die.'"

"You are Jenny. You must die."

"You too, Jane. Do it. Say it."

Jane's hands were different from Sukie's, and from each other: the bow hand thick and soft, the fingering hand over-developed and with golden glazed calluses on the cruelly used tips.

Jane said the words, but in such a dead determined tone, just reading the notes as it were, that Alexandra warned, "You must believe them. *This is Jenny.*"

It did not surprise Alexandra that for all her spite Jane should be the weak sister when it came to casting the spell; for magic is fueled by love, not hate: hate wields scissors only and is impotent to weave the threads of sympathy whereby the mind and spirit do move matter.

Jane repeated the formula, there in this ranch-house kitchen, with its picture window, spattered by hardened bird droppings, giving on a scrappy yard nevertheless graced at this moment of the year with the glory of two dogwoods in bloom. The day's last sunlight gleamed like a background of precious metal worked in fine leaf between the drifting twists of the dark branches and the sprays, at the branches' ends, of four-petalled blossoms. A yellow plastic wading tub, exposed to the weather all winter and forever outgrown by Jane's children, rested at a slight tilt beneath one of the trees, holding a crescent of filthy water that had been ice. The lawn was brown and tummocky yet misted by fresh green. The earth was still alive.

The voices of the other two recalled Alexandra to herself. "You too, sweetie," Jane told her harshly, handing her bubby back to her. "Say the words."

They were hateful, but on the other hand factual; Alexandra

said them with calm conviction and hastily directed the spell to its close. "Pins," she told Jane. "Needles. Even thumbtacks —are there some in your kids' rooms?"

"I hate to go in there, they'll start yammering for dinner."

Alexandra said, "Tell them five more minutes. We must finish up or it could—"

"It could what?" Sukie asked, frightened.

"It could backfire. It may yet. Like Ed's bomb. Those little round-headed map pins would be nice. Even paper clips, if we straighten them. But one good-sized needle is essential." She did not explain, *To pierce the heart.* "Also, Jane. A mirror." For the magic did not occur in the three dimensions of matter but within the image matter generated in a mirror, the astral identity of mere mute things, an existence added on to existence.

"Sam left a shaving mirror I sometimes use to do my eyes."

"Perfect. Hurry. I have to keep my mood or the elementals will dissipate."

Off Jane flew again; Sukie at Alexandra's side tempted her, "How about one more splash? I'm having just one more weak bourbon myself, before I face reality."

"This is reality, I'm sorry to say. A half-splash, honey. A thimble of vodka and fill the rest up with tonic or 7 Up or faucet water or anything. Poor little Jenny." As she carried the wax image up the six battered steps from the kitchen into the living room, imperfections and asymmetries in her work cried out to her—one leg smaller than the other, the anatomy where hips and thighs and abdomen come together not really understood, the wax breasts too heavy. Whoever had made her think she was a sculptress? Darryl: it had been wicked of him.

Jane's hideous Doberman, released by some door she had opened along the upstairs hall, bounded into the living room, the claws of his feet scrabbling on the naked wood. His coat was an oily black, close and rippling and tricked out like some military uniform with orange boots and patches of the same color on his chest and muzzle and, in two round spots, above his eyes. Drooling, he stared up at Alexandra's cupped hands, thinking something to be eaten was held there. Even Randolph's nostrils were watering with appetite, and the folded insides of his aroused erect ears seemed extensions of ravenous intestines. "Not for you," Alexandra told him sternly, and the dog's glassy black eyes looked polished, they were trying so hard to understand.

Sukie followed with the drinks; Jane hurried in with a two-sided shaving mirror on a wire stand, an ashtray full of multi-colored tacks, and a pincushion in the form of a little cloth apple. The time was a few minutes to seven; at seven the television programs changed and the children would be demanding to be fed. The three women set the mirror up on Jane's coffee table, an imitation cobbler's bench abandoned by the mechanical engineer as he cleared out for Texas. Within the mirror's silver circle everything was magnified, stretched and out of focus at the edges, vivid and huge at the center. In turn the women held the doll before it, as at the hungry round mouth of another world, and stuck in pins and thumbtacks. "Aurai, Hanlii, Thamcii, Tilinos, Athamas, Zianor, Auonail," Alexandra recited.

"Tzabaoth, Messiach, Emanuel, Elchim, Eibor, Yod, He, Vou, He!" Jane chanted in crisp sacrilege.

"Astachoth, Adonai, Agla, On, El, Tetragrammaton, Shema," Sukie said, "Ariston, Anaphaxeton, and then I forget what's next."

Breasts and head, hips and belly, in the points went. Distant indistinct shots and cries drifted into their ears as the television program's violence climaxed. The simulacrum had taken on a festive encrusted look—the bristle of a campaign map, the fey gaudiness of a Pop Art hand grenade, a voodoo glitter. The shaving mirror swam with reflected color. Jane held up the long needle, of a size to work thick thread through suede. "Who wants to poke this through the heart?"

"You may," Alexandra said, gazing down to place a yellow-headed thumbtack symmetrical with another, as if this art were abstract. Though the neck and cheeks had been pierced, no one had dared thrust a pin into the eyes, which gazed expressionless or full of mournful spirit, depending on how the shadows fell.

"Oh no, you don't shove it off on me," Jane Smart said. "It should be all of us, we should all three put a finger on it."

Left hands intertwining like a nest of snakes, they pushed the needle through. The wax resisted, as if a lump of thicker substance were at its center. "*Die*," said one red mouth, and another, "*Take that!*" before giggling overtook them. The needle eased through. Alexandra's index finger showed a blue mark about to bleed. "Should have worn a thimble," she said.

"Lexa, now what?" Sukie asked. She was panting, slightly.

A little hiss arose from Jane as she contemplated their strange achievement.

"We must seal the malignancy in," Alexandra said. "Jane, do you have Reynolds Wrap?"

The other two giggled again. They were scared, Alexandra realized. Why? Nature kills constantly, and we call her beautiful. Alexandra felt drugged, immobilized, huge like a queen ant or bee; the things of the world were pouring through her and reemerging tinged with her spirit, her will.

Jane fetched too large a sheet of aluminum foil, torn off raggedly in panic. It crackled and shivered in the speed of her walk. Children's footsteps were pounding down the hall. "Each spit," Alexandra quickly commanded, having bedded Jenny upon the trembling sheet. "Spit so the seed of death will grow," she insisted, and led the way.

Jane spitting was like a cat sneezing; Sukie hawked a bit like a man. Alexandra folded the foil, bright side in, around and around the charm, softly so as not to dislodge the pins or stab herself. The result looked like a potato wrapped to be baked.

Two of Jane's children, an obese boy and a gaunt little girl with a dirty face, crowded around curiously. "What's *that*?" the girl demanded to know. Her nose wrinkled at the smell of evil. Both her upper and lower teeth were trussed in a glittering fretwork of braces. She had been eating something sweet and greenish.

Jane told her, "A project of Mrs. Spofford's that she's been showing us. It's very delicate and I know she doesn't want to undo it again so please don't ask her."

"I'm *starv*ing," the boy said. "And we *don't* want hamburgers from Nemo's again, we want a home-cooked meal like other kids get."

The girl was studying Jane closely. In embryo she had Jane's hatchet profile. "Mother, are you drunk?"

Jane slapped the child with a magical quickness, as if the two of them, mother and daughter, were parts of a single wooden toy that performed this action over and over. Sukie and Alexandra, whose own starved children were howling out there in the dark, took this signal to leave. They paused on the brick walk outside the house, from whose wide lit windows spilled the spiralling tumult of a family quarrel. Alexandra asked Sukie, "Want custody of this?"

The foil-wrapped weight in her hand felt warm.

Sukie's lean lovely nimble hand already rested on the door handle of her Corvair. "I would, sweetie, but I have these rats or mice or whatever they are that nibbled at the other. Don't they adore candle wax?"

Back at her own house, which was more sheltered from the noise of traffic on Orchard Road now that her hedge of lilacs was leafing in, Alexandra put the thing, wanting to forget it, on a high shelf in the kitchen, along with some flawed bubbies she hadn't had the heart to throw away and the sealed jar holding the polychrome dust that had once been dear old well-intentioned Ozzie.

"He goes everywhere with her," Sukie said to Jane over the phone. "The Historical Society, the conservation hearings. They make themselves ridiculous, trying to be so respectable. He's even joined the Unitarian choir."

"Darryl? But he has utterly no voice," Jane said sharply.

"Well, he has a little something, a kind of a baritone. He sounds just like an organ pipe."

"Who told you all this?"

"Rose Hallybread. They've joined at Brenda's too. Darryl apparently had the Hallybreads over to dinner and Arthur wound up telling him he wasn't as crazy as he had first thought. This was around two in the morning, they had all spent hours in the lab, boring Rose silly. As far as I could understand, Darryl's new idea is to breed a certain kind of microbe in some huge body of water like Great Salt Lake—the saltier the better, evidently—and this little bug just by breeding will turn the entire lake into a huge battery somehow. They'd put a fence around it, of course."

"Of course, my dear. Safety first."

A pause, while Sukie tried to puzzle through if this was meant sarcastically and, if so, why. She was just giving the news. Now that they no longer met at Darryl's they saw each other less frequently. They had not officially abandoned their Thursdays, but in the month since they had put the spell on Jenny one of the three had always had an excuse not to come. "So how *are* you?" Sukie asked.

"Keeping busy," Jane said.

"I keep running into Bob Osgood downtown."

Jane didn't bite. "Actually," she said, "I'm unhappy. I was standing in the back yard and this black wave came over me and I realized it had something to do with summer, everything green and all the flowers breaking out, and it hit me what I hate about summer: the children will be home all day."

"Aren't you wicked?" Sukie asked. "I rather enjoy mine, now that they're old enough to talk adult talk. Watching television all the time they're much better informed on world affairs than I ever was; they want to move to France. They say our name is French and they think France is a civilized country that never fights wars and where nobody kills anybody."

"Tell them about Gilles de Rais," Jane said.

"I never thought of him; I did say, though, that it was the French made the mess in Vietnam in the first place and that we were trying to clean it up. They wouldn't buy that. They said we were trying to create more markets for Coca-Cola."

There was another pause. "Well," Jane said. "Have you seen her?"

"Who?"

"*Her*. Jeanne d'Arc. Madame Curie. How does she look?"

"Jane, you're amazing. How did you know? That I saw her downtown."

"Sweetie, it's obvious from your voice. And why else would you be calling me? How was the little pet?"

"Very pleasant, actually. It was rather embarrassing. She said she and Darryl have been missing us *so* much and wish we'd just drop around some time informally, they don't like to think they have to extend a formal invitation, which they *will* do soon, she promised; it's just they've been terribly busy lately, what with some very hopeful developments in the lab and some legal affairs that keep taking Darryl to New York. Then she went on about how much she loves New York, compared with Chicago, which is windy and tough and where she never felt safe, even right in the hospital. Whereas New York is just a set of cozy little villages, all heaped one on top of the other. Et cetera, et cetera."

"I'll never set foot in that house again," Jane Smart vehemently, needlessly vowed.

"She really did seem unaware," Sukie said, "that we might be offended by her stealing Darryl right out from under our noses that way."

"Once you've established in your own mind that you're innocent," Jane said, "you can get away with anything. How did she look?"

Now the pause was on Sukie's side. In the old days their conversations had bubbled along, their sentences braiding, flowing one on top of the other, each anticipating what the other was going to say and delighting in it nonetheless, as confirmation of a pooled identity. "Not great," Sukie pronounced at last. "Her skin seemed . . . transparent, somehow."

"She was always pale," Jane said.

"But this wasn't just pale. Anyway, baby, it's May. Everybody should have a little color by now. We went down to Moonstone last Sunday and just soaked in the dunes. My nose looks like a strawberry; Toby kids me about it."

"Toby?"

"You know, Toby Bergman: he took over at the *Word* after poor Clyde and broke his leg on the ice this winter? His leg is all healed now, though it's smaller than the other. He never does these exercises with a lead shoe you're supposed to do."

"I thought you hated him."

"That was before I got to know him, when I was still all hysterical about Clyde. Toby's a lot of fun, actually. He makes me laugh."

"Isn't he a lot . . . younger?"

"We talk about that. He'll be two whole years out of Brown this June. He says I'm the youngest person at heart he's ever met, he kids me about how I'm always eating junk food and wanting to do crazy things like stay up all night listening to talk shows. I guess he's very typical of his generation, they don't have all the hangups about age and race and all that that we were brought up on. Believe me, darling, he's a big improvement on Ed and Clyde in a number of ways, including some I won't go into. It's not complicated, we just have fun."

"Super," Jane said in dismissal, dropping the *r*. "Did her . . . spirit seem the same?"

"She came on a little less shy," Sukie said thoughtfully. "You know, the married woman and all. Pale, like I said, but maybe it was the time of day. We had a cup of coffee in Nemo's, only she had cocoa because she hasn't been sleeping well and is trying to do without caffeine. Rebecca was all over her, insisted we try these blueberry muffins that are part of Nemo's campaign to get some of the nice-people luncheon business back from the Bakery. She hardly gave *me* the time of day. Rebecca. She just took one bite of hers, Jenny this is, and asked if I could finish it for her, she didn't want to hurt Rebecca's feelings. Actually, I was happy to, I've been *rav*enous lately, I can't imagine what it is, I can't be pregnant, can I? These Jews are real potent. She said she didn't know why, but she just hadn't had much of an appetite lately. Jenny. I wondered if she was fishing, to see if I knew why by any chance. She may know in her bones about the . . . the thing we did, I don't know. I felt sorry for her, the way she seemed so apologetic, about not having an appetite."

"It really is true, isn't it?" Jane observed. "You pay for every sin."

There were so many sins in the world it took Sukie a second to figure out that Jane meant Jenny's sin of marrying Darryl.

Joe had been there that morning and they had had their worst scene yet. Gina was in her fourth month by now and it was starting to show; the whole town could see. And Alexandra's children were about to be let out of school and would make these weekday trysts in her home impossible. Which was a relief to her; it would be a great relief, frankly, for her not to have to listen any more to his irresponsible and really rather presumptuous talk of leaving Gina. She was sick of hearing it, it meant nothing, and she wouldn't want it to mean anything, the whole idea upset and insulted her. He was her lover, wasn't that enough? *Had* been her lover, after today. Things end. Things begin, and things end. All grown-ups know that, why didn't he? Caught as he was so severely, rotated on the point of her tongue as on a spit, Joe became hot, and walloped her shoulder a few times with a fist kept loose enough not to hurt, and ran around the room naked, his body stocky and white and two dark swirls of hair on his back suggesting to her eyes butterfly wings (his spine its body) or a veneer of thin marble slices set so the molten splash of grain within made a symmetrical pattern. There was something delicate and organic about the hair on Joe's body, whereas Darryl's had been a rough mat. Joe wept; he took off his hat to beat his head on a doorframe: it was parody and yet real grief, actual loss. The room, the Williamsburg-green of its old woodwork and the big peonies of its curtains with their concealed clown faces and the cracked ceiling that had mutely and conspiratorially watched over their naked couplings, was part of their grief, for little is more precious in an affair for a man than being welcomed into a house he has done nothing to support, or more momentous for the woman than this welcoming, this considered largesse, her house his, his on the strength of his cock alone, his cock and company, the smell and amusement and weight of him—no buying you with mortgage payments, no blackmailing you with shared children, but welcomed simply, into the walls of yourself, an admission dignified by freedom and equality. Joe couldn't stop thinking of teams and marriage; he wanted his own penates to preside. He had demeaned with "good" intentions her gracious gift. In his anguish he surprised Alexandra by getting erect again, and since his time was short now, their morning wasted in words, she let him take her his favorite way, from behind, she on her knees. What a force of nature his pounding was! How he convulsed, shooting off! The whole episode left her feeling tumbled and cleansed, like a towel from the dryer needing to be folded and stacked on some airy shelf of her sunny, empty home.

The house, too, seemed happier for his visit, in this interval before the eternity of their parting sank in. The beams and floorboards of this windy, moistening time of the year chatted among themselves, creaking, and a window sash when her back was turned would give a swift rattle like a sudden bird cry.

She lunched on last night's salad, the lettuce limp in its chilled bath of oil. She must lose weight or she couldn't wear a bathing suit all summer. Another failing of Joe's was his for-givingness of her fat—like those primitive men who turn their wives into captives of obesity, mountains of black flesh waiting in their thatched huts. Already Alexandra felt slimmer, lightened of her lover. Her intuition told her the phone would ring. It did. It would be Jane or Sukie, lively with malice. But from the grid pressed against her ear emerged a younger, lighter voice, with a tension of timidity in it, a pocket of fear over which a membrane pulsed as at a frog's throat.

"Alexandra, you're all avoiding me." It was the voice Alexandra least in the world wanted to hear.

"Well, Jenny, we want to give you and Darryl privacy. Also we hear you have other friends."

"Yes, we do, Darryl loves what he calls input. But it's not like . . . we were."

"Nothing's ever quite the same," Alexandra told her. "The stream flows; the little bird hatches and breaks the egg. Anyway. You're doing fine."

"But I'm not, Lexa. Something's very wrong."

Her voice in the older woman's mind's eye lifted toward her like a face holding itself up to be scrubbed, a grit of hoarseness upon its cheeks. "What's very wrong?" Her own voice was like a tarpaulin or great dropcloth which in being spread out on the earth catches some air under it and lifts in a bubble, a soft wave of hollowness.

"I'm tired all the time," Jenny said, "and not much appetite. I'm subconsciously so hungry I keep having these dreams of food, but when I sit down to the reality I can't make myself eat. And other things. Pains in the night that come and go. My nose runs all the time. It's embarrassing; Darryl says I snore at night, which I never did before in my whole life. Remember those lumps I tried to show you and you couldn't find?"

"Yes. Vaguely." The sensations of that casual hunt rushed horribly into her fingertips.

"Well, there are more. In the, in the groin, and up under my ears. Isn't that where the lymph nodes are?"

Jenny's ears had never been pierced, and she was always losing little childish clip-on earrings in the tub room, on the black slates, among the cushions. "I really don't know, honey. You should see a doctor if you're worried."

"Oh I did. Doc Pat. He sent me to the Westwick Hospital to have tests."

"And did the tests show anything?"

"They said not really; but then they want me to have more tests. They're all so cagey and grave and talk in this funny voice, as though I'm a naughty child who might pee on their shoes if they don't keep me at a distance. They're scared of me. By being sick at all I'm showing them up somehow. They say things like my white-cell count is 'just a bit out of the high normal range.' They know I worked at a big city hospital and that puts them on the defensive, but I don't know anything about systemic disorders, I saw fractures and gallstones mostly. It would all be silly except at night when I lie down I can *feel* something's not right, something's working at me. They keep asking me if I'd been exposed to much radiation. Well of course I'd worked with it at Michael Reese but they're *so* careful, draping you in lead and putting you in this thick glass booth when you throw the switch, all I could think of was, in my early teens just before we moved to Eastwick and were still in Warwick, I had an awful lot of dental X-rays when they were straightening my teeth; my mouth was a mess as a girl."

"Your teeth look lovely now."

"Thank you. It cost Daddy money he didn't really have, but he was determined to have me beautiful. He *loved* me, Lexa."

"I'm sure he did, darling," Alexandra said, pressing down on her voice; the air caught under the tarpaulin was growing, struggling like a wild animal made of wind.

"He loved me so much," Jenny was blurting. "How could he do that to me, hang himself? How could he leave me and Chris so alone? Even if he were in jail for murder, it would be better than this. They wouldn't have given him too much, the awful way he did it couldn't have been premeditated."

"You have Darryl," Alexandra told her.

"I do and I don't. You know how he is. You know him better than I do; I should have talked to you before I went ahead with it. You might have been better for him, I don't know. He's courteous and attentive and all that but he's not there for me somehow. His mind is always elsewhere, with his projects I guess. Alexandra, *please* let me come and see you. I won't stay long, I really won't. I just need to be . . . touched," she concluded, her voice retracted, curling under almost sardonically while voicing this last, naked plea.

"My dear, I don't know what you want from me," Alexandra lied flatly, needing to flatten all this, to erase the smeared face rising in her mind's eye, rising so close she could see flecks of grit, "but I don't have it to give. Honestly. You made your choice and I wasn't part of it. That's fine. No reason I should have been part of it. But I can't be part of your life now. I just can't. There isn't that much of me."

"Sukie and Jane wouldn't like it, your seeing me," Jenny suggested, to give Alexandra's hard-heartedness a rationale.

"I'm speaking for myself. I don't want to get reinvolved with you and Darryl now. I wish you both well but for my sake I don't want to see you. It would just be too painful, frankly. As to this illness, it sounds to me as if you're letting your imagination torment you. At any rate you're in the hands of doctors who can do more for you than I can."

"Oh." The distant voice had shrunk itself to the size of a dot, to something mechanical like a dial tone. "I'm not sure that's true."

When she hung up, Alexandra's hands were trembling. All the familiar angles and furniture of her house looked askew, as if wrenched by the disparity between their moral distance from her—things, immune from sin—and their physical closeness. She went into her workroom and took one of the chairs there, an old arrow-back Windsor whose seat was spattered with paint and dried plaster and paste, and brought it into the kitchen. She set it below the high kitchen shelf and stood on it and reached up to retrieve the foil-wrapped object she had hidden up there on returning from Jane's house this April. The thing startled her by feeling warm to her fingers: warm air collects up near a ceiling, she thought to herself in vague explanation. Hearing her stirring about, Coal padded out from his nap corner, and she had to lock him in the kitchen behind her, lest he follow her outdoors and think what she was about to do was a game of toss and fetch.

Passing through her workroom, Alexandra stepped around an overweening armature of pine two-by-fours and one-by-twos and twisted coathangers and chicken wire, for she had taken it into her head to attempt a giant sculpture, big enough for a public space like Kazmierczak Square. Past the workroom lay, in the rambling layout of this house lived in by eight generations of farmers, a dirt-floored transitional area used formerly as a potting shed and by Alexandra as a storage place, its walls thick with the handles of shovels and hoes and rakes, its stepping-space narrowed by tumbled stacks of old clay pots and by opened bags of peat moss and bone meal, its jerrybuilt shelves littered with rusted hand trowels and brown bottles of stale pesticide. She unlatched the crude door—parallel beaded boards held together by a Z of bracing lumber—and stepped into hot sunlight; she carried her little package, glittering and warm, across the lawn.

The frenzy of June growth was upon all the earth: the lawn needed mowing, the border beds of button mums needed weeding, the tomato plants and peonies needed propping. Insects chewed at the silence; sunlight pressed on Alexandra's face and she could feel the hair of her single thick braid heat up like an electric coil. The bog at the back of her property, beyond the tumbled fieldstone wall clothed in poison ivy and Virginia creeper, was in winter a transparent brown thicket floored, between tummocks of matted grass, with bubbled bluish ice; in summer it became a solid tangle of green leaf and black stalk, fern and burdock and wild raspberry, that the eye could not travel into for more than a few feet, and where no one would ever step, the thorns and the dampness underfoot being too forbidding. As a girl, until that age at about the sixth grade when boys become self-conscious about your playing games with them, she had been good at softball; now she reared back and threw the charm—mere wax and pins, so light it sailed as if she had flung a rock on the moon—as deep into this flourishing opacity as she could. Perhaps it would find a patch of slimy water and sink. Perhaps red-winged blackbirds would peck its tinfoil apart to adorn their nests. Alexandra willed it to be gone, swallowed up, dissolved, forgiven by nature's seethe.

The three at last arranged a Thursday when they could face one another again, at Sukie's tiny house on Hemlock Lane. "Isn't this cozy!" Jane Smart cried, coming in late, wearing almost nothing: plastic sandals and a gingham mini with the shoulder straps tied at the back of the neck so as not to mar her tan. She turned a smooth mocha color, but the aged skin under her eyes remained crêpey and white and her left leg showed a livid ripple of varicose vein, a little train of half-submerged bumps, like those murky photographs with which people try to demonstrate the existence of the Loch Ness monster. Still, Jane was vital, a thick-skinned sun hag in her element. "God, she looks terrible!" she crowed, and settled in one of Sukie's ratty armchairs with a martini. The martini was the slippery color of mercury and the green olive hung within it like a red-irised reptile eye.

"Who?" Alexandra asked, knowing full well who.

"The darling Mrs. Van Horne, of course," Jane answered. "Even in bright sunlight she looks like she's indoors, right there on Dock Street in the middle of July. She had the gall to come up to me, though I was trying to duck discreetly into the Yapping Fox."

"Poor thing," Sukie said, stuffing some salted pecan halves into her mouth and chewing with a smile. She wore a cooler shade of lipstick in the summer and the bridge of her little amorphous nose bore flakes of an old sunburn.

"Her hair I guess has fallen out with the chemotherapy so she wears a kerchief now," Jane said. "Rather dashing, actually."

"What did she say to you?" Alexandra asked.

"Oh, she was all isn't-this-nice and Darryl-and-I-never-see-you-any-more and do-come-over-we're-swimming-in-the-salt-marsh-these-days. I gave her back as good as I got. Really. What hypocrisy. She hates our guts, she must."

"Did she mention her disease?" Alexandra asked.

"Not a word. All smiles. 'What lovely weather!' 'Have you heard Arthur Hallybread has bought himself a darling little Herreshoff daysailer?' That's how she's decided to play it with us."

Alexandra thought of telling them about Jenny's call a month ago but hesitated to expose Jenny's plea to mockery. But then she thought that her true loyalty was to her sisters, to the coven. "She called me a month ago," she said, "about swollen glands she was imagining everywhere. She wanted to come see me. As if I could heal her."

"How very quaint," Jane said. "What did you tell her?"

"I told her no. I really don't want to see her, it would be too conflicting. What *did* do, though, I confess, was take the damn charm and chuck it into that messy bog behind my place."

Sukie sat up, nearly nudging the dish of pecans off the arm of her chair but deftly catching it as it slipped. "Why, sugar, what an extraordinary thing to do, after working so hard on the wax and all! You're losing your witchiness!"

"I don't know, am I? Chucking it doesn't seem to have made any difference, not if she's gone on chemotherapy."

"Bob Osgood," Jane said smugly, "is good friends with Doc Pat, and Doc Pat says she's really riddled with it—liver, pancreas, bone marrow, earlobes, you name it. *Entre nous* and all that, Bob said Doc Pat said if she lives two more months it'll be a miracle. She knows it, too. The chemotherapy is just to placate Darryl; he's frantic, evidently."

Now that Jane had taken this bald little banker Bob Osgood as her lover, two vertical dents between her eyebrows had smoothed a little and there was a cheerful surge to her utterances, as though she were bowing them upon her own vibrant vocal cords. Alexandra had never met Jane's Brahmin mother but supposed this was how voices were pushed into the air above the teacups of the Back Bay.

"There are remissions," Alexandra protested, without conviction; strength had flowed out of her and now was diffused into nature and moving on the astral currents beyond this room.

"You great big huggable sweet thing you," Jane Smart said, leaning toward her so the line where the tan on her breasts ended showed within the neck of loose gingham, "whatever has come over our Alexandra? If it weren't for this creature you'd be over there now; *you'd* be the mistress of Toad Hall. He came to Eastwick looking for a wife and it should have been you."

"We *want*ed it to be you," Sukie said.

"Piffle," Alexandra said. "I think either one of you would have grabbed at the chance. Especially you, Jane. You did an awful lot of cocksucking in some noble cause or other."

"Babies, let's not bicker," Sukie pleaded. "Let's have our cozy time. Speaking of seeing people downtown, you'll never guess who I saw last night hanging around in front of the Superette!"

"Andy Warhol," Alexandra idly guessed.

"Dawn Polanski!"

"Ed's little slut?" Jane asked. "She was blown up by that explosion in New Jersey."

"They never found any parts of her, just some clothes," Sukie reminded the others. "Evidently she had moved out of this pad they all shared in Hoboken to Manhattan, where the real cell was. The revolutionaries never really trusted Ed, he was too old and too square, and that's why they put him on this bomb detail, to test his sincerity."

Jane laughed unkindly, but with that toney vibrato to her cackle now. "The one quality I never doubted in Ed. He was sincerely an ass."

Sukie's upper lip crinkled in unspoken reproval; she went on, "Apparently there was no sincerity problem with Dawn and she was taken right in with the bigwigs, tripping out every night somewhere in the East Village while Ed was blowing himself up in Hoboken. Her guess is, his hands trembled connecting two wires; the diet and funny hours underground had been getting to him. He wasn't so hot in bed either, I guess she realized."

"It dawned on her," Jane said, and improved this to, "Un-came the Dawn."

"Who told you all this?" Alexandra asked Sukie, irritated by Jane's manner. "Did you go up and talk to the girl at the Superette?"

"Oh no, that bunch scares me, they even have some blacks in it now, I don't know where they come from, the south Providence ghetto I guess. I walk on the other side of the street usually. The Hallybreads told me. The girl is back in town and doesn't want to stay with her stepfather in the trailer in Coddington Junction any more, so she's living over the Armenians' store and cleaning houses for cigarette or whatever money, and the Hallybreads use her twice a week. I guess she's made Rose into a mother confessor. Rose has this awful back and can't even pick up a broom without wanting to scream."

"How come," Alexandra asked, "you know so much about the Hallybreads?"

"Oh," said Sukie, gazing upward toward the ceiling, which was tinkling and rumbling with the muffled sounds of television,

"I go over there now and then for R and R since Toby and I broke up. The Hallybreads are quite amusing, when she's not in one of her moods."

"What happened between you and Toby?" Jane asked. "You seemed so . . . satisfied."

"He got fired. This Providence syndicate that owns the *Word* thought the paper wasn't sexy enough under his management. And I must say, he did do a lackadaisical job; these Jewish mothers, they really spoil their boys. I'm thinking of applying for editor. If people like Brenda Parsley can take over these men's jobs I don't see why I can't."

"Your boyfriends," Alexandra observed, "don't have very good luck."

"I wouldn't call Arthur a boyfriend," Sukie said. "To me being with him is just like reading a book, he knows so much."

"I wasn't thinking of Arthur. Is he a boyfriend?"

"Is he having any bad luck?" Jane asked.

Sukie's eyes went round; she had assumed everybody knew. "Oh nothing, just these fibrillations. Doc Pat tells him people can live with them years and years, if they keep the digitalis handy. But he hates the fibrillating; like a bird is caught in his chest, he says."

Both her friends, with their veiled boasting of new lovers, were in Alexandra's eyes pictures of health—sleek and tan, growing strong on Jenny's death, pulling strength from it as from a man's body. Jane svelte and brown in her sandals and mini, and Sukie too wearing that summer glow Eastwick women got: terrycloth shorts that made her bottom look high and puffbally, and a peacocky shimmering dashiki her breasts twitched in a way that indicated no bra. Imagine being Sukie's age, thirty-three, and daring wear no bra! Ever since she was thirteen Alexandra had envied these pert-chested naturally slender girls, blithely eating and eating while her own spirit was saddled with stacks of flesh ready to topple into fat any time she took a second helping. Envious tears rose itching in her sinuses. Why was she mired so in life when a witch should dance, should skim? "We *can't* go on with it," she blurted out through the vodka as it tugged at the odd angles of the spindly little room. "We *must* undo the spell."

"But how, dear?" Jane asked, flicking an ash from a red-filtered cigarette into the paisley-patterned dish from which Sukie had eaten all the pecans and then (Jane) sighing smokily, impatiently, through her nose, as if, having read Alexandra's mind, she had foreseen this tiresome outburst.

"We *can't* just kill her like this," Alexandra went on, rather enjoying now the impression she must be making, of a blubbery troublesome big sister.

"Why not?" Jane dryly asked. "We kill people in our minds all the time. We erase mistakes. We rearrange priorities."

"Maybe it's not our spell at all," Sukie offered. "Maybe we're being conceited. After all, she's in the hands of hospitals and doctors and they have all these instruments and counters and whatnot that don't lie."

"They *do* lie," Alexandra said. "All those scientific things lie. There *must* be a form we can follow to undo it," she pleaded. "If we all three *con*centrated."

"Count me out," Jane said. "Ceremonial magic really bores me, I've decided. It's too much like kindergarten. My whisk is still a mess from all that wax. And my children keep asking me what that thing in tinfoil was; they picked right up on it and I'm afraid are telling their friends. Don't forget, you two, I'm still hoping to get a church of my own, and a lot of gossip does *not* impress the good folk in a position to hire choirmasters."

"How can you be so callous?" Alexandra cried, deliciously feeling her emotions wash up against Sukie's slender antiques —the oval tilt-top table, the rush-seat three-legged Shaker chair—like a tidal wave carrying sticks of debris to the beach. "Don't you see how horrible it is? All she ever did was he asked her and she said yes, what else could she say?"

"I think it's rather amusing," Jane said, shaping her cigarette ash to a sharp point on the paisley saucer's brass edge. "'Jenny died the other day,'" she added, as if quoting.

"Honey," Sukie said to Alexandra, "I'm honestly afraid it's out of our hands."

"'Never was there such a lay,'" Jane was going on.

"You didn't do it, at worst you were the conduit. We all were."

"'Youths and maidens, let us pray,'" quoted Jane, evidently concluding.

"We were just being *used* by the universe."

A certain pride of craft infected Alexandra. "You two couldn't have done it without me; I was *so* energetic, such a good organizer! It felt *won*derful, administering that horrible power!" Now it felt wonderful, her grief battering these walls and faces and things—the sea chest, the needlepoint stool, the thick lozenge panes—as if with massive pillows, the clouds of her agitation and remorse.

"Really, Alexandra," Jane said. "You don't seem yourself."

"I know I don't. I've felt terrible for days. I don't know what it is. My left ovary, before every other period, it really hurts. And at night, the small of my back, such pain I wake up and have to lie curled on my side."

"Oh you poor big sad yummy thing," Sukie said, getting up and taking a step so the tips of her breasts jiggled the shimmering dashiki. "You need a back rub."

"Yes I do," Alexandra pouted.

"Come on. Stretch out on the sofa. Jane, move over."

"I'm so scared." Sniffles spiced Alexandra's words, stinging high in her nostrils. "Why would it be just the ovary, unless . . ."

"You need a new lover," Jane told her, dropping the *r* in her curt fashion. How did she know? Alexandra had told Joe she didn't want to see him any more but this time he had not called back, and the days of his silence had become weeks.

"Hitch up your pretty blouse," Sukie said, though it was not a pretty blouse but one of Oz's old shirts, with collar points that refused to lie down, because the plastic stays were lost, and an indelible food stain near the second button. Sukie bared the bra strap, the snaps were undone, a pang of expansion flooded Alexandra's chest cavity. Sukie's narrow fingers began to work in circles. The rough cushion Alexandra's nose was against smelled comfortingly of damp dog. She closed her eyes.

"And maybe a nice thigh rub," Jane's voice declared. Clinks and a rustle described how she set down her glass and crushed out her cigarette. "Our lumbar tension builds up at the backs of our thighs and needs to be released." Her fingers with their hardened tips tried to release it, pinching, caressing, trailing the nails back and forth for a *pianissimo* effect.

"Jenny—" Alexandra began, remembering that girl's silky massages.

"We're not hurting Jenny," Sukie crooned.

"DNA is hurting Jenny," Jane said. "D'naughty DNA."

In a few minutes Alexandra had been tranced nearly to sleep. Sukie's awful-looking Weimaraner, Hank, trotted into the room with his lolling lilac-colored tongue and they played this game: Jane set a row of Wheat Thins along the backs of Alexandra's legs and Hank licked them off. Then they placed some on Alexandra's back, where her shirt had been tugged up. His tongue was rough and wet and warm and slightly adhesive, like a huge snail's foot; back and forth it flipflopped on the repeatedly set table of Alexandra's skin. The dog, like his mistress, loved starchy snacks but, surfeited at last, he looked at the women wonderingly and begged them with his eyes—balls of topaz, with a violet cloud at each center—to desist.

Though the other churches in Eastwick suffered a decided falling-off in attendance during the summer rebirth of sun worship, Unitarian services, never crowded, held their own; indeed they were augmented by vacationers from the metropolises, comfortably fixed religious liberals in red slacks and linen jackets, splashy-patterned cotton smocks and beribboned garden hats. These and the regulars—the Neffs, the Richard Smiths, Herbie Prinz, Alma Sifton, Homer and Franny Lovecraft, the young Mrs. Van Horne, and a relative newcomer in town, Rose Hallybread, without her agnostic husband but with her protégée, Dawn Polanski—were surprised, once "Through the Night of Doubt and Sorrow" had been wanly sung (Darryl Van Horne's baritone contributing scratchy harmony in the balcony choir), to hear the word "evil" emerge from Brenda Parsley's mouth. It was not a word often heard in this chaste nave.

Brenda looked splendid in her open black robe and pleated jabot and white silk cravat, her sun-bleached hair pulled tightly back from her high and shining forehead. "There is evil in the world and there is evil in this town," she pronounced ringingly, then dropped her voice to a lower, confiding register that yet carried to every corner of the neoclassic old sanctuary. Pink hollyhocks nodded in the lower panes of the tall clear windows; in the higher panes a cloudless July day called to those penned in the white box pews to get out, out into their boats, onto the beach and the golf courses and tennis courts, to go have a Bloody Mary on someone's new redwood deck with a view of the Bay and Conanicut Island. The Bay would be crackling with sunshine, the island would appear as purely verdant as when the Narragansett Indians lived there. "It is not a word we like to use," Brenda explained, in the diffident tone of a psychiatrist who after years of mute listening has begun to be directive at last. "We prefer to say 'unfortunate' or 'lacking' or 'misguided' or 'disadvantaged.' We prefer to think of evil as the absence of good, a momentary relenting of its sunshine, a shadow, a weakening. For the world *is* good: Emerson and Whitman, Buddha and Jesus have taught us that. Our own dear valiant Anne Hutchinson believed in a covenant of grace, as opposed to a covenant of works, and defied—this mother of fifteen and gentle midwife to sisters uncounted and uncountable—the sexist world-hating clergy of Boston in behalf of her belief, a belief for which she was eventually to die."

For the last time, thought Jenny Van Horne, *the exact blue of such a July day falls into my eyes. My lids lift, my corneas admit the light, my lenses focus it, my retinas and optic nerve report it to the brain. Tomorrow the Earth's poles will tilt a day more toward August and autumn, and a slightly different tincture of light and vapor will be distilled.* All year, without knowing it, she had been saying good-bye to each season, each subseason and turn of weather, each graduated moment of fall's blaze and shedding, of winter's freeze, of daylight gaining on the hardening ice, and of that vernal moment when the snowdrops and croci are warmed into bloom out of matted brown grass in that intimate area on the sunward side of stone walls, as when lovers cup their breath against the beloved's neck; she had been saying good-bye, for the seasons would not wheel around again for her. Days one spends so freely in haste and preoccupation, in adolescent self-concern and in childhood's joyous boredom, *there really is an end to them, a closing of the sky like the shutter of a vast camera*. These thoughts made Jenny giddy where she sat; Greta Neff, sensing her thoughts, reached into her lap and squeezed her hand.

"As we have turned outward to the evil in the world at large," Brenda was splendidly saying, gazing upward toward the back balcony with its disused pipe organ, its tiny choir, "turned our indignation outward toward evil wrought in Southeast Asia by fascist politicians and an oppressive capitalism seeking to secure and enlarge its markets for anti-ecological luxuries, while we have been so turned we have been guilty—yes, guilty, for guilt attaches to *o*missions as well as *co*mmissions—guilty of overlooking evil brewing in these very homes of Eastwick, our tranquil, solid-appearing homes. Private discontent and personal frustration have brewed mischief out of superstitions which our ancestors pronounced heinous and which indeed" —Brenda's voice dropped beautifully, into a kind of calm soft surprise, a teacher soothing a pair of parents without gainsaying a dreadful report card, a female efficiency-expert apologetically threatening a blustering executive with dismissal—"*are* heinous."

Yet behind that shutter must be an eye, the eye of a great Being, and in a premonition not unlike her father's some months before Jenny had come to repose a faith in that Being's custody of her even while her new friends, and those humanoid machines at the Westwick Hospital, fought for her life. Having herself worked in a hospital those years, Jenny knew how bleakly statistical in the end were the results obtained by all that so amiably and expensively administered mercy. What she minded most was the nausea, the nausea that went with the drugs and now with the radiation directed into her semiweekly as she lay strapped and swathed upon that giant turntable of chrome and cold steel, which lifted her this way and that until she felt seasick. The clicked-off seconds of its radioactive humming could not be cleansed from her ears and persisted even in sleep.

"There is a brand of evil," Brenda was saying, "we must fight. It must not be tolerated, it must not be explained, it must not be excused. Sociology, psychology, anthropology: in this one instance all these creations of the modern mind must be denied their mitigations."

I will never see icicles dripping from the eaves again, Jenny thought, *or a sugar maple catching fire. Or that moment in late winter when the snow is all dirty and eaten by thaw into rotten, undercut shapes.* These realizations were like a child's finger rubbing a hole in a befogged windowpane above a radiator on a bitterly cold day; through the clear spot Jenny looked into a bottomless never.

Brenda, her hair shimmering down to her shoulders—had it been like that at the beginning of the service, or had it come unpinned in her ardor?—was rallying invisible forces. "For these women—and let us not in our love of our sex and pride in our sex deny that they *are* women—have long exerted a malign influence in this community. They have been promiscuous. They have neglected at best and at worst abused their children, nurturing them in blasphemy. With their foul acts and unspeakable charms they have driven some men to deranged acts. They have driven some men—I firmly believe this—have driven some men to their deaths. And now their demon has alighted—now their venom has descended—their wrath hath—" As from the bell of a hollyhock a bumblebee sleepily emerged from between Brenda's plump painted lips and dipped on its questing course over the heads of the congregation.

Jenny tittered, to herself. Greta's hand gave another squeeze. On her far side Ray Neff snorted. Both the Neffs wore glasses: oval steel-rimmed grannies for Greta, squarish rimless on Ray. Each Neff seemed a single big lens, *and I sit between them*, Jenny thought, *like a nose*. An aghast silence focused upon Brenda, erect in her pulpit. Above her head hung not the tarnished brass cross that had been suspended there for years in irrelevant symbolism but a solid new brass circle, symbol of perfect unity and peace. The circle had been Brenda's idea. She took a shallow breath and tried to speak out through the something else gathering in her mouth.

"Their wrath has tainted the very air we breathe," she proclaimed, and a pale blue moth, and then its little tan sister, emerged; the second fell to the lectern, which was miked, with an amplified thud, then found its wings and beat its way toward the sky locked high behind the tall windows.

"Their jealouthy hath poithoned uth all—" Brenda bent her head, and her mouth gave birth to an especially vivid, furry, foul-tasting monarch butterfly, its orange wings rimmed thickly in black, its flickering flight casual and indolent beneath the white-painted rafters.

Jenny felt a tense swelling within her poor wasting body, as if it were a chrysalis.

"Help me," Brenda brokenly uttered down toward the lectern, where the crisp pages of her sermon had been speckled with saliva and insect slime. She seemed to be gagging. Her long platinum-blond hair swung and the brass O shone in the shafts of sunlight. The congregation broke its stunned silence; voices were raised. Franny Lovecraft, in the loud tones of the deaf, suggested that the police be called. Raymond Neff took it upon himself to leap up and shake his fist in the sun-riddled air; his jowls shook. Jenny giggled; the hilarity pressing within her could no longer be stifled. It was, somehow, the animation of it all that was so funny, the irrepressible cartoon cat that rises from being flattened to resume the chase. She burst into laughter—high-voiced, pure, a butterfly of sorts—and yanked her hand from Greta's sympathetic, squeezing grasp. She wondered who was doing it: Sukie, everybody knew, would be in bed with that sly Arthur Hallybread while his wife was at church; sly old elegant Arthur had been fucking his physics students for thirty years in Kingston. Jane Smart had gone all the way up to Warwick to play the Hammond organ for a cell of Moonies starting up in an abandoned Quaker meetinghouse; the ambience (Jane had told Mavis Jessup, who had told Rose Hallybread, who had told Jenny) was depressing, all these brainwashed upper-middle-class kids with Marine haircuts, but the money was good. Alexandra would be making her bubbies or weeding her mums. Perhaps none of the three was willing this, it was something they had loosed on the air, like those nuclear scientists cooking up the atomic bomb to beat Hitler and Tojo and now so remorseful, like Eisenhower refusing to sign the truce with Ho Chi Minh that would have ended all the trouble, like the late-summer wildflowers, goldenrod and Queen Anne's lace, now loosed from dormant seeds upon the shaggy fallow fields where once black slaves had opened the gates for galloping squires in swallowtail coats and top hats of beaver and felt. At any rate it was all so *funny*. Herbie Prinz, his jowly greedy thin-skinned face liverish in agitation, pushed past Alma Sifton and beat his way down the aisle and nearly knocked over Mrs. Hallybread, who like the other women was instinctively covering her mouth as, stiff-backed, she rose to flee.

"Pray!" Brenda shouted, seeing she had lost control of the occasion. Something was pouring over her lower lip, making her chin shine. "Pray!" she shouted in a hollow man's voice, as if she were a ventriloquist's dummy.

Jenny, hysterical with laughter, had to be led outside, where the apparition of her staggering between the bespectacled Neffs nonplussed the God-fearing burghers washing their automobiles at this hour along Cocumscussoc Way.

Jane Smart retired when her children did, often going straight to bed after tucking the two littlest in and falling asleep while the older ones watched an illicit half-hour of *Mannix* or some other car-chase series set in southern California. Around two or two-thirty she would awaken as abruptly as if the telephone had rung once and then fallen silent, or as if an intruder had tested the front door or carefully broken a windowpane and was holding his breath. Jane would listen, then smile in the dark, remembering that this was her hour of rendezvous. Arising in a translucent nylon nightie, she would settle her little quilted satin bed jacket around her shoulders and put milk on the stove to heat for cocoa. Randolph, her avid young Doberman, would come rattling his claws into the kitchen and she would give him a Chew-Z, a rock-hard bone-shaped biscuit to gnaw on; he would take the bribe into his corner and make evil music upon it with his long teeth and serrated purplish lips. The milk would boil, she would take the cocoa up the six steps to the living-room level and release her cello from its case—its red wood lustrous and alive like a superior kind of flesh. "Good baby," Jane might say aloud, since the silence in the flat tracts of the development all around—no traffic, no children crying; Cove Homes rose and retired in virtual synchrony—was so absolute as to be frightening. She would scan her splintered floor for a hole to brace her pin in and, dragging music stand and three-way floorlamp and straight-backed chair into place, would play. Tonight she would tackle the Second of Bach's suites for unaccompanied cello. It was one of her favorites; certainly she preferred it to the rather stolid

First and the dreadfully difficult Sixth, black with sixty-fourth notes and impossibly high, written as it had been for an instrument with five strings. But always, in even Bach's most clockworklike ringing of changes, there was something to discover, something to *hear*, a moment when a voice cried out amid the turning of the wheels. Bach had been happy at Köthen, but for his wife Maria's sudden death and the so *simpatico* and musical Prince Leopold's marriage to his young cousin, Henrietta of Anhalt, Bach called the little bride an "*amusa*," that is, a person opposed to the muses. Henrietta yawned during courtly concerts, and her demands deflected princely attention away from the *Kapellmeister*, a deflection that helped prompt his seeking the cantorship in Leipzig. He took the new post even though the unsympathetic princess herself surprisingly died before Bach had left Köthen. In the Second Suite, there was a theme—a melodic succession of rising thirds and a descent in whole tones—announced in the prelude and then given an affecting twist in the allemande, a momentary reversal (up a third) of the descent; thus a poignance was inserted in the onrolling (*moderato*) melody, which returned and returned, the matter under discussion coming to a head of dissonance in the *forte d♯-a* chord between a trilled *b* natural and a fingerstinging run, *piano*, of thirty-second notes. The matter under discussion, Jane Smart realized as she played on and the untasted cocoa grew a tepid scum, was death—the mourned death of Maria, who had been Bach's cousin, and the longedfor death of Princess Henrietta, which would indeed come. Death was the space these churning, tumbling notes were clearing, a superb polished inner space growing wider and wider. The last bar was marked *poco a poco ritardando* and involved intervals—the biggest a *D-d'*—which sent her fingers sliding with a muffled screech up and down the neck. The allemande ended on that same low tonic, enormously: the note would swallow the world.

Jane cheated; a repeat was called for (she *had* repeated the first half), but now, like a traveller who by the light of a risen moon at last believes that she is headed somewhere, she wanted to hurry on. Her fingers felt inspired. She was leaning out above the music; it was a cauldron bubbling with a meal cooked only for herself; she could make no mistakes. The courante unfolded swiftly, playing itself, twelve sixteenths to the measure, only twice in each section stricken to hesitation by a quarter-note chord, then resuming its tumbling flight, the little theme almost lost now. This theme, Jane felt, was female; but another voice was strengthening within the music, the male voice of death, arguing in slow decided syllables. For all its fluttering the courante slowed to six dotted notes, stressed to accent their descent by thirds, and then a fourth, and then a steep fifth to the same final note, the ineluctable tonic. The sarabande, *largo*, was magnificent, inarguable, its slow skipping marked by many trills, a ghost of that dainty theme reappearing after a huge incomplete dominant ninth had fallen across the music crushingly. Jane bowed it again and again—low $C^\sharp$-$B^\flat$-g —relishing its annihilatory force, admiring how the diminished seventh of its two lower notes sardonically echoed the leap of a diminished seventh ($C^\sharp$-$b^\flat$) in the line above. Moving on after this savoring to the first minuet, Jane most distinctly heard—it was not a question of hearing, she *embodied*—the war between chords and the single line that was always trying to escape them but could not. Her bow was carving out shapes within a substance, within a blankness, within a silence. The outside of things was sunshine and scatter; the inside of everything was death. Maria, the princess, Jenny: a procession. The unseen inside of the cello vibrated, the tip of her bow cut circles and arcs from a wedge of air, sounds fell from her bowing like wood shavings. Jenny tried to escape from the casket Jane was carving; the second minuet moved to the key of D major, and the female caught within the music raced in sliding steps of tied notes but then was returned, *Menuetto I da capo*, and swallowed by its darker colors and the fierce quartet of chords explicitly marked for bowing: *f-a aufstrich, $B^\flat$-f-d abstrich, G-g-e aufstrich; A-e-c$^\sharp$*. Bow sharply, up, down, up, and then down for the three-beat *coup de grâce*, that fluttering spirit slashed across for good.

Before attempting the gigue, Jane sipped at her cocoa: the cold circle of skin stuck to her slightly hairy upper lip. Randolph, his Chew-Z consumed, had loped in and lain near, on the scarred floor, her tapping bare toes. But he was not asleep: his carnelian eyes stared directly at her in some kind of startlement; a hungry expression slightly rumpled his muzzle and perked up his ears, as pink within as whelk shells. These familiars, Jane thought, they remain dense—chips of brute matter. He knows he is witnessing something momentous but does not know what it is; he is deaf to music and blind to the scrolls and the glidings of the spirit. She picked up her bow. It felt miraculously light, a wand. The gigue was marked *allegro*. It began with some stabbing phrases—dit-*duh* (*a-d*), dit-*duh* (*b♭-c♯*), dit dodododo dit *duh*, dit . . . On she spun. Usually she had trouble with these gappy sharped and flatted runs but tonight she flew along them, deeper, higher, deeper, *spiccato*, *legato*. The two voices struck against each other, the last revival of that fluttering, that receding, returning theme, still to be quelled. So this was what men had been murmuring about, monopolizing, all these centuries, death; no wonder they had kept it to themselves, no wonder they had kept it from women, let the women do their nursing and hatching, keeping a bad thing going while they, *they*, men, distributed among themselves the true treasure, onyx and ebony and unalloyed gold, the substance of glory and release. Until now Jenny's death had been simply an erasure in Jane's mind, a nothing; now it had its tactile structure, a branched and sumptuous complexity, a sensuous downpulling fathoms more flirtatious than that tug upon our ankles the retreating waves on the beach give amid the tumbling pebbles, that wonderful weary weighty sigh the sea gives with each wave. It was as if Jenny's poor poisoned body had become intertwined, vein and vein and sinew and sinew, with Jane's own, like the body of a drowned woman with seaweed, and both were rising, the one eventually to be shed by the other but for now interlaced, one with the other, in those revolving luminescent depths. The gigue bristled and prickled under her fingers; the eighth-note thirds underlying the running sixteenths grew ominous; there was a hopeless churning, a pulling down, a grisly *fortissimo* flurry, and a last run down and then skippingly up the scale to the cry capping the crescendo, the thin curt cry of that terminal *d*.

Jane did both repeats, and scarcely fumbled anything, not even that tricky middle section where one was supposed to bring the quickly shifting dynamics through a thicket of dots and ties; who ever said her *legato* sounded *détaché*?

The Cove development lay outside in the black windows pure as a tract of antarctic ice. Sometimes a neighbor called to complain but tonight even the telephone was betranced. Only Randolph kept an eye open; as his heavy head lay on the floor one opaque eye, flecks of blood floating in its darkness, stared at the meat-colored hollow body between his mistress's legs, his strident rival for her affection. Jane herself was so exalted, so betranced, that she went on to play the first movement of the cello part for the Brahms E Minor, all those romantic languorous half-notes while the imaginary piano pranced away. What a softy Brahms was, for all his flourishes: a woman with a beard and cigar!

Jane rose from her chair. She had a killing pain between her shoulder blades and her face streamed with tears. It was twenty after four. The first gray stirrings of light were planting haggard shapes on the lawn outside her picture window, beyond the straggly bushes she never trimmed and that spread and mingled like the different tints of lichen on a tombstone, like bacterial growths in a culture dish. The children began to make noise early in the morning, and Bob Osgood, who had promised to try to meet her for "lunch" at a dreadful motel—an arc of plywood cottages set back in the woods—near Old Wick, would call to confirm from the bank; so she could not take the phone off the hook and sleep even if the children were quiet. Jane felt suddenly so exhausted she went to bed without putting her cello back in its case, leaving it leaning against the chair as if she were a symphony performer excused from the stage for intermission.

Alexandra was looking out the kitchen window, wondering how it had become so smeared and splotched with dust —could rain itself be dirty?—and therefore saw Sukie park and come in along the brick walk through the grape arbor, ducking her sleek orange head in avoidance of the empty birdfeeder and the low-hanging vines with their ripening green clusters. It had been a wet August so far and today looked like more rain. The women kissed inside the screen door. "You're *so* nice to come," Alexandra said. "I don't know why it should scare me to look for it alone. In my own bog."

"It *is* scary, sweet," Sukie said. "For it to have been so effective. She's back in the hospital."

"Of course we don't really know that it was it."

"We do, though," Sukie said, not smiling and her lips therefore looking strange, bunchy. "We know. It was it." She seemed subdued, a girl reporter again in her raincoat. She had been rehired at the *Word*. Selling real estate, she had told Alexandra more than once over the telephone, was just too chancy, too ulcer-producing, waiting for things to click, wondering if you might have said something more subliminally persuasive in that crucial moment when the clients first see the house, or when they're standing around in the basement with the husband trying to look sage about the pipes and the wife terrified of rats. And then when a deal does go through the fee usually has to be split three or four ways. It really was giving her ulcers: a little dry pain just under the ribs, higher than you'd imagine, and worst at night.

"Want a drink?"

"Afterwards. It's early. Arthur says I shouldn't drink a drop until my stomach gets back in shape. Have you ever tried Maalox? God, you taste chalk every time you burp. Anyway" —she smiled, a flash of her old self, the fat upper lip stretched so its unpainted inner side showed above her bright, big, out-curved teeth—"I'd feel guilty having a drink without Jane here."

"Poor Jane."

Sukie knew what she meant, though it had happened a week before. That dreadful Doberman pinscher had chewed Jane's cello to pieces one night when she didn't put it back in its case.

"Do they think it's for good this time?" Alexandra asked.

Sukie intuited that Alexandra meant Jenny in the hospital. "Oh, you know how they are, they would never say that. More tests is all they ever say. How're your own complaints?"

"I'm trying to stop complaining. They come and go. Maybe it's premenopausal. Or post-Joe. You know about Joe?— he really *has* given up on me."

Sukie nodded, letting her smile sink down slowly over her teeth. "Jane blames *them*. For all our aches and pains. She even blames them for the cello tragedy. You'd think she could blame herself for that."

At the mention of *them*, Alexandra was momentarily distracted from the sore of guilt she carried sometimes in the left ovary, sometimes in the small of her back, and lately under her armpits, where Jenny had once asked her to investigate. Once it gets to the lymph glands, according to something Alexandra remembered reading or seeing on television, it's too late. "Who of them does she blame specifically?"

"Well for some reason she's fastened on that grubby little Dawn. I don't think myself a kid like that has it in her yet. Greta is pretty potent, and so would Brenda be if she could stop putting on airs. From what Arthur lets slip, for that matter, Rose is no bargain to tangle with: he finds her a very tough cookie, otherwise I guess they'd have been divorced long ago. She doesn't want it."

"I do hope he doesn't go after her with a poker."

"Listen, darling. That was never *my* idea of the way to solve the wife problem. I was once a wife myself, you know."

"Who wasn't? I wasn't thinking of you at all, dear heart, it was the house I'd blame if it happened again. Certain spiritual grooves get worn into a place, don't you believe?"

"I don't know. Mine needs paint."

"So does mine."

"Maybe we should go look for that thing before it rains."

"You *are* nice to help me."

"Well, I feel badly too. In a way. Up to a point. And I spend all my time chasing around in the Corvair on wild-goose chases anyway. It keeps skidding and getting out of control, I wonder if it's the car or me. Ralph Nader hates that model." They passed through the kitchen into Alexandra's workroom. "What on earth is *that*?"

"I wish I knew. It began as an enormous something for a public square, visions of Calder and Moore I suppose. I thought if it came out wonderfully I could get it cast in bronze; after all the papier-mâché I want to do something permanent. And the carpentry and banging around are good for sexual deprivation. But the arms won't stay up. Pieces keep falling off in the night."

"They've hexed it."

"Maybe. I certainly cut myself a lot handling all the wire; don't you just hate the way wire coils and snarls? So I'm trying now to make it more life-size. Don't look so doubtful. It might take off. I'm not totally discouraged."

"How about your little ceramic bathing beauties, the bubbies?"

"I can't do them any more, after that. I get physically nauseated, thinking of her face melting, and the wax, and the tacks."

"You ought to try an ulcer some time. I never knew where the duodenum *was* before."

"Yes, but the bubbies were my bread and butter. I thought some fresh clay might inspire me so I drove over to Coventry last week and this house where I used to buy my lovely kaolin was all in this tacky new aluminum siding. Puke green. The widow who had owned it had died over the winter, of a heart attack hauling wood the woman of the family that has it now said, and her husband doesn't want to be bothered with selling clay; he wants a swimming pool and a patio in the back yard. So that ends that."

"You look great, though. I think you're losing weight."

"Isn't that another of the symptoms?"

They made their way through the old potting shed and stepped into the back yard, which needed a mowing. First the dandelions had been rampant, now the crabgrass. Fungi —blobs of brown loaded by nature with simples and banes and palliatives—had materialized in the low damp spots of this neglected lawn during this moist summer. Even now, the mantle of clouds in the distance had developed those downward tails, travelling wisps, which mean rain is falling somewhere. The wild area beyond the tumbled stone wall was itself a wall of weeds and wild raspberry canes. Alexandra knew about the briars and had put on rugged men's jeans; Sukie however was wearing under her raincoat a russet seersucker skirt and frilly maroon blouse, and on her feet open-toed heels oxblood in color.

"You're too pretty," Alexandra said. "Go back to the potting shed and put on those muddy Wellingtons somewhere around where the pitchfork is. That'll save your shoes and ankles at least. And bring the long-handled clippers, the one with the extra hinge in the jaw. In fact, why don't you just fetch the clippers and stay here in the yard? You've never been that much into nature and your sweet seersucker skirt will get torn."

"No, no," Sukie said loyally. "I'm curious now. It's like an Easter-egg hunt."

When Sukie returned, Alexandra stood on the exact spot of grass, as best she remembered, and demonstrated how she had thrown the evil charm to be rid of it forever. The two friends then waded, clipping and wincing as they went, out into this little wilderness where a hundred species of plants were competing for sunlight and water, carbon dioxide and nitrogen. The area seemed limited and homogeneous—a smear of green—from the vantage of the back yard, but once they were immersed in it it became a variegated jungle, a feverish clash of styles of leaf and stem, an implacable festering of protein chains as nature sought not only to thrust itself outward with root and runner and shoot but to attract insects and birds to its pollen and seeds. Some footsteps sank into mud; others tripped over hummocks that grass had over time built up of its own accumulated roots. Thorns threatened eyes and hands; a thatch of dead leaves and stalks masked the earth. Reaching the area where Alexandra guessed the tinfoil-wrapped poppet had landed, she and Sukie stooped low into a strange vegetable heat. The space low to the ground swarmed with a prickliness, an air of congestion, as twigs and tendrils probed the shadows for crumbs of sun and space.

Sukie cried out with the pleasure of discovery; but what she gouged up from where it had long rested embedded in the earth was an ancient golf ball, stippled in an obsolete checkered pattern. Some chemical it had absorbed had turned the lower half rust color.

"Shit," Sukie said. "I wonder how it ever got out here, we're miles from any golf course." Monty Rougemont, of course, had been a devoted golfer, who had resented the presence of women, with their spontaneous laughter and pastel outfits, on the fairway in front of him or indeed anywhere in his clubby paradise; it was as if in discovering this ball Sukie had come upon a small segment of her former husband, a message from the other world. She slipped the remembrance into a pocket of her rain coat.

"Maybe dropped from an airplane," Alexandra suggested.

Gnats had discovered them, and pattered and nipped at their faces. Sukie flapped a hand back and forth in front of her mouth and protested, "Even if we do find it, baby, what makes you think we can undo anything?"

"There must be a form. I've been doing some reading. You do everything backwards. We'd take the pins out and remelt the wax and turn Jenny back into a candle. We'd try to remember what we said that night and say it backwards."

"All those sacred names, impossible. I can't remember half of what we said."

"At the crucial moment Jane said 'Die' and you said 'Take that' and giggled."

"Did we really? We must have got carried away."

Crouching low, guarding their eyes, they explored the tangle step by step, looking for a glitter of aluminum foil. Sukie was getting her legs scratched above the Wellingtons and her handsome new London Fog was being tugged and its tiny waterproofed threads torn. She said, "I bet it's caught halfway up some one of these fucking damn prickerbushes."

The more querulous Sukie sounded, the more maternal Alexandra became. "It could well be," she said. "It felt eerily light when I threw it. It sailed."

"Why'd you ever chuck it out here anyway? What a hysterical thing to do."

"I told you, I'd just had a phone conversation with Jenny in which she'd asked me to save her. I felt guilty. I was afraid."

"Afraid of what, honey?"

"You know. Death."

"But it isn't *your* death."

"Any death is your death, in a way. These last weeks I've been getting the same symptoms Jenny had."

"You've *al*ways been that way about cancer." In exasperation Sukie flailed with the long-handled clippers at the thorny round-leafed canes importuning her, pulling at her raincoat, raking her wrists. "Fuck. Here's a dead squirrel all shrivelled up. This is a real dump out here. Couldn't you have found the damn thing with second sight? Couldn't you have made it, what's the word, levitate?"

"I tried but couldn't get a signal. Maybe the aluminum foil bottled up the emanations."

"Maybe your powers aren't what they used to be."

"That could be. Several times lately I tried to will some sun, I was feeling like such a maggot with all this dampness; but it rained anyway."

Sukie's thrashing grew more and more irritable. "Jane levitated her whole self."

"That's Jane. She's getting very strong. But you heard her, she doesn't want any part of reversing this spell, she *likes* the way things are going."

"I wonder if you've overestimated how far you can throw. Monty used to complain about golfers looking for their balls, how they'd always walk miles past where it could possibly be."

"To me it feels like we've *under*estimated. As I said, it really flew."

"You work out that way then, and I'll retrace a little. God, these fucking prickers. They're *hate*ful. What *good* are they, anyway?"

"They feed the birds. And rodents and skunks."

"Oh, great."

"Some aren't raspberries, I was noticing, they're wild roses. When we first moved to Eastwick, Ozzie and me, every fall I'd make jelly out of the rose hips."

"You and Oz were just too dear."

"It was pathetic, I was such a housewife. You're a saint," she told Sukie, "to be doing this. I know you're bored. You can quit any time."

"Not such a saint, really. Maybe I'm scared too. Here it is, anyway." She sounded nowhere near as excited as when she had found the golf ball fifteen minutes earlier. Alexandra, scratched and impeded by (her sensation was) some essential and unappeasable rudeness in the universe, pushed her way to where the other woman stood. Sukie had not touched the thing. It lay in a relatively open spot, a brackish patch supporting on its edges some sea milkwort; a few frail white flowers put forth their attractions in the jungle shadows. Stooping to touch the crumpled Reynolds Wrap, not rusted but dulled by its months in the weather, Alexandra noticed the damp dark earth around it crawling with mites of some kind, reddish specks collected like filings around a magnet, scurrying in their tiny world several orders lower, on the terraces of life, than her own. She

forced herself to touch the evil charm, this hellishly baked potato. When she picked it up, it weighed nothing, and rattled:
the pins inside it. She gently pried open the hollow aluminum
foil. The pins inside had rusted. The wax substance of the little
imitation of Jenny had quite disappeared.

"Animal fat," Sukie at last said, having waited for Alexandra
to speak first. "Some little bunch of jiggers out here thought it
was yummy and ate it all up or fed it to their babies. Look: they
left the little hairs. Remember those little hairs? You'd think
they would have rotted or something. That's why hair clogs up
sinks, it's indestructible. Like Clorox bottles. Some day, honey,
there will be nothing in the world but hair and Clorox bottles."

Nothing. Jenny's tallow surrogate had become nothing.

Raindrops like pinpricks touched their faces, now that the
two women were standing erect amid the brambles. Such dry
microscopic first drops foretell a serious rain, a soaker. The sky
was solid gray but for a thin bar of blue above the low horizon
to the west, so far away it might be altogether out of Rhode
Island, this fair sky. "Nature is a hungry old thing," Alexandra
said, letting the foil and pins drop back into the weeds.

"And thirsty," Sukie said. "Didn't you promise me a drink?"

Sukie wanted to be consoling and flirtatious, sensing Alexandra's sick terror, and did look rather stunning, with her red
hair and monkeyish lips, standing up to her breasts in brambles, in her smart raincoat. But Alexandra had a desolate sensation of distance, as if her dear friend, fetching yet jaded, were
another receding image, an advertisement, say, on the rear of a
truck pulling rapidly away from a stoplight.

One of Brenda's several innovations was to have members of
the church give an occasional sermon; today Darryl Van Horne
was preaching. The well-thumbed big book he opened upon
the lectern was not the Bible but a red-jacketed *Webster's Collegiate Dictionary*. "Centipede," he read aloud in that strangely
resonant, as it were pre-amplified voice of his. "Any of a class
(Chilopoda) of long flattened many-segmented predaceous ar-
thropods with each segment bearing one pair of legs of which
the foremost pair is modified into poison fangs."

Darryl looked up; he was wearing a pair of half-moon reading glasses and these added to the slippage of his face, its

appearance of having been assembled of parts, with the seams not quite smooth. "You didn't know that about the poisonous fangs, did you? You've never had to look a centipede right in the eye, have you? *Have* you, you lucky people!" He was boomingly addressing perhaps a dozen heads, scattered through the pews on this muggy day late in August, the sky in the tall windows the sullen no-color of recycled paper. "Think," Darryl entreated, "think of the evolution of those fangs over the aeons, the infinity—don't you hate that word, 'infinity,' it's like you're supposed to get down on your knees whenever some dumb bastard says it—the infinity—and I guess my saying it makes me one more dumb bastard, but what the hell else can you say?—*think* of all those little wriggling struggles behind the sink and down in the cellar and the jungle that ended in this predaceous arthropod's—isn't that a beautiful phrase? —this predaceous arthropod's mouth, if you want to call it a mouth, it isn't like any of our ruby lips, I tell you, before those two front legs somehow got the idea of being poisonous and the trusty old strings of DNA took up the theme and the centipedes kept humping away making more centipedes and finally they got modified into fangs. *Pois*onous fangs. Hoo boy." He wiped his lips with forefinger and thumb. "And they call this a Creation, this mess of torture." The sermon title announced in movable white letters on the signboard outside the church was "THIS IS A TERRIBLE CREATION."

The scattered listening heads were silent. Even the woodwork of the old structure failed to creak. Brenda herself sat mute in profile beside the lectern, half hidden by a giant spray of gladioli and ferns in a plaster urn, given in memory this Sunday of a stillborn son Franny Lovecraft had once produced, fifty years ago. Brenda looked pale and listless; she had been indisposed off and on for much of the summer. It had been an unhealthy wet summer in Eastwick.

"You know what they used to do to witches in Germany?" Darryl asked loudly from the pulpit, but as though it had just occurred to him, which probably it had. "They used to sit them on an iron chair and light a fire underneath. They used to tear their flesh with red-hot pincers. Thumbscrews. The rack. The boot. Strappado. You name it, they did it. To simpleminded old ladies, mostly." Franny Lovecraft leaned toward

Rose Hallybread and whispered something in a loud but unintelligible rasp. Van Horne sensed the disturbance and in his vulnerable shambling way went defensive. "O.K.," he shouted toward the congregation. "So what? Well, you're going to say, this is human nature. This is human history. What does this have to do with Creation? What's this crazy guy trying to tell me? We could go on and on till nightfall with tortures human beings have used against each other under the sacred flag of one form of faith or another. The Chinese used to tear the skin off a body inch by inch, in the Middle Ages they'd disembowel a guy in front of his own eyes and cut his cock off and stuff it in his mouth for good measure. Sorry to spell it out like that, I get excited. The point is, all this stacked end to end multiplied by a zillion doesn't amount to a hill of beans compared with the cruelty natural organic friendly Creation has inflicted on its creatures since the first poor befuddled set of amino acids struggled up out of the galvanized slime. Women never accused of being witches, pretty little blond dollies who never laid an evil eye on even a centipede, die every day in pain probably just as bad as and certainly more prolonged than any inflicted by the good old *Hexenstuhl*. It had big blunt studs all over it, I don't know what the thermodynamic principle was. I don't want to think about it any more and I bet you don't either. You get the idea. It was terrible, terrible; Jesus it was terrible." His glasses fell forward on his nose and in readjusting them he seemed to press his whole face back together. His cheeks looked wet to some in the congregation.

Jenny was not here; she was back in the hospital, with uncontrollable internal bleeding. This was the sermon's undercurrent. Ray Neff was not here today either—he had accepted an invitation from Professor Hallybread to go sailing in Arthur's newly bought gaff-rigged Herreshoff 12½' across to Melville. Greta was here, though, sitting alone. It was hard to know about Greta—what she thought, what she wanted. Her being German, though her accent was never as bad as the people poking fun of it would have had you believe, put a kind of grid across her soul when you tried to look inside. Straight straw-dull hair, cut short, and amazing eyes the blue of dirty dishwater behind her granny glasses. She never missed a Sunday, but it may have been simply the unreflective thoroughness of her race, the German race, that admirable machine always waiting for a romantic demon to seize the levers.

Van Horne had been silent a while, pawing through the dictionary clumsily, as if his hands were gloves. Old Mrs. Lovecraft could now be heard as she leaned over to Mrs. Hallybread and distinctly asked, "Why is he using those filthy words?" Rose Hallybread looked exceedingly amused; she was a tall woman with a tiny head set in a nest of wiry gray and black hair frizzed way out. Her very small face was the color of a walnut, creased and recreased by decades of sun worship; what she whispered back was inaudible. On her other side sat Dawn Polanski; the girl had fascinating wide Mongolian cheekbones and smudged-looking skin and that impervious deadpan calm of the lawless. Between them she and Rose did pack a lot of psychic power.

Van Horne dimly heard the commotion and looked up, blinked, pushed his glasses higher on his nose, and apologetically pronounced, "I know this is taking plenty long enough but here, right on one page, I've just come across 'tapeworm' and 'tarantula.' 'Tarantula: any of various large hairy spiders that are typically rather sluggish and though capable of biting sharply are not significantly poisonous to man.' Thanks a lot. And his limp little buddy up here: 'Any of numerous cestode worms (as of the genus *Taenia*) parasitic when adult in the intestine of man or other vertebrates.' Numerous, mind you, not just one or two oddballs tucked back in some corner of Creation, anybody can make a mistake, but a lot of them, a lot of *kinds*, a ter*rif*ic idea, Somebody must have thought. I don't know about the rest of you gathered here, wishing I'd pipe down and sit down probably, but I've always been fascinated by parasites. I mean fascinated in a negative way. They come in so many sizes, for one thing, from viruses and bacteria like your friendly syphilis spirochete to tapeworms thirty feet long and roundworms so big and fat they block up your big intestine. Intestines are where they're happiest, by and large. To sit around in the slushy muck inside somebody else's guts—that's their catbird seat. You doing all the digesting for 'em, they don't even need stomachs, just mouths and assholes, pardon my French. But boy, the ingenuity that old Great Designer spent with His lavish hand on these humble little devils. Here,

I scribbled down some notes, out of the *En*-cy-clo-pedia, as Jiminy Cricket used to say, if I can read 'em in this lousy light up here; Brenda, I don't see how you do it; week after week. If I were you I'd go on strike. O.K. Enough horsing around.

"Your average intestinal roundworm, about the size of a lead pencil, lays its eggs in the feces of the host; that's simple enough. Then, don't ask me how—there's a lot of unsanitary conditions in the world, once you get out of Eastwick—these eggs get up into your mouth and you swallow 'em, like it or not. They hatch in your duodenum, the little larvae worm through the gut wall, get into a blood vessel, and migrate to your lungs. But you don't think that's where they're gonna retire and live off their pension, do you? No sir, my dear friends, this little mother of a roundworm, he chews his way out of his cozy capillary there in the lungs and gets into an air sac and climbs what they call the respiratory tree to the epiglottis, where you go and swallow him again!—can you believe you'd be so stupid? Once he's had the second ride down he *does* settle in and becomes your average mature wage-earning roundworm.

"Or take—hold it, my notes are scrambled—take an appealing little number called the lung fluke. Its eggs get out in the world when people cough up sputum." Van Horne hawked by way of illustration. "When they hatch in fresh water that's lying around in these crummy, sort of Third-World places, they move into certain snails they fancy, in the form now of larvae, these lung flukes, follow me? When they've had enough of living in snails they swim out and bore into the soft tissues of crayfish and crabs. And when the Japanese or whoever eat the crayfish or crabs raw or undercooked the way they like it, in they go, these pesky flukes, and chew out through the intestines and diaphragm to get into good old lung and begin this sputum routine all over again. Another of these watery little jobbies, *Diphyllobothrium latum* if I can read it right, the little swimming embryos are eaten first by water fleas, and then fish eat the water fleas, and bigger fish eat *those* fish, and finally man bites the bullet, and all the while these itty-bitty monsters instead of being digested have been chewing their way out through the various stomach linings and are *thriv*ing. Hoo boy. There're a ton of these stories, but I don't want to bore anybody or, you know, overmake my point here. Wait, though. You got to hear this. I'm quoting. '*Echinococcus granulosus* is one of the few tapeworms parasitizing man in which the adult worm inhabits the intestine of the dog, while man is one of the several hosts for the larval stage. Moreover, the adult worm is minute, measuring only three to six millimeters. In contrast, the larva, known as a hydatid cyst, may be large as a football. Man acquires infection'—get this—'from contact with the feces of infected dogs.'

"So here you have, aside from a lot of feces and sputum, Man, allegedly made in the image of God, as far as little *Echinococcus* is concerned just a way station on the way to the intestines of a dog. Now you mustn't think parasites don't dig each other; they do. Here's a cutie pie called *Trichosomoides crassicauda*, of whom we read, quote, 'The female of this species lives as a parasite in the bladder of the rat, and the degenerate male lives inside the uterus of the female.' So degenerate, even the Encyclopedia thinks it's degenerate. And, hey, how about this?—'What might be termed sexual phoresis is seen in the blood fluke *Schistosoma haematobium*, in which the smaller female is carried in a ventral body-wall groove, the gynecephoric canal, of the male.' They had a drawing in the book I wish I could share with you good people, the mouth up at the tip of something like a finger and this big ventral sucker and the whole thing looking like a banana with its zipper coming undone. Trust me: it is *nas*ty."

And to those who were sitting restless now (for the sky in the top panes of the windows was brightening as if a flashlight were shining behind the paper, and the hollyhock tops nodded and shuffled in a clearing breeze, a breeze that nearly capsized Arthur and Ray out in the East Passage, near Dyer Island: Arthur was unaccustomed to handling the lively little daysailer; his heart began to fibrillate; a bird beat its wings in his chest and his brain chanted rapidly, *Not yet, Lord, not yet*) it appeared that Van Horne's face, as it bobbed back and forth between his scrambled notes and a somehow blinded outward gaze toward the congregation, was dissolving, was thawing into nothingness. He tried to gather his thoughts toward the painful effort of conclusion. His voice sounded forced up from far underground.

"So to wind this thing up it's not just, you know, the nice clean pounce of a tiger or a friendly shaggy lion. That's what they sell us with all those stuffed toys. Put a kid to bed with a stuffed liver fluke or a hairy tarantula would be more like it. You all eat. The way you feel toward sunset of a beautiful summer day, the first g-and-t or rum-and-Coke or Bloody Mary beginning to do its work mellowing those synapses, and some nice mild cheese and crackers all laid out like a poker hand on the plate on the glass table out there on the sundeck or beside the pool, honest to God, good people, that's the way the roundworm feels when a big gobbety mess of half-digested steak or moo goo gai pan comes sloshing down to him. He's as real a creature as you and me. He's as noble a creature, designwise—really *lov*ingly designed. You got to picture that Big Visage leaning down and smiling through Its beard while those fabulous Fingers with Their angelic mani-cure fiddled with the last fine-tuning of old *Schistosoma*'s ven-tral sucker: that's Creation. Now I ask you, isn't that pretty terrible? Couldn't you have done better, given the resources? I sure as hell could have. So vote for me next time, O.K.? Amen."

In every congregation there has to be a stranger. The soli-tary uninvited today was Sukie Rougemont, sitting in the back wearing a wide-rimmed straw hat to hide her beautiful pale orange hair, and great round spectacles, so she could see to read the hymnal and to take notes on the margin of her mim-eographed program. Her scurrilous column "Eastwick Eyes and Ears" had been reinstated, to make the *Word* more "sexy." She had gotten wind of Darryl's secular sermon and come to cover it. Brenda and Darryl, from their position on the altar dais, must have seen her slip in during the first hymn, but not Greta nor Dawn nor Rose Hallybread had been aware of her presence, and since she slipped out in the first stanza of "Fa-ther, Who on Man Doth Shower," no confrontation between the factions of witches occurred. Greta had begun to yawn un-stoppably, and Dawn's lusterless eyes furiously to itch, and the buckles of Franny Lovecraft's shoes had come undone; but all of these developments might be laid to natural causes, as might Sukie's discovering, the next time she looked in the mirror, eight or ten more gray hairs.

"Well, she died," Sukie told Alexandra over the phone. "At about four this morning. Only Chris was with her, and he had dozed off. It was the night nurse coming in realized she had no pulse."

"Where was Darryl?"

"He'd gone home for some sleep. Poor guy, he really had tried to be a dutiful husband, night after night. It had been coming for weeks, and the doctors were surprised she had hung on so long. She was tougher than anybody thought."

"She was," Alexandra said, in simple salute. Her own heart with its burden of guilt had moved on, into an autumn mood, a calm of abdication. It was past Labor Day, and all along the edges of her yard spindly wild asters competed with goldenrod and the dark-leaved, burr-heavy thistles. The purple grapes in her arbor had ripened and what the grackles didn't get fell to form a pulp on the bricks; they were really too sour to eat, and this year Alexandra didn't feel up to making jelly: the steam, the straining, the little jars too hot to touch. As she groped for the next thing to say to Sukie, Alexandra was visited by a sensation more and more common to her: she felt outside her body, seeing it from not far away, in its pathetic specificity, its mortal length and breadth. Another March, and she would be forty. Her mysterious aches and itches continued in the night, though Doc Paterson had found nothing to diagnose. He was a plump bald man with hands that seemed inflated, they were so broad and soft, so pink and clean. "I feel rotten," she announced.

"Oh don't bother," Sukie sighed, herself sounding tired. "People die all the time."

"I just want to be held," Alexandra surprisingly said.

"Honey, who doesn't?"

"That's all she wanted too."

"And that's what she got."

"You mean by Darryl."

"Yes. The worst thing is—"

"There's worse?"

"I really shouldn't be telling even you, I got it from Jane in absolute secrecy; you know she's been seeing Bob Osgood, who got it from Doc Pat—"

"She was pregnant," Alexandra told her.

"How did you know?"

"What else could the worst thing be? *So* sad," she said.

"Oh I don't know. I'd hate to have been that kid. I don't see Darryl as cut out for fatherhood somehow."

"What's he going to do?" The fetus hung disgustingly in Alexandra's mind's eye—a blunt-headed fish, curled over like an ornamental door knocker.

"Oh, I guess go on much as before. He has his new crowd now. I told you about church."

"I read your squib in 'Eyes and Ears.' You made it sound like a biology lecture."

"It was. It was a wonderful spoof. The kind of thing he loves to do. Remember 'The A Nightingale Sang in Berkeley Square Boogie'? I couldn't put anything in about Rose and Dawn and Greta, but honestly, when they put their heads together the cone of power that goes up is absolutely *elec*tric, it's like the aurora borealis."

"I wonder what they look like skyclad," Alexandra said. When she had this immediate detached vision of her own body it was always clothed, though not always clothed in what she was wearing at the time.

"Awful," Sukie supplied. "Greta like one of those lumpy rumpled engravings by the German, you know the one—"

"Dürer."

"Right. And Rose skinny as a broom, and Dawn just a little smoochy waif with a big smooth baby tummy sticking out and no breasts. Brenda—Brenda I could go for," Sukie confessed. "I wonder now if Ed was just my way of communicating with Brenda."

"I went back to the spot," Alexandra confessed in turn, "and picked up all the rusty pins, and stuck them in myself at various points. It still didn't do any good. Doc Pat says he can't find even a benign tumor."

"Oh sweetie *pie*," Sukie exclaimed, and Alexandra realized she had frightened her, the other woman wanted to hang up. "You're really getting weird, aren't you?"

Some days later Jane Smart said over the phone, her voice piercing with its indignation, "You *can't* mean you haven't already heard!"

More and more, Alexandra had the sensation that Jane and Sukie talked and then one or the other of them called her out of duty, the next day or later. Maybe they flipped a coin over who got the chore.

"Not even from Joe Marino?" Jane was going on. "He's one of the principal creditors."

"Joe and I don't see each other any more. Really."

"What a shame," Jane said. "He was so dear. If you like Italian pixies."

"He loved me," Alexandra said, helplessly, knowing how stupid the other woman felt her to be. "But I couldn't let him leave Gina for me."

"Well," Jane said, "that's a rather face-saving way of putting it."

"Maybe so, Jane Pain. Anyway. Tell me your news."

"Not just *my* news, the whole *town's* news. He's left. He's skipped, sugar pie. *Il est disparu.*" Her *s*'s hurt, but they seemed to be stinging that other body, which Alexandra could get back into only when she slept.

From the wrathfully personal way Jane was taking it Alexandra could only think, "Bob Osgood?"

"*Dar*ryl, darling. Please, wake up. Our dear Darryl. Our leader. Our redeemer from Eastwick *ennui*. And he's taken Chris Gabriel with him."

"Chris?"

"You were right in the first place. He was one of those."

"But he—"

"Some of them can. But it isn't real to them. They don't bring to it the illusions that normal men do."

Har, har, diable, diable, saute ici, saute là. There she had been, Alexandra remembered, a year ago, mooning over that mansion from a distance, then worrying about her thighs looking too fat and white when she had to wade. "Well," she said now. "Weren't we silly?"

"'Naïve' is the way I'd rather put it. How could we *not* be, living in a ridiculous backwater like this? Why are we here, did you ever ask yourself that? Because our husbands planted us here, and we like dumb daisies just *stay*."

"So you think it was little Chris—"

"All along. Obviously. He married Jenny just to cinch his hold. I could kill them both, frankly."

"Oh Jane, don't even say it."

"And her money, of course. He needed that pathetic little money she got from the house to keep his creditors at bay. And now there's all the hospital bills. Bob says it's a terrible mess, the bank is hearing from everybody because they're stuck with the mortgage on the Lenox place. He did admit there may be just enough equity if they can find the right developers; the place would be ideal for condominiums, if they can get it by the Planning Board. Bob thinks Herbie Prinz might be persuadable; he takes these expensive winter vacations."

"But did he leave all his laboratory behind? The paint that would make solar energy—"

"Lexa, don't you understand? There was never anything there. We *imagined* him."

"But the pianos. And the art."

"We have no idea how much of that was paid for. Obviously there are *some* assets. But a lot of that art surely has depreciated dreadfully; I mean, really, stuffed penguins spattered with car paint—"

"He loved it," Alexandra said, still loyal. "He didn't fake that, I'm sure. He was an artist, and he wanted to give us all an artistic experience. And he did. Look at your music, all that Brahms you used to play with him until your awful Doberman ate your cello and you began to talk just like some unctuous *bank*er."

"You're being very stupid," Jane said sharply, and hung up. It was just as well, for words had begun to stick in Alexandra's throat, the croakiness of tears aching to flow.

Sukie called within the hour, the last gasp of their old solidarity. But all she could seem to say was "Oh my God. That little wimp Chris. I never heard him put two words together."

"I think he *wanted* to love us," Alexandra said, able to speak only of Darryl Van Horne, "but he just didn't have it in him."

"Do you think he wanted to love Jenny?"

"It could be, because she looked so much like Chris."

"He was a model husband."

"That could have been irony of a sort."

"I've been wondering, Lexa, he must have known what we were doing to Jenny, is it possible—"

"Go on. Say it."

"We were doing his *will* by, you know—"

"Killing her," Alexandra supplied.

"Yes," said Sukie. "Because he wanted her out of the way once he had her legally and everything was different."

Alexandra tried to think; it had been ages since she had felt her mind stretch itself, a luxurious feeling, almost muscular, probing those impalpable tunnels of the possible and the probable. "I really doubt," she decided, "that Darryl was ever organized in that way. He had to improvise on situations others created, and couldn't look very far ahead." As Alexandra talked, she saw him clearer and clearer—felt him from the inside, his caverns and seams and empty places. She had projected her spirit into a place of echoing desolation. "He couldn't create, he had no powers of his own that way, all he could do was release what was already there in others. Even us: we had the coven before he came to town, and our powers such as they are. I think," she told Sukie, "he wanted to be a woman, like he said, but he wasn't even that."

"Even," Sukie echoed, critically.

"Well it *is* miserable a lot of time. It honestly is." Again, those sticks in the throat, the gateway of tears. But this sensation, like that resistant one of trying to think again, was somehow hopeful, a stiff beginning. She was ceasing to drift.

"This might make you feel a little better," Sukie told her. "There's a good chance Jenny wasn't so sorry to die. Rebecca has been doing a lot of talking down at Nemo's, now that Fidel has run off with the other two, and she says some of the goings-on over there after we left would really curl your hair. Apparently it was no secret from Jenny what Chris and Darryl were up to, at least once she was safely married."

"Poor little soul," Alexandra said. "I guess she was one of those perfectly lovely people the world for some reason never finds any use for." Nature in her wisdom puts them to sleep.

"Even Fidel was offended, Rebecca says," Sukie was saying, "but when she begged him to stay and live with her he told her he didn't want to be a lobsterman or a floor boy over at

Dataprobe, and there was nothing else the people around here would let a spic like him do. Rebecca's heartbroken."

"Men," Alexandra eloquently said.

"Aren't they, though?"

"How have people like the Hallybreads taken all this?"

"Badly. Rose is nearly hysterical that Arthur is going to be involved financially in the terrible mess. Apparently he got rather interested in Darryl's selenium theories and even signed some sort of agreement making him a partner in exchange for his expertise; that was one of Darryl's things, getting people to sign pacts. Her back evidently is so bad now she sleeps on a mat on the floor and makes Arthur read aloud to her all day, these trashy historical novels. He can never get away any more."

"Really, what a boring terrible woman," Alexandra said.

"Vile," Sukie agreed. "Jane says her head looks like a dried apple packed in steel wool."

"How *is* Jane? Really. I fear she got rather impatient with me this morning."

"Well, she says Bob Osgood knows of a wonderful man in Providence, on Hope Street I think she said, who can replace the whole front plate of her Ceruti without changing the timbre, he's one of those sort of hippie Ph.D.'s who've gone to work in the crafts to spite their father or protest the System or something. But she's patched it with masking tape and plays it chewed and says she likes it, it sounds more human. I think she's in terrible shape. *V*ery neurotic and paranoid. I asked her to meet me downtown and have a sandwich at the Bakery or even Nemo's now that Rebecca doesn't blame us for everything any more, but she said no, she was afraid of being seen by those *others*. Brenda and Dawn and Greta, I suppose. I see them all the time along Dock Street. I smile, they smile. There's nothing left to fight about. Her color"—back to Jane—"is frightening. White as a clenched fist, and it's not even October."

"Almost," Alexandra said. "The robins are gone, and you can hear the geese at night. I'm letting my tomatoes rot on the vine this year; every time I go into the cellar these jars and jars of last year's sauce reproach me. My awful children have absolutely rebelled against spaghetti, and, I must say, it does pack on the calories, which is scarcely what I need."

"Don't be silly. You *have* lost weight. I saw you coming out of the Superette the other day—I was stuck in the *Word*, interviewing this incredibly immature and pompous new harbormaster, he's just a kid with hair down to his shoulders, younger than Toby even, and just happened to look out the window —and thought to myself, 'Doesn't Lexa look *fab*ulous.' Your hair was up in that big pigtail and you had on that brocaded Iranian—"

"Algerian."

"—Algerian jacket you wear in the fall, and had Coal on a leash, a long rope."

"I had been at the beach," Alexandra volunteered. "It was lovely. Not a breath of wind." Though they talked on some minutes more, trying to rekindle the old coziness, that collusion which related to the yieldingness and vulnerability of their bodies, Alexandra and—her intuition suddenly, unmistakably told her—Sukie as well deadeningly felt that it had all been said before.

There comes a blessed moment in the year when we know we are mowing the lawn for the last time. Alexandra's elder son, Ben, was supposed to earn his allowance with yard work, but now he was back in high school and trying to be a fledgling Lance Alworth at football practice afterwards—sprinting, weaving, leaping to feel that sweet hit of leather on outstretched fingertips ten feet off the ground. Marcy had a part-time job waitressing at the Bakery Coffee Nook, which was serving evening meals now, and regrettably she had become involved with one of those shaggy sinister boys who hung out in front of the Superette. The two younger children, Linda and Eric, had entered the fifth and seventh grades respectively, and Alexandra had found cigarette butts in a paper cup of water beneath Eric's bed. Now she pushed her snarling, smoking Toro, which hadn't had its oil changed since the days of Oz's home maintenance, once more back and forth across her unkempt lawn, littered with long yellow featherlike willow leaves and all bumpy as the moles were digging in for the winter. She let the Toro run until it had burned up all its gas, so none would clog the carburetor next spring. She thought of draining the sludgy ancient oil but that seemed *too* good and workmanlike of her.

On her way back to the kitchen from the gardening-tool shed she passed through her workroom and saw her stalled armature at last for what it was: a husband. The clumsily nailed and wired-together one-by-twos and two-by-fours had that lankiness she admired and that Ozzie had displayed before being a husband had worn his corners down. She remembered how his knees and elbows had jabbed her in bed those early years when nightmares twitched him; she had rather loved him for those nightmares, confessions as they were of his terror as life in all its length and responsibility loomed to his young manhood. Toward the end of their marriage he slept like a thing motionless and sunk, sweating and exuding oblivious little snuffles. She took his multicolored dust down from the shelf and sprinkled a little on the knotty piece of pine two-by-four that did for the armature's shoulders. She worried less about the head and face than the feet; it was the extremities, she realized, that mattered most to her about a man. Whatever went on in the middle, she had to have in her ideal man a gauntness and delicacy in the feet—Christ's feet as they looked overlapped and pegged on crucifixes, tendony and long-toed and limp as if in flight—and something hardened and work-broadened about the hands; Darryl's rubbery-looking hands had been his most repulsive feature. She worked her ideas up sketchily in clay, in the last of the pure white kaolin taken from the widow's back yard in Coventry. One foot and one hand were enough, and sketchiness didn't matter; what was important was not her finished product but the message etched on the air and sent to those powers that could form hands and fingers to the smallest phalange and fascia, those powers that spilled the marvels of all anatomies forth from Creation's berserk precise cornucopia. For the head she settled on a modest-sized pumpkin she bought at that roadside stand on Route 4, which for ten months of the year looks hopelessly dilapidated and abandoned but comes to life at harvest time. She hollowed out the pumpkin and put in some of Ozzie's dust, but not too much, for she wanted him duplicated only in his essential husbandliness. One crucial ingredient was almost impossible to find in Rhode Island: western soil, a handful of dry sandy sage-supporting earth. Moist eastern loam would not do. One day she happened to spot parked on Oak Street a pickup truck with Colorado plates; she reached inside the back fender and scraped some tawny dried mud down into her palm and took it home and put it in with Ozzie's dust. Also she needed a cowboy hat for the pumpkin, and had to go all the way to Providence in her Subaru to search for a costume store that would cater to Brown students with their theatricals and carnivals and protest demonstrations. While there, she thought to enroll herself as a part-time student in the Rhode Island School of Design; she had gone as far as she could as a sculptress with being merely primitive. The other students were scarcely older than her children, but one of the instructors, a ceramist from Taos, a leathery limping man well into his forties and weathered by the baths and blasts of life, took her eye, and she his, in her sturdy voluptuousness a little like that of cattle (which Joe Marino had hit upon in calling her, while rutting, his *vacca*). After several terms and turnings-away they did marry and Jim took her and his stepchildren back west, where the air was ecstatically thin and all the witchcraft belonged to the Hopi and Navajo shamans.

"My God," Sukie said to her over the phone before she left. "What was your secret?"

"It's not for print," Alexandra told her sternly. Sukie had risen to be editor of the *Word*, and in keeping with the shamelessly personal tone of the emerging postwar era had to run scandal or confession every week, squibs of trivial daily rumor that Clyde Gabriel would have fastidiously killed.

"You must imagine your life," Alexandra confided to the younger woman. "And then it happens."

Sukie relayed this piece of magic to Jane, and dear angry Jane, who was in danger of being an embittered and crabbed old maid, so that her piano students associated the black and white of the keys with bones and the darkness of the pit, with everything dead and strict and menacing, hissed her disbelief; she had long since disowned Alexandra as a trustworthy sister.

But in secrecy even from Sukie she had taken splinters of the cello-front replaced by the dedicated hippie restorer on Hope Street and wrapped them in her dead father's old soot-colored tuxedo and stuffed into one pocket of the jacket some crumbs of the dried herb Sam Smart had become, hanging in her ranch-house basement, and into the other pocket put the confetti of a torn-up twenty-dollar bill—for she was tired, boringly tired, of being poor—and sprinkled the still-shiny wide lapels of the tuxedo with her perfume and her urine and her menstrual blood and enclosed the whole odd-smelling charm in a plastic cleaner's bag and laid it between her mattress and her springs. Upon its subtle smothered hump she slept each night. One horrendously cold weekend in January, she was visiting her mother in the Back Bay, and a perfectly suitable little man in a tuxedo and patent-leather pumps as shiny as boiling tar dropped in for tea; he lived with his parents in Chestnut Hill and was on his way to a gala at the Tavern Club. He had heavy-lidded protruding eyes the pale questioning blue of a Siamese cat's; he did not drop by so briefly as to fail to notice—he who had never married and who had been written off by those he might have courted as hopelessly prissy, too sexless even to be called gay—something dark and sharp and dirty in Jane that might stir the long-dormant amorous part of his being. We wake at different times, and the gallantest flowers are those that bloom in the cold. His glance also detected in Jane a brisk and formidable potential administrator of the Chippendale and Duncan Phyfe antiques, the towering cabinets of Chinese lacquerwork, the deep-stored cases of vintage wine, the securities and silver he would one day inherit from his parents, though both were still alive, as were indeed two of his grandparents —ancient erect women changeless as crystal in their corners of Milton and Salem. This height of family, and the claims of the brokerage clients whose money he diffidently tended, and the requirements of his delicate allergic nature (milk, sugar, alcohol, and sodium were among the substances he must avoid) all suggested a manageress; he called Jane next morning before she had time to fly away in her battered Valiant and invited her for drinks that evening at the Copley bar. She refused; and then a picture-book blizzard collapsed on the brick precincts and held her fast. His call that evening proposed lunch upstairs at the snowbound Ritz. Jane resisted him all the way, scratching and singeing with her murderous tongue; but her accent spoke to him, and he made her finally his prisoner in a turreted ironstone fantasy in Brookline designed by a disciple of H. H. Richardson.

Sukie sprinkled powdered nutmeg on the circular glass of her hand mirror until there was nothing left of the image but the gold-freckled green eyes or, when she slightly moved her head, her monkeyish and overlipsticked lips. With these lips she recited in a solemn whisper seven times the obscene and sacred prayer to Cernunnos. Then she took the tired old plaid plastic place mats off the kitchen table and put them into the trash for Tuesday's collection. The very next day a jaunty sandy-haired man from Connecticut showed up at the *Word* office, to place an ad: he was looking for a pedigreed Weimaraner to mate with his bitch. He was renting a cottage in Southwick with his small children (he was recently divorced; he had helped his wife go belatedly to law school and her first action had been to file for mental cruelty) and the poor creature had decided to come into heat; the bitch was in torment. This man had a long off-center nose, like Ed Parsley; an aura of regretful intelligence, like Clyde Gabriel; and something of Arthur Hallybread's professional starchiness. In his checked suit he looked excessively alert, like a gimcrack salesman from upstate New York or a song-and-dance man about to move sideways across a stage, strumming a banjo. Like Sukie, he wanted to be amusing. He was really from Stamford, where he worked in an infant industry, selling and servicing glamorized computers called word processors. On hers she now rapidly writes paperback romances, with a few taps of her fingertips transposing paragraphs, renaming characters, and glossarizing for re-use standard passions and crises.

Sukie was the last to leave Eastwick; the afterimage of her in her nappy suede skirt and orange hair swinging her long legs and arms past the glinting shopfronts, lingered on Dock Street like the cool-colored ghost the eye retains after staring at something bright. This was years ago. The young harbormaster with whom she had her last affair has a paunch now, and three children; but he still remembers how she used to bite his shoulder and say she loved to taste the salt of the sea-mist condensed on his skin. Dock Street has been repaved and widened to accept more traffic, and from the old horse trough to Landing Square, as it tends to be called, all the slight zigzags in the line of the curb have been straightened. New people move to town; some of them live in the old Lenox mansion, which has indeed been turned into condominiums. The tennis court has been kept up, though the perilous experiment with the air-supported canvas canopy has not been repeated. An area has been dredged and a dock and small marina built, as tenant inducement. The egrets nest elsewhere. The causeway has been elevated, with culverts every fifty yards, so it never floods—or has only once so far, in the great February blizzard of '78. The weather seems generally tamer in these times; there are rarely any thunderstorms.

Jenny Gabriel lies with her parents under polished granite flush with the clipped grass in the new section of Cocumscussoc Cemetery. Chris, her brother and their son, has been, with his angelic visage and love of comic books, swallowed by the Sodom of New York. Lawyers now think that Darryl Van Horne was an assumed name. Yet several patents under that name do exist. Residents at the condo have reported mysterious crackling noises from some of the painted window sills, and wasps dead of shock. The facts of the financial imbroglio lie buried in vaults and drawers of old paperwork, silted over in even this short a span of time and of no great interest. What is of interest is what our minds retain, what our lives have given to the air. The witches are gone, vanished; we were just an interval in their lives, and they in ours. But as Sukie's blue-green ghost continues to haunt the sunstruck pavement, and Jane's black shape to flit past the moon, so the rumors of the days when they were solid among us, gorgeous and doing evil, have flavored the name of the town in the mouths of others, and for those of us who live here have left something oblong and invisible and exciting we do not understand. We meet it turning the corner where Hemlock meets Oak; it is there when we walk the beach in off-season and the Atlantic in its blackness mirrors the dense packed gray of the clouds: a scandal, life like smoke rising twisted into legend.

APPENDIX

Remarks upon accepting the National Book Critics Circle Award for Fiction for Rabbit Is Rich

GREETINGS TO the Book Critics and their lovely or handsome, as the case may be, satellites. I very much regret that I am unable to be in New York and to accept in person the award with which you have honored me. If it were merely a matter of flying for hours through the air, or snowshoeing across miles of undulating snowdrifts like Diane Keaton in *Reds*, or even riding down the paddle-wheel with which the New York Public Library supplies battered books to its sleepy patrons, I would indeed be with you, imbibing the good cheer that arises whenever two or three of the thoroughly well read gather and rest their strained optic nerves in delighted contemplation of one another's faces. But I am, alas, constrained to be elsewhere.*

So I must ask you to forgive my absence, and must put my editor, Judith Jones, to the embarrassment of reading these words, and to the additional embarrassment, at this moment, of reading a compliment to herself. For it is an incalculable comfort and encouragement to an author to have an editor so sympathetic, quick-witted, and indulgent as Judith, and to submit his manuscripts to a publishing house as constant and generous in its purposes as the firm of Alfred A. Knopf. The writing and publishing of books is of course a commercial enterprise, but one wherein the profit motive is oddly mingled with elements of the playful and idealistic. The very qualities that give a book enduring value can also be those that give it no immediate market value, and any writer must be proud to have as partner a business firm that accepts this paradoxical formula. This prize to the most recent of my books, all so lovingly produced by Knopf and so patiently kept in print, reminds me that to a writer publication itself is the great prize.

---

*I was being sued in Los Angeles, if you must know.

My wife, Martha, should also be thanked, not only for her many reassurances and suggestions in this specific case but for standing foremost in that band of intimates who surround with forbearance the homely and sometimes hopeless-seeming labor of concocting fiction. And in all seriousness I thank my characters, for coming to life as best they could and for enduring in resilient style the indignities I had planned for them. My native region of southeastern Pennsylvania, though nearly three decades have passed since I could claim sylvan residence, obligingly continues to warm my imagination with the impressions of humanity I received there, longer and longer ago— a land fertile for even the absentee farmer.

I treasure this award because it comes from fellow-workers in the fields of the written word, who risk deadlines, inky fingers, typographical error, and crank mail. In an age when, as in most others, it is easier to cry crisis than to describe peace, I am touched that you have singled out for this recognition an unsensational rendering of equivocal normal life, as it is led in middle age, by a man as ordinary as any American is ordinary.

1982

Remarks upon accepting the American Book Award for Fiction for Rabbit Is Rich

I WANT TO THANK the officials and judges of the American Book Awards via whom this honor has come to me; and let me thank as well the many people who have written me, apropos of *Rabbit Is Rich*, to point out that Janice could not be driving, as I have her do, a Maverick convertible, since the Ford Motor Company never made a Maverick convertible. Let me reassure these concerned multitudes that I have placed on order for Mrs. Angstrom a Mustang convertible, a car I know to be actual because I once drove one, with the wind in my hair and my foot to the floor. This real model, as opposed to the ideal but nonexistent Maverick, should be in use by the time of the paperback edition. Another correspondent has recently written me to say that on page 434 I have my chief character, early in the year 1980, take a cylinder of clove Life Savers from his desk; she, my correspondent, was a clove Life Saver freak and with sorrow informed me that the flavor hasn't been available since around 1972. Such are the perils of writing naturalistic fiction in an age of fantasy and imperial imagination.

Spring is the season of prizes in the arts, and this spring has been my season for prizes. But when I think of all those shyly hopeful springs when no boon or blessing came my way, and of all the fine books of fiction published in 1981 that have been shouldered aside by my own novel, I wonder, not for the first time, if the net discomfort and irritation generated by literary awards does not outweigh the total joy that accrues to their credit. Surely this smiling audience harbors more than one young heart ardently wishing that the gray-haired apparition at this lectern will, like the doddering Emperor Achon of Azania in Evelyn Waugh's novel *Black Mischief*, instantly perish under the weight of his newly bestowed crown. For our world of books, like most other worlds now, is the arena of an increasingly bitter struggle for space—for paper and cover cloth, for review space, and for the limited reading time that a busy citizen in this electronic age can afford. Though we literary folk can make a brave display in Carnegie Hall for an afternoon, we are not a symphony but a mob of one-man bands, one-person bands I should say, playing all simultaneously, and mostly unheard. The poets and fiction writers among us are in the retrograde business of spinning clouds, syntactical filament by filament, in an age when clouds can be had at the twist of a knob or the push of a button on an aerosol can.

To that young writer prizeless and restive in my audience I say: Have faith. May you surround yourself with parents, editors, mates, and children as tolerant and supportive as mine have been. But the essential support and encouragement of course come from within, arising out of the mad notion that your society needs to know what only you can tell it. This book of mine, and other books of mine, were begun and finished in that faith, and I accept this American Book Award as an unlooked-for but welcome sign from above that my faith was not altogether mad. Thank you, all.

1982

"Special Message" to readers of the Franklin Library's Signed First Edition Society printing of The Witches of Eastwick

NEXT TO the small Pennsylvania town in which I grew up there was an even smaller town called Grille, and in the middle of Grille, so I was told, a "witch doctor" practiced his mysterious arts. No shingle advertised the office, but the building was in plain sight; the sex of the supposed practitioner has been exorcised from my mind, but pow-wow doctors—makers of spells and animistic little cures—were an undoubted fact in Berks County not many decades ago, and may be yet.* It is

---

*By a coincidence truly uncanny, my Shillington High School classmate Barry Nelson, in the April 1984 issue of *Governor Mifflin Area History*, wrote at length of "Pow-Wows and Faith Healers in the Mifflin Area" just as my novel was being published. The "witch doctor" in Grille was identified as Harry C. Ohlinger, a Reading native and weaver by trade who died in 1955 at the age of sixty-two; he had lived in Grille, opposite the Center Hotel, since 1938, and had begun to practice his healing arts before then, at a farmhouse near Angelica on Candy Road, in Cumru Township. He was a Bible-reading, prayerful man, some of whose cures were simply traditional faith healing. Some were a bit stranger: "A woman who ran a farm in Maxatawny thought she had a jinx on her. He told her to put an ace of spades in a milk bucket, and milk a cow's milk into it. This broke the hex or spell." People lined up on his porch to see him, waiting two or three hours; he never charged money and was instead paid with "donations, whiskey, food, or knick-knacks." One satisfied customer recalled, "He cured my wife's back in three visits. He put his hand on your body, said something, and you could feel something happening." In Shillington, the widow of the pow-wow doctor Ellsworth Mohn remembered, "Ells would sit in front of you and he'd cup his left hand and hold it out like he was receiving something, holding it palm up. He took his right hand in a sweeping move across the inflammation in a catching motion, blew into the right hand, and slapped it into his upper hand. He would do this three times." Mohn always said his spells in "Dutch" (Pennsylvania German) and had learned how to pow-wow from a Mammy Bitting, also of Shillington. A sexual curiosity of the art of pow-wowing is that only a woman can teach it to a man, and vice versa. "The prayers are passed on by word of mouth. They must be memorized. There is no hexerei involved. The prayers are from the Bible." Yet some of the cures cited are distinctly elaborate: to cure a sick baby, a mother is instructed "to take the baby's shirt off, turn it inside out, and pinch it in the attic door over night." And: "Another story involved a small baby that cried constantly.

a land of gloomy hilltop forests and abandoned quarries and barns bearing hex signs; my grandmother was a great one for observing the minor superstitions, involving cats and salt, ladders and umbrellas. The supernatural never seemed far off, especially after the sun had set, and the friendly street I walked to school on every day yet had its quota of mysterious old women peeking out from behind their curtains, ready to pounce upon the child so careless as to set a foot on their little carpets of front lawn. I wonder, now, if the famous German discipline —for the presiding spirit of the land was certainly German, though its language was English and many of the place-names were Welsh—isn't maintained in large part by threats from the spirit world. At any rate, as a boy I ran scared.

New England, land of clear thinking, welcomed me to college. One of the very few books I bought and read on my own, in my four years at Harvard, was a translation of the French historian Jules Michelet's *La Sorcière*, entitled *Satanism and Witchcraft*. Michelet's romantic vision of the witch as the persecuted perpetuator of pagan nature-worship and a gentle rebel against the medieval church's tyranny stayed with me. To Michelet the decades since have added the reading of Huysmans's *À rebours* and Sylvia Townsend Warner's *Lolly Willowes* and those several novels by Muriel Spark that confidently touch upon the demonic. The 1960s saw witchcraft hit the media and go political. War protesters chanted and "tripped" and tried to put a spell on the Pentagon, and self-anointed enchantresses and warlocks from London to Los Angeles advertised their satanic commitments and supernatural powers; the gruesome climax came with the Manson murders of August 1969.

It is a curious fact of witchcraft study that, though members of contemporary cults and covens readily pose nude for the tabloids and fill volumes with their philosophy (in which astrology and health diets dance hand-in-hand with worship

---

The mother tried to quiet the child, but the crying got worse. Finally, in frustration, she said, 'Enough! I'm going to do something about this!' She placed a bucket of hot water in the middle of the parlor and placed a burning hot poker into the water while reciting a prayer. The next day a woman in the same town was scalded to death. This woman had visited the mother and had given the mother and her family something to eat. She was really putting a hex on them."—*1991*

of a Satan hard to distinguish from Santa Claus), and though such relatively recent episodes as the *fin-de-siècle* black masses in Paris that Huysmans described and the affair, in the 1670s, of the Marquise de Montespan—a mistress of Louis XIV's who attempted to secure his love with obscene rites—are undoubtedly historical, a fog of unknowing descends as the alleged Dark Age heyday of witchcraft is approached. Modern scholars like Norman Cohn (in *Europe's Inner Demons*) strenuously argue that there were *never* any covens or organized Devil-worship, that all confessions to the contrary were the product of torture or demented delusion. His opponents in this argument include Michelet, who was carrying forward certain earlier suggestions among nineteenth-century historians that witchcraft was an underground survival of the ancient pagan religions, and Margaret Murray, the Scots anthropologist whose book of 1921, *The Witch-Cult in Western Europe*, with its successor, *The God of the Witches* (1933), claimed, by the light of Frazer's *Golden Bough*, an extensive historical reality for the perennial rumors of witchcraft. While scholarly debates raged, modern British and American women were founding covens along the lines of Miss Murray's anthropology, and by 1970 (roughly the time of my novel), a Witches' International Craft Association had come into existence, along with a Witches' News Service, a Witches' Lecture Bureau, and a Witches' Anti-Defamation League. My heroines are not members of these organizations; their witchcraft is an intuitive and fitfully articulated collusion, sprung from their discovery that husbandlessness brings power. Witchcraft is the venture, one could say, of women into the realm of power. What women in the Middle Ages besides witches and queens wielded power that men needed to fear?

The ideology of my portrait descends from the impression of pathos and heroic subversion that Michelet communicated to a college student in the early Fifties. Many of the details of ritual and of the Devil's hollow appearance (for from the testimony of witch trials he would seem to have often been a man in a mask, with an artificial phallus) come from Margaret Murray's assemblage of evidence. The business of feathers and pins emerging from the mouths of the bewitched was suggested by the strange case of Christian Shaw, as described in *Witch Hunt: The Great Scottish Witchcraft Trials of 1697*, by

Isabel Adam. Books by Charles Williams, Richard Cavendish, Erica Jong, Pennethorne Hughes, Montague Summers, Colin Wilson, Peter Haining, Ronald Holmes, A. F. Scott, and others contributed to my picture. But I would not have begun this novel if I had not known, in my life, witchy women, and in my experience felt something of the sinister old myths to resonate with the modern female experiences of liberation and raised consciousness.

Moreover, I once moved to a venerable secluded town, not far from Salem, where there had been a scandal. I was never able to discover exactly what had happened—those old-timers who knew went vague and sly when pressed—but its aura, as it were, still hung in the air above the salt marshes, and haunted me. Among my literary debts let me acknowledge one to the French writer Robert Pinget; his novels admirably capture the spookiness of communities that hold in the crevices of faulty, shifting communal memory a whiff of sulphur, a whisper of the unspeakable. Emboldened by Pinget's example, I have tried here, in my own style, to give gossip a body and to conjure up human voices as they hungrily feed on the lives of others. The appetite is not trivial; we write and read novels to satisfy it.

1984

CHRONOLOGY

NOTE ON THE TEXTS

NOTES

Chronology

1932   Born John Hoyer Updike on March 18 in Reading Hospital, West Reading, Pennsylvania, the only child of Wesley Russell Updike and Linda Grace Hoyer Updike. (Father, born in 1900 in Trenton, New Jersey, is a former lineman for AT&T accumulating credits toward a state teaching certificate at Albright College, in Reading. Mother, born in 1904 in Plowville, Robeson Township, ten miles south of Reading, is a disciplined and hopeful writer of short fiction, submitting regularly but as yet unsuccessfully to *Collier's*, *The Saturday Evening Post*, and other popular magazines. The couple met in 1919, when both were students at Ursinus College, in Collegeville, Pennsylvania, and were married in Ithaca, New York, in August 1925, shortly after Linda Hoyer earned a master's degree in English from Cornell University. From 1926 through 1931 they traveled together for the phone company, living in hotels and rooming houses in Ohio and western Pennsylvania. In June 1931, after Wesley Updike lost his job in the Great Depression, they accepted Linda's parents' invitation to move in with them.) Called Johnny by his family and "Chonny" by their Pennsylvania Dutch neighbors, he is raised in Shillington (pop. 4,400), a town three miles southwest of Reading (pop. 120,000), the seat of Berks County. He, his parents, and his maternal grandparents live together at 117 Philadelphia Avenue, the home of Grandpa John Franklin Hoyer (b. 1863), a retired schoolteacher and onetime gentleman farmer financially ruined by the Crash, and Grandma Katherine ("Katie") Ziemer Kramer Hoyer (b. 1873), a farmwife made prematurely frail by Parkinson's disease. The two-story house of red brick and flaking cream-colored clapboards—built in 1900 and owned by the Hoyers since 1922—has a side porch, a red brick patio, and over the patio an abundant grape arbor hung with Japanese-beetle traps. At the bottom of the yard is an asbestos-shingled chicken house, a garden growing asparagus to sell at Shillington's Friday market, and, fronting on the back alley, a garage that is rented out to neighbors, as the family has no car. "Our lamps were dim, our carpets worn, our furniture hodgepodge and venerable and damp," Updike will remember. "And yet I never felt that we were poor."

1933 On his first birthday, family plants a dogwood sapling in the side yard. "This tree, I learned quite early, was exactly my age; was, in a sense, me," he will one day write. "The tree was my shadow." In September, mother takes job selling draperies at Pomeroy's department store, in downtown Reading, for fourteen dollars a week, leaving Johnny in the care of Grandma Hoyer.

1934 Through the influence of a Hoyer relative on the regional school board, father, now certified, is hired to teach seventh- and eighth-grade mathematics at Shillington High School (grades 7–12), a job he will hold for the next twenty-eight years. (His starting salary is twelve hundred dollars per school year, with which he supports himself, wife, son, and in-laws. In the summers he will eke out a living by working on town construction crews or as a manual laborer at Carpenter Steel, in Reading.)

1936 Mother quits job at Pomeroy's when, one morning on her way to the trolley stop, Johnny comes down Philadelphia Avenue crying after her.

1937 In September, enters kindergarten at Shillington Elementary School, which he will attend through grade six. There and at home shows a talent for drawing, and is encouraged by mother, who supplies him with paper, pencils, and paints. Working together at the dining table beneath a stained-glass lamp, the two design a cutout puzzle in the shape of a jack-in-the-box, the template for which is then printed in *Children's Activities* magazine, his first experience of "being in print."

1938 An attack of measles in February triggers the onset of psoriasis, a condition also suffered, to a lesser degree, by mother. "Siroil and sunshine and not eating chocolate were our only weapons in our war against the red spots, ripening to silvery scabs, that invaded our skins in the winter," Updike will recall. Because of his skin, he will dismiss all suggestions of his becoming a teacher, doctor, or other "public" professional. "What did that leave? Becoming a craftsman of some sort, closeted and unseen—perhaps a cartoonist or writer." With the anxiety of psoriasis comes another affliction, a stutter: "a distortion of the mouth as of a leather purse being cinched, a terrified hardening of the upper lip, a fatal tensing of and lifting of the voice." In the fall begins Sunday school at Grace Evangelical Lutheran Church, Shillington, where father, the son of a Presbyterian minister, is a deacon. Of his immediate family, only he and father are regular churchgoers.

1939   Begins making unaccompanied visits to the Shillington movie house, two blocks from home. "The theatre ran three shows a week, for two days each, and was closed Sundays," he will remember. "Many weeks I went three times." Fascinated by Mickey Mouse, tells family and playmates that he hopes one day to work as a Disney animator, a notion he will entertain until his late teens. Keeps scrapbooks of syndicated comic strips printed in the Reading *Times* and *Eagle*, including *Popeye*, *Dick Tracy*, and *Toonerville Folks*, and copies the drawings to learn the artists' techniques. Enjoys comic books and, especially, Big Little Books—chunky ten-cent volumes, each two-page spread a captioned comic-strip panel opposite a page of narrative text—a large collection of which makes up most of his childhood library.

1942   Mother hires neighbor Clint Shilling, a professional artist and member of the town's founding family, to give Johnny private lessons in drawing and painting. Shilling is also a fine-art conservator at the Reading Public Museum and Art Gallery, where Johnny and mother will spend many Sundays viewing the permanent collection—mainly nineteenth-century oil landscapes—and exhibits of new art by regional talent. Also takes piano lessons, and though he masters elementary music theory and sight-reading, he seldom plays for his own pleasure.

1943   At Christmas, Aunt Mary Updike, a lover of literature who had once been Edmund Wilson's secretary at *The New Republic*, treats the Shillington Updikes to a subscription to *The New Yorker*. The magazine, with its witty and sophisticated covers and cartoons, its light verse, humor, fiction, and criticism, instantly captivates him: "It *knew* best, *was* best." New York and *The New Yorker* soon become, in his phrase, "the object of my fantasies and aspirations."

1944   On weekends takes the twenty-minute trolley ride to the Reading Public Library and brings home mysteries

(Agatha Christie, John Dickson Carr), humor books (P. G. Wodehouse and the writers he has enjoyed in *The New Yorker*—James Thurber, E. B. White, Robert Benchley), and sometimes science fiction. In September, enters Shillington High School as a seventh-grader. Father is his math teacher for the next three years; he is also coach of the school's swim team, keeper of the cash box at sports events, and something of the faculty clown, friendly, self-deprecating, and popular with the students.

1945 Begins contributing cartoons, light verse, and movie reviews to the *Chatterbox*, Shillington High School's mimeographed student weekly. (By the spring of 1950, the end of his senior year, he will make nearly three hundred signed contributions to the publication.) In late summer, family is presented the opportunity to repurchase the sandstone farmhouse in Plowville in which Grandma and Grandpa Hoyer once lived and mother was born and raised. Although the house, called Strawberry Hill, is smaller than the Shillington residence, it sits on eighty-three acres of arable land instead of a half-acre town lot. Built in 1812, it has no indoor plumbing, is heated by a fireplace and a coal-oil stove, and, for the first year or so, is without electricity. On October 31, all five family members move into Strawberry Hill, which will be the grown-ups' home for the rest of their lives. Updike will later depict the farm as a "wearying place of work, weeds, bugs, heat, mud, and wildlife" where mother led the others in imposing order—"renovating the old stone farmhouse, repairing the barn, planting rows of strawberries and asparagus and peas, mowing a lawn back into the shadow of the woods." Father buys his first car —a balky 1938 Buick, prone to emergency repairs—for his and his son's commute to and from Shillington High. To a thirteen-year-old boy with New York aspirations, the move seems "less an adventure than a deprivation," a step backward in personal and family fortune.

1946 He and father join the Robeson Evangelical Lutheran Church, known as Plow Church, in neighboring Mohnton. Not yet old enough to drive, resentful of the loss of the Shillington movie house and the trolley cars into Reading, he finds escape and solace through reading, writing, drawing, and listening to the radio, especially to Boston Red Sox games. ("Ted Williams had made a dent in my consciousness before the war," Updike will remember, "but it was the '46 Sox"—led to the American League pennant by Williams's phenomenal hitting—"that made me a passionate fan.") In June works briefly in a local lens factory, and then devotes the first of four summers to cultivating the farm's strawberry patch, partly to meet a 4-H Club requirement but also to supplement the family's income. During the evenings writes first extended piece of fiction, a murder mystery featuring a suave Spanish detective. In the fall, begins after-school ritual of smoking, talking, and playing pinball at Stephens' Luncheonette, a hangout for his circle of classmates and the rendezvous for his ride home with father.

1947   In fall takes Shillington High School class in drawing and painting from teacher Carleton Boyer.

1948   In May, exhibits a drawing in a juried show of student art-work at the Reading Public Museum and wins a Scholastic Art Award. In fall revises light verse printed in the *Chatterbox* and sends poems, two or three at a time, to *The New Yorker*. Submits, in regular weekly batches, pencil roughs for gag cartoons to *The New Yorker*, *Collier's*, and *The Saturday Evening Post*. In November "It Might Be Verse" appears in *Reflections*, a bimonthly poetry journal published in Hartwick, New York. It is the first of a handful of high-school and undergraduate acceptances by small-circulation magazines including *The American Courier* (Kansas City, Mo.), *American Weave* (Cleveland, Ohio), *Different* (Rogers, Ark.), and *The Florida Magazine of Verse*.

1949   In fall elected senior-class president. Writes most of the text and photo captions for *Hi-Life 1950*, the school year-book. At mother's insistence, family visits the campuses of Harvard, Cornell, and Princeton Universities, and he applies to all.

1950   In spring accepted by Cornell and Harvard and decides on the latter, which offers a full-tuition scholarship. In June graduates from Shillington High School as co-valedictorian. Types his collected poems, 1941–50, and has them professionally bound into a black hardcover volume, its gold-stamped spine reading *Up to Graduation*. Spends the first of three consecutive summers as copyboy for the Reading *Eagle*, fetching coffee for the Linotype operators and contributing jokes and verse to Jerry Kobrin's local-interest column, "Reading in Writing." In September arrives in Cambridge, Massachusetts, with few definite plans beyond joining the congregation of Faith Lutheran Church. Tells parents he is dismayed by the paucity of Harvard's studio-art offerings and thinks he might major in English literature: "I've never read, after all, and now is the time. Besides, what else is there?" Assigned a room in Hollis Hall, one of the oldest dormitories in Harvard Yard, and a roommate, Christopher "Kit" Lasch, the future cultural historian and social critic. His first semester is crowded with required courses that leave little time for cartooning, though he does pull together a portfolio in time for the midyear staff elections at *The Harvard Lampoon.*

1951   In February elected to the Literary Board of the *Lampoon,* an undergraduate humor monthly (nine issues per school year) that, as Updike will later comment, "had begun in the 1870s as an imitation of *Punch*" but by the 1950s "was an imitation of *The New Yorker,* which suited me fine." With the May issue he immediately establishes himself as the *Lampoon*'s most versatile and prolific staff member. (By the time he graduates, in June 1954, he will have contributed more than 50 poems, 30 prose pieces, and 150 cartoons and spot drawings, as well as 8 cover illustrations.) At the end of the term is elected "Narthex" for 1951–52, the least of the magazine's three named editorial positions. He and Lasch agree to continue as roommates and are assigned a suite in Lowell House for the next two years. During the summer writes opening chapters of "Willow," a novel inspired by his Shillington boyhood; at the start of his sophomore year, he shows his work-in-progress to Albert J. Guerard, the head of the college's writing department, who refers him to a sympathetic but tough-minded English instructor named Theodore Morrison. "Professor Morrison wavered between having me rewrite what I'd done or letting me go ahead with it," Updike reports to his parents. "But he read and talked with me for about an hour, [then] agreed to let me forge ahead." As Morrison's special student, he is required to write at least three thousand words of "Willow" every two weeks. His other classes include Harry Levin's yearlong Shakespeare course and a semester of medieval art. In the latter he meets Mary Entwistle Pennington (b. 1930), a ponytailed, tennis-sneakered Radcliffe senior majoring in fine arts, with whom he forms a romantic attachment.

Raised mainly in Chicago, she is the daughter of the Rev. Leslie T. Pennington, a Unitarian minister, and Elizabeth Daniels Pennington, a former teacher of high-school Latin.

1952   In the winter studies Milton and, with Mary, takes Hyman Bloom's drawing class, Advanced Composition. In March abandons "Willow" to work on short stories with Professor Morrison. In June elected "Ibis" (second-in-charge) of the *Lampoon* for 1952–53. At the end of the school year, brings Mary home to Plowville to meet his family; she then returns to Radcliffe to graduate on June 15. After a final summer at the Reading *Eagle*, begins his junior year at Harvard. Continues his courtship of Mary, who lives with a roommate a ten-minute walk from Harvard Yard. Enrolls in Walter Jackson Bate's seminar on the history of literary criticism and takes classes in Spenser and in seventeenth-century English poetry. His writing instructor for the fall semester is Edgar F. Shannon, Jr., a Tennyson scholar who challenges him to write in strict poetic forms. In November hears Adlai Stevenson campaign for the U.S. presidency in Boston and, raised a "reflexive Democrat," carries placards for him near Cambridge polling places on Election Day. After Christmas, travels to Chicago to meet the Pennington family and to present Mary with an engagement ring.

1953   In the spring continues working on rhymed and metered verse, now with Professor Morrison. In April is one of eight Harvard juniors named to Phi Beta Kappa. Elected president (editor-in-chief) of the *Lampoon* for 1953–54. On June 26, he and Mary are married at the First Parish Cambridge, the Unitarian church in Harvard Square, in a service performed by Mary's father. As a gift from one of the Rev. Pennington's parishioners, the newlyweds take a four-day honeymoon at a private beach house in Ipswich, Massachusetts, thirty miles north of Boston. For the rest of the summer they work at Sandy Island Camp, a YMCA family camp near Lakeport, New Hampshire, where he runs the office and she the camp store. In July, receives two letters from William Maxwell, an editor of fiction and poetry at *The New Yorker*, each rejecting a poem but encouraging him to send others. In September, the couple moves into an apartment at 79 Martin Street, north of Harvard Square, and Updike starts his senior year. Later that month, Grandpa Hoyer dies at age ninety. Begins research for senior thesis, "Non-Horatian Elements in Robert Herrick's Imitations and Echoes of Horace," a yearlong project with advisor Kenneth Kempton. Takes courses in Anglo-Saxon and the Russian novel and writes short fiction for Albert J. Guerard. In December completes "Flick," a story about a former high-school basketball player struggling with young adulthood that Guerard thinks good enough for *The New Yorker*.

1954   Katharine S. White, fiction editor of *The New Yorker*, rejects "Flick," but Leo Hofeller, executive editor, suggests that Updike visit his office for a job interview. In April awarded a Frank Knox Memorial Fellowship, granting him a postgraduate year at one of several schools in the British Commonwealth; he chooses the Ruskin School of Drawing and Fine Art, Oxford University, which also agrees to take Mary as a part-time student. In June graduates *summa cum laude*, and he and Mary spend most of the summer at the Pennington family's summer cottage in South Duxbury, Vermont. On July 15, receives word that *The New Yorker* will publish his "Duet, with Muffled Brake Drums," a light-verse fantasy on the day that Rolls met Royce. ("From this poem's acceptance," Updike will later say, "I date my life as a professional writer.") By the end of the summer, Katharine S. White accepts four more poems and a short story, "Friends from Philadelphia." In August visits the *New Yorker* offices and meets William Maxwell but not the vacationing White and Hofeller. Later that week he and Mary sail from New York to Southampton aboard RMS *Caronia*, then settle into a basement flat at 213 Iffley Road, Oxford. There he rewrites "Flick," soon published in *The New Yorker* as "Ace in the Hole." In September signs an agreement granting the magazine first-reading rights in all his future writings.

1955   At the Ruskin School "paints onions and draws from the antique," and in the evenings reads Proust, Henry Green, and the Protestant theologians Kierkegaard and Karl Barth. Daughter, Elizabeth ("Liz") Pennington Updike, born April 1. In winter and spring, sells several poems and three stories to *The New Yorker*. On June 22, meets E. B. and Katharine S. White, who, traveling in England, make a special trip to Oxford to offer him a place on the staff of the magazine. Returns to New York aboard RMS *Britannic*. In late July rents a small temporary apartment at 126

Riverside Drive, at West Eighty-fifth Street, and on August 22 starts at *The New Yorker* as a writer for "The Talk of the Town." In compliance with the Reserve Forces Act of 1955, reports to the draft board; he is classified "4-F: Psoriasis." In September Grandma Hoyer dies at age eighty-three. On December 1, the Updikes move to larger apartment at 153 West Thirteenth Street, Greenwich Village.

1956   In January completes "Snowing in Greenwich Village," the first of more than a dozen short stories chronicling the increasingly troubled marriage of his characters Joan and Richard Maple. In April rereads "Willow" and again is moved to write a novel about his Shillington boyhood. Arriving early at *The New Yorker* every weekday morning, he drafts three pages of the book before turning to his current "Talk" assignment. At a lunch arranged by E. B. White, Cass Canfield, publisher at Harper & Bros., compliments him on his published stories and asks if, when the times comes, he might see his novel. By August, the end of his first year at the magazine, he is chafing in the harness of "The Talk of the Town." ("To concoct an anonymous fraction of it year after year loomed as fruitlessly selfless," he will remember. "It seemed unlikely I would ever get better at 'Talk' than I was at twenty-four.") By Christmas his novel, now called "Home," is almost complete.

1957   Second child, David Hoyer Updike, born January 19. One week later, Updike resolves to move his family to Ipswich, Massachusetts, and to continue writing for *The New Yorker* on a freelance basis. On February 9, during a weekend search for a suitable Ipswich rental, signs a one-year lease on "Little Violet," a two-bedroom lavender-shingled house near the corner of Heartbreak and Essex Roads. Shortly after arriving in Ipswich on April 1, joins the congregation of Clifton Lutheran Church, in neighboring Marblehead. Introduced to the game of golf by his wife's aunt, he is soon devoting several hours a week to practicing his swing at Candlewood, the Ipswich public course. Plays kitchen-table poker every other Wednesday night with five to seven male neighbors, a ritual that will continue, in one kitchen or another, for nearly fifty years. With Mary takes up the recorder—she plays alto, he tenor—and joins three or four other musicians to form a long-lived, ever-expanding local recorder society, learning and eventually publicly performing works by Purcell,

Handel, Pachelbel, and others. Finishes six-hundred-page draft of "Home," assembles slim collection of previously published poems, and gives Harper & Bros. the option on both. In late April, Cass Canfield accepts the poetry collection and assigns it to veteran editor Elizabeth Lawrence. In May, Canfield declines to publish "Home," thinking it "a very typical first novel"—a nostalgic childhood memoir that goes on far too long. Updike, stung by this criticism, conceives of a counter-novel—a brief and mildly futuristic "caricature of contemporary decadence," its protagonist a ninety-four-year-old man who leads a residents' revolt at an old-folks' home. He will finish a draft of the novel, "The Poorhouse Fair," by Christmas.

1958   Katharine S. White retires to Maine, and William Maxwell becomes Updike's fiction editor at *The New Yorker*. In January, Elizabeth Lawrence reports that Harpers is not convinced by the last third of "The Poorhouse Fair" and requests revisions. Updike withdraws the book and submits it to publisher Alfred A. Knopf, who accepts it as is. (The firm of Knopf will be his chief American publisher for the rest of his long career.) On March 2, receives advance copy of his poetry collection, *The Carpentered Hen and Other Tame Creatures*. Purchases a five-bedroom house, built in 1687, at 26 East Street, Ipswich, which will be his residence for the next twelve years. In May begins writing new novel, "Go Away," a high-school romance set in the Shillington and Plowville of 1947. Enjoys working with his Knopf editor, Stewart "Sandy" Richardson; also with the book designer Harry Ford, who gives "The Poorhouse Fair" a page and binding design that Updike will insist upon adapting for all his future Knopf titles. Begins ordering and revising short stories for his first collection, "The Same Door."

1959   In January publishes *The Poorhouse Fair*, which enjoys two weeks at number 16 on the New York Times Best Sellers list. Reads *On the Road* ("it's surprisingly good," he tells his parents) and writes a parody of Kerouac for *The New Yorker*. In February rereads the nearly completed first draft of "Go Away" and decides the book is "a mistake, a two-hundred-page and yearlong mistake, and would be best plowed under, leaving the material in the soil." In hopes of making up time lost on the aborted project, applies for —and in April is awarded—a Guggenheim Fellowship to underwrite a new novel, conceived as both a conservative answer to Kerouac and an expansion on themes first explored in "Ace in the Hole." Third child, Michael John Updike, born May 14. In August publishes *The Same Door: Short Stories.* ("An exciting brilliance pervades the sixteen pieces that make up this book," writes *The Saturday Review.* "All may be praised in superlatives without fear of fatuity.") In September finishes the first draft of his Guggenheim novel, "Rabbit, Run," and revises the manuscript through the end of the year. Now that daughter Liz is old enough for Sunday school, decides to leave the Lutheran church in Marblehead and, with his Unitarian wife, join the First Congregational Church in Ipswich, where the family can worship together. "A Gift from the City" included in *The Best American Short Stories 1959.*

1960   Delivers "Rabbit, Run" to Knopf on January 4. In winter spends five weeks with family in a rented house on Anguilla, in the British West Indies, a Caribbean holiday taken largely for the benefit of his psoriatic skin. There he writes several poems and five short stories, including "Pigeon Feathers" and "Home." In March rents a second-floor office in the block-long Caldwell Building, on South Main Street, Ipswich, where he will report six days a week through the summer of 1974. In April writes a memoir, "The Dogwood Tree," for Martin Levin's anthology *Five Boyhoods* (Doubleday, 1962), and a poem, "Seven Stanzas at Easter," for a religious arts festival at Clifton Lutheran Church. In May, *The Poorhouse Fair* awarded the Rosenthal Award of the American Academy of Arts and Letters "for a book of the previous year that is a considerable literary achievement." In July, in a conference room at Alfred A. Knopf, strikes obscenities from "Rabbit, Run" with his new editor, Judith Jones, at one elbow and a Knopf-appointed lawyer at the other. (Judith Jones will remain his Knopf editor for the rest of his life.) On September 26, attends Ted Williams's farewell game at Fenway Park and watches in fannish disbelief as his hero, in his final turn at bat, delivers one last home run. His account of the game, "Hub Fans Bid Kid Adieu," is published in *The New Yorker,* October 22. In November, *Rabbit, Run* published to very strong reviews. ("The merit of the book," writes Norman Mailer, "is in the dread Updike manages to convey" on behalf of Harry "Rabbit" Angstrom, "a young man who is beginning to lose nothing less than his good American soul.") The novel spends ten weeks on the New York Times Best Sellers list, peaking at number 14. Fourth child, Miranda Margaret Updike, born December 15.

1961 Newly fond of the Caribbean, spends a solitary week on the beaches of Puerto Rico, St. John's, and St. Croix. (In most of the following fifteen winters he will take a week-long "hit of sun," often alone, on Antigua, Aruba, St. Martin, Tortola, or, most frequently, St. Thomas.) Upon return begins "An Old-Fashioned Romance," planned as a short, lighthearted novel, set in the early 1950s, about a love affair between a black Harvard undergraduate and his white Radcliffe girlfriend. On March 11, "Translation," by Linda Grace Hoyer, appears in *The New Yorker*. It is mother's first published story; nine more will be accepted by the magazine through 1983. In July *The New Yorker* publishes "A & P," which will become Updike's most widely anthologized story and a standard selection for high-school literature textbooks. At the suggestion of editor William Shawn, begins to review books for *The New Yorker*. (His first assignment, forty-six hundred words on Dwight Macdonald's *Parodies: An Anthology*, appears in the September 16 issue. Over the next forty-seven years, he will contribute some 375 reviews and scores of unsigned "Briefly Noted"s to the magazine's Books section.) In September abandons "An Old-Fashioned Romance" and begins "The Centaur," a novel designed as a contrasting companion to *Rabbit, Run*, a study in adult duty and self-sacrifice instead of youthful impulse and self-gratification. As a favor to his friend and neighbor Bill Wasserman, editor of the weekly *Ipswich Chronicle*, begins a four-year masquerade as "H.H.," pseudonymous reviewer of local musical events. "Wife-wooing" included in *Prize Stories 1961: The O. Henry Awards*.

1962 In March publishes second collection, *Pigeon Feathers and Other Stories*. ("Updike is not merely talented," writes critic Granville Hicks, "he is bold, resourceful, and intensely serious. We hear talk now and then of a breakthrough in fiction, the achievement of a new attitude and hence a new method; something like that seems close at hand in *Pigeon Feathers*.") The book spends six weeks on the New York Times Best Sellers list—an unusual distinction for a story collection—peaking at number 13. In April, delivers

"The Centaur" to Knopf. In May begins research for a novel exploring the difficult presidency of Pennsylvania's James Buchanan (1857–61), but by Christmas will set the project aside. Teaches creative writing in Harvard's summer program, an experiment that confirms his distaste for the profession. In August, an affair with a woman of his Ipswich set precipitates a crisis that nearly ends both of their marriages. In November *The Magic Flute*, a prose adaptation of the Mozart opera with illustrations by Warren Chappell, published by Knopf Books for Young Readers. In late fall and winter, vacations with family in Antibes, France, and visits Naples and the ruins at Pompeii. "The Doctor's Wife" included in *Prize Stories 1962* and "Pigeon Feathers" in *The Best American Short Stories 1962*.

1963   In February publishes *The Centaur*, which spends ten weeks on the New York Times Best Sellers list, peaking at number 9. In April *The New Yorker* publishes "Giving Blood," a second Maples story. On May 1, in his Ipswich office, performs the story "Lifeguard," the poem "Earthworm," and other short pieces for freelance audio producer Laurence Lustig; the resulting LP, *John Updike Reading from His Works* (CMS Records, 1965), is the first of his many spoken-word recordings. Rewrites a section of the abandoned "Old-Fashioned Romance" as the long story "The Christian Roommates." Begins another long story, which, over the next eight months, develops into "Marry Me," a novel based closely on his adulterous affair. In September publishes second collection of verse, *Telephone Poles and Other Poems*.

1964   In January completes draft of "Marry Me," but with qualms both personal and artistic, sets the work aside. On March 10 accepts the National Book Award in Fiction for *The Centaur*; a citation by the judges—John Cheever, Philip Rahv, and Robie Macauley—calls the book a "brilliant account of a conflict of gifts between an inarticulate American father and his highly articulate son" that "readily takes on the risk of flamboyance in pursuing an acuteness of feeling." In April becomes, at age thirty-two, one of the youngest persons ever inducted into the National Institute of Arts and Letters. From May to August works on a short story about mother and Strawberry Hill that evolves into the novella "Of the Farm." In fall *The Ring*, a prose adaptation of Wagner's opera with illustrations by

Warren Chappell, is published by Knopf Books for Young Readers, and *Olinger Stories*, a selection of Pennsylvania stories from *The Same Door* and *Pigeon Feathers*, is published by Vintage Books. ("If I had to give anybody one book of me," Updike tells an interviewer decades later, "it would be the Vintage *Olinger Stories*.") Is surprised by an invitation from the U.S. State Department to act as cultural ambassador to the Soviet Union, where *The Centaur* is popular in Russian translation. In late October, he and Mary spend ten days in Moscow and Leningrad with fellow-ambassador John Cheever; together they drink vodka with various members of the Writers Union, including Andrei Voznesensky and Yevgeny Yevtushenko. For the next five weeks the Updikes and their Soviet and State Department handlers travel to Kiev and Tbilisi, then to Bulgaria, Romania, and Czechoslovakia. Upon return in December writes "The Bulgarian Poetess," the first of twenty short stories concerning the life and times of Jewish American novelist Henry Bech, unprolific author of the Beat-era classic *Travel Light*, whose reputation grows as his literary powers decline.

1965   Throughout the winter revises "Of the Farm," delivering the manuscript on March 1. In May publishes *Assorted Prose*, a miscellany collecting "Talk" pieces, humorous sketches, and book reviews, anchored by "The Dogwood Tree," "Hub Fans," and "Grandmaster Nabokov," the first of many appreciations of Vladimir Nabokov, "the best writer of English prose currently holding American citizenship." On the afternoon of Sunday, June 13, the First Congregational Church of Ipswich, built 1846, is struck by lightning and burns to the ground; Updike, making what will prove a five-year commitment, joins the committee charged with overseeing the design and construction of a new church building. In November publishes *Of the Farm*. ("In this, his fourth novel," writes *The New York Times*, "Updike has achieved a sureness of touch, a suppleness of style, and a subtlety of vision that is gained by few writers of fiction.") *A Child's Calendar*, twelve poems with pencil illustrations by Nancy Ekholm Burkert, published by Knopf Books for Young Readers. In Paris *Le Centaure* wins the Prix du meilleur livre étranger for the year's best novel translated into French. Donates his literary manuscripts, 1953–65, to Harvard's Houghton Library. (In

2009, Harvard will purchase the remainder of his papers from his heirs posthumously.)

1966　In August, resumes work on his Buchanan novel, but soon abandons it for a panoramic novel of contemporary Ipswich and "the way we live now." In September publishes *The Music School*, his third collection of short stories. The book occasions a long photo-essay in *Life* magazine ("Can a Nice Novelist Finish First?," November 4) in which Updike tells an interviewer that "my subject is the American Protestant small-town middle class. I like middles. It is in middles where extremes clash, where ambiguity restlessly rules." In November, at the request of the visiting Yevtushenko, Updike and playwright Arthur Miller accompany the poet during the New York leg of his first American reading tour. "The Bulgarian Poetess" wins the O. Henry First Award and is featured in *Prize Stories 1966*.

1967　Ipswich novel, now called "Couples," develops into an ambitious (and sometimes satirically sociological) study of the death of traditional institutions and the rise of "post-Pill" paganism. During a family vacation on Martha's Vineyard, is interviewed for *The Paris Review*'s "Art of Fiction" series, a transcription of which he takes pains to revise into a definitive artistic credo. During the previous August on the Vineyard he had responded to a British journalist's questionnaire asking where he stood on the Vietnam War. His conservative answer, now published in the book *Authors Take Sides on Vietnam* (Simon & Schuster), is widely criticized in the liberal press and in his own social circle. ("I am for our intervention if it does some good," Updike wrote. "The crying need is for genuine elections whereby the South Vietnamese can express their will. If their will is for Communism, we should pick up our chips and leave. Until such a will is expressed . . . I do not see that we can abdicate our burdensome position in Vietnam.") "My undovishness," Updike will later write, "like my battered and vestigial but unsurrendered Christianity, constituted a refusal to give up, to deny and disown, my deepest and most fruitful self, my Shillington self—dimes for war stamps, nickels for the Sunday-school collection, and grown-ups maintaining order so that I might be free to play with my cartoons and Big Little Books." Is commissioned to write two short plays: "Three Texts from Early Ipswich," a pageant to be performed in celebration of the town's Seventeenth-Century Day, August 3, 1968, and an adaptation of the Grimms' fairy tale "The Fisherman and His Wife," to be performed, with music by Gunther Schuller, by the Opera Company of Boston in the spring of 1970. These happy experiments in theater will lead him to recast his Buchanan novel in the form of a stage play. "Marching through Boston," a Maples story, included in *Prize Stories 1967*.

1968   In February *The New Yorker* publishes "The Wait," a lengthy excerpt from "Marry Me." *Couples* appears on April 2; Wilfrid Sheed, reviewing it on the cover of *The New York Times Book Review*, calls it an "ingenious" vivisection of "an authentically decadent community," a "fiendish compendium of exurban manners . . . described with loving horror." On April 10, the book enters the New York Times Best Sellers list, where it remains for thirty-six consecutive weeks, usually in the number 2 position, just below Arthur Hailey's *Airport*. On April 26 a portrait labeled "Novelist John Updike" appears on the cover of *Time* under the headline "The Adulterous Society." David L. Wolper, who will later produce *Roots* and *The Thorn Birds*, options *Couples* for $360,000, but the film is never made. From April to August writes the long poem "Midpoint," employing the meters of Dante, Spenser, Whitman, and Pope "to take inventory of his life at the age of thirty-five." Resolves to spend the 1968–69 school year in London with his family, partly to escape the distractions of celebrity, partly to escape a "Vietnam-addled America distressing in its civil fury." In September takes up residence at 59 Cumberland Terrace, on Regent's Park, and contributes occasional "Notes of a Temporary Resident" to the *Times Literary Supplement*, *New Statesman*, and the BBC's *Listener* magazine. In the Reading Room of the British Museum toys with his Buchanan drama, but again sets the work aside. In the fall takes a trip alone to Egypt. "Your Lover Just Called," a Maples story, included in *Prize Stories 1968*.

1969   In February writes fourth Bech story, "Rich in Russia," and begins to see the outlines of a possible Bech collection. Spends most of April in Morocco with his family, while, in America, *Midpoint and Other Poems* is published. Returns from London and, from June through December, writes three more Bech episodes for the evolving quasi-novel "Bech: A Book." In September *Bottom's Dream*, a prose adaptation of Shakespeare's *Midsummer Night's Dream* with illustrations by Warren Chappell, published by Knopf Books for Young Readers.

1970   In winter researches the life and presidency of James Buchanan at the Historical Society of Pennsylvania, Philadelphia. On May 7, at Boston's Savoy Theatre, Schuller and Updike's children's opera, *The Fisherman and His Wife*, receives world premiere under the direction of Sarah Caldwell. In June publishes *Bech: A Book*, which spends eight weeks on the New York Times Best Sellers list, peaking at number 7. Working from literal translations supplied by Slavists, fashions English versions of ten poems by Yevtushenko for the Russian's bilingual collection *Stolen Apples* (Doubleday, 1971). In summer travels in Japan and South Korea with fifteen-year-old daughter Liz, and on July 1 delivers talk "Humor in Fiction" at PEN conference in Seoul. From June to November, as relief from the recalcitrant "pastness" of the Buchanan material, writes the first draft of "Rabbit Redux," a present-tense sequel to *Rabbit, Run*. In late spring purchases a new, larger house for family at 50 Labor-in-Vain Road, Ipswich. Sells the house at 26 East Street to Alexander Bernhard, a corporate lawyer in Boston, who, with his wife, Martha Ruggles Bernhard, becomes part of the Updikes' social set. In October, Jack Smight's production of *Rabbit, Run*, starring James Caan, released by Warner Bros. Pictures to uniformly bad reviews. ("*Rabbit, Run* wasn't released," Caan quips to Updike's amusement. "It escaped.") "Bech Takes Pot Luck" included in *Prize Stories 1970*.

1971   In March delivers Rabbit sequel, and devotes rest of the year to writing short fiction and to shaping a new story collection. In February *Enchantment*, fifteen autobiographical vignettes by Linda Grace Hoyer, published by Houghton Mifflin. In November publishes *Rabbit Redux*, which spends seventeen weeks on the New York Times Best Sellers list, peaking at number 4. (Richard Locke, in *The New York Times Book Review*, calls the novel "a great achievement . . . I can think of no stronger vindication of the claims of essentially realistic fiction than this extraordinary synthesis of the disparate elements of contemporary experience.") In December, in Ipswich, Updike breaks his leg while playing touch football; spends a week in the hospital and three months on crutches.

1972 In March visits Venezuela as a weeklong resident at the American Venezuelan Center, Caracas, and lectures to an unappreciative audience on *Doña Bárbara*'s relation to the American Western. ("What the Third World does not want to hear about," Updike learns, "is parallelisms with the U.S.") Father dies, April 16, at age seventy-two; he is buried in Plow Church Cemetery, Plowville. Updike returns one last time to the Buchanan play, which he finds impossible to cut to playable length and so expands. ("Exhaustiveness is a novelist's method," Updike will later remark, "and what we have here is a kind of novel conceived in the form of a play . . . a drama [to be] staged inside the reader's head.") Writes a long miscellaneous afterword to the work, and delivers the typescript before Christmas. In October publishes fourth collection, *Museums and Women and Other Stories*. (William H. Pritchard, in *The Hudson Review*, writes: "He is a religious writer; he is a comic realist; he knows what everything feels like, how everything works. He is putting together a body of work which in substantial intelligent creation will eventually be seen as second to none in our time.")

1973 In winter spends four weeks with Mary in Anglophone Africa—Ghana, Nigeria, Tanzania, Kenya, Ethiopia—courtesy of the Fulbright Board of Foreign Scholarships. Attends a Pan-African literary conference in Lagos, and repeatedly presents an apolitical paper, "The Cultural Situation of the American Writer," to the consternation of politicized African writers' groups. Upon return, records uneasy impressions of Africa, Venezuela, and South Korea in the story "Bech Third-Worlds It." In spring and summer, writes first draft of "A Month of Sundays," a comic reimagining of Hawthorne's *Scarlet Letter* narrated by the adulterous Rev. Tom Marshfield, a latter-day Arthur Dimmesdale. On June 12, at commencement exercises in Harvard Yard, reads autobiographical "Apologies to Harvard," the Phi Beta Kappa Poem for 1973. Writes a personal essay on golf for *The New York Times*, and is soon asked to contribute pieces about the game to *Golf Digest* and other sports publications. In the fall, at the request of Knopf Canada, makes publicity tour of Toronto, Calgary, and Vancouver. Revises "A Month of Sundays" for delivery in the new year.

1974   In March, as a guest of the Australian Office of the Arts, delivers a speech, "Why Write?," at literary festivals in Sydney and Adelaide. Updike and Martha Ruggles Bernhard (b. 1937), their four-year acquaintance having become a deep attachment, decide to leave their spouses for each other. In June Updike moves from Labor-in-Vain Road to a studio apartment in Ipswich, and Alexander Bernhard moves out of the house on East Street. In summer publishes *Buchanan Dying*; the book receives few reviews, sells poorly, and soon goes out of print. In September, Updike leases apartment at 151 Beacon Street, in Back Bay, Boston, his "bachelor's accommodations" for the next twenty months. Throughout the fall, intermittently socializes with John Cheever, who, separated from his wife, is spending a year alone near Kenmore Square while teaching creative writing at Boston University. "Son" included in *The Best American Short Stories 1974*.

1975   In February publishes *A Month of Sundays*, which spends fifteen weeks on the New York Times Best Sellers list, peaking at number 6. In March, Updike assumes the remaining few weeks of Cheever's teaching obligation when Cheever, incapacitated by drink, resigns his position at Boston University. In April, at Berlitz in Central Square, Cambridge, begins a yearlong class in basic German, the language of his Pennsylvania forebears. In November publishes *Picked-Up Pieces*, collecting a decade's worth of speeches, essays, and humorous prose, the *Paris Review* interview, and some seventy book reviews. In November, undertakes experimental ultraviolet "light-box" treatments for psoriasis (PUVA therapy) at Mass General Hospital. "Nakedness," a Maples story, included in *Prize Stories 1975*.

1976   William Maxwell retires, and Roger Angell becomes Updike's fiction editor at *The New Yorker* for the rest of Updike's life. In winter, rereads the twelve-year-old manuscript of "Marry Me" and begins to revise it for publication. On the title page he labels the book a "romance," partly to highlight its Hawthorne-like allegorical scheme, partly to mark it as a thing apart from his other novels. In March, at Salem Court House, John and Mary Updike receive one of the first "no-fault" divorces granted by the Commonwealth of Massachusetts. In April and May, an abridged *Buchanan Dying* performed at Franklin and Marshall College, Lancaster, Pennsylvania. On May 21 is elevated from the 200-member National

Institute of Arts and Letters to the 50-member American Academy of Arts and Letters. On May 11 purchases 58 West Main Street, a red clapboard house in Georgetown, Massachusetts, and moves out of his Boston apartment. On June 28 is joined in Georgetown by Martha and her three boys, John (age twelve), Jason (eleven), and Ted (five). In this, the summer of America's bicentennial, Updike, Shillington's favorite son, agrees to be Grand Marshal of his hometown's Fourth of July parade. In October *The New Yorker* publishes "Here Come the Maples," the concluding episode of the Maples series. In November *Marry Me: A Romance* published to polarized reviews. Though it spends six weeks on the New York Times Best Sellers list, peaking at number 7, many critics call it redundant, sentimental, a mere "pocket version" of *Couples*. On December 8, delivers "The Written Word," the Frank Nelson Doubleday Lecture for 1976, at the Smithsonian Institution, Washington, D.C. "Separating," a Maples story, is included in *Prize Stories 1976* and Updike is given the series' Special Award for Continuing Achievement. "The Man Who Loved Extinct Mammals" included in *The Best American Short Stories 1976*.

1977   In February, revised edition of *The Poorhouse Fair* (1959), with a new introduction by the author, published in hardcover by Knopf. In March an abridged *Buchanan Dying* receives eight staged readings at the Institute for Readers Theatre, San Diego, California. In April spends a week in Toledo and Madrid with mother and daughter Miranda. In May publishes fourth collection of poems, *Tossing and Turning*. Embarrassed by the reception of *Marry Me* and determined not to be typecast as chronicler of "the adulterous society," plans an ambitious departure—a Nabokovian flight of fancy set in an imaginary sub-Saharan country and narrated by an elegant Muslim dictator with an aversion to all things American. In September delivers his speech "The Cultural Situation of the American Writer" to a receptive conservative audience at the American Enterprise Institute, Washington, D.C. On September 30, marries Martha Ruggles Bernhard at Clifton Lutheran Church, Marblehead. In October–November, the couple travels in Denmark, Sweden, and Norway at the invitation of Updike's Scandinavian publishers.

1978   Delivers African novel, "The Coup," on April 1. Arranges and revises his short stories of the last seven years, and writes "Atlantises" to round out the new collection. In November a thirty-minute film of "The Music School"— an actor's reading of the text accompanied by cinematic imagery—televised as part of PBS's *American Short Story* series. On August 9, Updike's son David, a Harvard undergraduate, publishes an autobiographical short story in *The New Yorker*; it will later be reprinted, with twelve other stories, in his collection *Out on the Marsh* (Godine, 1988). In the fall visits Jerusalem, Bethlehem, Tel Aviv, and Greece with Martha. In December, *The Coup* published to widespread media attention, including a front-page review in *The New York Times Book Review* and a long profile in *The New York Times Magazine*.

1979   On January 7, *The Coup* enters the New York Times Best Sellers list, where it remains for seventeen weeks, peaking at number 4. On March 12, Robert Geller's *Too Far to Go*, a two-hour made-for-television film based on the Maples stories, broadcast on NBC. Updike, who did not participate in the production, prepares a tie-in collection, *Too Far to Go: The Maples Stories*, published in paperback by Fawcett. In May delivers "Hawthorne's Religious Language," the annual Blashfield Address of the American Academy of Arts and Letters. When approached by James Forsht, editor of the U.S. edition of the French arts magazine *Réalités*, to write 650 words on a favorite painting, Updike responds with a series of nine such essays, his first sustained foray into art criticism. In June begins work on a third Rabbit novel, "Rabbit Is Rich." In October, *Problems and Other Stories* published. (In a front-page review, *The New York Times Book Review* calls *Problems* "a work of really awesome literary cunning. [It] won't be surpassed by any other collection of the next year, and perhaps not in the next ten.") Begins traveling to Europe with Martha every fall, usually for two weeks in Italy or France.

1980   In February completes the first draft of "Rabbit Is Rich." In June, after a reading at Case Western Reserve University, suffers crippling nausea; undergoes an emergency appendectomy at the Cleveland Clinic and is hospitalized for four days. In the fall visits London and the Orkney Islands with Martha. "Gesturing," a late Maples story, included in *The Best American Short Stories 1980*.

1981   In January delivers "Rabbit Is Rich." Returns to Venezuela for a second weeklong visit, during which he and Martha escape unscathed from a helicopter crash near Angel Falls. From June to December revises four previously uncollected Bech stories and writes three new ones to make "Bech Is Back," a second Bech book. On August 22, awarded the Edwin MacDowell Medal for outstanding contribution to American literature. In September publishes *Rabbit Is Rich*, which spends twenty-three weeks on the New York Times Best Sellers list, peaking at number 4. The BBC-TV arts magazine *Arena* and WGBH Boston coproduce "What Makes Rabbit Run?," an hour-long documentary featuring interviews with Updike at home, in Plowville, and in the offices of Alfred A. Knopf. "Still of Some Use" included in *The Best American Short Stories 1981*.

1982   *Rabbit Is Rich* awarded the Pulitzer Prize, the National Book Critics Circle Award, and the American Book Award in Fiction. In March, on Updike's fiftieth birthday, Knopf issues a revised edition of his first book, *The Carpentered Hen* (1958), with a new foreword by the author. In April "The Beloved," a long story of 1971 published only in excerpt in *The New Yorker*, printed by Lord John Press, Northridge, California, in an edition limited to four hundred signed copies. In May, moves to 675 Hale Street, in Beverly Farms, Massachusetts, his home for the rest of his life. On the second floor of the house an isolated suite of four small rooms, the former servants' quarters, becomes his new workspace. Spends the summer compiling and revising the contents of a third nonfiction collection. With Martha and her children becomes a parishioner at St. John's Episcopal Church, Beverly Farms. In October publishes *Bech Is Back*, which spends one week on the New York Times Best Sellers list at number 13. On October 18 *Time* magazine profiles Updike in a cover story titled "Going Great at Fifty." (This second *Time* cover painting, an oil portrait by Alex Katz, now hangs in the National Portrait Gallery, Washington, D.C.)

1983   From January to August drafts a novel about a modern-day devil who arrives in a Rhode Island seaport town to cultivate the powers of three young witches. On May 22 confirmed in the Episcopal Church by John B. Coburn,

Bishop of Massachusetts. In September publishes *Hugging the Shore: Essays and Criticism.* ("With this latest volume," writes Michiko Kakutani in *The New York Times*, "Updike has established himself, in his 'improvised sub-career as a book reviewer,' as a major and enduring critical voice; indeed, as the preeminent critic of his generation.") Leon Wieseltier, literary editor of *The New Republic*, asks Updike to write about the Fairfield Porter retrospective at the Museum of Fine Arts, Boston, the first of several exhibitions he will review for that magazine. "The City" included in *Prize Stories 1983* and "Deaths of Distant Friends" in *The Best American Short Stories 1983*.

1984   With series editor Shannon Ravenel, selects the contents of *The Best American Short Stories 1984* (Houghton Mifflin, October). *Hugging the Shore* wins the National Book Critics Circle Award in Criticism. In March visits Kenya and Egypt with Martha and thirteen-year-old Ted. In May publishes *The Witches of Eastwick*, which spends twelve weeks on the New York Times Best Sellers list, peaking at number 5. In September "The Roommate," a two-hour adaptation of the story "The Christian Roommates," televised as part of PBS's *American Playhouse* series. When approached by a would-be biographer for permission to write his life, Updike begins to plan, not an autobiography, but a series of six memoirs "tracing the inner shape" of his experience. The first of these, on the world of his childhood and his early impressions of life, appears in the Christmas issue of *The New Yorker*.

1985   In February visits Arizona with Martha and is deeply attracted to its austere landscape. In March publishes fifth collection of poems, *Facing Nature*. In April travels with Martha to Switzerland and Germany. In May *Selected Stories*, a three-hour, two-cassette recording of six stories chosen and read by the author, released as part of the launch of Random House Audiobooks; Updike performs "A & P," "Pigeon Feathers," "The Family Meadow," "The Witnesses," "The Alligators," and "Separating." Composes two further memoirs, one on his psoriasis and the other on his stuttering. Writes "Majesty," a second variation on the themes of Hawthorne's *Scarlet Letter*, this time from the perspective of a latter-day Roger Chillingworth. "The Other" included in *Prize Stories 1985*.

1986   "Majesty" delivered to Knopf, whose executives, con-
       cerned about confusion with a forthcoming biography of
       Elizabeth II, propose a change of title to "Roger's Ver-
       sion." In March travels with Martha and Ted in London,
       Oxford, and the rural south of England. Upon return, col-
       lects and revises his short stories of the last eight years. In
       late April visits Prague, and in July writes "Bech in Czech,"
       his first Bech story in five years. In September publishes
       Roger's Version, which spends fifteen weeks on the New
       York Times Best Sellers list, peaking at number 4.

1987   Plans to cap his "*Scarlet Letter* series" with the comic novel
       "S.," the confessions of Sarah Worth, a spiritual pilgrim
       who leaves her husband and daughter in New England to
       join the charismatic leader of an Arizona ashram. In April
       publishes *Trust Me*, his sixth collection of stories. ("It is in
       his short stories that we find Updike's most assured work,"
       writes the *Washington Post*. "Almost without fail they give
       pleasure, a quality not to be taken lightly.") On May 1
       delivers "Howells as Anti-Novelist," keynote speech of
       Harvard's two-day celebration of William Dean Howells
       at 150. In June, George Miller's film *The Witches of East-
       wick*, starring Jack Nicholson, released by Warner Bros.
       Pictures. ("It is not a movie I would see twice," Updike
       tells the agent responsible for the movie deal.) In August
       spends five days in Helsinki at the request of his Finnish
       publisher. In December elected chancellor of the Ameri-
       can Academy of Arts and Letters for the three-year term
       1988–90. "The Afterlife" included in *The Best American
       Short Stories 1987*.

1988   Writes three further memoirs—on his social conservatism,
       his Updike ancestry, and his sense of being a "self"—to
       complete the manuscript of his book "Self-Consciousness."
       In February an hour-long adaptation of "Pigeon Feathers"
       televised as part of PBS's *American Playhouse* series. In
       March publishes *S.*, which spends six weeks on the New
       York Times Best Sellers list, peaking at number 10. In April,
       during a visit to Northern Ohio University, in Ada, Ohio,
       visits the Wilson Sporting Goods factory, the inspiration
       for two short stories, "The Football Factory" and "Part
       of the Process." At the invitation of Knopf's Judith Jones,
       collects his art writings for publication as a large-format
       illustrated art book. "Leaf Season" included in *Prize Stories
       1988*.

1989   At New Year's begins work on a final Rabbit book, "Rabbit at Rest." In March *Self-Consciousness* published to strong reviews but modest sales. ("These memoirs," writes the *Chicago Tribune*, "take us inside Updike's mind in the way that biography almost never can.") In October publishes *Just Looking: Essays on Art*, and at the invitation of Robert Silvers, coeditor of *The New York Review of Books*, becomes a regular art critic for that magazine, contributing some fifty exhibition reviews over the next two decades. Mother dies of heart attack, October 10, at age eighty-five; she is buried beside her husband in Plow Church Cemetery. She leaves to her son the sandstone farmhouse and the land it stands on. She also leaves him her literary estate, including the page proof of *The Predator* (Ticknor & Fields, 1990), a second collection of autobiographical vignettes. Updike corrects proof and writes jacket copy, and his daughter Elizabeth provides line drawings as chapter openers. In a White House ceremony on November 17 receives the National Medal of Arts from President George H. W. Bush.

1990   In January delivers "Rabbit at Rest" and begins compiling a fourth collection of nonfiction prose. In the spring spends a week with Martha in Milan and visits the historic estate of Gabriele D'Annunzio. In September, takes the first of four golfing tours of the U.K. and Ireland with fellow-members of the Myopia Hunt Club, Hamilton, Massachusetts. In October publishes *Rabbit at Rest*, which spends seven weeks on the New York Times Best Sellers list, peaking at number 8.

1991   Rereads *Buchanan Dying* and, recalling his ordeal with that book, begins work on a comic novel that tells two mirroring stories: (a) an American professor of history remembers his untidy life during the mid-1970s and (b) interlards his reminiscence with pages from an unfinished project of that period, a life of President Buchanan. *Rabbit at Rest* awarded the Pulitzer Prize and the National Book Critics Circle Award in Fiction. In the fall visits London and Dublin with Martha. In November publishes *Odd Jobs*, collecting nearly a thousand pages of literary journalism and other writings. "A Sandstone Farmhouse" included in *The Best American Short Stories 1991*.

1992   In February, at the invitation of his Brazilian publishers, travels in São Paulo, Ouro Prêto, Brasília, and Rio. (Brazil,

Updike will later comment, "was a territory that lured me forward, into its luminous green depths, into its magical emptiness; it seemed one of the last earthly spaces that held room for the imagination.") On June 4 presented with an honorary Doctorate of Letters degree from Harvard University. In November, *Memories of the Ford Administration* published to mixed reviews and modest sales. "A Sandstone Farmhouse" wins the O. Henry First Award for best short story of the year and is featured in *Prize Stories 1992*.

1993   In June delivers novel "Brazil," a "magical-realist" retelling of the romance of Tristan and Iseult set in the slums of Rio and in the Brazilian backland. In April publishes *Collected Poems, 1953–1993*, gathering nearly all the poetry and light verse from his earlier volumes as well as more than seventy new and uncollected items. *Love Factories*, three uncollected short stories from 1988, printed by Eurographica, Helsinki, Finland, in an edition of 350 signed copies. In June he and Martha take a Harvard-sponsored cruise tracing the Mediterranean voyage of Homer's Odysseus. "Playing with Dynamite" included in *The Best American Short Stories 1993*.

1994   In January, *Brazil* published to mixed reviews and modest sales. "Grandparenting," a postscript to the Maples series, published in *The New Yorker*, February 21; the story is the capstone to a new collection of short fiction, delivered March 1. Revises, corrects, and expands the texts of the four Rabbit novels for a one-volume edition by Everyman's Library; writes long introduction to the collection, "Rabbit Angstrom," and in July hand-delivers text of the book to Everyman's London office. Begins "In the Beauty of the Lilies," an ambitious novel tracing one American family's relationship with God—and with Hollywood's false idols—across four generations. In November publishes *The Afterlife and Other Stories*. ("Marvelously moving," writes *USA Today*. "These tales evoke a certain peace . . . and a wonder at what an astonishingly graceful writer Updike is.")

1995   In May *Rabbit at Rest* awarded the William Dean Howells Medal of the American Academy of Arts and Letters for the most distinguished American novel of the last five years. In July, *A Helpful Alphabet of Friendly Objects*, a volume of humorous verse with full-color photographs by son David, published by Knopf Books for Young Readers. *Rabbit Angstrom* published in London and New York by Everyman's Library. "The Black Room" included in *Prize Stories 1995*.

1996   In January publishes *In the Beauty of the Lilies*, which spends five weeks on the New York Times Best Sellers list, peaking at number 9. In September, *Golf Dreams*—a collection of essays, poems, and fiction about learning, playing, and loving the game—published by Knopf. Records selections from golf book for Random House Audiobooks, the last in a series of "read by the author" cassettes that began with *Selected Stories* (1985) and continued with performances of *Trust Me* and *The Afterlife*.

1997   In February is presented the Campion Award, an occasional prize given by *America* magazine to honor the lifework of a distinguished Christian man of letters. Takes the first of seven consecutive March holidays on Gasparilla Island, in southwest Florida. Revises "Bech in Czech" and spends most of the year writing four additional stories for a final Bech book, "Bech at Bay." In October publishes *Toward the End of Time*, a postapocalyptic novel of the year 2020, in which a dying New England investment banker lives not in the present but in a variety of simultaneous realities. (Margaret Atwood calls the book "a little corner of hell as meticulously painted as a Dutch interior.")

1998   In April *A Century of Arts and Letters*, the history of the American Academy of Arts and Letters "as told, decade by decade, by eleven members," published by Columbia University Press. (The volume was conceived and edited by Updike, who also provided a foreword and the chapter on the period 1938–47.) On May 2, receives the Harvard Arts Medal for lifetime contribution to literature. Spends four weeks in China and Hong Kong with Martha, September–October, while, in America, *Bech at Bay* is published to strong reviews. ("Like the other books about Henry Bech," writes Jonathan Yardley in the *Washington Post*, "this is modest in size but generous with its rewards.") With series editor Katrina Kenison, selects the contents of *The Best American Short Stories of the Century* (Houghton Mifflin, April 1999), representing his work with "Gesturing," from

1980. On November 18, awarded the National Book Foundation Medal for Distinguished Contribution to American Letters. "My Father on the Verge of Disgrace" included in *The Best American Short Stories 1998*.

1999 In January "His Oeuvre," a final Bech story, published in *The New Yorker*. After rereading *Hamlet* and related scholarship and criticism, writes "Gertrude and Claudius," a prose "prequel" to Shakespeare's play. In September publishes *More Matter*, a fifth collection of essays and reviews. In October begins a novella-length postscript to the Rabbit saga, in which Harry's survivors, ten years after the events of *Rabbit at Rest*, "fitfully entertain his memory." In November, a revised edition of *A Child's Calendar*, with new ink-and-watercolor illustrations by Trina Schart Hyman, published by Holiday House.

2000 In January publishes *Gertrude and Claudius*. ("Shakespeare's plays have had many offshoots," writes Peter Kemp in *The Times* of London. "*Gertrude and Claudius*, though, stands in a class of its own: a superlative homage from one imaginative veteran to another.") In February *A Child's Calendar* named a Caldecott Honor Book. On July 18, Cameron Mackintosh's West End musical *The Witches of Eastwick*, with book and lyrics by John Dempsey and music by Dana P. Rowe, begins a fifteen-month run at the Royal Theatre, Drury Lane. Having viewed and reviewed the Jackson Pollock retrospective at the Museum of Modern Art in November 1999, continues his research on the lives of Pollock and his wife, Lee Krasner, and is inspired to write "Seek My Face," a novel about the New York art world of the 1950s. In October spends three weeks in Japan with Martha. In November publishes *Licks of Love*, collecting twelve short stories and the novella "Rabbit Remembered."

2001 In March *The Complete Henry Bech*, an omnibus edition of the three Bech books and their postscript, "His Oeuvre," published by Everyman's Library, London. On April 17–19, visits Cincinnati for the series of readings and interviews documented by James Schiff in his book *Updike in Cincinnati* (Ohio University Press, 2007). In May, publishes seventh collection of verse, *Americana and Other Poems*. While visiting stepson Jason on September 11, witnesses the fall of the World Trade Center from a rooftop in

Brooklyn Heights and records the horror as a "Talk of the Town" reporter. "Personal Archaeology" included in *The Best American Short Stories 2001.*

2002   In April the Updikes travel in Spain. With many of his early collections now out of print, revises short stories from 1953 to 1975 for republication in a definitive, omnibus edition. In November, *Seek My Face* published to mixed reviews.

2003   In January, *Karl Shapiro: Selected Poems*, edited with an introduction by Updike, published by Library of America. The Updikes visit Arizona for the month of March and, upon their return home, decide to buy a winter home there. In April is presented the National Medal for the Humanities by President George W. Bush. In spring begins writing the novel "Villages," conceived as an account of the life and times of a representative American male of Updike's generation. In September he and Martha spend two weeks on the Danube and in Prague. In November publishes *The Early Stories: 1953–1975*, with an autobiographical foreword by the author. ("Updike's artistry . . . is deeply and wholly seen," writes *The Atlantic*. "One reads through the plenitude with delight, expectation, and at all times gratitude.")

2004   In January purchases a condominium in Tucson and, with Martha, spends the first of five consecutive Marches there. *The Early Stories* wins the PEN/Faulkner Award in Fiction. In October *Villages* published to mixed reviews. At the invitation of Knopf prepares a second collection of illustrated art writings on the model of *Just Looking*. "The Walk with Elizanne" included in *The Best American Short Stories 2004.*

2005   In winter and spring, drafts a "9/11" novel about an eighteen-year-old New Jersey boy, the son of an Irish American mother and an Egyptian father, who, as a truck driver for a Muslim-owned furniture retailer, is slowly drawn into a terrorist plot. In November publishes *Still Looking: Essays on American Art*, with pieces on Copley, Homer, Eakins, Stieglitz, Hopper, Pollock, Warhol, and others.

2006   For three weeks in January, travels in the Hindu south of India with Martha. In June publishes *Terrorist*, which spends four weeks on the New York Times Best Sellers list

—Updike's first appearance there in more than a decade—
peaking at number 5. In September, a jury of Ann Beattie,
Richard Ford, and Joyce Carol Oates gives Updike the Rea
Award for his lifelong contribution to the art of the short
story.

2007   In winter travels with Martha in Cambodia and Thailand.
Devotes the rest of the year to writing "The Widows of
Eastwick," a sequel to *Witches* (1984) and a meditation
on youthful sins, abiding guilt, and the need for redemption. In May is awarded the Gold Medal in Fiction from
American Academy of Arts and Letters. In October publishes *Due Considerations*, a sixth collection of essays and
criticism.

2008   In January *The New Yorker* accepts what will prove to be
his final short story, "The Full Glass." Updike submits it
and seventeen other late stories to Knopf as the collection
"My Father's Tears." In February travels with Martha in
Egypt and Jordan. Everyman's Library offers to reprint,
for the first time in hardcover, *Too Far to Go*; Updike revises the text, adds the late story "Grandparenting," and
renames the volume *The Maples Stories*. On May 22, at the
invitation of the National Endowment for the Humanities,
presents "'The Clarity of Things': What Is American in
American Art," the thirty-seventh annual Jefferson Lecture
in the Humanities, at the Warner Theatre in Washington,
D.C. In June Library of America proposes a special edition
of "Hub Fans Bid Kid Adieu" to commemorate the fiftieth
anniversary of Ted Williams's last at-bat; Updike lightly revises the text and agrees to fashion a new preface and afterword for the book. In the summer begins research for, and
writes opening chapters of, "The Last Epistle," a historical
novel about the life of St. Paul. In September travels with
Martha in Latvia, Lithuania, Estonia, Finland, St. Petersburg, and Moscow. In October, *The Widows of Eastwick*
published, and Updike, though troubled by a persistent
cough, undertakes two weeks of publicity appearances in
New York City and on the West Coast. In November, believing he has pneumonia, is told by doctors at Massachusetts General Hospital that he is dying of stage IV lung
cancer. In November and December, keeps a journal in
verse of his hospital visits and prepares the manuscript of a
final book, "Endpoint and Other Poems."

2009   On January 2, files his last piece for *The New Yorker*, a
        review of Blake Bailey's life of John Cheever. Selects read-
        ings for his funeral service, including his own devotional
        poems "Earthworm" and "Seven Stanzas at Easter." Dies
        in hospice, January 27, in Danvers, Massachusetts. Funeral,
        February 2, at St. John's Episcopal Church. Leaves four
        posthumous books in proof: *Endpoint* (April), *My Father's
        Tears* (June), *The Maples Stories* (August), and *Hub Fans
        Bid Kid Adieu* (June 2010). He is cremated, and his ashes
        are buried privately. In July 2010, his children place a me-
        morial headstone, designed and carved by Michael Up-
        dike, near the graves of his parents and grandparents in
        Plow Church Cemetery, Plowville, Pennsylvania.

Note on the Texts

This volume presents texts of the three novels that John Updike published from December 1978, when he was forty-six, to May 1984, when he was fifty-two: *The Coup* (1978), *Rabbit Is Rich* (1981), and *The Witches of Eastwick* (1984). It also presents, in an appendix, Updike's remarks upon accepting the National Book Critics Circle Award and the American Book Award for *Rabbit Is Rich*, as well as a note on *The Witches of Eastwick* included in the deluxe, signed first edition of the novel.

THE COUP

The Coup, Updike's ninth published novel, was begun in the spring of 1977 and completed in March 1978. It was written at 58 West Main Street, Georgetown, Massachusetts, a red clapboard colonial-style house forty miles north of Boston where, from May 1976 through May 1982, Updike lived with his second wife, Martha, and her three boys by a previous marriage.

The novel had its germ in the author's brief encounter with Africa: in early 1973, Updike and his then-wife, Mary, spent four weeks in several countries on the continent—Ghana, Nigeria, Tanzania, Kenya, and Ethiopia—on a Lincoln Lectureship from the Fulbright Board of Foreign Scholarships. (Impressions of the trip made their way into the stories "Ethiopia," written in August of that year, and "Bech Third-Worlds It," written in December 1974; they also inform certain of the book reviews gathered under the rubrics "Africa" in *Picked-Up Pieces* [1975] and "The World Called Third" in *Hugging the Shore* [1983].) Some of the reading that Updike did in preparation for writing *The Coup* is detailed on the acknowledgments page of the novel, printed on page 3 of the present volume.

The Coup was published in hardcover by Alfred A. Knopf, New York, on December 7, 1978. Knopf also published a signed, slip-cased issue of the first printing, on special paper and in a special binding, limited to 350 numbered copies. A British trade printing, offset from the Knopf pages, was issued by Andre Deutsch, Ltd., London, in the spring of 1979.

The eighth printing of the Knopf hardcover, dated June 2003, is the text used here; it was the last overseen by Updike. On June 22,

2006, after inspecting the volume for typographical errors, Updike informed Ken Schneider, his editor Judith Jones's assistant at Knopf, that the corrections he had made to the seventh printing "check out perfectly—even the Cyrillics."

RABBIT IS RICH

Rabbit Is Rich was Updike's tenth published novel. In his introduction to *Rabbit Angstrom* (London and New York: Everyman's Library, 1995), a one-volume omnibus edition of *Rabbit Run* (1960) and its sequels *Rabbit Redux* (1971), *Rabbit Is Rich* (1981), and *Rabbit at Rest* (1990), Updike writes:

"Rabbit is rich, of course, in 1979, only by the standards of his modest working-class background. It was a lucky casual stroke of mine to give the used-car dealer Fred Springer a Toyota franchise in *Rabbit Redux*, for in ten years' time the Japanese-auto invasion had become one of the earmarks of an inflated and teetering American economy, and the Chief Sales Representative of a Toyota agency was well situated to reap advantage from American decline. As these novels had developed, each needed a clear background of news, a 'hook' uniting the personal and national realms. In late June, visiting in Pennsylvania for a few days, I found the hook in the OPEC-induced gasoline shortage and the panicky lines that cars were forming at the local pumps; our host in the Philadelphia suburbs rose early and got our car tank filled so we could get back to New England. A nuclear near disaster had occurred at Three Mile Island in Harrisburg that spring; Carter's approval rating was down to 30 percent; our man in Nicaragua was being ousted by rebels; our man in Iran was deposed and dying; John Wayne was dead; Skylab was falling; and Rabbit, at forty-six, with a wife who drinks too much and a son dropping out of college, could well believe that he and the U.S. were both running out of gas. Except that he doesn't really believe it; *Rabbit Is Rich*, for all its shadows, is the happiest novel of the four, the most buoyant, with happy endings for everybody in it, even the hapless Buddy Inglefinger. The novel includes a number of scenes distinctly broad in their comedy: amid the inflationary abundance of money, Harry and Janice copulate on a blanket of gold coins and stagger beneath the weight of 888 silver dollars as they lug their speculative loot up the eerily deserted main drag of Brewer. A Shakespearean swap and shuffle of couples takes place in the glimmering Arcadia of a Caribbean island, and a wedding rings out at the novel's midpoint: 'Life is sweet, that's what they say,' Rabbit reflects in the last pages. Details poured fast and furious out of my by now thoroughly mapped and populated Diamond County.

The novel is fat, in keeping with its theme of inflation, and Pru is fat with her impending child, whose growth is the book's secret action, its innermost happiness.

"My own circumstances had changed since the writing of *Rabbit Redux*. I was married to another wife, which may account for Janice's lusty rejuvenation, and living in another town, called Georgetown, twenty minutes inland from Ipswich. Each of the Rabbit novels was written in a different setting—*Redux* belonged to my second house in Ipswich, on the winding, winsomely named Labor-in-Vain Road, and to my rented office downtown, above a restaurant whose noontime aromas of lunch rose through the floor each day to urge my writing to its daily conclusion. Whereas Ipswich had a distinguished Puritan history and some grand seaside scenery, Georgetown was an unassuming population knot on the way to other places. It reminded me of Shillington, and the wooden house that we occupied for six years was, like the brick house I had spent my first thirteen years in, long and narrow, with a big back yard and a front view of a well-trafficked street. The town was littered with details I only needed to stoop over and pick up and drop into Mt. Judge's scenery; my evening jogs through Georgetown could slip almost unaltered into Rabbit's panting peregrinations three hundred miles away. In two respects his fortunes had advantage over mine: I was not a member of any country club, nor yet a grandfather. Within five years, I would achieve both privileged states, but for the time being they had to be, like the procedures of a Toyota agency, dreamed up. A dreamy mood pervades the book; Rabbit almost has to keep pinching himself to make sure that his bourgeois bliss is real—that he is, if not as utterly a master of householdry and husbandry as the ineffable Webb Murkett, in the same exalted league.

"Once, in an interview, I had rashly predicted the title of this third installment to be *Rural Rabbit*; some of the words Harry and Janice exchange in the Safe Haven Motel leave the plot open for a country move. But in the event he remained a small-city boy, a creature of sidewalks, gritty alleys, roaring highways, and fast-food franchises. One of *Rabbit, Run*'s adventures for my imagination had been its location in Brewer, whose model, the city of Reading, had loomed for a Shillington child as an immense, remote, menacing, and glamorous metropolis. Rabbit, like every stimulating alter ego, was many things the author was not: a natural athlete, a blue-eyed Swede, sexually magnetic, taller than six feet, impulsive, and urban. The rural rabbit turns out to be Ruth, from the first novel, whom he flushes from her cover in his continued search for a daughter. Farms I knew firsthand, at least in their sensory details, from the years of rural residence my mother had imposed on her family after 1945. Rabbit spying on Ruth from behind the scratchy hedgerow is both Peter Rabbit peeking from behind the cabbages at the menacing Mr. McGregor and I, the self-exiled son, guiltily spying on my mother as, in plucky and self-reliant widowhood, she continued to occupy her sandstone farmhouse and eighty acres all by herself. She did not, in fairness, keep the shell of a school bus in her yard; rather, the town fleet of yellow school buses was visible from the window of my drafty study in Georgetown.

"Though 1979 was running out, I seem to have worked at a leisurely speed: the end of the first draft is dated April 19, 1980, and seven more months went by before my typing of the manuscript was completed on November 23. Happily, and quite to my surprise, *Rabbit Is Rich* won all three of 1981's major American literary prizes for fiction (as well as a place in critic Jonathan Yardley's list of the Ten Worst Books of the Year). An invigorating change of mates, a move to a town that made negligible communal demands, a sense of confronting the world in a fresh relation cleared my head, it may be. The Rabbit novels, coming every ten years, were far from all that I wrote; the novel that precedes *Rabbit Is Rich*, *The Coup*, and the semi-novel that followed it, *Bech Is Back*, in retrospect also seem the replete but airy products of a phase when such powers as I can claim were exuberantly ripe."

Rabbit Is Rich was published in hardcover by Alfred A. Knopf, New York, on October 7, 1981. (An excerpt from chapter 1 had appeared, as "Rabbit Is Rich," in *Playboy* for September 1981.) Knopf also published a signed, slip-cased issue of the first printing, on special paper and in a special binding, limited to 350 numbered copies. A British trade printing, offset from the Knopf pages, was issued by Andre Deutsch, Ltd., London, in the spring of 1982. Deluxe, limited editions of *Rabbit Is Rich* were privately printed by the Franklin Library, Franklin Center, Pennsylvania, in 1985, and Easton Press, Norwalk, Connecticut, in 1993.

From late 1993 through mid-1994, Updike revised the texts of the four Rabbit novels for the omnibus edition *Rabbit Angstrom*, published simultaneously in New York and London by Everyman's Library on October 17, 1995. Updike wrote in the introduction to *Rabbit Angstrom* that "for this fresh printing, apt to be the last that I shall oversee, I have tried to smooth away such inconsistencies [in the series] as have come to my attention." The texts of *Rabbit Angstrom* were reprinted, with a few additional revisions by the author, in a two-volume trade paperback set titled *The Rabbit Novels* (New York: Ballantine Books, 2003). As Updike advised his bibliographer Jack De Bellis that these were the "least incorrect" versions of the texts, the 2003 text of *Rabbit Is Rich*, from *The Rabbit Novels, Volume 2: Rabbit Is Rich / Rabbit at Rest*, is used here.

THE WITCHES OF EASTWICK

The Witches of Eastwick, Updike's eleventh published novel, was begun in January 1983 and completed in August of that year. It was written at 675 Hale Street, Beverly Farms, Massachusetts, a "big white house with a view of saltwater" that Updike purchased in May 1982. (Haven Hill, as the ten-acre estate is locally known, was thirty miles east from his previous residence in Georgetown. It would remain Updike's home and workplace for the rest of his life.) Some of the experiences, landscapes, and literary works that inspired *Witches* are detailed in a note written for a deluxe limited edition of the novel, reprinted on pages 945–48 of the present volume.

The Witches of Eastwick was published in hardcover by Alfred A. Knopf, New York, on May 8, 1984. (An excerpt from chapter 1 had appeared, as "The Witches of Eastwick," in *Playboy* for May 1984.) Knopf also published a signed, slip-cased issue of the first printing, on special paper and in a special binding, limited to 350 numbered copies. Simultaneously with the trade edition, a limited edition was privately printed for members of the "Signed First Edition Society" of the Franklin Library, Franklin Center, Pennsylvania. A British trade printing, offset from the Knopf pages, was issued by Andre Deutsch, Ltd., London, in the summer of 1984. A deluxe, limited edition of *The Witches of Eastwick* was privately printed by Easton Press, Norwalk, Connecticut, in 2000.

The eighth printing of the Knopf hardcover, dated April 2007, is the text used here; it was the last issued during Updike's lifetime. On the flyleaf of his office copy of the first printing of the book, Updike listed the following corrections to be made to later printings of *The Witches of Eastwick*, all of which have been made here: 669.3 et seq., Maleficia [for "Malefica"]; 673.17, equilateral [for "isosceles"]; 681.10, run [for "from running"]; 683.12, two [for "ten"]; 701.14, plumber [for "contractor"]; 727.40, essence, [for "essence"]; 759.31–32, back (the engine also, oddly, was in the rear), start [for "back, start"]; 788.39, was, only on a chair, [for "was only on a chair"]; 815.14, wary, [for "wary"]; 817.15, tidily [for "neatly"]; 910.31, *D-d'*—which [for "*D-d'*, which"]; 922.21, *Hexenstuhl* [for "*Hexestuhl*"].

APPENDIX

The appendix presents three short texts by John Updike, two of them printed in 1983 and related to *Rabbit Is Rich*, the other printed in 1984 and related to *The Witches of Eastwick*.

"Remarks upon accepting the National Book Critics Circle Award for Fiction for *Rabbit Is Rich*" first appeared, under the rubric "On

One's Own Oeuvre," as "In acceptance of the National Book Award for fiction, on January 28, 1982, at the New York Public Library" in Updike's collection *Hugging the Shore: Essays and Criticism* (New York: Alfred A. Knopf, 1983). The text from the first printing of *Hugging the Shore* is used here, under a title supplied by the editor of this volume.

"Remarks upon accepting the American Book Award for Fiction for *Rabbit Is Rich*" first appeared, under the rubric "On One's Own Oeuvre," as "In acceptance of the American Book Award for fiction, on April 27, 1982, in Carnegie Hall" in Updike's collection *Hugging the Shore* (New York: Alfred A. Knopf, 1983). The text from the first printing of *Hugging the Shore* is used here, under a title supplied by the editor of this volume.

"'Special Message' to readers of the Franklin Library's Signed First Edition Society printing of *The Witches of Eastwick*" first appeared, as "A special message for the first edition from John Updike" in a deluxe edition of *The Witches of Eastwick* privately printed in the spring of 1984 by the Franklin Library, Franklin Center, Pennsylvania. It was reprinted—slightly revised, with an expansive footnote, and under the rubric "Literarily Personal"—as "A 'Special Message' for the Franklin Library's First Edition Society printing of *The Witches of Eastwick*" in Updike's collection *Odd Jobs: Essays and Criticism* (New York: Alfred A. Knopf, 1991). The text from the first printing of *Odd Jobs* is used here, under a title supplied by the editor of this volume.

This volume presents the texts of the original printings chosen for inclusion, but does not attempt to reproduce nontextual features of their typographical design. The texts are presented without change, except for the correction of typographical errors. Spelling, punctuation, even capitalization are often expressive features and are not altered, even when inconsistent or irregular. The following is a list of typographical errors corrected, cited by page and line number: 7.40, capital; 12.29, Splendors, Ellelloû; 109.10, 7-Ups; 126.3, "Freshman; 165.3–4, Sulieman,; 192.25, MacDonald's; 241.13, asked.; 262.36, trails.; 276.37, Three-Mile; 286.25, purselane; 342.27, house; 372.26, street.; 388.13, Lofty; 395.3, if off; 406.5, as as boring; 419.21, aglance.; 504.33, somewhat,; 577.29, Janice.; 723.8, Claus Oldenberg; 729.30, Tofrinal,; 845.4, hours; 865.34, he; 869.3, virture,; 873.8, *sanguines*; 873.17, *hatan.*

Notes

In the notes below, the reference numbers denote page and line of this volume (the line count includes chapter headings). No note is made for material that is sufficiently explained in context, nor are there notes for material included in standard desk-reference works such as Webster's Eleventh Collegiate, Biographical, and Geographical dictionaries or comparable internet resources such as Merriam-Webster's online dictionary. Foreign words and phrases are translated only if not translated in the text or if words are not evident English cognates. Biblical quotations are keyed to the King James Version. Quotations from Shakespeare are keyed to *The Riverside Shakespeare*, ed. G. Blakemore Evans (Boston: Houghton Mifflin, 1974). For further biographical information than is contained in the Chronology, see Updike's memoir "The Dogwood Tree: A Boyhood," collected in his miscellany *Assorted Prose* (New York: Knopf, 1965), and the six later memoirs collected in his book *Self-Consciousness* (New York: Knopf, 1989). *Updike*, by Adam Begley (New York: Harper, 2014), is a critical biography. *John Updike's Early Years*, by Jack De Bellis (Bethlehem, Pa.: Lehigh University Press, 2013), tells the story of Updike's life through age eighteen and relates it to the work. Selected print interviews, 1959–93, are collected in *Conversations with John Updike*, edited by James Plath (Jackson: University of Mississippi Press, 1994). In a sequel, *John Updike's Pennsylvania Interviews* (Bethlehem, Pa: Lehigh University Press, 2016), Plath collects interviews and literary profiles from 1965 to 2009. For further bibliographical information than is contained in the Note on the Texts, see *John Updike: A Bibliography of Primary and Secondary Materials, 1948–2007*, by Jack De Bellis and Michael Broomfield (New Castle, Del.: Oak Knoll Press, 2007).

THE COUP

5.33–34　*mal à l'estomac*] French: stomachache.

6.12–13　trans-Saharan traveller] The French explorer René Caillié (1799–1838), author of *Travels through Central Africa to Timbuctoo, and across the Great Desert, to Morocco, Performed in the Years 1824–1828* (1830).

7.28　*loi-cadre* of 1956] French legislative reforms that gave its overseas territories a greater degree of self-government.

9.15   the fabled Caliph Haroun ar-Raschid] Eighth-century caliph of Baghdad who plays a legendary role in *The Thousand and One Nights*.

9.23   Dienbienphu] The battle of Dien Bien Phu, March 13–May 7, 1954, ended in a Viet Minh victory over the French.

9.27   General Giap] Vo Nguyen Giap (1911–2013), commander of the Viet Minh army.

9.37   Bao Dai] Last emperor of the Nguyen dynasty (1913–1997), who reigned as emperor of Annam, 1926–45, and subsequently as chief of state of South Vietnam until ousted in 1955.

15.9   Nkrumah, Farouk] Kwame Nkrumah (1909–1972), Ghanaian independence leader and the first president of the Republic of Ghana, 1960–66; Farouk (1920–1965), the last king of Egypt.

15.29–30   *Der Spatz in der Hand . . . Dach*] German saying: The sparrow in your hand is better than the pigeon on the roof.

18.20   *pombe*] Swahili: alcoholic beverage, a word often used for beer.

19.9–11   call to first prayer, *salāt al-maghrib . . .* day has begun."] The Islamic day starts at sunset. Starting from midnight, the five obligatory Islamic daily prayers are *salāt al-fajr*, prayed at dawn before sunrise, *salāt al-zuhr* at midday, *salāt al-'asr* in the later afternoon, *salāt al-maghrib* after the sun sets, and *salāt al-'isha*, between sunset and midnight.

20.3   *piste*] French: track, tarmac.

21.16   MIRVed] The acronym stands for "Multiple Independently Targetable Reentry Vehicles," referring to nuclear missiles containing several warheads that could be directed toward a number of targets from a single missile.

22.8–9   "*N'alcoolisons pas . . . cela*,"] French: Let's not drink alcohol, the God of our people forbids it.

22.26   "Lumumba,"] Patrice Lumumba (1925–1961), a leader of the Congolese independence movement, was the first prime minister of the Congo, June 23–September 5, 1960. He was arrested on December 1 by troops loyal to Colonel Joseph Mobutu and shot on January 17, 1961, by Katanga secessionists led by Moise Tshombe, with possible CIA involvement in the assassination.

22.27   Stakhanov."] Alexei Stakhanov (1906–1977), a Russian coal miner in the Donets Basin whose exceptional productivity was praised by the Soviet government starting in 1935 as part of a campaign to speed up industrial production.

22.28   "Nasser, *da*, Sadat, *nyet*"] Gamal Abdel Nasser (1918–1970), president of Egypt, 1956–70, aligned Egypt with the U.S.S.R. and was decorated as a Hero of the Soviet Union; bilateral relations deteriorated under his successor

Anwar Sadat (1918–1981), president of Egypt, 1970–81, who expelled Soviet military advisors and withdrew from a friendship treaty between the countries.

22.29 Sholokov] Russian novelist and Soviet official Mikhail Aleksandrovich Sholokhov (1905–1984), author of *And Quiet Flows the Don* (1928).

22.29 *écrasez* Solzhenitsyn] Crush Solzhenitsyn, referring to the Russian writer and dissident Aleksandr Solzhenitsyn (1918–2008).

26.17 *galabieh*] Or djellaba, a hooded, loose-fitting garment covering the length of the body.

26.20 *tobol*] A type of drum.

26.23 *caïd*] Chieftain.

26.29 *dibia*] Diviner.

27.31 *tagilmust*] A long indigo garment comprising a turban and a face-covering, worn by Tuareg men.

30.7 Négritudinist] Négritude was a literary and cultural movement of Francophone African and Caribbean writers whose primary theorists and adherents included the Senegalese poet and statesman Léopold Sédar Senghor (1906–2001) and the poet Aimé Césaire (1913–2008), born in Martinique.

30.9 Valéry] The French poet Paul Valéry (1871–1945).

30.9–10 *Le Livre de Poche*] French publishing imprint ("The Pocket Book") of compact, inexpensive paperbacks founded in 1953.

32.15 *aftouh*] Desert.

34.9 FAO people in Rome] The United Nations' Food and Agricultural Organization has its headquarters in Rome.

41.4 *voitures*] French: cars.

45.9 *Dasein*] German: being, existence.

55.14 *barasa*] Rum.

57.21 *kaikai*] Distilled palm wine.

57.25 *lungi*] Sarong; skirt-like lower garment.

57.35 *boubou*] Robe-like garment worn by both men and women.

61.1–2 Plato's cave] See Plato, *The Republic*, Book VII.

68.24–25 *Mimosa ferruginea*] Rusty acacia.

70.5 *alghaita, kakaki, hu-hu*] Algaita, wooden oboe-like instrument originating in West Africa; kakaki, also a West African instrument, a long metal trumpet; hu-hu, a string instrument originating in China.

70.20 *kangas*] Colorful wraparound garments worn mostly by women but also by men.

73.18 General Thieu] Vietnamese military leader and politician Nguyễn Văn Thiệu (1923–2001), president of South Vietnam, 1967–75.

74.39 *Nouvelles en noire et blanc*] French: News in black and white.

75.36–37 the hardy *Hedysarum alhagi* eulogized by Caillié.] The "thistle of the desert" described by René Caillié (see note 6.12–13).

82.19 *ohwari*] Oware, West African board game.

84.24 *buibui*] Shawl-like garment.

85.1 Arthur Schlesingers] The historians Arthur Schlesinger, Sr. (1888–1965), whose books include *The New Deal in Action, 1933–1938* (1939), *Paths to the Present* (1949), and *The American as Reformer* (1950), and his son Arthur Schlesinger, Jr. (1917–2007), a speechwriter for Adlai Stevenson and John F. Kennedy, an official in the Kennedy administration, and author of *The Age of Jackson* (1945) and *The Vital Center* (1949).

86.26 "*Je vois.*"] French: I see.

89.4–5 *La chasse de la licorne* and other Flemish *menues verdures*] *The Hunt of the Unicorn*, seven tapestries comprising a late Medieval or early Renaissance series often referred to as the Unicorn Tapestries and currently in the collection of the Metropolitan Museum of Art; *verdures* refers to the ornamental background showing foliage.

90.13 Mr. Agnew] Spiro Agnew (1918–1996), vice president of the United States, 1969–73.

91.24 USIS] United States Information Service.

99.7 *Petrea volubilis*] Queen's wreath or purple wreath, an evergreen flowering vine.

100.25 the *banco* walls] Mudbrick walls made from a fermented mixture of mud and grain husks.

101.17 *zawiya*] Arabic: prayer room, a term used for a religious school in North and West Africa.

102.25 *Tallaqtuki*] Arabic: I repudiated you.

106.2–3 *Beneath the stars . . . Libya.*] From "The House-top: A Night Piece (July, 1863)," published in *Battle-Pieces and Aspects of the War*, by Herman Melville (1866). See Updike's note on page 3 of the current volume.

106.14 *reg*, *erg*, and *hammada*] Features of the Sahara Desert: a desert pavement, a high sand dune, and a rock plateau, respectively.

109.39 *douceur*] French: pleasantness.

111.30 mark of Cain or Ham] After murdering his brother Abel, the biblical Cain was condemned by God to wander the earth and was given a "mark . . .

lest any finding him should kill him" (Genesis 4:15). Ham was one of the biblical Noah's sons. His own son Canaan, because Ham had seen the drunken and
naked Noah asleep in his tent, was cursed to be "a servant of servants . . . to
his brethren." Ham has often been regarded as a black man because African
peoples were listed among his descendants in Genesis 10:6–20 or because,
according to a view first put forth in the fifteenth century, the descendants of
Canaan were black while those of his uncles Shem and Japheth (Noah's other
sons) were white.

114.6–7 Prophet Mr. Farrad Muhammad] W. D. Fard Muhammad, who
founded the Nation of Islam, a Black separatist religious movement, in Detroit
in 1931. He disappeared under mysterious circumstances in 1934. The movement was led thereafter by Elijah Muhammad (born Elijah Poole, 1897–1975)
from 1934 until his death.

116.13 Willy Mays] Hall of Fame centerfielder Willie Mays (b. 1931), who
played most of his Major League Baseball career for the New York and San
Francisco Giants baseball teams.

117.34 *Takbir!*] Arabic phrase for the proclamation of God's greatness, "Al-
lahu akbar!"

118.11–12 Московская . . . особая водка] Russian: Moscow . . . special
vodka.

119.20 Dinah Washington and Kay Starr] Singers Dinah Washington (born
Ruth Lee Jones, 1924–1963) and Kay Starr (born Catherine Laverne Starks,
1922–2016), popular from the 1940s through the 1960s.

121.11 Meroë] Prosperous ancient city in present-day Sudan, in the ancient
kingdom of Kush.

125.22 *Asseyez-vous*] French: Sit down.

126.9–12 Racine . . . Villon . . . Ronsard] French writers: playwright Jean
Racine (1639–1699) and the poets François Villon (1431–after 1463) and Pierre
de Ronsard (1524–1585).

128.5 Hudson's] Flagship store of department-store chain, a 25-story building
occupying a city block of Woodward Avenue in downtown Detroit.

128.34 *Nous buvons le pissat.*] French: We drink piss.

129.4 dingbat Daley] Richard J. Daley (1902–1976), mayor of Chicago for
twenty-one years, dying in office on December 20, 1976.

131.14 Messenger of Allah himself] Elijah Muhammad (see note 114.6–7).

132.4–7 the then recent Supreme Court decision . . . school] In *Brown v.
Board of Education* (of Topeka, Kansas), decided on Monday, May 17, 1954,
the Supreme Court unanimously ruled that segregation in public schools violated the equal protection clause of the Fourteenth Amendment and that

the doctrine of "separate but equal" set forth in the *Plessy v. Ferguson* railway segregation case (1896) had "no place" in public education.

132.22   *sous-officiers*] French: noncommissioned officers.

133.19–21   Nation of Islam took a mortal wound . . . Malcolm's killer] Malcolm X (born Malcolm Little, 1925–1965) was assassinated in Harlem by members of the Nation of Islam on February 21, 1965. Having broken with Elijah Muhammad in March 1964, he had made a pilgrimage to Mecca and had converted to Sunni Islam. Thomas Hagan, also known as Talmadge Hayer, a member of the Newark temple of the Nation of Islam, was indicted for the murder on March 11, 1965, along with two Black Muslims from New York, Thomas 15X Johnson and Norman 3X Butler. All three men were found guilty on March 10, 1966, and were sentenced to life terms. In an affidavit filed in 1977, Hayer admitted his involvement in the murder and stated that his accomplices were four men from New Jersey, not Johnson and Butler.

134.11   *caserne*] French: barracks.

134.11–12   *Aux Armes! Les Diables Jaunes!*] French: To arms! The yellow devils!

134.14–15   Dhū 'l Hijja . . . Muharram . . . Safar] Months of the Islamic calendar.

137.31–32   King Leopold] The Belgian king Leopold II (1835–1909), whose brutal and exploitive rule of the Belgian Congo was responsible for widespread atrocities and millions of deaths.

137.36   *la France, d'Outremer*] France's overseas territories.

139.6–7   General Faidherbe] Louis Faidherbe (1818–1889), governor of Senegal, 1852–61, 1863–65.

139.7   Hourst expedition] An expedition on the Niger River from Timbuktu to the Niger Delta led by the French military officer Émile Auguste Léon Hourst (1864–1940).

139.8–9   Colonel Toutée's famous diary] *Diary of an Officer of the Tunisian Expeditionary Corps* (1881) by Georges Joseph Toutée (1855–1927).

142.32   David Riesman] Influential American sociologist (1909–2002) best known for *The Lonely Crowd* (1950).

143.1   Daddy Warbucks] Industrialist who befriends Annie in *Little Orphan Annie*, comic strip created by Harold Gray (1894–1968) in 1921.

144.20–21   Géricault's painting of the raft of the *Medusa*] *The Raft of the Medusa* (1818–19), monumental painting by Théodore Géricault (1791–1824) depicting the struggle for survival on board a large raft by crew members of a vessel shipwrecked off the coast of present-day Mauritania in 1816.

148.16   Dahomey] Now the Republic of Benin.

148.21   *son-et-lumière*] French: sound and light.

148.32   *Je sais*] French: I know.

151.11–12   *Plus Haute Quarantaine*] Top Forty.

153.12   *la petite mort*] The little death, French phrase for orgasm.

156.1   *Prosnis', chernzhopyi!*] Russian: Wake up, black ass!

156.15–16   "*Eta chernaya pizd . . . sifilis.*"] Russian: "This black cunt is not so lively, eh?" "Calm down, they all have syphilis."

156.22–24   *Vive le peuple . . . décadent!*"] French: "Long live the people and the socialist and Islamic brotherhood! Crush the capitalist infamy, monopolized and very, very decadent!"

156.37   LA TÊTE QUI PARLE] French: The Speaking Head.

156.37   Мавзолей Эдуму Четвертого] Russian: Mausoleum of Edumu IV.

161.20–21   post-Sukarno] Sukarno (1901–1970), Indonesian nationalist leader and the country's first president, removed from power in the wake of an abortive 1965 coup in which he was implicated; the country's next leader, Suharto (1921–2008), became acting president in March 1967 and ruled the country until 1998.

161.26   street-plan cribbed from Baron Haussmann] From 1853 French civil administrator Georges-Eugène Haussmann (1809–1891) directed the radical transformation of Paris under Louis-Napoléon (Napoléon III), which included the destruction of many of the city's medieval streets and the creation of wide boulevards.

161.29   Rodin's *Balzac*] *Monument to Balzac* (1898), posthumous portrait of the French novelist Honoré de Balzac (1799–1850) by the French sculptor Auguste Rodin (1840–1917).

161.40   Ian Smith] Rhodesian politician (1919–2007), prime minister of Rhodesia, 1965–79, who defended white supremacist and non-majority rule.

162.35   Pound: Totalitarianism] The American poet Ezra Pound (1885–1972) supported the Fascist regime of Benito Mussolini in Italy in his writings and in anti-American radio broadcasts on behalf of the Italian government aired during World War II.

164.21–22   Guy Mollet's *loi-cadre* proclamation] See note 7.28. Mollet (1905–1975), Socialist politician who served as prime minister of France, 1956–57.

165.3   *minette*] French: a pretty, superficial young woman.

172.18–19   FERMÉ, закрыто, مغلق . . . *lu.*] Closed. . . . Open 9 A.M. to noon, 2 P.M. to 5 P.M. Entry tickets 50 *lu*.

173.1–2   *La tête du roi*] French: The head of the king.

173.4 Moscow Arts Theatre] Moscow Art Theatre, theatrical company devoted to innovative interpretations of the Russian repertoire, co-founded by the Russian director and acting theorist Constantin Stanislavsky (1863–1938), whose ideas form the basis of Method acting.

175.15 the Mahdi.] The messiah.

177.24 *mitrailleuse*] French: machine gun.

177.25 Berthier] The French engineer Emile Berthier, inventor of the family of rifles and carbines bearing his name that were used by the French army from 1890 onward.

177.38–39 "Colonel . . . *je présume.*"] Allusion to "Dr. Livingstone, I presume," well-known greeting of the Anglo-American journalist Henry Morton Stanley (1841–1904) on encountering, near Lake Tanganyika, the long-lost Scottish explorer and missionary David Livingstone (1813–1873).

178.31 Космос] Cosmos, Russian brand of cigarettes.

181.35 *disparue*] French: disappeared.

182.14 Doris Day] Film actor and popular singer (1922–2019).

183.40 Mungo Park] Scottish explorer (1771–1806), the first Westerner to explore the central portion of the Niger River, author of *Travels in the Interior Districts of Africa, Performed in the Years 1795–97.*

185.18–19 Afrikafreiheitswursthaus] German: sausage house of African freedom.

185.38 new Vice-President] Gerald Ford succeeded Spiro Agnew as vice president in the Nixon administration on December 6, 1973.

186.11 the Arabs with their embargo.] In retaliation for support of Israel in the 1973 Yom Kippur War, Arab oil-exporting countries instituted an oil embargo against the United States (among other countries), October 1973–May 1974, causing gasoline shortages, rationing, and a spike in the price of oil and gas.

187.15 like the ancient Tiberius] Roman emperor (42 BCE–37 CE; reigned 14 CE–37 CE).

193.12 *cinq et dix*] French: five-and-ten.

195.31 *baraka*] Divine blessing.

197.13–14 "Love Letters in the Sand."] Song (1931) by J. Fred Coots (1897–1985), words by Nick Kenny (1895–1975) and Charles Kenny (1898–1992), that was a hit for the singer Pat Boone (b. 1934) in 1957.

197.19 *képi*] French-style military cap with a flat, circular top and a bill.

208.16 Axum!] Or Aksum, ancient empire based in northern Ethiopia.

210.4   SAHAIR EL-CALAMAWY] Suhayr al-Qalamawi (1911–1997), Egyptian literary critic, fiction writer, and feminist activist. Updike met her when both writers delivered papers at the conference on Arab and American cultures sponsored by the American Enterprise Institute, Washington, D.C., on September 22–23, 1976. Her paper, from which the epigraph for chapter VII is taken, was later printed, as "The Impact of Tradition on Modern Arabic Literature," in the journal *Mundus Artium* 10:1 (1977).

212.7–8   "Love Me Tender," the youthful Presley requested] Elvis Presley's hit single "Love Me Tender" (1956) was a musical adaptation of a Civil War ballad.

212.8   "Cry Me a River," Johnny Ray begged] "Cry Me a River" (1953), song by Arthur Hamilton (b. 1926), a success when recorded by Julie Hamilton in 1955; the singer Johnnie Ray (1927–1990) had a huge hit in 1952 with "Cry," song written the year before by Churchill Kohlman (1906–1983).

212.8–9   "Qué Será, Será," Doris Day philosophized] In the Alfred Hitchcock film *The Man Who Knew Too Much* (1956), Doris Day introduced the popular song "Que Será, Será (Whatever Will Be, Will Be)," music by Jay Livingston (1915–2001), words by Ray Evans (1915–2007); her recording was a hit single in the United States and abroad.

212.12   "True Love,"] Song (1956) by Cole Porter (1891–1964) for the film *High Society*, in which it was performed by Bing Crosby (1903–1977) and Grace Kelly (1929–1982).

212.13   "Tammy."] Hit song (1957) for the actor and singer Debbie Reynolds (1932–2016) by Jay Livingston (1915–2001) and Ray Evans (1915–2007), featured in the film *Tammy and the Bachelor*.

212.15   "The Yellow Rose . . . Wanderer"] Popular American folk song; English-language version of "Der fröhliche Wanderer," song (1953) by Friedrich Wilhelm Möller (1911–1993) set to words by Florenz Friedrich Sigismund (1791–1877).

212.19–20   "A Whole Lotta Shakin' . . . Lewis] "Whole Lotta Shakin' Goin' On," hit recording in 1957 for the rock-and-roll singer and pianist Jerry Lee Lewis (b. 1935).

212.22–23   "The River Kwai March"] March composed by Malcolm Arnold (1921–2006) featured in the film *The Bridge on the River Kwai* (1957).

212.25   Oh Rose] "Oh, Rose Marie," doo-wop hit of 1959, written and performed by the a cappella quintet the Fascinators.

212.25   Secret Love] Song by Sammy Fain (1902–1989), words by Paul Francis Webster (1907–1984), from the film musical *Calamity Jane* (1953).

212.25–26   Queen of the Hop] Song by Woody Harris (1911–1985), a hit for Bobby Darin (1936–1973) in 1958.

212.26 Sugarfoot] Theme song of the television western *Sugarfoot*, 1957–61, composed by Max Steiner (1888–1971) for a 1951 film of the same name, with words by Mack David (1912–1993).

212.26 Standing on the Corner] Song from the musical *The Most Happy Fella* (1956) by Frank Loesser (1910–1969), a hit for the Four Lads in 1956.

212.26–27 Autumn Leaves] "Les Feuilles Mortes" (1945), song by the Hungarian-French composer Joseph Kosma (1905–1969), with words by the French poet Jacques Prévert (1900–1977). The English lyrics are by Johnny Mercer.

212.27 Naughty Lady of Shady Lane] "The Naughty Lady of Shady Lane," song (c. 1954) by Sid Tepper (1918–2015) and Roy C. Bennett (1918–2015), a hit for the Ames Brothers in 1954–55.

213.12 even for a namesake of Noah's grandson.] See note 111.30.

214.9–10 Crater Copernicus . . . Lacus Somniorum.] Prominent lunar crater and lunar plain, respectively.

216.23–24 theme song from *2001*, by Richard Strauss.] "Also sprach Zarathustra" (1896), Op. 30, tone poem by the German composer Richard Strauss (1864–1949).

221.24 *Petrea volubilis*] Queen's wreath or purple wreath.

222.20 "*Tallaqtukï. Tallaqtukï. Tallaqtukï.*"] See note 102.25.

223.25–26 *citron pressé*] French: pressed lemon, a kind of lemonade.

226.11 Didot fonts] Group of serif fonts developed in the late eighteenth and early nineteenth centuries by the French Didot family of printers.

226.14 Négritude] See note 30.7.

226.14–15 Gide, Sartre, and Genet] The French writer André Gide (1869–1951), whose many novels include *The Counterfeiters* (1925); the French existentialist philosopher, playwright, and novelist Jean-Paul Sartre (1905–1980); the French poet, essayist, and novelist Jean Genet (1910–1986), author of the novel *Our Lady of the Flowers* (1944).

230.38 *crapaudine*] Punishment used by the French military that was abolished in the early twentieth century. The man being punished would be placed on his stomach and have his legs and arms pulled backward until they touched, causing locked joints and muscle spasms.

233.6 *les joujous*] French: the toys.

234.5 *fool*] Fava beans.

234.8 *Wirtschaftswunderarchitekten.*] German: architects of the economic miracle, referring to West Germany's postwar economic recovery.

238.35 *Well-Tempered Clavier*] Collection (book I, 1722; book II, 1742) of keyboard preludes and fugues by Johann Sebastian Bach (1685–1750).

243.9–10   Delacroix skimmed the Maghrib] The French artist Eugène Delacroix (1798–1863) accompanied a French diplomatic mission to North Africa in 1832, and his travels there exerted a lasting impact on the subject matter of his works.

243.11   Josephine Baker, Sidney Bechet] Josephine Baker (1906–1975), African American dancer, singer, and actor who was enormously popular in France, where she spent most of her career; the saxophonist and clarinetist Sidney Bechet (1897–1959).

243.38   *sanza*] Small thumb piano, also known as a *kalimba* or *mberi*.

RABBIT IS RICH

246.5   George Babbitt] Protagonist of *Babbitt* (1922), satirical novel by Sinclair Lewis (1885–1951).

246.9   "A Rabbit as King of the Ghosts"] Poem by Wallace Stevens (1879–1955), published in *Poetry* magazine in October 1937 and collected in his volume *Parts of a World* (1945).

248.33   Prince Valiant] Long-running, syndicated Sunday newspaper comic strip created in 1937 by the Canadian cartoonist Hal Foster (1892–1982).

251.22   Skylab could fall on your head] Skylab, an American space station launched unmanned in 1973 for the conducting of scientific experiments, began losing altitude in orbit due to greater-than-expected aerodynamic drag caused by sunspot activity and its effect on Earth's atmosphere. The last of the three three-person missions sent to the station was completed in 1974. Although it was supposed to be transported back to Earth in the mid-1980s (by an as-yet-uncompleted space shuttle), Skylab could not maintain its orbit and disintegrated upon re-entry into Earth's atmosphere on July 12, 1979, with pieces of the station landing in western Australia. In anticipation of its descent in 1979 there was widespread speculation about where the wreckage would land and the damage it might cause.

253.29   Paul Dudley White] Pioneering American cardiologist and public-health expert (1886–1973), a co-founder of the American Heart Association.

264.35   Bowa] Philadelphia Phillies shortstop Larry Bowa (b. 1945), later the team's manager.

264.36–265.4   big salary? . . . Rose] After the 1978 season, the Phillies signed free-agent infielder Pete Rose (b. 1941), who had been a star with the Cincinnati Reds, to a four-year, $3.225 million contract.

269.14   *Manna mou*] Greek: My mother.

271.22–23   "How High the Moon"] Jazz song (1940) by Morgan Lewis (1906–1968), words by Nancy Hamilton (1908–1985).

271.24   "Puttin' on the Ritz"] Song (1927) by Irving Berlin (1888–1989).

274.36–40 "Stayin' Alive" . . . John Travolta theme song . . . Sweathogs from Mr. Kotter's class] The Bee Gees' hit "Stayin' Alive" accompanies the opening sequence of the film *Saturday Night Fever* (1977), introducing Tony Manero, a disco dancer from Brooklyn played by John Travolta (b. 1954). Travolta also belonged to the cast of the ABC television sitcom *Welcome Back, Kotter*, 1975–79, as one of the Sweathogs, the tough but sympathetic teenagers being taught in a Brooklyn high school by Mr. Kotter, played by Gabe Kaplan (b. 1945).

276.24–25 ALIEN . . . ALCATRAZ] Films from 1979: *Alien*, directed by Ridley Scott (b. 1937); *Moonraker*, James Bond movie directed by Lewis Gilbert (1920–2018); *The Main Event*, directed by Howard Zieff (1927–2009); *Escape from Alcatraz*, directed by Don Siegel (1912–1991).

276.31 Egyptian like Sharif] Omar Sharif (1932–2015), whose starring roles included *Lawrence of Arabia* (1962) and *Doctor Zhivago* (1965). He played opposite Barbra Streisand in *Funny Girl* (1968), directed by William Wyler (1902–1981), film about the comedian, singer, and actor Fanny Brice (1891–1951).

276.32 like Ryan O'Neal] Actor (b. 1941) who starred opposite Barbra Streisand in the comedy *What's Up, Doc?* (1972), directed by Peter Bogdanovich (b. 1939).

276.33 Woody Allen . . . Diane Keaton] Actor-screenwriter-director Woody Allen (b. 1935) worked with actor Diane Keaton (b. 1946) in eight of his films, including *Sleeper* (1973) and *Annie Hall* (1977).

276.37 Three Mile Island] On March 28, 1979, a pressure-valve malfunction at the Three Mile Island nuclear power plant near Harrisburg, Pennsylvania, resulted in a partial meltdown of a reactor core. There were no fatalities due to the accident, which released only a very small amount of radiation.

276.38 Somoza in trouble too.] In Nicaragua, the dictatorship headed since 1936 by members of the Somoza family was overthrown in July 1979 in a revolution led by the Sandinista National Liberation Front.

276.39 Florida killer] In 1976 John Spenkelink (1949–1979) was convicted of first-degree murder and sentenced to death by the State of Florida, prompting widespread objections to the penalty. He was granted last-minute stays of execution by a judge of the U.S. Court of Appeals for the Fifth Circuit and by Justice Thurgood Marshall of the U.S. Supreme Court, but both stays were vacated and Spenkelink was electrocuted on May 25, 1979. Executions in the United States had been suspended in the wake of the Supreme Court's decision in *Furman v. Georgia* (1972) but resumed after its decision in *Gregg v. Georgia* (1976) upheld the constitutionality of state death-penalty statutes. Spenkelink was the first man unwillingly executed in the United States after 1976; the convicted murderer Gary Gilmore (1940–1977) claimed he wanted to be put to death.

276.39–277.1   former leader of Great Britain's Liberal Party . . . former homosexual lover.] Jeremy Thorpe (1929–2014), leader of the Liberal Party (now the Liberal Democrats), 1967–76, was accused of hiring Andrew Newton, an airline pilot, to murder Norman Scott (b. 1940), who had claimed that he and Thorpe had had a two-year homosexual relationship in the early 1960s (before homosexual acts between consenting partners in private had been decriminalized) and had sold letters from Thorpe during the time of their alleged relationship to newspapers. On October 23, 1975, Newton shot Scott's dog with a handgun and threatened to kill Scott, but his gun appears to have jammed. Thorpe was acquitted of the conspiracy charges on June 22, 1979.

277.9   murder most foul?] Words spoken by the ghost of King Hamlet in Shakespeare, *Hamlet*, I.v.31.

277.25   records of a woman breathing] Songs on Donna Summer's album *Love to Love You Baby* (1975).

279.35–36   Polynesian in an old Jon Hall movie.] The American actor Jon Hall (1915–1979), raised in Tahiti, starred in films set in the South Pacific such as *The Hurricane* (1937), *Aloma of the South Seas* (1941), and *The Tuttles of Tahiti* (1942).

285.2   the Jeffersons] CBS television sitcom, 1975–85, developed by Norman Lear (b. 1922) as a spin-off of *All in the Family* (see note 316.31) and starring Sherman Hemsley (1938–2012) and Isabel Sanford (1917–2004).

297.2   Palmer . . . Nicklaus] Champion golfers Arnold Palmer (1929–2016) and Jack Nicklaus (b. 1940).

297.7–9   Aaron . . . Ruth's record.] Outfielder Hank Aaron (b. 1934) broke the long-standing Major League home-run record of Babe Ruth (1895–1948) on April 8, 1974.

297.34   Edgar Cayce] American faith healer, clairvoyant, and author (1877–1945).

297.37–38   Tibetan Book of the Dead] English title (from W. Y. Evans-Wentz's 1927 translation) of *Bardo Thodol*, Tibetan Buddhist text intended as a guide to the *bardo* (intermediate state between death and rebirth).

299.32   like a du Pont.] The wealthy du Pont family has exerted an outsized influence on social, political, and business affairs in Delaware. Its wealth derived from the gunpowder business founded by the French chemist Éleuthère Irénée du Pont de Nemours (1771–1834) near Wilmington, the forerunner of a global chemical and engineering corporation.

301.36   Fire Ozark] Danny Ozark (1923–2009), manager of the Philadelphia Phillies, was fired on August 31, 1979, during his seventh season with the team.

304.8   Bjorn Borg, and this skier Stenmark.] Champion tennis player Björn Borg (b. 1956) and skier Ingemar Stenmark (b. 1956), both from Sweden.

306.26   *Andy Mellon*] The financier Andrew Mellon (1855–1937), who served as secretary of the treasury in 1921–32.

307.26–27   Liz Taylor in *A Place in the Sun*.] Based on Theodore Dreiser's novel *An American Tragedy* (1925), the film *A Place in the Sun* (1951) was directed by George Stevens (1904–1975) and starred Montgomery Clift (1920–1966) and Elizabeth Taylor (1932–2011).

309.1   Ida Lupino.] English actor and director (1918–1995) whose prolific career included films such as *They Drive by Night* (1940), *High Sierra* (1941), and *On Dangerous Ground* (1951).

316.31   *All in the Family*] CBS television sitcom, 1971–79, starring Carroll O'Connor (1924–2001) as Archie Bunker, a working-class man in Queens, New York City, whose prejudices conflict with the views of his progressive son-in-law and daughter.

319.28   *Mangiamo, prego!*] Italian: Let's eat, please!

322.33–35   Carmen Miranda . . . Saludos Amigos movies.] Carmen Miranda (1909–1955) was a Portuguese-born Brazilian singer and actor known for her outlandish hats and colorful costumes. She starred in movie musicals such as *Down Argentine Way* (1940) and *The Gang's All Here* (1943), among the Hollywood films serving as a cultural complement to President Franklin Roosevelt's "Good Neighbor" policy, which sought to improve relations with South American countries. The Disney animated film *Saludos Amigos* (Hello Friends, 1942) comprised four short films with Latin American settings.

325.11   *mastoras*] Greek: masters, skilled artisans.

331.11–14   Carter's energy speech? . . . crisis in confidence.] In a televised speech of July 15, 1979, President Carter addressed the nation's energy crisis and outlined a plan to reduce American dependence on foreign oil. In what would come to be known as the "malaise" speech (a word not used in the address), he also pointed to a broader national "crisis of confidence."

337.4   Red Skelton] American comedian (1913–1997), a film actor and host of several radio and television programs bearing his name.

337.4   Buzz Aldrin] American astronaut (b. 1930), a member of the Apollo 11 moon mission in 1969 who, with Neil Armstrong, walked on the lunar surface, the first humans to do so.

337.19   Chappaquiddick] On the night of July 18, 1969, Mary Jo Kopechne (1940–1969), a political campaign worker, left a party on Chappaquiddick Island off Martha's Vineyard, Massachusetts, with Massachusetts U.S. senator Edward Kennedy (1932–2009). She died after Kennedy drove his car off a wooden bridge into a tidal inlet. Kennedy survived the accident and did not report the incident to local police until after Kopechne's body had been found the next day. He pled guilty to leaving the scene of the accident and received a suspended sentence. Irregularities in the investigation contributed to suspicions of a cover-up, and questions about the incident followed Kennedy for the rest of his life.

347.24 *Waltons*] CBS family drama, 1972–81, based on the writings of novelist Earl Hamner, Jr. (1916–2016), and set in rural Virginia during the 1930s and '40s.

354.28 Kent State Four] Thirteen unarmed students at Kent State University were shot, four of them fatally, by members of the Ohio National Guard on May 4, 1970, during a protest against the Vietnam War.

360.22 *engonaki.*"] Greek: grandson.

362.19 Peter Max] German-born American illustrator and graphic artist (b. 1937) whose psychedelic colors, simplified shapes, and neo–Art Nouveau lettering influenced design sense in the late 1960s.

363.19 *Reide, reide, Geile*] First line of a Pennsylvania Dutch nursery rhyme: "Ride, ride a horse." The remainder is given at lines 382.40–383.1: "Every hour a mile, / When it goes over the stump, / The baby falls down!"

366.5 *Jaws*] Film (1975), summer box-office hit directed by Steven Spielberg (b. 1946).

377.36–378.2 Charlie's Angels . . . Farrah Fawcett-Majors] *Charlie's Angels*, ABC television series, 1976–81, featuring a trio of female private investigators; Farrah Fawcett (also known by her married name Farrah Fawcett-Majors, 1947–2009) left the cast after its first season and was replaced by Cheryl Ladd (b. 1951).

378.20 G. I. Gurdjieff] George Gurdjieff (c. 1866–1949), Armenian-born teacher of mystical philosophy who settled in France after the Russian Revolution.

382.40–383.1 *Reide . . . nunner!*"] See note 363.19.

388.12–13 *Build thee . . . soul.*] See the fifth and final stanza of "The Chambered Nautilus" (1858), poem by Oliver Wendell Holmes, Sr. (1809–1894): "Build thee more stately mansions, O my soul, / As the swift seasons roll!"

389.28–29 AGATHA MANHATTAN MEATBALLS AMITYVILLE HORROR] Films from 1979: the thriller *Agatha*, directed by Michael Apted (b. 1941); the comedies *Manhattan* and *Meatballs*, directed, respectively, by Woody Allen and Ivan Reitman (b. 1946); the horror film *The Amityville Horror*, directed by Stuart Rosenberg (1927–2007) from a script by Sandor Stern (b. 1936), adapted from the "nonfiction novel" of the same name (1977) by Jay Anson (1921–1980).

394.39 pitcher like Jim Bunning] Hall of Fame professional baseball player (1931–2017) who pitched for the Philadelphia Phillies, 1964–67; later a U.S. congressman and U.S. senator from Kentucky.

403.8 attacked by that killer rabbit?"] After President Carter reported on April 20, 1979, that he had used a paddle to ward off a swamp rabbit swimming toward his boat near his hometown of Plains, Georgia, media accounts played up the story as a "killer rabbit" attack on the president.

403.22 blew up this old gent Mountbatten] Louis, 1st Earl Mountbatten of Burma (1900–1979), British naval commander, statesman, and cousin of Queen Elizabeth II, was killed on August 27, 1979, on his boat off the western coast of Ireland by a bomb planted by members of the Provisional Irish Republican Army.

408.8–9 the movie *2001*] *2001: A Space Odyssey* (1969), film directed by Stanley Kubrick (1928–1999).

414.21–22 cotton nighties . . . Time to Retire ad] Beginning in 1910, the Fisk Rubber Co. ran a popular series of "Time to Retire" advertisements featuring a young boy in nightclothes, holding a candle in his left hand and grasping a tire the size of his body with his right hand and arm.

417.34 *Edge of Night.*] *The Edge of Night*, soap opera on CBS, 1956–75, and ABC, 1975–84.

423.31 like that guy's on *Mad*] Alfred E. Neuman, mascot of the satirical comic book (and, later, humor magazine) *MAD*, 1952–2019, with a trademark gap-toothed smile and the tagline "What, me worry?" (sometimes "What? Me worry?").

428.3–4 movie about Encounters of the Third Kind] *Close Encounters of the Third Kind* (1977), written and directed by Steven Spielberg.

446.20 until ERA passes] The Equal Rights Amendment, forbidding the denial or abridgment of rights on account of sex, was proposed to the states by Congress on March 22, 1972, with a seven-year deadline for its ratification. After 35 states had ratified the amendment, Congress voted on October 6, 1978, to extend the deadline to June 30, 1982, but there were no further ratifications and the amendment did not go into effect.

450.19–21 nut take a shot . . . that Squeaky Fromme who used to lay the old cowboys for the Manson ranch] Lynette Fromme (b. 1948) pointed a gun at President Gerald Ford in Sacramento on September 5, 1975, before being restrained by a Secret Service agent. She was sentenced to life imprisonment for the attempted assassination. She had been a member of the counterculture cult led by Charles Manson (1924–2017), who inspired his followers to commit nine murders in the Los Angeles area, July–August 1969, allegedly in hopes of instigating a race war. "Manson ranch" refers to Spahn Ranch, a Southern California ranch occasionally used as movie sets where members of the cult lived in exchange for their labor in 1968–70, owned by George Spahn (1889–1974), who was reported to have had sexual relations with young women in the cult after Manson told them to do so.

452.29 Wankel engine] Rotary engine used in Mazda automobiles, invented by the German engineer Felix Wankel (1902–1988).

462.9–10 *What? Me Worry?*] See note 423.31.

473.8–9 *Beat the Clock* . . . Phil] Television game shows and talk shows hosted by the media personalities Merv Griffin (1925–2007), Mike Douglas (1920–2006), and Phil Donahue (b. 1935).

473.18 Carol Burnett reruns] *The Carol Burnett Show*, comedy and variety show on CBS television, 1967–78, hosted by Carol Burnett (b. 1933).

477.15 *The Watchtower*] Monthly magazine, founded 1879, distributed worldwide by the Jehovah's Witnesses religious sect.

485.6–7 Angels . . . since Farrah left."] See note 377.36–378.2.

485.26 CocoRibe] Liqueur of rum and coconut milk.

486.7–8 Pittsburgh . . . Family crap.] During their championship 1979 season, the Pittsburgh Pirates adopted the disco hit "We Are Family" (1979) by the vocal group Sister Sledge as a theme song.

487.7–8 gave the old Canal back last night."] Under the terms of the Panama Canal Treaty, signed by President Carter and Panamanian leader Omar Torrijos (1929–1981) on September 7, 1977, and ratified by a one-vote margin by the U.S. Senate the following year, the Panama Canal Zone ceased to exist as American territory on October 1, 1979, though the United States remained in control over the waterway and certain parts of the canal area, including military bases. The transfer stipulated that canal operations would be administered in a transitional phase by a joint U.S.-Panamanian Panama Canal Commission. The canal and its operations were wholly turned over to Panama on December 31, 1999.

491.19–20 *Dim all the lights sweet darling*] From Donna Summer's "Dim All the Lights," written by Summer (1948–2012) for her album *Bad Girls* (1979).

501.26–27 Earl Butz . . . 'He no play-a the game, he no make-a the rules.'] Remark made at a breakfast meeting with reporters by Secretary of Agriculture Earl Butz (1909–2008) on November 27, 1974, dismissing Pope Paul VI's views on population control. Butz had recently attended the World Food Conference in Rome and attributed the quip to the punchline of a joke heard there about an Italian mother disobeying the Pope by using birth control. Controversy ensued when the broken-English comment appeared in print, first in the New York *Daily News*.

504.28 Vatican Two.] Popular name for the Second Ecumenical Council of the Vatican, 1962–65, and its reforms.

505.33 Ann Landers] Pseudonym of Esther Friedman Lederer (1918–2002), author of a long-running syndicated newspaper advice column.

509.18–20   platinum flute . . . some Frenchman who had one.] The French musician Georges Barrère (1876–1944), who spent most of his career in New York City, was the first flutist to play a platinum flute in the United States; the French modernist composer Edgard Varèse (1883–1965) wrote *Density 21.5* (1936, rev. 1946) for him to play on this instrument.

511.34   Three Mile Island] See note 276.37.

513.20   CC and seven?] Cocktail made with Canadian Club whisky and 7 Up.

528.4–5   only claim to fame . . . May 4, 1970] See note 354.28.

528.8   '77 . . . Tent City] In May 1977, protestors at Kent State University objecting to the proposed building of a gymnasium annex on the site where four anti-Vietnam War demonstrators had been killed in 1970 (see note 354.28) pitched tents on campus on Blanket Hill and mounted an ongoing occupation that became known as "Tent City." A temporary restraining order led to the encampment's disruption and the arrests of 193 people on July 12, 1977. Opposition to the university's project continued throughout the summer and fall, including unsuccessful attempts to halt construction of the gym annex, which began in September.

533.36   Ilie Nastase.] Champion Romanian tennis player (b. 1946).

533.39–40   Donna Summer, something about a telephone] The song "Can't Get to Sleep at Night," written by Bob Conti (b. 1947) and Bruce Sudano (b. 1948), from Donna Summer's album *Bad Girls* (1979).

536.23–24   there is the God he is the apple of the eye of.] See Deuteronomy 32:10, in which God found Jacob "in a desert land, and in the waste howling wilderness; he led him about, he instructed him, he kept him as the apple of his eye."

537.16   *Stuck on you, stuck like glue.*] From "Can't Get to Sleep at Night" (see note 533.39–40).

541.40   *The Wild One.*] Film about motorcycle gangs (1953) directed by László Benedek (1905–1992) and starring Marlon Brando (1924–2004).

542.1   Alice Cooper] Stage name of Vincent Furnier (b. 1948), provocative rock performer known for his neogothic persona onstage.

542.18   *One night in a lifetime . . . night.*] And the later quoted lines *Babe it's gotta be tonight, babe it's gotta be tonight,* from Donna Summer's "One Night in a Lifetime," written by Pete Bellotte (b. 1943) and Harold Faltemeyer (b. 1952), from *Bad Girls.*

546.13   ERA] See note 446.20.

550.9   *Ecce homo.*] "Behold the man," Pilate's words to Christ before the Crucifixion, from the Latin Vulgate.

556.28 BREAKING AWAY STARTING OVER RUNNING and "10."] Films from 1979: *Breaking Away*, comedy directed by Peter Yates (1929–2011); *Starting Over*, comedy directed by Alan J. Pakula (1928–1998); *Running*, drama directed by Steven Hilliard Stern (1937–2018); and *10*, directed by Blake Edwards (1922–2010).

563.26 ABC eleven-thirty special report on the hostages] *The Iran Crisis: America Held Hostage*, program on ABC about the hostage situation in Iran hosted by the journalist Ted Koppel (b. 1940), which later became the long-running late-night news program *Nightline*.

572.6–7 the Hunt brothers . . . silver futures] In 1979, the brothers Nelson Bunker Hunt (1926–2014) and W. Herbert Hunt (b. 1929) began buying large quantities of silver bullion and futures contracts, pushing the price per troy ounce to record highs. In response to the silver bubble the Federal Reserve suspended trading in silver on January 17, 1980. On "Silver Thursday," March 27, 1980, prices collapsed in the metal's largest single-day decline. Each of the brothers went bankrupt, and their market manipulation led them to be fined $10 million each and to be prohibited from trading in silver by the Commodity Futures Trading Commission, along with payment of back taxes, interest, and penalties to the IRS.

575.11–12 occupation of the Great Mosque] On November 20, 1979, the Saudi militant Juhayman al-Utaybi (1936–1980) led several hundred armed men into Mecca's Grand Mosque and occupied the building, declaring his brother-in-law Muhammad Abdullah al-Qahtani to be the Mahdi, the Islamic messiah. In a battle that left hundreds dead and wounded, the Saudi military regained control of the mosque on December 4. Surviving insurgents, including al-Utaybi, were executed under orders of the Saudi authorities shortly thereafter.

578.3 Y-B] Yocum Brothers, a cigar manufacturing firm founded in Reading, Pennsylvania, in 1879.

584.21 Gervin for San Antonio] George Gervin (b. 1952), professional basketball player who spent most of his career with the San Antonio Spurs, 1974–85.

588.38–39 Guy Lombardo's brother now that Guy Lombardo is dead] Starting in 1929, Canadian-born bandleader Guy Lombardo (1902–1977) led his Royal Canadians orchestra in annual New Year's Eve broadcasts, first on radio and then on television as well. The Lombardo orchestra continued their televised performances on CBS for the two New Year's Eve programs following Guy's death, under the direction of his brother Victor in 1977–78 and his nephew Bill Lombardo in 1978–79. For the 1979–80 program CBS replaced the Royal Canadians with *Happy New Year, America*, hosted by Paul Anka and Catherine Bach.

592.1   Renée Richards] American tennis player (b. 1934) born biologically male who, after undergoing sexual reassignment surgery in 1975, was not allowed to compete as a woman in the 1976 U.S. Open. After a discrimination lawsuit against the United States Tennis Association ruled in Richards's favor, Richards was permitted to compete in the women's tournament the following year.

592.1   Steven Weed] Weed (b. 1947) was the live-in boyfriend of Patricia Hearst (b. 1954), the American heiress who was kidnapped by and then involved in the activities of the radical Symbionese Liberation Army during 1974–75. Her violent participation in her captors' actions and her subsequent trial—where the defense argued that her complicity had been forced—became one of the biggest American news stories of the 1970s. Convicted in 1976 for her part in an SLA bank robbery, Hearst later had her sentence commuted by President Jimmy Carter. She was pardoned by Bill Clinton in 2001.

592.1   Megan Marshack] Aide (b. 1953) to Vice President Nelson Rockefeller (1908–1979), who employed her as an assistant after he left office. She was with him at his Manhattan home when he suffered a fatal heart attack on the night of January 26, 1979, leading to speculation about the nature of their relationship.

592.2   Marjoe Gortner] Renouncing his religious faith and upbringing after becoming famous as a child Evangelical preacher (beginning at age 4), Gortner (b. 1944) was the subject of the documentary *Marjoe* (1972), after which he worked as an actor in movies such as *Bobbie Jo and the Outlaw* (1976) and *When You Comin' Back, Red Ryder?* (1979).

592.2   Greta Rideout] After Oregon removed legal immunity for husbands from rape charges in 1977, Rideout (b. 1955) accused her husband of rape in a case brought before a jury in the Marion County Circuit Court, the first time that a husband faced prosecution in the United States for an alleged rape of his wife committed while the couple were living together. An eight-woman, four-man jury acquitted John Rideout of first-degree rape on December 27, 1978.

592.2   Spider Sabich] Champion skier (1945–1976) killed by a gunshot fired by his lover Claudine Longet (b. 1942), a French singer and actor, in Aspen, Colorado, on March 21, 1946. Claiming in her defense that the gun had fired by accident, Longet was convicted of negligent homicide and served a 30-day prison sentence.

592.2   D. B. Cooper] Name given in media accounts of a man who hijacked a Northwest Orient Airlines flight from Portland, Oregon, to Seattle on November 24, 1971, with a bomb threat. Identifying himself as "Dan Cooper," he demanded four parachutes and $20,000 in $20 bills, which were given him after the plane landed in Seattle. Releasing the thirty-six passengers but keeping members of the crew on board, he then demanded that the plane be flown to Mexico City. While in the air he parachuted from the plane with the cash he had been given. His subsequent whereabouts, or even whether he survived the jump, remain unknown.

592.34 *ferhuddled*] Pennsylvania Dutch for confused, mixed-up, from the German verb *verhudeln*.

607.25 *Jaws II* ?] *Jaws 2* (1978), directed by Jeannot Szwarc (b. 1939), the first of three sequels to the 1975 film *Jaws* (see note 366.5).

613.8–9 "Send in the Clowns."] Song by Stephen Sondheim (b. 1930) from his musical *A Little Night Music* (1973).

615.4 Ipana] Toothpaste made by Bristol-Myers, introduced in 1901 and discontinued in the United States in the 1970s.

629.20–21 the du Ponts are king.] See note 299.32.

637.40–638.1 Jaworski went down flinging] Philadelphia Eagles quarterback Ron Jaworski (b. 1951) led a failed comeback in their playoff loss to the Tampa Bay Buccaneers on December 29, 1979, a defeat that knocked the team out of contention.

653.39 Congressional CC] The golf course at Congressional Country Club, in Bethesda, Maryland. Dr. Thomas, a Washington, D.C., physician, killed the goose near the seventeenth hole on May 3, 1979.

663.27–29 Andrews-sisters pageboy sings "Sentimental Journey" . . . Doris Day wartime Forties soul] The halftime show for Super Bowl XIV, "A Salute to the Big Band Era," was performed by Up with People, one of the musical ensembles organized by the nonprofit organization for young people of the same name, which were known for their wholesomeness and positive attitude. "Sentimental Journey" (1944), music by Les Brown (1912–2001) and Ben Homer (1917–1975), words by Bud Green (1897–1981), was the first of a long string of best-selling recordings by Doris Day. Released in March 1945, it became the unofficial homecoming song for soldiers returning from World War II.

663.32 Chattanooga Choo-choo] Hit record (1941) for Glenn Miller and His Orchestra, with music by Harry Warren (1893–1981) and words by Mack Gordon (1904–1959).

664.22–23 Bradshaw . . . Stallworth] Pittsburgh Steelers quarterback Terry Bradshaw (b. 1948) and wide receiver John Stallworth (b. 1952), both Hall of Fame players.

THE WITCHES OF EASTWICK

671.4 *Isobel Gowdie*] Scottish woman who confessed to practicing witchcraft in 1662. The quote is from *Ancient Criminal Trials in Scotland, Compiled from the Original Records and MSS., with Historical Illustrations, &c.* by Robert Pitcairn (Edinburgh: Bannatyne Club, 1833).

671.10 *Agnes Sampson*] Scottish woman who was tried as a witch in 1590 and executed in 1591. The quote is from *Memoirs of His Own Life, by Sir James Melville of Halhill* (1535–1617), edited by Thomas Thomson (Edinburgh: Bannatyne Club, 1827).

675.17–18 even Lynda Bird and Luci Baines.] The two daughters (born, respectively, in 1944 and 1947) of President Lyndon Johnson (1908–1973) and Lady Bird Johnson (1912–2007).

676.26–28 "The fag end of creation" and "the sewer of New England," Cotton Mather called the region.] In *Magnalia Christi Americana* (1702), book 7, Cotton Mather (1663–1728) called Rhode Island "that fag-end of the world." The second remark, often attributed to Mather, was made by the Dutch religious leaders Johannes Megapolensis (1603–1670) and Samuel Drisius in their letter to the Classis of Amsterdam, August 14, 1657.

676.29–30 soon-to-die Anne Hutchinson] Hutchinson (1591–1643), religious leader who, after her banishment from the Massachusetts Bay Colony for beliefs deemed heretical, moved to Rhode Island and later to a settlement near Pelham Bay in the present-day Bronx in New York. Along with members of her family and household, she was killed by Algonquian Indians in August 1643.

677.15–16 Great Swamp Fight in King Philip's War] In the summer of 1675, fighting broke out in New England between English colonists and an alliance of Wampanoag, Nipmuc, Pocumtuck, and Wabanaki Indians resisting colonial encroachment on their lands and sovereignty. (The conflict became known as King Philip's War after Metacom, or Philip, the sachem who led the Wampanoag resistance.) The Narragansett declared their neutrality while giving refuge to Wampanoag fleeing colonial incursions. Fearing that the Narragansett would join the Native alliance, the leaders of the United Colonies (Massachusetts, Plymouth, and Connecticut) decided to launch a preemptive attack. On December 19, 1675, about 1,000 colonial troops, along with 150 Mohegan and Pequot allies, attacked a fortified Narragansett village built in a swamp near present-day South Kingston, Rhode Island. After being initially repulsed, the colonial forces breached the settlement's palisade, set fire to its wigwams, and massacred those who tried to flee. Hundreds of Narragansett men, women, and children were killed, while the colonial forces lost about seventy dead.

677.18 the Hartford Convention of 1815] Meeting of Federalist delegates from New Hampshire, Vermont, Massachusetts, Rhode Island, and Connecticut in Hartford, Connecticut, from December 15, 1814, to January 5, 1815. The convention proposed the adoption of seven constitutional amendments designed to protect New England against southern and western domination by the federal government.

678.18 armless statue of Balzac by Rodin.] See note 161.29.

679.33 fragility of a Giacometti.] The Swiss-born sculptor Alberto Giacometti (1901–1966) is best known for his elongated sculptures of human figures.

684.18–19 *Ammophila breviligulata.*] American beachgrass.

686.37 Popper's études] *Hohe Schule des Violoncellospiels* (High School of Cello Playing, 1901–5), Op. 73, series of forty cello studies by the Austrian composer David Popper (1843–1913).

687.5–6 "Satisfaction" and "I Got You, Babe"] "(I Can't Get No) Satisfaction" and "I Got You Babe," hits in 1965 for, respectively, the Rolling Stones and Sonny & Cher.

687.6–7 wherever two or three teen-agers gathered together] See Jesus' words in Matthew 18:20: "For where two or three are gathered together in my name, there am I in the midst of them."

688.12 "*byelo.*"] Russian: white.

692.7 Heidi] Eponymous heroine of internationally read children's book (1880–81) by the Swiss author Johanna Spyri (1827–1901), later adapted for stage, film, and television.

692.24 *Kinder. Fünf*] German: children. Five.

694.16 v-and-t.] Vodka and Tab.

694.34–35 "Do I dare . . . upon the beach."] From the conclusion of "The Love Song of J. Alfred Prufrock" (1915), poem by T. S. Eliot (1888–1965).

700.10 Marisol] American artist born in Paris to Venezuelan parents (born María Sol Escobar, 1930–2016) whose work drew from Pop Art and folk art.

700.10–11 Niki de Saint-Phalle . . . 'Nanas'] The French artist Niki de Saint-Phalle (1930–2002) is best known for her large sculptural "Nanas," rotund women fancifully depicted in bold colors and energetic poses.

702.25 *beaucoup de rien*] French: a lot of nothing.

712.11 Peer Gynt] Eponymous hero of a verse play (1866) by the Norwegian playwright Henrik Ibsen (1828–1906).

714.5 Liberace] Polish American pianist, comedian, and showman (1919–1987), a notable interpreter of the classical piano repertoire in the popular style, and a pioneer of early television (1953–55, 1958–59).

715.8 a Calder or Moore] Large sculptures by the American sculptor Alexander Calder (1898–1976) and the British sculptor Henry Moore (1898–1986).

718.20 Webern bagatelles] Six Bagatelles for String Quartet (1913), Op. 9, by the Austrian composer Anton Webern (1883–1945).

720.16 Bellini] The Venetian painter Giovanni Bellini (1430–1516).

722.11 *Mia vacca bianca.*] Italian: My white cow.

723.8 James Van Dine] The American artist Jim Dine (b. 1935), known for his Pop works.

725.37 'Mood Indigo,'] Jazz standard (1930) first recorded by Duke Ellington's orchestra, with music by Ellington (1899–1974) and Barney Bigard (1906–1980), with words by Mitchell Parish (1900–1993) though credited to Irving Mills.

729.30 Tofranil] Trade name for imipramine, an antidepressant, manufactured by Mallinckrodt Pharmaceuticals.

729.31 *Either/Or*] *Either/Or: A Fragment of Life* (1843) by the Danish philosopher and religious thinker Søren Kierkegaard (1813–1855).

734.7 some perfectly harmless thing with Barbra Streisand] See note 276.31.

736.24 *Hogan's Heroes*] CBS television comedy, 1965–71, about Allied prisoners in a German POW camp during World War II starring Bob Crane (1928–1978) and Werner Klemperer (1920–2000).

742.27–28 Robert Joseph Auguste] French silversmith and goldsmith (1723–c. 1805) who made a crown and other regalia for Louis XVI's coronation and created silver tableware for courts across Europe, among other commissions.

744.23 Kienholz.] The American artist Edward Kienholz (1927–1994), known for his installations and assemblages.

744.27 *Vielfältigkeit*] German: diversity.

746.4 Queen Anne] Style of furniture that in its American manifestation flourished from the 1720s through the 1750s (though the English queen Anne herself reigned earlier, from 1702 to 1740), marked by graceful curves and simplified formal elements largely devoid of ornament.

746.10–12 those two Russkis . . . over there in Leningrad] Including significant holdings of works by Henri Matisse and Pablo Picasso, the respective collections of the Russian businessmen Sergei Shchukin (1854–1936) and Ivan Morovov (1871–1921) were expropriated by the Soviet government after the Russian Revolution and were later exhibited in the Hermitage in Leningrad (St. Petersburg), as well as in the Pushkin Museum in Moscow.

746.15 Jasper Johns] American painter, printmaker, and sculptor (b. 1930) whose signature subjects include targets, maps, American flags, and Ballantine Ale cans (see lines 747.3–10).

746.37 Petronius] Gaius Petronius, Roman author best known for *Satyricon* (late first century C.E.).

746.38 goat Rauschenberg put in the rubber tire] For *Monogram* (1955–59), one of the "combines" made by the American artist Robert Rauschenberg (1925–2008).

747.31–32 this entire sawed-off Dodge car he did] Kienholz's *Back Seat Dodge '38* (1964).

748.19 Mies van der Rohe] German-born modernist architect and designer (1886–1969).

749.9   John Wesley, no relation to the crazy Methodist] American artist (b. 1928), as distinct from the English cleric (1703–1791) whose revival movement within the Church of England provided foundations for the establishment of Methodism as an independent Protestant sect.

751.17   *Spartina patens*] Saltmeadow cordgrass or salt hay.

754.7–8   *Acer japonicum*] The full moon maple, native to Japan.

757.27–28   *empanadillas, calamares en su tinta*] Spanish: small stuffed turnovers, squid in ink.

759.12   Peds] Brand-name anklets.

760.19   Strad] Stradivarius.

760.23   Ceruti . . . Cremona too, but later.] Enrico Ceruti (1808–1883) came from a family of Italian instrument makers and was part of the renowned tradition of crafting instruments in the violin family that flourished in Cremona, Italy, as was Antonio Stradivari (1644–1737).

761.22   Nevelson] Russian-born American sculptor Louise Nevelson (1899–1988).

761.32   a wall like a Mondrian] The later work of the Dutch artist Piet Mondrian (1872–1944) is abstract and features rectilinear forms in bright colors divided by thick black lines.

767.17   surreal Arp shapes] The Alsatian artist Jean Arp (1886–1966) worked in a surrealist style for part of his career.

772.14   records . . . Joplin] As lead singer of the group Big Brother & the Holding Company, Janis Joplin (1943–1970) performed the traditional song "Down on Me" on the group's eponymous 1967 recording. The group's second album, *Cheap Thrills* (1968), included her renditions of "Summertime" (1935), song from the opera *Porgy and Bess* (1935), music by George Gershwin (1898–1937), libretto by DuBose Heyward (1885–1940) and Ira Gershwin (1896–1983), and "Piece of My Heart," written by Bert Berns (1929–1967) and Jerry Ragovoy (1930–2011). On her album *Pearl* (1971), backed by the Full Tilt Boogie Band, Joplin sang "Get It While You Can," written by Ragovoy and Mort Shuman (1938–1991), and "Me and Bobby McGee," written by Kris Kristofferson (b. 1936) and Fred Foster (1931–2019).

772.18   Tiny Tim] Stage name of the American singer and ukulele player Herbert Butros Khaury (1932–1996), whose career peaked in the late 1960s.

774.2   *Maleficia*] Latin: Wicked (a feminine singular form).

774.5   *a young French witch, c. 1660*] Updike's source is *The Black Arts: A Concise History of Witchcraft, Demonology, Astrology, and Other Mystical Practices Throughout the Ages* by Richard Cavendish (New York: Capricorn Books, 1967).

776.28 Greer Garson] British-born actor (1904–1996) who received several Academy Award nominations in the 1940s and won the Best Actress award for her starring role in *Mrs. Miniver* (1942).

777.38 Joan Baez] Folksinger and political activist (b. 1941).

782.35 first editions of Thornton Wilder and Carl Van Vechten] Thornton Wilder (1897–1975), American playwright and novelist whose most popular work of fiction was *The Bridge of San Luis Rey* (1927); Carl Van Vechten (1880–1964), American dance critic, photographer, and author of novels, including *Parties* (1930).

787.12 Rochester] Xerox Corporation, founded as the Haloid Photographic Company, had headquarters in Rochester, New York, from 1906 to 1969.

787.38–39 that Scotsman . . . lid of the kettle] A story told about the Scottish inventor James Watt (1736–1819), who in improving the design of the Newcomen steam engine contributed decisively to the Industrial Revolution, held that by watching a kettle boil he gleaned insights into the power of steam.

793.33–34 *Nil igitur mors est . . . habetur.*] "There death is nothing to us, of no concern whatsoever, once it is appreciated that the mind has a mortal nature." *De rerum natura* (On the Nature of Things), book 3, lines 830–31, by the Roman poet and Epicurean philosopher Lucretius (c. 99–c. 55 BCE), in the translation of A. A. Long and D. N. Sedley (1987).

794.3 *inane profundum*] Latin: deep void, phrase used by Lucretius in book 2, line 222, in the midst of a passage being paraphrased here.

805.29–30 an infinity of times, just as Nietzsche had conjectured] The German philosopher Friedrich Nietzsche (1844–1900) explored the idea of eternal recurrence throughout his writings.

805.32 *candida sidera*] Latin: bright stars. See Lucretius, *De rerum natura*, book 5, line 1210.

807.12 Kodály] The Hungarian composer and educational philosopher Zoltán Kodály (1882–1967).

808.26 Adlai Stevenson rally] Former Democratic governor of Illinois Adlai Stevenson (1900–1965) was the Democratic Party's presidential nominee in 1952 and 1956.

812.11 the woman in Peter, Paul, and Mary] The folksinger Mary Travers (1936–2009).

818.40–819.1 *Sator arepo tenet opera rotas*] The words of the Sator square, Latin palindromes written on squares of five lines (one word per line) that were thought to serve a protective function in antiquity and the Middle Ages; the phrase and variants were used in occult practices.

824.7 the blasphemous backwards words *Retson Retap*] *Pater noster*, the first words of the Lord's Prayer in Latin, read backward.

828.1 *Té para las señoras . . . favor,*"] Spanish: Tea for the ladies and the young lady, please.

829.12 Diana, Isis, Astarte.] Respectively, Greek goddess of the hunt, Egyptian goddess of fertility and magic, and a Semitic deity associated with sexuality and war.

829.35 Dragon Throne's] The throne of the Chinese emperor.

830.20 "Sha-ZAM!"] In the comic-book adventures of Captain Marvel, launched by cartoonist C. C. Beck (1910–1989) in 1940, the word that effects the transformation of orphan Billy Batson into superhero Captain Marvel.

838.22 Hindemith."] The German modernist composer and conductor Paul Hindemith (1895–1963).

842.6–7 "Livin' in the sunlight . . . time!"] From the song "Livin' in the Sunlight, Lovin' in the Moonlight" (1930), music by Al Sherman (1897–1973), words by Al Lewis (1901–1967), a version of which was recorded by Tiny Tim (see note 772.18) on his album *God Bless Tiny Tim* (1968).

846.29 *Kapellmeister*] German: choir director.

849.1–3 *The History of the Decline and Fall . . . Species.*] History (1776–88) by Edward Gibbon (1737–1794); novel (1774) by Johann Wolfgang von Goethe (1749–1832); study in natural history (1859) by Charles Darwin (1809–1882).

850.14–16 Dominican *sancocho* or Cuban *mondongo*, of Mexican *pollo picado con tocino* or Colombian *soufflé de sesos.*] Respectively, a beef stew; a tripe stew; chopped chicken with bacon; beef brain soufflé.

850.26 Toad Hall] In the children's novel *The Wind in the Willows* (1908) by the English author Kenneth Grahame (1859–1932), the home of Mr. Toad.

851.10 Lindner] The German-born American painter Richard Lindner (1901–1978).

852.38 Emily Brontë's inspired novel] *Wuthering Heights* (1847).

853.23 *Kojak*] CBS television series, 1973–78, a police drama starring Telly Savalas (1922–1994) as its eponymous detective.

854.7 *Friedrich Nietzsche, 1887*] From Nietzsche's *On the Genealogy of Morals*, translated from the German by Walter Kaufmann and R. J. Hollingdale (New York: Random House, 1967).

862.38 watch Archie Bunker."] Main character in *All in the Family* (see note 316.31).

864.20–21 *Es muy agradable . . . casa.*] Spanish: How very nice it is to have you again in this house.

865.5–6 A Nightingale Sang in Berkeley Square] Song (1939) by American composer Manning Sherwin (1902–1974) with words by English entertainer Eric Maschwitz (1901–1969).

866.2 How High the Moon] See note 271.22–23.

867.32 *Deseo beber!*] Spanish: I want to drink!

867.35 *huevos picantes*] Spanish: devilled eggs.

868.4–5 Wayne Thiebaud . . . cake] Cakes, pies, and pastry cases are among the subjects taken up by the American figurative painter Wayne Thiebaud (b. 1920).

868.13 *xu-xu*] Or chuchu: chayote squash.

868.34–35 Tom Wesselmann] American Pop artist (1931–2004).

869.18 Eva Perón's] Eva Perón (1919–1952), known as Evita, was the wife of Argentine president Juan Perón and a populist political figure in her own right.

873.6–7 *Hoc est enim corpus meum*] Latin: "This is my body," Jesus' words during the Last Supper repeated during the Eucharist, followed by "*Hic est enim calix sanguinis mei*," "For this is the chalice of my Blood."

873.17 *Emen hetan*] Here and there.

873.18–19 *diable . . . joue là*] French: devil, devil, jump here, jump there, play here, play there.

873.21–22 "Tinkletum Tankletum"] Ballad mentioned in an account cited in Margaret Alice Murray, *The Witch-Cult in Western Europe: A Study in Anthropology* (1921): "Isabell Shyrrie did sing her song called Tinkletum Tankletum; and . . . the divill kist every one of the women."

902.33 as if quoting.] See poem by the American poet E. E. Cummings (1894–1962) collected in the posthumous volume *73 Poems* (1962): "annie died the other day / never was there such a lay– / whom,among her dollies,dad / first("don't tell your mother")had; / making annie slightly mad / but very wonderful in bed / –saints and satyrs,go your way / youth and maidens:let us pray."

904.27–28 "Through the Night of Doubt and Sorrow"] Hymn with words (1825) by the Danish poet and novelist Bernhard Severin Ingemann (1789–1862), translated into English by Sabine Baring-Gold in 1867.

908.22 Moonies] Widely used term for members of the Unification Church, led by its Korean founder and self-proclaimed messiah, Sun Myung Moon (1920–2012).

909.13 *Mannix*] CBS television series, 1967–75, with Mike Connors (1925–2017) as the eponymous detective.

911.29 *Menuetto I da capo*] Musical directive to repeat the minuet part of the piece.

911.31 *aufstrich . . . abstrich*] German: upstroke, downstroke.

915.17–28 out of control . . . Ralph Nader hates that model."] The consumer advocate, activist, and presidential candidate Ralph Nader (b. 1934) rose to prominence with his criticism of the auto industry and its safety failures in the best-selling book *Unsafe at Any Speed: The Designed-In Dangers of the American Automobile* (1965).

922.21 *Hexenstuhl.*] German: witches' chair, the chair on which accused witches sat for interrogation.

924.1–2 *En-cy-clo-pedia, as Jiminy Cricket used to say,*] In 1956–57, *The Mickey Mouse Club* featured a series of educational, made-for-TV Disney shorts titled "Jiminy Cricket Presents . . . The Encyclopedia." In the natural-history "notes" that follow, Van Horne quotes from entries in the Encyclopaedia Britannica.

926.33–34 "Father, Who on Man Doth Shower,"] Hymn with words (1906) by the Anglican priest and hymn writer Percy Dearmer (1867–1936).

929.17 *Il est disparu.*] French: He's gone.

933.23 Lance Alworth] Football player (b. 1940), a wide receiver who played most of his professional career with the San Diego Chargers.

936.21–22 Chippendale and Duncan Phyfe antiques] Pieces designed by the English furniture makers Thomas Chippendale (1718–1779) and Duncan Phyfe (1768–1854).

936.39–40 H. H. Richardson] The American architect Henry Hobson Richardson (1838–1886), who contributed to the nineteenth-century Romanesque Revival in the United States; among his best-known buildings are Trinity Church in Boston and Sever Hall at Harvard.

APPENDIX

941.9–10 like Diane Keaton in *Reds*] In the historical romance *Reds* (1981), directed by and starring Warren Beatty, Diane Keaton (b. 1946) played the role of Louise Bryant (1885–1936), an American journalist in Russia during the 1917 Revolution.

943.15–16 page 434 . . . clove Life Savers] Updike revised the passage so that Rabbit's roll of Life Savers, clove flavored in the first printing of *Rabbit Is Rich*, were butter-rum flavored and thus not anachronistic. See page 635 of the present volume.

946.17–18   *Satanism and Witchcraft*] Subtitled "A Study in Medieval Super-stition," this reprint of *The Sorceress*, A. R. Allinson's 1905 translation of *La Sorcière* (1862) by Jules Michelet (1798–1874), was published by Citadel Books, New York, in 1939.

946.29   Manson murders] See note 450.19–21.

948.15   Robert Pinget] French novelist and playwright (1920–1997) whose books include *The Inquisitory* (1961) and *Someone* (1965).

*This book is set in 10 point ITC Galliard, a face designed
for digital composition by Matthew Carter and based
on the sixteenth-century face Granjon. The paper is acid-free
lightweight opaque that will not turn yellow or brittle with age.
The binding is sewn, which allows the book to open easily and lie flat.
The binding board is covered in Brillianta, a woven rayon cloth
made by Van Heek–Scholco Textielfabrieken, Holland.
Composition by Dianna Logan, Clearmont, MO.
Printing by Sheridan Grand Rapids, Grand Rapids, MI.
Binding by Dekker Bookbinding, Wyoming, MI.
Designed by Bruce Campbell.*

THE LIBRARY OF AMERICA SERIES

Library of America fosters appreciation of America's literary heritage by publishing, and keeping permanently in print, authoritative editions of America's best and most significant writing. An independent nonprofit organization, it was founded in 1979 with seed funding from the National Endowment for the Humanities and the Ford Foundation.

1. Herman Melville: Typee, Omoo, Mardi
2. Nathaniel Hawthorne: Tales & Sketches
3. Walt Whitman: Poetry & Prose
4. Harriet Beecher Stowe: Three Novels
5. Mark Twain: Mississippi Writings
6. Jack London: Novels & Stories
7. Jack London: Novels & Social Writings
8. William Dean Howells: Novels 1875–1886
9. Herman Melville: Redburn, White-Jacket, Moby-Dick
10. Nathaniel Hawthorne: Collected Novels
11 & 12. Francis Parkman: France and England in North America
13. Henry James: Novels 1871–1880
14. Henry Adams: Novels, Mont Saint Michel, The Education
15. Ralph Waldo Emerson: Essays & Lectures
16. Washington Irving: History, Tales & Sketches
17. Thomas Jefferson: Writings
18. Stephen Crane: Prose & Poetry
19. Edgar Allan Poe: Poetry & Tales
20. Edgar Allan Poe: Essays & Reviews
21. Mark Twain: The Innocents Abroad, Roughing It
22 & 23. Henry James: Literary Criticism
24. Herman Melville: Pierre, Israel Potter, The Confidence-Man, Tales & Billy Budd
25. William Faulkner: Novels 1930–1935
26 & 27. James Fenimore Cooper: The Leatherstocking Tales
28. Henry David Thoreau: A Week, Walden, The Maine Woods, Cape Cod
29. Henry James: Novels 1881–1886
30. Edith Wharton: Novels
31 & 32. Henry Adams: History of the U.S. during the Administrations of Jefferson & Madison
33. Frank Norris: Novels & Essays
34. W.E.B. Du Bois: Writings
35. Willa Cather: Early Novels & Stories
36. Theodore Dreiser: Sister Carrie, Jennie Gerhardt, Twelve Men
37. Benjamin Franklin: Writings (2 vols.)
38. William James: Writings 1902–1910
39. Flannery O'Connor: Collected Works
40, 41, & 42. Eugene O'Neill: Complete Plays
43. Henry James: Novels 1886–1890
44. William Dean Howells: Novels 1886–1888
45 & 46. Abraham Lincoln: Speeches & Writings
47. Edith Wharton: Novellas & Other Writings
48. William Faulkner: Novels 1936–1940
49. Willa Cather: Later Novels
50. Ulysses S. Grant: Memoirs & Selected Letters
51. William Tecumseh Sherman: Memoirs
52. Washington Irving: Bracebridge Hall, Tales of a Traveller, The Alhambra
53. Francis Parkman: The Oregon Trail, The Conspiracy of Pontiac
54. James Fenimore Cooper: Sea Tales
55 & 56. Richard Wright: Works
57. Willa Cather: Stories, Poems, & Other Writings
58. William James: Writings 1878–1899
59. Sinclair Lewis: Main Street & Babbitt
60 & 61. Mark Twain: Collected Tales, Sketches, Speeches, & Essays
62 & 63. The Debate on the Constitution
64 & 65. Henry James: Collected Travel Writings
66 & 67. American Poetry: The Nineteenth Century
68. Frederick Douglass: Autobiographies
69. Sarah Orne Jewett: Novels & Stories
70. Ralph Waldo Emerson: Collected Poems & Translations
71. Mark Twain: Historical Romances
72. John Steinbeck: Novels & Stories 1932–1937
73. William Faulkner: Novels 1942–1954
74 & 75. Zora Neale Hurston: Novels, Stories, & Other Writings
76. Thomas Paine: Collected Writings
77 & 78. Reporting World War II: American Journalism
79 & 80. Raymond Chandler: Novels, Stories, & Other Writings

81. Robert Frost: Collected Poems, Prose, & Plays

82 & 83. Henry James: Complete Stories 1892–1910

84. William Bartram: Travels & Other Writings

85. John Dos Passos: U.S.A.

86. John Steinbeck: The Grapes of Wrath & Other Writings 1936–1941

87, 88, & 89. Vladimir Nabokov: Novels & Other Writings

90. James Thurber: Writings & Drawings

91. George Washington: Writings

92. John Muir: Nature Writings

93. Nathanael West: Novels & Other Writings

94 & 95. Crime Novels: American Noir of the 1930s, 40s, & 50s

96. Wallace Stevens: Collected Poetry & Prose

97. James Baldwin: Early Novels & Stories

98. James Baldwin: Collected Essays

99 & 100. Gertrude Stein: Writings

101 & 102. Eudora Welty: Novels, Stories, & Other Writings

103. Charles Brockden Brown: Three Gothic Novels

104 & 105. Reporting Vietnam: American Journalism

106 & 107. Henry James: Complete Stories 1874–1891

108. American Sermons

109. James Madison: Writings

110. Dashiell Hammett: Complete Novels

111. Henry James: Complete Stories 1864–1874

112. William Faulkner: Novels 1957–1962

113. John James Audubon: Writings & Drawings

114. Slave Narratives

115 & 116. American Poetry: The Twentieth Century

117. F. Scott Fitzgerald: Novels & Stories 1920–1922

118. Henry Wadsworth Longfellow: Poems & Other Writings

119 & 120. Tennessee Williams: Collected Plays

121 & 122. Edith Wharton: Collected Stories

123. The American Revolution: Writings from the War of Independence

124. Henry David Thoreau: Collected Essays & Poems

125. Dashiell Hammett: Crime Stories & Other Writings

126 & 127. Dawn Powell: Novels

128. Carson McCullers: Complete Novels

129. Alexander Hamilton: Writings

130. Mark Twain: The Gilded Age & Later Novels

131. Charles W. Chesnutt: Stories, Novels, & Essays

132. John Steinbeck: Novels 1942–1952

133. Sinclair Lewis: Arrowsmith, Elmer Gantry, Dodsworth

134 & 135. Paul Bowles: Novels, Stories, & Other Writings

136. Kate Chopin: Complete Novels & Stories

137 & 138. Reporting Civil Rights: American Journalism

139. Henry James: Novels 1896–1899

140. Theodore Dreiser: An American Tragedy

141. Saul Bellow: Novels 1944–1953

142. John Dos Passos: Novels 1920–1925

143. John Dos Passos: Travel Books & Other Writings

144. Ezra Pound: Poems & Translations

145. James Weldon Johnson: Writings

146. Washington Irving: Three Western Narratives

147. Alexis de Tocqueville: Democracy in America

148. James T. Farrell: Studs Lonigan Trilogy

149, 150, & 151. Isaac Bashevis Singer: Collected Stories

152. Kaufman & Co.: Broadway Comedies

153. Theodore Roosevelt: Rough Riders, An Autobiography

154. Theodore Roosevelt: Letters & Speeches

155. H. P. Lovecraft: Tales

156. Louisa May Alcott: Little Women, Little Men, Jo's Boys

157. Philip Roth: Novels & Stories 1959–1962

158. Philip Roth: Novels 1967–1972

159. James Agee: Let Us Now Praise Famous Men, A Death in the Family, Shorter Fiction

160. James Agee: Film Writing & Selected Journalism

161. Richard Henry Dana Jr.: Two Years Before the Mast & Other Voyages

162. Henry James: Novels 1901–1902

163. Arthur Miller: Plays 1944–1961

164. William Faulkner: Novels 1926–1929

165. Philip Roth: Novels 1973–1977

166 & 167. American Speeches: Political Oratory

168. Hart Crane: Complete Poems & Selected Letters

169. Saul Bellow: Novels 1956–1964
170. John Steinbeck: Travels with Charley & Later Novels
171. Capt. John Smith: Writings with Other Narratives
172. Thornton Wilder: Collected Plays & Writings on Theater
173. Philip K. Dick: Four Novels of the 1960s
174. Jack Kerouac: Road Novels 1957–1960
175. Philip Roth: Zuckerman Bound
176 & 177. Edmund Wilson: Literary Essays & Reviews
178. American Poetry: The 17th & 18th Centuries
179. William Maxwell: Early Novels & Stories
180. Elizabeth Bishop: Poems, Prose, & Letters
181. A. J. Liebling: World War II Writings
182. American Earth: Environmental Writing Since Thoreau
183. Philip K. Dick: Five Novels of the 1960s & 70s
184. William Maxwell: Later Novels & Stories
185. Philip Roth: Novels & Other Narratives 1986–1991
186. Katherine Anne Porter: Collected Stories & Other Writings
187. John Ashbery: Collected Poems 1956–1987
188 & 189. John Cheever: Complete Novels & Collected Stories
190. Lafcadio Hearn: American Writings
191. A. J. Liebling: The Sweet Science & Other Writings
192. The Lincoln Anthology
193. Philip K. Dick: VALIS & Later Novels
194. Thornton Wilder: The Bridge of San Luis Rey & Other Novels 1926–1948
195. Raymond Carver: Collected Stories
196 & 197. American Fantastic Tales
198. John Marshall: Writings
199. The Mark Twain Anthology
200. Mark Twain: A Tramp Abroad, Following the Equator, Other Travels
201 & 202. Ralph Waldo Emerson: Selected Journals
203. The American Stage: Writing on Theater
204. Shirley Jackson: Novels & Stories
205. Philip Roth: Novels 1993–1995
206 & 207. H. L. Mencken: Prejudices
208. John Kenneth Galbraith: The Affluent Society & Other Writings 1952–1967

209. Saul Bellow: Novels 1970–1982
210 & 211. Lynd Ward: Six Novels in Woodcuts
212. The Civil War: The First Year
213 & 214. John Adams: Revolutionary Writings
215. Henry James: Novels 1903–1911
216. Kurt Vonnegut: Novels & Stories 1963–1973
217 & 218. Harlem Renaissance Novels
219. Ambrose Bierce: The Devil's Dictionary, Tales, & Memoirs
220. Philip Roth: The American Trilogy 1997–2000
221. The Civil War: The Second Year
222. Barbara W. Tuchman: The Guns of August, The Proud Tower
223. Arthur Miller: Plays 1964–1982
224. Thornton Wilder: The Eighth Day, Theophilus North, Autobiographical Writings
225. David Goodis: Five Noir Novels of the 1940s & 50s
226. Kurt Vonnegut: Novels & Stories 1950–1962
227 & 228. American Science Fiction: Nine Novels of the 1950s
229 & 230. Laura Ingalls Wilder: The Little House Books
231. Jack Kerouac: Collected Poems
232. The War of 1812
233. American Antislavery Writings
234. The Civil War: The Third Year
235. Sherwood Anderson: Collected Stories
236. Philip Roth: Novels 2001–2007
237. Philip Roth: Nemeses
238. Aldo Leopold: A Sand County Almanac & Other Writings
239. May Swenson: Collected Poems
240 & 241. W. S. Merwin: Collected Poems
242 & 243. John Updike: Collected Stories
244. Ring Lardner: Stories & Other Writings
245. Jonathan Edwards: Writings from the Great Awakening
246. Susan Sontag: Essays of the 1960s & 70s
247. William Wells Brown: Clotel & Other Writings
248 & 249. Bernard Malamud: Novels & Stories of the 1940s, 50s, & 60s
250. The Civil War: The Final Year
251. Shakespeare in America

252. Kurt Vonnegut: Novels 1976–1985
253 & 254. American Musicals 1927–1969
255. Elmore Leonard: Four Novels of the 1970s
256. Louisa May Alcott: Work, Eight Cousins, Rose in Bloom, Stories & Other Writings
257. H. L. Mencken: The Days Trilogy
258. Virgil Thomson: Music Chronicles 1940–1954
259. Art in America 1945–1970
260. Saul Bellow: Novels 1984–2000
261. Arthur Miller: Plays 1987–2004
262. Jack Kerouac: Visions of Cody, Visions of Gerard, Big Sur
263. Reinhold Niebuhr: Major Works on Religion & Politics
264. Ross Macdonald: Four Novels of the 1950s
265 & 266. The American Revolution: Writings from the Pamphlet Debate
267. Elmore Leonard: Four Novels of the 1980s
268 & 269. Women Crime Writers: Suspense Novels of the 1940s & 50s
270. Frederick Law Olmsted: Writings on Landscape, Culture, & Society
271. Edith Wharton: Four Novels of the 1920s
272. James Baldwin: Later Novels
273. Kurt Vonnegut: Novels 1987–1997
274. Henry James: Autobiographies
275. Abigail Adams: Letters
276. John Adams: Writings from the New Nation 1784–1826
277. Virgil Thomson: The State of Music & Other Writings
278. War No More: American Antiwar & Peace Writing
279. Ross Macdonald: Three Novels of the Early 1960s
280. Elmore Leonard: Four Later Novels
281. Ursula K. Le Guin: The Complete Orsinia
282. John O'Hara: Stories
283. The Unknown Kerouac: Rare, Unpublished & Newly Translated Writings
284. Albert Murray: Collected Essays & Memoirs
285 & 286. Loren Eiseley: Collected Essays on Evolution, Nature, & the Cosmos
287. Carson McCullers: Stories, Plays & Other Writings
288. Jane Bowles: Collected Writings
289. World War I and America: Told by the Americans Who Lived It
290 & 291. Mary McCarthy: The Complete Fiction
292. Susan Sontag: Later Essays
293 & 294. John Quincy Adams: Diaries
295. Ross Macdonald: Four Later Novels
296 & 297. Ursula K. Le Guin: The Hainish Novels & Stories
298 & 299. Peter Taylor: The Complete Stories
300. Philip Roth: Why Write? Collected Nonfiction 1960–2014
301. John Ashbery: Collected Poems 1991–2000
302. Wendell Berry: Port William Novels & Stories: The Civil War to World War II
303. Reconstruction: Voices from America's First Great Struggle for Racial Equality
304. Albert Murray: Collected Novels & Poems
305 & 306. Norman Mailer: The Sixties
307. Rachel Carson: Silent Spring & Other Writings on the Environment
308. Elmore Leonard: Westerns
309 & 310. Madeleine L'Engle: The Kairos Novels
311. John Updike: Novels 1959–1965
312. James Fenimore Cooper: Two Novels of the American Revolution
313. John O'Hara: Four Novels of the 1930s
314. Ann Petry: The Street, The Narrows
315. Ursula K. Le Guin: Always Coming Home
316 & 317. Wendell Berry: Collected Essays
318. Cornelius Ryan: The Longest Day, A Bridge Too Far
319. Booth Tarkington: Novels & Stories
320. Herman Melville: Complete Poems
321 & 322. American Science Fiction: Eight Classic Novels of the 1960s
323. Frances Hodgson Burnett: The Secret Garden, A Little Princess, Little Lord Fauntleroy
324. Jean Stafford: Complete Novels
325. Joan Didion: The 1960s & 70s
326. John Updike: Novels 1968–1975
327. Constance Fenimore Woolson: Collected Stories
328. Robert Stone: Dog Soldiers, Flag for Sunrise, Outerbridge Reach
329. Jonathan Schell: The Fate of the Earth, The Abolition, The Unconquerable World
330. Richard Hofstadter: Anti-Intellectualism in American Life, The Paranoid Style in American Politics, Uncollected Essays 1956–1965